JESSIE,

THE MORMON'S DAUGHTER.

A TALE OF ENGLISH AND AMERICAN LIFE.

BY THE AUTHOR OF "THE BLUE DWARF."

PROFUSELY ILLUSTRATED.

LONDON.
EDWARD HARRISON, EXETER CHANGE;
AND ALL BOOKSELLERS.

PREFACE.

THE MORMONS have now increased to nearly 400,000; they have carried their nefarious doctrines into every country in Europe, and have recruited proselytes in Asia and Africa. It is time that something were done to check their progress. In this work their blasphemous account of their origin, their abominable fabrication of a Bible, their cunning mode of proselytism, their lustful adoption of polygamy, for which system of legalized infamy they alone have left the confines of civilization, are fearlessly exposed.

Often in doing so we have had to enter into painful details—sometimes we have to indulge in disgusting descriptions; but who can expose such wickedness without entering into particulars, explaining their evil schemes and systematic delusions. In the end we have every reason to believe that education, enlightenment, and free discussion will destroy the evil, though we can scarcely hope it yet.

But something in the mean time should be done by law. Other recruiters for the social evil dens are punished, why should not the same law reach those who steal away the girls and women of England to fill their harems therewith. Education we have said will ultimately extirpate the foul blot; but in the mean time, those who are the guardians of the people should interfere. The impostors are abroad in the land; every month takes away many of their dupes from foreign shores. Again I lift the voice of warning. Beware of their arts. Enter not the circle of their fascinations; their charms are like those of the serpent, and lead to the death all that is holy and beautiful in this life, and all that can support the anxious soul in its moments of dissolution, and give it a happy and abundant entrance into the presence of just men made perfect.

THE AUTHOR,

JESSIE,

THE

MORMON'S DAUGHTER.

THE ASSASSINATION.

Book I.—THE MAN WITH TWO FACES.

CHAPTER I.

A MIDNIGHT MURDER.

A DREARY, dark, and extremely gloomy quarter is that in Manchester where once stood a street which we shall call Silver-street.

It was in a poor neighbourhood, and some years ago when corn was dear, when laws prevented food entering the land, and employment in consequence was scarce, a more squalid spot could not be conceived on the face of the earth.

Narrow streets, tall houses, murky and paneless—holes stuffed with rags supplying the place of glass—ill-dressed, gaunt men, pale and slatternly women, squalling children, were the natural consequences of the dismal poverty of a class which at the best of times is not too provident.

Were they provident, what a mighty change there would be.

What aristocracy could resist the power of a sober, well-fed, provident army of some millions of artizans.

But this quarter was also the abode of crime, of hideous crime in its every phase, sometimes the consequence of poverty, too often of defective education, sometimes of a native evil instinct.

Lawless men and profligate women dwelt here in unison, confederates and partners.

It is to this quarter that we must, under strange and most mysterious circumstances, take our readers, on a night which will be long remembered by certain parties in or near Manchester.

It was a little past midnight, and that part of the town was as a city of the dead—not a coach or cart wheel, not a human footstep, not a voice, not a dog baying at the moon, not even a dissipated cock cheated by its brightness into crowing! One might have fancied one's self amidst the ruins of a deserted capital.

The street to which we more particularly allude was peculiarly dark and narrow. Its houses, doubtless in their day of some importance, were tall, and thus added to the gloom. They, too, appear deserted; for not the faintest glimmer of a light was to be seen, which made the unearthly stillness almost awful.

Awful, yes!

In the placid meadow, in the calm seclusion of the country, such stillness would have been sublime; but in the vast emporium of commerce it was awful.

Suddenly a dark shadow appeared to flit along the wall as if seeking to hide its form.

It was that of a man in a cloak and slouched hat, who kept his head all the time turned cautiously over his shoulder, as if he feared that some one was following him.

Not the faintest trace of his countenance could be seen.

Suddenly he halted, and disappeared as if by magic.

And again all was still, though had any one been present they might have felt that the spirit of evil was brooding over the place.

A keen and practised ear too, might have heard a strange murmuring overhead, such as we have of a summer evening distinguished falling from the summit of a street in Venice—but then it was the whispering of lovers.

And this was not.

Then the click of a door might have been heard, a faint stream of light, and a man came jauntily forth.

He appeared to have no concealment about him, but strode along without hesitation as without fear.

But what is this phantom that crouches behind, creeping, crawling, like the slimy serpent of the forest?

It is the foulest spectacle that walks abroad, the hideous shadow of murder.

Thud!

The blow is evidently struck by one who understands what he is about.

The man fell upon his face, groaned, and lay utterly still.

Then the assassin opened a small dark lantern, and turned his victim on his face.

He was quite dead. The blow had been aimed with fearful accuracy.

The murderer listened cautiously, and then began rifling the pockets of the deceased.

He then cast cloak, hat, and knife on the ground, and walked away.

The fearful, the terrible deed was done.

Another murder was added to the list of those crimes which the law so vainly tries to check by means of strangulation.

We should almost be inclined to think that the first lawmaker was a Thug.

CHAPTER II.

THE BLUE DRAGON.

A cosy, respectable inn was the Blue Dragon, and much frequented in those days by most peaceable and decent individuals.

Its parlor was renowned for its conversation, especially on political matters.

Its frequenters were small tradespeople of a tolerable, well-to-do character, who, as evening drew in, leaving their spouses to take care of home, came here to enjoy the pleasures of a pipe, glass, and social conversation.

The oracle of the room was one Phineas Bristowe, a most sedate, not uneloquent, but at the same time, oily individual, who added to his business as a coal and corn dealer, that of preacher.

Now far be it from us to ridicule all those earnest zealots who leave their cobbler's, carpenter's, and other benches, in obedience to a call of the spirit; but we may be allowed simply to suggest that, as the professions of law and medicine require a long and consecutive training, so does that of teacher of the Truth.

But Phineas Bristowe was not of the same opinion. In the intervals of business he had obtained smatterings of knowledge, and had learned by heart or rote a very large number of quotations from the Scriptures, and this he thought amply sufficient to qualify him for the post of teacher of men.

And a fanatical and fierce teacher he was, dealing curses and damnation instead of blessings; and as usually is the case, rallying round him in consequence the ignorant, the weak, and the hypocritical.

Of middle height, under forty years of age, with narrow forehead, hooked nose, grey eyes that protruded from his face, a large and sensual mouth; this teacher of the gospel was accepted in that room as an oracle more by the loudness of his tones, than from any inherent talent in the man himself.

He had so long browbeaten the room, that people had got used to it, and would receive his castigations with rejoicing.

And, then, most of those present were elders of his church, or members of his peculiar congregation.

It was eight o'clock in the evening, and the parlor was tolerably full. Wreaths of smoke curled gracefully upward towards the ceiling.

The oracular despot, who sat in the easy chair beside the fire, was in the middle of an argument; his sayings were much enhanced in power by the fact that on this occasion he wore large green spectacles, which gave him an air of wisdom, in the same way we suppose, that large eyes are supposed to give the same quality to the owl.

Suddenly the door opened, and there entered the room a person on whom all eyes were instantly fixed.

He led by the hand a little boy.

Travel-stained, sunburnt, with moustache, long hair, and bushy whiskers, he yet, both in appearance and manner, looked a gentleman. His erect form, well chiselled face, and that indefinable something which can only be attained by long association with educated and polished society, was stamped upon him. There was something too of military frankness in his mien as he bowed gracefully to the company.

The boy was about eight. He too was slightly tanned, while, softened by youth, there was an unmistakable likeness to his father, as all at once decided the elder stranger to be.

His hair was dark, his eyes black, and his countenance tending to the oval, while the whole expression of his face spoke of candour and a generous nature.

"Will any gentleman inform me if Mr. Phineas Bristowe be present," said the stranger in a mellifluous voice.

The man in the spectacles rose as if by the action of a galvanic battery. His face seemed flushed with eagerness and surprise.

"That is my name," he said.

"May I, then, request the honour of your company to supper," replied the stranger ; "I have business with you."

"Pressing ?" said the other, hesitatingly.

"Very."

"Then excuse me, my friends ; I must join the gentleman," replied the preacher, but in such an odd, constrained tone of voice, that his friends and acquaintances exchanged curious glances.

Again the stranger bowed and left the room, followed by Phineas Bristowe.

The chambermaid was outside, ready to conduct them to a room where supper was ready laid.

Phineas stared.

"Good night, my boy," said the stranger, softly and gently.

The lad fondly embraced him, and then left the room with the chambermaid.

"I hope, sir," began the stranger, with a grave smile, "you will excuse the liberty I take; but I have been informed that from your official position in this neighbourhood, you may be able to give me some information I require."

"Anything within my poor means pray command," said the preacher, in the nasal tones he was wont to assume in the chapel.

"Let us first fortify the inner man," continued the stranger.

Phineas bowed ; and supper being hastily despatched, they filled their glasses, and turned towards the blazing fire.

They were in the month of April.

"I have," said the stranger. "returned to England, after an absence of fifteen years, in obedience to an extraordinary summons. Do you know Haddington Hall ?"

"Some eight miles to the westward ?" asked the preacher, musingly.

"Yes."

"I do."

"It is the property of Sir Thornley Haddington ?"

"I believe so.

"Well, my name is Marmaduke Haddington, heir to the title, if not to the estates, which are not entailed."

Phineas bowed.

"Now, I happened about fifteen years ago to have a deadly quarrel with my brother the baronet. The history of this quarrel I have no wish to narrate."

"And I wish to pry into no man's secrets, unless he needs consolation." replied Phineas.

"It is sufficient to say that this quarrel was caused, fomented, and brought to a climax by a white-livered knave, a canting, hypocritical scoundrel of the name of Beckford, a steward, secretary, and confidant of my brother. Now, I find that my brother is inclined to relent, is willing to take me by the hand, if I can but get the confession of this most monstrous and foul Iago."

"Which, I suppose, he will not give."

"I cannot find him. I went to Haddington. I found he had been ignominiously expelled the hall ; but I was told he had last been seen in this neighbourhood. Under these circumstances I inquired for some one who could guide me in my researches, and was referred to you. I was told that your visits to the haunts of poverty and crime were incessant."

Phineas bowed deprecatingly.

"I thought perhaps you might have fallen over him."

"His name was—"

"John Beckford."

"What kind of man ?"

"About your own height, but much thinner. He wore ruddy whiskers, his nose was hooked, but it was the cat-like green of his eyes by which none could ever mistake him."

The preacher mused, took a glass of wine, and rubbed his forehead.

At this moment the chambermaid came to the door, knocked, and informed Marmaduke Haddington that Master Henry would say his prayers to no one but his father.

"Excuse me, sir," said Marmaduke, with a glad smile, as he rose to follow the girl.

As the door closed behind him, Phineas Bristowe took off his spectacles to wipe his brow covered with big drops of sweat, and never did mortal eyes show such a cat-like expression. His countenance was livid, and hastily replacing the glasses, he drained two tumblers of port. Then he assumed a calm and placid look as he heard the other returning.

"May I be allowed to ask," said Phineas, when they were again seated together, "what your intentions with regard to this John Beckford may happen to be."

"I mean to make him confess—by fair means or by foul," replied the stranger, hotly.

"My dear sir," said Phineas in a reproving

tone, "you can scarcely expect me, as a minister of the Gospel, to acquiesce in any violence. It is totally out of my province."

"But if you will put me on the track of this miscreant," cried Marmaduke Haddington, "I promise to use none but persuasive means."

"I recollect during my career as a minister to have had the reprobate pointed out to me several times," said Phineas. "I am told he keeps a low gambling-house, or rather, they say, a magnificent hazard-table in one of the lowest streets of this quarter. If you will give me until morning, I will find his address."

"Sir, you have my most heartfelt thanks. You will remove a fearful load from my heart. But why leave me so hurriedly?"

"I intend making inquiries at once," replied Phineas Bristowe.

Marmaduke Haddington shook him warmly by the hand, and the preacher went out.

Why was it Phineas Bristowe tottered out of the room, nearly falling down stairs as he did so, and stood a moment in the passage, with shaking limbs and ghastly cheeks?

Nobody can possibly suspect. It is a deadly mystery.

No sooner was he in the street than he hurried to a small house close at hand, opened the door with a pass-key, and disappeared.

Ten minutes later an aged individual in a long greatcoat issued from the same *locale*, hurried to a livery-stables, and ordered out a post-chaise and four.

Half an hour later *two* post-chaises were darting along the highway in the direction of Haddington Hall.

Next morning early, Mr. Marmaduke Haddington received the following note:—

"*Silver Street. No. 13. Knock three times, at 12 p.m. The password is—'Starlight.'*"

And this was all!

CHAPTER III.

HADDINGTON HALL.

HADDINGTON HALL was a fine old Elizabethan mansion, one of those edifices built as if to endure against all time, and had been in posession of the Haddington family ever since the reign of that eccentric virgin, about whom historians have expressed such strange difference of opinion.

Its owner, as we have already been informed, was now Sir Thornley Haddington, a gentleman universally respected in the county; a magistrate, and more than once high sheriff.

For many years, however, he had lived in close retirement, issuing forth only on stated occasions when the duties of his office required him so to do.

From a gay and hospitable country gentleman he had become a silent, morose, and suffering invalid.

Besides the servants, none inhabited the hall, save his wife, and sister—a widow with an only son, universally considered the future heir.

Rumour spoke of a younger brother, a scapegrace and something more, who had mysteriously disappeared after trying to kill the baronet, at all events, after committing some monstrous deed which outlawed him from home for ever.

He had never since been heard of.

People said—and we all know what people will say—that his crime had been one of such a fearful and peculiar nature, as to have no name.

A nameless horror hung about his memory, and when he was spoken of, people shook their heads and looked very mysterious.

And now people began to cease to talk about him at all, and probably he would have been forgotten, but for certain events which we are about to record.

*   *   *   *   *   *

The baronet was very ill.

He lay in his chamber of state, attended assiduously by his wife and sister.

No hired nurse was ever allowed to come near him.

Lady Haddington was a pale, gentle, quiet, and evidently ailing woman of about forty. Every feature of her face denoted long suffering. You saw it in her eyes, in her wrinkles, in the corners of her mouth, but you saw at the same time, that the suffering was endured with angelic sweetness of character.

She never complained.

Mrs. Treherne, the sister, was a tall, dry, hard, bony woman, who looked as if she never could have shed a tear. Her small grey eyes, like those of a ferret, her unnaturally small mouth, her peaked chin, bespoke a nature selfish, grasping, and implacable.

She and her sister-in-law had very little communication one with another. There was something constrained and even fierce in their manner.

There was evidently some terrible secret in that house.

Until recently, until the sickness of the baronet, there had been no communication between the husband and wife for many years.

There appeared, however, now likely to be a relenting on both sides.

But Mrs. Treherne, the widow, was there.

The moment she discovered this fact, she never left them alone. On pretence of the delicate health of Lady Haddington, she constituted herself the head nurse, and though she allowed the wife to administer the medicines, she measured them out.

She slept on a couch in the room.

That is to say, if she ever slept.

She knew that the baronet had disinherited his brother, and any possible offspring he might have, in favour of her child.

She was not the woman to allow such a prize to slip through her fingers.

*   *   *   *

It was a little past ten.

The baronet slept.

The wife sat in an easy chair, watching her husband with eyes of anguish.

The sister sat at a distance, with a smile of scorn and triumph on her lips.

A gentle tap came at the door, and a woman entered.

In her hand was a note with which she walked across the room, and Mrs. Treherne took it mechanically and opened it.

Her face turned livid.

The attendant went out.

"What can he want—and at such a time?" she muttered. "But see him I must. All is still. He sleeps, and she is stupid with grief. No harm can be done in an hour. I will trust to my good star."

And she went out.

"No harm can be done in an hour!"

Every harm can be done. Ruin, desolation, murder, every crime can be done in less time, when there is fitting opportunity.

Aye, and good can be done, too.

The sister advanced towards the door.

"I shall not be many minutes," she said in a harsh voice, "only some orders to give."

"Thank you."

And the door closed.

"Merciful Heaven," gasped the poor wife, aloud, "oh! that he were awake, that in this dread hour I might convince him, as I hope to be saved and join him in heaven, that his brother was the victim of a most foul conspiracy, of which Beckford was the agent; that I might convince him how Marmaduke loved him, and at that very moment when this hideous tragedy was perpetrated, he was about to ask his consent to his marriage with poor Mary Dawson. Fool, fool! It was my fault. I did'nt know Thornley. I thought he might be offended at her humble station. Poor Mary—now in heaven—at least she left him one son to comfort and console. Would that I could die, if my death could convince Thornley that his brother was not only innocent, but the most devoted and loving of brothers. But it is too late; the wretched author of all this was far too cunning. That interview, when he begged me to intercede with Thornley, was so cunningly managed. My heart is breaking. Thank heaven, we shall be buried in the same grave!"

"Mary," said a sepulchral voice.

Lady Haddington placed her hand upon her heart, and caught up a glass of water.

"Did you speak, Thornley?"

"Mary, on your soul, as you live for heaven, as you deny Satan, is what you have just said true?"

"My husband, my beloved, my only loved," she frantically cried, snatching up a phial of prussic acid, infinitesmal doses of which were given to the patient, "bid me drink this, and with my dying breath I will swear—in presence of the dread Creator—that you have been deceived."

"Who by?"

"By Beckford."

"By who else?"

She held down her eyes.

"Finish your work," he said gently, but firmly.

"My beloved, it is my duty to the injured, or else I would not speak. I blush to say it. A part of the scheme was to prevent you're having direct heirs. Your sister coveted your inheritance for her son."

"Have you any proof?" he gasped.

Lady Haddington drew from her bosom a faded strip of paper.

The baronet held out his hand, he read:—

"*If all else fails, Beckford, she must be got rid of; but if he believes this story, they will be parted for ever.*"

"Merciful heavens," he cried, "come to my arms, my wife—*too late! too late!*"

And for the first time for fifteen years, the suffering wife and dying husband fell into each other's arms.

"But, hush!" he gasped, "*it is not too late.* Ring."

She obeyed.

A servant entered.

"Is Mr. Gibbons here?" he faintly asked.

"Yes, Sir Thornley."

"Show them all up," he replied.

"And now dearest, be calm. Do not excite me. I see it all. Heaven give me strength. Be silent, and watch."

His solicitor, the vicar, and curate, who had been sent for for a very different purpose, now entered.

"Bolt the door," said the baronet.

"Not a word, gentlemen, I have no time to lose," he added, turning to the new arrivals. "Have you my will?"

"Yes, Sir Thornley."

"Then, while the soul clings to the body, I am master. Write a codicil."

"Certainly, Sir Thornley."

There was nothing heard for some minutes but the dictation of the dying man, and the scratching of the lawyer's pen.

"And now, gentlemen, you are perfectly aware that I am of sane mind, that I have strong reasons for so doing."

"We are," they all cried.

"This letter, in my sister's handwriting—you, Gibbons, can compare it—is valid reason enough. If she disputes the will, produce it in court."

"Thornley!"

"Mary, has she not separated man and wife for fifteen years—did she not slay the innocent unborn—am I not a childless man, and shall I not be avenged?"

"Vengeance is mine, saith the Lord, I will repay," said the rector.

"True, true—but I feel faint. Read to me. I have done with the world. Wife, my own martyred, angel wife, take my hand. And now, Dr. Manders, the prayers for the dying."

And amid the choking sobs of his true and faithful partner the prayers were read in solemn and awful silence.

The door had been unbolted.

Mrs. Treherne entered hurriedly.

"Hush!" said the curate.

The widow glared at the dying man and his wife, and approached on tiptoe.

She saw even then that something had happened—but she feared nothing.

He was dying.

The solemn words were continued, and then the baronet opened his eyes an instant, looked at his wife with intense fondness, and closed them again.

He was dead.

"Some of your foolish nonsense, Lady Haddington," the sister began.

"Mrs. Treherne," said the rector, gravely, "at the last moment, when the soul was flitting, there was a holy and heavenly reconciliation. Heaven be thanked for all its mercies. And now let Lady Haddington be removed; she has fainted."

With a cold glance of contempt, Mrs. Treherne rang a bell beside her.

Two domestics appeared.

"Remove Lady Haddington to the Blue Chamber," she began.

"To the Orange," said the rector, quickly; "I am one of the executors under the will. Let the turret-bell be tolled at midnight, for Sir Thornley Haddington has departed."

Mrs. Treherne stood pale with astonishment and passion. The Orange Room was never occupied by any but the dowager ladies of the house of Haddington.

She was alarmed at this, even more than at the strange and inexplicable reconciliation of husband and wife.

CHAPTER IV.

THE GAMBLING-HOUSE.

LITTLE or big, great or small, carried on in cellars or in palaces, the hells which spread devastation and slaughter through the land are all the same. They may be squalid or splendid, they may be frequented by drunken middle-class men or blacklegs and nobles, they level all.

'Tis the same haggard, miserable, wretched look everywhere.

Pale faces, bloodshot eyes, quivering lips, the very soul fluttering on the mouth, wild exultation, and the very bottomless depths of despair, all are to be seen alternating on the coun, tenances of those who follow in the train of the worst vice ever invented by the strange imagination of man.

For this vice, whatever the other foul propensities of our nature, is of our own making.

The man in the cloak and hat was punctual to his time.

He knocked thrice, at brief intervals, at the door of the miserable house, and a wicket opened.

But no light could be seen, nor did any one appear.

"Who knocks?" said a thick voice.

"Starlight!" was the reply.

Like magic the portal flew wide open, and a passage was revealed. The man shuddered, but recovering himself, entered. The door closed behind him.

"Follow me," said the thick voice.

A faint glimmer of light now guided them on their way.

A second door was reached.

The guide rang.

It opened, and a few whispered words were exchanged.

The porter then made way for the stranger, and pointed to a green baize door.

The stranger passed on, pushed against the new impediment, and stood almost dazzled by the scene. Next moment he had glided among the throng of gamblers unnoticed, unperceived.

In the time of which we speak, the taste for gambling was at its very height. Men who had made fortunes by the war, appeared as anxious to lose them on the hazard of the dice, as they had been anxious to acquire the means they now so idly squandered.

Besides, in all great commercial cities there is a gambling element which must be satisfied somehow.

So the Greeks, who risk hundreds of thousands on a rise or fall in the price of corn, will also hazard hundreds of pounds on a card.

We could tell some strange stories of this kind —perhaps we may in the course of our narrative.

The room was large and well furnished. A chandelier illumined it over head, while other lights were fastened against the wall.

There were men of all ranks that may be found in a great commercial city present.

There were bankers, merchants, brokers, agents, blacklegs, and professionals.

But the stranger had no eye for any of these. He walked carelessly about, as if watching the game, but in reality in search of one well remembered face.

He could see it nowhere.

He examined every official connected with the establishment, but not one presented the slightest resemblance to the person sought.

The stranger's brow grew dark, and with affected carelessness he sat down and ventured a few pounds on the chance of the game.

As he rather wished to lose, it was rather singular that he did lose.

Having thus satisfied his conscience, and paid his footing, he went up to an attendant who was laying out a costly supper.

"Is not Mr. John Beckford here to-night," he said, pouring out a glass of wine.

"No, sir."

"Oh, indeed—I am sorry for that. I came here on purpose to see him."

"He is not always here, sir. He was to-night called away to London on particular business; he will be here the day after to-morrow."

"Oh, never mind," said the stranger, "I will call in again. Seems to be a deal of play."

"Pretty well, sir."

"Good night."

And with a careless mien the stranger moved away, passed out of the door, gave each of the guides or porters a handful of silver, and issued into the open air.

*   *   *   *   *   *   *

Who has not heard the distant, faint hum of the supernumeraries on the stage, low, distant, and hollow, as they do the mimic shouting of an army advancing in battle array, and who has not noticed how quickly the rumours increase, until it gushes forth, a terrible, an awful, almost a real shout?

So it is with the *vox populi* when murder has been done.

At dawn of day two workmen proceeding to their daily avocations, found the body of the unfortunate man lying on its face in the street, not twenty paces from the fearful den of Mammon.

"Murder!" was the cry.

Then came others rushing in hot haste, and as if on the very sky the fearful deed had been written in letters of blood, the whole city took it up.

Murder!

It was the talk of every place where men do congregate in less than two hours after the first discovery of the body.

Meanwhile, the officials had raised him up, and drawn by we know not what terrible instinct, had taken the corpse to the Blue Dragon, where the clothes were at once recognized.

"Our lodger!" cried the landlord.

"Poor child!" said landlady and chambermaid in one voice.

Then they looked at the face, as the head shook from side to side on the shutter, and they could not recognize it.

The features were eat away by some fearful corrosive substance.

Besides the knife, vitriol had evidently been used.

They bore the body into a large room used as a club-room, and—Heaven forgive him, for it was his nature—the landlord began at once to think of lowering his liquor, in expectation of the vast concourse of people who would be rushing to the house.

Suddenly a child, half clad, pale, and agonized, appeared at the top of the stairs.

"What is the matter," he cried; "is my pa come home yet?"

There was a dead, a fearful silence. Not one in that rude crowd dared answer the questions of that poor boy who had awakened from his sleep, disturbed by the noise, and found his only parent, beside whom he always slept, absent.

"Your pa's all right," suddenly said a soft and consoling voice, as Phineas Bristowe, with a meaning and warning glance at all around, ascended in the direction of the lad. "Put on your clothes, and I'll take you to him."

"The good man—"

"The worthy man—"

"Just like Phineas."

Such were the exclamations of the crowd, as the preacher ascended to where Henry stood.

Henry dressed eagerly, and as he did so, Phineas spoke.

"Your father has been detained," he said; "but he will explain all. Do you know where he put his pocket-book?"

"No, sir; but that's all the baggage he's got," pointing to an open trunk.

Phineas searched it all over, and found nothing, not a scrap which could identify the owner. But his hands clutched a purse, which he unhesitatingly thrust into his pocket.

Then he took the boy by the hand, and led him through the busy throng.

All made way with more respect than they would have shown to a king.

Was not that boy the child of the murdered man, and as such was he not the subject of legitimate British curiosity?

And then there were many with genuinely feeling hearts in their bosoms.

"We shall want you, sir," said an officer respectfully.

"Why?"

"You saw the gentleman last night, and your evidence will be important."

This was whispered.

"Certainly; I will but leave him in the care of *my daughter Jessie*, and then return."

The officer bowed.

But this is not the place to introduce Jessie to our readers. She will require a whole chapter to herself, for is she not our heroine, JESSIE, THE MORMON'S DAUGHTER?

And such a heroine!

CHAPTER V.

THE INQUEST.

IT happened that the inquest could not take place that day, the coroner being engaged elsewhere.

In the meantime it was said that the murdered man was no less a personage than Marmaduke Haddington, or, as he would have been styled, Sir Marmaduke Haddington, baronet, heir of Haddington Hall.

Imagine the excitement.

A man, who, had he lived but forty-eight hours longer, might have been the undoubted heir of one of the finest mansions in the county, and an estate of £20,000 a year, to be found assassinated in the streets of Manchester.

Rumour with her hundred tongues was at once alive, and when at twelve the next day the inquest was opened, it was with difficulty an open space could be kept near the doorway to permit ingress and egress.

The coroner took his seat, the twelve good men and true were sworn, and the beadle in a hoarse voice called for silence.

The coroner made a short speech, and then called the two labourers who had first discovered the body.

They simply deposed to the fact, and to their running for help.

Then came the landlord, landlady, and chambermaid.

Their evidence puzzled coroner, jury, and public.

They all swore to the clothes of the deceased, but all three, though examined separately, declared that there was something, they could not tell what, which made them unwilling to take oath as to the identity of the body.

"What is that something?" said the coroner, almost angrily.

"Don't know," said the landlord.

"Don't know," said the landlady.

"Don't know," said the chambermaid.

"Very strange," exclaimed the coroner. "I suppose it's this atrocious vitriol has so changed him. It has singed his hair and whiskers. It has, indeed, disfigured him. But we shall see. Call Mr. Phineas Bristowe."

The preacher entered, and was sworn. He took the oath in the most solemn manner.

"Look at the body," said the coroner.

Phineas advanced, and the sheet was removed. He gazed at it with awe and reverence

"Have you ever seen that person in life?"

"I have."

"When?"

"Night before last."

"Tell us what you know about him."

Phineas told what many present knew, and then went on:

"When we were alone, he told me, to my great amazement, that he was Sir Thornley Haddington's long lost brother; that hearing of his brother's illness, he had returned to England, as he was next heir, and wished me to intercede with somebody, to obtain an interview with his angry brother. I expressed myself surprised, but yet, as a minister of the Gospel, agreed to fulfil his wishes. I then retired, and intended going over to Haddington, when the news came of the baronet's death."

At this moment an officer produced the letter giving information relative to the Silver-street gambling-house.

"This is strange;" said the coroner, "who could have sent him there? I recollect some strange rumours about the habits of Mr. Marmaduke Haddington. At all events, I impound this document; it may lead to a discovery of the den of infamy near which this awful crime was committed. Next witness."

In walked the boy, deathlike in his paleness, only supported from falling by a child of his own age, all golden curls and blushes, who, as he tottered along, whispered words of comfort and condolence.

It was Jessie; but we cannot pause to describe her here.

"Well, my little man," said the coroner, kindly, "do not cry. I am very sorry to see you here, but it cannot be helped. I suppose you say your prayers?"

"My—my—my—" and he sobbed aloud, while scarcely a dry eye could be seen in the room. "my father taught me to say them every night."

"And you knowing what an oath is, would not tell a lie?"

"I don't know what it is—" said the boy, pushing back his dark curls, and looking proud even amid his tears.

"I mean, that having sworn to tell the truth, you will answer every question truly."

"Shall I tell you the story of Ananias," replied the boy in a low tone.

"That will do—swear him."

Amid the most profound silence, and even awe, the child was sworn.

"Your name?"

"Henry Thornley Haddington."

"Your parents?"

"Marmaduke Haddington—and Mary, his wife," he continued sobbing, "she has been dead two years; and he—"

His eyes fell on the white sheet, he closed them, and shuddered.

"How old are you?"

"Ten, sir."

"Where were you born?"

"At Madras, in India."

"Well, my little man, I am very sorry to force you to do anything so painful, but you must view the body. Don't be afraid."

"I never was afraid of my pa, living; and I'm sure I shan't be, dead," sobbed the boy.

They raised the sheet timidly, and as he pproached, the humming of a large fly was distinctly heard in the room.

The boy clasped his hands wildly, and gave a shriek which pierced the very roof.

"Be calm, my boy, and tell me if you ever saw that person before."

"NEVER," passionately cried the lad; "that is not my father. How cruel! why have you told me that he was dead? It is not a bit like him."

"These are his clothes—but stay, give the lad a cordial."

One of the breathless audience fetched a small glass of noyeau. Henry gladly drank it.

"But, my lad, the wicked men who killed him, have burnt his face with vitriol."

"I never saw that man before. He has got my father's clothes on; but see, by all the love I had for him, by the dear hope that he lives, I swear on my solemn oath, that is not my father."

"What makes you think so?"

Calmly now the lad walked up to the dead body and turned down the sheet.

"My father was stouter, better looking, and had much darker hair."

The interest was intense. All looked at one another. The coroner and jury were puzzled. The boy's genuine grief, now so quickly subsiding, utterly puzzled them.

At this moment a terrible bustle outside attracted attention.

"Make way! make way!" said the officials.

"Where is he—let me see him, my dear, my beloved brother?" shrieked a lady in deep mourning, but with every mark of rank and fashion about her.

The coroner rose.

"I have the honour of addressing—" he began.

"I am Mrs. Treherne, sister to the late Sir Thornley Haddington. A fearful rumour has reached my ears—my youngest brother."

"Compose yourself, madam. There appears to be a doubt. The son of Mr. Marmaduke Haddington positively denies the identity of the body."

"Son!" said Mrs. Treherne, with a stare, "my poor brother Marmaduke was never married."

"Who dares say that?" cried a firm but shrill voice.

"I do, sir."

"My name, madam, is Henry Thornley Haddington, and my father only two nights ago showed me his marriage certificate," cried the boy, indignantly.

"My good little boy," said the widow, gently, "if it be true, indeed, I shall welcome you to my heart. But as I never heard of any such marriage, please to tell me where it—"

"I don't remember," cried Henry, bursting into tears.

"I should think not."

A thrill of horror went through the crowd. Mrs. Treherne felt she was losing ground.

"Pray let me see my dear brother," she said, casting up her veil, "and this matter can be discussed afterwards."

She was sworn. She then advanced towards the body with half-averted head.

Then she glanced quickly round, and rushed back wildly.

"I could swear to him amongst a thousand," she said.

"Do not believe that wicked woman," cried Henry, indignantly, "who says my father and mother never were married."

And they did not. Great is the power of the innocent.

The verdict was:—

"We find that the crime of wilful murder was

A MORMON MIRACLE.

committed (*by some persons unknown*), on the body of a gentleman, supposed to be Sir Marmaduke Haddington, but which there is no evidence to prove."

Who was right? The poor boy who refused to believe these mangled remains to be those of his father; or the sister, who had known him from his birth.

If not Marmaduke Haddington, who then was he?

If not Marmaduke, where, then, was the father of the boy, and why was he left alone.

The coroner bade them calmly reconsider their verdict.

The jury retired; and while they were absent, Mrs. Treherne requested Phineas Bristowe to take care of Henry until his claims were properly sifted.

Henry retired without making the slightest resistance.

After an hour of intense excitement, the jury returned with a verdict still unsatisfactory.

"We find a verdict of wilful murder against some person or persons unknown, committed on the body of a gentleman, supposed to be Sir Marmaduke Haddington."

And they refused to alter their verdict. But what cared Mrs. Treherne : she knew the contents of the will ; she had the estates ; all she wanted was the title.

CHAPTER VI.

READING THE WILL.

IT is not our fault if this be a dismal history, made up, too, of terrible and wild adventures by flood and field. We invent nothing.

Even in recording, exposing, and explaining the foul and wicked mystery of Mormonism, that filthy blot upon the civilization of the age, we shall neither exaggerate nor extenuate.

It would, alas ! be impossible.

We shall simply bring to light fearful and horrid crimes.

Some have mildly alluded to this blot on the sects of our day, as a mere excuse for excuseable polygamy.

That is bad enough ; a crime in the eyes of God and man. But this horrid iniquity is but another name for indiscriminate prostitution.

Talk of the mysteries of a Turkish harem, they are as nothing to what we shall evolve in the course of our narrative.

Our details will necessarily be somewhat prurient, but the whole system is one of pruriency.

We approach the subject with horror, but a stern sense of duty upholds us.

No one who reads our pages in earnest, but will reject the plague spot on our civilization, unless he be a hardened profligate wanting a new sensation.

We shall have enough to tell our readers of the melancholy order. Let them, then, excuse us if we spare them the funeral.

It is over ; and in the library of the hall are congregated the lawyers, the rector, the curate, Lady Haddington obscure in an arm chair, Mrs. Treherne in the front place triumphant, scarcely caring to conceal her pride.

And her arm is round the neck of her son William Treherne, the heir expectant of the whole of this mighty fortune, a vicious, mischievous, cruel little boy of eleven, already the terror of the hall servants.

Behind stand some distant relatives, poor relations.

Round the doors stand the whole domesticity of the castle.

They all loved their old master, and above all their suffering mistress ; but alas ! for poor human nature, they were but too ready to throw up their caps for the victor, let that victor be King Richard or King Henry.

The lawyer majestically waved his hand for complete silence.

This was the will, divested of its legal phraseology :—

"I Thornley Haddington, being of sound mind and body, do hereby, for reasons which I do not think it wise or prudent to explain—reasons which would horrify all who heard—disinherit of all real and personal property, my brother, Marmaduke Haddington, his heirs, and assigns. I do not even leave him a mourning-ring. Let the title suffice."

Mrs. Treherne's eyes flashed fire, the domestics held down their heads.

"To Lady Haddington I leave the dower house and five hundred a year."

Lady Haddington did not even raise her head.

"My estates in England, Scotland, and Ireland, my personal property of all kinds, I hereby devise to my sister, Martha Treherne, in trust for her son, William Treherne, on condition that he takes the name of Haddington on coming of age."

Again the lady's eyes flashed, and the lad looked haughtily around.

The domestics tried a faint cheer, it was a failure. Mrs. Treherne smiled. They were in imagination already dismissed.

Then followed liberal legacies to all his domestics.

A cheer followed this announcement.

" Really—" began Mrs. Treherne.

" Allow me, madam, to finish," said the lawyer, bowing very stiffly.

Mrs. Treherne trembled, and leaned back in her chair.

" Then follows a codicil," said Mr. Gibbons, " signed by the late Sir Thornley, on the night of his death."

" Some imposture," cried Mrs Treherne.

" Madam," said the lawyer, "I drew the codicil myself, in the presence of our worthy vicar and his curate."

Mrs. Treherne's teeth chattered. A strange, vague, and mysterious dread was upon her. She leaned back in her chair, and drew her ill-favoured son close towards her.

The lawyer read the codicil out, in a slow and measured voice.

"I, Thornley Haddington, do hereby, in the presence of competent witnesses, revoke every clause in the above will, except such as regards my servants, and do hereby declare that the whole of my property, real and personal, is left to my dear wife, in trust for my brother Marmaduke, his heirs and assigns—reserving to herself an income of five thousand pounds per annum, during her natural life.

"To Mrs. Treherne I leave an annuity of two hundred pounds a year, for her life, and that of her son, with the dower house ; and may she live long to repent the deep injuries she has done me and mine."

" By heavens !" cried Mrs. Treherne, starting up, pale, haggard, and with clenched hand, " this is either a forgery or some foul and malignant falsehood has been told to my brother."

" Madam," said the lawyer, coldly, " you are accusing both myself and these gentlemen."

" The law will decide between us," she continued, actually foaming at the mouth with impotent rage.

" As you please, madam," replied the lawyer, coldly. " I have the late Sir Thornley's instructions with regard to that. This letter will satisfy you as to his reasons."

And he held before her eyes her own note, addressed to Beckford, the former steward.

With a shriek, more like the cry of a lunatic than a sane person, she fell back in convulsions, and was removed from the room, still clinging to all she loved on earth, her son.

Then burst forth from the servants a hearty cheer that was with difficulty repressed.

CHAPTER VII.

THE PREACHER'S HOME.

PHINEAS BRISTOWE lived in a detached cottage a little way out of town.

It was a neat eight-roomed house, and on the inside was a model of cleanliness and good management.

It was tenanted, in addition to its master, by his wife, Jessie, and a servant girl named Susan.

Mrs. Bristowe was a pale, thin, wretched looking woman, of about thirty. She had once been very handsome, but some corroding sorrow had done the work of time. She glided about the house without speaking, except in answer to a question. Her face wore a look half wan, half terrified, and though when her husband was present she tried to look cheerful, it was always a failure,

He was stern and merciless in his manner to her, ordering her about like a slave.

She never complained.

If she ever shewed the slightest inclination to resist, one bend of his shaggy eyebrows, one glance at her child, was enough.

To Jessie his manner was patronizing, not affectionate.

Jessie was about nine years old, though indeed she looked a little more.

Never did pen do justice to female beauty. It is possible to describe almost everything else ; but round woman there is a something which it is not possible to define.

We may say that she had a high pale brow, shaded by golden curls ; we may tell you that her eyes were filled by an expression of exquisite softness, when not kindled by instantaneous fire ; we may add, that her face was the most winning and intellectual that ever secured the heart of man, and that to this she united a figure of the most graceful proportions, forming a combination of elegance fitted for a sylph : we may describe her rosy cheeks, her ruddy lips, revealing pearly teeth, and then you will have no idea of Jessie.

Let us, then, wait until she is a woman, ere we strive minutely to describe her. We shall have opportunities enough.

It was some evenings after the coroner's inquest. Henry, broken-hearted, but firmly satisfied that his father was alive somewhere, was listening to the prattle of the little girl, while Phineas Bristowe, by the side of the fire, sat with lowering brow, gazing alternately at his wife and the burning coals.

The poor meek, placid woman was sewing, scarcely ever raising her eyes from her occupation.

The domestic, a strikingly handsome girl, came in and out, exchanging strange glances with her master as she did so.

With lustrous black hair, eyes of the same hue, floating as it were in liquid fire, her face was one of those which irresistibly attract the voluptuary. As far as could be judged, her figure was faultless.

She looked, when she exchanged glances with Phineas Bristowe, the incarnation of volupty.

Presently she placed a cloth upon the table, and laid supper.

All this time no conversation took place.

"Make haste with your suppers," suddenly said Phineas, in a harsh, grating tone. "I want you all in bed. I expect to have visitors presently."

"Am I included in this request?" said his wife, meekly, and yet half sarcastically.

"Certainly," he continued, "my business is private. Susan will wait on my friends."

There was a faint flush on the woman's pale and cadaverous face, that went up to the very roots of her hair. She looked at Phineas, and was about to speak.

A terrible scowl, and a menacing though almost imperceptible glance at Jessie restrained her.

As soon, then, as supper was over, she rose, took the two children by the hand, and retired without a word.

Susan cleared away the supper things, and placed a bottle of spirits on the table. She then coolly mixed two glasses, and seating herself familiarly by her master's side, looked strangely into his face.

We have said that she was beautiful, but it was the beauty of the fiend.

There was an expression on her lips, which made even Phineas Bristowe lower his eyes.

"How much longer?" she hissed, rather than said.

"Bide your time," he replied rather evasively.

"Phineas," said the girl savagely, "I have loved you. When I first knew you I was, at all events, innocent in deed. By solemn promises and by arts infernal you have corrupted me, body and soul—*but where is my reward?*"

"I have promised, and I will fulfil."

"When?"

"I cannot say. I am not ready to leave this part of the world yet."

"Phineas Bristowe," continued the girl, rising and standing before him in menacing beauty, "recollect that I know you—that I could with a breath expose and ruin you. Think not I will much longer waste my youth and beauty here. You have given me to eat of the fruit of the tree of knowledge—I know my value. You have sown the seeds, be careful that you reap not the whirlwind. You have taught me the might, the magic power, of charms I little dreamed were made to tempt mankind. Make me wait much longer, and I will find another lover."

"Hush," said the other in a husky tone, taking her hand as if he would have drawn her nearer to him, "come here."

"No," she said, tauntingly, while she bent her eyes upon him in a way that maddened him, "never again until you have a right."

"Syren—sorceress," he said, rising with a flushed countenance, "what is the meaning of this?"

She looked at him calmly, nothing but the heaving of her beautiful bosom showing that she was moved.

"It means that I will submit no longer to the degradation of being *her* menial. You have taught me that love is the only real bond uniting man and woman—that marriage is a mere form. Well, so be it. I am, then, your wife far more than she is. Treat me henceforth as such, or we part for ever."

Phineas wiped the heavy drops of perspiration off his brow. This man could not be said to love. He had no conception of the meaning of the word. But he had conceived a violent passion for this girl, which perhaps might have faded away, had she not every now-and-then taken such freaks as this in her head.

"Susan, do not be foolish. The promise I have made I will keep. But you must be patient. I expect daily, hourly the message from the holy city. Then will all change, and I shall be free. Hush! away at once. I will speak to you presently. Do not go to your bed."

And he hurried her from the room.

He then opened the door, and admitted a figure wrapped in a cloak, her face concealed by a heavy slouched hat.

Phineas closed the door.

He then turned, and stood face to face with Mrs. Treherne, but Mrs. Treherne, so pale, so wan, so haggard, he could not restrain a sudden start.

"What is the matter?" he said.

"Lost! ruined! betrayed!" she replied, in hollow tones.

"How mean you, madam?"

"I mean that Sir Thornley is dead, the will has been read, and everything is left to Marmaduke Haddington and his children."

"But has he any?"

"Lady Haddington knows where the marriage took place—at least so she says," hissed Mrs. Treherne.

"Well, what then?"

"My son must inherit," she continued. "Thanks to you, Marmaduke Haddington is out of the way."

"Hush, madam, for mercy's sake," gasped the other.

"The boy must follow," added the woman.

"Madam," said Phineas, recovering himself by a terrible effort, "I have done much to serve you; but now you have lost the prize, *who is to reward me?*"

"Lost the prize! You are mistaken. Let this boy be removed, and I will soon get rid of Lady Haddington. My son, then, is sole heir. Phineas Bristowe, or rather—"

"Hush! madam—in mercy, hush!" he said, in tones of abject terror.

"During twelve years do you think I have been idle. I have saved thousands. Continue to serve me, and I will overwhelm you with riches."

"What am I to do?" he gasped.

"Ere the dawn shed its light on earth, let my son be heir!"

"What will you give me?"

"Two thousand pounds. Come to me ere dawn at the dower house, tell me all is over, and it shall be paid."

"It shall be done. But fail me not. Ere to-morrow, I must be far away."

"You pledge yourself to have no mercy?"

"I will have none," said Phineas, with a horrid grin. "Be at the lower window of the dower house at midnight: I will be there."

Mrs. Treherne rose, and without another word, went out.

Then Phineas Bristowe, pale, cadaverous, and with the heavy perspiration pouring down his face, called Susan, in a whisper, and bade her once more fill their glasses.

Then took place a conference between that pair, that demons might have shuddered to have listened to.

And as Susan listened to his plans, her eye lit up with unholy fire; nor did she now reject the proferred caresses of her master.

When they had taken two large tumblers more of brandy, both rose. Despite the spirits, their faces were white, of that colour seen but seldom except on criminals ascending the scaffold.

They opened the door leading to the upper chambers. All was hushed and still.

Slowly and cautiously they went up stairs.

Then wild cries were heard, and down presently they came running, with hair on end and ghastly faces, and straining eyeballs.

Neither spoke, but they acted in deliberate unison.

They dragged all the furniture they could lay their hands on, piled it with the girl's bedding, pieces of wood, broken boxes, and other inflammable things, to the bottom of the staircase, poured over it a quantity of turpentine and then, setting a lighted candle on the whole fled from the house, nor halted until they reached the entrance of a copse, at about a quarter of a mile distance.

They could see that the cottage was already wrapped in flames.

CHAPTER VIII.

RESURGAM.

WE must now change the scene to a spot which may or may not be familiar to such of our readers as were born in the earlier part of the present century.

It is in the great metropolis.

The hour is midnight. In other parts of London there may be people about; but here near the human burrow we are about to visit, all is still.

A narrow archway, not much more than four feet high, leads into some den of darkness, to which Erebus appears as light. But towards this spot every now-and-then, certain mysterious figures are tending. They all halt at the archway, look down it, utter some cabalistic word, and disappear.

Presently, two figures appeared, creeping along the wall towards the arch.

"Can this be the place?" said one, in a husky tone.

At this moment, a link appeared, carried in the hand of a dwarfish lad, revealing a narrow passage, about sixteen inches wide, and fenced on either side by old barrel staves, broken iron hoops, and rotten palings. Within this was what has been called a curious arrangement of puddle-holes, dung-heaps, cabbage-stalks, brickbats, and broken bottles.

"Does yer vant Master Sharp?" said the lad.

"Yes, my boy."

"Make haste, then," continued the other, a short, stunted, blear-eyed London boy, with every mark upon him of misery and intemperance, "they're a-coming it blessed strong to-night, and must shut early."

The pair—a man and a woman—made no reply, but followed the boy up another turning, until they halted at a low, square brick building, the door of which was open.

A man whispered to them; they shewed a card, and were at once admitted.

The door then closed.

They were in a kind of chapel, but a chapel fitted up in a way that would have astonished any but the knaves and dupes by which it was filled.

It was hung on all sides with alternate strips of white and black, so as to entirely conceal the windows.

At one end was a rude altar, round which stood a number of beetle-browed, thin, cadaverous-looking men, in white neckcloths and black clothes, excepting only one, who wore a long white surplice.

This was a man of about thirty, tall, swarthy, with terrible black eyes, and a look before which any moral woman must have quailed.

And yet the female part of the audience were nearly all young and rather good-looking girls.

They were seated on benches round the chapel, the centre being wholly taken up by a square kind of table, on which lay what appeared a corpse, covered by a white pall.

This was railed off, and surrounded by wax tapers.

The scene of blasphemy which follows—with other licentious scenes with which we must pollute our pen—let us not be blamed for, they must be exposed.

Beside the priest sat a man and woman, evidently absorbed in grief.

Then began the high priest in the white surplice.

His voice was musical, but vulgar. What his words were, we dare scarcely say. We but give some.

"Believe! believe! believe! or ye shall all be accursed. I come, the prophet of the true faith, to call you to the fold. Come! oh! come to Him; he has appointed for you a city flowing with milk and honey. This is the advent of the true Messiah. The book has been found, and the truth first discovered. Oh! do not delay—his chariot wheels are waiting for you. Come! come! come! And ye, my sisters, shall know that in the new Canaan ye shall not, as here, be slaves and toilers, but revel in delights and joys unknown to the worn out and rotting world. I am sent by the great and the good prophet, to whom the Lord has revealed himself, to summon you to Zion. All who follow the counsels of the elder shall be saved. You have come, as you think, to witness the burial of our sister. I say that ye have not. She is not dead, but sleepeth."

The congregation rose, half terrified, half incredulous.

"Be seated. It is given to me to raise the dead, to cure the blind and the lame."

Then, amid an awful stillness — the very beating of hearts being heard—the high priest approached the centre of the hall.

"Behold, all! that you may know she is dead."

And he pulled away the cloth, revealing, as he did so, the perfectly nude form of a most lovely girl, of about seventeen, to all appearance, however, quite dead.

A groan of anguish burst from all. The girls held down their heads—some in real shame, some to keep up the pretence.

The men looked on with greedy eyes.

Then some fell on the ground, sprawling and writhing, and uttering the most horrible blasphemies.

The priest slowly and methodically passed his hands over the whole person of the young girl, quoting Scripture, with disgusting levity, all the time.

The death hue on her face appeared to fade, and with a deep sigh, a heaving of the bosom, and a strange, startled look, the girl rose up on her elbow, almost as lovely, and quite as nude, as Venus rising from the sea.

The priest cast the cloth over her; and, amidst the most frantic and terrible excitement, started off with an impious hallelujah.

There was no doubt, whatever, that a very large proportion of the audience believed in the miracle.

They had been prepared for weeks, by the most wild and blasphemous announcements, for anything which could possibly happen.

The elders treated it as a matter of course; and, when several females had borne off the supposed reanimated corpse, gave utterance to some half-hour of the most vile blasphemy in his own praise.

"And now," he said, "let all depart in peace, save the elders and the elect. All who have been this night converted will join the first happy band about to seek the new Zion in the new country."

The door was opened, and the awe-stricken congregation departed.

There remained only seven elders, or apostles, or priests, and as many young and good-looking girls.

There were also the couple who had arrived last.

One of the elders walked deliberately towards these two.

"Well," said the elder, in a solemn tone, "you came to scoff—do you remain to pray?"

"Aye, verily," replied the other, and bowed low.

"And you wish to give your whole soul to the good cause?"

"Aye, verily."

"And thy sister, also?"

"Aye, verily," said Susan, with such a look at the elder as made him start.

The new converts to the saints were fitting diciples: they were Phineas Bristowe and Susan Mendip.

"Come, then, and ye shall witness the secret mysteries of the saints."

And he bade them follow him towards the altar. ——————

CHAPTER IX.

THE BAPTISM.

THIS is not the place to explain fully the doctrines of the rampant sect of imposters, knaves, lunatics, and wretched dupes, known to the world as Mormons. We shall have ample opportunity in the course of our narrative, to reveal their foul secrets and infamous hypocrisy.

We must let their deeds, however, speak as much as possible for themselves.

Disguise it as they may, the real aim of the whole thing is the debauchery of young women, and the installation of a system before which the harems of Turkey become scenes of pastoral innocence, and Plato's filthy propositions with regard to women, in his boasted republic, are almost moral.

We suspect that the first founder of the sect must have had some indistinct notion of grafting thus much of Paganism on a bastard Christianity.

The doors were made fast, and then the thin mattress on which the girl who had, in the eyes of the congregation, been restored to life, was removed, thus revealing a large tank full of water.

The women adjourned to a side room, to which an elderly female beckoned them

"Wilt join them," said the high priest to Susan, fixing on her at the same time, a burning glance.

"In what?" replied the girl, whose eyes had for sometime been fixed on the erect and stalwart form of the elder.

"Baptism," he continued.

"What am I to do?" she said.

Phineas Bristowe looked livid, and wanted to check the conversation. He began to have a strange dread of this man.

"Our sister has not yet been received into the church," he observed.

"We force no one," said the elder coldly, "we only summon the sheep to the fold, in the name of the Lord."

At this moment the seven girls led by a matronly-looking woman came forth, actually stripped to their last garment; they walked awkwardly, and seemed half inclined either to laugh or cry, they did not know which.

They had been told that in appearing thus before elders of the church there was no indelicacy. So said Plato, when he wished youths, and maidens to exercise naked in the gymnasiums. But the innate sense of modesty engrafted in all women, made them abashed. They did not dare to refuse, and yet doubtless if they could have gone back they would.

But their minds had been excited by the rabid picture of the joys that awaited them when once partners of the elect, which could not be until they had been formally received into the bosom of the church.

The women were promised every spiritual and physical joy the imagination of the preachers could devise. We know, ourselves, how revivals have been made use of to rouse evil passions, and how sadly they have brought religion into disrepute.

And the men.

"What reward have men who have faith to forsake their rebellious and unbelieving wives, in order to obey the commandments of God? *An hundred fold of wives in this world,* and eternal lives in the next."

Such are the words of one of the twelve apostles of the new religion.

There was a small ladder beside the tank, up which the bevy of lovely girls hurriedly ran as if eager to leap into the water, and thus hide their shame.

Then the elder approached, and opening a book, went through a hideous paraphrase of the ordinance of baptism, standing beside the tank, and feasting his eyes on the loveliness of the unfortunate and shivering girls.

During the proceedings, he ventured, unblushingly, on such assertions as the following:—

"The way of truth is so plain that a fool can point it out as well as anybody. Let those who are considered fools by their neighbours and relatives come to us—we will make them kings and priests.

"Let a man come to me, believe my gospel, and preach it, and all his sins shall be forgiven. He shall have riches, honours, and all the wives he wishes for in this world."

Presently the ceremony over, the girls hurried away to dry and clothe themselves; and when the elders followed them, they found a superb banquet laid out, with wines and spirits in abundance.

The girls had quite recovered, and looked with eager eyes, at the unaccustomed display of luxuries.

What followed it would be impossible to describe. Under the influence of the generous liquids, scenes ensued only to be comprehended by those who have seen a secret love-feast, a night forest revel at a revival or camp-meeting, or who has read the narratives of Louis XV.'s orgies in the Palais Royal.

And yet these girls had no conception of what in the future they had to endure.

Toleration is the great bulwark of our happiness and greatness. But cannot blasphemy and gross indecency be prevented?

We punish the recruiters for foreign brothels, cannot we restrain the crimps of prostitution on a scale so mighty as this?

CHAPTER X.

RETRIBUTION.

PHINEAS BRISTOWE was one of the few at the time of which we speak, who had been let into the mystery and true objects of the Latter-Day Saints, or Mormons.

This sect, which went about promising to its votaries salvation, a residence in the New Jerusalem on earth, and a seat in Paradise beyond the grave, never in its secret councils pretended to make their future residence other than a huge harem.

Phineas whose soul was steeped so low in bestiality, as to have fitted him for a Turk, with all his nameless vices, jumped at a religion which promised him unlimited indulgence in his passions.

He had been long in correspondence with Christian Whitmer, the elder, who had enacted the farce of resurrection ; and now that England was becoming too hot to hold him, he was glad to join a gang, whose chiefs when not " thieves, swindlers, and cut-throats," were knaves, imposters, lunatics, and silly and credulous enthusiasts.

He and Susan Mendip had been long preparing for flight.

Every penny he had saved in the world had been transmitted to an agent in London.

Hence his journey to the metropolis.

Christian Whitmer had introduced them to the residence of a respectable widow, who let lodgings.

Here they took apartments.

Whitmer had lived in the house some ten months, during which he had passed as a humble minister of the Gospel.

The widow and her daughter Mary, a handsome girl of about nineteen, had been quite won by his piety.

Without affrighting their ears by any heterodox opinions, Whitmer painted in glowing colours a country inhabited only by the elect, where none but sincere believers should congregate.

Mary listened to his rude eloquence with a charmed tongue.

Both mother and daughter had made up their minds to become pilgrims to the New Jerusalem.

Then came Mr. and Mrs. Phineas Bristowe, or, as they were called in London, Mr. and Mrs. Fenton.

By a previous arrangement, they made with the preacher one family.

All was ready for a ship-load of emigrants to start on their way.

Phineas was deeply anxious. A vague, but terrible presentiment of evil prayed on his mind. Christian Whitmer yielded to his representations, and a start was at last decided on for the next day but two.

Phineas Bristowe went out directly after breakfast to visit his agents.

It was his intention to turn all his money into bank-notes and gold, and to strap them round his person.

With this view he went out alone.

Christian Whitmer remained with Susan.

He had been seated, reading, when Phineas left the room, but no sooner was his back turned than he rose.

" Sister," he said, in a hollow voice, " I can bear this suspense no longer. You cannot love this man. Listen to me. It is my hope to be, if not chief, in the new nation we are about to found, at least one of its chiefs. You are too beautiful, too lovely, to be the companion of a being like Phineas Bristowe, say but the word and you shall be my queen."

Susan looked at him from under her eyelids. He was a fine man, above six feet high, and tolerably well-proportioned. Certainly, with a woman of her character, there could be little difficulty in deciding between him and Phineas.

" One of your queens !" she said smilingly and yet sarcastically.

" Susan, it is the law of our church, as it was

in the days of Abraham, that we take more than one wife, for no woman can be saved but through her husband ; but you will be my first, my chief, my only one."

She looked at him half in admiration, half in scorn, ere she replied.

" I take your pledge," she said, " but mind you, fail me not—I am no weak girl."

" No ! but a glorious woman. Glory and wealth shall be yours. You shall revel in palaces, and all around shall be your handmaids."

" And Phineas—how is he to be deceived ? The man loves me in his way."

There was a cold, odd glitter in his eyes.

" We can leave him behind."

" He is very rich."

" Ah ! " cried Whitmer with a sudden flush, " very rich is he ! Where is his money ?"

" He has gone to fetch it," she replied.

" Are we friends—do we understand one another ? " whispered the apostle in a low tone, glancing uneasily over his shoulder as he did so.

" We do."

" Then we must have the money first, and then leave him behind. Look here," continued Whitmer, taking a printed paper out of his pocket.

" What is it ? "

" The 'Hue and Cry,' " said Whitmer, fixing his eyes upon her with a meaning smile.

The girl turned pale, snatched the printed paper from him, and read.

It contained a full description of the person of Phineas Bristowe and Susan Mendip, and a reward for their apprehension.

Even this bold woman trembled and turned pale.

" Susan," said the elder in a low tone.

" Whitmer," she replied.

" Can I depend on you ?"

" You can."

" Then let us first secure his money, and then while I secrete you, I can give him up and claim the reward."

" And you will be faithful to me," said Susan, putting her soft arms round his neck, and allowing him to kiss her freely.

" I will, and to you only."

At this moment the door was burst open, and the widow and her daughter entered, the one red with passion, while the countenance of the other exhibited every token of the most abject despair, mingled with indignation and grief.

" Hoity toity !" said the widow, " fine goings on. Please to take youself off mum, don't allow no make-believe wives, no grass widows here. I'll tell your poor silly husband all about you when he comes home. As for you, Mr. Whitmer, I'm glad I see's through your deceptions—so please to pay up your bill and move."

" But, my good woman—"

" Don't good woman me," replied the widow ; " leave my house, you vagabond swindling—"

" Be cautious, madam," said the elder, in a stern and solemn tone ; " what you say is actionable. I shall not allow one of the saints to be insulted in this way. As to leaving your dirty, flea-bitten house, I am too glad."

" Leave it, then, at once."

" Oh ! mother," said the poor girl, clutching with her right hand the elder's wrist, and with her left her mother's hand, while her eyes were fixed with a most beseeching meekness on the Latter-Day Saint " for my sake—"

" Dare you to defend him ?"

" Unhand me," said the man, angrily.

" Let him go," shrieked the widow.

" Oh ! mother—he said he loved me—he promised to marry me, and—and—"

" And what ? " cried the poor widow, turning ghastly pale.

" I believed him," said the girl, bowing her head, and turning crimson to the temples.

" Let us go," said the elder, rather uneasily.

" Go," gasped the wretched girl, " and leave me. Oh ! I am punished, indeed. I was to be married to him directly we got out, and—and—in three months I shall be a mother."

The high priest uttered an indignant exclamation as he angrily pushed the girl from him. Mary became insensible. The mother fell upon her knees, forgetting in her great love for her child, all thought of anger, while Susan looked on coldly and unmoved.

" This is no place for us," said Christian Whitmer, taking hold of her arm, " let us go."

" Whither ?" cried Phineas Bristowe, advancing into the middle of the room, and glaring like a demon at the pair.

He saw at a glance how things stood. The instincts of his nature made him cling to Susan with intense earnestness. He was resolved, then, to combat for her to the last.

" Whither," repeated Whitmer, coldly; " shall I tell him Susan ?"

" Yes," said the girl, with brazen audacity.

And still in presence of these savage and selfish brutes, the mother tried to restore to consciousness her insensible child.

" To claim the reward for your apprehension," hissed Christian Whitmer in his ear.

" Ah !" said Phineas, feeling for a pistol, " that wretched girl has betrayed me."

" No—read," replied Whitmer, and with a fiendish grin, he pointed to the other's name in the " Hue and Cry."

With a wild cry, that rang through the whole house, Phineas turned and fled.

Whitmer and Susan, hand in hand—not like our first parents, but like fiends of hell—slowly crept down stairs.

Some hours later, there were in that house, side by side on a bed, a dead girl, a breathless babe, and a lonely and broken-hearted old woman.

To quote the words of Mackay, " A lustful and depraved apostle," had passed that way.

And such scenes are of daily and hourly occurrence in the land. Can no means be found to check the leprous progress of a scourge which carries in its track ruin, desolation, and death ?

Alas ! nothing but exposure can be of any use, and this the Press alone can accomplish.

CHAPTER XI.

THE FLIGHT.

HOUNDED to death!

It matters little what the deed and what the crime, the fugitive flying from punishment and suffering feels himself just as much aggrieved.

Phineas Bristowe, rushing from the miserable cottage of the widow whose hearth his comrade had made desolate, regarded himself as a victim of society.

His many crimes, his hypocrisy, his wretched past, all in his eyes were swallowed up by the thought of the base ingratitude of Susan and Christian Whitmer.

But if his hand was against every man, every man's hand was against him.

He was an outlaw, a felon, his life forfeit to the justice of his country.

Whither, then, should he fly? Where should he hide his head—he, assassin, adulterer, and thief?

In England he could not be safe.

He had heard dimly, by report, of this new Zion about to be erected into a new nation, and he knew, from what he had seen, that no amount of moral iniquity would unfit him for the citizenship of the holy city.

The huger the sinner, the more mighty the saint.

Like many another knave and imposter, he resolved to hide the scarlet robe of crime beneath the white tunic of religion.

But how to reach the promised land ?

His name was in every mouth, his description in every newspaper.

He knew not how it could be, but in the handbills which stared him in the face at every corner, crimes he believed utterly buried in oblivion, or secreted in his own bosom, were alluded to.

A penny broad sheet laid bare the naked monstrosity of his existence.

He must bury himself in some far distant land, where even his features should be unknown.

But how ?

No coach or waggon was safe, while, doubtless, every seaport was well watched.

The man, with his multitudinous vices, had the indomitable energy of great criminals.

He started on foot that very night for Liverpool. He dared not ask his way, and steered by the stars. He never showed himself by daylight, hiding in outhouses, barns, or on haystacks.

He lived upon raw vegetables torn from the fields, on berries, on one or two loaves stolen from bakers' carts.

If any met him at night, they gave him a wide berth, so appalling had became his look, so fearful his voice, so terrible his manner.

Market girls, whom he robbed of eggs and butter, spoke of him in an undertone for years after, and used his name as a scarecrow for children.

He glared at them as they passed with a malignant scowl, but hurried on, more terrified at the sight of a little child than all mankind were with him.

Ah! ah! 'tis a fine thing is crime—so jolly—so productive of happiness.

Men may sneer, but virtue is its own reward, and even in the very absence of the suffering which follows one.

Ragged, footsore, dirty, the very picture of degraded crime, Phineas Bristowe crept one dark

THE SECRET PASSAGE.

midnight into the huge city of Liverpool. His weary task seemed only begun. Now that he had reached the goal of his wishes, what should he do?

To obtain a passage on board a ship was most hazardous. What disguise could he assume? A sailor it would be vain to pretend to be. His thin, cadaverous face rendered a jolly farmer out of the question.

He was as far off safety as ever.

Did he remain without shelter until daylight, in all probability his race would be run.

Creeping, crawling, keeping in the dark shadows, he gained a cluster of narrow streets near the port of this mighty *entrepôt* of commerce, whence pour forth those thousands and hundreds of thousands, who would find occupation enough here, were England better governed.

A red light suddenly streamed across the wanderer's path.

Looking up, he saw that it came from behind the narrow curtains of a small beershop.

He listened. Not a sound came from within

He placed his trembling, nerveless hand upon the latch, and opening the door, peeped in.

A stumpy, hideous, leering Jew slept in an arm-chair behind the counter.

Phineas Bristowe saw that he was alone.

He was armed, and being utterly desperate, walked in and cast himself upon a bench.

"S'help me Mo!" said the Jew—and if an educated Jew be a gentleman, a low Jew is the incarnation of blackguardism—"dish ish a nyche vay to enter a chent's house."

"Give me food and drink," replied Phineas, in a tone so hollow, so awful, the man started.

"Mine got!" he said.

"Don't be alarmed—I have plenty of money."

"De monish is vergoot, mine frensh, but s'help me Mo! if you didn't just frighten Ishacs a bit. Ain't you been dead, mine frensh, and somebody forgots to bury you—eh?"

"None of your jokes," said Phineas, grimly.

The Jew handed him a ham-bone—he was not particular—some bread, and a quart of beer, which the other devoured most ravenously. While he did so, the Jew watched him attentively; and as his eyes took in every feature of the haggard, bearded, ragged, dirty fugitive, he glanced furtively at a bill.

"That will do," said Phineas, in a more natural voice, as he pushed away the bare bone and empty quart-pot. "I feel better. A bowl of punch and a pipe—"

"Don't shell spurrits," replied the Jew, "but to oblige a frensh, I getsch shome."

"Thank you," said Phineas, looking at him now with a coolness that astonished himself, "I'd rather not. Look you, Mr. Devil's-dust, or whatever your name may be, I don't mind telling you as a friend that I am the man for whom a paltry one hundred pounds' reward is offered on yonder bill—but," here he played with a pistol, "beware! The man who attempts to take me dies. I am a desperate man. But let any one get me safely on board ship, and I will give him five hundred pounds."

"Mine gosh—five hundred pounsh!" said the Jew, who had turned pale at the sight of the pistol, but whose dirty yellow face became livid at the thought of the golden prize, "ish it a fact?"

"If you read the bill, man, you will find that I am not accused of robbery. Whatever money I have about me is my own. I will honestly pay you the sum I have said, if you will get me secretly on board some vessel—hide me till the ship starts, and then leave me to myself."

"I vilsh do it—mine gosh—let me shee de monish," said the Jew as he opened the bar, and signed to the other to follow him into a little parlour, on the table of which stood a bowl and every material for punch.

"I have it all safe here in good notes of the Bank of England," continued Phineas, thrusting his left hand into his bosom, while with his right he clutched his pistol.

He then counted out five hundred pounds, and laid it on the table.

The Jew greedily seized the notes, and examined them with a scrutinizing eye.

"No mishtake," he said, with a hideous grin.

"Hand over," replied Phineas, sternly.

"Eh!" cried Isaacs, with a convulsive clutch at the crisp, though flimsy paper, "couldn't I shust keep a hundred pounsh?"

"If you like; but now to business."

"Dere is a fynsh ship shails to-morrow. De mate ish von frensh of mine. If you like—goshe on poard at vunce—eh?"

"I must be rigged out better than this," replied Phineas.

The Jew was prepared for every emergency. He then explained that the mate, "who was a friend of his," would wink at anything he did, and that if he liked to go on board, he could at once be concealed in the hold. The ship was almost in ballast, having only some two or three hundred barrels of porter below, with ballast and water.

About an hour later, Phineas, carrying a heavy sack of biscuit, while the Jew took charge of a keg of rum, crept out of the house, and made their way towards the port.

The vessel, a very large brig, had not hauled out into the stream, but was quite ready for a start.

The hatches were still open, though they would be battened down at daylight.

The watch on deck was asleep, and the Jew was able to creep on board, and descend the hatchway to the hold undiscovered.

He then produced a dark lantern, and with a terrified and anxious look, slipped between the sides of the vessel and some well-packed barrels, until they reached the bulkheads, which divided the cabins from the hold. Here was a narrow space not more than sufficient for one man.

"Be shtill, and don't shneeze, till you're out at she," said the Jew, in a strangely alarmed tone.

"I will be cautious," replied Phineas, with a shudder.

"De monish," continued the Jew.

Phineas paid over the notes, which the other clutched with frantic but silent exultation.

And so they parted.

Phineas was alone in the dark and gloomy hold of a ship, the destination of which even was unknown to him. This was an omission which struck him at once.

His tongue stuck to the roof of his mouth as he made the reflection, and he tried to call the Hebrew back.

But all he heard was a low chuckle as Isaacs hailed the sleepy watch.

What if even now he was going to betray him, and claim the reward?

Mechanically he turned a small spigot in the keg of rum, filled a horn by feeling with his fingers, and drained it to the last dregs.

In a few minutes he lay insensible on the floor.

It was hours, many hours, ere he awoke to consciousness again, and when he did so, he heard strange noises near him, and a scampering in all directions as he sat up.

Ah! ah! he was alone in the hold, with a keg of rum, a sack of bread, and a myriad of rats—and the hatches were on.

The motion told him, too, that they were out at sea.

———

CHAPTER XII.

A FEARFUL RESOLVE.

THE constitution of Mrs. Treherne's mind had always been very different from that of her late brother. Grasping, selfish, moody, and saturnine, she appeared to live only for what she could grasp at.

She had married for gold.

She was now selling her very soul for the same glittering dross.

As she walked that dower house of a night alone, she revolved in her mind more of crime than would have sufficed to stain the soul of a professional conqueror.

Mistress of Haddington Hall she intended to be, while that her son should be heir, was fully decided in the secret cavities of her brain.

But how?

Even the most active and energetic are compelled to descend to reflection as to the means.

Mrs. Treherne, suspicious in the extreme, had, after paying the heavy bribe she had promised to Phineas Bristowe, been suddenly struck with compunctions of conscience, not at the crime, but at the extent of the reward.

The deep sensation caused by the destruction by fire of the preacher's cottage, served her purpose. An inquest was held upon the matter, and a most minute search was made for any human remains. But not the remotest trace of any were found.

The examination clearly proved that the house had been set on fire purposely, and the clever detectives said, from the sitting-room.

It came out of course publicly in the course of the inquiry, that no human remains were among the charred wood and burnt bricks.

Then Mrs. Treherne knew that she had been deceived by the man in whom she had trusted.

He was, however, far away, and nothing was to be done but depend on her own exertions.

The dower house had been the ancient dwelling-place of the Haddingtons in days of yore, and though it had fallen to decay, and been chiefly rebuilt in a modern style, one noble room remained.

It was the picture-gallery.

The pictures themselves had been removed to the hall, but the gallery was untouched.

Here this evil woman would walk up and down of an evening, ruminating, thinking, plotting for hours.

She would stride from end to end of the gallery in perfect silence, but the hour came when she was loquacious enough.

Philosophers say that fish are mute by reason that they drink nothing but water. We have known many human beings who could never speak until they imbibed a certain quantity of the juice of the grape. Hippocrates says that it does a man good to get drunk once a month— Horace, that water drinkers never could write poetry.

Now we know not if Mrs. Treherne had ever consulted Hippocrates on the point, but this we do know, that she improved upon his receipt.

Mrs. Treherne drank daily.

Always in secret.

It was the only antidote to still the baleful sensation of her dead heart.

At nine, her son, and one female domestic, retired to rest. She then entered the gallery, locked herself in, opened a cupboard, and pulled forth a bottle of brandy.

She took a small glassful, and then walked slowly up and down, until she felt the need of further stimulants.

Gradually her visage began to glow, her eyes to flash, and her whole countenance to assume a diabolical expression.

Ha, ha! it is the demon of the drink at work, and it works well in woman.

"Avaunt thee, boy!" she cried out, at last— "thou art like thy father, it is true! But what matters that? Children have ere now been born out of wedlock. Marmaduke was never married—she may say it, if she will, but I know better. At all events, I will risk nothing. Better at the bottom of the sea or in the depths of the grave, than to wander in outcast poverty! Ah, ah! I will be very kind!"

And with a hideous laugh, she drained the burning drink once more.

"Where is he?—where can he have gone? That woman may know all, and take him to her. He must be found! 'Tis clear," she continued, taking up a copy of the very "Hue and Cry" which had so disturbed Phineas Bristowe, "the wife and husband have fled different ways. This is maddening! Marmaduke carried on a correspondence with her, that I know. Let her but find the child, and we are lost! No—but my task would be the harder."

Again she drank.

"What is to be done, whither shall I go? Ah! I have it," and she laughed long and loud. "Joe Galpin is the man. Away, then, to London. He must find them, or——"

And a demoniac smile passed over her haggard face.

"That man Phineas has played me false. I fear me more than once. Why have I never seen his wife?—and why does that child remind me of—"

She did not finish the sentence, but drained hastily another glass, clutched a candle, and tottered to bed.

But not to sleep. There is no calm slumber for the evil ones of this earth.

That is one of their worst, most bitter punishments.

And she dreamed a dream so like reality, it will serve to illustrate a portion of her early life.

In the days when she was young, and oh! how lovely, she had in the very pride of her girlhood, married Mr. Treherne, not for any love she bore him, but merely for his money.

She did more than not love him, she abhorred him.

It is a wicked and an evil thing for a woman to do, to marry when she loves not; to lavish caresses when her heart spurns and loathes, for surely it must one day be discovered.

But worse, she loved another, wildly, passionately, hopelessly.

There is a strange and perilous beauty in cripples. The younger brother of Mr. Treherne, relative to whom we have a most astounding and tragic story to tell, was not more than four feet and a half high. He was a dwarf and a hunchback.

His face was perfect as that of Apollo. His golden hair fell over a massive brow of dazzling whiteness—his soft blue eyes spoke of the most pure and yet passionate love—his mouth had the smile of an angel.

So humble, so gentle, so conscious of his infirmities.

His soul was as noble as his face was beautiful. There was not an atom of the crookedness of his body in his soul.

Mr. Treherne was a jolly, fox-hunting country gentleman of good estate, but without any of those fascinating qualities which a woman desires who is not satisfied with an honest man who looks to his home and children, without depriving himself of those amusements native to his sex and character.

But Mrs. Treherne, at that age, lived only for love. Her soul burned with the most ardent passions; and the frank caress of a husband who looked upon her with pride as the head of his house, sufficed her not.

She wanted some one to whisper soft nothings in her ear, to paint passion in glowing colours, to talk of forbidden joys, and woo her to them.

Her bosom was a volcano.

All this she thought she had found in the poetic soul of the hunchback.

Ha! what is this sight that makes her eyeballs glare wildly, her heart to stand still, her flesh to quiver, and her burning love to turn to hate?

A beauteous girl of twenty, pale and in tears, is seated on a bench in the park. Her dress is genteel, but lowly, but everything bespeaks the lady.

At her side is the hunchback, his face crimson with blushes, his eyes beaming with love as he listens to some terrible confession.

She has drawn near, she hears it.

The confession is indeed no uncommon one, a story of sin and shame, which it is our duty at a future time to record, but it touches deeply the heart of the noble hunchbank.

A pause, and then the maiden casts herself at the feet of the cripple, who raises her up, clasps her in his arms, and their lips meet in one wild, passionate, and intoxicating first kiss of love.

The demon has entered into the soul of the other, and she vows revenge, and when she vows, desolation and death are sure to follow.

Panting with rage, passion, and bitter regret, Mrs. Treherne woke, nor could she sleep for a long time, as she dwelt on these feverish images of the past.

CHAPTER XIII.

A DUEL IN THE DARK.

BITTERLY did Phineas Bristowe curse the haste which had made him enter that dark, gloomy, and subterraneous den without a light of any kind. He knew very well that his eyes would have gradually become accustomed to the darkness; but then, what of the rats? and besides, he was so habituated to smoking that he could scarcely do without it.

In his rage and despair he felt about, until his hand alighted on one of the porter-barrels.

By desperate exertions he contrived to take off one of the hoops with which to defend himself against the vermin which infested the hold.

Then he took a seat, and ate.

He had taken care to see to the position of the water casks.

His supply of water could not fail.

He ate his fill, and then disposed himself to think, a task above all unpleasant to one whose career had been so foul as his.

Suddenly he gave a terrific start, and almost shrieked.

He clearly heard the sound of another human breath, mingling with the plashing of the water on the sides of the ship.

A cold sweat burst out over his whole body, his hair appeared to stand on end, his breath came and went in fitful puffs, now stopped, now gasping.

He listened with all his ears, and presently detected its presence at no great distance.

He went on his hands and knees, after feeling for his pistol, and then began crawling towards the sound.

But the passage was too narrow.

The barrels, as he advanced, were placed nearer to the bulkhead.

He applied his ear to the slight opening, and listened.

The breathing appeared more and more distinct.

He determined to know at once the meaning of this joint occupancy of the hold.

Holding on the barrels, and feeling his way with extreme caution, Phineas Bristowe, who all the time scarcely dared to breathe, crept towards the centre of the vessel, underneath the hatchway.

He had put his spectacles in his pocket as useless.

When he reached the centre of the hold, a faint glimmer of light became visible.

It made the darkness appear more thick below.

Phineas Bristowe crossed the hold, still cautiously feeling his way with his hands. The ship was rolling and pitching under the influence of half a gale of wind.

In two or three minutes, however, he had reached the other side.

By the faint glimmer from above, and his eyes also becoming gradually used to the obscurity, he saw that there was no aperture between the barrels and the sides of the vessel, except by climbing over one barrel which stood on end.

Phineas bent his head over this, and distinctly saw—rapturous delight—that the other, whoever he might be, had a lantern.

He was doubtless a hunted fugitive like himself, and therefore there must be sympathy between them.

He resolved to seek his companionship and the use of his light.

He was about to climb over the barrel, when he perceived that it was empty and could be removed.

A transverse bar, about three and a half feet from the ground, kept the water hogsheads in place.

Clutching his pistol from instinct, and with his heart beating wildly, he stooped beneath the bar, and the ship just then giving a heavy lurch, he fell headlong forward.

Before he could rise, with a wild and savage cry a man burst from a place of concealment at the end, and flew at his throat.

"Who are you, what want you? Die, wretch, or speak?" cried the other in terrible tones.

Phineas Bristowe fell helpless back without a word.

The man mumbled some inarticulate words, and turned to fetch a small lantern which hung from a hook in the bulkhead.

Phineas rose to his feet.

He would have fled; but a fearful fascination held him still.

He must know the awful, the unearthly truth.

The man turned towards him, and these two stood in presence, face to face, pale as death, ghastly—and next instant both equally horror-struck.

Phineas felt his knees giving way beneath him—if he fell, he knew that he was lost.

The other stared at him with a glance which seemed to denote the maniac.

The face of this one was thin, white, and haggard. It had been close shaven, but a stunted beard and moustache made it look still more terrible.

A fiery red wig surmounted the crown.

"Ha! ha! ha!" he cried, "rare games. Are we already in hell that the foul fiend himself comes here to torment me? Speak! tell me, art thou Lucifer?"

Phineas backed slowly.

The other, his hand on one of his pistols, glared fearfully at him, gnashed his teeth, and slowly followed.

With a sudden and quick movement, for which the other was quite unprepared, Phineas knocked his lantern to the ground, and fled.

With a howl of rage, the other, just as the vessel was evidently struck by a huge wave that shook every timber, fired his pistol.

Phineas had expected this, and himself pulled the trigger.

The other was too quick for him.

The two pistols went off at the same time, and both fell to the ground.

With hushed breath, crawling along the planks, Phineas sought his shelter. He had been wounded in the arm.

He easily bandaged this up, but his mind had received a terrible shock.

The face of the maniac was ever before him.

A craving to see him when at rest came over his soul. He knew him, and yet he knew him not.

He listened with the most profound attention, but he could not even hear him breathe.

Then came another horror.

He might perhaps have killed him.

If so, the consequences would probably be terrible. At the end of his journey his presence must be discovered, as well as the disgusting evidence of his crime. The dead body decom-

posed, the pistols, the bullet, would all speak trumpet-tongued.

Decomposed! Yes, truly. But might not this breed some terrible fever?

Ha! ha! ha! They would both be found dead, the murderer and his victim.

A terrible fear came over the soul of Phineas Bristowe, and he resolved at any price to discover the truth.

But his purpose received a sudden interruption.

A sudden bustle on deck, a stamping of feet, a clanging of ropes, a hurrying to and fro, a fearful pitching and rolling of the vessel,—made him suddenly aware that something serious had happened.

The ship had evidently been attacked by a sudden and terrible storm.

He became really ill, and laid for some time helpless and stupified.

Then he drank deeply of rum until he slept—and this again, and again.

When he again awoke the ship was still rolling from side to side, but the worst of the storm appeared to have passed away.

Then Phineas again listened for his mysterious companion. He could not hear a sound, nor could he see a light.

He now once more clutched his pistol, and with every precaution he could use, crept round to the place of concealment of the other.

It was easily found.

Feeling with extreme caution he soon perceived that the barrel had not been replaced.

Surely the man was dead.

He prepared to crawl under, when, with a yell of triumph, the other flew at him.

Few words passed, but a deadly struggle ensued in the dark.

The maniac had Phineas Bristowe by the throat.

The preacher was so taken by surprise, that he struggled faintly.

"Ha! ha! ha!" shouted the maniac, as Phineas's arms relaxed, and he fell back. "I have you now, fiend—devil! Never again shall you torment my soul! But let me look at him."

And again he sought his light.

"Help! murder! help!" shouted Phineas, who had shammed, leaping to his feet.

And he rushed towards his hiding-place, shrieking at the top of his voice.

He had lost all control over himself.

"Ha! ha! ha! devil!" cried the infuriated maniac, "have I been cheated? Have at you. I will drain every drop of blood in your veins but you shall die!"

Phineas was silent as the grave. Abject terror taught him cunning, and instead of rushing to where his food and drink were, he climbed up a ladder, and struck wildly at the hatchway.

A faint light streamed through a chink.

With a knife he slit the tarpaulin through the opening in the wood.

One terrible heave with his shoulders, and the hatchway flew upwards.

Phineas leaped on deck frantically, the maniac the moment the light became visible, rushing after him.

Then commenced a terrible chase round the decks, which, however, at length ceased from sheer exhaustion.

Both at the same moment stood still, and both looked fearfully around them.

How awfully still was the ship.

Not a soul appeared on board. The masts were cut away, and the rigging hanging over the side.

The rudder was entirely gone, and she had sprung a leak.

As far as they could see, lay before them the heaving and illimitable ocean.

"Curses be on my fate," said the preacher, with a furious glance at the maniac, who stood with folded arms at a little distance, calmly contemplating the magnificent prospect.

"Curse not," he said, in a solemn tone, "for we are about to die. May heaven forgive you, as I do."

And the mysterious companion of Phineas Bristowe's seclusion, the companion of his still more awful ocean vigil, disappeared in the direction of the captain's cabin.

CHAPTER XIV.
AN OLD FRIEND.

No sooner was the resolution of going to London come to, than Mrs. Treherne determined to carry it out at once.

This woman, in the course of a strangely diversified career, had passed through scenes of the most extraordinary nature.

Despite her intense desire to interfere between her brother and his wife, she could not refrain at times from visiting London.

This woman had three passions, lust, avarice, and gambling.

Truly hers was an evil nature.

The woman who waited on her, and in whom she exclusively confided, was left in charge of the son.

This woman will be described at a future time.

No other attendant was allowed to sleep in the house, though two came for occasional service.

Alone, Mrs. Treherne entered the coach which was to take her to London.

She was very plainly though well dressed—she had the instinct of a lady who never wore gaudy finery, and disguised herself still further under a widow's cap.

She joined the coach at some distance from home, at a place where she was not known.

Her movements were necessarily mysterious.

She started about eight days before Phineas Bristowe's escape from Liverpool.

There was no one inside when she started—a matter she rejoiced in, as she preferred quiet, just then, to companionship with her fellows.

Her journey to London took place without an event of any kind.

She took up her quarters in a small inn near the Strand.

No sooner had night come than she hastened forth, wrapped in a cloak, and with a hat over her eyes.

She took her way towards the lower quarters of Westminster, then the abode of vice of all kinds.

She required no showing the way.

The man she was about to visit had served her in many ways during life.

Mrs. Treherne was much richer than people supposed her to be,—and much of her wealth this man knew the secret of. He had served her well at very critical periods of her existence.

He was well aware of deeds which would have led her to the very scaffold.

And what did she not know of him?

Passing by the abbey, she made her way to the Almonry,* then a low rookery, inhabited by the most wretched and abandoned characters.

Few women would have ventured to tread the precincts of that neighbourhood at night, knowing, as Mrs. Treherne did, the character of the inhabitants.

But Mrs. Treherne had no fear; it was a feeling unknown to her energetic and masculine nature.

In the centre of the Almonry was a small shop, down two steps—a kind of receptacle for miscellaneous rubbish, old napless hats, shoes guiltless of soles, and often of uppers—garments, male and female, of the most indescribable nature—old iron, tin ware, pictures, clocks, brass rods—a medley of apparently useless rubbish.

Over this presided a little, thin, blear-eyed man, of about seventy, so wizened, and apparently so old, as to be incapable of motion. The whole of his garb was not worth a groat, while the hairs on his head would not have spoiled the beauty of a virgin's chin.

He was bent double, and coughed incessantly, especially when trying to speak.

"And what, my little lady, can I do for you?" he said in a cracked voice.

"I want to see Joe Galpin," she replied imperiously.

"Joe Galpin? Heaven have mercy on us, haven't heard of him for years!" answered the old man, shaking his head.

"Rueful Reuben," she continued, sternly, "it is of no use deceiving me! Joe Galpin is here, and see him I must! Ring the bell, and say: 'Our Sal' is here!"

The man's eyes flashed with peculiar fire as he rose, rang a bell close to his hand, and after waiting two minutes, whispered something up a tube. The answer came instantly.

"Be pleased to wait one moment," said the old man, with extreme civility.

He then bustled across the shop with alacrity, and closed the door.

This done, he returned to where he had been seated, and after diving in among a lot of old iron, took up a strange-looking handle. This he inserted into a hole and turned it. As he did so, the heavy fireplace and the wall above moved bodily on one side, and revealed a long passage.

* The Eleemosynary, commonly called the "Ambry." The first printing-press ever seen in England, was set in this Almonry under the patronage of Esteney, Abbot of Westminster, by William Caxton, citizen and mercer. The house in which he is said to have lived, called the "Reed Pole," and long an object of attraction, is described by Bagford as a brick building, with the sign of the "King's Head." It stood on the north side of the Almonry, with its back to the back of those on the south side of Tothill-street, and fell down, from sheer neglect, in November, 1849.

The old man took up the candle which alone illumined his shop, and passed down the passage but without turning his back to the lady, who, despite her evil passions and scowl, was still a handsome woman.

The old man looked at her with the utmost veneration. He had been a rare profligate in his youth, and tried to conjure up the memories of old.

At the end of the passage a staircase in tolerable good repair, with a coarse carpet, became visible, while Mrs. Treherne could see that the inner door of this house was sheeted with iron and covered with bolts and bars.

There was a light above, and with a low bow Rueful Rueben left the lady to find her way alone.

She walked forward, as if the place were familiar to her, until she reached the first landing.

She then entered a room in which at a desk was seated a man of about fifty, hale though slightly grizzled, his face expressive of cunning, duplicity, and wretched avarice. And yet he was not one of those misers who slave to amass gold merely for the sake of amassing.

He had a little villa somewhere, of a most luxurious class, to say nothing more; we may perhaps find ourselves there ere long.

"To what, my dear madam," he said rising, "do I owe this honour?"

"I want your services."

"They are always yours," he continued, placing a chair close to his hand.

"For a consideration," she continued, with a bitter sneer. "But never mind. That I am willing to pay, you know. Now listen to me. Sir Thornley Haddington is dead. Do not interrupt me. He found me out on his death-bed, and left all to his brother."

"Good gracious me, I thought—"

"All failed. One hour undid the work of years. But Marmaduke is out of the way—"

"Then, madam, I do not understand—"

"Sir, he has left a son, a boy about ten. I contrived to keep him back for a day or so, but now he has disappeared, and has fallen into the hands of a woman who probably knows all. She will intrigue with my sister-in-law, and I shall be ruined."

"What can I do in all this?" said the man, with a strange look.

"You have cunning, enterprise, and plenty of agents. You must find the woman, and by fair means or foul, take from her the boy."

"And what do with him?"

"He must not stand between me and mine," she replied in a hoarse tone.

"Madam," he said in firm but respectful accents, "what am I to have?"

"A thousand pounds."

"'Tis poor pay for so great a risk. I may have to spend money in abundance."

"Here is two hundred pounds as earnest money," continued Mrs. Treherne, giving him a roll of notes. "Spend it freely; but let the deed be done. When you find the boy, let me know; I will reflect on his fate."

At this moment a bell tingled thrice.

Joe Galpin put his ear to a pipe and as he did so turned pale and looked uneasily at Mrs. Treherne.

"I must ask you to retire for a short time," he said hastily. "A person whom I *must* see is coming up, he might know you again if he ever met you."

"I can go into the next room," replied Mrs. Treherne, with something like a blush on her face.

The man hastily rose, and taking a key, went out upon the landing. He then opened a door, and giving Mrs. Treherne a taper, ushered her in. She heard the key turn as he retired.

"Fool," she said with a cold smile, "as if I had forgotten."

And hastening to the side of the room, which was handsomely furnished, she applied her eye to a small bit of thick glass, that however gave a dim view into the next room.

Her ear was at the same moment brought into contact with an opening that allowed every word that passed to be distinctly heard.

Scarcely had she done so, when she covered her face with her hands, and looked even more haggard and wild than we have ever seen her.

"Merciful heaven," she muttered, "can the grave give up its dead!"

CHAPTER XV

THE COLONEL.

A HANDSOME man, of about forty years of age, with, however, a dissipated, jaded, and to use a common phrase, a rather seedy look, had entered the room, and cast himself, as if utterly weary, into a chair.

"Ah! ah! Joe," he said, with a bitter sneer, "so you perceive I am not dead."

"I see it," replied the other, in slightly tremulous tones, "to what—"

"There, none of your long phrases! Hand me the brandy-bottle, and you shall know everything,"

Joe pointed to a cupboard behind the visitor.

"Hang it, you're mighty polite to an old friend—might have helped me," said the other, rising at the same time and bringing forth the bottle and glasses; "but never mind, years make great changes in us all. Here am I, after ten years of foreign travel, as poor as Job."

"I should never have thought it!" replied Joe.

"Luck, sir, luck. I always was unlucky. I have tried every part of the world, and failed everywhere."

"But you understand the cards, dice, and chances as well as most men."

"I thought so—but hang me if I do. Just been utterly fleeced in Paris, and so have come to you for assistance."

"My dear colonel," began the other, hurriedly, "really times are very bad, and—"

"You skulking imitation of a Greek Jew," said the other, angrily, "I don't ask you for money, except a guinea or two, as a loan. I want information, and what's more, I want to give you some news."

"As to a few guineas, of course they are at

your service, and with regard to information, why anything I know—"

"You will give in exchange for what I know," said theother, draining more brandy; and then he added, "What of 'Our Sal?'"

The man started, and then to divert attention, filled *his* glass, and drank.

"Sir Thornley is dead, and she lives alone in the dower house," he added.

"Any money?"

"Why?" said the other, in a hesitating way.

"Don't try to hum me, Joe; that's enough. She has some, and must share it with me. Is she as handsome as when—"

And he looked significantly towards the next room.

"She is still a very fine woman," said Joe Galpin.

"Oh, well, that's something to know. Alone in the dower house—humph! Must have money; if she don't recollect old times why—"

He said no more.

"What was the news you were about to afford me?" continued Joe Galpin, anxious to change the subject.

"The Hunchback is coming home. He has made another fortune. He wants to find his daughter," said the stranger, with a peculiar smile.

"Humph!"

"What has become of her?"

"Don't know,"

"Really, no hum."

"Really."

"Then look to your skin. He more than half suspects something."

"What?"

"That I shall keep to myself until I learn more. So give me the promised guineas, and let me go."

"I shall see you again soon," said Joe Galpin.

"Are you afraid of your money?" cried the other, fiercely; "because if you are, keep it."

"Oh, no, not at all! But I should like to know how you get on."

"Oh! don't be alarmed," said the other, with a sardonic grin; "when I'm togged I'll come and see you at H—"

"Hush!" gasped the other, in low, hollow tones.

The colonel went out laughing.

Joe Galpin shook his fist after him, and then went to let Mrs. Treherne out.

She walked into the room, set herself in the chair so recently occupied by the stranger, and hastily drained a glass of brandy.

"That man must die," she said, in hoarse tones, "the world is not wide enough for both."

"What man?" gasped Joe Galpin, "there has been no man here."

Mrs. Treherne pointed, with a sardonic grin, to a faint chink in the wall.

"You forget," she continued.

"Well," he answered, doggedly, "what of him, then?"

"Leave him to me. He shall come to the dower house, and welcome. But what of the hunchback? if he comes, and learns the truth, then am I lost beyond all hope. He never sus-

pected me. But this wretch knows all. And then you talk of her and the girl. I thought them dead."

"They are both living."

"How I am cheated, robbed, betrayed!" she cried. "I pay fortunes away to gain my end, and now, after all these years, spectres rise to cross my path, to embitter my existence, and make life hideous. Where are they?"

"Shall I tell you—"

"Speak, man—"

"Make it worth my while, and ere that man lands in England, all your enemies shall be out of the way."

"I double the reward," she said hoarsely.

"You had better leave it all to me," he continued rather anxiously.

"I must know. Vague suspicions fill my soul with awe. Let me know the worst."

Joe Galpin looked her full in the face, and said two words.

Mrs. Treherne shrieked in mortal agony.

"Fate! fate! fate!" she cried, and drained a whole bumper of brandy.

CHAPTER XVI.

THE FUNERAL VAULT.

Out into the night they went, three poor penniless wanderers.

Mrs. Phineas Bristowe had overheard the whole of the plans of her husband. There was a secret between them which alone kept her his slave. She had his secret now, and one would make him subservient to her. But there was another which fired her soul with such dread horror, that it alone accounted for her wan and haggard appearance.

Phineas Bristowe and Susan were only waiting for Jessie to grow up a woman to trade upon her beauty.

Mrs. Bristowe, or Cornelia, as we shall often have reason to call her, knew well of the illicit connection between the preacher and his servant-girl. But this she utterly scorned. She despised them both, and was only chained by a link now broken.

She hastily wrote on a scrap of paper certain words, and then lowered the children into the yard by a bed-rope. To descend herself was easy.

When the two intended assassins rushed up they found the rooms empty, but on a table was a slip of paper with these words:—

"*Fly while there is time. I have heard all, and go to the nearest magistrate.*"

This explains their alarmed and precipitate flight.

Meanwhile Cornelia and the two wondering children took flight—the latter knowing not why nor wherefore. She simply said that something dreadful had happened, which she would explain when they were older.

That night they slept in a barn, and next morning, by the sale of her wedding-ring, she was able to procure them a hearty meal of bread and milk, fortified by which they pursued their journey.

AN UNEXPECTED RECOGNITION.

Mrs. Bristowe appeared to have little motive in taking any particular direction, and yet she was very careful as to the turnings, examining sign-posts, and asking the way in towns.

A watch followed the wedding-ring, and in this way a long journey was performed; how much time it took she never could tell. Sometimes they were hospitably entertained at a farm and stopped a day or two. But nothing bent the woman from her purpose.

At length her eyes seemed to brighten, and her pace to increase. She held a child in each hand, and though night had long since fallen, she hurried on her way. It was a fearfully dark night. The clouds seemed to press down upon the earth, and all betokened the approach of a heavy storm. The children looked up towards her face, though they could not see it, in great alarm.

"Mamma," said Jessie, "I saw a light yonder, why not seek shelter?"

Mrs. Bristowe halted, and looked up at the sky. It was terribly gloomy, and yet she was scarcely conscious of what she did. The children, however, alarmed at the coming storm, led her gently through an open gateway, and up a path deeply shaded by trees, until descending a rather rapid slope, they reached a dark and gloomy arch, beneath which they took shelter.

Still the poor woman remained wrapped in a kind of ecstacy.

Suddenly, with a terrific thunderclap, the storm commenced. The rain fell in torrents, and all were thankful for the shelter thus opportunely afforded them.

"Mother," presently whispered Jessie, "do you know where we are ?"

"No, my child."

"It is a churchyard."

"What !" gasped the poor woman, shaking as with the palsy, "has then my very instinct brought me here, and this—hush ! some one comes. This way, my children ; breathe not, speak not, for who can come into such a place at midnight with good intent."

They retreated, clinging to the woman, and just able to distinguish two approaching figures, one of whom held a lantern in his hand.

It was pitch dark beneath the arch, but the woman, groping with her hands, and as if familiar with the way, led them on, muttering to herself strangely all the time.

"What means this—the grating open ? Am I doomed to behold some fearful desecration of this temple. What can they want ? Move slowly, my children, be cautious—you have never done any harm. Be not then alarmed, when I tell you that we are in the burial vaults of a church. The dead cannot harm you, but the living may. Be silent, then, as death."

She could distinctly hear the footsteps of the men advancing, and just as she concealed herself behind a pillar, they entered.

Heaven only knows how she restrained a fearful shriek, as she recognized the parties.

One was very old. He was dressed in coarse habiliments covered by clay, while on his head was a dogskin cap. His face was puckered and covered with stray hairs, which had apparently deserted his chin. At a glance any one could see that he was a grave-digger.

The other was a tall, coarse, good-looking man of about forty, evidently a gentleman born, but with a reckless and unprincipled expression of countenance.

"And this, Roger, is the old place," he said, rapping his boot with a riding-whip. "Hold up the candle, and show us the coffin."

"You was allays a fearful ne'er-do-well," replied the sexton in a low, hushed tone ; "but my heart misgives me. What you want to do, is sacrilege."

"Pooh ! pooh !" cried the other, "take a drain of the brandy, man. I tell you the coffin is empty. I want to convince you of this."

The sexton took the bottle from the other's hand, and drained a goodly draught.

The gentleman then advanced to a leaden coffin, and laid down the lantern they carried.

It was rather an extensive vault, and contained the mouldering remains of several great families in the neighbourhood. Some were ranged round on shelves, but the one in the centre still lay upon heavy trestles.

It was a custom of the family to which that coffin belonged, for the last to lay thus in the centre of the vault, until space was required for a new comer.

The sexton, as if resolved to take no part in the proceedings, seated himself on an old stone coffin in a corner, lit his pipe, again applied himself to the brandy-bottle, and muttering some indistinct words waited.

"Ha ! ha !" laughed the other, looking at the coffin with a sneer, while he prepared a chisel, mallet, and screw-driver, 'Sacred to the Memory of Lionel Treherne.' Funny, very ! when I saw him alive not three months ago. But there's rare games afloat. Fool ! to let me know that this coffin contained the secret of his life."

Mrs. Bristowe was close to Jessie. She now kneeled, and, clutching her arm, whispered slowly in her ear.

"Lead the boy out of the vault. If you see me flying, slam the grating, and turn the key the moment I am out. Go—our lives depend on caution."

The fugitives were behind a pillar to the right of the entrance, and far nearer the doorway than the sexton and his companion. They were, too, in complete darkness, so that the children, terrified and alarmed at what they had seen, crept, with their hearts in their mouths, towards the grating.

There they stood spell-bound.

The gentleman had now also lighted a pipe, and was hard at work chiselling all round the coffin, where the lid had been soldered to the body.

His instruments were sharp and keen, and his tools of the very best quality.

The task was soon completed, for the fellow was an apt workman.

Then he burst into a hoarse laugh.

"See, neighbour Roger, how the world is gulled." And as he spoke, he tipped over th coffin, from which fell, first a lot of stones bricks, and hay, and then a thick parchment packet.

"Found it, by the Lord !" cried the man, as he rushed towards it.

But, with a wild shriek, a figure burst from behind a pillar, stooped, clutched the parchment, and with a terrible cry of exultation, fled towards the door.

"Damnation !" yelled the desecrator of the sanctuary, while Roger let fall pipe and lantern. "After her, or she will raise the whole country."

A slam, a click, a sharp turn of a lock, and they knew they were prisoners.

"Woman—devil—whatever you be—give me back what you have stolen," shouted the one, while Roger trimmed the almost extinguished lamp,

As he raised it up, the colonel found himself face to face with Mrs. Bristowe, haggard, ghastly. with wildly flashing eyes.

But the grating was between them.

"Stolen !" she said, hoarsely; "it is mine, man of evil and of blood !"

"Cornelia, by all that's infernal !" he gasped, and rushed with all his might against the door. "But stay, in the name of God, and I will tell you a secret you would give your soul to know."

But it was too late; the woman had fled with all her strength once more out into the stormy night, leaving the colonel and the sexton prisoners in the vaults of St. Nicolas, the parish church of B——.

She secreted the parchment in a pocket, took the children by the hand, and fled as fast as their little legs would carry them,

About an hour later, she halted at a roadside inn, open for carters and market people.

She had a few shillings left, with which she determined to procure a night's rest. She accordingly hired a bed, gave the children bread and cheese and ale, which they had scarcely consumed ere they lay side by side in a sound and heavy sleep.

She then trimmed an oil lamp, and broke the seals of the parchment, which was directed to herself.

Out fell several guineas and a roll of notes.

These, poor as she was, she pushed on one side. She was devoured by a desire to know this awful secret from beyond the grave.

There were a number of parchments in the parcel, but these she regarded not.

It was a letter in a well-known handwriting that she snatched at.

For half an hour she read it with wavering breath and burning cheeks.

Then she fell on her knees, her eyes streaming with tears, her bosom heaving with rapture, her old strange beauty stealing back again under the influence of happiness.

A mystery of her girlhood, hitherto impenetrable, had been solved.

"Oh! my darling child, my Jessie, now I can look upon you without shame—my angel, my darling."

And rising, she kissed the girl, after which she continued the reading of this strange voice from the tomb.

But what the wondrous secret was, time only can show.

CHAPTER XVII.

THE MIRROR IN THE DESERTED HALL.

AGAIN that weird-like woman walked the picture-gallery; again she strode backwards and forwards between one of the windows and a table which supported a brandy-bottle and glasses, but her step was slower, her eye less lowering, her face brighter and more smiling than usual.

Opposite to her, and illumined only by a small lamp, was a strange old mirror.

It had certainly served some purpose once, but what that was was hard to be told.

Two glasses had been joined together, so as to form a triangle, the point of which rested on the mantelpiece.

They both reflected now only the door of an adjoining chamber, except when Mrs. Treherne walked up to them and surveyed her somewhat stern and singular beauty.

It seemed to satisfy her, for her eyes became languishing, and her bosom heaved, as only the bosom should heave of a passionate woman who waits a lover.

Now she expected a burglar, and had expected him nightly for some time.

At length the period of her watching seemed likely to terminate. The clock struck twelve, and though Mrs. Treherne had not indulged so freely as usual in brandy, yet she appeared weary.

"He comes not," she said, stamping her foot upon the ground; "will he always tarry, and drive me thus to madness. But I must stay these wild beatings of a heart that burns with hate or love as fiercely. I will to bed, and steep my soul in sleep."

She turned, and glided noiselessly from the room.

And the dim, forsaken mirror, o'er which many a stately throng had gleamed, which had looked down so calm on wine-cup and song, was alone; for the song had left no echo, and the wine-cup had long since been quaffed, and hushed in the grave were the silvery voices that had laughed in its presence.

But, hark! there is a footfall without. A heavy step approaches one of the windows, and then, after a deathlike pause, some one can be heard at work at the shutters.

The housebreaker knew his trade, for the shutters soon flew open, and he was at work on the glass.

Oh, dim, forsaken mirror, why dost thou now but give faintly back the quiet stars and the sailing moon on her solitary track?

The glass soon yielded, and using considerable caution, the man unbolted the window, pushed it open, and entered the long silent picture-gallery.

"That was well done," he said in a low tone, "and now, where the deuce does the old cat hang out?"

At this moment a door opened with violence, and he saw, *reflected in the mirror*, a room elegantly furnished, a warm fire, a superb collation, and a magnificent woman in evening costume looking at him with a beaming smile.

"Welcome, Colonel Meadows," said a rich but slightly sarcastic voice.

"Curses light on my betrayer, what is the meaning of this?" cried the man, darting towards the window.

"Fie! fie! afraid, and of a woman," continued the other.

"Is that you, Julia, and alive," whispered the man.

"Julia, and alive," she replied.

"Then here goes," said the other, and he muttered to himself, "better a live rendezvous than a burglary, and perhaps a—"

What, he did not say, but closing the shutters carefully, he advanced towards the room, where, her face actually wreathing with smiles, stood Mrs. Treherne, by the aid of art and her maid looking a superb woman.

"This is a surprise," said the man addressed as Colonel Meadows. "Why, Julia, you look handsomer than ever."

"Do I," replied the artful woman, accepting without hesitation his passionate embrace; "and you are not changed."

The colonel led the widow to a couch, after closing the door, and burst out laughing.

"That I should wish to see you is not surprising; but how the deuce could you have expected me?"

"John," said Mrs. Treherne, bending her eyes, with a strange smile, on his face, "unknown to you and Joe Galpin, I was in the old house of the Almonry that night, and heard your conference. Be not alarmed. I am not angry. I came in search of a confidant, a friend, a devoted and earnest assistant. I intended to have used Galpin, but when I heard of your intended visit, I determined to make friends with you again; and that if you would dare something for me, to reward you beyond your expectations—surely beyond your deserts."

And this woman drew his really handsome head towards her, and kissed his forehead. He pressed his lips to her neck.

For awhile their thoughts wandered to the past, many years ago. It was a scene like this, suddenly come upon, that had killed Mr. Treherne.

"And can you still love me?" said the captain, continuing to feed on kisses which were not repelled.

"How can you doubt me," sighed Julia.

The colonel scarcely knew what to answer, so filled a bumper for both, and pledged her in sparkling wine.

Let us cast a veil over the next hour, devoted to love and recollections of the past, and then rejoin them more calm and collected. He supporting her magnificent but yielding form in his arms, she looking with luxurious eyes up into his face.

"John," she said, "if you will be true to me, if you will devote your whole energies to my service, I can soon be at the head of twenty thousand a year as guardian to my son, with untold wealth in ready money, at my command."

"The deuce you can—how so?"

Mrs. Treherne calmly explained her views.

"You infernal temptress," he said, in tones half jocular, half real, "and what is to be my reward?"

Julia held down her eyes.

"I have always been wholly yours," she said with the faintest possible blush; "do all I want, and everything shall be yours—as well as this hand."

And she placed her jewelled fingers in his.

She was still looking down, and saw not the strange gleam which flashed through his eyes.

Next minute he was on his knees, thanking her with an earnestness which was scarcely feigned. He was comparatively poor, and the prospect of handling so much wealth, was a temptation he could not resist.

"And you will devote all your energies to my interests?" she said.

"I will, on my soul—on my honour!"

"Then are we victorious."

"Not so sure of that," said the colonel, moodily, "for the Hunchback is alive, and about to return to England."

Julia turned deadly white under her rouge, and looked at him wildly, almost madly.

"Lionel Treherne!" she hissed forth in husky and dry accents, "then am I lost for ever."

"Julia," continued the other, rather harshly, "if you have nerved your soul to wade through crime to rank, and wealth, and honour, then why should you fear that little spawn of the devil? He is but one more to slay."

"Slay Lionel Treherne!" she shrieked, "never!"

"Then you still love the wretched cripple who spurned your advances, and threatened to expose you," sneered the colonel.

"Love him, no," she said more calmly," but do not talk of him and murder. I never believed in his death. I knew that the hour would come, and that the avenger of blood would pursue me—but no more of this. I am undoubtedly yours, so let this subject be talked of no more, except when absolutely necessary."

"As you will."

"You know, Meadows, that your peerage only requires money to revive it. Be my devoted slave, and it shall be. Nothing shall stop me. I have resources you little dream of; but Haddington Hall must first be mine."

The colonel's eyes flashed fire. The burning ambition of his youth, the dormant peerage, had been suddenly revived in him, and like his Julia, he was ready to wade knee-deep in crime to attain it.

That night, this new Lady Macbeth and her lord made a compact at which fiends might have wept.

By a strange turn of the wheel of fate, their first enterprise was directed against Jessie, he Mormon's Daughter.

CHAPTER XVIII.

NIGHT ON THE PATHLESS OCEAN.

"I CANNOT, and I will not die," shrieked Phineas Bristowe, gazing out upon the wide sea, blue, soft, and undulating, but treacherous. "Can nothing be done to save us from this horrible fate?"

A strange gurgling noise under his feet made him start,

The ship was fast settling down into the ocean.

With a hideous yell, with a blasphemous cry, Phineas Bristowe leaped upon the bulwarks.

Not a sail, not the faintest trace of land.

Phineas sprang again on deck, and in the terrible anguish of his evil soul, cursed and swore, and prayed alternately, in the most frightful manner.

"Curse not, lest you be cursed," said a deep voice near him, and looking up, he saw his late companion wrapped in one of the captain's pilot-coats, a fur cap over his ears, shading indeed nearly all his face, which was further concealed by a huge wrapper or comforter. "Cease your moanings, and aid me, so that we escape."

At the last words, Phineas Bristowe bounded to his feet.

The stranger who in the hour of danger, and under the influence of the mighty ocean before him, appeared to have recovered his lucidity, while at the same time, he had apparently lost all animosity towards the preacher, now in a few brief words explained that the crew, in the hurry of departure, had put out all the boats, but finding the jolly-boat unnecessary had left it floating astern, with its mast stepped, and its sail in the bottom.

They had only to load it with food and biscuit, and steer a little northerly of west, to make some part of the coast of America.

Restored to life and consciousness, the preacher showed that he could work with a will, and in less than twenty minutes, water, biscuits, and other provisions were placed on board.

The stranger took the helm, and sternly bade Phineas go forward.

Scarcely had they gone two hundred yards from the ship, when a loud noise made them turn round.

The decks had blown up, by the mere force of the sea.

Then the stern rose, then fell, followed by the bow, and with a terrible roar and splash, went head foremost into the sea.

Barrels, casks, pieces of wood, hencoops, and other things floating around, in a few minutes was all that remained of the goodly ship, which a few days before had been the centre of so many hopes and fears.

And thus they were launched upon the vast ocean, with no other guide save the polar star, upon which the supposed maniac kept his eyes fixed with unerring glance during the night, while the sun guided him by day.

He slept it is true at times, but one of those weary, startled sleeps which are not to be entrapped.

Several times Phineas Bristowe would have crept aft during his slumbers, to steal the rum, which the other had taken under his especial protection, but a start, a growl, and a clutch at a pistol, would drive him back to his lair.

For some days the sky continued blue, the sea gentle, the wind fair, but almost imperceptible.

Their provisions began to give out, and their water waxed very low.

The stranger was rigid in his adherence to rations.

He never spoke to Phineas, but issued his orders by signs.

On that vast ocean, emblem of eternity and power, they appeared mechanically to have laid aside their former bitter enmity.

At all events, it was so with the master. Phineas often indulged in a muttered curse and a savage scowl at the man, who, having the water, spirits, and biscuit to his hand, did not eagerly devour all he could reach.

Had he dared, he would have shot his master.

But who could guide the boat to a port?

Smaller, and smaller grew their rations of food and water—lower, and lower became their hopes. Still there was the same unnatural calm upon the waters. If this continued, they must surely perish from the slow progress of starvation.

"Let us enjoy what remains," said Phineas, one day, "and then the devil take the rest."

The maniac drily handed him the water-cask.

Phineas held it to his lips. It was empty.

Then the man at the helm began to sing. He was decidedly delirious from fever. He had eaten nothing for a whole day, but sat brooding over his own thoughts. Every now-and-then the preacher would see a wild, glittering eye fixed

upon his own countenance, and he began to tremble. He was no match for the other, who, moreover, was armed.

Resolved, however, to sell his life dearly, he clutched his unloaded pistol, ready for a deadly struggle.

He made up his mind at the first hostile demonstration from the maniac, who evidently in his lucid moments was calm enough, to eject him from the boat, or perish in the attempt.

His eye rested greedily on the keg of spirits and the remains of the biscuit.

And still no wind.

They were not in a torrid zone, but without a breeze, with scarcely even a breath of air, their sensations were intensely those of suffering.

The maniac sang louder and louder, and his eye grew more wild every minute.

Suddenly he leaped to his feet, and glared at Phineas with a wild and savage glance.

"Wretch!" he shrieked, in a voice that made the welkin ring, "I have thee now."

And he stood up in the boat, preparatory to making a rush at the preacher.

Phineas turned, as if to fly, and as he did so his astonishment may be conceived when, within two hundred yards, he saw a large brigantine, which lay almost becalmed on the waters. Its approach unperceived was easily explained—it was painted a light green, which did not show at a distance.

Phineas Bristowe did not hesitate a moment, unaware that the maniac had fallen back in the boat, foaming at the mouth, headlong he plunged into the sea, and struck for the vessel.

Fifty grim visages watched him over the bulwarks, and when he approached the brigantine, a life-belt and rope were thrown him. Weary and exhausted, it was as much as he could do to use them. When they drew him on deck, he clutched the rope with the energy of death.

He had fainted.

When he recovered, he was in a dark and gloomy hole, surrounded by berths. On numerous chests sat a collection of sailors of all nations, but without exception characterised by one feature—villany of expression. He gazed wildly around, and for a moment fancied himself in Pandemonium. Then, slowly, recollection came. He remembered all, even to the plunge in the sea.

He remembered that he had left the maniac alone on the wide, wide ocean.

Then he felt his body, and as he did so, could with difficulty restrain a volley of curses.

They had given him a change of clothes, but had taken his belts with over two thousand five hundred pounds of notes and gold in them.

A thrill of horror passed through his veins. He was on board a pirate, ruined, naked, and without a hope in the world.

Such was the result of his many crimes.

But he dared not remonstrate. Never had he seen such a fearful set of cut-throats. Still, nature is imperious, and he was compelled to speak.

"Water!" he muttered.

"Water, my honey," said a great, big fellow with a terrific pair of whiskers; "is it whater ye want? take holt."

And he handed him a panniken of weak grog.

"And now, I guess, Mister Stranger, a'ter liquor you'd feel mighty wolfish," continued a thin Yankee.

Phineas nodded.

They brought him biscuit and salt pork, which he devoured with avidity.

"And now, my man," said one in authority, "if you'll just get up, we'll put you ashore in an hour. The *Flying Fish* is entering the harbour of New York."

Mechanically, Phineas Bristowe obeyed. He was helpless as a child. To make any resistance was folly. His miserable state of poverty rendered him unusually humble, while the robbery of his wealth clearly explained the character of his associates.

He crept out of his berth, and crawled on deck, after pulling on a decent outer coat, handed to him by one of the crew.

They were running up close to the land, and amid a crowd of shipping.

But he had no time to admire the beauties of nature, for as he advanced mechanically towards the quarter-deck, he was addressed by so strange an individual, that his whole attention became at once absorbed.

"Wull, copperas nose, and how's yer mother's son—spec yer drank more salt-water nor was good for yer constitution. Wake-snakes and walk-chalks, man—this here child ain't a-gwine to eat yer."

Phineas looked up, and saw standing before him a man about six feet high, with black hair, coal-black eyes, a huge hooked nose, and withal a rollicking cast of countenance. He was dressed more like a fisherman than a sailor, with high boots, and as he gazed at the preacher with one eye closed, Phineas thought he had never seen anything so awful in all his life.

"Wull, stranger, hopes yer feel better. Guess I'm mighty busy now; gwine to warp in thar; meet yer in the evening at this here diggens. Ax for Fussy Foster, and say Captain Brandt sent yer."

And he thrust a card into the other's hand.

Phineas muttered some incoherent reply, and mingled with the crowd of sailors, who were all too busy to attend to him or his miseries.

CHAPTER XIX.

NEW YORK.

IN half an hour more he was in the streets of New York, almost as naked as he was born, and without a penny in his pocket.

His hair was thick and matted, his beard and moustache were beginning to grow, his face was whitey-brown, his eyes set deep in the sockets, his bones protruded from his cheeks, while his whole aspect was wild and fearful.

Except his pilot-coat descending to his knees, his clothes were mere rags, and his shoes almost dropped off his feet.

In this way he wandered about until he reached a splendid street, which he afterwards knew to be Broadway. Everybody but himself was either well dressed, or happy, or busy, and by keeping on the curb he was not jolted more than once a minute.

Mechanically he moved on until his progress was checked by a slight crowd. A carriage stood before the door of an hotel. In it was already seated a tall, striking looking man, while a splendidly dressed woman, holding up her dress so as to show the contour of a beautifully shaped leg, encased in the most delicious of silk stockings, was just about to join him.

As she placed her foot on the step, Phineas, with a low cry, sprang foward; and touched her on the shoulder.

"Susan," he said in a low tone, "for the love of God, hear me!"

With a stare that would have adorned a woman of quality, the girl turned round and looked him full in the face.

"Fellow," she said, "I don't know you."

She leaped in as she said so, and the carriage drove off.

Stupefied, thunderstruck, mad with rage and despair, Phineas hurried away. Suddenly he recollected the slaver's card.

"Beauchamp House, New York."

He went up to a lounger, and with a humble mien showed the card, and asked the way.

"Wull, you are green, you are," said the fellow, squirting out an ocean of tobacco-juice on the other's toes, "that's the diggens."

And he pointed across the road to a magnificent hotel, fitted up, it could be seen, even from without, in a most gorgeous style. Phineas Bristowe looked about incredulous.

"Fact," said the lounger.

Desperate as he was, there was nothing for it, but to try, so he walked across the road, and ascended the steps. He found himself in a magnificent anteroom. A waiter advanced in an insolent way.

"What you want, sar?"

"This is Beauchamp House?"

"Yes, sar—Besham House, sar—what you want, white niggar?"

"Fussy Foster, from Captain Brandt," said Phineas, desperately.

"Eh—massa," replied the darkey, with a submissive bow, "dis way."

And casting open the door of a superb apartment, a kind of coffee-room of oriental magnificence, he led the way to where the captain of the slaver sat before a well laid-out lunch in company with a gentleman in black.

"Sit down, sir," said the captain, with a grin.

Phineas, his eyes starting from his head, unable to speak, his sick and hungry soul fainting at the sight of such a feast as he had never seen before, obeyed a sign from the captain to fall to.

When he had satisfied the imperious calls of hunger, during which time the captain eyed him with grim satisfaction, the other spoke.

"And now, blast you, sir," said the slaver, with a dark frown, "how dare you take a gentleman for a thief? Do you think I'm one of yer roaring catamount horse-thieves? Why didn't yer ax for your money—eh? Now look you yar, you yaller-looking monkey—for three straws I guess I'd kip it. Der yer think cos a gentleman deals in black cattle—"

"Hush!" said the gentleman in black.

"Shut up thar—thunder! I'm clar here away. I say, der yer think cos I'm a coast a Africa coaler," he added with a grin, "I'd kip yar darty money. Stranger, I guess no how. Thar, count yer shin-plasters and gold, and be damned to yer."

"It is unnecessary," said Phineas, trembling with joy.

"I guess it ain't," replied the slaver, drily; "and now make tracks, or I'd not be sure of my temper, with such a black-looking scran."

Phineas needed not twice telling, but, his heart beating with tumultuous emotions, rushed from the hotel.

CHAPTER XX.

AN INDIAN FIGHT.

VAST as are the changes which time has wrought in the different parts of the great continent of America—as nothing to what inexorable time will bring about—few places exhibit more the pitiless progress of civilization than a certain spot in Ashtabula County, Ohio, to which we shall not more particularly allude.

At the time of which we speak, in the early part of the present century, the whole surface was one forest, hunted by the prowling panther and the no less savage Indian, who lay in wait to take advantage of any unguarded moment to sally forth and deal desolation round upon the whites.

Their opportunities in this neighbourhood were, however, few, as the forest-borders were seldom visited by any but large parties of explorers and hunters, whom it would have been unsafe to attack.

We must now transport our readers thither, on a memorable night, which has much to do with the establishment of what its votaries call the new religion, and which we denominate the Great Imposture.

It was within an hour or two of night, and at the mouth of a dark and gloomy glen so overspread by trees and undergrowth, that in all probability the light of the sun had not penetrated since the Creation.

A party was camped at the mouth, in the primitive fashion of all American hunters.

A triangle had been erected from which depended an iron kettle, and round this four stalwart youths in hunter's garb were stretched, with their rifles between their knees, waiting for the evening meal to be completed.

They were all tall, coarse-featured lads, but not wanting in either intellect or acuteness, while one, whose name was Joseph, added to this the cunning of a fox. The others, Hyrum, John, and William, were less markedly characterized.

All were smoking, while Joseph, in deep contemplation fixed his eyes on the heavens, as if in secret communion with some spirit of the air. This youth was enthusiastic, ambitious, and devoured by every passion known to humanity.

He lusted with all his soul for power, wealth, and woman.

And he was poor, unlettered, and ignorant.

This, to the bold and energetic, is as nothing.

And this youth was both, with the most unbounded self-sufficiency, conceit, and ambition.

Suddenly, Hyrum set up a cry, and all started up.

"What's up?" said Joe, with manly gravity.

"Look!" said Hyrum.

He pointed to the waters of Lake Erie, a broad, inland sea, majestic and imperious in the storm, when its angry billows lashed its rugged shores, but beautiful as a sleeping tiger in its hour of repose.

A small canoe, impelled by a tiny sail, was breaking the waves, with one figure in the stern, while behind, stretching out with all the energy of an eager chase, were four canoes, full of armed Indians, racing as for a prize.

"Joe," said Hyrum, with a queer pucker of his huge face, "if that arn't a gal!"

"Eh!" cried Joe, his sallow face lighting up.

"Them Injine's arter no good," said Hyrum.

Joe rose, clutched his rifle, and with great strides began to make towards that part of the lake where it appeared that the solitary fugitive might be expected to land.

His stalwart brothers followed him at a rapid pace, like fearless hunters as they were.

They had nearly half a mile to go, and necessarily, as they left their elevated position, lost sight of the actors in the scene which so much interested them.

They knew that night would soon fall, and that there was no time to lose.

In a short time they reached the confines of the woods, an open and green space sloping down thence to the lake.

The scene was now terribly exciting. The canoes were almost neck and neck, while the fugitive had taken down the small sail, trusting to a paddle. But the case was hopeless. The Indians must reach the small canoe, and ere it came to land.

"Thunder!" said Joe, who was a tall, gaunt lad, of about seventeen, "what's to be done? Its a tarnation fine gal."

And his little grey eyes glistened as he wiped the sweat off his lofty forehead.

"Shute!" said Samuel.

"No," replied William, calmly—he was a mere hunter, little given to sentiment, but eminently practical, "it is a girl, the Indians won't hurt her. Let's wait till night, track 'em, and then release her."

All bowed to this advice, as the best under the circumstances, and falling on their knees watched the progress of events with intense interest.

The girl, for such the fugitive undoubtedly was, suddenly ceased rowing, and folding her arms, appeared to resign herself to her fate. But still the canoes continued their headlong course, and at last one, slightly lighter than the rest, gained ground, when a warrior, who had stood upright in the bows of the next, made a tremendous headlong plunge, went out of sight, and rising, laid his hand quietly on the girl's shoulder.

The chase immediately ceased.

The girl was a prisoner.

The Indians then held a brief conference, and four of the boats returned slowly the way they came, while that to which the prisoner belonged approached the shore.

Its occupants landed. They were ten in number, and well armed.

The brothers glanced at one another.

Joe nodded.

" Not yet," said William.

The Indians, wholly unsuspicious of the presence of danger, the hunters having made their fire with charred wood, fastened their boat, and without in any way confining her motions, marched in a direction which took them close to the hidden hunters.

Not one even drew a breath.

" By heavens !" said Joe, when they had disappeared in the forest, " a white gal."

" And darned handsome, eh! Joe ?" added Hyrum, with a chuckle.

Joe made no answer, but leading the way, struck upon the trail of the Indians, which they took no pains to disguise. Their followers, however, kept at a most respectful distance.

Every now-and-then Joe looked with ecstacy at the mark of a tiny and lovely foot. He was intensely excited. Something seemed to tell him that he had fallen on his fate.

Presently night fell, as it always does in America, without warning, and they found themselves in utter darkness.

But at the same time the faint glimmer of a distant light, proclaimed that the Indians had halted. Extreme caution had now to be used, as the Custalogas were a cunning race, and kept a careful look out over their watch-fires.

It became necessary to crawl step by step, halt, and listen. No ear is so keen as that of the red Indian. In his instincts, and habits, he partakes more of the nature of the wild beast than any other race.

By dint, however of the utmost patience and caution, they at length succeeded in coming within sight of the camp.

Some wood-coals had been lighted, over which a youthful warrior was broiling a mess of game.

The rest reclined around in various attitudes, while one stood facing the girl, slightly bound to a tree.

She was about sixteen, tall, slim, and yet powerfully made. Her face was handsome, and yet masculine, probably from exposure to the open air, but her eyes had a power and rich voluptuous languor, that made the heart of Joe beat wildly.

She was dressed like a half-caste, in a tunic or hunting-shirt, leggings, mocassins, and wore a cap of deerskin.

By her side was a small rifle.

She appeared more intent on examining the fine proportions of the young Indian chief before her, than occupied with her own position.

His speech was long, cunning, and full of Indian flowers of speech, the purport however was as follows : —Her father was a great warrior, his wigwam was a mighty one, and contained much riches. It was time that the greybeard retired from active life, and went back to his settlements. They knew he loved the singing-bird, his only daughter. If then he would give up his wigwam and all it held, they would restore his daughter ; if not she had the very worst to expect, and then, death.

" Well, I declare, young speckletoes," said the Amazonian damsel, " that's plain speaking, and

Captain Reardon, my father, is not very likely to convene. I says no ; but you can just ask him."

The eyes of the Indian rolled significantly.

" I am the Yellow Bear," said the young chief ; " the pale faces have robbed me of my inheritance ; they are destroying the woods, and taking away the hunting-grounds of my people. I can stand idle no longer. My braves have risen in their might, and the first trophy they must have is your father's wigwam. You must yield it to us, or die."

" I'll die fust !" cried the girl, resolutely.

" What says the singing-bird—shall the greybeard die, too ?"

" Catch 'un," said the girl, with an undaunted mien.

The warriors sprang to their feet in a whirlwind of passion, raised their tomahawks—at that moment four sheets of flame flashed before their eyes, and as many warriors fell, never to rise again.

Then came a fifth—it was the girl's.

This was followed by the rush of four huge forms from the brake right upon the camp.

They loaded as they ran.

But the Indians vanished like magic, crying out, in words unintelligible to the girl—

" The money-digger ! the money-digger !"

" Well, that's friendly," said the girl, patting Joe on the shoulder as he unfastened her cords, and was indeed an unnecessarily long time about it.

It gave him an excuse to clasp her buxom waist, and to feast his eyes on a bosom of the fairest proportions, as revealed by her disordered dress.

At length, however, she was free, and Joe would have asked for explanations.

" Make tracks," said William, coolly, " the whule bilin' 'ull be down on us like smoke, if yer don't hook it. Whar do yer live, miss ?"

" Follow me," replied the girl, and loading her rifle, she led the way in a direction that took them past their own camp. Here they halted ten minutes to recruit themselves.

The flesh-pots of Egypt were too much for them.

They devoured the stew, but scarcely had finished before they knew that the Philistines were on their track.

A goodly benefit would it have been to society if they had slain the lot.

CHAPTER XXI.

THE BLOCK-HOUSE.

IN a deep, secluded valley, through which meandered a small river towards the lake, was a block-house of considerable extent, which had been erected some years back by Captain Simon Reardon.

It was situated where the river took a bend, almost meeting at one point.

Except a narrow strip, guarded by a gate, the block-house was on an island.

Captain Simon Reardon was an inveterate hunter, and at the same time an enthusiast with regard to the history of the ancient Indians.

As the axe of the hardy pioneer cleared, and the ploughshare turned up, the earth of the valley, he

A MORMON MIRACLE.—(*See page* 13.)

foll constantly upon the remains of America's past history, as connected with her cherished heartstones and sacred groves, spots hallowed by noble deeds, and the graves of a lost nation.

Numerous skeletons, jars of earthenware, thin sheets of brass, covered with hieroglyphics, turned up, and the delight of the recluse was great.

He collected a perfect museum of curiosities.

Then came a pale, anxious, inquiring youth, called Solomon Spaulding, whose whole soul was given to the elucidation of the history of his native country. With him it was a passion which

know no bounds. He examined the old man's museum with care, and then fired, inspired by all he saw around, himself a religious enthusiast, he began to uncoil, page by page, and leaf by leaf, a wild, visionary romance, intended to explain the advent of the first race of human beings in America.

This book he read evening after evening to the old man and his daughter.

Captain Reardon was delighted, and in the exuberance of his feelings promised his daughter in marriage to the young enthusiast.

Little did he imagine by what strange means he was laying the foundations of a new religion.

Now, Solomon Spaulding was a sedate book-worm, a man in whose eyes a woman was very well as a useful piece of furniture, but not a being to devote your whole soul to—yes, such, fair readers, was his idea when first he saw her.

But all flesh is weak, and before he had been in the block-house a month, he loved Emma with all the energy of a simple and generous heart.

Alas! Emma was a girl full of health and spirits, far better disposed for a frolic than for study, better suited to a tramp through the woods, a tiger hunt, or a night's salmon spearing, than to mend a scholar's shirts or nurse his children.

Emma was as wild and as free as a colt.

Still, having never seen any other man save him and her father, she had not rebelled against the decision which made her the student's wife, and she even submitted to his embrace, allowed him to call her his love, and even was herself a little tender—in fact, did all kinds of foolish things which lovers will understand without our description, and which no description will convey to the mind of any one else.

Now, Solomon had fallen sick, and in the goodness of her heart Emma had gone up the lake to fetch some simple medicines which his case required.

The captain sat by the fireplace in his huge kitchen, cleaning his rifle, while Solomon, pale, cadaverous, and gaunt, despite his illness was poring over and correcting his wild and singular manuscript.

It was evening, and though the bold Emma had not returned, they did not feel in any way uneasy. They were used to her wanderings, and then, nothing had been seen of red skins for some days. Be it remarked, that with all their reverence for the early Americans, they had a most wholesome dread of their descendants.

When the sun had fallen beneath the horizon some two or three hours, the veteran raised his head.

"I say, Solomon, little Em should be here."

"Yes—as thou sayest," replied the solemn young man.

Alas! solemnity and virtue, and even seldom solid *moral* qualities have much influence with the girls.

A blockhead with a smart pair of whiskers will out-weigh the thoughtful man of genius at any time.

The proverb, "That all is not gold that glitters," is little understood by women, who hence are such worshippers of power.

There was a brief pause, during which the two men communed with their own thoughts.

Then a wild shriek was heard, and the words of some one in mortal agony.

"Father! Father! come, or we shall surely be slain."

Captain Reardon flew to a terrace on the left side of the gateway, followed by several labourers and hunters attracted by the shriek; they at once understood the state of affairs.

Close to the stockade that instant halted Emma and the four white youths, while twenty yards behind came whooping, howling, and yelling, some fifty or sixty savages thirsting for their blood.

The white youths turned, levelled their rifles, and fired. At the same instant, a heavy volley from the terrace was poured into the Indians.

Then the gate flew open.

"I've been took," said the excited girl, embracing her father, "but these are my saviours."

"Welcome, my sons," cried the old man, warmly, as he closed the heavy gate.

And the serpent entered this new garden of Eden.

CHAPTER XXII.

A SIEGE.—A DELICATE NIGHT ADVENTURE.

THE Indians no sooner found that their prey had escaped, than they retreated towards a small belt of wood that crossed the valley beyond rifle-shot.

As usual, they withdrew after a check, only, however, to plot and devise some means of carrying out a bloody revenge.

Several of their young men had been slain, which would of course rouse within them the very worst passions of their nature.

But an instant attack was not to be expected.

Captain Reardon accordingly, having placed some of his men as sentries, invited his guests to follow him into the vast kitchen to which Solomon had already retreated.

A sturdy handmaid hastened to spread the evening meal, while Emma, in hearty accents related how she had been taken by the Indians, and released through the courage and devotion of the four young men.

The thanks of the father were hearty, and expressed in suitable terms, after which they sat down to feast, the zest of which was heightened by their terrible run through the woods.

Solomon, being an invalid, sat by the fire, the veteran occupied one end of the table, surrounded by his dependants, Emma sat at the other. Joe was close to her side.

Before they had been five minutes at table, a keen observer might have remarked that Joe eat his food with his left hand, while Emma used the right.

The others were out of sight.

The flushed faces of both, and the downcast eyes of Emma, showed that the hands were not idle, if the lips were.

Captain Reardon and Solomon, *apropos* of the savage Custalogas raging without, were discussing antiquities. No wonder they could not see an inch before their noses.

The three brothers, Hyrum, John, and William, were very hungry, and looked chiefly at their plates, though now-and-then they glanced uneasily at the lovely countenance of the girl, upon whom Joe made such audacious advances, that at last she was obliged to take away her hand.

"Don't be silly," she said.

Alas! Joe was learned in the ways of woman, so he took her by the hand once more, squeezed it, and whispered something in her ear.

Emma laughed and blushed, had he been a

timid lover, in all probability she would have frowned.

After supper, the captain proposed a bowl of punch, a proposition which was met with loud applause. Joe, however, modestly offered to take a turn round and visit the sentries.

His offer was accepted, and Emma volunteered to show him the way round the outworks. The blockhouse itself, which was two-storied, occupied the centre.

It was a calm night, a seductive breeze played through the trees, the stars looked down smiling on this naughty earth, and Joe and Emma turned, not towards the stockade, but the orchard.

Had Solomon Spaulding been anywhere within hearing, he would, as they entered the orchard, have heard something very much like that peculiar sound which emanates from a kiss.

Then followed a deeply interesting conference, after which they hastily visited the terrace, and reported all still.

They then re-entered the house, in time to taste of the second bowl of punch. They found Solomon and Reardon in deep argument, and the three brothers drinking deeply and smoking like furnaces.

Joe filled a bumper for Emma, which after some hesitation, she drank off. Her eyes now sparkled with redoubled brightness. So did those of Joe.

They then again went out unperceived, and scarcely were they out of the house, than Joe caught her in his impassionate embrace, and kissed her lips wildly.

"Don't! don't!" said the girl, upon whom the terrible storm of passion swept for the first time. "I am very wrong. You know that *he* is to be my husband—and I musn't, it is wicked."

"He," cried Joe, wildly, "never! I love you. I am not what I seem. To others I may be rough, but there is that within me says I shall be great and mighty. My soul is too big for my body. I am young—my brain whirls with wondrous things. Listen to me, Emma, my Emma, give up this slave of the lamp, this mere bookworm, be mine body and soul, my wife, and I shall do wonders. Yours the star to guide me on my way. Refuse, and I become once more the wretched wanderer of the wild forests and woods."

"But my father,—Solomon,—no, no, I cannot listen to you," she faltered.

"I have a vast idea germinating in my brain. I have seen, and I have heard. I know that that which is taught as religion, is not true. I," he cried, with an enthusiasm of a fanatic, for he was then half sincere, "will rear a creed that shall be one around which those may gather who would retain the pleasures of life, and yet worship and reap the benefits of their devotion. A new dispensation is coming, but only the inspired must know. Oh, Emma! of my soul I love you; and I say unto you, that the word has gone forth and it must be obeyed, that you shall be blessed in me as a husband. What saith the law, that ye shall desert all, and cleave unto your husband."

Joe caught her in his arms, and pressing his lips to hers, the wild, passionate, ignorant girl forgot all but the tempter and love.

"I will be yours," she said.

Then followed a whispered conference, after which they thoroughly understood one another. There was, however, one proposition against which Emma rebelled a long time, but alas! when once a woman has made a false step, the road downwards is easy enough.

CHAPTER XXIII.

THE DELICATE NIGHT ADVENTURE CONTINUED.

WHEN they re-entered the kitchen, things were still in the same state, though the party had been reinforced by all the sentries and outliers save two.

Nothing had been seen of the Indians, and their very silence appeared ominous.

It was agreed that all further potations should cease, and that the whole garrison should at once go into the open air, and taking up such positions as were best calculated for comfort and repose, be ready, rifle in hand, for the first attack, which was sure to take place during the night or at dawn of day.

All readily agreed to this, and clutched their rifles.

Emma yawned, and kept her seat.

"Art tired, child?" said the veteran, smiling.

"Yes, father," faltered Emma, with a faint blush.

"Well, to bed, lazy one. The Indian war-whoop will soon enough arouse you, when please God we've licked the ryptiles, let us have a jolly breakfast."

"Very good, father," she continued; "would you like some coffee to keep you awake?"

"Capital idea, gal," he said, laughing, and he went out, followed by the whole party.

Every man was left to his own device as to the selection of his sentry-box. The captain chose the terrace, so did most of the men, a girl being appointed to bring round the coffee. Hyrum, John, and William seated themselves behind a wood pile.

Joe leaned against a ladder, not twenty yards from the wood-pile. The ladder was exactly under a window with white dimity curtains, behind which burned a light.

It was now very dark, and when this light went out, nothing was to be seen or heard in the whole stockade but the dark shadows of the trees and buildings, and the whistling of the wind.

But the demon of illicit passion stalks abroad by choice at such times.

Hyrum had watched Joe, and wondered at his selection of a position. He had his suspicions, but said nothing. Presently, about one in the morning, a girl brought round hot coffee, which, as the night was very cold, was most welcome.

The girl brought a can for the four brothers.

Hyrum drank his mug, and then walked over to the ladder to give Joe his. As he expected, no Joe was there. He looked up. The light was out, and the window was shut.

A diabolical idea of hate and jealousy swept over the soul of Hyrum. He had so constantly noticed the good fortune and superiority of Joe, that in his heart he envied him. He had seen and noticed the absorbing attraction between the two new lovers.

Tell us not that love at first sight is impossible. Generally in the case of a man it is but a simple ebullition of passion, but woman is often subjugated at once when the fatal individual comes.

Hyrum had noticed the looks of the two, had seen the electric shocks, the mesmeric kind of attraction which had seized upon them both, and had done so with feelings of extreme bitterness.

A kind of demon seemed to possess him.

He determined to expose the guilty pair.

Creeping into the house, now wholly abandoned by all save Solomon, who had stopped to watch in the kitchen, and the coffee-girl who was outside, he looked around him. All was still as death, and the kitchen was empty. Not even Solomon was there.

Hyrum clutched his rifle, and went up a narrow stairs. At the top was a dark passage. Up and down this could be heard a heavy step, which Hyrum at once guessed to be that of Solomon Spaulding.

The lad hesitated. Had this man suspicions? If so, his brother's life was in danger.

With slow and cautious steps he retreated, and leaving the house unnoticed, turned round, and sought a position under the window occupied by Emma Reardon.

Hyrum was a solemn thinker; he was in the habit of loading a pipe, placing his back against a wall, and then communing profoundly with himself. On this occasion he had much to occupy his mind. The lad had fallen deeply in love with the beautiful wild girl of Ashtabula, and had had serious intentions of proposing.

On the face of the wide earth there is nothing more sacred than the love of a genuine and manly youth—not the mere animal instinct which drives the herd of half-grown boys to follow in the trail of every girl they meet, but the pure unadulterated devotion of a heart which knows no guile.

No; Hyrum, whatever his subsequent faults, on the present occasion was sincere. The bold spirit of the girl, the romantic circumstances under which they had met, the poetry of the landscape which surrounded them, had awakened within him one of those earnest, genuine, and devoted passions which taking root in boyhood, nurtured by circumstances and nature, become in some the undying thought of a life.

What real man but has in some secret corner of his heart a memory of youth, a faded flower, but still fragrant, not a skeleton, but a statue all redolent of beauty, truth, and innocence, which when he thinks of, he feels a smile ineffably sweet radiate over his hardened countenance, which carries him back on magic and resplendent wings to the days of his youth?

Sophisticate as we may we are better in our youth, than when we grow older. We are less hard, less cruel, less selfish—more sincere and single-minded.

Hyrum sucked at his pipe, thought and thought again, until Nature, in all probability, asserted her privilege, and he went to sleep.

It must have been so, for the next thing he knew was that a terrific uproar had taken place, guns were exploding, the awful Indian yell filled the air, and a general call to arms took place.

"Thunder!" he cried, as a heavy weight fell on him suddenly, and looking up, he found that his brother had alighted on his shoulder.

But Hyrum had no eyes for him—what he saw was the form of Emma, in more than *deshabille*, watching with deep anxiety the progress of her lover.

"Git out," said Joe, in no very excellent humour.

"Jist expect I wants to," replied Hyrum, sullenly.

"That you?" continued Joe, with a slight blush.

"Expect it ud better been me than her father," answered Hyrum, who was awfully colloquial when he liked.

"It's the work of the Lord, and I am his humble servant," began his brother.

"You be cussed," cried Hyrum, "it's the devil is up now. Don't yer yare the pop-guns. There's some sport about, enuff to make yer leave off thinking of gals."

And the two young men made for the terrace, where a terrible conflict was taking place between the garrison and infuriated red skins.

Such was the first of the many amorous exploits so renowned and frequent in a land of virtue and decency, for which became afterwards famous General Joseph, prophet, inventor, and high-priest of the Mormons, or Latter-day Saints.

He had not, however, yet discovered a wholesale system of seduction, nor had he invented his female cattle-market.

CHAPTER XXIV.
GERMS OF THE FUTURE.

IT is not our wish here to describe at any great length an Indian fight. We shall, as we proceed in our records of the fearful sufferings of the deluded dupes of Mormonism, have to delineate certain scenes of this kind on a grand scale.

This engagement was not, however, without its excitement and its episodes. The Indians rushed madly to the assault, and though continually repelled by the unerring rifles of the whites, returned again and again to the charge.

But the stockade of the old border chieftain was too well built to feel the attacks of the painted savages, who at length beat a sullen retreat, and one hour after sunrise the very last of them had disappeared beneath the leafy arches of the forest.

Captain Reardon, however, was an old soldier, and not easily to be deceived. He resolved to refresh his men by means of a hearty breakfast, and then to scour the woods, two experienced hunters acting as scouts, lest the red skins should venture on an ambuscade.

Emma Reardon, dressed in most coquettish style, her beautiful eyes evidently suffused with tears, but whether shed at the sight of the dangers endured by her friends or from any other cause, we cannot at present decide, had prepared a magnificent breakfast. There was flesh of deer, and turkey, and goose; there was fish from the lake, Indian corn-cakes, coffee and whiskey in abundance. All did justice to the fare, and none more so than Joe Smith, whose little gray eyes twinkled with satisfaction at the sight of so much goodly fare.

If ever there was a mere animal nature, it was that of Joe Smith.

After breakfast the intended expedition took place, but by some unaccountable accident, Joe had a great splinter in his foot, which wholly incapacitated him from walking. The unsuspicious captain suggested a poultice and a day's conversation with Solomon Spaulding.

To this Joe was nothing loth.

Cradled in rude and savage hills, whose deep ravines and narrow gullies he had explored inch by inch, his soul had not failed to be slightly touched by that awe which grandeur always inspires. There were strange germs in this man's soul. Like Mahomet and Joan of Arc (to desecrate these great names in connection with one so vile), he had yearnings from his youth upwards to be something, which yearnings properly directed had perhaps made him great in the paths of honour and virtue.

And yet one who could contrive so foul an imposture, who could bring to his aid blasphemy and the most audacious misuse of divine names and things, who could found a sect on the basis of promiscuous sexual intercourse, must have had a natural bias towards evil.

But Joe could do nothing like anyone else. When he could have had a pig or a goose for asking, he preferred stealing it; and though he had not the least idea as yet how—he had come to the resolution to be a mighty leader among men.

He had a deep reverence, like many another spouting and inveterate ranter, for money; and as he had not as yet hit upon the idea of the tabernacle, he took the simplest way to find gold.

Joe had since his infancy been a money-digger.

On every spot where a rumour of hidden treasure was rife, there was Joe. But as yet he had found nothing.

Some other plan must, then, be hit upon.

He knew not why, but the antiquarian researches of Solomon had awakened in his bosom a certain amount of awe; and when the sick student spoke of the early history of America, and asserted that the Indians were the descendants of the lost tribes of Israel, his excitement became great.

"You seem interested," said the student, with a faint blush; "shall I read you the imaginary history of the early settlers, which I have written during my seclusion here?"

"It would delight me," replied Joe.

With all the delight and ardour of a young author, Spaulding unlocked a heavy desk.

"This is the clean copy for the press," he said, pointing to one sealed up, "but this is the same."

And turning the leaves in a feverish way, he began to read.

It was a wild and extravagant religious novel, in which Mormon and his son Meroni played the principal part. It was written in a biblical style,

and professed to detail the arrival of the first settlers in America—the lost tribes of Israel, who came from Jerusalem by land and sea, and who now are the wild and savage red skins.

Much mention was made of the Lamanites.

Joe listened with awe and rapture. The heavy sweat poured in pearly drops from his brow. As he wiped his head with his rude kerchief, he revolved scheme after scheme, but could come to no conclusion.

A wild inspiration was in the lad's inmost soul, an inspiration at which Lucifer might have smiled, but it took no form as yet.

Joe's sensations of admiration were the greater that he could not read.

The reading was interrupted by the return of the scouts and hunters. The Indians, it was reported, had lost heart, and departed.

Joe and his brothers, who were some distance from home, determined at once to venture through the woods next day, and for this purpose decided on starting at daybreak.

With this view, after a hearty supper, crowned by a huge bowl of punch, of which all partook freely, they retired to rest, the four brothers thanking Reardon heartily for his hospitality, while the generous old man declared himself deeply indebted to them for saving his daughter, and begged for an early visit, when he would be able to fix a day for his daughter's wedding.

All promised.

Next morning, the four brothers left the stockade, and commenced their march.

They had not gone more than a mile down a deep gully, which the sagacious William had selected, when Joe gravely cried a halt.

"He was not going home with them," he said, "at all events, then."

"Why?"

He could not say, but they might go alone, or wait for him there, just as they pleased.

All, except Hyrum, believing in one of his mad treasure-digging expeditions, shrugged their shoulders, and already feeling the effect of his determination and superior talents, yielded to his wishes.

Joe smiled, and lay down to rest.

At dark he left them, nor did he return until late, and then he was not alone.

Under his arm was a parcel sewed in canvas, and by his side was Emma.

She had eloped with Joe from the tender arms of her father, and the affections of her affianced husband.

But the necessities of our narrative compel us to leave General Joe, and follow in the tracks of the men whom we left in New York.

We shall find them by introducing certain new characters. Much of the misdeeds of the Mormons must be related in the forms of episodes as we proceed.

CHAPTER XXV.

A HAPPY HOME.

RICHARD BROWN was a native of one of our most fertile western counties. At an early age he had been seized by a desire to visit foreign parts, and his first adventure was on board a vessel sailing for New York. He shipped as cabin boy.

This one voyage was enough for him. No sooner had he set foot upon the soil of the republic than he determined to reside there permanently.

We have no space to record his upward battles in the world, but shall take him at the age of thirty-four, well to do, prosperous, and full of hope for the future.

He had a store of his own, and employed several clerks; he owned a warehouse on one of the quays, and several vessels which traded with the interior and along the coast.

He was said to be making money with extreme rapidity, and all the marriageable ladies above a certain age, began to set their caps at him. Of course, lovely damsels of from seventeen to twenty-one never do such things. It is the men who run after them.

Now, Richard Brown was a tall, portly, handsome man of his years, which were few for one so high in the world's favour, but business had so absorbed him that the idea had never crossed his mind how much more agreeable his home would be, were there a smiling, young, and pretty face to greet him on his return, to say nothing of numerous little Browns on a graduated scale.

His home was elegant, neat, and warmly tended by a lively housekeeper of about thirty, the widow of one of his clerks, killed in his service.

A very enticing widow, too, and she knew it.

Strange that this fact never struck Mr. Brown.

He was in everything away from his counting-house one of the most simple of creatures. His heart was without guile, and it never struck him that those glossy brown ringlets, those dark brown eyes, those dimpled cheeks were periodically shining, glistening, and smiling upon him for the desperate purpose of reducing him to subjection.

Ambitious, wily, amorous Mrs. Pigott, was to him an upper servant, with whom he was on the most friendly terms—no more.

Sheep's-eyes, sighs, looks, cast-down glances, and blushes, were all lost on the cold-hearted Dick.

His time had not come.

But one Sunday afternoon, when after a very hard week's work Richard Brown had ventured upon a solitary rural walk, his fate met him.

It had been very hot. The sun, however, was obscured by clouds. But it was a sultry day. By some instinct or fatality, Dick Brown had a silk umbrella, which was the more fortunate that towards the afternoon it promised rain. Dick looked up at the sky, and smiled at his own foresight.

Alas! poor victim.

He was following a very retired and unfrequented path across some fields, which presently brought him to a small, bubbling, rippling stream, crossed by means of large stones placed at short distances just above the pellucid waters.

Dick raised his eyes, and his face became crimson.

As far as he could judge, the stream was being crossed by a tall, handsome girl, who, totally unconscious of the proximity of a male individual was showing a little more of a leg and ankle than is usual in public, even when the said leg or ankle is encased in the most spotless of white hose.

Spell bound, Richard Brown followed, and just as the lady reached the other side—she was dressed in white, with a thin silk scarf, a chip bonnet, and feather—the rain came on.

"Allow me," said Richard Brown, bounding to her side by an impulse he could not resist.

The young person looked up, blushed, was excessively confused, and cast down her eyes again.

But she did not refuse the proffered umbrella.

The shower was very heavy, so that they were glad to take shelter beneath a dense grove of trees, which in addition to the umbrella, completely screened them from the rain.

"I am afraid, Miss," said Dick, "that it has set in for the evening."

"I hope not," cried the other, in a startled tone, "for I must go through with it, then."

Dick thought he never had seen any one so beautiful. She was a tall girl of about eighteen, with jet black hair, dark eyes, an oval and somewhat olive complexion, with an expression of considerable intellect and power—just now heightened into beauty by her excited state of mind.

"Impossible! you would be soaked through in five minutes, even with my umbrella," continued Dick; "and now I think of it, the clouds do look a little lighter. Let us wait half an hour."

The young lady acquiesced, and the conversation became more general. She was very lively, witty, and had read much. Her conversation was agreeable, even fascinating. The half-hour passed away like five minutes.

"I really must go," she said with a sigh, "there is no prospect of a change."

"But why in such a hurry. If we wait awhile the stage will pass yonder on the high road in an hour," replied Dick.

"In an hour," she gasped, "I shall be ruined."

"How so," he said with genuine interest.

"I am apprentice to a dressmaker, Madame Selous; and if I stop out after eight, she will dismiss me, and I shall forfeit my premium," she said, with a deep blush.

He had noticed that neatly as she was dressed, her things were all very plain. He calculated that she was poor.

"I know Madame Selous," he continued, "she works for my housekeeper, Mrs. Pigott."

"Are you Mr. Richard Brown?" said the young girl, blushing still more crimson.

The merchant smiled, and drew himself up to his fullest height.

"That is my name."

"I must wish you good-bye, and thank you," she said in a low tone; "the poor milliner's apprentice is no fit companion for you. You would be laughed at if seen, I should be pointed at. Thank you once more for the last time."

"If I let you go," cried Dick, heartily, "may I be—well never mind, Miss—what's your name?"

"Eliza Simmons,"—very faintly.

"Now look you, Miss Eliza Simmons. I'm

Dick Brown, worth I suppose some hundred thousand dollars, perhaps more. I am thirty-four years of age, single, and never saw anybody half so handsome or charming in my life. I'm a plain, outspoken man. If you will have me, here I am ; and if you won't, I'm d—d if I ever marry. Say, will you place yourself under the care of my housekeeper to-night, and to-morrow —well, to-morrow we will see ; and besides," looking at his watch, " *it's nearly eight o'clock !*"

Eliza Simmons looked wildly at him, and would have fled in real alarm.

But there was something so open, manly, real, and genuine in his manner and expression, that she could not be angry.

"You can't expect me, sir," she said, " to take so hasty a proposition seriously,—our different stations in society."

" Fiddlesticks ! my father was a half-starved farm labourer. I know all you would say. Well, I shall love you no better in six months than I do now. I know my heart, however. It has spoken once and for ever. Eliza Simmons, you have the happiness or misery of an honest man in your hands—say the word."

"But it's so absurd."

"Excessively sensible — cut dressmaking — employ Madame Selous yourself, eh ?"

The eyes of the girl flashed fire.

"Besides, only fancy the scolding," he said, half imploringly, half jokingly, " *it's eight o'clock !*"

"I will not accept so sudden, so strange an offer," she faltered ; "but if Mrs. Pigott will give me a bed, I will accept it, and ask her to make my peace to-morrow with Madame Selous."

Dick Brown made no reply ; but as at that instant the rain ceased, he took her arm, and, hurrying along, caught a return vehicle on the highway, which put them down, in a very short time, at his own door.

Dick Brown was a little pale as he descended from the vehicle, and caught sight of the widow on the top of the steps.

"My good gracious !" she said, with uplifted hands, " Master, and Lizzy Simmons !"

"Poor girl, yes," cried Dick, hypocritically. "Caught in the pelting storm—afraid to go home. Give her a warm supper and a bed, and after breakfast send for Madame Selous. *We* must talk to her."

"She's a dreadful old tigress," replied the unsuspicious Mrs. Pigott ; "but I dare say you can bring her round, sir."

"I dare say I can," said Dick, drily.

Next morning Dick sat gravely reading his paper ; Lizzy blushing, and her heart palpitating, tried to eat ; Mrs. Pigott did the honours of the breakfast-table with the dignity of the future mistress, when Madame Selous was announced.

"Ah, vot I see !" she cried, with a wicked glance at Lizzy, " my runvay 'prentice. A mees, I send you vay, I stop you—"

"Madam," said Dick Brown, severely, " hold your clatter, and take the measure of Miss Simmons for the most magnificent *trousseau* your *atelier* will afford. On Saturday, Miss Simmons becomes Mrs. Brown."

Mrs. Pigott shrieked, Lizzy fainted, and Ma-

dame Selous became perfectly cringing and servile in her attentions.

And thus Lizzy Simmons became Mrs. Brown, and for five years lived with as full a share of happiness as is given to us mortals here below to enjoy.

Then came—but we must not anticipate.

CHAPTER XXVI.
MARRIAGE AND MYSTERY.

MATRIMONY is a mystery, which those who have had the most experience of, understand the least. It is notorious that those matches made under the most sunny auspices, where on both sides there is every promise of happiness, are often the most miserable.

Too much is expected on both sides, and both are disappointed.

There are two roads to happiness in wedlock.

The first is where two people of an unimpassioned nature seriously select each other as partners for life, calmly, without any very great expectations, and travel on together for years, serenely, quietly, without any emotion that makes the heart beat wildly or even irregularly.

The second is the true marriage, where two hearts, irresistibly impelled towards each other, meet in a furnace, as it were, of affection, and become fused into one, where thought, being, soul, desire, are all in common ; where the man, impelled by resistless force, yields his whole heart unto a woman, who, in turn, responds by all that deep devotion, ardent love, strong sympathy, and fathomless affection which is the glory and pride of the sex.

Such a union is like a mingling of gold and silver ; the contrast of strength and weakness, of manly vigour and feminine dependence, is more beautiful, however, than anything which colour can effect.

Now, the marriage of Richard Brown and Eliza Simmons belonged to neither of these categories. Dick was a man of business, absorbed in the cares of a multifarious trade, proud of his wife and his home, delighted to return of an evening to his domestic gods, and to see the lovely woman presiding at his table. Nothing gratified him more than the smile on her face, or the sparkle in her eye when he brought her home rich presents, or a ticket for the opera, or theatre, or public ball.

But never, though he could not see it, was more ill-assorted couple.

Mrs. Brown was a woman of ardent soul, devoured by nameless desires. She craved after the impossible, after the unknown. She fancied that she should have been the wife of a great poet, actor, or painter, who would have comprehended her soul.

Alas ! as no man is a hero to his valet, how few are but ordinary mortals to their wives.

"Who could love a man she saw use a bootjack or wear a nightcap ?" cries a despairing Frenchwoman.

Mrs. Brown would sit for hours with a novel or a poem before her, which she saw not, or read not, her eyes fixed on vacancy, her mind far away, dreaming—seated on the borders of a vast ocean, across which her soul would fly, far, far away into the dim obscurity of some unknown region, as yet unexplored.

Out, out into the dark waste of waters would she sail in search of something, she knew not what.

By day, by night, this sensation was on her soul. A dead, heavy weight pressed upon her heart, a weight of actual woe, felt more acutely that she could not share it.

She saw a doctor, but he could do nothing for her. It was mental, purely mental. But her conscience is clear, she has done no evil.

Woman! thou hast married a man without feeling affection for him, and the craving of thy soul is love!

Many women (like Mrs. Richard Brown had for five years) pass through life unaware of the volcano in their own bosoms, happy and innocent, because untempted.

Mrs. Pigott had not left on the marriage of the merchant. She had so contrived by assiduity, by making herself useful, by taking all household cares off the hands of Eliza, as to render herself indispensable.

One evening—it was Mr. Brown's whist evening at his club—Mrs. Brown was alone. She knew not why, but she had not asked anybody to tea. She was even more melancholy and meditative than usual. She had resolved to fill several pages of her journal. These mystic, un-understood women, write their thoughts in ledgers. In time, like other old ledgers, too, they go to the butterman.

Suddenly Mrs. Pigott entered, dressed for out of doors.

"Going out?" said Mrs. Brown.

"Yes," replied the housekeeper; "I am going to hear the most wonderful preacher ever known. He has discovered a new dispensation, a straight road to heaven. It makes one so comfortable to hear him."

"Indeed," cried Mrs. Brown, whose whole soul craved for excitement and novelty, "I think I shall go with you."

Mrs. Pigott clapped her hands. A flash of pleasure brightened her brown eyes.

In a few minutes, Mrs. Brown, who was always full dressed, was ready. She was now a magnificent even voluptuous-looking woman. Ease and good living had done their work.

Three-and-twenty, her face rather pale, but with a most perfect contour, a faint but healthy blush, her teeth white as pearls, and her eyes wild and languishing, no man ever passed her unnoticed.

And this woman it was, superbly dressed, who entered that evening the chapel of the Latter-Day Saints. It was a great evening it appeared. Christian Whitmer was to preach to the people, who came in crowds.

Mrs. Brown and Mrs. Pigott, who had reserved seats, took up their places in front of the preacher.

It is not our province to fill our pages with the blasphemy which falls like poison-drops from the lips of these preachers. Suffice that the discourse for the evening was on Joe Smith and his early career. After numerous wild quotations from Scripture and incoherent phrases, such as occur

in the Book of Mormon,* he began to expatiate on the inspired nature of Joe Smith, of whom he said:—

"When somewhere about fourteen or fifteen years old, he began seriously to reflect upon the necessity of being prepared for a future state of existence; but how, or in what way to prepare himself, was a question as yet undetermined in his own mind. He perceived that it was a question of infinite importance, and that the salvation of his soul depended upon a correct understanding of the same. He retired to a secret place in a grove but a short distance from his father's house, and knelt down and began to call upon the Lord. At first he was severely tempted by the powers of darkness, which endeavoured to overcome him, but he continued to seek for deliverance until darkness gave way from his mind, and he was enabled to pray in fervency of the spirit, and in faith; and while thus pouring out his soul, anxiously desiring an answer from God, he at length saw a very bright and glorious light in the heavens above, which at first seemed to be at a considerable distance. He continued praying, while the light appeared to be gradually descending towards him; and as it drew nearer it increased in brightness and magnitude, so that by the time it reached the tops of the trees the whole wilderness was illuminated in a most glorious and brilliant manner. He expected to see the leaves and boughs of the trees consumed as soon as the light came in contact with them; but perceiving that it did not produce that effect, he was encouraged with the hopes of being able to endure its presence. It continued descending slowly, until it rested upon the earth, and he was enveloped in the midst of it. When it first came upon him, it produced a peculiar sensation throughout his whole system; and immediately his mind was caught away from the natural objects with which he was surrounded, and he was enwrapped in a heavenly vision, and saw two glorious personages, who exactly resembled each other in their features or likeness. He was informed that his sins were forgiven. He was also informed upon the subjects which had for some time previously agitated his mind—namely, that all the religious denominations were believing in incorrect doctrines, and consequently that none of them was acknowledged of God as His church and kingdom. And he was expressly commanded to go not after them; and he received a promise that the true doctrine, the fulness of the Gospel, should at some future time be made known to him. After which the vision withdrew, leaving his mind in a state of calmness and peace indescribable."

He then coolly and solemnly recorded Joe Smith's interview with an angel, "*a little above the common size of men in his age;*† his garment was perfectly white, and had the appearance of being without seam," who pointed out to him where the new Bible was to be found; and, after a series of wild, rudely-eloquent, and rhapsodical appeals for the truths of the new book, concluded in some such words as these:

"Why do I summon you, my beloved brethren, and, above all, my dear sisters? I summon you in the name of our great prophet and leader, to whom, on the 21st February, 1831, Jesus Christ himself in person said, 'Hearken, oh! ye elders of my church, who have assembled yourselves together in my name, even Jesus Christ, the Son of the Living God, the Saviour of the world. Behold, verily I say unto you, I give unto you the first commandment, that ye shall go forth in my name, except my servant Joseph Smith, junior.' And they went forth, and he remained to be our stay and our support. Verily I say unto you, there hath not been one since St. John who is so great. Did he not translate the Book of Mormon from hieroglyphics,

* For example "Ye are likely unto they—Do as ye hath hitherto done—I—the Lord delighteth in the chastity of women, I saith unto them—I who ye call your king, &c."

† The words of Orson Pratt, one of the twelve apostles.

A DRAWING-ROOM SCENE.

the knowledge of which was lost to the world; in which wonderful event he stood alone, an unlearned youth, to combat the worldly wisdom and multiplied ignorance of eighteen centuries, with a new revelation, which would open the eyes of more than eight hundred millions of people, and make plain the old paths. And the power of God has held him up against the power of hell and earth, and verily I say unto you, that now the new dispensation is known, none shall be saved unless they come unto Joseph Smith, who has witnessed the visions of eternity, who has beheld the glories of the mansions of bliss—who has seen the regions and misery of the damned. I say, then, let all see and know the goodness and glory of God, for as sure as ye come unto us, so sure as you lay your burden at our feet, shall you have joy and happiness unutterable in this world, and eternal life in the next.

"The God that others worship, is not the God for me.
He has no parts nor body, and cannot hear nor see.
    But I've a God that lives above,
    A God of power and of love.
A God of revelation—oh, that's the God for me!
Oh, that's the God for me! oh that's the God for me!"

Some terrible denunciations, certain wild and entrancing promises of earthly joy and repose, certain visionary outlines of terrestrial happiness, with vague allusions to the future, followed, the whole delivered in the most burning language,—language that made the heart beat wildly, the cheek turn pale, and the eyes of his votaries brighten.

"Come in, and be introduced to him," said Mrs. Pigott, as they rose.

Eliza made no reply. She had listened with open mouth. The preacher's eyes had been fixed on her from the first. His ardent and fiery glances had exercised a magnetic kind of influence over her. All these imposters had availed themselves of what was true in mesmerism, and turned it, like A. Dumas, to account. Like most imaginative women, talent and eloquence of any kind had a deep grasp upon her mind. Hence the ease with which certain ministers of the Gospel have drawn women from the paths of virtue. Spiritual ecstacy is too often followed by more mundane emotions.

Mrs. Brown followed her, conducted like one in a dream, and was scarcely conscious, when the housekeeper invited Christian Whitmer to call, of what she had done. But that night she slept not. A strange and awful presentiment weighed upon her mind.

CHAPTER XXVII.

BIGAMY.

WHEN Phineas Bristowe rushed forth from the hotel with all his money restored, he was more nearly going mad than at any of the worst periods of his trials.

A reprieve from death has often been the cause of insanity.

Phineas rushed along, regardless of where he went, until wearied and exhausted, he sat down in a retired place.

Wiping the perspiration from his brow, he became more calm, and at once secreted his treasure.

Then he waited until he found a conveyance, and returned into the heart of New York. It would be difficult to say which thought occupied him most, joy at the recovery of his money, or the prospect of vengeance on Susan and her ravisher.

His first visit was to a superior class of ready-made warehouse, where with a smile he recounted his mishap, and requested that the very best of everything should be shown him.

He rigged himself out in a showy but rich style, slipped on a common suit, and having purchased a portmanteau, followed a porter to a respectable hotel recommended by the clothiers.

Before an hour had passed, Phineas Bristowe had indulged in a warm bath, a bottle of spiced wine, and a light supper, after which he retired to a luxurious bed, in which he slept the sleep of the just.

In the morning, after twelve hours of complete rest, and a breakfast such as is rarely seen out of America, the preacher felt all his burning passions revive within him.

He sallied forth, armed, without any particular aim, but determined to make himself familiar with the localities of the place.

He pretty well recollected where he had seen Christian Whitmer and Susan.

They had been at the entrance of a princely hotel, a circumstance which puzzled Phineas. He was not aware of the kind of dust thrown in the eyes of the dupes of Mormonism.

It was a splendid day, and before he had been long abroad the street became thronged. Men hurried hither and thither intent on business, while others strolled about looking at the shops and the beautiful women who were beginning to throng them, and the not less beautiful girls who were the presiding divinities.

But though Phineas Bristowe was seldom indifferent to a close examination of female loveliness in any form, he was now insensible.

His eyes were fixed on a carriage which stood before the hotel of the previous day, and which he fancied he recognised.

The carriage-way was so crowded that vehicles could only proceed at a walk.

When the expected couple, accompanied by two girls very well dressed, chiefly in white, came out, Phineas Bristowe was able to follow them with ease.

Susan was radiant.

She had a white crown upon her head, which denoted her intention of becoming a bride that day—and a virgin bride too!

Phineas tottered for a moment, and then followed.

To his amazement they did not drive off to any obscure chapel of their own persuasion, but halted before a respectable church.

The preacher clutched his loaded pistols, and followed the bridal party, which in the church had become rather numerous.

He hid himself in a corner of the church behind a pillar. A frantic rage took possession of his soul. He would kill them both as they retired triumphant from the altar.

His agony was intense. The bride was exceedingly lovely.

Phineas now first understood the magnificence of the creature he had hitherto seen clothed only in the humble garb of service. His face was deadly pale, his lips were white, his teeth clenched, and his eyes rolled wildly in their sockets.

He looked the very demon of vengeance.

The service was over, and they retired to sign their names. Phineas looked at the priming of his pistol.

A hand was laid on his shoulder.

He turned quickly, and a tall, youngish woman, with the remains of great beauty, concealed by dirt, rags, and a hungry expression of countenance, peered right in his face.

"Which do you hate?" she said huskily.

"Both," he replied mechanically.

"Ha! ha! ha!" she gasped, "don't kill them; follow me, and I'll show you how to be avenged."

"Who—what are you?"

"Follow me, and you shall know. Nan, I seek not to deceive you. There is no torture imagination can conceive, which I would not inflict on them. Death would be mercy. Come."

Phineas Bristowe reflected. Assassination in open day would be fatal to himself. Delay would only make revenge the sweeter.

The woman, as if satisfied that he would follow her, strode out of the church without looking back. Phineas did not lose sight of her.

Soon, to his astonishment, he found himself threading a labyrinth of dark, narrow, and muddy streets, as filthy and hideous as any in the old country. Cries of rage, laughter, the most hideous blasphemies, snatches of horrid songs, assailed his ears from the open doors of slimy and half-ruined houses.

They were in the quarter of poverty, destitution, crime, and death—the Five Points.

Suddenly the woman darted up stairs, followed by Phineas, who could scarcely keep his footing on the greasy and repulsive-looking planks. At every storey, men and women in actual rags, begrimed with dirt and smoke, half naked and hungry-looking, thrust their heads out, to stare at the stranger.

Phineas would gladly have retreated, but that would have been to show fear.

At the summit of the house the woman halted, and threw open a door that scarcely stood on its hinges.

A small tallow candle, hastily lighted, exhibited a room utterly devoid of furniture.

There were the four bare walls, the very window-panes being replaced by rags and straw, while everywhere the evidences of rain were visible.

"Behold man! This day in the church, with his carriage and pair, this man was married. He is my husband, and this is *my* home. Ha! ha! ha! do you not see the revenge we have in store?"

"Then she is not his wife?" cried Phineas, wildly.

"I am his first and lawful wife," said the woman, in a hollow tone, as she tore down a piece of the wainscoting, and took out some papers, "and I am dying of hunger."

"Why did you not say so before?" gasped Phineas; "let us leave this place. Why did you bring me here?"

"That you should see my misery, and be present while I secured the means of vengeance. Ha! ha! ha! how she will crouch in agony, and how I shall triumph over her."

Phineas turned to go, and by great good fortune reached the street unmolested. He did not like the situation in which he found himself. The man was a natural coward. He could tell that he was in a neighbourhood to which St. Giles's in London was safe, as New York was then the refuge for the destitute, the vicious, the offscourings of all Europe.

The woman, however, entered a miserable-looking eating-house, and called for food, which she ate ravenously.

"Can you spare me a little money," she said, in a hesitating manner, "that I may appear decently in the streets?"

Phineas Bristowe, who would not have given to a beggar to save her life, a penny, eagerly pressed gold upon her, gave his direction, and made an appointment for the next day.

Sweet indeed is revenge to the heart of most men.

The wild desire raged within his soul, until it scorched. Bigamy was severely punished in those days, when the United States had not departed so much from its primitive simplicity as it has now.

Seven years in a cell, for a man like Christian Whitmer would be worse than death to some.

His wild and fierce passions would be as scorpion-whips to lash his soul.

CHAPTER XXVIII.

LE PREMIER PAS.

MRS. RICHARD BROWN retired to rest that night with a weight upon her soul. Her evening at the chapel had aroused strange dreams within her, and the dark and piercing eye of the preacher was never out of her thoughts.

She could not sleep.

While her good and faithful husband was wrapped in peaceful slumber, dreaming, if at all, of argosies and Dutch consignments, of his quickly-increasing dollars, and perhaps of his handsome wife, she tossed restless, feverish, and unquiet.

Where a green and placid oasis had so long been, up had risen a volcano breathing flames and suffocating smoke.

The path of life, so still, so tranquil, had become rugged, boisterous, and full of asperities.

She panted for breath as she lay; there was a sinking of the heart, a dull lowness of spirits, accompanied by an inclination to weep.

She burned for the morrow.

Now, Eliza Brown had no thought of any evil; she merely hankered for the unknown and incomprehensible — for what she had not.

Like many another young woman she felt a nameless want.

It is painful, indeed, to be tied to one you love not, who has no sympathies in common with your own, who cannot quench the fire of soul which is within you. But why marry without love? The error brings its own punishment.

Darkly, drearily, sadly passed the long hours until dawn came, when she woke, haggard and unrefreshed. She sat down to breakfast in silence.

"You are not well," said Richard, glancing his eye over his paper at his wife.

"Nothing," she replied, quietly, "only I did not sleep very well last night. A day's quiet will put me to rights."

"Had you not better see Dr. Watts?" continued the husband, anxiously.

"Oh no! it is nothing. You mustn't spoil me," she added, laughing—but *not* that silvery ringing laugh which was so peculiarly her own.

Richard Brown dived into his paper, and shortly after walked down to his office calm, his mind full of business, happy and contented.

Proud indeed should be the wife whose husband, while carving out her and her children's fortunes, gives his honour wholly into her hands.

A doubt of Eliza, would in his mind have been sacrilege,

Under Mrs. Pigott were all negro servants,

without exception devoted to their mistress, who was very kind to them.

Mrs. Pigott was tart, suspicious, and exacting, not one of the domestics liked her. On this occasion she announced her intention of going out marketing. She would, she said, afterwards visit her mother.

Eliza Brown sat in a small and excessively handsome furnished room. It was adorned with pictures of considerable value, and possessed a harp and piano. Music she had studied under the very best teachers that money could afford, and yet she liked it not. Her soul of late had not been attuned to harmony, everything grated upon mind and ears.

There was a chord without tune somewhere.

She had dressed herself with unusual care. In general, her attire was very simple.

But now a dark velvet robe defined as she sat the contour of her splendid limbs, while a stomacher of lawn scarcely concealed the bursting beauties of an admirably shaped bust. Her pallor was all gone. Her skin was white as the driven snow, but the centre of her cheeks were roseate and blooming. Her lips were as ruddy as health could make them. Her eyes shone with terrible vivacity.

"What is the meaning of all this?" she cried, struggling with her own secret impulses. "Why am I not content? Why do shadow-processions of events cross my path—why do I stumble and halt as one in a dark place? What could be more kind, more generous, more devoted than the behaviour of my husband? And yet am I like the imprisoned bird panting for air and liberty. And yet do I feel like some long imprisoned sufferer eager to leave his cell, or as a sojourner on some pleasant island, who, wearied of the silken monotony of happiness, would launch out upon the dark sea of doubt. Why am I not happy—why do I ever thirst for that which is not, cannot, never will be? My fate is settled. I am to live the ordinary life of woman; be the head of the house, to receive my husband's friends, to dress in fine clothes, and visit my equals, to read, talk, and play. What more would I have? *What more would I have?*" she repeated, clutching her hands over her head. "Why all, everything, the glowing sympathy of a soul all love and passion, a poetic, ideal existence, eternal converse on the beautiful and true, wanderings through the vales and over the hills of lands consecrated by fame, anything but the tame, quiet, passionless existence to which the respectable married woman is doomed. I do declare that I would rather be a trull, bedizened in faded silks, in second-hand plumes and borrowed flowers, the plaything of an hour, than the licensed companion of a man whose calm and passionless existence drives me mad, and whose sterling worth makes me blush with shame."

And striding across the room she pressed down the bands of her jet black hair upon her massive forehead.

"I have seen a worse face than that, the observed of all observers in an opera-box, but Ha! ha! ha! my husband is a simple merchant, totally unsuited to such a place, and yet, were I to speak the word—were I but to whisper a desire, all this and much more would be mine."

An impatient gesture, a walk, and then she began again.

"Alas! why do I deceive myself? It is nothing of all this I want, but love—only love, the undying devotion of a heart all my own, which utterly removed from all the vulgar cares of life, would sit in passionate communion with my soul for ever. But hush! be still thou truant beating heart—let me drown my senses in harmony."

And wildly she struck the harp, which gave forth a wail of sad and almost unearthly music.

"I will sing unto the Lord," said a seductive voice; "sing praises in His name. To every thing there is a season, and a time to every purpose under the heavens; a time to weep, and a time to laugh; a time to mourn, and a time to dance. When I gaze on so much beauty and so much grace, I could say, 'Let her kiss me with the kisses of her mouth: for thy love is better than wine.' Pardon me, fair lady, but if my tongue goes too fastly, believe me that I mean no offence—only a brotherly greeting."

And before Mrs. Brown could recover herself, he had implanted a kiss upon her forehead.

Timid, trembling, with downcast eyes, as shamefaced as a school-girl of sixteen, that woman sat in the presence of the bold, handsome and cynical apostle of the new faith. She felt that his eyes were upon her, and she dared not look up.

"It delighted me much, my sister," he said, taking her burning hand in his, "to see you at the meeting of the saints. Where two or three of *us* are gathered together, there is the spirit. To us has been revealed the truth, as taught by our great prophet who translated the book of life from an unknown tongue. And we declare, that an angel came down from heaven and brought the plates, which we saw."

"Did you see them?" cried Mrs. Brown, clasping her hands. "Is it possible that I am honoured by the presence of one who has conversed with the Lord?"

"It was necessary to convince us," said Christian Whitmer, humbly; "we were all hard to believe, a stiff-necked and unbelieving generation. So, at the earnest request of Joseph himself, the Lord appeared unto us, to certify to the truth of the book, and we know that all who believe shall be rid of their garments of blood, and dwell eternally in the heavens."

Mrs. Brown's eyes opened with wonder and ecstacy.

"Sister," continued Christian, "forasmuch as the heart of man is hard and difficult to convince, are we compelled to seek our converts amongst the fairer and softer sex. For one man who will join Zion, there are a dozen women."

Mrs Brown raised her eyes with a startled expression. The words rather sobered her.

"But I understand marriage to be one of your most sacred sacraments."

"So it is, the holiest of the holy, the joy of this life, and the preparation for the next. But, forasmuch as no woman can be saved except through a believing husband, the saints have so ordained, according to the commandment of the Lord, that whereas every man shall have a wife, who shall be unto him a carnal wife, the mother of his children and the head of his household, so the elect of grace among the sex shall, until such time as all mankind be turned to the right way, be the spiritual wives of the elders, and so shall they be saved."

For an hour he poured forth a torrent of such jargon, interlarded with scriptural quotations, by which he sought to prove that there was no happiness in this world, and no hope for the next, except in a belief in the Latter-Day Saints.

Mrs. Brown was subjugated, overpowered, overwhelmed more by the impassioned voice of the man than by his words. Then he changed his tone, and began to develop his own personal feelings. Without alarming her, or wounding a delicacy as yet untainted, he allowed her to see by his looks, his sighs, his grave aspect, that he was her devoted slave, and took his leave suddenly, wringing her hands as if he dared trust himself no longer with her.

Mrs. Brown covered her face with her hands, and buried her head in the soft cushions. She was in a perfect whirl of excitement. She remembered scarcely a word of what the preacher had said, but she felt the pressure of his hand, she saw the roll of his dark lustrous eye, and the kiss on her forehead burned like a coal.

Meanwhile, on the threshold of the boudoir stood, eyeing her with malignant satisfaction, the widow, who all these years had bided her time.

"At last," she muttered, and glided away.

CHAPTER XXIX.

CASTING OUT DEVILS.

A SUMMONS came to Christian Whitmer from the saints in Jackson County, Missouri, to join them with as little delay as possible. He had already sent on the main body of his dupes, who were to meet him in Kirkland, Ohio. He waited but to grasp at one or two richer victims, who would bring large treasures to the stores of the sect.

This caused him unlimited leave.

Susan had from the first, when consenting to aid the views of her husband, insisted on a firm, tangible, and legal marriage. She insisted, too, on his abstaining from any attempt to increase the number of his wives, all which Christian Whitmer solemnly pledged.

He, however, constantly pleaded business to leave her, and in this way contrived to visit Mrs. Brown every day.

The infatuated young woman, her brain on fire, her wildly impassioned nature raised to fever heat, her heart a vacuum before, readily believed the new doctrine taught by the preacher.

The belief in latter days prior to the second coming of Christ to reign on earth for a thousand years, is general with a large class of persons. On this idea the Mormon elder worked, straining every ordinary event of the day into a sign and portent. Teaching the old and the new, basing his doctrine upon stray passages from the Bible, asserting personal inspiration from God, promising possession of the earth all temporal power and glory, and the blessing of heaven upon true believers, he only exaggerated and caricatured the conduct of many another popular exponent of truth.

Mrs. Brown believed. Her soul bent in earnest and devoted belief. She was convinced that the truth was in this man.

Then Christian Whitmer gave her clearly to understand that she must give up her unbelieving husband, and fly to Zion, where she could be regenerated.

She started from this with abhorrence. What! leave her good, kind, devoted, tender husband, the man who had raised her from the dust, who had devoted his whole soul to her, and whose only regret, most good-humouredly expressed, was that he had no children—no, never.

"You love this man of Belial," said Christian Whitmer, coldly.

"No; but I respect, I venerate him," she faltered.

"Let him, then, be converted," continued the elder. "Bring him into the true church."

"He has expressed the most intense horror of your doctrines," cried the young woman.

"Then let him die in his sin," said Christian Whitmer, coldly; and then he added, taking her two hands in his, "I had not thought this. I had thought that one possessed of such lofty genius, of such noble aspirations, would have been an ornament and rich chaplet unto Zion. I had hoped that the humble person of the teacher of truth was not indifferent to you. I had begun to picture to myself a home in our Jerusalem, of which you were to be the hope, the adornment, the delight, and the joy—for oh, sister Eliza, I do—it is useless to disguise it longer—I do love thee."

The wife was startled. But she had long allowed the deadly poison to enter her soul. The first drop is the pollution.

And now as he spoke, her eyes flashed, her bosom heaved, her cheeks flushed, and then, as he continued in burning language to paint his passion, she slowly raised her eyes to his, swimming in tears of anguish and of joy.

"And you will be true unto me?"

"For ever!" said the wily elder, who was using the most dangerous weapon of destruction given to man—religious fervour.

But doubly accursed are these wolves in sheep's clothing, these deadly and dastardly hypocrites.

"Then I am thine, wholly thine," cried the infatuated girl.

"We are not safe here," replied the preacher, hastily. "Will you meet me this evening? I have to cast forth devils to-night from two women, after that I will see you alone. I have much to say."

She pressed his hand, they cordially embraced, and parted.

Nobody is more easily deceived than the good. That night, after tea, the wife spoke in calm and almost smiling accents to her husband.

"What are you going to do, Dick, to-night?"

"Stop at home with you, dear," he replied, slightly surprised.

"Well, but I wanted to hear a new lecturer, a religious lecturer, and then to call upon Mrs. Elton, who has sent word she is unwell. I suppose, Mr. Dick, I must send you out to whist," and she laughed.

"You impudent hussy," cried Dick, laughing, "why didn't you say so before I took my boots off?"

"I didn't think of it, but if you don't like—" she began.

"Don't like, my pet! Why you know, you dear darling, that there is nothing on earth I would not do to please or gratify you. Mrs. Pigott, just ring for Scipio to order the carriage."

Tears almost came to her eyes as she turned away. Had she wept, she had been saved.

Mrs. Pigott rose, and ordered the carriage. Mrs. Brown went up stairs to dress.

About half-past six she drove to the chapel used by the Latter-Day Saints in New York. A fearful, a hideous ceremony was going on. None but the initiated were allowed to be present.

The chief prophet had engaged to cast out devils.

A man had to be ordained to the priesthood; but alarmed for his reign on earth, the devil resisted.

"When we laid hands on him," said Christian Whitmer, on a subsequent occasion, "*the devil entered him;* but the power of Jesus Christ in the holy priesthood was stronger than the devil; and after all the endeavours of the powers of darkness to prevent us, we ordained Brother —— to the office of a priest in the Church of Jesus Christ and the Latter-Day Saints."*

But the devil was not to be done, so he entered a sister. "The devils kept coming for several hours. As fast as one lot was expelled, another lot entered. At one time we counted twenty-seven came out of her. How was it they could acknowledge the power, and yet would damn our power, damn our gospel, and tear and bite? The sight was awful, but it has done us good. I may as well say that the devils told us they were sent, some by Cain, some by Kite, Judas, Kilo, Kelo, Kalmonia, and Lucifer. We cast them out thirty times, and had three hundred and nineteen devils."

Could not the stocks, ducking-stool, and cart's tail be revived for such of those saints as are not fit inmates for a lunatic asylum?

Mrs. Brown listened with awe. She was spellbound; and when the chief priest prayed earnestly, and with seeming sincerity, that the demon might be removed; when Christian Whitmer rebuked the devil for indecent language, for calling him "d—d old captain;" and when he solemnly asserted that he himself had once wrestled seven hours and a half with Lucifer, and added numerous blasphemies, which we refrain to repeat—she believed.

* Word for word from a Mormon newspaper; and this scene occurred at Leamington Spa, Warwickshire, England.

Nothing is too absurd, even the violation of all human decency and common sense—even the ludicrous, for the credulous mass of ignorant fanatics.

The meeting closed with prayer and a general announcement that Satan had received "a goodly licking."

The audience gradually dispersed, not however before many poor dupes had been added to the list of the church.

Mrs. Brown joined the preacher, and shortly after left the chapel, closely wrapped up and leaning on his arm.

A darkly muffled figure, and then a second one, darted from an archway, and dogged their steps.

But the infatuated pair saw them not; they were in the full swing of a new-born passion, which is blind, deaf, and implacable.

They little thought of the clouds which were gathering round their devoted heads.

CHAPTER XXX.

A PANIC.

A HOT, sultry morning. Mrs. Brown slept heavily, and when she woke, could scarcely conceive but that all that passed was a dream.

She was in her own room, and alone.

A clock on the mantel-piece told her that it was twelve.

It was nearly four hours later than usual. Her husband, for the first time since her marriage, had breakfasted alone.

But she was rather glad of it. She could with a certain amount of calmness survey the events of the previous day, and look into the depths of the future. Her countenance was flushed and heated. She knew not whether to be glad or sorry at the course events were taking.

She did feel a strange, odd sinking of the heart, a twitch which will invade us when we have done ill. But then the flattering unction was laid to her soul, that as she had married for money, she could not but love some day.

If her husband was displeased, the law gave him his remedy in divorce.

We have great respect for the American people, more for their institutions; but the liberty with which the marriage tie can be dissolved is a crying evil.

American women, especially the southerners, who have many of the vices of their own negroes without their virtues, look too often upon marriage as a roving licence to go about the world independent of public opinion and morality.

If they indulge in any of those irregularities, such as flirtation, or even a little adultery, why what matter, if they cannot get a divorce, they have a separation.

They talk of French girls becoming emancipated by marriage—not half so emancipated as the yellow-skinned, gaunt-bodied, and languorous-eyed women of the south, who, were justice done in this world, would often wait upon their own striking, elegant, and even handsome half-caste girls.

If separation does take place between North and South, the negroes will certainly in the end be the masters, and the whites the slaves.

The clock struck twelve. At two her husband would be home to dinner. She had only just time to dress. She rang a bell, and when the attendant came, gave her the necessary orders.

She had a headache, was not well, but would try to come down to dinner.

Slowly, methodically, with the most consummate art she dressed herself. Never had she looked so thoroughly, so awfully beautiful. It was a sight to see her dress, a sight that would have delighted many a heart.

She descended to the drawing-room, and gave her orders; looked in upon the dining-room, saw that all was right, but stared at the sight of five plates.

When, however, she learned that the two head clerks were coming, she made no remark. Her husband had used her to sudden invitations, and in her native gaiety of heart company to her was always a relief.

They came precisely at two. Mr. Brown entered hastily, and begged that dinner might be hurried, as a sudden pressure of business had fallen upon them. He had brought his clerks with him to lose no time. He scarcely spoke to his wife, who presided at the table in her usual quiet, demure, and ladylike manner. The conversation was of protested bills, a tight market, and prognostications of a coming commercial panic.

"Many will go, sir," said the head clerk.

"Yes; it is to be hoped that my house has not been built upon sand," replied Mr. Brown, gloomily.

The clerk started at the tone in which this was said. Even his wife looked at him curiously, but he avoided her eye.

"I am not uneasy," continued Mr. Richard Brown, "oh! no. I know the stability of my affairs; but one can never be sure. I have been so happy, so contented, so tranquil, so solid, and firm for five years, and then so confident and believing, that I have never examined so closely as I otherwise should. Who knows? all the while enemies may have been undermining me, traitors deceiving me!"

"Sir!" cried the head clerk, while Mrs. Pigott and Mrs. Brown exchanged anxious glances, "you are unnecessarily alarming yourself. Whatever happens, your house is built upon a rock, and cannot fall. I stake my whole year's salary, that so safely have you done business, that the most terrible panic would do you no harm, nor touch your stability or happiness."

"I hope not," said Mr. Richard Brown, gravely; "but take a glass of wine. I must return at once to the office. Every book, every account in the ledger shall be overhauled before I sleep this night. I shall set my house in order, and be prepared for the worst."

As he said this he rose hurriedly, and though Mrs. Brown with anxious and beseeching looks implored an interview, he shook his head, and hurried away.

"What can be the matter?" cried Mrs. Brown,

"he looked so wild, so strange. I never saw the like before."

"I have heard strange rumours abroad," said Mrs. Pigott. "Banks are breaking, merchants smashing, and every sign of a commercial panic coming on. Fortunately, nearly every penny my master has, is invested in English securities."

"How do you know?" asked Mrs. Brown, with a keen, quick glance.

"Did you not notice that when he read you his will?" continued Mrs. Pigott.

"I had forgotten," said Mrs. Brown, with a flush.

She recollected that will. He had left her every penny he had in the world unconditionally.

But time was wearing away apace. Her spiritual visitor was coming at half-past three. Mrs. Brown passed to her bed-chamber, and from her chamber to her boudour.

The chief priest was received coldly.

A shade of compunction had fallen on her soul. But the man was wily and eloquent. He remained in conference with her until half-past five, when Mrs. Pigott knocked discreetly at the door. Oily, polite, and unctuous as she usually was, she was more so than common on this day.

"Master cannot return to tea, he sends to say. Will Mr. Whitmer join us?"

"Cannot return!" cried Mrs. Brown.

"You recollect what he said at dinner?"

"Oh! yes; of course Mr. Whitmer will stay."

They adjourned to the dining-room; tea was made; general conversation ensued. Christian Whitmer was very shrewd. Mrs. Pigott he saw was not a friend, so he was extremely careful how he behaved. He spoke of Zion, of the New Jerusalem, and launched forth into those unmeaning and irrelevant quotations from Scripture which serve to cover so much ignorance in certain ministers of the Gospel.

Big-sounding words, without any signification, are often preferable in the eyes of the vulgar to simple common sense.

About half-past nine, Mrs. Brown and Whitmer being alone—Mrs. Pigott had gone out to order supper—a violent ringing came to the bell.

Mrs. Pigott, after a moment, hastened in.

"Please, mum, master ain't very well, his work ain't finished, and should be much obliged if you would walk down to the warehouse for an hour."

Mrs. Brown and the preacher exchanged glances.

"Certainly," said the former, rising to conceal her pique and vexation. "Who brought the message?"

"Father Brown."

"I will go at once," replied the wife. "I am sorry to be so unceremonious, but I must leave you, Mr. Whitmer."

The preacher smiled, muttered something about her duty to her husband, and took his leave.

CHAPTER XXXI.

DARK WATERS.

It was now a dark and gloomy night. After the sultry heat of the day, the night-wind blew cold and fitful. And yet Mrs. Brown went out on foot. The carriage would not have been ready under half an hour.

Her guide was an aged black, who carried a lantern in one hand, a heavy stick in the other.

He was devotedly attached to his master, whom he had served ever since soon after his arrival in America.

Mrs. Brown it was strange, had never taken such particular notice of everything as she now did. The houses, the shops, the lamps, a passing dray or hackney coach, every door she passed, every bell that tolled, rested upon her memory.

She walked like one in a dream.

At length they reached the deserted quay on which her husband's warehouse was situated.

Two huge buildings occupied one side of a narrow street. Then came a wooden house of some extent, built right out over the water, for the convenience of landing and embarking goods. It was in the same state in which it was when Richard Brown bought it fifteen years before of Julius Hoffman, the Dutchman said to have been a smuggler and slave-dealer.

It was quaint in the extreme, with regular penthouse eaves, small windows, and a great crane hanging out from a huge loft which often contained merchandise to a marvellous extent.

The floor on a level with the ground was a vast warehouse, with an office partially partitioned off at the end.

The door was ajar, and as Father Brown, the negro, led the way, Mrs. Brown noticed that the entrance was choked up with bales of cotton. But these past, there was an open space.

Mrs. Brown thought, as she followed the negro, that she heard a step behind her, but turning and seeing nothing, she dismissed the idea.

"Is that you, father?" said a voice, so deep, so hollow, so strange, that the wife stood spellbound.

"Eos, massa, Missa Brown here."

"Very good. Good night, father; shut the door. Come early in the morning."

And still it was the same deep, hollow, and cavernous voice.

Mrs. Brown, scarcely conscious of what she did, advanced slowly towards her husband. He was seated over a small fireplace, warming his hands. A small table with tea-things, such as he was accustomed to use in his bachelor days, was beside him.

His head was bent towards his knees.

A small, flickering tallow candle alone illumined the whole warehouse, blackened and aged by time. The roof without being lofty, appeared so, in the faint glimmer, while the dark beams, carved and painted, grinned down upon her.

A chill wind blew up through the chinks of the flooring.

"What is the matter, Richard?" she said, gently.

Slowly, and as if unwillingly, he turned round. Gracious heavens, what a wreck! His face pale, his hair matted, his eyes bloodshot, his lips quivering, his whole expression that of utter despair—he looked so wan, so woeful, so utterly unlike himself, that Eliza almost shrieked.

"Surely," she said, "you have not allowed business to affect you thus."

And still he spoke not, but looked, oh! with what an inscrutable glance, right into her eyes.

"Do you know what this day is?" he said, in a husky whisper.

"No."

"Five years ago, on a Sunday, I met, near a pebbly stream, a poor but lovely girl, whom in my blind infatuation I took to my heart, and made the queen over all my possessions. I was an old fool, but I was very happy. They were very pleasant years, and had I my time to come over again, I should do it again—yes."

"What is the matter?"

"I loved her—oh! how I did love her. I worked hard, I slaved, I heaped up riches, that she might hold up her head among women, and in case of my death, this paper," holding out a parchment, "makes her my sole heiress. Woe is me, 'tis a bright world, and I thought without a speck, but now all is dark."

"In the name of heaven, what possesses you?" cried the terrified woman, who, close to the parchment, saw a cocked pistol.

"It was a pleasant dream, while the old man thought that the young girl loved him, but, alas, the awakening was bitter."

"Richard—Richard, speak plainly to me, or I shall die at your feet!"

And she kneeled wildly to him, with clasped hands.

"Yes—yes—very—very beautiful! That explains the mad infatuation," he continued, with a glazed and leaden eye, though his expression would have drawn tears from a dumb animal; "but I was wrong—very wrong. I should not have taken her so by surprise. How could I expect a child to know her mind."

And now, hiding his face in his hands, the strong man wept.

"Husband—Richard——" she began.

Slowly—very slowly he raised his head, and turned his haggard countenance towards her, as fixing his dim and almost sightless eyes upon her, he spoke once more.

"How many husbands would you have?" he said, this time coldly and sternly.

"What?" she faltered.

"You forget last night. I never left you; I was in the house where you supped with Christian Whitmer. *I saw all—all*, mind you woman. I was with you at supper! Ha, ha, ha! how many husbands would you have?"

And he laughed wildly, while she fell prostrate at his feet senseless—as much in look a corpse as any that ever went forth to the grave.

"Shall I kill her now?" he said, looking at her with an awful expression of countenance, which, however, relaxed suddenly to the softness of a woman's.

"Oh! what have I done!" he cried, as he bathed her face with vinegar, "that this awful punishment should fall upon me? Eliza—my

THE BARBER FINDING JESSIE AND HENRY.

wife, my beloved—awake ! Let us fly—let us seek some distant spot on earth, where the wicked are not, where we may be alone—away —away—away from the evil world, and where in mutual forgiveness and love—"

He stopped. She breathed ; she opened her eyes, and looked him full in the face.

"You heard me, Eliza ?" he said, blushing crimson with very shame.

"I did—I refuse ! How," she continued, rising and confronting him, very pale, very white, but awfully resolute, "could we live to-

gether. I never loved you, Richard. It is not my fault. I was grateful to you—I looked upon you as a dear friend, but that is all. Now we know one another, and we cannot ever, from this moment, dwell together. I must go forth—"

"To this man ? never !" said Richard Brown, clutching a pistol.

"I will go forth alone with my shame and my guilt," she continued, without appearing to notice the threatening demonstration. "I came to you poor, and I will leave you so. Death will soon bring rest—"

Her husband caught her wrist wildly, and dragging up a huge trap, pointed to the turbid, swelling, tossing waters beneath. He held up the candle, which disclosed a deep, dark chasm.

"There," he said, "is peace! Eliza, what I have suffered this day has deprived me of all love for life; and yet, if you would go where your fearful sin should never be known, to some old world city in Holland, I will again strive to live, and forget—"

He shut his eyes, and covered them with a hand, as if to shut out a horrid vision.

"If not—if you can never look me smilingly in the face again, let us die. 'Tis but a leap," he said, with a fearful calmness, "and all is over."

"Die!" she shrieked, "no, no! I cannot, will not die. Ah! there is help."

"Where, cockatrice?" he gasped, and turned round to where her hand pointed.

There was the preacher, with his pistol in his hand, surveying them with a cold and glittering eye.

With a wild and savage howl he thrust his wife on one side, and utterly regardless of the fact that Whitmer was armed, stepped back to take a spring.

Horror of horrors! he had forgotten the trap, and fell, thrusting out his two hands just in time to save himself. With these he clung despairingly to the flooring.

His eye fell upon his wife, who was kneeling, with clasped hands, within one single yard.

"Save me! save me!" he cried, in the first impulse of alarmed nature.

The preacher advanced towards him with the pistol in one hand, the will in the other.

"Too late, sir," he said, with savage emphasis, "you know too much."

Richard Brown looked at his wife. The glance was one—oh, God! could she ever forget it—was a mixture of reproach, of love, of the most undying self-denial.

"Save me, Eliza!" he faintly ejaculated.

"Save him! save him!" shrieked the woman.

The wretched man, whose eyes were starting from his head, whose struggles were now purely physical, looked ardently into his wife's face, as if to ask her if she meant what she said.

"Here, Richard, take my hand; Christian Whitmer, take the other side. Good Lord! be quick."

"He or I," said the preacher, hoarsely; "if that man lives we are ruined."

"I will save him—his life is mine; then I am yours," she gasped.

"You shall not," bitterly cried the preacher; "his life is mine."

And he stooped with the intention of unclasping the wretched victim's hands.

"Wretch! be thou accursed," said Richard Brown, as with one awful look at his wife, he, of his own accord, let go his hold.

One fearful splash, and all was still. The preacher darted to a side window, but he could neither see nor hear anything of the broken-hearted and murdered husband.

Mrs. Brown was speechless with horror. It was only when Whitmer had poured a goodly dram of brandy down her throat that she revived.

"Where is he?" she gasped.

"Dead, and you are free," he replied. "Come, come, be calm, and let us lay our plans."

*   *   *   *   *   *

Next morning a strange event took the whole of New York by surprise.

Mr. Richard Brown, after selling his entire business to Messrs. Peat and Rolt, his two ex-head clerks, for a large sum, payable by bills running over five years, had, it was said, sailed in the night for Europe, to settle his affairs there.

No one was at all surprised when it was found that to provide against accidents, the merchant had left everything, even the proceeds of the business, to his wife.

Mrs. Pigott alone wondered. She had expected a very different catastrophe.

But she held her tongue and waited. She had, however, strong suspicions that something wrong had occurred.

CHAPTER XXXII.

JESSIE FINDS A FRIEND.

THE conditions proposed by Mrs. Treherne to Captain Meadows, previous to her consenting to marriage, were indeed hard. She was willing, she said, to trust him to a certain extent, but other things were to be done at once.

Mrs. Treherne lived in hourly dread of a terrific explosion.

No one but herself knew the frail tenure by which she clung to honour, repute, and life.

Her past existence had been one long episode of horror. Her crimes were of such a nature that we gladly put off their record.

The first duty of the colonel was to find the wife of Phineas Bristowe and the two children. From motives which we cannot as yet explain, she desired to have them both in her possession. But to track the fugitives was no easy task. The devoted mother, for such she was, not only to Jessie, but to the boy, had used every device that maternal instinct could suggest to defeat their wicked and unholy machinations.

But evil men have long arms, and Joe Galpin, who was now the colonel's most obedient servant, had correspondents in every great town and every seaport in England.

He was said to be the safest and most extensive fence in the three kingdoms.

Burglaries and robberies were carried on on a larger scale then than now. With all their boasted acuteness, the officers of those days were not so efficient as our present police.

Among other of Joe Galpin's correspondents was one Josh Rackshaw, master of a smack which ran between London and Bristol. This individual dealt ostensibly in fish and such articles; but there were shrewd suspicions afloat as to the occasional contents of his hold.

It was said—mind you, it was only said—that for miles around the repute of Josh was known, and that for days before his departure, he would receive mysterious visits in his private domicile, after which strangely heavy little kegs and barrels would go on board.

Now, Joe Galpin had furnished this personage, merely by way of keeping good his word with the colonel, with a full description of the fugitives.

But no one ever thought that poor Mrs. Phineas Bristowe would ever trudge all that way from Manchester.

But she did, and for the very reason that it was a long way off.

And, then, she was not so poor as people imagined. The parchment parcel which had found its way so mysteriously into her hands, contained a goodly sum in gold and notes.

So Mrs. Bristowe, after a long and wearisome journey, took up her residence in a small and busy street in Bristol. Her intention was to open a shop in the stationery and general line, so that she might earn her living, and give up her wealth to the education of the children.

Since reading the confession contained in the letter, which she had so eagerly devoured, a great change had taken place in the feelings of the young woman, which reacted on her *physique*. Her pallor decreased, her cheeks filled out, and ere three months, in her neat black dress, she looked a most presentable-looking person.

Her business became quite thriving, and her children the admiration of the neighbours.

Opposite to Mrs. Bristowe's shop was that of Peregrine Grundy, barber and bird-fancier.

There was not such a man for a clean shave or a cut in all Bristol, while for canaries and bullfinches he was celebrated over the whole town.

A queer-looking card was Perry. Short, stout, with a bullet-shaped head denuded of all superfluous hair, with a flat nose, and little grey eyes, an arm all muscle, he looked what he had been—a prizefighter. Now, Perry was not like most of the fancy, in heart a thorough rough and blackguard, but a very decent fellow, so when he had punched one or two heads, and been duly punched in return, he retired into private life.

Wishing for occupation, he became a tonser and dealer in birds.

Now, Perry was vastly fond of the fair sex. It so happened, then, that as the widow began to thrive, both in person and pocket, his eyes were perpetually aimed in that direction. It came about, soon after, that Perry was always in want of a sheet of note-paper, or a pen, or a halfpennyworth of wafers, or a few shirt-buttons, a pennyworth of pins, or some little domestic article in which Mrs. Bristowe dealt.

He became quite familiar, and gave the children some young birds. This necessitated personal attendance whenever he could spare time. What could children know about birds: he must show them all the ins and outs of the fancy. And the mother smiled, and got quite to like the rough-mannered, odd-looking, queer-speaking Perry.

And Perry knew this, and was all the more timid, respectful, and abashed.

Yes; he the fighting man, who had thrashed Joe Spuggins in thirty-seven minutes, and was a kind of local Tom Sayers.

And so, in utter disgust at his own timidity, Peregrine Grundy periodically punched his own head.

"Nice child, that 'ere," said his regular customer, Josh Rackshaw, one day while being shaved, pointing through the open door to where Jessie was standing in conversation with Henry.

"Werry," replied Perry, turning to his strop, and energetically plying his razor as before.

"I suspect, strangers to these parts?" continued the owner of the smack.

"They is," said Perry, seizing him rather roughly by the nose, "hangels gin'rally is."

"Ain't much acquaintance with them fish," continued Josh Rackshaw, gruffly. "Seem pretty children—"

"Cherrybims," said Perry, "mother a hangel of light, which is my opinion; welcome to yours, Josh, eh?"

"And where does this here torch as has set your heart on fire hail from?" continued Josh, quietly.

"Don't know, mysterious, seen better days, sich a stunner," said Perry, half annoyed by the questions, and still unable to resist the temptation of talking about her.

"Seem to know her, Perry," laughed the other.

A one-eyed gunner was Josh Rackshaw. Under another name he was said to have been a slaver, not to say a bit of a pirate, but having lost one peeper, and parted company with his larboard fin, he had determined to stay nearer home, watch over his wealth, and increase his store in a less dangerous way.

And this partly because he was a widower and had one daughter, Polly Rackshaw.

"Ever since she arrived quite promiscuous in that shop, which, to my hies, is the beautifullest in Bristol."

"Ha! ha! ha! soon be Mrs. Grundy, I suppose, this Mrs. What's-her-name?" laughed Josh.

"Bristowe is her name," said Perry, with a blush that went up to the very roots of his hair.

Josh turned to put on his neckcloth, and as he did so made faces at himself in a glass. That night before he indulged in his evening rummer of spirits, he wrote a brief note to Joe Galpin, having done which he considered he had performed his duty, and got gloriously drunk accordingly.

Several days passed without any change. Perry still continued his visits, and always was so respectful to the mother, and so polite and attentive to the children, that Mrs. Bristowe got more and more to like him.

One evening, a very cold, dismal, and dark evening it was, Jessie and Henry had gone out together. After their school-hours they were in the habit of going of little errands for their mother, who could never stir abroad, until her shutters were closed.

It was eight o'clock, and the children had been gone double their usual time. Mrs. Bristowe stood at her door, and looked anxiously up and down the street. Peregrine pretended to be deeply engaged in smoking his pipe, but he actually squinted along the blackened tube, until he squinted himself into the belief that something was the matter.

"Anything the matter, missus?" he said, running over the road, and touching his cap.

"Nothing the matter, Mr. Grundy, only the children have been a very long time, and I am growing anxious."

"Where is they gone?" said Perry, planting his cap firmly on his head, and emptying his pipe of the hot ashes by knocking it against the wall.

Mrs. Bristowe gave him the requisite information in a faltering voice, and the young man hurried away as fast as his feet could carry him.

He was away an hour, and when he returned, he was heated and appalled. He told the terror-stricken widow that not a trace of them had been seen anywhere. They had not been to any of the places they were directed to.

"Great God!" cried Mrs Bristowe, "then have my enemies found me."

"Enemies," said Perry, tucking up his sleeves, while he turned cold all over, "where are they, let me look at them—won't I—well, never mind, what I would do if I had 'em here. But what do you really think, missus."

"Lost, ruined, betrayed! Some wretch has tracked me to this humble home," she said, with clasped hands and streaming eyes, "and they are gone—gone from me for ever."

"My!" gasped Perry, turning pale, "there's a downy cove been a pumping me about you— don't I deserve it!"

And with his two fists he dashed his head about, in a way, which had it been inflicted upon anybody else, might have been calculated to lead to a breach of the peace.

"Who—where is he—what was he like?" she gasped.

"Mum," said Perry, with a dry smile, "it's all my fault; but blow me if I don't give it un. If so be they're in Bristol, I'll find un. Now, missus, if you takes on, I'm a dunner."

"I will be patient," said the wretched mother, clasping her hands once more; "go, God bless you."

And having armed himself with a stout stick, Peregrine Grundy went forth upon his journey; by that kind of intuition which is given sometimes to the most simple, he at once suspected Josh Rackshaw as the guilty author of the abduction.

CHAPTER XXXIII.

PERRY TAKES AN APPRENTICE.

MANY have doubtless read Sala's smart and lively account of a Bristol ship-chandler a hundred years ago. Now, Josh Rackshaw called himself by the same name, but to this trade he added that of "mine uncle."

Situated at the corner of a lane, every other house in which was ruined and dirty, let out in tenements to single men, single women, families, sailors, or anybody who sought such humble shelter, Josh Rackshaw's establishment was double. The corner house was that devoted to the pawnbroking business, while that in the main street was used as a store.

Josh sold things without number. His capacious warehouse contained an assortment of almost everything usually required in a seaport town.

Old quadrants, sextants, stuffed birds and monkeys, aged compasses that had been to the Indies and back, sou'-westers, cracked barometers, huge silver watches, cutlasses, pikes, rusty guns, old coats, sail-blocks, draught-boards, broken chessmen, loadstones, leathern buckets, Dutch clocks, and other things innumerable, blocked up the store. Hams, cheeses, tallow candles, were piled on shelves or suspended from the ceiling; while amidst the whole, his one eye peering about with a sly and cunning glance, stood Josh Rackshaw.

Peregrine Grundy entered as calmly as he could, just in time to catch the glance of a very pretty face peering from behind an apology for a window.

"Go to bed," said Josh, gruffly. "Ah! who'd a thought it, my son. Why what brings you so far from home?"

"Them children's lost," replied Perry, in a dry tone.

"Eh! don't say so; them pretty children?" cried Josh.

"Yes, and you know it, old un. Now none of your capers with me. You never came axing questions for nuthin', I know. Come, where are they? tell us at once, or it'll be wuss for you."

"Good lud! the man's drunk. What were those children to me?" said Josh, with a bluster of manner not lost upon Perry, who again caught a glimpse of the pretty face.

"Don't know, and don't care; but harkye, Mister Josh, I'm an old hand. The young lady is up to your tricks, so if yer don't give 'em up, *what do you say to a search-warrant?*"

Josh stepped back quite livid, and glanced rapidly round towards a blunderbuss, just in time to catch a last glimpse of the same pretty face.

"Polly, you hussy," roared the angry ship-chandler, "will you go to bed?"

The feminine intruder hastily fled, and the slamming of a door announced her departure.

"I tell you what, you skulking son of a gun," continued Josh, "if yer don't clear out, I'll have you taken into custody."

"Give up the childer, and I'll shake hands," said Perry, insinuatingly.

"Damn the children and you too, what the devil do you think I know about them? I tell you what it is, Mr. Grundy, it's my opinion you're after no good," cried Rackshaw, seizing, in his passion, a large rattle, which, however, he had presence of mind not to use; "so if yer don't hook it, I'll call the watch, as sure as my name is Josh Rackshaw."

"*Which it ain't!*" said a strange, cracked, and mysterious voice, that made Perry start, and Josh grind his teeth.

"I here for no good! why you bloody old receiver," cried the angry barber, "where do you keep your stolen goods?"

"*Under the counter,*" said the cracked voice— "*look alive—that's the place. Old Rack's a—*"

"Will you leave my shop?" roared Josh, foaming at the mouth with rage, as he took down his blunderbuss; "if you don't, may I be hanged if I don't let fly, and swear you attempted to rob me."

"*Hang him up, damn his eyes!*" croaked the mysterious voice, which Perry now found was that of a hideous old parrot, perched in a cage at the back of the shop.

Bursting out into a forced and yet hearty laugh, Perry looked keenly at Josh.

"I know them kids is here. I'm not a werry poor man, and if I don't git a search-warrant, my name ain't Peregrine Grundy: I'll spend every penny I have but I'll find 'em. Good night."

And the barber went out, leaving Josh in a state of mind bordering on frenzy.

Peregrine walked away with a chill at his heart. He expected that Josh was watching him, so he lit his pipe and strolled homewards. He, however, almost immediately returned, after luckily meeting with a sharp lad named Pike, whom he despatched on an errand to Mrs. Bristowe.

"Tell her to shut up, and wait. I'll be home as soon as possible."

Poor Peregrine Grundy little imagined the interval which would occur before he would return to his own home.

Pike was directed to return with all due diligence to a public-house nearly facing the pawnbroker's, in a room of which Perry ensconced himself. The ex-fighting-man was known there and respected, so when he proposed to smoke and drink at an open window upstairs, no questions were asked.

Perry had a first-rate view of the store, and also up the narrow lane in which was situated the pawnbroking establishment.

He soon saw that Josh Rackshaw was shutting up, and in a great hurry, too. A rough-looking, shock-headed Irishman was helping him; and no sooner had the old fellow placed a padlock on the door, than he hurried away.

Now Perry Grundy had made up his mind to get into the house, but how, was an important consideration. He really had not the remotest conception how it was to be done, and yet he had made up his mind to it as fully as ever soldier made up his mind to glorious victory.

Perry had his eyes about him, and he noticed that a great many people went up the narrow alley facing him: he noticed, too, for Perry was observing, that they were generally males and females in couples; and he remarked also, that the women appeared to be of the class known as "unfortunates," while the others were of almost all grades in the social scale.

Now Perry was sober, and not likely to indulge in low society, especially with Mrs. Bristowe's pretty face ever before his eyes; but as he gazed and gazed at the groups standing at the corner, or pacing up and down, or standing at their doors, a brilliant idea struck him.

"Pike, my boy," he said, as the boy came into the room, "you can do a pot—eh?"

"Can't I—just," grinned the ugly boy.

Yes; Pike was ugly. We regret to say it—we regret for his sake and our own too. Short, with a head of hair like a door-mat in a fit, with eyes that looked obliquely down his nose, with a mouth that disclosed jagged and saw-like teeth, with a sallow, freckled complexion, pallid from insufficient food, with clothes that dropped off him from sheer force of mending, with a huge pair of holey shoes, made for a large man, and fitted on by means of dirty straw, with a half-vacant, half-cunning look, Tom Pike, beggar, errand-boy, crossing-sweeper, had never been suspected of dishonesty.

"And a half-quartern loaf," said Perry.

"Try me—just!" replied Tom.

"And some cheese," continued Perry, smiling.

Tom looked at him, as he rang the bell, with a dim notion that he was a most mighty philanthropist.

A girl came with a light, and took the order, not, however, without staring at Tom.

"And now, Pike, yer rogue, just listen to me. You knows old Rackshaw?"

"Don't I—old Tenpenny—"

"Well, Pike, I'ze going to wisit him," said Perry. "I got werry pertikler business there—only yer see, Tom, I doesn't want to see *him*. So, Tom, if yer sees him coming, just you whistle as I know yer can whistle, and I'll be ready. What's the young fool looking at?"

"Yer ain't a-going to rob him—eh?" faltered Tom.

"There's one for your nob," said Perry, gravely, hitting him smartly on his matted hair. "No; but the infernal thief stole them childer—you know!"

"Don't yer do that again," cried Tom, blubbering, but whether at the blow or the information, it is hard to say. "Poor little hangels! Oh, ain't he a rascal, that's all!"

"Now yer seems to hunderstand," said Perry, "I'll continuate. Just you whistle, sharp too, if yer sees him—once quick if he's alone, and once for every cove as is along with the old thief. Now eat away, young un—I'm off. By-the-way," he said, lingering and looking very grave, "did yer ever shave a feller?"

"No—never."

"Could you do it?"

"Well, master, I'd try anything," grinned Tom Pike.

"Now I believe that 'ere young devil would. I ain't the leastest doubt in life as he'd try for to use my werry best razors as if they wur old knives. I'm werry nigh certain as he'd take my rig'ler customers by the nose, and shave 'em right off. Tom, you're a wonder. Well, Tom, so as if I doesn't turn up in the morning—nor to-night—get you home to my place. You'll find a suit of barber's boy's clothes in the three-cornered cupboard, Tom. Put 'em on; mind yer washes yer face and combs your hair—and says you, 'Master's gone to town, what can I do for yer.' And mind you," said Perry, solemnly, "mind yer does it slow, Tom—don't cut their pimples right off, Tom, and mind their noses. I werrily believe the young imp as is laughing there ull do it, too. *But who's to cut their hair?*"

And Perry groaned.

"I will, won't I just," said Tom,

"Don't," cried Perry, faintly; "or if yer does, draw it mild. Leave em a lock or two."

"Won't I," grinned Tom, almost frantic with delight. "But suppose they says I've murdered you, and took the business?"

"You precious young warmint," grinned Perry, and then taking out a card, which in the exuberance of his feelings he had printed when he first started in business, he wrote on the back in his rude way:—

"*Gone away on business. Back soon. Tom Pike, my man, will hact in my habsence.*

"PEREGRINE GRUNDY."

Handing this to Tom, he went out, muttering to himself—

"Won't there be a few shindies and cut chins; my hies! what a lot of county crops I shall see in my streets."

And Perry sighed at the very thought of such desecration of his important art.

CHAPTER XXXIV.

THE SEARCH-WARRANT.

THE opening of the barber's shop on the following morning, was an event long remembered in that neighbourhood.

Mrs. Bristowe had not been to bed all night. She sat up waiting, that dreary province of womankind. Her eyes were scarcely ever off the shop of Peregrine Grundy, and yet somehow a short stunted figure had contrived to creep in about midnight.

It was about six when she was enabled by the growing daylight to distinguish what was passing, and then she rubbed her eyes, as if she thought that somehow she had deceived herself.

The shutters had been taken down, and the door was wide open, so that she could distinctly see all that was passing.

Before a glass stood a short stunted figure, that of a lad neatly dressed, with a clean white apron on, who having evidently bestowed remarkable pains on his rebellious shock head of hair, was now either endeavouring to shave himself, or practising on his beardless chin, for the benefit of others.

Had not her very soul been warped by sadness, grief, and melancholy, Mrs. Bristowe must have laughed, but as it was, she cast a shawl over her head, and ran across.

"Where is Mr. Peregrine?" she said, sinking into a chair.

With his left hand the boy handed the card written on the previous night to the speaker, and then wiping away the soap-suds, turned rapidly round, and asked the bereaved mother if he could do anything for her.

"My!" cried Tom, "if it ain't Mrs. Bristowe."

"Where is Mr. Grundy?" she continued; "has he heard anything of the children?"

"Hush!" said Tom, closing the door, and in a low whisper telling all he knew, which with the exception of having seen several persons go into the house of Josh, and himself having been ejected the public-house at midnight, was not more than has already been related.

"And you have not seen Mr. Grundy," continued Mrs. Bristowe, "since he entered the house?"

"I hasn't," said Tom; "it seems as how he expected to be some time, seeing for he told I to keep shop."

"I must go to the magistrates. I must and will find my child. Merciful Heaven! they will not take from me my babe, my only joy, my hope, my stay, the child of my—" and ere she could say more she sobbed aloud.

Tom Pike, endeavouring to wipe away an imaginary tear, thrust the soap-brush into his eyes, which made him bellow lustily, which proceeding, however, was speedily quelled by a cry of astonishment.

"Mum, you're wanted."

Mrs. Bristowe started up, and to her astonishment saw a postchaise, with four horses, the postilions covered in mud, standing at her door, at which a well-dressed gentleman was knocking.

With a wild cry, Cornelia hurried across the road, and dashing open her own door, was followed by a slight figure, dressed in a heavy cloak, and slouched hat.

The carriage then drove away.

Tom Pike stared with open eyes, nor could he attend to business, even when a customer came, until a hearty curse made him aware of his carelessness. He then in a dignified manner began operations.

A 'cute boy was Tom. By a kind of intuition he scraped the chins of his new master's friends, with a lightness of touch and an ability which astonished no one more than himself.

About eight, the carriage came again, now with only two horses. Mrs. Bristowe was handed in, and the whole party drove off, and the place knew her no more.

But that afternoon a couple of officers, accompanied by two most respectable solicitors, and a strange gentleman in dark clothes, and a very precise white choker, presented themselves at the shop of Mr. Josiah Rackshaw.

He was not in, but the rough individual who on the previous night had put up the shutters, was behind the counter.

"Want Mr. Rackshaw," said the strange gentleman, blandly.

"Then by the powers ye must find him," cried the Hibernian attendant.

One of the men who had kept in the background, here leaped over the counter, and collared the Irishman, at the same time exhibiting his search-warrant.

But before they completely overpowered him, he succeeded in ringing a bell with violence.

Then a rush down some stairs was heard, and Josh hobbled into the shop. Ugly as he usually was, he was uglier still from the application of a huge patch of black plaister to his sinister and sightless eye.

"Well, what's the row?" he said in a blustering way.

"Search-warrant," said the other officer, blandly, making signs to several other men on the opposite pavement, who now took charge of the entrance to the pawnbroking establishment, while one joined them in the shop.

"And what der ye think I cares for your sarch-warrant, Muster Cheeseman? Fire away! Fine liberty of the subject! Sarch the house from top to bottom, and then you won't find nothing, that's all!"

There was an odd twinkle in his eye which the lawyers did not like. They looked at one another with a doubting air.

"Perhaps you'd like to sarch my smack 'Betsy,' he sneered.

"That is being done," said the police-officer, drily.

Josh Rackshaw turned slowly round, and gazed full in the other's face.

"You don't mean for to say that any white-livered scoundrel has dared to touch my 'Betsy.' Well, I wish I had him on board the 'Polly-wash,' that's all;" and then he added, with a vindicative scowl, "but I should fancy the 'Betsy' is standing under heavy sail about Porloch Bay, just now—she sailed before daylight this morning."

"The revenue-cutter is ready," whispered one of the lawyers, and then vanished.

Josh stood still a moment, as if struck dumb, and then recovering himself, led the way upstairs, muttering curses, not loud but deep.

They searched the house from top to bottom; they poked into every place that human ingenuity could suggest; and all they found were bales of goods, except that in a bedroom near the top of the house, was a very pretty young girl of seventeen, who had evidently been weeping.

They examined her closely, but she knew nothing. Her manner was evidently that of one in abject terror.

The officers and their employers retired utterly discomfited, amidst the ill-suppressed glee of the old ship-chandler, who, however, the moment their backs were turned, mounted a powerful horse, and rode off in the direction of the southern coast at a fearful rate.

CHAPTER XXXV.

A PRETTY GIRL'S BED-ROOM.

MEANWHILE, what had become of Peregrine Grundy?

No sooner had he left the house in which Tom Pike was ensconsced, than he strolled across the road to where a group of young girls in tawdry finery were standing speaking in laughing and joyous tones.

"Well - how are ye?" said Perry. "Jolly? Which, now, of you heifers has a top room?"

Some laughed, some told him to mind his own business, they wanted none of his "imperence," while others said they had top rooms.

"Well—supposes we drains," said Perry, producing a bright, new gold coin—the barber was a man of money—" and then we can talk business."

As he said this, he winked knowingly and wickedly at a rather good-looking but saddened girl of seventeen, who nodded. He then led the way to the bar of the public, ordered a large supply of liquor, and left the house with the girl under his arm.

They were soon in a dirty bedroom at the very summit of the house.

"Now, look you here," said Perry, bolting the door, and putting a sovereign into the hands of the girl, "would you like to yarn one or two more of them yellow boys?"

The girl stared at him with open mouth.

"Can't you speak, my beauty?"

"What is I to do?" gasped the miserable and miscalled votary of pleasure.

"Nuffin, old gal. But, do you see, I'm partial to smoking, 'specially on tops of houses. Now don't you laugh. Will you be my friend, and I don't know what I won't do for you?"

"Will you take me from this cursed den?" she said, in a tone which satisfied Perry that he had made a right selection; "will you let me go away, and perhaps be taken home? If I could only dress decently, and get my box and things—oh! I'm sure they would never know anything of the past."

"I will. Now gal, I tells you frankly, square and right up, I am a-going on a dangerous errand—a very dangerous one—so here's two more of them shiners. Do you stay here till I come back, and if I don't, why yer carn't wait, but take my advice and hook it."

With these words he opened the garret window, and left the unfortunate girl amazed, utterly bewildered, and yet rejoiced.

Once outside, Perry found that he had undertaken a very difficult task. The roofs of the houses were slanting, and very worn. He had to tread with the utmost caution, now crawling, now walking erect along a parapet, and now forcing himself along by main force over a congeries of stacks and chimneys that almost gave way in his hands.

At length, however, he reached the roof at the extreme corner of the street, and he knew that he was near the end of his journey.

Had not the way he had come been extremely dangerous, Peregrine Grundy would doubtless have had his journey for his pains; but it never entered into the brain of any sane person to fancy that ought mortal would front almost certain death to reach that position.

The roof of the pawnbroking establishment was flat, and exhibited not even a trap; but that of the warehouse was slanting, and had a large garret window. It was barred with iron, though the panes of glass had all vanished by slow degrees.

Perry had borrowed of his old acquaintance the landlord, a pair of pincers, a small crowbar, a dark lantern, a saw and a pick-lock, which the landlord *said* had been left in his charge by a celebrated cracksman lately deceased.

Perry trimmed the lamp, and fixing it on the edge of a parapet, between which and the window was a deep gutter, he took his crowbar in hand. To his surprise and delight, the bars and their supporting wood-work were so rotten that he with ease penetrated into the room, which had evidently been deserted for years. It was half an inch deep in dust and fallen plaster, so that though he stepped cautiously he raised so heavy a cloud as almost to choke him.

Again a door stood in his way. This he soon mastered, and was next minute on the landing.

The whole interior of the house was gloomy and poverty-stricken, as if Josh Rackshaw had added to his other vices that of avarice, an insatiable desire for money for its own sake.

The first room to his left, was also empty, so with a slow and deliberate step he descended the stairs.

On the next landing were two doors. That to the left, opened on a kind of store-room, while that to his right, he at once discovered to be a bedchamber.

This he determined to explore, as it had at one end a kind of dressing-closet.

Just at that moment, Perry heard the sound of a rapid footstep ascending the staircase.

He looked around. Nothing in the way of concealment offered itself, except the cupboard, which was hung with female apparel.

Hastily shutting his lamp, he drew himself as much within the cupboard as possible.

It would not quite close, and Perry could see all that passed, without being seen.

A very pretty girl, well made, with black hair and eyes, entered the apartment, with a bed-room candle in her hand, *and locked the door !*

Perry, as he would have expressed, felt "all-overish." He scarcely dared to breathe, look, or think. He was in what might truly be called an awfully perplexing predicament.

Locked up, and with a charming girl too.

She set down her candle, and threw off a thin shawl that covered her shoulders. This revealed a well-fitting dress and a glowing bust.

Perry shut his eyes.

She was standing before her glass, and loosening her frock.

Perry could have groaned.

She let it fall at her feet, and stood admiring herself in her stays and petticoats.

Perry didn't shut his eyes. In his position what man would have done so ?

"Heigho !" she sighed, as she smiled complacently on her own rosy cheeks, glossy hair, and exceedingly handsome neck and shoulders. "What's the use of being well made and good looking, I should like to know," she continued, "if one never is to have a sweetheart? Father shuts one up so, I never see anybody. I wonder who that good-looking fellow was who came here to-day."

"Meaning me," thought Perry, not a little gratified.

"And who father was so awful snappish to. I wanted to stop. He looked good humoured."

"Ain't she a sweet hussy."

"Well, it's no use sighing. But if father does go on this way, why I expect it 'ull be a case of Gretna Green, some of these days. If I only could find a bold young chap suited to my taste, wouldn't I. I ain't going to be mewed up this way, I know. Well, it's no use repining, and it's no use admiring my white neck and shoulders, though I may as well as nobody else can, so here goes to bed," and she began to unlace her stays.

"Don't," said Perry, bobbing his head out of the cupboard, but looking modestly on the ground, "I can't stand this here no longer."

The girl looked wildly at him, shrieked, and fainted. Poor Perry was now utterly bewildered, but in this emergency, regardless of how much her modesty might suffer when she recovered, seized a water-bottle, raised her in his arms, and bathed her face, her neck, and shoulders.

In a few minutes she opened her eyes.

"Don't be frightened, miss, I ain't no thief nor robber, but a respectable tradesman as pays rates and taxes."

"Are you ?" gasped Mary Rackshaw, gazing at him with wondering eyes.

"Yes, miss ; and if so be as you'll just" here he coloured to the eyes, "dress yourself, I'll tell you all about it."

With a deep blush, Mary leaped from his arms, ran behind the bed with her dress and shawl, to the manifest relief of Perry.

"And now, sir, if you please, I should like to know how you came to be hid in my bedroom ?" said Mary, in very pretty confusion.

"It's a long story," replied Perry, scratching his head.

"Then, sit down," continued Mary, pointing to a chair, while she took a stool. They were thus about three or four feet apart.

"Thankee, miss," said Perry, "but now I'm seated, I don't know where to begin. Your father is not my friend, and perhaps you won't like—"

"Did you come here to do anything wrong ?" said Mary, with a pretty pout.

"No," cried Perry, energetically, at the same time in his enthusiasm hitching his chair nearer to her, "it's all about the children."

Mary turned pale.

"Ah !" said Perry, hitching up to within a foot and a half, "does yer know anything about them ?"

"I do ; but tell me all. My father says—but never mind—tell me the truth."

"I will, so help me Bob !" cried Perry, hitching close up this time, and taking her hand in his.

And he did, but somehow or other he did not very strongly allude to his sentiments with regard to the supposed widow. He merely dwelt upon his affection for the children.

"But what do you suppose to be my father's motive," said Mary, very gravely, "for taking them away ?"

"Don't know—paid for it, I suppoge," continued Perry.

"And if," said Mary, with a sigh, "I assist you to release these children, you'll let my father alone ?"

"As long as he leaves them," retorted Perry.

"You promise ?"

"For your sake—"

"For my sake ?" cried the girl, blushing deeply, and endeavouring to take away her hand ; "you'll soon forget all about me."

"I won't," said Perry, passing his right hand slily round her waist.

"Oh ! I've heard all about you men," whimpered Mary, "what token will you give me ?"

"That," said Perry, and he implanted on her lips a kiss, which having never received one before, except from papa, utterly bewildered the young lady.

"Don't," she whispered faintly, but at the same time leaning on his shoulder in such a languishing way as to necessitate a repetition of the offence.

"And you will love me a little bit," she continued.

"If you saves these here children from the clutches of them fellers as wants 'em, there's no saying what I may not do," cried Perry, energetically.

THE MURDER AT THE OLD FERRY.

A brief pause ensued.

"I don't know," said Mary, releasing herself firmly from his grasp, "much of the world; but I do know there is a deal of wickedness in it. But if you are deceiving me, I will never believe any one again. You oughtn't to be here, and I ought not to listen to you; and then father," she added with a shudder, "threatened to horsewhip me if I went near them."

"Horsewhip!" said Perry, looking quickly at the handsome shoulders, now concealed from view.

"Well, never mind, come with me," cried the girl, with a flushed face and beating heart, leading the way towards the door.

This she carefully opened, and began descending the stairs.

Perry, bewildered by the terrifically sudden impression which he had made on the girl's susceptible heart, knew scarcely what he was about.

He had presence of mind, however, to secure his stick and pistols. His tools he had slung inside his coat.

Down, down they went until they reached the

level of the shop, which was parted off by a strong iron railing from the house.

Mary turned away her head, and pointed to a dark, slimy-looking door, leading to the cellar.

"Down there!" groaned Perry, "oh, miss! how could you connive at such cruelty."

"I!" cried the poor girl, bursting into tears, "I connive at cruelty. Merciful Heaven! if you knew all that I have suffered, and how in this terrible prison I force myself to gaiety, you would not speak thus. For what I have done to-night, I shall surely die."

"No you won't," said Perry, breaking off the ponderous lock with one twist of his crowbar, "but here goes,"

And seizing the candle from her hand, he led the way down.

A faint, close, oppressive odour of damp straw, of mouldy boxes, of vermin, rats and mice, and snails, came up the dark staircase, and when he reached the floor, his horror knew no bounds.

Despite the noise, the two children, had wept themselves to sleep in each other's arms, on a pile of dirty straw.

Henry lay with his head upon a deal box, heavily asleep, but his face ghastly; while Jessie, with her glorious curls veiling her classic beauty of countenance, was pressed close to him, her arm round his neck in a kind of half caressing, half protective attitude.

"Beautiful little darlings," said Mary.

"Hangels," replied Perry, as he wiped away a tear, waking them with the other.

But they did not move.

"Drugged!" gasped Perry, who had seen such things during his fighting experience.

Mary trembled like a leaf.

"We must carry them," said Perry, sternly.

One shrill whistle at some distance made Perry start. He listened with the deepest attention. One—two—three.

"Curses on them," he muttered.

"What is the matter?" said Mary.

"Your father, with two men," continued Perry, clutching his loaded pistol.

"In the name of the daughter," said Mary, passionately, "spare the father's life."

"I will," replied Perry, moodily, "but I must escape with these blessed babies," and returning his pistols to his pockets, he doubled up his heavy fist with a stern compression of the lips.

"Mercy," said the wretched girl.

"Them's the critturs wants mussy," replied Perry, sternly; "go a-hind yon tubs, and leave all to me. In a scrimmage a woman 'ud best be saying her prayers."

In an agony of fear and terror, Mary retired to the spot indicated, quite out of sight.

Perry placed himself in the deep gloom beside the steps, and having his lantern safe, blew out the candle.

"Sold, by Satan!" yelled Josh, at the top of the stairs, "somebody's been here. Come along."

And with a hop, skip, and a jump, he was on the floor of the cellar in a moment. He had a candle in his hand, and saw Perry, but the boxer was too quick for him. One heavy blow, planted right on his sinister eye, sent him rolling senseless into a distant corner.

"Now then, any more on you?" said the gallant barber.

"Two," cried a husky voice, as a couple of men with crape masks faced him, the first levelling two pistols, one at Perry, the other at the children.

The barber stood aghast at the horrible threat, indeed so utterly did it unnerve him, that he saw not a cudgel raised in the air, and which descended on his head with stunning force.

Down fell Perry, like a lump of lead.

"Kill him, cut his d—d throat," yelled Josh, getting up.

"Kill me fust," cried Mary, rushing forward, and raising the insensible Perry in her arms.

"Oh!" said Josh, suddenly becoming calm, a sign of deadly resolution in this man, "so you're in it, are you. Never mind. Go upstairs; we'll settle our little business another time."

"I won't go up to be flogged," replied Mary, resolutely.

"Egad, I should think not," laughed one of the masked ruffians.

"Mind your own business, colonel. You go girl," continued Josh, with flashing eyes, as he clutched the stick he used as a support.

"You shan't murder them," said Mary, in a loud voice.

"Nonsense," cried the man with the pistols, in a somewhat soft and persuasive tone, "no one shall be harmed. As soon as the children are restored to the parents from whom they have so infamously been stolen, he shall be set free."

"You swear it?"

"On my honour as a gentleman," said the other, raising his jewelled hand, and taking hers.

With a sigh, a lingering glance at Perry, and a defiant one at her angry father, she went slowly up to her bedroom, locked herself in, and wept all night.

In the morning, Josh entered just as she had finished dressing. In his hand was a riding-whip. His face was convulsed with passion, the ropy veins were swelled almost to bursting, while his one eye rolled fearfully in his head.

Mary turned slowly round and faced him. Her countenance was ghastly pale. Her form seemed to have dilated. Her eyes flashed liquid fire.

Josh stood aghast.

"Well, have you murdered him?"

"Who—what—the barber?" he gasped, "what is he to you?"

"I love him," she said coldly.

Josh raised his whip, but ere he struck, retreated. She had a pistol in her hand.

"Strike," she said, "but as surely as you do, I will shoot myself, and denounce you with my dying breath. Understand me; you are my father, and as your daughter, I will remain in your house, so long as you treat me with propriety. But henceforth we are as strangers. If you have murdered that young man, I will leave you. But beware how you attempt to touch me again. I am no longer a weak and silly child, but a woman."

Utterly overwhelmed with astonishment, Josh Rackshaw left the room amid a torrent of execrations.

Mary was not the first girl whose whole nature had been changed by sudden and irresistible love.

She did not believe that her father had deliberately murdered Perry, and therefore was determined to discover his whereabouts, and if possible, to save him.

CHAPTER XXXVI.

THE FERRY-HOUSE.

MEANWHILE poor Jessie and Henry had been removed by the agency of Colonel Meadows on board the smack.

They had originally been secured and gagged while walking down a dark and narrow street. On their arrival in the house of Josh Rackshaw, they had been drugged and placed in the cellar, from which, senseless and unconscious, they had been removed to the smack.

Here they were secreted in the hold, a matter of unnecessary precaution, as the vessel put to sea instantly on their arrival on board.

The sensations of the poor children on coming to themselves may be conceived, not described. Unable to comprehend where they were, in almost total darkness, with the flooring moving uneasily under them, they were at first panic-stricken.

They shrieked terrribly.

Then a man, raising a kind of trap, descended a ladder, and stood before them.

He was a man of about thirty-five, short, stumpy, and pitted with the smallpox. His face was hard and unfeeling. In his left hand was a lantern, in his right, a ropes-end.

"Well, now what's to pay?" he said, brutally, "who's a-hollering?"

The children were still, they scarcely breathed. Their wan, pale, and haggard faces were fearful to look at, their eyes were sunk deep in their sockets, and their expression was one of fixed horror.

The ruffian raised his rope, but, as if thinking better of it, lowered it again.

"Come on deck," he said gruffly.

The children tottered after him, and in a few minutes were, still clinging one to the other, upon the deck. They gazed in wonder and alarm around. They were on the wide and open sea. Nowhere was anything visible but sky and water. The wind was blowing very nearly a gale.

At a signal from the man, the children crawled into a boat which was on deck, and were covered up by a sail.

They could not eat. They felt as if they were dying, but so helpless that they seemed to care little for anything.

Towards night the wind abated, and they were glad of some tea and biscuit. Then again they cowered under the canvas, and conversed in low, hushed whispers.

They could not for a moment conceive why they had been taken from the guardianship of their good, and kind mother. After an affectionate and whispered conversation, they fell asleep.

And thus the time passed until they reached the river Thames, when they were taken into the cabin, and furnished with the means of washing and tidying themselves.

When they came once more on deck, they found themselves at anchor in a small bay. A boat awaited them, into which they were lifted without any unnecessary words.

Both were too terrified to demand any explanation.

No sooner were they landed, than the man who had already threatened to use the rope to them, led them up a slope of sand and grass, after which they found themselves on the edge of a vast extent of marshes.

Not a house of any kind was in sight.

At the end of half an hour, however, they reached a small creek, where stood an old ferry.

A ruined house formed the habitation of the ferryman.

It was composed of red brick.

"House!" shouted the man, in a loud, commanding voice.

A moment or two of delay took place. Then a door opened, and a woman appeared. Without a word she entered the boat, and pulled it across. The man entered it, and signed to the children to follow.

The house on the other side was, as we have said, in ruins. It had been large, and at some former period had been used for some manufacturing purpose. Its kitchen was of considerable dimensions. A small but neglected quay showed that barges had stopped there in former days. There was a large chimney, too, which threatened to topple over at the slightest breeze.

The man and woman had a conference, carried on in a low whisper, after which money was exchanged, and the sailor departed.

The woman, a little, short, bony, ill-looking woman of about forty, dirty, slatternly, and evidently habituated to drink, now seated herself, with a pipe in her mouth, and a glass of gin. Then casting a handful of gold and silver into her lap, she began greedily to count it.

"I'm so hungry," said Henry, in a whisper.

Jessie patted his forehead, and tried to hush him.

"What are you mumbling about?" said the woman, in an angry tone.

"Please, mum," replied Jessie, in a low, humble, winning voice, "the little boy is hungry and thirsty."

The woman looked strangely at the child. She was as ill-favoured a specimen of womankind as anybody could wish to see; her countenance was sullen and repulsive, while she was abominably redolent of gin, and yet something had moved her.

"Hungry!" she cried, "good lud! look in the cupboard, and see what there is."

Jessie curtsied, and hastily obeyed. She found some fat bacon and a basket of eggs, some coarse bread and raw onions.

She looked timidly at the woman.

"Help yourself—don't be bashful," she cried, helping herself to another glass of gin, and watching the child with a strange interest.

Jessie took down a dirty, half-rusty, old frying-pan, and after some further search found some paper and rags. With these she cleaned the cooking utensil out until it shone. Then she cooked the bacon and eggs, which she placed upon the table, with a very questionable cloth, but still neatly, and as if she had been quite a little woman.

"Ha! ha! ha!" laughed the woman, "shouldn't I like you for a servant. It's cooked first-rate. I'll help myself." And with a heartiness of manner quite unexpected, she joined the children in a substantial meal.

"Well, if you ain't a-mugging of yourselves," said a coarse voice, which startled all, while a dog, a snappish cur, came bounding and yelping in.

"Is that you, Jim?" replied the woman, carelessly.

The other did not reply, but seating himself, began unbuttoning his gaiters.

He was a man of about five-and-twenty, short, thickset, with a low forehead, heavily arched eyebrows, short brown hair, a thick lip, and heavy chin—the very type of a low pothouse poacher.

The game laws, bad as they are—a vile tax for the exclusive amusement of the rich—do no greater evil than that of fostering in almost every township and village of England, a set of idle, dissolute fellows, who, from the fact of following an unlawful calling, become callous to the perpetration of things even more objectionable.

Better exterminate every partridge and pheasant in the land, than endure the intense demoralisation caused by game laws and poaching.

"Where does them brats come from?" said Jim, as he concluded his operations, and helped himself to a thick slice of bacon and an egg.

"What's that to you?—there paid for," replied the old woman.

"Darned if I don't think they're out of the 'Betsy,'" continued the youth, scowling at the children, who luckily having satisfied their appetites, had skulked into a corner.

"Might have guessed worse."

"Well, if there going to stay here," said the man, "I'm to have some of the plunder, I suppose?"

"And what for, James Belton?" continued the old woman, fiercely. "This is my house, and I shall do what I like in it."

"You do pretty much," said the man, sulkily. "Hast got any money?"

"Not for you," cried the virago, rising and standing before him with clenched fists, "you lazy, skulking hound. I tell you what, Jim, if you don't pretty soon clear out, I'll make you. I'm getting tired of keeping such an idle, ne'er-do-well. Because you married my daughter, and killed her—"

"Mother!" he cried passionately, "take care—"

"I don't say you murdered her," continued the hag, in fierce accents, "except by your cruelty—so there's plain English for once; so the sooner you go, the better."

"Im a-going soon enough. I expects the 'Betsy' wants a hand—there's sutthen up, and the sooner I gets out of this den, the better. I'm to meet Jones to-night; but I can't go to the 'Silver Key' with ne'er a penny."

"Earn one, then," said the woman, hoarsely.

He looked at her under his eyes, and glanced at the gun which he had laid down, and a wicked expression of countenance startled the observant children.

"I only want half-a-crown," he said in a milder tone.

"No—get out!" shrieked the woman, draining off some more gin.

"I've got one, please, sir," said Jessie, holding out one, which her mother had given her for some purpose; "you're welcome to it."

"Well, that's jolly," cried the man, with a hoarse laugh, as he took the money; "never larn to be stingy, like that old tabby."

And taking up his gun, and whistling to the dog, he went out.

"Have you got any more?" said the woman, as soon as he left—greed and avarice sparkling in her eyes.

"No, ma'am," replied Jessie.

"Well, go out, and look about. When you are hungry, come in and make tea. I'm going to take a nap; but mind you, you won't run away?"

They exchanged glances.

"If you don't promise, I'll lock you up there," said the woman, fiercely, pointing to the loft.

"We will not run away," they said, looking her full in the face with those truthful and beautiful eyes.

"Go!" she said, huskily. "Go!" she added, as they closed the door, "go, or I shall become mad. Were are *my* children? Where my poor Mary's babe, with the blue eyes and the rosy cheeks—all—all—in the cold churchyard, and I a lone and miserable woman. Why is it I feel so dark to-day? Why do I feel that I could weep as I gaze at those two children. Well—well, its no use fretting," and drinking off another glass of gin, she sank back into an uneasy slumber.

The children thought that they had never seen so desolate a region. On all sides spread a sandy and grassy plain, composed of coarse, tufty herbage, while not a hillock was to be seen even on the banks of the river.

It was a lazy, slow, idle river, creeping along with very little regard to the impatience of travellers, or the health of sojourners on its banks. It swept along with a majestic flow, like that of a prosy Chancery barrister, or pompous chairman of quarter sessions. Its banks were reedy and slimy with mud. It looked something like the banks of certain rivers in the lowlands of Texas, except that no alligators floundered thereby.

Not a house in sight, not a welcome steeple speaking of some quiet yet secluded hamlet.

The children looked abroad with a sense of weary sorrow. They felt they must be a very long way from home; and why had they been brought to this secluded den, away from every sign of civilization.

Weary at last of wandering abroad, they took their way to the ruined hut, which, for the moment, they were almost tempted to call home.

CHAPTER XXXVII.

THE MURDER.

THEY found the woman still asleep, but as she had alluded to tea, Jessie with that inherent tidiness which was part of her nature, began to 'make tea.'

The kettle was boiling on the hob, and the little girl already knew where to look for the teapot, so she took it from the cupboard, and with Henry's assistance the necessary preparations were soon made.

But still the woman slept, not comfortably, not well, but uneasily, with heavy breathing, and sighs as of one in pain. Her eyes opened at times, though it was evident that she saw not.

Jessie touched her gently on the arm.

"Who is there? you shall not have it," she exclaimed, starting up. "Ah! have I been sleeping? —come back already—but I see it is late. Will you make the tea, little girl?"

"I have made it," said Jessie.

"What a good little girl," cried the woman, with a stare. "Well, pour it out, and then you must go to bed, I see you are tired."

Jessie took her seat, and as she had often been accustomed to, when her mother was ailing, presided at the tea-table, much to the admiration of the woman, who drunkard and bad as she was in many other ways, was subjugated by the voice of innocence and youth.

Heaven only knows what pre-visions of coming ill, what dark shadows of gloom, were weighing on her soul as she sat watching their gentle and fond caresses.

At length she seemed to crave once more that stimulant, which she was ashamed to take in their presence.

She pointed to a ladder.

"You must sleep as best you may in the loft, let down the trap and fasten it, for Jim is dangerous when he is drunk. Be careful with the lantern," and, with a muttered something, she hurried them away.

They ascended the ladder to find themselves in a large loft, filled by lumbering old boxes, some bundles of hay, and other things. Of the hay, they proceeded to make their bed, with the assistance of two coarse and ragged horsecloths.

First they prayed.

This was a duty they never omitted, nor ever failed to find relief and satisfaction in.

They then spoke in whispers of home, of their hopes of escape, and of their many plans for finding those who were so dear to them, and whispering and talking they fell asleep.

They had turned a large and thick bar, which thus effectually secured the trap.

At what hour they knew not, but they had slept some time, they were aroused by a noise below. Listening anxiously, they knew it to be Jim, the son-in-law, who had returned from his booze.

Hardly knowing why, they held their breaths, and peered down through some of the many holes and crannies of the loft.

Then they saw James Belton enter the shanty. His gun was still in his hand, and his little cur followed him. He was very much intoxicated, his hair was matted and tangled, his eyes bloodshot, and his words almost unintelligible.

"I will—hic—I will have money, darned if I don't—money—I won—der—where—where the old devil keeps it. She must tell me."

There was but the flicker of an expiring candle and the flare of the dying wood embers.

But the children could see enough to alarm them terribly.

He laid his gun against the wall, and took off his cap.

He glanced around. But no probable hiding-place appeared before him.

He looked stealthily at the woman.

"Greedy old tabby," he muttered, "can't spend it herself, won't give it a fellow. Where the deuce does she put it. I maun have it, and I will. I'ze spent all—lost money at cards, and I maun go back. Dang it, where can it be?"

The woman slept in her chair. It was her usual custom. She had a bed, but scarcely ever used it. Jim had never been able to make this circumstance out.

Greed and avarice sharpened his intuition.

He now noticed that the chair was always carefully preserved in the same place.

A smile of rejoiced cunning passed over his soddened and sulky face.

He looked at her fixedly. She was in a sound and heavy slumber.

He drew her away gently, chair and all, from where she sat, and so gradually—for drunkedness is very cunning—that he did not wake her.

He was some time about it.

As he finished, the candle went out, and he had to look for another.

He knew where they were kept, and soon procured one. He lit it, and approached the spot. His heart beat wildly with savage gladness.

There was a round tile under the matting, which had moved away with the chair, that had recently been taken up.

Jim stooped down, drew out his knife, and tried to raise it.

"Touch it, and I fire," shrieked a fearful voice close to him.

He turned, shaking as with the palsy, and there stood his mother-in-law, with his gun in her hand at full cock.

She was ghastly pale, but her eyes rolled in her head with exasperation and fury. She looked like a tigress ready to defend her young; and in such a nature, gold was even more precious than nearness of blood.

"Put down that gun," he said with a savage glance as he clutched his knife.

"Get out, leave the house," screamed the woman.

"Now I tell you what it is," cried the ruffian, fixing his eye upon her, "I means to have my halves of this money, I'll divide fair, but if you ain't agreeable, why I'll have all—so choose, and choose quickly."

"My money!—no, not a penny. I will die first. It is all I have. I am getting old, and won't be murdered in a workhouse—no, I won't, to feed such lazy, idle, good-for-nothing beasts as you. Let you have my money to guttle and swizzle, and deceive young girls,—no, never, that I won't. I tell you, I'll die first."

"Then die," yelled the ruffian, making a dart at her.

She fired. But he struck up the gun.

The children shrieked, till the welkin rang again.

The shot struck the roof close to their heads.

They were fascinated with horrible curiosity.

He dashed the gun to the ground with a fearful laugh.

"And now, ma'am," he said, with savage calmness, " I'll have it all."

He clutched her by one arm.

She saw not the knife.

She flew at his face with a yell, and scratched him furiously.

Then came several blows with all his brutal might and strength, a moan, a fall, a heavy groan or two, and all was still below.

The children shrieked with unabated violence.

"I'm a-coming to you," he said, in a deep, hollow, husky voice, that froze them with terror, "don't be in a hurry."

Then he turned to the table, and helped himself from her spirit-bottle.

His hand shook as with the palsy, his face was white, his teeth chattered, and his eyes were ever turned away from the thing on the floor.

That once immortal being was a clod.

Few like to look upon the dead—none, hardly, on the violently slain, save the callous, obdurate, and systematic assassin, or the reckless and soulless conqueror or trampler on his country's liberties; a hangman, a Francis II., a Louis Napoleon.

This man, vicious as he was, shuddered at the deed done. There is a reaction so rapid in these cases that probably, had the choice been given, he would have sneaked away penniless to have had her sitting alive in the arm-chair.

But now for safety and flight.

Safety could only be purchased by slaying the witnesses of his crime.

Flight to be of any use must be instantaneous.

He stooped to search the hiding-place, and to his delight and surprise found over a hundred pounds, the savings of the wretched woman since her husband's death had given her the ferry. The money was in various coinages, which he thrust all into a leathern bag at his side.

Then he rose and wiped the heavy perspiration from his brow.

The children only moaned.

"Come you down, will you."

No answer.

"If yer don't come down, I'll come up and cut yer accursed little throats."

No answer.

The infuriated ruffian knit his brow, and with fearful deliberation ascended the ladder.

But the trap resisted his efforts. The children in their agony had piled everything they could upon it.

The ruffian shrieked with rage.

He could see that a faint streak of dawn was appearing, a grey dimness, precursor of the true light.

These little witnesses would betray him, even more than that stark, stiff body on the ground.

The children must die.

He tried all his strength upon the trap in vain, it would not budge an inch.

With a demoniacal glare he descended the ladder, and sought his gun. He loaded it heavily with duck-shot, and having pointed upwards, again addressed them.

"Come down, or I'll shoot," he said, with a fearful oath.

No answer, not a sound to betray their whereabouts.

With a savage recklessness he fired. But he knew by the sound in vain.

The children had succeeded in overturning two bundles of hay on the loft, and instinctively ensconced themselves upon it. The balls and shot fell harmless.

They clutched each other's hands, and with eyes upturned to heaven, neither spoke nor breathed. They were scarcely conscious of what passed. But they felt that to move would be fatal to their safety.

Their faces were awfully pale.

After the shot, some minutes of stillness ensued, and then their little hearts almost burst with agony, their hands fell helpless, their blood ceased to flow, the very agonies of death were felt, as the hoarse, harsh, hollow voice of the murderer fell upon their ears close to them.

"Come out of that, you whelps," he said, peering in through a narrow window of the loft, "or by —— I'll shoot."

They gave one fearful shriek, that rung wildly through the air.

"Just hold on a minute," said a hearty voice at some little distance, "we're a-coming."

The assassin fled, already seeing the gallows before his eyes.

And he knew those voices well.

CHAPTER XXXVIII.

THE GOOD DIVINE.

AND still the children shrieked wildly.

The men dashed into the house, and one fell over the prostrate form.

The other rushed to the fire, stirred the embers, and lit a candle.

They were two gamekeepers, who, on the lookout in the neighbourhood, had heard the fearful cries of the children.

They gazed at one another speechless with horror.

The man who had fallen over the murdered corpse was covered with blood.

And still the children shrieked.

"Be quiet," said one of the men, "there's nobody here wants to hurt you. Which way has he gone?"

They could not answer, but they could be heard removing the hay.

"Can't raise the trap," said Henry.

The man ascended the trap, and pushed it upwards.

Then the two children came down, trembling, half dead with fright, and scarcely fully convinced that they were acting rightly.

But the men, rough customers though they were, spoke softly to them, and casting a cloth over the body, questioned them as to what had passed.

They told their story minutely.

It was now daylight, and it was agreed that one of the keepers should start to the nearest town, about three miles off, and fetch a constable. The children begged to be taken too, but the man promised to bring a cart for them.

So they went out into the open air. They could not stay in the house with the body.

It was a glorious morning, the birds carolled high in the heavens, the dew sparkled gloriously on the grass, but the children saw nothing but one another.

They were utterly powerless even for speech.

The whole course of their life for some days had been so fearful, closing up too with this fearful and hideous tragedy, that they were even more bewildered than horrified.

Presently they heard the sound of approaching wheels, and turning round saw a common market-cart approaching, in which sat the gamekeeper, two constables, and a gentleman in black.

This was a clergyman, and magistrate who had at once consented to accompany the party.

He descended from the vehicle, and approaching the children, spoke to them in a kind and conciliatory way, which at once caused them to burst into tears.

"There's good children," he said, "tell me all about it. Be calm, and I dare say we shall manage to make you comfortable,"

Jessie looked him full in the face.

"Will you send us back to mother?" she said eagerly.

"I will do everything in my power," replied the other. "But of this shocking affair?"

Jessie, not without considerable emotion, told the story of the murder.

The constables and gamekeepers exchanged glances.

They knew their man, and had already in their own minds spotted their game.

This preliminary once settled, the magistrate, after a hasty glance at the scene of the murder, left the hut in charge of the constables, and himself returned to F—— in company with the two children.

He had made up his mind.

Until such time as they were called for in a court of law, they were to reside with him.

He had sufficient knowledge of the world to be aware that they were children of tender growth and nurture.

Imagine the change of feeling which came over Jessie and Henry, when, after passing through the hands of a kind old housekeeper, they were seated at the rev. doctor's breakfast-table, in the enjoyment of every comfort and luxury.

The past seemed a horrid dream.

Doctor Philpott then let them tell their stories in their own way.

He took minute notes of every particular, and the very next day, in addition to a full account of the murder, there appeared in the papers an advertisement describing Jessie and Henry.

For many days there came no answer, at all events, not from the right parties.

Everybody, however, who had lost a child, wrote to demand additional particulars.

One morning they were on the lawn in front of the house, looking fresh, rosy, and happy once more.

Jessie was springing up fast to be a tall and most lovely girl.

Henry looked a manly little fellow.

Their trials had aged them, without leaving any painful mark behind.

They were seated on a bench, while the doctor, already excessively fond of them, viewed them from an open window.

He was a childless widower.

He had lost some little ones in days gone by, and to find himself suddenly the guardian of these lambs—as he would say—was both painful and pleasing.

He would gladly have adopted them, but then he knew that others had fairer claims.

Whence comes this sudden noise?

Hark!

A postchaise is dashing furiously up towards the house.

It halts.

A lady descends from it. She is in black, and veiled.

The children rise in great agitation.

The doctor hurries on to the lawn.

"My children!" she cries.

She raised her veil.

"I don't know you," said Jessie, in an astonished tone.

"The bad woman," cried Henry, with horror depicted on his countenance.

"Gracious heavens!" she continued, "is it then true, that my children know me not? Has suffering and absence so changed them?"

"You ain't my ma," said Jessie.

"Go away," cried Henry.

"Pray, madam, may I ask an explanation of what I hear," said the doctor, in a bland tone.

"Sir—"

Another and another. Two more postchaises, as if running a race of life or death, came dashing up towards the house, and both halt before the door.

A lady descends from each.

They are both in black.

"My child — my angel!" shrieks the first, towards whom Jessie runs wildly, and is clasped in her mother's arms.

Henry advances more timidly, but the other lady, whose face is strange to him, but yet very kind, clasps his two hands, and gazes with earnest attention in his face.

"Your name?"

"Henry Haddington."

"Child of my wronged brother!" cried Lady Haddington, "behold in me your aunt—your guardian, the protector of your name and fortunes."

"And pray who is this other lady?" said the doctor, turning round.

But the third lady had moved rapidly away, and was driving off.

The doctor saw that there was a mystery.

It would take the combined force of a pen and pencil much more powerful than ours to describe the scene of explanation, rejoicing, and excitement which ensued.

The doctor came in for his full share.

He asked them in, and, having at once made the ladies aware that he could not part with his young charges until the affair of the murder was settled, he could do no other than invite them to take up their residence with him.

And thus was the fearful crime of James Belton made the means of restoring the children to the arms of their legitimate guardians.

CHAPTER XXXIX.

A WONDROUS ADVENTURE.

MEANWHILE, what had become of Peregrine Grundy?

Polly Rackshaw never faltered in her decision. She held little or no communication with her father.

He was sullen.

She was determined and calm.

"Give me back my love," was her answer to every one of his advances.

"I know nothing of the fellow," he would reply.

Mary did not believe this.

But what could she do.

She had saved a little money.

This put an idea in her head, and she determined to carry it out.

She would go forth into the world, and seek him.

One evening, then, she made up a bundle, and passing quietly through the pawnbroking establishment, found herself in the street.

Perry had told her his address.

She determined to visit the barber's shop.

This was easily found. Peregrine Grundy had taken care to describe his whereabouts, to prove that he was what he professed himself to be —a respectable tradesman.

Mary Rackshaw was little used to the streets. Her father's jealous and watchful care made him keep her pretty much a prisoner.

Still, by judicious questioning, she was able at last to reach the desired locality.

Nearly all the shops were shut.

That of the barber was still open, and was easily distinguished by a few coloured lights, which Perry was fond of indulging in.

Mary advanced towards it with a beating heart. Should her fears prove incorrect, and the young man be safe at home, how should she explain her visit?

Well, she resolved to be of good cheer, and bear it bravely out. Had he not promised to love her always, and had she not a right, then, to visit him?

As she drew near, she heard voices. Her heart beat more quickly still.

At last she reached a point where she could both see and hear without being seen.

A boy with a red shock head of hair was standing with his back to the wall, while a little stout woman, with a huge cotton umbrella, a vast bonnet of most fantastic dimensions, and a very red pock-marked face, was seated on a chair before him, evidently in a great rage.

The boy wore the apron of a barber. In one hand was a razor, and in the other a strop. He, however, looked petrified with terror at sight of the brass point of the umbrella, which was every now and then violently in propinquity with his nasal organ.

"Now you young savagerous ruffin, I knows as how you've been and killed my nevvy—salted him in a barrel, and sent him off to the Heast or West Hindies—eh?"

"Mum—"

"Now don't acerberate me, you rampagous young ruffler, you mammiferous cut-purse. I know you've been and gone and done it—and I as his heirs and assigns, do insist upon a true and pertikler history. Did you cut his throat?"

"Mum—"

"Now I knows you've done it," she continued with a furious poke, "only confess—"

"But mum—"

"Confess!"

"Listen, mum," shrieked Pike, dropping his razor and strop, and making a dart at the mantelpiece, whence he took a card, which he thrust into her hand.

The fat old lady placed the umbrella between her knees, hunted up from her pocket a variety of indescribable articles, always to be found in old maids' pockets—took from among them a pair of spectacles, and read the note with the eye of a judge.

"Humph—queer—tell me all about it."

"I can!" said Mary, entering hurriedly, to the awful discomposure of the old lady, and the great relief of Pike.

"Wait," he said, "till I puts up them 'ere shutters, and we'll have a cup of tea."

"No thank you."

"With rum in it," continued the boy, insinuatingly.

"*With rum in it,*" said the old lady, with deep sigh, "what is this world a-coming to? Well, since you are so perlite, we'll take a cup of tea—*with rum in it.*"

"Werry good," said the boy.

And he put up the shutters. Then he proceeded in a most recondite way, with the assistance of Mary, to prepare tea, run out for a new loaf, and some nice butter, not forgetting the spirituous liquor to which allusion has already been made.

The tea with the rum in it, was pronounced perfect, and then Mary Rackshaw was called upon to tell her story.

She told it clearly and distinctly.

"Strange! but it's my opinion, as Mrs. Grundy, his heirs and assigns—and so on—that the said Peregrine Grundy, my nevy, will return. It ain't likely as he's killed. So—what's to be done? This bit of property is waluable, and it ain't to be supposed as this precious young wagerbone, as makes tea with rum in it—" here the old lady looked at the hob very hard, still more hardly at the kettle, and then at some glasses—just obliquely.

"Rum-and-water," said Pike.

"Just a leetle taste—as makes tea with rum in it, is fit to be entrusted with the stock in trade, and the whole tenement—except under supervision. So, young woman, as you takes an hinterest in my said nevy, I his heirs and assigns, do request you to look after Mr. Imperence here. Thank you, a little more sugar, there's a good boy—too much water, just a taste more of rum."

"I should be most happy," said Mary, with a blush of pleasure, "but I'm afraid my father—"

JOE'S WIFE MAKES A DISCOVERY.

"Your father," said Mrs. Grundy, severely, "I wish I had him here."

"He is my father. As you wish it, I will come. But cannot you madam—"

"Grundy, of Bath—occasionally wisiting this part, being myself employed in the bonnet line, first fashions, and so on—will look in now and then. And you, young man, recollect the orful responsibility of your situation. Master and man all in one, and so no more from yours at present —here's the coach—"

And with a jerk, something like a curtsey, she made her exit from the room, and was next seen running in great haste after a Bath and Bristol coach, which was in no very great hurry to escape from her.

After some further conversation, Mary likewise retired to her sad and solitary home, determined to leave no stone unturned to discover her dearly-beloved Perry.

His danger, the recollection of the strange way their acquaintance had been made, the uncertainty as to his fate, had awakened in her bosom a flame not very likely to be extinguished.

CHAPTER XL.

THE WHIRLPOOL.

IT is very much against our own inclination that we leave our favourite Jessie to follow in the track of the founder of the new religion, which has so devastated the homes and hearths of so many simple people in so many different lands.

Though the study be not pleasant, it may not be unprofitable; and if it deters one from accepting the abhorrent tenets of the great modern imposture, we shall not have striven in vain.

Joseph Smith returned with his young wife—for he really did marry the girl who had so foolishly eloped from her father—to the residence of his parents.

The change was one which told at once upon the health and spirits of the young girl. She found herself surrounded by a sordid, grovelling, and ignorant set, that forcibly contrasted with her own once happy home.

Father, mother, and children lived in the most squalid misery, arising partly from idleness, partly because their bad character prevented any of the neighbouring farmers from employing them.

Indeed, such was their evil reputation, that they at length removed to an abandoned shanty in the mountains, added to it a rude log hut or two, and lived almost wholly by hunting, and certain less lawful proceedings.

Joe Smith became intensely thoughtful and abstracted, held himself aloof from his family, rarely even communicating with his wife.

No doubt his whole soul was bent upon the imposture which he afterwards so successfully carried out.

His absences became numerous, long, and mysterious.

He was always going to the forest.

The district in which they lived was wild in the extreme, though at no great distance spread fertile plains, dotted with villages, homesteads, and farms.

Had the elder Joe Smith and his sons followed their trade honestly, they could have gained a most respectable living.

They were blacksmiths, gunsmiths, and knew every department of their trade.

One night Joseph Smith, who was exceedingly erratic in his proceedings, rose suddenly from his chair, and, muttering something about the forest, left the house.

No one took any notice of his proceedings, so used were they to his manner.

One, however, was less scrupulous. His young wife, upon whom a heavy cloud had fallen, had resolved in her own mind to fathom the mystery of his proceedings.

Dark and gloomy thoughts hung upon her soul. Strange suspicions had already crossed her mind. Certain comforts and luxuries to which she had long been a stranger had suddenly appeared in their shanty. Money, too, appeared oddly plentiful.

The Smiths wore better clothes every day.

Joe Smith was not unkind to her, but he was neglectful and abstracted.

Though her feelings had much altered, she still clung to him as her husband; and the idea that any other woman was the partial cause of his absence was madness.

When a wife becomes indifferent on this point, her affection is wholly gone.

Under these circumstances Emma Smith, the future prophet's wife, had determined to follow him on his next journey, and, at any risk, arrive at a distinct conclusion.

This occasion seemed a remarkably auspicious one. Joe Smith was unusually grave, thoughtful, and abstracted. He had been shut up in his hut alone all day, and now went forth with a grave and solemn step.

Over his shoulder hung his rifle.

The wife had provided herself with stout shoes, a flask of corn-juice or whisky, a biscuit or two, and a brace of pistols.

As she glided forth from a cluster of trees, and followed in the slowly retreating track of her husband, her manner was calm but determined. She had fully made up her mind to the worst, but wished to know it.

Alas! how often has a wife repented such Eve-like curiosity.

Better live in ignorance than have the heart scorched and withered with fatal knowledge.

The man trod heavily and deliberately, so that the more tender girl had no difficulty in following him.

And then her bringing-up had not been so delicate as to make the forest or mountain any very great obstacle in her eyes.

She saw at once that Joseph was on his way towards a high and rude mountain district, covered by an almost impenetrable forest, so that unless she kept pretty close to him she might easily chance to lose him.

Her forest education now served her in good stead.

With all the caution and stealth of an Indian she tracked him.

Once or twice he halted, and looked back, as if he suspected that somebody was following.

Emma darted behind a tree, but so cautiously and noiselessly, that every time he came to the conclusion that he was deceived.

Once he levelled his gun and fired.

But not a sound escaped the lips of the daring wife.

Joseph from that moment appeared satisfied that his ears had deceived him; and, as if eager to make up for lost time, dashed forward through the undergrowth at a more reckless pace, so that his wife was able to follow him with difficulty.

Presently, on reaching the crest of a hill, a dark and gloomy valley appeared beneath them.

There was not a glimpse of moon or stars. A perfect Cimmerian darkness enveloped all nature. The very trees looked misshapen columns, obelisks, and other monumental blocks of stone, except that the wind made them creak and groan everywhile to add to the horrors of the place.

The roaring of a torrent did not detract from the effect.

And now Emma Smith knew where she was, and shuddered with awe.

Below, in that black darkness, was the Cauldron Lynn.

Women are never without a taint of superstition. As they are more religious than men, so have they a tendency to exaggerate.

She had heard fearful stories whispered of compacts with evil demons; and she knew that from his boyhood Joseph Smith had been said to search for hidden treasure by means of unhallowed practices.

What then was she going to witness.

Again she shuddered; but this time because she had lost all sight of her husband.

For a moment she felt inclined to shriek lustily, but forbore, lest all her labour should be in vain, to say nothing of the dread she entertained of the anger of her husband.

Like all enthusiasts for good or evil, Joe Smith was terribly passionate.

And yet her position was a fearful one. Alone in that terrible place, without the slightest means of finding the back track, what were her chances unless her husband came to her assistance.

Alone! Good heavens! those dense and gloomy forests abounded with the wolf, the panther, and the grizzly bear.

A horrible dread came upon her soul, and she shrieked aloud.

But nothing by way of answer reached her ears save the gloomy echoes of her own voice in that almost pathless forest.

She kneeled, and sent up a wild and passionate prayer to heaven, for in heaven alone could she hope for assistance, by man she was abandoned.

Hark! what comes in answer to her wild and incoherent cries.

Despite the roar of the torrent below, her forest ears cannot be deceived.

It is the growl of a bear, which is to be heard approaching rapidly.

Dear is life, and only remembering that her husband had disappeared under an archway of trees, close in front of her, Emma Smith rushed headlong in the same direction, and was next minute rolling down a steep hill.

Then she became temporarily insensible.

When she came to, she was in utter darkness, while the torrent roared close at her feet.

Awful was the shudder that came over her. She knew well the character of the waters which swept so near her.

A mountain torrent had, by incessantly wearing away a rock upon which it fell, dug a deep excavation, in which the water seethed and boiled unceasingly.

In the course of time, the basin becoming thin, an orifice was perforated, and then another, until the whole of the water rushed down a precipice in that way.

Many had fallen into the Cauldron, and been whirled down until they had been literally dashed to pieces.

In the darkness and gloom was it not very easy for the same to happen to her?

Then she listened for the bear, but the din of the waters was so great that she could detect no other sound.

Her desolation was fearful. Afraid to move lest she might be plunged into the whirlpool below, she might at any moment be attacked by the fierce beast which had caused her such terror.

In the hope of discovering the nature of the ground, she stretched out her arms.

On one side she touched the roots of trees.

On the other, horror of horrors! the damp edge of the Cauldron Lynn, the very spray of the fall, now she found wetting her.

Her heart appeared to leap to her mouth, for another three or four inches, and all had been over.

What should she do?

A bright idea struck her; quick as thought she drew a pistol and fired in the direction of the seething and boiling waters.

Who has not felt how much worse the fear of what may be almost always is, to what is the reality. To stand as it were on the brink of doom, with an unknown danger before us, is something truly awful—while, who has not trembled at the thought of peering into unknown depths of gloom and terror.

Emma felt almost inclined to close her eyes as she fired, but fortunately took courage and awaited the result.

The flash of the pistol illumined the darkness, visible but for a second, but that second contained a life.

She saw close to her feet, and plunging into unknown depths the sweeping, seething waterfall, but she also saw, or fancied so, the terrible grizzly bear of the forest, gazing at her with a strange and puzzled look.

Behind her was an ascent, up which she fled for a few minutes, and then halted, dazzled, astounded, and yet comforted. In the new intensity of her feelings, she forgot everything but the sight before her.

CHAPTER XLI.

THE CAVE OF MORMON.

She was at the summit of the cascade, just where it poured clear off a bed of rock into the mighty depths below.

Just beneath was a narrow ledge, washed with eternal spray, but still admitting of passage by a bold human footstep.

Across this path fell a vivid blaze of light, while, every now and then, sparks and flashes, could be distinguished.

Emma was satisfied that she had penetrated her husband's secret.

At any other moment she might have hesitated, but now she had no compunction. The bear, for a moment dazzled by the pistol flash, would soon follow her.

Sooner brave her husband's fearful passion, than be torn to pieces by the king of the American forest.

With a trembling heart, she adventured on the ledge, but to her great delight found the task neither a difficult nor a dangerous one, and in a few minutes she was landed on the other side, and stood almost in the mouth of a deep excavation, once, no doubt, a channel for the seething waters.

The cave was below her, and brilliantly lighted up. At the back was a large charcoal fire, while in the wall, were fixed several flaring pine torches.

The furniture of the cave was peculiar.

On one side was a large table covered with small elongated brass plates, " which had the appearance of gold. Each plate was not far from seven by eight inches in width and length, being not quite as thick as common tin."

Before these sat Joseph Smith in his shirt sleeves.

He was engraving on these plates the most mysterious series of signs.

An eye-witness says: " It was in fact a singular scroll. It consisted of all kinds of crooked characters, disposed in columns, and had evidently been prepared by some person who had before him at the time a book containing various alphabets, Greek and Hebrew letters, crosses, and flourishes. Roman letters inverted or placed sideways, were arranged and placed in perpendicular columns; and the whole ended in a rude delineation of a circle, divided into various compartments, decked with various strange marks, and evidently copied after the Mexican calendar, given by Humboldt, but copied in such a way as not to betray the source whence it was derived."

Before the future prophet and impostor, were several grammars and other books, with the alphabet open in all cases.

The man appeared to take a letter from one, and a letter from the other, without any order of preconcerted rule.

As far as Emma could see, the characters were small and beautifully engraved.

Emma could not make it out.

She little imagined that her husband was fabricating a Bible on which to found a new religion.

She then perceived that there was another person in the case. A thin, gaunt, little man, with heavy moustache, shaggy hair, and a rude set of habiliments, while his face was cadaverous, and his eyes hollow in the extreme.

He was printing from a little hand-press, with great care, some narrow slips of paper.

Then Emma Smith knew that she stood in the presence of forgers, driving their unhallowed and illegal trade in the depths of the wilderness.

" Well, how gets on, Joe?" said the printer, who was no less a personage than Simon Rigden, the future right hand of the prophet.

But before we record the answer of General Joe, let us explain how these worthies met.

The first real advantage which accrued to Joseph from his marriage with Emma Reardon, *was learning to read.*

The young man had unhesitatingly confessed his ignorance to his wife, and applied himself to supply the deficiency with the most unwearied industry.

Had he used one half the energies he wasted on imposture in a good cause, he might have been a great and good man.

The only use he made of his learning was to shut himself up, and learn the manuscript he had stolen from Spaulding by heart.

He also studied hard at the Bible, and easily finding among his neighbours the wild theological works of certain of the more extravagant Puritans, his head became, in three years, a store of biblical knowledge.

Then it was that he resolved to have visions' and found a new religion on the Book of Mormon, which he had contrived to write out in a coarse but legible hand.

A difficulty staggered him.

His coarse and vulgar penmanship never would be received as inspired.

Dispirited, angry, full of prodigious designs, he went out into the forest.

The cave he discovered when in chase of a wolf, but that was not the place of his meditations.

He had selected a spot of calm and sequestered beauty, where a grove gave pleasant shade from the sun, and where a murmuring brook that swept past his feet made sweet music, while it also ministered to his wants.

Here on a pleasant bank, where grew fragrant flowers, would sit the nascent impostor, poring over the manuscript of the Book of Mormon, and committing whole pages of it to heart.

And the place was called the Hill of Cumoral.

When he had learned whole passages, he would shout them out to the inanimate woods and forests.

One day he was seated, the book before him, ranting, raving, pouring forth a mixed jargon, extracted partly from the romance, partly from passages of the Bible, twisted to suit his own meaning, when a loud laugh startled him from his employment.

" Thunder ! " said a hilarious voice, " if this ar don't beat cockfighting. Preaching to the crows, eh! stranger."

Clutching his rifle, Joseph Smith, pale with rage, started to his feet, to confront the sneering face of a man of middle height and age, also armed with a rifle, and with pistols protruding from his belt.

" What do you mean ?" said Joe, fiercely.

" Nuthin," replied the other, " only hearin' you a shoutin, I kim up and listened."

" Who, and what are you ?" continued Joe, scarcely able to articulate with rage.

" My name is Simon Rigden, said the other, " printer, engraver, and minister of the Gospel— and, stranger, I've got a copy of that 'ere book in my pocket."

And he pointed to the manuscript.

Joesph Smith felt as if shot. All his hopes, aspirations, were now cast to the ground.

At first he determined to end all doubt by shooting the other, but he had sense enough to know that the struggle might be doubtful.

And then the magic words uttered by the other decided him more than anything.

Printer, engraver, and minister of the Gospel.

What a perspective did this not hold out.

" Can you shoot," said Joe, abruptly.

" Can't I," replied Rigden, with a covert smile.

" Let me see you," continued Joseph, with that air of superiority which so often influenced his dupes.

Rigden looked around. On a rock about eighty yards distant stood a small, strait tree, the stem of which was not much more than a quarter of an inch thick.

" I can hit that," said the printer, quietly.

" So can I," replied Joe, and with unerring

aim, he poured forth his volley, and the spurting bark showed that he had succeeded.

The other volley followed, and the same result ensued.

"Drove the pin, by heaven!" said Joe, using a favorite locution of target-shooters. "And now sit down and tell me what you mean by saying you've seen that book before. I think, if we can be friends, I can shew you a way to fortune."

Simon Rigden then explained that a very short time previously Solomon Spaulding had come to an employer of his, one Patterson, with his manuscript, which he wished published as a romance.

But Patterson said that it would only sell if brought out as a true history.

This Solomon Spaulding declined to authorise.

A long correspondence ensued.

During the time Simon Rigden, then an itinerant Campbellite preacher, thinking it might be useful to him in connection with his sermons, copied the book in secret.

Then Solomon Spaulding died, and soon after, Patterson.

The relatives of Spaulding destroyed his copy as worthless.

"Ah!" said Joe Smith, with a deep sigh of relief, "Spaulding dead—the manuscript destroyed —all is well."

"What mean you?" cried Rigden.

Joe Smith took him by the button of his coat, and in a long and eloquent discourse displayed all his views.

The other listened, first with awe, then with incredulity, and at last with admiration.

"Creation of God," he said, "if it could be, it would be prime.

"It shall be," cried Joseph, "I will teach a new dispensation. I will earn a name before which that of Mahomet and every other prophet shall pale. I will found a new religion and a new people, who shall gather together from the uttermost ends of the earth. I tell you, stranger, that this book is but a means to an end. Let me breathe into your ears my real secret : I am inspired, but this history of the past will be my Koran. Now, Simon Rigden, are we friends, or shall we stand at ten paces and decide who is the better man?"

"Friend, admirer, disciple," said Rigden, with considerable eagerness.

And these two consummate knaves shook hands. They thoroughly understood each other.

They put all their resources together, and established in the cave, to which they gave the name of Mormon, an *atelier* where Simon could forge notes, while Joseph Smith fabricated his bible.

The border notes in those days were easily imitated and more easily passed with a rude and partly unlettered people.

Joe and Simon therefore reaped a rich crop in this way, taking care, however, to issue them at some distance from home.

*   *   *   *   *   *

"The plates are nearly finished. In four days they shall be buried on the Hill of Cumoral. That will be a task of some labour, Master Simon, and of course we cannot touch them until the turf has grown again : then for fame and fortune."

"Or martyrdom," said Rigden, gravely.

"What matters. Look you, Simon, I was brought up in ignorance and vice, but I feel that in me which says that if I had been educated and placed in a more fortunate position, I could have been anything I wished. Since I have read, thoughts burn within me which consume my soul. I am ambitious of fame, and rather than win it no other way, I will obtain it by death."

"You're a wonder," said Rigden.

"Am I?" cried Joe, listlessly, "but I've done for to-night. Sleep you, while I go forth and pray on the Hill of Cumoral."

Rigden looked strangely at him, as if he could not understand so odd an admixture of knavery and credulity.

Joe Smith passed out without any further words, and so wrapped was he in his own thoughts that though he almost brushed past his terror-stricken wife, he did not see her.

CHAPTER XLII.

THE VISITATION OF THE ANGEL.

OUT into the dark forest the prophet stalked, rifle in hand, treading its mazes as if every avenue were familiar, and at no great distance behind him his wife, keeping him in sight with the utmost difficulty.

So nerved was she to the worst, that she scarcely sought to disguise her presence.

This, probably, prevented her discovery.

The over-cautious are the oftenest betrayed.

Away towards the hill and grove of Cumoral stalked the man of busy thoughts, his brain working eternally with his awful schemes and his visions of glory, influence, and unlimited power over the female sex.

Foul was the slander upon religion when Joseph Smith dared to found his sect upon the pure creed of Christianity, of which virtue and chastity are as corner-stones.

The polygamy-built religion of Mahomet would have better suited his real view.

But it was necessary to delude his dupes, and he used the name of The Saviour.

The darkness was fading away, and a faint light, that of the moon peering through the open glades of the forest, as they approached the grove, over which lowered the Hill of Cumoral.

Crossing the brook, Joseph Smith halted, and appeared for a long time to be kneeling in prayer.

The wife, disgusted, terrified, and alarmed at all she had heard, would willingly have burst upon him and upbraided him with his conduct, but she was alone with him in that dark forest.

Kneeling behind a tree, at a distance of about thirty yards, she watched his movements with intense curiosity.

Was he not wholly playing a part? Was he partly impostor, partly enthusiast, partly rogue, and partly fool?

Then he rose and set light to a small pile, and again fell upon his knees.

Scarcely had he done so, than there glided

between himself and the fire a figure in white raiment, with a chaplet of flowers round its head, arranged so as to represent a glory.

And with the fire throwing out the delicate form, it looked very much like one.

Emma shuddered, and a great fear fell upon her soul, as her husband rose and looked fixedly at the figure, waved his hands several times, and seemed to pass them over its face.

The figure stood in an attitude fixed and immovable as that of a statue.

"Who art thou?" he then said.

"An angel of the Lord," said the figure, in accents which went to the heart of Emma Smith.

"And who am I?"

"His well-beloved servant."

"What is my duty on earth?"

"To love and restore—to pardon and punish—to announce the coming of Him to reign a thousand years upon earth."

"And when shall the bright day come?"

"Soon—soon. But enough for to-day."

"Enough, bright spirit—you may depart," said Joe, and the figure turned with a smile, and—*after shaking hands with Joseph*—took its way through the forest.*

Cold drops of dewy sweat upon her brow, her limbs shaking under her, the wife glided through the forest a little way, then crossed the brook, and darted on the way taken by the figure.

She was not long ere she saw her moving slowly along, humming to herself a hymn of praise.

Next minute, Emma Smith, with flashing eyes, with arms outstretched, stood facing as lovely a specimen of girlism in the very dawn and bud of womanhood as her eyes had ever fallen on.

Of middle height, dressed in pure white, with no head-covering but a chaplet of white flowers, with an oval face of pure red and white, lips slightly parted in alarm, with golden curls waving over her shoulders, with eyes of blue starting in terror, she seemed about to shriek for assistance.

"One word, and you die," said the other, sternly, as she cocked a pistol.

"Who and what art thou?" murmured the alarmed maiden.

"The wife of the man with whom you have been playing your tomfooleries in the forest," continued Emma.

"Wife!" said the maiden, clasping her little hands in utter and genuine woe—"wife!"

And she sank on a bank with her head bowed between her knees.

"Why should the word so touch you?" cried Emma, in bitter scorn.

"Because I am his wife!"

"Girl—say that again—that I may nerve my soul to the dread task imposed upon me—that I may rouse myself to the dread and fearful duty. When were you married to him?"

"I am his spiritual wife—we were married by the altar in the grove."

"*Spiritual wife!* Ha! ha!" laughed the other, bitterly, "so that is his idea—the villain. Girl, you seem innocent and light-hearted—sin, I believe, has not yet touched your soul. Tell me your story, honestly, frankly, and I will then judge you."

"I will," cried the girl, in artless accents, which went to the soul of the injured wife. "About two months since there was a mighty preacher came to Little Manchester down there, and he preached a revival sermon. It was awful to hear. Everybody was to go to a wicked place, and suffer eternal fire, because we were all full of sin. I listened to him with terror and alarm. I didn't feel very wicked before, but I do believe it made me feel wicked ever after. I seemed to fancy that if we are all to be sent to the wicked place but those who were the elect, I might as well be wicked as not, and cried, and sobbed, and fell into hysterics. When I came too, I found that man"—this with a shudder—"holding me in his arms outside the church, and whispering to me I should be saved. I said I was very much obliged to him, and so I was, I'm sure."

"Then he drew me away, and told me that he was a great prophet, only his time was not come, but soon would; and that he had long been looking for one as innocent as I was to become his guardian angel. He said that no woman could be saved except through her husband, but that he could not make me his wife until he started on his great pilgrimage to convert the world."

"I should think not," muttered the wife.

"Still," she continued, "he said I must be converted and taught my duty as a high priestess of the new faith, and made nightly appointments to meet me at the grove of Cumoral."

---

* It is painful to recur to blasphemy and imposture, but the Mormons must be exposed. We place in a note Joseph Smith's account of this vision four years after. He doubtless intended to allow his disciples to behold him in communion with angels after a little practice.

"Four years ago, while alone, two singularly beautiful personages appeared to me, and announced themselves as messengers from the throne of God, sent to reveal to me that I had been chosen to make known to man the errors of their faith—a faith which was offensive in the sight of God—and teach them the truth of the plan of salvation, which had been lost for ages through the stubborn wilfulness of man. I had long been troubled in my mind at the sinfulness of my own heart before that hour; but no sooner did these messengers announce to me the mission I was to fulfil, than all doubts ceased, and I felt my heart rising in adoration before my Maker. A few days passed, when I began to feel that I was past sinning—pride entered my heart, and I gloried not at the good I should accomplish, but at the honour and fame my mission would bring me. Then I began to be again miserable, when the angels re-appeared, who chided me for the wickedness of

my thoughts, forgave them, and then told me that the records of the Lost Tribes of Israel were buried in the Hill of Cumoral, where they were deposited fourteen hundred years ago by Moroni, the son of the Prophet Mormon, having previously engraved them on plates of gold, the Prophet Mormon assuring his son Moroni that, after the lapse of fourteen hundred years, a Gentile nation should recover them, and, through the truth of their prophecies, be turned to the true worship of God. The angel gave me the directions by which I could find the spot indicated, and with joy I hastened to lay bare the holy treasure. On the west side of the hill, where the storms of ages had beaten against it, I dug down by the side of an immense rock, where, below the surface about two feet, I laid bare a square marble box, so firmly cemented that water could not penetrate its interior. At the sight of the box, I knelt in prayer and adoration to the great Jehovah, and my heart was melted by divine love. With reverence, I laid my hand on the lid, when it flew open by an invisible hand, and beneath I saw plates of shining gold, covered over with strange characters, and on the tops of these lay two thick glasses set in a rim of gold. At the sight of the golden

"And you went?" asked the wife, with a searching glance.

"I went," continued the other, bending down her head.

"What happened?" coldly continued the wife.

"He met me. 'Hail, Sophia! elect lady!' he said, 'favoured of the Lord! Angels send thee greeting, for thou art exalted above other women, who henceforth shall do thee reverence.'"

"Ha! ha! ha!" laughed Emma.

"'The heavenly hosts even now surround thee,' he continued, 'rejoicing that thou art worthy of this exalted honour. Thou lackest faith, Sophia, or thou wouldst see and acknowledge the presence of the heavenly visitors.'"

"Wretched impostor!" muttered the wife.

"I believed him, and since then three times a week I have met him, and—and—" she could say no more, but fell weeping on the other's neck.

"Poor child," said Emma, whose rancour all vanished. "Vile profligate! Oh, how am I punished. To leave my father's home for such a man. I see all his schemes as in a mirror—but if truth can prevail—never mind. Well, poor child, you fell a prey to this man."

"I did."

"Well—go thy ways home. The worst may not be. See this man no more. I have now a hold upon him. Can you walk?"

"Yes," she said faintly.

"Here, take this flask," giving her a small bottle of brandy and water, "it will help you on your journey. Have you far to go? By-the-way, where do you live?"

"At Little Manchester—two miles distant."

"I shall remember. Here we part—better, perhaps, never to meet again."

The excited wife then wrung her hand, and darted into the deep recesses of the forest.

The girl had told her that she should once more visit the grove.

She too had resolved to be there.

CHAPTER XLIII.

THE PROPHECY.

It was a lovely evening when Emma Smith, after a long day's rest in her cottage, took her way towards the forest once more.

She knew her way now with confidence, for she had noted every track that could guide her.

Her husband had not returned, which made her confident that he would be at the rendezvous.

She left it purposely late, as the girl had told her that he never came before three in the morning, that being the hour at which she could easiest escape from her home without arousing the suspicions of her family.

Emma, then, did not hurry herself. Like most women, she was very impulsive, and though burning with vengeance and hate, had made up her mind to no particular course of action.

She walked along, with her small rifle in her hand, in a dreamy state of mind.

Presently she sat down to rest.

The sun was setting in all its glowing glory behind a row of mighty trees, the pillars of ages, and sending a softened light through their boughs over the rich, prairie-like sward, dotted with flowers that gave everything a purple hue. Birds still fluttered and twittered and sung in every bush, squirrels chirruped over head, and the sand-hill crane's shrill whoop could be heard in the distance, with the gobbling of the wild turkey flying to roost. Crickets gambolled at her feet, nor was the musical frog of the prairie silent.

And the heavens were cloudless.

Emma thought herself a girl again, and laughed aloud, so utterly did the scene take her away from the dread present to the happy and delightful past.

But suddenly all the stern reality came back to her heart.

Past—present—future.

What hovers above and flaps his wings?

Is it the hideous carrion-vulture gloating over its prey; or is it the fluttering of the wings of that dread angel which rarely comes without casting at least its shadow before.

Alas! it is the angel of death indeed, the angel of sin and woe.

With weary and exhausted frame, dreading she knew not what, full of dark forebodings of what was to come, she rose and dragged herself through the forest towards the fatal rendezvous.

No longer was she the light-hearted girl, but the stern woman, implacable, vengeful, her heart seared and scarred to the very core.

Was not her husband an impostor, a forger, and a ruthless seducer.

---

plates my heart became steeled by avarice, and I resolved to use the gold; but no sooner was the thought born in my heart, than an invisible hand struck me to the earth, and the ground gathered over the box and its contents. The air became filled with whispering voices, while cloud-like forms flitted around me. Ever and anon balls of fire hissed above me, while fiery serpents shot athwart the sky, and the sun paled in their fiery light. These died away, when the hosts of heaven with their golden chariots and myriads of purified spirits, led on by the Patriarchs and Prophets, passed before me, among whom Mormon, the last of the Prophets, paused and addressed me thus:—

"'Take heart, O Joseph; for in thee shall the prophecies be fulfilled; and thou shalt, if thou overcomest the evil in thine own heart, reign among us.'

"The words of Mormon comforted me; and when this procession had passed, darkness fell around, and groans and shrieks filled the air. Trembling with affright, I looked around, and, approaching, I saw Satan and his fiends amidst clouds of flame, the smoke of which rolled high o'er the heavens. And as they drew near and encompassed me wild cries and blasphemies rent the air, I threw myself in the dust and besought aid from the great Jehovah. A moment passed, when a rushing sound, as of many winds,

was heard, and Satan fled before the angel who stood before me, crying:—

"'Arise, O Joseph! chosen Prophet of the Lord, who delighted in thee, inasmuch as thou hast turned to him, and scorned the evil! arise and go thy way, for, notwithstanding thou hast sinned in thy heart, when thine eyes beheld the word which was shown thee, thou shalt yet abide four more years in the world before thou shalt possess it. Go thy way, and sin no more!' With these words he left me, and I returned sorrowing to my home. Did you know all the bitterness and sorrow I have borne during those four years, you would think more leniently of me now, for there was time enough for me to reflect upon the glorious mission I had delayed by the sinfulness of my heart, and to fortify it against a repetition. Four years to day the angel appeared to me while in the field at work, and said:—

"'Arise! beloved of the Lord! and bring forth the word of thy God, and proclaim it to the world!'

"As I, at the command, went forth, the heavenly messenger went before me, and I stood over the place where it was entombed, and when I had thrown out the earth, the lid of the marble casket flew open of itself, and there, as I had seen it before, were the precious contents."

Little did she imagine how his very cold audacity and utter recklessness were to be his means of success.

Some paint him as second to none who died for his belief. He—a vicegerent of God and tavern-keeper—a prophet of Jehovah, and a base libertine—a minister of religion, and a general—a ruler of tens of thousands, and a slave to his own base, unbridled passions—a preacher of righteousness, and a profane swearer—a drunkard, a mayor of a city, and a bar-room fiddler—a judge, and a reckless invader of all social rights!

But we must leave his character to develope itself, and return to our narrative.

Slowly, reluctantly, she sped towards the rendezvous—she knew not why.

Leaden weights were upon her feet, such as we feel in dreams, when we would fain run but cannot.

And still she moved onwards until, after several long and thoughtful rests, she came in sight of the grove of Cumoral.

Then she sat her down to reflect for the last time, ere she took up her position near the spot where she was to meet her husband.

The night was calm and blissful. Paradise itself, in the great day when man first trod within its precincts, could scarcely have been more serene—perhaps scarcely more beautiful.

Everything was soft, serene, and lovely.

And yet was there a strange odour—in reality a reflection of the mind—in the air—a sickly odour of blood it might have been.

Strange how the past waits upon us afterwards. How we remember, when the event has occurred, that which otherwise we never should have noticed.

" I thought there was something strange " is a common expression, *apres coup.*

And this is no imaginary thing. When any striking event has occurred, we do remember things previously unnoticed most distinctly and positively.

Mrs. Emma Smith at last heard a heavy footstep she knew too well, crashing through the underwood.

She was within thirty yards of the prophet's 'altar,' behind some peccan bushes.

She peered out.

It was her husband, with his long rifle in his hand, stalking towards the trysting place.

He had crossed the brook ; he had laid down his rifle against a tree ; he had looked upward with his usual devilish hypocrisy ere he knelt, when a light white figure, all bespattered with mud, burst from the grove beyond and confronted him.

" Beast, liar, contemptible and unmanly coward, at last I find thee. Beast, did I say ? Thou art worse than the animals of the field who pursue their instincts ; for thou, who hast been taught better, who hast intellect and power, thou art indeed the very fiend. Ha ! ha ! ha ! wife, quotha, spiritual wife, thou bibbing drunken suborner of female virtue. I spit upon thee." *

" Have you been drinking, Sophia ? " said the astounded prophet.

" Drinking ! " she shrieked, rushing at him in

the wildness of insanity, " not bread, not water has passed my lips since I have heard thy crimes."

" Crimes ! you foolish girl."

" Foolish, mad, worse," she shrieked. " Would that these little hands had strength for murder, you should not cumber the earth an hour longer."

" Dearest girl," cried the prophet, who believed her under an attack of temporary insanity, " come rest your head here, and you will soon be better."

" Now, thou most audacious beast, go to thy wife," she yelled forth rather than said, for in truth she was approaching madness.

" Wife," said Joe Smith, this time with a start, " what mean you ? Who dares say I have a wife, any wife, save you ? "

" Everybody,—'tis wafted on the wings of the wind," she laughed aloud, *" has she not a father, and looks he not for the ravisher ?"*

" Ah ! " cried Joe, really alarmed, " who dares say this ? "

Sophia saw that she had struck home. She followed up her advantage.

" Ha ! ha ! your craven soul is filled with dread, —coward, thief, forger ! "

" Forger ! " gasped Joseph Smith, with a countenance black as night, as he clutched her arm, " what mean you, speak, or—"

" You wouldn't strike poor Sophia," she said, looking up into his face with almost something of the old, old look, " strike a poor girl ? "

" By the heavens above I will, if you explain not the word *forger.*"

" Strike, then," said Sophia, tearing herself from him, " strike, and you shall know the endurance of a woman's will. . I will NOT explain. But be in no hurry, Joseph Smith, the chosen of the Lord. The wretched girl has no shame now, she is ruined and an outcast, nothing can make her worse ; and she will whisper to the people, a great prophet and his first disciple live in a cavern near the great boiling waters, and they print such pretty notes, and such odd-looking plates, won't you go and see : and Joseph Smith, they will hang you on the nearest tree, and the world will lose its new high-priest, ha ! ha ! "

" D———n," yelled Joseph Smith, as she turned to go, " come back and explain yourself, or by the living—"

" God of Mormon," laughed Sophia.

All this time Mrs. Smith, paralyzed, knelt behind the peccan bush, mumbling incoherent prayers.

" Come back, I say," roared Smith, snatching up his rifle.

" Good bye ! I'm not afraid—come back with father and mother, and brothers and sisters, to see my new husband—Ha ! ha ! ha ! "

And the poor half-mad girl, who had never gone home, turned towards that sacred spot, never so dear as when we have forfeited all claim to it.

With a wild execration, Joseph Smith snatched up his rifle and fired.

" Take that," said the ferocious ruffian.

A shriek, a double shriek, for it had an echo, filled the air, and Sophia, the prophet's victim, fell forward on the ground.

In a moment she turned and rose in a sitting attitude.

---

* She had evidently been taught quaintness of language by the prophet for his purpose.

JESSIE VIEWING THE PARK SURROUNDING HER MOTHER'S MANSION.

Her countenance was more beautiful than ever. A calm and placid smile replaced her bitter and fierce expression as she gazed upon the prophet, who stood stunned, horror-stricken, and ready to flee.

He too had heard that second shriek, so distant and yet so near.

"And this is death," she said calmly, and almost tenderly, "death. Joseph Smith, I thank thee. Thou hast saved me from much evil. I bear thee no malice; but woe unto you if you desist not from evil, for the day is coming and the reaper. To the dying is given to see into futurity. Come nearer, Joseph."

"Sophia, in mercy's sake forgive me! some demon tempted me. Let me examine your wound."

He knelt.

"It is useless; raise me up. Joseph, with all your faults I loved you, and I love you still. 'Tis better, then, to die, than live to be neglected, forgotten. or cast upon one side with indifference, as I should surely have been. But listen, Joseph—my hours are numbered, nay, my minutes

Repent, give up this fearful scheme of yours for establishing a false sect upon the ruins of truth and honesty."

She paused and looked straightforward, as if her eyes saw into the very depths of futurity.

Emma Smith crawled nearer.

Joseph Smith himself shuddered, and actually shed a tear.

Weep on. Not an ocean of such drops shall wash out this blood-stained deed, this ever-crying, everlasting stain upon thy humanity.

Her eyes closed.

She whispered, but they heard every word.

"Hush! do you hear them coming,—armed men in thousands. Why are their faces blackened? Hush! do you hear him—he is trying to speak to the mob. On they rush; in vain he strives to fly. I cannot see his face. Ah! 'tis Joseph Smith, the prophet. They fire. He falls, *shot through the heart!* Oh Lord my God!"

Let the reader mark these words at a subsequent period of our history.

And Sophia closed her eyes, and died.

CHAPTER XLIV.

THE REGULATORS.

How Emma Smith got home she never knew, but she recollected that she had tore along at a tremendous pace, had fallen exhausted, and then had fainted.

The next thing she knew was when she woke in her bed in her own solitary hut.

Courageous in some things, Emma Smith wanted the sterling moral courage which makes women home-heroines, and men great.

The death of Sophia had utterly demoralized her. At first she burned for revenge.

But how?

To denounce the truth would be to bring destruction on her own race, and, then, bad as any man may be, does a woman ever utterly give up the husband she once loved?

She resolved, as many a wiser woman has done in a better cause, to remain silent, and devour her grief. It was a rude and terrible task, but one to which she resolutely nerved herself.

She knew her absence would excite no comment. She made no secret of her earnest desire to discover the secret of her husband's absence; and as in that singular community of the Smiths nobody asked any questions, and everybody was free to go or come as they pleased, she was pretty safe from any denunciation, unless, indeed, she betrayed herself.

But Joseph Smith came not. She dressed herself carefully, tidied her cabin as only a woman can tidy it, and adorned herself with scrupulous neatness and care.

She then went to her household work with her usual industry.

Once she tried to sing, but it was a miserable failure, and she tried no more.

She never closed her eyes, lest she should in a vision see that dreadful spectacle which was for ever fixed on the retina of the brain.

Murder never dies. To those who have ever seen it committed its memory is eternal.

And Joseph Smith came not, nor did she see trace of him for many days. She learnt even to converse on the subject with the family, but coolly, not with the anger of a woman slighted and scorned; so deep had the iron of fear entered into her soul.

The rest upbraided him, for they missed his money, but she merely sneered.

Smithville, as the neighbours called the eyrie of the brood, consisted of six scattered log-huts in a little clearing, reached only by two rugged paths, known but to woodmen, hunters, and trappers. They were very rough for horsemen, so that visits were rare even in a country where every man of any substance owned a nag. A more solitary, deserted, accursed den never was fixed upon for human habitation.

The clearing was a plain, about a mile in circumference, with here and there a tree A small grove stood near the six log-huts, many of the trees barked, while others had been cut down. The view was bounded by the forest-clad hills above this little tableland.

The whole was wrapped, one Sunday morning, in a deep fog, such as often rises upon such spots early in the day.

Emma, who had not quite forgotten her Sunday, though so long the associate of men who feared neither God nor man, was leaning pensively out of window, watching the dismal scene, and thinking of another view from that old blockhouse where perhaps her father still mourned for her. A soft but not unpleasing sadness fell upon her soul. She had fallen upon that peculiar phase of mind when only the pleasant part of things is remembered.

As she leaned forth she could almost fancy she was still a child in that wild and snowy region where she had been born, and where each Sabbath morn, she had been summoned to the simple village church near which reposed the ashes, ever sacred, of a mother.

Hark! it is a tinkling bell which rouses her, and which makes her start with astonishment, alarm, and horror.

A man of apparently gigantic proportions appeared in the fog, waving his hands in all appearance to companions behind, and agitating as he moved a little tinkling bell.

By his costume she knew him to be a shepherd of the plains; but ah! what is this one—two—a dozen—a hundred—horsemen, who come now galloping, screeching, yelling round the house.

"Kim out ye reptiles," shouted one, as they surrounded the hut, "kim out, or we'll fire the lot."

A wild crew of farmers, labourers, townsmen, storekeepers they were, and all armed with guns, knives, and pistols. Mexican blankets, ponchos, common blanketcoats, broadcloth, velveteen jackets, high boots, shoes, spurs, and no spurs, steeds sixteen hands high, ponies that left a man's legs upon the ground, were all there, while every man halloed in a different tone, but at the top of his voice.

Every door opened as if by magic, and every man, woman, and child rushed forth, while the elder Smith, not without some rude dignity, asked their business.

"Joe Smith, by thunder!—and Joe Smith we'll have, as sure as my name's Silas Meldrum."

Emma nearly fainted. This was the name of the brother of the murdered Sophia.

"What d'yer want with my son?" continued the elder Smith.

"What do we want—I'll tell you, old alligator. We want to skin him alive, he and a low, mean, skulking Yankee been and shoved about more "shin-plasters,"* ner never were seen in these h'yar parts afore, and it don't convene to the eternal fitness of things to stand it nohow; so whar is he?"

"Ask his wife," said the elder.

"Which is the critter?"

"I am," said Emma, coldly, as she advanced into the midst.

There was a dead silence.

"I have not seen my husband for three weeks," she said, "and never know to a minute when he will return. He generally hunts a month."

Loud execration burst from the men, but no one doubted her word: Her manner was so earnest.

"They're all jist as bad," said Silas Meldrum, in a voice of thunder, "tie up the men, and give 'em thirty-nine."

With an expedition which seemed to denote considerable experience in this peculiar style of executing Lynch law, the Smiths were seized, tied up to trees, and switches being cut, the executioners turned to their chief for orders.

"Forty lashes, save one," he cried.

"Save him!" shrieked Emma, wildly, she knew not why,—at all events, why she used these particular words.

All turned in the direction of her outspread arm, and saw—the fog was slowly rising—two mounted figures seated calmly on their horses, surveying the strange scene.

"Them's them," shouted the shepherd, who had guided them to the village.

To dash at their horses, to mount amidst shouts and execrations, to menace the fugitives with instant death, if they did not surrender, intending fully to slay them if they did, was the work of an instant, and away went fugitives and hunters at a rattling pace towards the hills.

"Well, Joe's done us a good turn oncet on a way," said Hyrum, with a laugh; "I fancy I feel them fellows a-switching. Untie us, girls, and let us go to breakfast."

"And Joe," said Emma.

"Catch a weasel asleep," replied Hyrum.

Meanwhile, Joseph Smith and Simon Rigden, who had come down on a visit to the farmer's paternal home, laden with the spoils of the surrounding neighbourhood, had, to use an American phrase, "made tracks."

They guessed at once the nature of the visit paid by the regulators, and knew that, if captured, their lives were forfeited.

They knew the hills, and the fog moving but slowly, they were able to keep within it for a time, though the pursuers never wholly lost sight of them. There were men behind as daring and as reckless as themselves, burning with desire for vengeance.

* Bad notes.

The issue of bad money in the Border States of America was attended often with fatal and dreadful consequences.

It was accepted by ignorant woodmen, boatmen, and labourers, who, when they took it to an irascible storekeeper, received, perhaps, a shot in exchange.

Terrible fights and quarrels had been the consequence of the audacious paper issue of Messrs Joseph Smith, Rigden, and Co.

These notes fell like a moral blight on the community.

Nobody dared to take small notes without having them examined by the schoolmaster or other authority.

This engendered a state of things intolerable in a country where small notes form a necessary of existence.

The regulators determined to rout out the coiners and forgers, and punish the ringleaders with death.

The shepherd had identified Joe and Simon, so that the hounded and hunted men now rode for life.

Away—away—over piles of stones, over fallen trees, down deep gullies, into dark bottoms, the abode of bears and panthers, under the echoing arches of the forest, through marsh and dell, where lived the hideous alligator,—away dashed the pursued and the pursuers, the former silent, the latter shouting at the tops of their voices, and encouraging one another by view-halloes, oaths, and execrations, such as would scarcely be understood if introduced into these pages.

The fugitives were striving by might and main to get out of sight of the others, and to this end they strained their generous steeds—stolen by the way—to their utmost speed.

Whip and spur were used without mercy. The horses foamed at the mouth, fumes as of fire burst from their nostrils, their flanks reeked with sweat, and they seemed, as they bounded along the rude acclivities and declivities of the mountain, to be actuated by superhuman strength.

"'Nation fine brutes," said Rigden.

"Mighty," replied Joe, "but they must go faster."

They were within a quarter of a mile of the edge of the dark ravine.

The regulators came dashing up with loud cries of joy.

The fugitives could not escape.

The pursuers had divided, and would close round them near the Cauldron Lynn.

"Ah!" said Joe, at last, as their pursuers, though still heard thundering down the open glade, were concealed from view.

He said no more, but leaped from his horse, followed by Simon.

Both then *seated* themselves on the edge of a wide shingly descent on the edge of the ravine, and, just as the others came in view, started off at full speed, like players down a Russian mountain.

With mingled oaths and laughter the pursuers also began to dismount, and while several imitated the extraordinary mode of descent adopted by the fugitives, others began running down by the assistance of the trees.

Joe and Simon were not more than twenty

yards a-head, sliding at a pace which spoke volumes for the capacity of their leathern continuations, the impatient regulators were whooping and yelling one another on, laughing with frantic delight at the prospect of tarring and feathering their victims, when suddenly Joe and Simon rose to their feet, gave a fearful cry of defiance, and plunged to the left, right in the direction of the boiling, seething cauldron.

Fearful were the yells which ensued, they were to be baulked of their revenge after all.

Away—away, the fugitives thirty feet a-head amid the trees—and the white sheen of the waterfall a-head glistening in sight, its roar deafening their ears.

Shot after shot was fired in the hope of maiming them—but in vain.

The pursuers are good runners. Some cast away their guns. It is useless.

With an awful shout of defiance, Joe and Simon plunge head long at the waterfall, and when the panting, raging, execrating crowd comes up, nothing is seen but something dark turning wildly round in the eddying waters below.

The path discovered by Emma Smith is nowhere to be seen.

CHAPTER XLV.

HOME.

THE villain who committed the horrid murder on the poor old woman at the ferry was soon tracked and brought to justice.

On the evidence of the children he was found guilty.

But they were taken out of court before they knew this.

They never were told during youth at all, that the penalty to him was death.

Weakest of all punishments. Man must dare imitate the Almighty, and, unable to give life, must arrogate the power of extinguishing it.

All murder, murder, murder.

The trial over, it was necessary to return home, and to leave the good divine, who parted from them with visible regret. They promised, however, to correspond.

Henry and Jessie would not think of being parted, and as for mysterious reasons the ladies were the best of friends, even as sisters, they readily agreed to travel in one postchaise.

Now this reminds of the earnest requests made to us by several of our correspondents—to whom all thanks—to let them into the secret of the contents of the parchment which Mrs. Bristowe found in the coffin.

We freely declare that we respect these correspondents. That tale is the most extraordinary ever told in the whole range of modern narrative; but, readers, we are sorry to say, you must wait our will and pleasure. All in good time.

The journey was long and pleasant. Lady Haddington was in raptures at her discovery of him whom she felt satisfied was her husband's lawful heir, the son of *his* murdered brother.

Mrs. Bristowe—we need make no secret of the matter—was beyond measure enraptured at having once more folded in her arms the angelic little Jessie.

Nor, indeed, did her satisfaction seem mixed with the least alloy. Of Mr. Bristowe she never spoke one word.

Jessie had whispered something of him once, but a dark frown on her mother's face repelled her.

"Never mention *that* name again, child. I will tell you all when you are a little older."

With many tears, with many smiles, with tender kisses, and most passionate vows, those children, so long companions in joy and in misfortune, separated about thirty miles from Haddington Hall.

The elders had settled a most intimate and continual correspondence.

They had formed a league against the common enemy, and but for cogent reasons to be hereafter explained, would have arranged for all four to live together.

Crack! crack!

Away went the postchaises; and Henry and Jessie were parted, alas! to meet but seldom again, except after trials which scarce could be expected to leave them an atom of their former elasticity, purity, or youthfulness of spirits.

As in duty bound, we follow Jessie.

No sooner were they alone than Cornelia clasped her wildly in her arms.

"My angel—my darling—never again to part," she said.

"I hope not, mother," said Jessie, smiling through her tears; and then she added with becoming gravity, "at least not till I marry Henry."

Cornelia laughed, a merry, ringing laugh such as she had not heard for many years, at least issuing from her own lips.

"Why, you silly puss, Sir Henry Marmaduke Haddington, Baronet, will be too great a man for you," she said.

Jessie looked grave, turned pale, and nearly fainted.

Ah, little sorrows are big ones to little people, and we should indeed be careful not too deeply to wound their tender susceptibilities. Govern them we must somehow, but oh! let us not be stern—the world will be all that, perhaps more, and the bright era of youth is short.

"My darling, I did but joke," said Cornelia, eagerly clutching Jessie to her breast.

"Don't joke about him," replied the lovely child, looking tenderly up into her mother's face with a glance which never, never in all after years was forgotten.

A cold shudder passed through the poor mother's frame.

Already her baby-girl's heart was portioned off from herself, and such a look as that spoke of undying faith and truth.

"Can you keep a very great secret, Jessie?" she said.

"I can do whatever you tell me mother," was the reply.

"The day may come, child, when it need be no secret; but one who has a right to command us, wills it so. Until then, I give you leave—breathe not a syllable—whisper it not—even to Henry—

boys cannot keep secrets—his mother knows it, dear—and heaven bless you."

"It shall never pass my lips."

Cornelia told her the secret in seven words—seven magic words, which will be repeated in good time.

With a wild shriek of joy, Jessie threw herself into her mother's arms, and wildly embraced her.

For some time as they road along nothing was said.

They were winding down hill. Before them lay a lovely park, encircling an old, rather gloomy, but most picturesque looking Elizabethan mansion, round which stood some superb ancestral oaks.

Several pretty cottages, a neat villa or two, were at the side of the road to the left.

"Well, Jessie, you see your home," said Cornelia, smiling.

Jessie looked out, opening her great eyes to their full extent.

"Is it that pretty cottage all over honeysuckle?" she said joyously.

"No."

"Then it must be the one all covered by ivy?" she continued.

"No—try again."

"Not that great, tall, ugly white house?" said Jessie, half inclined to pout.

"Wrong again, miss."

"It can't be one of these cottages," said Jessie, looking a little, just a little, disappointed.

"No, my dear child. What see you to your right?" continued Cornelia.

Jessie looked timidly in her mother's face.

"You don't mean that grand castle, mother?" she said faintly.

"I do."

"Then, mother, you are—" and Jessie hesitated slightly.

"What, my dear?"

"A servant."

"No, you proud, haughty little puss, that house, that castle, as you call it, is—well, I must tell you—yours!"

Jessie sat in utter stillness, unable to speak, and yet, though hearing, unable to understand.

"What, ma'?"

"My dear child, you promised to ask no questions."

Jessie smiled, kissed her mother, and said no more.

She had noticed with some surprise that while residing with the worthy divine, her wardrobe had taken a remarkable change. Her dress, though simple, was of the richest material. She was now habited in a robe of black velvet, with a cloak and hood of pink satin, lined with white. Her hat was of the most deliciously sensitive leghorn, with white feathers; so that, after all, it would have been absurd to suppose she was going to a cottage.

Once for all, it is no use. Was ever poor author so pestered. Another letter. I cannot reveal my secrets even with the promise of such a bribe, and from a young lady, too, who says she is a *petite brune*, with blue-black eyes!

———

CHAPTER XLVI.

JESSIE AT HOME.

———— Lodge (we must still be more and more mysterious) lay before her as she slowly drove up towards the lawn, but she saw it not.

They had left the postchaise about a quarter of a mile from the park-gates, and entered a barouche, drawn by four superb horses.

No sooner had they entered this, than they advanced slowly towards the lodge.

And why?

The road was so crowded that they could not advance, and the people were all shouting and waving their hats, and crying, "Welcome home!" in a manner that fairly astounded Jessie, and seemed, though it pleased, not at all to surprise Cornelia.

She smiled and bowed, and bowed and smiled, as if she had been used to it all her life.

Jessie gave it up; and, except that she wished Henry was there to see, made no more mental effort about the matter.

Then came the hall. Servants stood in rows on each side, who bowed respectfully as Cornelia, leading Jessie by the hand, passed proudly, but with a kindly bow, through their midst.

It was no use. Jessie had read all the fairy tales in the "Young Girl's Best Companion," but there was nothing like this.

For once, reality went far beyond what the imagination could have conceived in its very highest flights.

Then Cornelia told a superb-looking lady—Cornelia's own lady, Jessie soon found—that she should not want her this time, for she would change her own things for dinner, and even wait upon her little child.

"Don't be affronted, Foreman," said Cornelia, kindly, "you shall have her all to yourself to-morrow, I promise you."

The maid thanked her with a curtsey, and the mother and daughter went up-stairs.

Cornelia's bed-room seemed to Jessie to be just such a one she should have imagined the Queen might have slept in—not large, but furnished with such exquisite taste.

It was on the first floor, all the reception-rooms being on the ground-floor, and *all* the servants' rooms above.

We shall not pause to describe the bed-room. We shall have to do so under more painful circumstances.

They dressed, and were ready long before the dinner-bell rang, so that they were not in a hurry.

"I want to show you something," said Cornelia, with a smile.

"What is it, mother—"

"Come and see."

Cornelia led the way, and pushing open a door upon a side corridor that was at the back of her mother's room, Jessie stood still in amazement.

It was a room nearly as large as her mother's, but the walls were of white satin, fluted to the centre, where a lovely rosette of pink satin gave *eclát* to the whole. The ceiling was adorned by the most chaste of paintings; the furniture was all in that peculiar French style, mother o' pearl and ebony, which is so startlingly beautiful; the tiny bed was hung with curtains—

But—why does Jessie start?

Over the mantel-piece is her own portrait. It is her very image.

"Oh, mamma—who did that—"

"Curious again—all in good time you shall know," said Cornelia. "Well, how do you like your room?"

"Beautiful," cried Jessie — "but, ma'— I'd rather sleep with you, as I used to do."

Cornelia turned away to hide a strange expression of her own still beautiful eyes, accompanied by a faint blush.

"My child," she said gravely, "as you grow older you will understand things you do not understand now. In the position in which you are now placed, self-dependence is essential. But be not alarmed—you will be near me. Close your eyes and give me your hand—don't open them until I say, 'Now.' Step forward twice."

Jessie obeyed.

"Now!"

She opened her eyes; she was in her mother's bed-room, and very far from the door.

"Why, ma' its magic," she said smiling.

"Not quite, child,—but I must say it looks very like it," replied Cornelia, who seemed even happier than her wondering, happy, and delighted child.

They now descended to dinner, which they took in great state, such having always been the custom at ——— Lodge. Jessie did not eat much, but she sat up like a little queen, and was dignified and polite and condescending, to the infinite delight and amusement of her mother.

After dinner they drank one another's healths in a dignified kind of way.

Then candles were brought, but not lit, in the withdrawing-room, and all the servants retired.

Cornelia gazed with heavenly delight on Jessie.

"The night is lovely, child. Foreman is longing to speak with you. It is my custom of an evening to be alone for some time—it is a habit, dearest, but I will explain another time."

This was said hastily, hurriedly, as the speaker rung the bell, and then laid herself down on a rich couch near the fire.

Foreman appeared.

"Now, Foreman," she said, "I trust my dear child to you for two hours. Introduce her as becomes the future mistress of this house to all. Show her the conservatory, the aviary, and, if you wrap her up well, the lawn. I will ring for lights and tea when I rise."

And kissing Jessie, she lay down again.

The drawing-room was now dark and gloomy. The tall windows gave scarcely any light, the more that the trees waved gently to and fro. At a sign from Cornelia, Mrs. Foreman closed the shutters.

Jessie, curious but puzzled, went out, leaving her mother alone.

With a light bound Cornelia leaped from the couch, and bolted the door behind them.

Then, in the gloom hardly illumined, from the open door of an adjacent room there came rushing towards her a figure not taller than Jessie, whom she clasped wildly to her heart.

"Are you happy now, my joy?" she said.

"Too happy," whispered the figure.

The rest of the words were lost in the soft murmur of passionate kisses.

CHAPTER XLVII.

FIRST NIGHT AT HOME.

When Jessie went forth to the servants' hall, guided by the proud and happy Foreman, she at once delighted the hearts of all.

The attendants in that house were selected with care from the neighbouring tenantry, not so much for their showy accomplishments, as for their honesty and fidelity, which, as their superiors were kind, unexacting, and unhesitatingly good, proved the right method in the end.

Everybody loved Cornelia. They had heard faint rumours of her terrible misfortunes and trials, but none knew exactly what they were.

There was an extraordinary fact whispered abroad with regard to the birth of Jessie, which though said in low tones and by way of question, was never asserted as a fact.

Still, everybody knew that there was something strange connected with her.

When, then, she entered the room, in which on this occasion all the servants were collected, and did so without her hat and cloak, her extraordinary beauty made a rare impression, and from every side rose cries of " God bless her! "

Much struck by their kindness, Jessie made a little speech, which though a little theatrical and savouring of her friend the barber, was genuine in intention.

The applause was tremendous, and Jessie was no ways surprised that cake and wine was handed about, and that she, though she had dined, had to partake of it.

Then her mamma's health was drank, amid loud cheers and applause.

" I thank you," was all Jessie could say, and hurry from the room with Foreman, to hide her tears.

She was taken to the conservatory, to the aviary, and, wrapped in shawl and hat, to the lawn, whence she could survey the surrounding park in the dim, rising moonlight. This however, was only for a moment.

As she re-entered the house, the bell rang for lights and tea, and Jessie gladly hurried to rejoin her mother,

She found her thoughtful, almost sad, but she reanimated at the sight of her child, and a cheerful, happy hour or two did they spend until bed-time, chatting, laying out plans for the future, studies, picnics, visits to remarkable places, and introduction to neighbours of her own age.

" And when shall I see Henry?" said Jessie, archly.

Cornelia's brow contracted slightly, and she glanced nervously towards the music-room adjoining, looking nervously and anxiously right over Jessie's head. She was seated at her feet on a stool.

" Soon, my dear girl; but Henry must go to school, to college, before he is a man, and knows his own mind. You are both children, and I am very wrong even to let you talk of what it will be time enough to think of these ten years."

Jessie sighed deeply

" I am not angry, child," and then to herself, unconscious of the child's presence, " 'tis fate. If *he* would be as faithful – boy as he is – what glorious victory."

" Over whom ?" said Jessie.

" Was I talking in my sleep ? then it is time to go to bed. Come, dearest—my sweet privilege it is to guard you to your rest."

And ringing for lights, the mother and child retired to the room of the latter.

Jessie undressed slowly, glad to keep her mother near her as long as possible, prayed earnestly, and got into bed.

" Now, Jessie," said she, in earnest tones, " do not forget what I say. The light above—"

It was a beautiful soft lamp almost touching the roof.

"—Never goes out. If you feel unwell at any time, touch this silver knob close to your hand. If any of the wretches who have persecuted me were to renew their machinations, pull this iron one with all your strength. It alarms every servant. If they were a dozen, they could not escape. But be not uneasy, dearest ; this is only done as a matter of precaution. Good night, pleasant dreams, and Heaven bless you."

They embraced, and after examining the fastenings of her door, Cornelia disappeared, but not by that form of exit.

And Jessie was alone once more.

Jessie was happy, bewildered, puzzled, astonished, and almost incredulous. Could all this be true ? Could she, the whilome inmate of a cellar, of a ship's hold tenanted by rats, the hider in the loft, be really lying there in that room of state, surrounded by dozens of obedient menials, and by every luxury that wealth could devise,—above all, the equal, to all appearance, of Henry her —

What ?

That was very nearly a terrible slip, but, no matter, we will curb our pen.

And then she thought of Henry, and this took up a good deal of time, especially as she was, as little girls and young ladies ever are when wanted to retire, not a bit sleepy.

And, then, just as she began to go off into a doze, she noticed that her window was closely barred with iron, and she noticed,—yes, it must be really true,—two fierce eyes gleaming through those bars, eyes fixed, as she fancied, with vindictive malice on herself.

What was she to do ?

She did not like to wake her mother, on the first night of her arrival, on a mere fancy ; so she did not move, but watched the man with the most fixed attention.

Yes ! it was a man, and she felt certain she had seen his face before, but still she was clearly aware that any attempt of his upon the bars would be simply hopeless.

They were thick and strong.

Hark ! what is that ? It cannot be a mouse, no, nor a rat ! Not likely, in that splendid room. It is a something scratching against the door. Somebody is doing something to the lock.

Jessie, her heart beating wildly, raised her hand with the intention of pulling the silver knob gently ; but as at this moment the door seemed to give, convulsively she pulled the iron knob.

A shot, a shriek, and then a fearful ringing of bells followed.

" Lie still," whispered the voice of her mother, close to her ear, " all is safe. You see, dearest, I am not alarmed."

She turned, and her mother's lips were close to hers, how, in her confusion she could not tell.

" Now shut your eyes, dearest, and cover yourself over until I speak."

Jessie did so, and heard a rush of steps—one through her own room —and then she heard—her door was wide open now—her mother speaking.

" You see that my warnings with regard to my child were necessary. Who is the traitor ? "

A man who had been working at Jessie's door was here raised up ; he was quite dead.

A secret bolt, set in motion by the picklock, had shot him through the heart.

" Don't know him," said every voice at once. Cornelia knit her brow.

" Don't know him ! Are there then secret ways into the house. Take the wretch away—lock the body in the strong room, and send round, even now, for coroner, constable, and jury to be here ere twelve o'clock. I cannot rest until I find out who it is."

" Whoy," said a rough assistant lad to one of the servants, " if it ain't Joey—Suky's sweetheart."

There was a wild agonising shriek from among the women, and a girl, rather good-looking than otherwise, rushed forward, and fell on her knees before Cornelia.

" Wretched girl," said she, sternly, " is this, then, your handywork ?"

" Mine ! " gasped the girl, looking with mingled awe and disgust at the corpse—" the man has been prowling about a-making up to me these four days. Every time I went across to the dairy he would speak to me—wanted to come in, but I said no, it was forbid. I can fancy now what he wanted. I never liked un missus, that I didn't."

Cornelia looked around, and her eye suddenly caught a white face, glittering eye, and quivering lip.

The likeness to the dead man was fearful.

" Seize Andrews—bind him—hold him," she said, pointing to a new domestic, who by great exercise of influence had got into the house.

" Madam, I will confess all," said the guilty wretch, " that man "—a bursting sob,—" is my youngest and favourite brother. Curses on her—"

" Silence. Secure him in the Blue Room alone. I will examine him there."

And he was dragged one way, while the corpse was taken another.

" Guard him well until the morning," added Cornelia, who then glided into her daughter's room.

She found Jessie lying in the bed, with her eyes shut, and deadly pale, her limbs quivering with terror.

" What is it, mamma ?" said the poor girl, as she returned Cornelia's warm embrace.

"The same wicked enemy who has been our persecutor before. But never mind, darling, you are well guarded, you have nothing to fear."

"But the man at the window!" she continued with a shudder.

"What man?" gasped Cornelia. "Speak up, my child, every syllable is gold."

Jessie described him as well as she could, adding, that she had a faint recollection of having seen him before.

Cornelia listened with deep attention.

"Where do you think you saw him?" she said tenderly.

"In the cellar at Bristol," replied Jessie.

Cornelia gave a faint shriek, and then begging Jessie to seek repose, wheeled an arm-chair beside her, intimating her full intention to watch that night over the slumbers of her darling babe—as all mothers are so fond of calling their children, even when they have outgrown their teens.

We are not alluding to that class of mothers who conceal their daughters' ages, and keep young women short-coated and in trousers to make themselves appear juvenile, they are too silly and contemptible for notice; but those fond parents whose imaginations make them see the babe once at their knee, always a babe.

Jessie soon slept and soundly. She was very weary, and her mother's presence giving her confidence, she fell into the land of dreams and alone.

CHAPTER XLVIII.

THE STRONG ROOM.

ANDREWS, the new servant, was taken to the strong room, and thrust in with no other companionship than a flickering tallow candle and a jug of water, from which he at once took a long and eager draught.

He was in a burning fever.

Tempted by the demon lucre, which destroys more souls than any other lust, he and his brother had entered upon a fearful scheme for a great reward.

Already was he a prisoner, his brother dead.

His brother too, some fifteen years younger than himself, whom he had so much loved, the last legacy of a dying mother.

Andrews could have knocked his head against the wall with rage, fury, and despair.

Was all the wealth his employer offered him worth that life he had seen ebb before him?

Moody, sullen, and woeful he sat, wrapped in his own dismal thoughts, until he thought he should go mad with very loneliness.

In the extremity of his despair he drew forth a pipe and tobacco, by way of doing something to pass the weary hours.

The candle still flickered, but it could not last long. When that was out, he knew he should be wholly in the dark, alone with his regrets and his wicked thoughts.

And still, despite the innate wickedness of the man, in this the first burst of his regrets and sorrows, his chief thought was for his brother.

Once or twice he seemed to doze off, and then to wake with a start.

What would he not have given to have known that that part of his awful dream was untrue?

And now the candle-wick rose up in one high flame, spurted, and went out with an ominous hiss.

He was in total darkness.

A shudder came over his frame. That room was without windows or chimney. The air was close and thick—did they mean to abandon him altogether to his fate?

Strange though, that though he smoked unceasingly, the room did not seem so very close after all, considering the acrid vapour from his pipe.

He began to believe in some mysterious means of egress.

Suddenly—he never could tell whether he had been to sleep or not—he heard something move with a click like that of a bolt being shot.

He started, for a great fear came over him: they had killed his brother, why should they not kill him?

A cold perspiration burst out over his whole body.

"John Andrews!" said a low and rather threatening voice.

"Who speaks?" he faltered.

"No matter. One who has a right to judge you. You have joined in a foul conspiracy against your employers. You know the law is severe on this point."

"Of course I know it," he said sullenly, "but what care I? You have murdered my brother, do with *me* as you please."

"Because your brother has perished are we inclined to be merciful, if you will only answer certain questions."

"I am ready."

"Who is your employer?"

"What shall I get by revealing this?"

"Impunity for the past, reward for the future," replied the voice. "Do this, or the law shall take its course."

"I am in your hands—" but what further passed at this interview will be discovered in the course of our narrative.

Next morning John Andrews was nowhere to be found; and in the course of the day a coroner's inquest decided that the brother had died from an accident while attempting to commit a burglary at —— House.

After this, double precautions were taken, and for a time Jessie was able to pursue her studies in peace.

Jessie showed the utmost aptitude in her studies, and never did mother enjoy happier hours than when the lovely girl stood beside her, reading, or sat at a table earnestly pursuing her writing-lessons.

Her drawing-master was her delight.

Short, almost to deformity, with a slight hump, golden ringlets, and a massive forehead, Monsieur Edouard, as he called himself, was as devoted as the mother in his endeavours to advance the young pupil placed under his charge.

He seemed never happy, but when, about two o'clock, he glided into the young girl's studio, and bending over her, stood guiding her eager fingers in their favourite task.

Favourite she knew not why, except that she liked the master.

JEALOUSY.

Eternal mystery, of which the famed story of Abelard and Heloise is but one exemplification; that the pupil generally takes most readily to that which is taught by a favourite master.

But why in these modern times—why not exclude male teachers altogether from the institutions of the young?

The corrupting influence of foreign dancing, music, and other masters is scarcely yet known to the full. Great scandals are always hushed up, if not for the sake of the house, for the sake of the young ladies.

Cornelia never left her daughter's side for one moment more than she could help. She lived in constant dread. A cold-blooded enemy was ever at work with the stealth and perseverance of the hound which hunts the poor negro to his lair, and which certain humane writers would adopt in the case of poachers in this country.*

Cornelia knew her danger well; but defended as she was, she had little dread. Still she, determined never to relax her vigilance until death removed her enemy, or a husband undertook the guardianship of Jessie.

---

* Mr. John Meyrick, in *House Dogs and Sporting Dogs,* (Van Voorst) proposes that, for the purpose of tracking poachers, bloodhounds should be employed. Is Mr. J. M. an Englishman, or a relative of Legree, the southern slave thief?

CHAPTER XLVIII.

DEFEAT.

THE intense hatred felt by Mrs. Treherne against the lad whose proved legitimacy would ruin the hopes of her son William, took its origin purely in her desire to behold her offspring inherit Haddington Hall and its princely rent roll.

But her hatred of Jessie, though to a certain extent interested also, took its origin in the strongest impulse of a woman's nature.

A woman who, in the plenitude of a devouring passion, casts herself like a famished wolf into a man's arms, and is repulsed, though ever so kindly, never forgives and never forgets.

The nature of Mrs. Treherne was inherently bad : as a girl she had not resisted the fierce impulse of her passions,—she had been a faithless wife,—and was now a profligate widow.

More than one had shared her orgies, but chiefly the colonel, whom she had promised to marry ; but one burning spot appeared stamped upon her heart, and that was the rejection of her advances by one whom she had loved to very madness.

Amid all the blandishments of satisfied love, no woman ever forgets a deadly affront of this nature. Why, therefore, she should bear such fearful hatred to Jessie is however quite unconceivable.

At least, it appears so.

William, who was ailing, but who already tyrannised over his mother to a terrible extent, had gone to bed, and Mrs. Treherne, as was her wont when violently agitated, walked to and fro in the picture-gallery.

Her brow was dark as midnight. A terrible struggle was going on in her mind.

The colonel had pledged himself to remove the two fatal obstacles which stood in the way of her wealth and happiness.

If he did so—should she marry the colonel, or cast him on the troubled sea of life, to fight his own battle with the world?

Mistress of Haddington Hall, and of another fair domain she coveted as much, could she not marry some man of more note?

But then, the colonel might become dangerous. He was a man who cared little for what he did, when his passions—lust and avarice—were concerned.

So, Mrs. Treherne could not make up her mind, —but, like many of her impulsive and terrible disposition, waited the course of events.

Suddenly, just upon dawn of day, the clatter of horses' hoofs were heard in the distance.

Mrs. Treherne placed her hand upon her heart.

"Who comes—what news—is he successful, or has he failed?"

Such were the thoughts which crossed her busy mind as the horses hoofs clattered along a distant road, and then suddenly ceased.

She opened a window, and looked out into the gloomy night. Her view was here bounded by the park fence.

Her portion of the park was separated from the other by means of a plantation of dark firs. Such had been the custom for years,—there nearly

always having been some obnoxious person whom it was thought wise to separate from the rest of the family.

Along a narrow pathway she could see him coming, walking his horse now, as if caution were requisite.

He was alone.

"Alone—again defeated—but no, he would not dare—he has rode forward to tell me that she is coming, that I may glut my revenge upon that face which has worked such mischief. My wishes prosper here, at least."

The colonel dismounted, fastened his horse inside a rude stable always well provided with provender for his use, and darting across a narrow space of green sward, entered the window.

He was pale as death, and heavy drops of perspiration dropped from his brow.

"Wine!" he gasped.

Mrs. Treherne rushed to the refreshment-room, where supper was always laid, filled a goblet, and returning eagerly, gave it to him.

The colonel drank it slowly, as if to gain time, and then laid it down with a deep sigh.

"The news! the news!" she cried impatiently.

"All lost!" he replied. "George dead, and John Andrews taken. I escaped by a miracle."

"Close the window," she answered hoarsely, "and come into the supper-room. We can there discuss the matter. Fate is against us as yet, but come what will, I must succeed. Failure is utter ruin."

And without one word of pity for the fate of her wretched instruments, this dark and dreary woman took her way towards the supper-room.

The Colonel closed the shutters, and, not without an inward shudder, followed her.

Had he have perished, would he have received one jot more sympathy?

He thought not.

Was it, then, worth while to serve this woman with the blind fidelity he had hitherto done? At all events, it would be beyond measure unwise to show any faltering now that her blood was up.

The stake he was playing for was a great one, and, after all, she might be sincere.

It was broad day when the conference ended.

Mrs. Treherne retired to her apartments, and the colonel adjourned to an inn, which served as his head-quarters on such occasions.

About twelve in the day he made a ceremonious call—such being his custom.

While at lunch with the widow, it was announced that a man wished to see the colonel on imperative business.

They exchanged glances.

"Show him into the library, and the colonel will join him," said the widow.

"Remain here, William," she continued, as the servant retired. "I want to speak with the colonel."

"Shan't," said the precocious heir; "if he makes love to the missis, I can make love to the maid. Bother stopping here—Mary is up-stairs."

Mrs. Treherne blushed crimson, the colonel laughed, but rather bitterly.

Mary was a plump, rosy girl of seventeen, who, while she allowed the boy to make love to her, spurned the addresses of the libertine colonel.

William flounced out of the room.

"If you don't curb that boy he'll break your heart," said the colonel, quietly.

"Curb," cried Mrs. Treherne, sharply, "perhaps your lordship would like to try the experiment of curbing me. We are both of the same blood."

The colonel bowed gallantly and led the way towards the library, where pale, haggard, and covered with dust, stood John Andrews.

"Escaped!" said the colonel.

"No," gasped the man, "they kicked me out in the dark. Oh, sir!—oh, madam!—why did I join in this wicked enterprise? I am ruined, lost, undone; my brother is dead, and I am completely at their mercy."

"Whose mercy!" sternly said Mrs. Treherne.

"I don't know. I have never heard the man's voice before, but I shall never forget his last words."

"What were they?"

"*Go; and thank your stars that a desire to screen your guilty employer saves your life, which otherwise had been forfeit.*"

"And what do you now propose to do?" said Mrs. Treherne, with a dark and angry flush.

"Into whose service can I go now, except yours, madam. I have no character; who will accept me, ignominiously dismissed from —— House."

"Sit down; tell your whole story; and we shall see," said Mrs. Treherne.

A long conference took place; and it finally was decided that John Andrews should take up the provisional position of Mrs. Treherne's butler, until some future plan of action was decided on.

With Mrs. Treherne, failure was only a signal of renewed exertions.

CHAPTER XLIX.

THE STRANGE MEETING.

WILLIAM TREHERNE, the long-supposed heir of the house of Haddington—provision had actually been made for his changing his name—delighted in all such amusements as were in any way compatible with cruelty.

He never went out without a gun. He was not actuated by any of that pure fondness for field sports which is the natural result of a country education and habits of energy and activity, thus making sport noble and inspiring—but he loved to kill purely for killing sake.

He adored to witness the death agony of any animal, though the moment it was dead he would spurn it with scorn. He killed merely for the sake of killing.

His nature was cruel in the extreme; and it mattered little to him what it was he tortured.

Of course he was not brave, and would have shrunk with terror from any thing or any one who could have turned against him.

In his tricks he was chiefly abetted by a lad of the name of Jack Finch, who, with a spiteful little terrier named Fox, would generally be found at his heels.

Their favourite scene of amusement was an extensive rabbit-warren at the extremity of the dark firs, where, though near the road, they were able to carry on their depredations and cruelties without let or hindrance.

Jack Finch had a pet dog, a cur, as ugly an animal as any man or boy might wish to see, but which both William and Jack were right fond of.

The dog is a noble animal, but it is a well-known fact that this style of animal will very often take after its masters. A regular devil was Dusty Bob, up to every kind of mischief which its masters could desire.

Now, poaching and smuggling are very naughty things, but, like very many other naughty things, will not easily be checked as long as man is man, and this terrestrial earth affords us such irresistable temptations.

We do not pretend to defend any impropriety of any kind—very far from it; but there are things which, knowing to be wrong, we either smile at, or only mildly disapprove.

One of these is poaching.

If you are not a high game-law parson, an inveterate preserver of pheasants and partridges, do you not heartily, all of you, side with the breaker of the laws?

And would not you, if you had been William and Jack—at least had you have been in their place—and had caught such a poacher too?

They started about eleven, on murderous thoughts intent, both bending under the weight of double-barrelled guns, and rapturous with delight at the prospect of a general slaughter of the innocents.

The rabbit-warren was a rough plain, cut here and there by small gullies, and covered every here and there by bushes and furze.

The boys had secretly laid one or two man-traps, which they had no right to do, the warren belonging to Haddington Hall. But Lady Haddington seldom came that way, knowing from the gamekeepers that it was a favourite resort of her nephew.

Away dashed the boys, doubly delighted at the prospect of a *battue*, and of capturing some poor devil in the iron fangs of their infernal machine.

They had crossed the hedge and palings dividing the warren from the dowager park, and were in all the exultation of sport, when Dusty Bob opened mouth lustily, and darting away, disappeared down a small declivity, whence, in another moment, proceeded the most fearful shrieks.

The boys pricked up their ears. Their man-trap had done good service, though manifestly on this occasion the sufferer was a female.

The boy-sportsmen hurried forward with their guns at full cock.

Their most savage instincts were aroused. They turned pale with rage and excitement. Their eyes flashed fire, and, by way of encouraging Dusty Bob, they both fired in the air.

Again the dog yelped and barked, while the shrieking continued.

Rushing headlong down the slope they soon found themselves in presence of the victim.

It was a very handsome, dark-eyed girl of thirteen, tall and well-proportioned for her age, whose torn habiliments, blood-stained hose, and bare feet, showed both the suffering she endured, and the efforts she had made for her own delivery.

She was kneeling now, and keeping the yelping cur off by means of a switch.

William Treherne had all his mother's evil instincts. At first, mere delight at having captured a victim, made him halt and lean on his gun, while Jack Finch laid down and shrieked with laughter.

" Good gentlemen, do let me loose; I've been here since daylight. My feet are quite sore, and my ankle is nearly broken. I must beat this nasty little cur."

"Oh! oh! oh!" shrieked Jack Finch, lying on his back, and kicking his heels high up in the air.

"Ain't you ashamed of yourself?" said William, with assumed gravity, "you idle, thieving gipsy you."

"I ain't a thief; I only came to pick flowers and roots for grandmother," cried the girl.

"Flowers and roots! How many rabbits have you snared, eh?" laughed Jack.

"Do let me go," said the girl, in a beseeching tone.

"Flog you first," cried Jack, in pure exuberance of cruel fun.

The eyes of William Treherne flashed fire. The proposition suited the ferocious young libertine. With a devilish sneer on his face he approached the girl.

"It will be better than a whipping at the cart's tail," he said, laying his hand rudely on her shoulder, to tear away her scanty cotton dress.

The girl looked at him, and saw in his eyes the most coldblooded and remorseless cruelty. The proposition, vile as it was, had delighted him. He saw that the girl was beautiful, and he had an ulterior object in view.

At sixteen years of age, William Treherne was a little Faublas—that prototype of Don Juan having commenced his adventures at fifteen.

"Now, my dear, it's no use resisting. Those pretty hands of yours must submit to be tied. I mean to flog you, and when I mean a thing, I do it."

"Beware!" she said, "I am a gipsy, and death will be too little punishment for such a crime."

"No! no! now give us a kiss, and I won't hit very hard," laughed William, while Jack screamed with laughter.

"Unhand me."

"One kiss—two, and for every kiss, one blow the less," said William, catching hold of the helpless girl,

"Take that," she cried, and struck him across the face with the switch, leaving a wale on either cheek.

"D——n!" cried the young ruffian, striking her violently with his fist.

The girl shrieked, the dog barked, snapped, and jumped at the girl—Jack Finch still kicked his heels and roared.

"Up, Jack, and strip her," said William, white with rage, and taking out a knife he began to cut a thick switch, "I'll tan her gipsy hide that its redness shall hide the brown."

Jack Finch ceased laughing, and rather unwill-ingly prepared to exchange his part of spectator, for that of actor in the scene.

The girl gave a wild despairing cry, as Jack approached with a sullen determination to obey his master, more alarming even than the passion of William Treherne.

"Back—back, I warn you," she cried.

"Strip the ——," roared William, whose switch was cut, "I am ready."

"So am I," said the voice, as clear as a bell, of some one close at hand, and ere William could strike one blow, there rained upon his head and chest such a volley of well planted hits, as laid the foundation in five minutes of two as excellent black eyes as any young gentlemen ever desired.

Forced to defend himself, William dropped his switch, and fought with desperation, all the time calling on Jack to come to his assistance.

"If he do," said a thick, chuckling voice, "I'll give un such a hiding as he'll remember."

William here fell, and it was a picture to see little Henry, not more than thirteen, rushing with victorious glance to release the young girl, aided by the gamekeeper, who had accompanied him to the scene of battle.

The girl was released, nearly fainting from exhaustion and fright, just as Mrs. Treherne and her maid came up on one side, and Lady Haddington, accompanied by Henry's tutor, on the other.

"My poor murdered boy!" cried Mrs. Treherne, in frantic tones.

"Great hulking coward," said the gamekeeper, bluntly, "first to beat a girl, and then to be thrashed by a child. If master had'nt a stopped me, I'd a whipped un like a hound, I would."

"So," cried Mrs. Treherne, wild with rage, as her boy rose and stood sullenly by her, wiping his face, more bathed in perspiration than in blood, "this is the bastard who is to rob my child of his inheritance."

"This, madam," said Lady Haddington, calmly, "is, if his father lives not, the future lord of these estates,—Sir Henry Marmaduke Haddington, Baronet."

"We shall see."

"We shall," said the boy, quietly. "This, mamma, is the bad woman who tried to persuade the jury that my papa was never married, and that it was his body was found murdered in the streets of Manchester."

"Come away, or I shall shoot him," muttered William.

"And, more, you will please to stop away," said Henry, sturdily, "until you have publicly begged this child's pardon. My mamma tells me that all I behold from here is mine. George," this to the gamekeeper, "you will see that these boys do not trespass on the rabbit-warren until I give them leave."

This was said with such calm determination, that everybody started. His sufferings and sorrows had aged his character. The air of noble justice, of severe decision, with which the words were said, struck all of them with awe.

Not one but felt that it was the master who spoke. Lady Haddington turned away to hide a tear of gratified pride,—Mrs. Treherne, a scowl of the most malignant hate and malice.

"I shan't ask your leave," said William, "I know who is master here."

"You have my orders, George," replied Henry, with the stately air of a little Louis XIV; "will you come to the hall, miss?" he added, turning to the girl, "my mother will have you refreshed, and sent home. Where do you live, and what is your name?"

CHAPTER L.

THE GIPSY GRANDAM.

At this instant the bushes close at hand were pushed on one side, and a new actor appeared upon the scene.

This was a very aged woman, almost bent double with years.

She had originally been very tall, but the accumulated years had told upon a frame to all appearance originally of iron strength.

Her countenance proved that in early days she had been strikingly handsome, though now every feature was furrowed and wrinkled. Her nose was hooked and marked in expression, her dark grey eyes flashed with the fire of youth, and as leaning on a tall, straight, but knotted stick, she faced the whole party, she looked like some ancient Druidic priestess, new risen from the grave.

All started, from various emotions, for nearly all knew her.

"So," she said, striking her staff angrily into the yielding earth, as she fixed her gaze menacingly on Mrs. Treherne, "the young wolf shows his fangs early. Strike my grand-daughter! Better have died as he raised his switch. Madame Treherne, in days gone by, when you were a young girl, you insulted and flouted me, because I knew your secret."

"Woman," gasped Mrs. Treherne.

"I am not about to betray you," continued the other, with a chuckle, "the time is not yet come. But you, whelp of an evil race, beware! Look but at my child again, profane her but with your thoughts, and you shall see how an old gipsy quean can avenge herself. I thank you, son of Sir Marmaduke. You have acted like the bright man you will be—like your father's son. Take the word of one who knows much, but says little; your father is not dead—and she well knows it."

Pointing to Mrs. Treherne, who stood pale and speechless from passion.

"Come, Lola, thank the young gentleman, and let go his hand. We may serve the house-dwellers, but we cannot be their friends or their equals. Come, I say."

"But, grandmother," said Henry, with ready wit and coaxing manner of genuine unsophisticated youth, "Lola wants rest, refreshment, and a new dress. Mother will not let her go until she has recovered from her fright."

"A chip of the old block—just like his sweet father, heaven bless him," chuckled the old woman, "a rare job had I to keep him from the camp; a pretty face or a neat ancle had always more charm for him than a fox hunt. Well, young sir,

for once, I will accept invitation, the more that I would speak to you and Lady Haddington both, of that which concerns you. And now go," she said imperiously, to Mrs. Treherne, and then clutching William by the arm—Jack Finch was away behind a hedge—"raise but your finger to touch my Lola, and I will have you scourged by those that will take care the law touches them not. Go."

And to the amazement of all, Mrs. Treherne took her son's hand and hurried away, her face no bad image of an ancient fury.

At a sign from Henry the gamekeeper went forward.

"Meg," said Lady Haddington, gravely, "I know not what secrets of my sister you may know, but I pray you, for my sake, to use your power gently. My husband's family has been kind to you and yours, forget not his memory."

"May heaven be his home, my lady," cried the old gipsy mother, "what you say is true. But beware of *her*. There is no more bitter enemy in the world than Margeret Treherne."

"Hush," cried Lady Haddington, "let the children go forward. Show the way, Henry."

Henry politely gave his arm to the little gipsy girl, an act which made both their elders bite their lips, but from very different motives. Lady Haddington was slightly annoyed at the familiarity between the heir of the house of Haddington and the ragged gipsy, while the aged crone was vexed to notice the flush of pleasure which suffused the cheeks of the outlawed child of nature.

As they walked towards the house, a long conference took place between the lady and the old woman, which ended in mutual assurances of support.

Henry had found a friend not by any means to be despised.

He had made another, whose undying devotion was to be his in many a terrible struggle with his enemies.

Poor, simple-hearted Lola.

The old gipsy and her granddaughter were hospitably entertained at the hall, and at night-fall were allowed to depart, according to their invariable custom.

Except in attendance upon certain great occasions on the heads of the house of Haddington, the old crone had never slept under a roof.

Next day, Mrs. Treherne publicly broke up her establishment, discharged her few servants, shut up her house, and departed, as she announced, for Germany, there to educate her poor, defrauded son at one of the cheap German universities.

But, two or three days after, Cornelia received an ill-written scrawl, which was intended to place her on her guard.

"*She ain't gone at all. She may hang out some where else, but she comes to the Dower House every night. She's up to something. She suspects me, so I'd best keep out of the way.*"

Despite every failure, despite the danger of her proceedings, it was quite clear that Mrs. Treherne had not resigned her schemes against the peace and happiness of Henry and poor Jessie.

CHAPTER LI.

BIGAMY.

We return to New York, to our friends Phineas Bristowe, Christian Whitmer, Susan, and Eliza Brown.

The widow of the merchant, though apparently inconsolable for the loss of her husband, soon in reality forgot her grief before the blandishments of the villanous high-priest of Mormonism.

She had already agreed to accompany him to his new residence with the elect, and had promised to devote her wealth to carrying out the great designs of the prophet.

It is true that Christian Witmer, between his two wives, as he called them, found himself considerably puzzled.

He was quite sure that, in her present state of mind, she would not, for one moment, accept the convenient and abominable doctrine of spiritual wifedom, however tamely, quietly, and degradingly some women might bend beneath the demoralising yoke.*

She had made a fearful and an awful sacrifice, but it was with the idea that she was to be the exclusive companion of the treacherous and avaricious priest for life.

She madly, wildly, blindly loved the man who had recklessly destroyed her peace of mind for ever.

The bare suggestion of sharing his affections with another, and that a first wife, would have driven her mad with humiliation and jealously.

Not so Susan.

Her failing was greed and ambition. Could Christian Whitmer have clearly shown her any permanent advantage in his connection with Eliza Brown, she would have submitted to it without a murmur,

She had gained her point.

Her sway over Christian was unbounded,—it was the sway of an energetic, powerful, though coarse mind over one of which the mainspring was vanity and conceit.

Susan despised, while with savage impetuosity she loved Christian Whitmer.

It was pure animal passion, however, without one redeeming point of refinement or sentiment.

He gave her every luxury which the money of his many dupes could command.

But something must be done. The elders at head-quarters were clamorous for his arrival, and the wretched creatures whom he had brought from England and Wales, were crying out for the promised land.

He hardly knew what to do. When they set out, Susan and Eliza would inevitably be brought in contact, and the unpleasant circumstance was sure to be revealed that there were two Richmonds in the field.

What was to be done?

They were alone. Christian Whitmer had been all day out on business relative to the departure of the saints to Nauvoo—so he said—though his time had been chiefly spent in a *tête à tête* with

charming Mrs. Brown, who had accompanied him to one of those suburban retreats where *dejeuners* are served with unsurpassed luxury to the rich and luxurious denizens of the mighty city of New York.

The hour was approaching when his departure could no longer be delayed.

They were to join a caravan of new converts and recruits to the faith of Joseph Smith, at the end of the week.

Susan, like all persons who have come suddenly into possession of pecuniary resources, to the use of which she was not accustomed, was ludicrously extravagant and luxurious in her ideas of dress.

Christian Whitmer, who was a Turkish pasha in his ideas of women, took especial pleasure in her decorating herself.

Her peculiar taste promised him some variety in the harem which is the sole sincere belief of the Mormon elders.

If he could not turn the heads of his fellow-quacks with envy, he could sun himself in the full blaze of her beauty, set off by gaudy finery.

Christian Whitmer would have enjoyed the presence of a *corps de ballet* for his own individual amusement.

He lay luxuriously on a couch, with a long cherrystick pipe in his hand, while Susan stood before a glass, adjusting a superb new silk dress which had that evening been brought home by the dressmaker, and which displayed arms, legs, and bosom rather more even than modern ball-room etiquette considers justifiable.

She looked really magnificent in her finery, and she knew it.

She never wearied admiring herself in 'the mirror, before which she stood, and when she caught the eye of the Mormon elder gloating as it were upon her lovely form, she smiled with gratified vanity.

" How beautiful !" he said, casting his eyes up to the ceiling in unaffected ecstasy.

" La ! nonsense."

" Lovely !" continued Christian.

" What—the dress?" said the silly woman, with an affected laugh.

" No, you, you adorable angel," cried the deluder, " come and kiss me."

" Shan't !" said Susan, showing her white teeth, " get up, if you want one."

" You cruel, naughty Susan," lisped the Sybarite, rising with affected languor, " I suppose I must come and fetch it."

" No," she cried, and rushing towards him, she kneeled by his side, and folding him in her snowy arms, gave him kiss for kiss.

Suddenly the door flew open with a bang, and some persons entered the room.

Susan rose to her feet, with a brow as black as night, but otherwise completely self-possessed.

Christian muttered something not very flattering to the intruders, and then rose also to his feet.

" Phineas Bristowe !" said Susan, with a flush, and yet, a scornful smile, " pray to what do I owe the honour of this visit ?"

" D——n," cried Christian, turning deadly pale, as a lady who accompanied Bristowe unveiled herself.

---

* We regret to say that we have letters before us written by women, defending the immoral doctrine of polygamy.

" Shall I ring, and have these people turned out," said Susan, scornfully.

" Ye-e-es—no— I think—" stammered Christian.

" Ring, you shameless trull," said the woman, in accents choked with passion, " and the officers who wait without will appear to take this man in custody."

" For what?" cried Susan, whose choler was rising.

" Bigamy," replied the other, coldly, " that man was married to me in the State of New York, madam ; so he was to you. What you are you now know, but I am his wife ; and unless he at once gives me his arm and leads me away, I will see at all events that he is exposed to the world in all his naked deformity."

" Jane," began the wretched man, who had lost all courage, " I thought you were dead, indeed I did."

" And wished it. Our children *are* all dead, Heaven be thanked. They died of cold, wet, and hunger ; and I should have died, but that I found you out, and made this man my friend."

Bristowe bowed, and showed his sharp, file-like teeth.

" This man hated you, because you took from him his splendid prostitute—"

With a cry of rage Susan flew at the angry woman, and in one moment a contest ensued which we almost despair of rendering in all its true colours.

'Tis seldom that woman in her sober senses so far forgets herself, as to decend from the weapon which is peculiarly her own, to that which she possesses in common with all animals of a feline nature ; but when she does, dire is the shock, terrible the conflict.

Susan was a powerful girl, but Mrs. Whitmer, though weakened by suffering, was of a wiry frame, and animated by fury both against her husband and his shameless paramour.

Their hands were in an instant amidst one another's hair, and dire would the tussle have been, if the two men—we are almost ashamed to write it—screaming with laughter, had not separated them.

" I'll tear your eyes out," said Mrs. Whitmer.

" Yours ain't worth touching," cried Susan.

" Silence," said Christian, who had contrived to catch a glimpse from Susan, and to exchange glances with her, " and I will settle matters so that peace shall be permanently restored. Silence, and if you are not agreable, why then you shall do just as you please."

" What is it?" said Susan, with a wink seen only by Christian.

" I listen," observed Mrs. Whitmer.

" Mr. Phineas Bristowe," began Christian Whitmer, gravely, " under the impression that I was a widower, I took from you one to whom you were attached, honourably married her. I now find that my wife being alive, that marriage is null and void. Under the circumstances I have humbly to apologise for any wrong I have done. Jane, there is my hand, forgive and forget. Mr. Bristowe, you are a man of the world like myself. The least said is the soonest mended. What say you, Susan, will you take his hand?"

Oh, what a fool is man. Phineas Bristowe grinned a ghastly smile, and took the hand which the syren placed in his with the most entrancing and bewitching smile.

Mrs. Whitmer, upon whose shattered frame and weakened mind suffering had done its worst, burst into tears and fainted.

An attendant was summoned, and the lady removed to a bed-chamber.

" Dismiss the officers, and let this most happy catastrophe," said Christian Whitmer. " be celebrated in a glorious supper."

Bristowe was never proof against any carnal temptation, and going outside, at once dismissed the officers with a good earnest of future favours.

A supper was then ordered of the most expensive and luxurious character.

Mrs. Whitmer, unused to the attentions lavished upon her by her husband, was easily induced to be guided wholly by him.

A grand festival to her was something so new that she could scarcely credit her eyes.

Bristowe seated beside Susan was intoxicated both with wine and love. Susan darted glances at him which awakened in him the memory of those days when she was all his own.

Whitmer was tender in the extreme to his poor wife, herself suffocated with joy, and in the excitement of the moment, forgetful of how she degraded herself by associating with a creature so abandoned and debased.

And the supper continued, the champagne corks flew about wildly, and ere midnight, every one of them were to all appearance utterly overcome with liquor.

*　　*　　*　　*　　*　　*

All was as still as death in the great hotel in the Broadway in New York.

Every inmate had gone to rest.

It wanted a few minutes of daylight. The grey dawn was creeping in through the uncurtained window of a large bedroom in the house where the supper took place, and where two people slept soundly.

Suddenly one moved, and a female form rose with dishevelled hair, and, as the hand pressed to the brow denoted, aching head.

She gazed around her wildly, as if totally unconscious of her whereabouts.

She seemed striving to recollect the events of the preceding night, which had been temporarily obliterated by the wine which she had been tempted to take on the exciting occasion of her reconciliation with her husband.

Suddenly she recollected that she was not alone, and the long-deserted wife actually blushed at the thought of having her husband at her side.

Suddenly she gave a wild and sudden start.

" Heavens!" she cried, darting from the bed, " it is *not* my husband!"

With a violence and energy astonishing in one so weak, she shook the sleeper's arm.

" All—right—Su-Su-san. Wantsh to sleep— eh," grunted the tipsy man.

The woman sank into an arm-chair.

It was Phineas Bristowe !

He was dead drunk.

Mrs. Whitmer dressed herself with a calmness which it would have been horrible to behold.

The man was again in a sound slumber. He was totally unconscious of her presence.

Her face was of the whiteness of chalk. She saw clearly now, how herself and Phineas Bristowe had been duped by the infamous pair.

There were two bells in the room, one for a chambermaid, the other for boots.

At any hour of the day or night you can have attendance in a first-rate American hotel.

Mrs. Whitmer rang for the chambermaid, who came in ten minntes.

She was a smart, good-natured, coloured girl.

Mrs. Whitmer put a golden eagle into her hand as she closed the door.

"Girl," she said in a hoarse, hollow voice, "you look good-hearted—you will not betray me. Where is the gentleman who has been staying here sometime, with whom we supped last night?"

"Went away last night," replied the girl.

"I thought so," gasped Mrs. Whitmer, "he was my husband—and that fine madam was his trull. He drugged me last night, and put me to bed with yonder drunken beast. Find me a bed-room, and never let him know that I passed the night with him, and I will reward you. Call him to breakfast at ten."

"Never say not one word, missus," cried the coloured girl, "I see'd them peoples a-sniggering when they paid the bill. My! the wickedness ob de white folk, golly!"

And without another word the chambermaid led her to another bedroom, received a heavy fee for her services, and going down stairs made a sleepy clerk enter the new tenant with a number in a book.

At ten she sat before a glorious American breakfast-table in a private room.

Phineas Bristowe, who had been told that the lady waited breakfast for him, came down very dandified in his dress, but very white, feverish, and fishy about the eyes.

As he entered the breakfast room, he gazed around with an air of half anger, half surprise.

"Where the devil are they got to?"

"Of whom do you speak?"

"Of Mr. Whitmer and Susan."

"Gone—bolted last night. It means Mr. Bristowe that we are two dolts, whom these two wretches have deceived and are now laughing at."

"Thunder!" cried Bristowe scratching his head, as if hardly yet awake ; "then who the deuce did I sleep with last night?"

"Mr. Bristowe," said Mrs. Whitmer, coldly, "you will please to recollect that I am a lady. You drank so much last night—I believe we were drugged—that you have taken leave of your senses. Let us, however, refresh ourselves and then I mean to follow up the miscreants."

"Well, I don't care," muttered Bristowe to himself, "I know I did. I thought it was Susan, and hang it, I could not have dreamt it."

Then he spoke aloud.

"I will track them to the death," he continued savagely. "They shall pay dearly for this scurvy trick. I see it all now. But I hope I have not kept you waiting, you look ill."

"I never exceeded two or three glasses of wine before," she said, coldly, "and I am sure they put something in that wine. My head aches in the most fearful manner. But I live now only for revenge."

The two now sat down to breakfast, and during this meal which continued for some considerable time, they matured their plans of revenge.

Mrs. Whitmer had lost all idea of being restored to her husband. There was now a barrier between them, known only to her, to him and his paramour, which sternly forbade all future intercourse.

It was now necessary to find out the precise track of the Mormons, both being fully resolved to follow like Red Indians on their trail.

CHAPTER LII.

ON THE SCENT.

PHINEAS BRISTOWE was pretty well aware of the haunts where Christian Whitmer, when not engaged in his favourite employment of woman hunting, loved to pass his hours.

Christian was essentially low in his tastes.

The dullest tap-room was to him a perfect elysium.

At all events he could there be whatever he pleased.

Every where else, especially among educated men, he was sure to find his level, but here, by the expenditure of money, he could always be king.

There are men who would rather be the king of a jerry-shop, than the ordinary member of a respectable parlour.

Phineas Bristowe well knew that several of the Mormon agents were in the habit of visiting a certain establishment in disguise. They were not likely to fall in with any of their dupes in this quarter, as most of those who join the Mormon imposture, are, in the first place generally sincere.

Men talk of the dissipations of London and of Paris but if any one wants to see dissipation on a grand scale, glittering with gold and jewels, let them go to New York and New Orleans.

There vice, though in the former city, somewhat concealed from public view, is arrayed in purple and fine linen.

Everything is lavished, which can cheat and delude the senses.

The temples devoted to the priestesses of Venus are perfect models of a peculiar style of art, and their denizens, as false, treacherous and hollow-hearted, as any even of the Parisian ladies of the *demi-monde*.

How far superior the general morals of the Americans are to those of any other country, may be judged of by the fact, that there no writer is yet found to idealise ladies of easy virtue, and to erect them into a romantically sentimental class.

But Phineas Bristowe did not intend to search for his intended victim in the palaces of vice.

On the same evening, when the adventurer found himself *tête à tête* at breakfast with Mrs. Whitmer, instead of the fascinating Susan, he dressed himself with extreme care.

His object was not to be known or even noticed

JESSIE AND HENRY AT DOVER.

He then cast off his respectable garments, and furnishing himself with an emigrant-looking suit from a second-hand clothes shop, he added a huge pair of whiskers, a slouched hat, which with the use of some walnut-juice dye to his hands, gave him a most sinister appearance.

In his pockets he slipped a pair of small pistols, which, with a short Spanish dagger, formed no contemptible protection.

Mrs. Whitmer wished him luck, and bade him be careful, as any failure on his part, might cause their vengeance to be baulked.

Phineas Bristowe smiled. He was not the man to throw a chance away, or to run his head into any unnecessary danger.

It was dark when he sallied forth from the hotel, leaving the wretched and deserted wife alone.

He sauntered slowly along with a pipe in his mouth, in order at once to assume the aspect of a man who was wandering about to pass away the time, though all the while he was glancing keenly to the right and left.

Like the man in the Victoria melodrama, he never " thruved a chance avay."

The locality to which he was wending his way was one not ostensibly known to the police. Like their compeers on this side of the water, those gentlemen had convenient eyes.

Nothing destroyed the range of their vision so much as golden spectacles.

Strangely enough everybody else was perfectly familiar with the locality.

It was the pet meeting place of all the rowdies in New York.

If ever there was a hell upon earth, that was it. It required the united efforts of a Frenchman, a Jerseyman, and a New Yorker to effect its establishment.

Going down a narrow turning, and another, and another, Phineas Bristowe found himself opposite what appeared to be the back of a large warehouse.

In front of it ran a long, deep, and dark area.

A narrow flight of steps led downwards to a door, at which Phineas tapped in a peculiar way.

The door opened at once, and a tall burly man hastily surveying the new arrival told him to enter, and closed the door with a bang.

The sound of voices, of music, the rumour of a large body of persons speaking at once, fell on his ear, but it was only after passing through two other green baize doors, that the whole Pandemonium came into view.

It was a vast cellar, the walls of separation of which had been replaced by one or two stout square pillars of stone, and some twenty or thirty of iron, strong enough, to all appearance to sustain the weight of a mountain, and yet tapering elegantly from roof to ceiling.

On each side of the vast cellar were rows of private boxes, with iron bars and curtains.

At the open window of each of these, sat at this early hour of the evening, a girl arrayed in all the magnificence of Cyprian toilette.

All were handsome, some even beautiful, but with the ineffable mark upon their brow, which sin without shame ever stamps.

They were of all countries, even the East furnishing its quota.

There are Americans who trade in white slaves quite as readily as in black.

The hold of a ship in the Mediterranean is as secure as a cell in Virginia.

But the day and the hour is coming. Who knows but that the Black Washington who is to avenge his race, may not be now studying the plans for a great free black state in America.

It must come to this.

At the further extremity of the room was a stage, just as in a theatre.

It was a music-hall.

Not a respectable, reputable and soul inspiring locale, such as Westons and the Oxford, but a music-hall for rowdies and fast New Yorkers, where no decent female ever set her foot.

The body of the hall, except where four bars supplied refreshments of every kind to the visitors, was filled by little tables, at every one of which men sat, smoking, drinking, and playing cards.

Poker, yucca, brag, and other American gambling games were alone popular.

Those near the private boxes indulged in coarse and vulgar jokes with the women, who laughed heartily.

The songs on the stage passed off in nearly dumb show, but the ballets, being a little more *outré* than is allowed on any stage were vociferously applauded.

Many may recollect the riots at Naples, when the ladies of the corps and ballets were ordered to wear drawers.

Well, no police decree of that kind had found its way into Rowdy Hall.

Phineas Bristowe glanced hastily at the inmates of the private boxes, and having selected one to his fancy, whispered to a black waiter.

The front of the private box glided on one side and he was admitted; the syren smiling on him just as she would have smiled on any one else.

Phineas could now by sitting a little back, see everything that occurred without being seen, while he could leave the box by a back passage if he liked.

He ordered refreshments, which were placed on a table on a level with the cushions of the box and then examined every person within range with a keen and observant eye.

Not one countenance did he recognize.

He began to be afraid that he had come for nothing.

It was however early as yet, and they might come later.

He turned therefore to his companion and entered into conversation. As he expected, from the glance of her eye, when he first saw her, she was intelligent and even witty.

The conversation warmed, and for a time Phineas Bristowe lost all knowledge of what was going on. The girl made him laugh heartily. She had been an English servant, but endowed with the fatal gift of beauty, had fallen by degrees until she found herself in this scene of splendid misery.

There was a slight tone of bitterness in her remarks which is common with her class when speaking of themselves.

This interested Phineas.

Suddenly he started as a familiar voice fell upon his ear.

Yes, there at a table not five yards from him was Christian and three companions just seating themselves and giving their orders to the waiter.

A dark and bitter smile passed across his face as he drew back.

Despite his disguise, he might be recognized. A recognition would not be without danger, as Phineas knew his companions to be Mormons, not of the race of dupes but leaders in the van of the foul imposture.*

"Do you know those men?" whispered the girl in a husky tone, her face pale under her rouge, and her eyes flashing fire.

"I do."

"Are they friends of yours?"

"No."

"Acquaintances?"

"No."

"Bitterly detested enemies," said Phineas in a tone not to be mistaken.

"Do you see the man with the goggle eyes?" she continued.

"Christian Whitmer?"

_____

* Those of our readers who unfortunately have Mormon friends or relatives should induce them to read these revelations. They will do good service to the cause of truth.

" Yes."

" Well ."

" That man it was brought me here. I lived with him when he was married. His wife fell ill, the doctor gave her up ; he promised me marriage. I believed him—she died—but he left me to ruin and shame."

" Died ! Mrs. Whitmer is alive and well. I breakfasted with her this morning."

" Then he is a bigger villain than I thought him, for this young person that died was married to him, I know. I believe he poisoned her."

" Ah ! was there any suspicion ?"

" None."

" Where was she buried ?"

" Would you do it ?" said the girl with flashing eyes.

" I would do anything to punish him."

" What has he done to you ?" asked the girl with a keen and searching glance.

" Taken from me the only woman I ever loved." said Phineas hoarsely.

" Then will I trust you. But no more of this serious talk. Let us watch them. Do you know where Christian lives ?"

" I do not. It is to track him that I came here."

The girl, who was always called Molly in that establishment, pulled a wire, and in a few minutes a little negro lad came to the back entrance of the *baignoire.*

Molly pointed out Christian Whitmer to the lad, and whispered a word or two.

" Give him a dollar," she said.

Phineas obeyed, and the boy disappeared with a bow and a grin.

CHAPTER LIII.

THE VAMPIRE.

MEANWHILE the curtain on the stage had drawn up for a ballet and all eyes but those of one or two inveterate gamblers were fixed upon the scene.

It was oriental in magnificence, and Phineas himself, despite the fierce emotions which filled his soul, was entranced.

He never lifted his eyes from the stage.

Suddenly Molly touched his arm.

" What is it ?" said Phineas without moving his head.

" Look across, just by the footlights, there is a man there who seems curious about you."

Phineas started as if stung, and glanced across with blanched cheeks, so quick is terror.

A low, despairing cry burst from his lips, as he fell back in the box.

There, thin, pale, gaunt, but with eyes that burned like coals, was his companion in the hold of the emigrant-ship, and whom he had left floating, a dead body in an open boat upon the pathless waters of the ocean.

Twice had he seen him dead.

Merciful Heaven ! what could be the meaning of this. Was it a vision, a phantom of his diseased brain ?

" What is the matter, are you ill ?" said the girl rather scornfully.

" No, but 'tis the fiend himself. Twice have I seen him dead."

The girl stared, and Phineas rousing himself looked again.

There he stood, motionless, his face ghastly pale, his eyes fixed on Phineas with a terrible expression, but without making any motion to come near him.

" Can we leave this place ?" whispered Phineas.

" Yes, but there's nothing going on upstairs till midnight."

" Upstairs ! what's that ?"

" The house, the most splendid place in all New York. But you must sport your money freely."

" Hang the money ! let us go."

" Come."

" No, no, no."

Phineas Bristowe had made a slight motion as if to rise, when the other with a fierce and maniacal glare, had exposed the barrel of a pistol which could just be seen from between two of his fingers.

" You are very changeable," laughed the girl.

" I will remain here. I must speak with that horrible man, I must know—"

" What ?"

" Whether he be human, or a hideous vampire."

" He looks mad to me."

" I wish to heaven he were," continued Phineas, who shook in every limb, and whose schemes of vengeance against Christian Whitmer were utterly forgotten in presence of the fearful danger which menaced him.

Why was this man there.

How had he tracked him, and what was the motive of this desperate hostility.

There was only one explanation of his determination to pursue him to the death ; but this was too horrible to be credited. He should himself go mad if he could believe this—as then indeed he could understand the awful expression of hatred which filled that man's whole countenance.

And then if this were so, it might not be madness after all, but only the expression of a deadly and fearful hatred.

There came over him, as he brooded over the past, and as vague, dreamy, and indistinct, the future presented itself to him, a fearful chill, a cold perspiration bathed him from head to foot.

And still Christian Whitmer and his friends continued their play.

Molly caught the eye of a girl in an opposite box, and a rapid exchange of signals took place. In the exercise of their degraded calling, these girls have often need to communicate with one another unbeknown to their male companions.

The girl replied with a smile and a laugh.

Phineas Bristowe, in the meantime, had leisure to recover himself slightly.

A conference took place between himself and Molly.

The man smiled. The idea suggested by the girl just suited his fancy.

But how to escape the vigilance of one he mentally called the vampire.

His eye never wandered from that box.

In the meantime he saw a black waiter bring a scrap in writing to the Mormon elder, who, after reading it, turned towards one of the boxes and nodded.

The girl to whom Molly had telegraphed looked radiant with delight.

She only knew, however, that some fun was to be expected.

Presently Christian Whitmer threw down his cards and strolled across to the box whence the message had come.

It was to invite him to join herself and a friend or two at supper.

Molly whispered the welcome intelligence in the ears of Phineas.

"But that infernal man. He's mad, and a chance shot might take effect."

Molly pulled a string, and they were instantly in total darkness.

A shutter had glided down from above, along two well oiled groves.

"This way," she said, taking his hand, "follow me, and do not say a word."

Phineas Bristowe, trembling like one about to take his place on the scaffold, clutched at her soft hand and followed.

She cast open the back door of the box, and entered a narrow passage, faintly illumined by a lamp at the further end. Turning rapidly to the right, she came upon a winding iron stairs.

"Go up," she said.

Phineas obeyed, and the two were soon on a landing.

"Have you a ten-dollar note," she began.

Fear, and the hope of revenge, drove from the soul of Phineas the hideous demon of avarice.

"I have."

"Lay it on the clerk's book as we go in," she replied, and rang the bell.

The door opened, and a livery servant ushered them into a hall, where sat a red-haired youth, with blear eyes and the faintest trace of a moustache, before a large ledger.

Phineas laid down the ten-dollar note.

The clerk smiled, took from a number of small pigeon holes an embossed card, wrote on it some scrawling letters, and handed it to Phineas.

He read.

"Molly—Number six."

Then came a date.

Phineas Bristowe looked inquiringly at the girl.

"It means," she said, with a bitter smile, "that you have bought me for twelve hours."

Phineas bowed, and showed his white Carker-like teeth.

Molly now led him through a gilt door-way into the saloon of the nefarious establishment.

CHAPTER LIV.

THE SALOON.

THE saloon differed in no way from the drawing-room of a large foreign *hotel* or palace—two words meaning the same thing—except in size. It was gorgeously furnished with soft and silky carpets, candelabras, chandeliers, and rich hangings.

Couches, arm-chairs, settees were placed round the room, the centre being reserved for such as chose to indulge in a dance to the music of a full rich-toned pianoforte.

The women wore ball-dresses, and except that they shot fiery and meaning glances at the men who occupied the room, they would not at a first glance have been told from the members of more fashionable if not more frivolous society.

If women were better educated, more capable of sustaining conversation, less given to mere showy accomplishments, men would not seek the fascinating society of the Aspasia's and Lais' of the day.

These women use every art to win men to their feet, even to enlisting the powers of evil, eloquence, and humour into their service.

Phineas Bristowe stood with Molly leaning on his arm, transfixed with surprise.

His somewhat coarse emigrant garb excited no notice. Disguises were common in that place.

"Come," said Molly, "I am going to order supper in a private room—that fellow will never find us. Who is he?"

"No matter," replied Phineas with a shudder —his fixed intention to refuse the expense of a supper at once frustrated—"I hate him. Where is our room?"

"I have asked Christian Whitmer to join us with a friend."

"The deuce you have – there will be a fight."

"No—he shall not know you. I mean to give him a regular fright. He shall not forget Molly in a hurry!"

And with a sardonic grin on her face, the girl passed across the splendid saloon, through a large supper-room and to where another stair-case led upwards.

In a few minutes they were ushered into a superb apartment, adorned with mirrors and furnished in the same gorgeous style as the rest of the house.

It must be remembered that New York is the residence of the sweepings of every capital in Europe, fraudulent bankrupts, forgers, thievish trustees, runaway clerks, and other rogues who have done swindling on a large scale.

The reputable and honourable residents form a large proportion of the population.

The rich rowdies and loafers count, however, by tens of thousands.

They are the supporters of such dens as that which we are describing.

There are more such places in England than our social reformers believe.

Many a legislator must smile at the grave speeches made on certain occasions by men, who are the supporters in secret, if not of such habitations, of others of a more select and secluded character.

Vast, indeed, is the hypocrisy of modern society.

Molly took Phineas into a bed-room, and by the artful combination of a few colours which she used mysteriously in some part of her toilette, so disguised him, that he started himself when he looked in the glass.

They again returned to the supper-room, where they found Christian Whitmer in high glee with his lady friend.

He had won largely at cards and was disposed to be liberal.

He insisted upon being at the expense of the supper, to which no objection being made, Molly went out to give orders.

She soon returned, followed by waiters bearing plates, dishes, glasses, and bottles in abundance.

They then retired, the girls agreeing to do the honours without assistance.

To this agreement the men made no objection.

The two girls exchanged some rapid signs.

CHAPTER LV.

THE SUPPER.

THE hour was verging towards twelve and still the orgie continued.

Christian Whitmer was getting very intoxicated.

The others though elated, were able still to distinguish what they were about.

Superb fruits were on the table, of which Molly and her friend partook freely.

Christian Whitmer laughed at them, and continued to pour out wine.

When nobody else drank he plied himself with it.

"Jolly," he said holding up a glass, "aint it awful jolly. I tells you what gals, it aint half so jolly though as last night. Such a lark—what's the matter—eh—toothache?"

This was Phineas, who at the recollection had made a hideous grimace.

"Tell us all about it," said Molly's friend.

"So I will, ain't done laughing yet," continued Whitmer.

And in a long rambling way he told his story. The man, though a sot, had coarse humour, and the catastrophe of the affair excited shouts of laughter in the girls.

"Took the young one and gave him the old woman," screamed Molly, regardless of the dark scowl on Phineas's face. "But never mind, here's your health old boy."

A bumper was filled and drained freely by Christian, who now sat helpless on his chair, his eyes half closed, the very picture of an utterly brutalized drunkard.

At a sign from Molly, Phineas and the girl slipped behind a screen.

She retreated to the bedroom,

Christian Whitmer fell asleep, but nodding forward, his head hit the table.

"Eh, well what is it?" he cried, "what all gone? shabby, doosed shabby, nice lot—drink old boy, drink—soon be back."

And by great exertions he filled another glass.

At this moment a door creaked and a tall figure in white came gliding into the room. It made not a sound on the carpet. It wore a long night-dress, just like grave-clothes, a close cap, indeed nothing could be seen but a white cadaverous face and two fierce glaring eyes.

"Who, and what art thou?" said Christian Whitmer with chattering teeth.

"The spirit of thy dead wife, Sally Palmer," replied the white figure.

Christian rubbed his eyes, opened them again, and drank a glass of wine.

"Accursed thing," he said in a voice half sarcastic half terror-stricken, "what means this visit. She of whom you speak is long since buried in the cold church-yard."

"Her spirit walks until her murderer is brought to justice."

"Murderer," gasped Christian, his hair fairly rising on his head, his face ghastly white, "how dare any one accuse me of such a crime?"

"I do."

"'Tis a false and wicked lie, she died of apoplexy," cried the other in a low tone.

"Dost know this bottle?" said the figure holding up a small vial, partially filled by some nearly colourless fluid,

"D——n," roared Christian starting to his feet and snatching up a desert knife, "this jugglery shall cost you dear."

And half sobered by the terrible memories of the past, he rushed towards her.

He was caught however by two strong arms, while the figure stood motionless before him.

"Unhand me! who the deuce are you?" he said in husky tones.

"Be quiet, be perfectly calm, or I will fetch the police," said Phineas in his natural tones.

"In the devil's name where am I, and by what fiends am I tormented?" he gasped.

"So you took Susan, and left me the old woman," said Phineas crushing his arm in an iron grasp.

"And you poisoned your wife, and promised to marry me," exclaimed the white figure.

"Look at me Christian Whitmer, and see to what degradation a man may drag a woman."

"Molly Stanford—"

"The same, you recollect me now. Now I have long wished to leave this country, to go where my errors are not known. Give me the money to do that and I will forgive you."

"And you will be silent."

"Silent as the grave."

"How much do you want?"

"Two hundred pounds," said Molly slowly.

"Two hundred devils."

"Murder, bigamy, attempted assassination in a—" began Molly.

The wretch sat down and wiped his clammy brow. Money was the keystone of his arch. His craving for gold, even overpowered his lust. Big drops of perspiration poured down his cheeks.

"If I must, I must—come to me tomorrow," he began.

"I know you well man," she said contemptuously, "if you have the money it is about you. There is no fear of being robbed here. What you give, you will give freely, and," she added with a laugh, "I will give you a receipt."

Christian dived with his left hand into the recesses of a mysterious pocket, and drew forth a pocket-book.

With many a groan he counted out the money in English notes—notes that represented many a nefarious transaction—many a poor widow and orphan robbed.

When he had placed it in the girl's hands, he rose.

"Now I suppose I may go."

"You'll make me a present," said Molly's friend.

Christian would have refused with an oath, but he felt completely powerless.

He gave her the smallest note he had, and then moved to the door.

"I must go with him," said Phineas, with a sarcastic smile, "my friend and I have some business matters to settle."

Christian Whitmer opened the door with a muttered oath.

The Vampire stood in the door-way with folded arms.

"Hell and furies," said Phineas, falling back as from a blow.

"You can go," remarked the stranger with a polite bow, addressing the Mormon elder, "I know you not, but this most foul and wicked wretch dies this night."

Christian Whitmer bowed ironically to Phineas, and was about to wish him good night, when it suddenly flashed across his mind that the other was possessed of money, and if made a friend, might yet prove useful.

He touched his forehead.

"Mad," said Phineas, desperately.

"And if I am mad, wretch," began the other, "whose fault. I sometimes think I am, or else I should recollect who and what I am. But I have only to kill you and then I shall remember. Come wretch."

At this instant Christian grappled with him from behind, Phineas made a rush and ere he was aware of it, his arms were pinioned.

"Ring," said Phineas.

The girls really alarmed obeyed, and one or two servants came.

"This man is a maniac got loose," said Phineas, "his fancy is murder. I charge you to hold him until we escape, or we must appeal to the authorities."

Now the house had the greatest objection to any contact with the authorities. Despite, therefore, the fearful struggles of the maniac, they caught him firmly, and held him so until the two others had made their escape.

Then with a thousand apologies they set their prisoner loose by a small private door, leading through dark and narrow lanes, where he could never find his way in the day time.

Christian Whitmer would have shaken off Phineas, but that gentleman was obdurate.

He showed his pistols, and declared that they must come to an explanation that very evening.

Christian Whitmer finding that nothing else was to be done gave way. He invited his companion to accompany him to his hotel.

What the consequence of this alliance was we shall learn as we progress in our narrative.

CHAPTER LVI.

ILLUSIONS.

DESPITE the joy which Jessie felt at being reunited to her mother, despite her satisfaction at finding herself in a station in life which opened to her such bright prospects for the future, the young girl was not exactly happy.

She did not see enough of Henry.

There was a strange mystery about her mother which she could not fathom.

She was thoughful, abstracted, and at times there was visible a strange constraint in her manner.

Despite the park, the pony, the carriage, the drives through every part of the country; despite the fact that very little effort was made to force knowledge upon her, her cheek grew pale, her eyes dim, and her walk lost much of its youthful elasticity.

Child thou art verging on that mysterious world, which becomes known to some so much earlier than others. Vague feelings she did not understand filled her soul, she could hear the first dim flattering sound of that sweet music which comes softly across the deep ocean that separates girlhood from womanhood.

Like the solitary Crusoe of the desert island she could see in the far off distance a glorious light on a distant hill top, but she could not feel it.

But her soul was attuning itself to love, which soon must flood and overflow every other sensation of the heart.

Jessie only knew that the society of Henry was inexpressibly dear to her.

But she hesitated to speak of it, for fear of wounding her mother's feelings.

But however unwilling a parent may be to allow that the health of a beloved child is affected, there are those fortunately always ready to open our eyes.

The dwarf, who appeared to be the tutor and council general of the establishment, whispered warnings in the mother's ear.

Inexpressibly alarmed, she at once sent for a physician of eminence.

He examined Jessie with the utmost attention, conversed with her, and then retired to a private room with the mother and the dwarf, called by Cornelia always, Monsieur Edouard.

"How old is the young lady?" he asked.

"Just upon thirteen."

"Humph! seems older. Were she not so young I should unhesitatingly say that she was fretting—that is, that the course of true love did'nt run smooth, you know," continued the physician with a bland smile.

The mother and the dwarf exchanged glances.

"Ah!" cried Dr. Rummidge, "I see that there is some little justification for my suspicion."

"She is very much attached, from very peculiar circumstances, to a youth of her own age—but I cannot think—"

"My dear madam—the female sex is made up of many and subtle organizations. The affections are always powerful, and in some the nerves are very sensitive at an early age. Little Miss Jessie is fretting about an imaginary hero, personified in the young gentleman alluded to. My decided prescription is the sea side and the young gentleman."

And the doctor blandly took a pinch of snuff.

"In the meantime we must give this romantic young lady some tonics—"

"It shall be done at once," cried Cornelia, herself a little agitated.

"My dear madam, we must be cool, very cool.

I should advise a residence of six months at Dover, better than Brighton—all glare, sun and noise—invite the young gentleman, and without altogether interfering with their studies let them have as much of one another's society as they like—baths, drives and walks. When the autumn comes she will be stronger in mind and body."

The physician took his fee, stopped to dinner, and left early.

Cornelia sat down and wrote a long letter to Lady Haddington.

The dwarf superintended the packing with a very grave and rather mournful face.

The letter to Lady Haddington was sent off by a special messenger.

The answer came just after breakfast.

Cornelia had noticed with a pang that Jessie scarcely touched her morning meal, and that she rose from it listlessly and with pallid cheeks.

" Well, Jessie, what have you particular to do to-day," she said affectionately.

" Much as usual, mamma—my lessons, my music and painting, and then a drive out with the two cream-coloured ponies," replied Jessie with a smile that was brimful of gratitude.

" Well, my dear, I think you had better adjourn your lesson to-day, and help Foreman to pack."

" Why, mamma ?"

" We are going to the sea-side. Lady Haddington has written to Dover for a house, and we are going on a visit."

Jessie looked hard at her mother. She was very pale and ready to faint.

" Henry is to be there," she gasped.

" He is, my child."

" Oh, mamma," sobbed Jessie, a flood of tears bedewing her cheeks, " you are too good."

" My dear, your happiness is my first thought—the duty of my life."

" But it seems so ungrateful, mamma, to be so happy to leave this beautiful home. But I really cannot help it."

" We do not make our own hearts, child. It is perfectly natural that you should desire to see one so dear to you as Henry. So dearest go, bid Foreman pack. Tell her we shall stay six months."

Jessie again embraced her mother, wiped her tears, and sped away on her pleasant duty.

The dwarf glided into the room.

" You must be doubly careful," he said, " she must be never out of your sight. Mrs. Treherne has not left the country. This pretended absence is but a blind to some infernal plot. Be wary, careful, and never trust any strangers."

" I will watch my treasure with the heart and eyes of a mother," said Cornelia.

Next morning a heavy travelling carriage left ——— hall for the celebrated watering place and ancient city of Dover.

CHAPTER LVII.

THE " OSPREY."

CIRCUMSCRIBED by lofty hills, peculiar in shape, Dover can never become a magnificent suburb of London, like Brighton, but it is infinitely more

agreeable and pleasant as a residence, while the society is delightful.

It is a little select and exclusive, but once set your foot within the magic circle and nothing can be more pleasant.

For walks, for drives, it is inimitable.

But we must think more of our narrative and leave description to its proper place.

The meeting between Jessie and Henry was affectionate in the extreme, though on his side unattended with any of that exquisite manifestation of sensibility which so peculiarly characterized the lovely child.

Henry was still in manner and heart a boy, but nevertheless devoted to Jessie.

But Jessie was disappointed. She had a vague sense of something wanting.

Still she had too much good sense to manifest in any way her belief in his shortcomings, and satisfied to be with him, made herself a mere girl again, and entered freely and heartily into all his amusements.

She went out to sea in a boat with him, went fishing, drove a pony chaise against his, climbed Shakespear's cliff, visited the Castle, and won from him the characteristic remark, that he wished he had a brother like her.

Those were halcyon and summer days, alas ! too bright to last.

In general, Lady Haddington and Cornelia accompanied the young people in their excursions, except on the sea—to which both ladies had an insuperable objection.

They, however, on these occasions watched them from a drawing-room on the Marine Parade with powerful telescopes,

A special crew had been selected from amongst the jolly fishermen and boatmen of the port with strict orders to be extremely careful and never to go out of sight.

At other times, the young people would row about in a small boat, never, however, leaving the shore, or going above fifty yards from the front of the house.

One or two servants stood about or lounged on seats, or lay on the sands, apparently unconnected with them, but ever on the watch.

An odd little man with a very good basket of fruit for sale, would often waylay them, and win them to spend money, which at last grew into a daily habit, so that at last his arrival was looked for with regularity.

They seemed to have a strong body-guard enough in all conscience.

About a month after their arrival in Dover, a new watcher made his appearance.

He was a sailor, and by his countenance any one could see that he had been a voyager to hot countries.

His face was bearded like the pard; his cheeks, chin, and upper lip were one mass of hair.

A stylish straw hat, blue jacket and trowsers, with a red flannel shirt, made him easily recognizable, except that he always passed rapidly with a hasty glance upward at the balcony, and then took up his post at some little distance.

His chief occupation consisted in smoking a short clay pipe and throwing pebbles into the water.

Sometimes he would take a boat and row about, always keeping a respectful distance from the young people.

At last he was noticed, and the telescopes were set to work upon him.

But neither of the ladies noticed anything about him to connect him with any one they had ever seen. They thought no more of him. He was evidently an idle tar, spending his money while waiting for another berth.

A new subject of interest drew off their attention.

"I should like to be a sailor," said Henry one morning as they stood gazing out upon the sea.

"Why?" cried Lady Haddington in a somewhat alarmed tone.

"If only to own such a craft as that," he replied, "look at it Jessie."

They all gazed in the direction pointed out by Henry, and there truly lay as lovely a schooner yacht as any one could wish to have gazed upon.

The hull was long and low, with very slight bulwarks revealing the white and polished deck, with a handsome brass swivel gun. The masts tapered high and raked aft with considerable elegance, while every sail was white and new, in admirable keeping with the rigging and flying gear.

"It is beautiful," said Jessie, "one might go round the world in it."

The ladies themselves could not help admiring it, and at the urgent request of Henry it was resolved if the yacht remained in Dover, that they would find out the owner and request permission to visit it.

Henry, however, like most boys of his age was for an immediate examination of the vessel on the outside.

A pleasure boat lay handy, and their crew were always within ten minutes hail.

On the beech stood the strange sailor smoking his pipe and looking curiously at the yacht.

The ladies walked down to the beech.

The boat was prepared for a launch. Her small crew were quite ready.

Henry and Jessie climbed on board.

"Going out to that ere yacht?" said the dark sailor touching his hat, while he turned away to cough.

"Yes," said Henry.

"May I be so bold," he continued, "if so be 'taint no 'fence, just to ax to be runned out? I think I knows the craft."

Henry turned towards the ladies.

Cornelia with a grave smile nodded her head affirmatively.

"Come on board my hearty," said Henry, who was in great spirits.

Mumbling some words of which no one exactly understood the significance, the strange sailor leaped on board, and with the evident claims to superiority which appertains to the sailor of the long voyage, took the helm.

The sloop glided with a graceful motion off the shingle, and in another minute floated.

Her sails were soon trimmed and on a wind she headed almost for the yacht.

But the strange sailor seemed not to desire too near a contact with the beautiful schooner. He sailed up near enough to obtain a good view and then steered round at an extremely respectful distance.

Not a soul could be seen on board. The schooner swung gently to her anchor like some huge bird floating on the waters.

"Mighty queer yacht," said the sailor of the long voyage.

"A spanker," said one of the crew, "looks as if she could run into the wind's eye."

The strange sailor made no reply. His whole attention was fixed upon a man who suddenly appeared leaning over the bulwarks.

"Come on board, my young master," he said, in a hoarse voice, that made Jessie and Henry turn round and the strange sailor start again.

"No," said the dark seaman gruffly; and without further parley, he headed for the shore.

The ladies were at the balcony, the men servants were lounging about in various attitudes, while the fruit and sweetstuff-man was surrounded by a party of juveniles, to whom he was vending his wares at a very low rate indeed.

The children went straight to the house to take lunch.

The strange sailor walked straight up to the little man, whose odd appearance had more than once struck him.

Very short, stout, and thick-set, his whole form was enveloped in a great coat, that descended to his heels. Huge lacquered spectacles, red whiskers, and a broad brimmed hat completed his strange appearance.

As the sailor approached, and seated himself on the bench beside him, the children hurried away. They were used to the little man, but in presence of the stranger they were timid.

"Friend of them ladies," said the strange sailor, with a jerk of his finger towards the balcony.

"Why do you ask," replied the other.

"Well done, old sourkrout—all right and above board—ship-shape and so on. I only asked a question, vich, if answered, information might follow."

"I am a friend of theirs—of the children above all," said the little man.

"So am I," said the strange sailor, with a very peculiar smile.

The little man eyed him with a half suspicious glance.

"Your name," he said, curtly.

"Yourn," said the sailor.

"My name matters not. I see you are trifling with me."

"Bles yer 'art," laughed the man of the long voyage, "nuffin so very absurd. Harkee, friend, if so be you is, I dare say you've heard my name."

"Let me hear it now."

The sailor whispered it laughingly in his ear. The little man caught his hand in his two and rung it with singular energy.

"You know'd it then," said the sailor, dashing away a tear, "she has spoke'd of me."

"Knew it, of course we do. As you have been so frank with me, I'll tell you who I am."

And the little man whispered something in the other's ear.

The sailor had stooped to listen, and he did not raise his head for some minutes. He sat as if

A STRANGE PAIR IN THE CABIN OF THE " OSPREY."

pondering the truth of what he had heard, and when he did raise his head there were tears upon his cheeks.

"No," he said, " it aint possible."

"It is."

"Then God bless her—and now we understand one another. A bit of news. Who do you think hangs out on board yon schooner?"

"I don't know."

"Rackshaw !"

"What !"

"Rackshaw—Bristol—he has stole the young 'uns," continued the sailor.

"The accursed fiends are on our track," said the little man ; " but see, is not that a boat from the schooner ?"

"It is."

"Will you follow the crew, or whoever leaves the boat, and join me by-and-bye."

"I will."

An address was agreed on, and then the two separated, the sailor to saunter, with a short pipe in his mouth, towards the esplanade, where the boat appeared likely to land, the little man to dive into the streets at the back of the marine parade.

CHAPTER LVIII.

IL CONDE.

On the balcony of a house, at a considerable distance from the Marine Parade, stood watching the boat that was coming in from the schooner, a tall and gentlemanly-looking foreigner.

His countenance, with its olive complexion, jet black whiskers and moustache, was that of a Brazilian.

His eye was dark and penetrating.

Little was known of him in Dover, except that he was rich, kept numerous servants, owned a beautiful yacht and lost his money freely at the club, to which he had brought unexceptionable references.

He gave his name as Il Conde del Blanco, chamberlain to his majesty the Emperor of the Brazils.

He spoke English with fluency which he incidently explained by announcing that his mother was an Englishwoman.

The dark sailor looked keenly up at the window without however pausing, and then seating himself carelessly on some timber at a little distance, watched the boat coming ashore.

It was pulled by four sailors, while a stout man in a straw hat, sat in the stern sheets.

The man landed, and walked strait up to the house, where stood the count in the open balcony.

The seaman with the black beard gave a low shrill whistle.

He saw it all at a glance.

The boat took its way back in the direction of the schooner.

The dark seaman entered a public-house, bought some bread, took a stiff jorum of brandy, and prepared for a long watch.

It lasted until nightfall, when the steersman of the boat, rather unsteady in his walk, came forth, and took his way towards the old town.

The stranger followed him after hailing a boy and bidding him follow also.

On nearing the port, the yachtman went into a public-house.

The sailor followed, and wrote two or three words in pencil on a scrap of paper.

"Take that," he said giving an address, " and you will get a shilling."

The boy nodded and ran away with a smile. He was evidently delighted.

The dark sailor entered the large taproom of the public-house, at this hour not much frequented, and found the yachtman ordering some fresh grog and a pipe, though evidently the worse for drink.

"Well shipmate," he said, hic—, fixing his dull fishy-eyes on the new comer, "going to refit."

"Yaw," said the sailor in a deep sepulchral voice, which made the other start.

"A mounsheer—drat you," cried the tipsy man, with a snap of his fingers

"Nein !" replied the other.

"What then ?"

"English."

"Why the devil then do you talk Dutch ?"

"Cape."

"Why hang you, you're as chary of your words as a sea lawyer."

"Tongue."

"What ?"

"Cut."

"Who by ?"

"Savages."

"So you can't speak two words can't you. I only wish I had you on board my craft I'd soon teach you to talk plain, my fine fellow d——d if I would'nt."

"Try."

"Will you ship ?"

"Yaw."

The yachtman, who was really in a passion at the other's monysyllables, angrily replied that if he shipped with him, he'd better look out for squalls, as the first excuse he'd teach him to speak up.

"Yaw."

"I tell you what it is, if you can't slip. no more jaw tackle than that you'd better stuff a pipe in your mouth and say no more. I go on board at twelve, you can go with me if you like."

"Yaw."

The yachtman started, frowned, and then his hot brandy-and-water coming in, took a heavy gulp to hide his indignation.

But the room began to fill. It was the rendezvous of the real and pretended sufferers from poverty, who attempt at watering places, to get a living out of the charitable and good-natured.

Never give to beggars, say the cold-hearted and cold-blooded centralists, who do everything by rule, and who mete out charity as Hudibras did

"Pots of ale
By geometric scale."

But a penny, given with a kind word and a smile often gives more satisfaction to the real unfortunate than a whole meal handed over by an insolent relieving officer.

There came the Italian organ grinder with his pockets well laden with coppers, and his white teeth grinning at the prospect of a good meal ; the eternal Polish refugee, whose wife is always in an interesting situation, which reduces him to sell steel pens ; the well dressed Hungarian who has just received a letter from Perth, and who has a good silk umbrella which he is ashamed to pawn, and who is dying with hunger. It is to be remembered that this gentleman never speaks to the same party twice, and if you tell him to call on you at any address, never comes. There were the usual lame and blind, but not one of those who beg from sheer necessity.

They do not spend their earnings in festivity or drink.

About an hour after the room was tolerably full, a fresh arrival took place. This was a little fantastically dressed man, with a slight hump, who carried in his hands a little three-legged table, and a small box.

He glanced timidly around the room as if he feared he was an intruder.

"Well," said the yachtman, who was still further on the way towards intoxication. "what are you, a man or a monkey ?"

"A poor Brazilian who gets a living in an honest vay," replied the dwarf in good English, but with a slight foreign accent.

"How is that?" continued the other, brutally.

"You are not my master," said the man, wiping his forehead with an old cotton handkerchief.

"Why, cuss you, you're only a monster. Do you dare to bandy words with me? If you don't speak up, I'll smash you into a pancake."

"Nein," said the dark sailor.

"Why you tramping piece of jaw tackle," cried the other in a rage, "would you dare to interfere?"

"Yaw," cried the other thrusting out a hard and sinewy fist, and placing it in very near juxta-position to the yachtman's nose.

He turned very red in the face but gulping down his resentment, ordered another glass.

"Would you like to see what I do?" said the little man, humbly addressing his brave defender.

"Yaw! yaw!" said the dark man.

The little Brazilian placed his table on the ground in the centre of the whole party, and opening his box, commenced with his lithe and practised fingers a series of tricks with cards, with handkerchiefs, with coins, with hats, all so wonderful that the audience were struck dumb with astonishment.

Not one of them had ever seen anything like it before.

"Why, you son of the devil—you reg'lar little imp—what's your name?" said the drunken yachtman.

"Don Herrera."

"Well, b——t you, Don 'Era, if you'll come on board our yacht to-morrow, and do a bit of conjuring I'll give you a sovereign."

The little man bowed humbly.

"The gentleman says so now, but if I come perhaps he may turn me away."

"Do you think I want to cheat you? Do I look like a cheat? What the —— are you all laughing at—eh?"

"I'd rather have some money now."

Again the dark sailor raised his fist and struck the table.

"Now," he said.

"Oh, my fine fellow," muttered the yachtman, "if I don't marry you to the gunner's daughter, my name aint——. Well, never mind."

At the same time he cast a crown on the table.

"You see I pay the fellow in advance. Remember—six o'clock to-morrow—on board the 'Osprey'—schooner-yacht lying off the Marine Parade."

"I will be there," said the little man.

"You'd better."

"Eat," said the dark sailor.

"Yes, signor," replied the little man, with a smile and a nod.

The dark sailor rang, and in his odd way ordered a steak for two, which the two demolished a short time after with great apparent relish, after which they conversed as best they might; the little man, however, retiring early to bed.

"Twelve," presently said the dark man, touching his hat to the yachtman.

"Twelve what?" grunted the other in reply.

"Clock."

"Oh, you remember that, do you. Well, where's your traps?"

"None."

"Have you got any money?"

"Yaw."

As if utterly unable to control himself, the other rose and staggered out of the house, after getting his new recruit to light a lanthorn, and lead the way.

They took the direction of the beach, and soon were close to the water.

A small jolly-boat stood off about twenty yards.

"Boat a-hoy," said the yachtman.

"Who is that?"

"Schooner 'Osprey.'"

"All right," was the reply, and next minute the jolly-boat was beached.

"Who's this, skipper?" said one of the men.

"Who? —— if I know. But he's a messmate as can keep a quiet tongue in his head. Pull away—I'm sleepy."

The skipper sank in the stern sheets, the four men pulled away, while the dark sailor took the tiller in hand.

"Pretty cool fellow," said the skipper, with a grin of astonishment, "to squat down beside the skipper."

"Skip—," cried the other.

"Yes, and be —— to you. What did you think I was?"

"Cook."

The other muttered some incoherent words, and clutched at the dark man—the crew tittered audibly.

The dark man thrust the drunken yachtman back on his seat, and pointed to the water.

"Quiet."

"Quiet, you son of a b——h," roared the skipper.

"And if I don't?"

"Over," cried the other, holding him with his left hand as in a vice.

The man said nothing, but darting a ferocious scowl at the sailor, closed his eyes and said no more until he was on deck.

He then hesitated a moment, as if about to wreak his vengeance, but overcome by drink, sought his bunk forward with the men, after ordering the new sailor to keep deck watch for the remainder of the night. This was the only way he could devise to annoy the imperturbable seaman.

"Yaw," said the other, with a grin.

The skipper shook his fist at him, and retired almost choking with passion.

CHAPTER LIX.

THE SCHOONER "OSPREY."

ALL was still on that brightly-polished deck. The boat rode quietly at anchor, while the sea, though never at rest, was as calm as the mighty heaving of distant waters would allow it to be.

The night was dark in the extreme. The

clouds hung low and seemed to portend a coming storm.

The town looked like a picture of fairy land, with its bright lamps shining in long rows, reflected magically in the water.

The strange sailor with an odd sort of a chuckle again loaded his pipe, and leaning over the taffrail, gazed down at the black waters.

He appeared alone in possession of the vessel.

There was a grave and solemn glance in his eye, as gazing earnestly at the shore he endeavoured to make out the position of the house in which the children slept.

Suddenly he turned away impatiently, and was surprised to see a light streaming up the companion-way.

Curiosity overcame every other consideration, and cautiously descending the steps, he came in full view of the cabin.

It was very large, unusual space having been devoted to it, and admirably fitted. It had cushions, sofas, mirrors, and sideboards, with a large dining-table in the midst.

But the dark sailor saw neither the trappings, nor the gilding, nor the rich array of ornaments.

His eyes were fixed upon a richly rounded arm, revealed by the fall of a sleeve.

It was a plump, white, dimpled arm, and of course belonged to a woman.

She was young, and as far as one could judge by the glimmer of a side face, very pretty. But she was very sad, and though she read a book with attention, she seemed scarcely to be aware of what she was doing.

The leaves remained unturned for a very long time together.

Her thoughts were far away.

The dark sailor rubbed his eyes. He could scarcely believe his senses.

An idea flashed through his brain, and was then dismissed as almost too absurd for belief—and yet—

Yes, it must be.

" Mary," he whispered.

She turned with a start and gazed him full in the face.

The other held his finger up to his lips.

" What do you mean ? " she said.

" Safe—"

" Yes, but what do you want ? There is no one here, but I can obtain assistance in a moment."

" Oh ! "

" Now go away, sailor. My father is on board, and I'm surprised at your impudence."

" Eyes," said the dark man.

" What ? "

" Lips," cried the other.

" The man's mad," said the girl, rising.

" And so, Mary, you do not know me ? " he continued, with a deep chuckle.

With a suppressed cry like that of a wild creature from which its young had been torn, she leaped to his arms, and for five minutes nothing could be heard save the passionate embraces of this strange pair.

Then they conversed in whispers for about an hour, after which, numerous embraces, whisperings and kisses having been duly disposed of, the dark sailor went on deck.

It was with the energy of a Bounaparte that he now loaded his pipe and walked the quarter deck of the " Osprey" as if he had been its owner.

Several times he halted, and standing still had a hearty laugh all to himself. He appeared to think something a very good joke, though what it was we are truly at a loss to say.

While he was walking day broke, and away in the eastern sky rose the glorious orb of morn, which science says is decreasing in heat and light by a slow and gradual process which ultimately must end in extinction.

It will, we hope, last our time.

About half an hour later the whole range of waters was flooded with golden rays that danced merrily on the sparkling waves of that placid and seductive sea.

About an hour after the skipper came on deck followed by the whole of the crew, a band of some ten as ill-looking foreigners as ever stepped on the deck of merchantman or yacht.

The dark sailor braced himself up for a contest.

" Well," said the skipper advancing towards the dark sailor, " you're taking it pretty easy. Aint you going for to swab the decks ?"

" Nein !"

" What ! you tarnation ill-looking monkey, why, aint you shipped aboard this here craft.

" Yaw !"

" Now look you here Mr. Yaw and Nein if you don't slip your jaw-tackle, you and I'll have one of the smartest rows ever you see. I'm master in my own ship, and what's more, I mean to be, so just you set too and swab them decks."

The dark sailor made no reply, but stepping forward suddenly, caught hold of a stout French lad, a cabin boy, and holding him firmly by the nape of the neck, pointed to the bucket usually employed to haul water on board.

" Swab," he said.

" Seize the villain," cried the skipper, still suffering from his inebriation of the previous night, " knock him down. Mutiny by the powers of darkness."

Several of the crew rushed at the dark sailor, who, using the French boy as a propeller, knocked two down, and then making a rapid motion with his left hand, sent the skipper flying into the scuppers with a fearful yell, the effect of which was not much diminished by the stream of blood which spurted over his nose.

Then clutching a handspike, he retreated with flashing eyes until he suddenly brought up against the capstain.

" No," he said.

" My pistols," roared the infuriated skipper as he rose from the deck.

" Yaw," said the dark sailor levelling a Colt's revolver straight at his head.

" Ha ! ha ! ha !" laughed the skipper, diving behind the men, " a very good joke, Yaw and Nein. Well, you are a plucky fellow. If ever I want a mate you're the very identical fellow for me. Get your breakfast."

And he turned away towards the cabin with a dark scowl which proved how fearful was the hypocrisy of his soul.

The dark sailor grinned, and as the crew made no hostile demonstration, held out his right hand, while in the left he showed several silver dollars, and making a significant motion towards his mouth, signified that they would at a future time drink to their mutual better acquaintance.

The men shook hands with him all round, and seating themselves on the forecastle prepared to enjoy their morning meal.

The dark sailor by his performance on that occasion rose greatly in the estimation of the seamen of the "Osprey."

If he had the strength of three he could eat for four.

The way too he pulled at the rum bottle when it came round after the black mixture which passed for coffee, was something which excited the admiration of all.

The French boy rubbed his shins and grinned from ear to ear.

The dark sailor was in an hour the pet of all on board.

CHAPTER LX.

PARLOUR MAGIC.

It was the afternoon of the same day and the two young child lovers were standing hand-in-hand gazing out upon the sparkling and ever heaving waters of that narrow channel which separates two worlds.

For France and England are two worlds, as different as Europe and America on its first discovery.

Our morals may not be very much better than those of our Gallic neighbours—they say we are a hundred per cent more immoral—but our manners are widely different; and when one compares the sleek, oily, false but insinuating Frenchman, with the bluff, manly, though rougher Englishman, one is proud of one's own country.

There is one thing to be said in favour of the French. We never heard of any weak and silly enough to turn Mormons.

There may be from among the filthy scum which rises on the surface of French low society, certain men who have played the part of the deluders in this most insensate folly; but even French peasants are above being the dupes of Latter Day Saints.

The yacht was still the point of attraction with Henry, while Jessie looked up at him with a tender and inquiring glance.

But at fourteen a boy thinks more of his hoop, his boat, his pony, his bat, than of any sweetheart.

And quite right too.

But don't the dear girls look down upon such poor deluded creatures with eyes of contemptuous pity.

Even those whose juvenile hearts beat for beauty, are not spared by the immolators in crinoline.

"Aint she a darling?" said the boy, suddenly.

"What, dear?"

"The schooner yacht," replied Henry, proudly, using the proper word.

"It is a pretty vessel," said Jessie.

"Should'nt I like to go on board," continued Henry.

"You can if you like, my little man," said a deep base voice close to his elbow.

They both turned and saw a handsomely dressed and most imposing foreigner standing close at hand.

Henry's eyes sparkled with delight.

The two ladies, the guardian angels of the children, were close behind on an iron seat.

"Thank you, sir," replied Henry.

"I have a little party on board this evening—just my own family, to witness the tricks of a most wonderful little conjuror," he continued, in a gentle tone.

"Would'nt you like to go, Jessie?" said Henry, in animated tones.

"If it pleases you," she replied, with one of her heavenly smiles.

"Shall I ask mamma?" continued Henry.

"Yes, my little man," said the foreigner, who waved his hand to the crew of a handsome cutter, who were about five-and-twenty yards from the shore.

A small boat with one waterman was just about to put off from the beach.

There was one man in it. A wee man. In fact the timid little Brazilian conjuror.

A pleasure-boat capable of carrying at least twenty persons was also making ready for a sail.

Lady Haddington and Cornelia heard the lad's demand without surprise, and after cautioning him to be very careful, gave him leave to go with Jessie.

A man servant, however, must accompany them: John, too, who was an expert swimmer.

A sign was made to him, and when he came up, strong instructions given.

John walked behind Henry to where the foreigner stood.

"Please, sir, misses says she's very much obliged, and if you have no objection to my going with them, they're quite welcome."

The Count haughtily bowed, and replied that the ladies wishes were commands.

He then led the way with that proud humility which is the characteristic of the foreign noblemen.

The boat was ready.

Two sailors assisted the whole party to enter.

The footman went forward.

The foreigner placed the children beside him in the stern sheets.

He conversed with them in affable and friendly tones.

The children were delighted, though at times certain harsh notes struck upon their ears.

The conjuror advanced slowly towards the schooner, but considerably ahead of them.

The pleasure-boat stood out to sea, with a number of people on board.

The "Osprey" had an awning spread over the whole of the deck.

The little conjuror had climbed up the sides of the "Osprey," and discharged his waterman before the four-oared cutter came alongside.

The pleasure-boat passed away to seaward with a red pennant flying at the masthead.

On reaching the deck of the Osprey the young

people found that a table had been set upon the deck, or rather the companion hatch had been turned into a table, while seats had been placed around.

It was all under the awning.

The front seats were arm chairs, in which sat the foreigner, the children, two dark gipsy-eyed girls, and a young lady, suspiciously like the one the dark sailor had kissed on the previous night.

At a sign from the foreigner the crew made a circle behind.

At one end of the circle stood the skipper, his eye fixed more upon the dark sailor than upon any one else.

The dark sailor leaned with folded arms against the bulwarks.

As soon as all were seated, the Brazilian conjuror stepped forward, leaped on the table with the agility of a monkey, and bowed to the audience.

Henry curled his lip disdainfully.

He would rather have examined the schooner and have had a sail.

But the little man placing his three-legged stool before him, began almost immediately such a number of such extraordinary tricks as to rivet the attention of all.

While doing so he kept up a continual clatter of words.

"Well, my little friends," said the foreigner, "I think we have had enough of this."

It was growing dark, and as on this part of the deck there were side awnings, several lanterns served fully to illumine the scene.

"One more trick, my good sare," remonstrated the conjuror, "an' you sall say it is vonderful."

He kicked the three-legged table from before him, and took from a green bag two double-barrelled pistols.

Henry's eyes glistened. Fire-arms were equal favourites with yachts.

The little conjuror cocked the pistols.

"Now you see, mine frens', I have change everyting into everyting else. I do more wonderful ting. Vat yer name, signeoir?" with a low bow to the foreigner.

"Il Conde del Blanco."

"Your name, mine fren'," addressing the skipper.

"Jacob Lutzen," said the other with a grin. He had been infinitely amused with the conjuror.

"And Herr Yaw and Nein."

"Joe," said the dark sailor.

"And you, mine pretty miss," addressing the handsome young woman.

"Mary."

"Well now, you, I wave my pistol once—twice—tree times, and presto the Conde del Blanco become Colonel Meadows; Jacob Lutzen, he be the rascally stolen good receiver, Rackshaw; Joe become Peregrine Grundy; and you all but one, very fine collection of double-skilled knaves and villains."

All stood petrified with astonishment, rage, and horror.

"Seize the little imp," roared Colonel Meadows with a fearful oath.

"I'll settle the wretch," screamed Rackshaw, drawing a cutlass.

"Two can play at that game," said Peregrine Grundy, dashing off his huge whiskers and moustache.

And he knocked the skipper down with one well planted blow of his fist.

Dire was the confusion. The colonel gave confused orders, the men rushed round him, Mary pulled Henry and Jessie away towards the cabin, while the little conjuror stood calmly surveying the scene with his pistols still levelled.

"Tumble up boarders," he cried in a loud and shrill voice.

And before any of the party could recover from their surprise the crew of the pleasure-boat leaped on the deck of the schooner, and mastered every man who made resistance.

"Ha! ha! ha!" said the dwarf, with a shrill and hollow laugh, "so this persecution is never to cease. Do you think, insensate fool, that these children came on board here like lambs to the slaughter—Jessie, Henry, look at that man. Read in his countenance the villain he is. Colonel Meadows, let me warn you. The next attempt you make on these poor children shall be fatal. I know you well; I know the full catalogue of your crimes."

"Sir, by what authority," began the other recovering himself; "I say, by what authority have you dared to erect yourself into a judge of my conduct."

"Authority! by the rope that hangs round your neck. Remember Leopold Treherne—remember Cornelia Lester.

The colonel bowed his head and was silent.

"I am going on shore," continued the dwarf. "On my arrival I shall report your attempted rapt of these children to the authorities. It will be your fault if you wait the arrival of the ten-gun brig, which lies yonder. As surely as you are in sight, as surely shall you be arrested as a pirate. Come, my children."

"Come Mary," said Peregrine Grundy, taking the girl's hands.

"Dare to touch her," cried old Rackshaw, rising and rubbing his head.

"I cannot leave my father," said Mary, sadly, "goodbye Perry. You must go without me—"

"If I do may I be——"

Mary shook her head.

"You ar'nt a going to take her by force from her father," sneered Rackshaw.

"No, I ain't a going to do no such thing. I'm going to take her out of the hands of a murderous, thievish hound, a forger and thief, to take her to her father."

The old skipper dropped down like a dead man on the deck, and before Mary could recover from her astonishment, she was in the boat with the dwarf, Perry, and the child lovers.

Jessie was quite calm, but Henry's eyes flashed and his mouth was closed sharply.

He wanted to know what it all meant.

"Ask Lady Haddington," said the dwarf in his low sweet tones.

"Oh, Perry!" cried Mary, crying and sobbing, "what did you mean? My father—"

"Is living. I'll tell you all about it, its a precious queer yarn. I've been round the world since you and I met in the old bedroom."

And Perry looked very sly as he spoke, not

exactly in Mary's face, but just round about her neck and shoulders.

Mary blushed and said no more.

That night a conference was held at which it was decided to remain in Dover for the rest of the season, then break up their establishment suddenly, and retire altogether to some retired locality, where Henry and Jessie's education could be attended to, without giving any clue to the inveterate enemies who pursued them with such undying hate.

Next day in Dover, a rumour flew through the town that the rich Brazilian Count had vamoosed, yacht and all, without any warning to his servants or landlady.

CHAPTER LXI.

THE RETURN HOME.

TOM PIKE was in the shop.

"How that boy's grow'd," said Mrs. Grundy, as periodically she came in search of news from her nevy.

He had been gone two years, and nobody in Bristol, among those who knew him, ever believed that he would come back.

And yet nobody attempted to disturb Tom Pike in his business.

On the contrary—his polite manners, his wish to oblige, his admirable style of shaving and hair cutting had won for the house a numerous *clientele*.

And then the rent was paid regularly, and the receipts given in charge to Mrs. Grundy.

This female had taken a partner in business, which circumstance enabled her to be much oftener in the shop than otherwise would have been the case.

Her visits were generally paid of an evening, towards tea time, on the slack days of the week when Tom Pike could afford to do the amiable.

They had never given up the rum in the tea.

It had been their calumet of peace, and no change had yet been made in their arrangements.

Their universal topic of conversation was the absent Perry.

Mary used at one time to come in, but she was often absent from Bristol.

She was very sad, and had ceased almost to hope for the return of Peregrine.

She mourned him as she would have a lost husband.

Then she left Bristol, she told them, for a long journey, begging that if Perry returned he might be told that she had never been unfaithful to his memory.

They were both very sorry to lose her, especially as Mary was never weary of hearing the full details of the disappearance of Peregrine.

As far as he thought it judicious, Tom Pike had told the story to his customers, who were delighted to hear it repeated, and always seemed to think it a very good joke.

"It was my fixed of intentions, announced to my brother on his dying day, never to neglect my poor Perry, and I always hoped to live to leave him a very tidy little sum, which, though I say

it as shoul't not say it, have been the savings of a honest life—and honesty, Tom, as the pocket-book says, is the best of policies—seeing which I have never insured my life, thinking it unnecessary. And now to think of his a-going away into furrin' parts; its against all nature, and I don't understand it."

"He never went of his own accord, nohow," replied Tom Pike.

"They do say there is such thing as pressing, but not benown to my knowledge, never see'd nuffin of any such outlandish proceedings, and under conviction, don't believe in it."

"Don'tee, mum."

"I don't, as I was a-saying, I did hope to survive to leave my money to nevy. Well, if I can't, I can't. I may mention, that, under the circumstances, I shall leave it to the business."

"But, mum—"

"Silence is the bettermost part of discretion, as the pocket-book say, so allow your elders my dear young friend, as the methody parson said to the boy at the crank, such is life and everything is for the best, in the best of all possible worlds."

Tom Pike bowed.

"When you reaches the age of reason, it is my fixed intention to consider you as in the place of my nevy, God bless him, and I hope he may live till the age of Methuselah."

"Thankee, that's hearty," said a well known voice, speaking with considerable emotion and heartiness.

"'Ooray," shouted Tom Pike.

"Oh," said the old lady, and clutching her umbrella convulsively, she looked hard at Perry, and prepared to faint.

"Don't," cried Tom, pouring some rum in his hurry more down her neck than into her capacious mouth.

"All right," said Perry shaking them both by the hand, "com'd home and brought a wife with me."

"Perry," exclaimed the ancient Mrs. Grundy in tones, awful from their seriousness, "I fancies you've been in furren parts. I've read books, and I've heard tell, that them benighted creatures fancies themselves all Adams and Eves. I hope Perry—"

"Ha! ah! ah!" laughed the joyous barber, "come in, Mary. All serene and shipshape—hooray."

And as the blushing Mary tripped in all white favours and lace, the delighted barber gave a regular view-halloo, which made the old rafters shake again.

"And now, Tom Pike, my boy," said Perry, "I thank you from my 'art. You're just the honest boy I thought you, and the people says as you cuts and shaves like the barber of the King of Spain, what ruled his master. I'm delighted to hear it; for I makes you a present of past, present and future, the money made, the money in, the money owing, and the goodwill of the business for your natural life—amen."

"Oh!" said the boy.

"Perry, my child," began Mrs. Grundy.

"Aunt, I've married a fortin'. I retires from the scrapery trade, but shall be werry 'appy to give my friend Pike a morning call; and so if you'll shut up, and come along, blow me if you shant have such a tightener as you aint seen for many a month of Sundays."

*   *   *   *   *

Two days later there stood behind the counter of the marine store and general shop of Mr. Rackshaw, a stout burly young man, who apparently by way of heightening his importance, wore spectacles.

But a keen eye might have detected that the glasses were only at the side of any character suited to defective sight.

The front ones were common glass.

There was an odd smirk on the face of the youth as he occasionally walked up the shop and conferred with certain parties in a back parlour.

He also several times entered the pawnbrokery office where he gave succinct directions on certain matters, with the air of one who is used to command.

About eleven o'clock a heavy fly or hackney-coach stopped at the door, and a man in a dog's-skin coat and sou'-wester descended hastily from it.

In one hand he clutched a huge cudgel, in the other a carpet bag.

The young man behind the counter began to whistle in the most provoking manner.

The man in the dog-skin coat entered the shop hurriedly, as one who is master of the situation.

He went straight up the shop, and prepared to raise the flap to go behind the counter,

"Hollo! more free than welcome," said the young man, slapping it down again, "what can I do for you, swag?"

"Why you infernal impostor," cried the man in the dog-skin cap, "how dare you stand behind my counter?"

"Good gracious, Sam," said a youth with a theatrical start, turning towards an assistant who appeared in a mysterious manner, "fetch a policeman, the man is mad."

"I tell you what my joker," cried the old man furiously, "you'll get yourself in a pretty scrape directly. This is my house, and where is my servant?"

"Sir," said the youth, "I have no wish to hurt the feelings of an individual with whom I am not acquainted; but I beg to inform you that this establishment is the property of Mr. Peregrine Grundy, the husband of pretty Mary, the daughter of William Rackshaw, so long successfully personated by his brother-in-law, Joseph Spinner."

"It's a lie—a confounded lie," shouted the infuriated ruffian.

"Will you walk in?" said the young man, taking off his spectacles and revealing the good-humoured countenance of Peregrine Grundy.

The old man, utterly overcome by news which to him seemed incredible, followed the young man.

He was powerless to resist.

The ex-barber showed him into a room, where at a table, on which was displayed expensive cut decanters, with every luxurious wine that

the art of man has contrived to extract from that royal fruit the grape, sat Mary and a tall, thin, gaunt and tanned man of most venerable appearance.

The ex-pawnbroker sank with a groan upon a chair.

"So," said the tall man rising, "this is the account I receive of your stewardship."

"Mercy!"

"Mercy! Did I not leave you a pretty little child and its fortune. Did I not believe that, as its uncle, I could trust you? Did I not bid you accumulate my capital until my return, or until my daughter married, and did you not sign this bond?"

And the old man struck the parchment with his outspread hand.

"I did."

"And what shall be the fate of the unjust steward?"

"William Rackshaw," said the other humbly, "I confess all. The temptation was too much for me. I freely resign all. I go forth a wanderer on the face of the earth. I have my vessel —that is my own. I ask no more."

"But there are charges against you which I cannot allow to pass unnoticed."

"William Rackshaw, be merciful. The day was when you and I were little boys together. Farewell, may we never meet again in this world."

"But, Henry and Jessie?"

"Are free from me."

"You swear?"

"There I will give you information, that will baffle all future attempts."

And with muttered words, the astounded and terrified ruffian explained all he knew.

The result will be seen in the sequel.

CHAPTER LXII.

MORMONISM.

WE could wish to cast a veil upon the fearful enormities of the atrocious sect, which, despite all effects of exposure, is carrying desolation and sorrow into the homes of England, but the scourge is raging with redoubled violence.

We are conscious of doing our duty, or the very nauseousness of the subject would deter us from the task.

Let not the foul apostles of Mormonism fancy that their ribald anonymous letters have any influence upon us.

We regard them with the same indifference as we do the furious diatribes launched against us in the chapels of the deluded Latter Day Saints.

If we turn from the constant exposure of Mormonism to other times a little more agreeable, it is from a desire to spare our readers.

Besides, the exigences of our narrative are such that we go not where we will.

Sing, as ye may, poets and prose writers of the bay of Naples—praise as ye will the intense and admirable beauties of foreign parts—we have seen in England, Scotland, and Wales, scenes of unrivalled loveliness—scenes which are as much

THE RENDEZVOUS.

worthy of being sung, as any that ever was chronicled in rhyme.

So seemed to think a traveller, who, descending from the top of a stage-coach, took his way across the fields to the lovely sea-port town of T——

He was a stranger in the land, but withal so affable and well-spoken, that the jolly driver of the Tally-ho, John Jones, gave him not only all the latest information with regard to the locality, but indulged, as old wheezy coachmen would sometimes in those days, in a goodly budget of gossip by the way.

The coach was bound for T——, but having to stop at a lodge leading to a certain aristocratic establishment situate on the way-side, the coachman advised the traveller to walk across by a cross-cut and put up at the Dolphin until the arrival of the coach with his luggage.

From certain words which fell from the honest coachman during the progress of his discourse the traveller highly approved of this plan, and away he trudged with considerable vigour across some meadows, over a stream, and down by a hill-side until the town, or rather, to be more correct, the village came in sight.

Not a soul had he met on his way, though he had noticed many houses embowered in trees, with rich and plenteous orchards, and every sign of plenty and comfort.

T—— is a pretty place. Fishing town,

watering-place, and rising business town, it has for some time attracted the attention of the searcher after health, and, we are sorry to say, in common with many other parts of Wales, it has felt the curse of Mormonism.

It is with deep regret that we say it, but the fact is notorious, that Wales is the hot-bed of Mormonism.

Why ?

Because education has not spread, because the march of intellect has not yet reached the denizens of the otherwise happy principality.

And yet T—— was celebrated for its schools.

They were, however, schools of high repute, kept by ladies and gentlemen of first-class education, and frequented by the youth connected with the *élite* of the county.

To this place the stranger came, to all appearance his luggage consisting of a stick.

He entered the parlour of the Dolphin, however, with the air of a man who felt himself to be of importance, and at once ordered refreshment.

"I will dine, and, if possible, take up my quarters for a few days—"

The landlady to whom he spoke was a very bonny dame of about five-and-thirty, buxom, rosy, smiling, and a widow; but being also a thrifty dame she glanced imperceptibly at the traveller's dusty garments and boots with a smile slightly derogatory to his gentility.

"I was recommended," continued the stranger; "to the Dolphin by the worthy driver of the Tally-ho, who will presently be here with my luggage."

Bright was the smile on the rubicund countenance of Mary Jones, who was shrewdly suspected in the village of a sneaking kindness for John Jones, himself a hale widower of forty.

A very fit couple to come together, doubtless, a reader might say, for who should be fitter for matrimony than those who have tasted of its sweets ?

Away Mary Jones bustled to prepare the dinner, none the less readily that the traveller ordered first a bottle of her very best wine, and then, in his most respectful tones, begged the landlady to assist him in drinking it.

"I desire to remain here some time," he said; "but should wish first to learn something of the neighbourhood."

Poor Mrs. Mary Jones smiled and curtsied, and we fear thought much less just then of John Jones than she had done since the death of her dear departed, such is the influence of plausible manner and a good address upon that most susceptible of all organs, the female heart.

There was an unctuous smile upon the stranger's face as he crossed his hands—we are afraid upon his stomach—and said grace, which appeared to the woman really marvellous.

"Fish," he said, as she raised the bright and shining cover.

And it was fish.

"If there is one thing I like more than another," he said; "it is——"

Here he wiped his lips with his white napkin.

"Beautiful trout," put in the landlady.

"It is trout," continued the stranger.

The dame curtsied, and the stranger rose.

"If there is one thing I dislike more than another," he said, in grave and dulcet accents; "it is to be seated while a lady is standing. I have the misfortune," he added, taking the dame's hand in his, "to be myself alone in the world. Since the time of my dear departed saint, I can scarcely see a lady without dropping a tear. Pray be seated."

And in a moment Dame Mary Jones found herself seated by the side of the stranger, who rang the bell.

"Bring me in a hot plate and a knife and fork," said the unctuous stranger to the bare-legged handmaid who came hastening in, but in tones so paternal that the sight of the two at dinner excited scarcely surprise on the part of the servant.

There was no resisting him. So the landlady dined with him, took wine with him, and about an hour after dinner, when the third bottle of port was brought in, was seated beside the traveller with her hand in his, and a very red face.

"I hope," said the traveller, with that uplifting of the eyes, and that strange pressure of the hand which is peculiar to the wolves in sheep's clothing, who go about seeking whom they may devour; "I hope that this neighbourhood is pious."

"Oh, lawk, sir, yes; we've two Church of England places of worship."

"I account them not; they are as it were sons of Belial."

"I begs pardon: well, then, we have a Methody, a Wesleyan, and a Ranter."

"They are better. Are there no more ?"

"One Simon, the cobbler, has started a class in a barn, as he calls Latter Day Saints, but I've never been near them."

"There will we go, sister Mary," said the stranger; "for I have heard that they are very good people; that they are humble and meek in a stable is as nothing, for the lowly shall be exalted."

"Amen," said the really pious woman.

"And the neighbours, are they poor ?"

"Very, except one family, and them people knows very little about except that they go to church once a day on Sunday, and never speak to nobody in the village."

"Proud and rich," said the traveller, casting his eyes up towards the ceiling. "Are they many ?"

"A lady and her son, a mother and her daughter. Such a beauty."

"Verily a carnal child. Describe her unto me."

"A child in years, but a woman in manner. Her hair is like a golden guinea."

"And they live—"

"At Haythorne Lodge, where John Jones,"—here the landlady blushed—"was to stop with their hampers and the strange travellers. But that puts me in mind—where can John Jones be ?"

The traveller made no reply, but, pouring out a bumper of wine, gave it to the agitated landlady to drink.

"Verily, sister Mary, you are agitated. Drink this good wine, it will do thee good," and the traveller, handing the glass with one hand put his arm round the buxom waist with the other.

Ah! if we were but to go by results we should fancy that Eve tempted Adam with a bunch of grapes, except that we recollect that cider is as intoxicating as wine.

When the traveller, emboldened by success, imprinted a kiss upon her buxom lips, she made no resistance—such is the frailty of poor human nature.

"Well, I'm dommed if that ain't cool! Missus, I'm ashamed of you! Sir, you're no gentleman!" bellowed the burly driver of the Tally-ho, entering the room, his whip in one hand, and a steaming glass of brandy-and-water in the other.

The landlady gave a little feminine shriek, and would have fainted, but somehow she could not contrive it.

"Swear not at all, my friend," said the traveller with consummate gravity. "I did but imprint upon the cheek of this good dame a chaste salute. I am a humble member of the Church of God, a preacher of the Word, and was but persuading our sister here to enter the fold."

"The Devil you were! Well, I tell you plainly what it is, I don't like them there sisterly and brotherly kisses."

"Mr. Jones, I'm surprised at you. The gentleman has been very polite."

"Cursed polite!"

"He asked me to keep him company, being himself a lone widower."

"Is he?" said John Jones, sarcastically. And then he added, seeing that the landlady looked really annoyed, "but I suppose it's all right. Am I allowed to join the party?"

"Pray be seated," said the traveller. "Have my boxes and packages arrived safe?"

"All right, sir," replied the coachman, lifting his right finger with professional rapidity to his forehead.

"Then pray join us. Will you join us in wine, or shall we warm the inner man with more potent liquor?"

"I likes brandy," said John.

"I think a glass will temper the chilliness of the wine," observed the traveller.

Mrs. Mary Jones, rose and, we are sorry to say, not walking in a very matronly and becoming manner, left the room and returned shortly after with the brandy.

"What time will you take tea, sir?" said the widow, with a curtsey.

"Whenever you like if made with your fair hands."

"I have a friend, a Miss Matilda Crunch," began Mrs. Jones.

"Old Mother Bristleback," growled the coachman.

"Old? why she ain't above four years older than me," said Mrs. Jones, bridling up. "As I was a saying, she's a confidential governess in a first-class ladies' establishment. She is coming to tea. If I might presume—"

"Let us have the honour of her company by all means," said the traveller.

"Ha! ha! ha!" laughed the coachman, with a regular fat chuckle that shook his ponderous

sides. "She's a good 'un, she is, but t'other—pushete," uttering an indescribable sound; "but you shall see, I won't say nothing, only if you wanted a wild cat for a menagerie she'd do beautiful."

The traveller smiled, and, after one or two sips at his brandy, went up stairs to prepare for the evening's amusement.

At tea-time he was dressed with extreme care, and was the very model of a preacher such as suits the fiery and highly-spiced tastes of the Spurgeon-hunting class of the community.

He was all in black, with a white neckcloth; a highly-starched stand-up collar, dark whiskers, and spectacles, the whole brought to a climax by a most solemn and sanctimonious cast of countenance.

Thus he was introduced to Miss Matilda Crunch as the Reverend Obadiah Simcox, of Smithville, United States of America.

CHAPTER LXIII.

THE UNDER-GOVERNESS.

THERE is no more praiseworthy vocation than that of devoting oneself exclusively to the education of the young. It is a sacred, a solemn, and a most responsible undertaking.

No one ought to venture on it without due deliberation, and with a capacity for the profession.

It is abominable that education should in any way be left to quacks and incapables; much more so that it should too often be the resource of the idle, profligate, and dissolute.

Miss Matilda Crunch was an old maid. It is the favourite theme of those who hold the pen to satirise this class of ladies, though why, it is perhaps hard to say, except that their own sex blame them for preserving the one virtue for which single ladies are chiefly admired.

Not that we venture to affirm that all so-called old maids are, by reason of that appellation, chaste—by no means! We should otherwise be strangely put to, to discover mothers for a great many apocryphal nieces and nephews with which the world abounds.

Now as to what category Miss Matilda Crunch belonged will be seen in the course of our narrative.

Miss Matilda Crunch called herself assistant-governess in the highly respectable ladies' school kept by the Misses Crumptons.

Now, as her duties consisted solely in taking out the boarders for walks, escorting home day-scholars, and mending clothes which had come to grief, our readers may give her a more subordinate appellation.

Be this as it may, at the tea-table of Mrs. Mary Jones she was a very important individual.

She spoke as the representative of the boarding-school.

Mrs. Jones looked up to her with reverence, and considered her coming to tea on half holidays—Wednesdays and Saturdays—as a great honour.

The Rev. Obadiah Simcox, as was the duty of a minister of the Gospel, was profoundly polite to Miss Matilda Crunch, though when he caught a comic expression of disgust on the jolly countenance of the coachman, he as nearly as possible exploded into a loud laugh.

Matilda Crunch was tall, spare, not to use the vulgar word scraggy, suspiciously red about the nose, and adorned with eyes that when irate might not have disgraced a hungry hawk.

Now there are many married women thin, ugly, and cross-grained; but they never excite the same remarks as virgins of the same age, simply because society feels that having done their duty in the world they should be allowed quietly to settle down into calm, unnoticed individuals.

"And how is all at the establishment?" said Mrs. Jones, after mixing her own and her friend's tea with rum.

"The establishment is, materially speaking, in a most prosperous way," said Matilda Crunch, with a groan.

"I hope nothing is amiss spiritually?" cried the minister, with an alarmed look.

"Oh! my good sir, it is not for me to say, but all is vanity. Our establishment is eaten up with that great and deadly sin. Our young ladies are carried away by all the wild fashions of the great city, even to the utter neglect of their immortal souls."

"Do they dance?" said the reverend, with a groan.

"They do."

"Do they sing?"

"They do."

"And play upon ungodly instruments?"

"I am sorry to say they do; and the worst of all is one lately introduced—a child of singular beauty—called Jessie——"

"Jessie what?" said the preacher, turning very red in the face.

"I don't know—I never heard. I only know that her mother is called Cornelia."

"Are you ill?" cried the landlady, as she noticed the preacher turn deadly pale.

"No, no—give me a little rum—only agitation. I once had a daughter called Jessie, and, strangely enough, my wife's name was Cornelia. Thank you—but the mother of this girl does not live at the school?"

"Oh no, sir. They live at Haythorne Lodge. There are two ladies. Miss Jessie has a cousin called Henry Haddington—"

"D———n!" muttered the preacher, but in so low a tone that none heard him.

"He attends classes at the rector's, and the two always return in the same carriage."

"I suppose they are very rich?"

"Immense; and as some folks are able to see no merit in anything but gold they are the pets of the school, the country, and the parsonage. I know what I know, but I can't help saying that the girl is truly lovely."

"And the lad—"

"A Adonis," said the spinster, energetically.

"And the girl a Venus," added the other with a smile.

"Yes, we're celebrated for our beautiful girls all over the country. I told you once," said the governess, with an odd smile.

"What!" cried the traveller.

"Nonsense," said Mrs. Jones, blushing and mincing.

The coachman grinned, the subject was changed, and the tea being removed soon after, spirits were introduced.

"Mind smoking?" said the coachman, with a nod.

"I like it; it promotes the flow of intellect," replied the traveller.

"I make it a rule," said the old maid, "never to do anything injurious to the harmony of society."

The coachman, who had heard this phrase twice a week for several years, immediately filled his pipe and ordered some brandy-and-water.

A game of whist was proposed, followed by supper and more grog, so that the traveller had no further opportunity of conversing with the assistant-governess on the interesting subject of the school.

At length eleven o'clock arrived, when the house, being orderly and well-conducted, did what every orderly and well-conducted house should do—closed.

The coachman buttoned up his coat, put on his comforter, and wishing the others good evening, retired to conduct the governess home, not without strong misgivings as to the propriety of leaving the somewhat luxurious traveller in company with his affianced wife.

Now the traveller had very different designs, but at the same time he had no objection to as many strings to his bow as fortune chose to give him, so the moment worthy John Jones turned his back he entered upon a learned discourse on the miseries of single blessedness, throwing out hints, not mysterious but loud, of his desire to enter again the holy bonds of matrimony, if he could but find a lady disposed to take pity on him.

Mrs. Jones blushed, and appeared by no means averse to a serious consideration of the matter.

The consequences will be explained hereafter.

CHAPTER LXIV.

THE BOARDING-SCHOOL.

THE establishment of the Misses Crumpton was on a very extensive scale, and was patronised not only by the neighbouring gentry but by the most distinguished families from every part of Great Britain.

It had a high reputation, and to have been educated at Moreton House was a very fair introduction to certain circles of society.

The most rigid references were exacted from all who aspired to the honours of an entrance, while a discipline as severe as that of a Sacre Cœur convent was carried out in reference to the male creation.

The professors were all old and ugly, while

even the male attendants were taken from the lame, the halt, and the blind.

All the ladies who held office under the superiors were sedate and grave as Sisters of Charity.

Not a poem, not a book any way resembling light literature, was allowed in the house, which explained the avidity with which the bigger girls devoured questionable French novels and immoral English ones with an avidity which was no wise surprising.

A judicious assortment of amusing works for leisure hours would have remedied this; but the very suggestion would have frightened the Misses Crumptons out of their senses.

In fact, we may tell the story of the education of these young ladies in some such words as Byron describes that of Don Juan :—

" The languages, especially the dead;
The sciences, and, most of all, the abstruse;
The arts, at least, all such as could be said
To be the most remote from common use:
In all these he was much and deeply read;
But not a page of anything that's loose,
Or hints continuation of the species
Was ever suffer'd, lest he should grow vicious."

Now it might be asked, how did the elder girls in this school become possessed of such works as those alluded to ?

Well, they all had ample pocket money, and there was in the house a black-eyed, lively girl of about nineteen—a servant with a sweetheart who subscribed to a circulating library to please his charming Kitty.

The catalogue was smuggled into the school —the serpent entered the Garden of Eden.

Let us take our readers within the charming circle of those who are to be the mothers of England.

Be not alarmed.

We are going to make no general attack on the most virtuous women in the world, or upon the most admirable system of education.

We must not, however, disguise from ourselves that there are exceptions to the rule.

To a certain extent this was the case at Moreton Hall. How, has only partially been explained.

We must now introduce our readers into the interior of the school, and describe it in such a way that subsequent events may be clearly understood.

The school was surrounded on all sides by high walls, which, in addition to protecting the court-yard and house, served to conceal a large and well laid-out garden, which served the young ladies for recreation and exercise.

A pretty flower and fruit garden, near to the establishment, was bounded by a lawn, of some extent itself, skirted by a small *bosquet*, or thicket of various trees, underneath which were seats and swings.

The lawn on the side of the garden was occupied by the younger ladies engaged in play, nursing their dolls, or making for them fantastic articles of clothing, in anticipation of those days when they should be similarly occupied with their own offspring.

The elder girls were scattered beneath the shade of the laburnums and other trees forming the thicket.

Some were swinging, some talking, while one group, concealed from view by the wavy boughs of a tree, surrounded a girl, who, with flashing eyes and ruddy cheeks, was reading out some pestilent novel of the fast school to the great delight of her hearers.

Every now and then they cast suspicious glances towards an arm-chair, where sat Miss Matilda Crunch, her whole mind and attention given to the unfortunate juveniles whom she kept under the strictest discipline.

Of course a number of young ladies, all very nearly arrived at years of discretion, could by no possibility come to any mischief—of course not.

But who are these two seated in a little arbour apart from the others, in earnest conversation ?

One is a tall, elegant, graceful English girl. She is five feet two, that happy medium for a woman which lends such charms to the unformed girl, such becoming dignity to the more voluptuous woman.

She was chastely dressed in a blue and white silk dress, with wide sleeves, while on her head was a hat of the finest Leghorn, unadorned except by a simple white ribbon.

Her face was dazzlingly fair, soft, white, and purely translucent; her forehead, not so low as to bespeak want of intellect, was not massive enough to be masculine. Her almond-shaped eyes were shaded by deep, silky eyelashes, that shaded their excessive brightness; while her lips, parted as if in wonder, showed her white and beautiful teeth.

Like a bursting waterfall of gold fell the flood of rich auburn hair upon her shoulders.

Her whole aspect was that of pure innocence and youthful beauty.

Her companion was much older, and very different.

She was taller than the fair girl—very tall she appeared.

Her figure was slight, excessively well proportioned, and being well displayed by a dark and low-cut silk dress, revealed the budding beauties of what promised to be a most voluptuous form—when love and passion should have further ripened it.

She was dark. Her hair and eyes were jet-black, with a piercing expression in the latter which struck her companion with a kind of awe.

Her face, though very beautiful, was of the heavy Napoleonic style of face.

She was a French girl, and had come from Paris armed with the most unexceptionable references, both from her own country-people and from English families.

Her name was Julie De Lorme.

She had been telling Jessie her history.

She had no mother; her father was rich; but his views were those of an old noble of ancient days. His son would inherit all his fortune, while she must either marry a man for his money, turn governess, or enter a convent for the remainder of her days.

"Mine is a sad fate ! You at fifteen, a mere child in age, have owned to me that you love. What, then, must be my feelings at eighteen ? I sigh for love, I live for love, I pant for love;

it burns my very soul, and yet I know not what it is. I have seen no man except our ugly old teachers to speak to."

"My Henry—"

"Is a boy. When you are a woman he will be a man, and as your favourite, Scott, says 'high and perilous adventure is not Henry's fate. He would never have been his celebrated ancestor Sir Nigel, but only Sir Nigel's eulogist and poet. I will tell you where he will be—at home, my dear, and in his place; in the quiet circle of domestic happiness, lettered indolence and elegant enjoyments of Waverley and honour. And he will refit the old library in the most exquisite Gothic taste, and garnish its shelves with the rarest and most valuable volumes; and he will draw plans and landscapes, and write verses, and rear temples, and dig grottoes; and he will stand in a clear summer night in the colonnade before the hall, and gaze on the deer as they stray in the moonlight, or lie shadowed by the boughs of the huge old fantastic oaks; and he will repeat verses to his beautiful wife, who will hang upon his arm, and he will be a happy man.' "

"And she will be a happy woman," laughed Jessie, unconsciously continuing the quotation. "But you are mistaken, Julie, Henry is a man of action and enterprise. There is more beneath his still and quiet manner than you would believe."

"It may be so, but your English boys seem to me all very childish," said Julie.

"Fancy."

"When I have a lover, and I will have one," continued the energetic French girl, "I will have a man, one I can look up to and admire."

A long and piteous tale had the romantic young lady told to Jessie, full of sighs and interjections, with here and there a sorrowful episode, until Jessie had, from very pity, learned to love her.

Jessie had been sent three times a week to the school to finish her in her French, and to improve her music. As she and Julie always spoke in the former language, the first object was admirably obtained.

After a few days the two young ladies became inseparable.

And yet, had this schoolgirl friendship been strictly inquired into, it would have been found that the whole of the advances had come from the elder girl. Jessie was too timid, too gentle, too retiring to force herself upon one so much her senior.

And then a secret monitor, one of those gentle warnings which come to us so distinctly and yet so faintly as to take no body or form, seemed to tell her that the connection was not one that she should have entered upon so lightly.

Julie was bold, audacious, and spoke of love in a crude and masculine way, which often shocked Jessie.

But then the other knew as well how to temper the fire of discourse with some sentimental change, to open the tender flood-gates of the heart by a tale of grief and sorrow. She had suffered much in her youth, and the sympathetic soul of Jessie excused all her faults because of the sorrow of her youthful days,

passed under the supervision of a hard stepmother.

"I certainly should not like a convent," said Jessie, after a pause. "I should think any position better than the four walls of a prison house."

"You are right; and yet," cried the other, with one of her light laughs, "if all we read in story books be true, lovers are not wanting even in convents. There, my little prude, don't be angry, only look at *la grande* Edith, how she turns up her eyes to the ceiling, and clasps that letter to her lips. She is in love."

Jessie looked, and saw a girl she had often noticed, but rarely had spoken to—

Edith De Lancy was a tall girl of eighteen, very pale, with deep blue eyes, flaxen hair, and a sorrowful, but kind and gentle cast of countenance.

She was timid, retiring, tender-natured, incapable of much exertion, but loving, faithful, and true-hearted.

She had finished her studies, except amusing herself with music and singing, but no one came to take her away. She dined with the ladies, and never went out except in a carriage, accompanied by one of the Misses Crumpton.

Beside the arbour in which the two girls were seated was a small round spot of grass, occupied by a statue.

It was sheltered and lonely, being overhung by trees.

A garden arm-chair filled up one corner, and to this spot Edith de Lancy took her way.

CHAPTER LXV.

THE RENDEZVOUS.

EDITH sat down, and, unconscious that she was observed, took from her bosom a letter, which she first kissed, then bedewed with her tears, and finally read.

Jessie would have retired, but Julie made her a sign to remain.

"You see," she whispered, "what love can do. It turns that tall, gawky girl into quite a beauty. While she reads the mad rhapsody in her hand she looks quite heavenly."

"She is beautiful," replied Jessie.

"They say she is very rich," continued Julie.

"Her father is one of the richest baronets in England," replied Jessie.

"I would lay my life," added the romantic French girl, "that her lover is poor."

"Why?"

"Because she seems so broken-hearted," replied Julie.

Jessie smiled, and owned that the guess was tolerably reasonable.

"We ought to befriend her," added Julia, clasping her hands, her dark eyes flashing with excitement.

"But how can we? Besides, we ought to know nothing whatever about it. Should we even be seen looking at her now it would bespeak an unfair amount of curiosity."

Julie smiled, and turned away her head to

avoid the other seeing something very like a grimace.

Suddenly she turned back again, and laid her hand upon the other's arm.

"What is it?" whispered Jessie.

"Some one is climbing upon the wall."

Jessie looked in the direction indicated, and saw that a ladder was being fixed against the wall of the enclosure. The first impulse of Jessie was to go away, under the impression that she really had no business there, but a strange, unaccountable impulse compelled her to remain.

Presently the ladder appeared fixed, and for a moment all was still.

The two girls watched with intense anxiety.

Edith de Lancy continued still moodily the perusal of his letter.

Then a head was seen to rise above the wall, and Julie de Lorme was obliged to thrust her handkerchief into her mouth to prevent her laughing, while Jessie placed her hand upon her heart, unable to speak, sit down, or articulate a sound.

It was the young lover of Jessie—Henry Haddington.

Now, as he could see Jessie every day, his object in thus clandestinely visiting the school-ground looked remarkably suspicious, and so Mademoiselle Julie seemed to think.

"It's Monsieur Henri," she said, with a suppressed giggle.

"I know it," replied Jessie, very pale, but very calm.

Henry looked about him carefully, and perceiving no one in sight but Edith, looked downwards, and appeared for a moment in conference with some one.

He then descended. Julie looked graver, and Jessie smiled.

In a moment more another head rose above the wall, that of a young man in the costume of a naval officer.

He was about four-and-twenty. His fine oval face was skirted by silky black whiskers, his eyes, black and piercing, were beaming with excitement and happiness, as they fell upon the sad figure of the contemplative maiden.

"Edith," he said, in a low, but distinct whisper.

"Charles?" gasped the young girl, leaping to her feet, and next minute they were clasped in one another's arms.

"Come away," said Jessie.

"They will be found out," replied Julie, in a hoarse voice, her eyes fixed, with a basilisk glance upon the handsome sailor.

"Then we must let them know we are here," continued Jessie, speaking loud. "I will not play the eavesdropper."

And she stepped out upon the lawn. Julie followed her with a pout.

"I wish you to know," said Jessie, "that we are aware of your presence in the garden. I will add that I am surprised at my cousin Henry mixing himself up in an affair of this kind."

"You are, Jessie," replied the young officer, taking off his cap with a profound bow, while Edith clung in a terrified way to his arm.

"He is my husband," she said, after a few moments.

"My name is Jessie," continued our heroine, "and if, indeed, you are husband and wife, I cannot doubt that you are cruelly parted. But beware, the governess has looked several times this way: if you are found there will be a terrible noise, and the school will be ruined."

"I will but speak a few words to my wife," said the young man, "and then I will go."

"Married?" said Julie in a hoarse and unnatural tone, "so young and so handsome!"

"They are a well-matched pair," observed Jessie.

Julie made no reply. The young officer was leaving. He bowed low to Jessie and went away, his departure being assisted by Henry, who little thought in what tragic affairs he was mixing himself up.

Edith turned towards the two girls, and taking a hand of each begged them not to betray her.

"If you only knew my history," she said.

"Tell it to us," cried Julia.

"The younger girls are going in to lunch," said Edith, "you stop with me. I can have anyone to dine with me when I please; hitherto I have desired to be alone, but now—"

And her eyes brightened up as she turned towards Miss Matilda Crunch.

"Will you be kind enough," she said, "to inform the Misses Crumpton that Miss Julie and Jessie will dine with me at four?"

Miss Matilda made a low obedience. Miss Edith was to be humoured in all things consistent with her safety.

They now all returned to the arbour, and seating themselves Miss Edith, as we must still call her, began to tell her story.

CHAPTER LXVI.

A STORY OF A HEART.

I AM the only daughter of Sir Edward de Lancy, the oldest baronet, I believe, in the whole roll of the kingdom.

It is not my wish or intention to speak harshly of my father, whose character, however, I must develope more by circumstances than remarks.

He was the only son of Ireton de Lancy by his first wife, who died shortly after giving birth to this child.

My grandfather was passionately fond of his wife, and for many years refused to be comforted. He even refused to see his child, who grew up apart from him among strangers.

In time, however, grief wore away, and at length my grandfather, wearied of loneliness, married a second wife, one of the kindest and best of women.

Her first act was to bring home the child who had been so long exiled from his father's home, and from that hour until the day of his death she never treated him in any other way than as her own child.

To her also a son was born, who was twelve years younger than my father.

It may have been because of his early exile from home, or because of other causes, but my father never liked his brother, my uncle Walter.

The difference of age, of itself, was enough to account for a want of sympathy.

But I am afraid my father hated him.

My father was sole heir to the baronetcy and the estates, while my uncle inherited only a very moderate income and his mother's fortune.

He went into the navy, married early, won distinction, and had one son, Charles.

My father did not marry until after his father's death, and then to the beauty of the country.

My mother was—is—as good as she is beautiful.

But she had one fearful fault in my father's eyes.

She never had a son.

After my birth she never had a child.

My father, I am told, has never smiled for years on this very ground.

He was never what is called cruel to my mother; but he was cold, harsh, and repellent.

He was polite in the extreme, and, before strangers, showed all due deference and affection.

But the want of a son rankled in his bosom all the more that he knew my cousin Charles, the son of his brother the admiral, was his heir.

Any allusion to this circumstance drove him mad, and his only happiness, I am sorry to say, appeared to be derived from the fact that father and son were both on an unhealthy West Indian station.

My father gave his mind much to politics, and represented his county with *eclat*.

He was a strictly honourable man and devoted himself to the interests of his constituents with great energy.

During the session, my mother's health being very delicate, we avoided town, and resided at Brighton.

The air agreed with my dear mamma, and I was always fond of the sea.

I was past eighteen. You smile. I am nearly twenty years of age now.

It was in July. We had been out for a drive on the Lewes road, when there suddenly came a thick darkness over the sky. Every sign became visible of a coming storm, and we hurried towards home.

I never before or since ever saw such lightning or heard such thunder.

The coachman could scarcely hold the terrified horses, which reared and galloped and evinced every desire to bolt.

My mother sat up as white as a sheet, while I nestled in her bosom.

It was an open barouche, and neither the coachman or footman could close the carriage. It was as much as they could do to keep their seats.

"It is going to rain; we shall be wet through," said my mother, with a shudder.

"A fearful shower is coming on," cried a voice near us. "Ladies, the storm is increasing in violence. Will you allow me to offer you the shelter of the barracks."

We accepted, without the slightest hesitation, this offer, and, before we were conscious of who had assisted us, were in a large warm room in company with several officers in the army, and some gentlemen in plain clothes.

"Lady de Lancy," said the gallant colonel of the regiment, "this is indeed a lucky chance. Sir Walter de Lancy, Mr. Charles de Lancy."

But the admiral had leaped forward and taken my mother's two hands, while Charles was shaking hands with me.

It was a most delightful and romantic meeting, and made, necessarily, a strong impression upon two young people.

From that day the admiral and his son became constant visitors to our house.

We were very happy.

I and Charles were affianced before we had known one another a week.

Then came my father, whose rage at the return of his brother and nephew to Europe knew no bounds.

He treated them with haughty and stern politeness, bowed them out, and the same evening took us off to London.

We resided in Grosvenor-square.

My father gave my mother strict injunctions never to be at home to his relatives.

He said not a word to me. It would, I fear, under any circumstances have been useless. My heart was wholly gone.

As a matter of course, Charles found me out without the slightest difficulty. My father's address could not be concealed.

Letters, such letters as I believe lovers only can write, poured in upon me two or three times a day; and at last, moved by his earnest entreaties, I consented to see him.

We met every evening in the enclosure of the square of which I had the key, and in an hour of frenzy—he expected every day to sail for foreign parts—I agreed to marry him.

He put up the banns in a pretty village near London, and one morning, after leaving a note for my parents, I went out.

I took a hackney coach and met him at the appointed place. He seated himself by my side, and in a state bordering on delirium—half happy, half alarmed—we took our way to the church.

Everything was ready, even to the witnesses, and in less than twenty minutes we were man and wife.

I took my husband's arm, and prepared to leave the church, when a loud noise was heard, and my father, with several servants and two officers, entered the sacred edifice.

He was pale with rage. He clutched my arm and dragged me away. Before Charles could explain himself, and claim his rights, I was torn away, thrust into a carriage, and brought here.

I have never seen or heard from my family since I have been in this place, and began to fear that I was about for the future to remain here when I saw my husband.

"Since the day of your marriage," said Julie, with an odd smile, "you have never once seen your husband?"

"Never!"

PEEPING TOM.

"Then you are a wife only in name," continued Julie De Lorme.

"That is all," said Edith, with downcast eyes, her cheeks suffused with radiant blushes.

Jessie opened her eyes wide, but said nothing.

"And now, what do you mean to do?"

"To join my husband. He is with his ship here, but has written for leave of absence. That once obtained he will provide me with a home."

"And you mean to stay here without seeing him?"

"No."

"What mean you?"

"He will visit me almost every night until all is ready for my flight. My room is concealed by a thicket. I can easily open my window."

This was said with a charming confusion that made the young girl's features quite lovely.

Julie laughed an odd, dry, peculiar laugh.

"And when does Leander pay his first visit to Hero?" she said.

"To-night; but come to dinner. We can talk at our leisure."

An hour later Jessie left for home, after a promise of strict secrecy.

Henry accompanied her. He said not a word about his share of the adventure.

———

CHAPTER LXVII.

A MYSTERY.

It was nearly midnight. The sky was clear and bright, stars twinkled in the blue heavens, and a soft and gentle wind sighed through the trees.

It was a night for a stroll by the seaside, or beneath the leafy arches of a forest, but not for a rendezvous of love.

The very stars themselves seemed to look down with disapproval on the clandestine nature of the business.

And the trees seemed to be whispering something as they laid their heads together highly unfavourable to the interview.

And yet what more proper than that a young husband should be stealing to the arms of his lovely and expectant wife?

Pity, sigh our fair and pitying readers, that a husband should be compelled to be thus seeking happiness by stealth.

But the course of true love never did run smooth, and what truer love is there than that consecrated by matrimony?

Edith had every luxury which she could wish for. Her room was in a projecting wing at a considerable distance from the sleeping apartments of the other girls, whose dormitories were in a well-ventilated wing at the back.

She had a piano, a collection of well selected books, and permission to read up to any time she thought proper.

An attendant slept in an outer room

Edith had given her several glasses of wine.

Love is a wonderful sharpener of women's wits. There is a French tale entitled—"How girls learn what is what." We fancy that the little god Cupid is the most successful teacher.

Then Edith ,to pass away the time, played the piano, but sadly out of tune.

This failing, she tried to read.

But, and we appeal to every young lady who has known what it is to wait the coming of a favourite swain, what, in such a case, is the use of reading?

The one feeling absorbs all others—we read without seeing, without understanding.

Edith sat at her open window.

The hour of his coming was to be midnight. Never had the time passed with such fearful slowness. The very minutes appeared to be interminable.

Then the clock of a neighbouring church began to strike.

Edith drew a long breath.

Then she distinctly counted twelve.

She could have counted the beatings of her own heart had she been so inclined.

And still he came not.

Hark, what noise is that? it surely is the sound of human footsteps, advancing slowly, but still distinctly and audibly.

Edith seemed to feel the burning kiss of her passionate young husband on her lips.

She clasped her hands, closed her eyes, and listened.

Still a sound, but, instead of nearer and nearer, receding farther and farther.

What could it mean?

And then the sound altogether ceased.

Edith leaned out, and, bending her head low, listened with the eager ear of the watcher.

Not a sound.

With a strange dread upon her soul she stepped across the iron balustrade of her window, and slid out into the garden.

Scarcely knowing what she did, she ran through the shrubbery towards the spot where she expected her husband to cross the wall.

She even ventured to call him by name, but no answering voice came to console her wildly beating heart.

Had his presence been discovered by one of her father's emissaries?

This uncertainty was, indeed, very dreadful. Still, hoping against hope, she wrapped a thin shawl over her head and waited.

But he came not.

The clock struck one, and, wearied and heartsick she turned towards her chamber.

What new mystery is this?

Her chamber window is closed.

She pushes against it; it does not yield. The thick, curtains are drawn inside.

Edith felt ready to faint. What fearful combination of circumstances had taken place? In what way could she possibly explain this strange, almost terrible event?

Could her attendant have arisen, and, fancying her in bed, have closed the window?

How, then, could she explain her presence in the garden.

Chilled to the very heart, fainting with shame, terror, and despair, she sank at the foot of a tree, and, shuddering all over, closed her eyes.

In no way that she could conceive could she think of any rational explanation of this most strange mystery.

The want of faith in Charles de Lancy she ascribed to any cause but his own fault.

Poor Edith knew, in her own person, the sweets and bitters of a first rendezvous.

She had thought of nothing else all day. She doubted not that he had done the same.

But if, indeed, anything had occurred to prevent his coming, why had her chamber window been so unaccountably closed.

She felt as if she should go mad.

It was a warm night, and at last she sobbed herself to sleep.

She appeared to have slept only a few minutes when she was awoke by the chill of the dawn, and the loud chirripping of birds on all sides.

She rubbed her eyes and started to her feet.

Her chamber window was wide open.

Dizzy, puzzled, exhausted, she crawled into the room.

Why does she start back, still more pale and haggard, still more wan and trembling than before?

Her long locks hang down, wet with the dew, her eyes start from her head.

A dark frown settles on her brow.

Had she been dreaming?

No.

She had passed the night in the garden, and yet her bed had been occupied.

Two persons had slept in it.

A bottle of wine she had provided for her husband had been emptied.

Two glasses had been stained by wine.

A flush of indignation, of scorn, of contempt, passed along the young girl's face.

Her husband had been there.

But who had taken *her* place?

The very thought made her blood tingle and rush to her head, blinding her vision for a moment.

Had Charles de Lancy joined in the trick against her?

How could she tell?

A sickness, a deadly faintness came over her soul, and she would have fallen, but it was in the direction of the bed.

A convulsive shudder passed through her frame, and, seating herself in an arm-chair, she burst into tears. Then she roused herself, dried her eyes, and sat herself down to think.

What should be her course of action?

Believe her husband wilfully guilty she would not.

She must, however, be sure of what she did. Could she prove any one guilty she felt within herself that no revenge could be too fearful.

That she had been thus maliciously deprived of her husband's society she might look over, but that while she was shivering in the garden another——

The thought was maddening.

Plotting, thinking, her weariness overcame her, and she slept. When she woke she was calmer.

She was very pale, but she dressed herself with extreme care. She endeavoured, as much as possible, to avoid appearing as if anything extraordinary had happened.

About one she went out into the garden.

On the lawn was pacing up and down a young girl.

Her cheeks were flushed, and her eye flashed with a triumphant glance.

It was Julie de Lorme.

Edith started back as if she had trod upon a rattle-snake on the pathless prairies.

She had yet to learn that a woman is often possessed of a sting worse than that of any serpent.

Julie stopped and advanced as if to offer her hand.

"Cockatrice!" said Edith, with a smile of superb contempt.

"Oh," cried Julie, standing back, "so you've guessed it, have you? I hope you enjoyed your moonlight stroll."

"Wretch," said Edith, biting her lips until the blood came, "I will expose you!"

"Keep my secret," replied Julie coolly, "and I will keep yours. Another time do not open your mouth so wide to one who is quite as weary of solitude as you are yourself."

"But what villanous trickery? I will expose you both."

"Mrs. de Lancy," said Julie, with her cold smile, "your very good natured but very silly husband knows nothing. Keep your own counsel and I will keep mine."

And the audacious girl turned away, leaving Edith nearly mad with rage.

How could she expose the profligate girl without ruining her own prospects.

But in a few days she should be her own master, and then a full confession would be in her power.

Edith smiled. To the best of women a little revenge is sweet, especially when it is in a case of love-larceny.

But she would take care that Charles should not again be inveigled by any syren.

She turned pale.

She had only arranged with him for the one rendezvous; how could she arrange a second?

Suddenly the thought struck her that Jessie might be able to assist her.

But Jessie would not be there that day.

She must wait and bear all the terrible fever of suspense. At all events she would not witness the sneering and complacent smile of her rival.

She retired to her chamber, and came forth no more.

One only thought consoled her, the idea she hugged to her bosom, that revenge was sweet.

And thus the day wore away.

CHAPTER LXVIII.

THE BOARDING SCHOOL.

THE traveller having satisfactorily secured the friendship, to say the least of it, of Mrs. Mary Jones, the buxom landlady of the Dolphin, began to lay himself out for his other schemes.

The conversation with Miss Matilda Crunch had set him thinking.

One of the objects he had chiefly in view was to secure the person of some resplendent beauty.

Jessie, according to all account, was just what his imagination had figured to himself.

But how to obtain a sight of her.

He, after some hesitation, determined to write to Miss Matilda Crunch. This plan he at once carried out, but penned his epistle with extreme care. While leaving her to infer that his sentiments were very tender he begged her to second him in a plan which might be conducive to his interests in life.

He proposed for a short time to pass for a cousin just arrived from America, and in this character to gain admission to the school. His wish was to deliver some lectures on America to the young ladies.

Miss Matilda, who for some years had been dying to change her name, and who saw in this plan some hope, readily agreed.

She obtained leave for her cousin to call.

He was received in the state drawing-room by the two Misses Crumpton in person.

Matilda Crunch, humble and retiring, stood in the background.

"Good morning, sir," said Miss Crumpton, rising

from her chair, and curtseying with great dignity.

"We understand you wish to visit your cousin Miss Matilda Crunch, our esteemed assistant."

"If I might meet with your approbation," replied the traveller, with a low bow.

"Well, sir;—we, that is, my sister and myself, are not in the habit of permitting male visits to our establishment, but at the same time we think that a little judicious relaxation of rule, in the case of one so highly esteemed and regarded, cannot but be productive of good. Supposing we say, then, once a week, for one hour, in this room."

"Thank you, madam," said the traveller, humbly.

"I am deeply obliged," repeated Matilda.

"I have travelled much," continued the stranger. "I have wandered through every part of North and South America. I have hunted buffalos, crossed a wide and deep stream on the back of an alligator—"

"My dear sir,—fie!" said the eldest Miss Crumpton, gravely; "don't you think that statement slightly—shall we say—hyperbolical!"

"No, madam," continued the other. "I have seen more wonderful things than that. In crossing the stony desert beyond the prairies, on the back of an elephant, I and my companions drove a whole troop of tigers into a river and drowned them."

The sisters exchanged glances.

Matilda turned very pale.

"But it is not necessary to enlarge upon all I have seen. My reason for mentioning the matter was that, in these days of progressive enlightenment, it is necessary that even young ladies should be well informed on every topic, and I thought that my experiences might be embodied with advantage in a series of lectures."

"Sir," said Miss Crumpton, with awful gravity. "I have the word of Miss Matilda Crunch to the statement that you are her cousin; I can see that you are a gentleman of very varied talents; but, sir, I am sorry to observe—I can equally perceive—addicted to saying that which is not—"

"Madam."

"You perhaps forget that, for the proper discharge of our duty to the numerous young ladies confided to our charge, it is necessary that we should be well informed on every topic; now our books teach us that Waterton story of riding on the back of an alligator is untrue, that elephants and tigers are inhabitants of Asia and Africa only; and so," rising. "we wish you a very good morning, and decline your lectures."

So saying, the virtuously indignant ladies sailed out of the room.

"Oh, sir ——"

"Couple of starched old tabbies," said the traveller, very red in the face, "of course I was only joking."

"You should never joke with the head of an establishment like this, and, after what has happened, I think you had better stay away. I can see you on Wednesday and Saturday."

"All is not lost, my dear madam. I will explain more fully when we meet again. My brain teems with a great and glorious future, which, madam, if you can but comprehend, you shall share. To-morrow night I will explain."

Matilda Crunch looked down, blushed, giggled, and, after promising to meet him, accepted a chaste salute, and then they parted.

CHAPTER LXIX.

A NEW AGENT.

THE rage and fury which filled the bosom of the Mormon agent at the immediate discovery of his shallow artifice was unbounded.

His purpose in England was both to make proselytes and to make money, both for himself and the band of impostors he so worthily represented.

He had even dared to aspire to filling his harem from the body of young and fresh beauties of a boarding school.

Nothing is too young, too pure, too sacred for the maw of a Mormon elder.

Nothing can equal the infatuation of the silly dupes who are led away by them.

The women in this country who go forth to join them do so with their eyes open.

They know that they go only to swell the concubines of a Mormon harem.*

* We insert a letter, the original of which is in our possession. As is the case with every dupe-letter written from Utah, it exhibits great simplicity, ignorance, and want of education. We must also premise that no letters are allowed to pass the post-office but what are read by elders:—"it is with pleasure I take my pen in hand to address a few lines to you. but I *supose* that you think by this time we have *forgoton* you, or that we never intended to write any more, but we have not *forgoton* you, nor I dont expect we ever shall at least we dont feel inclined to do that, and as for writing we have been *puting* it off from time to time thinking that we should have *moar* news to tell you. I *supose* that before this letter reaches you that you have heard that we have arrived in Utah, at least —— is back in the states but she *or* repented staying *their* by the way she writes to us. she says if she sells all her *close* she will come next year. the reason she stayed beyond was her Mrs *perswaded* her to stop and she promised her a great many things *if she wand* stay but I dont supose she will full fill one of them. we like *hear rerry* much, this is the Conntry where a poor man can get rich you can be your own master and show you independance to a good advantage. most every man out *hear as* a farm of his own and *as* plenty of stock such as horses *mulles oxern* Cows sheep and so on and so forth, and a man can get these things if he is *industrious* and Brigham Young is a *good* man, and I think every one loves him out *hear* their is good land out hear, they have some coal here and plenty of wood, Farming is the chief business out here we had a *rerry* pleasernt Journey out here far better than what I expected we had forty wagons and a boat one hundred and fifty head of cattle with us the Indiande are *rerry* peacable if you do not *intearfear* with them will not with you I never felt afraid of them nor they with me. I *goast* to go and shake hands with them and talk to them as well as I could some understand Englash language *rerry well* we never had any *dearths* in our train and everything went *rerry* orderly. —— is married to a man by the name of —— he is an American she is second wife she is *rerry* happy and comfortable the *larst* letter she wrote to me she said that she had not repented the step she had *takern*, HE IS VERY WELL OFF he as got a large farm plenty of Stock he keeps his carriage horses *mulles* so on and so forth, and above all that he is a good man he is *rerry* intelligent he wanted me but I *thort* that I *woud* have one nearer my own age I am not married yet, although I might have been time and again I was once engaged to a young man he was very rich but his riches was a curse to him I found out he was very fond of drink and so I *woud* not have him he was a merchant he made me several very handsome preserents, and they are valuable I might have had *a relatiee* of his he

To any right-minded English woman or girl the very idea must be utterly infamous.

What then must be the state of mind of those who go with their eyes open into the mighty brothel, the Sodom and Gomorrah of America.

They must be of the same deluded class of those that follow the procuresses of London, Paris, and Brussels.

Weak, silly, and vain moths flying to the flame!

But this man was baulked at the outset. While under the impression that he was ear-wigging a couple of silly old maids, he, to use a common phrase, "put his foot in it."

But did this man despair?

By no means.

He had measured human credulity, and he knew it to be boundless as the ocean.

To him the whole world was made up of knaves and fools.

To calm his agitation, however, he first took a stiff glass of brandy-and-water, lit a cigar, and then strolled down towards an unfrequented portion of the beach.

He required to be cool and collected to think over his plan.

There were forty girls, from fourteen to eighteen, in the school.

He had made up his mind to carry away ten of the loveliest.

He was all the more resolved to do so that he had been snubbed and insulted.

The man's soul was made up of venom, lust, and hate; and the more he deserved anything which another might inflict the more he loathed the inflictor.

His determination was to ruin the school by some great scandal.

He had made up his mind that the scandal should burst in such a way that it should not be hushed up.

But with all his talent for scheming, with all his villanous art and devilry, he could as yet devise nothing.

It is no fiction that when we are bent on mischief the devil is always ready at our elbow.

He is always there, and requires to be driven away—not summoned by unholy incantations.

The "devil" is generally but the evil desires of our own hearts.

But sometimes he is bodily active in our behalf.

If he had selected an infernal instrument, a pair, indeed, of plotters of most foul wickedness, he could not have outdone the two he now threw together.

A stream cast itself, at some little distance from the town, through a mass of rocky lumps into the sea.

Above the rocks was a deep pool.

A man in humble garb, his back turned towards the traveller, was lazily casting his rod into the water.

The traveller strolled towards him, and, seating himself on a stone, looked at him listlessly. Presently his attention was attracted by the man himself.

About twenty, slightly made, of elegant form, not to be concealed by coarse habiliments, his face was one which to certain tastes was perfection.

His features were very small and regular, the skin white and fair; his whiskers silky and black, his hair the same.

He was a very handsome, though effeminate young man.

But the strange, languid, but still lustrous eyes, seemed to say that if effeminacy were there it was the effeminacy produced by debauchery and excess.

Those eyes were surely never seen but on the face of one of the children of night, the favoured sons of Lucifer.

"You'll know me again, old one," he said presently with a laugh. Such a laugh! it must have gone to the heart of a woman who only judged by outward show.

"Well, perhaps I shall. Have a cigar?"

"Don't mind," replied the youth, throwing down his rod; "this work's devilish wearisome."

"Why do you fish then?"

"Why," said the other, puffing away at his half-lighted cigar, "were you ever, my good fellow, so doosed hard up that you hadn't a shot to fly with—no bacca, no lush, no grub, and, worse than all, no money, eh!"

"Well, I cannot say that I ever was."

"Well, I tell you, then, if you ever were you'd be glad to fish for want of something better to do."

"It's slow work," said the elder.

"Slow!" cried the other, lying back and

---

is a good man but I do not like him, I have plenty of offers but I do not want to get married yet the winters are very long out here but the Folks seem to enjoy themselves very much in the dance dancing is fashionable here, and they have splendid musice the halls in the Citty are large and commodious and fixed up in excelent stile you wood be suplised if you was to see them when taken all things into consideration it is suprising to see what a beautiful Citty this is knowing what a short time the people have been here to build and what ill convernances they have been put to in getting the things to build with I have been to twelve balls this season and expect to go to more I have been to two where Brigham Young was I have seen him dance I am going up to his house this afternoon, I am acquainted with a young maman (woman?) that his teaching school for him so I am going to see her she says that she as been into Famileys in the states where their has been only one wife and their as been more discord in that Family then what their is in the whole of his Family she says they are united and happy they are going to build a splendid Temple out here and some large halls this summer, we here that the states are in a dreadfull confushion and I expect they will be they have killed a prophet of the Lord and they will have to suffer for it we believe that Brigham Young will yet be presedance of the united states, Joseph Smiths prophecies are being fullfiled every day I wish that you was hear you wood enjoy yourself verry much and you would do well you had ought to make up your mind and come Father his going to take up land and is going farming he thinks that you and him wood do well togeather you must make up your mind to come if you ever go to R—— call upon M—— and tell them we are well and wood like to hear from them Give our love to Mrs —— and to all enquiring Friends give our love to uncle—and when you write let us know how they are getting on I hope he is doing better give my love to —— I hope she is better and married by this time I must conclude we all send our love &c &c

"P.S.—We often have the Indians come to our door they paint their Faces red and their hair is black."

We apologise for the length of this letter, but we must give everything we can explanatory of the Mormons.

laughing; "so it is; but do you see those four perch in the grass there? Well, that and all I catch this afternoon will be my dinner. Tick's up."

"May I inquire what your profession may be."

"You're mighty curious, old gentleman; but as your cigar is very good, and I see one or two more, I don't mind telling you."

"I've plenty of cigars, and money, too, for all that."

"A mighty stupid thing to say to a starving man," said the other, with a devilish twinkle in his eye.

"Not a bit," replied the elder, drawing out a pistol, "I always provide against accidents."

"Ha! ha! ha!" cried the other, laughing still more heartily, "well, what say you to the sock and buskin."

"A goodly profession, but bad for the pocket. What line do you take?"

"Hamlet, Othello, Romeo, the Dog of Montargis—anything, comic or serious."

"Humph," said the Mormon, laying his hand upon his arm, "there is a part you might play with profit."

"What is that?" cried the other, eagerly.

"That of a young foreign nobleman on his travels, with plenty of money in his pockets, and nothing to do but to make love and flirt with the girls."

The youth's eyes flashed fire.

"Are you jesting me? If I thought so, pistol or no pistol, I'd knock you on the head and throw you in the pool."

"My impetuous young gentleman," said the Mormon, coolly. "I am not jesting. I never jest except with my intimate friends. If you will light your cigar and listen I will endeavour to explain myself in a way which shall be mutually satisfactory."

The other lit his cigar and listened attentively.

Half-an-hour later they parted, apparently with a thorough understanding. The traveller returned to his inn and dined, the angler shouldered his rod and went away whistling gaily.

CHAPTER LXX.

PEEPING TOM.

NEXT morning a square, official looking letter, with three large seals, came addressed to the Reverend Simcox, who opened it eagerly in presence of his worthy friend Mrs. Jones, who was making tea for him.

"My goodness," he said, letting it fall.

"My gracious, what is the matter!" said the buxom hostess.

"Who would have thought it. I find that some kind friend of mine in Paris has appointed me travelling tutor to the young Viscount de Florac, a gentleman who, on coming of age, will have an income of forty thousand a-year."

"My gracious."

"He is travelling in search of me, and wants to find a quiet hotel here where he can put up for a time."

"I am afraid my house would not be good enough for him," said Mrs. Jones.

"My dear madam these rich young noblemen have no nonsense about them. Besides, I am directed in this letter to inculcate humility, and to look after his health and moral habits. Where could I bring him to a more thoroughly homely and comfortable place. I engage your best bedroom for him, another for his valet. We can have this room for meals. He will be here to-morrow;"

Mrs. Jones leaped up. Her face was very red. Though her inn was often used by respectable families as an hotel, she had never yet had a count with forty thousand a year.

"My dear madam, let us finish our breakfast," said the Rev. Mr. Simcox, mildly. "You will have ample time to prepare. I am quite sure that, in so well ordered a house as yours, there will be very little to do."

Mrs. Jones looked radiant with delight, and yielded readily to the wishes of the arch impostor.

The scheme he had devised was one of the most devilish ever imagined, and never could have entered the brain of any but a fiend in human shape.

But there is nothing to which the love of power, lust, and avarice will not drive some men.

As delighted and radiant as if he had done a good action, the Rev. Mr. Simcox went out after dinner. He strolled away towards a certain walk, where, by common consent, Miss Matilda Crunch was to pass with the school.

He had not long to wait.

In less than half an hour he saw the head of the column advancing preceded by Miss Matilda Crunch, and a very pretty blue-eyed girl of sixteen, who always, by direction of the Misses Crumpton walked with the governess.

It was a wide, shady walk, with seats.

The traveller sat a little back, where he could see them all.

His grey eye took in the whole bevy of beauties at a glance. He thought he had never seen so much loveliness before.

But he starts and turns pale as, next to the governess, he descries a fine, handsome, young woman arm in arm with a lovely child.

It was Edith and Jessie, henceforth inseparable.

The man turned away as if to avoid being seen.

In two years more she will be glorious; fit, indeed, for the high priestess of the new and false religion.

The whole school passed without even glancing at him once.

What did they care about an ugly middle-aged man?

Poor girls! They little imagined, some of them, how much he thought about them.

Giving them an advance of a hundred yards, he rose and followed them.

They were going quite out into the fields.

At length they reached a large meadow beside a running stream. It had the additional merit of having a shady grove on one side.

It was entirely unfrequented.

Indeed it was private, and intruders would have been instantly warned off.

The young ladies were free from all intrusion, as the Misses Crumpton paid rent for the use of the field.

They, accordingly, ran about without fear of being overlooked.

Some played hoop, others hide and seek, some battledore, while others put together beautifully made fishing-rods; others, again, ran races, and all enjoyed themselves freely, in the full conviction that no one belonging to the male sex could overlook them.

Miss Matilda Crunch seated herself in a shady place, and, pulling out a novel, began to read.

The traveller crawled through the hedge, and, by the exercise of considerable ingenuity, contrived to pass into the grove unobserved.

Several of the bigger girls were taking off their shoes and stockings, preparatory to crossing the stream to a small but beautiful meadow.

A young and ruddy girl was tripping down towards them with a pitcher of milk.

Full of fun, and high spirits, the elder girls rushed towards them, with all the freedom of Naiads.

The Mormon elder lay at full length in the grass, like a snake and serpent as he was.

His eye fell upon Julie, who was disporting herself even with more freedom than the presence of girls only should have allowed.

The Mormon pitched upon her at once as a victim easily to be led away.

Idiot! She could have twisted him round her little finger.

Presently he saw a bevy of the younger children, who were playing hide-and-seek, approach his way.

With a hasty movement he retreated towards the upper end of the field, where the girl afterwards saw him in conversation with Matilda Crunch.

Before, however, they marshalled for the walk back he had returned in the direction of the town, more than ever determined on carrying out his infernal schemes.

But first of all he had made up his mind to secure Jessie.

This was necessary to his ultimate success in his great scheme of life.

Besides, if something he suspected turned out to be true, it would be thousands of pounds in his pocket.

CHAPTER LXXI.

THE VISCOUNT DE FLORAC.

It was about twelve o'clock the next day that Mrs. Jones and the Rev. Mr. Simcox were in conversation at the window of the parlour.

Both were in a deeply anxious state of mind.

The Rev. Mr. Simcox was exceedingly anxious to catch a glimpse of his pupil.

The good hostess was in what is called a fidget.

If he only would come in a carriage and four. What a triumph over the Red Lion.

But there is a noise and clatter in the street.

He is, indeed, coming. Ah! well, not so bad after all. He is in an open carriage, a phæton, with a pair of horses.

A postilion is driving, while his valet is seated on the box.

He has no luggage; of course that will come by the wagon.

Out rushes Mrs. Jones. The valet, however, opens the carriage before her, and a slight young man, wrapped in a fur cloak, steps out.

He bows gracefully to the landlady, and inquires in dulcet tones for the Rev. Mr. Simcox.

That gentleman steps hurriedly forward, and with a low bow introduces himself.

Will his lordship take lunch?

His lordship consents, and a very neat and tempting collation is laid out.

The valet retires to the kitchen to indulge in more humble fare.

The viscount looks at the door.

The traveller screws up his eyes and makes a sign for caution.

"How do you like me?" continues the youth complacently.

"First rate—splendiferous, as we say in the United States," replied the other.

"Well, let us eat and drink, now. We can talk presently."

And the two worthies, luxurious and sensual in everything, continued their meal, after which, lighting cigars, they strolled forth into the town.

At this moment an open carriage whirled past, in which sat Jessie and Henry.

"What a lovely creature," said the Viscount de Florac.

"She is," replied the traveller, drily; " but you must not even look at her."

"Why?"

"In the first place she is a child; and, secondly—"

"You have marked her down for yourself. Why not say so?"

The other muttered something inaudible, and the subject was changed.

The viscount and his tutor walked towards the sea-shore. Already there was a rumour in that little provincial town that a rich young French nobleman had arrived.

All the young ladies' hearts were in a flutter.

It is a sad, sad truth, that genius, good qualities, nobility of character, even manly beauty, go for little with the fair bevy of unmarried girls, when rank and title stand near them. Not that all young women are selfish, wild-minded, and silly, but how many out of a hundred are capable of a disinterested passion that looks only to the man loved and not to the lining of his pocket.

The state of modern society, the necessity for money, the fierce competition in dress, outward appearance at the expense of comfort, health, and peace of mind, is at the root of the evil.

Every man ought to marry irrespective of his money status.

Marriage is the true state of the human race.

I would not allow any but married men to hold a situation of trust or responsibility.

A married man is more trustworthy, safer, and more to be depended on than single ones.

Young men should be dismissed from every post public and private, if at twenty-five they had not a wife.

It is sheer hypocrisy to talk about the social evil when the tendency of the age is to increase it.

"A single man without encumbrance" is the tone of thousands of advertisements.

Give increased employment to women, encourage marriage, discourage mere life for show, and the social evil will diminish.

It can only be eradicated when sin shall cease to be.

The beach was crowded. It was a lovely day, and the visitors came down to enjoy the breeze and the sight of the curling waves that broke in rolls of fretted silver on the shore.

There were young ladies and old ladies, nursery-maids and children, while several schools of young ladies, in all the pomp and circumstance of the latest fashions, made up a scene which would have warmed the heart of an anchorite.

It is good to enjoy life, and cold is the heart, indeed, which does not view the delight of the young with pleasure.

The Count de Florac, throwing away his cigar, sauntered along in conversation with the traveller, but never allowing any woman to pass without a glance of his dark and glittering eye.

Presently they approached some bathing-machines, near which was a group exclusively composed of girls.

The Rev. Mr. Simcox nudged his young friend.

The viscount drew himself up to his fullest height, and began stroking his slight moustache.

The girls were seated on the beach, some on camp-stools, some on the ground, forming a circle round the amiable Matilda Crunch.

Jessie had just joined them, and was in earnest conversation with Edith.

Julie sat apart with an opera-glass in her hand. This was chiefly directed towards the distant figure of a naval officer.

Suddenly the viscount, passing very close to her, touched her as if by accident. She started, turned pale and red, and sank on the ground, gazing with open mouth at the retreating figure.

"Do you know that young lady?"

"Slightly," observed the viscount, drily.

"But what think you of my plans?" said the traveller.

"Charming," replied the viscount, with a strange smile. "One or two of them are very lovely."

The traveller rubbed his hands, and the two continued their walk.

CHAPTER LXXII.

MATRIMONY.

Two nights after her severe and painful disappointment Edith de Lancy took up her station in the garden at an early hour.

Her young husband was punctual to the appointment, even to being before his time.

It was a dark night, and Edith trembled so that she could only take his hand and lead him forward.

She answered no questions until he had gained her chamber through the window.

He was about to close it.

She checked him.

"Wait," she said, her bright eyes suffused with tears.

The young officer looked at her with surprise.

"Charles," she said, looking down upon the ground, "do you know where I passed the last night?"

"In these arms," he cried, with an astonished look.

"On yonder grass, at the foot of that tree," replied Edith.

"But my dear girl——"

"I speak the truth, Charles."

"In the name of Heaven explain yourself, my darling!"

"My meaning is, that your foolish wife, anxious about your not arriving, went out into the garden, and when, hopeless and weary, she returned, this window and the shutters were closed."

A red flush covered the young man's face as he sank into a chair.

"You were not alone——"

"I was not—but——"

"How could you be deceived?" said the young maiden wife, reproachfully.

"My darling Edith," he cried, starting up, "whoever it was blew out the light and refused to speak. I was hurried away before daylight. I confess I did think your fears very silly. But, my dear girl——"

"Enough," said the blushing girl, "but promise me you will never speak to this bad girl."

"I don't know who she is even."

"Then I will tell you," said Edith, quickly.

"I am sure I do not want to know," replied the young man, pressing his lips to her burning cheek.

Now this was not exactly true, for he was vastly curious; but, of course, he was too much of a diplomatist to say so to his young wife, who, though she tried her best not to be angry, was sorely vexed in her own heart.

Women scarcely ever forgive even an involuntary infidelity.

* * * * *

And thus passed a whole week, during which all this extraordinary series of intrigues went on, unnoticed, undiscovered, under the shade of night.

Alas! poor moon, called by poets the chaste and the cold, what sins does not thy rule conceal, which makes night truly hideous.

Jessie came three times a-week to the school; sometimes with her mother, sometimes without, but always carefully and well guarded.

The young officer appeared in no great hurry to take his wife away.

Was it because he could enjoy the society of his wife without let or hindrance, or was he curious to discover who was the mysterious Egeria who had so strangely passed for his wife on the first memorable occasion?

THE DUPLICITY OF MISS CRUNCH.

But his wife never alluded to her, and the lady herself gave no sign.

The Viscount de Florac continued to waylay the young ladies on their walks, and his persistence excited their attention.

Their curiosity was roused. Fatal gift above all others—especially for women.

The traveller continued to pay his court to the widow at the inn, and to the antique maid out of doors, contriving, too, to keep both in the dark as to his double dealing.

For reasons best known to himself he kept out of the way of Jessie and her mother; the latter he had not yet seen.

He knew that she was rich, and inhabited a splendid residence of her own—purchased since her arrival at the watering place.

But he bided his time.

CHAPTER LXXIII.

AN EXPLOSION.

A FORTNIGHT had passed.

The Misses Crumpton had, on a certain Wednesday, organised an evening—half musical, half dance—to which such of the parents and relatives as inhabited the neighbourhood were invited. The Misses Crumpton so far departed from their established rule as to include in the invitation the traveller and the Count de Florac.

The wealth of the latter, his gay equipage, and his very gentlemanly bearing, were the talk of the town.

The officers of the man-of-war were included in the invitation.

Lady Haddington and Cornelia consented to be present with Jessie and Henry, the latter now a midshipman in the navy.

No one could resist his earnest solicitations to be allowed to follow that noble profession.

He had just put on his uniform for the first time.

The concert was to be carried on by the more advanced pupils, assisted by the teachers.

A wondrous player on the violin, a little, short, hump-backed man, had also volunteered his services.

The company began to collect at an early hour.

The ladies of rank and title were honoured with front seats close to the performers.

Chairs were placed for all the others, except that at the back standing-room was left for any who might be too late to obtain a seat.

The room was very full.

The last arrival was the Viscount de Florac: he was accompanied by his tutor.

The viscount was dressed scrupulously in the Parisian fashion, far too effeminate for our taste, but pleasing in the eyes of the frivolous.

The tutor wore a black frock coat, a very high white choker, dark green spectacles, and a curly brown wig.

His face was as white as if it had been whitened by artificial means.

He glanced quickly round, and while the viscount, with well-bred impudence, pushed up towards the front to have a good look at the audience, he drew back.

He was not at all ambitious of publicity.

Still he contrived to place himself in a position to see without being seen.

A kind of niche, from which a statue had been removed for fear of accidents, was covered by a curtain.

Behind this he crept, and glared out upon the gay and festive scene.

He could scarcely restrain a cry as his eye fell upon the splendid form and figure of Cornelia, once so thin, so pale, so wan. He could hardly believe his senses.

What had happened to bring about so wondrous a change? No hypothesis which his brain could conceive could explain it to his mind.

But all voices are hushed. The busy hum of whispering school girls is heard no more. Parents and guardians look around with warning glances as the wonderful violin player steps forward to the front.

A low, wild howl, like that of a wild beast, but so faint, so indistinct, so suddenly checked as to excite no great attention, whirls round the room.

Does the grave give up its dead?

And Jessie is by his side, looking on admiringly, wonderingly, affectionately.

Now is the dread mystery revealed, and out from the house totters the traveller, glad to hide his head at the inn, under pretence of a sudden and severe sick headache.

A wild and wondrous song, as it were, is sung by the magic violin, which soothes and charms every listener, and then, as the player appears about to finish, Jessie advances to the front of the orchestra, and a voice rich, full, and mellow, takes up the strain.

The musician continues a low melody, which is as entrancing as the song, and then he, too, after one burst that seems to wing every listening soul to heaven, sits down.

The applause was genuine and sincere, and as Jessie came to her mother's side, Cornelia could scarcely restrain her tears of gladness and of joy.

The concert which followed was pleasing and agreeable, but nothing occurred to mar the effect of that glorious achievement.

Then came the ball, which had long been impatiently expected by the young ladies. Poor little dears! the society of the male creation was a thing so long denied them that they thought it something wonderful.

How many hearts were lost and won that evening it would be a hard thing to say.

At eleven the younger ladies retired at a signal from the teachers.

The parents began to move, and at last none remained save the elder girls.

The Viscount de Florac had danced with all who were old enough for the honour.

Several had blushed immensely while so doing. We are almost afraid that the wicked youth had been squeezing their hands.

He was now away, and all save Julia and Edith were discussing his merits.

Edith had retired, pleading a headache. Julia had smiled strangely. That peculiarly constituted young lady did not believe the husband story.

She was the very personification of a modern fast young lady.

All was now still, when, to the astonishment of all, a loud knocking and ringing came to the door.

In rushed a servant.

"What is it?" said one of the heads of the house, rising from her seat.

"Please ma'am Sir Edward de Lancy, and Sir Walter de Lancy, both in a towering passion."

At this moment the brothers entered the room.

"I tell you, sir," shouted the former, "that I will have the young villain hung. To dare—"

"But, brother," began the admiral.

"Sir Walter de Lancy," said the elder, "I have long told you."

"Gentlemen," said the Argus of Moreton House, "may I be allowed to ask what is the matter. To what do I owe the honour of this untimely visit?"

"Zounds, madam! what is the matter?—to what do you owe the honour of this untimely visit? Why, madam, infamy is the matter, ruin is the matter, hanging is the matter," shouted the infuriated baronet.

" Sir—"

" I tell you, madam it's all true."

" What, sir ?"

" Why, a man's in my daughter's bedroom, and has slept there every night for nearly a month."

The two Misses Crumpton shrieked, Matilda Crunch fell back and nearly fainted.

I am sorry to say that the young ladies giggled.

By stepping back into the shade they had contrived to remain unnoticed, and in this way were enabled to listen to the whole scene.

" Sir," began the elder sister, " I scorn your assertion. It is an abominable and wicked calumny. Your daughter shall not remain a moment longer in this house."

" I should think not, ma'am, and I believe no respectable female will when they tell their parents what they see," roared the infuriated baronet.

" Follow me, sir," said Miss Crumpton, pale with rage.

The baronet did follow. His brother, who was much calmer, kept as close to him as possible. The school girls crept up as close as they could without being seen.

Miss Crumpton thundered at the door.

A few minutes' silence followed, and then a key was heard turning in the lock.

The door opened, and there blushing, rosy, pretty Edith appeared, leaning on the arm of Charles de Lancy, the young naval officer.

" Now, madam," shouted Sir Edward.

" Merciful heavens !"

" The depravity of human nature."

" The wickedness of girls."

" Silence !" said Charles, pushing Edith gently back, " I will not hear one word against my wife and cousin. We have been married six months. Separated by an unjust decree I have only just discovered her residence. While preparing a home for her I have every right to visit her wherever I find her. Sir Edward I regret that an unjust and unkind dislike of your only nephew should have compelled us to resort to a course which I know to have been erroneous. Had I been treated differently I would have waited your pleasure ; as it is I beg to say that, asking nothing of you, wishing nothing of you, I will protect and claim my own wife before the whole world."

" Sir," began the baronet.

" They are married, brother," said the admiral, gravely ; " would to Heaven they were not. I would sooner have cut my right hand off than it should have happened. But we cannot unmarry them. As for you, sir," continued the admiral, " here are your sailing orders. You are appointed captain of the Firefly, with important despatches for the admiral at Malta. This will teach you to be skulking when you ought to be thinking of your profession."

" I am always ready to do my duty," said the young man gravely but sadly.

" I will go with you. Father, I cannot leave my husband, but before we part, perhaps for ever, embrace your child. I have done wrong, I know ; but oh, my father, I did so love him !"

The baronet turned away.

" Sir Edward I have erred," said the young sailor, " but not your only child. Forgive her, Sir Edward."

" Young man," replied the baronet, in a husky tone, " I will forgive all. I will become reconciled to those I have, perhaps, too long been estranged from, on one condition."

" And that is, Sir Edward ?"

" That you leave my child in England until you return. I am called to London on urgent business, but Lady de Lancy can join her in this most respectable establishment."

A loud hem from the Misses Crumpton.

" Do, Charles," whispered Edith.

" Sir Edward anything to win your favour," said Charles, heartily.

" Come along Walter," said the baronet ; " hang it, man, let us go and drink a bottle of wine. After all I think we're two old fools. I beg your pardon—at all events I am one. Ladies, many apologies. In the morning I will bring Lady de Lancy to visit Mr. and Mrs. Charles de Lancy, unless, indeed, Mrs. de Lancy would like to come now."

Edith made a motion as if to advance, but Charles pulled her back and closed the door.

All the big girls giggled ; what about, I really cannot say.

The brothers went away arm in arm, not a whit less astonished than any one at the strange, mysterious, and unexpected issue of what appeared about to be a tragic comedy.

Next evening, after certain family arrangements, Charles and Edith parted.

" My dear husband," said Edith, at last, " are you very curious ?"

" Why ?"

" Because I want you to do me a favour without asking why or wherefore."

" Well, my dear girl, I will."

" Thank you, dearest. My request is contained in this note ; and now—"

But why endeavour to depict a scene as impossible to paint as to gild refined gold.

Once on board, Captain Charles de Lancy, to whom Henry was appointed a midshipman, opened the note.

" *I am curious to write a tale. Find out for me at Malta the History of Paolo Dumourier and Teresa Dunbar. I want the most minute particulars. I will read you the tale and the riddle when you return.*"

CHAPTER LXXIV.

A PERILOUS ADVENTURE.

BUT we must leave the demon of desolation and ruin at work in the Welsh watering place ; must leave Jessie and the school to the working of revenge and every evil passion, to introduce certain personages necessary to the development of our narrative.

We have not forgotten the Mormons.

One of their demoniacal agents is at work in the peaceful valleys, whence they draw the largest amount of their dupes.

At no very great distance from the scene of

the vile plots of the traveller and his accomplice, the Viscount de Florac, is a wild and ragged shore, skirting a savage bay, little frequented in the day time by any but the most impoverished class of fishermen.

Every now and then a revenue cutter would just poke its nose into its mouth, cautiously, and as if afraid to venture too far, but it would soon sail away as if the examination were worse than useless.

And yet it was a great smuggling crib.

Wise legislators, clever statesmen have been for many years under the impression that smuggling has long been entirely given up.

It is a grand mistake.

Until very recently it was very common, and, to an extent, almost fabulous.

It can never be stopped except by being rendered useless.

Free trade, in the modern acceptation, is the only way to ruin—the old free trade.

But at the time of which we write it was carried on very extensively. There are plenty of persons living, and not old people either, who have made their fortune in the contraband trade.

On a bare and naked cliff, with nothing to indicate fitness for the habitation of man or beast save a square field, surrounded by a wall of loose stones, was a small, low hut.

Built in an exposed position, it was low, and its roof protected from the pitiless winds by large and heavy stones, placed here and there.

One chimney served the whole habitation.

It was out of all ordinary traffic, though from close to it could be seen several villages, lofty hills, and lovely forests.

Its only known inhabitant was an aged crone, of a most sullen and savage character, who came from nobody knew where, obtained permission to build this cot, rented a square field of land for vegetables, and was, it was rumoured, the widow of some pirate of the sea, who had perished miserably.

Her talk was always of storms and shipwrecks.

A few shepherds, a wandering angler, and a persevering artist, had occasionally obtained admission to her hut at times, and had always left with the impression that the old woman was mad.

Under no pretence whatever would she allow any one to pass the night in that dismal hut.

Several times travellers, from sheer curiosity, wished to remain. But she sternly ordered them away.

And yet people had sworn that noises had been heard in the hut at night.

It was a dark and gloomy night. A heavy breeze was blowing directly on the shore.

Not a coast-guard but was snugly housed.

Who would venture in that neighbourhood on such a night, with a revenue cutter outside?

Below, along the beach, and sometimes over the rocks, half way up the cliff, was a path used by adventurous travellers.

To save a long detour, two men, with guns upon their shoulders, are making their way along the shore.

The waves dash right up to the narrow pathway in wreaths of foam.

The travellers begin to lag.

"I wish we'd stopped at the inn," said the Viscount de Florac, one of the sportsmen.

"So do I," cried the Rev. Mr. Simcox. "Brandy-and-water is better than the taste of the briny waves."

"It would'nt do to go back," continued the viscount.

"I can't stand it much longer," continued the other; "my feet are sore, my knees shake under me."

"Look."

"Where?"

The Viscount de Florac pointed towards the distant opening between two lofty rocks which formed the entrance to the bay.

It was a grand and noble sight.

The night had been gradually getting darker and darker, until at last it sank like a funeral pall upon the whole scene; but at this moment, as if by a stage transformation, the huge veil lifted, and a strange light pierced through a vast cavernous orifice.

It was the rising of the moon in a small, clear patch of the heavens.

And, clearly defined, every spar and rope distinct, against the distant horizon, was a large schooner, coming right in for the shore.

Three lights, in a triangle, were suspended from its bows, below the martingale-guy.

A gun flashed at the same moment, and then the panorama changed as if by magic.

A cloud had passed before the moon.

At the same moment a ruddy glare fell upon the water at no great distance in front.

"Smugglers, by the Lord!" said the Viscount de Florac.

"The devil! We had better make ourselves scarce," whispered Mr. Simcox, in a low, trembling voice.

"If I do may I be extinguished!" cried de Florac. "We are drenched, cold, and hungry; and I bet you a crown if there's a smuggling job on we are treated with attention and politeness."

"Why so?"

"Ah! that is my secret," said de Florac.

The traveller made no reply.

"Follow me, say nothing, and make no resistance if disarmed," whispered the viscount.

They now advanced along the pathway, using some caution. For a moment or two nothing could be seen but the dim and ruddy glow of a fire on the water; but soon a number of voices became perfectly distinct.

The viscount stood still, and gave a shrill and prolonged whistle.

A dead silence followed.

"*Hoop toy!*" cried the other, "*ben culls are coming—one toq.*"*

"*Hoop toy!*" replied a hoarse voice, and then six or seven men rose from the ground, and the two friends were all but carried forward by their rude hands towards the fire.

---

* Gipsy and Welsh smuggler slang. "Look out! friends are coming,—one a stranger.

They were then loosened, and found themselves in the centre of an excited but silent group.

The Viscount de Florac stood surveying them with a look of profound impertinence.

The Rev. Mr. Simcox trembled like an aspen leaf.

A stout, burly, and rather ill-looking ruffian, with a dark frown, habited in a guernsey, high boots, and red cap, stood in front of them. A pair of ominous-looking pistols, beside a dirk, showed that he had the means of carrying out any deadly purpose ready to his hand.

"Whence came you, and what do you want?" he said.

We give a translation. The whole conversation was carried on in slang.

"We come from hunting; we want fire, bread, and a roof."

"How came you a *ben core* to patter slang?"

"It is my mother tongue. Are you a master?"

"No," opening his eyes.

"I am." He lowered his voice to a whisper. "A crossed dirk and a red bowl awaits those who disobey."

The burly man took off his red cap and bowed low, with absolute intense reverence.

"But your friend."

"Shall be initiated."

The schooner could now be hardly seen, and the chief, after bidding two members of the gang show the strangers to a fire, give them refreshments of every kind, and all necessary attention, they themselves made off to the water's edge.

CHAPTER LXXV.

THE SMUGGLER'S CAVE.

AN aged woman bade the two friends follow her.

They turned a kind of rocky wall, stooped low through an arch clearly at high tide covered by the sea, then entering a vast natural cave, soon found themselves in a rude chamber, where fire, a supply of cold meat, and steaming grog was readily placed before them.

The Rev. Mr. Simcox, who was very white about the face, took a bumper, and then sat down with a sigh of relief.

The old woman stood beside the fire and began patting the head of a frail-looking lad of thirteen or fourteen, who was looking vacantly at the smoke.

"I am terribly afraid, my good friend Simcox," said the Viscount de Florac, helping himself to a huge piece of beef, "that you are an arrant coward."

"Sir?"

"Viscount if you please."

"Viscount be —— ! No more a coward than you are," blustered Simcox.

"Well, if so," said the other, with provoking coolness, "the matter is very easily settled. I call you a coward, and I repeat the accusation!"

"Sir!"

"You continue to insult me ——"

"Sir!"

"By addressing me with a want of courtesy, with a familiarity altogether unbecoming the relations of master and pupil ——"

"D ——n, Sir!"

"Don't swear, I'll knock you down ——"

"Mr. ——"

"Naturally aggrieved, you insist on pistols. That respectable old lady, I am sure, will oblige us. Shall it be before or after dinner? I should say after, for as sure as I take a pistol in hand it will be your last meal, so you may as well enjoy it."

"Don't be a fool," said the Rev. Mr. Simcox, meekly, "and just explain to me how the deuce you mean to get out of this hobble?"

"Hobble?—what do you mean? I fancy it is the most delightful piece of luck!"

"How so?"

"Humph! I fancy that some of our projects carry at their end a rope long enough to hang us both. Should we fail, or be discovered, there can be no doubt that these people would be of immense use to us."

"They might be; you are right! The schooner would be first-rate."

"Then I begin to see reason re-assuming its sway. Captain Poswaithe is very obliging to his friends."

"So you know the smuggler?"

"I do."

"The deuce you do? And pray what jargon is that you were talking ——"

"That you will have to learn," said the Viscount de Florac drily.

"How so?"

"You must be initiated," replied the other.

"In what?"

"The ancient and honourable society of the enemies of all law and jurisdiction."

"The advantage?"

"First, the trifling advantage of being allowed to leave this place alive."

"What?"

"If you refuse to take the oath—and that of secrecy as well—you will never be permitted to go away."

"What a cut-throat lot! What on earth made you drag me here?"

"Simply because I wished you to become one of us. In whatever part of the world you may be it will serve you. Every Mormon should join."

"Again ——"

"Should you ever fall into trouble—should the clutches of the law fall upon you, every cull is bound to be your friend."

"But the initiation?"

"I can tell you nothing. I dare not violate the secrets of the prison-house."

The Rev. Mr. Simcox made a wry face; but being, to a certain extent, a philosopher, and being convinced that he was in for it, and could not help it, he resigned himself to his fate.

He accordingly ate heartily, drank the same, and then, in imitation of the viscount, started a pipe.

Presently a man entered the room.

He was a good-looking man of about forty,

but with the mark of the beast distinctly upon his face.

He shook hands with the young man, and spoke to him in an unknown dialect for some time.

He then turned to the other.

"So you've violated the secrets of the craft, my tulip. It'll cost you pretty dear."

"I am ready to pay anything in reason."

"My good man, all that you have is ours; but in the event of your becoming one of us, of course it will be different."

"If not?"

The captain drew a table-knife coolly across his throat.

"Sir," said the Rev. Mr. Simcox, hemming slightly to clear his throat, "I should have preferred entering your honourable society without compulsion. I should have been pleased to join you of my own accord; but, as it is not to be so, I am delighted to do so on any terms you may propose."

"Very good."

"First-rate," added De Florac.

"And now to refresh. The run is complete; my men are hard at work. While they are finishing we can sup. So-ho! there!"

The aged crone of the hut—not the one who had waited on the strangers—here entered, bearing a steaming joint of boiled beef and carrots, which made Simcox and De Florac simultaneously lay down their pipes.

The very sight of this goodly English fare quite renovated their appetites

For eating, drinking, and love-making, to say nothing of fighting, commend me to the dwellers in this tight little island.

Other people pick a bit. We eat.

The captain helped them copiously, and, for the nonce, the utmost harmony prevailed.

Suddenly a loud shout proclaimed that the immediate business of the night was over.

The goods were all stowed away.

"Come!" said the captain, rising.

A cold shudder passed over the frame of the Mormon elder. He felt as all do when about to try the unknown. A dread comes over us always when about to face that which we do not understand.

The Viscount de Florac looked as solemn as a parish clerk.

But when the tutor's back was turned he thrust his tongue in his cheek and grinned.

CHAPTER LXXVI.

THE INITIATION.

IN a large chamber of the cave, lighted by a dozen or so of torches, were collected in every variety of attitude, costume, and with every shade of countenance, a band of men whose very appearance indicated their lawless occupation.

Smuggling may be the most venial of offences against the law, but, like poaching, you never know where you may be led to.

Smuggling has been too often the cause of murder.

It always appears to combine a little bit of piracy.

Habitual defiance of the law is productive of a harsh expression of countenance.

Though many believe themselves not to be doing wrong, they know that they are doing something illegal.

Some sat on projecting pieces of rock, some on the ground, some had chairs or stools.

All had pipes or glasses.

The captain took his seat in an arm chair at the head of a large coarse deal table, round which sat the immediate crew of the schooner.

The captain lit his pipe with becoming gravity, and took a heavy pull at his glass.

"Brother pals, prigs, and free traders," he began, "I have called you together for an important purpose, that of receiving a new member. He is willing to take the oath, and to run all the risks."

A loud shout followed.

"Who presents him?"

"I do," said the Viscount de Florac.

"On what ground?"

The young man replied in the slang dialect he had already used.

"Aspirant, stand forward!"

"I am here," said the traveller, beside whom stood his pupil.

"Your name?"

"Simcox."

"Your trade?"

"My profession is that of a humble preacher of the Word of God."

A murmur of astonishment and incredulity passed round the room.

"It is true," said the viscount.

"Swear, Simcox."

The young man administered the oath, which, horrible, blasphemous, and ribald, he took without a shudder.

Of what use would it be to print it? They would only use one as vile, as horrible as that which is in use now.

"Blindfold him," said the captain.

The viscount and one of the others who stood near him at once proceeded to perform this office so effectually that in a moment he was utterly incapable of distinguishing a speck of light.

"The cup."

A goblet was placed in his hand.

"Drink! 'tis the blood of life!" said the captain, in a hollow tone.

With a cold shudder the Rev. Mr. Simcox drank, and as he did so a fearful clang stunned him: a cloth was cast over his head; he lost all sense, except that he was being hurried away upon men's arms.

Then all was still.

When he came to himself he could not hear a sound.

Yes—hark! What is this?

He listens with bated breath.

'Tis the wash of rising waters.

With agony stinging him to the very heart, he tore off his bandages.

He was in total darkness.

Stretching out his hand he felt the cold and clammy wall.

He stooped, and touched water.

In an agony of terror, he found a seat, and contrived to sit with his feet out of the water.

What was to be done?

His first impulse was to shriek, and implore the mercy of his tormentors.

But if, for some inscrutable reason, they meant him any injury, this was useless, for not a sound came in reply.

There was the echo of his own voice—that was all.

Then he wiped the cold and clammy perspiration from his brow.

As he did so a long wave washed his feet.

Then he remembered that the tide was rising.

The whole affair was, then, a mockery; and, as a punishment for discovering his secret, they had doomed him to this hideous death.

Up rose the water.

It was to his calves.

He felt around, but there was no spot higher than that which he occupied.

Again he shrieked frantically.

But nothing but the dull echo, and the splash, splash of the water, came in response.

In an awful frenzy, half mad, he clasped his hands in a wild appeal to heaven.

All his sins—the fearful catalogue of his crimes—came like a vision of judgment to his soul.

He howled with terror.

Buried alive!

It is at such moments as these that men feel all the force of crime.

There was no hope.

The water was up to his knees.

It was rising very fast. His lower extremities were cold and clammy.

Again he directed wild appeals for mercy—now to heaven, now to his persecutors.

Then, to hear him curse, blaspheme, pray, whine—all in tears.

No patient martyrdom was his.

There must be faith in the soul which meets death with calmness.

Ah! it is to his middle. His whole body is getting numbed, the air is getting close and confined, the rising water is forcing it upwards, and he feels a thick, choking, sensation.

Then again he roared for help.

"Hollo! what cheer, messmate?" he heard far away in the distance.

He looked up; and at the very summit of a long flight of steps, cut out in the side of a vast cavern, the whole floor of which was one sheet of water, he saw the captain and the Viscount de Florac standing.

Without a word he rushed up the steps, and followed the two men into a small hut.

"Welcome, brother," said the captain with a grin.

"Twice welcome," added the youth.

"May both of you be ——," he began.

"Silence," said the captain sternly. "You are now one of us—be satisfied; and now to business. The night is far gone, but it will be much better to wait for dawn. This gentleman tells me that we may be able to understand one another. Anything for an honest penny—

while, as a matter of course, for a brother I shall work cheap."

"Humph!" replied the traveller, who could not refuse the temptation to join them in a stiff glass of brandy, after his adventure in the cavern, "I don't know. I want a man I can trust and a swift vessel on a certain night, but when that night will be I cannot say."

"I'm your man."

The three villains, for such they were, now had a long conversation, after which it was agreed that the schooner, on its return from every voyage, should report itself to the reverend brother, and be always at his command for special service.

A vessel had for some time been chartered to take an exclusive cargo of Mormons to the States. On the sailing of this vessel much of his future plans depended.

He was in active correspondence with the whole gang of impostors, who were going about the county picking up fools and dupes to people the New Jerusalem.

Let all who are likely to be duped wait until they have read our revelations of Mormon life in its native hideousness.

CHAPTER LXXVII.

ABSENCE.

JESSIE felt her boy lover's departure intensely.

Henry had such a fierce desire to try the sea as a profession, until his coming of age gave him other duties, that no one thought of opposing him.

Least of all Jessie.

She saw that, though his affections were wholly hers as a boy, that he felt none of that intense and passionate love which she already understood but too well.

Her heart had spoken, and she loved, child as she was, once and for ever.

But then she knew that her lover—her future husband—should be a man

But what a comfort and consolation she found in the society of Edith de Lancy, the wife of her young lover's captain.

Julia she had ceased to associate with.

That young lady had grown moody and silent. She kept apart from the rest of the scholars.

A new and strange system had been adopted in the school.

Miss Matilda Crouch would, on several occasions, take out a single young lady at a time, on the plea of companionship for herself, and mental improvement to the juvenile.

This was a favour which had only been accorded to the elder girls—young ladies supposed to be able to take care of themselves.

The Rev. Mr. Simcox and his friend, the Viscount de Florac, continued to meet the school out.

On the plea of their having been invited to attend the concerts and balls of the establishment, they allowed themselves to speak rather freely to the young ladies.

The viscount was very reserved in his attentions. He paid no noted respect to one more than another.

But a strange change had come over the school.

Several of the elder girls might have been noticed to lose all their gaiety and light-heartedness.

They were to be seen in corners, devouring letters with intense earnestness.

The pallid hue of sickness and care replaced that of health.

The Misses Crumpton began to be uneasy. There appeared to be an epidemic threatening the school.

There was an epidemic.

It was of a nature, however, usually greeted with gratification in well regulated families.

Four months had passed since the departure of Captain Charles de Lancy and Henry.

Several letters had been received from them.

At last a large packet was received.

Mrs. de Lancy at once intimated her intention to give a grand party.

Her husband was expected home every hour.

The party was hailed without any enthusiasm.

The spirit of the school was gone.

But Mrs. Charles de Lancy appeared wholly indifferent to the want of fervour on the part of the school.

She appeared in most admirable spirits.

Jessie could not make her out.

There were some things secret even from her dear young friend.

Julie appeared to grow worse and worse.

Her attempts to a reconciliation with Jessie were met with a resolute opposition.

Mrs. de Lancy was firm against all the cajolery of the syren who had deprived her, on a memorable occasion, of her husband's society.

Julie grew very uneasy. She continued to receive letters almost every day.

And every day she renewed her efforts upon Jessie.

*   *   *   *   *

Meanwhile the Rev. Mr. Simcox had not been idle.

He had insinuated himself into the obscure little congregation of Latter-Day Saints, and had preached to them the abominable new doctrine.

He had revealed to them the mysteries of Mormonism.

Many converts had joined the church.

A large party of infatuated dupes had agreed to follow the fortunes of Joe Smith.

They waited but the arrival of a Mormon emigrant ship to depart.

One which was about to take in a party at Bristol was daily expected to call for them.

At length its departure from Bristol was announced.

The Mormon flock were bade to keep themselves in readiness for immediate departure.

Everything was packed up ready, but not without a certain amount of secrecy, under pretence of the persecuting character of the Gentiles.

The Rev. Mr. Simcox and his chief agent had doubtless their reasons for the secrecy in question.

In the afternoon of a memorable Wednesday, long remembered in T———, the day was magnificent.

A hot breeze came up from the sea.

Clouds redolent of storm covered the horizon.

Towards the afternoon the large brig might have been seen beating up towards the bay.

In its wake was a schooner yacht.

It did not resemble the Osprey in colour, but there were those who would have sworn to its identity with that vessel.

Towards evening the two vessels anchored and made all snug for the night.

Every precaution was taken in case the night should turn out dirty.

*   *   *   *   *

Mrs. de Lancy, to whom her father, now that a reconciliation had taken place, was excessively liberal, had done things upon a very grand scale.

She had invited several of the relatives of the pupils.

There were to be tea, a dance, an early supper, and then, on the retirement of the younger pupils, the festivities were to be renewed.

CHAPTER LXXVIII.

THE SOIREE DANSANTE.

LIGHT were the steps, and merry the laugh, of the majority of the guests, especially the younger ones, on this memorable occasion.

A band had been provided.

Among the guests were the Rev. Mr. Simcox and the Viscount de Florac.

The latter was peculiarly volatile. He danced with all the leading beauties of the school, and made love to them desperately.

Miss Matilda Crunch trembled.

The Misses Crumpton looked rather serious, and made a mental note not to invite him again.

Jessy danced with a young girl of her own age.

Her's was the poetry of sentiment.

She could not endure a polka or a waltz with any one save her affianced husband.

Mrs. de Lancy, aided by her mother, saw to the comforts of the guests.

Everything passed off admirably.

Julie was in exuberant spirits.

Once or twice she exchanged a rapid word with the Viscount de Florac, upon whose arm she leaned with marked tenderness.

Several of the girls turned pale and bit their lips.

At length supper was announced, and so admirable were the arrangements that everything went off well.

After supper the more youthful part of the community, such as really were of tender years, retired.

The rest adjourned to the large school-room,

THE DEAD BRIDAL.

which served as a ball-room on the present occasion.

The musicians began to tune their instruments.

"Ladies and gentlemen," said Edith, suddenly, as she motioned the musicians to pause, "I think our friends here should adjourn for twenty minutes to the supper-room. In the meantime, just by way of passing away the half hour, what say you to a story? I can promise you one of a most thrilling character."

"Yes! yes! bravo—delightful," was the cry.

The musicians bowed their thanks, and retired.

A circle formed round the fair speaker.

The elder ladies, including Lady Haddington and Cornelia, were accommodated with chairs.

The gentlemen stood upon one side.

A bevy of girls, nine in number, had drawn together to the back of the room.

Jessie took a stool at the feet of Mrs. de Lancy.

Julie, with a pout of disdain, seated herself on a sofa facing the Viscount de Florac.

This young lady was quiet, but evidently, from her colour, slightly agitated.

"I am not very practised as a story teller," said Edith, "so have written out my narrative. I had placed this story in my evening's programme."

General applause followed, and then she began in a voice as clear as a bell.

CHAPTER LXXIX.

WOMAN'S REVENGE.

"THE scene of my tale is laid in Malta," she began, spreading out her manuscript with her soft white hand.

Julie and the Viscount de Florac exchanged a sharp electric glance.

Both turned a little pale.

Julia fanned herself in a peculiar way with her ivory fan, which she used with all the dexterity of a Spanish *prima donna*.

The Viscount de Florac played with his watch-chain.

A covert fire lit up the eye of Edith.

No one appeared to notice this by-play. Everybody was settling himself down to listen comfortably to an interesting story.

"Malta is a very curious place. I might take up hours of your time by a mere outline sketch of its early history, and also with an elaborate description of its shape and form.

"But I have, like the celebrated knife-grinder, a story to tell, and I wish to tell it as briefly and succinctly as possible.

"In the Strada del Santa Maria lived, some years ago, a jeweller.

"He was a man of considerable wealth and very peculiar habits.

"He had lost his wife when she was very young, and been left with an only daughter, Teresa.

"His name was Dunbar, for though domiciled in the East from childhood, he was a Scotchman by birth.

"Of his origin, previous history, and of the causes which brought him to the East, nothing was known.

"He was a man of morose manners, excessively saturnine, devoted to his business, and possessed of but one desire in life—to make money.

"But, miser though he was, he did not love money for its own sake.

"In his youth he had suffered much, and his poor wife's death had been accelerated from want of necessaries at a critical time.

"He was determined that his daughter should never know the same misery and wretchedness.

"She was young, she was beautiful, and he loved her as his life.

"She was very young, not more than fifteen, but she was quite a woman. The eastern climate ripens early, and kills, too, as quickly.

"The house they lived in was old. It had been built with more regard to architectural beauty outside than comfort within.

"It was, however, safe.

"There was no entrance, except from the shop, which was small, and guarded by a heavy iron door.

"Except a narrow space on the counter, which could be closed by an iron gate, the shop was shut off from all communication with the house, by iron railings.

"Here sat Signor Dunbar from morning till night, doing business.

"He was well known to have a splendid stock of jewellery, precious stones, and curiosities at his finger ends.

"He was the idol of our English officers in both army and navy.

"He advanced them any amount of money, at a good, but not usurious, rate of interest.

"But, then, he never lent but to perfectly solvent characters.

"He had the rent roll, resources, debts of every family, whose scion applied to him for assistance.

"He never risked money for large prospective profits.

"His plan was moderate profits and certainty.

"A man who insured his life, found special favour in his eyes. But he never objected to a large outlay of jewellery, on which the profit was very great.

"Every night he entered in his books, the profits of the day, and gloated with delight on his approach towards the sum which was to be the final fortune of his petted child.

"He made up his mind to a million sterling.

"His wish was not an unreasonable one; he had some years before inherited the savings, fortune, and estates of an elder brother. All this he had put into money, and lent out on mortgages, through an eminent solicitor in this country.

"And Teresa Dunbar, what of her?

"Unconscious of the splendid fortune which awaited her, she grew up in retirement, like a petted bird in a cage.

"The old man was approaching the acme of his hopes.

"He would then remove to England and find a husband for his Teresa from among the noblest in the land.

"His wealth would enable him to select one worthy of her.

"Worthy of her! Hers was a subtle, cunning, and artful nature, that deserved no such love. She regarded her confinement in that old house as refined cruelty on the part of her father.

"She had the best teachers that money could procure, every luxury that wealth could command.

"But she was a prisoner.

"Her soul burned with fiery and fierce passions.

"She almost hated the old man, whose life was one long martyrdom to her future position in society.

"She was petulant, dissatisfied, and even sulky at times.

"'Be patient, my bird,' he would say, 'the time is coming quick when we shall see our home—when you shall be as free, rich, and noble as you could wish.'

"'I want to be free here, in this sunny clime, not in that cold and distant clime of which I have read until my blood runs chilly in my veins.'

"And the old man reflected that perhaps she wanted society of her own rank and age, so he proposed that she should go to school in England, until he could settle his affairs and follow.

"She refused. No, she would stay with him.

"Then she changed her mind.

"Why?

"We shall see.

"Teresa lived on the second floor of the old-fashioned house, which had been fitted up with every comfort for her sole use.

"Here she took her lessons, played music, read, or oftener sat musing, as young girls will do upon whom the mysterious influence of the great master passion is falling for the first time.

"She would sit at the open casement, thinking, watering her flowers, feeding her bird, and listlessly leaning on her elbow, which was well-shaped, though dark.

"One day she was singing when she heard, at no great distance, a heavy sigh.

"She raised her head, and saw glaring at her with a fierce pair of eyes, a good-looking youth about sixteen or seventeen years of age.

"He was leaning out of a window about six feet above hers.

"He was dark, he was full of fire and spirits, and the solitary young girl thought she had found that which she was in search of.

"He bowed low—she smiled.

"There was in ten minutes no restraint between them.

"The youth confessed that for some days he had been watching her from his chamber, unseen and unnoticed, that a wild and terrible passion had filled his soul, and that the sigh which had startled her was the irrepressible bursting of his heart to speak his love.

"Her pupil dilated, and she asked him, in feverish accents, if he could not come near her, as their conversation might be interrupted.

"His eyes flashed, and he at once suggested that by means of a ball of twine, which he had, a rope ladder might be placed between the two rooms.

"The wayward, impulsive, and passionate girl nodded.

"The ball of twine was cast to her, and in a few minutes the youth was by her side.

"Her youth, her untutored passions, her solitary life, may have been some excuse for her forwardness.

"But she was ruined.

"Some hours later, after her father had wished her good-night, they began to talk more calmly.

"He spoke of marriage.

"He knew of her wealth.

"But how was it to be done? He was the son of a noble, ruined by the French revolution. He was poor; he had nothing but his talents, a fair education, and a determined will.

"Her father would never agree.

"Then flashed across the girl's mind the plan which her father had suggested for her going to school in England.

"Her father had never interfered with her reading.

"She knew all about Gretna Green, and the general ease of marriages in England.

"She proposed the scheme to Paolo. She would yield to her father's wishes,—she would agree to come to England. Once there, their marriage was an easy affair.

"But money!

"She could get any quantity.

"Paolo yielded, and, like *Romeo* from *Juliet's* chamber, went not until morn.

"Teresa, eager to carry out her plans, complained the next day of illness, and expressed a belief that the change to England, and the attendance of her great medical men, would benefit her.

"The doating father agreed at once.

"He spoke in terms of passionate fondness, and after explaining that a ship would start in a few days, on board which an English family were going to England, he said she should accompany them.

"He would follow as soon as he could wind up his affairs.

"'And now,' he added, stroking down her dark hair, 'I wish my child to understand me.

"'I was very poor in my youth. I was excluded, from no fault of mine, from my father's patrimony. I married a young and beautiful girl. She suffered much, and when you were born I vowed that you should never know that want which had caused me so much misery.

"'I determined to be rich. I am rich, rich by hundreds of thousands, and these, by that will,'' pointing to a piece of parchment, tied with red string and sealed by many seals, which lay on the table before him, 'everything is left to you.'

"Teresa stammered forth her thanks, and after some further conversation, hurried, guilty, and lost, to the arms of her lover.

"She told him all. He smiled, and said that she was treasure enough without the money.

"But in his heart of hearts it was the money he coveted.

"Young as he was, his soul lusted for wealth. It was his mania. He loved women, but no woman in particular. He had a raving passion for power and wealth, and already had committed crimes from which many a hoary galley-slave would have started aghast.

"He did not tell his thoughts.

"But he vowed that Teresa should be his without fear of her wealth being taken from her.

"How was this to be done?

"Alas! in that man's soul were devices so devilish that they would have surprised a fiend.

"It was arranged that Paolo should accompany Teresa on board the ship to England in the modest position of a student.

"He was English, though born abroad, and speaking every European language fluently.

"Every preparation was made to enable Teresa to perform her journey with comfort and *éclat*. Her *trousseau* was something wonderful.

"She had a rich order on a London banker.

"But there was one thing necessary yet to unite her closely to Paolo.

"She must commit a crime.

"True, she was guilty in the eyes of morality or towards virtue, but she had done nothing to bring her within the meshes of the law.

"She had, fond of show, money, and wealth as she was, expatiated on the beauty of certain diamonds, necklaces, and other jewels, which were to be her's when she came out into society.

"He, like a fiend, whispered in her ear that

such things were an absolute part of a girl's *trousseau;* that, being her own, why did she not take some of them with her, to adorn her at balls and parties, which, even at school, with her great means, she could command?

"She yielded.

"Her soul was not of that constitution which resists temptation.

"That night they opened her father's jewel chest, and *she* took from it such ornaments as were of most value.

"The next day she went on board.

"At evening time they sailed, the young scholar having come on board.

"But what had passed between twelve at noon and six in the evening?"

Edith drew a long breath, the Count de Florac's lips quivered, and Julie hid her face in her fan.

The whole audience listened attentively. The earnest manner of Edith more than words, had succeeded in deeply interesting all.

Even those who objected to some of her details could not muster courage to interrupt her.

"The jeweller, as soon as his daughter had departed from his home, at once resolved to hasten after her.

"He had fancied that he should not miss his child for a month or so.

"But no sooner was her back turned than he felt an aching void.

"He determined, then, at any sacrifice, to follow her, and that with as little delay as possible.

"He closed his shop, and began making an inventory of his goods preparatory to his departure for England.

"He was in his own room, where he kept his valuables, his ledger, his accounts, and correspondence.

"The book in which he entered all his transactions was before him.

"The costly box containing his choicest jewels, that which his daughter had robbed, was before him.

"He was in act of opening it.

"Something strange in the lock appeared to puzzle him.

"At length it flew open, and his keen and practised eye at once told him that it had been disturbed.

"A fearful groan of anguish passed his quivering lips, and then he bowed his head upon the table.

"No one but his daughter could have had access to it. "The thought was madness.

"'Robbed! robbed! by my child,' he cried.

"At the same moment a step was heard, followed by a cry of anguish.

"He had been struck by a dagger between the shoulders.

"Next morning the house was broken open by the police, and the whole tragedy discovered.

"Whom to suspect?

"The daughter had parted from her only parent at the ship's side.

"No one knew of any enemy he could fix on, yet the house was not robbed.

"The will and all the valuables were found intact.

*   *   *   *   *   *

"The young girl reached England, and though hearing of her father's death, still entered a school.

"She refused to marry her betrayer.

"She knew the value of her immense fortune.

"Besides she had taken a fierce dislike to her lover, who was as worthless as he was wicked—as wicked as he was worthless.

Edith ceased.

————

CHAPTER LXXX.

A VILE PLOT.

"Is that all?" said the Viscount de Florac, with a sneer on his pale face.

"No; for let me tell you that Teresa changed her name, and is now called Julie de Lorme, while the assassin calls himself Viscount de Florac."

A fierce cry from the viscount was followed by a rush towards the door. Julie sprang to her feet brandishing a small dagger, while all the company were wild with terror and astonishment.

But at this moment there darted forth from the doorway two officers, who seized the supposed viscount, while a tall, thin, gaunt, spare man sprang from behind some thick curtains and confronted Julie.

"Father!" shrieked the unhappy girl.

"Yes, your injured, betrayed, and disgraced father. That wretched assassin stabbed me in the back, and for nearly a year I hovered between life and death. His punishment is in the hands of the law, yours in mine."

And with a stately step he dragged the half-fainting girl away.

The officers removed the murderer, whose trembling lips, glazed eye, and horror-stricken countenance, sufficiently betrayed his guilt.

At this moment Captain Charles de Lancy and Henry entered hurriedly, while from an opposite side in rushed an upper servant with terror depicted on her countenance.

"What new calamity?" said the elder governess, who had stood for some minutes speechless with terror and astonishment.

"Nine of the young ladies have eloped, leaving notes in their rooms," said the terrified girl.

The sisters looked wildly round.

"Where is Louise?" gasped the younger Miss Crumpton.

"Gone."

The poor woman fainted. The pretty, unassuming, blue-eyed girl who walked with the under governess, was her own child. She had been married when very young, but had concealed her marriage, thinking the miss better in a high class school.

The uproar was now awful. Parents, whose children were in bed, insisted upon their being woke up, and dressed.

They would not allow them to remain an hour in the house.

"Ruin, utter ruin!" said the elder sister. "Where is Matilda?—help my poor sister."

"Please mum, Miss Matilda's gone too," said the upper servant; "she went with the parson gentleman."

All this time Lady Haddington, Cornelia, Captain Charles de Lancy, Henry, and Mrs. Charles de Lancy, were hurriedly preparing to leave. They were aghast with horror and disgust, and, above all, anxious to remove Jessie from the contamination of Mereton house.

Fearful was the confusion that ensued.

Carriages were wildly called for in all directions.

Those of Lady Haddington and Cornelia were before the door. The whole party squeezed into them. Mr. and Mrs. de Lancy, with the latter's mother, were to accompany them on a visit.

Their home was soon reached, and all gladly bounded from the carriages.

A sharp, shrill cry, resounded from half-a-dozen lips.

"*Where is Jessie?*"

But no Jessie was to be seen. Each of those in the three several carriages had supposed her in the other.

JESSIE HAD DISAPPEARED.

CHAPTER LXXXI.

THE SEARCH FOR JESSIE.

MEANWHILE, dire was the uproar and confusion at the school.

The police had carried off the Viscount de Florac.

Julie had gone with her father, without giving a glance at her old lover.

The visitors had all retired.

It now transpired that while Edith was taking her extraordinary revenge on Julie, the nine girls alluded to had taken advantage of the intense interest with which the story was listened to to slip out one after another, reach their apartments, and write a note.

After this they slipped out, assisted by the very girl who, once they were off, gave the alarm.

She was, it is true, bewildered at the simultaneous elopement of nine, but avarice overcame every other consideration.

But imagine the horror of the two wretched ruined heads of the school, when they read the notes.

Every letter said the same thing. Something had occurred which rendered it impossible for them to stay any longer in the school. But under the protection of Miss Matilda Crunch, and trusting to the honour of the Viscount de Florac, who was about to make instant reparation by an immediate marriage, they thought it best to withdraw from Mereton House.

Such was the tenor of every letter.

The accomplished and cunning villain—this worse than Don Juan—had, by means of bribery and his forked tongue, succeeded in deluding nine girls into the belief that he was about to marry them.

And not one had discovered the other's secret.

Here was a fearful and horrible scandal, one enough to ruin the reputation of a hundred schools.

And then poor Louise.

She thought herself an orphan, brought up in the school by the charity of friends.

Her mother studiously avoided giving any ground for suspicion.

She did not even show her any greater indulgence than any other child.

But she confided her to the care of Miss Matilda Crouch.

But vanity and avarice had turned her head.

The Rev. Obadiah Simcox had promised her the head position in his household. He had succeeded in converting her to the true church.

He had also crossed her palm, not with silver, but with gold.

While the sisters were bemoaning the hard fate, a tremendous knock at the door startled even the servants, who were packing up.

They opened hurriedly.

It was Captain Charles de Lancy, Henry, and the Dwarf.

All were all as white as ashes.

"Had any one seen Jessie—"

"No."

Not a soul in the house but answered the same.

At this moment a beachman passed by.

"Beg parding," he said, "but be ye looking for a young lady?"

"Yes, my friend," replied the Captain, motioning to his companions to be still.

"Well, I saw nine go on board a big brig bound for Meriky," he said, "and I see one carried on board in a faint like."

The house faced the sea, on a high terrace, overlooking humbler dwellings.

It was morning.

"There they be," said the beachman, pointing to the offing.

All looked, and away in the distance could be seen the brig and the yacht.

"Their names—"

"The Nauvoo brig, from Bristol, and the Hosprey yacht—"

"We must after them," said Henry, whose stern, compressed lips showed how deeply he felt the dreadful occurrence.

"We must," said the Captain, gravely, "but we must have Admiralty authorisation first."

"How long will that take," cried Henry.

"We can telegraph and see," replied the youthful officer, with a grave smile, for he knew too well the character of official people not to be sadly afraid.

Of course our readers know that we allude to the clumsy old telegraph used by our naval authorities before the present wonderful invention came into practice.

They telegraphed full particulars, and then went home.

Cornelia was in a raging fever.

Lady Haddington was heart-broken.

But it was fearful to see the agony of the Dwarf. Jessie, to be safe, had remained at home under the impression that with her mother and Lady Haddington she was quite safe.

He seemed now to blame himself for all that had occurred. He wept bitterly, and refused to be comforted.

Captain Charles de Lancy, who, considering that he had returned from a four months' journey to the society of a young wife, was marvellously chivalrous and ready, suggested that he should accompany them on their contemplated journey.

"No," he said, shaking his head mournfully, "heaven knows how gladly I would accompany you, but my duty is clearly marked out. My post is here, but I will procure you documents which will authorise you to act for her mother."

The captain bowed.

"She is ill—delirious—you know something of her history; I will tell you more while we are waiting the verdict of the doctors. But Henry, when you find Jessie, not a word. I have most urgent reasons for what I say."

And the Dwarf told his story and hers not completely, not fully, but as much of it as he thought wise and proper.

It was, indeed, an extraordinary one, and one which, when fully developed, will startle and amaze our readers.

They heard him with silent awe and wonder.

Both shook him heartily by the hand, and Cornelia, being in the charge of Lady Haddington and the doctor—who promised a favourable turn—it was then agreed to seek for further information by a visit to the inn.

Mrs. Mary Jones looked considerably confused and chop-fallen when her visitors arrived.

The Rev. Obadiah Simcox had scarcely paid any bill during his whole stay. The Viscount had not asked for his.

Both appeared so exceedingly flush of money that to have presented an account would, so Mrs. Jones thought, have looked like an insult.

Many travellers would like to be treated with such consideration.

Her weeping and lamentations were now something awful, though John Jones giggled and sniggered, especially at the backsliding of Miss Matilda Crunch, that most pious and chaste virgin.

Mrs. Jones could tell them little more than they knew, and that was so coupled with regrets and personal sorrows that they left hopeless of any more satisfactory result.

Having heard from a messenger that no despatch had come, they determined to visit the prison.

CHAPTER LXXXII.

MASTER PAOLO.

A SIMPLE call upon a visiting magistrate produced the requisite order, and in great hope they all hurried to the small prison of the town.

The order was simply to admit them to see the prisoner.

A fee from the Dwarf of a rather liberal character enabled them to see him alone.

He was in a cell about four feet wide and ten long, by as many high.

He sat on a seat at the extreme end, his legs chained to a heavy transverse bar. In the prison dress, pale, haggard, and with a wild, anxious look, none of those who had seen him in his more fashionable garb could, by any possibility, have known him to be the same person.

"What do you want?" he said savagely. "Am I to be made a show of? I won't be insulted."

"We come not to insult you. We come for information—"

"Oh—you want me to criminate myself. What can you say against me? That I seduced nine lovely girls—what of that?"

His listeners shuddered.

"We want no details on that matter," said the Dwarf sternly, "we come for information relative to your vile accomplice—"

"Ha!" said the other with a long drawn breath, and he added, grinding his teeth, "Could you hang him?"

"That could I," cried the Dwarf, in his impetuous way.

"I hope so. The villain—you have his name?"

"No."

"His name is Phineas Bristowe—"

"Heavens!" cried Henry.

"Curses light on the fiend," shrieked the Dwarf, "and he has been within my grasp for months. Hang him—yes, had he ninety lives."

"But what shall I gain?" said the prisoner, sullenly, "by anything I say? I am a hopeless prisoner, without a friend, charged with crime committed in a foreign land."

"For which you will be tried in Malta—if the people don't tear you to pieces," said Captain de Lancy, sternly.

The prisoner turned pale. Some fearful reminiscence seemed to make him writhe in agony.

"Merciful heavens, why so?—I committed no crime. I only struck the old man in self-defence," he cried, "why take me back there?"

"Because such is the law. Now, remember," continued Captain de Lancy. "I make no promises, but make a clean breast of it—and we shall see what may be done."

The young man thought a moment, and then told that part of his story which referred to himself and Phineas Bristowe, since their meeting at the watering-place.

They thanked him, placed money in his hands, and left with a promise to apply for his trial to take place in England.

Before following him, however, let us stay a few minutes with the prisoner.

The gaol was small, but well built and airy.

On the principle that those who have a short time to live should, at all events, enjoy some immunities and favours never granted to lesser criminals, the prisoners for a capital offence, like the condemned felon, always enjoy certain privileges.

This was not departed from in the present instance.

The Viscount de Florac had the best ceil in the gaol.

But his ankles were manacled, still without interfering too much with his movements.

His window was level with his head when he stood up.

Could he have stood upon his chair, he could have looked out.

But the manacles upon the ankles were principally for this very purpose.

The window was square, and well secured by iron bars.

They looked too thick for a giant to have broken, and the Viscount de Florac had very little idea of being freed from his chains.

His whole aspect was gloomy, dark, and hopeless. He seemed to have done with the world.

He was ghastly pale.

No sooner were their backs turned than a cold, sardonic smile passed across his countenance.

"Take me back to Malta," he said, between his set teeth. "Oh, no! no! no! If they but knew. And yet they will do it—it is just like them. But here is a power which enables me to defy them all."

And he unwound his curly hair, taking from a heavy tress, almost like a woman's, a small glass bottle.

He opened it.

The stopper was in one hand, the bottle itself in the other.

A faint almond-like smell pervaded the whole cell.

The prisoner smiled a smile so wan, so hopeless, and yet so fiendishly triumphant, that his own mother must have shuddered at him.

"Ha! ha! ha!" he said aloud, "they think to have me, but I have them—ha! ha! ha! 'tis a fair world and a brave, but better to die thus than dangle by a rope in mid air."

"Hist—Paolo!" said a low hushed voice from without.

The viscount replaced the stopper in the bottle and carefully concealed it.

"Who is there?"

"Teresa."

"Where?"

"Outside."

The window of the cell, for the purpose of light and air, was situated in a narrow lane that skirted the prison.

"So you have not deserted me?"

"Deserted you—heaven forbid. You have been my whole thought since that wretched girl betrayed and ruined us."

"Why did she do so?" asked the Viscount de Florac, a little sarcastically.

"How can I account for a woman's tortuous ways?" said the other, a little huskily.

"Well, no matter; why have you come?"

"To compass your escape."

"How?"

"What need you?"

"A file."

"It is here," she replied, as she glided it in through the bars.

"A bottle of vitriol."

"I have not forgotten it."

"A small saw."

"Catch it."

"Thanks my brave girl—there is a good time coming yet."

"How long will you be?"

"The hour?"

"Two."

"Midnight will see me free—perhaps the hour of ten."

"I will be here."

"Had I but a flask of generous wine," added the viscount.

"It has been thought of," replied Julie de Lorme.

The viscount caught at it eagerly, and drank a large draught.

"That restores me," said the young man. "Now leave me to work. I must listen with all my ears."

"Ten!" replied the voice.

And then all was silent, save when the low, rasping sound of the file could be heard—grit—grit—grit.

Presently the gaoler came on his afternoon rounds.

He brought some meat, bread, and water.

"I drink nothing but wine," said the Viscount de Florac, with a scornful smile.

He had hurriedly concealed all his unlawful possessions.

"May be," laughed the gaoler, "but that ain't allowed here."

"What is the price of a good bottle?" replied the Viscount.

"Hast any money?"

"You have my purse — it contains seven pounds—for each pound you can bring me a bottle"—continued the other.

The gaoler shook his head.

"You must give me the money with your own hand."

"Hearkee, my man. No one saw me searched but yourself—arrange with the searcher. I will sign a fresh paper leaving out the seven pounds. Let me have seven bottles of good wine and they are yours."

The prisoner had, on his arrival, been carefully searched, and a list of his things made out.

In the hurry of the night arrival no one had read it.

The viscount had signed it disdainfully.

The gaoler hurried away to fetch the wine.

In half an hour he ventured with the bottle and the list.

The prisoner turned on one side to read it. As he did so a sardonic grin crossed his face.

In his trade of an adventurer he was up to many tricks.

He wiped his pen carefully.

He dipped it, not in the inkstand but in a little phial he had taken from his belt.

He signed in a large bold hand.

The gaoler thanked him and folded up the paper.

We may here mention that when produced to the justices it was found without a signature.

It was blank in all but the handwriting of the gaoler.

The covetous functionary could give no explanation, and was discharged.

Meanwhile the prisoner, having got rid of his manacles, had risen to his feet and commenced upon the window.

The bars were thick, but the vitriol was burning, the oil was soft, and the saw truly tempered.

The task went bravely on. He felt double vigour under the influence of the generous wine, and long before eight o'clock had got rid of one bar.

Then he heard the round coming.

He hastily replaced the bar, sat down with the manacles on his feet, and folded his arms.

"Well, ole fellash," said the gaoler, "how dosh yer find'sh yourself?"

"Tollol," replied the viscount.

His keeper was drunk, dead, beastly drunk.

The viscount had a great mind to knock him down.

"Allsh shryht," said the gaoler; "now prisoner—shleep."

Then he bent low, telegraphing over his shoulder to where his subordinates were outside.

"Comsh—smoksh—pipe—shoon—"

And slammed the door.

The viscount laughed grimly. If there was one thing more than another he missed in prison it was tobacco.

An excellent slave, but a bad master, is the Virginian weed.

When ill, when care is worrying us, when we vainly seek an escape from a great difficulty, what so consoling, what so pleasant as the fragrant whiff?

But the young smoker of modern times, puffing, blowing, and spitting, ere his bones are set, is paving the way to death.

No wonder that, in the present census, women predominate by half-a-million.

They neither smoke, nor turn day into night, nor gamble, nor follow any of the devices which lead speedily unto death.

Their errors, when they have errors, are charming ones.

Ere nine o'clock the window was free. But the Viscount de Florac wore the prison dress, and he thought it better to wait.

———

CHAPTER LXXXIII.

MR. JOHNSON'S SUPPER.

ABOUT a quarter past nine, when all was still, when boys had ceased to whistle, and girls to quarrel, when the officials of the gaol had collected in the stone kitchen, to talk over pipes and beer, of the ludicrous dereliction of duty of the chief goaler, did Paolo, Viscount de Florac, hear a scratching noise at his door.

Then after some difficulty a key was inserted in the door, and the wicket opened.

The chief gaoler winked at Paolo.

In his hand was a lamp, which he laid on a kind of side shelf.

He was very much intoxicated, but he was able to do what he wanted.

He dragged in a small table and a stool.

Then followed a basket.

Last of all he closed the door.

"Now, olsh boy, laysh the cloth," he said, staggering to a seat, "we'll enjoy ourselves."

The Viscount de Florac could scarcely believe his senses. He, however, rightly judged that the head gaoler, on the strength of the seven pounds, had been enjoying himself, and in that state of maudlin generosity which, with some people, is the offspring of drink, had determined to share his enjoyment with the author of his own extra treat.

De Florac could scarcely help laughing in the other's face, but forbore to do so in consideration of the promised treat.

The drunken man seated himself with great pomposity on his stool, put his pipe in his mouth, and surveyed the whole scene with extreme unction.

He was a stout little man, with a brown frock coat, red waistcoat, and one of those queer cocked hats, in more civilised parts of the world peculiar to Greenwich and Chelsea pensioners.

His nose was rubicund, and his little grey eye twinkled with undisguised merriment and enjoyment.

He appeared to expect Viscount de Florac to do the honours and himself to look on.

The viscount, utterly regardless of the presence of the head gaoler, had shaken off his manacles.

Mr. Johnson was perfectly indifferent to the fact.

He had, at that moment, a notion above fetters.

Paolo dived into the basket and brought up a pie.

"Pigeon!" said Johnson, with a hiccup.

Knives and forks, glasses, two bottles of wine, cheese and bread followed.

"Eat," said the gaoler.

"Drink!" cried the prisoner.

And he poured out two stiff bumpers. He had need of all the artificial stimulant he could obtain to nerve himself for his enterprise. The gaoler was in that foolish state of drunkenness when a man will take all he can get.

The viscount having heartily devoured a goodly portion of the pigeon pie, lit his pipe.

Mr. Johnson smoked with extreme gravity. He had evidently come primed with something he had to say, but could not recollect it.

At length he seemed to catch it by the tail.

"More money?" he said, closing one eye.

"Yes."

"How moosh?"

"What for?"

"Hearkee, friend Flurrie—Hayrick or whatsomever your name is—you'r—jolly good fellish—"

"Thank you."

"I'm good-hearted chap, mind you—donsh like see shen'man hung—so it struck me as you would like to boltch!"

"The very thing I mean to do."

"Now'sh, yer see, nutchin for nutchin, I am willinch to risk my place, and all that sort of

THE RESCUE.

thing, if, yer see, you can downsh with the dust."

"How much?" said De Florac, musing."

"You shee's Mr. Hurric, you shee, there's me and my missish, yer see, and four little Johnsons, yer see, and it ain't much amongst ush."

"How much?"

"I thought I said—shousand pounds, yesh, I did say shousand pounds."

"Well, Mr. Johnson," said the Viscount de Florac, gravely, "I'll think about it. You must be aware that I do not carry such a sum about me, but I dare say it can be managed. To-morrow I will give you my answer, so now—hurrah! and another bumper."

The gaoler accepted the draught, but it proved too much for him. He drained it to the last dregs, and fell back insensible, muttering something about "shousand pounds."

The viscount at once took off his coat, hat, and vest, after which he denuded him of his unmentionables, which he himself donned.

He then, in pure mischief, dragged the drunken brute to his own vacated seat, leaned him against the wall, placed the manacles over his legs, and, as a last indignity, standing on his shoulders, vaulted through the arched window into the lane.

He had heard the welcome voice of the girl, who had really saved his life.

He caught her in his arms, and embraced her

wildly. Men are rarely ungrateful just when their lives have been saved.

In danger, the doctor is my dear friend.

In doubt, my dear sir.

In convalescence, "Well docter—did'nt expect to see you."

"Come," whispered Julie.

But ere they could move from the spot a startling interruption took place.

"Come—I'll come you, you artful hussy,—who should a man come with, but his own lawful wife, I should like to know. Ugh, you drunken brute."

"Betsy," said a solemn hollow voice, from some unknown quarter; "I'll swear that's Betsy —ors right."

De Florac understood the situation in a moment, and turning sharp round, grinned horribly in the face of the goaler's wife, who no sooner saw his countenance, than she shrieked violently.

"Ors right," grunted the distant voice.

"Ugh—you brute," said the Mrs. Johnson, for whose interests the goaler had so recently been pleading, "I can see it all—ruined—lost, undone."

And, losing no time, she ran to the door of the prison, rang the bell, and, in one moment announced to the astonished warders the escape of this principal prisoner.

A general rush took place to his cell,—when, to the wild surprise and increased astonishment of all present, they found, seated in the prisoner's place, Mr. Johnson the gaoler.

As no explanation could be got from him, the delinquent was taken to bed, while Mrs. Johnson effaced every sign of the night's festivities, leaving behind, however, the file, the saw, the vitriol, and the oil.

Strange as it may appear, no rumour of the orgie passed the prison gates.

Mrs. Johnson was a good general, and out of her matron's place had saved money.

But, as we have before remarked, this did not save her husband.

In the meantime the officers were in chase of the fugitive.

They returned ere morn without tale or tidings of him, and yet his fate was not many hours a secret.

CHAPTER LXXXIV.

THE HAUNTED HOUSE.

"WHITHER are we going?" said the Viscount de Florac, as they had gained the shelter of a silent and unfrequented street.

"To my father's house," replied Julie.

"What?"

"I mean what I say. He has forgiven me, and is quite ready to consent to our marriage, after which he proposes to visit America. He has conveyed all his treasure there."

"Forgiven you—wishes to be friends with me?" said de Florac, clutching her by the arm, and looking full in her pale and excited face: "what does this mean?"

"It means that my father loves me to distraction—that once alone with him I explained all, our mutual affection, my detestation of marriage for mere fortune's sake—and, after an arduous struggle, he yielded."

"Teresa, you then affect to love me?"

"Can you doubt it?"

"I have doubted it."

"Why?"

"I have seen your eyes fixed on others—and then, why the deadly hatred of this English girl?"

"The man she loves did notice me once, and had I encouraged him would have been glad to have dallied at my feet. But the fool was married—enough of this, however—what say you to a journey to America, the land of the free?"

"I care not where it is, so that I have love, riches, happiness," replied the viscount.

"You shall have all; but we will to the warm and sunny south. That is my dream—to be waited on by slaves—to be really and truly master—to have no law but one's own will; that to me is happiness—"

The viscount smiled. Perhaps he thought that with such a husband she would find that she would have some other master besides her own will.

But he did not reply. He was puzzled. He knew not what to think of this sudden change on the part of an old man he had not used too gently.

He knew very well the fascination of the syren, but he knew also the power of revenge.

What to think he knew not.

Several times he determined to shake off his companion and flee, but then there arose the mighty difficulty as to leaving the country.

It was not to be done without money.

And then there were one or two places already, at his age, too hot to hold him: one of these was France; another was Italy.

While debating, therefore, the proper course in his mind, he reached the threshold of his destination.

It was a dark and gloomy night. Deeply-charged clouds sped with fearful rapidity across the horizon, portending a tremendous and immediate storm.

The wind howled through the tall trees, and waved their huge boughs about like the arms of a windmill.

The young girl had opened a gate leading to an avenue of trees.

They were tall, thick, and gloomy, and led towards an old house, long since doomed to destruction.

It was for sale, and was to be pulled down by the buyer.

The Viscount de Florac knew it well, as well as its fearful reputation.

"Why has your father chosen Castle Gloom for his residence?"

"Because it suits his ideas. He has bought it, and, until he rebuilds it, chooses to dwell there. It is an odd fancy, truly; but who can fathom the heart of man?"

"Would I could the heart of woman!"

"'Tis easy—"

"As to decipher hieroglyphics."

"Why so?"

"Let a woman say or do what she will, there is always something behind she does not reveal."

"You are learned in women."

"I have lived more than most men of my age," he said, with a fatuitous smile.

"'Tis well for you," replied Julie, with a sneer.

"Why so?"

"Is it not happiness to enjoy life, and have not you enjoyed it?"

"I have, and mean to enjoy it more. But hark you, Julie—why this cold, sneering, dissembling tone? In what way are you deceiving me; to what are you leading me?"

"Why ask a woman whom you do not believe?" she said quietly.

"I ought to believe you," he replied, with a deep sigh; "and yet I feel as if you were like all your strange and vacillating race since Eve—a bitter deceiver."

"Paolo superstitious!" she said.

"No, not superstitious; but, girl, like most men of my character, I am a fatalist. No rope, no water, will or can kill me; but I have a terrible dread of fire."

"Why so?"

"A gipsy—"

"Ha, ha, ha!—a gipsy. So you believe in old wives' tales?"

"And so would you if you knew this one," replied Paolo, angrily.

"I will laugh no more. What said she?"

"The other night I was wandering alone, musing of the future—"

"And of Julie."

"And of Julie, as you say. Suddenly there appeared before me an aged woman, bent double. She called me by my name—my real name"—here he shuddered fearfully—"and, after telling me of things I thought buried in oblivion, warned me that rope would not hang, water would not drown, but that fire would at length burn me."

"Paolo," said the young girl, pausing on the threshold of the house—"your real name, what is that?"

"A secret that dies with me."

"Surely you must have done strange deeds to fear that your name should be known!"

"Strange deeds!—yes. But, Julie, give me a home and love, and my name shall ring yet for good and glory. I am not naturally evil. I have been much tempted—but no matter. How the old house frowns!"

It was an old house—of what time or age, or architecture, few cared to ask. It had once been the manor house, but had long since been abandoned. The mouldering timbers of the windows and doors almost yielded to the touch, and the affrighted sparrows, who had sought therein a shelter for their brood, escaped with a shrill chirp into the night air.

A fearful tale of crime and murder reddened its walls.

Not the meanest peasant would live in it.

It had fallen to decay, and, as the wind moaned and hurried through its glassless casements, the ignorant might well be excused for fancying the place was haunted.

The door leading to the hall was still entire, and as Julie raised the knocker and awoke the echoes, the whole building seemed to groan.

Presently the door swung open and the old man stood before them.

"Come in," he said.

Hand in hand, they entered, and the door was closed behind them.

The old man opened a side door, leading to a room which had once been the library, but which had long since been abandoned to the bats.

A rude fire burned in the hearth.

A table, on which were some refreshments, filled the centre of the room.

Three chairs were arrayed around it.

The old man seated himself and bade them do likewise.

Both obeyed.

The Signor Dunbar was tall, thin, haggard; the face gave token of great physical and mental sufferings, while a keen and restless eye marked a nature keen, observant, and relying on itself.

There was power, secretiveness, and passion, in that lofty forehead.

His mouth exhibited a hard and remorseless nature.

He wore a dressing-gown and fur cap.

"Young man," he said, "my daughter has revealed to me the past. Of that I have little wish to speak. Enough that you have rudely rifled the precious casket of a woman's honour—enough that in a moment of phrenzy, you wished to take a life which was useless to me, but which assured you both riches and power. Enough—I want no words. You love my daughter."

"I do."

"You wish to be her husband?"

"I do."

"'Tis well, none other would have her. We are going to America. According to the customs of that land, shall you be wed this night. Are you willing both?"

"I am."

"Yes, father."

The old man rose, and, opening a door, there entered one whom both recognised as the American consul.

He was a judge in his own country.

He had the power to marry.

The ceremony was brief. A paper was signed. The bride and bridegroom put their names—and, the official having received a large fee, bowed low and retired.

CHAPTER LXXXV.

THE DEAD BRIDAL.

The old man rose and saw him out, then returning, he poured forth wine, and the three drank.

"Now," he said.

"What sir?" asked the viscount, for under this name he had married.

"Allow me to conduct you to the bridal chamber," said the father hoarsely.

Julie looked appealingly at him.

"Take your husband's arm—he seems strangely dilatory for a young lover. When I was wed— Ha! ha! ha! I tarried not 'till I was alone with her. I loved and no witness could interrupt my happiness."

He grinned horribly a ghastly smile.

Julie turned pale.

The viscount looked from one to the other.

"Who is the dupe," thought he? "the old man meditates some treachery. But, let us humour him."

He bowed gallantly to his wife and led her after her father, who bore a lamp.

He halted before a room at the back of the house, looking out upon a stream.

It was rudely furnished.

A low wooden bedstead and a chair was all its furniture.

"You must fain, young people, put up with this to-night," he said, with his odd smile; "you shall have better accommodation to-morrow. In the evening our ship sails for the land of the free."

And, hurrying away, he closed the door.

Julie cast herself weeping into her husband's arms.

She writhed in agony.

"What is the matter?" he said.

"Oh Paolo!" she replied, "will you love me, be true to me"—

"I will,—but why this agitation?"

"Paolo," she whispered in his ear, "my father's forgiveness is all a sham. He is satis-fied with the marriage—but he wants a widow for his daughter."

"Fiend of hell?" began De Florac, "I half suspected this."

"Hush! He expects you to sleep. Then I am to open the door and let him in. But I never mean to do it. I wished to be your wife, and I shammed consent. Here!"

And she placed a pistol and a dagger in his hands.

Her eyes flashed, her face flushed, her whole mien was that of one who had come to an awful determination.

She looked a Lucrezia Borgia and a Beatrice Cenci all in one.

The Viscount de Florac took the arms.

"Now, I am safe."

"Yes—my love, my life—and, at last we may be happy."

"Ha! ha! ha!"

"What fiendish laugh is that?"

As he spoke, a heavy key turned in the lock, and an iron bar was heard falling without.

Paolo rushed to the window.

It was barred with iron.

"Ha! ha! ha!" shouted a maniacal voice; "little dears—rob and kill your father, will you? Pretty turtle doves—caught in a trap, caught in a trap, my precious darlings. The old man is going, going, going—and you will burn, burn, burn!"

"D—n, what does the old wretch mean?"

"Father, father, surely you will not kill my husband?" gasped Julie.

"Both, both! serpents, vipers, toads! ha! ha! ha! you thought the old man was going to forgive—wait, and you shall see."

And they heard him going away—silent, pitiless, without a word.

They rushed at the door, but it was strong and defied their utmost efforts.

"Vile wretch," said the viscount wildly, "this is your doing."

"Oh, say not so, Paolo, I did but jest. If we must die, let us not quarrel; but, surely, he will not be so cruel."

The viscount made no reply, but proceeded to examine the room in search of some weapon, or something which could be turned into a weapon in order to burst open the door.

Meanwhile the old man, after effecting some preliminary arrangements, descended to the ground and closed the door behind him.

His face was horrible to see, so clearly was madness and revenge there wildly mingled.

Not wishing to strike a light, and fatigued with his exertions, he threw himself down upon the grass near the shrubbery, and, by the aid of the moonbeams, partook savagely and like one famished of some of the dry and scanty provisions he brought out with him.

But the change of scene made him shudder; he felt an icy chillness come over him, as he arose and sought the purling brook, on which the moon streamed serenely, and drank deeply of its pure water.

He feared for a moment to allow the air to descend on his parched head; he listened to the distant lowing of the cattle—to the barking of a dog in the village; and, like a being scouted by the world—loathsome to the sight of honest men—he entered the lone copse, and threw himself upon the cold grass to pass a night far more wretched than imagination can picture.

But he lay with the moon streaming upon his careworn face, till the passing cloud floated over the face of the same, and then he fell asleep; but not even then to rest. He started from a brief repose, cold and miserable, and, muttering upon the fate he was enduring, he again sank to sleep.

But why that cry—that moan? it bespoke a fear of consciousness in itself worse than death.

He dreamed it was true. He slept, but it was, as it were, the last effort of nature; it was a forced sleep of agony.

Suddenly he awoke.

The hall was in flames. The old, the dry, the antiquated building was burning, crackling, roaring like a furnace.

"Ha! ha! ha! ha! ha!" roared the old man, who was surely mad, for within that fearful blazing pile was his only child and her husband; "so they would have killed and robbed the old man, would they?—ha! ha! ha! I have them now. They will hurt me no more."

At the moment a wild shriek, a terrible yell of despair, rose upon the night wind.

"Ha! ha!" he laughed, "so they begin to feel the fire. A jolly bridal this—who comes? —but no, there is no sound."

Another roar was distinctly heard.

The worm-eaten pannelling of a vast chamber had caught.

"Ah!" he exclaimed, "the old house is doomed.

"Where are they now? he comes not."

He parted his long grey hair from his forehead, and muttered incoherent imprecations upon their devoted heads, as he calmly awaited the end.

A roar was distinctly hear, the furniture was burning quickly, and though he did not behold it, the flames leaped madly from the gothic windows, and the wood cracked with sickening violence.

"Ah ! it burns well—it has caught the library ! I hear the door falling !" and he looked down the stairs as the flames burst forth in violence, and a scream of terror arose in the building.

"Again !" he cried.

He ran to the window, as a confused murmur of voices was heard, and the sound of horses' feet came upon the night air.

The whole of one wing of the edifice was in a blaze, and reflected far and near.

The truth was too evident ; a passing traveller had alarmed the village.

He knew that hundreds might flock to the spot, but he would not quit his post.

The first to arrive on the spot were Captain de Lancy, Henry, and a body of villagers.

They were on their way to the brig, which was starting in chase of the emigrant vessel.

Attracted to the fire by some irresistible impulse, the captain at once recognised Mr. Dunbar.

"Good heavens !" he cried, "what is the meaning of this?"

A fearful yell of utter dismay and despair burst from the burning pile ere he could reply.

"Man !" said the captain, clutching the arm of the jeweller, "what is this ? Who is within yon house ?"

"My daughter and her husband !" yelled the other. "Ha ! ha ! ha ! it is of no use, you can't save them ; they are burning on earth, while down, down, below hell awaits them !"

Bidding some of the peasants take charge of the maniac, the captain looked around, saw a large beam of wood, and, himself setting the example, it was directed with terrific force against the doorway.

The doorway gave way with a crash.

The hall was full of smoke, but as yet no fire had reached it.

Captain de Lancy, followed by Henry, entered, and shouted loudly to any who might be within.

But no response came.

He then endeavoured to ascend the old stone staircase.

But the smoke and flames poured down with awful fury.

There was no chance of saving the old Manor House.

They reluctantly retreated, but made another effort on another side.

"Back ! back !" suddenly shouted some of the spectators.

The captain caught his midshipman by the arm, and retreated quickly.

The roof had caught fire, and the lead, used so much in the olden time, was flowing down in fiery flakes.

Nothing living could be within that vast and all-consuming furnace.

Captain de Lancy turned away with a deep sigh, once more to interrogate the madman ; but in the confusion he had contrived to give his captors the slip, and was nowhere to be seen.

The officers in chase of Paalo now came up, and being informed that he had perished with Julia in the flames, returned to make a report according to the evidence.

Captain de Lancy and Henry Haddington went on board.

CHAPTER LXXXVI.

THE FIREFLY.

THE small sloop of war commanded by Captain de Lancy, and to which our hero, to his very great delight, had been appointed, was one of the swiftest vessels in the service.

Nothing, then, could have been easier than to have overtaken the delinquent Mormon emigrant brig.

But how ?

They knew that she was bound for America ; but they also knew that she might, in the hope of blinding them, have changed her destination.

The deluded apostles of the new religion have, in general, selected New York as their port of debarcation ; but there was no particular reason why, under the fears of pursuit, they might not hurry elsewhere, and, escaping into the interior, thus effectually bar all fear of discovery.

It behoved them, then, to be cautious, to keep a strict look out, to speak every vessel coming in a contrary direction, and to be guided by circumstances.

The young midshipman was perfectly wild with excitement. Nothing kept him up but the strict discipline so essential to naval glory, and the personal kindness of the captain.

Henry, though still a boy, loved his dear friend Jessie with an earnestness and warmth which wanted but a few years to fan into a flame that would last with his life.

Never laugh at boyish love. In after years it may turn out that that which was timidly expressed in days gone by was a mighty and a real passion which has left traces upon every future transaction.

Master Henry had begun to smoke his cigar, and often, in the recesses of the cabin, casting off all the restraints of rank, the commander and his subordinate would talk of the dear absent one.

The orders of the Admiralty were to bring back the vessel wherever they found it, in order that the abductors might be tried for their crime.

Our readers must, however, be pretty well aware how vain was the hope to fall in with that one particular vessel in the vast expanse of the great ocean.

Still those interested did not despair.

Night after night the young captain and his midshipman walked the deck in earnest conversation, but ever watchful of the horizon.

The look-outs were indefatigable.

Twenty pounds was promised to the first who discovered the brig.

All hands were to be treated sumptuously.

For several days the weather was fine in the extreme.

A wind on the starboard quarter sent them bowling along at a gallant pace.

For two days they had carried on a fine nine-knot breeze, to the delight of captain and crew, but, towards the evening of the second day, it began to increase in strength.

The atmosphere became dense, the clouds appeared to frown down upon them, the stiff top-gallant breeze increased to a gale, and hands were called to take in the mainsail.

This made her ride easier for a time, though she still plunged terrifically.

Then from the dark and murky clouds the rain began to fall in such fearful torrents as are rarely seen in any but tropical districts, though in North America it does " pour a few."

The sailors said that every drop was the size of a musket ball; and the ceaseless, never-dying shower flashed and hissed as it cut up the black and tumbling sea.

The Firefly flew before the sudden and furious gusts. It required all the presence of mind of two old salts at the wheel, aided by a quarter-master, to keep her from broaching too.

But it was still daylight, if daylight there could be in such a storm.

"The Nauvoo," shouted the look-out, and every eye was bent in the direction indicated; "two points on the weather-bow!"

Yes, there she was; now lifted on a wave, now sinking into the trough of the sea.

All who had seen her, in fact, now recognised her, some by one thing, some by another.

A loud shout ran through the vessel.

But this was no time for shouting. Dark night was coming on, and the wind was increasing fast. They lowered the main-topsail, furled the fore and mizen-topsails, clewed up the fore-sail, doubled the watch on deck, and scudded on in the darkness and obscurity of the wild and troubled ocean; but the fast increasing gale compelled them to have everything furled fore and aft, and the ship was almost under bare poles.

'T was not without some reason, for the wind
  Increased at night, until it blew a gale:
And, though 't was not much to a naval mind,
  Some landsmen would have turned a little pale,
For sailors are, in fact, a different kind,
  At sunset they began to take in sail,
For the sky showed it would come on to blow,
And carry away, perhaps, a mast or so.

Nobody went below. The captain stood on the quarter deck holding on to a brass stancheon. Henry clung close to him. Their eyes were as much as possible directed towards the spot where the Nauvoo had been seen, but, from some cause or other, not a trace could be discovered.

The probabilities appeared to be that she had taken in all sail, and was scudding under bare poles.

But all surmise was useless. They must wait the coming morn. The fury of the storm was such as can only be described in the words of an eloquent sailor.

" Sir," were the words of Henry, to one of his superior officers, " when I stood by the weather rigging of the mizenmast and saw the stupendous mountains of ink that rolled towards us, black, heaving, crested and terrible, with the pale green lightning bursting behind them, and revealing the sharp outline of their ridges, as it shot through the cloudy sky, then the thunder followed, peal on peal, as if its very sound would have ploughed the ocean up; and then came another deluge of blinding rain, while the wind blew in one unceasing and unvarying tempest. The dead lights were shipped, and the hatches battened down till our people below were almost suffocated; the pumps were kept at work, and the strong ship rose and fell like a cork on the stormy sea, one moment pitching with bows under water, and the next, rolling till her channels were buried and her yard-arms dipping in the foam."

The lightning flashed with a vividness which would not be understood in this country by the most elaborate description.

Bolt after bolt shot athwart the sky—bright, broad, and blinding—while the thunder rolled with majestic roar.

All was drenched.

Everything dripped with rain and spray.

And thus the night passed.

CHAPTER LXXXVII.

THE STORM CONTINUED.

TOWARDS daylight the wind began to fall, but the swell of the mighty ocean was still fearful; the sloop was kept as steady as possible by a small amount of sail, but, as usual, pitched and tossed with twofold violence.

The awful motion of a vessel when the wind has ceased and the waves still run mountains high, is something indescribable.

Now the vessel pitches bows under, and shakes as if the masts were about to jump headlong overboard—then up she goes, the stern settling down into an apparently bottomless abyss, then she gets into the trough of the sea, and rolls; Lord, how she does roll, until the yards *touch the water*, now on one side, now on the other.

Not a soul can move about the deck. The men are lashed at the wheel, and those on deck hold on to the belaying pins.

Still, though such was the case on board of the Firefly, the captain and Henry contrived to crawl up to the crosstrees, and with the ship's best telescope to look around.

Not a trace of the Nauvoo was to be seen in any direction.

The captain and the midshipman descended to the deck in silence.

A fearful dread was upon their souls.

The storm had been so fearful that surely the Nauvoo could not have set sail and escaped.

She must, then, have foundered with all hands.

It was a fearful alternative to think of.

Henry was pale as ashes; his teeth chattered, and his whole frame quivered.

The captain himself, satisfied that the look-out had been correct, quietly ordered the reward to be paid, and extra grog distributed to the men. Double the usual allowance was given, in consideration of the sufferings they had gone through.

Captain de Lancy then drew Henry down stairs, and made him lie down, after giving him a composing draught from the medicine chest.

The poor boy, weary, exhausted, and broken-hearted, soon found in nature's sweet restorer that balm which, under such circumstances, it alone can give.

The captain seated himself, and seemed deeply absorbed in thought.

He, too, fell at last into a deep slumber.

When he awoke the ship had ceased labouring. There was evidently calm water and a light breeze.

Henry opened his eyes at the same time.

Captain de Lancy ordered breakfast, of which he made Henry partake.

In answer to questions, the steward informed them that two remarkably heavy showers of rain, without a breath of wind, had beaten down the sea.

A bright sky and a light wind followed.

Thus much the steward, but as he handed round biscuit and toast, and served the broiled ham, the captain saw that he was, to use a familiar expression, itching to speak.

"Have you anything particular to say to me, Minship?" he said.

"Well, sir, I don't know," said the steward, with a sidelong glance at Henry.

"Speak out—what is it?" cried Henry, eagerly. "I beg your pardon, sir."

"Not a word. Tell the news, Minship," continued the captain kindly.

"Well, sir, the men have seen something, they can't make out what, something long and dark—perhaps a spar, perhaps a boat—a long way off, and Mr. Preston has headed for it," said the steward.

"Tell Mr. Preston to step down and join us," replied the captain. "Mr. Haddington, be still. There is plenty of time. Eat your breakfast. That done, we will go on deck."

Henry filled his cup, and forced himself to swallow a mouthful or two.

"Well, Mr. Preston," said the captain to the first lieutenant, "sit down. What is the news about some sign of a wreck?"

"Well, sir, Ben Bunk, who got the twenty pounds, was on the look-out just now, and came down to tell me he thought he could see something a long way off. I lent him a good glass; he went up, and now says it's a boat. He's conning the vessel right towards it."

"That's right," replied the captain, who caught an almost imperceptible glance from the first lieutenant; "take a cup of coffee—there's plenty of time."

The lieutenant bowed.

"Steward, the cognac. Just a taste after this coffee, youngster," addressing Mr. Henry with all professional gravity. "I dont want to set you a bad example, but, after the night we have passed, you must just take a sip."

And he filled a large wine glass for each.

When Henry swallowed his it nearly choked him.

He could not make out the captain's motive at the time, but he soon did.

On, on sped the vessel, running gently through the glassy and tiny waves.

Henry's face was flushed and anxious. He could see that something serious was about to happen.

Suddenly a terrific shout, a shout of joy, a shout of triumph, such as only English throats could give utterance to, startled all.

The captain and lieutenant exchanged glances.

Henry flew on deck like a madman.

The captain and lieutenant followed scarcely less eagerly.

The sight which met their gaze was marvellous.

The day was magnificent. Every man on the ship, though one watch should have been below, was on deck. Rigging, tops, even cross trees, were everywhere crowded.

The hammock railing was one line of human heads.

Henry bounded to the gangway, and there, down upon the glassy waters, was a large boat.

At the bottom of the boat with dishevelled hair, with ghastly pale countenance, lay Jessie, senseless, and, to all appearance, dead.

"She lives!" said the doctor, who bent over her.

"She lives!" shouted the whole crew, in one triumphant chorus.

"She lives!" gasped Henry, as he caught her in his arms, and rushed headlong towards the captain's cabin.

"Here's a pretty kettle of fish," said Captain de Lancy, with a grim smile.

The lieutenant bowed, and then gave some directions to his subordinates, which being promptly obeyed, order was once more restored in the ship.

"How shall we steer?" said the lieutenant.

"For New York," replied the captain; "we are but two days off, and we must get a servant for our young lady."

The lieutenant bowed again.

"Tell Mr. Henry Haddington, as soon as the doctor has made his report, to come to me."

In about ten minutes the young midshipman came on deck, his face radiant.

"Well."

"Out of danger, sir."

"Then thank God. And now, Mr. Haddington, leave her in the doctor's hands; duty must be attended to. I must make no jealous young gentlemen on board. You will dine with me at three; but, if Miss Jessie be better, you can see her. We shall be anxious to hear her story."

Henry bowed low and joined his messmates, who received him with a hearty welcome, that went to his very heart.

The news that they were bound for New York was alone delightful.

About two Jessie came to her senses, and,

being fully prepared for the interview by the doctor, was clasped in the arms of her own dear Henry.

Her story was strange and wonderful indeed, but incoherent. It was only at a later date that those interested could fully understand it.

We must, therefore, give it in our own words.

CHAPTER LXXXVIII.

THE NAUVOO EMIGRANT SHIP.

The arrangement between Paolo and Dr. Obadiah Simcox, or, more properly speaking, Phineas Bristowe had been, that the former should induce as many of the unfortunate girls who peopled the school to elope with him.

Each was to believe herself the chosen one.

It was only when on board that they were to be undeceived, and initiated into the abominations and infamies of Mormonism.

Bishops may defend it, and philosophers excuse it, but the bane of Paganism, Islamism, Mormonism, and every other false polity, has been polygamy.

It is the curse of the Turks, and has made them the foullest nation on the face of the earth.

And the sooner they are extirpated from the face of the earth the better.

Even if they be replaced by the blackleg Greeks.

Anything is better than the foul and vicious religion, the degraded morals, of the followers of Mahomet.

Where polygamy exists women must be degraded to the level of mere animals.

Charles II. was a polygamist. Hence the filthy morals of the Restoration.

Do not quote the superabundance of women in this country. Supply our colonies properly, and take into consideration the army and navy, and we shall find the sexes nearly level.

Nature has, therefore, decided the question for us.

The unfortunate girls, who each expected to be a countess, and who had yielded to the importunities of the sham viscount, only with a view to this consummation, and to escape the monotony of school life, were to have the Hobson's choice of being one of the wives of a Mormon elder, or to be no wife at all.

Acquainted, as Phineas Bristowe was, with the general weakness of the sex, and also with their natural clinging to even the name of virtue, he felt that the name of wife would go a long way.

Where so many, who should have known better, had, with their eyes open, consented to be the under-wives of Mormon elders, what could be expected from feeble girls.

We have heard ourselves a woman of thirty-seven own her intention, before a daughter of eighteen, to become the second or third wife of a Mormon elder.

She could see no harm in her handsome daughter doing the same.

Phineas Bristowe was sufficiently fearful of his companion, the so-called viscount, to have no intention of trusting him; but when he saw how things were going he determined to act for himself.

He had completely won over the silly Miss Matilda Crunch to his views.

By her aid it was that he succeeded in the confusion in entrapping Jessie, over whose head a thick shawl was thrown.

She was carried to the beach insensible.

The night was pitch dark.

The nine wretched victims of a vile compact were so closely veiled that no one could recognise them.

Each had the same password.

It was only when they unveiled in the cabin specially provided for them that they recognised each other.

Their astonishment was something ludicrous. They were all ready to sink with shame, sorrow, and despair.

But, like many others, they veiled their feelings under immediate laughter.

Explanations followed.

Then all knew that they had been deceived by the same atrocious villain.

Some fainted, some shrieked, some sat down in sullen defiance.

All felt that death itself would only be a too happy release.

And there they sat, with glazed eyes, ghastly faces, and parched lips, until long after the ship was on its way.

At this juncture the door opened, and the sleek, smooth face of Phineas Bristowe protruded itself.

All glared at him with concentrated fury.

He took no notice.

The hypocrite knew that in the worst of troubles, in the very depths of despair, in the jaws of death, women always fly to religion with the utmost eagerness.

They are not always at such times able to discriminate between true piety and that false parade and mockery of religion which is the common counterfeit of knaves and impostors.

Phineas Bristowe at once raised his voice with that hypocritical whine which has been borrowed from the sincere but affected Puritan.

He told them that a great misfortune had occurred.

His pupil had been, he believed, falsely accused of crimes of which he was even personally ignorant.

He, himself, would indeed vouch for his truth and honour.

He was an accepted apostle of the new light.

Then Bristowe, with that power of misrepresentation, which was his great forte, began a lecture on Mormonism.

He dwelt with anxious fervour on its miracles and prophecies.

He solemnly vouched for its divine origin, and the inspired character of its teachings.

These young girls, accustomed to the quiet teachings of a worthy and simple preacher of the Gospel, were bewildered.

THE EMIGRANTS.

Their astonishment knew no bounds.

But their curiosity was roused.

An inward monitor told them that, after what had occurred, they would be better suited to the nefarious atmosphere of a Mormon harem than to associate with the reserved and modest of their own sex, in moral England.

Fine morality which enveighs with so much interested bitterness against those who scourge the vices of the day.

According to their theory, let well alone; allow the glaring immorality, the degrading vice, which crawls just beneath the surface of society, to have full swing—offend not the nostrils of gentility by painting society as it is.

Allow the venomous dry-rot of Mormonism to prey upon the vitals of our peasantry.

For fear of hurting tender consciences allow these hardened hypocrites to pretend that their zeal is only for religion.

No! painful, disagreeable, and nauseous as the subject is, it must not be said that all have shrunk from painting the corroding vice of polygamy.

Do those who fulminate against our exposure in such strangely bitter words wish that the great social crime of the day should be secretly encouraged?

It is time that things should be called by their right names.

Clothed in the word *Traviata*, our aristocracy and royalty rush to witness the trials of a prostitute; but attack the professors of polygamy in plain language, and the friends of the institution are up in arms.

Phineas Bristowe at last touched tenderly, gently, with intense caution, on spiritual wifedom.

His hearers were slightly startled.

But then the thing sounded so simple that they were not particularly alarmed.

He did not, for one moment, allow any of his real meaning to pierce.

A late traveller says there are no grog shops, brothels, or Traviatas in Utah.

Of course not.

Where a man has as many wives as he pleases; where an elder can always deprive an inferior of a wife; where a man can take his wife's daughter, if he pleases, what need of official brothels?

The whole town is one great pest house of adultery and promiscuous intercourse.

Having thus awakened the minds of the unfortunate girls to some sense of what was coming, he withdrew just at the right moment

Matilda Crunch, with a most demure and grave face, now entered and announced herself as the matron who was to attend to their wants.

She had become a thorough disciple of Phineas Bristowe.

But then she was to be his first and only real wife.

Poor woman.

She little suspected the real character of her infamous suborner.

Sitting down among them, the ex-governess, who had been learning all the cant of Mormonism by heart, entered with zest into their discussions.

She explained to them all that was obscure in the talk of Phineas.

What could they do?

They were moral outcasts from their own sphere—their parents would have nothing to do with them. With that logical quickness which makes all women repel those of their own sex who commit one fault, and admire the man who commits a hundred, they would be pointed at by many, perhaps, scarcely better than themselves.

What could they do?

And so they floundered into the utmost depths of degradation by consenting to become dupes of the Mormon imposture.

CHAPTER LXXXIX.

JESSIE.

SEVERAL mornings had passed. The brig, upon which all sail had been clapped, was keeping steadily on her course.

The yacht schooner had never lost sight of her.

Repeated signals took place between the two vessels.

On several occasions there came visitors on board the brig to spend the evening.

They were ushered mysteriously into a kind of general cabin.

That generally appropriated to the captain was never opened to the public.

It appeared inhabited by some mysterious personage.

A black servant, a girl, was alone allowed admittance.

The nine female neophytes of Mormonism were on the quarter deck.

The other Mormons, Welsh peasants, their wives and daughters, deluded from their pleasant hills and healthy homes, were scattered about the main deck.

There had been a slight gale in the night, but the day was now clear, bright, and beautiful.

There was not a trace of cloud in the pure blue sky.

Not a trace of foam could be seen on the bright blue sea, which shone around hot, waveless, and still as an ocean of molten crystal.

Its surface seemed to vibrate in the rays of the sun, though the season was not at its height, and under the burning glare those girls thought with a deep sigh of the cool and pleasant autumn days, the shady trees and stubble fields at home, when the grain is gathered on the breezy uplands, and the bordering coppice becomes tinged with russet brown.

It has been truly said that, in such moments, there are thoughts which steal over us, and win us from ourselves.

All the girls were silent.

They leaned over the bulwarks and looked down upon the placid waters.

Not one but would have given many years of their coming life to have been then by their mothers' side.

Suddenly they all started.

A voice, melody itself, but wild, wailing, and bursting with sadness, burst upon the awful stillness of the ship.

The words of the song could not be understood, it being in some foreign tongue.

But it was a wail of anguish, that, all could tell.

And then came the notes of a harp, played with exquisite power and taste.

All eyes were turned towards where Phineas Bristowe and Matilda Crunch walked in silent dignity.

But they offered no explanation.

They seemed, indeed, gratified by the effect produced.

The girls whispered among themselves, and then agreed to send a messenger to those in authority to request an introduction.

It would be something to dispel the monotony of the journey.

They were politely received, but their request was for the moment declined.

That, the unblushing Phineas Bristowe declared to be the great secret of the Mormons.

It was their shibboleth, their kaaba, their corner-stone.

The girls were compelled to be satisfied.

But, even credulous as they were inclined to be, they put no faith in the absurd statement of Phineas.

Some said they recognised the voice.

"Who is it?" cried one of the daughters of curiosity.

"Well, I think it's Jessie."

All started with horror. That fair, devoted, generous-hearted girl to be a victim of foul Mormonism was too bad!

They shuddered, and relapsed into silence.

It was Jessie.

In the confusion of that terrible night she had been abducted by Phineas Bristowe and his bland accomplice, Matilda Crunch.

There is nothing some women will not do in the desperate hope of a husband.

The old maid was one of this rather numerous class.

Phineas had promised her, to use a French expression, "mounts and marvels."

What his exact views were, with regard to Jessie's future, it would be difficult to explain.

He had a vague idea that she might prove useful.

Youth, beauty, and innocence combined were rarities in the great pandemonium of prostitution.

Let us for a moment enter the cabin.

The Nauvoo brig had been chartered at Bristol for the conveyance of a rich cargo to New York, as well as a passenger ship for Mormon emigrants.

The invoices showed a large stock of jewellery, watches, diamonds, and other portable property.

The demand for these things in New York is immense.

The profit is enormous.

The Mormons were not averse to making money by any means.

The cargo had been insured to the very utmost of its value.

The Mormon emigrants had, under the advice of the elders, turned all their property into money.

New York, they were told, was the proper place to supply themselves with goods.

The ship itself was the property of the Mormon corporation.

The great advice of Joe Smith and B. Young to the saints has always been, "increase the funds."

With a view to making the insurance of the ship as large as possible, its fittings had been very expensively carried out.

The cabin was furnished like a boudoir, with paintings all around, costly furniture, and contained a harp and piano.

It was tenanted only by Jessie and the dumb black girl who waited on her.

Jessie was now fifteen and a few months, just verging on the mysterious confines of womanhood.

Every day she appeared to increase in beauty.

She was very pale.

Her large, lustrous eyes showed traces of suffering and sorrow.

But she did not despair. Her's was a noble and trusting heart. Above all, she trusted in One in whom none trust in vain.

They could but kill her body.

Pervert her from her cherished affections, turn her from the friends she loved, touch her pure and noble soul, they could not.

She was brave among the brave.

She knew not fear, in the ordinary sense of the word.

And yet she knew that she must be prepared for the worst.

Jessie had not been put in possession of the mysterious history of her youth.

She never could be.

The subject was not one to be revealed to the pure of soul.

But she knew enough to be aware of the monstrous wickedness of Phineas Bristowe.

Warning voices had dinned into her ears to beware of him above all men—and that man her reputed father.

Jessie knew enough of human nature to be aware that the possession of her person might materially assist Phineas in any plots he might have to carry out against her mother.

But why all this trouble, patience, and expense to obtain possession of her person?

Why this splendour by which she was surrounded?

It was useless to waste her energies in vain attempts to fathom the course of events.

She determined to bide her time, and, to beguile the weary hours, devoted herself to arduous study.

There were numerous books, in a well-appointed library.

Then she thought of her music, and found solace in song.

And thus the time passed.

CHAPTER XC.

THE LIFE BOAT.

WHEN nearly at the end of their journey it was that the weather changed.

Jessie had noticed that a perceptible difference had taken place in the nature of the interviews between the officers of the schooner-yacht and the leader of the Mormons.

They used to come every evening, spend an hour or two in carousing, and then return to the Osprey.

They never went empty-handed.

Small boxes, little bales, and bags were handed down into the boat.

But now the supper-table was disturbed by quarrels.

Jessie could have overheard every word had she been so disposed.

One night a sentence so startled her that she was obliged to rise and listen.

"But I *will* save the women," said the voice of Phineas, who was greatly excited by drink.

"Curse the women!" replied a voice; "there are plenty more where they came from."

Jessie was startled, and, unable to resist the temptation, advanced to the door and listened.

To her astonishment she found that some one had left the door ajar.

This was Juba.

Of Juba, more anon.

Jessie peered through with extreme caution.

At a table set out with provisions, wine,

brandy, and tobacco, sat Phineas Bristowe, and three men in the garb of sailors.

" I shall save the women," repeated Bristowe, " if the men go to the bottom."

"How do you propose to do that 'ere," sneered one in the garb of the better sort of seamen. If so be as we had had a gale of wind we might have done it."

"We must spring a leak," said Bristowe, "and then we must take all the women first—except that precious old maid—and say we'll come back for the men."

"But yourself—"

" I'm all right ; don't fret about me," said Phineas, with a knowing look.

The other, who was, indeed, the smuggler captain, smiled scornfully.

"Is all the cargo on board ?" he asked.

" All."

"Everything valuable," replied Bristowe.

At this moment the vessel gave a lurch. Away went plates, dishes, glasses, and bottles.

A loud shriek was distinctly heard.

A man came down to say that a sudden squall had struck the ship, but that she had righted.

The revellers rushed on deck, Phineas Bristowe looking very white and terrified.

Jessie was horror-struck. She understood sufficiently of their conversation to be aware that some infernal plot was in progress, though what its exact nature was she could not say.

She understood that the valuable cargo was being removed ; that the ship was to be deserted ; and that, at all events, a portion of the crew was to be abandoned.

The dreadful glances interchanged by the men sufficiently betokened how fell was their purpose.

But now all was changed.

Wrapping a cloak round her, and passing hastily through the public room, Jessie crept up the companion way, and, stooping low, looked out upon the awful scene which presented itself with earnest and admiring eyes.

The sky had changed from blue to black, heavy clouds rolled apparently from every point of the compass, the sea was wild with foam, and yet the gale had not commenced.

In the south-east the sky was clear and cloud-less, whilst, in the opposite direction, dark, heavy, purple waves rolled over each other, more unnatural in appearance owing to a lighter cloud covering the curling fluid as if with a veil.

Shooting from this dark heap of clouds, some few were separated and rose to a higher region of the air, in which they were dissipated and blown out like mares' tails, passing rapidly over the convoy ; whilst on the water, and about a mile from the ships, the sea appeared as if covered with a thick, white haze, before which seemed a dark line of black.

As this was evidently no common squall ; the hands were turned up, the topsails lowered and made as secure as possible, the yards were squared, the jib hauled down, and the fore-topmast staysail set, the Nauvoo lying at this time with her starboard broadside to the approaching storm.

Jessie had never seen a sight like this ; and much as she had read in books of fiction, of waves rolling mountains high, of storms, of dangers, of perils encountered by seamen, she was by no means prepared for the silent approach of the enemy. There was evidently much apprehension on the countenances of several of the seamen.

It was nearly a calm, with the squall coming gradually up as if to burst upon them ; and from the manner in which the dark cloud had blown over them, the immense rapidity with which it swept aloft, it was most evident that it would be a serious storm.

In the hurry and confusion of the scene, Jessie was quite unnoticed.

She was, therefore, able to follow, without any difficulty, all the events as they progressed.

About half-an-hour after Jessie took up her post the storm burst upon the ship, and then no pen can tell, no words give the most faint outline, of the tremendous force with which it assailed them.

Jessie still gazed as if spell bound.

It was now quite dark ; the night had completely closed in ; the rolling sea, with its white head, came rushing higher and higher ; above, no moon shone to cheer them, or exhibited the lamp of night to guide them on their way.

At this moment Jessie perceived that Phineas Bristowe and the strange sailors, were approaching the cabin.

She dived below, and gained her own private cabin.

The others came tumbling down.

"Well," said the smuggler captain, taking a bottle of brandy.

"Give me a drain," replied Bristowe, who was very pale.

"Drink, and decide ; you are now master. The gale changes all—"

"Can the schooner carry all hands."

"She can—"

"Then we will save all. It will look better. Not a soul suspects the removal of the cargo ; we shall obtain great credit if we save all ; and the insurances on the ship will be, together with the cargo, an enormous profit."

"Well, just as you like," said the smuggler, surlily.

"How far off is the schooner ?"

"Close under our lee."

"Then I will spring the leak," continued Phineas, still more pale than before ; "you presently advise the skipper to try the pumps."

"All right," replied the smuggler, who again went on deck.

"Juba," said Phineas.

The negress came forward and bowed her head.

"Have my lifeboat put out and swung behind, as you know nothing can strand her ? At all events I will be sure of Jessie."

Juba bowed and went on deck.

Then Phineas Bristowe raised a trap in the deck, and, taking a lantern and an augur, went down into a dark space beneath the lower deck.

He was below a quarter of an hour.

When he came up his face was livid and his teeth chattered.

He laid down his lantern, again drank brandy, and then approached the cabin.

Jessie stood calmly awaiting his arrival.

"Come," he said, in husky tones, "the ship is in danger. Take nothing with you; it will be enough to escape with our lives "

Jessie stood still without replying.

"Why do you not speak, girl?"

"Where are you taking me?"

"Why do you ask? Have I not a right to take you where I please?"

"No."

"How so?"

"You have no right."

"Am I not your father?"

"You are not."

"Wretched girl—who has put this folly in your head? If I am not your father, who is?"

"I don't know."

"This is idle now. Follow me."

Jessie knew that to resist was hopeless, and accordingly took her way towards the deck.

The crew were still working at the pumps.

The boats were all out.

Jessie was let down into a kind of lifeboat of peculiar construction.

Phineas Bristowe returned towards the cabin to fetch Juba, and a small, but valuable package.

When he returned no boat was to be seen.

In the haze and mist he could see nothing but the schooner yacht.

The lifeboat had disappeared.

Mad with rage and disappointment, he rushed to the other boats.

In a quarter of an hour all had left the ship.

In half-an-hour she had sunk.

BOOK II.

THE PRETTY HORSEBREAKER.

CHAPTER I.

HOME.

THE return of Jessie to England was a triumphal march.

They made no stay in New York. The punishment of Phineas Bristowe was adjourned to a more fitting opportunity.

Besides, all were eager to see England once more, the land where all had so many ties and affections.

Jessie recovered with marvellous rapidity.

Nothing interfered with her at all but her anxiety about her mother.

Her dear Henry was, at all events, near her, and this, to her mind, was almost more than anything else.

If one could imagine the possibility of twin souls divided between two bodies it would have been in the case of Jessie and Henry.

There appeared no possibility of any difference or disunion between them.

Jessie was now a woman.

Love had unveiled its fairy mysteries to her, and she knew that for life Henry was all in all to her.

But Henry was still a lad.

He loved Jessie, but it was with more of a sisterly affection than anything else.

But his heart was warm indeed, and it required but a spark to light up a flame.

Fair and sunny was the passage home, and ere many days the whole party were landed at Portsmouth.

Cornelia and the whole party, so anxious with regard to Jessie, had taken up their residence in London, as the most central place where to hear of their arrival.

We draw a veil over the reunion of those who loved so much.

Captain de Lancy obtained three months leave of absence, and during this time Henry came to live with his family.

They had selected a retired part of Chelsea as a rendezvous. In those days it was not the densely populated district it is now.*

The house was an old one.

It stood in a garden, leading down to the Thames, and was quite out of the way of all fashionable visitors.

Captain de Lancy and his wife had gone down to Wales, to enjoy their retarded honeymoon.

The residents in the old Chelsea house were Cornelia, the Dwarf, Lady Haddington, Jessie, and Henry.

They had ample attendants to guard the house.

---

* Chelsea: A manor and village on the banks of the Thames. In a Saxon charter of Edward the Confessor, it is written, "Cealchylle," in Doomsday-book "Cercehede" and "Chelched," and in documents of a later, though an early date, "Chelcheth" or "Chelcith." Sir Thomas More, writing to King Henry VIII., subscribes his letter "at my pore howse in Chelcith." Norden's etymology, in the opinion of Lysons, is best supported by fact: "It is so called," he says, "from the nature of the place, whose strand is like the chesel (ceosel or cesol), which the sea casteth up of sand and pebble stones, thereof called Cheseley, briefly Cheselsey, briefly Chelsey as is Chelsey (Selsey) in Sussex." The manor is said to have originally formed a part of the possessions of the Abbey at Westminster; but nothing is known with certainty of its history till the time of Henry VII., when it was held by Sir Reginald Bray, from whom it descended to Margaret, only child of his next brother, John, who married William, Lord Sandys This Lord Sandys gave it, in 1536, to Henry VIII., from whom it passed to Katherine Parr, as part of her marriage jointure. It was subsequently held by John Dudley, Duke of Northumberland.

The old Manor House stood near the Church, and was parted with by Henry VIII. to the ancestors of the Lawrence family, from whom "Lawrence-street," Chelsea, derives its name. The new Manor House stood on that part of Cheyne-walk between the "Pier Hotel" and Don Saltero's coffee-house.

This now extensive parish, at one time the Islington of the west end of London, was famous at first for its Manor House, then for its college, its botanic garden, its hospital for sailors, its gardens, its waterorks, its buns, its china, and its custards.

"—————— dead,
Or, but at Chelsea, under custards read."—GAY.

Recent events had put them on their guard.

Now, attached as Henry was to his friends and even to Jessie, it cannot be supposed that he could devote his whole time to them.

He was young, and must necessarily wish to enter into the amusements of youth.

With a view to his passing his time pleasantly he had received letters of introduction from his captain to several of his intimate friends.

For several days Henry was content to stroll about the garden with Jessie, to read with her, to listen to her playing, but soon it was evident that he was moped.

Youth is the season for enjoyment—and for enjoyment of a peculiar kind.

Henry had that passion for field sports which goes so far to elevate the race of Englishmen.

One morning after breakfast Henry announced his intention of presenting some of his letters of introduction.

The Dwarf gave a quiet smile, Lady Haddington looked alarmed, Cornelia looked quickly at Jessie.

Jessie smiled too.

"Quite right," said the Dwarf, "you must not be always tacked to the women's petticoats, Henry."

"Oh," replied Henry with a blush and a laugh; "it is not that, but I've seen so little of London—and then it is time I used my captain's letters."

"Be careful," said Lady Haddington, "of strangers."

"And of your friends," observed Cornelia.

"Upon whom do you call first?" said Jessie.

"I thought of Lord Lionel Thynne—he is a young sailor," replied Henry.

Soon after he went out, leaving them all anxious and uneasy.

The Dwarf, however, earnestly begged them to be no ways uneasy.

"As to expecting a lad like him, high-spirited, and verging on manhood, to be happy moped up here—it is folly," he said; "he must, at any rate, see the world. If he be sterling, it will not harm him. If he be weak and foolish, alas! seclusion would not save him."

Jessie sighed, and made no reply. She, poor girl, could not see why he could not be satisfied with that same quiet existence which made her so happy.

But it was in vain to repine—so she resolved to pass away the day in study.

Towards the evening she went out into the garden, and stood gazing out upon the placid waters of the Thames.

Soon she uttered a sharp cry of pleasure—which brought all her friends from a neighbouring bower to her side.

"Here comes Henry," she said, much confused at her own impulsiveness.

They looked out.

It was Henry indeed, in a smart rowing boat, manned by two watermen, making for the landing place of the garden, accompanied by three companions.

But ere we land him, we must explained how he had reached so far.

CHAPTER II.

LORD LIONEL THYNNE.

HENRY HADDINGTON, to speak the truth, bounded into the carriage which was to convey him to town with something of the alacrity of one who is escaping from temporary confinement.

His was an ardent spirit that required excitement.

Some natures are so constituted.

Happiness is found in a variety of ways.

One will find it in knitting stockings in a chimney corner, while another will be dashing through a foaming sea in an open boat to save life.

Some find it in the chase, the pursuit of finny fish, hard and dry study, gallantry, or any other of the multifarious pursuits of life.

Henry's was one of those natures which require excitement.

To him life, as it is generally understood, was a sealed book—and yet a strange, vague and mysterious warning seemed to tell him it had charms.

He was about to lift the mysterious veil which separates the existence of the schoolboy from that of the man.

Would he be one whit the happier?

No.

Remain in your childhood mood as long as you can. Love your books, your doll, your playthings, your music, your studies as long as you can—for all else is vanity.

Be children as much as you may, for—children! though the sterner pleasures of manhood be not without their sweets, they are mingled so with bitters as to have a taint of earth.

Now, childhood is heavenly.

But Henry was no philosopher; he was not, even very partial to books.

What he coveted was society, life, action, and soon, perhaps, love.

Young Lord Lionel Thynne, though his father, a first Lord of the Treasury, lived in great style in one of the squares, had chambers in the Temple simply because they overlooked the water.

He was about one-and-twenty, of middle height—the perfection for a sailor—stoutly built, with dark hair and eyes, and an almost swarthy complexion. Some women declared him to be eminently handsome, while others shrank with terror from his penetrating glances.

He was elegantly dressed.

A thin man with spectacles, grey hair and a soft bland smile, sat at breakfast with him, as did also a young rubicund, jolly-looking lieutenant, famous for his capacity for imbibing copious quantities of liquor, and for his taste for low life.

The thin man was a Captain Grossmith, but in what service he had acquired his title no one knew.

He was the inseparable companion of Lord Lionel Thynne.

The one was rich, and the other poor.

Captain Grossmith was ready to do anything for his patron.

They were seated at breakfast.

It was twelve o'clock. Everything which could tempt the appetite was on the table, and the three men had been luxuriating over their feast for some two hours.

"What's to be done?" said Lord Lionel, "I feel monstrous hippish, it's too early for the club, too early for little Polly, and vastly too early for cards."

And he yawned.

At twenty one he was *blasé*, used up, and all because he had abused life instead of enjoying it.

"A game of skittles?" said Lieutenant Rouse.

"My dear Rouse, decidedly you are going down—low, my dear fellow—low—*in the daytime.*"

Lieutenant Rouse puffed away at his cigar, and took a bumper of sparkling hock.

He did not like being called low, but he couldn't offer to quarrel with his rich brother officer.

"Yesterday morning, as I was coming into town," began Captain Grossmith in a drawling tone of voice, "I saw in a shop, *somewhere*, the most charming bit of innocence that I have fallen upon for some time—delightful."

"Young?"

"Sixteen."

"Pretty?"

"Fair, golden curls, blue eyes, just a trifle of roses in her cheek."

"Made up?"

"No; modesty itself."

"By Jove!" cried Lord Lionel, "if I were not just now so spoony about Polly I'd think of it—but no," with a yawn—"I can't be bothered with too many, but keep her in your eye, my worthy Panderus of Troy."

"Ha! ha! ha!" laughed the other, with a slight hectic flush of the face, "You are a little too hard, Lionel. A friend can't do a friendly act but he must be maligned. I rather fancy I shall keep my information to myself.

"Just as you like," said the young nobleman with a perceptible sneer.

At this moment a firm but modest knock was heard at the door.

A servant entered with a letter.

With a hasty apology Lord Lionel broke it open.

"By Jove!" cried he with some little animation, "what's he like, Williams?"

"A very handsome lad, my lord."

"A cub, introduced by Captain de Lancy," said the juvenile nobleman.

At this moment, Henry. who was tall for his age, entered with an air of modest dignity, which struck all present favourably.

"I am most happy to make your acquaintance —am I to say Sir Henry?"

"No, my lord. I firmly believe my father to be alive."

"Then Mr. Haddington. I am to sail with you next voyage as first—sit down, we are now young gentlemen together. These are my friends, Captain Grossmith and Lieutenant Rouse. Do you smoke?"

Henry bowed to the gentlemen present.

"Well!" he said, "my captain has taught me to dissipate so far."

And he took up a cigar, while Lord Lionel filled his glass with sparkling hock.

With a faint blush, Henry drank it off.

He had now time to observe the room. It was spacious and handsomely furnished, but the style was what might be called the sporting. On all sides were foils, gloves, sword sticks; while on the walls were pictures of horses, dogs, and ballet girls in the most seductive of attitudes.

"You are amused by my ornaments?" said the young nobleman.

"I should have expected to see more of ships and boats," replied Henry.

"Oh, I've plenty of them in my bed-room and in my nautical album. Are you any hand at the gloves?"

"Will you try?" said Henry, quietly.

Up jumped the two.

At last there was some chance of excitement. Lord Lionel was very strong, while his hangers-on never ventured to beat him.

Besides, he was a very good hand, and in all probability would punish the raw one.

Henry had taken lessons in the school of adversity.

He rose quietly, and picked out a pair.

The table was pushed back, and a clear space made.

The friendly combatants stripped as far as was necessary.

Lord Lionel hit out with both science and strength.

But he could not touch Henry.

Lord Lionel's hot temper was at once up, and he begun to try some nasty hits.

Henry planted a rapid couple of blows on chest and nose.

"That will do," said the young noblemen. with an affected laugh; "it will not do for a young gentleman to be thrashing his commanding officer."

Henry smiled, and laid down his gloves.

"Foils, or single stick?" continued the young nobleman.

"Middling," said our hero, carelessly.

Now Lord Lionel Thynne, who was quarrelsome in the extreme, had devoted some considerable time and study to sword exercise, and prided himself on being rivalled by no man.

He was also a dead shot.

But Henry had been taught by the Dwarf, who, under the most amazing circumstances, had learned to be the first swordsman of his day— to fence with unrivalled art.

He took up his sword and mask, and Lord Lionel winced.

The air with which he did it betrayed one who was very far from being a novice.

"I doubt I must avoid quarrelling with you," he said, in a tone of slight irritation.

"I hope we shall never have cause," observed Henry, gravely.

Their swords, or rather foils, crossed rapidly, and in a moment it was evident that two first-rate hands were at work.

Lord Lionel used every effort that science had

taught him to enable him to touch the other, but without effect.

Henry was again his master.

At the end of ten minutes Lord Lionel's sword flew from his grasp and fell against the wall.

The hangers-on—the parasites—looked very much astonished.

Lord Lionel, on taking off his mask, was very pale.

"I had not known you so accomplished, Mr. Haddington," he said, rather coldly, "or else I had not tried conclusions with you. But never mind," he added more jovially, "I will take my revenge another time. I was up late last night."

"Whenever you please, my lord; and now I will ask another glass of wine," said Henry, wiping the perspiration from his countenance.

"Say you," cried Lord Lionel, gaily; "and then what say you to a row up the river to Putney before dinner?"

"With all my heart," cried Henry.

"But no more experiments," continued Lord Lionel; "we'll have watermen this hot day. You will dine with us at eight—"

"Well, as you wish; in fact, I should be much gratified," said Henry, frankly.

This decided on, they all rose and, walking down to the water's edge, there found a boat of his lordship's. Two watermen hastened down from a public house, and in a few minutes they were launched upon the water.

CHAPTER III.

ON THE RIVER—MAGNETISM OF JESSIE.

THE four men, though of different ages and very different characters, were equally prepared to enjoy themselves.

We may say that all were votaries of pleasure.

Lord Lionel Thynne found it in the pursuit of innocence and virtue, in winning from woman her honour, and in the inordinate love of cards, racing, boating, or anything which created feverish excitement.

Captain Grossmith found it in any dissipation which cost nothing. His object was to make money by means however disreputable.

Lieutenant Rouse cared for nothing but drink, smoke, and the society of the very lowest of the other sex.

His happiness was found chiefly when he could sneak away from his patrons.

Henry, whose mind was hitherto totally unperverted, found it in any manly exercise.

He tossed back his long hair as he inhaled the refreshing breeze and, throwing away his cigar, found pleasure in looking about him.

The others talked, without even looking to the right or left.

For them scenery, public buildings, the busy life of the great river—the noblest commercial river in the world, yet now converted into a sewer above and below London—had no charms.

The sweet flowing stream about Richmond and Twickenham, the pastoral and pretty at Pangbourne, would have amused them even less.

Oh silver-streaming Thames,* oh silver-footed Thamesis;† or, as Denham says:—

"O, could I flow like thee, and make thy stream
  My great example as it is my theme;
Though deep yet clean, though gentle yet not dull,
Strong without rage, without o'erflowing full."

When will modern science and sanitary commissioners make of the mighty stream an ornament and glory unto London.

But instead of admiring the waters bridges, and public buildings, the conversation of the trio turned on the amusements of London!

At the request of Lord Lionel, who had his reasons, nothing was said to shock the modesty of Henry; but he heard enough to let him be aware that the town contained more mysteries than he as yet suspected.

They purposely coloured the scenery rather highly.

Henry began to believe that he had seen nothing.

It was agreed that after dinner they should visit one or two of the amusements of London.

Henry, however, requested leave to call and just hint that he should be late, as such was not his usual habit.

Lord Lionel tapped him on the shoulder with a smile.

"What a good boy we are!" he said.

"Not at all; but I do not like to give those about me unnecessary pain," replied Henry, warmly.

"Perfectly right," said the young nobleman.

The conversation was now changed, until they were abreast of the garden in which stood Jessie, and distant about ten yards.

"What a lovely girl!" said Lord Lionel enthusiastically.

Henry turned in the direction indicated.

"That is my cousin. I must land here," he said, with a smile.

"By Jove! I'll land with you and be introduced."

"I shall be most happy to introduce you to my future wife," said Henry, with a rapid but meaning glance at the other two.

Lord Lionel stared.

He had thought Henry much more green than he appeared to be, despite his ability in fencing and boxing.

"Just land us," said the young nobleman. "You chaps can see how dinner gets on; we'll be with you precisely at eight. I suppose we can have a trap?"

"You can have my carriage, if that is what you mean?" replied Henry.

At this moment they landed, and the two parasites, rather piqued, made off, vowing vengeance against the cool impudence of their new acquaintance.

Lord Lionel was such a perfect gentleman, that when he was introduced to Jessie and the ladies, not one but what was pleased with Henry's new acquaintance.

How little could they imagine the fatal and bitter enemy he was ultimately to prove.

He conversed pleasantly and agreeably with

* Spenser   † Middleton, and Herrick.

LOTTY.

the elder ladies, and with the most marked courtesy towards Jessie.

"I am deeply grateful to Captain de Lancy," he said, "for introducing me to one whose acquaintance, I hope, will be so agreeable to myself and my friends."

"I am glad you are pleased with him," said Lady Haddington, with a gratified smile.

"I am afraid you will not be pleased with me," replied Lord Lionel.

Jessie looked keenly at him with her clear, blue eyes.

"Why?"

"Mr. Haddington has promised to return with me to dinner, and I cannot let him off his engagement."

The ladies looked rather serious.

Jessie plucked a flower, and began pulling it to pieces.

"The fact is, that I and Mr. Henry will, in all probability, have to sail together for several years, and I want to introduce him to some messmates. We shall have several friends, and, as I dare say you are early people, I have ordered my people to make him up a bed; but I am his elder officer, and will take as much care of him as if I were Captain de Lancy himself."

The ladies smiled at the earnestness of the juvenile officer.

Jessie took Henry on one side, and put her arm caressingly in his.

Lord Lionel's eye flashed with unwonted fire.

The young lovers walked away out of sight.

Lord Lionel continued his conversation with the elder ladies, but a keen observer might have detected how he longed for the re-appearance of Jessie.

Round she came, leaning on Henry's arm.

They were both smiling and laughing.

Any little pettishness she might have shown as to his temporary desertion had all now disappeared.

"What a remarkable pair!" cried Lionel, involuntarily.

"They are." said Cornelia, warmly. "They are made for each other."

"Engaged, I suppose," replied Lord Lionel, with a smile.

"Indeed, it is no secret. They are to be married as soon as Henry is of age."

"Indeed."

Such was the single word spoken by Lord Lionel; but, in his heart of hearts, he at once resolved that Henry should never become of age.

Presently the carriage was announced, and the two young men left the house, Henry delighted at the prospect of an evening's amusement, Lord Lionel panting under the burning fire of a passion as rapidly conceived as it was delirious.

He was engaged in marriage; he had a most fascinating establishment at the west-end, where dwelt a girl he had hitherto adored.

"And had he quite forgotten Julia?
And should he have forgotten her so soon?
I can't but say it seems to me most truly a
Perplexing question; but, no doubt, the Moon
Does these things for us, and whenever newly a
Palpitation rises, 'tis her boon,
Else how the devil is it that fresh features
Have such a charm for us poor human creatures!"

CHAPTER IV.

LONDON BY NIGHT.

THE dinner, or rather supper, was the acme of luxurious extravagance. To describe it would require the pen of a Lucullus or a Soyer. It was furnished by a celebrated cook.

The dishes were numerous, and their names unpronounceable.

They were, however, delicious.

They seemed never to weary.

Washed down by the most delicious wines every new dish seemed to give a new appetite.

Even Henry gave way to the strange influence of mere material delights.

Delights that only pall, but which, if rashly indulged in, become absolutely disgusting.

He laughed, joked, and drained his glass with the best of them.

About twelve he was sufficiently far gone to be initiated into the mysteries of London life.

They all put on great coats, and sallied forth into the open air.

Lord Lionel took the arm of his youthful prey.

Burning with desire to possess Jessie, than whom no beauty had ever struck him so much, Lord Lionel had determined either to make

Henry utterly unworthy of the happiness which awaited him, or to remove him mercilessly from his path.

He doubted not that a very little would be required to turn the scale in favour of the probable heir to a dukedom.

Oh! for the pen of a Dryden or a Pope to describe the great city at midnight.

How comparatively noiseless are the streets where the car and the hoof, and the quick stepping foot, and the loud voice was not long since intermingled in the stir of life—there now is quiet.

"A deadness mantles round the midnight scene!"

Where are the busy thousands that during the day have made it so full of life?

"Some, weary of woe, are lapped in sleep,
And blessed in dreams, whose day-life was a curse;
Some, heart-rack'd, roll upon a sleepless couch,
And, from the heated brain, create a hell
Of agonising thoughts and ghastly fears;
While Pleasure's moths, around the golden glare
Of princely halls, dance off the dull wing'd hours,
And oh! perchance, in some infectious cell,
Far from his home, unaided and alone,
The famished wanderer dies."

Suddenly our party, who had been following the Strand, and had crossed Leicester-square, emerged upon the Haymarket—that sink of London iniquity—one blaze of life and light.

It is in vain that we boast of our civilisation, of our efficient police, and of our desire to promote morality and virtue, while such a pest house disgraces our vast metropolis.

Here in gilded saloons and *cafés*, in gin shops redolent of oil of vitriol and turpentine, sulphurous ether and grains of paradise, in every imaginable den that the reckless love of money can produce for the profligate, the silly, and the young, congregate painted women, with insolent eye and heated brow, dressed to fascinate and deceive, but foul, vile, and degraded as the lowest trulls that haunt the purlieus of St. Giles's, or the arches of the Adelphi.

Brazen, shameless, with but one desire, drink —for money is only subordinate to this—yet do these hideous painted sepulchres devour the substance of our choicest youth, corrupt their morals, and ruin their health.

Why?

Because men without brains, or men without hearts, call spending a night in this noisome den seeing life!

Seeing death rather.

And the police allow these things, though every house is more or less carrying on an illegal traffic.

An honest onslaught on these sinks of impurity would soon send the keepers of them to Whitecross-street, and the girls to Bridewell.

But we are told the police have their reasons for not putting them down.

Doubtless.

But what is this?

A *café* shining with mirrors, surrounded by crimson benches and marble tables, where lounge men in peculiarly shiny hats, heaps of sham jewellery, many of them with a strong Jewish caste of countenance, in conversation with fashionably-dressed girls—fine, some handsome, some striking, some almost beautiful, but all with the mark of the beast upon them.

None are pretty, because prettiness necessitates, at all events, a semblance of innocence, which not one there possesses.

All the men are smoking, some of the women are taking refreshments.

But not many, for there has not yet been an arrival of flats.

What, then, are these men?

Animals kept by these painted butterflies; drones that feed on the garbage cast to them by these hired prostitutes; things utterly without a name.

The English language has no word sufficiently low to describe them.

They are chiefly foreigners, or Jews, though a superficial eye might mistake them for men of substance.

The girls fawn upon and caress them.

They first make them their fancy men, and then become their slaves.

These beings are blacklegs and thieves, and yet men of decent family and good position shake hands with them, and are hail fellow, well met.

Men, who are at other times ornaments to society, associate with this scum, doomed to die in a garret.

"No voice to sound
Sweet comfort to his heart, no hand to smooth
His bed of death, no beaming eye to bliss
The spirit hovering o'er another world!"

The arrival of Lionel's party, accompanied by so handsome a youth as Henry, created a sensation; and when, at a large table at the end of the room, expensive refreshments were ordered, with unlimited cigars, a crowd of harpies came round.

Four or five of the best dressed of the syrens of the quarter seated themselves unasked.

One came close to Henry.

She was about seventeen, and the day had been when a more beautiful and seductive creature never existed. She had been, not quite two years before, innocent and happy, in the quiet home of her father.

She was a curate's daughter, and, but for evil instincts, might have grown up to happiness and respectability.

Asked in marriage by a respectable young tradesman, she had preferred listening to the lying promises of a young gentleman who spoke of marriage but to win her love and ruin her reputation.

She fled with him.

Fool!

When a man means marriage he acts openly and honourably.

In three months Christine was upon the streets, a celebrated nymph of the pavè.*

But did she accept her position, as many do, with quiet resignation? Not at all.

She hated and loathed those she fawned upon and caressed. She had ruined more young men than any girl of her age. She wrung their purses dry, and cast them from her with scorn.

The moment the youth's money was spent she showed herself in her true colours.

*Pronounced pavay.

She laughed him to scorn, explained her tactics, and laid bare the native hate and ferocity of her skeleton heart.

The victim left her disgusted with himself, and distrustful of all women.

This girl, who was called Christine, saw at a glance that in Henry she had found a novice, and she at once proceeded to play her cards as usual.

Lord Lionel, whom she affected to respect because he was generous, without attaching himself to her car, gave her an imperceptible nod.

Christine at once examined Henry a little more keenly.

She saw his noble head, his eyes redolent of truth and goodness—she read his whole soul.

She seemed scorched to the very heart.

Had she have acted otherwise in the opening of her career might not such a companion have been her lot in life?

But she subdued her regret, and began to play her deep and subtle game.

She saw, at once, that it would not do to alarm the native sensibility of the youth.

"And you find pleasure in such a place as this?" she said, in silky tones.

It was the tiger putting forth its velvetty paw without showing the claws.

"Indeed I don't know."

"Don't know?"

"Fact," said Henry, laughing, "it is very different to anything I have ever seen before, but it is very lively."

"So it's your first visit?"

"It is."

"I dare say it won't be your last?"

"I don't know. I shall join my ship in a few days, and when I return to England I shall marry, so my wild days will not last very long."

"Marry!" said the girl, with a pout and a frown, "it's ower soon."

"Well, I don't know; I've been engaged since I was a child."

"Do you love her very much?" half sneered Christine.

"Yes."

"What would she say to your being here?"

"She knows it."

"Knows it! Why, surely, how can that be?"

"I told her. As I mean no harm in coming here, why not?"

Christine stared at him with open eyes. This was something new, fresh, extraordinary.

A strange suspicion crossed her mind.

"Will you help me to some champagne?" she said.

Henry served her gallantly, and drank himself. Their hands met.

Henry's cheeks grew crimson as she pressed them, and looked straight into his eyes.

A quick and peculiar wink passed between Lord Lionel and Christine.

The latter became pensive and thoughtful.

"Are you going to the saloon?" she cried suddenly, in a whisper, addressed to Lord Lionel.

"As you like," replied the young nobleman, "but what say you to S——?"

This was carried.

CHAPTER V.

A NIGHT HOUSE.

In a street off the Haymarket is a dark-looking shop front, which at night, in all probability, might pass unnoticed by any but those bound to visit its interior.

A dark, heavy door closes all entrance to all but the initiated.

On knocking a wicket opens, and a huge, ugly, villanous, pock-marked face becomes visible.

If known to this Cerberus the door itself turns upon its hinges, and you are in Sam's.

It is a long room, one more in the shape of a French *café*, with cushioned seats, mirrors without end, marble tables, and a bar, behind which the favourites of this honourable house are admitted.

Oh, know, ye innocent wives, whose husbands are detained at their club, that here it is that many a well-known merchant, legislator, or man about town, spends his night drinking the vilest of diluted compounds, at unheard of prices, basking in the smiles of faded and be-rouged beauty, elbowed by blacklegs, Greeks, and bullies, until health fails, pallid cheeks ensue, and the falling grey hairs proclaim that in these dens of crime have been sown the seeds of death.

Christine had taken Henry's arm, and, as her chief wish appeared to be to monopolise him for a while, she cared little where she went.

On entering this disgraceful den she led him to a vacant table at the end of the room.

Her eyes shone with unusual brightness; there was something strangely grave in her mien; she appeared thoughtful.

Lord Lionel and his party went behind the bar.

"She's playing a deep game," said Lord Lionel, with a smile.

"Who, and what is he?" asked one of the girls.

"A baronet and heir to sixteen thousand a year," said Lord Lionel maliciously.

The girls exchanged glances and looks of vexation. They had, with the natural instinct of their degraded natures, stuck to the lord while they neglected the commoner.

They could see that Henry and Christine were engaged in earnest discourse.

This looked serious.

In all probability they were discussing settlements. A youth like that would be led to do anything by a girl so facinating as Christine—or, as the other girls called her, Polly Clarke.

Lord Lionel Thynne watched them with a cold and saturnine air.

If he could but make Henry rush into the toils of the syren he should have the way made easy for him.

But it would not do to be in too great a hurry.

He must first get tolerably into the good graces of Jessie, and this could only be done through the mediation of Henry.

What his real views with regard to the girl were he did not know himself.

He was engaged to be married to a rich and noble heiress, but it was not likely that he would hesitate much where his passions were concerned.

If marriage was to be Jessie's price, he almost fancied he would be disposed to yield on that point.

Afraid that Christine might hurry on events too much, he strolled towards the spot where the two were in earnest conversation.

They ceased speaking as he came near.

This looked suspicious, and he bit his lip.

"Well, I'm tired of this. Do as you like, but I shall go up to Lotty's, to supper," he said.

"Supper!" laughed Henry, "why, I should have thought it more like time for bed and breakfast."

"Ha! ha! ha! but we be boys who turn night into day, and day into night. Wait until we are aboard ship, keeping watch and watch. Come, what say you?"

"I am ready for anything."

"And you Christine?"

"Too happy to be your lordship's guest," she said, curtseying.

In ten minutes more they were in cabs, bowling away in the direction of St. John's Wood.

Henry and Christine occupied one to themselves, and it was not without emotion that the young man found himself seated next one so charming, to all outward appearance, as the lovely girl beside him.

They were alone.

He could feel her perfumed breath fanning his cheek.

She had placed one arm round his waist, and with the other held his hand.

She did not offer to speak.

In the half dark of the coming morn her shadowy outline looked absolutely beautiful.

Strange, new, and overwhelming sensations took possession of him. A dreamy languor overcame him, so powerful that he closed his eyes.

Then a strong *apre* and pungent kiss fell upon his parted lips.

Henry gently disengaged himself.

"Do not be offended," she said, in low, gentle, murmuring accents.

"I am not offended," he faltered forth in reply.

"And be careful, we have arrived. Rely upon it, my gentleman has some design on you. You make moderate love to me, and I'll find out."

The cab stopped, and Henry had just time to assure her t... he would follow her advice ere they got out and followed Lord Lionel to the door of one of those quiet, rural, secluded, but wicked retreats to which silly lads, middle-aged rakes, and antiquated vol...aries take their favoured odalisques.

A smart ring at a door brought a rapid answer.

It was four o'clock in the morning.

But the slaves of the lamp f luxury must be ever ready at command.

Lord Lionel had brought with him Captain Grossmith, Lieutenant R use, Henry, and three ladies.

He entered the house, and, opening the door, a handsomely furnished double drawing-room was exposed to view.

A man stood waiting for orders, a little weasoned, lanthorn jawed Frenchman, the very image of servility, rapacity, and avarice.

"Souper, milord?"

"Yes."

"For all?"

"Of course. Where is your mistress?"

"In bed."

"No," cried a voice, joyous, ringing, and full, and at the same moment a superb woman entered the room.

CHAPTER VI.

LOTTY.

THIS was Lord Lionel's last fancy, one that had lasted nearly six months, and appeared likely to last longer if one might judge by the fascination she still exercised over him.

Lotty was about nineteen, tall, full grown, and exceedingly voluptuous in form for her age.

Her shoulders were magnificent, beautifully rounded, and shown off by a superb blue velvet dress, which she had hastily donned.

Her hair was glossy black, and hung in massive curls round her head.

Her low, white forehead surmounted eyes of vivacity and energy, swept and softened by long flowing eyelashes.

Her face was faultless, her coral lips a bow, and her chin massive enough to be richly voluptuous.

Her mien and walk was queenly.

No one would have suspected her of being a courtezan; or have imagined that she was one of what modern slang so strangely calls the "pretty horse-breakers."

"But why was she so?"

That, as she has an extraordinary influence on the fortunes of Henry and Jessie, our readers may learn at a future time.

Her history was not even suspected.

How she came under the protection of Lord Lionel Thynne was, in itself, a tragic romance.

As she walked into the room she took Lord Lionel's hand with heartiness, bent her head slightly and scornfully to the women, and with haughtiness to the men.

Lord Lionel then introduced Henry.

Lotty was peculiarly gracious.

"Who is he, and why do you bring out one so young?" she said, aside.

"Oh, it's young Sir Henry Marmaduke Haddington: he's my sub—I must make a man of him."

There was something strange in the way Lotty looked at him as he spoke.

"Have you ordered supper," she said, to change the conversation.

"I have. In the meantime will you sing?"

Lotty smiled languidly, and turned towards the piano.

Henry, with natural politeness, turned to attend her music.

Lotty smiled on him, and began a brilliant air.

Henry was lost in wonder. The soft, youthful organ of Jessie had filled him with delight; but the rich, learned, and voluptuous tones of the pretty horsebreaker took him unawares.

Henry but yesterday was a boy; he was quickly learning in this voluptuous atmosphere that he was a man.

As Lotty sang she turned often towards him—not so much with a view to try the influence of her dark and piercing eyes, as to see how he was affected.

Henry knew scarcely which way to look.

All the others were playing cards!

Christine even, though she every now and then watched her prey with the glance of a spider, could not resist the temptation.

Lord Lionel Thynne was in unusually good spirits.

He turned his card with a loud laugh.

"Play away, Lotty," he cried; "this is delightful!"

"But I weary you," said Lotty, addressing Henry. "You would prefer to join them?"

"Oh, no!" he replied warmly, and with a sincerity which was unmistakeable. "I would far rather listen to you—all night!"

A faint flush passed across that superb face, a brightness of the eyes illumined her countenance, and she continued.

This time she played, and very loudly, too.

"How long have you known Lionel?" she said, under cover of the music.

"Since yesterday."

"Ah!—no longer? Strange that he should bring you here!"

Away went the music, a loud and noisy peal, but exquisitely played.

"Well, he offered to show me a little of the life of London. I little dreamt of—"

Lotty looked mournfully at him.

"And of which you will soon sicken. I must talk more to you," she added.

Supper was here announced, and, at a sign from Lotty, Henry gave his arm to the mistress of the house.

She placed him next to her at supper. Lord Lionel gave her one scrutinising glance, and then took the head of the table.

It is, unfortunately, true that much of that wit, repartee, and humour—wit, repartee, and humour, without coarseness—has been driven from the *salons* and tables of the great, to be replaced by a rigid dulness and etiquette, of which, unfortunately, the most moral court in Europe has set the example.

But must virtue and morality be necessarily accompanied by dulness?

Certainly not.

As surely as you prevent the lighter order of amusements, and discountenance genial intercourse between the sexes, so surely you will be supporting secret immorality.

In the purlieus of the great city, in the *petites maisons* of the Cyprians of the hour, society, as there constituted, is free from all restraint, without being tainted by license.

It was markedly so in this case.

The conversation turned on art, on poetry, on

music, the drama, and was sparkling—full of anecdote and fun.

Henry was amazed, as well he might be, comparing them with the dull, namby-pamby absurdities of good society.

When supper was ended Lord Lionel proposed retiring.

The hint was taken.

Captain Grossmith, the lieutenant, and the ladies hurried to leave.

Henry was told that a bed had been provided for his accommodation.

He bade Lotty and Lord Lionel good night, and retired to his chamber.

His head was hot from wine and general excitement.

He hardly knew what to think of what he had seen.

If this was vice, it presented itself to him under auspices which did not shock him as much as he expected.

Coarse, rude, ostentatious vice must always be offensive.

Hence the disfavour with which filthy pictures and boldly impure novels are received.

But there are many works, by eminent writers, far worse than these, rejected by society, as there is much of profligacy concealed beneath a bright and flowery exterior.

Well, Henry was tired, and resolved to put off thinking about it at all until to-morrow.

CHAPTER VII.

NIGHT AT LOTTY'S.

THE apartment to which Henry was taken by an attendant, not very much inferior in attraction to her mistress, and who, while she yawned and gaped, could find eyes enough to admire the handsome youth, was excessively rich in its decorations.

A large four-post bedstead was hung with rich curtains.

Rich hangings and pictures studded the walls.

Every luxury that ingenuity or wealth could devise was lavished on that apartment.

It was the best in the house.

A lamp, that diffused a soft and lambent light stood on a table.

Iced water and a flask of wine were by the bed-side.

A little fire burnt in the stove.

"Is there anything else you want?" said the female attendant, with something very much like an impudent leer.

"Nothing."

"Oh!—very well."

"Good night miss," continued Henry, who, as she stood in the middle of the room, felt rather uncomfortable.

"Good night, sir," said the girl, turning herself round until her hoops trembled again—"not even a kiss."

This was muttered.

"Selina," cried the imperious voice of one accustomed to be obeyed.

It was Lotty.

Selina slammed to the door, and hurried away.

Henry hastened to undress and go to bed. He was in a whirl of astonishment, if not of pleasure, but he was weary.

No sooner had he laid his head on his pillow than he was sound asleep.

He slept, he dreamed, he slept, as he afterwards knew, for hours.

Then he awoke.

And still the fire burned in the fire-place, and the lamp gave its undiminished light, looking as if it had been fresh trimmed.

Henry felt as if he had slept for hours, so refreshed was he, and was about to ring when something arrested him.

It was a rattling at the end of his bed.

"Are you awake?" said a soft voice he knew full well.

"Yes, madam."

"Then be still. I wish to speak with you most particularly," said Lotty, coming round to the bed, and taking possession of an arm chair close to his head.

Henry stared at her with open eyes.

"Where is Lionel?" he said.

"Lord Lionel went away with his friends," replied Lotty coldly. "He will return for you at four, to go up the river in a boat. It is now past twelve."

"Past twelve!" cried Henry, "and you have not been to bed?"

"I have not."

"Why so?"

"That is my secret. You may know it and you may not, everything depends on circumstances; but, as I have urgent reasons for knowing why Lord Lionel brought you here, and is so attentive to you, I have come to ask you to explain."

"I really can't say."

"Will you simply tell me all that has passed since you have known my lord?"

"I will if you wish it."

"I do wish it."

"It is very simple. I had a letter of introduction to him from Captain de Lancy."

"Indeed."

Henry then briefly told his story, up to where Jessie was mentioned.

"Jessie—Jessie what?" cried Lotty eagerly.

"I scarcely should tell you, but her name is Jessie ——"

"Heavens! and her mother?"

"Cornelia ——"

"Merciful Providence. Is Jessie very beautiful?" continued the other, leaning towards Henry and clasping his hands.

Henry gazed rapturously at her beautiful form.

"Speak, I implore you."

With a faint blush Henry drew forth a small miniature of Jessie.

Lotty grasped eagerly at it.

"Henry Haddington, as you love Jessie and your future happiness, have no reservations from me. I can, and will be, your friend. Tell me your history, plainly, briefly, and on the word of a much injured, and most foully wronged woman, I pledge myself to be your best, your most powerful friend."

" And Lord Lionel ?"

"Must know nothing."

" Why ?"

"Never mind. Take my word for it, the less he knows the better. He is young, thoughtless —well, we shall see."

" Will he not be offended if I tell you what I keep from himself?"

" Let him be offended."

" But—"

" Young man," said Lotty, turning crimson to the neck, " I don't know if you suspect any near connection between myself and Lord Lionel."

" Well," stammered and blushed our unfortunate hero.

" You mean that you suspect me to be his mistress," said Lotty.

" I did."

" Then know that I am nothing to him. He chooses the world to think so—so do I. But the sole tie which binds us is one, that, when known, the world will indeed be startled to hear."

" Pardon me, madam—"

"There is no need. The position I occupy I have sought. No one thinks any better of me. But the world shall know—the world shall know."

" What ?"

" Never mind. Tell me your story, and one day I will tell you mine."

Henry prepared to begin, and then turned very red.

" I have already revealed a secret I had pledged to keep, in telling you her name.

" No matter, your secret shall be kept. But waste no more time."

Henry, thus tempted—and she took one of his hands in hers, so beautiful and lovely—told her briefly all his previous history.

" Thank you; and now, Henry Marmaduke Haddington, mark my words. If you would be happy with Jessie ; if you would avoid terrible evils, of which you little dream, let me be your friend. Tell me all, but keep our friendship a secret. To be of use to you our alliance must not be suspected. Be friends with Lord Lionel. Come here, see me often, but never let our interviews be revealed."

" But, dear madam, why ?"

" I understand your doubts," she said, sadly, "but this meeting is perfectly providential . Believe in my devoted affection, and oh, Henry Haddington, trust me !"

Henry knew not what to do.

She held his hand in hers, and, stooping low, kissed his forehead.

He would have drawn her nearer to him.

" I will trust you with my life," he murmured, trying to reach her lips.

" 'Tis well," she said, sadly, " but remember Jessie. She might disapprove our contract if thus sealed."

And, rising, she drew aside the curtain.

" Dress yourself," she said, quietly, " and, when ready for breakfast, ring."

Kissing his hand, with tears in her eyes, she went her way.

Here were a series of mysteries.

She was living with Lord Lionel Thynne as his avowed mistress, and was not his mistress. First mystery.

She wanted to be his disinterested friend. Second mystery.

Her affection for him was evidently very great, but she would not allow him even to kiss her. Third mystery.

Our young gentleman, whose ideas were forming very fast, rose rather sulkily from his bed, and proceeded to dress himself with extreme care.

Presently Selina knocked at the door, and announced that Lord Lionel and Madame were waiting breakfast.

Fresh mystery.

But Henry did not try to unravel this. He had never been so hungry, so he put his curiosity on one side, and went down to breakfast.

Lord Lionel, in elegant morning costume, and Madame Lotty, in the same, at once seated themselves at the breakfast table, which was as ceremonious as one might have been in Belgrave-square.

Lotty was insipid in the extreme.

Lord Lionel was dull.

Henry was puzzled.

After breakfast Lord Lionel rose and wished Madame good bye.

" Happy to see you, Mr. Haddington," said Lotty, extending two fingers.

Henry took them, bowed, returned thanks, and wondered at the duplicity of women.

Lord Lionel smiled.

CHAPTER VIII.

ON THE RIVER.

" AND now for Chelsea !" cried Lord Lionel, with the heartiness of a boy. " I have stolen you away, so what do you think I've done ?"

" Don't know."

" Sent up a note; said you would make a round of calls, and at four o'clock my boat would be ready to take them a pic-nic journey."

Henry smiled.

" They are not very fond of the water."

" Oh, mine is a regular barge," laughed Lord Lionel, " with plenty of room, an awning, a band, and all that sort of thing."

" Well, if they like it, I'm agreeable," said Henry, laughing, and thinking Lord Lionel one of the best fellows in the world.

The vague, mysterious, odd suspicion he had began to entertain against him appeared to fade away in the light of day.

He even began to doubt the wisdom of the agreement he had entered into with Madame Lotty.

But on this subject his lips were sealed.

His lordship's phaeton took them with extreme rapidity towards Chelsea, and before the time mentioned they had alighted, and in one minute were with the ladies in the drawing-room.

They were dressed ready, to Henry's great delight, and no little astonishment.

" We have seen the boat," said Lady Haddington, with a smile.

"Quite safe," laughed Jessie.

"Especially with a crew so gallantly officered," said Cornelia.

Lord Lionel bowed, and would have offered his arm to Jessie, but *les convenances* forbade that.

Besides, Jessie quietly sidled up to Henry.

Lord Lionel took the two elder ladies, in defiance of the popular prejudice about the ass with the two baskets, which a man with a lady on two arms very closely resembles.

The young lover followed, smiling and happy.

Jessie was even more light-hearted than usual.

But on the soul of Henry had fallen the burning heat of woman's love, and his arm trembled as he walked by her side.

Such feelings are generally contagious.

Jessie trembled violently.

The others were ahead, and out of sight.

They were pacing down a shady avenue towards the water.

"Oh, Jessie!" cried Henry, in a thick and husky voice, "how I do love you!"

And he pressed her to him.

Jessie trembled, but did not reply.

Henry let go her arm, slipped his arm round her waist, and, drawing her gently towards him, kissed her rosy lips.

"You musn't," said Jessie, faintly.

But it was too late. They had exchanged the first kiss of love; they had sealed their fate by the first burning kiss of passion.

Like a guilty thing Jessie turned away, followed by Henry, half terrified, half proud of his achievement.

They were being called, and their running drew all attention from the state of confusion they were both in.

It was a lovely evening. The boat was broad of beam, with a large awning, and ten rowers, each with one oar. A servant in livery stood prepared to look after the refreshments.

Lord Lionel saw to the ladies' seats, placing them so as they could command a view of the river.

Jessie he placed beside Henry, so that she sat facing himself.

Then the serpent began his seductions. Lord Lionel knew that he was handsome, and an excellent talker. He could narrate adventures which had happened to him, and adventures which had not, with equal zest, imperturbable good humour, and aplomb.

He could draw to tears, or move to laughter, almost just as he pleased.

As Henry wanted them to like his new friend, he gave him full swing.

At intervals a wind band performed with great effect, and the servant handed round refreshments.

In this way the time passed gaily, and it was dark when they returned.

As the chaloupe glided down the placid river, Henry, who had his hand over a rail concealed in part by the awning, felt it gently touched by a soft hand.

He felt a paper placed quickly in it, and he instinctively clutched it within his own.

The hand then squeezed his, and he heard the grating of a light boat against theirs. Then all was still.

Henry was the first to land, give his assistance to all the others eagerly, and then, the boat being discharged, led the way towards the house.

Lord Lionel still kept beside the old ladies.

His great purpose was gained. He had obtained access to the house. He trusted to himself to do the rest.

Henry made some hasty excuse and went out of the room.

He was eager to read the letter.

When he had done so he turned very pale, but, with a resolute mien walked up stairs to the library, where he was sure to find the dwarf.

CHAPTER IX.

THE RIVER PIRATES.

THERE were wild bulls in England in the reign of Queen Anne, says Macaulay, and so there are now, for that matter, though not in such abundance.

In the days of James we are told that the river was infested by a set of pirates, who, under pretence of searching for arms or delinquents, rummaged every boat that passed.

The forms of society have changed, but the pirates exist still, and, at the time of which we speak, were in full play.

We fear we are revealing secrets, but the stern exigencies of our narrative compel us to divulge what, we fancy, was not known even to the police or coast guards of the time.

People fancy that smuggling has become a very old story.

We are sorry to say it was never riper than at the time of which we speak.

We do not allude now to the common thieves.

Not even to the common *river pirates*, who plundered ships and small craft at night.

Not even to the *night plunderers*, consisting of watchmen, who formed in gangs of five or six, and used to lighten small craft.

Not even the *heavy horsemen*, who used to go on board either by connivance or under the pretext of selling some articles, having peculiar dresses, which had pockets all round, and bag bladders and pockets affixed in various parts, which they filled with sugar, coffee, cocoa, or any portable article, and who, in the night, would plunder more largely, and were rowed by what were called game watermen, who were always ready to receive what was thrown to them.

Not even to the mudlarks, scuffle hunters, copemen, who now, like the others, are nearly extinct.

No--to none of these do we allude, though at one time numbering eleven thousand, and robbing property to the value of half a million sterling.

Let our readers follow us, and they will see what we mean.

Towards the mouth of the Thames, at a place which shall be nameless, is a wharf, where some hundred of barges load with hay and different other articles for transport up the river.

THE RAT CELLAR.

They go to London and above with the tide.

Their crews are a wild and strange people, totally apart from all others, and with a very different notion of morality or honesty.

They are not very highly paid, and consider it fair to pick up a shilling in the best way they can.

How they do so will presently be seen.

Beside the wharf were several cottages and one low public house.

It was composed of one large room and a loft.

The large room served the purpose of a tap-room, parlour, bar, cellar, and everything else.

The owner and his wife slept in the loft, when they did sleep.

This was a rare event.

One thing certain, they never closed.

The public room was surrounded by barrels and kegs, full and empty, while the middle was taken up by a small table and chairs.

These were perpetually occupied by the heterogeneous population of the barges.

They slept on board.

But, while in port, they spent their earnings, legal and illegal, on shore.

The night was bleak and cold; a stiff easterly breeze came rushing from seaward, the clouds closed around them like a pent house, and no

162

JESSIE, THE MORMON'S DAUGHTER.

man could possibly see further than for a small radius around him.

The crew of all the boats were in doors enjoying themselves. They were too busy to note the weather.

Men and women were equally bent on killing time, by eating, drinking, and card-playing.

One man, however, did not join the revellers. He was outside on the wharf, pacing assiduously up and down.

Under his arm was a telescope.

He wore a thick pilot coat, and a sou'-wester.

Every now and then he turned an impatient glance seaward.

He could sweep the distant horizon with his night glass.

Despite the blackness of the night he could make out one or two large vessels, chiefly colliers, passing up the river.

The tide was running like a mill race.

But still he walked up and down, exhibiting, it is true, continual signs of impatience, but never giving up his post.

Suddenly there appeared in the black darkness—in the far off distance—something like a star.

It kept bobbing up and down, however, and was speedily joined by two others.

Then it vanished.

The man with the night glass went inside, and soon returned with a blazing torch, which he held carelessly in his hand, lighting his pipe thereby.

Then he cast it on the ground near a heap of straw, which flared up in the wind, and could be seen from a long distance.

After he had let it burn for a few minutes, the man stamped it out.

Presently there could be heard the rush of a vessel through the water close at hand.

" Hoarse o'er her side the rustling cable rings,
The sails are furled, and, anchoring, round she swings;
And gathering loiterers on the land discern
Her boat descending from the latticed stern.
'Tis mann'd,—the oars keep concert on the strand,
Till grates her heel upon the shallow sand."

The persons who came on shore on the present occasion were many.

All but one were sailors, and he wore the disguise of one of the gallant fraternity.

He was a stout built man, with a pea jacket and a sailor's red cap.

But he wore spectacles.

He landed with the others, and, entering the house of entertainment, made for a small table by a deserted fireplace.

Here, at his request, he was served with victuals and drink, while the other arrivals, joined by several of the bargemen, went to work outside.

At what?

The large schooner which had brought up in so mysterious a manner was loaded with tobacco and cigars.

She had an assorted cargo besides.

This latter was to be seen by the custom-house and pay duty.

The rest was to go up in the various hay and other barges, which could land it in packages at the rendezvous of the smugglers.

The men were well paid for their trouble, and never split.

There is this quality among smugglers—they rarely peach. Talk of honour among thieves, it is absurd. There is always a king's evidence in a gang ready to save himself by betraying others.

This affair settled, the materials of the run fairly distributed among the barges, the captain of the schooner introduced the former look-out to the stranger, who wanted, for peculiar reasons, to enter London, not in triumph, but upon top of one of the barges.

A bargain was soon struck, and the schooner went away to be boarded higher up by custom-house officers, who found nothing not mentioned in her papers.

The stranger, who gave his name as Brown—which name, with Jones and Smith, rules the directory—intimated, after a copious meal and a pipe, that he should like to sleep.

The bargeman, a rough and ready customer, whose name was Bob, said that he should start in an hour, so that the traveller could either climb on top of the hay, or take his cabin.

Mr. Brown preferred the hay, having had some experience of cabins.

Bob told him he might do as he liked, upon which the stranger climbed up as best he could, pulled a tarpaulin over him, and resigned himself to slumber.

Nor did he rouse up until it was broad day, and the barge had gone as far as the tide would let them.

They took up their quarters at a water-side inn, made themselves very comfortable until pursuing their journey, and in time came to their destination.

CHAPTER X.

THE DOTTED SPOG.

A CONSIDERABLE way above Westminster Bridge, on the south side of the river, is an inn, which we shall not more particularly indicate than by the euphonious name appended to our chapter.

The Dotted Spog overlooked the river, may, indeed, have been said to face the river, as more customers frequented it on that side than on any other.

A rude and much worn flight of steps led from the water to the ground floor, which included the tap-room, bar, and bar-parlour.

Above this was a room, with a bow-window overlooking the river, frequented by the better sort of visitors.

The whole was ancient, mouldy, and, to all appearance, mouldering to decay.

But the landlord, Peter Trufit, said it would last his time.

A jolly, grizzly pated Charon he was, as he stood, pipe in hand, on his own steps, watching the barge as she rounded too close to his own door.

"Old Bob Rust for a pound," he said, to some one behind him.

A fine guess, seeing that that worthy was visible to all who wished to see him.

Five minutes later he might have been seen, after giving his boy a friendly tap on the head to keep him civil, pulling ashore, accompanied by the spectacled stranger already alluded to.

The two ascended the steps slowly, and a few words were interchanged between the landlord and Bob, after which Peter Trufit became obsequious in his turn.

"Friend of captain—wants to stay a day or so?"

"Certainly; a month if you like, sir; this way."

"But let us have a drain first," said Mr. Brown.

"With pleasure. What will you take, sir?" said Peter Trufit.

Every one ordered his favourite beverage, after which Mr. Brown, having ordered a sitting room and bedroom, was led up stairs to the former by the landlord himself.

"And now," said Mr. Brown, "will you oblige me with a small carpet-bag I left below, dinner—beefsteaks and onions—sharp, in an hour; a stiff jorum, and a telescope."

"A what, sir?" cried Peter Trufit.

"A telescope."

"Certainly sir."

And Peter Trufit retired, believing his new arrival to be a rum customer indeed.

In a few minutes he returned, followed by a rubicund and stout girl of nineteen or so, at whom Mr. Brown stared till she giggled, unbeknown to Peter, who was a little deaf, and a little blind when it suited him.

He then handed the traveller the required articles, and retired.

Up jumped the stranger, and, fixing the telescope to suit his eye, looked eagerly across the river.

He had scarcely done so when he was startled by something.

He rubbed his eyes and looked again, and, as he did so, a fiendish smile of demoniacal exultation swept across his countenance.

What was it he saw, reader?

Jessie, leaning with affectionate solicitude on the shoulder of Henry, who was seated in somewhat of a thoughtful mood on a stool beside her.

They were, evidently, in deep consultation.

Mr. Brown put down his spectacles and his telescope, wiped his face, rubbed his hands, and drank off his brandy and water at a draught.

He then rang for more.

As soon as it was brought, which it was by the rubicund maiden, who had to endure some toying from the stranger, he sat down, opened his carpet bag, and began to write.

A horrible and savage grin rested upon his countenance.

He had taken a pocket book forth and examined it carefully.

He then directed letters, and went out and posted them himself, though the distance to the post-office was great.

He then returned, and, after eating, imbibing, smoking, and gossiping away the day, went to bed considerably the worse for liquor.

His next day was spent in the same manner, until, towards evening, when informing the landlord that he might be late, he went out.

Top-boots, spectacles, a large shawl round his neck, a huge bludgeon in his hand, he looked the stage bailiff of other days.

But we must precede him in his journey.

CHAPTER XI.

THE RECEIVING HOUSE.

LONDON contains more mysteries than any other city in the world.

There may be more desperate and hideous crimes in Paris, and on the continent generally, because the nature of the foreigner is more ferocious than ours.

But, despite the generosity and nobility of the English character, take it in the aggregate, crime makes worse ruffians of Englishmen than of any other.

The wretched character of the homes of our poor, the dens in which they live, the crowding together of families and the sexes, the unwholesome exhalations of the older, undrained houses, driving men to public houses to spend their evenings, is one of the main causes of this.

Poets and satirists have sung the praises of mine inn in contradistinction to home, or, at all events, as a very good substitute for it when abroad; and there is a comfort, a cleanliness, a geniality in the hotel, and a respectability in the company which authorises, in some measure, such an opinion.

But it is otherwise with the gin shop and beer house, where needy men do congregate from noon till night, from night till morn, for the purpose of amusement and refreshment at the least possible cost.

Indecent songs, equivocal stories, tossing, card playing, carried on with little regard to strict honesty—the system of over-reaching another being considered smart—blunts the sensibilities, and paves the way to errors less venial or excusable.

Theft is the readiest way of replenishing the pockets of an idle man.

To theft the Bedouins of society resort.

But of what use would theft be if there were no receivers of stolen goods?

The putting down of 'fences' and receiving houses are the first steps towards discouraging theft.

But this the police either do not or will not understand.

The extinction of crime, I have no doubt, they think undesirable.

But the abolition of fences is contrary to their theory.

These fences are, to a certain extent, in collusion with the police.

They give up, every now and then, certain unfortunates.

The fence who deserts a pal never allows the circumstance to become known.

He contrives to appear exceedingly disconsolate and regretful at the accident.

But he is nearly always the betrayer.

Thieves will not generally believe this, but so it is.

The traveller, for a purpose which will be understood as we proceed, was desirous of making acquaintance with one of this numerous fraternity.

He had, accordingly, announced his intention of visiting him by letter.

Judah Sol, as the individual in question was popularly designated by the fraternity, resided in a narrow, dirty, dismal street, somewhere out of Holborn.

The traveller strode slowly up the street; he looked neither to the right nor the left.

He was aware of the position of the house.

It was a marine store shop. Flaming bills announced that within the highest price was given for old rags, bones, and grease. A doll with a black head and white petticoats swung, as from a gallows, to and fro in the wind, and, to make the resemblance more exact, creaked hideously in the night air, being suspended by a rusty chain.

An odour of filth poured forth from this den.

Its obvious trade, encouraging, as it was, to river thieves, was the least part of its profit.

Servant girls, apprentices, costermongers—whose barrows are convenient shelters for such unconsidered trifles as lead, iron, glass, knives, and candlesticks—are the chief open customers, but at night comes the higher branch of visitors.

The traveller, or, as he called himself, Mr. Brown, entered and looked around him.

The shop was, however, such a heterogeneous mass that, for a moment, he stood dumbfounded.

Such a pile of apparent rubbish he had never seen before.

"Vell, my frient," he heard some one say, "vat I do forsh u?"

Mr. Brown peered further down the shop, and there saw the speaker.

He was a little, old man, standing on tip toe, with spectacles on his nose. He was pockmarked, nearly bald, with a peaked chin, and a sinister expression of mouth, on which hovered the signs of half a century of crime.

"Mr. Judah?"

"Yesh."

"Can I speak with you in private?" asked Mr. Brown.

"Bishness?" said the Jew.

"*Toy ben rog*," replied the stranger, in a whisper.

"*Rog!*" said the Jew.

"*Rog ben toy*," continued the new arrival.

The Jew took off his greasy dog skin cap, and led the way into a small back parlour.

He then motioned the other to a seat.

"Vat ish the bishness?" said the Jew.

"We are quite private?" replied the other.

"Qvite."

"Then, Mr. Judah, plain English is the best. I want two men experienced in burglary, men who will stick at nothing. I will pay them handsomely if they do their work well."

"*Snik*," said the Jew.

"What?"

"*Snik*," he repeated, drawing his hand across his throat.

"Yes."

"Then I have justs de ting, mine frient."

"I am lucky."

"They are te two most pig plackards in town; but two shentlemen as understands bishness."

"Can I see them?"

"De fee ish ten pouns," said the hideous little monster, holding out his hand.

Mr. Brown, with a slight grimace, placed the money in the other's palm: the fence then rose.

He took a key and opened a door of communication between the shop and the upper part of the house.

He then led the way up a steep flight of stairs, towards the first floor.

But he did not stop there.

He went still higher up, opening a door at every flight.

At last he reached a large square store room on the very top of the house.

It was surrounded with shelves piled up with goods.

Placing his hand in a mysterious way against one of the shelves, he caused it to revolve and then reveal a door.

At this door he knocked in a peculiar way.

It opened, and they found themselves in a tolerably large room, rudely furnished.

In the centre was a table, at which sat two men.

They were playing the classic and popular game of put.

Bottles, tobacco, and pipes, covered one side of the table.

Near a small fire-place, on the hob of which sung a kettle, was a woman leaning her face in her hands.

The Jew closed the door, and bowed low to the two men.

"A shentleman on bishness," said the Jew, in a cringing way.

"Curse business," said a stout, ill looking ruffian about thirty. "Let us finish our game."

"Goot bishness," continued the Jew.

"Wait?" cried the other, savagely. "I can't win a game. This ere cove is the devil."

His companion, a young man with a slouched hat, made no reply, but, continued quietly playing his cards.

"That's enough," he said, with a fearful oath, "and now, curse your old carcass, what is the nature of your business?"

"This shentleman will explain," said the Jew.

The man turned towards Mr. Brown. The younger one raised his eyes.

Brown started back.

The young one rose to his feet.

"No?"

"Yes."

"It can't be?"

"The devil."

"Who'd a thought it?"

"Phineas Bristowe, as I'm a living man," cried the youth.

"The Viscount de Florac as sure as eggs," cried the traveller.

The woman gave a shrill scream.

The traveller turned towards her.

It was Julie.

* * * * *

The escape of the Viscount de Florac and his mistress, Julie, had been little less than miraculous.

As the flames reached their height, as they

began to give up all hope, a trap opened, and the gipsy woman, whose daughter had been protected by Henry, stood beckoning them downwards.

At the iron gate of a cellar looking on the river they found a boat.

In this way, amidst the noise, bustle, and confusion, they easily contrived to escape.

How and why the gipsy had appeared to save them at that exact moment of time will appear at a future period of our narrative.

CHAPTER XII.

BURGLARY.

THE greeting between the Viscount de Florac and Phineas Bristowe was hearty.

The latter intimated, on the retirement of the Jew, that the affairs of the saints were progressing with marvellous good fortune ; that the saints were becoming numerous ; that the whole continent of America was about to adopt the new religion.

"And my nine wives ?" said de Florac, in a low whisper.

"Well."

"Julie, we have private business to speak of. You had better go to bed."

"Eh? What?" she said, rising, with a scornful yawn.

"Why don't you go to bed ?"

"Just the thing I want," replied Julie, who, with a surly "good night," opened the door, and retired.

"You were going to say—" said the viscount, as soon as her back was turned.

"They are all well—married," added the preacher, with a chuckle.

"So much the better," continued the viscount. "And now, what is your business ?"

"My business is one likely to put money in the pockets of all concerned in it."

"Good," said the fat man.

"Hem," said de Florac.

Phineas Bristowe then explained under what extraordinary circumstances Jessie had escaped from him.

How, to his utter astonishment, he had afterwards seen her in the streets of New York.

Now Jessie was, under most peculiar circumstances, heiress to an immense fortune.

Any risk or trouble they might take in getting possession of her person would be amply repaid by the reward.

He proposed, once more, to get Jessie secretly in his power, and then to make a safe bargain with her friends.

He would take a large sum to set her free, and leave her henceforth unmolested, or he would detain her a prisoner.

"But she is your own child ?"

"Heaven knows," said Phineas Bristowe, with a hypocritical shrug.

"How so ?"

"Her story is the most extraordinary and mysterious ever conceived," said Phineas. "But now to business."

"That's it," said the elder ruffian.

"Well, I intend, the first dark evening, to make an attempt on the house."

"Any swag ?"

"They are very rich, and the house is splendidly furnished," continued Phineas Bristowe. "Besides that, I will give a hundred pounds for the night's work."

"Done," said the professional burglar.

"And now to business again," said de Florac. "I wish to speak with you in private."

"All right," said the cracksman, pulling away at his pipe, while Phineas and de Florac moved towards the door by which Julie had retired.

"Do you return to America?" whispered de Florac.

"I do."

"When ?"

"As soon as Jessie is in my power I shall leave this country for ever. Our prophet, Joe Smith, has traced gigantic plans ; I am to aid him, and, if you choose—"

"I shall go."

"But Julie ?"

"Must go with me."

"Why ?"

"She is the sole heiress to her father's wealth. He has sent it all to America, at least I think so. Once there she must marry me legally. I can then think what is to be done."

"Right. And now, to arrange our plan. This man—"

"Has the reputation of being the ablest cracksman in England."

"Then let us consult him."

The consultation did take place, and the three soon after parted, to all appearance, satisfied with each other.

CHAPTER XIII.

A GLOOMY ADVENTURE.

THE night selected for the nefarious attempt on the lonely house in Chelsea was dark and tempestuous.

The two burglars had been with the traveller for forty-eight hours.

A minute outside survey of the premises had been carefully made.

The burglar pronounced the house to be not easily broken into.

The reward, however, was great, and he was willing to persevere.

The mansion appeared as if inhabited by wealthy people, and, while willing to aid him in his endeavours, the others gave him free leave to monopolise the whole of the plunder.

Dick, as the ruffian was called, smacked his lips with considerable gusto. He had a kind of professional pride in his occupation.

So had Jack Ketch, or Dun, as he used to be told.

There is no accounting for tastes.

They rowed up and down the river, entered the garden at night, assured themselves there were no watch-dogs, and studied the ground as a general might a field of battle.

On the night in question, being sufficiently prepared, they took a final inspection.

This was about a quarter of an hour before the return of Henry and his party.

A small boat lay under the bank, concealed by an overhanging bush.

Close to this they remained for some time in anxious consultation.

Then they went across to prime themselves with brandy before entering upon their dark and dangerous enterprise.

In the meantime the family returned, took supper, and, when Lord Lionel went away, retired to rest.

All was still as death within, though something of a storm raged without.

The night was pitchy dark.

Clouds spread right and left, and the antique trees in the garden quivered in the stiff night breeze.

Not a light was visible in the whole house.

The calm within appeared unnatural during that fierce conflict of the elements.

Presently a distant rumbling indicated the approach of a thunder-storm.

Not a craft of any kind could be seen on the surface of the river.

Doubtless the Thames police were creeping about, although, perhaps, tempted by the gloom to seek refuge where a warm fire, and a hot, steaming glass gave more of creature comfort.

But what is this gliding silently and still across the waters?

A boat!

A boat manned, too, by three men!

It makes its way to the landing place unguarded by rails.

The boat is made fast to the shore, and the three men land.

They were all masked.

Each clasps some weapon or instrument necessary to the perpetration of his crime.

The professional burglar has a large sack for what he technically calls "the swag."

They listen for any sound, rather from habit than anything else, for the storm, which increases in intensity, drowns every other noise.

They are soon in the deep shadow of the mansion, at the door which opens on the lawn.

They produce a dark lantern, and examine the door.

The burglar looks keenly at the lock, and shakes his head.

"What's the matter?"

"Patent."

"Curse it!" said De Florac, "what is to be done?"

"Try the window," replied Dick.

They moved on one side, and examined the shutter. It was very strong.

Again a parley took place.

The professional burglar became very thoughtful.

"I don't like it," he said.

"Why?"

"Take hours. But I see only one way."

"What's that?"

"Look," said Dick, pointing to a small fanlight over the doorway.

"Well."

"I can cut the glass clean out if you will creep through."

"I will try," said De Florac, not without a slight grimace.

The burglar now, aided by his companions, and by a rustic chair they brought from the lawn, ascended to the oblong pane of glass over the doorway, which he began cutting with a diamond.

Practice makes perfect as the woman said, who, having carried a calf up a hill every day as it grew, was able at last to carry a cow.

The glass was out in a very few minutes, and deposited with care on the grass.

Viscount de Florac took a dark lantern, and, opening it slightly, peered into the hall.

All was still.

He crept through with extreme care, and, after considerable twisting and turning, succeeded in falling inside.

He then, without difficulty, found the library door, and treading, without fear, on the soft carpets, opened a window, and undid the fastenings of a shutter.

The three cold blooded villains were now in the house.

What was next to be done?

The least alarm might be dangerous.

Phineas said that they must bind or gag any one who resisted, but that, in case of a struggle, the silent knife must do the work.

Do not let us be told that the villany of this man is exaggerated.

Crime may decrease as far as the number of criminals may be concerned, but crime increases in intensity.

In a highly cultured state of society this must always be, especially where there is such vast disparity in wealth.

Where, as even in this land, the wealthy classes try to cast the burden of taxation off their own shoulders.

That it is true the state of things on rural parishes sufficiently testifies.

When a cottage goes to decay, is not the tenant mildly told to go to the next parish?

And people say that the poor are not interested in having a vote.

Had the masses votes, and had sense to resist the wretched temptations of bribery and intimidation; if they would but once choose a bold, free, and independent parliament, excluding, as much as possible, landed proprietors, they would find at once the tremendous difference.

In twenty years means would be found of employing everybody.

Poor rates would fall to nothing.

But, in the meantime, the burglars are in the hall, looking about them.

The carpet on the stairs is thick and soft.

They need fear no discovery from the sound of their footsteps.

They prepare to ascend towards the upper rooms.

How do they propose to discover the room occupied by Jessie.

By the test of Cinderella.

Phineas Bristow swore that, if her shoes were outside the door, he should know them in a minute, as she had the smallest and prettiest foot in all the British isles.

Viscount de Florac gave a short, dry laugh.

A strange, an appalling sound startled them from their fancied security.

Ere they could tell what it was a terrible voice shouted to them to surrender.

They looked up and found that they were confronted by armed domestics headed by Henry himself.

Close to them on the stairs was the dwarf, his arms quietly folded.

Phineas Bristowe gave a wild yell, and flew down stairs, followed by De Florac.

The baulked burglar made a desperate attempt to stab the dwarf with a knife.

A short sword dagger flashed in the dwarf's hand, and wounded him in the wrist.

With a savage cry he, too, fled.

The three men reached the bottom of the staircase almost together.

In their terror they looked not before them.

An awful cry of anguish followed. They had fallen through a yawning gap extending the whole length of the hall.

With an awful clang it closed over them. Maimed, bruised, and, in the agonies of pain they were in, they found themselves alone in total darkness.

"B—t you!" growled Dick, after a few minutes, "here's a pretty plant! Where's the glim?"

"Here," said De Florac, faintly.

___

CHAPTER XIV.

THE RAT CELLAR.

GROANING piteously De Florac, who, fortunately for him, had not loosed hold of the dark lantern, withdrew the slide which had hitherto closed it, and held it on high.

They were in a large, deserted cellar, the walls slimy with vermin and filth.

The floor was covered with fresh straw.

It had evidently been placed so as to break the force of their fall.

They had, then, been expected.

How had they been betrayed? Who had set their deadly enemies on their track?

They lay, in utter anguish, turning this over in their minds.

Phineas Bristowe, who was stout and corpulent, had fallen headlong, with difficulty preventing his brains from being knocked out by stretching out his hands.

He lay, as it appeared, insensible on the straw.

Dick the burglar was crawling on his hands and knees, and crying out that his leg was broken.

The viscount had seen the yawning abyss in time, and had, by a desperate leap, escaped with a fearful shaking and a sprained ankle.

For a time none spoke; but presently, by a law in nature, no sooner was the lantern set down than they began to crawl towards it.

Soon they sat, a hideous trio—pale, ghastly, bleeding—round the light.

All simultaneously put their right hand to their pockets, and felt for a brandy-flask.

They found them safe.

A drain of the fiery liquor seemed to rouse their energies.

"Somebody's split," said the burglar.

"It must be," said Phineas.

"But who?"

"Humph!" continued Dick, "you and her wern't the best of friends, you know."

"Her?" said Phineas.

"Her?" said the viscount.

A pause ensued. The three men glared at each other with cold and glittering eyes.

In the minds of the mean, the dastardly, and the corrupt, the innately depraved and unscrupulous, the feeling of revenge is the strongest in nature.

Hence the deeds of a Nero, a Napoleon, of a James II.

Hence the magnanimity of a Cromwell, a William of Orange, a Washington.

"I'll cut her —— throat!" said Dick, with a blasphemous cry.

"Roast her!" said the priest, a cruel of all cruel races.

"Leave her to me," replied Paolo, with a smile, so bitter, cold-blooded, and savage, that the others shuddered.

"Well, you know your own business best," said Dick; "but, as you seem able to move, just look about. Ain't there no door?"

Paolo rose to his feet, took the lantern in his hand, and peered round the vault.

"None," he said, in an awful tone of voice.

"None?" repeated the others, echoing his words.

Again dead silence prevailed, and then the other two, by a desperate effort raising themselves up, examined the cellar.

A doorway had recently been bricked up. The traces of the mortar were clearly visible.

They were in a living tomb!

A howl of pain, anguish, and despair burst from the three wretches.

They were immured in a vault to die of hunger!

The light of Heaven, the blue sky, the green fields, were for ever shut out from them.

A burning thirst seemed suddenly to catch them.

They flew for refuge to their brandy-flasks, but this only made the matter worse—their parched lips became on fire.

A glare of insanity appeared in their eyes.

They looked at each other with a fiendish and exulting smile.

Then they gazed upwards.

The roof overhead was of wood.

Of course, if they raised their voices, they must be heard by those above.

The domestics could not be a party to this demoniacal plot.

No disinterested being could join in revenge so fearful as this. No servant, however well paid, would be silent while human creatures were being starved to death.

But the victims forgot that they were outlaws, upon whose head a price was set, and that there are those who consider any punishment light for such criminals.

The servants might, probably, be actuated by

an immoderate, an unscrupulous, a remorseless zeal for the cause of virtue.

Look back to the crimes of history.

Let us instance Scotland.

Its story abounds with frightful tales, with vindictive massacres and assassinations.

But they were regarded as sacred duties, as exquisite pleasures, by the perpetrators.

What were, then, those wretches that they should excite pity?

They were wretched outlaws condemned beforehand by the law.

Had not a Highland tribe, having been affronted by the people of a parish near Inverness, surrounded the parish church on a Sunday, shut the door, and burned the whole congregation alive? While the flames were raging the hereditary musician of the murderers mocked the shrieks of the perishing crowd with the notes of his bagpipes. A band of Macgregors, having cut off the head of an enemy, laid it, the mouth filled with bread and cheese, on his sister's table, and had the satisfaction of seeing her go mad with horror at the sight. They then carried the ghastly trophy in triumph to their chief. The whole clan met under the roof of an ancient church. Every one in turn laid his hand on the dead man's scalp, and vowed to defend the slayers. The inhabitants of Eigg seized some Macleods, bound them hand and foot, and turned them adrift in a boat to be swallowed up by the waves, or to perish of hunger. The Macleods retaliated by driving the population of Eigg into a cavern, lighting a fire at the entrance, and suffocating the whole race, men, women, and children.

When civil strife was raging good men were found to excuse the massacre of Glencoe because the victims were thieves. No usual appeals for mercy could be brought to bear with regard to outlaws, whose lives were forfeit to the law.

Some such fearful thoughts must have been passing through the minds of the three burglars.

Though these instances were unknown to them, they were familiar with others.

An awful howl of rage burst from them.

Again they drank deeply from their flask of brandy, and sank down, mad, intoxicated, and blaspheming.

Some of the brandy was spilt, and Paolo let fall the lantern.

The straw ignited, and the three infuriated ruffians were compelled to jump up, and rush to the extremity of the vault to escape burning and suffocation.

But a savage delight came to their souls.

If they were burnt the house would, probably, catch fire, and the inmates perish with them.

The straw burnt furiously, however, only for a few minutes, and then again the cave relapsed into darkness, except where a glow in the centre indicated where the straw had been.

All three appeared at the same moment to notice that a square space in the middle of the vault was untouched by the fire.

All made a rush forward despite the most blinding smoke.

It was a grating over a dark abyss.

Then all was darkness, and the three exhausted ruffians, choked, blinded, mad with drink, sank down upon the ground to seek a heavy and fearful slumber.

In a few minutes nothing could be heard but the heavy breathing of the sleepers.

Yes!

Hark!

What is it?

An odd pattering to and fro might have been soon after detected.

It was the rats gathering from afar to the loathsome feast, which guilt and crime, and avarice and lust, had prepared for them.

And still the three men slept the sleep of of gross inebriety.

The rats might soon be counted by hundreds.

How they came up, whence they issued, what signal had brought them, altogether was a mystery.

Why do crows and vultures collect upon a coming battle field?

Why do sharks follow a ship which contains the dead or dying!

These are mysteries which not even the naturalist can explain.

CHAPTER XV.

JESSIE'S PLOT.

THERE was more sense in Jessie's little finger than in the whole body of many young women of her age.

She knew Henry's character thoroughly. She understood at once, and for ever, that he was not a quiet, stay at home bird, but that he must be amused.

A writer has recently asserted that drunkenness is as much an illness as consumption, and no more to be blamed.

This senseless apology for the grossest and most debasing of vices can only come from the mouth of one steeped to the eyes in the love of drink.

But the pursuit of pleasure, a fondness for excitement, a desire to be doing always, is a native characteristic.

Now Henry was one of those natures which requires in youth the excitement of cricket, boating, field sports, and some engrossing occupation, in manhood a profession, in the prime the strife of politics.

In the navy he found an object to employ him.

But he was now on leave of absence.

Jessie saw at a glance that the quiet, secluded, almost humdrum life of home, which to her was so charming, would not suit him.

He had, as much as possible, tried to be satisfied with it, but he had failed.

He had found a change in the society of the bustling and active Lord Lionel Thynne and his friends.

But, then, Jessie did not like Lord Lionel Thynne.

It was very unreasonable, was it not? I have no doubt that many of my young lady readers will think Jessie a great fool.

THE DETECTED ROUE.

Was he not a lord, second son of a duke, very handsome, rich, and the relation of a minister?

What more could she want?

Poor young ladies. It is too often upon such premises that you lay the foundations of a life-long misery.

Jessie was acute, had penetration, and an intuitive knowledge of character.

She saw, as clearly as she saw the sun at noon-day, that Lord Thynne was not the sort of companion suited to guide the inexperienced and warm-hearted Henry.

But, then, she would not say so for the world. This would look like coercion.

She did not want him tied to her apron strings.

But she did want to wean him, as much as possible, from the habit he had now got of spending all his evenings and most of his nights with Lord Lionel.

Nobody else objected to this. Lord Lionel was his superior officer, would soon sail with him, and no possible harm could happen to the young midshipman in the lieutenant's society.

So did not think Jessie.

She, therefore, quietly suggested that Henry should occasionally bring home his friend, that Lady Haddington should give parties, and oh! wonder of wonders, her birthday was next Monday.

No. 22

Her birthday!

Of course this was a day on which she could do just as she liked.

She determined to give a ball, and, what was more, a fancy dress ball.

Lord Lionel Thynne was specially invited by a letter in Jessie's own hand.

The libertine had felt a bounding sensation at the heart he had not experienced for some time.

His passion for Lotty was by no means extinguished—for a very good reason.

But he could find room for more than one affection, and for Jessie he felt one of those fierce, absorbing, and terrible passions, which visit, for their sins, the hearts of the wicked.

It is not to be supposed that, because Lord Lionel was a debauchee, living in a constant turmoil of wild pleasures and vices, that he was incapable of a real, true, and genuine passion.

He was a man to live, as long as he could, a life of dissipation, but ready, at the proper moment, to surrender to youth, beauty, and innocence.

Lord Lionel Thynne really loved Jessie.

He felt a boy again. He saw in her the means of breaking with his more unprincipled associates.

He was heir-apparent to a dukedom, his elder brother being sickly and unmarried.

He would marry, abandon his evil ways, become a public man, and keep up the time-honoured name of the Duke of ——.

He would keep open house, enter Parliament, win a great name, and utterly give up the Capuan life he was leading.

Shade of our great mother Eve! how often has the bright eye of a lovely girl induced men to make similar good resolutions?

But making and keeping good resolutions are not quite the same thing.

The invitation received by Lord Lionel, in the handwriting of Jessie herself, appeared to him to be a sign of her having particularly noticed him, and not unfavourably.

He was wild with hope and excitement.

He looked down with pity on the mere boy who asserted that Jessie was to be his wife.

As a rule, he would have been quite right. Very young girls generally look up to men who are considerably their seniors, just as some women of thirty are fond of mere boys.

But what Jessie was we shall see in much more intricate and dangerous positions than that in which she is now placed.

Henry, as soon as the ball was decided on, gave up his whole mind to it.

It was not only an occupation, but it was an occupation which pleased Jessie.

In the first place, there were invitations to be written, and these were not a few.

The name of Lady Haddington was not unknown in society.

She it was who, in another year, was to present Jessie at court.

And then Lord Lionel Thynne pleaded in a most humble way that his mother and sisters might be invited.

He had contrived to learn that Jessie was heiress to twenty thousand a year.

As no one of his family but himself believed his elder brother to be seriously ill, such a match was no mean one even for the second son of a duke.

Lord Lionel communicated the intelligence to his mother and sisters.

They were delighted at the idea. It was charming, rural, unsophisticated.

A fancy dress ball, too, given at such short notice, was supremely charming.

They were sure they should like Jessie. They would be gentle, kind to her. They would not crush her with too much protection.

They would recollect that she was to be their dear sister.

Poor Jessie little expected to be so highly honoured.

The fact of the Duchess of —— accepting the invitation made the ball quite the fashion, and several ladies called upon Lady Haddington to beg invitations for their friends.

Every body saw that it would be a perfect crush.

But the old house was quite equal to the occasion.

CHAPTER XVI.

THE FANCY DRESS BALL.

THE old house at Chelsea was very large, and, though no such affair had come off within its precincts since the days of stupid, obstinate, and silly Queen Anne, there was ample space.

Every room on the ground and first floor had been hastily decorated and fitted up. A vast tent covered a very large portion of the garden —all the centre, indeed.

There were no tall trees except at the sides.

This division of the reception rooms was, above all, beautiful.

Lamps of variegated colours had been arranged among the shrubs and small trees with great good taste.

All was a blaze of light, except where, towards the end, a terraced walk had been left in shadow.

It overlooked the river.

The general refreshments and the supper-room were served in gorgeous style.

Harry was chief ordainer of the feast.

At an early hour the carriages began to arrive. England is not exactly the country for fancy dress balls. They are seen to more effect where the climate allows them to take place wholly in the open air.

But the good taste and judgment of the givers of the feast gave glorious zest to the scene.

Jessie, who was now full grown, and in the very zenith of her beauty, came down attended by a train of pages to receive her guests.

They were chiefly little girls, whose mammas had begged that they, as a favour, might be present.

Jessie wore the superb costume of Mary Queen of Scots, when she was, however, Queen of France.

Her purple velvet robes, her crown of pearls, her collar and diamonds, became her well.

Henry, as the youthful king, looked radiant with pride and happiness.

Lady Haddington, Cornelia, and the dwarf, looked on them with perfect amazement.

Never had they seen so fair a couple.

It seemed almost superhuman beauty.

Henry had never looked so singularly hand-some.

Why?

As he took her hand to lead her to her seat he seemed for the first time fully to realise the nature of the love which was creeping on his soul.

A throne had been erected for the royal couple.

But, as the guests began to arrive, they rose to receive them with a calm and quiet dignity which amazed all beholders.

To possess dignity suited to a prince it is not always necessary to be born on the steps of the throne.

They came not in crowds, but in droves—kings, and princes, and banditti: Charles the Seconds, Lady Jane Greys, Marie Antoinettes, flower girls, Italian beauties. Henry the Eighths—men and women of all races, and every variety of costume.

But all bowed to the throne of youth, of beauty, and assumed royalty.

It was a perfect levee.

The Duchess of —— came early. She was accompanied by her daughters: three swarthy, handsome, but portionless girls.

At all events portionless for the daughters of a duke.

Lord Lionel Thynne wore the costume of a naval officer of the line of Charles II.

The ladies wore superb court dresses.

They had been waiting for this. The musicians struck up for a dance.

A general dispersion took place—some moved towards the ball-room, some to where the cards attracted their notice.

Lord Lionel bowed low to Jessie.

"It is the privilege of royalty, even of female royalty," he said, "to choose a partner, but may I humbly suggest—"

"Our royal husband," replied Jessie, sweetly, "has laid his commands on us, but the next dance we command your hand."

Again Lord Lionel bowed low, while Henry very rudely laughed. It was very rude, but he could not help it. The gravity of Jessie was so inimitable.

Lord Lionel smiled. He had heard the soft, almost plaintive, tones of Jessie. They had gone to his very heart. He could not believe for one moment that one so queenly, so superb, so beautiful, so clearly able to pick and choose where she pleased, would be satisfied with a mere boy.

The dance began, and many crowded to see the graceful couple.

Lord Lionel had selected a very beautiful girl, and had contrived to be near them.

He himself was struck with the loveliness of both, and for a moment his heart failed him.

"And now, Henry," said Jessie, when the dance was over, "you must now leave me, and see to others. Already I have noticed how people have looked at us."

"What matter."

"All the young ladies are jealous of me," said Jessie, demurely.

"And all the young men of me."

"Well, jealousy is a bad feeling, and we must not encourage it; so, Monsieur mon roi, go, make yourself agreeable to the company, and when the clock strikes one you can take me down to supper."

Again a fresh orchestra had struck up a fresh piece of music.

Lord Lionel was proudly advancing to where they stood.

Henry turned quickly away.

Both sighed.

Ha! ha! love is advancing the siege with wild rapidity. There is jealousy in the camp.

Who, at their age, has not felt a pang to be parted even for a moment.

Bright visions, beloved hours, memories even fresh and cheerful when the head is bowed, and the heart cold, and the hairs grey, have ye not, even then, your charms?

Does not some pleasant note, some sunny glance, some exquisite moment of bliss, burst up from the far off mirage of our youth at times, and give us both pain and pleasure?

Youth is better than beauty: who preserves the first longest is happiest.

Jessie gave her hand to Lord Lionel, while yet her eyes followed the half lingering step of Henry, the glance cast over his shoulder as he walked.

"Thanks, your majesty," said Lord Lionel.

The music was a waltz.

"Is your majesty ready?"

"Her majesty is sorry to say that our dance must be the next one. Her majesty never waltzes," replied Jessie.

"Then will your majesty deign to walk through the grounds?" said Lord Lionel, not at all sorry for the change in their arrangements.

Jessie bowed courteously, and took his arm.

There was a flush on the young officer's face, a mingled look of hope and fear, a wild, anxious glance, which should have alarmed Jessie.

But, above all things, she was not vain.

Lord Lionel kept her in constant conversation. He admired this, he asked questions about that; he drew her attention to some of the more remarkable ornamentation of the grounds until he came to the terrace.

It was entirely abandoned.

"And here," he said, drawing her gently beneath a falling curtain of verdure formed by admirably arranged creeping plants, "you behold the reverse of this gay and festive scene."

"Where?" said Jessie, smiling, despite herself, at his somewhat forced enthusiasm.

"On this still and silent river. All here is still. Even our riot and music has failed to attract from the busy haunts of men. See how calmly the deep waters flow. Miss Jessie, this is a fit emblem of two existences."

"You are poetical, my lord."

"Yours and mine. You have hitherto lived in a calm and happy world of your own creation, while I have sought the battle of life. You, with books, music, and dear friends, have had your life flow onward like this calm and solemn highway."

"Not quite."

"In part, then, while I have existed in a merry and bustling medium like that within," he continued, lowering his voice.

"Men generally do."

"Because men have no guiding star. Now, young lady, I have often thought that the perfection of human existence, the acme of human happiness, the state of being nearest to that of the fair Paradise where our first parents dwelt, is in the conjunction of two such lives, in the cohesion of two such existences. In a word, dear Jessie, I, the heir to a dukedom, with a splendid career before me—with rank, honour, power, ready to be showered on me from all sides—love you, Jessie! And oh, if I could but hope that our futures were to be mingled! If our hands were to be joined there might be happiness for you; there would be for me joy, glory, and happiness unutterable! Why do you turn away, dear girl? I am abrupt; pardon the violence and energy of my new-born passion! Say you are not angry."

"My lord," said Jessie, in a tremulous voice, she in vain struggling to speak steadily and firmly, "if you are in earnest, and not jesting—"

"Jesting! Heaven—"

"Not jesting with a young and inexperienced girl, I thank you—"

"Thanks: oh, no! 'Tis I—

"Listen, my lord. If you are jesting the cruelty is undeserved. I will, therefore, take you in earnest, and believe that you are serious."

"I am."

"In that case again, my lord, I thank you from my heart, but—"

"Oh, Jessie, Jessie!" began the nobleman, in accents of genuine alarm.

"My lord."

"Miss ——, I beg pardon."

"Listen to me calmly one moment. Had I suspected that Henry's friend intended any such address I should have carefully avoided this interview, for I regret—"

"Be careful; do not drive me mad. I have been thoughtless. The world thinks me feeble; but this first passion of my life is capable of giving me new heart, new courage, new life. Let my mother speak to you—my sisters, they know of my hopes, of my love, and sanction it."

"It would be vain," said Jessie, firmly, 'my mind is definitively made up. I shall always be happy to see you as the friend of Henry Haddington, but I must beg that you will not compel me to refuse seeing you by again renewing a topic which must be ever painful to both."

"You refuse me?"

This was said in a tone of wonder.

"I do."

"You refuse me?"

His voice was raised much louder, as if passion were assuming its sway.

"My lord, I say, once for all, that I thank you, but must decline your kind offer," said Jessie, whose eyes began to flash.

"One moment," cried Lord Lionel, wildly, and, strange to say, dashing away a tear.

"My lord—"

"You love another?"

"This, my lord, is very unfair."

"I know you do. Henry Haddington introduced you as his future wife.

"Well, my lord?"

"'Tis true, then; I thought it a boyish joke. Pardon me," he said, bowing low, to hide his pale face and bitter expression of countenance, "had I have believed him I should have spared you this pain, and myself much unnecessary humiliation."

"There can be no humiliation, my lord, where there is no crime," said Jessie, gently.

The poor girl pitied him.

"But this will be talked of. I shall be laughed at," began Lord Lionel.

"How so, my lord?" said Jessie, looking him full in the face with those deep eyes of hers.

"You will keep this a secret?"

"From every one."

"From Henry?"

"From him most of all."

"And meet me as if nothing had happened?"

"Yes."

"Jessie, you are an angel. Go, join the revellers, leave me awhile. I will return soon. They must be searching for you?"

Jessie held out her hand. He started, pressed it to his lips.

She was gone.

CHAPTER XVII.

THE BROTHERS.

"Gone! refused, and by a little girl, I, the proud heir of a dukedom, a man capable of vast design, and ready to win fame and honour at the cannon's mouth, or in the senate, for the woman I love, refused! ha! ha! refused, and for a beardless boy who knows not the meaning of love's sacred fire. Refused, too," he added, slowly, "*by the only woman I ever loved.*"

He strode angrily along the gallery.

"But this must not be. I will be revenged, revenged, revenged!'

"How?"

Lord Lionel Thynne started, and, looking up, saw before him the figure of an odalisque, but so closely muffled in her veil that he could not discern her features.

"Who crosses my path?" he said, angrily, laying his hand upon his sword.

"Ha! ha! ha!" laughed the other.

"Surely I know that voice?'

"You do."

She unveiled, and the pretty horsebreaker of St. John's-wood stood before him.

"You here?"

"Why not?"

"But"—

"You seem to forget, my Lord Lionel Thynne, what I once told you, that I had means of introduction into good society you little suspected. I am here, and have been here all the evening."

"Why?"

"To watch you."

"To watch me," he cried, with a strange glitter in his eye; "for what?"

"Do you forget your oath, my lord?" she replied, with bitter sarcasm.

"No, by Heaven!"

"I heard all," she answered coldly.

"Well, but I must marry some day, and this girl—"

"Is too good, too pure for you."

"What know you of her?"

"That matters not. I came here with other views. *He is here.*"

The young nobleman started back as if struck. His face was deadly pale, his eyes started from his sockets, he stared wildly and terribly around.

"So, my lord, that oath which you took, under such fearful circumstances, that oath which, in some things, you have kept—"

"Yes! yes!"

"Because I can act weakly the oath is not yet fulfilled. You took it voluntarily, you took it freely. I demand its fulfilment before you enter upon any new scheme—even of domestic love and the affections."

"And if I refuse?"

"What!—an English gentleman and officer break his oath?"

"I do not intend that, but still I may not wholly neglect my future happiness."

"Then you no longer profess to love me?" she said, looking up.

"I love you as much as ever I desire you, passionately—but—but—"

"You love this girl better?"

"I would make *her* my wife."

"You offered to make me your wife?"

"Yes," stammered Lord Lionel.

"You never meant it?"

"I did, but—"

"But, what?"

"I did not know then."

"That is true, but, when you took that solemn oath, you knew, and yet that man yet lives."

"He is—"

At this moment a tall, pale figure, in the costume of the Spanish Grandee, raised the curtain of creeping plants, and peered with a listless eye upon the scene without.

With a stifled cry the young woman hid her face in her veil and fled.

"My lord marquis, you here?" said Lord Lionel Thynne half respectfully, half affectionately.

"Ah, Lionel, how are you? I was invited and came to see this pearl of beauty."

"What think you of her?"

"Pretty, but insipid. Who was that just left you?" he continued.

"Pardon me," said the other, in the same signs of confusion.

"Say no more, my brother. I thought I knew the voice. I pry into no man's secrets. But I never see one beauty in woman now. I once

believed in beauty, in heavenly love, but now—"

"My lord, you never tell your sorrow," said the young sailor, with animation.

"Because we are no longer Ly and Tom, brother Lionel," replied the elder brother.

"But the respect I owe—"

"There used to be no respect between us, but only love."

Lord Lionel bowed low. His very heart strings seemed ready to burst.

"Do not excuse yourself, Ly. I am going to Paris to-morrow to consult the physicians there for my peculiar malady. When I return, if I feel better, I will tell you all.

And the marquis turned his handsome, pale face towards the garden, shook his brother's hand, and re-entered the parterre.

Lionel heard him give a deep sigh like a sob.

"D——n! I think that woman is damning me body and soul," said Lord Lionel, wildly. "Peculiar malady. By Heavens, when he returns, I will have an explanation!

When he returns! Thus it is with human beings, always procrastination.

CHAPTER XVIII.

A MODERN HELL.

WHEN Jessie parted from Lord Lionel Thynne it was with the firm belief that, though he had shown some little anger at what had occurred he had received his rejection in a nobler spirit than she had expected.

There remained the future position of Henry with regard to Lord Lionel, and Jessie, had she have exercised her own judgment, would have brought about a complete estrangement between Henry and the young nobleman.

But there were two very strong reasons against this.

In the first place, the most remote hint to the young midshipman would have been a breach of promise to Lord Lionel.

And then Jessie was the soul of honour.

In the second place, it would not have been wise to have produced a breach between two officers of the same ship.

Her lips were, then, sealed.

She could not give the faintest hint of what she wished.

When then, two days afterwards, an invitation came to Henry to join a party of friends, she did not say a word.

It was a late invitation, so that they spent the whole of the day together.

Henry always devoted a certain number of hours a day to genuine study.

Because he had joined the navy that was no reason to be in ignorance.

Every man gains by study.

Makes him discontented with his real position.

And very properly.

Henry, however, loved study heartily for its own sake, and was forming a choice library to take on board with him.

He had mastered such languages as were useful to him, French and English. He could even enjoy Latin and Greek, but his chief love was for the modern.

His very great favourites he read out to Jessie in the garden, and Jessie read them out to him.

These were her hours of real and genuine happiness.

It had no alloy.

At nine a smart cab, which the inexhaustible kindness of his guardians had sent up for him, was at the door, and, in full dress, Henry drove off to join the party of young men.

There were several strangers present, to whom Henry was formally introduced.

The most prominent of these was one Sir Thomas Plimmery, a gentleman whose hooked nose, protuberant eyes, and scant grey hair, seemed to proclaim him one who had seen something of the great battle of life.

He was about forty, but a very dissolute life about town made him look much older than he really was.

He was a noted gambler, and his introduction, upon the present occasion, seemed ominous of some peculiar scheme.

He was not generally encouraged at evening parties of fast young men.

He had nothing to lose, and was in the habit of winning very often.

He was not even a gentleman.

But he had fought several duels, and had always come out victorious.

This opened all such doors as those of the chambers of Lord Lionel to him.

As he was introduced to Henry he showed great deference.

This put our youth immediately on his guard. He was not suspicious, but the over politeness of a man like Sir Thomas Plimmery was too great a bait to swallow.

It was a wine party—all drinking, smoking, and talk.

Henry didn't like it much, but he wanted to see the life of people of his own age.

Gradually, as he warmed with wine, he got more used to it.

When, about one, a general sally was proposed, he heartily seconded the motion.

Coats, hats, sticks, were speedily found, and Henry, taking, as usual, the arm of Lord Lionel, followed the more noisy members of the party.

They proceeded, however, with unusual civility. No assaults were committed on the watch, no bells were rung, no public house entered for the usual lark.

They were in St. James's.

A very large house was before them. The whole party halted.

It was quite a palatial mansion.

The young men went in slowly, two and two.

"What place is this?" said Henry, who was rather elevated.

"A club-house. Such fun," said Lord Lionel, laughing.

They went in.

Poor Henry, Heaven help him, was in one of the famous hells of the West-end.

On his conduct this night, in all probability, depended his whole future existence.

On ascending a staircase they were ushered into a most splendid room, where many persons were at supper. The magnificence of the room, the brilliant looking-glasses in massive frames, the sumptuous lamps and wax candles, the many tables laid out with costly plate, and the general good humour, happiness, and zest with which all enjoyed themselves, struck Henry with surprise.

He was invited by some of his companions to partake of some of the highly-seasoned dishes; and their rich spiced and savoury flavour gave the greatest zest to the champagne and claret, which passed round with marvellous rapidity.

There was general conversation, tolerably decorous, on politics, scandal, and passing events.

Henry began to think London a wondrous fine place indeed.

The supper was cleared away, and, in a few minutes, Henry found, to his amazement, that he was in a gambling house.

They were, indeed, in Fishmonger's Hall; the great *crock*-odile mart for gudgeons, flatfish, and pigeons.

This nefarious house, the expenses of which were considerably over a hundred pounds a day, despite the low price of the wines, made always huge profits.

The waiters, several times, had a thousand pounds at the end of the season divided amongst them.

A million of money has, on one or two occasions, changed hands in a single night.

Many men staked ten thousand pounds at a single throw.

They were about to play *rouge et noir*.

Henry looked very serious; but then the wine was working more and more in his head.

"Be careful," said Lord Lionel, and strolled over to where a knot of men were conversing round a fireplace.

Henry remained looking on with the fascination of a bird caught in the toils of a serpent.

Rouge et noir, red and black, fortunately now expelled from this island, except where low ruffians, imitators of the old hellites, keep secret houses, is a game all in favour of the bank.

Besides this, the croupiers and dealers are always selected for their adroitness in all the mysteries of the black art.

They are knowing at sleight of hand tricks, at rouge et noir.

A word on the game. It is a modern game, named from the table, which is covered with red and black cloth.

The croupier sits on one side, the dealer on the other.

Six packs are shuffled and dealt round to the parties to shuffle and mix.

He then removes the end cards into the various parts of the three hundred and twelve cards, until he meets a picture card, which he places upright at the end.

The game then commences. To Henry it appeared very simple.

He timidly ventured a card on the red.

"Voltre jeu est il fail—it is, the game is ready—rouge gagre."

Henry was lost, he did not understand a word. He left his stakes.

In twenty minutes a murmur went through the room.

" Young man," said Sir Thomas Plimmery, coldly, "take up your money if you can. You have won twenty thousand pounds."

Staggered, puzzled, scarcely knowing what he did, Henry thrust the money in his pocket.

" You're in luck to-night," said one of the others.

"I did'nt know," replied Henry, simply; "I thought I was losing."

"Faith, you took it very coolly. The bank did'nt. They are as savage as bears."

"They can have it back if they like," said Henry, who was now quite cool.

"Back !" cried one or two ; "mad—green—not to be thought of."

"Play ecarte ?" said one.

" I'll try," replied Henry;" " I have played."

So he had during some of his boyish wanderings with gipsies.

Besides, it was a favourite game of the dwarf, who, without being a gambler, was fond of whist, ecarte, and piquet.

They moved away from the rogue et noir table and sat down in a further corner.

Henry was pitted against one of the youths of the party.

They began for ten pounds. Henry had his pockets so full that he was ashamed to say no.

They began to play.

He won several games. The young man threw down his cards, and Sir Thomas Plimmery took them up.

He sat facing Henry with a cold, still, impassible countenance.

There was silence in the room.

It was a kind of projection from the large hall, and could hold about a dozen people.

Several of those present were there on purpose to see the rook pluck the pigeon.

Sir Thomas Plimmery took the cards in his hand with the air of an old professional.

Henry had had time to cool more than people fancied.

He was excited to the last degree, but in no ways intoxicated.

"A bumper of claret," he said, quietly, to a waiter who was passing.

" What do you play for ?" said Sir Thomas Plimmery, with an ill-disguised sneer.

" What you please."

"A cool hundred ?" said Sir Thomas.

Our youthful hero bowed.

They cut for deal.

Henry lost.

One of the chief means of winning at this game is to turn up a king. Sir Thomas turned up a king.

" How lucky."

Very," said Henry.

They played ; Henry scored one. The other was his equal because of his king. Henry dealt.

He did not turn up a king.

The other scored, and was one a head.

Again Sir Thomas Plimmery turned up a king to the astonishment of all present.

Henry smiled complacently, but his eyelash trembled, and his eye glittered slightly.

The claret came, and he drank it off with great coolness.

He lost the game, but did not offer to pay his loss.

"Double or quits," said the rook, with a perceptible yawn.

It was really not worth while to play with such a greenhorn.

He really felt for him.

" With pleasure," said Henry, with a smile ; " my deal : now I am going to cut up a king."

" What do you mean, sir ?" cried Sir Thomas, colouring.

"That unless this extra card is taken from the pack," showing one, the edges of which protruded from the side, " I really must cut up kings as well as you."

" Do you accuse me of cheating, sir ?" cried Sir Thomas, furiously.

" I beg to state," said Henry, with perfect calmness and self-possession, " that with these cards I could turn a king every time if I liked."

A dead silence prevailed in that group; they all saw that the insult was deadly.

Some pitied the unfortunate youth, who could be no match for Sir Thomas Plimmery, roué and duellist.

Some were pleased. The discovery was so damning to their set that the offence could only be washed out in blood.

" I want no evasion, sir," yelled Sir Thomas, drawing general attention from all quarters.

Lord Lionel Thynne came hurrying up.

" What is the matter ?"

" Don't interfere. This friend of yours has dared to insinuate that I have dealt unfairly," he cried, in a hoarse voice.

" Is this so, Henry ?" said Lord Lionel mildly.

" I mean to say, my lord," replied Henry, firmly, " that this pack was taken by Sir Thomas Plimmery out of his sleeve; that the pack which was first on the table is in his breast coat pocket; and that every time he turned the king he shifted the cards to obtain it by unfair means. If that is not cheating I don't know what is."

Pale, his eyes starting from his head, the detected roué flew at Henry.

But Henry was now very tall and sinewy ; he caught the other firmly by the throat, and cast him back to a considerable distance, but not until he held in his hand the proof of his cheating.

He exhibited the pack of cards he had taken from his pocket.

A head of the house came bowing up.

" Are these cogged cards yours ?" said Henry, showing him the pack which contained what is technically called " the old gentleman," a card larger than the others.

" No, sir ; I think not."

Sir Thomas Plimmery came up boiling with rage.

" Your card, sir ; here is mine."

" I will neither take yours nor give you mine," said Henry, quite coolly. "I have proved you a blackleg and a cheat; I will not fight with you. If you dare to speak with me in a private place I will horsewhip you, and if in a public place I will give you in custody. But, if any *gentleman* is aggrieved by what I have done, I shall not shrink from half a dozen encounters."

This was said with such calm dignity that Sir Thomas slunk away, and Henry, on all sides, received the hollow and false congratulations of the crowd.

Next day every really useful charitable institution received a sum of money from an anonymous benefactor.

It was from Henry's winnings.*

CHAPTER XIX.

WOMAN.

LORD LIONEL THYNNE had so arranged his conduct, on that memorable evening, as to merit rather the gratitude of Henry than any other return.

Nobody suspected, at least strangers, that the whole affair was a diabolical plot on the part of Lord Lionel Thynne to rid himself of a rival he detested.

We wish not to extenuate the criminality and iniquity of Lord Lionel.

But we plead extenuating circumstances.

Eve tempted Adam in Paradise, and since then, somehow or other, women have been at the bottom of every trouble.

Now Lord Lionel Thynne had conceived for Jessie one of those mighty passions which make a man's whole existence.

He loved her truly, devotedly, sincerely.

In his way it is true.

For he would have sacrificed his own feelings to have made her happy.

This is the true test of love, but one few men can stand.

He burned with anxious desire to possess Jessie—to make her his wife—to adorn her almost superhuman charms with diamonds and precious stones—to present her at Court—to walk, proud and erect, with her upon his arm.

To win her smiles he was ready to do any gallant achievement.

He could have given up all his evil associates, have abandoned the navy, and settled down as a country gentleman aiming at political eminence.

He forgot one compact, from which no good resolution could release him.

He felt he could, indeed, do anything but give Jessie to another.

Lord Lionel stood upon the summit of a hill, from which he could look down upon two roads.

One was the broad, open road, which leads to dishonour and destruction.

The other was the arduous way, which leads to glory and renown?

A woman was to turn the scale.

Why a woman?

Why should man, the first created and noblest of human and other beings, the king and lord of the universe, bow the knee, worship a being inferior to himself in intellect and power?

What is woman that we should make her the chief goal of all our wishes?

Wherefore should we toil in youth to win her smile, and in every stage of life be influenced by her magic charms?

Why should the poet be truly able to exclaim—

> How dreary, alone,
> The world would appear
> If women were none.

Why should versifiers din into our pleased and gratified ears that—

> Without their smile
> Life would be tasteless, vain, and vile;
> A chaos of perplexity;
> A body without a soul 'twould be.

We allow them to say it because it is true, because woman is the last and best of all God's works.

Lord Lionel Thynne had loved more than once. His connection with Lotty was of a nature almost too brutal to be told, and yet the time must come, hesitate as we may, when this and other revelations must be made.

But never, never, never, in the whole course of his strange and eventful life, had such a feeling come over him as that he experienced for Jessie.

It was more than love.

It was more than passion.

It was a wild, delirious dream, such as haunts the soul day and night, night and day, like a leash of furies pursuing the shadow thought of murder through an overcharged brain.

Lord Lionel felt that, to win this girl, to set the seal of possession on the wings of desire, he would peril a universe.

Lord Lionel, however, knew not what to do. The refusal of Jessie was a blow from which, in the case of most men, there would have been no appeal.

A gentleman, when once his proposals are negatived, is apt to retire hurt, pained, but with no bitter or vindictive feeling against the woman who declines his addresses.

But though in position and by education a nobleman, Lord Lionel Thynne had none of the instincts of a real gentleman.

In his earlier boyhood he had taken advantage of his rank and social position to ruin the peace and happiness of several humble families.

To the young and vulgar Don Juan these triumphs were things of mighty congratulation.

What to a heartless boy is the life-long misery of a parent, of a father and mother, or of the fair victim herself.

Later Lord Thynne had conceived much stronger passions.

The passion of his life was Jessie.

---

* One or two correspondents want to know when we return to the Mormons. We have devoted anxious care and deep research to a complete investigation of the whole foul iniquity, but we must not neglect Jessie's early life. Her conduct later would not be understood if we hurried over her youthful trials.

THE MYSTERY OF A NIGHT.

But what was to be done?

Henry had not a suspicion of the truth. Neither by word or hint had Jessie given him to understand that there had been any proposition of a nature adverse to his claims made by his new friend.

Lord Lionel Thynne then, to a certain extent, had the game in his own hands.

His first task was to detach Jessie's love from Henry.

This was not an easy task though.

But it was one which a man like the young nobleman was likely to compass.

But Jessie was no mere impulsive girl to be carried away by mere rumours.

She must have convincing proof of the infidelity of Henry before she would allow herself to be deluded into any act derogatory to the dignity of her love and fidelity.

But not Mephistopheles himself had a more diabolical capacity for plot than Lord Lionel Thynne, and, aided by his friends Captain Grossmith and Lieut. Roose, he doubted not his complete success.

But he must be complete master of the situation.

S—— races were coming on. The ducal mansion was in the neighbourhood.

The duke was too busy to leave town for more than an hour.

The marquis was on the continent.

Lord Lionel Thynne made a formal demand for the use of his father's house for ten days.

It was given.

He then invited Henry and all his family to D—— Park.

A Lady Maud Leslie, a Scotch aunt, would play propriety.

Jessie was delighted.

They were going to leave London, and once more breathe the glad and free air of the country.

Henry was pleased, too. He began to be rather wearied of London.

His adventure at the gambling house had slightly changed his views.

But, then, he had not seen enough of life.

A change, however, was desirable, so Henry came down to S——, not saying—

> " There, in close covert by some brook,
> Where no profane eye may look,
> Hide me from day's garish eye ;
> While the bee, with honeyed thigh,
> That at her flowery work doth sing,
> And the waters, murmuring
> With such concert as they keep,
> Entice the dewy, feathered sleep."

CHAPTER XX.

TREACHERY.

D—— PARK was a beautiful specimen of an English aristocratic residence.

It was vast in its proportions, and was provided, of course, with every comfort and luxury that modern civilisation can conceive.

The park was magnificent, and enclosed in a ring fence.

But we have little time for reflection or description.

Ours is a story of action, and actions crowd upon us so rapidly that we have little time for any observations.

Lady Maude Leslie, the Scotch aunt, who, at her nephew's urgent request, had consented to preside over his splendid hospitalities, was a very handsome widow, of thirty-five, but not looking a day older than nine and twenty.

To this age she would have owned, but there was a slight impediment.

She had a daughter.

Such accidents will happen, even to such splendid and youthful specimens of humanity as Lady Maud Leslie.

And this daughter, with the fair, golden-tinted hair of her country, the exquisite complexion combined, a majestic form, and a face full of sweetness and nobility, that left her no chance of remaining unmarried.

Lady Maud Leslie might have taken counsel from some of the ladies who, in the census-paper, put themselves down the same age as their daughters.

But in society this would not do.

It was this lovely girl, the vision of beauty, so fair and serene, that Lord Lionel Thynne had brought all the way from Scotland to use against Henry in his plot on Jessie.

The young nobleman had resolved to win Jessie as his bride.

If——

But win her he would, if not by fair means, by means as foul as imagination could conceive or mind invent.

The plot he had now devised may seem incredible to those who know not the intricacies and wickedness of the human heart.

But once lay down the proposition, that a man loves without hope, and there is no scheme too desperate for his diseased and excited imagination.

Lord Lionel did the honours in splendid style.

No expense was spared.

Everybody brought their own special body-servants with them, and there were rooms for more.

On the morning of the first day the whole party congregated on the lawn.

The park was before them where to choose.

A splendid awning had been erected on the lawn.

It was open only on the side towards the park.

Here, on that genial summer day, they had come out to breakfast.

Adela Leslie was seated next to Jessie. The young girls were already friends ; at all events there was one link to bind them.

They both loved.

In the whole world there was not another such a being to Adela as Lord Lionel Thynne.

She adored him.

She had a right to do so.

She was his affianced wife.

The betrothal had taken place when the girl was in her cradle.

She had been educated to love Lionel, and well had she learned her lesson.

Lord Lionel was utterly indifferent. He was one of those men who are sure never to love a wife imposed upon them.

He had been not at all unwilling, at some future time, to make her his wife, but he should never love her.

But now all was changed.

The one burning spot upon his soul was to possess Jessie.

Her rare and majestic beauty made him fiercely desirous to make her his wife.

But how was this to be ?

By sacrificing Adela.

What cared he if his designs were gratified ?

Adela was a simple, not very strong-headed girl. Her love was meek, obedient, and devoted.

She would do anything in the world for Lord Lionel Thynne.

He had told her to rise at six.

She rose at six, and met him in the park.

Had he have told her to have come to his room she would, in all probability, have done so.

She knew no harm.

She was soon to be his wife.

They wandered in the park.

It was summer, and summer in the woods, of which poet may sing, and writer write for ever, and yet all is not said.

Summer in the woods ! There is music in the very words. A rustling of green boughs, hanging their gorgeous garlandry over our heads; a humming of bees, who have known no other dwelling than the wild solitude of a flowery forest; a lisping of waters, welling away in sunshine and in shadow; a thousand voices, all blending into one rich harmony, reach our ears in the beautiful name of summer. The young spring has mellowed into the full maturity of her beauty, and the last finishing touch has been given to the landscape. The sky is of a deeper and darker blue; there is a richer flush on the cheek of the wild rose; and a lighting up of a newer joy on the countenance of every flower, as if Morning had left a warmer blush to settle down upon the scene, and mantle it in one fond embrace.

Adela was inexpressibly happy.

She was leaning on the arm of the only man she had ever loved.

He was looking at her with eyes of affection. It is true that he said nothing; but, then, in love, what is more eloquent than silence?

They have lost all trace of a pathway. They are in a copse, where they have caught sight of the wild thyme, purpling the ground, and scattering around its aromatic fragrance.

They gaze upon the variegated tints of liverworts and mosses, which spread their rich carpeting over the ground, with fringe of every hue and size, shining in red, and brown, and gray, and scarlet, beneath the bronzy gold of the prickly furze and the pale hue of the broom.

"Adela."

"Lionel."

"How like you my father's home?" he continued. "Much."

"What think you of the young couple you saw last night?"

"They seem nice little people."

"He is, above all men, my best and dearest friend. He is going to sail with me soon. They are engaged to be married, and will be married as soon as he is of age. Now I want to make this place as agreeable to them as I can, for I like them. Will you help me to do so now as surely you will when sole mistress of D—— Park?

"I?"

"My brother will never marry. His health is very delicate. He begins already to speak of me as his heir."

"Poor fellow."

"He is a noble fellow," said Lionel, sadly, "though I cannot make him out at times. Well, let that pass. What I want you to do is very simple. I want you to treat Henry as a brother, while I treat Jessie as a sister."

"That will be capital," said Adela, clapping her hands.

"I will prepare Henry for it. He will be quite happy so that you talk to him about Jessie: I can talk to her about you."

Adela, smilingly, joined heartily into the plan; and then, after some further strolling about, returned to the house.

Lord Lionel's heart smote him a little. The innocent loveliness of Adela had roused in his mind feelings which, but for his wild passion for Jessie, might have ripened into love.

Her *abandon*, her familiar, affectionate way of leaning on his arm, the glance of her blue eye fixed lovingly on his, the frank, innocent way in which she allowed him to encircle her waist, and to kiss her rosy lips, roused in him feelings, which, could she have suspected it, would certainly have scared little Adela Leslie.

But she loved him with her whole heart, and she was to be his wife.

CHAPTER XXI.

MORE TREACHERY.

IT was after breakfast, and all signs of the meal had been cleared away.

The elder ladies had congregated in a group evidently prepared to chat, and enter upon some of those trifling works of the needle which take up so much of the time of the fair and not unlaborious sex.

Lady Haddington, Lady Leslie, and one or two other guests were in this group.

Adela, Jessie, two sisters, and Miss Malcolm were standing apart.

Lord Lionel, Henry, and two young gentlemen suitors—despite very moderate incomes—suitors for the hands of the two sisters, rose and went out on the lawn.

The day was magnificent.

"Lunch at one, and then to the races," said Lord Lionel. "What say you to a rustic ramble: eh, gentlemen?"

All were agreeable. The suitors of the Miss Malcolms, who were very shy, sailed up to their respective mistresses.

"Now, Henry, allow me to request you, as a *preux chevalier*, to take charge, and guard from all harm, Miss Adela Leslie, the future Lady Lionel Thynne. I will do the same with Miss Jessie. Do you sound my praises as I sound yours."

Henry, laughingly, took the arm of Adela, who was evidently pleased, as could be seen by her laughing eyes.

"Charming girl," said Lord Lionel, following in their track.

Jessie looked keenly at him. Was he playing a part, or was he sincere?

"An amiable and very fascinating girl," replied Jessie, gravely. "Did I understand you rightly when you said 'your future wife?'"

"Yes!"

"I am glad of it"

"Why?"

"Because I think you will be happy."

"You hesitate?"

"No."

"Jessie, if I may dare to use that honoured name, I know you wonder at what appears my fickleness. Allow me to explain——"

"My lord, it is not needed."

"For my own gratification. I have been betrothed to Adela from fifteen years old."

"My lord?"

"I am serious. She was one year old when the wise resolve was come to. She is heiress to a vast property, once in our family, and this arriage will re-unite the disjointed parts. I never could see the justice of this arrangement. Well, I met you. I had made up my mind to please my friend, that, *some day*, I might consent to this marriage. Again I say, then I saw you. All my resolves were at an end. I loved you——"

"But, my lord, is this kind?"

"You rejected me. What my sufferings were I will not venture to say. But I am no fool. I resolved that none should ever know what mania possessed me. I returned to my allegiance to poor Adela, and, I dare say, as time go, shall make a very good husband."

"As times go," said Jessie, mournfully. "And you would marry a poor girl who loves you, while you did not love her?"

"Love me? I doubt that. 'Tis but a question of habit."

"My lord?"

"Look when she was upon the sward with Henry. How happy a child she is. Can a little girl like that know what love is? I think not."

"Youth, my lord," said Jessie, "decides nothing one way or the other. But I have no wish to probe your secrets. Let us join your future bride."

"No easy task at the rate they are going," said Lord Lionel, with a covert sneer.

Jessie looked up at him. She could not understand him There was a strangeness in his tone which puzzled and annoyed her.

He had professed to give up all hope of her.

Of course he was a gentleman and a man of honour, and she was bound to believe him.

Wandering slowly along, they lost sight of Henry and Adela.

"After all," began Lord Lionel, with a hearty laugh, "Henry is but a boy."

"My lord!"

"And that he should play hide and seek with a pretty girl is quite natural."

"My lord," said Jessie, almost sternly, "I will not hear a word against my cousin Henry. He has taken Miss Leslie with him simply to please you. He would rather be with me."

And Jessie, under pretence of picking flowers by the way-side, removed her arm from that of the young nobleman.

He bit his lip and turned very pale.

Unless he could rouse the jealousy of Jessie his whole plot must fail.

He, however, saw that, at that moment, he must change his tactics.

He speedily, therefore, joined the other young people, and wandered about until lunch time. When they returned homeward Lord Lionel had his young affianced bride upon his arm, while Henry walked with Jessie.

Lord Lionel was very silent. He knew scarcely what to do.

If he could not use the present opportunity, when would another occur?

His imagination, however, was totally at fault.

And thus the day passed, and nothing was done.

Towards evening, after the race was over and the whole party had dined, Lord Lionel retired.

Under the circumstances all the gentlemen had declined to sit over their wine.

They preferred to join the ladies in the drawing-room overlooking the lawn.

Lord Lionel retired to his library to commune with himself. There, after an hour's deep consideration, he hit upon a plan which he thought would be certain not to fail.

He looked at himself in his glass.

To win one woman he was about to offer up the sacrifice of angels.

CHAPTER XXII.

VILLANY.

ADELA LESLIE was a mere child, pure in thought, innocent, yet she loved Lord Lionel with a love which knew no discrimination. She looked up to him with even as much awe as affection.

There was nothing she would not do to please and gratify him.

This Lord Lionel knew.

Having seen carefully to his toilette he descended to the withdrawing room.

Adela was not there. The other couples were engaged round a table, the ladies working, the gentlemen admiring their work.

The elder ladies were engaged in conversation.

Lord Lionel saw, by the direction of his aunt's eyes, that Adela was not far off.

He turned into the spacious music-room, and there she was, leaning by an open window, and looking out upon the splendid park.

Lord Lionel crept slowly up to her and passed his arm round her waist.

"Is that you, Lionel?" she said, without turning round.

"Yes," he said, drawing her to him and imprinting a burning kiss on her purest of lips.

"There, that will do, I am not your wife yet."

"I wish you were," he replied, in tones of deep and earnest passion.

"Why?"

"Why?" he said, looking into her eyes with a glance which could not be mistaken even by one young and innocent.

Adela held down her head.

"It won't be long," she said.

"Not long," he replied, in a gasping tone, "not long! an age. Here have I to wait a year because they say you are too young. And I, who love you passionately, who pine for you to be mine, who long with evident desire to press you to my panting heart, all my own—must wait. It is maddening to think of. Sometimes I think of marrying in secret even if they were not to know it."

"Lionel, you are my lord and master. Cherished wife of your bosom, I ask no joy greater. If it were necessary to your happiness that we should wed in secret, instead of openly, I would not say nay."

"You heavenly angel!" cried Lord Lionel with a delight not all feigned, as he pressed the half-frightened girl to his heart, and swept her lips with a tempest of kisses. "It shall be so, and no later than to-morrow."

"To morrow !" she faintly murmured, her feelings somewhat overpowering her.

"Would, love, it could be to night !"

She opened her eyes, which had been closed under the influence of delirium, and looked him fondly, oh, so fondly in the face.

He whispered something in her ear.

She made no reply, but, like a frightened bird, nestled in his bosom.

A fearful smile, such as Mephistopheles might have envied, passed across his countenance, and, after some further delay in conversation, they rejoined the others in the drawing room.

Lord Lionel Thynne had succeeded in presuading the fond and loving girl that she was, to all intents and purposes, his wife by the solemn contract their parents had entered into.

She had listened to the fatal sophistry of this evil man, and had decided to admit him to her chamber.

CHAPTER XXIII.

THE MYSTERIES OF A NIGHT.

IT was eleven when the ladies retired to rest; the gentlemen remained behind some time longer. They were now joined by Captain Grossmith and Lieutenant Rouse, who had their bachelor quarters in some quiet nook in the house.

D——House was spacious in the extreme, and could have afforded accommodation for a very much larger number of visitors.

The bedrooms appropriated to the ladies were in a special corridor.

It was illuminated all night by a bright and beautiful row of lamps.

The floor was wholly concealed by a rich Turkey carpet.

Lady Haddington's room was on one side; opposite it was that of the Lady Cornelia.

Jessie's room was next to her mother's; on the opposite side was that of Adela.

There was dead silence at twelve in the whole house. The revellers below could not be heard in the upper parts of the mansion.

Jessie had retired with her mother, who always contrived to find a room which communicated with that of her beloved child.

Cornelia, tired and complaining of a headache, went to bed directly, leaving Jessie in the care of Lucy, her own tiring woman.

Lucy was an excellent servant, highly recommended for fidelity and ability.

She appeared very fond of Jessie.

Lucy was young, black-eyed, and full of spirits. Her tongue never flagged as long as any one would listen to her.

She was ceaseless in her talk. As she never ventured on scandal, her young mistress listened to her with a playful earnestness which delighted the girl.

It was midnight, and Jessie, in an undress which any of her lovers would have been in raptures only to have witnessed, sat before the glass.

Her long, curly tresses lay in a shower of gold over her shoulders Lucy—combed and brushed them for the night.

Jessie was, she knew not why, thoughtful, so that, though Lucy rattled on as usual, her words conveyed no meaning.

Suddenly Jessie started.

On the lace worked pin-cushion a letter was fastened.

She rose and took it in her hand.

It was in a delicate female hand.

Jessie opened it.

"*Deluded girl,*" it said, "*you believe in the fidelity of man. The lover for whom you sacrifice so much will pass the night in the arms of another, one who has seduced him from his allegiance to the pearly queen of beauty.*"

Now Jessie was as little disposed as any one to believe in scandal.

Besides, to that moment such had been her purity and innocence, that no child could have had a soul more thoroughly a blank page, as far as conceiving the reality of passion.

A wild, terrible conception of the reality flashed through her brain.

Henry, deluded, led away—she would not believe him the seducer—was about to violate the hospitality of that house, disgrace himself, and insult those whose roof sheltered him.

Her own wrongs she thought least of.

And yet, devoted as she was to Henry, she could not imagine his thus betraying her.

Was it the act of the generous youth she had so much loved ?

"*Hide in the alcove at the end of the passage, and, as the clock strikes one, you will see him seek her chamber.*"

Lucy stared at her mistress, whose teeth chattered, whose face was deadly pale, and whose compressed lips and agitated manner sufficiently indicated her great mental anxiety.

"Are you ill, ma'm ?" she said.

"No, but I shall not go to bed. I shall read and write for an hour or two."

"But you look ill, miss."

"I wish to be alone, Lucy," said Jessie, very gently but very firmly.

Lucy rose, and, after turning down the bed and lingering a few minutes, went her way.

Then Jessie stood up. She looked a woman avenged. She looked like some virgin priestess upon whom the first breath of insult had fallen with a deadly blow.

She was quite white.

Her teeth chattered violently.

She took an opera cloak and wrapped it closely round her.

On a side table was a small flask of some exquisite cordial, forwarded by the thoughtful care of a mother.

Jessie slowly poured out a glassful and drank it off.

A slight pinky colour came to her ghastly cheeks.

Her eyes gave forth an awful brightness.

Her bosom heaved as if the heart-strings within must have burst.

It was frightful to see her.

In that young and innocent heart had entered the burning, scorching fire of jealousy.

She would see and be convinced, and then— what then?

A moment the thought flashed across her mind that she would not seek to penetrate the mystery.

But, then, Henry might be maligned.

Out into the passage she went, peering with extreme caution around.

At the end of the passage was a female figure supporting a lamp.

Behind this was a thick curtain.

Jessy had not noticed it before.

She made towards it now, and, drawing it on one side, saw that it concealed a niche.

She hid herself in the drapery.

A damp, cold perspiration broke over her whole body.

She quivered as with the ague.

To be watching at night, like a guilty thing, was enough.

But to be a spy on her lover.

Every now and then Jessie felt ashamed of her position.

She would return to her room; she would go to bed; she would bury her head in her pillow, and in sleep find that relief which is only to be wooed by the happy and the innocent.

Hark!

She can hear footsteps.

Where Jessie stands she has a view of the whole passage, but the light, being most brilliant at her end, the rest is in deep gloom.

Still that form creeping along, feeling his way along the wall, as if in darkness, is, she at once knows, Henry.

But somebody is behind him.

But still it is Henry.

Her knees shake under her; she totters; her eyes become sightless, and she sees no more.

In a few minutes, when she came to, all is still as the grave.

With a trembling hand, with a heart turned to stone, she totters towards her room.

As she came out she had noticed that Adela's room was ajar.

It is now shut.

She tries it. It is firmly bolted inside.

With a white, chalky face, she enters her own room and fastens it behind her.

Her own face frightens her. She blows out the light and crawls to bed.

There, in bitter agony of woe unutterable, she weeps herself to sleep.

But sleep cannot last for ever.

As morning broke she opened her eyes, and, by natural impulse, stretched forth her arms.

A faint, double cry burst forth, and Jessie and Henry are clasped in one another's arms.

But only for a moment.

Burning with blushes, wild with fear, utterly unable to comprehend the truth, Jessie releases herself.

"How came you here?" she whispered, half hiding her head under the bed-clothes.

Henry devours her charms with a greedy eye.

"For the love of mercy!" she continued, explain yourself and go.' How came you here?"

"I don't know," said Henry, in a tone of intense bewilderment, mingled with passion.

"Don't know?"

And Henry put her hand in his frenzy to his burning lips.

"Hush, Henry. I heard last night that— that—you had a rendezvous with that girl Adela. I watched; I saw you go to her room, and I woke to find you here—

"Rendezvous—Adela—go to her room?" gasped Henry.

"Yes."

"Never. I drank too much last night, and asked them to take me to bed. Adela is to be Lionel's wife. I swear to you, Jessie, on my soul, I have never thought of any but you. My own darling beloved, I care not what accident has won for me the dear delight—

"Henry!"

"My own Jessie!"

Jessie spake in a low tone. She saw by Henry's glance that he was innocent. The revulsion of feeling was terrific; it nearly drove her mad. She longed to clasp him to her heart, and say how dear he was to her, and how delighted she was to find him innocent, but an instinctive dread was upon her.

She shook with fear.

He shook with happiness.

"You love me, Henry?"

"With all my soul."

"Henry, do leave me. I am in your power. The slighest move and my mother may awake. Oh, do leave me! I am your own little wife that is to be: do not remain until you make me blush to look you in the face."

"To have you thus in my arms, to clasp you to my heart, and then to have to leave!" said Henry, huskily.

"Have mercy on me!" said Jessie.

His wild and fearful transport of passion had communicated itself to her.

She felt she was lost.

"Henry, have mercy on me! I love you from my soul—but go, or I never will be your wife— I will never look you in the face again. My good, my noble Henry, have mercy on your own poor Jessie!"

"Bless you!" cried Henry, slipping from the bed, and hurrying on his clothes.

CHAPTER XXIV.

MARRIAGE.

"Well and nobly done!" said a voice close to him.

He looked up, as did Jessie, and, to his and her astonishment, there stood Lotty.

Jessie could have fainted.

"My dear girl, don't be alarmed. I am a friend; I will prove that to you. Thank Heaven you have been saved from a diabolical plot."

"A plot?"

"A plot?" repeated Jessie.

"Yes. Henry, who was well plied with drink last night, was to have passed the night with Adela, while Lord Lionel came here."

"The ruffian !" said Henry.

"He is all that," replied Lotty, gravely. "But let there be no scene. If you will take my advice, Henry, you will get out of this scrape quietly. You now know your friend Lord Lionel?"

"I do."

"But public scandal will be as disagreeable to you as to him."

"That is true."

"Leave me with Jessie," continued Lotty, "and, when you meet Lord Lionel in the morning, be guided by me."

"I will."

"And now, hurry to your room," continued Lotty, whispering a few words.

"Good morning, Jessie."

Jessie whispered a reply, though shivering as with the ague, and Henry hurried away, wild with passions of a very varied kind.

He now faintly began to understand the part that Lord Lionel had been playing.

Still he had a doubt.

He was ashamed to confess it, but he had a vague and indistinct recollection of having joined, the night before, in some plot derogatory to his and Lord Lionel's future wives.

The young nobleman had persuaded him that they were as good as married.

Their future wives were, indeed, their wives before Heaven.

Wild with champagne, Henry could recollect yielding to this disgraceful temptation.

But why should Lord Lionel have conceived the infamous plan of changing rooms?

It was too terrible to believe.

It must be a fit of jealousy on the part of Lotty, nothing else.

To cool his heated brow Henry, after fully equipping himself, went down stairs, and finding the hall door open, went out into the park.

Under the shade of some dark firs Henry saw Lord Lionel walking up and down in a state of great excitement.

Henry became alarmed, and determined, at any price, to come to an understanding, or, at all events, to be convinced of the truth of the assertions made to him by the pretty horse-breaker.

Lord Lionel was deadly pale. The reflection of a bitter regret appeared upon his countenance.

He had no sooner seen Henry than he came up to him with quick strides.

"Well," he said, abruptly.

"Well, my lord."

"A pretty couple we are."

"How so?"

"How so?"

"I repeat, how so?"

"Why, don't you remember our villanous plan last night?" cried Lord Lionel.

"I do."

"Well?"

"Brutalised by drink, I did agree to a plan at which my soul revolts now. But, luckily, my nefarious views were frustrated," said Henry, quietly.

Lord Lionel started back with a wild and astounded expression of countenance.

"How so?"

"A guardian angel passed the night with Jessie."

"Her mother?"

"No, Lotty."

"D——n!" cried Lord Lionel. "How on earth did she come here? How dares she to enter my father's house?"

"Of all this I know nothing; but I do know that she has saved me from a crime. I should have cursed myself for all my life. I can now look Jessie in the face without a blush."

"Henry, you are right. I was mad last night, but I am a man of honour and a gentleman. Will you serve me?"

"How?"

"I intend marrying Adela this very day. Our union is known to be settled. Will you take horse and ride to London? I cannot leave my guests. With a letter from me you can obtain a special license. Will you go?"

"With all my heart," cried Henry, clasping his hand. "This is the resolve of a man of honour and a gentleman."

"She is my espoused wife, Henry," said Lord Lionel gravely. "I took advantage of her innocence and love. I must now at once do my duty. Come to the library and I will write."

Henry followed, completely convinced that all his suspicions with regard to Lord Lionel were utterly unfounded.

To write a note to Lady Haddington, to scrawl a few lines to Jessie—requesting her to be bridesmaid to Adela—and to mount his horse and away, was a very short work for Henry.

He had sense enough to know that Lord Lionel must be made to act honourably and justly while he was in the humour.

He lost no time, and, by twelve o'clock, had reached a small village near D—— House, at an inn of which he was to meet Lord Lionel.

*   *   *   *   *

It was evening. The superb saloons of D—— House were lit up with great splendour. A number of hasty invitations for a carpet dance had been sent out on all sides. The company came crowding in, and early, too, as the whole affair was to be commenced extempore.

At least two hundred persons were collected from the neighbourhood, and included visitors to the races.

Lady Leslie did the honours with extreme dignity.

But why did not Lord Lionel appear, and why had Adela got so unfortunate a headache?

Presently Jessie and Henry came in arm in arm. Some sly remark of the young rogue had set her blushing like a peony.

Then open flew the folding-doors dividing the great dining hall from the suite of saloons.

"Lord and Lady Lionel Thynne," said the groom of the chambers in a loud voice.

The *coup de theatre* was terrific. A buzz of astonishment went through the room.

Pale, with slightly swollen eyes, the almost baby wife—radiant, however, with happiness—followed, where her husband led her to her mother.

Lady Maude Leslie stood pale and irresolute. The crowd stood back a little.

All saw that it had been a clandestine affair; though all knew it was but anticipating a settled arrangement.

"Now, Lady Leslie," said Lord Lionel, in his brusque and coaxing way. "you must not be angry If you will engage people to marry when so very young, you must not wonder if they get married.

"This is infamous," whispered Lady Leslie, "but I will not allow it. Adela is a mere child. She shall not be your wife for two years if I can prevent it"

"Too late," said Lord Lionel, in a very low tone, "wedded and bedded."

And he led his young wife away to present her to the wondering and admiring group.

Every propriety had been violated, it is true, but the affair was so very romantic that, while the elders frowned, all the young people were delighted.

Jessie knew not what to think. Henry had ventured on no explanation to her.

About eleven she retired to bed. She was utterly wearied, and suffered from a violent headache.

Cornelia wished her good night, and, quietly dismissing Lucy, Jessie remained alone.

Next minute she was joined by Lotty, whose lips were firmly set, whose brow was contracted, whose face was white as that of a ghost.

"Is this true?"

"What?"

"That Lord Lionel is married?"

"Yes."

"Ah!" said Lotty, with a deep sigh, "the wretch, the traitor! Still there is some shame left in that cold and wrinkled heart."

"What you said yesterday cannot be true," said Jessie, looking down.

"It was. In the morning Lord Lionel found himself with Adela. She is his affianced wife, and he could not very well avoid marrying her. Besides—"

"What?"

"He can rid himself of her easier as his wife than as his cousin."

"You describe a monster."

"Such he is."

"I thought you loved him."

"I love Lionel Thynne!" almost shrieked Lotty. "I hate, I loathe him. He little suspects that I am tracking him as the bloodhound tracks the black slave. Let me but find out one foul secret—let me but tear from his heart that which has been my ruin, and I would kill him with my own hand."

Jessie looked horror stricken.

"Ah, girl, did you but know—and when you are old enough you shall know—all I have suffered and have yet to suffer, you would pity me. Indeed, I demand your pity. I have authority over you."

"You?"

"Yes. You will be surprised, I dare say, but so it is," she continued. "Sit down and I will tell you enough to give me a claim to your sympathies if not to your affections."

*   *   *   *   *

It was eleven when Lucy came to call Jessie. Her mother would have entered her room but the door was locked on that side.

Lucy knocked, but no answer came.

She had a latch-key, however.

She entered with precaution, and, advancing to the window, opened the curtains slowly.

Turning round, she gazed at the bed.

It had not been slept in.

Not a sign of Jessie was to be seen. Without a doubt she was not in that room.

To give the alarm was the first thought of Lucy, who was petrified with alarm and grief.

The confusion which ensued may be more easily imagined than described.

The evidence of both Cornelia and Lucy proved satisfactorily that she had gone to her room.

How, then, and in what way could she have disappeared without leaving one trace behind?

Lord Lionel Thynne and his bride had started on their wedding tour, leaving Lady Maude Leslie in charge of the house.

The guests were departing.

The sudden marriage of Lord Lionel had broken up the party.

But how, in that well-guarded house, from a room so secure as that in which Jessie had been expressly placed, could she have been removed thus silently and in secret.

All remained petrified with horror and astonishment. No one could do anything but lament. Not an idea suggested itself by which to trace her.

The Dwarf, who had mysteriously appeared that morning in the house, suggested that information should be given to Bow-street, and to the police of every seaport in the kingdom.

It was poor comfort, and yet it was all that could be done.

Henry was in utter consternation; Cornelia was wild with horror and alarm; Lady Haddington knew not what to think.

CHAPTER XXV.

PHINEAS BRISTOWE.

MEANWHILE we have left Phineas Bristowe, Paolo, and Dick, in the most desolate of all cellars.

Our readers are, we suppose, too perspicuous to suppose for one moment that we have any intention of leaving them there.

No.

The time for punishment is not yet come.

But how are they going to escape? This is a mystery which we suppose our readers have solved in their own way.

For some hours after they had discovered the yawning pit by means of the blazing straw they remained in utter silence.

They were horror-struck, and deprived of all power of motion.

Phineas was the first to speak.

FURNISHED APARTMENTS.

"Well—thunder—this won't do. How are we going to get out of here?"

"*Carajo!*" said Paolo, "how should I know? When they let us out."

"We may wait along enough for that. They have got us safe, and, be sure, they will keep us."

"You don't mean to say they are going to starve us outright," said the burglar, in a hollow tone.

"That I do, unless we get out by the sewer," replied Phineas.

"Sewer?—where?"

"Down that hole."

"Why the —— did you not say so before. Come along. If it's a sewer I know its depth."

And the burglar crawled to the edge of the black pit.

He could hear a rush of waters below, but he could also hear that it was upwards from the river.

"Tide's up," he said; "we must wait till it goes down."

"Who's got a light?" replied Paolo.

"I have," said Dick.

"Then here's oil. I had quite forgotten that I had a flask."

"Fire away," said the burglar, eagerly.

In five minutes more they could once again gaze upon their different countenances, pale, ghastly, and hideous.

Then they looked down.

They first tore up the grating.

The water was not more than a foot from them, black, murky, and filthy.

No 24.

It was now nearly still.

They watched it with eager eyes, for in that hideous canal lay their only hope of safety.

Those above were pitiless.

They were doomed by them to the most hideous and horrible of all conceivable deaths.

Presently Dick lit a pipe. After so long a fast it appeared a superhuman delight.

The others were not slow in following his example.

Thus half an hour passed.

Then the tide began slowly to turn.

They all thought, as they sat gazing at that Stygian pool, that they had never before seen or conceived such a scene of filth and horror.

It was perfectly hideous.

But to them it appeared delightful: it was the means of escape.

Slowly at first, and then more rapidly, until at last it ran quite swiftly, the stream settled down.

They judged it at last to be about up to their knees.

Dick, with a carelessness which showed considerable experience, dropped into the sewer.

He then held the light for the others to descend.

In two minutes they were wading along, almost choked by the hideous exhalations of a London sewer.

But they had no great distance to go; in a few minutes more they were in the open air.

It was dark night.

The tide was getting lower and lower every moment.

They could see a glimmer of light in the window of the Dotted Spog on the other side of the water.

But no boat.

Yes, there is one close at hand, and, by great good fortune, it is their own. Even the oars have not been removed.

With the delight almost of reprieved criminals, they enter the skiff and pull across to the opposite bank.

A church close by strikes midnight.

Peter Trufit stands upon his steps. The fat girl is shutting up.

"Hallo, who comes?" he said.

"All right," replied Phineas Bristowe, as they ascended the steps.

Peter lifted up a lantern which he held in his hand, and, at the same time, threw open the door of his house.

"Mudlarks, by gum," he cried.

"Shut up," said Phineas, gruffly, "and, while we clean ourselves a bit, get us a roaring hot supper. Never mind expense."

"We aint eat a bit since we left here," continued Dick.

"Carambo!" cried Paolo.

Peter still stood with his eyes open, while the others pushed passed him and went up stairs.

Phineas took them all to his room, and in five minutes the whole were stripped and getting rid, with marvellous celerity, of the mud, filth, and dirt which they had picked up during the adventures of the two nights and days.

A box of clothes was opened, and each man took what he liked.

In a quarter of an hour they descended, roaring with laughter.

A supper of steaks and chops smoked on the board.

Peter, as soon as he recovered his senses, set to work with prodigious energy. He outdid himself.

He joined them at supper at their own request.

Never in his whole life had he witnessed such feats of gormandising.

It was something awful to contemplate.

Three hungry men, after a fast of forty-eight hours.

"More! more!" they cried, like the three horse-leech's daughters.

Then came grog and pipes.

For about two hours every faculty was given up to the refection of the inner man.

"And now for business," said Phineas, striking the table with his hand.

"Business," repeated Dick

"Yes, business," said Paolo, huskily.

Peter, who was slightly inebriated, was removed by the stout party.

The three others were also slightly intoxicated. They one and all tried to whisper to the fat chambermaid.

But she eluded their attempts, and took her master away.

"The first question to be considered is," said Phineas, "who betrayed us."

"Exactly," said Dick.

"So," replied Paolo, with a savage and sullen scowl.

"First," continued Bristowe, "we must have been betrayed, that's certain."

Dick nodded his head.

"What's your opinion?" added Phineas, addressing himself to Paolo.

"Julie."

"Why?"

"She's cut up uncommon rough for a day or so," put in Dick.

"If it's her it's all over," said Paolo, gloomily, "I'll cut her throat."

"Sarve her right."

"Let us do nothing in a hurry," cried Phineas, "my move is—examine the question first, and decide afterwards."

"Good."

"Agreed."

"And then—same terms to be continued—who will follow me again? Be sure they have left that house. But I'll follow them. Not only will I carry out my plans, but I will be revenged."

"We're your men," said both the others.

This decided on, they all contrived to find a resting-place on the floor or chairs, and there lay until the day was far advanced.

CHAPTER XXVI.

FURNISHED APARTMENTS.

IT was three o'clock in the afternoon when a hackney coach stopped before the house of the Jew receiver.

The confederates descended hastily therefrom, and entered the shop.

The Jew welcomed them heartily.

"How's madam?" said Paolo, hastily.

"Never sheen her," replied the Hebrew. "Shust rings the bell, and my little Juda, she take up what she wants."

"She has not been out?"

"No, s'help me Mo."

"Not written any letters?"

"Cantsh shay—aint shent any out," replied the receiver.

The three confederates exchanged glances. They saw at once that their surmises with regard to Julie must be erroneous.

They all seemed relieved.

Without a word they went up stairs. On entering the room they found her seated quietly reading a book. She was very pale and wan.

"Well," said Paolo.

"It is not well," replied Julie, rising. "I cannot, and I will not lead this life any longer. I shall die. Don't tell me about danger. Take a respectable furnished house and you will be in less danger than here with this Jew. At all events, I can then breathe the fresh air, and enjoy some sign of life. Two more days of this dreary solitude will kill me."

"She's right," said Phineas, after a moment's reflection. "It is necessary to our plans that we have a house of our own. What say you to this? I will take a house as master; you and Julie can be my son and daughter-in-law, while Dick would look grand in livery.

"Haw! haw! haw!" cried Dick, laughing, "anything better than this hide-and-seek game."

"Anything," said Julie.

"As you will," replied Paolo.

Next day Phineas Bristowe, made up with consummate tact by the united efforts of Dick and Paolo, went forth with the object of seeking a house.

He looked immensely like a ranting "Methody" parson.

His choker was irreproachable, his spectacles alone looked pious.

Phineas took his way towards the New-road, and, after a careful examination, found a house which to all appearance suited him.

The whole or part of the house was to be let furnished.

Phineas knocked at the door, a knock both conciliatory and imperative.

An odd little woman came to the door.

"You let furnished apartments, madam, I believe?" said Phineas, blandly.

"I do—walk in, sir—single, sir?—only for yourself, sir?" began the "body!"

"I am single," said Phineas, with a wave of his white hand which displayed his diamond rings to advantage.

The little woman bobbed.

Phineas took a chair.

"I am a minister of the Gospel," he said, deprecatingly; "a humble apostle of the truth. I have a son married. He is anxious to see something of London before starting for America. I request the whole house. I expect an afflicted child of mine."

"Widower?"

"Yes."

"Widow myself; can feel for you, sir."

"I am that sorrowful being, my dear madam," continued Phineas. "This afflicted child of mine is not quite right in her head, but we hope and trust that change of air and scene may do her good."

"It is to be hoped—"

"I have also a man servant, an honest, worthy fellow, but rather rough."

"Good."

"Now, madam, what shall we say?"

"How long?"

"By the month. Won't bind myself to more. Depends on the doctors."

"Three guineas a month, and extras," said the little old lady very sharply, just as if she had not asked enough, and was ready to put on an extra pound at half a minute's notice.

"Humph."

"Sir?"

"Every attendance, clean linen, so on," said Phineas, gravely.

"If plate and linen required, ten shillings extra," replied the woman.

With an odd twinkle of the eye Phineas pulled out his purse.

The plate and linen had decided him.

"My dear madam, your furnishing plate and linen will save me from unpacking. Will you be kind enough to give me a memorandum for ten pounds? I am a stranger in town, and can give no reference until I see my bankers; then, if you wish it—"

"Not at all necessary," said the dame, clutching the crisp new bank note.

She then hurriedly drew forth a desk, and proceeded to write a receipt.

"What name?"

"Walker."

"Sir?"

"The Reverend Thomas Walker," continued Phineas, with intense gravity. "A very awkward name, my dear madam. Little naughty boys will make fun of it, but this is a world of woe, and we must put up with greater sorrows than that. Are you alone, madam?"

"No, sir. Why?"

"I feel slightly fatigued. Wine—but no, I think a small drop of brandy would revive me."

The old woman rang the bell, and, in a moment, a starved-looking girl of about fifteen made her appearance. She looked the image of hunger, gaunt, livid, and yet showing that with care and attention she would be a good-looking girl.

"As I am as it were already a lodger," said Phineas, "I will take lunch. Girl, will you order a couple of bottles of stout, a nice, crusty new loaf, a pound of cheese, and a bottle of the best brandy."

The girl stared, took the money, and yet stood still.

"Go!" said the odd little woman in a low, strange tone. The girl hurried away.

Phineas Bristowe felt puzzled. The little woman had shown such strange emotion at the sight of money that he at first had judged her to be a miser.

A suspicion now crossed his mind that she was in abject poverty.

Genteel poverty, with every outward sign of having money, but penniless.

The worst, most miserable and wretched poverty of all.

He was determined to see.

The lunch was laid with remarkable alacrity. Phineas, while appearing to be examining one or two very superior engravings on the wall, watched them.

Their eyes glistened with a wild glare at the food on the table.

"Quite ready, sir," said the widow.

"Thank you. That's capital. Very good choice, my girl : join me, of course," cried Phineas. "Can you draw a cork, my girl?"

"Yes, sir," in a low tone.

Phineas helped the widow first, and then, as if from mere distraction, piled up the girl's plate with bread and cheese.

"You mustn't mind me," he said, with a benevolent smile, "the girl wants her lunch."

And he gave it to her, with a glass of beer.

She hurried away down stairs with a wild and wolfish look in her eyes.

The old woman looked at him with a strange and startled expression.

"You have penetrated my secret," she said, almost choking.

"What secret?"

"That I am starving!"

"My dear madam, if so it rejoices my heart, as a Christian minister, to have fallen upon you in your time of trouble. Pray say no more. If our coming to you is useful I rejoice in it."

"You have saved us from death," gasped the widow.

"Nay, madam."

"Yes. I am an officer's widow. I have no friends in the world. My sole resource is letting lodgings. My pension does not pay rent and taxes. For six months I have had no lodgers."

"Bless my soul ! but eat, madam."

"I will, presently. We have lived Heaven knows how. I could neither sell nor pawn my goods for fear of not being able to let when the time came. But had you not entered my house to-day like an angel of light—"

"Oh, madam !"

"We must have perished, or I must have parted with our sole means of existence. My child—"

"She is your daughter."

"She is. I am compelled to let her pass as a servant.

"Be not ashamed, madam. All is for the best. I shall stay with you at least a month, and, even should I leave, will try and be useful to you. Now, pray eat, madam, or you will spoil my lunch. Call up your daughter."

"No. Let her never know that I have revealed my fatal secret. She would die. She is a girl of high spirit. Oh ! had you seen her before this awful trial fell upon us—she was beautiful."

"And will be again," said Phineas, with paternal affection.

"I hope so."

A heavy shower of rain coming on, Phineas Bristowe contrived to learn the widow's whole story.

He went away an hour later rubbing his hand.

It appeared to him that he had fallen upon a fine tool.

Mother and child were starving.

Could they possibly resist the force of such temptation as he could throw in their way ?

CHAPTER XXVII.

THE THREE PIPES.

NEXT day the whole party were installed in the widow's house.

They found themselves surrounded by every imaginable comfort.

The gratitude of the widow was deep and illimitable. She had expended a considerable portion of the money advanced in procuring many things previously deficient.

No sooner were they installed than it was determined to proceed at once to business.

Paolo, Phineas Bristowe, and Dick the tumbler all decided to go into the country.

Mary, the widow's daughter, could wait upon Julie in their absence.

Julie was, or professed herself to be, perfectly satisfied.

The plan of the three confederates was to venture into the neighbourhood of the old house at Chelsea, and there, by cautious but judicious inquiries, to discover what had taken place since they had been trapped.

Their plans were, however, upset by an unexpected accident.

Julie was very fond of reading.

One of her favourite pastimes was the study of that erudite chronicle of fashionable movements, the *Morning Post*, of Jeames and Jenkins, notoriety.

It lay before her at breakfast.

"Your birds have flown," she said, with a slight sneer.

"What birds?" said the supposed Viscount de Florac.

"What birds?" repeated Phineas.

"*Lord Lionel Thynne,*" she began to read, "*is entertaining a fashionable and select party at D—— Park during the races. Among others we have heard the names of Lady Haddington and the young heir of that ancient house, with other members of the family.*"

"Whew !" said Paolo

"The devil !" replied Phineas. "But, never mind, it saves a deal of trouble. We must start at once. Have her in my possession I will."

Paolo's eyes glittered.

Julie looked at him over the paper. Her face was cold and impassable.

Paolo took no notice, but rose from the table to dress.

In a few minutes it was arranged that each of the three should start separately.

The simultaneous arrival of three such men in a village like D—— might excite suspicion.

There were numerous conveyances, both fast and slow, during the races.

Each man was to disguise himself in his own way, and they were to meet at the first beershop to the right hand in the village, to wait each other's arrival.

"Julie" was to be the password.

They then separated, each man his own way. To avoid exciting any suspicion they were compelled to dress away from the poor widow's house.

Besides, they knew of celebrated dressers—regularly in the pay of thieves and burglars—who would do the make-up wonderfully.

At that time there were a great many German refugees in this country—all political, romantic, and smelling of tobacco.

Phineas Bristowe determined to do the ultra-smoking German. At all events, he was not likely to be forced to speak if he did this successfully.

The dresser he called upon to officiate acquiesced, and in twenty minutes Phineas emerged into the open air a perfect stage German—slouched hat, huge meerschaum pipe and all.

His beard and moustaches were perfect forgeries in their way.

"My eye, what a Guy!" saluted him as he walked.

Phineas smiled benignantly.

Such observations made him perfectly satisfied that he was safe from any discovery even should he unfortunately fall in with any one who knew him personally.

He little imagined the terrible trial in store for him.

We must follow him in his remarkable adventures before we attend to Messrs. Paolo and Dick the tumbler.

Phineas walked slowly and placidly towards the coach office where started the vehicle for D——. In his left hand was a large black carpet bag.

His right was wholly taken up with his huge pipe.

Presently, irresistably attracted by a showy gin-shop, he went in.

He pointed gravely to a bottle.

The man placed Hollands before him without a word.

A further proof that he took him for a foreigner was, that he gave him no change out of a shilling.

The Mormon elder chuckled hideously with delight.

He took another glass, and paid another shilling for the sole pleasure of being cheated.

He then went his way.

When he reached the coach-office it wanted only ten minutes to the time of starting.

Phineas laid down the exact money, and received an inside place.

He clambered up quickly, and entered the vehicle.

He thought he should have fainted.

He was face to face with two genuine, real, live Germans, dressed very much like himself.

There was no possibility of mistaking their physiognomies.

Phineas Bristowe was now dreadfully alarmed. A cold perspiration burst out upon his skin. Every minute he expected they would speak.

It was dreadful.

What could it be?

Presently the coach started, just as he had determined to get out and go outside.

Then each German pulled out a large pipe, and began gravely to load it.

Phineas did the same. It was the best thing he could do.

All three began to smoke in silence. They proved very Dutchmen for taciturnity.

The silent Prince of Orange was nothing to them.

Phineas felt relieved.

They were evidently two surly brutes; perhaps bound for the races—thimble riggers, and were afraid that he would spoil their little game.

He determined to be calmly dignified, and not at all familiar.

He closed his eyes for a few minutes, and smoked away in a kind of doze.

Then he slowly opened one eye.

He nearly spoke, so great was his surprise and astonishment.

Both the other Germans had one eye closed, and were peering at him, out of a corner of the other, with the most odd and scrutinising expression.

A cold shudder came over Phineas. He was in the most fearful state of dread.

He had heard of such things as detectives, who enjoyed torturing a victim as Indians do their prisoners at the stake.

This continued silence, too, was so oppressive and horrible.

Had he but known one phrase in German he would have blurted it out at any risk.

The stream down his back was as cold as icicles.

He had a great mind to be taken ill and stop on the road.

They were ascending a hill at that pace such as only English stage-horses can attain to.

Phineas almost thought he would leap out. He began to be frantic with terror.

There was a fearfully stern look about the men as they advanced on the road.

Heavens! what a relief. The milestones began to show that he, at least, was nearly at the end of his journey.

At the top of the hill was the village.

The race-course was several miles off. There were special conveyances to this place in the morning.

The coach stopped to change horses at a large inn at the entrance of the village.

Phineas hastened to descend from the vehicle, and hurried away so fast that he forgot to give the coachman his expected shilling.

He walked forward as fast as his leg would carry him; and, without either turning to the right or left, made for the first beer shop he could see on the right hand.

Two heavy, lumbering steps could be heard behind him.

They were dogging him. The infernal blood-hounds of the law, or the persevering friends of Jessie, were on his track.

He very nearly made up his mind to cast away his carpet bag and fairly run.

But this would be too violent and tragic an end to the scene. He determined to carry on to the last.

The beer-house—by name the Green Dragon—was reached; and, turning quickly in, Phineas darted into the best room which was vacant at the moment.

He was about to close the door when the figures of the two Germans stood close to him, pushed the door, and entered likewise.

Phineas knew that all was up.

"It is that cursed Julie," he muttered, wiping his hot and fevered brow.

"Julie!" said one German.

"Julie!" cried the other.

The three stood aghast.

"Well, I'm d——d," said Phineas, "if I did not think you were officers."

All roared with laughter. The dresser had, while he was about it, made them all up as Germans, and not one had suspected the *super-cherie* until they all uttered the password at the inn.

But all had been so terrified that they gladly rang the bell and ordered refreshments in the shape of tea and such fare as the house provided. They likewise engaged beds.

CHAPTER XXVIII.

MYSTERIOUS.

ALL the next day the three men kept within doors. They spent money freely, and were accordingly accommodated with the exclusive use of the room they had at first occupied.

Here they sat smoking and drinking until the dusk of the evening.

They then paid their bills; and, taking their carpet bags, went on their way.

They had contrived to learn the exact position of D—— Park.

It was two miles distant, and they, accordingly, made quickly in that direction.

They had made up their minds to the most extreme caution in their way of proceeding.

They were amply provided with every implement appertaining to a house-breaker.

Their heavy carpet bags contained also their own clothes, with which to return to their residence in the house of the poor widow.

About a mile from the village they found that a small grovy lane led in the direction of the Park.

They determined, at any risk, to take this way, as more likely to avoid observation than following the regular highway.

A lantern was produced, and served to guide them partially.

They were in a lovely lane, with high hedges on each side.

Any other eye than that of the three murderers would have rejoiced at the scene before them.

At every step they fell in with some exquisite little flower.

There was the centaury, with its small, pink, star-like bloom; or a cluster of crimson hare-bells.

Here the stately foxglove reared its long stem, hung with a profusion of pink, pendant flowers; while the velvet leaves of the colt's foot appeared in the distance like broad patches of sunshine; and the bright green of the spreading fern added to the beauty and picturesqueness of the scene.

These are again over-topped by crab trees and bushes, running ragged and wild, and hung with the glowing fruits of the forest, on which the birds will feed in the dark months of winter, when the insects have betaken themselves to their hiding-places, and sunk into their long sleep, from which they will not awaken until the warm breath of spring is again abroad.

Look upward amid the land of leaves; see how the wedded boughs

"Make net-work of the dark blue light of day."

But it is night now; and, had it been day, none of these men would have cared for the beautiful scene before them.

What an awful stillness reigns around, except where the tramp of their feet is heard!

Then a gentle wind stirs amid the branches, sounding sweet, and low, and solemn, like whisperings from another land.

But what is this?

The lane ends abruptly; a lofty stile seems to stay all further progress.

Hark!

'Tis a watch-dog at no great distance. They are near a farm house.

Every caution is now necessary. The light is put out, and they cross the stile slowly and with exceeding caution.

Still they hear the bark of the dog.

They can now see the farm out-houses, and other buildings.

They knew the direction of D—— Park; and they knew, therefore, that they must pass some little distance to the back of the farm.

They can see a plantation of tall trees waving their tall boughs in the distance.

They turn in this direction.

They are crossing a field of stubble.

Paolo (Viscount de Florac) leads the way.

They make as little demonstration as possible. The sight of three men creeping along a field at that time of night would, of course, be considered suspicious.

At length they reach a high kind of hedge.

It is thick with hazel and other trees.

Paolo, leaving his carpet bag a moment and clutching his stick, begins to force his way through it.

They appear to fancy themselves on the edge of the park.

Suddenly a loud curse is heard, followed by the fall of a heavy body.

They stand still, transfixed with horror and alarm. In the stillness and silence of that night they are afraid the cry will be heard at the farm-house.

"Paolo," says Phineas, in a low tone.

No answer.

"Be careful," suddenly they hear from a considerable distance; "it's a quarry, you can get down safe enough."

Much relieved, they begin to crawl through the hedge with their burdens, one holding the lantern in advance.

In another minute they are on the edge of a quarry, the side of which slopes down to an extent of about twenty feet.

Prepared by the experience of their guide they contrive to reach the bottom in safety.

They are in an extensive stone quarry, apparently. from the grass growing around, long since deserted.

A halt was decided on.

But where should they conceal themselves? A hasty glance round the quarry soon showed them that, as usual, many deep recesses had been cut in the rock, some of which had been used either as tool houses or habitations.

They gladly sought shelter, and, after some refreshment and a brief consultation, agreed to leave their bags there, and advance on their way unencumbered.

About an hour later, after a deliberate smoke, they rose to their feet, and began their journey anew.

Not a trace of moon or stars was now visible in the sky.

Clouds, in dark, heavy masses, had been slowly sweeping up until all was dark as pitch.

A chilly wind seemed to portend rain.

The three men smiled grimly.

They left the quarry by a regular road, which took them to the edge of the plantation.

The highroad passed between the quarry and the trees.

The very highroad they had sought to avoid.

Hark!

What is that dismal, fearful sound?

A sound of clanking chains at no great distance from them.

They stand still and listen. They peer eagerly out into the darkness.

"There! there!"

"Where?"

Phineas Bristowe guided them to where, on a huge gallows, swung three men in chains.

"Diavolo!" cried Paolo.

"Hem," said Dick, settling his cravat.

"I remember now," observed Phineas Bristowe, coolly, "three fellows for highway robbery. More fools they. Come along."

And, crossing the road, he climbed over the ring fence which encircled the park.

CHAPTER XXIX.

THE PARK.

THEY were now in the utter gloom and darkness of the plantation.

But they could see, at some little distance, the clear, open park.

In a few minutes they found themselves on its outermost edge.

About a quarter of a mile distant lay the splendid mansion of the Dukes of ———.

Between where they stood and the house was a large grassy, open space, interspersed with trees.

They can see lights flickering in the said palatial mansion afar off.

They are determined to cross the park, prowl round, and trust to the chapter of accidents.

They advance with cautious steps, as part of the park being preserved, gamekeepers are almost sure to be met.

About two hundred yards in front of them is a small lake.

They do not discover it until they are on its very edge.

But, at the same moment, they become conscious of the presence of a fourth party.

A dark figure clothed from head to foot in black, is a little ahead of them.

It glides along without the slightest noise.

No sound of steps can be heard, though they all listen attentively.

They say nothing, but all eagerly follow it. These are desperate men, who, even if they had believed in supernatural agencies, were not easily terrified.

The figure is making straight for the castle.

They follow with extreme caution, their very hearts in their mouths.

What can be this dark and shadowy form, and what can it be doing at this unseemly hour alone in the park?

They fell half inclined to come up with it, but it moves so swiftly that it would be a race if they did.

They are now close to the mansion, which, except where a few lights may be seen on the second floor, is all in darkness.

At the corner of the building is an ornamental tower covered with ivy.

Towards this the dark figure makes its way, and disappears.

The trio plunge after it, and, cautiously using a lantern, see an open door before them.

It is almost entirely concealed by the ivy.

"This is fortunate," said Phineas, in a low tone; "at all events, we have access to the house —one point gained."

The others made no reply, but followed him into the interior of the tower.

The ground floor was like a vault.

In the corner was a spiral staircase.

Phineas began ascending slowly.

It went up a considerable distance, and then opened upon a narrow corridor, constructed, apparently, in the thickness of the wall.

They all listened cautiously, but heard nothing for some minutes.

Then a low, murmuring sound attracted their attention.

Phineas groped along the wall, and soon saw a sliding panel, scarcely shut.

He peered through into a superbly furnished bedroom.

It was by the exercise only of the most terrible amount of nerve that he refrained from uttering a loud cry.

On a chair was Jessie, in earnest conversation with a very beautiful woman.

Phineas drew back.

He whispered low to his companions.

"Gag and secure her," he said; "I will take care of Jessie."

The panel was well oiled, and glided in its groove without the slightest noise.

Lotty's back was to this secret entrance.

Jessie was looking full in her face.

Lotty was urging her to something she evidently did not approve of.

"No. I believe every word you say, but that does not convince me I should be right to yield to your advice.

"But, Lotty—"

At this instant a rich shawl was thrown over the head of Lotty, while Phineas, taking advantage of Jessie's sudden terror, thrust a handkerchief in her mouth, and bore her away.

A hasty glance round the room showed that no real valuables were about.

The trio hastened to decamp, leaving Lotty insensible on the ground.

They descended the stairs rapidly; luckily for them Jessie had fainted.

They lost no time.

In a quarter of an hour they were in the quarry, under shelter of the excavations.

In their extreme haste they had not noticed that they had been followed with all the patience of a sleuth-hound.

Phineas took a small bottle from his bag, and poured something into Jessie's mouth.

She was no longer insensible, but made no effort to speak.

In a few minutes she lay on the ground, the very image of death.

The men made a small fire, and lay down to rest.

It was daylight when they awoke.

They all now changed clothes, placing their foreign disguise in the carpet bags.

Then Phineas, once more in the costume of a clergyman, issued forth on an expedition.

He had not far to go.

There were several inns and posting houses on the road.

He had given full instructions to Paolo and Dick the tumbler.

When Jessie awake she found herself alone with these two.

Paolo looked at her with a glance which froze her with terror.

It was not threatening, however.

"You are in my power," he said, still looking her full in the face, "but, mark me. Give me a solemn promise of silence until we reach a house we are taking you to, and I will spare you."

Jessie knew enough of the terrible reputation of Paolo de Florac to suspect the nature of his threat.

"I promise to be silent," she said, with a shudder. "Indeed—"

"Swear," cried Paolo.

"Why?"

"Then I can believe you."

"If you cannot believe my word you cannot believe my oath," said Jessie, firmly.

"I believe her," put in Dick, who had been watching her attentively.

"Do you?" sneered Paolo.

"I does," said the burglar doggedly; "and, what is more, I mean to say this. If you tries to do her never so little harm, I'll punch your head as soon as look at you."

"The deuce you will?"

"I will. I don't know what your little game is; but d——n me if I'd see such a girl as that hurt."

"A pretty fellow you are. But nobody wants to hurt her," said Paolo, with a malicious grin, "so shut up."

"And nobody ain't agoing to hurt her, neither," said Dick. "No, my little dear, I'll take precious good care of that. But until I know what master's orders is, you won't scream, or holler, or anything of that ere—eh?"

"I will not," said Jessie, firmly, and giving the rough burglar a grateful look.

"Come along, then," he continued.

Paolo said not a word, but took up his carpet bag, and seemed to wait.

"You just go on first," said Dick. "I ain't agoing to let you walk behind with that ere stick."

Paolo scowled at him, but went on first.

They soon reached the highway, and stood leaning against a gate.

In a few minutes a postchaise became visible.

It drew up, and Paolo and Jessie got in.

Dick, who now wore his livery, took his seat on the box.

Away drove the postillion.

About ten minutes later a horseman, well wrapped up and defended against the night air, galloped up, and continued on his way until he came in sight of the postchaise.

He then slackened his pace, and, keeping in the background, contrived, however, not to lose sight of the vehicle.

He did not. On reaching London he observed that it halted at an inn and set down its passengers on the pavement in front.

The postchaise drove away, and the footman hailed a hackney coach. All got inside and drove off to the house in the New-road.

CHAPTER XXX.

JESSIE A PRISONER.

THE astonishment of Jessie at finding herself in the presence of Julie was something almost ludicrous to behold.

Julie stared at her with a look of cold and defiant disdain.

Jessie made no attempt at entering into conversation with her, but looked at her with extreme pity.

Julie spoke in a whisper with the others.

She had prepared Mary for Jessie's arrival, and

AN UNEXPECTED FRIEND.

had, according to the instructions of Phineas Bristowe, indicated that she was slightly mad.

She now signed to her to follow.

Jessie obeyed.

Julie led the way upstairs to the very top of the house in utter silence.

She threw open the door of a room, motioned to Jessie to enter, and, when she had done so, closed the door upon her.

Jessie found herself in a large bedroom, receiving light only from the roof.

It had no look-out.

It was meanly and poorly furnished, but for that Jessie cared not. The sorrow near her heart was the reflection of what her mother and Henry would suffer.

She had no fear for herself.

She was brave, in the first place, and then, in the second, she felt satisfied that there was nothing to gain by her death.

Murder is not committed without some object to be attained.

But how long was she to be confined, and where was she to be taken to?

They had already tried to abduct her to America, for what purpose she could not conceive.

She knew something of Phineas Bristowe, which rendered his conduct inexplicable.

Presently there came a gentle knock at the door.

" Come in !"

" I can't."

" The door is fastened outside."

A key was turned, and the daughter of the house appeared.

A few days of abundance in the way of food had produced a wondrous change in her.

She looked quite pretty and interesting. Indeed, Jessie was quite struck by her appearance, though she wondered at the startled expression of her countenance.

"Will you take some tea now, please?" she said, in a timid voice.

"With pleasure," replied Jessie, "I am quite faint after my long journey."

"I hope you find your room comfortable?" continued the young girl, anxiously.

"Well," said Jessie, with a quiet smile, "I've seen worse, and I've seen better."

"I dare say, Miss."

"But poor prisoners must not be choosers. I dare say I should find a cell in Newgate still worse."

"Prisoner!" cried Mary, gently. "Oh! don't say so, Miss. I wouldn't think of it."

"Young girl," said Jessie, in her quiet, commanding way, "go fetch my tea. If you are in league with those wicked wretches down stairs you will betray me—that can do no harm. If you are not, obtain permission to stop with me awhile, and I will tell you the truth."

"I will," replied Mary, with glistening eyes.

She said no more, but went slowly downstairs, wrapped in deep thought.

About a quarter of an hour later Jessie heard the rattle of tea things, and a knock at the door.

It was the footman who had taken her part.

She was about to thank him, when he made an hideous grimace, and made a sign over his shoulder.

Then Jessie knew that somebody was listening.

Dick retired and shut the door.

She heaved a deep sigh, for either the young girl had betrayed her, or her stern guardians suspected her tenderness of heart.

Jessie took her tea—which was very nice, with several tempting knick-knacks—deliberately.

She was not going to despair, not she. She would not give way to despair and groaning; while there was life there was hope.

Had not Julie and Paolo escaped from the terrible fire at T——?

Could she not escape from the abominable gang who persecuted her?

When she had quite done tea she put the things outside, and, lying down on the bed, prepared to rest.

But, first, she pushed a bolt on the inside of the room.

A deep blush came across her countenance as she recollected a recent adventure to which leaving her door open had subjected her.

They had not provided her with lights, so, as the darkness drew in, she could only lie down on the bed and think.

Under the circumstances this was not a very pleasant amusement.

But she could not sleep. There is a state of mental excitement which utterly drives away slumber.

And yet Jessie felt that she must have dozed off slightly once or twice, for she suddenly and unexpectedly found herself counting twelve.

As she did so she saw a light coming streaming into her room.

Quite startled, she sat up on her bed.

It was from the skylight.

Jessie had not undressed. She darted off the bed and looked about for some means of defence.

She determined not to scream until she saw what was the character of the intruder.

The skylight appeared gradually to be removed, and then the light was lowered slowly into the apartment.

It was held by a female's hand.

"Miss—young lady—are you asleep?" said a soft, earnest voice.

"No. Who is it?"

"Mary, the girl who came up about tea. Take the light."

Jessie stepped forward and took it. Mary, at the same moment, slid down, and alighted on a chair, which Jessie hurriedly brought to her assistance.

"Oh, Miss, I was so vexed they wouldn't let me bring up your tea. They said I was too soft-hearted for one who—who—who—"

"What?"

"Well, Miss, they say——"

"Do tell me."

"That—that——"

"What, girl?"

"You are mad! But I don't believe it."

"I am not mad," said Jessie, quietly, "though I do wonder that I am not. Sit you down. But, first, tell me how you got here."

"I sleep in the next room. They have persuaded mother to lock me in. But I was determined to see you, so I got extra candle, pushed up my skylight, and crawled along the roof here."

"You are a brave girl: and if, after hearing my story, you will help me to escape, my friends will reward you handsomely."

"We are poor, very poor. Until these people came we were literally starving," said Mary.

"They will be kind to you while it serves their purpose," said Jessie, sadly.

"They have been very kind. They seem very good, especially the old gentleman."

Jessie shuddered.

"Listen to my story, and then you will find this man to be a monster so hideous that you will shudder at the recital!"

And Jessie told her story. It took her a long time, and when she had finished it was day-dawn.

"And now, girl, aid me to escape, and neither you nor your mother shall ever know want. Your mother shall come and live on our estate, and you shall be my companion and friend!"

"We are alike," said Mary, with glistening eyes, "let us go at once."

"No. You and I must escape together in the night. Your mother is older than you are, and may not believe all I say, and yet it is Gospel truth. The moment my flight is discovered they will flee. Your mother then will be convinced."

After some further conversation Mary agreed

to be guided in everything by Jessie, and took her leave to snatch some little rest.

The new lodgers, however, were not early risers, so that she could count upon some rest.

CHAPTER XXXI.

A DEATH-BED.

THE next evening Phineas Bristowe, Julie, and Paolo held a consultation.

They thought it high time to take their departure.

Nothing could be done with Jessie until she was safe in the lock of the Mormons.

In Nauvoo city they could defy the writs of any civilised Government.

It was determined, then, to start as soon as they could find a ship.

It was arranged that Phineas and Julie were to assume the garb of Quakers.

Paolo would try and get a passage as one of the crew.

It was determined to pay a visit to France, and sail from Havre. There was, in this way, less fear of detection; besides, in those days, there were no extradition laws.

Julie, like a true woman, determined to lay in a respectable stock of clothes.

Paolo and Phineas let her have fifty pounds.

She laughed and told them she would be the best dressed Quakeress in all America.

"Verily," she said, "after visiting St. Paul's Churchyard thou shalt not know me."

She took a hackney coach as soon as she was out of the house, and drove hurriedly away.

She gasped for breath.

In her hand she held a paper, which she had been clutching in her hands since breakfast time.

"Drive to the Temple," she said.

The Temple reached, she discharged the vehicle, and turned within its musty purlieus.

The advertisement was directed to herself, and implored her to lose no time in calling to see her dying father, who would forgive all.

The address was Mr. Knowles, —— Temple.

She soon found the name on the door, and in an agony of expectation rang the bell.

The door was opened by a tall, portly, and very respectable looking gentleman.

"Is this the residence of Mr. Knowles?" she said, in a quick, hurried tone.

"Yes."

"My name is Teresa Dunbar," she said, still more eagerly.

"Come in."

She found herself, after pacing through an ante-chamber, in a handsomely furnished lawyer's office.

There were chairs and desks for several clerks, but they were, momentarily, absent.

"What of my father?" said Julie, *alias* Teresa.

"Hum. Mr. Dunbar had reason to believe that you perished in a dreadful fire."

"But here I am."

"Hum. Mr. Dunbar is very ill."

"The more reason I should see him."

"Hum. He has been ill some time. At first he was delirious in an hospital."

"But now?"

"Hum. He recovered his senses, and put the whole of his affairs in my hands."

"But why trifle with me, sir?"

"Hum. I have not trifled. Young lady—for I have no reason to doubt your statement—you father is very ill indeed."

"But where?"

"Hum. He must not be agitated. Still, if you will be guided by me, you shall see him."

"When?"

"Hum. In five minutes."

The gentleman rose, and pushed open the door. He held up his finger.

"Alone! alone! always alone," said a well-known voice. "Is it to be always the same?"

"No, my friend," said the lawyer, entering the room, and motioning to Julie to follow slowly, "not alone. I have been attending to your business."

"Well? well?"

"Yesterday I sent an advertisement to all the papers—"

"Well?"

"This morning—"

"Is she alive?"

"Yes."

"Thank Heaven, then, I am not an assassin. But where is she?"

"Near—"

"Let her come, for I am fast going. If she delays I shall not see her before I die."

With a wild cry Julie threw up her veil, and sprang forward.

The old man gave a shrill grasp, and caught her in his arms.

But he could scarcely speak.

He was fast going.

The lawyer, who had sheltered him in this strange place at his own request, left them together.

A very brief explanation followed.

"You escaped—and that wretched young man?"

"Is dead," said Julie, coldly.

"So much the better," gasped the old man. "Julie, you are rich, very rich, much richer than you believe. You will now marry a nobleman—a gentleman—you may be a duchess if you like."

"But, father—"

"Hush! call in my friend."

The lawyer came.

"The will!—the will!" gasped Dunbar.

The lawyer produced it. Dunbar jealously examined the seals.

"Take it, Julie," he said, "it is all your own."

Julie took it mechanically.

"This worthy gentleman will be your adviser, your friend—but I have left you everything absolutely, without control of any kind, my darling child."

"Oh! my good father," said Julie, sobbing.

The lawyer had to draw her gently away.

She started, and looked upon the bed.

He was dead.

Julie fell back in an arm chair in a paroxysm of grief—assumed wholly. She was laying her plans at the time.

"My good girl," said the lawyer, "I am an old bachelor, but my housekeeper will gladly be of every assistance to you. Until you take your own house command mine. With a fortune like yours I shall take a splendid estate to prepare for you, but in the meantime—"

"I thank you, sir," she replied, rising and turning her back on the dead, "and I will accept your offer with pleasure. I will make your home my home this very night, or to-morrow at latest. But I have some poor persons in my humble abode whom I must see alone. I came out in a desperate hurry for money. If I do not return my landlady will commit suicide—or something dreadful."

The worthy lawyer—and an excellent man he was, though of a much abused race—opened his long purse, and took out a roll of notes.

"Will a hundred pounds be of any service?"

"Ample, my dear sir. Your address?"

He gave it. Julie returned towards the bed, as if she would have cast herself on it.

"No! no!" she sobbed, "I will not give way. Pardon me, sir, I am weak. But I will be strong—very strong."

And she sobbed hysterically.

"My dear young lady, your father was very old and ailing."

"And I away. But I must not give way thus. My starving protegès are waiting for me—adieu."

And, conducted to the door by the bowing lawyer, she went out.

"Poor girl!—excellent heart—happy to have her in my house," muttered worthy Mr. Knowles.

Had he seen the awful look upon her face, as she got outside, he would have formed a very different opinion, and have shrank from all contact with her as from a venomous reptile.

Julie took a cab, and hurried away.

Whither?

We shall soon, perhaps, discover.

It was nearly six o'clock when she drove hurriedly up to the door of the widow's house.

Phineas and Paolo, with rather scared faces, were looking out of the window.

CHAPTER XXXII.

A PLANT.

"WHERE have you been all this time?" said Paolo, in a moody tone, as she entered; "where are your purchases?"

"I have made none. Oh! Paolo."

"What?"

"I have seen—"

"Who?—what?—the devil?"

"No."

"What, then?"

"My father."

"D——n," cried Paolo, "then it's time to go."

"No; he's, he's—"

"What?"

"Dead."

"Dead?"

"Yes, and left me everything."

"Hooray!" cried Paolo, wild with delight; and, as he spoke, he caught hold of her two hands as if he were about to dance round the room.

"Paolo, I am weary. He only died to-day. I must rest. Besides, one of the partners is coming here to tell us all about it."

"About what?"

"About the will," said Julie, sitting down. "I got a hundred pounds," producing the notes.

Paolo gasped for breath.

"How much is his fortune?"

"I don't know. Something immense by the manner of the lawyers.

"Allow me to congratulate you," said Phineas, advancing with low bows.

"Thank you. And now to order a delicious little supper," continued Julie. "I am wild to know all about it."

"So am I," said Paolo, who really was so overwhelmed at the prospect as scarcely to be able to speak.

"We must be married by licence to-morrow somewhere," said Julie, with her most seductive smile; "that marriage is of no use in law."

"I know," replied Paolo, falling from the seventh heaven.

"Now do not be downcast," said Julie, cheerfully; "you must assume another name—anything very, large—marquis—duke if you like—my riches will make everything go down, and who will dare, in our splendid mansion in Park-lane, or our palace in the country, to take you for the notorious Viscount de Florac."

"We should be safer in Spain or Italy," replied Paolo, moodily.

"As you will," said Julie; "but now for Mr. Knowles."

She rang the bell, and, giving to the widow five pounds, ordered supper for four.

"Will you see to some really good wines?" she said, addressing Phineas Bristowe.

The Mormon elder, in his heart, favoured the good fortune of Paolo, and mentally determining to obtain a good clue, readily agreed, and went out.

In an hour he had sent in several dozens of first-rate wines.

The widow and Mary laid the supper.

Dick saw to the wine, to ice, and to all other accessories.

At eight a very genteel brougham drove up to the door.

The widow announced Mr. Knowles.

He was a middle sized man, with red hair, a curly set of whiskers, a white neckcloth—quite a jolly looking lawyer.

He shook hands heartily with Paolo and Phineas, who were both immensely polite.

"Very sudden," he said, shaking his head; "here to-day and gone to-morrow. La! very; but there is a second side to the question"

"Yes," said Phineas, wagging his poll with intense professional gravity.

"Ah! me!" added Paolo.

"The estate is very great," continued the lawyer.

"Mr. Knowles," said Julie, with great dignity, "we will talk of this by and by."

"As you please, Miss."

"I have ordered a little supper. I really feel a dread of entering on business," she continued.

"Very natural," said the other.

"So let us sup first."

At this moment the folding door flew open, and the exquisitely laid out supper appeared before them.

"SUP"—

So said Dick, who stood napkin in hand, ready to officiate.

He got no farther for an instant. A violent cold seemed to attack him on the instant. The contortions of his visage were hideous.

"PER!"

He got it out with great difficulty.

The lawyer followed Julie, who was taking the head of the table. Paolo was close to his side. Phineas Bristowe, pushing Dick on one side, advanced towards a seat facing the lawyer.

"Vich vine?" said Dick, in an audible whisper.

"Port and sherry, and then champagne," whispered Phineas. "Mind you put on the hock just as I call for it."

"Vich is hock and vich is champagne?" said Dick, pointing to the two tubs of ice.

"Why, you fool," cried Phineas, going out into the passage.

"It's Forrester, the hofficer," said Dick, slamming the door of the room; "and there's a lot more outside."

Phineas almost fell.

"Follow me," said Dick.

Away they ran, while a fearful scuffle took place in the supper room.

A thundering knock came to the door, and, when Mrs. —— opened, in rushed half a dozen Bow-street officers.

As Dick closed the door on the supper room the supposed lawyer caught Paolo by the throat, and, before he recovered his senses, had him handcuffed.

The young man trembled like a leaf. One glance at Julie told all.

Her look was demoniacal, triumphant, like that of a fiend."

"Wretch!"

"Thus," she said, "I rid myself of the enemies of my father."

"You were my accomplice."

"I told you so," said Julie, turning to the officer. "Sir, I have been the slave of these men for months. It was useless to leave them; as long as they were loose my life was not safe. But do not let the others escape."

"Take this fellow off to Newgate," said the officer, as the runners entered; "two of you can manage him."

Paolo made no resistance, but he gave Julie one look. She returned a haughty and insolent smile.

"We shall meet again," he said.

"I hope not," replied Julie.

The officer and his followers rushed upstairs after Dick and Phineas, who had obtained a considerable start. They examined every room as they passed, and found no one in any of them.

The birds had flown. Nor were Jessie and Mary any where to be seen.

CHAPTER XXXIII.

THE ESCAPE.

WHILE Julie had been carrying out her nefarious scheme for the betrayal of criminals not a whit more guilty than herself, a great change had taken place in the fortunes of our heroine, Jessie.

No sooner was the supper laid out than Mary, with the advice and consent both of the widow and Dick the tumbler, took up a small tray of very choice things to Jessie.

She took, also, a small bottle of wine.

The story of Jessie had so preyed upon the mind of Mary that she could think of nothing else.

To her young and romantic mind, the whole seemed like a ghastly narrative in a book.

She thought of it all day, and she dreamed of it at night.

Every consideration of self was merged into that of compassion for Jessie's sufferings.

Creeping upstairs, so as not to be heard by Paolo or Phineas, Mary knocked gently at the door.

She unlocked and Jessie unbolted it at the same moment.

Jessie stared at the neatly laid out supper.

Mary smiled.

"What is the meaning of this?" said Jessie, who was very pale.

"Well, Miss, I've been thinking we'll never get such another opportunity again. They've got people to supper; they're too busy to think of us. We could easily slip out."

"We?"

"Yes."

"You don't mean to accompany me?"

"I do."

"But your mother?"

"Write a note and drop it in the post the moment we are out."

"But how do you mean to escape?"

"At the bottom of the stairs, above the kitchen where mother and Dick sits, is a door. It is always open. It leads into a yard. In this yard is a door opening out into a narrow street."

"Let us go at once."

"But, supper?"

"Put it in yonder basket and take it with us. I could not eat it now."

"As you like," said Mary, boldly.

They now began with beating hearts, pale faces, and sparkling eyes, to prepare themselves for their journey.

Whither?

This Jessie did not know, unless, indeed, she went home. Somebody would be there to communicate her arrival to her disconsolate family.

But the first consideration was to get out of the house.

They put all they could in the basket, and then, with beating hearts, went down stairs.

Mary tripped lightly down, singing all the while.

Jessie, poor girl, crept like a shadow against the wall.

They reached the parlour floor, however, and were passing out into the yard when a loud rat-tat came to the door.

With a bound they were in the yard, and opened the back door.

Two gruff looking men stood close to the door. The men looked at them.

"Well, my little dears," said one, "and where are you going?"

Mary was more used to the streets of London than Jessie.

"Mind your own business, fellows," she said; "can't one go of an errand? Never answer such people," she added in a loud, confidential whisper to Jessie.

The two Bow-street officers grinned, but, having no orders about these young parties, allowed them to pass unmolested.

The two girls hurried on for some little time in the direction of Islington.

Not Islington of to-day, but forty years ago— a very different thing.

They held the basket between them, and in his way they advanced on their road until they were quite out in the fields.

They had not seen anyone for some time. It was getting very late.

Fortunately the night was light.

Not a house was visible in any direction.

In a field at no great distance they could see a large hay stack.

They made their way towards it.

It was an enormous haystack, one side of which was much higher than the other.

A large quantity had been removed on the one hand. This made a kind of shelf to be reached without much difficulty.

The two girls clambered up.

They now saw that a short ladder stood in such a position as to allow them to climb to the very top.

It was very snug up there, some small quantities having been taken out of the centre.

They ascended by the ladder.

This they drew up after them.

Having thus fortified themselves against any fear of interruption, they proceeded to take refreshment.

They were both very faint and weary.

Having supped they said a short prayer, and lay down to sleep.

Mary, the household drudge, was in a sound slumber in a moment.

But Jessie in vain wooed the capricious deity. She gazed upwards at the lovely sky, and thought.

Where was Henry? Where was her mother? Where were all those she loved and honoured? Should she ever see them again?

All these were speculations which tired and wearied her brain.

Her chequered fortunes, her many and severe trials floated through her young imagination like painful dreams of the past.

Suddenly she raised her head slightly.

Two men had just clambered a style, and entered the field.

Jessie bowed her head. She was not at all alarmed. They had nothing about them to tempt evil doers.

Alas! poor Jessie, you have youth, innocence, and budding charms, to violate which would delight any lustful ruffian.

The men make straight for the haystack, and, clambering up, cast themselves wearily on the hay. They are panting with some terrible exertions.

"Curses light on Julie," she heard a well-known voice say, to her utter horror and astonishment.

"She blowed us," replied Dick.

"Of course she did," continued Phineas. "I long suspected she hated Paolo, but I did not think that she would betray him thus. It was a dead plant."

"Well, master," replied Dick, "and what does yer mean to do?"

"Dick," said Phineas, "you are a man of energy and decision. If you will stick to me I will yet make your fortune. I have money and I can get more."

"How."

"If I once get that girl safe over in America her mother will give any money for her. I am sure of twenty thousand pounds. That's about the child's income for one year."

"That gal?"

"Yes."

"I'm your man. But you wont ill use her?"

"Ill use who?"

"The gal."

"What do you mean?"

"Well, she's very pretty."

"D——n man!" cried Phineas Bristowe, "she's my own child."

"The devil."

Jessie shuddered from head to foot.

"What put that in your head?"

"Why you see that ere young chap's got some such notion, I know," said Dick.

"I have done many things which wont bear the light," remarked Phineas, with a hypocritical whine, "but never will I allow that child to be harmed."

"Good!"

"And now for business."

"Good again."

"I must have her in my power or I am lost," continued Phineas.

"All right."

"Now I know she has gone off in the direction of the Hall. Her mother is there; and all sorts of offers have been made in the papers on condition of her restoration. Her mother, I know, is at home."

"Good."

"Now I know not how she will get there, but get there she will. We must follow. If we overtake them, well and good. If not, something will turn up."

"Right again," said Dick, who was half asleep.

"Which is our best way?"

"Keep on this road ten miles till you come to a cross road that leads to the———; follow your nose for one hundred and odd miles, and there you be, right as ninepence. Now, master," he added, yawning terribly, "I'm tired. Let's sleep."

———

CHAPTER XXXIV.

A HUNDRED POUNDS REWARD!

THE horror, the terror, the agonies endured by Jessie were something to be remembered during the whole of her future life.

She moved not; she scarcely breathed; but, as soon as she was sure that the two men were in a sound sleep, she gradually awakened Mary.

By signs (she kneeled up), by pressing her hand upon her lips she contrived to keep her silent.

She then pointed downwards.

Mary gazed in speechless horror.

Jessie then made signs to her not to speak whatever might be the temptation.

And thus they watched until the sun was high in the Heavens.

About eleven the two men woke, and, after a brief conference, descended from the hay stack, and commenced the journey.

Mary looked at Jessie inquiringly.

Jessie told her all, and then added her determination to follow in their track, instead of getting a head, until she reached home.

"But how shall we live?" said Mary, in a scared tone.

"I have money," replied Jessie, "so now to breakfast."

They had remains of veal pie, and cold fowl, and wine, but they had no water.

They took about a spoonful of wine to give them courage, and then began their journey.

At the first brooklet they slaked their burning thirst, and added water to their wine.

Which was very good for little children, though wine is spoiled by water.

They now felt stronger, and keeping a cautious look out a head, proceeded onwards.

"Mary."

"Yes, Miss Jessie."

"I've been thinking—"

"What?"

"Well, I'm afraid we shall not go long this way. If stopped by constables we can give no very clear explanations. Besides, it does seem odd two girls travelling alone."

"Well?"

"I think I shall dress as a boy, and dye my face and hands like a gipsey."

Mary laughed.

"You must dye me, too."

"I can then say I belong to Berkshire, and am taking sister home from service," continued Jessie.

Mary agreed to everything.

They soon came upon one of those small towns which surround London in all directions,

and Jessie boldly entered a ready-made clothier's shop and looked about her.

"I want a suit for this girl's brother," she said; "he's employed in the fields. It's for Sunday."

"How big is he, Miss."

"Well, about my height," said Jessie, after a moment's thought.

A plough boy's Sunday suit was now brought out, and, after some discussion, bought and paid for.

It was made up into a bundle.

They went out and continued on their way.

At the door of a small ale house they saw a donkey, very aged and forlorn, with a wisp of straw on his tail.

A countryman was praising its points.

"Cheap as dirt at ten shillings," said the owner.

"Give you eight," said a tall, gawky youth.

"That's enough," cried the owner, "let's say no more about it. I'll make sassages of it first."

"Aint the first," grinned the yokel.

The owner of the donkey made a dive at him, but brought up as he saw Jessie hold out the ten shillings.

He stared.

"Buy him?" said he.

"Yes," replied Jessie, handing him the money, and taking hold of the halter.

The lookers-on laughed; but Jessie cared not, and marched away in triumph.

They were soon in the open country once more, and turned at once into a thicket.

Mary sat down and screamed with laughter.

Jessie began gravely to undress.

This was easy enough.

But to dress.

This she found rather more complicated than she expected.

But Mary, laughingly, came to her assistance, and at last she was dressed, her hair fastened up in her cap, and her face and hands smeared with a mixture of wine, earth, and berries.

Mary dyed herself in the same way.

A bundle was then made, and, by great exertions, Mary contrived to get on the animal's back.

They had never thought of a saddle.

They now felt much safer, and, indeed, to see that plump lad leading the donkey with one hand, and clutching a stick with the other, one would have thought them a very well matched couple.

Presently they saw a roadside inn before them.

Again they looked cautiously about, but, alas! saw their danger too late.

Their deadly foes were reclining on a bench on the side of the road opposite to the ale-house.

"Hoo!" said Jessie, giving the donkey a good blow in the flanks.

The ancient quadruped moved not one iota the quicker.

Mary kicked, but in vain.

They were compelled to pass at a slow and deliberate pace.

The two men continued drinking and smoking,

their eyes never removed from the direction of London.

The fugitives, with wildly beating hearts, proceeded on their way.

A sharp turn suddenly caused them to lose sight of their foes.

"They knew us," said Jessie.

"But why not stop us?"

"We should have screamed and denounced them," replied Jessie.

"We're lost."

"No," said Jessie, quietly leading the donkey through a gap in the hedge, "they will give us a good start, to get us out of hearing. Lie down here, and hold the donkey's tail down."

"Why?"

"He can't bray then. I will keep watch," said Jessie, smiling at Mary's astonishment.

Nothing more was said.

Jessie peered through the hedge.

About half an hour elapsed, and then she saw the two men tramping along at a rapid pace.

"They can't have gone far," said Dick, "if it is them."

"I'm sure of it," replied Phineas, "I knew the artful young wretch's eye in a moment."

And they hurried past.

Jessie watched them out of sight, and then slowly retraced her steps towards the inn.

A crowd was before the door. A mounted messenger had just put up a large placard headed A Hundred Pounds Reward.

"Two noted burglars," said the mounted messenger.

And he read the bill aloud.

"They're just gone by," said Mary, hastily, before Jessie could stop her.

"When?—when?" cried several.

"They were smoking and drinking on yonder bench just now," she continued.

"Blowed if they wer'nt," said the landlord, slapping his thighs, "what an ass I was not to see it."

"You allers was a fool," added his better half "now you've been and lost a hundred pounds."

"Have I?" he said, taking down an old blunderbuss: "come along. Whose game?"

About five volunteered, and away they sped upon the road.

"Here they be," he shouted, like a madman, "a coming back."

They were close at hand. They had guessed Jessie's trick, and were returning.

"Surrender!" cried the fat, valiant beershop-keeper, levelling his blunderbuss.

Without a word the two men bounded into a field.

The landlord fired, and then an increasing crowd set up a chase.

"Betrayed! and by them," said Phineas, as, heading low along a hedge, he made for a dense thicket.

"I seed a Bow-street messenger with a big bill," said Dick.

"Oh!"

This was all that Phineas could say, for the tremendous pace at which they were going was utterly destructive of all powers of conversation.

They could hear their pursuers along the road; they could hear others darting through the hedge.

"I see 'em," shouted the mounted messenger; "a hundred pounds atween us if we catch 'em."

"Hurrah!" said the mob.

"Fight," said Dick.

"Yes," replied Phineas.

Their pursuers were now about fifty yards behind them, while they were on the edge of a dense thicket.

They made a dart for it, and disappeared.

When the pursuers came up they could not see any trace of the malefactors.

The mob, however, agreed to guard the thicket while the mounted messenger rode off for the assistance of constables.

CHAPTER XXXV.

MAN HUNTING.

IN the meanwhile Jessie and Mary, satisfied that, for the present they were in no danger of pursuit, hastily pressed onwards, determined, at all events to get on the road as far as possible.

The knew the road now without need of further asking.

Jessie felt sorry to have betrayed the other fugitives.

But she really could not help it.

It was her or them.

With what deep anxiety Jessie now looked forward to the moment when she should once more be folded in her mother's arms.

One or twice she felt inclined to take the stage-coach and hurry home.

But she was afraid that their youth and sex might subject them to stricter inquiries than would be pleasant.

She determined, then, to proceed as she had originally decided.

*		*		*		*

But she was not as safe as she suspected. The bitter enemy of her peace was on her track, and in a more savage humour than he had ever been in before.

The watchers round the thicket were, like all Englishmen, easily roused up to spirit where there was a prospect of a hunt—especially a man hunt.

And, then, these two were notorious criminals, or else who would offer one hundred pounds reward for their apprehension.

They, therefore, stationed themselves, armed with sticks and staves, at every place where any one was likely to attempt to escape.

This lasted about an hour.

It was very hot. The sun and the shadows are at play on the edge of the forest, now tracing between them dark and golden lines, and now letting in a gush of glittering sunshine, and even sinking again into the blackness of shadow.

Having nothing else to do, the rustics sit down and rest themselves.

MRS. TREHERNE'S VISIT TO JESSIE.

And still the officer does not return with the promised assistance.

Presently there is a stir in the bushes, and a man in the dress of a gamekeeper appears to two of the scouts.

He makes signs for silence.

The scout approaches nearer. He is followed, at a little distance, by two companions.

"What is the matter?" asks the gamekeeper, who was now followed by a companion, both issuing forth into the open air.

"Two murderers have hid in the thicket," said one of the rustics.

"When?"

"Joe"

"Tummus"

"It's them."

"Where?" said one of the scouts.

They had not said a word about the reward. Clever fellows.

"You see that tall oak," said the first gamekeeper, pointing down a long and picturesque vista of the wood.

"Yes."

"There's two rummy looking coves hid up in that tree."

"Armed?" said one of the scouts.

"No, footsore and weary."

The three rustics exchanged glances, clutched their sticks and began gliding behind trees and bushes towards the oak in question.

No sooner were their backs turned than the

gamekeepers exchanged anxious glances, and stooping low along a hedge, took to their heels as fast as they dared go.

About a quarter of an hour later several mounted Bow-street officers rode up.

A loud shout caught their ears; and, dismounting from their horses, they rushed towards the noisy scene of action.

They found two men, half naked, struggling with three of the scouts.

The two men did not say a word.

On the approach of the officers the struggle ceased.

The men pointed to their mouths.

They were gagged.

On their release they drew a long breath.

"Darned fools," said one, scarcely able to speak from passion. "Why, you Jem Lock, don't you know me?"

"Joe!" shouted the astonished rustic. "But where's the murderers?"

The Bow-street officers listened:

"Two ruffians caught us here asleep," said one of the men, "and robbed us of our clothes and guns."

"The deuce—how long ago."

"Half an hour."

The discomfited rustics now explained their meeting with the gamekeepers; and, after a few oaths and recriminations, the whole party set off in pursuit of the bandits.

But the country was so intersected with cross roads and lanes that not a trace of the two men could be found.

But the officers did not give up.

They proposed to hunt the fugitives over the kingdom.

*   *   *   *   *

The worst feature against their success was the great command of money possessed by Phineas.

Little suspecting how near the enemy were, the supposed boy and girl hastened on their way.

They had no fear of molestation now from their chiefly dreaded foes.

As Jessie had fortunately a moderate supply of money, they were able to live well on the road, and to obtain comfortable shelter every night.

They advanced, however, very slowly. They were no great walkers, and the donkey was very little use to them.

He was aged, and found luxury by the way to rest.

Still, at the end of the fifth day, they knew that they were not far off from their longed-for destination.

The country appeared familiar to Jessie. Even Mary fancied she had seen it before.

Towards evening, very fatigued and weary, they reached a roadside inn.

It was a very old-fashioned, but comfortable place.

As usual, the arrival of the two rustics on a donkey excited a considerable amount of attention.

But the gentle manners of both disarmed all unkindly suspicion.

Jessie called the chambermaid on one side— as she had done at every place—and revealing her sex, at once, without difficulty had obtained a bed-room for the two.

She hinted at her story, and, as such persons can generally tell a lady from her manners, her statement was believed.

They wished, they said, to avoid observation, and would like their tea in their bedroom.

It was a large comfortable room, looking out on the highway.

They sat down at the open window, and enjoyed their tea.

In the course of conversation, Jessie had alluded to her being near home, without betraying herself.

It was twelve miles distant.

The chambermaid had spoken to the landlady, whose eyes at once flashed with excitement.

"As sure as fate it's Madam's lost child, that the country's all grieving about!" she cried.

"Miss Jessie ——!" cried the girl.

"I'm certain of it. But don't worry the children. Jack will be home presently, and he shall ride over at daybreak."

This was spoken in the bar.

Something dark seemed to glide along the passage.

It was Jessie.

She entered the yard, and, going to the stable, as was always her habit, looked after the donkey.

As she passed the window of the tap-room, on her way back, she saw two men eagerly devouring bread and cheese.

They wore the dress of carters, but Jessie knew them at once.

They were Phineas Bristowe and Dick the fumbler.

The window was open, but the yard was so dark that they could not see out.

"I know it's them," said Dick. "I know'd the moke."

"Lucky for us they got that donkey. We should never have traced them otherwise," savagely replied Phineas.

"Pretty kittens," said Dick.

"I'm getting sick of this. That girl is an evil demon. She invariably gets me into a scrape."

"Not her fault."

"Perhaps not. But, Mr. Dick, I've an idea?"

"What is it?"

"I've lost the co-operation of Paolo; but I have great things to execute—but I'm sick of all this risk. My plan is to go in for a great stake. Mrs. Treherne lives close here. Now if we could get Henry Haddington into her hands, as well as Jessie, we could make a fine haul."

"How so."

"It's a long story; but it is sufficient for you to know, that if, by means of Jessie, we can trap Henry into the hands of Mrs. Treherne, there will be no reward too great for us."

"I'm your man, wherever money is to be made," said Dick.

"I propose to go over to her to-night.

"They are safe up stairs. They won't stir until morning. By that time she will have decided what we are to do. Touch the girls here we cannot."

"All right," said Dick?" "art ready?"

Phineas rose, and the two went out of the room.

Jessie prepared to follow them, and, at any peril, learn the exact nature of their infamous plans.

But it was too late to communicate with Mary. She might lose sight of them.

Already they were outside the house.

CHAPTER XXXVI.

THE OLD HOUSE.

FOR many more years than anybody could recollect a house had stood about a hundred yards from the highway in a narrow valley.

It was surrounded by dark firs.

For many a long day, though handsome and spacious, the house had been uninhabited.

The owners had lost nearly all the adjacent land, and were living abroad in obscurity.

It was out of the way—it was in want of repair—it was too big: such were the answers to all the attempts made to let it by the agent.

When, therefore, a family who declined to give any references, but who agreed readily to the rent asked, were willing to do repairs, and paid rent in advance, they were allowed at once to take possession.

The family was composed of a lady and gentleman, and a lad of between seventeen and eighteen.

They had two servants only.

They were a surly and silent couple, who thought of doing all the errands and making all the purhases of the family.

The house had been made habitable, and such rooms as were necessary had been repaired and furnished.

The best room was the old library, denuded of books, but still bearing marks of its former distinction.

Here sat the lady and gentleman.

They were sitting after dinner.

The youth was on a stool, playing with a couple of dogs.

His glance was surly in the extreme.

"So you saw Phineas in London?" said the lady.

"I did; and, in case he had any news, gave him our address."

"A great folly," said the lady, sternly; "I always objected to your going to London."

"If you think I am going to be cooped up here always," sneered the gentleman, "you are very much mistaken."

"I know. While I am devoting every energy of my life to the great end, all you think of is amusement."

"You make so little progress."

"I keep back that my bark may be worse than my bite. They no longer suspect my being in England. Give me but the chance."

"Every time we have tried we have failed," sneered the colonel—for, of course, it was this unprincipled agent of Mrs. Treherne who was addressing her.

"Yes," said the lad, savagely; "and I know this, that if this life lasts much longer I'll run away for a soldier."

"Fool!" cried the mother, who, much as she loved her son, could not bear to be resisted. "I should do well if I let you go.

"Do you know what you are throwing away?"

"I am sure I don't."

"Revenge and wealth. If my plans succeed you will be head of the house of Treherne and of Haddington."

"If!" sneered the boy.

"You will not only crush the youth who has deprived you of rank and fortune, but you will take his mistress."

The youth's eyes glistened at this promise.

His eyes looked up at the clock, and he smiled.

Leaving the two others to continue their conversation, which was always devoted to plans against Henry, he walked slowly out of the room.

He had made an appointment with a certain village beauty, and the reference to Jessie reminded him of it.

She was to be in the copse of dark firs at the back of the house about this time.

There was a small door on that side, formerly used by servants, but of which the young roué had the key.

He took his way quickly in the direction, and let himself out.

We have already recorded the fact that it was a dark night. The wind howled through the tall trees with a wild and moaning sound.

The dark, heavy clouds threatened rain.

Master Edward Treherne began to fancy that his amorous hopes were likely to be disappointed.

Just, however, as with a muttered curse he was about to return into the house, he saw a dark figure approaching.

"Is that you, Maria?" he said, advancing.

"It is so cold," said a soft, female voice.

"Come on quick," replied Edward; "give me your hand. I thought you were not coming."

Before the female could answer a loud ring was heard at the front entrance of the house.

"What the deuce is that?" said Edward.

"Two very ill-looking men," replied the female voice. "They frightened me out of my life."

"Come in!" said Edward, hurriedly.

He seized the girl's hand, which trembled as she took his. She, however, followed him into the house.

They were in a dark passage.

"Be careful of the steps," said Edward; "I must leave you a moment to get a light."

He then slowly felt his way upward.

The other followed slowly and cautiously.

She trod so lightly that no one could have heard her.

There was a considerable bustle at the end of the long passage, in a kind of hall.

Edward hastened to see what it was as he recognised his mother's voice.

The figure glided into the first open door, from which a light issued.

It was the library, which the others had just hastily quitted.

There was a screen in one corner, probably intended for use in colder and more severe weather.

The light figure glided behind and crouched up breathless in a corner.

The very next instant the whole party came back, escorting in Phineas Bristowe and Dick the fumbler.

Edward, in his anxiety to learn the news, had apparently forgotten his fair friend.

Phineas and Dick seated themselves: and, while the lady of the house called for refreshments, wiped their heated brows.

"To what do I owe the honour of this visit?" said Mrs. Treherne, gravely. "Your conduct towards me has not been such as to warrant your coming thus unceremoniously."

"Madam," said Phineas, meekly, "I knew, very well, that my good fortune has not been able to keep up with my good wishes, but——"

"What now?"

"If I put both Henry Haddington and Jessie in your power," he replied.

"Who is this?" said Mrs. Treherne, pointing to Dick.

"A friend of mine who has been unfortunate. He's devoted to your interests," replied Phineas.

"Indeed!" observed Mrs Treherne. "On what conditions?"

"He desires to leave this country for America. If we succeed in carrying out your former great designs of winning for your son Edward Haddington Hall—and, by his marriage with Jessie, —— Hall also for him—surely it will be worth your while to reward us handsomely."

"It will," said Mrs. Treherne, eagerly. "Name your price."

The colonel never spoke a word. The very idea of the cub Edward, as he called him, inheriting all this property was gall and wormwood to him.

"Madam," said Phineas, "I know that you have saved large sums of money. My old bargain holds good, I trust. My friend will be satisfied with a thousand pounds."

"Thousand devils!" said the colonel, angrily.

"Sir," put in Phineas, "Mrs. Treherne knows well the value of our aid. Jessie is now in our power. We are willing to give her up to you on certain conditions."

"Well?"

"Once she is in your possession, cannot you compel her to aid you in your plans against Henry?"

Mrs. Treherne and the colonel exchanged glances.

"One word, madam," said Phineas. "I have something for your private ear."

"Why?" asked the colonel, with considerable anger of manner.

"Be true to me—betray me not," whispered Phineas, turning to Mrs. Treherne. "For——"

Here he stooped low to whisper a sentence which made Mrs. Treherne almost shriek with horror and rage.

At the same moment another incident occurred which, for an instant, startled the whole party out of all thought of further conversation.

The person behind the screen leaned forward to catch the whispered words of Phineas Bristowe.

The screen gave way and fell forward.

Jessie, in her boy's dress, stood revealed before them. Phineas knew her in a minute.

"Jessie, by Heavens!" he cried, with a cry of bitter disappointment and rage.

Mrs. Treherne caught her by the arm.

"And this is the girl who, with that other impostor, is to rob my brother's family, and my late husband's family, of their estates?"

"Who and what I am you know," replied Jessie, in a voice which she forced herself to render calm.

At this moment Edward entered. He had searched the room below, the offices below, and found nobody.

He stared wildly when he saw Jessie.

"Who is this?" he inquired, with a puzzled air.

"Your future wife: embrace her," said Mrs. Treherne.

"Keep off, at your peril," cried Jessie. "I hate, I loathe, I scorn you. Your touch is pollution."

Edward almost whistled. He understood now.

"Girl!" said Mrs. Treherne, sternly, "you came here by your own consent; you leave this house married to my son, or you never leave it alive."

"I will die before I be the wife of one I despise and hate," said Jessie, forgetting her costume.

Mrs. Treherne rang a bell very sharply.

A middle-aged woman appeared on the threshold.

"Take this girl to the Blue Room," said Mrs. Treherne; "confine her closely until clothes are prepared for her."

Martha, such was the woman's name, stared wildly, but made no observation. She was used to obey orders without questioning them. Jessie, with her lovely countenance, beaming with faith and hope, shook her head and followed.

"I shall make no resistance," she said, with scorn.

CHAPTER XXXVII.

NEWS OF JESSIE.

THERE was great mourning at —— Hall.

Thither all the friends of Jessie had returned after the dreadful blow they had received by her strange abduction.

The had set to work agents innumerable, but not one of the party could as yet start upon the search themselves, for Cornelia was, to all appearance, dying.

Every day letters were written backwards and forwards.

Lotty had, in confidence, told Henry all she knew about Jessie.

But that was not much.

Still they did not suspect anyone save Phineas and his satellites.

Lord Henry Thynne was hardly likely, just married, and on his wedding tour, to trouble his head about one who had despised his advances.

Still, her disappearance from D—— House was a mystery, and on the very day of the adventures recorded in the last few chapters it had been determined to act as if Lord Lionel Thynne had some hand in the abduction.

Henry had determined to follow on his track in some disguise that could not be penetrated.

About five in the morning the house was startled by a loud ringing at the principal entrance. It continued for several minutes in a way that designated that the messenger had some excuse for his apparent rudeness.

Henry was the first to rush down. He was followed by several servants.

But he had opened the door before them, and found that the messenger was the ostler at the Roebuck Inn.

"What on earth is the matter, Martin?" said Henry, somewhat impatiently and angrily.

"Well, please, sir, missus thinks," began the ostler, in a stammering kind of way, "that a young lady—"

"Well?—what?—speak out, man," cried Henry, wildly.

"Is the young lady as is lost," continued Martin.

"Gracious Heavens! where is she?" cried Henry.

By this time several servants were in the hall, while the dwarf appeared on the staircase.

"At our house, please, sir," said the ostler.

"Put four horses to the barouche," cried Henry, wildly. "Pardon me, my friend" (this was to the dwarf), "but I am half mad."

"Be calm, Henry. Let me question the man."

He did so, and the ostler, who had heard all from the chambermaid, told the story.

They were frantic with delight, for no one had the least doubt about the identity of the fugitive with the long lost Jessie.

The servants, despite their over eagerness, had a carriage ready in a marvellous short space of time.

Henry and the dwarf got in with the ostler, whose horse was knocked up.

The horses flew along, as if aware of the glorious mission on which they had started.

Henry had never looked more excited, and yet happy, in his life than he appeared now.

Both he and his companion were too excited to speak.

They sat wrapt in their own individual thoughts.

Henry had no doubt whatever, but the dwarf, more used to disappointments, was deeply anxious.

Youth is apt to be sanguine, one of its brightest privileges.

On! on sped the horses, galloping under the gentle influence of whip and spur, until, at last, the Roebuck is in sight.

They have just come up a steep hill, and are on its crest: about half a mile in the valley below can be seen the red bricks of the inn.

The ostler rises and makes a waving signal.

Away, wildly they dash downwards, until the crowd round the doorway can be seen.

In another instant the horses are reined in.

A wild cry assails their startled ears.

"I don't know! Where is she? What have you done with her?" sobbed a female voice.

With a convulsive shudder, a terrible prevision of ill, Henry leaped from the carriage.

Mary, her eyes red with weeping, her face swollen from a night spent in tears, is held by the landlady.

"What is the matter?" said the dwarf, trying to be calm.

"Last night, sir," said the landlady, "we saw this girl go up with the young lady in disguise of a boy, and this morning, when we got up, she is sighing, and moaning, and calling for Jessie!"

"Come in here," said the dwarf, motioning the landlady and chambermaid to follow him into the parlour.

Henry and Mary came too.

"Now, my good girl," said the dwarf, "tell me all about it."

Mary then explained that Jessie, fancying she had seen their pursuers on the road, had gone down stairs under pretence of looking after the donkey, and had not returned.

"What were the men like?" said the landlady.

Mary described them with extreme minuteness.

"The wretches!" she replied, "they were in the tap-room last night, and went away early. I heard Master Meyrich say he thought they were after no good."

"Did he see which way they went?" asked the dwarf.

"He lost them on the road leading to the Dark Fir House."

"Who lives there?" continued the other.

"Don't you know them?" cried the astonished landlady.

"No."

"The old Mrs. Treherne, sir. Sir Marmaduke Haddington's sister."

Henry and the dwarf exchanged a terrified glance.

"She must have overheard something," said Henry, "and determined to follow those fellows to that house. This is too horrible. If Jessie is in that house, and has come to any harm, I will no longer have any mercy on those who have no mercy on me. The law shall decide between us."

"Amen!"

But now it became a question as to what should be done. To proceed openly to the house was to put the aggressors on their guard.

After an earnest conference they came to the resolution to dissemble, and try and meet foul and horrible treachery by the force of courage and cunning.

At this moment a messenger was to be seen galloping at a terrible rate down the hill away from the direction of —— House.

"What new misfortune does this bode?" said the dwarf.

"Good Heavens!" cried Henry, impetuously; "Cornelia!"

"Hush!" said the dwarf, wildly. "For Heaven's sake do not suggest."

The messenger was now close at hand. He rode straight up to Henry, and placed a letter in his hand.

"From Jessie."

He tore it open eagerly.

"*I am where it will be with difficulty that you can find me,*" it said, "*but if you will come alone to a cross road called the Sister Elms—which any one will show you—a young girl will guide you to me. You have only to say 'Jessie.'*"

"This is not her handwriting," gasped Henry.

The dwarf took the envelope and letter.

"The direction is in her writing," he said, after a careful examination; "but be not alarmed, I understand it all."

"What?—what?"

"She has written to you, and the letter has been abstracted.

Henry struck his forehead with his hand.

"No matter, I will be there. I will risk anything to see her.'

"We shall see about that," said the dwarf, drily.

"Now for calm consultation and breakfast. I will then explain to you my plans in full."

Henry groaned in deep anguish of spirit, and then, as usual, gave way to his more experienced friend and counsellor.

CHAPTER XXXVIII·

THE GIPSIES.

MEANWHILE Jessie had been removed to her room and locked in by the officious guardian selected for her.

As yet there was no sign of any practical cruelty.

They wanted her to be the wife of the hated young Edward.

This, of course, she knew she could not be—she would die, but not marry one she loathed and detested.

But she little knew the determined character of those into whose hands she had fallen.

They would hesitate at nothing which would enable them to carry out their plan of aggrandizement.

The window of the room occupied by Jessie looked out upon the dark fir plantation.

She was loftily enough situated to see that over the dark firs was a hill, apparently covered only by furze.

A dark-looking square building occupied the centre of the view.

But it was useless to watch now, at that late hour of the night, where none could be moving.

She was about, then, to retire to rest, after locking her door, when her attention was irresistibly attracted.

Suddenly, on the summit of the hill, which was not two hundred yards distant, a slight flame became then visible.

The fire was against the wall of what soon appeared to be the ruined remains of a farm house.

The fire blazed up, and made the little picture distinctly visible.

There was a triangle of sticks, a cauldron hanging from it, and two figures—one light and active, the other seated on the ground.

Jessie's heart began to beat wildly. Who were those people?

Why were they there at this hour of the night?

She knew that they must be gipseys, and some gipseys had proved the friends both of Henry and herself.

A wild hope flashed across her mind.

It was an old woman and a young one evidently.

Supposing that it' turned out to be the old grandame and her beautiful daughter.

Jessie had often, in her happier hours, amused herself in the gipsey camp. The girl had been a great friend of hers.

There were two massive wax candles on the table.

She lit the one which, as yet, had remained useless, and taking them to the window, placed them one on each side.

This done, she stood exactly between them.

Then a strange, sharp, shrill cry, like that by which smugglers in the Pyrenees convey sounds and signals for miles in the mountains, passed her lips.

At that still midnight hour it seemed to fill the whole circumambient air.

The young figure clasped her hands.

The elder started to her feet.

Then both, after casting fresh fuel on the fire, disappeared in the surrounding darkness.

Jessie returned her candles to their original position on the table in the room.

She waited.

But she heard nothing but the soft soughing of the wind and the music of the waving tree tops.

Then a slight rustle might have been distinguished by a keen and attentive ear.

"Who sounds the gipsey's call at this unhallowed hour?" said a soft and silvery voice.

"'Tis I, Jessie."

"Our darling, our mistress," said—

"I know it was her," replied Jessie. "Heaven, in its infinite mercy, be praised."

"Silence," said the silvery voice, "there are others up in the house. But be of good cheer, mother and I are near, and no harm can come to you."

"Heaven shower its choicest blessings on you," replied Jessie, in a low but distinct tone, "for I feel now as if I were safe."

And she closed the window, and soon after laid down. Utterly exhausted and wearied with physical fatigue and mental emotion Jessie soon slept soundly.

She seemed to fancy that, as some one knew for certain where she was, her escape had become a matter of certainty.

Poor girl, she had many, many trials to come, by sea and by land, in England and on the wild, illimitable prairies.

When Jessie awoke it was about mid-day. She found, beside her bed, a fitting costume for a young lady, which she gladly substituted for the unbecoming garb her safety had induced her to adopt.

She then rang for her breakfast.

The calmness and self-possession of Jessie utterly astounded her aged attendant.

She began to put the room to rights as soon as she had laid the breakfast properly.

"My lady will join you in a few moments," said Martha, with a smile.

"What lady?" replied Jessie, with a scornful smile.

"Madame Treherne, the mother of the heir of Haddington," said Martha.

"And who, pray, may that be?"

"Mr. Edward, to be sure, though Lady Haddington do snub him," replied garrulous Martha.

"While Sir Henry Marmaduke Haddington lives," said Jessie, calmly, "Mr. Edward can never be heir."

"Does he live?" cried the old woman.

"Mrs. Treherne may have caused the murder of the father, but the son lives to succeed and avenge him," said Jessie, sternly.

"Oh, don't ee talk of murder," cried Martha, much agitated, "missus wouldn't do it."

"She is capable of any crime to carry out her fiendish purposes," said Jessie. "If ever crime sat on the brow of woman it does on hers. The boy will be as evil as his mother."

"Don't ee say so, don't ee say so," cried Martha.

The door was pushed violently open, and Mrs. Treherne entered, livid and trembling with rage.

"Girl!" she shrieked, "how dare you thus calumniate me to my servants?"

"Madam, I cannot calumniate you; your conduct to myself and Henry has been such that nothing I could say could equal the plain truth."

"Leave us," said Mrs. Treherne.

Martha went out.

"So, girl, instead of submissiveness, and a humble disposition to obtain my forgiveness, you defy me."

"I defy and hate you."

"Beware!"

"I fear you not. Rather than become the bride of that ill-favoured and wicked boy, you call your son, I will die of absolute starvation."

And, as she said this, she rose, pale but sublime in her beauty and undaunted resolution.

"We shall see. But, I tell you, girl, that if I will a thing it must be done. I am no puny, whining girl, but a strong and determined woman."

"So am I."

"So much the better for you, and the worse for your husband."

Jessie's lips curled.

"But, mark my words. To-morrow night, without resistance, without any appeal to the clergyman who will perform the ceremony, you will marry my son by special license, or—"

"What?" said Jessie, coldly.

"You shall be glad to ask for marriage on your bended knees."

"Why so?"

"You shall suffer the last indignity a woman can suffer as punishment for your obstinacy," replied Mrs. Treherne, hoarsely.

"And you," said Jessie, blushing up to the eyes, "call yourself a woman; you dare, a mother, and a relation of my own."

"Girl!" cried Mrs. Treherne, with blanched cheeks, "what mean you?"

"You know, and know well. And yet, with all this, you dare to threaten me in a way that no man would do except under the influence of madness. But I fear you not. My friends know where I am."

"I give you free permission to write to them, and will myself send the letter," said Mrs. Treherne.

"You will?"

"Write and tell this impostor boy where you are," she replied, "and let us see if one will dare come here to face one so foully outraged as myself."

Jessie eagerly wrote a brief note, informing Henry Haddington where she was, and then directed it.

"You will send this?" she said, unable to believe her senses.

"I will, this very instant."

And, in reality, glad to get away from the victim of her avarice, and ambition, and hate, she hurried from the prison apartment.

CHAPTER XXXIX.

THE PLOT.

MEANWHILE several of the more faithful adherents of the family had been sent for by the dwarf and Henry.

They came for the purpose of watching the House of the Lone Firs in such a way that nobody should go in or out without their knowledge.

Henry had determined to be at the rendezvous, and to act according to circumstances.

Her friend and guardian angel was to follow with others at a distance.

It was terrible to wait so long, but to show themselves before the time in the neighbourhood would have, in all probability, spoiled all.

Henry, however, could not remain still.

To allay his feverish impatience he took his rod, and followed the stream in an opposite direction.

It was only an excuse, however, to commune with his own thoughts.

About a mile from the inn, on a pleasant road leading to a neighbouring town, was a very pretty cottage, or, rather, house. In front was a lawn, laid out with very superior taste and judgment.

The house was two storeys high.

The stream was clear and pellucid at no great distance from the house.

Henry now recollected that this was the residence of the Reverend Jonas Faraday, vicar of S——, the town close by, a living which, when of age, was in his gift, if he could prove himself the heir, but was now in the gift of the widowed Lady Haddington.

He walked into a small bunch of trees, and began to set out his fishing implements.

Just as he did so he heard the trot of a horse on the road in the direction from which he had come.

On how little sometimes hangs the fate of nations and of families.

Henry mechanically, by some mysterious impulse, concealed himself.

The horseman came in sight almost simultaneously. It was the colonel.

Henry felt a cold shiver pass through his frame.

He was, he at once saw, bound to the house of the Reverend Jonas Faraday.

What for ?

Of course they were about to force Jessie into a secret marriage.

A perspiration like an icy shower-bath broke over the whole frame of Henry.

The colonel rang the bell.

A servant came.

He took the colonel's horse and led him round towards the stable.

The colonel walked up the gravel way towards the house.

He was at once admitted ; the Reverend Jonas Faraday making it a rule never to refuse to see visitors.

Henry cast away his rod, and, crossing the road, bounded over a quickset hedge, and, in an instant, was in the vicar's grounds.

Did Henry for one moment fancy that he was about to play the eaves-dropper ?

If he did, he knew that, under the terrible circumstances in which he was placed, he was justified in using any means to save his beloved and persecuted bride.

He moved hastily along the thicket, and, in a few minutes, found himself close to the open window of the vicar's library.

The vicar had just risen to receive his strange visitor.

Henry panted with excitement. He cared not much whether or no he heard what passed, but still he would gladly have eased his own burning agony.

The vicar took his seat in his arm-chair close to the open window.

The colonel occupied another.

" Can we be overheard, reverend sir ?" said the colonel, in his most dulcet manner.

" Not a soul ever comes this way when I am at my studies," replied the vicar. " But if you wish—— "

And he rose as if to close the window.

Henry's heart beat very wildly this time.

" No; that is quite sufficient. The air is quite refreshing," said the colonel.

The vicar bowed.

" Shall I offer you any refreshments," said the vicar.

" I thank you—no. I have come to consult you on a very serious and delicate matter," began the colonel.

" I shall be most happy to give you my advice," said the vicar, with a low bow.

" I sent up my name."

" You did, colonel."

" Perhaps you are not aware that I am engaged to Mrs. Treherne ?"

" I have heard so."

" I have allowed that matter to be deferred, as my claim to the dormant peerage of —— is about to be decided."

Again the vicar bowed.

" But I still take a deep interest in the business concerns and family matters connected with Mrs. Treherne."

Again the grave and impassable vicar bowed.

" You are aware that she has a son ?" said the colonel.

" I am aware that she has a son."

" You are, perhaps, not aware that he is a rather unmanageable young cub ?"

" I have heard serious complaints of his behaviour to respectable young women."

" Indeed !"

" And should have complained to his mother, but that she does not do me the honour to attend my church," said the vicar, mildly.

" I did not know his vagaries were so widely known. Well, it is to be hoped they will now cease."

" Why ?"

" He is about to be married."

" Perhaps it may correct his errors. But I know not," said the clergyman.

" It must, it shall."

" Is the young lady agreeable ?"

" She cannot help herself !"

" But then—— "

" Hearkee, Mr. Faraday, though a clergyman you are a man," said the colonel.

" What then ?"

" This future stepson of mine has seduced a girl of high family and great expectations," said the colonel, sadly.

" This is awful—this is terrible !" replied the vicar.

" But I discovered it. It appears that he really loves this girl. Under these circumstances we have hurriedly procured a special license. We have, to spare the girl's feelings, consented to a private ceremony. There will, in this way, be no scandal."

" But, as nothing is known, why not have the marriage public ?" said the clergyman, his pale face becoming scarlet.

" Neither she nor the boy will marry at all unless we consent to privity. They will take their wedding tour, and then announce their marriage."

" I am strongly opposed to anything clandestine," said the vicar. " What say her friends ?"

" They will not see her until she is married," replied the colonel, " in mercy to her."

" I will do it. Under the circumstances it is my duty. The girl's ruin might otherwise be on my head. When will you require my services ?"

" To-morrow night. A carriage will come for you. Say nine o'clock."

HENRY'S INTERVIEW WITH THE GIPSIES.

The vicar bowed.

The colonel rose, and, thanking him in enthusiastic terms, they shook hands.

In a few minutes more the colonel might have been heard galloping off.

CHAPTER XL.

COUNTERPLOT.

No sooner was he out of sight than another visitor was announced.

The vicar, who had taken up a favourite book, sighed, put it down again, and told them to admit the fresh disturber of his peace.

It was Henry, who was ghastly pale and extremely agitated.

"Excuse my intrusion," he said; "excuse my abrupt way; but I have heard the whole of your conversation with the vile and unprincipled colonel!"

"Sir," said the vicar, his pale face flashing with honest indignation, "then allow me to say you have done a very mean thing, whoever you may be."

"Mr. Faraday," replied the other, almost haughtily, "when I tell you that Colonel L—— has lied to you in every word—has engaged you to join in a rape and abduction! when I tell you that the wretched victim whom they are striving to immolate is as spotless as an angel, and my affianced wife, you will understand that, following the colonel like a bloodhound, I spied into his secrets !"

"But who are you, and who is the victim ?" gasped the bewildered vicar.

"My name is Sir Henry Marmaduke Haddington," said our hero, mildly.

"Heavens ! And the lady's ?"

"Jessie, the daughter of Cornelia and —— "

"Merciful Father ! And I was about to be led into this awful plot. They surely could not believe that I should have tamely submitted."

"They have no scruples."

"They could only have killed me," said the vicar, with a sublime smile.

Henry wrung his hand, and a long conversation followed, after which Henry returned towards the inn, while the Rev. Jonas Faraday issued forth on one of his old and well-known pious errands.

He walked some little distance, and then entered by a path through a small orchard a cottage, the door of which was opened to him by a dark-eyed girl, of about eighteen, who cast her eyes down upon the ground as he spoke.

"Margaret, I have come to speak seriously with you," he said gravely, but in a tone of exquisite mildness.

*   *   *   *   *

Meanwhile Henry had returned to the inn, and informed the astonished dwarf of all that had passed.

He heard with mingled disgust and satisfaction.

To what state of mind did they hope to reduce Jessie that they dared to send for such an one as the Rev. Jonas Faraday to go through the ceremony ?

It was, to say the least, a mystery not very easily solved.

But they must have patience.

But time was fast flitting, and Henry and the dwarf prepared for their journey.

They had everything ready, and were about to give the word when the old gipsey and her daughter entered.

At any other time both Henry and the dwarf would have been glad to have seen them. They were now in the way.

"Be not so hasty," said the elder gipsey. "We are those you ought to welcome."

"Why ?"

"We come with news from Jessie !" replied the aged crone, with a smile.

Henry took her hand.

"Forgive me if I seemed impatient," he said. As he spoke he closed the door, and bade the two be seated.

"Ha, ha !" said the old woman, laughing. "There is magic to a young heart in a woman's name. But I was not angry with you. The dove is in the hands of the hawk. It is natural you should strive to release her."

"And I will, or perish," said Henry, solemnly.

"But let us understand one another," replied the old crone, "that our flaws may not clash. There is ample time. Nothing can be done to-night."

"Why not ?"

"Tell me all you know, and I will explain further," replied the woman, with the obstinacy of age.

Henry gave a clear though brief account of all that had passed.

Both the crone and Zerlina listened with attention and strict silence.

"It is now nine. 'Tis not ten minutes to the Two Elms, and she will be there only at midnight."

"But every moment—— "

"Hurry is worse than delay. Do you wish to save Jessie certainly and surely ?"

"You know I do."

"Well, let one of you write all you wish to say to Jessie, while the other procures me a short rope about fifty feet long, and some twine about the same !"

"What for ?" said Henry.

"Do as she tells you," replied the dwarf. "I will write while you do so. You can add a postscript."

Henry wondered and obeyed. He went out, took the ostler and a dog-cart, and drove off to the town. With great difficulty he procured what the gipsey had ordered.

He would not have minded had he have seen any use in what she demanded.

All this time he had not taken the slightest notice of Zerlina.

A tear stood in the eyes of the lovely gipsey girl, who would willingly have died for him.

When he returned he informed the gipsey that all she had asked for was ready.

She smiled, and bade him be of good cheer.

"We will now go and meet this false messenger of an accursed race," she said, fiercely.

All rose and prepared to follow her. She was agitated. The dwarf gave her his arm.

Henry took hold of the hand of Zerlina, which trembled in his grasp.

But he never so much as noticed it.

What was the poor gipsey girl to him that he should think of her, and Jessie, too, in more than mortal peril.

Presently they stood under a wide-spreading oak.

"Yonder," said the gipsey, "are the two elms. I see a girl is seated on a stile beside them."

"But there may be an ambuscade," whispered the cautious dwarf.

"No. He can go. They wait at some distance. Hold the girl firmly by the arm and bring her here."

Henry walked firmly forward, in a careless kind of way, too, as if he meant to pass the two elms.

"Jessie," he said, in a low tone, as he passed.

"I am the messenger," replied the girl, rising.

"From whom ?"

"From the young girl in the ruined tower."

"Who told you so ?"

"One who loves me," replied the girl mournfully.

"Girl," said Henry, taking her arm and drawing her away, "if you are honest, no harm shall be done to you. But I have my reasons for not going with you now."

The girl made no resistance whatever.

Presently they stood once more under the wide-spreading oak tree.

The gipsey produced a dark lantern and turned it on. The girl stood pale, trembling, and dumb.

"So," said the gipsey scornfully, "having been the victim of the bad woman's cub, you now become her tool—her willing tool."

"No," gasped the girl, with tears in her eyes, "indeed not. But, having promised, I came here to avoid exciting suspicion. Listen."

She told her story.

All listened in wild and almost incredulous amazement.

But Henry believed her, and said so.

A mutual explanation took place, and then they separated.

"Ten minutes before the sun rises over yonder hill," said the gipsey, "be here those who love Jessie. A gipsey boy will bring you to where I shall be."

CHAPTER XLI.

A LA BLONDIN.

It was a lovely morning.

The dawn had not yet quite broke.

It might have been cockcrow, but it was not quite dawn. Aurora, with her bright and rosy fingers, had not drawn the sable curtains of night.

They still made network of the dark blue light of day.

It was now September—the month so disliked by all game, and so loved by man.

> "The roses of summer
>   Are past and gone,
> And sweet things are dying
>   One by one.
> But autumn is bringing,
>   In richer suits,
> To match with his sunset,
>   His glowing fruits.
> And the flowers the dewdrop
>   Deserted now,
> For the richer caress
>   Of the clustering bough."

Henry, who has not taken off his clothes, has called the dwarf, who is pale and haggard.

There are recollections in his life—to be told only when we publish the awful mystery contained in the coffin parchment—which make him pant with dread.

He knows what fierce passions will tempt men to, and what, therefore, Jessie has to dread.

And he knows, too, the character of the fierce fiend in whose clutches she is now.

Mrs. Treherne, worst of all, malignant, ambitious, avaricious, and lustful.

The colonel, licentious and avaricious to the last degree.

As to Edward Treherne, *alias* Haddington, they knew him to be that worst specimen of humanity—a profligate boy.

They went forth into the open air armed. They would not, could not trust their lives in the keeping of the wretches they had to deal with.

They hurried to the spot where the old crone had appointed them to be.

A gipsey boy awaited them.

"Follow," he said, and darted into the great wood of the dark firs.

They were soon at the back of the house inhabited by Mrs. Treherne and her unfortunate prisoner.

They saw a window, at a very great height from the ground, open.

A strong iron balcony was in front of the window, commanding a splendid view.

Suddenly Jessie appeared, and Henry was about to address her when the gipsey placed his hand upon his lips.

"Wait."

"Why?"

"See!" and she pointed to Zerlina, who was ascending a huge and lofty fir which faced the window.

All held their breath in anxious astonishment.

None could make out what was about to happen.

When quite opposite to the window, Zerlina whispered a few words to Jessie, who disappeared.

Then Zerlina produced a bow and arrow, and, taking an assured and steady aim, shot through the open window. Then Jessie came forth and held the arrow up in her hand.

She undid a ball of twine which had been fastened to it, and one end of which Zerlina held.

The amazed spectators began to have some vague perception of the truth. They held their breath with perfect awe.

Then Jessie began to haul up the ball of twine, and presently the spectators saw the end go across.

Jessie having caught hold of an end of it, proceeded to fasten it to the iron balcony.

She took several turns under the guidance of the gipsey girl.

The old crone then told the dwarf and Henry to approach nearer.

They saw two gipseys climbing the tree in which sat Zerlina.

They proceeded to fasten the rope to the tree with as great a strain as their strength could give it.

It was as nearly taut as any rope ever is under the circumstances.

Then Zerlina looked below with a quiet and proud smile.

Jessie quickly hid her face in her hands in fearful awe.

Henry shuddered, and would have cried out, but his tongue clove to the roof of his mouth.

The gipsey girl, who wore short petticoats—indeed, the regular costume in which she exhibited at fairs—took from the tree a pole, and started on her fearful and perilous journey.

Why was it that Zerlina was able to walk so calmly?

She had not the slightest symptom of fear.

Everybody held their breath, while a cold perspiration poured over their bodies.

Jessie began to peer through her fingers as soothing words passed the lips of Zerlina.

Then, with great difficulty, all repressed a cry as the gipsey leaped into the balcony.

"I will go, too," said the dwarf, in a low hasty tone.

"But you will perish!" replied Henry, in amazement.

"No—let him go!" said the aged gipsey.

And the dwarf began to climb upwards until he reached the extended rope.

His body was light, and the strength of his arms very great. He did not attempt to imitate the mode adopted by Zerlina; but crawled along the rope by mere exercise of muscular force.

He soon reached the window, without undergoing half the danger which had been the lot of Zerlina.

He then waved his hand to them below, let go the rope, and closed the window.

Henry felt more easy now. Jessie had now near her two devoted friends, and no serious harm could come.

They all now, as the day was breaking in earnest, departed, Henry to prepare for the evening, the aged gipsey crone and her party to keep watch in the forest.

As they all took their several ways a young sportsman, who had wandered that way, and who had stood watching them with amazement and delight, hurried the way he came, whistling to his dogs and shouldering his gun.

CHAPTER XLII.

WEDDING BREAKFAST.

JESSIE'S delight, at finding herself restored to the protection of some, at least, of her friends, was beyond all bounds. She kissed them both, laughed, and played such wild antics that they were alarmed for her sanity.

Soon, however, she calmed down, and began to ask questions. She felt quite hurt that she had not seen Henry.

"But he saw you," said the gipsey, with a low smile, "and he was happy."

"True," whispered Jessie. "And now, before we are interrupted, tell me all."

An explanation ensued, and then they examined the room for the means of hiding the dwarf and the gipsey.

The room was a large, old-fashioned one, with a good-sized alcove containing the bed.

At each end of the bed were two sorts of cupboards, concealed by heavy curtains.

They contained lumber and boxes.

As soon as they heard any movement in the house—which was not very early, from the habit all had of imbibing prodigious quantities over night—they each retired to their hiding place.

Jessie always kept her door bolted, nor would she even open it when she heard the voice of the old servant Martha.

They were able, in this way, to secrete themselves safely.

About ten the aged servant came with the breakfast things.

Luckily the dame had a large idea of the capacity of the human frame with regard to food. If she had ever heard that we require six pounds of solids and liquids per day, she evidently thought that it must be taken all at once, like a pill.

Her supply of bread, coffee, cold fowl, tongue and ham, was something wonderful.

"You appear to think me possessed of a wonderful appetite," said Jessie, with a smile.

"The young, and the rich, and the happy always like plenty of choice," she mumbled. "But, while I'm wasting time in talk, my old man will be wanting his breakfast."

And she hurried away.

Jessie again closed the door, and bolted it before she called her unexpected guests to their merry meal.

Neither of them could help laughing.

"Hush!" said the gipsey, who was the first always, according to the habits of her race, to think of danger.

And she pointed to her lips and the door.

As soon as a hearty meal had been made the two guardians returned to their hiding place.

Jessie opened the window and threw the bones of the fowl to a dog she had noticed occasionally wandering round the back of the house.

Presently Martha came to bring a couple of large band-boxes.

She took no note of the extraordinary breakfast Jessie appeared to have made.

"Look you here, miss," she said, "these are your wedding dresses."

"I do not want them, and I shall not put them on," replied Jessie, with extreme coldness.

"I say, minx, that you will," said Mrs. Treherne, entering upon the footsteps of Martha.

"How so, madam?"

"If you will not put them on, with Martha's aid," she replied, "I will send up two ploughboys to help you to dress. We shall then see what your ladyship will say."

"I will put them on myself if I am not disturbed," said Jessie.

"No one will come near you until the ceremony," replied Mrs. Treherne, with a sneer, "except to bring your dinner."

"What ceremony?" asked Jessie, with provoking calmness.

"Your marriage, this night, with my son," replied Mrs. Treherne, sternly; "mind you, nothing can prevent it."

"No minister of God will force a girl against her will."

"Refuse, and you know what awaits you," replied the fury.

And afraid she should lay violent hands on Jessie, she hurried out of the room, banging the door to.

"That I could have ever believed I loved that woman," said the dwarf, wiping the cold perspiration off his brow.

Jessie stared, but did not venture any remark.

Zerlina advanced, opened the boxes, and began to lay out the bridal dresses, which were handsome

As there was really now no danger, both

Jessie and the gipsey girl could not help amusing themselves admiring and trying them on.

And thus the day passed, and night came slowly on.

CHAPTER XLIII.

THE CHAPEL.

THE old house of the Dark Firs had witnessed many a strange scene in its day, especially in the olden time.

Under Catholic and Protestant rule both it had been the refuge of the oppressed.

Its chapel had witnessed mass celebrated at night at the peril of the lives of those who officiated and those who heard.

It had also seen the more simple ritual of the reformed church.

It had had many strange and thrilling vicissitudes.

It had seldom been the theatre in feudal times —when it was the castle of a stern baron—for such a scene as it was to witness that night.

A young girl to be dragged to the altar, and swear the most solemn of vows to one she loathed and detested.

It was horrible to think of.

But Mrs. Treherne and the colonel went to work in a systematic kind of way which marked their utter callousness of heart.

The colonel and Mrs. Treherne were actuated most by avarice and ambition.

But Edward was chiefly by hate.

Ha! ha! ha! she detested him, she loathed him, she preferred the youthful impostor who had invaded his undoubted rights.

But what would that avail her when, after the ceremony, they were left alone together in the bridal chamber, she almost a child, he almost a man.

His fierce desire to possess her was such that he had resolved to curb all signs of hate until by and by.

He little knew Jessie. He little knew either the penetration of her mind or the character of her heart.

She utterly and irredeemably despised him, and would have done so if forced into a hated union.

She would have treated it as a farce, and have stabbed him to the heart as the vile violator of woman's purity had he approached her.

So is every man who marries a woman, weak, and frail, and yielding, against her will.

No slave market presents a worse scene than parents selling their children for gold or rank.

It was about nine.

The old chapel, which had not been used for years, had been prepared roughly for the occasion.

It was musty, dirty, and ill suited to the occasion.

It was impossible, at so short a notice, to half light it up.

But both Mrs. Treherne and the colonel thought it best not to make it too bright.

The colonel had gone to fetch the vicar.

Mrs. Treherne had ascended to Jessie's room, where, by the most horrible threats, she again tried to induce her to yield her consent.

Jessie remained calm, cold, and motionless.

She drove the wretched syren of the house of Haddington nearly frantic by her contemptuous silence.

"I warn you that, if you say a word, if the minister is fool enough to listen to you, you shall to-morrow crawl on your knees, and beg to be my son's wife," she yelled.

Jessie smiled.

"I would not were I dishonoured. I would sooner be that painted thing without a name than your son's wife," she replied.

Mrs. Treherne rose from her chair as if to strike her, but she thought better of this.

"Wretch!" she said, "ten minutes will decide your fate. I hear that the minister has arrived."

And she motioned Jessie to precede her.

With a cold and haughty smile Jessie did as she was bid, leaving the foaming dame to follow her in her own way.

She found Martha, her husband, and Edward Haddington awaiting them in the old chapel.

"My dear Jessie," said Edward, advancing with a bow.

"Keep back, sir. I am not yet that foul and lost being, your wife," she said.

Edward turned ghastly pale, and would have retorted angrily, but that he heard advancing steps.

In the gloom a small group approached.

"My Lady Treherne," said the voice of the colonel. "I bring our worthy friend the Reverend Jabez Faraday, who has consented to contract this marriage."

"Who else?"

"His clerk and a trusty witness," replied the colonel.

"And now, as the hour is late, and I have much else to do," said the clergyman, "let us proceed."

"With pleasure."

"Are the contracting parties here present?" began the minister, in a solemn voice.

"They are," said Mrs. Treherne.

"Let them come forward," he continued. "Which is the young gentleman?"

"I am."

"The young lady?"

"That am I," said Jessie, "and I proclaim this marriage to be attempted to be forced upon me. I hate and loathe this man, and all his set."

"And I solemnly forbid the banns," said the ringing voice of the dwarf.

The clergyman dropped his book, the colonel stood petrified, Mrs. Treherne tried to fly, Edward actually cried with rage.

"Who forbids the banns?" said the clergyman.

"I do. This is a foul and unnatural outrage," said the dwarf, "this wretched boy, in his wild desire to become possessed of property to which he has no claim, is here to do this foul and unnatural deed in defiance of oaths."

"What say you, sir?" mildly responded the Reverend Jabez Faraday.

"Let me go," said the colonel.

"Let me go," repeated Mrs. Treherne.

Henry had thrown off his disguise as the clerk of the parson, and stood beside Jessie ready to champion her again to the world.

Zerlina stood in the background.

"No,' said the dwarf, "there are officers within call. I am not going to allow this foul outrage to pass unpunished."

"A word," said the clergyman. "I came here perfectly aware of what was about to happen. By some means or other this license has been obtained in blank; I have, therefore, filled up the spaces with the names of Edward Treherne and Margaret Percy—come forth."

And behind, from the darkness of the chapel, came a glowing, blushing, rather gaudily dressed girl.

Edward turned pale with rage. His mother looked at the girl with scorn and hate. The colonel smiled. He was delighted with the turn affairs had taken.

"Who and what is this girl?" said Mrs. Treherne, fiercely.

"A decent and respectable girl who, under the influence of this young man's tongue, has acquired a right to be called his wife."

"Never."

"I won't."

"Edward," said the girl, "is this the way you keep your promises?"

"Promises! you never expected me to keep them," said Edward.

The girl began to cry.

"Unless Mrs. Treherne gives her instant consent," said the dwarf, sternly, "I will call in the officers and give the whole party into custody for the 'repeated' abduction of Jessie, as well as the attempted—"

"Hush," said Mrs. Treherne, who had never looked once at the dwarf, once so loved, who now appeared to be the arbitrator of her fate.

She then said two or three words in a whisper to Edward.

"I am ready to keep my promise," said Edward, loudly; "in fact, I was only afraid of mother when I said different."

"The guardian assents," said the clergyman, mildly.

"I do," said Mrs Treherne, with an awful gulp.

The clergyman performed the ceremony without further delay, and the daughter of the village shoemaker was daughter of the House of Treherne.

"And now," said the dwarf, "I once more leave you. Once more, for family reasons, I decline to call in the assistance of the law. My forbearance will last no longer. Next time I shall call for a stern and awful reckoning."

And they left the house.

Henry took Jessie's arm.

The dwarf gave his to Zerlina, the gipsey girl. She was very sad.

The bridal party remained alone.

"So, girl," said Mrs. Treherne, clutching her by the arm, "you have contrived to gain your infamous end—but do you think I will ever recognise you?"

"Let me go, madam," said the girl, "you hurt me."

"Leave her to me," said the son; "she is my wife, and I like her."

The mother let her go.

"You like her," she said, with a cold glitter in her eyes that was awful to gaze at; "then like her, but no child of hers shall ever inherit my fortune. So choose between us.'

"Madam," said the girl, humbly, "I did not seek your son. I was a poor but honest girl when first I knew him. I cannot help if he promised me marriage, and under a promise—" She looked down.

"And what to me are the love amours of a boy and cobbler's daughter?"

"Mother," said Edward, who was fascinated by the presence of his really pretty wife, "do not insult her. If you do I will go from this house to-night, and, throwing myself on the mercy of my cousin Henry, I will never return."

The colonel and that bold, bad woman exchanged glances.

"Well!" she said, "since it must be so, it must, but no thanks. I must have time to reconcile myself to this downfall of my hopes. Go, order supper; perhaps over the feast I may learn to like my—*daughter!*" she said, and the heart of the poor shoemaker's daughter sang with joy. Edward let her out.

He knew in what poverty she had lived, and that such a supper as his mother and the colonel liked would be to her a wonder.

"She must die," said Mrs. Treherne, leaning heavily on the arm of the colonel.

"Die?"

"Yes, die! Do you think that I will allow any such base born wretch to usurp my place, or that I will yield obedience to my boy's wife if I can help it?"

"You say nothing of *him*," said the colonel, with a sneer.

"Don't you, then," she cried, with the glance of a tigress. "I won't stand it."

"I thought you had forgotten," he replied, more tenderly.

"Forgotten! A woman refused, and by a wretched cripple—do you, then, think, in the whole measure of the world's capacity for ill, there is a meed of pain that can be measured out severe enough to punish a man who has had the priceless jewel of a woman's love offered to him, and refused it."

The colonel's face flushed up.

"This to me?"

"To you! Why, man, dare you compare our coarse fancies to such a love as that has been? Say no more."

"I see you hate him. If you only knew—"

"What?"

"That which I can tell you of him."

"Speak!" she cried.

"Well, I will undeceive you on one point. I am not the father of—"

"Silence! Breathe it not. I know what you are going to say, but say it not if you would not have your tongue blistered. I know what it all encloses. The racking belief that such a thing might be a probability has nearly driven me mad."

"Let us change the subject. What of this girl?"

"She dies. I will not one day breathe the same air with her."

"But we must be cautious. People will talk."

"Who can talk? She has a bedridden old cobbler for a father."

"How know you?"

"Pshaw. Do you think an intrigue like this could be carried on unknown to me? Had I, however, have suspected, then a convenient dose of poison would have ended all."

"But Edward—"

"The boy has got his toy, that is all he cares for. But he will soon pall with such a baby face. He is a Treherne."

"A Haddington," said the colonel.

"If you will, and, as soon as I can show him advantages to be gained, he will be on our side."

"Do you think so?"

"I know it. Is he not my son?"

A long conference ensued, and then they went up from the chapel to the room where the happy and delighted young couple were watching the preparations for supper.

The girl was in ecstacies. She was not only an honest woman but a lady.

Her happiness beamed through her eyes.

She was radiant.

Really pretty, she now looked beautiful.

But neither youth, nor beauty, nor happiness made any difference to this second Lady Macbeth.

She sat down to supper with her, the venom of her heart distilling at the time.

She took wine with the girl she had doomed to death, and such a death!

DISEASE OF THE HEART!

The girl was glad to retire early with her husband—if only to get away from the enraged crone.

The colonel and Mrs. Treherne remained together to plot and curse.

CHAPTER XLIV.

THE WHITE-HAIRED STRANGER.

It was some few days after the events recorded in the last chapter that two men of villanous mien might have been seen advancing along a road in a very retired part of the country.

They wore the aspect—or, at all events, bore the costume—of pedlars, and yet looked better calculated to lighten others of loads than to carry them themselves.

They were Dick the Fumbler and the indefatigable Phineas Bristowe, upon whom impunity had brought the usual curse of recklessness.

They had left the house of the Dark Firs with the conviction that they had carried out the views of the Colonel and Mrs. Treherne, and that, at an appointed time, they should receive their full reward.

They had made an appointment with her in a certain place in London, where they could be more easily concealed than anywhere in the country.

There were quarters in London and Liverpool where the appearance of two such men would excite neither notice nor comment, while, to the more unsophisticated countryman, they everywhere looked suspicious.

They were sulky with one another; but they knew not why. Perhaps they were dissatisfied with themselves.

Nothing makes a man more thoroughly detest his neighbours than when he has done that which should make him utterly disgusted with himself.

It is just retribution.

"I don't like this 'ere kind of work," said Dick, in a surly tone, "a constantly cutting about and never nothing done."

"What do you mean?"

"I means what I says," replied Dick, still more surlily.

"And that is?"

"I gets nothing."

"Have you not as much to eat and drink as you please?" asked Phineas Bristowe, assuming a dictorial tone.

"Yes."

"Money in your pocket?"

"Yes."

"Well then?—what then?"

"I tell you what, master, that aint the thing. Anybody, who aint a fool, can get enough to eat and drink and have a few shillings in his pocket. But what I wants is to feel the shiners in handfuls, to clutch 'em—to eat gold, if I like—to drink for a month, with a pretty girl on both sides of me! Ha! ha! ha!"

"You are luxurious," smiled Phineas Bristowe. "In a few days—"

"Yes, it's always a coming; but the day never comes. I'm tired."

"As soon as we arrive in London," said Phineas, "we shall receive the reward for which we have long aimed."

"And you trusts that 'ere queer-looking 'oman?" said Dick.

"I do because I have secrets of hers which would hang her."

"Whew!" said Dick, with a long whistle. "That's the game, is it? You're a artful card, I sees. But look here? Here's a public. I'm dooced thirsty."

"You always are," groaned Phineas, who, however, made no objection to so reasonable a proposition.

The house was one of those rural and sequestered places much frequented by carters and tramps.

A bench under each window—there was one on the side of each door—invited repose.

On the bench farthest from them was a man resting himself, whilst consuming the contents of an earthen jug. He was travel-stained.

He was old. His long white hair hung upon his shoulders. He looked calm and venerable.

A quick, sharp eye alone betrayed his attention to any outward object.

He glanced once at the travellers as they approached, and only once. He then dipped his nose in his jug, and became abstracted.

Dick went in and fetched a pot of beer.

Phineas began to open the small pack he carried on his shoulders, and which contained nothing more valuable than provender for the wayside.

But the provender was good. There was a cold fowl, some nice slices of exquisite ham, neat little loaves of white bread, and other delicacies calculated to tempt the appetite and incite to drink.

"Better fare this than in Newgate," said Phineas, with a grin.

"What makes you think of that?" replied Dick with a start, and a cautious glance at the stranger, who sat utterly immovable.

"I was thinking of our juvenile friend, Count Paolo de Florac," said Phineas, tearing off a wing.

"Ha! ha! ha! a very good joke," said Dick, stuffing in a mouthful of savoury ham; "I never thought of him."

"But he's thought of you," remarked the white-haired stranger very drily.

"Oh!"

"Ah!"

This from Phineas Bristowe and Dick the fumbler with an energy so ludicrous as to make the stranger smile.

He arose and advanced towards them, unmindful of the cautious way in which they clutched their thick cudgels.

"You spoke of my friend Paolo," he said, with a benevolent smile.

"Your friend Paolo?" replied Phineas Bristowe interrogatively.

"He calls him his friend," said Dick in feigned admiration.

"He is my friend, and I hope you are disposed to be his, or else—" and the stranger smiled very significantly.

"What," said Phineas Bristowe, not without some little inward trepidation, "what if we were not?"

"Yes, what?" added Dick the fumbler, blurtingly.

"Well," said the stranger, stroking his chin caressingly as he looked up towards the sky, "well, if you didn't—"

"What then, man?" cried Phineas impatiently.

"Yes, what, then?"

"I'm to act according."

"Sit down, sir," said Phineas, in a more bland tone, "and then let us understand one another."

"Not here," replied the venerable stranger; "patrols are apt to pass—there's a large reward for your apprehension."

They shuddered.

"Fill a can and come into yonder wood. We can talk safely."

Dick had a large can always ready in case of emergencies. He filled it with strong ale, and the two made the best of their way to a stile, leading by a path through the fields to a small wood.

They had scarcely entered the field when they heard the steady trot of a horse.

Peering through a hedge, they saw an officer riding at a tolerably fast pace towards the alehouse.

Phineas and Dick shivered with terror at their narrow escape.

They now rapidly made tracks for the wood, which was on the side of a somewhat steep eminence.

Ere they saw any more of the patrol they were securely concealed in a small and comfortable clearing.

All sat down on the grass, and wiped the heavy drops of perspiration off their brows.

"Whew!" said the venerable stranger, with a heavy asthmatic agitation of his chest, "the devil."

"A close shave," said Phineas.

"A buster!" remarked Dick the Fumbler, emphatically.

Again they heard the trot of the patrol, and saw the summit of his hat moving along the road.

He cast wary glances to the right and the left.

The three men watched his movements with intense interest.

He seemed undecided what to do, but at last rode off as if he was persuaded that no suspicious circumstances had presented themselves.

The three men still, however, held their tongues. They were afraid the breeze should carry their voices on the wings of the wind.

The venerable stranger pointed to the great can of beer in the safe custody of Dick.

Dick nodded, and produced a pint pot, which he had probably abstracted in some moment of thoughtlessness.

They drank in silence.

No sound was now heard save the murmuring of the wind in the tree tops, and the twittering of birds in the hedge rows.

"Now then, ancient party," observed Dick, "I should like to know who and what you are?"

"Well, my kiddy," said the other, with a smile, "my name is Zosh Bloke."

"Thunder!" cried Dick, with an oath; "that's a lie!"

"Thank you for your politeness," observed the other in the most unmoved manner, at the same time lifting off his venerable wig, and showing a short, stubly stock of red hair, entangled—to use a vulgar expression—like a dog in a fit.

"By gum," said Dick, with a grin, "but you did it fine—splendacious."

"Then, our Richard, I never do it otherwise. There's never an officer in London I couldn't hoodwink, I can tell you."

"So you seem, friend," said Phineas Bristowe; "but that does not explain to this child the reason and cause of our meeting in this singular manner."

"Old friend," said Dick.

"Well, sir, it's easy explained. I'm known to all the faculty in London. I pass as a distressed father, or a widowed mother, or a 'torney's clerk—just as the case may be. Now, this here lad as is took sends for me as his blessed parient, and werry affecting our meeting was."

"I should like to have seen it—uncommon," said Dick.

ESCAPE OF BRISTOWE.

"I shouldn't," observed Phineas Bristowe, drily.

"Well, it was a sight, especially for a father," continued Zosh Bloke.

"What then?"

"Well, our mutual friend, Paolo, no ways likes the lodgings provided for him; so, you see, he means to get out."

"How?"

"That he leaves to you."

"To me?"

"Exactly."

"But how can I do it?' cried Phineas, in an exasperated tone; "I know nothing of the interior of Newgate."

"You will," he says, "if you don't get him out."

"Will I?—how so?"

"He'll betray you as sure as fate," added Zosh.

"How can he?" savagely asked the enraged Mormon.

"He'll publish a full confession — tell all your little games about Mormonism—reveal every fact of your history—give forth all your numerous aliases—and, in fact, publish a true and particular biography of so and so, *alias* so and so, *alias* so and so—with a full, true, and particular account of his past and future life, which will not be long, as Tyburn—"

"Stop, you infernal monster," cried Phineas, in an exasperated tone. "What can I do to help him?"

"There thou saidst?" said Zosh. "On that subject I am authorised to confer with you seriously."

"Go on sa," said Dick the Fumbler, rubbing his hand.

"Well, speak out and explain yourself," said Phineas.

"With pleasure," said Zosh Bloke.

"Proceed."

"The soul of business is money. Now, I am willing and agreeable to assist Master Paolo in an escape from Newgate, but, as you must be well aware, such an attempt is not to be carried out without a deal of personal risk. Now, I have a great regard for my worthy friend Paolo; but, as a natural result of that faculty implanted in us by nature, I have a very serious preference for my own particular carcass, as the lawyers say in their writs, confound 'em—de *hàré yer karkass.*"

"Of course! of course!" said Phineas, with an impatient wave of the hand.

"Now, I am willing to allow that for a consideration," he continued, "I am always ready to serve my fellow creatures. So the wish of Paolo is, that you should advance the necessary money to induce me—"

"Induce the devil! I've no money," said Phineas, angrily.

"In the case of a refusal his instructions are that I should" (here the stranger played with the butt end of a pistol) "give you both in custody."

There was a pause. They looked at one another.

"How much does he value his cursed carcass at?" said Phineas.

"At five hundred pounds which is my regular price," said Zosh.

"Five hundred furies! I wont give a farthing," said Phineas, furiously.

"Then," said Zosh, rising, "you not only run your neck in a halter, but you lose the certain share in a splendid operation."

"What is that?"

"Well, a *certain party,* who betrayed *certain parties,* has come into possession of *certain property,* which the said *certain party* was to divide with the other certain parties."

"The deuce!"

"The viscount told me to say as how she had started on the splendid—jewellery, pearls, diamonds—and if you would just help to get him out he would go smash in revenge and glory."

"Done," said Phineas, "you shall have the money. But how—"

"Don't ask, that is my business. My word is my bond, vich Mr. Richard here knows. So, business settled, let us be jogging."

———

CHAPTER XLV.

AN AWKWARD PREDICAMENT.

"Hush!" said Dick, in a low tone, "I sees 'em. There's a dozen on 'em."

"Who?—where?—what?"

Dick pointed to where three mounted constabulary were halting at a gate, while half a dozen rustics, armed with pitchforks and poles, were opening for them.

"Follow," said Zosh, bounding like a panther into a thicket.

The side of the hill where they had been sitting might have been about fifty feet in height. At its base was a very dense mass of willows, through the centre of which ran a small stream.

The head of the stream was a pond, so overshadowed by trees that it could scarcely be ever day in that locality.

They crept through the willows, and, shivering with terror, stooped low under the trees.

A loud shout proclaimed, in a few minutes, that the place they had selected as a camp had been discovered.

They had left arms and baggage behind them, especially the beer.

Then they came dashing, madmen like, through the bushes.

Zosh Bloke crept on his hands and knees under the dark and lowering trees.

They were at the head of the pool. A heavy bush, being accidentally pushed aside, showed what appeared to be the mouth of a sewer.

Zosh thrust his head in.

"All right," he said, and began crawling upward.

The others followed.

It was evidently a kind of sewer to carry off the surplus water from some lake or pond on the top of the hill.

It was now hot weather, and there was no water.

It was close, mephitic and now that they were all in it, horribly dark.

There was scarcely room for a man's body to pass.

They could not crawl upon their hands and knees but like serpents.

Should it grow narrower? There was not the slightest hope of their being able to go backward.

They shivered with horror.

Zosh Bloke, who went first, moved very slowly.

Phineas Bristowe began to puff and blow at every movement he made.

He was between the two, and they intercepted the air.

They were afraid to speak lest they might be heard.

Dull sounds from behind informed them that their pursuers had not given up the search.

Should the pursuers discover the sewer they were lost.

Suddenly Zosh Bloke lay down with a groan. This allowed a slight current of air to pass to Phineas, who aroused himself enough to venture on a whisper.

"What's the matter?" he said, in a tone of awful agony.

"I'm fainting!" said Zosh Bloke; "curses light on Paolo!"

"For mercy's sake," whispered Phineas, "don't you faint!"

"Taint likely. As if I cared about you!"

gasped the wretch. "But to die here like a badger in a hole—"

"Try again," said Phineas, in a hollow and terrified tone.

"What the h—ll's the matter?" said an awful voice behind them.

It was Dick, who had heard and comprehended the controversy.

No answer was given him, as at this very moment an odd sort of gurgling sound was heard close above.

They both listened attentively.

It was Zosh Bloke swallowing the contents of a small flask.

"What are you doing now?" said Phineas, with a shudder.

"Poisoning myself. Always carry it about with me—never be taken alive, nor die by starvation."

"Poison!" was re-echoed by two awfully alarmed voices.

"Heavens!" cried Phineas, "what poison?"

"Brandy!" chuckled the other, once more slowly advancing.

Phineas gave a sigh of relief.

In a few minutes more Zosh again halted suddenly.

Again Phineas addressed him in fearfully alarmed tones.

"Hush! Do as I do, as you value your life," he said; "there are dangerous people near."

Then Zosh advanced a little farther, and a sudden burst of light upon the head of Phineas Bristowe announced that he had crawled out of that horrible upward sewer which might have been their tomb.

Then Phineas Bristowe peered forth. Horror of horrors!—

He was in Haddington Park; and he, of all others, had not recollected this ancient water-way, by which the surplus water of the fish-pond was carried away in wet weather and in the winter season.

But this was little matter in presence of another danger.

On the other side of the pond was collected a party, who had sought the shade of the trees to guard against the sun, which was hotly shining on this summer day.

The party—he knew them all at a single glance—consisted of Jessie, Henry, Cornelia, the Dwarf, Mary, and Lady Haddington.

They were seated on rustic seats, reading and conversing.

Phineas groaned inwardly; and one thought of what he might have been, but for his crimes, passed over his seared and hardened conscience.

There was not one in that group whom he had not injured.

An energetic grunt from below warned him to proceed.

He crawled out like an adder from his hole; and, following in the muddy track of Zosh Bloke, disappeared behind some trees.

The two fugitives were now together, and were soon rejoined by Dick.

They were all hideous to see, as they once more stood in the light of the glaring sun.

They were about to make a detour through the park when they were startled by the simultaneous rising of the whole party on the other side of the fish-pond.

At the same moment the constabulary, followed by the rustics, burst upon their view from several points.

Henry hurried to meet them and ask their business.

He struck his forehead with his hand when it was explained.

The three saw, from his passionate gestures, that he knew at once who the police were in pursuit of.

Zosh Bloke, a man fertile in resources, led the way.

They cautiously and slowly descended that very hill which they had ascended under such horrible circumstances.

Zosh Bloke had his idea.

His companions, who saw his determination, followed him without any observation or hesitation.

They were soon at the bottom of the hill.

At the edge of the wood, near a field of stubble, a carter stood whistling as he held three horses.

Dick the Fumbler actually grinned with delight.

He saw the plan in an instant, as did Phineas.

Zosh flew like a tiger at the man's throat, who, however, had time to shout out "Thieves!"

"Murder!"

"Take that, you foolish churl," said Phineas Bristowe, knocking him down with his huge clerical fist.

Then the three men mounted, nothing daunted by the cries and threats from above.

The officers had now seen them.

Their imprecations were fearful, as they saw the three ruffians galloping away on their own horses.

The fugitives paid no attention whatever to the others.

They galloped away furiously for dear life, with very little regard to what those behind them thought of their proceedings.

The fellow (Zosh Bloke) was himself a criminal of the deepest dye, though his person was not well known to the police; but his association with the two well-known ruffians would cause inquiry.

Out! out! upon the high-road they turn, and gallop furiously on towards London—the refuge of the desperate, the poor, and the struggling men of genius.

CHAPTER XLVI.

A GREAT DECISION.

WHILE these merciless villains are galloping on the highway, ready at any moment to commit crimes even of greater atrocity than any they have hitherto perpetrated, we return to pleasanter scenes.

The shock given to all in the park of Haddington, by the startling arrival of the ruffians in that peaceful and secluded spot, was awfully fearful.

All returned to the house; and armed servants were sent forth in all directions to take the disturbers of their peace, dead or alive.

Then the whole party remained in the mansion.

This system of persecution could not long be endured; something must be done to obviate it. All were of this opinion.

Some said one thing—some said another. At last Henry claimed silence.

"Something must be done," he said, in grave and earnest tones; "but I only see one decisive and positive remedy."

"What is that?" said Cornelia, with eagerness.

The dwarf watched him eagerly and gravely.

"The remedy I propose is, perhaps, a selfish one," he continued. "It may sound so, but I say it not in selfishness."

"What is it?" said the dwarf, gently. "Speak out, my boy."

"She is guarded like the treasure that she is, but she is not guarded enough, nor at all times."

A half-smile passed over the lips of all save Jessie, who blushed rosy red to the very roots of her hair.

Something in the eyes of Henry had told her all.

"Do not smile, or I shall lose courage. You all know how dearly I love Jessie. Give her to me as a wife. Give me the right to guard her night and day, and I defy them all: they shall not snatch her from me, not while there is a breath of life in this body!"

The dwarf and Cornelia exchanged glances.

Mary drew Jessie gently away towards an open window.

"Do not hesitate!" cried Henry. "Something tells me she is on the brink of a greater danger than ever befell her before. Let her be my wife, and not one hour will I be away from her side until her enemies are no longer able to persecute her. They are many, and they are utterly unscrupulous."

"The boy is right," said the dwarf; "and then, he is a man of knowledge," he added, with a smile.

"He is my own brave boy," replied Cornelia, "and deserves his wife."

"Nobody asks the old woman what she says," observed Lady Haddington, gravely.

"Because," cried Henry, embracing, "I know my mother will refuse me nothing."

"You are right, my dear son," she said, warmly.

"But what say you to this my own dear, darling Jessie?"

Blushing, her eyes downcast, above all not daring to meet the passionate gaze of Henry, Jessie came back leaning heavily on the arm of Mary, now her companion, with the consent of the mother, who had been removed to a beautiful cottage in the neighbourhood.

Jessie stood there, beauty incarnate.

A halo of love seemed to encircle her lovely form.

"What says Jessie?" said the dwarf, with his softest and sweetest tone of voice, a voice that ever thrilled through her with a strange sensation of delight.

"What says Jessie?" repeated the sadder tones of Cornelia.

She was her mother, and to part from a child is always grievous.

Happy if the dear child thinks, in after times, of—

"Pictures of the happy home, the sisters kind and free
That laughed, and played, and knelt with her around a mother's knee;
Her father, with his faltering voice, upon her bridal day,
When trustingly, though mournfully, he gave his child away.
All these, and tenfold more than these, upon her soul rushed back,
Keeping her madly-tortured heart impaled on memory's rack;
And when, at last, like those of old, her eyelids slept for sorrow,
'Twas but to wake, and feel renewed, such hopeless pangs to-morrow."

But Jessie had no such doubts. But still, with that native modesty which is woman's greatest charm, she stood trembling and irresolute.

"Have you any doubt or fear?" said Henry, taking her hand.

She raised her lovely eyes, and looked full in his face.

There was a glance of undying confidence, which he alone of all understood, and he alone could understand.

"I don't know," she said, in a tone so low it sounded like music afar off; "I don't know what to say. I am so young, so inexperienced, that I would gladly let others—"

"Do you love him?" said the Dwarf and Cornelia in one breath.

"*Mother!*" with such an accent, she replied, looking at her almost reproachfully, at all events sadly.

"I know you do, darling," she said, with tears in her eyes.

"But she has not answered the question," said the dwarf, in a very grave and anxious tone. "Young ladies do not always know their own minds, and if afterwards——"

"*Father!*"

This burst from her so suddenly, so wildly, that though she would if she could have checked the words it was too late.

Cornelia looked wildly round at all present.

Lady Haddington smiled.

The dwarf stood like a statue, unable to move or speak.

"And did your own heart," he said, in tones of deep and fervent rapture, "tell you this. Surely you, Henry——"

Henry smiled, and slowly shook his head.

"I always knew it," cried Jessie, passionately, "from the first moment that——"

She stopped, blushed, and trembled, she could say no more.

"Go on," said the dwarf, catching her to his breast.

"Ever since," stammered poor Jessie, blushing still more, "the day when I first saw you and dear mother together."

"Mysterious law of nature," said the dwarf, reverently. "it is impossible to deny thy great and marvellous powers!"

"But, father, it was this—I saw how much mother loved you."

Here Cornelia began to blush herself.

"Yes, I am your father. Dearly beloved and darling girl, it may never be your fate to know the reason for my mysterious secrecy. But it must be so no longer. You can only be married to the world as the only daughter and heiress of Leopold Treherne, the heir of Treherne Hall, and Cornelia his wife!"

"Treherne!" said Jessie, quite bewildered.

"Yes, child. Behold in me the younger brother of that man who was once the husband of Mrs. Treherne, the sister of Henry's grandfather!"

"Then Henry is my cousin!" she faltered forth.

"Yes, and let me take a cousin's privilege," said Henry, advancing.

"No," interposed Leopold Treherne, "not until she has fully and freely consented to be your wife.'

"Must I?" faltered Jessie, whose waist was already encircled by the arm of her dear cousin and future husband. "Then, if I must, father, mother dear, I must."

And half laughing, half crying, she fell, nothing loth, into Henry's arms.

And this was the formal betrothal of Henry Marmaduke Haddington and Jessie Cornelia Treherne, the real heiress of that noble house.

Then the elder ladies retired for awhile, taking Jessie and Mary with them.

"And now," said the dwarf—as, during many a day, we must continue to call him—"we must have some serious conversation, Henry. I must already claim a father's right to advise and control."

"Always, sir, until that real father shall come to share your power," cried Henry, warmly and impetuously.

"Your marriage must be public. To save you from much persecution and misery I have withheld from you the most important secret of your life."

"Sir!"

"You know the bitter enmity which Mrs. Treherne bears towards you," continued the dwarf, making him sit down on a chair beside his ottoman.

"I do, sir."

"She knows you to be the heir, but believes that you have not the proof," he continued, sadly.

"But I am—"

"You are. I have in my possession the certificate of your mother's marriage and of your own baptism, continued the dwarf. "To yourself I can swear.'

"Merciful Heaven, I thank you!" cried Henry, passionately.

"Now these proofs must be openly produced before your marriage. This will bring a host of hornets round you," he added; "be, therefore, doubly careful."

"I will."

"For reasons unnecessary to explain now you will have against you Mrs. Treherne, the Colonel, and Phineas Bristowe, if not others. All, therefore, I have to say is — be watchful and careful. Go nowhere at night or in the dark. Once married, you shall go abroad with such a retinue as shall defend you against all enemies. Besides, your marriage shall be so public that few who are interested in injuring you will dare to come forward afterwards."

"Public," said Henry, almost sadly. He almost thought a public marriage a desecration of the beauty of Jessie.

"It must be so before the whole world," replied the dwarf.

"How long will it take?" said Henry, rather mournfully.

"An age for a young love," replied the dwarf, "a month."

"A month! Why, surely that is too long?" continued Henry.

"I have the settlements, invitations—everything to do. The very milliner, the dressmaker, will cry fie you for thinking of it under. My dear boy, when once you are married you will learn, I hope, to enjoy her society, so be reasonable now."

Henry was very much inclined to curse lawyers, milliners, dress-makers, tailors, and the whole tribe that follows in a wedding train, but he felt his conscience prick him.

They had given him the priceless treasure. Was it not unkind and ungenerous to complain, and thus show ingratitude?

"Heaven bless you for what you have done, my dear father!" he said.

"But that I have a daughter such as Jessie I would say, 'I wish I had such a son.'"

And hand in hand they went out of the room to dress for dinner.

To say that Henry was supremely happy was to say little. He was in Heaven.

Jessie wished to be alone to cry, but Mary would not leave her.

When they met at dinner they were both most elegantly dressed.

Henry had never shown such a painstaking toilette.

They ate their dinner in comparative silence. The hearts of all were too full for speech.

They had forgotten all about the remorseless fugitives.

CHAPTER XLVII.

THE WEDDING DAY.

NOTHING was now thought of but the wedding.

Lawyers, dressmakers, *modistes*, began to arrive at the hall. In consideration of their enemies, and of their implacable persecution, it was arranged that etiquette should be partly departed from, and that Jessie and Henry should reside in the same house.

We are not quite sure whether this was or not a wise arrangement. Familiarity is, above all things, against the fervency of love. The more fact of being deprived of each other's society is an incentive to the desire to be united.

But so long and sincere had been the affection of Henry and Jessie that they complained not that continual familiarity bred contempt.

They were never happy except in each other's society.

Alas! how long will this virgin purity of love continue?

They were careful not to venture out of sight of Haddington House, under any circumstances.

It was no drawback to their genuine happiness that Mary nearly always was with them to play propriety.

In Jessie's case it was rather an advantage, as, when they were entirely alone, the ardent young husband was always making tiresome allusions to a certain night which Jessie professed herself anxious to forget.

Mary was already sufficiently versed in the science of love to be able to understand that the lovers desired to be alone.

She always kept, then, a *leetle* behind, under some excuse or other.

Meanwhile preparations were going on for the wedding with the utmost rapidity.

The minister who was engaged to marry them was a clergyman high in the church.

The bridesmaids were the *élite* of the rank and beauty of the neighbourhood, all a little older than Jessie.

Perhaps there might have been a slight heartburn about this. But, then, Jessie was such a dear girl.

What did Henry and Jessie care about the lawyers?

What cared they about settlements, seeing that both of them were minors—infants in the eyes of law?

It was a glorious satisfaction to be able to say good bye to musty parchment, and to run out to the lawn to wander, like Adam and Eve, in the first innocent, happy days of Paradise.

And the day approached.

The day came.

It was a glorious September morning, a bright sky above and summer green beneath, when, at early dawn, the preparations began.

All the tenants, labourers, and humble neighbours had been invited to lunch, dance, and supper in a vast back lawn, usually used as a bowling green and cricket ground.

Tables were laid out under, a wide awning impervious to wet, and so stretched out to poles as to afford complete shelter in case of a shower.

But the sun shone gloriously above as if in honour of the bridal.

As the marriage was to be by special license the great banquetting room was fitted up as a kind of chapel, and here, about one, the guests had began to collect.

The ladies who were to surround Jessie on what is familiarly called the trying occasion, including her mother, Lady Haddington, and the ladies' maids, collected in the magnificent drawing-room.

The happy Henry, with his friends, was to enter from the adjacent library.

The real chapel, which was close to the great banquetting hall, was too small for the ceremony, so many would have been excluded from the gay and festive scene.

Jessie, though pale and trembling, was lovely in the extreme.

She was exquisitely dressed, under the superintendence of her mother and a *posse* of milliners.

A Frenchwoman pronounced her to be *magnifique, superbe.*

The bridesmaids looked on her with perfect awe. The idea of a young thing like that being a wife.

It was really something quite wonderful.

They all sagely remarked that it was "ower young;" just a month or two, and she would have been as old as they.

That was a very plain way of saying a thing, was it not? I really do not know if you understand.

All went down at length, save Jessie and her mother, who, naturally enough, wished to have a moment alone with her daughter.

Jessie fell upon her knees and asked a blessing.

Cornelia gave it to her darling with all her soul, her eyes wet with tears of mingled joy and sorrow.

And a mother's blessing is always a good and pleasant thing.

"Come then, my dear," she said, and covering her eyes with her handkerchief, she led the way down stairs.

As she began descending the great staircase leading to the hall Cornelia thoroughly recovered herself.

"Give me your hand," she said, "it is the last time we shall have been like two girls together."

No answer.

Cornelia turned sharp round.

No Jessie!

"Jessie," she cried, "where are you? The hour has arrived when you must prepare for your great trial."

No answer.

"Jessie!"

Then in a slightly startled tone, as she returned on her way toward the bedroom, expecting to find her weeping.

But neither on the staircase, nor in the bedroom could the slightest sign of the young bride be discovered.

Cornelia gave a wild cry and fainted.

It was an awful wail of anguish that rang through the whole house—startling its echoes, and striking the hearers with awe.

First among those who bounded up the stairs were Henry and the Dwarf.

Their agonised faces sufficiently showed they were prepared for anything.

At the sight of Cornelia insensible on the ground the Dwarf became frantic with alarm. His first thought was for his adored wife.

In a few minutes she was aroused, and was able to give a clear and short account of what had happened.

Those who were in the secret at once knew the meaning of what had taken place.

None had entered the room but the Dwarf, Henry, and Lady Haddington.

The rest had kept back from politeness.

The Dwarf whispered a few words to Henry and he at once went out.

His face was pale with terror and anxiety.

He directed a servant to fetch Doctor Graham.

In an instant a gloomy rumour ran through the house. Everybody looked uneasy and alarmed.

The doctor came and was admitted into the apartment.

Then the Dwarf and he held a conference for a few minutes.

Then the doctor went forth, and with a grave face announced that there would be no wedding that day. The excitement—fit—so sudden—very serious affair—better to-morrow—hoped so at all event.

And so cleverly was it done that nobody thought of asking who was ill. The doctor, of course, referred to Mrs. Leopold Treherne, or Cornelia, as we call her.

The disappointed crowd thought it was Jessie.

The guests were compelled to take breakfast, however, while the humbler people were requested to eat as if nothing extraordinary had happened.

What was intended for the evening was given them to take home with them to use as they pleased.

By three o'clock there were none in the house but those who were in the secret of the truth.

A special message had been despatched to Bow-street for every officer who could be spared at any cost.

Then inquiries began among the confidential domestics.

But on such a day of bustle, and anxiety, with so many carriages and strange servants about, it was impossible to take any very particular notice.

Still, some one recollected that a carriage, with the windows down, drove off from the servant's door about the time of the unexpected explosion.

This was a clue. The council retired to consult.

CHAPTER XLVIII.

A STRANGE LETTER.

THERE were three hypotheses to go on.

First, it might be an attack from the three ruffians to whose persecution they owed so much suffering.

Secondly, it might emanate from Mrs. Treherne

Then the dwarf paused for a reply.

'There is another, and more dangerous enemy to be apprehended,'" said Henry, in a low and mournful tone.

"Good Heavens, what?' cried the dwarf, wildly, "what new and dreadful complication do you insinuate?"

"The wild and ungovernable passion of Lord Lionel Thynne."

The three stood aghast. Horror kept them speechless.

Henry then related, in as few words as possible, without compromising himself or Jessie any way, the designs of Lord Lionel Thynne against his future wife.

He said he believed that he had married in a moment of impulse and irritation against Jessie.

While yet his hearers were unable to say a word a servant announced that a stranger wished to say one word in private to Henry.

With one bound he was in the hall, and beside a booted and spurred messenger, who bowed low.

"Mr. Henry Haddington," said the man, respectfully.

"The same."

"This letter, sir, is for you. No answer."

Henry tore it open with frantic eagerness.

"*Allow an old friend to congratulate you on approaching happiness. My heart is still scared and scorched. The Bear of D——, weary of his hastily married baby-wife, is furious at the news—and vows awful vengeance. This is from a friend. If you say one word to Jessie's mother she will know who I am. The word is Lotty the Little. But, as you wish for happiness, say only that I have appeared mysteriously to warn you with regard to Lord Lionel Thynne. I will tell all in due time, when perhaps the world may know the wrongs of Lotty the Little.*"

Henry mused deeply as he went up stairs, and at last came to the conclusion that the only way to avoid awkward explanations was to show the letter itself.

Its injunctions for secrecy, then, would be at once acceded to.

He entered the library, where they were all collected, and found them waiting anxiously.

"I fear that I have been right in my supposition," he said, in his low, soft tones.

"How so?"

"I have received too late—a warning. It is anonymous, but none the less to be respected," he said.

"Who is it from?" asked the dwarf eagerly, holding out his hand for the letter which Henry held.

But Henry did not offer to give it to him as he expected.

"Mrs. Treherne," he said, "this letter says if I say two words to you you will know the writer directly."

"And what are those two words?" said the sorrowing mother.

"Lotty the Little."

"Heaven!" gasped Cornelia.

"My beloved wife," cried the dwarf.

"Lotty the Little."

"I don't recollect."

"Give me the letter," said Cornelia, wildly and passionately.

Henry gave it to her to read, which she did with a devouring curiosity which was shown in every lineament of her face.

"My God! my God!" she said, "what mysteries do environ me. I know who it is.

But, until I know more of her connection with Lord Lionel Thynne, I will not say."

"It is no evil one," said Henry, very gravely, "I am sure."

"Still there is a mystery, and I like not mystery. But now for Jessie. What think you?"

"I think that we should be guided in part by this communication," said the dwarf, "but I will still pursue the others myself to London. You, Henry, take an officer with you and follow the lead."

"I will," replied Henry, sternly, "and, should he prove to be the traitor, his life shall pay the forfeit."

"Leave him to the law," said the dwarf; "all you have to do is to prove the abduction. We shall then have him wholly in our power."

"But he may again—"

"No. Hitherto, for Jessie's sake, I have been merciful. But I will have no more mercy. I will strike a blow that shall startle all who dare to attack my child. She shall herself go into court and narrate her wrongs."

"It is best," cried Cornelia.

Before such a decision what could Henry do but bow his head.

It was then determined to await the return of the officers who had been summoned from London.

The frantic state of our hero may be imagined. And this was to have been the first consummation of Love's young dream.

*   *   *   *

Meanwhile on, on for London are the hunted fugitives rushing.

They know at once that it would be madness further to attempt to keep on the patrol horses.

They were sure to be recognised ere they had gone a few miles.

All that they could hope for was that they might get out of sight of their pursuers by these means.

If this alone were secured, they would have done something.

The artful Zosh Bloke kept ahead, peering carefully to the right and left.

Presently he saw that they were coming to a cross-road. He at once made up his mind.

"I know where we are," he said; "leave the horses here. I will take you across a country where no patrol can follow us."

Neither Phineas nor Bristow were at all disposed to dispute the advice of their experienced companion.

They dismounted at once, and, backing the horses, allowed them to go their own way, which was naturally enough to the nearest patrol, where their presence excited the greatest consternation and alarm.

Everybody at once thought that the three officers had been murdered.

The whole patrol was in a fearful uproar at once.

Nobody knew what to do or what to advise.

Presently, however, one mounted a fresh horse and rode back upon the road to ascertain the fate of his companions.

He soon met them running along accompanied by a mob.

As soon as they heard what had happened, an officer, who had been one of the three, gave his orders.

"Ride back; give directions to scour the country in every direction. They are for London. Pass the word from every station. Be sure their game is London. But, as sure as my name is Darby, no London policemen shall capture them three wagerbones."

He was a very clever man was Mr. Darby, but he did not know what a customer he had to deal with in the person of Zosh Bloke.

He thoroughly comprehended the plan upon which the officers would hit. They would guard every highway and byeway to London. Therefore he would not go to London at all in the way the constabulary expected.

Zosh Bloke knew that they were near a small seaport, whence fishing smacks sailed to London.

On board one of these boats Zosh Bloke determined that they should take their passage as poor men.

And so they did, glad beyond measure to exchange their hunted life for the rough deck of the oyster smack.

In this way they arrived, after a long journey, safely in London—the refuge of the hunted bandit.

They went straight to the somewhat mysteriously situated house of Zosh Bloke, where that worthy entertained them in a luxurious style that rejoiced the hearts of the two sensual men.

But, then, he knew well they could afford to pay for it.

A long conference now took place as to their future proceedings, Zosh Bloke being chosen the arbitrator.

Phineas Bristowe sighed for the flesh pots of Egypt, and no less for the blue, grey, dark eyes of his Mormon harem.

What were all of them doing in his absence?

This was not a very comfortable reflection to the elder.

He determined therefore, on reflection, to return to America.

After some trouble, Zosh Bloke being away, Phineas succeeded in making a disciple of Dick the fumbler.

Many a coarser and more impudent villain than the housebreaker has entered the confederacy.

This will be seen when we give a real picture of Mormon life.

Its untold horrors are boiling on the ear and tongue—longing to be uttered.

Before Zosh Bloke returned it was determined that, all business settled, they would go over to America, at all events until things blew over, and home became comfortable.

Zosh undertook to get them safe off, if paid.

As the price was set upon their heads, they could not but accept so liberal and considerate an offer.

Next morning Zosh Bloke went to see Paolo.

The same evening the Viscount de Florac was in the company of his old comrades.

How he escaped from Newgate he refused to tell. He was bound, he said, by an oath never to tell.

JESSIE IN NAUVOO.

Then Phineas Bristowe confirmed him in their intention of at once leaving the country for America.

"Not I—nor you," said Paolo, savagely striking his fist on the table, "until I have the dowry of my wife."

Phineas Bristowe shuddered at the ferocity of his glance.

"I have a few things to settle," said Phineas; "but you cannot get the dowry without the wife."

"I mean to have both." he said, with a hideous grin; "but out of these I shall find the way to punish her."

"She deserves it," said the Mormon elder sarcastically; "but I question if she will stand a plurality of wives.

"Stand!" said Paolo, savagely. "I'll teach her to betray me unto death."

And, after some preliminary arrangements, the three villains retired to mature their atrocious plans.

BOOK III.

NAUVOO.

CHAPTER I.

JOE SMITH.

EVEN the partisans of Joseph Smith allow that from 1820, the period of his first vision, up to 1823, Joseph suffered himself to be carried away by the world's current, and committed faults which his panegyrists attribute to the weakness of youth, and the corruptness of human nature.

He himself admits, in his autobiography, with something like compunction, that he yielded to temptation and to the gratification of divers appetites culpable in the sight of God.

However, he felt, he said, remorse for his conduct, and one night, the 21st of September, 1823, after he had retired to bed, he supplicated the Almighty to forgive him his sins, and to make known to him by some manifestation in what light he appeared to the Omniscient.

A "Personage" then appeared to him in the midst of light, brighter than mid-day, simply clad in a flowing robe of spotless whiteness.

The dazzling messenger, calling him by name, said he had been sent by God to him, and that his name was Nephi; that God had a work for him to accomplish; that his name (Joseph's) would be blessed and accursed through all the nations of the earth; he likewise told him that there was in existence a book, written on gold plates, which gave an account of the first inhabitants of the continent of America, and of their origin.

He added that it contained the fulness of the Gospel of Jesus Christ, as it was given to His people on this land.

He further said there that there also existed an instrument which consisted of two smooth three-cornered diamonds, set in glass, and the glasses were set in silver bows, which were connected with each other much in the same way as old fashioned spectacles; that these glasses, being attached to a breastplate, constituted what is called the Urim and Thummim, and would be found deposited with the plates; that the possession and use of these glasses constituted a Seer in primitive times, and that God prepared them for the translation of the Book.

He then quoted several prophecies from the Old Testament, and many passages from it and the New, and ended his discourse by warning Joseph that, whenever the time should come for his receiving the plates, the breastplate, and the Urim and Thummim, he was to show them to no one, save such as God might indicate, on pain of death.

Twice again did the same Personage appear that night, repeating exactly the same things; and, as he was on the point of departing, enjoined Joseph to be actuated, in his desire to obtain the plates, by no other motive than that of glorifying God; and also to be proof against the temptation of selling them in order to satisfy his own wants. The cock crew, and day broke.

Joseph rose without having had time to sleep. He went to his work with his parents, when the same Personage he had seen during the night appeared to him a fourth time, repeating the same things, and enjoining him to communicate all to his father. Joseph obeyed; and his father told him that it was all from God, and that he must go and do as the Heavenly Messenger had commanded him. Joseph at once left his work, and went to the place where the messenger had told him that the plates were deposited.

Near the village of Manchester, in Ontario County (State of New York), is an eminence higher than any other in its neighbourhood, and known to the Mormons by the name of Cumorah. On the western side of this hill, a little below the summit, under a stone of considerable dimensions, the plates were found deposited in a stone box.

The lid was thinned off towards the edges, and raised in the centre in a kind of globe, which rose above the surface of the soil. Joseph, after removing the earth which covered the edges, raised the stone with a crowbar, and found the tablets, the Urim and Thummim, and the breast-plate.

The box was formed of stone, held together at the corners by a kind of cement.

Two stones were placed cross-ways at the bottom of the box, and upon these stones were the plates and other relics. Joseph attempted to take them out, but was prevented by the Heavenly Messenger, who again told him that the time had not yet arrived, and that he must wait four years from that time. The divine envoy added that Joseph must present himself at the place of deposit in a year from that day, and that he must keep the same rendezvous every year until the time had arrived for him to take away the plates.

Joseph obeyed the commands of the Angel, and every year met him at the appointed spot to receive his instructions as to what the Lord wished done, as well as revelations as to the manner in which His kingdom must be governed in the latter days.

The 22nd of September, 1827, the heavenly messenger delivered to Joseph Smith the plates, the Urim and Thummim, and the breast-plate;

ou condition that he would be responsible for them, and that he would preserve them carefully until such time as he should be again asked for them.

The Urim and Thummim consists, states Joseph Smith's mother, who had seen them, of two transparent stones, clear as crystal, set in the two rims of a bow. By this instrument Joseph was enabled to understand the characters on the tablets, to see to any distance, and to obtain revelations upon every kind of subject he desired.

The plates had the appearance of gold. They were about seven inches wide by eight long, and their thickness was not quite that of an ordinary sheet of tin. Egyptian characters were engraved on both sides of each plate, and the whole was bound in one volume, like the leaves of a book, closed by three clasps; its thickness was six inches. One portion of the plates was sealed up. On those which were not sealed there were small characters of letters, skilfully cut.

"The whole book," says Joseph Smith, "by its shape, denoted the antiquity of its origin, and displayed some ability on the part of the engraver."

The breast-plate or pectoral was of pure gold, according to the statement of Joseph's mother, who had seen and touched it. It had four golden straps, of which two were intended to attach it to the shoulders, and the other two to fix it on the hips. These straps were exactly the breadth of two female fingers, and they were pierced with several holes at the ends, by which to fasten them. "This article was worth five hundred dollars at least," adds the Prophet's aged mother.

But this is not the place to tell the history of Mormonism; we wish rather to describe it in its every phase—to tell of how it works.*

Let it suffice that, by lying, imposture, false revelations and threats, Joe Smith succeeded in getting his Bible printed and circulated.

He began to preach, and his sheer impudence gave him disciples.

At last he collected a host of people around him, some who believed and some who did not believe—some dupes, some tools and willing satellites.

It is to one of his scattered colonies that we must now direct the reader's kind attention.

On the borders of one of the many fertilising streams of one of the richest districts of America was a newly built village. It would rather be described correctly as a hamlet of scattered houses.

Joe Smith lived in a small white log hut on the top of a hill, whence he commanded a view of all around.

It was a beautiful land, and, could the Mormons have been satisfied with practising there a merely spurious and absurd form of Christianity, none would have interfered with them or their prophet.

It was their own monstrosities brought all upon them.

In the depths of the valley, near a mill

stream, is a pretty little stream, with a neat cottage by its side: a nice garden runs from the front to the very edge of the river. It is a pattern of comfort and cleanliness perfectly Dutch.

It is the dwelling of a sincere Mormon couple, believers in the Divine interpretation.

They had not yet had the fearful atrocities of the system unveiled to them in full.

And yet the prophet had given hints of polygamy.

But, as yet, he has only thrown out gentle suggestions.

It is a seed cast into the ground to ripen more fully.

The prophet is not yet civil and military dictator.

The miller, a young man of ardent fancies and weak head, has joined the Mormons solely for the sake of conscience.

He bid his young wife believe the doctrine of Joe.

They loved one another too much to take notice of the specious arguments in favour of polygamy.

It mattered not to them if the idea were right or wrong. They felt quite sure they would not practise it.

Strong, especially so the wife, in her own strength of mind, and equally confident in the love of her husband.

Yesterday—but, alas! not to-day.

Eliza Wilmot stands at the entrance of her cottage with an infant babe in her arms—her eyes half dimmed with tears.

She is receiving into her gentle breast the first arrow of sorrow.

Where she stands she can see two figures though they cannot see her.

One is a young girl, neatly clad, of elegant form. reading.

The other is her husband, leaning across a hedge and watching the beautiful girl with anxious and even ardent eyes.

Eliza Wilmot is realising the probability of her husband loving another.

She has felt the first bitter sting of Mormonism.

But still the girl read on, and of her Eliza Wilmot has no fear. She has no fear because the girl has told her her story.

She believed her before, but thought her prejudiced against the Mormon chiefs and their doctrines.

But she believes all now—yes, every word, and she has made up her mind.

Nothing sharpens the female faculties like jealousy—and how can polygamy exist without jealousy?

In the Turkish harem, where a beautiful and lovely girl obtains the caress of her master once in a lifetime, fearful tragedies are the result of the system. How, then, can it be believed that, among the votaries of a sect professing to be Christian beyond all other sects, and asserting its claims in the name of natural law, of the written law of the Bible, and recruited from a class of women peculiarly strong in feeling on this tender point, the foul blot can exist without fearful results?

* The above is a favourable account, derived principally from Mormon sources.

This girl, who loved her husband and whose husband loved her, already felt the blight of the hideous scourge upon her. She was one of the first victims of the doctrine of polygamy.

Promiscuousness of sexual relations, or community of women, has existed, though rarely, among several people, as the Tropobanians of Ceylon. It still exists, in a certain degree, among a few savage tribes. According to natural law philosophers argue that it is not unlawful.

Polyandria—or a system of many husbands—has existed among several nations; and Cosca informs us that in Britain the father and sons, whatever their number, had often but one wife among them.

Even at this day we know that polyandria is practised by a tribe in the Himalayas, as is also the case among several savage tribes in the Pacific.

Polygamy, which is an immense step beyond community of women and polyandry, toward the true ends of society, has existed from the earliest historical periods amid several nations, some of them possessed of a certain degree of education, as a state of things lawful, natural, and sanctioned by religion. It is to this day still lawfully practised throughout a great part of the world. But it must be borne in mind that it everywhere seems restricted to a limited number of rich people.

Must we, with certain jurisconsults, admit that polygamy is not contrary to nature, and come to the same conclusion on this point with St. Augustine himself? Perhaps not; but we must first come to an understanding about the word nature, and distinguish between the social and the animal nature of man. If man be nothing but an animal, superior to other animals only by his instincts and passions, well and good; all he has then to do is to give himself up entirely to the laws of his animal nature; to live after the fashion of brutes; to couple at random, or according to his convenience; and to abandon his little ones, the fruit of these promiscuous relations, to the care of their mother, or to nature. But if man, as we believe and maintain, is, according to the fine definition of a celebrated philosopher, an intelligence served by organs; a soul in a body; if his intelligence be everything, and his body a mere instrument, a purely material envelope, then is his nature other than that of animals—it is that of intelligent beings, and it is in this noble nature we must go and search for the laws which are to govern him, and not in that which he has in common with the dog, the bull, the ram, the cock, the crocodile, or the fish.

The husband heard the step of his wife, and hurriedly concealed himself. He could be heard the next minute chopping away as if nothing had happened.

Still the young woman advanced.

Her face was very pale; tears stood in her eyes; her lips were compressed and set.

The girl sat totally unconscious, gazing at the softly flowing river.

The young mother sat down beside her.

"Girl," she said, in a low whisper, "you must go from among us."

"Why?" she replied, almost mechanically, without moving.

"Because my husband loves you, and, under the new light, can make you his wife."

The girl started.

She had heard of the custom, but she, at all events, believed that the marriage was facultative on the part of the women.

"He cannot force me?"

"I am terribly afraid he will," replied Eliza, mournfully.

"Never," said the girl, firmly. "I will die the death first!"

She raised her head.

It was our own dear Jessie, the Mormon's daughter, now in the very haunts of the nefarious and vile imposture.

But how she came there—her strange and wild adventures—must now be told.

CHAPTER II.

A BRIDAL TOUR.

THE honeymoon, even where a couple are no exceedingly attached, and where love has had no very great share in the matrimonial contract, is generally one of the pleasantest times of our lives.

Casting off all care and thought for to-morrow, we are content to enjoy the present. Away from all worry and business, the very earth we tread on is brighter than of yore, the sky more sunshiny and glorious, the air more lambient than usual.

But, when marriage is the offspring of true and mutual love, the honeymoon is a paradise of bliss and joy.

Not so with Lord Lionel Thynne and his weak but fair young bride.

Lady Thynne was one of those soft yielding natures which, if they cannot inspire our respect, at all events rouse within a manly breast every feeling of pity and love.

She adored, she worshipped her husband, and it was this very adoration and worship that made her unhappiness.

Her husband scorned her for her very love.

His was not a nature to be satisfied with so easy a conquest. He despised her for the very fault which he in his wicked designs against Jessie had led her into.

Still he was not insulting, did not descend to reproaches, neither said nor looked anything painful: he was what, to a true-loving woman's heart is worse—indifferent.

He yawned over the breakfast table; he read article after article in the morning paper; he sauntered down to a game of billiards while she was dressing, and perhaps only came back when luncheon was announced.

Lady Thynne remained with her maid, scarcely ever giving herself the trouble to dress, because well aware that she would dress in vain.

After lunch Lord Lionel, more because his wife was pretty and well-dressed—of course she was richly dight, but she had good taste, which

is rarer than wealth—than from any other
motive, took her for a walk or a drive.

Ladies, be always pretty and well-dressed. It
is astonishing how attentive it will make the
generality of husbands.

Then they dined, and little Lady Lionel, as in
duty bound, went through the ceremony of
leaving him alone to take his wine. He generally contrived to have in a male companion to
assist him.

She then saw no more of him until he came
to bed.

It was, indeed, a very ominous beginning of
married life.

It promised little for a calm, happy, and pleasant
future.

They had reached a fashionable watering-
place, where, the hotel being good, the company
excellent, the wine ditto, and the billiard-table
first-rate, he announced his intention of abiding for some time.

His worthy little wife saw that he was
pleased, and so endeavoured to be satisfied herself.

But his only amusement was a solitary afternoon's drive.

I suppose she thought this was a way men had
got.

She certainly thought it a very inconvenient
and unpleasant way for them to have. But she
complained not.

Two days passed pleasantly enough. Lord
Lionel Thynne was unusually gracious and
smiling.

We suppose that he had been winning at
billiards.

Her ladyship cared not so that he smiled.

He took her out for several drives. On the
morning of the third day, however, there was a
change in the atmosphere.

They were at breakfast. She was reading a
letter from her mother. He was absorbed in
the study of his morning paper. He read it
with the listless air of a man who reads simply
because he has nothing else to do.

Because, in fact, he has no better companion
than his wife.

There are a great many people like Lord
Lionel Thynne. But then why, in Heaven's
name, do they encumber themselves with a
wife?

"Shall I give you another cup of tea,
Lionel?" she said.

"Thank you, yes. The coffee is not good.
D——!" he added, raising his voice in an acme
of terror and rage.

"Lionel!"

"I beg your pardon," he said, between his
set teeth, "it was a sudden pang—and then—and
then—a favourite horse of mine, which is backed
to win a thousand, is taken off. I must start for
London directly."

"Directly?" she said, faintly. "Why, I shall
be an hour—"

"You will remain here, Adela. My business
is with jockeys and horse dealers. I must travel
post haste. I shall be back to-morrow."

And rising with one more hasty apology, he
hurried out.

Poor Lady Lionel sat petrified with astonish-

ment. All this flurry, hurry, and excitement
about a horse was strange.

She took up the paper to see the horse's
name just as the rattling coach and four
horses passed the window.

She paused at the column which her husband
had been reading.

Then she read as follows:—

"We have great pleasure in announcing the
immediate marriage of Henry Marmaduke
Haddington, Esq., heir to the title and estates of
Sir Marmaduke Haddington, with Miss Jessie
Treherne, only daughter of Lionel Treherne, Esq."

A deadly sickness came over the whole frame
of Lady Lionel Thynne. A fearful suspicion,
which at times in the dead hours of the night,
in the weary watches of the day had filled her
soul, became confirmed.

When Lord Lionel woke, in the night before
their marriage, and found her in his arms he
had looked astonished.

He, she was quite sure, had expected to find
some one else.

She saw it all now, and guessed even the
whole of the nefarious plot by which Jessie was
to have been his victim.

And yet Lady Thynne was loth to believe it
of the man who had sworn to love and cherish
her for her whole life.

But how could she doubt it now?

Why had he hurried away?

To prevent, if possible, the coming marriage
of Henry and Jessie.

What could she do?

To write to them was to betray her lord
and master, and this, however deeply she might
be wronged, she never would have condescended.
She would much rather have died

What, then, was the true course for a deserted wife?

To bide her time and wait.

Still she would write to her husband, and
gently hint something, which would show him
that her suspicions were aroused.

With a pale and tottering step she walked to
a side-table, and began writing a letter.

She duly sealed it and directed it to him at his
club.

Then she ordered the carriage, and, in the
society of her lady's-maid, drove about the
whole day, the observed of all observers—the
admiration of young and old.

Meanwhile Lord Lionel Thynne, his soul
animated by every bad passion that afflicts
humanity, was hurrying off to town on the
wings of the wind. He drove like a madman—
paying unheard of prices to the astonished post-
boys.

In three days Jessie—whom he still passionately loved—whom he adored with fierce passion
and desire—was to be married to another, and
that other Henry.

This was equally galling to his pride and
passion.

He adored her, and he hated him with fierce
intensity.

What he should do, what means he should
adopt, how he should compass his evil desire,
he knew not; but that he would prevent the
marriage he had made up his mind.

Hate and lust—which is not love—will drive man to more evil than any two other feelings known to the human breast.

And it was in this mood Lord Lionel reached London.

CHAPTER III.

THE LONDON REPORTER.

THE whole country rang with the news of the coming wedding. That two such lovable and lovely beings should become husband and wife seemed so natural that all applauded.

It did seem strange to some that they should wed so young, for, of course, the true reason was a mystery to all; but as they were rich, and in possession of every want in life, there were not the same reasons for waiting that existed with others.

Where two young people are suited to each other, in Heaven's name let them marry young—ere the world has cooled their souls, or sin found an abiding place.

The danger, and it is a great one, of early marriages is, that two persons of utterly different characters should come together—a young man with an old woman, or something equally incongruous.

And let everybody recollect, that let fortune smile or frown as she will, it is on marriage the happiness of your life depends.

For good or for ill it seals your worldly fate for life.

The whole country rang with the preparations.

There was talk of it on the roadside; and, Heaven knows, every village tap-room rang with the news.

The "Red Stag," kept by Bully Betts, was no exception to the rule.

On the night but one before the wedding this was particularly the case. There had been nothing else all day.

The huge and ponderous landlord, who was known by the popular—if not euphonious—name of Bully Betts, set the example, and he stood with his back to the fire.

The tap-room was a kind of kitchen, of rather large dimensions, with here and there a coarse deal table.

From habit the regular customers congregated about the empty fireplace, the wide mouth of which the landlord almost concealed with his capacious person.

Poachers, farm labourers, even servants from the hall; a very mixed crew, indeed, filled up the room.

A country cross-road stage, about seven in the evening, deposited a dapper individual at the door.

His costume was peculiar. He wore shabby black, brushed very much, but, withal, very clean. His linen, though worn, was scrupulously correct. His gloves, though rusty, had no holes in them, while his boots exhibited signs of considerable acquaintance with the cobbler.

On his nose was an ancient pair of spectacles.

His hat had a jaunty, devil-may-care look about it, entirely caused by the way it was worn upon the side of his head.

In his hand was a small bag.

With this he entered the village ale-house and sat down, ordering supper and a pint of Cooper.

There was a dead silence in the room; any one, with half an eye, could see that the new arrival was a Londoner—and country folks have an instinctive dislike of a Londoner.

Why?

Really there is no explanation possible, except that he is cleverer, more knowing, better informed than themselves. It's a pity to say so, but it's true.

The stranger laid down his bag, and, taking an easy and *nonchalant* position, began drinking his beer, which had been brought while supper was preparing.

"Is it far to Haddington Hall?" he said, in a general way.

"No;" said Bully Betts.

"I'm glad of that," resumed the stranger, with a smile.

"Why?"

"Because I've to walk over in the morning," continued the other.

"What for?"

"To give an account of the interesting event for the morning papers," said the other, with a look of importance.

Everybody exchanged glances. They had all heard of the far-famed reporter for the morning papers, but they had never seen one before.

Even Bully Betts allowed his rigid countenance to relax into a smile.

"Oh," he said, "but it don't take place to-morrow."

"I know that; but I wish to see the grounds and house a day before hand," said the special reporter. "I understand it is a very fine old place."

There was a chorus of voices at once chanting its praises.

There was not such another place in the kingdom. It was worthy of the place and of the people who lived there.

"Bless my soul!" said the reporter," "why it's a wonder."

It was a wonder, of course. The seven wonders of the world were nothing to it in the imaginations of these rustics.

"I must go over to-morrow. Can I have a bed now, and a trap in the morning?" said the reporter, quite cheerfully.

"Of course," replied the landlord; "you can have anything here."

"Then," cried the facetious London gentleman, "I'll take a roast nightingale for supper—sharp!"

The audience laughed heartily at the exquisite sharpness of the Londoner. Cries of "Had him there" were bandied about.

"No, he hadn't," said Bully Betts, savagely. "I meant anything in reason. Now roast nightingale for supper ain't reason. Young man, don't go for to crack jokes with me. I'm hot. They calls me Bully Betts."

"Do they? and a devilish good name for you. I should think," said the other, coolly. "My name's Felix Mortimer; but I've licked better men than you."

And he took the attitude of a fighting man in such a way as to assure all present that he knew what he was talking about.

Bully Betts foamed with rage. He did not like being bearded in his own den. And then people did think so that his fight was all bounce. He trusted to his size.

"Have you?" he said, doggedly. "Well, if you're civil you won't fight with me."

"I'll tell you what I'll do," said Felix Mortimer, Esq., winking at the company; "I'll lick you, kiss your wife, and sleep with the chamber-maid for a rump-steak and dozen."

The rough audience roared at this coarse challenge.

The landlord looked at him with an awful expression of countenance.

"You're a rum 'un," he said, relaxing into a grin, "that you are. But let's have no quarrelling. What say you, sir, let's be a gallon of ale and say no more about it?"

"No," said the reporter; "I'll be what you like all round—and the very best. Hooray! my paper pays."

The cheering which followed was tremendous, and, from that moment, any opposition to the Londoner was out of the question.

It was early the next morning when, after a hearty country-inn breakfast, where, if French rolls and good coffee are wanting, you have delicious butter, eggs, milk, and tea, the stranger leaped into a gig and drove towards Haddington Hall.

He had appointed to meet one of the inferior servants, at another little beer-shop, who would guide him.

The man was to his time, and gave him full directions how to view the park and grounds unobserved.

The reporter thanked him, paid him handsomely, and allowed him to go away. The services of every servant were in request on this important and festive occasion.

The reporter was invited very civilly to join the festivities in the kitchen the next day, which invitation he accepted with a grin.

But whose fault is it that representatives of the press are too often reduced to this inferior hospitality?

Their own.

The beer-shop where he put up his horse and gig was close to the park palings, and Mr. Felix Mortimer entered the park by a small bath-way with ut any difficulty.

_____

CHAPTER IV.

THE SERPENT AND THE GIRL.

MR. FELIX MORTIMER was very pale. Perhaps this style of approaching a house was new to him, perhaps it was derogatory to his feelings—very probably. Mr. Felix Mortimer, after all,

did not look like one of those scavengers of the press who pick up information down the kitchen steps as area sneaks do bottles and brooms.

He looked a higher-class man—one who, at all events, was admitted to the hall, or a lower table.

But then there is always something unpleasant in approaching any man's house in a secret, underhand, and paltry manner. Even the amourous gallant, in search of female beauty, feels ashamed, especially when coming away.

Felix looked about him as if man-traps and spring-guns were spread over the whole surface of the park.

But the path through a kind of wood was clear and well defined.

Presently he could see the house—at all events, one end of it—an end almost without windows.

He paused, and looked curiously at the ancient pile.

He could see the stables, the out-houses, the dairy, and many other of the offices. Not a soul, however, appeared stirring.

He sat himself down upon a bank screened by some bushes.

As he did so he heard a light step at no great distance.

They say that Satan always gives us opportunities. He is always providing the wicked with the means of carrying out their wickedness. So says the moralist.

Say, rather, that the wicked man turns everything to his purpose.

Felix Mortimer pressed towards the spot whence the sound came.

He saw a very dainty lass tripping along with mincing step, and a ludicrous attempt at fine ladyism.

Believing herself wholly unobserved, she was practising.

She was about nineteen, with jet black eyes, raven hair, a _nez retroussé_, and rather thick and sensual mouth—the very woman Felix Mortimer could have wished for.

She was slightly dressed, with a green silk parasol.

The simplest student of human character would have put her down as an under lady's-maid in the first glory of her elevation from a lower rank in the hierarchy of domesticity.

Felix Mortimer, with a strange gleam in his eyes, took off his spectacles and advanced to meet the young lady.

"Excuse me miss—young lady," he said, with a low and polished bow, "but I am very fortunate in meeting you."

"Sir, I really don't know you," she said, in a mincing tone, intended to imitate some of her fine lady acquaintances.

"I am under the painful necessity of adding that I am in the same unfortunate state of ignorance; but I am sure that, if yould listen to me, you would understand and appreciate my motive."

"I am in a great hurry, sir. There is much to be prepared for the wedding."

"Then I am fortunate enough," he said, "to fall upon one of those who will personally witness this interesting ceremony?"

"I shall be present," replied the girl, with a significant toss of the head.

That girl believed that, if she liked, she could have passed for Jessie.

"Indeed! Now, then, allow me to introduce myself to you as Mr. Felix Mortemar, representative of the whole daily press of London, sent down here to collect all the information for them regardless of expense."

"Indeed."

"Now, miss," said the energetic reporter, placing her hand in his, and allowing five remarkably bright sovereigns to fall in her hand, "I need scarcely say that, if you will aid me in my duties, I shall be eternally grateful."

He had not miscalculated her character.

Her eyes flashed, her cheeks flushed, and her whole mien showed extreme agitation.

"Sit you down, miss," said Mortemar, pulling out a pocket-book, "and I will explain myself more fully."

She sat down on the fragrant bank nothing loath. She was one of those to whom money was a great temptation.

It must ever be so to the poor.

He then told the same story as he had at the road-side inn.

"I will tell you all I can," said the girl.

"Thank you; but what I want is to see—"

"You must ask the steward."

"No. I don't mean to trust everybody. I want to have only one confidant, a discreet, pretty, amiable girl, who will, from her goodness of heart, aid me."

The girl simpered.

"Now enable me to enter the house unperceived, conceal me somewhere all night, and I will make the five pounds fifty."

The girl's bosom panted with excitement. Fifty pounds was a real fortune.

"Your papers are very rich," she gasped.

"They are. Don't you see there's a good many of 'em, and they don't stand about expense when a high family is concerned. It interests the whole country."

"Do it?" said the girl; "but I dare not assist you."

"Why?"

"There is no place where I could hide you," she faltered.

"Do you sleep alone?" he said, placing his arm round her waist, and freely pressing her towards him.

The resistance was very weak. Had he not forced money upon her, and, therefore, was he not, to a certain extent, allowed to take liberties?

"Of course I do—but—"

Here she blushed violently.

"Honour," said the reporter, gravely; "besides, for further safety, I shall come in the disguise of a woman."

The logical conclusion did not seem very clear to the girl.

Felix Mortemar pulled out his purse and shook the golden coin.

"Tin from my employers," he said, in an insinuating tone; "and now, if you will aid me in this important affair, you shall have this little watch as a keepsake from me."

"You will be a gentleman?" she whispered, with downcast eyes.

"Honour," he said, with, however, an audacious glance, which the girl, if she understood it, chose not to appear to do so.

"What time will you come?" she continued.

"What time will you have finished your duties?" he asked.

"Eleven," she said, rising.

"Eleven then be it. Where?"

"Here. I must meet you and guide you to the house."

And thus they parted. Another serpent sorely tempted another Eve.

The man put on his spectacles, rubbed his hands, and, as if desirous of keeping out of sight, hastily left the park.

He returned to the place where he had hired his trap.

At dusk of evening he left on foot.

About a hundred yards on the main road he met a post-chaise; there was an exchange of signals at once between the young man and the driver.

The post-chaise pulled up and Felix Mortemar, Esq., entered.

The post-chaise continued on its way.

It halted at last at a house on the other side of the park, and, when the gate was opened, a most respectable-looking lady in mourning alighted and entered the inn.

CHAPTER V.

THE COURT DRESSER.

THOUGH the new arrival was not very handsomely dressed there was an air of respectability about her—nay, even a commanding air, which imposed upon the landlord and landlady.

"Thank you kindly," she said, as she was ushered into a room. "I will just take a glass of ale and a biscuit, and then walk up to the hall."

"To the hall—walk?"

"Yes. I never venture to go to the door in a post-chaise, though I am dresser to the royal family. It looks assuming. I shall walk up to know what time they will want me to-morrow."

Court dresser. It was to their rustic minds an awful trade.

They were profuse in their attention.

"I thank you kindly. Now, good people, I shall start. If I'm not back by twelve they will have given me a bed, which is very likely, seeing I have so many to dress."

"Very likely," said the landlord, "they be werry hospitable."

"I'm glad to hear it. I shall pay for a bed whether I use it or not, and let my driver and the horse be well attended to. Have you money, Joe?"

"Yes, mum," said the driver, who was passing along the passage.

"If I don't come back pay my bill and your own, and come round in time to take me to H—— house. I cannot stop for the ceremony—so

THE HON. MR. STANLEY AND THE COUNTESS OF SIDONIA.

very busy. Such is life! Here a wedding, there a funeral."

And, with a melancholy wave of the hand, she walked forth from the house.

She stepped leisurely along until once more the park fence was reached; with a stride and a bound she was immediately out of sight.

The supposed woman now examined closely the priming of a pistol, which she placed again in her bosom.

Then she waited under a tree.

Exactly as the clock struck eleven a figure came tripping towards her.

"Where are you?" said a low voice.

"Here, my charmer," cried the other, advancing, catching her round the waist, and kissing her.

"Don't, you horrid old thing," said the girl.

"Ha! ha! ha!" said Phelix Mortemar; "you you really took me for a woman?"

"I did for a minute. But be careful, the Dwarf, I mean Mr. Lionel Treherne, will soon go his rounds, when we should be in a pretty pickle," she said.

"The Dwarf, eh?"

And the reporter's voice trembled.

"Yes; he examines every door and window every night. I verily believe he never sleeps. He's a walking about everlasting."

And all this while she was leading him towards the back of the house.

A staircase, once probably used for a variety of clandestine purposes, had been exclusively appropriated to those who slept in the garret—all female servants.

Of this the girl, whose name was Maria, preserved the key.

She opened it cautiously. The door led into a long gallery.

She listened with deep attention.

Not a sound could be heard.

"Hush!" he said, suddenly.

"Go up, right to the top. I will follow. Number 17," whispered the girl, giving him a key. "It is the Dwarf on his rounds."

He wanted no second telling, but glided up the stairs as light as a ghost.

Maria lingered behind; respectfully bade the Dwarf good night, and slowly ascended the stairs.

In certain minds avarice, the lust of gold, the worship of the slightest approach to wealth is such that it utterly obscures the mental vision.

This girl knew nothing of the man who had tempted her, nor could she have any proof of the reality of his purpose.

But he had given her gold.

She must have known, by the man's eye, how little sincere he was in his promise to herself. She knew that in his hands she was helpless, and that for gold not only was she about to betray her employers, but to sell her own honour.

And yet she hesitated not.

And this Maria was not wholly evil. She did only what hundreds of girls do every day from sheer ignorance and defective education.

In far too many parts of England chastity, among the lower orders, is regarded as a very minor virtue.

It is, alas! too true, and one scorching blot upon those who profess to be teachers.

Reading, writing, sewing, and every useful art, are taught before morals.

But these teachings will not make girls virtuous.

They are allowed too much liberty at the very age when they are least able to take care of themselves.

From thirteen to eighteen the supervision of parents should be incessant.

If after that they cannot take care of themselves, no parents can.

But, at the time we speak of, going out by themselves, indiscriminate intercourse with young people of either sex should be, as much as possible, discouraged.

It is not the parents who find out all that their children do. But others know that scarcely one girl survives this foolish and wicked carelessness.

The sham woman reached number 17 without being disturbed. She opened the door hurriedly and went in.

Her—we will use the word as long as the dress is retained—face was pale in the extreme, but evidently, by the expression, more from extreme agitation than terror.

Presently the key turned in the door, and Maria, looking somewhat confused, entered.

She quickly locked the door behind her.

She then removed a cloth from a table near the window, and disclosed a very nice supper, with bottles of ale and one of wine

"Why Maria, love, you're quite a darling," said the other, gallantly.

Maria blushed, and this time did not call him a horrid old woman when he embraced her.

*   *   *   *   *

Maria, who overslept herself in the morning, and whose eyes were slightly swollen with weeping, left the sham-woman alone in the bedroom.

She said she could find her way about in the bustle without being noticed.

In fact the crowd of visitors, servants, assistants, and attendants speedily became so great that anybody once within the building could circulate with perfect safety.

Felix Montague, as he called himself, had examined the house with the most intense care.

He perfectly recollected where the servants staircase formed a junction with the passage leading to the ladies' chambers. He soon saw, too, that everybody was busy in front of the house.

His proceedings were not, therefore, likely to be interrupted.

He crept down stairs with all the caution and stealth of a Thug.

He contrived by sauntering about, by pretending to be busy, to gain a room, where Jessie's trunks were being packed up.

Here, when an opportunity offered, he concealed himself.

Hours passed.

At last the door between that room and Jessie's bedroom was thrown open.

Then came the conversation between Jessie and her mother.

Cornelia, aware that she was behind time, hurriedly led the way.

Jessie turned to take one girlish look at the glass, and, as she did so, a frightful female figure appeared instead on the mirror.

Ere she could cry a handkerchief was passed across her face.

She was insensible.

The sham-woman snatched her up in her arms and hurried down the passage in a direction opposite to that followed by Cornelia.

The servants' staircase was utterly deserted.

She gained, without interruption, the copse where he had met Maria at.

A postchaise awaited her.

He thrust her in, and the post-chaise proceeded at a leisurely pace until the postillions came to a cross-road. Then away they darted at all the speed they could command.

About twenty miles further on they met a private carriage.

The post-horses were discharged.

The private carriage made the best of its way towards London, where only a girl of Jessie's remarkable appearance could, by any possibility, be concealed.

And then, in all probability. it would be the last place they would look for him.

They entered London at night, and drove to a house which, to all appearance, was shut up.

It was the private mansion of the profligate young man who, though called Felix Mortemar in these chapters, has been, doubtless, recognised as Lord Lionel Thynne.

Having effectually secured his prey in safe hands he started at a rapid rate for the watering place where his wife was.

He found her cold, indifferent, and utterly incredulous.

She would not believe that he had been detained all this time on mere sporting business.

CHAPTER VI.

THE TEMPTER.

MEANWHILE the ill-used and much persecuted Jessie had come to her senses.

She found herself in a large and rather well-furnished room.

It was a bed-room, furnished somewhat in the style of France. The bed was in an alcove, concealed by curtains.

The rest of the room might have been a drawing-room.

Everything was old-fashioned, but good. But the windows were barred with iron, while, worse than all, they looked out only on dead walls.

There could, then, be no hope of assistance from that quarter.

Now many girls in Jessie's predicament would certainly have given way utterly to despair under the circumstances; but Jessie had already been so often tried in the furnace of affliction that she was not so downcast as would have been expected.

She had a bold, firm, and courageous heart, and she dreaded nothing from any one save by the exercise of some foul and horrid treachery.

Jessie was a woman.

She now understood thoroughly the nature of the sacrifice that was asked of her; and, like a true woman, she determined to die rather than submit to the foulest indignity that could be put upon one of her sex—that of submitting to the caresses of a man she hated.

We scorn and despise those who sell their bodies to the highest or first bidder in the public streets.

Truly it is the acme of human degradation and the culminating point of vice and iniquity.

But how much better is the woman who sells herself for life to a man whom she does not love for mere position or money.

The union of the sexes is only excusable where real love exists.

Under any other circumstances it is, beyond description, gross and repugnant to nature.

The whole love that was in the heart of Jessie was lavished upon Henry.

She had not the faintest, the most remote corner in her heart for anyone else.

We do not allude to the natural affection which she experienced for her relatives.

Jessie sat herself calmly down to examine the situation.

Of course she knew in whose power she was. A kind of instinct had told her all along what she had to expect from Lord Lionel Thynne.

A fierce and burning passion like his could not be very easily concealed.

Jessie had read to the depths of his very soul.

But hers was a nature which rose with her dangers and misfortunes.

She had sat some time in deep thought when a key grated in the door, and two women entered.

One was stout; had been handsome; but was so disguised by dress and ribbons that it was rather difficult to fix upon her precise age. It was clear that she painted, which accounted, probably, for the fact that she never blushed.

This was the celebrated Madame Denise, of aristocratic notoriety.

This infamous woman, of a class, we hope, rapidly disappearing from the face of the earth—at all events in this country—had been patronised by the great of this earth.

Her senses were palled by crime.

She could not understand how any woman could resist rank and gold.

Every manifestation of dislike on the part of the young and beautiful she looked upon as mere hypocrisy and waste of time.

But then it was clever, and it made the yielding more delightful.

She was accompanied by a young woman—a kind of attendant.

"Well, my charming miss," said Madame Denise—the infamous wretch was a domiciled Frenchwoman—"and how do you like your apartments? I hope you are comfortable?"

"Comfortable!" cried Jessie, with an air of lofty scorn, to which Madame Denise was unaccustomed; "comfortable! when I know in what infamous hands I am."

"Infamous!" cried Madame Denise, with a somewhat hollow laugh.

"Yes, madame, infamous. Are you not the wicked agent of a wicked man?"

"You have been brought here by a friend who wishes to make you happy."

"Happy," said Jessie, looking her keenly in the face; "by a friend! Madame, Lord Lionel Thynne, a married man, took me, as you may see, from almost the foot of the altar to bring me here. But think not I fear him. I have friends; and the sole heiress of a noble house, with a fortune of twenty-thousand a-year, is not to be secluded and inquiry stifled, as may be the case with some of his wretched victims."

Madame Denise and the girl exchanged strange glances.

"In the first place," said the woman, "I know no such person as Lord Lionel Thynne."

"You cannot expect me to believe you."

"In the next, I have been assured that you sought to leave your husband, who had just taken you to the altar."

Jessie smiled scornfully.

"Then I know that you are a poor girl, raised by charity to an elevated position."

"Woman, think what you please. I warn you. Let me once escape from here—and no feeling of mock shame shall restrain me—I will appear in any court in the land to have you punished."

"I came here," said the other, coldly, "to let you know that this is your servant. She will take your orders. In this room you remain until the gentleman returns."

And much nettled, and a little alarmed, the procuress went out.

"What will you take?" said the attendant—a young, ugly, and surly-looking woman.

"Breakfast," replied Jessie. "I do not mean to be downcast. But, girl, I know not, and I care not, who you are. I know this, however, that you are equally criminal with your employers, and will be punished equally."

"I am a servant, and bound to obey my mistress," said the girl, sullenly.

"Obey in all things lawful," said Jessie; "but not where crime exists. Aid me to escape and you shall be amply rewarded."

The girl shook her head, and went out to prepare the young lady's breakfast.

And thus the day passed and night came, and with it the sound of revelry, which, up in that prison chamber, sounded a mockery indeed.

CHAPTER VII.

THE COUNTESS SIDONIA.

THE house in which Jessie was now incarcerated was at no very great distance from Hyde Park. We could be more particular in our description, even with regard to our infamous procuress, but the law of libel is very tender.

The dead walls at the back merely separated her from a mansion of aristocratic renown.

It was the residence of the Countess Sidonia.

The Countess Sidonia was a lady of prodigious wealth, who had suddenly appeared as a star of the first magnitude in the orbit of London society.

She had taken a splendid mansion, and had it furnished on a scale of unusual magnificence.

She had introductions to one or two noble families through the Spanish embassy.

Her wealth, beauty, and charms did the rest.

While waiting for the regular London season she had determined to inaugurate her arrival in London by a splendid *fête*.

It was nearly upon the close of Parliament, but there were enough of the *beau monde* in town to cause a great display.

Everybody was wild to see the Countess Sidonia, whose beauty and loveliness all had heard so much of.

Young as she was the countess, having a duenna in the shape of a Spanish marchioness, poor but proud as Lucifer, gave a dinner to a select party.

They were chiefly foreigners, though one or two old English diplomates figured amongst them.

Everything was done in a style which reminded them of the days of really good eating.

People really only eat now. They used to dine. But the art of dining went out with hair powder and good old port.

After dinner it was, however, that the crush began, and that everybody had an opportunity of gazing on the wondrous beauty of the lovely Countess Sidonia.

There she stood, beside a capacious arm chair, receiving her guests with a queenly grace which won every heart.

She was superbly beautiful, rich, and twenty.

It may be inquired how many hearts she took by storm that night?

One or two in particular.

As the fortunes of Jessie were wondrously affected by the events of this night we must, to a certain extent, be minute.

There were hundreds of persons in that brilliant assembly, crowding these superb saloons, whom the Countess Sidonia had never seen before, and would not recollect, in all probability, if she saw them again.

But there were one or two, more particularly introduced to her, she was not likely to forget.

The vast mansion in which the ball was given was peculiarly built.

The dining room, library, and domestic offices filled the ground floor.

The first floor had seven reception rooms, opening one into the other.

At the back of these were the private apartments of the Countess.

They consisted of a bed-room, sitting-room, and boudoir.

The bed-room was a superb specimen of the upholsterer's art.

The sitting room, opening on a balcony, and looking out on the park, was on one side; the boudoir, discreet, and looking out only on a court, was on the other.

The entrance to the sitting-room was from one of the saloons, but the key turned in the door marked that this was private.

Among the late presentations to the Countess Sidonia were two young men.

One was the Honourable Mr. Stanley, an *attaché* to an English embassy, a young gentleman who, from some considerable residence on the continent, had imbibed somewhat fantastic notions of women.

He was twenty seven, tall, handsome, with expressive black eyes, that no modest woman could stand the brunt of for a moment.

He actually started as he gazed on the countess with a sensation of pain.

How could he have lived so long and not known this splendid and voluptuous beauty.

A wild and sudden resolution swept across his soul.

The eyes of himself and the countess met, and, when he asked her to dance, she readily accepted.

The Honourable Mr. Stanley was a man of the world. He did not venture to alarm the resplendent beauty by coarse flattery, but with that delicate tact which intercourse with good society alone can give he succeeded in pleasing her.

She left him to receive some fresh arrivals, satisfied that he had made a favourable impression.

In general the Honourable Mr. Stanley would have been satisfied, and would have spent the rest of the evening in some agreeable and satisfactory manner.

But now he wandered about, lost in thought.

Though there was something warm and voluptuous in the manner of the Countess Sidonia he attributed it to her country.

She was, he understood, Spanish.

He was a younger son, with no prospects but his profession.

The Countess Sidonia was enormously rich. He had seen that the liking had been mutual.

A man like him was not likely to waste much time in reflection. He did not think long, but came to a determination which did more credit to his head than his heart.

He now became quite at his ease, and sauntered alone with the easy air of a man of fashion and a gentleman of large experience.

CHAPTER VIII.

THE RUSSIAN PRINCE.

AMONG the new arrivals was a young Russian. He wore the superb uniform of his regiment, having that day, he said, been presented to his majesty.

He was a good looking man, with, however, such a profusion of red beard, whiskers, and moustache, as to render him, in the eyes of most of the ladies, a perfect fright.

Women like a martial appearance, but not a mere sticking out of a door mat.

He bowed low to the countess, and, addressing a few words of French, passed on to allow others to be presented.

He seemed struck by the magnificence of the apartments, gazed admiringly at everything, and not least at the host of pretty women by whom he was constantly surrounded.

He was the only Russian present, that embassy being out of town.

It was soon known that he was a Russian prince, Ironbliski by name, and even the Countess Sidonia herself, surrounded as she was by so many noble names, felt some delight at the arrival of a real prince.

She had sent out so many blank invitations to "dear friends" that she had not the least idea she had invited him.

At all events she was very much obliged.

But the prince appeared himself not the most amiable or polite of individuals. He never spoke to anybody, but sauntered alone looking here, there, and everywhere.

His special attention was paid to the refreshment room. There he drank off two bottles of champagne.

But they did not make him a bit more sociable or amiable.

The ball continued. The Countess Sidonia could not resist the appealing glance of the Honourable Mr. Stanley, whose eye had truly something agreeable in it.

It was a waltz—of all dances to a woman the most entrancing, and not at all despised by men. Well may Byron say :—

"Endearing waltz! to thy more melting tune
Bow Irish jig and ancient rigadoon;
Scotch reels, avaunt! and country-dance, forego
Your future claims to each fantastic toe!
Waltz—waltz alone—both legs and arms demands;
Liberal of feet and lavish of her hands;
Hands which may freely range in public sight,
Where ne'er before—but pray 'put out the light,'
Methinks the glare of yonder chandelier
Shines much too far, or I am much too near;'
And time, though strange, waltz whispers this remark,
'My slipping steps are expert in the dark.'
But here the man with due decorum halts,
And leads his long end petticoat to waltz."

They looked the handsomest couple in the room, and, as he pressed her waist, there was an unmistakeable look of languor about her which inspired the *attaché* with most audacious hopes.

The Countess Sidonia was indeed a votary of Terpsichore, and would have thoroughly enjoyed the dance but for a slight accident.

As she started she caught the eye of the Russian prince fixed on her with a look of unmistakeable rage, jealousy, and an indescribable expression.

Still the countess was not a woman to make herself miserable about trifles.

She fancied, and her woman's heart beat with satisfaction as she thought so, that two men had really fallen in love with her on the same evening.

Was it not delightful?

The Countess Sidonia's first object in life was a princely marriage.

She was not a woman to value money for its own sake, or to devote her life to acts of charity and good works.

Her charity began at home.

Quiet, and calm, and beautiful as she looked, her bosom was a volcano of passions.

In the luxurious volupt of the dance she soon forgot the scowl of the Russian, and, the waltz over, she made a sign to the band.

They played "The Roast Beef of Old England."

The Honourable Mr. Stanley had pleaded for this, as he then secured the right to take her down to supper.

Here, on the first introduction to the lady, was a second distinction.

At least twenty young men envied him his good fortune, and, knowing her reputed wealth, began to see visions of Stanley becoming the head of a new house, having a country palace of his own, and founding a great name.

The demeanour of the countess, even at supper, was calculated to encourage the idea. The fact was, she had been carried by storm, and, when the honourable *attaché* squeezed her hand under the table, made no resistance.

He then, as they rose from table, whispered a few words.

"I shall always be happy," she replied, with a gracious bend.

Soon after the brilliant assemblage disappeared.

CHAPTER IX.

A SCENE.

It was three o'clock in the morning, and the Countess Sidonia was alone in her bedroom.

She had dismissed her maid.

She was but partially undressed.

She had burned to be alone that she might give way unchecked to the delicious sensation which was filling her soul.

The fervent attention of the handsome *attaché* had produced a correspondent effect upon her impulsive and passionate soul.

She loved.

Born of a southern clime, her veins were filled by a blood to which ours is cold.

It comes hotly through the veins like molten lead; it scorches the brain, and reduces every part of the frame to a state of dry fever.

Her eyes flashed with a brilliancy she could not but herself admire.

"That that man loves me," she said, looking at herself in the glass, and admiring, with a soft complacency that only made her all the more beautiful, her own lovely shoulders, eyes, and countenance, "I am sure; he is evidently a gentleman of rank and fortune. But, then, is he rich?"

She thought a moment.

"But what matter! If I thought he could love me for my own sake I would gladly resign my fortune to his hand."

A sigh.

"But how to tell? A man's heart is inscrutable. They are all selfish, insidious, and exacting —hateful in the extreme."

Her eye flashed.

"Have I not found them so? Have I not reason to curse the whole race?"

A deep, deep sigh.

"And yet what true woman can live without their love?" she continued.

A pause.

"Not I. But this will never do; three o'clock in the morning, and not to bed! Where will be my bright eyes to-morrow? Laying in bed in the morning will not give them to me."

She rose and began to undress.

It is not our wish to penetrate too far the mysteries of a lady's night toilette, though perhaps we might say as much about it as most people, but we will say that not Venus herself could have presented more attractions than she did in the course of her transfer from her rich silk dress to a more light and airy costume.

At length, after a slow and somewhat tedious process, she appeared ready for bed.

The soft rays of the night lamps shed their lustrous rays round the superbly-furnished chamber.

It was an abode of love and loveliness.

The presiding goddess crept into bed, and laid her head upon her pillow.

Too much accustomed to contract her thoughts to be very wakeful, she at once prepared for sleep, which is seldom denied to the selfish.

She laid her head on her pillow, heaved a heavy sigh, and in a moment would have been asleep.

But what is this?

She distinctly hears strange noises.

To the right the heavy breathing of a man, accompanied every now and then by something very like a snore.

To the left a whispered conversation.

The noise from the boudoir was regular and steady.

That from the sitting-room was low, hushed, and whispered.

What was to be done?

A cold, shivering sweat burst out from the quivering limbs of the lovely countess.

Was she surrounded by robbers?

In that case she stood a poor chance, as her servants lived on another floor.

Was she beset by lovers?

A balmy feeling of content came over her as this idea filled her mind.

She was not afraid of half-a-dozen, though, sooth to say, she would rather just then have had one.

Still there was no time to be lost.

She glided from the bed, slipped on a wrapper which lay at its side, and was about to approach the bell when she was stuck dumb and motionless.

"One moment, lady," said a deep, stern voice.

She raised her head.

It was the Russian prince. It was, indeed, a lover, but not the one she expected, certainly not the one she wished.

"One moment."

"Prince, this outrage!"

"Outrage," he said, in a voice that made her shiver to her very marrow bones, "what outrage can there be in a husband's presence in a wife's chamber?"

"Have mercy on me," gasped the countess.

She knew him now.

"So, Julie, you sold me to the police," said the Viscount de Florac, in furious, hissing tones, "and thought to deceive some other infatuated fool."

She covered her face with her hands—not in terror, but to think.

She could still hear the steady breathing in the boudoir.

"Will you speak?"

"Paolo," she said, raising her lovely and fascinating eye to his, "what would you have me say?"

"Answer me."

"But you have condemned me unheard."

"Was it not patent, clear as noon day?"

"No."

"Cockatrice, dare you deny that you betrayed me?"

"I deny nothing," she said, in a firm voice, "but ask you now what you seek."

"To spend this night in your arms—to-morrow we will consult further."

"Sir," she said, quickly, "you dare not—you are an outlaw. In the morning my servants will find you."

"What then?"

"My reputation."

"Am I not your husband?"

"Are you not an outlaw ?"

"Who made me so."

"Not I.'

"Who, then ?"

"Your own crimes."

"Beware that you tempt me not. Already for your foul betrayal has your fate been decided by those you so avenged."

"My fate !"

"Know you not the fate of traitors ?"

"Not being a traitor, I cannot guess."

"Shall I tell you ?"

"Yes."

"DEATH !"

The soft breathing ceased.

"Monster !" she said, in a loud voice, "I utterly contemn and despise you. Not content with the gross insult you have put upon me you now threaten. Help !"

"Now then."

Then came in sight Phineas Bristowe and fumbling Dick.

But at the same moment—not much to the embarrassment of the Countess Sidonia—appeared the Hon. Mr. Stanley.

"Vile wretch," said Paolo.

"What seek you here ?' cried the *attaché*, half awake.

The Countess Sidonia profited by the confusion to ring a violent peal on her bell.

"Help !—murder !—thieves !—fire !" she cried, in thrilling tones.

"We shall meet again !" said Paolo, pale with rage and terror.

Without another word he and his two accomplices turned and fled.

Stanley would have followed.

"Stay," said the Countess Sidonia, in tones half beseeching, half tender, "think of my reputation. Conceal yourself. My servants are coming.

The *attaché* hastily returned to the snug boudoir.

The Countess Sidonia hurried in the direction of her saloon, where she now met several half-dressed servants.

"Call the police," she said, quickly, "the burglars were concealed about. They have just fled my chamber. Quick !"

The servants stood horror-stricken and irresolute.

One, more bold than the others, ran down to the hall.

The front door was wide open, and two policemen were coming up the steps.

The valet told them what had happened, and the guardians of the night intimated their intention of instituting a search.

One remained at the door, to summon further assistance.

The other went up to the saloon of the Countess Sidonia.

"I am glad you have come," she said.

"Please my lady," said the honest guardian of the night, "will you be kind enough to tell me all you saw."

"I was retiring to rest, my good man," said the countess, very coolly, "when I heard a noise in my private room. I passed in and saw three men. Frightened, I at once rang my bell, and

cried murder. They fled, and that is all I know about it."

"Oh."

"I will now leave the house in your hands, satisfied that I am safe, and, as I am very fatigued, retire to rest."

"Shall I watch with your ladyship ?" said a favourite attendant.

"No."

This was said very drily indeed, and as she said so the countess bowed and re-entered her own sitting room.

CHAPTER X.
MR. STANLEY.

SHE was heard to lock the door.

The Honourable Mr. Stanley fell at her feet.

"Angelic woman," he said, "can you excuse my boldness—my indiscretion ?"

"Sir," replied the countess, "rise and explain your object in being here."

"To tell you I love you."

"You might have waited a more fitting opportunity."

"Madam, you are so lovely, so angelic, so surrounded by admiring friends, how could I have hoped, except by mere chance, to have approached your footstool ? I was so dazzled, so delighted, so enraptured, that I determined, even if I mortally offended you, to learn my fate to-night."

"You have saved me from the infamous enterprise of one who has been my persecutor long," began the Countess Sidonia.

"To whom do you allude ?"

"The Russian Prince. I had retired to rest," said the Countess Sidonia, with a charming blush, "and was just about to sleep when I heard the breathing of a man who slept—"

"I slept," cried Stanley.

"Yes, slept; and very soundly, too. Scarcely had I recovered from my terror and astonishment when I heard whispering in the next room. I rose to ring the bell when the Prince caught me by the hand."

And the Countess Sidonia blushed charmingly.

"You forgive me, then ?"

"I forgive you," she said, offering her hand, which he took, and did not resign, "for Heaven knows what my fate would have been but for your opportune awakening."

"I thank, then, my stars, charming countess, that my audacity went so far, and now —"

"We must think of your leaving."

"But the police—the servants ?"

"True ; what is to be done ?"

"Hear me."

"Hear what ?"

"Lady, I love you. I am of good family, but a younger son. I have, however, only five lives between myself and a noble peerage. Apart from the fact that I am not rich I am sure you would not ask one of nobler family or birth. Say, dear lady, that I am not wholly indifferent to you."

"You are not," said the Countess Sidonia,

looking at him with a tender and languishing eye.

"Bless you," he replied, keeping her hand in his, and slowly passing his arm round the voluptuous waist of the impulsive young woman.

"I am very rich. My late husband—"

"A widow?"

"Yes, but the widow of a man who was to me a father. He left me my property wholly at my own command. Mr. Stanley, I shall be frank with you. I think I shall like you, and I can only say that if on inquiry, if on further acquaintance I see no reason to change my views I shall, perhaps—"

"Angel!"

He had his arm quite round her waist now.

"And now, that you have wrung from me this much, retire, I pray you.

"Can you give me a sight of the gates of paradise," said the ardent lover, gazing at her lovely bosom, "and send me forth?"

He drew her to him gently.

"But, Mr. Stanley, you forget yourself. I am not—consider my people—leave me."

But the Honourable Mr. Stanley was an experienced man. He saw that both the pride, affections, and passions of the Countess Sidonia were enlisted in his favour.

He had conceived a sudden, wild, and real passion.

Her riches were well known.

He had determined to marry her, but he could not bring himself, now that he clasped her in his arms in her own bedchamber, to leave her.

And he did not leave her.

Next morning about twelve the Honourable Mr. Stanley—who really had never left the house—contrived, by a little manœuvring, to be introduced into the countess's breakfast room just as she sat down alone.

"I am at home to no one," she said, significantly to the female attendant.

And then the happy and enraptured lovers were once more alone.

CHAPTER XI.

A MEETING.

MEANWHILE what had become of the three fugitive burglars?

They had fled as if Satan himself had been behind them, cursing, as they did so, their evil fortune, one another, and everything in creation.

Paolo took the lead. He was lighter of foot than the others.

There was no need for words.

They had already a rendezvous arranged.

Paolo opened the street door, and, darting into the street, was soon lost to view.

Dick the fumbler was not quite so fortunate. He ran with tremendous force against a policeman, knocked him down, rolled over, nearly knocked his own eye out, and then, starting to his feet, set off again at a terrific pace, followed by the infuriated constable.

The door remained wide open, but no Phineas Bristowe made his appearance.

That worthy, in a mental state of trepidation, blundered up the principal staircase—luckily avoiding that by which the servants descended—and found himself in one of the upper rooms recently vacated by a servant.

He entered this quickly, and the instinct of self-preservation guiding his every faculty, he opened the window, and darted on to the roof.

He looked around him.

London by night, from the top of a lofty house, exhibits one of the strangest of all strange appearances. Distant towers, steeples, domes looming up in the darkness, houses of all heights, shapes, and sizes, chimney pots, dog vanes, dove cots, rabbit hutches, everything lumbering, old, and useless—clothes drying; here and there a lighted window, where affection in hired service watched over sickness—all may be seen.

But Phineas Bristowe regarded not this.

Safety was all he dreamed of.

He looked below.

A dark, well-like looking court separated him from a lower house, one of a row, that had their backs to the more princely mansion.

But to his right a slippery roof descended to the summit of the other house, which was surmounted by a lead.

To glide down this slope, at the risk of being precipitated below, was the work of a moment.

He was on the lead.

A kind of sentry box in one corner enclosed a stair head.

The door was open.

Phineas Bristowe, still in fear and trembling, descended with cautious steps and slow.

The top landing was dark.

But on the second a light streamed from under a doorway.

The key was in the door.

Phineas Bristowe slowly undid it.

He entered. A lamp burned upon a table, while on a chair, full dressed, slumbered a beautiful maiden.

Phineas almost uttered a cry.

It was Jessie!

Placing one hand upon her lips in a waining attitude, he shook her gently.

She started to her feet.

"You here?"

"Hark, girl, as you value our lives," said Phineas, in a tone of genuine alarm.

"But —— "

"Jessie, this is no time for explanation. Suffice that, escaping from a neighbouring house for my life, I entered here. Led by a light, I open a door, and find you. Can you tell me where we are?"

"In an infamous house."

"You are a prisoner?"

"I am."

"Will you venture anything for liberty?"

"All."

"Then follow me."

"Where?"

"Where you please."

"To my mother?"

ESCAPE OF PHINEAS BRISTOWE.

"Jessie, I am tired of this life. If your mother will forgive me we may be happy yet."

"But you are not my father," she said, with a cold firmness that startled him.

"Not your father," said the other, in tones of astonishment, "why?"

"That we cannot discuss now. Take me to my mother."

"I will, and she shall determine my future fate. I am your father, Jessie, and as such shall always treat you. Come."

Jessie followed. But what was this terrible secret? What did it mean that more than one person claimed to be her father?

It was the most acute mental lecture that could have been inflicted on a gentle, loving, and sensitive girl.

Clutching a poker, Phineas descended the carpeted stairs.

Every landing had its bright lamp.

They soon reached the hall, which was furnished in a style which bespoke the rank and wealth of the supporters of the house.

How is the social evil to be checked, even to

be preached against, while legislators and noble-men support such establishments?

The social evil is the worst, most damnable, most atrocious blot on civilisation; but let us not attack merely the poor outcasts and hungry votaries of pleasure, who, famished and ill, crowd our streets—living sepulcres—but strike at the root.

Large rewards for the exposure of the higher class of brothels might defy the systematic bribery by which such places are able to live.

The eye of justice and of law should not be blind to the excesses of the rich while so severe on the errors of the poor.

Let us begin at the beginning.

There were men who came to that house who, while they would not have given a hundred pence to save a poor girl in the streets from starving, would have given a thousand guineas to debauch a pure and innocent girl.

A porter slept in a cosy arm chair, ready to admit any friend.

"Undo the bolts," whispered Phineas.

Jessie began with trembling hands to undo the fastenings.

Phineas stood over the porter with his poker poised in mid-air.

Jessie drew two bolts, and was turning the rather ponderous key.

The porter awoke.

"What's your game?" he said, with a startled glance at the man.

"I will split your skull," replied the Mormon, to whom terror gave courage.

"Will you," said the other, rising.

The door opened. Phineas struck at the porter, who rang a bell furiously, while cursing the other, whose blow had caught him on the arm.

Jessie darted into the street, and Phineas quickly followed.

A hackney-coach was passing, into which they entered, and were quietly driven from the scene.

———

CHAPTER XII.

MEANWHILE Henry and the other friends of Jessie had not been idle.

The girl, who had been the victim of Lord Lionel Thynne, confessed all except his passing a night in her room.

The detectives confirmed the fact of a sham reporter having come down in the neighbour-hood.

Henry at once determined to follow in the track of Jessie, while the Dwarf, without indi-cating his movements, went also on her track.

It was easy to find the residence of the young married couple.

Henry knew hardly how to act.

He determined, therefore, to be guided by circumstances.

He took a rapid conveyance to London, and started on his way.

He had plenty of money, and was well provided with arms.

He determined to learn the fate of Jessie from Lord Lionel Thynne, even at the pistol's mouth.

He knew that Lord and Lady Lionel were at B——. at the —— Hotel.

Thither he made his way, and, arriving late at night, put up there.

As early as was consistent with common politeness he inquired if he could see my lord.

"He is breakfasting with my lady," said the attendant.

"Show me up," he replied, sternly.

The waiter took him up, and, knocking at the door, announced a gentleman to see Lord Lionel.

The young nobleman was fully prepared. He had seen Henry arrive on the previous night from the billiard-room.

"Ah. this is delightful," he said, "is it not, Lady Lionel? To what do we owe the pleasure of this unexpected visit?"

Lady Lionel smiled her welcome and listened.

"I am on no journey of pleasure," said Henry, restrained with difficulty by the presence of the lady.

"What then?"

"Jessie has been foully stolen from me on our wedding day, and I am on a journey to find her; nor shall I rest until she is restored to me, and the infamous ravisher punished."

"Poor Jessie," said Adela, watching her husband. "How very shocking."

"But why have you come here? This is a long way off," said Lord Lionel.

"I will tell you my reasons, my lord, when you shall have leisure to speak to me in private," replied Henry.

Lord Lionel hurried at once from the room, followed by Henry.

"I knew it," said Adela, with a cold and bitter smile. "I shall meet Colonel Harcourt this very afternoon. I will be revenged!"

And she took up the paper.

Meanwhile Henry had followed Lord Lionel into a private room.

"You speak in such a tone," said Lord Lionel, "I am compelled at once to ask your meaning?"

"I mean, Lord Lionel, that you are a cold-blooded villain!"

"Sir?"

"A cowardly outrager of all that man holds dear in nature!" began Henry.

"Sir?"

"I accuse you of stealing away my bride! I ask you, as you value your life, to restore her to me?"

"I am not in the habit of listening to threats," said the young nobleman.

"All this, my lord, is evasion," cried Henry, whose fiery passions were getting the better of him, "and if you will not speak I will find a way to make you!"

"Sir, to a civil question I might have returned a civil answer, but as you have insulted me I can but request you to name a friend. We must meet no more but at the pistol's point!"

"At once?"

"As soon as you please. But I have to find

a second. I suppose you will do the same. I shall not leave the hotel."

And with a haughty bow Lord Lionel Thynne left the room.

Gasping for breath, Henry went into the open air.

Fight! It was what he wanted above all things. But where, in that strange place, should he hope to find a friend?

He was nearer one than he thought.

CHAPTER XIII.

THE DUEL.

WITH a sullen brow and an aching head he went forth.

The hotel faced the sea, and, to cool his fevered skin, he leaned over the parapet.

A great many people were there, watching a beautiful frigate that lay at anchor at no great distance.

Among the other spectators was a young man in the undress uniform of a midshipman.

A bright idea struck Henry.

"May I ask the favour of a word with you, sir," said Henry, with a bow.

"Certainly," replied the midshipman, with a smile.

"My name is Henry Marmaduke Haddington, of Haddington Hall, ——shire. I am a midshipman on board the —— with Captain —— de Lacey."

"I know him well," said the midshipman, heartily.

"Then you must respect him," replied Henry.

"I do, indeed."

"Then, sir," said Henry, handing his card, "you will not object to help me out of a serious difficulty."

"My dear fellow," replied the young officer, taking his arm, "I am quite at your service; though I must candidly say that my governor keeps me so demualy close I cannot do any thing in the money line."

"The service I ask of you," said Henry, "is a much more serious one."

"Explain."

"I am about to fight," began Henry.

"To fight?"

"Yes."

"Serious?"

"In mortal combat. I have been insulted in the most deadly manner."

"How so?"

"My affianced bride was abducted from me on the morning of my wedding."

"The devil!—that was awkward."

"I have followed the criminal. He refuses to give up the place of concealment. I have insulted him; he is about to challenge me."

"His name?"

"Lord Lionel Thynne."

"D —— a!"

"Sir!"

"The villain. You are more fortunate than

I am. I know him well. I was once under him. I have a shrewd suspicion that he trifled with a beloved sister's heart."

"Your name?"

"I am usually called Lord de Lorne," said the midshipman, quietly.

Henry shook him by the hand.

"My father is a duke, it is true, but with a deuced large family. My sister, like myself, has a small perlieu."

"I am proud, my lord, to make your acquaintance; and, as I certainly shall never be able to sail with Lord Lionel, I hope I may be transferred to your ship."

They were now at the hotel, which entering the young midshipman sent word that he should be in all day, and wait Lord Lionel's convenience.

In an hour a gentleman entered. He was a young officer from the garrison.

A mighty fine opinion of himself had Captain Cregan.

"You are Mr. Haddington?" he said, in a rich Cork brogue.

"My name," replied Henry, "is, I have every reason to believe, Sir Henry Marmaduke Haddington, Baronet."

"I fancy you said believe, sir?"

"My father's death has never been satisfactorily proved," said Henry, haughtily.

"Well, then, by the powers we'll consider him dead. Sir Henry, you decline, I suppose, to apologise?"

"I do, sir!"

"You know the alternative?"

Henry bowed.

"My friend," and the captain laid a very heavy stress on the word friend, because he was a lord, "Lord Lionel Thynne observed to me that perhaps you were without a second? There's plenty of our fellows will be glad to help you out of a difficulty—indeed, happy to oblige a gentleman always."

"My friend Lord Charles de Lorne will arrange all preliminaries," said Henry, half inclined to smile.

The captain—who had seen a lord before, but never spoken to one—bowed low, and retired with the naval officer towards a window.

In a few moments the captain retired.

"Sir Henry," said the young nobleman, smiling, "I fancy we are all pretty green in such matters. He knows nothing and I know nothing; but I've got a capital pair of duelling pistols at my rooms."

"I will, then, ask the favour of a loan of them."

"With all the pleasure in life, I was about to say," replied Lord Charles de Lorne, "but you know I do not mean that."

Henry gave a sickly smile.

"We are to meet on the Castle Hill in two hours from this."

"When and where you please. I will but write one letter in case—"

"Now care killed the cat, and down-heartedness is always bad in serious cases like this. You are in my hands. You will write a short letter, drink three glasses of wine, and take my word for it, we shall crack a bottle to our better acquaintance about six."

Henry made no reply, but followed quietly to the other's lodgings.

He wrote his letter, drank three glasses of wine, as advised, and then, calling a coach, departed for the scene of action.

CHAPTER XIV.

THE GROUND.

UNDERNEATH the castle walls was, in a secluded corner, a ditch, which seemed made for the awful purpose to which it was now to be put.

Dark, secluded, out of the way of foot passengers, it was further shaded by tall trees that waved from the opposite side.

The wall was here a hundred feet in height.

The grass grew high in the dank and moist soil.

It looked a place for murder to lodge in.

Many a grave might have been dug in that gloomy hollow, and the world have been no wiser.

Lovers like shady walks and umbrageous vistas in the forest; but no lovers would have ventured here.

It was deadly in its aspect.

Henry and Lord Charles de Lorne were first upon the ground.

They looked about them with something of suspicion. It looked like a place designed for mortal combat.

By a kind of irresistible impulse they spoke in low and hushed whispers.

Then came a sound from some distant bushes, then voices, and Lord Lionel Thynne and Captain Cregan were in sight.

No attempt was made to settle the matter without an appeal to arms. The feelings on both sides were too hot to admit of explanation or apology.

They were placed in position by their respective seconds.

Lord Lionel Thynne was the first to fire. In his agitation he missed his rival.

Then Henry, with a deadly purpose in his eye, took aim and fired.

As he did so Lord Lionel tossed up his hand and fell upon his face.

Captain Cregan gave a shrill whistle, and the regimental surgeon came rushing through the bushes.

Henry stood transfixed with horror.

The fearful revulsion of feeling which succeeds all such deeds was already on his soul.

To take life is so horrible that the worst murderer always repents, almost ere the deed is done.

Much more one of noble and generous feelings like Henry Marmaduke Haddington.

He stood like a statue, deadly pale. His eyes were fixed on vacancy.

" Come."

" Is he dead ?"

" I cannot say. But we had better leave this We shall have both to keep in seclusion."

" I must wait till I hear the verdict of the surgeon."

Lord Charles de Lorne stepped forward.

" Well ?" he said.

" Severely wounded," said the surgeon, " but not, I believe, mortally. All will depend on one moment."

He was already extracting the ball.

" Here—it is out. With care he may live ; but it will take long nursing and time."

" Hush !" said the wounded man, sitting up, " I know my danger. Not a word more. Where is Henry, I must and will speak to him ?"

They exchanged glances.

" He must not be agitated."

" Best humour him."

Lord Charles de Lorne returned to where his principal stood, still in the same statuesque position.

" He is very badly hurt, and wishes to speak to you ?"

Henry made no reply, but strode quietly to the side of the wounded man.

" Alive !" gasped Lord Lionel, who had been raised against a sloping bank.

All stood back. Henry kneeled beside the wounded man.

" Henry," he whispered, his fixed eyes almost death-like in their expression, " forgive me, and I will tell you the truth."

" Where is Jessie ?"

Lord Lionel whispered her address.

" Say I am dying—that she had better fly at once. My papers will, if used against her, ensure her transportation. If she hesitates say you will search the vaults."

" The vaults !"

" She will know my meaning."

" But how have you behaved to Jessie ?"

" Like a brother. I know not why I took her away. She is as pure as the unborn babe. And now, another favour."

" What is that ?"

" Go forward, tell my wife the truth, but say to all others that I have had a fall. Gentlemen, it is my wish," he said, raising his voice, " that this affair be treated as an accident. And now, Henry, Heaven bless you. May we never meet again except as friends. I shall never forget this lesson, should I, indeed, live."

" I forgive you," said Henry, taking his offered hand, " and, when time shall have proved your sincerity, shall be prepared to hail you as a friend."

Lord Lionel bowed his head

Henry and Lord Charles de Lorne retired, leaving the surgeon and Captain Cregan in charge of the patient.

They galloped back as quick as possible to B——. They had good horses.

They went to Lord Charles de Lorne's lodgings, and thence to the hotel.

It was time.

Lady Adela Thynne was writing a letter in answer to one from a mysterious profligate who had pursued her with his audacious addresses.

She was promising to meet him that evening.

Henry entered with as composed a face as

possible.

Lady Adela rose to meet him with a blanched face—blanched from sheer terror and shame.

"My dear Lady Adela," he said, gently, "I have a painful duty to perform."

"Painful duty?" she gasped.

"I and Lord Lionel have had a very serious quarrel."

"Yes—yes," she gasped.

"We have fought."

"He is dead!" she wildly cried; all her woman's love gushing on her soul.

"No."

"Bless you! But—"

"He is slightly wounded, and he sent me forward to say—"

"He sent you?"

"Yes."

"How can that be?"

"We have shaken hands, our cause of quarrel being removed, wholly removed," he added, significantly.

"Thank Heaven!"

"Lord Lionel wishes the affair to remain a profound secret for this reason. You will be told of an accident, a fall from a horse; be not, therefore, shocked or alarmed when he arrives."

"I thank you," said the young wife, solemnly, "for you have given me back my husband. I hope he will live to be grateful to you for giving him back unto himself. Farewell!"

They left her.

What an agony of tears was that she shed, as, falling on her knees, and raising her lovely streaming eyes to Heaven, she tore into infinitesimal morsels the damning letter she had been writing!

With what an agony of dread and hope she leaned forth from the window to watch for her wounded husband!

He came at last; but he was insensible.

That night, and many more, she watched his flickering breath.

CHAPTER XV

MADAME DENISE.

Lord Charles de Lorne, whose ship was in the roads for some weeks, had leave of absence; and he now asked Henry's permission to follow him in his search for his beloved Jessie.

With the frankness of his age Henry had told him the outline of his story.

Lord Charles de Lorne was enthusiastic at once in the cause of the lovely heroine of our narrative.

Henry, after wishing him to detail his hopes, at once admitted him of his party; and, taking post-horses, dashed at a rapid pace towards London.

It was ten at night when they reached their destination.

They put up at an hotel, dressed deliberately, took some refreshment, and, ordering a hackney-coach, drove to the celebrated Madame Denise's.

They were fully aware of the character of the house they were going to.

They knew, also, that admittance could only be gained by stratagem.

This is why they had dressed themselves with care ere visiting the house.

On arriving at the house their youth and general appearance at once obtained them admission to the hall.

They gave their cards to the hall-porter, whose left arm was in a sling.

Their cards were passed through a grating.

Next minute they were ushered into a superb apartment, furnished not only in a luxurious, but a voluptuous, and even gorgeous style.

Lord Charles de Lorne stared at the extreme beauty of the pictures, the subjects of which were indelicate to the last degree.

Henry saw nothing. His whole mind was fixed on something else.

Madame Denise entered quickly, her very sweetest smile on her face.

"What can I do for you, my dear sirs? Delighted to make your acquaintance. I have some dear darlings."

"Silence, infamous woman!" said Henry, clutching her by the arm; "I come from Lord Lionel Thynne."

"Unhand me, sir!"

"He is dying."

"I know him not. Unhand me! or I shriek for assistance."

"Do so," said Henry, in a low, hissing whisper; "we can then have in the officers to search the vaults."

Madame Denise fell back in a chair, gasping for breath, utterly annihilated with horror and alarm.

"What seek you—what want you?" she gasped.

"The young lady brought here by Lord Lionel. Let me see her at once, or, by Heavens, I will have the house pulled to pieces!"

"Alas! my dear sir, what you wish is utterly impossible," she sobbed forth.

"Why?"

"She has fled."

"No falsehood! Oh, Heavens! If anything has occurred to her there is no punishment—" began Henry, frantically.

"I swear to you her escape is a mystery. She was aided in it by a middle-aged man with spectacles, who broke my porter's arm with a poker. Call him in."

Lord Charles did so.

When ordered by his mistress he told his story in a plain and straightforward manner.

"Phineas Bristowe, by Heavens!" gasped Henry. "But how did he get in?"

"From the roof. We found traces of him in the dust and dirt. He had slided off the great house at the back. As I live, sir, I know no more."

"Show me her room."

"I am too ill," said Madame Denise, ringing a bell.

The hard-featured attendant entered.

"Show this gentleman the room from which

the young lady escaped with the parson," said Madame Denise.

Henry rushed up stairs.

Lord Charles de Lorne's face was crimson. He had scarcely heard a word that passed.

His eyes were fixed upon the glowing busts and naked figures in the pictures.

"I hope, my lord," said Madame Denise, with a smile, "that this little occurrence will not deprive me of your visits."

"Certainly not," stammered the youth; "I will come alone."

"Look here," said Madame Denise, rising, and removing a small curtain.

Lord Charles saw what looked like the glass of a peep-show.

He peeped through, turned red and white, and retreated hurriedly.

"I will come," he said, in a rather husky voice.

He had seen some half a dozen most lovely women, in a series of most lascivious attitudes, as they came out of the bath.

It was quite early for business. They were preparing for the evening's amusement.

Presently Henry came down looking pale and wan.

The tales of all parties in the house were too consistent to be doubted.

CHAPTER XVI.

THE rage, fury, and despair of Paolo—Viscount de Florac—when he fled from the house in which he had seen Julie enthroned in all her loveliness and wealth may be conceived, not described.

Though he knew not what measures he should adopt to bring about his ends he was determined on revenge.

His was a nature not rarely induced to give up a bad resolution.

It was about as difficult as to make him keep to a really good one.

The three confederates had returned to their old haunt at the old fence's.

On the night of the attempted burglary and rape Paolo and Dick the fumbler reached home first and determined to smother all thoughts of their discomfiture in a jovial supper.

They procured an ample supply of provender from a neighbouring night house.

Beefsteaks, onions, and unlimited beer.

Homely fare, but to be despised by none.

They had reached that happy state when a pipe and a glass of grog is beatitude.

Then in came Phineas Bristowe with Jessie.

With a significant glance he imposed silence on his companions, and led her through to the rooms occupied formerly by Julie, now Countess of Sidonia.

He then returned to his companions rubbing his hands.

"Ah! ah!" he said; "I, at all events, have done business. To-morrow I sail for America. Once there I shall command fortune's smiles for ever. Those who go with me share with me."

"I shall go," replied Dick the fumbler.

"Not I," said Paolo. "I will never leave England until I have my revenge of that woman."

"Revenge is sweet," observed Phineas; "but she is powerful. That woman loves another, and nothing will give her greater pleasure than to hang you out of the way.'

Paolo ground his teeth with impotent rage. He felt too truly the correctness of the other's words. She did hate him, all the more so that she had once dearly loved him.

Alas! that such opposite feelings should exist between two people once lovers.

Paolo was consumed by passion. His fiery imagination had been roused to madness by the wealth and luxury of the *soi-disant* Countess of Sidonia.

He writhed with infuriate rage at the thought of being supplanted by the aristocratic and handsome Englishman.

He coveted her—her person and her money.

He risked life in the attempt; but what, to a desperate man, is life?

As soon as he had fully determined upon this course of action, and intimated as much to his companions, Phineas declared his intention of taking rest.

Early in the morning the Mormon elder and Dick the fumbler started.

Jessie went with them without resistance.

She had written a letter to her mother which she was allowed to post with her own hand.

It enclosed one from Phineas.

He had declared to Jessie that he had proposed terms upon which Jessie was to be given up and never more molested.

He would wait for an answer at a stated place, which he had named.

They travelled by stage coach, as Jessie had no desire for a rescue.

In this way they reached Bristol.

They took lodgings at no great distance from where vessels sailed from.

The house was an inn, a respectable old inn of the ancient school.

A bed-room and sitting-room were set apart for Jessie. Phineas and the fumbler preferred taking up their quarters in the tap-room.

Phineas, as soon as they were safely located, went out to look for a ship.

To his great delight he found one in fact chartered by the Mormons.

He had no longer any fear as to the consequences. He could get on board without any difficulty.

We need scarcely say that Phineas Bristowe had not the slightest intention of restoring Jessie to her mother unless under circumstances of the most unexampled barbarity.

In the cavernous depths of his evil heart he had schemes that might have served for models to a Mephistophiles.

They were always working within his brain, whence they leaped forth *cap-à-pie* to destroy and curse.

The vessel was to sail in ten days. It was necessary, therefore, to be particularly careful all the time they remained in Bristol.

The least false step, and all was lost !

Jessie began already to be impatient, and Phineas and Dick the tumbler held long consultations.

Jessie on one or two occasions went out for a drive in an open carriage.

She had been again allowed to write to her mother. One day she received an answer from her and Henry, herself, and the dwarf would be with her as fast as they could possibly get together.

One day Jessie, very elegantly dressed, rode through the streets with Phineas Bristowe by her side.

A loud cry made him turn round.

Phineas looked wildly in the same direction.

"Ooray," said a well known voice

And Jessie saw a respectable looking man, a pretty woman with a young baby, and a little girl about three, all standing staring at her with open mouth.

It was Perigrine Grundy and his wife Mary.

"Stop," said Jessie, her face flushing with delight.

"Drive on," cried Phineas, huskily; "I dare not be known here. It is as much as my life would be worth. Who are they? You can visit them alone."

Jessie waved her hand to them, and then turning towards the Mormon elder, told all she knew of their story.

Bristowe, in his heart, cursed the day he ever came to Bristol—but he made no remark.

But he also made up his mind.

CHAPTER XVII.

TOM PIKE.

That night they removed into private lodgings. No sooner had they done so than the two confederates came to a final resolution.

They would endure no more danger from Jessie.

The lodging they took was composed of the whole of a furnished cottage.

Behind was a yard.

They announced their intention of making considerable purchases previous to their departure for America.

They were particularly anxious to pack their perishable articles in a careful and scientific manner.

This accounted for the assiduity with which they devoted themselves to carpenter's work.

When not out buying the needful things for their colonisation projects they were hard at work, almost day and night hammering away.

Jessie went out for no more drives.

Phineas Bristowe represented his own dangers in so terrible a light that it was impossible for her not to be alarmed.

For ten years she had called this man father, and he now positively asserted his claim to that title.

She certainly could not wish to hurt him.

She knew for certain in her more serious moods that he was not her father, but at the same time she dare not act as if he had no claim whatever on her affection.

She consented, after receiving her mother's letter, to remain indoors.

Meanwhile Phineas Bristowe was meditating one of the fowlest acts of treachery we have yet had to record.

In order to be prepared for the arrival of those who might interfere with his nefarious projects he sent Dick the tumbler abroad, to act as a spy.

He was utterly unknown to Peregrine Grundy, and could, therefore, easily deceive that worthy individual.

Dressing himself with scrupulous care as a countryman, Dick the tumbler made his way to the shop of Tom Pike.

That worthy was now quite a man in appearance, doing a thriving business, and looking forward to being married.

The respectable appearance of the so-called farmer quite delighted him.

"Young man," said he, after the operation of shaving had been performed, "I am a stranger to this city."

"So I should suppose."

"Why?"

"Well, sir, you do look a countryman."

"Do I?" grinned the other.

"Yes, ee do."

"And so I am; so I wants to ax you some advice," continued the other.

"With pleasure."

"Well, my missus, like the rest of 'em, is getting dissatisfied with old things, so she's given me these here old spoons to sell, and then I'm to buy new ones, real modern patterns."

"Yes."

"Now, can you tell me where this can be done?"

"Can't I just," said Tom Pike, with a hearty laugh, "and close by, too."

The farmer looked exceedingly gratified, and readily agreed to the other silversmith shop in order to guide him to his friend's establishment.

He did so, and was formally introduced to Mr. Peregrine Grundy.

The business was soon transacted, and then the gratified farmer offered to stand treat to Tom Pike.

"I should like you to join, sir; but business is business," said the farmer

"It's my time for a pipe," laughed Peregrine, in return, "though to-night I'm rather busy."

"The old story," said Pike.

"Yes."

"No sign of the gal?"

"None."

"Have you looked out sharp?"

"Yes."

"She ain't left Bristol?"

"Not by sea."

"Ah, I wish we could catch 'em."

"We will," said Peregrine. "I'm dead on to that villain, Bristowe. I means to have the pleasure of throttling him myself."

"Gumption," said Pike.

"To-night Mr. Henry and Co. arrive, and

then we'll take care nobody goes on board that ere Mormon ship I'll be bound."

"Do you think they're going by that ere ship?" asked Pike.

"I know it. They've taken berths."

This was all said as they crossed over the road to the public.

Dick the fumbler chuckled heartily. He had already found out all he wished to find out, and a little more.

How on earth were they to sail by the Joe Smith, bound for New York.

It was an ugly job; especially now that Henry and Jessie's other friends were expected to arrive.

After spending an hour with Peregrine Grundy and Tom Pike the farmer retired promising to call again in a few days, as he liked their way of doing business.

Phineas Bristowe launched out in curses not loud but deep when he heard the report of Dick the fumbler, whose successful scheme alone saved them from being immediately discovered.

What was now to be done?

After a considerable debate it was agreed to let things take their course in the usual way.

CHAPTER XVIII.

THE letters written by Jessie to her mother were allowed to be sent purposely to mislead the unfortunate members of her family who were left behind.

They were all posted in London, so that all clue to her real position was lost by this artful contrivance.

Henry was raving mad when he received a letter from his old friend, Peregrine Grundy, announcing that Jessie had been seen in Bristol, accompanied by the incarnate fiend Phineas Bristowe.

The dwarf, Cornelia, and Henry immediately set off, post haste, to the celebrated sea-port.

After seeing Peregrine they put themselves in communication with the police.

This was two days before the vessel was to sail.

From that moment Henry and Peregrine never lost sight of the ship. They watched it carefully day and night.

But nothing conspicuous could they see.

Goods went on board, passengers came and went, but no trace of Jessie or her abductor.

It was the night before the departure of the Joe Smith, and Henry and Peregrine were walking up and down, smoking a cigar.

The night was dark.

It was about nine.

The port was deserted, save where a cart now and then came down and deposited its burden.

The Joe Smith, being about so soon to sail, was the only vessel nearly ready. Every effort was being made to get it prepared for sea.

Its complement was nearly in.

At daybreak it went away.

Some large packages, which were to occupy a position on the deck, were alone to be received,

A little after noon two men came in sight, driving a sort of truck, on which was a large black box, not unlike a huge coffin.

Henry approached, with his usual caution, and saw only two strange faces.

The long box was marked —

"Glass. With care. This side up."

Henry sighed deeply, and let them pass; and yet could he but have known how very near he was the object of his anxious and delirious search.

The packet was hoisted on deck with care, and left by the two men.

Again the two resumed their weary watch.

Daylight broke, and the usual train of emigrants came on board, old men, younger couples, and children. all about to leave their country under the influence of one of the most hideous delusions which ever disgraced a civilised country.

Then began the casting off of ropes, and all the bustle and activity of a sailor departing for the long voyage.

But not a sign of Jessie, nor of her infamous persecutors.

Henry began to believe that they had discovered his presence in Bristol, and had hence been scared away.

He determined to redouble his exertions, but still did not object to Peregrine going out with the vessel and returning with the pilot boat.

Peregrine did not know what to make of the whole affair. He somehow thought that they were being chiselled—done—flabergasted—how, he could not for the life of him make out.

To go out with the boy gave him time to think.

He was awfully unhappy.

To the connection with Cornelia, Jessie, and Henry, he owed the whole of his present happiness, and gratitude was the first inspiration of the glowing heart of Peregrine Grundy.

Not to interfere with the duties of the sailors and the business of the pilot, Peregrine seated himself apart from the rest of the passengers.

Near him was an Italian, with a tall, slim-made bear, evidently very savage, for it was chained and muzzled, while the Italian kept it quite close to him, holding a chain in one hand and a stout stick in the other.

Peregrine had seen the bear go on several days before, evidently very reluctantly, uttering strangely horrid cries as its master dragged it along and beat it with a stick.

To avoid annoying the other passengers the Italian had taken a state cabin for himself and the bear.

The animal was tired, and threw itself on a pile of spare sails, while the Italian lit himself a cigar.

"Queer couple," thought Peregrine, and then he added, "You and your fellow passenger going to America?"

"Yes," said the Italian, with a very slight accent, "I can do noting in de ole country, and I try de new."

"Hem! Not a bad idea."

"You go to—"

PAOLO AND JESSIE.

"Not I."

"Ah! why then are you on board the Joe Smith?"

"Why, you see, I expected somebody to go by this ship whom I wanted to catch. But—damn 'em!—though every officer in Bristol has been on their track, they have as yet baulked us!"

"De debil!" said the Italian, giving the bear which had started up a smart rap; "dat very onloky."

"Deuced unlucky—carrying off a beautiful young woman—they deserve to be hanged."

"Exactly," said the Italian.

Peregrine then, in the exuberance of his feelings, told the whole story to the Italian, who shook his head.

"Ver horreed," he remarked.

By the time this confidential confabulation was over, the pilot was ready to leave the vessel. His cutter hove in sight, and Peregrine walked rapidly up and down the deck, carefully examining the passengers.

But those he sought were nowhere to be found.

Disconsolate and sad, Peregrine descended the side of the brig, which immediately set all sail, and was soon a good distance from the cutter.

Peregrine gazed mournfully at the receding vessel with the captain's glass.

"Good Heavens!" he cried, suddenly.

"What?"

"Pilot! pilot! we must catch that ship— there is the girl I have been in search of."

Yes, there was Jessie up in the rigging, waving a long scarf aloft to attract attention.

"Impossible!" said the pilot. "Have no power—besides, she has the weather gage of us now—we should never catch her with this breeze."

"Put back, then, in the name of God!" said Peregrine, hurriedly. "There is a quick sailing man-of-war in the harbour. By Heavens, these villains shall be caught!"

The Pilot willingly agreed to this, and late in the afternoon they reached Bristol.

But nothing could be done that night.

It was too late.

They were completely outwitted.

The phrenzy of Henry, of Cornelia, and of the Dwarf, may be conceived but not described.

Even when Jessie was in the power of Lord Lionel Thynne, they did not feel such awful dread as now.

CHAPTER XIX.

A MARRIAGE.

BEFORE we return to Jessie—now bound at last for a Mormon settlement—let us explain one circumstance which had a marvellous effect upon her fortunes.

Certain events which had taken place had rendered it advisable that the marriage of the Honourable Mr. Stanley and the Countess Sidonia should be celebrated without delay.

The Countess Sidonia, with all her sudden passions, was not a woman to place herself in the power of any man.

She herself proposed to make him a present on the wedding day of a hundred thousand pounds, the remainder of her vast property to be settled on herself.

A very brief legal document was all that was necessary to do this, as the Countess of Sidonia, while owning one large estate just purchased, had every farthing besides in the funds.

The Honourable Mr. Stanley was perfectly satisfied with this arrangement.

It made him a rich man.

He was no reckless spendthrift, though a man of pleasure.

He at once looked out for an estate on which to invest his hundred thousand pounds, and found one valued at about one hundred and fifty.

This he did not mind, as he felt satisfied his wife would not begrudge him more cash when she knew the safe use he was going to make of it.

As their acquaintance had been so very short, and the Countess Sidonia had no intimate private friends in England, it was determined to have a very quiet, retired marriage in a secluded village near London.

A certain village inn was selected for the ceremony. They even resolved to spend the honeymoon—alas! already nearly half over by anticipation—in the same locality.

It was on the banks of the Thames, with a pretty garden running down to the water.

Here, with a small, a very small, retinue of servants, they took up their quarters for the few days before the private marriage could take place.

The happy day soon came round which was to merge the Countess Sidonia into Mrs. Stanley, and no one more gladly hailed it than Sidonia.

She had no fear that, despite his having won her without marriage vows, the Honourable Mr. Stanley would desert her.

She knew that though he really did love her, that love was also not uninfluenced by her money.

And the Countess Sidonia was eagerly desirous of changing her foreign name into an English one.

They went to church accompanied by a few of the most intimate friends of the bridegroom, his own sisters acting, with pleasure, as bridesmaids.

They were married.

They returned to the inn to breakfast, and the ex-countess Sidonia—she insisted on dropping the title—with a sweet smile of pride and happiness, handed her husband *two* hundred thousand pounds in new notes.

Her husband's eyes flashed with delight and genuine gratification.

The guests began to disperse, and, at last, there only remained a worthy solicitor, who had been all life devoted to Mr. Stanley.

He, desirous of settling his affairs, and of completing the purchase money of the estate, asked leave of his wife to speak a while with his lawyer.

The ex-countess Sidonia was watching, with an amused eye, the antics of an Italian and a bear—a dancing bear—in the garden.

"You will find me in my room, Alick," she said; "but do not hurry, settle your business with Mr. Crowther."

The two gentlemen retired.

Mrs. Stanley, after a few moments, became thoughtful, and, turning up a side passage, ascended to her room by a back stairs.

She then opened her door, and, entering, was about to close it, when she found that the bear had followed her. Before she could cry out she was caught in its arms; she remembered nothing more.

A handkerchief was applied to her nose, and she fainted.

They carried her down, crossed the garden, entered a boat, and crossed the river.

When the Countess Sidonia came to herself, she found herself inside the bear skin, her mouth gagged and muzzled, and Paolo Viscount de Florac standing before her.

"Woman," he said, in an awful voice, "I give you fair warning. I never mean to part with you again; and before that man shall possess you——"

A faint chuckle made him raise his whip.

"I will kill you. So understand me. Submit to your fate until on board ship, or, as I live, I will slay you. I am already condemned to death, nothing can happen worse. So you are warned. If I die with you—you shall still die."

And by this terrible threat, and the occasional use of the stick, the young ruffian contrived to get her on board the Mormon vessel.

But the husband was not so blinded as he expected.

Julie contrived to scrawl on a large sheet of paper with charcoal three words, which she thrust into the hand of the boy who had played the part of bear before herself.

"*Five pounds reward! Go to my husband, give this—Infamous rival—gagged me, America.*"

And, now, how was it that Jessie had been smuggled on board the Joseph Smith?"

Phineas Bristowe had been in the habit of sending on board every day, packages addressed to himself, under another name, at New York.

The last he sent was a large box, well furnished with holes, and admirably ventilated.

Inside this was a mattress.

On that mattress lay Jessie.

She had been drugged, and so arranged that she lay like a dead body.

Then Phineas and Dick arranged for a passage on board the pilot boat.

They easily got on board without being noticed, and, at once, taking the great box down into the state room, released Jessie.

No sooner did some powerful smelling salts bring her to her senses than she flew on deck, run up the rigging, and made wild signals of distress.

Paolo looked on with a derisive and chuckling laugh.

The signals of the poor girl were seen, but the result is already known.

No one interfered with her until she came down from the rigging, when Phineas Bristowe said to her, in his hard, hypocritical way,—

"I shall be able to make better terms on the other side of the water; there," pointing to Bristol, "I am not a free man."

"There is a law in America," replied Jessie, with a look of scorn.

And she went down stairs to her own room. It was a state-room, opening upon the saloon, in which the leading passengers were to dine.

"Jessie," said a strangely familiar voice from an adjacent berth.

"Who is there—what is it?" replied the young girl, considerably puzzled.

"It is I, Julie—the victim of an infamous plot," said the voice. "Undo the fastenings."

Jessie drew a bolt, and Julie appeared.

"At least we are two," she said; "now I defy their malice. You come in here," she continued.

Bewildered and astonished, not knowing how to act, Jessie obeyed, and found herself in what appeared intended for the captain's cabin.

"I know not what these villains mean," continued Julie; "but do you insist on being with me?"

Glad of female companionship, and won over by a pitiful tale told by Julie, Jessie agreed to be her companion.

Neither Bristowe nor Paolo raised any objection.

They had them now secure, and that was all they cared about.

They had days and days to lay their plans, and yet there was danger, as their pursuers might induce more than one man-of-war to take up the chase.

If they reached America before them, their position might be serious indeed.

Once in the United States, they feared nothing.

But for several days they did not even see a sail, though more than one pursuer was on their track.

Lord Lionel Thynne and Henry were the principal ones.

We shall see with what success.

CHAPTER XX.

PAOLO AT WORK.

The Joe Smith, meanwhile, dashed rapidly on before the easterly gale, which blew favourably from the very first, speeding them on their way to the mountains and prairies of the great republic.

But soon the favourable gale appeared to show signs of changing.

Every stitch of canvas was set, and the vessel rolled and laboured heavily, as the rising gusts caught her, and drove her with increased speed through the foaming waves.

The wind was rising rapidly.

At the same time, the barometer was falling.

The captain frequently cast anxious looks behind him, and then dived down into the cabin, to consult his barometer and charts.

Even the tough old sailors looked serious at the tremendous banks of clouds which were rapidly rising astern and on every side.

And Jessie and Julie—what of them?

No hope—not one single ray of sunshine on their path.

Alone on the ocean.

Alone in the world.

None but enemies around them.

Their few friends separated from them by leagues of boiling surf.

"O! this is dreadful," Jessie would cry, "this horrible confinement—death itself would be preferable!"

"Do not despond," Julie would reply; "we shall yet escape from these ruffians. I feel, I know it."

"Alas!" said Jessie, weeping, "I see no chance of delivery, no hope."

"Hark!" cried Julie, "what is that?"

They listened intently.

It was the loud, bellowing voice of the captain.

"All hands reef topsails."

Up crowded the active and willing seamen, and soon one reef was taken in the straining sails.

Still onwards tore the Joe Smith through the heaving and boiling waves.

She almost seemed to fly.

The masts bent and groaned before the blast.

The wind still continued rising.

The captain and mate were standing on the poop with Phineas Bristowe.

The captain looked aloft at the straining spars.

"I must soon take another reef in," he said.

"Nothing of the kind," said Bristowe; "keep all the sails on her. Let her fly before the breeze, far from the land we have left."

"Yes," said Paolo, who then came up, "keep her going, captain—keep her going; we want to arrive at our destination."

"Yes," grunted the skipper, "but it would hardly help you to have the masts blown out of her."

Nevertheless, he gave no further order to reduce sail; and on dashed the Joe Smith, as if urged by all the demons of the blast.

Fiercer roared the storm, and louder roared the wind and waves.

The captain looked more anxious than ever; the mate was also very serious.

The sailors were congregated together in groups, muttering in low tones, and looking to windward, —they were not afraid, but discontented.

Presently, Jessie and Julie were again alarmed by the same hoarse bellowing, "All hands reef topsails."

It was the captain's stentorian voice giving this fresh order.

This time, two reefs were taken in, and now even Phineas did not object.

He began to be alarmed for his own safety.

There were many ominous signs to alarm the Mormon elder.

One was the anxiety of the mate and captain, and the serious looks of the old tars.

Another was the fact that the carpenter of the ship might be seen every half hour sounding the pumps.

But as yet there was no water inside the ship.

All was safe so far.

The good ship did not leak a drop.

Onwards she dashed, all the wild night, before the waving storm.

Her timbers creaked, and her masts groaned and bent like reeds before the blast.

All the passengers were either very ill, or too much frightened, to remain on deck.

Jessie and Julie had been persuaded by the stewardess to undress and go to bed.

Jessie was not sea-sick. It was not her first sea-baptism.

Julie suffered dreadfully.

She seemed at times almost fainting from fear and pain.

The stewardess was alarmed, and went to the captain for medicine.

The captain was in the saloon with Paolo and the mate.

"One of the ladies is ill," said the stewardess.

"Ill, eh—sea-sick, I suppose?"

"Yes, captain; but worse than I have ever seen anyone."

"Well, I will give her a composing draught. Bring me the medicine chest."

It was brought.

"Lend me a hand, young fellow," he said to Paolo, "with these bottles, will you?—the confounded rolling and pitching of the old barque makes doctoring difficult work."

Paolo complied.

"What are you going to give them, captain?" he said.

"O, a sleeping draught—laudanum, I think—there's nothing like sending the poor things to sleep."

"Well, give her a good strong dose; she will want it such a night as this."

"All right," said the skipper.

Suddenly, a diabolical thought came into the head of Paolo.

"Captain," he said, "give them both a dose; the other is just as sure to want it before long."

"Well, if you think so, I will."

He proceeded to mix another draught.

As he finished, Paolo purposely knocked the captain's speaking trumpet off the table.

"What's up, youngster? I wish you'd be careful," said the skipper.

"I beg your pardon," said Paolo.

At the same time, he took up the laudanum bottle, and poured some into each of the tumblers.

Before he had time to replace the bottle, the captain had picked up the telescope.

"What are you doing with the bottle?"

"Having a drink myself."

"Why so?"

"Because I shall never sleep through this infernal din, otherwise."

"By God!" said the skipper, "you have taken a pretty dose."

He held the bottle up to the light—it was more than half empty.

"Why, it is enough to send you to sleep for a week."

"I have a strong constitution," said Paolo, calmly.

"I should think so."

No more was said on the subject; but Paolo gave a triumphant smile.

"At last," he muttered, "proud beauty, you are in my power!"

"Here," said the captain to the stewardess, "take this to the ladies, and see they take it."

A man, at this moment, called out to the captain down the skylight.

It was the chief mate.

"Another squall coming up, sir."

"Does it look like mischief?"

"Black as thunder."

"Wind."

"Yes sir, wind and rain."

"I'll be on deck in a minute."

"Just put these bottles back in the chest for me, sir," he said to Paolo; "I must get on deck, and see about taking in more sail."

He left, and went on deck in a hurried and anxious way.

Paolo was now alone.

He took up the laudanum bottle, and placed it in his pocket.

Then he closed the medicine chest, and locked it carefully.

"I may as well make all safe," he muttered. "Master Bristowe may be in the way ; I will ask him to have a glass of grog with me, to keep his spirits up ; this will do the rest :" and he concealed the bottle in his pocket.

He went on deck.

He found Phineas seated on a hencoop near the binnacle.

The Mormon appeared in great terror at the violence of the wind and waves.

Nevertheless he had his eyes about him.

He was seated on a part of the ship immediately above the cabin window of Julie and Jessie.

"Come down, man, and have a glass of grog, instead of sitting there as if you were going to be swallowed up by one of those big waves."

"O Lord, don't mention it!" said Phineas, looking with horror on the raging mountains of water astern.

"Come down in the cabin ; we shall have rain directly."

At this moment big drops began to patter down upon the deck.

Phineas rose, and walked down the companion-ladder into the cabin.

Paolo followed him, with a cynical smile.

"Steward!" he shouted, "bring some tumblers, brandy and hot water."

The steward appeared with the brandy.

"No hot water, sir," he said, "the galley fire is put out by the sea, and we shan't be able to light it till the gale is over."

"Never mind," said Paolo ; "we must e'en drink it cold, good Phineas."

"O Lord!" cried Phineas, "what a storm ! and the galley fire out, too—what shall we do for breakfast ?"

Paolo laughed.

"Breakfast!" he said; "who talks of breakfast ? why, we shall all be at the bottom of the sea before morning."

"Good heavens !—is there really any danger ?"

"Danger? I should think there was."

"You don't mean to say we shall be all drowned ?"

"Of course we shall—why, Phineas, you ought not to be alarmed—one of the Lord's chosen, eh ?"

But Phineas did'nt seem to see any comfort in this.

He poured out two stiff tumblers of brandy.

He drank his own, as also did Paolo, in deep silence.

Then he repeated again, and again.

"Do you really think there is danger, then ?"

"Of course there is."

"What does the captain say ?"

"There he is, you had better go and ask him."

He pointed up the skylight.

The figure of the captain could be seen leaning against the mizen-mast.

He was talking to the mate, and looking anxiously astern at the weather.

"I think I will do so," said Phineas.

Accordingly he rose, and blundered up the companion-ladder, as well as the violent lurching and rolling of the ship would allow him.

CHAPTER XXI.

PHINEAS TRICKED.

WHEN he was gone, Paolo produced the laudanum bottle, and poured a large dose into the glass of Phineas Bristowe.

"There !" he muttered, "I think that will send the old boy to sleep."

He looked towards the cabin, in which were Julie and Jessie.

Then he rose and tried the door.

It was locked on the inside.

He was prepared for it, and did not seem at all discomposed.

He could hear the regular breathing of the two girls through the door.

He went to the steward's cabin, where there was still a light burning.

The steward was there with his wife, the stewardess.

He readily found an excuse for disturbing them.

"Steward, can you give me a little lemon ? This brandy of yours, is rather raw and strong."

The steward gave him the lemon.

He turned to leave them. Turning round, he said, casually, to the stewardess,—

"By the way, how are the ladies ?"

"Oh, better sir, thank you," was the reply ; "they both went to sleep very soon after I gave them the medicine."

"They took it, then ?"

"Oh, yes, sir ; the younger lady did not take so much, but the other took all hers, and was asleep in ten minutes."

"Indeed," said Paolo, carelessly; "I am glad to hear it—poor things ! they need sleep, I am sure."

"They do indeed, sir."

"Good night," he said.

"Good night, sir."

Paolo reseated himself at the cabin table.

Soon Phineas Bristowe came down, glad to be once more out of the roaring wind and rain.

He looked pale, and terribly frightened.

"Well," said Paolo, "what news ? what sort of a night is it ?"

"O, bad, very bad—the storm is dreadful."

"What says the captain ?"

"Nothing. I cannot get a word from him."

"Come, come, never mind," said Paolo ; "fill your glass, and drive dull care away."

He filled his own, and Phineas's.

Phineas drank his off, glad of anything to drive away his fears.

Paolo watched him drain his glass, and smiled grimly.

"What if the dose should have been too strong ?" he thought. "Well, never mind if it is. It will be only one the less in the world."

This was the way in which the hardened reprobate regarded murder.

"Come, Phineas, my boy, fill your glass again; let's have a song ;" and he filled both glasses, and struck up,—

> "Come, landlord, fill a flowing bowl,
>   Until it does run over,
>   For to-night we'll merry be;
>   To-morrow we'll get sober."

Even Phineas, ruffian as he was, recoiled from this defiant ribaldry and insolent defiance of heaven.

The howling storm raged and roared; heaven's artillery had just begun its dull rumblings; and the gigantic waves seemed to grow bigger and bigger.

And yet this man could sing.

Phineas, bad as he was, was quite staggered.

"How can you sing?" he said. "Why, we may all be drowned before morning."

"Well, never mind, we'll drown care now, ha! ha! ha!" and he laughed long and loudly at his own joke.

"Don't make such a noise," said Phineas, "you will wake the ladies."

Paolo smiled.

He knew there was little fear of that.

Again he filled the glasses, and said,—

"Wake the ladies! not for worlds, old boy. Here's their jolly good healths, especially the little one, eh, you old rascal?"

He gave Phineas a dig in the ribs, and refilled his glass.

"Nice girl, isn't she?"

"Who?" said Phineas.

"Why, Jessie, of course."

"Jessie!"

"Yes, Jessie; the little girl in that cabin," pointing with his finger, "that you are so fond of."

"Mine is there, but she is under the loving care of a father."

"Loving care of a fiddlestick," said Paolo, mockingly.

"Mine is a pure, holy, and godly love," continued the Mormon, casting up his eyes.

"Yes, no doubt of it," said Paolo; "that's what your taking her to Utah for, you old rascal, is it? Well, look out that Joe Smith does not see her, or he will be having a pure, holy, and godly love for her also."

"Joe Smith!—Jessie!" gasped the Mormon, in alarm. "No!—never!"

The powerful opiate now began to take effect on him.

He could hardly keep his eyes open; the lids seemed of lead.

His speech was thick and his head nodded.

It was evident to the cunning and unscrupulous Paolo, that he would soon be in a deep, insensible slumber.

"Come, have another glass," he said, filling Phineas's tumbler.

Phineas drank it.

He was getting intoxicated.

This fact, with the laudanum, must soon reduce him to utter helplessness.

"Let me see," said the other, "what was I saying?"

"Oh, I was talking about Jessie."

"Jessie," said Phineas, drowsily, "what about her?"

"I was saying how fond you were of her."

"Do you know," he continued, "I begin to think I shall be fond of her, too."

"You!" said Phineas, in sleepy, drunken astonishment. "You! you villain!"

"Yes, I—why not? Am I not a good-looking fellow, and isn't she a pretty girl? What more natural? eh, you old sinner?"

Phineas grew pale with rage.

Paolo, knowing he would soon be quite helpless, determined to torment him still farther.

"She is a beautiful girl—isn't she now?" he continued. "I never saw a more beautiful bust and figure for so young a girl. How old is she, Phineas?"

"What's that to you?" was the surly reply.

Phineas had now the greatest difficulty in keeping his seat.

His eyes closed several times, and it was with a great effort he again opened them.

"What's that to me?" said Paolo. "Why every thing to me. Because I love the girl, and mean to have her."

Phineas, drunk and almost insensible as he was, turned livid with rage.

"I mean to have her," Paolo continued, "I tell you, and to-night—this very night—eh, Phineas?"

The Mormon looked at him with his dull and fish-like eyes.

"Which is her cabin, by-the-bye? I forget. Do you know?"

Paolo rose, as if about to seek the door.

Phineas, blind with rage, rose also to prevent him.

He staggered forward a few paces, and then fell heavily to the floor.

The drink and laudanum had produced their effect.

Paolo gazed at him, with a mocking, triumphant air, for a minute.

Then he went to the steward's cabin, and knocking, said,—

"My friend here, on the floor, has been drinking too much; you had better move him to his cabin."

The steward came out, and between them, they lifted the insensible form of Phineas, and took him to his berth.

"He is very intoxicated, indeed," said the steward.

"Yes," replied Paolo, "he was so frightened, that he would have drank a gallon if he could."

CHAPTER XXII.

PAOLO AND JESSIE.

LEAVING Phineas in a state of utter insensibility, Paolo mounted the companion-ladder and went on deck.

The storm raged with greater fury than ever.

The captain and mate were gazing anxiously first at the black masses of clouds, which were still rising and scudding over their head; then at the bending masts, and then at the mountainous waves, which rolled and tumbled after them.

"Well, captain," said Paolo, "what do you think of the night? is there any danger?"

"No immediate danger at present; but if this sea continues rising, we must heave to, or we shall have a big roller over the stern, and be swamped."

"Yes," said the mate, "she can't scud like this much longer, the sea is rising fast—we shall have to heave her to, I'm afraid; then we shall feel the storm in earnest."

Paolo paid but little attention to what they said.

He was thinking too much of the project he intended to carry out.

Jessie was asleep, so also was Julie—both sound asleep—drugged—Julie, especially, had taken a large dose and would not wake. That was certain. And as for Jessie, if she did wake, the roaring of the wind and waves would drown any slight noise or disturbance.

Never was villain and ruffian more cold-blooded than this Maltese outlaw.

He descended into the cabin again. He went to the door of the steward's birth. All was still, no light could be seen.

Nothing could be heard but the howling of the tempest.

The vessel rolled and lurched so fearfully that he could hardly keep his feet.

But this did not, in the least, turn him from his purpose.

He went to the door of the girls' cabin, and listened attentively.

He could hear the sound of their regular breathing.

They slept calmly, peacefully—the sleep of innocence and youth.

Then he went on deck.

He well knew the port-hole which opened into their cabin.

The mate and captain were standing aft by the binnacle.

The darkness of the night concealed him from their view.

He climbed quickly over the bulwark, and holding on by the rail, crawled along the spar which was secured outside the vessel.

The spray of the sea dashed over him, and almost wetted him through.

But he heeded it not.

He was determined to attain his object; and that at all hazard.

The brandy he had drunk seemed to increase his determination.

He arrived at the port-hole, which he well knew.

He tried it.

It was not locked.

Jessie, who had so carefully locked and bolted the door, had forgotten the window in the port.

He opened the window and listened.

All was silent.

Slowly and cautiously he passed in.

The cabin was lighted by a dim oil lamp, suspended from the deck above.

He looked around him.

In a raised berth, at one extremity of the cabin, was Julie—his supposed wife.

He approached her and gazed fixedly at her.

She was fast asleep.

He touched her gently.

This appeared to have no effect on her, as she still slept on.

He then shook her, still she remained completely insensible.

"Good!" he muttered, "she is safe at all events."

Then he advanced to the other end of the cabin.

Jessie was reposing in a low berth, concealed by curtains.

He drew them aside, and gazed on her sleeping form.

The violent rolling and lurching of the ship had discomposed the bed furniture; her night dress was partially drawn aside, revealing the exquisite symmetry of her bust.

He bent down, and imprinted a kiss on her snowy neck.

She sighed softly, and murmured "Henry."

Paolo also smiled, but it was the smile of the fiend gloating over his victim.

Again he kissed her, still she did not wake.

The calm placidity of her countenance made even this ruffian pause.

Still she slept calmly on.

At last, grown bolder, he clasped her in his arms.

She struggled faintly, and again murmured the name "Henry."

The vessel lurched and rolled more violently than ever.

The wind roared with increased fury, and Paolo could hear the big waves foaming and roaring.

But nothing moved him from his fell purpose. The man had the instincts of a demon and a satyr. Unfortunately there are too many like him.

He was a fit pupil of the Mormons.

He watched Jessie for some moments, and then again kissed her forehead, eyes, mouth, and neck.

Suddenly she opened her eyes, and saw before her the form of a strange man.

And that man not Henry.

She disengaged herself, by a violent effort, from his arms.

She screamed violently.

But Julie slept a death-like sleep, and the howling of the fearful storm drowned her voice altogether ere it reached the deck.

"Leave me—leave me!" she cried. "See yonder where your wife sleeps. Surely she must wake."

"She will not wake. I hate her, and I love you—have long loved you—and I will have you mine!"

"Never!" cried Jessie, rising, and drawing her clothes around. "If man and woman desert me, heaven will not!"

Paolo sat down upon a chair, and looked at her with a half-sneering, half-admiring, expression.

"You are very beautiful, Jessie," he said, "and if I thought you would marry me, I might be disposed to listen to reason."

"Marry you! Never,—monster! Have you not a wife already? and are you not the most merciless wretch in existence? I would sooner die!"

"Die? Oh, no! No death for you, my love. I adore you; and I mean, when we reach Nauvoo, to place you at the head of my establishment."

Jessie made no reply. The laudanum was again producing its effect.

He rose, and advanced towards her.

"Heaven have mercy on me!" she said; "for if not, I am lost!"

Paolo, with flashing eyes, and a calm but terrible smile, kneeled beside her couch.

Suddenly, as if by a special interposition of Providence, there was heard loud shouting and tramping of feet overhead.

The vessel strained and heaved on the tremendous waves.

Then her stern sunk in the deep trough of the sea.

Then there was a loud roaring noise of rushing water.

An enormous wave had broken close astern of them.

When the immense waves broke, the danger was great. She was pooped.

On it came—rushing—roaring.

It was upon the ship.

Close astern, it towered up above, its white crest foaming, roaring, and boiling.

For one moment it remained, as it were, suspended over her.

Then it dashed with its full fury over the stern and quarter-deck.

Paolo still knelt beside Jessie.

He heard the rushing dash of the boiling wave as it rushed over the ship.

Then there was a loud crash, and a torrent of water burst into the cabin through the stern windows.

The dead lights, which secured the windows, were torn into a thousand pieces.

The torrent of water carried all before it.

Paolo, Julie, and Jessie were swept helplessly before it.

On, on, it went, bursting down the bulkhead, between the ladies' cabin and the saloon.

Jessie was washed right out on deck before she recovered her consciousness.

The roaring wave had done her a double service.

It had saved her from the hateful advances of Paolo.

It had also, by its cold, restored her to her senses.

Paolo seized hold of part of the rigging, and was soon in safety.

Julie and poor Jessie would not have fared so well, had it not have been for two of the sailors, who each laid hold of one of their dripping forms, and bore them in safety to the fore-cabin.

Then it was that Jessie recovered sufficiently to comprehend and remember the peril from which the friendly wave had saved her.

She burst into tears.

Should she never be freed from these persecutions and outrages?

And Henry—what of him?

Alas! she knew nothing—feared everything.

She could not know that he was even now in swift pursuit, in the splendid sloop-of-war, Firefly.

She feared she should never see him again.

She wept bitterly at the thought.

And then she remembered Lord Lionel Thynne, and shuddered.

She knew well that he also would pursue her with unrelenting ardour.

Hers was, indeed, a sad prospect.

CHAPTER XXIII.

THE STORM.

THE deck of the Joe Smith presented a fearful scene.

The water rushed backwards and forwards, sweeping everything before it.

Water-casks, hencoops, spars, chairs, tables, cabin furniture, and anything else in its way, were torn up, and dashed backwards and forwards, as she rose and fell in the trough of the sea.

The captain, mate, and sailors had taken refuge in the rigging, till the water should have flowed off the deck.

Paolo had also placed himself in safety.

A dark object was dashed swiftly by the place where the captain and mate were.

It struggled in the water with frantic energy.

They soon discovered that it was a man.

Between them, they seized it, and dragged it up in the rigging.

It was Phineas Bristowe.

Five minutes more, and it would have been all over with him.

He was half drowned as it was.

The cold water had but half aroused him from his drunken, drugged sleep.

He gazed stupidly around him, clinging tightly to the rigging, in abject terror.

"There! hold on, man!" said the skipper; "you are all right now."

The water had now nearly left the deck, and the skipper and mate descended.

"We must heave her to, Mr. Mate," said the captain. "If she should ship another such sea, it would be all up with her."

"If she's hove to, she'll strain and labour a deal more," said the mate.

"Can't be helped," was the reply—"it must be done. The sea is still rising, and we shall be pooped in another hour, if we scud before it."

The Joe Smith was dashing through the water at a fearful rate.

She must have been going at least twelve knots before the hurricane.

"Station the men, Mr. Mate, and heave her to."

"Ay, ay, sir."

It was done.

"All ready, sir."

"Very well," replied the captain, taking his place near the wheel.

He watched the waves, which rolled up astern, long and anxiously.

The proper time to heave to is immediately after a large wave has passed.

There is then usually a succession of smaller ones.

At last an enormous roller was seen coming up astern.

THE PRIVATE DETECTIVE.

Onwards it came, towering above the ship—a perfect mountain of water.

It seemed as if about to break.

The captain looked anxiously at the water.

If it should break over the ship, it would be almost certain destruction.

On it came with a swift rush.

But fortunately it did not break.

It raised the vessel on its foaming crest, and bore her up—up as if to the very clouds.

Then it passed from under her, and instantly broke into roaring foam.

If it had been one moment sooner, it would have overwhelmed them.

The captain gave a sigh of relief.

The immediate danger was passed.

"Hard a starboard!" shouted the captain, to the man at the wheel.

The vessel readily obeyed the helm, and came up to the wind.

"Haul in on the starboard braces!"

It was done, and she rapidly came up to a point close to the wind.

The only sail she had set was the close-reefed main-topsail and storm-staysail.

But even this scanty canvas heeled her over frightfully.

They now felt the full fury of the storm.

The wind howled and roared through the rigging, and each succeeding gust seemed as if it would tear the masts out, or capsize her.

She pitched and laboured fearfully in the tremendous sea.

It was impossible for even the sailors to keep their feet.

Frequently heavy seas struck her with tremendous force on the bow and broadside.

On these occasions, she would reel and tremble fearfully in every joint.

"She strains frightfully," said the mate.

The captain made no reply.

He looked anxiously, first to windward, and then at the straining and heaving vessel.

"Sound the pumps," he cried, "let us see if she is still tight.

The carpenter, with difficulty, dragged himself along the deck with the sounding rod and line.

All waited in breathless silence for his report.

Their fate hung upon it.

If she sprung a leak in such a fearful storm, she must be lost.

He sounded the well carefully,—slowly.

Then he drew forth the rod.

He examined it deliberately; then, with pale face, he turned towards the quarter-deck, and shouted,—"Two feet of water in the hold!"

All seemed horror-struck at the dreadful news.

The captain was the first to recover. "All hands to the pumps!" he cried.

The seamen crowded around them, and commenced to pump as well as the violent pitching and labouring would allow.

It was a struggle for life and death.

They worked in silence for an hour.

Phineas Bristowe and Paolo took their turn.

Even the captain, mate, and steward threw off their coats, and took their spell.

After an hour's hard pumping, the carpenter again sounded.

All awaited the verdict in breathless silence.

With pale face and trembling hands, he again drew up the rod and examined it.

"Three feet of water he said!"

In spite of all their efforts it had gained a foot on them.

The sailors seized the pump handles, and worked furiously.

They pumped like madmen for another hour.

Then they threw themselves exhausted on the wet deck.

Again the carpenter sounded.

All again waited in breathless anxiety.

"Four feet of water in the hold!"

Once again they started to their feet, and rushed with renewed fury at the pumps.

The vessel was now obviously settling down in the water.

She was less lively, and shipped seas more frequently.

She was fast becoming water-logged.

The storm gave no sign of abatement.

"If this lasts for another two hours," said

the captain to the mate, "it is all over with us."

"All over, indeed," said the mate, with pale face. "Shall we put her before the wind?"

"Impossible," was the reply; "with all that water in the hold, she would be swamped in five minutes."

Still the exhausted crew toiled wearily at the pumps.

Another hour's hard work, and again the carpenter was sounding.

"Five feet of water in the hold!"

It came like a death-knell to their failing strength and spirits.

Another two feet, and she would sink.

The dawn was now just beginning to break.

It revealed the full horrors of the scene.

The black and gloomy clouds, the roaring, boiling, foaming ocean on all sides, and their labouring, straining vessel, fast settling down in the water.

"There may be a change for the better when the sun rises," said the captain.

"It is our only chance," replied the mate; "but an hour and a half more like this, and it is all over."

The ship gave a heavy lurch to starboard, and two or three waves broke right over her.

She lay like a log on the waters.

"Go and look at the barometer," said the captain to the mate.

He descended for that purpose, and returned, looking a little more hopeful.

"It is rising slowly," he said.

"Thank God!" replied the captain; "we have one more chance."

"Give the men some brandy," he added.

A bucket of brandy was brought out, and each drank as much as they pleased.

Some drank nearly a pint at a draught, but it had no effect on them.

The tremendous labour of the pumps prevented their getting drunk.

"Work away, boys! there is hope yet," cried the skipper, encouragingly.

And they did work, like furies, for another hour.

Again the pumps were sounded.

"Six feet of water in the hold!"

One more foot—perhaps, less—and she must go down.

The sun was now just rising.

The captain and mate now threw off their coats, and taking each a long draught of brandy, seized the pump handles.

"Work away, boys!" he cried. "If we can only keep her afloat for another two hours all will be right. The glass is rising fast."

These words of hope put new life into the exhausted sailors.

They toiled on savagely, as never men toiled before.

They were working for life.

They pumped on, without cessation, in silence.

Not a man left the pumps, or spoke a word.

Breath was too precious to be wasted in conversation.

Still they worked on.

The sun rose red and angrily.

The wind blew, sometimes in gusts more furiously than ever, but sometimes there was a slight lull, which enabled the vessel to right herself.

This gave them a better chance at the pumps.

Another hour passed.

Again the carpenter sounded the pumps.

The captain looked anxiously to windward.

The clouds looked as threatening as ever.

"Five feet and a half of water in the hold!" said the carpenter, examining the sounding rod.

"Work away, boys!" cried the captain, to the sailors—who had left off pumping in despair—"Keep her afloat for one more hour, and we are saved."

They again seized the pump handles, and toiled wearily on.

Their spirits seemed utterly prostrated by the tremendous labour.

The captain and mate consulted together in a low tone of voice.

"It is our only chance," said the captain.

He and the mate then took their places at the lee-braces.

"Put her before the wind," shouted the captain, to the man at the wheel.

"Hard up your helm."

It was done, and the ship payed off from the wind.

They hauled in the weather-braces, and squared the yards.

On she dashed, lumberingly and heavily.

She contained so much water, that her deck was scarcely above the level of the sea.

The waves made a clear breach over her.

But the men could pump better now that she was before the wind; because she was on an even keel.

They took no heed of the water, which was sometimes up to their waists—but pumped steadily on.

The captain poured brandy in a tin pot, and handed it to them, one by one.

This gave them fresh strength, and they pumped with renewed force.

Another hour had now passed.

Again the carpenter sounded.

All waited anxiously for his report.

"Five feet and a half water in the hold!" he said

"Hurrah!" cried the captain, "the water has not gained on us."

"Drink, boys, drink, more brandy, more brandy, and work like horses, and we are saved."

And they did drink, and that deeply.

There was but half a foot of water between them and death.

If the water gained another half foot, they were lost.

It is true, the storm was not now quite so violent.

But their strength was failing fast.

The draught of brandy put new energy in them, and once again they seized the handles, and worked fiercely on.

Another hour passed.

Again the carpenter sounded the pumps.

Again they all waited anxiously for his verdict.

"Five feet and a quarter of water in the hold!"

They had gained a quarter of a foot.

They might yet be saved, if the storm did not increase.

More brandy was served out, and once again the exhausted crew pumped on.

It was now broad daylight, and the fury of the storm seemed to have spent itself.

But there was danger that their strength would fail under such tremendous work, or that the gale might again rise.

If such were to happen, all would be over.

Clank, clank, went the pumps, as they worked for dear life.

After another hour, the well was again sounded.

"Four feet and three-quarters in the hold!"

They had gained half a foot.

If they could gain another foot, they would be safe.

They now took a few minutes' rest, which their exhausted condition rendered necessary. Then again, stimulated by brandy, they seized the pump handles, and toiled on bravely.

As day came on, the wind abated with great rapidity, and by twelve the sea began to go down, admitting of efforts being made to stop the leak.

After about an hour of hard work, a sail was passed under the bottom of the ship, which materially aided the desired object.

Again there was but three feet of water in the hold.

The men now pumped in watches—half lying down.

Ere night it would have been difficult to have believed that old ocean had ever been lashed up to such extreme fury.

They were sailing before a fine breeze towards their destination.

Julie and Jessie were once more in their cabin They had hinted enough to Bristowe to make him watch Paolo.

He, however, kept sullenly out of sight.

CHAPTER XXIV.

A MORMON COFFIN.

THE Mormon emigrant ship, after its numerous perils, was now in sight of Boston, to which port it had preferred going, for the simple reason that its course towards New York was suspected.

All understood one another on board that vessel, save the two victims of the hate of Paolo, and the ulterior designs of Phineas Bristowe.

If Paolo had not injured the unfortunate, though wicked Julie, he would not so much have hated her.

He knew that he was the first and primary cause of her downfall.

A man always hates or despises the woman he has ruined.

If he could, he would ever after shun the very sight of her.

How often has this strange hate gone to the length of murder ?

Why is it that men seldom like their illegitimate offspring as well as their rightful children ?

They have done them a wrong.

But now the question was to land Julie and Jessie, without giving them an opportunity of communicating with the officers and others, who would at once board the vessel on its arrival.

Very little favour was shown to a vessel devoted to Mormon immigration.

The better class of Americans, as fine a race as ever lived, hate and abhor the iniquities of this degraded sect.

On a voyage from England to America, some are sure to find out the atrocities of the system, and to repent their having ever joined.

Hence a pure Mormon ship has always a condemned cell.

A cell where they can confine those who have shown themselves restive to the authorities of the infamous and lecherous elders.

Very many of the unfortunates, deluded into a belief in the doctrines of Mormonism, are carried away solely by the religious enthusiasm instilled into them by the rude but artful eloquence of the preachers.

It is only after a time that they begin to read the true character of the apostles of sin, vice, and iniquity.

Then would they gladly escape from the toils of their teachers, as the frightened beast would from the toils of a snake.

But to return to the heroic Jessie and the unfortunate Julie.

No sooner had the first look-out announced the approach of land, than Paolo and Phineas Bristowe had a conference together, despite their secret hatred.

It was part of the trick of these men to be learned in scientific delusions.

Julie was fond of wine, and had persuaded Jessie, after the fearful storm, to take some to revive her drooping spirits.

Julie was careful not to take enough to disgust or alarm her companion.

She had had difficulty enough already to get over her objection to her society.

But Julie was unhappy, and that was already sufficient to excite her sympathy and condolence.

Jessie knew the connection could not last long.

Paolo and Bristowe, after a very short confabulation and conversation, sent in a more than ordinary tasty lunch to the two girls.

They partook of it—as people do on board ship —by way of pastime.

In half-an-hour after, they were fast asleep, and in an hour laid out for dead.

Then two coffins—coffins purposely prepared by the Mormons for their victims—were brought out, into which the inanimate bodies were placed in the presence of several witnesses.

Then it was announced to the appalled crew and passengers that the two prisoners in the state-cabin were no more.

The crew would probably have murmured, but the majority were dupes of the sacrilegious creed of Joseph Smith.

Every preparation was now made to receive the officers of the customs.

No sooner were they at anchor than the majority of the passengers hurried away to the Mormon depot at Drove Point.

The elders who had charge of the dead, alone remained behind.

No hindrance whatever was attempted to be placed in their way.

The officials were used to their disgusting vagaries, and gladly got rid of their enactors.

They were allowed to take away the unfortunate girls in a barge.

They were at once taken to the residence of a Mormon elder.

They, of course —when they came to, with severe head-ache, and a sense of long sleep—never suspected the horrid trick played upon them.

" How could we have been landed ? " said Julie, thoughtfully.

" I don't know."

" Drugged, of course."

" Do you think so ? "

" I am sure of it."

" They are very cruel men. But in this great and free country surely we shall be liberated," cried Jessie, mournfully.

" My girl, these men are playing for a great stake, and will spare no means, lawful or unlawful, to compass their wicked ends. They have agents and friends."

" But we shall travel by public coach," said Jessie.

" I doubt it."

There was silence, broken shortly after by the entrance of several blacks, bearing a copious breakfast—a sight, even in their deplorable condition, not to be despised.

They had not tasted food for fourteen hours.

They spoke to the blacks, but they gave no answer.

" Poor slaves of a dominant race !" said Julie ; " they dare not speak."

" Would, sometimes, that I were a black slave," replied Jessie.

" Oh no ! "

" Why not ? "

" Henry, then, would surely not marry you," said Julie, laughing.

" I shall never see him again," she replied, " after all I have endured. After the sufferings I have gone through, I shall surely die. and not a soul that lives will know where to find my grave."

" Eat," said the more matter-of-fact Julie, " you will be better."

————

CHAPTER XXV.

THE PRIVATE DETECTIVE.

IT would take up too much of our space to record the journey of the man-of-war and the yacht.

It is sufficient for the purposes of our narrative to state, that they reached New York almost about the same time.

Lord Lionel Thynne had written a most energetic letter, promising never to interfere with Jessie again.

Though Henry did not believe the tardy assurance he had received of the good-will that Lord Lionel Thynne felt towards Jessie and himself, he took the advice of his captain, and forbore to quarrel with him any more.

They took up their residence at different hotels, of course.

Lord Lionel shewed himself ostentatiously in all the fashionable resorts, with his wife upon his arm.

What a happy little woman she was!

If men only knew with what ease they could distribute happiness to their wives and children, how much less of misery there would be in the world!

How often have we seen the eye beam, and the colour come at one kind word!

It is the best and easiest delight that soul can give to soul.

Most women would prefer from the man they love, a kind, a gentle word, to the fondest, most passionate caress.

And Adela—good, kind, pretty, little Adela, believed all this sincere.

Not so, Henry Haddington and his gallant captain.

They could no longer confide in a man who had behaved with such extraordinary duplicity.

After a long discussion, they determined on their course of action.

They had heard, that in New York, as in more civilized towns, there existed a race of men, whose sole employment was to pry into the affairs of others—for a consideration.

They were, in fact, private detectives—a race which may have their uses, but of which, happily, the number are few.

Henry and the captain, under the advice of an eminent New York solicitor, who advised them, of course only as a man of business, determined to call in the services of Monsieur Dubost.

He came.

They were at breakfast in a private room. They were too full of sorrow and care to enjoy the splendour and comfort of the public life of a New York hotel.

Paris cannot shew better.

The room was neatly but plainly furnished. Nothing was forgotten for comfort, from spittoons to rocking-chairs.

A sable waiter introduced the celebrated Monsieur Dubost.

They expected, from his name, to see one of those bright specimens of a mouchard so often to be found in Paris.

He might have been of French parentage.

He was a decided Yankee now.

He bowed his way in, however, with considerable evidence of deference and humility.

He was a tall man, thin, cadaverous, without the slightest evidence of whisker or moustache. His hair was thin and spare, turning towards grey. His eye was keen and sharp.

"Sit down, sir."

"Yees, sirree," in a sharp nasal twang, as he took a chair at some distance from the naval officers.

He then placed his hat upon the ground. Into his hat he then dived, and picked out several pieces of paper, and on which he began at once to scribble notes.

"I guess you gents mean business," he said, in a shrill, squeaking voice.

"We do" said the captain.

The private detective kept diving all the time into his hat with marvellous rapidity.

"I guess you'll tell us slick straight off its natur'," said the detective, examining mysterious little packets, one after another, and replacing them in his hat, after a cursory survey.

"Of course."

The captain, as more likely to impress the man than the youngster, spoke, and told his story.

The man listened attentively.

Humph! One man was to watch the movements of my Lord Thynne. A real live lord—no gammon, no mistake.

A real live lord.

Humph! Unusual in a free country to annoy the movements of a British nobleman—but still, if a man were handsomely paid, it might be done—humph!

"Money in reason is no object," said Captain de Lancy, with a smile.

The man made a note on a piece of paper, and handed it to the captain.

He smilingly examined it.

The sum was agreed on.

Monsieur Dubost returned it to his hat, and took out another.

"I understood," he began.

Another dive after a little packet.

"What?"

"Something about my friends, the Mormons," he continued.

"Friends?"

"Yes, friends. I guess, sirreee," he said, with strange pronunciation of the word "sir," which is peculiar to Yankeedom, "you'd call 'em friends too, if they'd a been an' taken off your wife and only daughter. Thunder, I love 'em!"

"You have suffered from them?"

"Wall! I guess, sirree, that if you'd a been and had a respectable business, a pretty wife, a happy whum, and a darter yer prized as the apple o' yer eye, and them blamed vagerbones had took all away, you'd understand—thunder!"

And, in his great excitement, he took out half-a-dozen pieces of paper and made several rapid notes.

"If you will take something, I will explain our views a little more fully," said the captain.

"Thank you, sirree," replied Monsieur Dubosh, "a little brandy cold."

The liquor was brought.

Captain de Lancy told his story minutely, and explained that, in the search for Jessie, Henry would accompany any one who undertook this part of the task.

"Good, sirree," said the man, rising, "he as shall watch the lord, I spec will be ater him in less than no time. Him as will go with the gentleman is yar. Back in half an hour."

And, with a low bow, he crammed all his papers into the everlasting hat, clapped it on his head, and retreated, leaving the two friends in a state of wonder, not unmixed with hope.

CHAPTER XXVI.

THE MORMON RETREAT.

EVERYBODY has heard of the Underground Railway, in America—a name given to a system of escape, organised by quaker philanthropists and others, to assist fugitive slaves escaping from their masters to Canada.

A similar system prevails with regard to the dupes and victims of Mormonism, who are thus hurried from place to place under the very noses of the authorities.

The almighty dollar has too many worshippers in America, to make any thing difficult where there is money to back the transaction.

Julie and Jessie were transferred swiftly and secretly from their prison in Boston, to a similar one elsewhere, without the slightest hope of any interference on the road.

Jessie and Julie had now nothing to hope for, but in their own strength of mind and determination of character.

They, in whispered conversation, for the waggon they travelled in contained many dupes or victims, encouraged one another to the most determined resistance.

Jessie had seen already too much of the world not to dread the worst.

She had less fear, however, of Phineas, than she had of Paolo.

She knew all the unmitigated ruffianism of this man, from personal observation, and the story Julie had unfolded on the journey.

She hated him, as she would have hated a noxious reptile endowed with the knowledge of right and wrong.

Exhausted nature sought, in sweet sleep, refreshing repose—and thus they came to their journey's end.

How they never knew.

They found themselves in a mansion, with apparently no look out toward any main road or street.

Its back looked out upon a large and gloomy garden, with very high walls.

Beyond, were high wooded hills, in the far-off distance.

What chance of escape was there here?

And yet is hope so wonderful and great a thing that it never wholly deserts the human breast.

They were, at all events, not alone.

They were on the first floor, and had the sole range of three rooms. There were numerous others on the same floor, but they were locked, and though both made every effort to open them, their efforts were wholly unavailing.

Again their attendants were silent blacks, who refused to answer any questions that were put.

They waited on them with scrupulous care, but retreated at once their necessary service done.

The girls had no resource but conversation and a piano, upon which, being very splendid musicians, they amused themselves.

Once or twice Julie played, while Jessie accompanied, or they sung duets together.

On one occasion, just as they had concluded a magnificent air, Paolo and Phineas Bristowe entered, accompanied by several attendants.

"Follow me," said Paolo, savagely.

"Whither, wretch?" replied Julie, with a look of fearful hate and scorn.

Two powerful men took her by the arms, and led her away, utterly helpless.

"Why could you not keep quiet, Jessie?" said Phineas, in gentler tones. "I am compelled to remove you from hence."

Jessie smiled one of her superb and lovely smiles, as she rose to follow him.

"Friends have heard us," she said, "or you would not be so alarmed."

Phineas Bristowe replied only by a dark and angry scowl.

"Follow me," he said, bluntly, and Jessie, without hesitation, obeyed.

As she passed through the doorway, the two black attendants threw a thick veil over her head, that effectually deprived her both of sight and speech.

She was then hurried below, towards the basement story of the house.

CHAPTER XXVII.

MADAME DUQUESNE.

SHE had been heard, but not by friends.

Lord Lionel Thynne was driving out in the outskirts of New York, with a very fast Englishman, of middle age, whom he met at the hotel.

Captain Septimus Rowan belonged to no regiment in particular, but it was enough that he had been in the army for him to be a respectable man —so that he found, when he presented himself, in tolerable form, at the hotel, that he was willingly received into general company.

As he was fond of billiards, knew New York well, and was amusing and chatty, he soon ingratiated himself into the good graces of Lord Lionel Thynne, and became his constant and favourite companion.

They played billiards together, walked together, and in the morning, before Lady Thynne was visible to the public eye, drove out together.

They were a well-matched pair. To hear them rattle on about women, one would have said, What a fearful pair of roués!

A roué is the most wretched of all human beings, without knowing it, as he looks upon women only as instruments of his gross pleasures, without reference to the relations of mother, sister, wife.

Alas! he never knows what he loses.

One day they drove into an old Dutch suburb of New York, where there were still houses surrounded with gardens.

On their return home, they drove slowly, the horses being warm, and just as they came abreast of a great mansion, built in the antique style, they halted.

"What is it, my lord?"

"Do you not hear?"

"No."

"Not that superb voice?"

"I think—yes—very fine."

"It is glorious. I never heard its equal but once. I could swear it was the same."

"Impossible."

"But it is."

"How so?"

"What is that house?"

"I don't know—but I can soon find out," replied the captain.

Lord Lionel was silent, and drove slowly off. He was very thoughtful.

That voice was the voice of Jessie, that he could swear.

He would have known it amid a thousand; he felt it thrill through his veins like fire.

He suspected already what that house was; but how to obtain admittance!

It must be done.

But he was not the man to confide his real plans to any one.

He determined to act wholly for himself.

He was a cold and cautious actor where his passions were concerned.

They never got the better of his discretion.

He scarcely spoke until he returned to the hotel, and threw the reins to the well-drilled and obedient grooms.

"Would you try and find out what that house is, captain?" he said.

"Certainly," replied Captain Septimus Rowan, with a bow.

And away he walked, stick in hand, with the true half-pay strut and swagger.

Lord Lionel Thynne would have stared to see him enter the office of Monsieur Dubosh, and give, instead of asking, information.

He was the private detective employed to watch Lord Lionel.

In a few minutes, another gentleman, a sleek, well-dressed, well-to-do looking citizen, entered the inn where Henry and the captain were at lunch.

They saw at once, by his face, that he had good news.

"Well?" said the captain.

"News."

"Good!"

"Found her."

"How?"

"Young gentleman, that is a part of my business which I never reveal."

"I beg pardon."

"Not at all."

"But the news?"

"I know the house in which the young lady is confined," continued the detective, whose patronymic on the present occasion was Johnson.

Henry rose.

"Be calm, sir. We must deliberate."

Henry sat down, pale and anxious.

"The house she occupies has been long suspected as a crimping house for the Mormons at times; but is well known as the country residence of Madame Duquesne."

"Who is Madame Duquesne?"

"Well—a very accommodating lady, who will never ask her boarders for a certificate of marriage," said Johnson.

"This is dreadful. My poor, poor, Jessie!" said Henry, in agonized tones, "when will thy persecutions end?"

"They will not dare mix her up with the infamous company of the house," said Captain De Lancy. "You know their object to be money, and nothing else but money."

"Yes, yes," said Henry; "but how, Mr. Johnson, do you propose to act?"

"Well, sir, you see, it's a difficult job," he replied, scratching his head.

"Never mind."

"But you see."

"Is it money?"

"Well, sir, you've been so very liberal, I don't hardly like to say yes."

"Never mind money."

"Well, you see, it aint everybody can get into Madame Duquesne's. Leastwise, only in certain company."

"Explain your meaning."

"You see, you must be introduced by well-known ladies," he began.

"No matter, the means."

"Well then. I'll introduce you to two ladies, first-raters. They must suspect nothing. You must say, heard tell of their beauty, and heard tell of Madame Duquesne's—and you want to sup there."

"Well! well!"

"I leave you to act for yourselves. I will get assistance and a search-warrant. So if you give the signal, in I come smash through the windows, and if the young lady is there—"

"If—"

"Well!"

"What?"

"It aint professional—but if you won't use the information, I don't mind telling you how we found her out."

"On my word of honour, nothing shall pass my lips," said Henry.

"Does Lord Lionel Thynne know her voice?" asked Johnson, knowingly.

"Yes," replied Henry, with compressed lips.

"Then he says he heard her singing this morning, at the back of this very house——"

"Singing?"

"Well, sir, aint that a good sign?"

"True, true."

"Now, sir, you know what to do."

CHAPTER XXVIII.

NEW YORK LIFE.

WHAT motive it was made Lord Lionel Thynne get rid of his friend, Captain Septimus Rowan, he could not even explain unto himself.

It was a kind of instinct

He then went up stairs, and found his wife at her toilette.

"How well you look," he said, with a soft, hypocritical smile.

"Perhaps I do," she replied. "If so, it is because I am happy."

"You look so, ducky. By the way, could you manage to do one day without me," he continued, kissing her white shoulder.

"It's a long time."

"True; but, dear, you know I must join at times in manly sports. I have heard of a party going up the Hudson, for a day's shooting. They leave in about an hour—they will be back to-morrow evening—what say you?"

"Leave me all night," said Adela, with genuine horror.

"Well, darling, it seems hard, does it not? But if you really cannot——"

"Lionel, I am a little fool, I know. But I don't want you tied to my apron strings. Be careful, and come back as soon as possible."

Lord Lionel kissed her, and after some talk, went out.

He felt a kind of dull remorse at deceiving that loving child; but his fierce passions soon got the better of his good feeling.

Adela was very sad. What he had said might be true. But a woman once deceived, is not easily deceived again—at least, not wholly.

She had heard him give an order in the hall, to George, to fetch his shooting tackle, and bring it ashore.

That was something.

But then his great and sudden hurry to be away from her, a hurry he had not manifested for some days before—days which appeared like a second honeymoon.

How often is a man more kind when he is deceiving than when not.

Happy, good, and contented husbands are so often indifferent.

It is a fatal necessity however, which women would do well to understand.

We must leave poor Adela racked by doubt, and follow Lord Lionel Thynne.

A quiet French *valet de place*, at once informed his lordship of the character of the house from whence the lovely voice had emanated.

Lord Lionel heard him with incredulous and angry astonishment.

"It is vare true," said the valet.

"But the lady, whose voice I heard, could not have been in such a place."

"Vare mooch fine lady go dere—yes—me lord."

"How to gain admittance?"

"Most take one lady."

"Indeed—but——"

"I show you one vare bootifool lady—she vare fond of go to Madame Duquesne. She fust-rater."

"Get a hired vehicle," said the profligate nobleman, scarcely concealing his disgust.

The *valet de place* gave an ignoble grin, bowed, retired, and in a few minutes more they were rolling together towards the abode of the fine lady.

She occupied a small neat house in a retired street, and was certainly very handsome and voluptuous looking.

She received the English lord with the utmost respect and delight.

"You may go," she said, in the most supercilious tone, to the valet.

He bowed.

"Here, fellow," cried Lord Lionel, taking out a hundred dollar note; "mind, if you breathe a word of what has passed, I'll find some means of having revenge."

The man bowed obsequiously, after seeing the note, and went out delighted. To what lower depth of degradation can humanity fall?

The woman was his wife.

"And now, *mon chere ami*," began the courtezan, who was in complete *deshabille*, "have you come to spend the day? I like to spend the day. A *recherché* dinner here, and then at dark a carriage, and a drive to Madame Duquesne's, supper, and ——"

Her voluptuous eyes said the rest.

Lord Lionel Thynne acquiesced.

"First, then, I will dress—at least, when I have ordered dinner. You can smoke, or read, or look out of window."

"I prefer to help you to dress," said the volatile Lord Lionel.

"Thank you."

It was dark, when a close carriage, one of those mysteriously affected to this special purpose, drew up to the door.

It was a one-horse brougham.

They nestled inside, and drew up the blinds. Lord Lionel could not afford to be seen.

The blinds, however, enabled you to look out.

They dashed along the road at a considerable pace; but a two-horse brougham passed them on the road.

"The sisters Leona," said the woman, whose name was Lucie.

"Who are they?"

"Friends of Madame Duquesne," laughed Lucie, with a tap with her fan.

"Oh!"

"Now, do you know, my gentle lord, that I have a habit, when I take a friend to Madame Duquesne's, of keeping that friend to myself."

"But ——"

"Listen. I do not mean that you should not move about and enjoy yourself; but I don't allow any other lady to monopolize your attention."

"Certainly."

"That understood—move about, speak, laugh, joke, play cards, do as you please; but I'll watch you get into no mischief."

"Thank you. Mischief enough yourself."

"Yes," she said, with a sigh; "but I was not mischief once."

"What then?"

"A good and faithful wife."

"The deuce!"

"You may laugh, but nothing is more true. My husband deceived me with low wretches I would not have touched with the hem of my dress. I swore to be revenged—and I am what I am."

ADELA AT MADAME DUQUESNE'S.

"And your husband ——"

"Takes hundred dollar notes from noble lords for a special introduction," she said. with bitter sarcasm in her trembling voice.

"What?"

"'Tis true."

"He your husband?"

"In name. We are total strangers. I am now reckless. He has fallen as low as man can fall. I treat him as I would a dog. But I have a sweet revenge."

"What is that?"

"The wretch loves me."

Lord Lionel Thynne shuddered. Much as he had seen of life, this was too horrible.

But he only laughed.

He could not afford to show his disgust and repulsion at them both.

CHAPTER XXIX.

MADAME DUQUESNE.

A QUIET old place, to all appearance, was this temple of pleasure, the favourite resort of the wealthy voluptuaries of New York.

But every night, at dark, the scattered neighbours see carriage upon carriage arrive, and set down the well-dressed and the lovely daughters of night.

All knew what style of house it was. But it was better here than in the heart of the city. It was well-conducted, and nothing was said.

Lucie gave a peculiar knock and ring, upon which the door opened, and the brougham drove off to a stable, well aware its services would not be required for hours.

Then a number whispered up stairs, was quite enough to bring it to the door.

They ascended a dimly-lighted staircase, and entered a room, which more resembled the gambling rooms at Baden-Baden than anything else we could describe.

There were well-dressed men, beautiful women, card tables, music, wine, and every kind of refreshment.

The whole set off by a rich, pungent perfume, which left nothing to desire.

And yet where was the pleasure of all this glitter and feverish excitement?

Nobody ever yet could tell, and I am quite sure nobody ever will.

Lord Lionel Thynne took the arm of Lucie, and walked about.

There were many rooms. Some for hazard, some for cards, and some for dancing.

They went to the latter.

Imagine, when Lucie pointed out the sisters Leona dancing, the dismay of Lord Lionel.

They were dancing with Henry and Captain de Lancy.

It is true, that Henry and his superior officer were very serious, but the public set that down as English gravity.

Lord Lionel turned scornfully away.

"So, my lord, how is this I find you here?" said a voice of not inconsiderable attraction.

He turned.

"Madame Duquesne," said Lucie, with a courtesy; "and I leave you in her care, while I go speak to a friend."

"Mrs. ——"

"Hush!" said the woman, leaning her arm on his; "my London name is unknown here."

"Can I speak with you alone?"

She smiled.

"None of your nonsense," he said; "I can put a thousand in your pocket."

"Pounds, not dollars," she replied, with a greedy expression.

"Yes."

"Follow me," she answered; and raising a curtain, she pushed open a sliding pannel, closed it again, and they were in a lovely boudoir, receiving no light except from the top, and most magnificently and erotically furnished.

"Only your own few," he said, with a smile, "are admitted here."

The eyes of this noted Messalina flashed almost indignant fire.

"You used to be one of them."

"Never mind. I came to talk of business. Do you want a cheque for a thousand?"

"Of course I do. I think of retiring soon. I am sick of ——"

"What?"

"Never mind what; go on."

"The money is easily earnt."

"Speak."

"Bring to me here, place in my power, that girl whose voice I heard this morning, and the money is yours."

She turned ghastly pale.

"What know you of that voice?"

"I know her well—and, by heavens, there are others here who know it too!—those English gentlemen with the sisters Leona."

"Ah!"

"They will not offer money."

"What then?"

"They will appeal to the law and police."

"Who is she, then?"

"An heiress, and the affianced wife of the younger man," said Lord Lionel.

"And you will give me a thousand pounds?"

"I will."

"Draw on your bankers at once."

"Before I see her?"

"My lord, my word is as good as yours. If you do not get her, you can write by the same ship to stop the order."

He took up a pen, and wrote upon a stamped paper, which she laid before him, the necessary draft.

She took it, with a dulcet smile.

Then she pressed a bolt, took up a lamp, and a dark stairs was revealed.

"Her friends heard her singing," she said, "and were afraid."

"The deuce!—who are they?"

"How should I know?—I never ask."

"So they took her to the vaults. Don't shudder —they are as warm and easy as my boudoir; only nobody, who did not know, *could ever find them.*"

Lord Lionel followed her impatiently.

They soon reached a kind of corridor, with a strong door at one end.

The corridor was paved with flagstones.

Madame Duquesne pointed to one, and showed a slight dent in the side.

"Put your finger to it."

It rose with ease, and revealed a stairs descending to another chamber, from which the same warm, pungent, aromatic odour arose that Lord Lionel had noticed at the top of the stairs.

"Go, and joy go with you! You had better bring her up to the boudoir. They both sleep," she added, with an infernal smile.

He descended eagerly, and as he did so, the paving stone closed over him with a dull clang.

The woman smiled a hideous and painful smile. It was frightful to look at.

"There you remain, my lord, until the thousand pounds is paid - if not longer," she said.

And she turned away.

"As if the others would not pay me better," she added, as she ascended the stairs.

She was soon in the boudoir again, and in a few minutes she was about to re-enter the saloon.

A dull murmur reached her ears.

She opened a small hole.

A fearful uproar was in the place.

The police had burst in in large force, and all the people were leaving in a hurry.

Madame Duquesne knew at once that her house was ruined.

With a calm determination, worthy of a better cause, she opened a large box, took forth a small ebony casket, containing all her savings in notes, shares, and securities, and hurriedly returned the way she came.

She had friends in New York, and a vessel sailed for Havre, before daylight.

CHAPTER XXX.

THE SEARCH.

WHEN Henry and Captain de Laney found that there was no visible communication with the back of the house and the front, they determined to act with vigour.

Henry went to the front, broke a pane of glass, and putting his mouth to the heavy shutters, gave a shrill whistle.

At once a man rushed over, and gave the peculiar knock and ring.

The door opened.

In rushed at least thirty policemen, and detectives, who took possession of the house.

The gay visitors ran off in all directions.

Henry and Captain de Laney remained complete masters of the situation.

But where was Lord Lionel Thynne?

They had both seen him in company with the woman Lucie, but when she left he had not accompanied her.

They must make a fresh search, and, in the meantime, the police were directed to bring back the young woman.

But she knew nothing, save that Madame Duquesne seemed to recognise her noble admirer, and had called him on one side.

The police all declared that Madame Duquesne had not gone out the front way.

But she had disappeared. She was nowhere to be found.

When it was found that Madame Duquesne had disappeared, of course the police made no difficulty as to an elaborate search of the house taking place.

Henry tore through the place like a madman. Every stair was ascended, every door opened, every cupboard examined.

But no Jessie.

Every trace of the Mormons had also utterly disappeared.

They had, in all probability, taken the alarm, and, favoured by their diabolical ingenuity, and extraordinary luck, had escaped.

It was no use doubting the matter; so, after a wearisome and hopeless search, the police were left in possession of the house, and the others left, in despair at their bad luck.

But where was Lord Lionel Thynne?

All asked themselves this question, though none were able to give a favourable answer.

He had been seen to go in, but no one had seen him go out.

That, however, was of little consequence now, as it was clear that it was the Mormons who were in possession of Jessie.

The rage, despair, and frantic agony of Henry, may be conceived, but not described.

It was in vain for his friend to endeavour to moderate him.

He would not be comforted.

Consolation, even the consolation of religion, will not come all at once. Time is the only true comforter, and restorer of the mind, as nature's sweet restorer, sleep, is of the body.

At length, however, they succeeded in inducing him to listen to reason.

All knew now where the Mormon emigration was tending, and there was no doubt that Jessie would be taken to swell the body of the elect, in this great Agapemone of Prostitution.

All they had to do, then, was to follow in their track.

This Henry decided to do.

The task was, however, not altogether an easy one for them to carry out.

The Mormons went about armed unto the teeth, and in great force.

To travel in small bodies was not possible, for already their great unpopularity had commenced.

Not only were they guilty of ensnaring away the wives and daughters of respectable farmers and labourers, but they laid hands upon what some people consider even more sacred property—they stole chickens, fowls, pigs, and other domestic articles, without compunction or remorse.

Their neighbours at first despised, then feared, and at last hated them.

There was one consolation, at least, to the mind of Henry.

Jessie was not in the unhallowed hands of Lord Lionel Thynne.

He knew scarcely why, but he had not the same fear of Phineas Bristowe, as he had of the libertine and unprincipled nobleman.

CHAPTER XXXI.

A MORMON CELL.

MEANWHILE, the police, having fastened up the entrance, and assured themselves that the house was deserted, proceeded, as policemen will, to regale themselves on the many good things which the guests had left behind them.

They occupied the deserted saloons, and were soon so well employed, that, what with good eating, wine, and laughter, they became utterly oblivious of their calling.

Then a shape, which none had seen before, flitted across the room.

It had a lantern in its hand.

It entered the boudoir.

As it gazed mournfully around, it shook its head.

It was a woman—in fact, Lady Thynne, who, on the watch for her husband, had entered the house with the police unperceived.

She knew that he had not gone out. She knew that he must be still somewhere within the mansion.

Her jealous imagination—jealous in the just and fair point of view—made her at once believe in his being with Jessie. He would have come out had he not found her.

She looked upon their search after the young

girl as merely superficial, and was firmly convinced that she was still concealed within the house.

Of course she knew nothing of the secret machinations of the Mormons, whose infernal ingenuity in fraud and falsehood she had yet to learn the extent of.

She passed through the boudoir and descended the stone stairs.

She soon reached the paved corridor, from which opened up so many doors.

They were all open now, and disclosed the neatly-furnished cells of Mormon victims.

But they were empty.

Not knowing what to think, she went out into the garden.

Her jealous rage passed away, like a flash of lightning.

She began now to feel a strange kind of fear for her husband.

Let either a husband or wife, who have once loved, find the other in danger, and the old feeling must bubble up.

The Lady Adela began to be seriously alarmed. What had they done with him?

She knew Henry to be incapable of a bad or ungenerous action.

But there might be others concerned in the matter, who might not be so nice.

She went out into the garden, we have said, and looked up at the house. But not a trace of light was visible.

She returned slowly towards the house, and as she did so, a faint moan fell distinctly upon her ear.

She looked wildly and warily around her, and listened.

Again a low, fearful moan came distinctly to her.

She searched along the house, but could make out no window, not even a grating.

She re-entered the villainous mansion, which, like many a similar one in this country, reeked with crime.

She walked slowly along the passage, and again carefully examined every cell.

Not the faintest trace of any living being could she see.

It was a dreadful state of suspense to endure.

She left the lantern in a cell, and recollecting that the moan had seemed to come from below, lay flat upon the stones.

Then she plainly and distinctly heard it again.

Once more the lamp was had recourse to, and she examined the ground with extreme care.

With a cry of joy, she saw that one of the flags was a trap. A jagged, broken hole enabled her to insert her finger and raise it.

A dark pit opened before her. Steps led below. With the heroic courage of a wife, she descended, and soon found herself in a small and handsomely-furnished bedchamber.

These chambers emitted no sounds whatever from within.

Of course the poor young girl never imagined the atrocious aim to which they were put.

On a sofa, gasping for breath, but now slightly recovering, lay her husband. He was in a fit

from sheer rage. When he saw that he was not alone in the apartment, he flew towards her, with a yell.

" Wretch!"

" Husband!"

" Adela," he gasped, "is it you who have saved me from death?"

" It is."

" My own dear, generous girl!"

" How came you here?"

" I know not. Some friends tempted me to this villainous den. I was first drugged, then robbed, and finally cast here to die. Come away; I feel as if I were in a grave."

Adela said nothing for a moment.

" The house is in the hands of the police," said Adela, after a while. "What is to be done? I don't want to be seen."

" Can we not escape by the garden?" he replied, eagerly.

" Come," said Adela; and going out, they searched the garden round.

A small door, that by which Madame Duquesne had escaped, was found open. It led down to a kind of creek or bayou. Several boats were there, but without oars or skulls.

They were compelled to work round, and gain the highway, which, after following for about a mile, brought them to where a cabman stood drinking.

For the promise of a handsome fare, he drove them swiftly into New York, to their hotel, where we leave them for the present.

CHAPTER XXXII.

THE MORMON CARAVAN.

By dint of considerable enquiry, by questioning right and left, the young officer and his captain found out the probable route that the Mormon caravan would take.

They did not travel from New York as they did in more thinly-peopled districts.

They excited as little observation as possible, knowing themselves to be obnoxious to the feelings and sentiments of the better class of the community.

Besides, Phineas Bristowe and the Viscount de Florac, had their own reasons for not exciting particular observation.

They, therefore, sent forward the great body of the dupes by a boat, as far as they could go, and themsleves, taking the ferry, crossed over to the mainland, and hiring two light waggons, made an appointment, and started separate ways.

Phineas Bristowe still continued his solemn assurances to Jessie, that, as soon as he could come to terms with her relatives and friends, she should be restored to them.

All he asked was immunity for the past, and a slight provision for the future.

This Jessie coldly promised him.

On any other topic she declined to converse with him, but, seated back in the waggon, remained wrapped in deep thought.

At the time of which we speak, the saints had no local habitation, bad as their name was. They were scattered over the face of the land, preparatory to the time when they should be summoned to gather together, and journey to Zion, the New Jerusalem of their hopes.

The saints, then, while hurrying towards their coming head-quarters, were occasionally able to find hospitality at the house of a friend.

If not, they were compelled either to put up at an inn, or trust to the hospitality of a wayside house, where they took very good care to say nothing about their disgraceful and abominable doctrines.

Jessie, who, strange to say, had no dread of Phineas Bristowe himself, nor dread of others when in his company, never said a word to throw doubt upon his assertions.

There was one thing she knew. Henry was on her track, of that she was certain—something told her it was so.

Phineas Bristowe, for very obvious reasons, chose all the unfrequented ways possible; went round, indeed, to avoid highways, and put up, if possible, rather at the wooden shanties of the half-ignorant back-woodsmen, than in the houses of respectable and well-to-do farmers.

His own deficiencies had less chance of being found out.

Besides, he knew he might venture on sounding sometimes his host, or, at all events, his wife or daughter.

Jessie soon found that her journey was not to be so peaceful as she could have wished—she had again to endure and suffer.

CHAPTER XXXIII.

THE NIGHT AT DOU'S CREEK.

THEY had travelled all day along a very bad road, in the hope of reaching a small village, well-known to Phineas as a station of the Mormons—a halting place for the saints.

But the roads were heavy from rain, and the two wretched hired hacks done up.

In this predicament a halt was declared.

It was quite dark, and Phineas Bristowe, considerably annoyed, descended from the shaft, mounted a bank, and looked around.

Soon his researches were rewarded by the appearance of a light at no great distance.

"House!" he cried.

"Hilloa! who's thar?"

"Strangers—lost their way—cattle used up. Can you give us a bed?"

"Don't knoa, stranger—let's look at yer," said a jolly voice. "Perhaps I mout, and perhaps I mout'nt."

"Come, Jessie," cried Phineas Bristowe, guessing, from the other's tone, how much more influence she would have than he could expect, "get down, and let us enter the house."

As he spoke, he saw a kind of road, and allowing Jessie, wrapped in a thick woollen shawl, to go first, he drew the wearied steeds along.

"Woll," said the man.

"Please sir," answered Jessie, rather frightened at his tone, "our beasts are tired out, and we would be glad to rest awhile."

"Thee shall, as sure as I'm no Dutchman. A rather guess, young 'un, this 'ere kind of life don't shute yer constitution. Come in."

"Thank you."

"Come in—who's the old 'un?"

"Father," said Jessie, who had, after some hesitation, agreed to call him by this name along his whole journey.

"Oh!"

They entered a regular log hut, of rude character, but considerable dimensions; one-half was divided into two compartments, and Jessie could see that both had beds in them.

"Woll—I guess you're considerable slick looking girl for a Britisher," began the man, who was about forty, good looking, but rough in speech and manner.

"How do you know I am English?" said Jessie, with a smile.

"My! woll, that 'ere beats creation. Woll, all you Britishers hos sich a pertikler barr, at the ond of yer tongues, like, there's no mistaking you; that's a fact."

"Just as we know an American in England," added Jessie.

"Oh, yes, I spect yer does! Don't yar such English at the court uv Queen Victoria, eh? that's a fact."

"I believe you are right," said Jessie, who, but for the entrance of Phineas Bristowe, must have laughed outright in the Yankee's face.

"We are much obliged," began Phineas, "for the accommodation. I expected to have reached Neatsville."

"You ain't a ——Mormon?" said the man, with a fierce glance.

"I don't know anything about Mormons," said Phineas, quietly; "but I was told to rest there, on my way up country,"

"That's right—most people du stop thar. Woll, my gal is out, so young woman, if as how yer likes, the inner room's your'n; the old 'un can cotton to the settle."

"I thank you."

"You are very kind."

"Thunder!" said the other, in a loud voice. "You're in a tarnation hurry, anyhow. Ain't yer got no teeth in yer head—eh? And don't yer ever eat nothin,—eh?"

"We have provisions in our van," began Phineas, in a kind of whining tone.

"Provisions—beg yer pardon, young lady—but provisions be spifflicated. This here night you sups with old Jacob Squash—and I only wishes, for your sake, as how my old woman—old Squash I calls her—and Em'ly Squash, and Jane Squash, were to whum, they'd make you kinder more welcome than I have."

"I'm sure you are very, kind," said Jessie, resting her soft hand on his arm.

The backwood farmer smiled, and commenced bringing out all the good things which his rather extensive batchelor larder afforded.

These Jessie, with great neatness and despatch, placed correctly on the table.

"Now I guess," said the farmer, watching her sylph-like movements with delight, "you're what my old father used to call a young lady. He was a Britisher, he was. Woll, he used to say as how you ladies had a knack a doing things slick—anyhow, I see he was about right."

"Your father was an Englishman?"

"He war."

"But his name was'nt Squash."

"No more ain't mine," said the other, with a broad grin, "it's only my nick——"

"What?"

"My nickname. My name's Beckford."

"The deuce it is! And what part of England did you come from?"

"My father, I guess, were a kind of what you call tenant uv old Sir Marmaduke Haddington, the werry old 'un as was."

Jessie almost started. Phineas Bristowe, whose back was to the farmer, turned deadly pale. He knew the man now. He had before suspected.

"Woll, you see stranger," said the garrulous backwoodsman, "father he had a oldest son—my brother, you see—but he got to be a big man, and guess father did'nt think he war a dootiful son—so father sloped, and here I is, his descendant and executor. But now, stranger, fire away."

Supper was now hailed with pleasure by all parties—Jessie would gladly have been alone to have thought over the revelations of the farmer.

As soon as it was ended, she retired to rest, and closed the door.

Phineas Bristowe lit a pipe, scarcely knowing what he was doing.

The farmer bustled about.

CHAPTER XXXIV.

A MORMON MIRACLE.

Soon they were all ready for bed.

"Good night, stranger," said the farmer, in a jolly good-humoured tone.

Phineas could have sworn it was the voice of his old neglected father.

"Good night, bro——" began Phineas.

Rat! tat! tat!

A very gentle timid knock, as of one who was afraid to knock louder, or whose physical powers would not allow him to do so.

With a kind of good-humoured growl, the farmer went to the door.

"Spect it aint an inn," he said.

A gaunt, spare man, with hollow eyes, and cadaverous features, entered.

"A glass of water and a shakedown," he muttered; "I am very ill."

The good farmer gave him some cider, and assisted him to a seat.

He slightly wetted his lips, and then rejected the liquor with disdain.

"Sleep," he muttered.

"Help me to lay him on the bed," said the farmer to Bristowe.

Phineas did so, and soon the man lay on the bed, utterly exhausted.

Finding he did not wake, he took a large bearskin coat, wrapped it round himself, and lying down before the fire, was soon in the sleep of the just and the good.

Phineas could not sleep for some time. As he gazed upon the features of the sleeping man, big drops of sweat came bursting over his face and neck.

He was gazing, as it were, on the features of his dead father.

For this was his own father's son.

The cause of their separation will appear at a future period.

At last, he too slept on the long settle beside the fire, nor woke until glad day had long since been heralded by chanticleer.

He found the farmer and Jessie busily employed setting out the breakfast things in the most friendly manner.

One glance sufficed to show him that he had nothing to fear from any words on her part.

"Now, stranger," he said, to the man who lay on the bed, "break'ast."

No answer.

"I say, old feller, had a mighty tall sleep," continued the farmer.

No answer.

"Then I'm darned if I don't shake a little life into you—Golly! the man's stark, stone, staring dead!"

"Dead!" repeated Phineas.

"Dead!" faltered Jessie.

"Dead!" said Jabez Squash, as he called himself; "I wou'nt a had it happened."

"Who said dead?" cried a voice that made Phineas shudder. "There are none dead, save those whom the Lord has called unto himself. Ah! our brother has indeed been called unto heaven; but there is a power on earth to loose and unloose, to bind and unbind—and I am a humble instrument of that power."

"Ay're yer?"

Phineas drew Jessie into the chamber he had recently occupied. He shook, as with a palsy, with terror and guilty shame.

"I am. This man who appears unto you dead only sleepeth," said the preacher, unmindful of the other's tone, or the wild gleam of his eye; "and if you will have patience, I will show unto you the power of the saints. After one short prayer, he shall arise and walk."

"Shall he?"

"He shall. Stand aside, and behold the triumph of truth and of faith."

Phineas shuddered.

"Shall I?"

"Our deceased brother."

"Hearken, Muster Preacher," said Squash, with something like a grin. "I suppose you ain't pertikler to the complaint."

"Certainly not."

"It mout be measles."

"It might," said the preacher, rather uneasily.

"It mout be cholera."

"It might—but——"

"Well, you see, if it ain't no difference to you, stranger—I never did see a corpus brought to life—resuskicated, I thinks you call it; but then, d'ye see, before I believes in the bringing to, I must be sure of the going off. I believes, from yer mug, as how yer might revive this here corpus—but to make shure, yer see, I gives his neck a chop with this here axe—off it goes, and——"

"I'll be darned if yer do!" cried the supposed corpse, bounding from the bed, and making immense tracks through the door, for the open country.

The missionary would have followed.

"You low, long legged skunk, you pot-bellied abortion of a Latter-Day Saint, you foul spawn of Satan—go! But let another Mormon elder enter my house, and he leaves it not alive. Go, lest, in my just rage—but first hearken. You know, you skulking hound, that I have daughters. Let me but hear that you have spoken to them, and I'll skin you alive, and then burn your blamed village about your ears."

And thus warned, *Christian Whitmer* slunk out, followed by the revilings of the justly-enraged farmer.

"I can't help it, miss," said the farmer, when he came in, and found them at breakfast, very pale and hurried. "Take your breakfast. Do not let that horrid scene make you uncomfortable."

"Oh, dear no! I was certainly a little startled at first."

"Ah, miss, you don't know! These wretched Mormons give us no peace. We are almost obliged to lock our children in. It is not safe to let them go to a dance or a frolic. My old 'ooman gen'rally stops at whum with me, but now the old 'uns must go to take care of the young 'uns. Cheer up, miss—and may heaven keep you from these blamed vagabones."

"Amen!" said Jessie, heartily, not daring to look at her companion.

Phineas here rose, and thanking the farmer for his generous hospitality. hurried to saddle his two hacks. Nor did he appear at all easy in his mind until he had started on his way, though the farmer gave him a hearty invitation to come again.

CHAPTER XXXV.

CHRISTIAN WHITMER AGAIN.

"You must not mind what that prejudiced man says," remarked Phineas, after they had proceeded some distance from the log hut.

Jessie made no reply.

"There can be no doubt," continued Phineas, "that in all sects, religions, and parties, there are black sheep—why not, then, in the true one?"

"Silence," said Jessie, quietly. "You know very well that I am not to be deceived. It is no part whatever of our compact that I am to listen to heresy, falsehood, and deceit."

He turned away very pale, and bit his lips till the blood came.

No conversation passed for some time. Jessie was thinking over the strange fortunes she had endured for years, and wondering when Henry would be on her track. That he would be so, there admitted no doubt. And her little heart throbbed, and her cheeks flushed, as the thought filled her mind.

The village or collection of log huts. called by the euphonic name of Dou's Creek, was about five miles distant.

They could see the distant hills which crowned the habitations.

They were steep, wild, and precipitous, and covered by stunted pines.

They looked in the distance like a black and wavy mass. Smoke rose from some of their summits, the smoke of the wild charcoal burners of that district.

They were ascending one hill after descending another, when Phineas suddenly turned his head.

A band of horsemen were coming at full gallop along the road. Their mad and furious gestures proclaimed the intensity of their rage. They were waving rifles on high, and they seemed to call on them to stop.

Suddenly a rifle was levelled in the direction of the waggon. Phineas Bristowe coolly halted, and drew up his waggon by the wayside.

The horsemen soon were up to them, and surrounded the waggon. with angry gestures.

"What want you?" said Phineas, calmly, addressing the supposed Jabez Squash.

"What is the matter?" added Jessie, in her softest and mildest tones. "Surely nothing evil has happened in this short time."

"My daughters, my little ones, my children, have been lured away by the wretched Mormons!" cried the father, whose affected Yankeeism, faded away under the influence of genuine sorrow.

"Merciful heavens!—But we know nothing about them," cried Jessie.

"I don't know that," said the man doggedly, "take him away. I will examine them separately."

Phineas Bristowe was removed by the orders of the leader, by which title he was unanimously recognized, as being the injured party in this case.

"Before I answer any questions," said the girl, with calm dignity, "will you explain what your charge is against us?"

"First, I think you Mormons—I know you are going to the settlement. Second, it is strange you should have come last night to sleep just when there was an empty bed."

"Well?"

"In the next place, my little ones went to a frolic last evening—it lasted all night. In the morning, when mother woke from a nap, both were gone, coaxed away by a fellow in spectacles, just like that chap."

"Well?"

"Now, if you had nothing to do with it, you know something about it. If I find it so, I am damned if I don't flay you and him alive."

"You will not. You will not lay a finger either on him or on me, John Charles *Beckford*."

"What? Say that again. Did I say that to you last night?"

"No, you said that your family name was *Beckford*; that is all."

"Then, how know you?"

"No matter. Can you keep a secret?"

"I can. Speak!"

"My name is Jessie Cornelia Treherne, and I am the affianced wife of Henry Marmaduke Haddington, sole heir to the honours of that noble house," she said, calmly.

"Heavens!" he cried, doffing his cap; " can this be true? But Henry Marmaduke Haddington —why not Sir?"

"Because until his father's strange disappearance is explained, or death proved, he will not assume the baronetcy."

The man's brow cleared up, as if by magic, as he heard her speak.

"And when shall you see Master Henry again?" he said, respectfully, forgetting for a moment his own sorrows.

"Soon I hope," she said, with a sigh. " But ask no explanations. I shall rest in the Mormon village some days, for so I choose. Now, be guided by me wholly for a few days—and if your daughters are among the Mormons, I will trace and restore them."

"I care not, if they have disgraced themselves," said the other, passionately.

"Trust in Providence. Hang about the village —watch me—and trust me to find some means to communicate with you."

"Heaven bless you!" he cried; and then assisted her to take her seat once more.

He rode off, and in a few minutes returned with Phineas Bristowe, who was surprised to behold the deference with which Jabez Squash treated Jessie. The whole cavalcade, at a whispered word from Squash, rode off.

"Those girls *must* be restored at once, before ruin overtakes them," said Jessie, quietly.

"Must—why?"

"Do you forget who they are? If nature is not wholly dead within you, ——"

"Nature—what mean you?"

"Hush! Do not attempt to deceive me. Phineas Bristowe, *alias* ——"

"Silence! Not a word. Girl, you are right. They are of my blood, and they shall be saved," said the other, huskily. " I have done much evil, but I have not yet lost all feeling. My own flesh and blood shall never suffer. But, Jessie, we must be cautious, very cautious. If my brethren thought I had betrayed them, I should be lost."

"Can I do anything?"

"I suspect Christian Whitmer. He is already my enemy. I must, therefore, be cautious, very cautious. See, yonder comes a lad mounted on a donkey. Send him to—to Squash's—say that if he comes at midnight, close to the northern end of the village, you will, if his children be there, conduct him to them. Let him be well-armed, but come alone."

The girl hastily wrote a note, and fastened it by means of knitting cord.

It turned out that the boy was a help of the good farmer's, going to his work, who willingly took the note.

CHAPTER XXXVI.

A SMALL MORMON VILLAGE.

THE harem system, where eighty wives or more lived under one roof, or divan—the parent wigwam —had not, at the time of which we speak, been introduced.

Mormonism, in its open defiance of the world, was not the hideous thing it is now—shameless, reckless, vile—beyond power of description.

When we come to Nauvoo, and the City of the Salt Lake, our readers will fully comprehend the reason w y we have neared the subject gradually, with repugnance and hesitation.

But even in its early days, when polygamy was restricted to two, or, at most, three wives, it was revolting enough.

A man may here keep a wife, and concubine under the same roof, in the shape of a governess, or servant, or companion; but the woman knows it not; or even, if she suspects it, and, for her own dignity's sake, or the happiness of her children, declines to make a scandal thereof, at least, she avows it not.

Let us enter Dou's Creek, and see the picture it represents.

It was a village of about thirty houses, built without much regularity, but the doors always looking towards a common centre.

There was always an affectation of Arcadian and patriarchal simplicity about the Mormons, which seems as suitable as it might be with a congregated mass of London pickpockets and street-walkers.

In the centre were held the games, dancing, wrestling, running, and such like.

There were several empty houses, which had belonged to Mormons, who had been forwarded to the upper settlement as they were ready.

At the door of the principal house, stood Christian Whitmer, and the man who had pretended to be dead. They leered at Jessie, with a strange and dangerous expression.

Phineas Bristowe smiled scornfully.

Jessie, at his desire, now alighted, and looked around her.

She saw dismal huts, listless-looking men, slatternly women, and a crowd of children playing about the lawn, or hanging round their mother's feet at the doors.

But nobody took any notice of the poor defenceless little creatures.

They were common property. And we all know to what the system of common property leads.

What is everybody's business is nobody's business.

But Jessie had little time now to examine the scene, as Phineas Bristowe, for reasons of his own, was eager to get her inside a hut; hurried her out of the van, placed their worldly goods in the house, and left her there without locking the door.

'Twas the advantage of being truthful. No one could doubt that bright and sunny face.

Talk of merely beautiful features—a truthful, honest face is worth it all.

The hut into which Jessie had been ushered, was a mere log house, requiring no further description, but its back-window had a look out upon those mysterious pine-clad hills they had seen from afar off.

Jessie sat down upon a large deal box, and gazed musingly at them.

Meanwhile, Phineas Bristowe, his teeth set, and his brow knit, had walked up to Christian Whitmer.

THE SHOT FROM THE HUT.

"So, sir!" he said, in a menacing voice.

"So sir, to you!"

"You remember our last meeting, I suppose?"

"Guess I do."

"And you are not ashamed?"

"Of what?"

Phineas was deadly pale.

"What has become of Susan?"

"Inside there."

"And Mrs. Brown?"

"Inside there."

"Hum! That affair last night was a narrow escape for you.'"

"Rather," said Whitmer, looking at his accomplice.

"Now, Whitmer, it's our interest, as elders, to be friends, and, on one condition, I will."

"What's that?"

"You saw that girl?"

"I did."

"She must be respected."

"Ha! ha! ha!"

"She is too good *for us*. Besides, she is a great card—a very great card."

"How so?"

"I can make thousands by restoring her to her friends. While, if I were to try to keep her, we

should bring round us a hornet's nest, which would
do us more harm than you can conceive."

"But the thousands?"

"You shall have a fair share."

"Then friends we are."

"I want you to do another favour."

"What is that?"

"I want Jessie to take her meals with your
people, while the hut is being done up for her accommodation."

"Certainly."

"But as she is not a Mormon, and never is
likely to be ——"

"I understand, old fellow—all correct and
proper."

"I will fetch her, while you go speak to the
women," continued Phineas.

Christian Whitmer turned away, with a strange
scowl upon his selfish, brutal, and malignant
countenance.

Phineas Bristowe, who believed in him just as
far as he could see him, turned away in mute and
stern disgust.

Bad as this man was, he could see the utter
rottenness of the other's soul.

Jessie was quietly watching the hills from her
open window.

"Jessie," said Phineas, seriously, "I am
about to do that which will place my life in jeo-
pardy."

"Indeed!"

"To have a chance of success, I must dispose
of Whitmer."

"How?"

"I must intoxicate him. You know him not.
On the faintest suspicion of the truth, do you
know what the wretch would do?"

"What?"

"Jessie, you are a brave girl, and, as I live,
shall come to no harm."

"Thank you."

"Well, now, reflect. This man has taken
these two young girls as his handmaidens."

"I understand," said Jessie, with a rosy blush.

"If, by our means, he is deprived of them,
what will he do?"

"I cannot say."

"He will want you in their place."

The pupils dilated, the nostrils widened, the
face flushed; but there was no fear.

"You will not allow this," she said.

"I will not. But he may appeal to the community," said Phineas.

"What then? I can but die."

"Die! No, brave girl, you shall not die.
But now, while you take lunch with his wives, I
will amuse him."

"His wives?"

"Yes, Jessie; and you must show no repulsion, or there will be danger. Come—you are
courageous enough, I know, to face this imaginary
and temporary danger."

Jessie followed him, with an aching heart.
Scenes of a nature so extraordinary that she
could scarcely credit them were passing daily
before her, like the pictures of a diorama.

She seemed, despite herself, mixed up in all.

Christian Whitmer stood at the door of his
house, which, as a specimen of Mormon primitive architecture, is worthy of a few words.

Actually living in the house with him, he had
but two wives.

The others were scattered about, or had been
transferred to Mormons of inferior rank.

The house was circular in form, tolerably well
built, and somewhat capacious.

On entering from the front, you found yourself
in the parlour, kitchen, and receiving-room,
coarsely but abundantly furnished.

Still nothing was in its place.

There was no presiding, guiding female hand in
the locality.

Three open doors revealed the mystery of Mormon family arrangements.

They led to three bed-rooms.

That in the middle was the bed-room of the
husband, those on each side the respective bed-
rooms of the two wives.

Who has not, who has gazed at the sleeping
faces of a happy husband and wife, felt that truly
they were united until death us shall part, and
hoped that even then, in another sphere, they
should be united in all purity and love.

But Mormonism destroys all the gentle solaces
of matrimony; takes from it its romance, its
thousand delicate and untold mysteries, its sweet
confidences, its pure undefiled and joyous intercourse.

No whispered prayer at night—no bending in
joy unutterable over the first-born—no sense that,
when the nuptial door is shut, care is shut out
with it, and that two, united as one, shall lie in
the intense enjoyment of one feeling more powerful than any other—that both are again safe on
this one night, and that peace and happiness shall
reign again triumphant for one half-day.

The Mormon wife sneaks to her husband's
couch like a guilty adulteress, ashamed that the
other should know; or, brazenly proud of the temporary preference shown her, stalks there in open
day.

Faugh! a bishop may reasonably defend the
institution among savages, but let it not be tolerated
among those who profess to be civilised and
Christians.

CHAPTER XXXVII.
POLYGAMY.

THE two wives looked keenly at Jessie, and
their pale, sallow faces flushed.

Pale, sallow faces!

And so it was. After their discovery of the
wretched deceit of Christian Whitmer—when
they came to know that, legally married once, he
could not marry them—the two handsome and
vain women sank by slow degrees into slatternly
household drudges.

Instead of seeking—pure voluptuaries, as they
both were—to earn at least his favourable notice
by increased care in dress, in manners, and in
general behaviour and appearance, they began
quarrelling, backbiting, slandering, and lying to
the man, one against the other, until he became fairly disgusted.

Instead of, as Mormons in theory expect, women vying for the men's smile, by every feminine act of coquetry and cajolery, they fight for him.

No soft blandishments, no tender assiduity, no sweet, welcoming smile.

No; but a keen, suspicious eye cast for his first look. Vulgar triumph on the part of the one who obtains it—bitter despondency, despair, and hate in the bosom of the disappointed one.

In the Turkish harem poison, irritant cosmetics, the bowstring, or the suffocating pillow, do the work.

The mysteries of the Mormon harem are yet untold.

That will come!

It is of no use mincing the matter. The grosser part of love is so intimately connected with the more ethereal passion—the great purpose of nature so bound up with the tender affection which exists between husband and wife—that one cannot exist without the other.

Never, then, can love exist where a man distributes his favours indiscriminately.

Utah! Desert!—Desert!

Thou art without love!

Thou shalt go, then, to thy fall as surely as did the cities of the plain—Sodom and Gomorrah—for ye, too, have dethroned love, and set up lust in its place.

Accursed be he who first set forth, then, this gospel of evil, and tried to erect a creed and a government, where the affections are unknown, and the animal passion reigns triumphant, as in a pigsty or a rabbit warren.

"Who is this?" said Susan, the former servant and mistress of Bristowe.

"Who, indeed?" said the once sprightly and beautiful Mrs. Richard Brown.

"What's that to you?" he answered, in a savage tone; "at all events, you'd better treat her well. She's ——"

"Jessie—oh, heavens!" said Susan, covering her face with her hands.

"It is Jessie," replied Phineas Bristowe, gazing with surprise, not unmingled with disgust, at the poor creature he had once so adored.

"Fear not," said she, turning with a scornful smile to Eliza; "we have nothing to fear."

"That's lucky," sneered Christian Whitaer, whose cold, glittering eye, however, was never off Jessie.

"Come along," said Phineas, who noticed this with an uneasy feeling.

And away they went, at some distance, to a secret drinking shop known only to the elect.

There are no beer shops or brothels in Utah, says a recondite writer.

No brothels! Merciful heavens! How can there be, when, with greedy eye, every girl who arrives is devoured and bought or taken by some elder or priest. What need of small brothels, when the city is one huge sink of iniquitous prostitution.*

No beer shops! The Mormons meet and drink

in bodies. They drink at home. There is plenty of company.

"So, Jessie," said Susan, in a very humble tone, "you have come here."

"Very much against my will. But, still, not to join you."

"Then why?"

"I may not say—I may not explain anything. I have promised, on certain conditions, not to reveal his secrets, and I never tell an untruth."

"How is your mother?" said the young woman, still quite humbly.

"She was very well, and, I daresay, would be now, but that I was torn from her arms on my wedding day," replied Jessie, quietly.

"Wedding day! Married! Who to?" asked Susan, quite excited, as young women are apt to be, somehow, at the very thought of a wedding.

"I am not married. I was to have been to Mr. Henry Marmaduke Haddington, the heir of the house of Haddington," continued Jessie.

Then the women exchanged mysterious and significant glances.

"This is very extraordinary," said Susan. "Your mother, then, is ——"

"At home, in her own house."

"What a dreadful old wretch that Phineas Bristowe must have been!" began Susan, spitefully.

"The less *you* say about him the better," said Jessie, mildly.

"Very well. Now, Eliza, ain't you going to lay the cloth for lunch?" said wife No. 1.

"Shan't."

"And, pray, why not?"

"Only because I shan't," replied wife No. 2, testily.

"It is your turn. I waited yesterday," continued Susan, in the tone of one who knew that she was right, "and you know it."

"Well, and what of that?"

"You know very well it is turn and turn," said Susan, with a meaning look.

"Girl," said wife No. 2, "do you hear this? This is what this infamous and degrading belief has brought us to. I, who was a worshipped wife, who had a home and a large fortune, being fool enough to make all over to him, am now reduced to be a household drudge. Never be the second wife of any man. It is terrible—it is frightful. I cannot endure it. I shall some day go mad, or kill him, or kill myself."

"No loss to anybody, I'm sure," said wife No. 1. "You know that he still loves me, and only keeps you out of charity."

"You lie, you wretched trull! He's afraid of your temper," cried No. 2, fiercely. "I was no cast-off mistress, but an honest woman, when that wretch betrayed me with his honeyed tongue."

"Honest woman!"

"Hush!" cried Jessie, who had been so overwhelmed with this aspect of a Mormon interior, that for a moment she could not speak. "Do not, for Heaven's sake, degrade your womanhood by quarrelling thus. Is there anything I can do for you?"

"No—never mind! you are an angel," said Susan, wiping her eye.

* As we proceed, we shall prove every assertion we make, step by step.

"I'll do my work," added ex-Eliza Brown, sullenly, "only I don't like being ordered about."

A hollow truce ensued—such a hollow truce as would ensue, where two women with such cause of mutual detestation and abhorrence had to live together.

If Othello could kill his wife on mere suspicion—if women, in history and song, have perilled their souls, because they have heard that a lover or husband was unfaithful—what can you expect from ignorant, passionate, unguided women, who daily see the act of infidelity before their very eyes?

The really degraded and shameless of their sex are those who calmly endure it.

They deserve to be sold by auction in the slave bazaar of Constantinople.

Eliza Brown now rose, spread a table, laid upon it a simple repast, with cider, and the three, rather to pass the time than anything else, began to eat.

A shrill succession of squalls interrupted them.

"Cuss them brats!" said Susan.

"Hang them!" muttered Eliza Brown.

But both rose to fetch their children. They had something of the maternal instinct left. But it is a mysterious law of nature, that the love of a father for his child influences to a great degree that of the mother.

Now, as a man who has several wives, and a vast number of children, cannot unless he selects some victim of gross favouritism—love his children as a father should, this insensibly reacts on the mother.

Now, it is notorious that among the Mormons very little affection exists between parent and off-spring.

When we come to the Salt Lake, we shall elucidate this in full, and show how foul a blot on the earth is the creed which destroys that golden link, forged in heaven itself, which binds a parent to a child, and a child to a parent.

They gave them the necessary nourishment, and then cast them on the bed as mere animated bundles, without value.

And thus passed a wretched and miserable day. Bickering without end, disputes about whose turn it was to do this, and to do that, varied by visits from women, curious to see the girl who had just been introduced into the settlement.

Jessie saw with what greedy eyes she was devoured by young and pretty girls, who, finding her prettier and younger than themselves, felt a cold chill of alarm go to their hearts, as they reflected on the known fickleness of their husbands.

Could the demon himself invent greater torture for the heart of woman?

But Jessie went on cheerfully doing any work that she saw wanted to be done, dusting up the room, nursing the babies, undressing and redressing them, and making herself such an angel of light in the place, that every heart turned toward her.

"She's too good for any here," said one.

"Perhaps she's for the Prophet,"

"The old wretch!"

"I wish he had been strangled at his birth."

"The ugly beast!"

"I wish I had him here."

Such were the ideas of the women with regard to worthy Joe Smith.

There are always two sides to a question. It is very well for men, whose whole souls are filled with lust, to applaud the man who discovered so easy a way of satisfying their indiscriminate passions—but let the women speak.

At last they went away, and soon after tea-time, Phineas Bristowe returned, thanked the two wives, and took Jessie to his own house.

"Jessie," he said, closing the door, "I must leave all in your hands. I have left Whitmer sleeping. I am a little more sober than he is—but I gave him—hic—laudanum—all right. I could not help it, gal."

"Speak on."

"You will save these girls; I know you will. But you will return here?"

"I will."

"I know you will. Now, when you see their father—tell him that I have—hic—hic—requited his hos—hos—hos—pitality—and that the best favour he can do me is to forget me utterly—utterly."

"Why?"

"You know why, girl."

"But——"

"It's useless."

"One word——"

"Girl, if you move me to passion, I shall—the drink—forget."

"Go on."

"'Tis now quite dark. See you, up in the hills there, a faint, glimmering light?"

"I do!"

"The girls are there.

"But how am I to reach them? How shall I ever find that desolate spot?"

"Listen! You must cross the river ford at the back of the village. You must then keep a mountain path—recollecting, whatever you or your companion may fancy to the contrary, to keep to the right. If you take one turning to the left, you are lost."

"I will remember."

"And now I must go. Be here at dawn of day. Whatever you do, do not betray me."

"I will not."

And as she spoke, Phineas Bristowe vanished, leaving her alone in the dark.

It was already very late.

Standing beneath a tree, holding his horse, she saw the stout figure of a man.

She guessed at once that it was the so-called Jabez Squash.

Without a moment's hesitation, or fear, she bounded through the open window, and walked straight towards the stranger.

"Is that you, girl?" said a husky voice.

"Yes, I am before my time, so are you," replied Jessie.

"Girl, I am a father; and this is one of those foul wrongs a father never forgives. I would scourge the foul lepers, who invade the peace of families in this way, until they died."

"You must be very calm," said Jessie, firmly, "or I can, and will do nothing."

"I will be calm, little angel—only tell me, are they safe?"

"They are. I have found out where they are, and alone," she continued. "But I only found it out under a pledge of solemn secrecy. You must swear that, if I give back to you your children, you will never, *under any circumstances*, reveal the secret, which has been confided to me, that they may be saved."

"Give me back my little ones," he said, "and I solemnly swear all you ask."

"It is well. Now look. Do you see yonder light under the pine grove?"

"I do."

"There sleep your children, alone and unguarded."

"Let us go."

"Be not so impatient. The way is difficult and dangerous. I have [directions so minute," she continued, "we cannot miss it; but how to cross the river!"

"My horse," replied the anxious father.

Jessie mounted, and the stout farmer, who knew the ford well, led her across, and in a few minutes they were on the other side, in perfect safety.

He then, by her direction, hoppled 'his horse, and started up the the gloomy and narrow path on foot, guided by the sure foot and keen eye of Jessie.

CHAPTER XXXVIII.

ROSE AND BLANCHE.

THEY were twins.

At seventeen, it was seldom the lot of man to gaze upon two such pure idealities as were these two lovely girls.

They were innocence and candour itself.

Of their beauty it is unnecessary to speak, when we say that, taking into consideration the size of the neighbourhood, they had more lovers than there are leaves on an autumn tree.

Of course the eyes of the Mormons were upon them.

These wretches prowl about, cunningly instilling a word here, another there, insinuating, creeping, crawling, making false and lying statements, which, however, wrapped in the tinsel eloquence of these men, imbued with scriptural quotations, make impression on the young and tenderer sex.

Girl, when one of these noxious vermin comes near you, if you have not the courage to cast him off at once, go to the nearest pastor, and if he be a true Christian, he will hear your story, and in one short hour, easily save you from perdition in this world, and punishment in the next.

Fellows in the sanctified garb of preachers, real wolves in sheeps' clothing, had watched when the girls were alone—had called for a drink of water, and left at the door "Holy Crumbs of Comfort for Sinners;" little poisonous tracts, containing all the venom of Mormonism under the form of Scripture.

Then they had ventured to speak.

They had told of the spiritual joys of Zion and the New Jerusalem.

Unfortunately, the girls were ill prepared to resist the temptation. The regular preacher they attended was one of those wild enthusiasts who, all doctrinal, spasmodic, and Spurgeonic, have no time for precept and proper teaching.

This man prepared more souls for the evil leaven of Mormonism than he would like to have had known.

They were always in a spiritual fog about religion.

The Mormon tracts and teachings put them in a perfect ferment.

The Mormons told them to reveal nothing unto their parents, until the moment of spiritual grace came unto them. Then all might be told.

And it did come.

At the frolic, Christian Whitmer presented himself with some friends, and, while poor Mrs. Farmer Squash dozed off, invited the girls to a great revival preaching, to take place at daybreak.

"Only listen to the good and great men who will preach," said Whitmer, "and your souls are saved."

"But ma!"

"They shall know all."

"Father!"

"I will be the messenger."

We need not repeat the promises, the lies, the nasal twisting of texts, which were brought to play to influence the two poor girls. In the hands of unscrupulous men, the Bible is the most dangerous of instruments.

The twins yielded.

A waggon was in readiness, the girls were placed inside, and Christian Whitmer, with the deliberate intention of proving an alibi, played the disgraceful trick to which we have given prominence.

The girls had not gone far before they repented, and begged to be set down.

But their conductors had strict orders not to listen to them.

They drove by ways known almost wholly to themselves.

The girls began, now it was too late, to weep, to cry, to entreat.

It was in vain. They were in the hands of men who knew no mercy, where beauty and innocence were concerned.

The wolf shows more mercy to the lamb, the tiger to the gazelle, than the Mormon animal to his prey—woman.

It is horrible, it is disgusting, but it is, alas, true!

Mormonism means—empire if we can; but woman anyhow.

The two trembling girls clung together.

An awful and undefined dread came over their souls.

Their very danger lay in the utter and pure innocence of their hearts.

They knew no evil—no, not so much as Eve knew ere the serpent beguiled her.

Their souls were sheets of white paper—their hearts had never beat.

And yet they feared.

They saw, now that their fears were excited,

that the men who guarded them were savage and resolute.

They became, therefore, themselves necessarily silent and watchful.

Had the poor doves have known all !

There were three men. Two were middle-aged men, friends of Whitmer, and well paid for the expedition.

The third was a blear-eyed fellow, short, stumpy, ugly, broad-shouldered, with already three wives.

"It's a pity they are not three," he said, with with an oblique glance at his two companions.

"Why ?"

"They are very pretty."

"It's no go, Redfern," said the elder of the two fellows; "one of them's for Christian Whitmer, and we toss for the other."

Redfern scowled angrily, but made no reply. His passions were roused, and he was a man seldom known to hesitate in their indulgence.

But he said nothing. He, however, like the parrot in the story, thought the more.

They proceeded until they reached the foot of the hills, in a very different direction to that by which Jessie was ascending.

They got within about the same distance, however, with the van, and then alighted.

"Where are we ? and where are you taking us to ?" said Rose, who, by virtue of half an hour, was the elder born.

"We are obeying orders. Our chief will be here in a very short time.

"Chief !"

"The chief priest."

"Heavens, Blanche, they are Mormons !" said Rose, in a tone of horror.

"What then ?"

"Father says they all ought to be hung," replied Blanche.

"Does he ?" scowled Redfern. "He'd better keep a civil tongue in his head, or I'll know the reason why."

The two girls made no reply; his manner was enough to terrify any one; nor did they speak until, by paths known only to themselves—paths they had in part made—the men reached the hut.

"This is the house of true believers—enter, and be not alarmed, none will hurt you. Await here, in prayer, the coming of the angel."

And, after pointing out provisions, lamps, and other necessaries, they went out.

A bolt and padlock turned outside, informed them that they were close prisoners.

To describe the woe, the repentance, the anguish, of these two charming girls—models of innocence, and purity, and love—would, indeed, be a vain endeavour.

They loved one another. Except their parents, they had never yet seen in these wild districts any one to move their hearts.

This, then, was their only consolation—they were not parted.

Poor consolation, when we know the nature of the beings we now write of.

How all abhor the vices of Charles II. and Louis XV. of France, who elevated lust into a kind of altar, to worship at.

But what were these men, vile as they were, to a whole community of panders, bullies, and profligates ?

They feared and doubted, and feared and hoped, until, exhausted by weeping and the previous night's frolic, they slept.

The window panes were replaced by holes left by strong wooden bars, so that there was as little chance of their escaping by the window as the door.

They slept soundly for hours, until, indeed, the deepening shadows showed them that night was approaching.

They lit a lamp provided for them, and impelled by a desire common to us all, began to partake of some food.

In romances of chivalry, and, indeed, in many modern novels, it is always a mystery how the hero, heroine, or some other leading character, does at times do stupendous deeds, for days and weeks, under circumstances when to obtain food is impossible.

But in real life, the most romantic bride would feel faint, indeed, before the end of her journey, if she did not partake in earnest of the wedding breakfast.

They supped, and then sat talking in low, hushed whispers.

Why were they left so long ?

What was the meaning of their being abandoned thus in this lonely place up among the mountains, the wild haunt of bears and wolves—at best, of savage charcoal burners ?

It was about nine o'clock.

They sat interlaced in one another's arms upon a kind of couch, a picture of angelic sweetness lovely to behold—a picture not often given to man to gaze on ; for they lay in all the abandon of nature, innocence, sisterhood, and girlhood.

Suddenly a cold shiver went through their veins, and they seemed transfixed to stone.

A fierce, hot breath could be heard distinctly through the wooden bars.

Rose slowly looked up, adjusting her dress as she did so, and saw two gleaming eyes peering on her.

"What is it ?" said Blanche.

"A wolf or a bear, by the eyes," said the girl, innocently.

"Ha ! ha ! ha !" laughed the coarse voice of Redfern—he was wonderfully amused—"wolf—bear ! Open the door, my pretty ones."

"No—go away !" they cried.

"I won't. I say, pretty ones, what ankles ! Ha ! ha ! ha ! Didn't think any one was looking, did you ? Oh ! oh ! oh !"

"Go away."

"Open the door, or I will break through the bars, I say," growled the man.

The girls fell down in an attitude of prayer, and clasped their hands.

The man struck at the wooden bars with a ponderous axe.

And still the girls prayed fervently.

CHAPTER XXXIX.

THE SEARCH.

No sooner had the farmer and Jessie entered on their perilous undertaking, than they observed the most exact silence.

They knew not what difficulties might stand in the way, nor what treachery might be afloat.

The farmer carried in one hand a short rifle, while by his side was an axe, and in his belt a brace of pistols.

No man knew better how to use them.

Jessie carried a dark lantern.

"What is your guide, that you look so often on the ground?" he said.

"I look for the trail," she replied, with an amused smile.

"You seem very confident."

"I am quite sure," said Jessie. "I have good reasons to be sure. When you know them, you will understand why I am certain."

The farmer became even more thoughtful than before.

They were walking along a most dangerous path. They had entered upon it almost unawares.

A narrow ledge of rock skirted a precipice of some thirty feet, sheer down to a tributary of the larger river below.

Above them a similar rock went, as it appeared, perpendicular up to the heavens.

"Be careful—in Heaven's name, be careful, girl! I should never forgive myself if the slightest mishap ——"

"Follow me. Speak not! Look!"

And suddenly halting, Jessie pointed to the figure of a man, with a rifle on his shoulder, to all appearance following the same track as themselves on the opposite side of the valley.

"What can it be?"

"Hush! sounds travel quick in these hills," said the farmer.

"Where can he be going?"

"If I thought he were going to the hut," said the father, "I would shoot him as he walks."

"And meet your children with murder on your soul." said Jessie.

"Better murder than ——"

"What?"

"Never mind, girl; go on, in Heaven's name"

They advanced at a rapid pace until they came face to face with a sharp point of rock.

A path went up both sides.

Jessie turned to the right.

"But this is the way, girl," said the farmer, rather impatiently. "I can see that fellow is gaining on us.

"This is the way."

"Why so?"

"Because I know it is. Believe me, and, as you love your children, doubt me not a moment."

The other bowed his head, and in his heart bemoaning his fate at the necessity of being guided by a weak girl, followed.

Jessie was careful, from that moment, to turn rapidly every corner they came to, and in this way at last, reached a terrace, whence the hut could be discovered at the distance of a hundred yards.

The light in the window burned plainly a moment, and then a dark substance concealed it from their view.

"'Tis a man."

"Stop!" whispered Jessie, clutching his arm, "creep up gently."

Again he yielded, and arrived just in time to see the man shiver the bars, with his ponderous axe, to pieces.

He gave no second blow, the heavy fist of the backwoodsman struck a blow, which felled him, like an ox, to the ground, bleeding and insensible.

At the same time the girls inside gave a loud cry as the door opened.

"Don't hurt us! We never did any harm to any one. Dear father and mother."

Silence was the only reply to their frantic words.

"Who is it?" they said, still afraid to open their eyes, or rise from their knees.

"Rise, there is no fear," said a soft and dulcet voice, close to them.

"An angel from heaven to save!" they cried, in one voice.

"I guess she is, gals," said the farmer, in a jolly voice—his old American voice again—"a splendiferous fust-class, entire angel, and no mistake."

"Father!"

"Yes—I guess it is fayther.! A pretty nice kipple of gals you is!"

"Do not scold us father, we have suffered so," began Rose.

"Don't, father."

"I will not, my darling, but let us away. There is danger in this place."

"That horrid man ——"

"He won't trouble you just yet."

"Wunt he?" yelled a frantic voice outside. "Somebody's been and broke the secret; so"—and the heavy bar fell across the door outside—"just stop thar till I brings up the people."

The farmer rushed to the window and saw the stumpy form of Redfern, dashing down the pathway by which he had came.

With a deep sigh, he levelled his rifle—a rifle that never erred—and a flash and a shriek gave at once token of his victory.

He then dashed through the open window, opened the door; and, led by Jessie, who alone knew what she was about, all went as rapidly as possible down the pathway towards the ford.

Jessie, as soon as this was reached, gave the message of Phineas.

"Strange," said the man.

"Not at all."

"Do you understand him?"

"Yes——"

"Then why not explain?"

"I may not. But the time will come, is coming, when I may. Farewell! never forget me, if you do him."

"Forget you, girl—Miss Treherne," he said, "never!"

"Forget you!" cried the two charming girls, "not if we lived a thousand years."

"Go, the least alarm might be dangerous. That man was, I hope, only wounded—go."

They had forded the river. A hasty farewell was exchanged between them, the farmer hurried away. Jessie hurriedly returned to her hut, crept in at the window, and closing the window, tried to sleep.

She could not.

She thought of Henry; of Henry, at all times; of Henry, one night when——

Well, reader, if you cannot guess which night she particularly remembered, you know very little of the warm impulses of an innocent girl's heart.

CHAPTER XL.

THE WARNING.

In the morning there was dire uproar in the Mormon village.

The secret retreat and hiding-place of the Mormons had been broken into, and two most lovely girls taken therefrom.

Rumour at first accused Redfern; but, about ten, he crawled into the village, bleeding, faint, and nearly dead.

All he knew was, he said, that while wandering about the hills, and keeping watch over the neophytes, he had been felled to the ground and shot.

By whom he could not tell.

He had lain for hours, until the blood was partly staunched, and then he had contrived to make his way to Dou's Creek.

Christian Whitmer looked keenly out of his bleared, bloodshot, and half-closed eyes at Phineas.

"Never look at me, man," said the Mormon elder, coldly.

"Why?"

"I had no hand in the release, though I'm glad of it."

"Why so?"

"They are too near neighbours."

"Ha! ha! ha!"

"I tell you they are too near neighbours; see what comes."

All turned in the direction to which his arm pointed.

A horseman entered the village. He was a stalwart youth about nineteen, armed with rifle, pistol, and axe.

He held out a letter.

Phineas took it.

"Read it out," said the youth.

"I shall do as I please," replied Phineas.

"Better, I guess."

Phineas turned his back.

"I will read it out when you are gone, and then will send an answer."

"Kain't be done, stranger. Must jist take an answer now."

"Friends," said Phineas, "this is the insolent message which is sent to us :—

"'*To the b—— Mormons of Dou's Creek.*

"'*This is to give warning, that if ye don't clear out in one week, bag and baggage, from this country, the Regulators will be down upon you. Kill—burn—slay—will be the cry of*

"'THE REGULATORS.'"

"We have no answer to give. We will appeal to the law."

"You'll think better of it," said the youth, with a dark frown.

"No."

"Take a fule's advice, and du," said the lad, who was not murderously inclined.

"No—the law."

"The law will do you mighty little good," said the lad, kindly.

"We will try it. Go."

The other rode off, waving his rifle over his head in token of defiance.

An immediate council was now decided on. Messengers were sent off at full speed to other small settlements, and all agreed to concert together for the common defence.

It is quite certain that if, in the first instance, the Mormons had been treated with a little less violence, and not indiscriminately slaughtered, as they were in some instances, they would not have had so many followers.

Martyrdom is the very worse use to put a quack to.

It makes his fortune.

Now the Mormons were genuine quacks, and sought martyrdom.

If one or two had been punished for cruel abduction by the cart-tail, the branding-iron, and the treadmill, a stop would have been put to the vile heresy far more effectually than by all the burnings, shootings, and slaughterings possible.

The abduction of the children of the farmer was patent. A jury would have found the villains guilty without hesitation, and the evil would have been, to a certain extent, stopped.

But the regulators thought otherwise, and the terrible war between civilisation and Mormonism began.

CHAPTER XLI.

NO ESCAPE FROM MORMONISM.

That night a conference was held of the leading Mormons, who came, in obedience to the call, from far and wide.

Joe Smith himself had been sent for, but the prophet had not arrived.

His authority could alone finally decide the course of action to be adopted.

Meanwhile, the women careless, listless, and indifferent, lounged about, gossiped, attended to such necessary household duties as they knew must be done, or sat at their doors, in moody silence. There was no generality among them, they did not dare trust each other with each other's secrets.

Eliza sat apart.

She was suckling a little child under a tree, a little way from the village.

As usual, she was contemplating flight.

There could be no object in detaining her.

But there was.

Once free from the infamous yoke of Mormonism, would she not speak out?

But still what could detain her?"

Ah! ha! ha!

The dagger, the sack, the rope.

None are allowed to leave the unhallowed fraternity. Many innocently believe that they may leave when they please.

THE MORMON RETREAT.

They are fearfully mistaken.

Once a Mason, always a Mason; once a Mormon, always a Mormon.

Not that we compare the two fraternities.

The bleaching bones of hundreds of returning and repentant dupes, murdered by fellows in the disguise of Indians, attest the truth of what we urge.

The Mormons know it well, and hence their fear of publicity, their love of hole and corner meetings.

They hesitate at nothing.

The few who have escaped their fangs, have given us pretty revelations.*

* Even those hoodwinked by them say enough.

So Eliza Brown sat by the wayside, just out of sight of the village, on a seat under a tall, spreading oak, uncared for, and alone.

She was, truly, "that wretched thing, a wife in name, but without the love or the protection of her husband."

She sang mechanically to her child, for she loved it not.

Love was dead within; it was in the grave of that murdered husband of whom she never thought without a shudder.

She had not killed him, it is true, but was she not the guilty cause of all?

She knew she was.

"Lullaby, Lullaby—poor fatherless child—

would it not have been a mercy if you had died?"
The child looked up.

"Had it have been his child—my own injured
Dick, my Richard, husband, lord—instead of the
child of this wretched and miserable outcast, I
might have loved it—but I was a fool."

"Lady," said a voice that made her thrill with
terror.

She looked up, and saw a venerable man, in a
broad-brimmed hat, a white blanket coat, and who
leaned upon a staff. He looked wan and aged,
and full of sorrow.

"What want you? I have no money; you have
come to the wrong place," she said.

"No money. I ask for none. Only give me
shelter, bread, and a cup of water."

She rose.

Hospitality is one of the crafty tricks of the
Mormons, who, while acting up to the devices of
the devil and his imps, profess all the virtues of
Christianity.

"Follow me, good father," she said, I can give
such comfort as my slender home affords."

He bowed, and followed meekly and humbly.

They were soon in her house. The wife No. 1
was out, so that Eliza had it all her own way.

She gave him what the larder afforded; waited
on him, gave him meat and drink, never offering
once to sit down.

She waited like a servant, and he never once
said, "sit down."

When he had quenched his hunger and thirst,
he laid his staff on one side, cast himself on a
bench in the room, and, drawing his hat over his
eyes, slept.

When Christian came in, and told both his
wives to go to bed, and be hanged to them, he saw
nothing of the stranger.

All was silent in the hut.

Eliza Brown, uneasy, uncomfortable, in a strange
fever of horror and dread, watched.

Then the pilgrim rose, cast off his hat, and she
saw—she expected it,—

HER HUSBAND.

An awful gleam was on his face, as he, clutching
a dagger, walked on tiptoe to the door of the
chamber where Christian Whitmer slept.

Eliza declared afterwards, that she could not
have moved any more than if she had been in a
dream.

She was spell-bound.

He opened the door—no noise, save an odd sort
of gurgle, was heard, and he came out, blood upon
his hands and face.

He found himself face to face with his guilty
wife.

"And will you not slay me?" she said. "Death
were sweet from you, my own Richard."

He looked keenly at her.

"No," he said, "your punishment shall be to
live."

"To live!"

"Come—I can tell you no more now," he said,
hastily.

She followed.

"And the child?" he said, staring wildly at her.

"'Tis his," she replied, in a tone of the utmost
disgust.

He glared still more strangely at her, but made
no reply.

Out into the village, passed the huts into the
high road, where, at some distance, a light cart
awaited them.

They entered together, that strange pair, neither
speaking a word.

Off they drove.

It was a dark and tempestuous night. The wind
blew in fierce gusts. The rain began soon to fall,
so as to blind the driver.

On, on, they went towards the settlements,
leaving Mormonism, they hoped, for ever behind.

Richard Brown was silent. His great revenge
—his punishment of the man who had wronged
him—had, at last, come about.

But the woman.

Alas! poor Eliza. He was thinking of how he
was to make her feel all that he had suffered since
that fatal day when she and her paramour plunged
him, as they thought, into the fangs of death.

She rode by him, fancying that there was sublime forgiveness in man, as there so often is in
woman.

Alas! poor woman, the heart and soul of man
is differently constituted.

Their fate may be alluded to at a different time.

CHAPTER XLII.

THE PROPHET.

THE Mormons waited, in a fever of impatience
and dread, for the arrival of the prophet.

Indistinct rumours had reached their ears of
great preparations which were being made, for the
purpose of carrying out the threats of the Regu-
o rs.

They had organised a system of scouts to watch
the proceedings of the Mormons.

The best, the most affectionate wives and
daughters, were watched with jealous care; it was
impossible, after the misadventure of Rose and
Blanche, to trust the best women of them all.

Now, it is not to be expected that men exposed
to the daily dread of losing that which is dearest
to an honest man, of all his possessions, should
reason calmly.

The law provides but very feeble remedies for
such misdeeds.

The seducer, the man who takes away the
honoured wife of your bosom, under some foul
and specious pretence, may be slightly punished.

But not as an indignant husband or father could
wish.

Then we must not be surprised if the foul blot
of Mormonism and polygamy has been the means
of introducing, into peaceful communities, the
terrible judgments of Judge Lynch.

It is the only weapon in the hands of an indignant populace.

To the extent of ducking and flogging, it might
be introduced with advantage here.

Whenever a Mormon touter introduces himself
into a peaceful and happy neighbourhood, let the
elders of the people hold a meeting, and—well, we
will not be very minute—give him his deserts.

All the men in the Mormon village were congregated together, irresolute and undecided.

They, at all events, were cleaning their rifles, in case they were required.

It was night. They were in a large kind of barn illumined by pine knot torches, that shed a ruddy, Rembrandt-like hue on all those dark, gloomy, and saturnine faces. They sat smoking, examining the locks and barrels of their rifles, and talking in whispers.

The fearful state in which Christian Whitmer had been found had filled them all with consternation. Susan had been able to explain that an old man had come there in search of a night's hospitality, and had departed stealthily, it was supposed, with Mrs. Eliza Brown.

Christian Whitmer was too ill to give any explanation His wound was such as to require the utmost attention.

Evil as he was, he now experienced the devotion of woman. Susan loved him not, but as he was ill and well-nigh perishing before her eyes, she nursed him with all the devotion which the sex will show even to strangers.

He was insensible from loss of blood.

While they were discussing the best means for preventing such accidents for the future, the news came that the prophet had arrived.

He entered stealthily and carefully.

He had no wish to be a martyr in order to show the truth of his doctrines.

He lived in continual fear and dread of the just retribution which was likely to befall him. Joe Smith, however, assumed, as he entered the barn, that air of suavity and dignity which imposed upon his dupes.

All rose to greet him with real or mock respect, as there were those even among the men who believed in him and his teachings.

He took his seat at the end of the barn.

One of the most noted of the village told him all that had occurred.

He made out, however, the Mormons to be the injured parties, and spoke of two converts—sisters who had entered upon the path of salvation—been torn away by the ravening Gentiles.

And now, he added, the persecution of the faithful was about to commence.

Joe Smith rose, and in his coarse, vulgar, and blasphemous corruption of Scripture, spoke in solemn tones of the duty which rested upon the faithful.

They were to remain at their posts.

He would write to the governor of the state, and claim the protection of the law.

The law must and would protect them, but if it would not they must protect themselves.

He advised that if satisfactory arrangements were not made before the eve of the last day fixed by the Regulators, they should act for themselves, and defend by force of arms their homesteads and their homes.

They were to send their wives and little ones into the mountains.

"But ultimately we must leave these here diggens. The Gentiles is jealous of the righteous peoples who are in favour with God. They would keep us in anguish of spirit and cruel bondage. But fear not!—has not He said, 'I will take ye to me for a people, and I will be to you a God, and ye shall know that I am the Lord?' Fear not! for the day is coming, and the hour is at hand, when we shall live in Zion. If the heart of man was not so hard, we should now be in the New Jerusalem; but you must work, you must save, you must collect gold, silver, and precious stones, that ye may build a tabernacle unto the Lord, around which may be congregated all that are faithful in spirit and in truth."

"But these people are mighty angry—there will be blood spilt," said one.

"And do yer hope to found the true Church of the Latter-day Saints without blood?" cried the prophet, in an angry tone.

The speaker slunk abashed before the anger of the high priest.

"Who is to be our general?" asked another.

"Who is your head man?" asked the prophet.

"Christian Whitmer."

"And where is Christian Whitmer?" repeated Joe Smith.

They told him what had happened, and as the story continued, the prophet turned pale with fear. How soon might not the same fate be his?

He hastily adjured the Saints to be watchful, promised to do all he could for them, said he would be always amongst them in the days of trouble, and then retired, to see Christian Whitmer.

Jessie was in the sick man's hut when the prophet entered slowly.

His lubricous eye—always cast about for new food for his devouring passions—fell upon her, and she actually quailed.

"Who is our sister?" he said, making as if he would have chucked her under the chin.

Jessie drew back, with the utmost scorn depicted on her countenance.

"My daughter," said Phineas Bristowe.

"Hath she been sealed?"

"No."

"Why is that?"

"She is not one of us."

"Then why is she here?"

"I am striving to teach her the true faith," said Phineas, evasively.

"It is time she understood," replied Joe Smith, sternly; "let her join the Saints, or at once leave the tents of the New Israel."

"I ask nothing better," said Jessie, "for since I have been here, I have seen nothing but imposture, crime and villainy."

"Dare you speak thus of the believers in the only true prophet?"

"Joe Smith!"

"Yes."

"Accursed," said Jessie, with flashing eyes; "accursed was the hour when he was born. Better had he been stifled, like some hideous, misshapen monster, than have lived to deal misery and wretchedness broadcast over the land, and to ride roughshod over morality, virtue, and truth—"

"Hold, blaspheming girl!" cried the prophet, "I am the Lord's anointed, of whom you speak. And now, girl, know this—with your opinions it would be idle to allow you to go abroad. Ere a month is over you shall be my wife—if you will, my favoured wife."

"Better dead, or tied living to a dead carcase," said Jessie, with a look of repulsion.

But Phineas Bristowe drew her hastily away to her own hut.

———

CHAPTER XLIII.

A STRANGE MEETING.

MEANWHILE, events were occurring elsewhere of strange importance to the course of this true and faithful history.

The Mormons had, on their departure for New York, divided themselves into several parties, so that those who had good reason to fear pursuit might defeat the machinations of those in their rear.

Phineas Bristowe, as has been seen, had started on his way alone with Jessie.

Paolo had done the same with Julie.

These two, though they hated and detested each other, still thought it wise to keep up a semblance of friendship.

They were to meet in the valley of the Styckell, where Joe Smith temporarily held his court.

The great body of the Mormons, having no really unwilling victims amongst them, travelled in a caravan, as ordinary emigrants.

On the way they refrained as much as possible from letting their true character be known.

They, however, tried on all occasions to pick up a stray convert or so.

Sometimes they succeeded, but their plans were in general laid so cunningly that none suspected.

Henry and Captain de Lancy, under the advice of the chief detective, made up their minds to follow in the track of the person whom, after some inquiry, they found to resemble Phineas Bristowe.

They were at the hotel. It was the last evening of their stay. At day break, provided with a guide, and accompanied by an officer bearing a warrant, they were to start on their way. By pushing on, they were sure to overtake a waggon, even though it had the start of them.

Henry and Captain de Lancy were in a nearly deserted smoking-room.

A gentleman sat near a fireplace reading and smoking a cigar.

M. Dubost was ushered in, went up to the stranger, which he did after bowing to his old employers.

A brief conference took place.

Then M. Dubost approached Henry and Captain de Lancy.

"I reckon, genl'men," he said; "this stranger yar, is upon about as wild a goose chase as ere of you. He, too, has missed a gal—his wife—and I know for cert'n she aint landed in New York. Maybe she was a passenger in that ere almighty fine Mormon ship."

The gentleman now introduced himself as the Honourable Mr. Stanley, and in a few clear sentences explained his story.

"But are you certain that the abduction of your wife ended in a forced voyage to America?" said Captain de Lancy.

"I have a good reason for it," said the young diplomatist.

At this moment a packet was placed in the hands of Henry.

It bore the handwriting of Jessie.

Henry tore it open wildly, and saying he would be back shortly, hastened from the room.

It was a long account of the journey, but without any allusion to the infamous conduct of Paolo.

Jessie felt that even though his outrage was miraculously prevented, a lover would not like to dwell on such a subject.

But she told how she had found Julie on board, and how she had been taken from the arms of a husband to whom she was devotedly attached.

She, too, was being carried into the Mormon territory, though she was not to accompany her.

Henry started. He knew scarcely what to do. At all events, he determined to consult Captain de Lancy ere he acted.

The Honourable Mr. Stanley appeared to be a gentleman, though rather one of the worldly class.

Still he was a man who evidently deserved a better fate than to be wed to the vicious and bad Julie de Florac—alias, the Countess Sidonia.

He sent a servant down to Captain de Lancy, to request his attendance on most important business, for half an hour.

He hoped Mr. Stanley would wait, as the business might possibly turn out to affect him.

Captain de Lancy hurriedly left his new acquaintance, who had told him the whole story of his acquaintance with the Countess Sidonia, her enormous wealth, her unexampled generosity.

"The Countess Sidonia is the infamous Julie," said Henry, after a few words.

Captain de Lancy coloured up to his eyes. He had never forgotten the deceit practiced upon him by the charming sinner.

"This man must be told all," he said.

"So I thought, but wished to consult you," replied Henry.

A consultation took place, after which the bell was rung, and the Honourable Mr. Stanley was requested to take wine with them in a private room.

He hurriedly joined them.

"Have you heard of my wife?" he said.

"I have," replied Captain de Lancy. "Pray be seated."

"But ——"

"Your wife is in this country. She came over in the same vessel as the young lady we are in search of."

"You rack me—where?"

"Mr. Stanley," said Captain de Lancy, with all a sailor's frankness, "may I be allowed to ask you a very delicate question?"

"You may."

"Did you marry the Countess Sidonia only for her wealth, or were you influenced by her beauty, her accomplishments, and supposed virtues?"

"Supposed virtues?"

"I ask you a question, Mr. Stanley," said Captain de Lancy, gently but firmly.

"I will answer you with all the frankness you could wish. I fell in love with her at first sight. When I found she was wealthy, I was delighted, as I am poor. But I would not have married her for the wealth of the Indies had there been anything against her moral character."

"She was taken away from you on the day of your marriage," said de Lancy, drily.

"She was."

"Thank your stars, then, that you have a loophole. Be calm—listen to my story—and when I have done, decide. My hand or my sword's point are equally at your service."

"I will listen," said Stanley, who was very pale.

And Captain de Lancy told him all.

"And you are sure," said Stanley, from whose brow and hair the huge drops of perspiration fell in rapid rotation, "that it is the same woman?"

Henry handed him a page of Jessie's letter, to read.

"Merciful Heavens! but she is married to this ruffian!" gasped Stanley.

"It may be so," said de Lancy; "but we have no proof."

"I will track the wretches to their lair," cried Mr. Stanley. "I thank you. I am unmanned, and cannot keep you company. One glass of wine. Do not think me angry or vexed with you. You have done right—quite right. But I have been a blind fool. A woman, who—but never mind."

And wringing both their hands, he hastily left the room.

CHAPTER XLIV.

ON THE ROAD.

PROVIDED with a guide, and accompanied by a clever detective, with an official warrant which, on a pinch, could be backed by the sheriff of any county in any state of the Union, Henry and Captain de Lancy started on their journey.

Both wore broad-brimmed straw hats, and in general costume bowed quite to the customs of the country.

The waggon driven by Phineas Bristowe had no particular mark about it, but still, with slight interruptions and delays, they were able, thanks to the keen power of cross-examination possessed by the officer, to follow it accurately.

Wherever they had halted, the beauty of Jessie had been the theme of universal remark.

All said that she travelled with her supposed rather readily and willingly.

Then they knew that she had made some promise, which she was unable to break.

Henry burned with impatience.

On they went, not at a sufficient speed to satisfy the impatient lover—that was impossible—but quite rapidly enough for the cattle they bestrode.

One day, they heard that Phineas Bristowe had passed that way four days before, on the way to a Mormon settlement situate at the foot of some well-known hills.

The heart of Henry beat high with hope, as they urged their horses to their utmost speed.

They scarcely halted for food or refreshment of any kind.

At length, night fell upon them while following a pathway across a half-cultivated prairie.

"My horse is done up," said the detective.

"And mine," replied the guide.

"And mine," added Captain de Lancy.

"But we cannot camp here," interposed Henry, with a deep sigh.

"We must, if nothing better turns up," said the detective; "but yonder, behind those trees, I saw a light—we may obtain shelter."

Henry made no difficulty. They had done that day all that human nature and horseflesh could do, and rest was indispensable.

The guide, who knew the country tolerably well, dismounted, and soon found the pathway leading to the house, which being the only one in that region, the reader will not be surprised to learn was that of the so-called Job Squash.

The farmer soon came to the door, attracted by the loud barking of his dogs.

Henry advanced, and intimating how fatigued they were, demanded hospitality.

"Well, I guess it aint Job Squash as 'ull turn most men from his door—but jist speak up, and tell us who yer be, and what your business are."

"My name," said our hero, "is Henry Marmaduke Haddington, but ——"

"Hoorah! all right!" shouted the farmer. "Come, gals, here's Jessie's friend and the grandson of my honoured lord and master."

And the whole party followed Henry, whom the farmer literally dragged indoors.

"But how do you know me?—and who knows Jessie?" cried Henry.

"All," said the family, in one voice.

"Who knows Jessie?" cried the farmer; "why we all know Jessie. My two gals know Jessie—my old woman knows Jessie—and I know Jessie. And so you are Master Henry Haddington, are you?"

"In Heaven's name, explain yourself!" cried Henry. "We are in pursuit of my affianced wife, who has been carried off by that black-hearted villain, Phineas Bristowe, alias, John Beckford."

"Merciful Heavens!" said the farmer, sinking in a chair; "and was that my big brother?"

A storm of enquiries now ensued, and after some considerable difficulty, something like an explanation took place.

"Now I understand," said the farmer, after he had sent the women to an outhouse to prepare supper, "why he allowed Jessie to save my children. He is not, then, wholly bad. He has, to a certain degree, repented."

"Do not believe it, sir," cried de Lancy, warmly; "you must tear him from your heart. He has only taken this poor girl away from home and her friends, to torture us and get money."

"And Jessie must be rescued."

"She shall! She shall!" said the farmer, wiping the big drops of perspiration from his

brow; " but if you can, be merciful to John—
do. Take her away—take her to England."

" Let him give up Jessie," replied Henry;
" and I, for my part, will forgive him all."

" He shall," cried Beckford; " the girl saved
mine. If I die, she shall be rescued. But do
you know that to-morrow evening we attack the
village ?"

" Heavens! and in the fight what may not
happen ?" said Henry.

" There will be no women there," replied
Beckford, " if they mean fighting. These Mormons will remove their wives and other valuables."

" Where?"

" I think I could say—but Jessie, Jessie, why
did you make me take that oath ?"

And in answer to their eager enquiries, Beckford
explained Jessie's brave and heroic conduct.

All admired it, and all understood the reserve
of the farmer.

A bright idea struck Henry. He hurriedly left
the hut. The farmer guessed his errand, but made
no objection.

He had gone to interrogate the girls, who were,
however, only able to give a general explanation
of the locality of their place of imprisonment.

Henry determined, therefore, to make one of
the attacking party on the village, trusting to
learning from some of them the real position of
the women.

Mr. Beckford looked uneasily at Henry, as he
returned to his room.

" They do not remember the road," he said,
with a deep sigh.

Supper now was brought in, and conversation
became more general, every one of the party announcing their intention of taking part in the
attack on the Mormon village.

About forty constituted the band of Regulators,
while the adult males among the Latter-day Saints
were about thirty.

But then they would be entrenched.

CHAPTER XLV.

THE ATTACK ON THE VILLAGE.

It is not our intention seriously to defend the
practice of taking the law into our hands. It is a
practice fraught with danger to individuals and the
commonwealth.

But as there are certain noxious vermin who are
only to be rooted out by poison and such violent
remedies, so must the apostles of prostitution and
adultery be treated in a different way from anybody else.

In this country we would give them over to a
jury of indignant English matrons of the ultra-
chaste school, and should have no fear but they
would give them a lesson to be remembered.

Still, we believe if the vile juggle, deception,
and blasphemy of Joe Smith had been allowed to
run out, men only taking care to guard against
the rape and abduction of their daughters, it
would scarcely have numbered so many disciples,
nor had so many big books written about it.

But now the imposture is so rife that it is impossible to supply the antidote.

There was scarcely a farmer or labourer in that
scattered neighbourhood who had not suffered in
some way from the nuisance of Mormonism.

Women and young girls had been subjected to
the nauseous temptations of the elders.

Then they were such idle thieves. Rather than
work hard and honestly, they took whatever they
could find.

Now, in an agricultural country, where everything lies so open and exposed to larceny, this
was a very powerful argument for getting rid of
them.

So it was decided to smoke the rats out of their
holes.

Beckford, who had been the immediate cause of
the congregation of the Regulators, showed on the
following day no weakness.

He had resolved personally to take no part in
the hand-to-hand conflict.

He, however, in the first place, provided provisions in abundance for all, fed their horses, and
feigning lameness, stayed at home to superintend
the preparations for the evening festivities, " ater
them blamed Mormons were all killed or smoked
out."

It was two in the afternoon when, under a
bright American sun, the mounted regulators
went forth in all that reckless variety of costume,
or rather absence of costume, so characteristic of
the backwoodsman.

There were coats with the fur out, and coats
with the fur in, blanket coats, frieze coats, grey
coats, wideawakes, tall white beavers, black hats
with white bands, and white hats with black bands,
gaiters, knee breeches, ponchoes, capes, great
coats, jackets ; with rifles, muskets, carbines,
blunderbusses, every species of fowling-piece, both
ancient and modern.

There were long beards, and short beards, and
no beards.

There were English, Irish, Scotch, German,
and genuine descendants of the old stock who had
fought for independence and liberty—all filled
with the same utter detestation of the Mormons.

The outrage on the two girls had aroused the
neighbourhood to an unusually excited state,
though the feeling had been long smouldering.

All felt how soon the same might occur to themselves.

None were safe.

Wife, widow, maid—it was all the same to the
ferociousness of these lecherous knaves.

Quackery has descended to many tricks, but in
modern times no quackery ever went so far before
as to invent a religion, in order to procure a number of prurient-minded men an unlimited amount
of wives.

Among those who rode with the Regulators
there was one exception to those who were belli-
cosely inclined.

This was the officer.

What was about to be done was illegal, and he
would have no hand in it.

The Mormon village was situated on the banks
of the river.

It was surrounded by thickets, mounds, and hillocks, whence a good view could be obtained.

One or two rode forward as scouts, and returning in a few moments, informed the others that the Mormons were prepared.

They had thrown up stockades.

Sentries stood at the narrow gaps left between these rude fortifications.

A conference was now held.

It was agreed to send forth a flag of truce before any blood was shed.

This even was only decided by a bare majority, the others being for instant annihilation.

Henry was chosen.

He placed a white pocket-handkerchief on the end of his gun, and trotted deliberately towards the frail fortifications.

Two men came from the village.

"What's yer want?" said one, a tall, thin man, with wavy hair.

"I come as a messenger from the people of this county," replied Henry.

"What is your message?"

"First, that you surrender up your arms."

"Well."

"That you harness your horses, mules, and cattle, and leave the spot at daybreak."

"Go on."

"That you marshal all your women, and let them freely state if they are with you of their own free will."

"Go on," said the Mormon, with flashing eyes.

He was clearly an enthusiast.

"That you give up a young lady named Jessie Treherne, illegally detained amongst you," he went on.

"And if we refuse?"

"We must make you succumb to force," said Henry, rather staggered by his calm demeanour.

"Then to the God of Battles we entrust our cause. We fight under the banner of the Lord. Our cause is just and righteous. Who are ye, that you should tell us to leave our houses and our land at your bidding? This spot is ours by the inalienable right of purchase, and we will maintain that right unto the death. As for our women—our wives—they are not to be made a laughing-stock to strangers."

"But your village is a refuge for kidnappers and abductors," said Henry.

"People say so. I, for one, deny it. There are no women here but those who have cast their lot with us. There were none, I mean, for now none are here but men."

"But Jessie?"

"I know nothing of her."

"Old man," cried Henry, "you may be a husband and a father."

"I am both. Three wives, seven sons, and as many daughters have I been blessed with; and yet have I journeyed a long way to do battle for the Saints."

"Old sinner!" thought Henry.

"It is useless wasting more words. We attack no one—we are on our own ground. If attacked, we shall defend ourselves, and Heaven help the right!"

"Amen!"

And Henry rode away.

He told his comrades the determination of the Mormons to defend themselves.

The Regulators shouted.

They were rejoiced.

It was exactly what they wanted.

Apart from their desire to rid the country of the pestiferous sect, they liked fighting.

It was part of their nature.

The village was defended naturally at the back by the river, and on one side by a complicated system of dykes and ditches.

It could be attacked only in front, and on the right of the assailants.

Every man dismounted, hoppled his horse, and crept up as near as possible.

Then several sharp cracks and wreaths of blue smoke proclaimed that the work of destruction had commenced.

Men of the same race, citizens of the same country, were engaged in a conflict such as on a larger scale disgraces the land of Washington now.

The Regulators were fighting at a disadvantage.

The Mormons had planted their stockades with considerable ingenuity.

They could see without being seen.

It was only when several were wounded, one dangerously, that the Regulators saw how tedious a siege they had engaged in.

A general draw off took place.

It was resolved, after some deliberation, to storm the village in three columns.

Henry and Captain de Lancy kept closely together. They never lost sight one of the other.

"Down," said Henry, suddenly tripping his commanding officer.

"Henry!" cried de Lancy, severely.

"I beg your pardon, sir," replied the youth, pointing to a bullet which had entered a tree— "that ball would have passed through your heart."

"Hem," laughed the naval officer, "I suppose in prairie warfare all is fair, but don't do that on board ship."

"I would do much to save your life, sir."

"I know it, my boy. But look yonder!"

He pointed with his finger to where, stealing along the edge of a wood, some thirty armed men were about taking them in flank.

It was a reinforcement of Mormons.

CHAPTER XLVI.

A FIGHT.

A SIGNAL, previously agreed on, brought the whole party together.

They were now outnumbered.

They had hoppled their horses at a distance, and now were congregated in a little valley.

On each side of them were small hills, not more than thirty feet high, with a tolerably stiff slope on the other side.

It was determined to act on the defensive until the strength of the Mormons was really known.

Crawling up cautiously, the whole party lay

flat on their faces on the side of the village, or on the side of the reinforcement.

Utter stillness prevailed.

Every man clutched his rifle with a firm determination to do or die.

The Mormons in the village suddenly uttered loud shouts of rejoicing.

They had made out the new arrival.

They believed the attacking force scared away, and in a rash moment rushed forth to meet them.

A deadly volley of forty rifles—and a dozen Mormons bit the dust.

Dragging the dead and wounded within the stockade, the Mormons, who were now united, appeared to deliberate.

In a few minutes they came forth, singing psalms and hymns, and uttering cries of vengeance.

With a loud cry they rushed towards where the Regulators were outlying.

A heavy platoon discharge from both sides ensued, and then they closed.

Butt end of guns, knives, tomahawks, began to do their work.

The Mormons were very superior in number, but wanting in energy.

Still numbers will have their weight.

The Regulators, at a signal from their chief, made for shelter.

They hid behind trees, rocks, and piles of cut fire-wood.

Every man proceeded to load, glad to regain a little breath.

Henry and Captain de Lancy stood side by side.

" Well," said the captain.

" Well," said Henry.

" Slightly wounded," replied de Lancy, smiling.

" Ditto," repeated Henry.

Both spoke truth. They had received slight flesh wounds, nothing more.

Close to them, three or four of the farmers were in close confabulation.

The words " fire," " burn them out," " tar and feather," were distinctly audible.

Then a lad hurried away in the direction of the horses. In a few minutes he returned, leading one which, not being mounted, had excited the attention of the Englishmen.

Two stone jars were slung on each side.

Bundles and kegs surmounted these.

Henry watched their proceedings. They began by twisting together dry grass, Spanish moss, pine knots, and other inflammable articles, which they first soaked in turpentine and other combustible material, which had been probably brought for the use of Judge Lynch.

When they had prepared a tolerably good-sized infernal machine, another conference was held, after which two of the party disappeared at the rear of the camp.

The rest then began a fire so incessant, so well sustained, so deadly, that the Mormons were not able to show themselves.

But they returned the fire with equal alacrity.

Little harm, however, was done on either side.

The afternoon was hot and sultry. A steady breeze blew from the west side of the village, that protected by the dykes and ditches.

The Mormons were now in front, and on the eastern side, upon which the Regulators poured an incessant discharge of rifles and musketry.

Half an hour passed.

Then from the easternmost hut—and they all nearly touched—uprose a volume of smoke, black as ebony, and then a column of bright and lurid flame.

A wail of horror burst from the Mormons.

Many of them casting down their arms, began to make frantic endeavours to save their furniture.

The Regulators loaded once more, and stood ready for action.

A proposition was made to exterminate the whole apostate race.

But humanity prevailed.

Those who threw down their arms were to be saved.

Night fell rapidly, and the infernal machine having at once set fire to the hut in such a way that to extinguish it was utterly impossible, in another moment, the whole body of huts began to take fire.

" Surrender, Mormon dogs !" cried a stentorian voice. " All taken with arms in their hands shall die. Come forth, or ye shall be shot like dogs !"

No reply came.

" Once—twice—thrice !" shouted the Regulator; " you have but while I repeat those words to come out—once—*twice*—THRICE !"

And the Mormons, utterly cowed and dispirited came crawling forth in ones and twos, until the whole body were prisoners in the hands of the triumphant and victorious Regulators.

Night, which in America comes without warning, suddenly, as if by the magic fall of a curtain, had now fallen, and the burning huts made an illumination, which could be seen far and wide.

It was indeed a strange scene, to contrast by the lurid light of the flames the different countenances of the Mormons and the backwoodsmen.

The former were sullen, dejected, and gazed upon the destruction of their property with feelings which may be easily conceived.

The Regulators felt nothing but joy and delight, They had at last rooted out the obnoxious vermin, with the loss of one killed and seventeen wounded.

The Mormons were pinioned.

" And now, you infernal G—d darned kettles of iniquity, you tin pots of larceny and rape, you almighty horse thieves and *im*-posters whar's the women ?"

No answer.

" Whar's the angeliferous British gal as saved the *tu* daughters of Squash from that almighty vermin, Christian Whitmer ?"

The Mormons exchanged glances.

" I see yer luks. Now I tells yer what, if yer don't tell us right away slick, I calculate it'll be wuss for you."

No answer.

" I'll lick the whul lot on yer, until the blood runs down yer backs."

JESSIE AND THE PANTHER.

"Do with us as you will," said the old enthusiast; "we will not betray our women into your hands."

"Flog'um!" shouted twenty angry voices.

"Hold!" cried Henry, "one moment. Old man, will you abide by this? Take me alone to where the women are. Let me speak to them, and if any are detained against their will, they shall be allowed to come away freely."

The Mormons whispered.

"There are none detained. Even the English girl is with us by her own free consent," said the old man. "But you are hard to convince. If you will, you may come—and my brethren will remain as hostage for your safe return."

And still the flames burnt high, and the dry logs and shingle cracked in the blast.

"I accept," said Henry.

"And mind yer, old feller," cried one of the Regulators, "yer see them hickory sticks the boys is cutting. Be mighty quick, for if the youngster aint back safe at twelve, be sure there'll be thunder to pay."

The man, whose arms had been unpinioned, made no reply, but signing to Henry to follow him, walked straight to a ford which led to the mountains.

CHAPTER XLVII.

POLYGAMY.

He did not take the same path as that by which Jessie had led the farmer to the rescue of his two lovely and innocent daughters.

He strode up a steep hill-side on the opposite side of the ravine—apparently the same by which Redfern had approached his prey.

It was a bleak, arid, and miserable-looking place.

Stunted pines grew between huge boulders, ragged vegetation peered up through stones and flints, and far away stretched a kind of desolate and bleak moor, where nought was heard save the cry of the sandhill crane and buzzard.

It was such a scene as might have excited the soliloquy of Manfred.

They were, indeed, withered pines—all withered, trunks stripped and barkless, branches lifeless—done by a single winter.

Well might the misanthrope, in his anguish, compare himself to such a scene.

> "To be thus—
> Grey-haired with anguish, like these blasted pines,
> Wrecks of a single winter, barkless, branchless,
> A blighted trunk upon a cursed root,
> Which but supplies a feeling to decay;
> And to be thus, eternally but thus,
> Having been otherwise!"

"Young man," said the Mormon, in a stern and yet sorrowful tone of voice, "know you what you have done?"

"In what way?"

"Look!"

And he turned and pointed to where the lurid flames rose from above the smoke, making the whole adjacent country one vast mass of darkness.

"Well, sir," said Henry, "but why have your people provoked this?"

"How have they done so?"

Henry laid his hand upon his arm, and told, as briefly as he could, of the outrage on Farmer Squash, *alias* Beckford.

"Bad," said the man, fervently; "if these deeds are done, the Saints will be in bad odour. I have three wives, but they came willingly, and are happy and contented. But how have my people hurt you?"

Henry told him all he knew of Phineas Bristowe and Jessie.

The man was silent. Henry spoke in a deep, feeling way, which made the other think. Perhaps a thought struck him for once, that there was more of evil than he believed in the sect to which he belonged.

But the man, though old, was wedded to his one darling idea, polygamy, which, whether in Turkey or Utah, is just the same.

The men like it.

The women do not.

This man, Tobias Johnson, who aimed at being one of the great elders of the church, had been first drawn into the sect by the promise of an unlimited number of wives. This, with a little preaching and hypocrisy, had fairly hooked him.

> "I know not if he had domestic cares—
> No process proved connubial animosity:
> Four wives and twice five hundred maids unseen
> Were ruled as calmly as a Christian queen.

> If now and then there happen'd a slight slip,
> Little was heard of criminal or crime;
> The story scarcely pass'd a single lip—
> The sack and sea had settled all in time,
> From which the secret nobody rip—
> The public knew no more than does this rhyme.
> No scandals made the daily press a curse,
> Morals were better, and the fish no worse."

If we would state in a few words the real and genuine objection which women have to the institution, we must do so in verse. Byron has had the audacity:

> "Polygamy may well be held in dread,
> Not only as a sin, but a bore;
> Most wise men with one moderate woman wed,
> Will scarcely find philosophy for more;
> And all (except Mahometans) forbear
> To make the nuptial couch a ——"

He then audaciously adds—"Bed of Ware."

> "The fair sultana err'd from inanition;
> For were the sultan just to all his dears,
> She could but claim the fifteen-hundredth part
> Of what should be monopoly—the heart.
> It is observed, that ladies are litigious
> Upon all legal objects of possession;
> And not the least so when they religious are,
> Which doubles what they think of the transgression.
> With suits and prosecutions they besiege us,
> As the tribunals show through many a session,
> When they suspect that any one goes shares
> In that to which the law makes them sole heirs.
> Now, if this holds good in a Christian land,
> The heathen also, though with lesser latitude,
> Are apt to carry things with a high hand,
> And take what kings call an imposing attitude,
> And for their rights connubial make a stand
> When their liege husbands treat them with ingratitude.
> And as four wives must have quadruple claims,
> The Tigris hath its jealousies like Thames."

But this is a digression.

When they had reached what appeared to be the summit of the valley, Tobias Johnson paused.

"Thus far I have shown you all. But now, young man, if you would go further you must trust wholly to me, and be blindfolded."

"Why?"

"I dare not reveal our secrets."

"May I trust you?"

"You may, as I have a soul to be saved."

Henry stood still, and allowed his eyes to be securely bandaged.

CHAPTER XLVIII.

THE MORMON REFUGE.

The sectaries of Joe Smith, who had never forgotten his original trade of a forger and horse-thief, were perhaps better acquainted with the secret nooks and hiding-places of the country than even the trappers or hunters.

In this way they dared to compare themselves to the early Christians, or to the persecuted Puritans and Covenanters of our own country in its days of darkness and intolerance.

As well might the banditti of Italy and Spain lay claim to our sympathy, because they have, from time immemorial, been compelled to hide in caverns, forests, and fissures in rocks.

It was near one of these that Henry had now arrived.

The old man took him by the hand, and bidding him tread fearlessly, and without any dread of danger, led him onwards.

He was evidently turning him round and round once or twice, to make him lose all recollection of his original position.

Then he halted.

Henry felt a cold kind of rush of air, as if he were passing through a damp archway.

"Three steps down," said Tobias Johnson.

Henry stepped as told.

"Four up."

Again he obeyed.

In this way he appeared to move about for about ten minutes, when a loud hum of voices fell upon his ear.

"What news?" burst from a chorus of female voices—"what news?"

Henry's bandage was removed.

He was in a large vault, lit up by an abundance of pine torches, the black smoke of which hung like a cloud from the roof.

On the floor were some hundred women and children in a variety of attitudes.

Some stood sullen and insensible, some nursed their offspring, some wept, some knelt in agonized and anxious prayer.

The degree of estimation in which each husband stood might easily be guessed.

But all cried for news.

"The home of the Saints is no more—the Saints are themselves all prisoners.

A wail of anguish rose to the roof.

"Who is this?" cried a tall, bony virago.

"A gentile."

"What does he here?"

"Duck him!"

"Hang him!"

"Silence!" shrieked the old man; "if you but lay your finger on him, every one of the Saints will perish."

The women fell back in horror.

"Hear him. He will explain his errand."

Henry waved his hand, and advancing where all could see him, he began in his soft, thrilling, and musical voice.

"I came principally to seek from amongst you my young affianced wife, stolen from me by a wretch named Phineas Bristowe. In the next place, I came to say that if any of you are detained here against your wills, you are to come with me. You shall be free."

Half a dozen rose hurriedly, and advanced towards him.

"Henry Haddington!" said one, clutching him by the arm.

"That is my name."

"Your are too late. The moment Phineas Bristowe saw the flames, he took horse with Jessie, and has been over the mountains this hour."

"Which way?" he gasped.

"To follow is impossible," she replied, "But I think I can tell you where he is gone."

"Speak woman."

"To Spas Creek—the residence of Joe Smith," she answered, in a low whisper.

"This on your word as a woman."

"Of a woman who knew her mother—and one who always pitied Jessie. Ask no more, I will tell you nothing. Go, and may fortune attend you."

And Susan fell back into the ranks, as had already done the few who, in a moment of sudden excitement, had stood out from the rest of the Mormon matrons.

They were lost beyond all redemption.

At least, among the Latter-Day Saints they went by the name of wives.

What would they be called anywhere else?

Several witnesses confirmed the statement, that as soon as Phineas Bristowe saw, by the outburst of the flames, that the Saints were overpowered, he announced his intention of at once starting on his way to inform the prophet of what had happened.

Henry was reluctantly compelled to yield to the force of evidence, and believe.

Tobias Johnson, who had shown no evidence of any triumphant delight at the disappointment, now approached, and Henry again submitted to be blind-folded, and was in due course led back to the outer world.

Nor did he ever once think of looking back to ascertain the position of the place of refuge to which their own villanies and impostures had driven the believers in the blasphemies of Joe Smith.

The fury of the Regulators, at the return of Henry without Jessie, knew no bounds, and but for his own earnest interruption, it would have gone hard with the Mormons.

"And now, I guess, yer ramping hoss-stealing alligators," cried one, "make tracks; and let me tell you, for one, if I ever see one of you villains anywhere 'bout arter this, I makes no bones on it—I shutes."

"And I—and I!" shouted twenty voices.

The Mormons were unbound, and then, unable any longer to restrain themselves, nearly all the Regulators fell upon them with hickory sticks, which sent the miserable, homeless, outcast wretches flying to the hills, with curses, not loud but deep, upon their lips—and burning desire for vegeance in their hearts.

Then all mounted their horses, and turned towards the farm-house of Charles Beckford.

Henry, in a low, despairing mood, rode behind, in conversation with Captain de Lancy. The former now saw but little hope. Phineas was about to remove hence to a place far beyond the reach of ordinary law, being in a new settlement, on the very verge of the Western Prairies.

The Mormons already were thinking of making their permanent residence Nauvoo, but many in the prevision of future troubles, had already gone west.

It was to one of these distant, and almost uninhabitable quarters, that Joe Smith had retired, as he said, to meditate and reflect on the word of God, and where Phineas was dragging the unfortunate Jessie, whose marvellous and wonderous beauty was the theme of all beholders.

And who more dangerous than the hoary villains who first preached polygamy as a duty in a Christian land?

The Far West! Like most Englishmen, Henry had a very vague idea of what this genuine name meant.

Out West, is an indefinite term, whose limit

has never been circumscribed, and never can be fairly reached until civilisation, marching on with its measured stride, has set its foot upon every inch of ground between the Atlantic and Pacific shores.	At the time of which we write, however, the States which form the eastern and western boundaries of the Mississippi were the chief theatre of emigration, though many a bold trapper and backwoodsman began to feel the atmosphere oppressive with the breath of numbers, and to yearn for still deeper solitudes.

On their arrival at the house of Farmer Beckford, as we shall henceforth call him, the girls rushed wildly out to meet the party.

"Jessie!" they cried, seizing each a hand of Henry, as he dismounted from his horse.

"Gone!" he replied, in choked accents.

CHAPTER XLIX.

FLIGHT.

PHINEAS BRISTOWE, under the specious pretence of being purely a preacher of the word and a non-combatant, had gone up to the place of refuge, to take care of the women and nurse the wounded men.

But no sooner did the crack of rifles ring in the air, than he crawled out, saddled two powerful horses, kept in stables at the rear of the cave, and then, being ready for the worst, climbed up where he could get a good view of the scene of action.

He had a powerful glass, and could make out every phase of the proceedings.

His delight knew no bounds, when he saw a prospect of the Mormons winning the day, for though he was well aware, that after the combat they would have to leave the country, still it would inspire the general population with respect.

But suddenly a column of smoke, succeeded by a towering outburst of flame, informed him that the Mormon settlement was doomed to destruction.

Then he knew that the Regulators were at last victorious.

He could hear their wild and victorious shouts.

He guessed, that by the application of torture of some kind, the Regulators would find out where Jessie was concealed.

He determined to be beforehand with them.

More than once he had fancied that he could made out the form of Henry.

His decision was soon come to.

The track of the regular Mormon caravan lay about a hundred miles to the south, and he knew, by the rate of travelling they must adopt, that he should be in time to catch them.

Such had been the arrangement with Paolo, who was hurrying upwards with Julie.

He re-entered the cave, took Jessie on one side, told her the infuriated mob would soon be there, and that he, at least, would fall a sacrifice.

"Fly then!"

"But Jessie—come with me still, and I swear to you by all that is sacred, you shall write to your friends, and make your own terms for me. All I ask is pardon for the past."

"Would I could believe you!" she said.

"You may, upon my soul!" he cried.

"I will," she continued, rising thoughtfully; "but why go farther—why not retreat?"

"The mob have destroyed the village, doubtless they have slain all the people.	I have no resource but to fly—come!"

Jessie followed.

They reached the stable by a winding passage. But not unnoticed.	Susan watched the actions of her old lover with scorn and hate.

'Tis ever so.	No medium in woman—bitter hate, or passionate love.

The horses were powerful and well chosen.

But Phineas Bristowe scarcely knew the way.

It is true, that every Mormon commonly possesses a private map of all the routes to Nauvoo, and this he had in his pocket.

But the night was intensely dark.

This he did know, that a path led down the side of the hill towards the river, and then a rude kind of highway took them partly on their way.

His present object was simply to get away from the infuriated mob.

He cared not for awhile where he concealed his head.

All he cared for was, that he should be at a distance from that scene when the mob arrived.

The path was narrow and steep, so that Phineas Bristowe had at first to trust nearly wholly to the sagacity of his horse—which trod with extreme caution on his way down.

Jessie followed close behind.

In this way they contrived, though the *trajet* was a very long one, to reach the road in comparatively a short space of time.

But the road was ill defined, and extremely difficult to follow.

There were no tall hedge rows or towering trees, to indicate on the darkest night the way to be followed, while numerous ruts every now and then almost brought the horses to their knees.

It was a cold, bleak, bitter night, and apparently no hope of shelter.

But Phineas Bristowe cared not.	He had a strong impression of the kind of shelter he would have found, if he had been given over to the hands of the young heir of the house of Haddington.

They were obliged to proceed with extreme caution, as, from want of a moon, they could not make out any of the dangers that beset their path, while by walking they were enabled to trust to the sagacity of their noble steeds.

Presently Phineas drew rein.

"What is it?" said Jessie.

Phineas dismounted and listened.	He stooped towards the ground.

He could clearly hear horses' hoofs clattering roughly, with headlong speed, along the road.

He dared not do so himself.

Ere he mounted, he looked wildly around.	At a considerable distance to the left of the road was a dark and gloomy wood, apparently of vast extent.

It might be the abode of the snake, the bear, and the panther.

But of two evils he choose the lesser.

Man just now, in his estimation, was the greater evil.

He was well armed. He had the means of lighting a fire with ease.

Mounting once more, he selected a spot where the plain seemed pretty level, and seizing Jessie's bridle, turned towards the wood.

" Where are you taking me?" said Jessie.

" Hush! we are pursued," he whispered. " If I am taken now they will kill me."

Jessie made no reply.

Why should she ever be made a party to the crimes and follies of others—she, the innocent and pure?

But what this man said was plausible, and she wished not to have his death upon her head.

" If you stand by me now, Jessie, like a brave girl," he said, " it shall be your last trial."

" I will do so."

" Henry is in America."

" I know it! I know it!"

" I saw him."

" Where?"

" In New York——"

" But——"

" There I could make no terms for myself."

" Was he well? How did he look? Tell me I beg, I pray you?"

" Well—he is now on your track. Not so near as to be with these ruffians, but near enough for me to communicate with him as soon as we are in a place of safety."

" Thank heaven!" cried Jessie.

" Now ride," said Phineas, as they came beside a struggling row of trees.

A long level meadow stretched before them.

The night was dim but not always dark. Ragged clouds flew over the sky, now concealing, now revealing, the pale face of the half-hidden moon. Occasionally great drops of rain would patter down, and the wind surge in the pine trees.

That, and the soft turf under their feet, drowned the noise of the horses' steps.

The trees grew thicker.

The branches of the pines met above her over this strange road, casting strange and changeful shadows on the narrow way.

At some moments, everything would be shrouded in total darkness—again the cold moon would sail forth, gazing down through the tossing foliage, as they flew along.

The wood was not far ahead of them now.

Again it was black dark, but they abated not their speed, trusting to the sagacity of the noble animals who bore them.

They had ridden, perhaps, a mile, when they again heard the sound of at least two horses in pursuit.

But they were on the skirt of the vast forest now, where no human eye, even that of an Indian, could follow at that time of night.

Phineas walked the horses gently along through a deep grove of pines, and noticing that here and there the forest was free from underwood, continued on his way into the very depth of the forest.

About an hour later, he cried a halt.

They were in what appeared a narrow gulley, overgrown completely with trees, so thickly,

indeed, as to make the spot more like a cavern than anything else.

Phineas dismounted.

He amply provided himself with necessaries. A small lantern was trimmed and lit.

He then saw that they were in a dried-up water course.

In some places heavy banks, intermingled with roots, overhung the small stream.

This formed a kind of small cave.

Phineas took two large horse cloths from the horses, and giving them to Jessie, bade her make some sort of a bed with them.

Here he intended remaining until morning.

Then he led away the horses, and hoppling them after the American fashion, left them, certain that they could not stray very far.

He afterwards drew forth some provisions, and, with some difficulty, prevailed on Jessie to eat.

He gave her, too, brandy qualified from a pool close at hand.

He himself took a deep draught without any mixture of water.

Then he wrapped himself in a cloak, and soon both slept soundly, after the harassing fatigues of that day and night.

It was morning when Jessie awoke.

Gliding away towards the pool which Phineas Bristowe had indicated to her, she performed her ablutions, sent up a fervent prayer to heaven for herself and all she loved, and then returned to where the Mormon—sullen, with bleared eyes and face bloated by evil passions—was rising to go in search of her.

For a moment he thought she had fled.

But when he saw her come, radiant in her beauty, though very grave and pale, his sullen face brightened, and he welcomed her kindly.

They breakfasted, and, the horses being caught, proceeded on their journey.

CHAPTER L.

THE PANTHER.

PHINEAS knew that the route he was in search of lay to the south, and therefore across the forest. This he clearly ascertained by an examination of the map.

He had no guide, however, but the sun, and the forest was so dark, entangled and thick with briars, that their progress was very slow.

As they advanced, it grew more dense, and it was with extreme difficulty that he could urge their horse through the trees.

Often they had to dismount, and lead them.

Strange noises assailed their ears at times, noises that did not tend to reassure them.

Phineas was pale with terror, and yet the instinct of self-preservation made him prepare for the worst.

One barrel of his fowling piece was loaded with slugs, the other with three balls.

Whatever came of it, he determined to use his firearms if attacked.

Jessie rode on in happy unconsciousness of this kind of danger. She scarcely heard the murmuring voices of the forest. Her mind was far away.

Suddenly the horses snorted, reared, and drew back, their forefeet fixed firmly in the ground.

" What is it ?" said Jessie.

" Some wild beast," replied Phineas, trembling in every limb.

Decidedly Jessie was a heroine.

" Let us dismount and fasten the horses. They will otherwise run away with us."

Phineas did so, and could scarcely succeed in fastening them safely to a tree.

Jessie then patted them on the neck, talked to them, and tried to soothe them.

Magical is the power of the human voice, indeed, for they were still directly

" A panther ! a panther !" said Phineas Bristowe, in terribly fearful accents.

" Where?" said Jessie, very white and blood-less in the face, but still calm and collected.

Phineas pointed to the bough of a tree right in their path.

The panther was crouching, as if ready for a spring at the foremost horse.

With a silent prayer, Jessie took the gun from the other's hand.

Fortunate it was, that the dwarf had encouraged her to practice at a mark with Henry.

She looked steadily at him, took aim, and fired one barrel.

The panther gave a horrid growl, and stood still irresolute.

She had slightly wounded him with the slugs.

" Fire," mumbled Phineas, hiding his face in his hand; " fire the other barrel."

Jessie did so, just as the ferocious animal sprung into the air with the intention of striking the first horse.

But the aim was too true. The cougar fell half way, and crawled into a thicket.

" Brave girl !" cried Phineas, recovering him-self—" let me load again. My hand has been very shaky, of late—very shaky."

But Jessie had sunk on a bank, in a fainting fit. She was utterly exhausted.

Phineas, however, occupied himself with loading, and in a few minutes, no animal reappearing, was able to assist Jessie to rise.

Not a word passed.

The horses seemed to be aware that victory had remained to the human species.

They no longer showed any sign of terror.

CHAPTER LI.

A SHANTY.

AGAIN the fugitives continued on their way through the dark and gloomy forest.

Towards evening they began to see signs of a clearing of considerable extent.

Then they came upon a trail, evidently much frequented by travellers.

They followed it the more readily, that it began to rain.

Presently they saw a rude kind of shanty, from which swung a sign denoting that it was an inn.

They advanced at a rapid pace, drew rein, and entered the house.

A slatternly woman stood behind a kind of bar —an Indian sat smoking by the fire.

As they entered, he neither moved nor raised his head.

A boy took their horses, and led them behind.

They then enquired if they could have supper and a bed for each.

"Well," said the woman, throwing open a side door, " the young woman can lie down there in the straw, and you can sleep by the fire."

" That will do," said Phineas ; " and now, give us the best grub you've got."

And he followed Jessie into the room which was to be her dormitory.

The rain now beat wildly in the one small window, and on the roof, which was just above their heads ; the wind roared around the corner of the house, swinging the little sign of the hedge tavern, with a harsh creaking ; the pine trees all about whistled and shrieked.

Phineas and Jessie thought themselves fortunate in escaping the storm, even in such a place.

A warm supper once partaken of, a rough bed was made for Jessie—towards whom the woman was tolerably kind, and she retired to rest.

Phineas Bristowe filled a pipe, ordered a stiff glass of grog, and sat down opposite the Indian who, apparently, had never moved.

He was not an ordinary looking Indian.

He was of moderate height, well-made, very dark, but with features so regular that few would have fancied him, except from his colour, to be a genuine Redskin.

He was handsomely dressed, with deer-skin leggings adorned by scalp locks, mocassins, a tunic of leather profusely adorned with beads and silver ornaments, while his head-dress was evidently that of a chief.

His rifle stood by his side, while a knife and tomahawk depended from his belt.

He was smoking and drinking whiskey from a horn.

When Phineas sat down, he was calm, cool and collected.

He scarcely noticed his presence.

Presently, as if by accident, his eye fell upon the white man—and as it did so, a gleam of ferocity, unutterable crossed his countenance.

" Wet night," said Phineas, thinking he had better say something.

The Indian grunted out something unintelligible, drained his whiskey, and ordered more.

" Give me your gun, knife and tomahawk," said the woman : " none of your drunken Indian rows for me."

The other submitted to be disarmed, with a savage gleam in his dark eye.

He then took the whiskey, and drained it to the very dregs.

Phineas Bristowe went on smoking quietly—perfectly unconscious of the fearful peril he stood in.

The cougar would have been welcome as a domestic cat, in preference to the being who now sat before him—had he but have known.

Had he but have suspected there was no spot

of earth too distant—no retreat too lonely—for him to have sought, rather than have remained one moment in his company.

But Phineas Bristowe knew nothing, suspected nothing.

Then with a fearful growl, or rather grunt, he flew at Bristowe's throat.

He had him down, with his hands round his neck, until he was black in the face.

A horrible gurgle in the throat of the Mormon elder, brought the woman to his assistance.

A traveller at that moment entered.

Between the two they dragged the Indian off, and threw him out of doors.

It was time. The angel of death was hovering right over Bristowe's head, but declined to strike

It left him a few more years for repentance yet.

"Where is he—what's the matter?" he sputtered, as soon as they had poured some brandy down his throat.

"Gone—how are you?"

"Better."

"I'll have none of them Injines no more," said the woman.

"More brandy," said Phineas.

They gave it to him. He lay down directly after, and went to sleep.

So utterly stupefied was he by the quantity of brandy he had taken that, despite his pain, he slept.

In the morning, when he awoke, he found Jessie waiting breakfast for him.

She had heard of the attack on the previous night.

"How do you feel?"

"Sore."

"Are you much hurt?"

"A little."

"Can you get up?"

"I will try."

And with the assistance of Jessie, he rose, and having partaken of a hearty breakfast, prepared to depart.

While paying his money a thought seemed to strike him.

"The Indian?"

"Cum'd in this morning early, tuk his traps, and sloped," said the hostess.

"Humph!"

After a short and thoughtful pause, Phineas Bristowe changed the subject.

"I want to reach the great trunk road from New York to Illinois," he said.

"Going west?"

"Yes."

"Well," said the woman, with a sleepy expression of countenance, "you must cross the forest due south."

Phineas looked dark.

"Ye can go back about fifty mile," said the woman.

"Well," said Phineas, "I can't do that; I'm in a hurry."

"Then you must cross the forest to Neatsville," said the woman.

"Is there any track?"

"An Indian trail," said she.

"That will do. Come, Jessie, time is going fast; we have a long road."

And paying his bill, he went out.

CHAPTER LIII.

LOST IN THE FOREST.

It was now about ten o'clock. A great portion of the day was before them.

Phineas Bristowe, after the successful encounter with the *cougar* or panther, felt rather less alarm at the presence of the denizens of the forest.

He trusted the gun, however, to Jessie.

"I'm a very poor shot," he said, with a faint attempt at a laugh.

Jessie shuddered, but believing it to be her duty, she took the gun and slung it by her side.

The forest was nearly as dense as ever, but Indians and others had crossed so often, as to have left a tolerably distinct trail.

Phineas had been told that he could easily cross the forest in a day.

He rode on, therefore, without pressing his horse to any very great speed.

He reserved it for a moment of pressure or sudden danger.

It was a lovely morn. Not a sign of a human being was in sight but themselves. The wavy forest, the sighing of the wind, the sky above, alone occupied the attention.

Jessie was awed.

There is a feeling of immensity comes over us as we gaze upon the vast American woods, which nowhere else is experienced.

Jessie experienced this.

Around, even when they rode to the summit of some steep hillock, nothing could be seen but the wavy tops of green trees, stretching out like an ocean of leaves into the far illimitable.

Above, when she gazed amid that awful stillness, she might well have cried,—

"Oh! thou beautiful
And unimaginable ether! and
Ye multiplying masses of increased
And still increasing lights! What are ye? What
Is this blue wilderness of interminable
Air, where ye roll along, as I have seen
The leaves along the limpid streams of Eden?
Is your course measured for ye? Or do ye
Sweep on in your unbounded revelry
Through an aeriel universe of endless
Expansions, at which my soul aches to think,
Intoxicated with eternity?"

Jessie was essentially of a poetical tone of mind.

She had stored her memory with many a masterpiece of those gigantic minds, which made up the galaxy of English glory.

Forgetting all her troubles and sorrows, carried away by the feeling of her situation, every now and then she would burst forth, like a singing bird, and fill the woods with harmony.

"Rather dangerous here," said Phineas.

"Why?"

"Indians."

"There are no inimical Indians so low down as this," replied Jessie.

"Don't know. I rather fancy that fellow last night was pretty inimical."

"Yes, but he had been drinking."

"I don't know that," said Phineas, with a shudder. "I rather think that was an excuse. But never mind, it makes me ill to think of it. See, we have a mile of pleasant turf, let us trot."

And, as if anxious to escape reflection, he trotted forward.

They went on this way, alternately trotting and walking, until the sun had long passed its meridian.

They were then on the edge of a small stream.

The horses were tired.

Phineas drew rein and dismounted.

An ample meal was soon spread out on the grass, of which both gladly partook.

There is nothing like the American forest for sharpening the appetite.

This done, they started on their way again.

About an hour before dusk they reached a denser part af the forest.

The trail divided into two.

One seemed just as beaten as the other.

Phineas Bristowe was utterly at a nonplus. He knew not what to do. He had asked no questions as to any such contingency.

"This is dreadful;" he said, "who knows?— one way may carry us miles into the depths of the forest."

"But both are frequented."

"True."

"Trust to the horses."

"In an ordinary case I would do so," said Phineas, "but there is this difficulty."

"What?"

"The path to the right goes due south—that is our direction."

"Well!"

"The other bends to the eastward."

"To the south, then," said Jessie.

On they advanced, at a very slow pace, however, for the road, or rather bridle-path, began to be very indistinct and overgrown by trees.

They had evidently taken the wrong turning.

"We must retrace our steps," said Phineas Bristowe, in a trembling voice.

"But we shall never reach the ford before dark," replied Jessie. "Better halt."

"Halt here—no."

"We shall lose our way!"

"No," said Phineas, who spoke in a wild, bewildered way; "come."

And turning his horse's head, he endeavoured to return the way he came.

But ere they had gone night had fallen. It was not even a starlight night. It was black, or rather, to use the poet's words,—

"It is a fearful light!
No sun, no moon, no lights innumerable—
The very blue of the enpurpled night
Fades to a dreary twilight. Yet I see
Huge dusky masses; but unlike the worlds
We were approaching, which, begirt with light,
Seem'd full of life, even when their atmosphere
Of light gave way, and showed them taking shapes
Unequal, of deep valleys and vast mountains,
And some emitting sparks, and some displaying
Enormous liquid plains, and some begirt
With luminous belts, and floating moons, which took,
Like them, the features of fair earth; instead,
All here seems dark and dreadful."

"Phineas," said Jessie, in an earnest tone,

"we have provisions, blankets, the means of making a fire; let us camp till morning."

"Fire will bring Indians."

"It will keep off wild beasts."

Phineas was off his horse in a moment, and soon busily engaged in collecting fuel by the light of his lamp.

A fire was soon made in a kind of hollow, the horses hoppled, and the camp, to use an American phrase, made as comfortable as possible.

But Phineas was not at his ease. The memory of the fearful attack of the previous night had not passed away from his mind.

He thought deeply and long.

"Jessie!"

"Sir."

"I wish to have some serious conversation with you," he began.

"I shall be very happy."

"Jessie, I have been all day thinking over my past life. I am not going to enter into any of the many regretable circumstances with which it has been connected, but I wish to ask you one or two questions."

Jessie started.

By some strange delusion, as she fancied, a kind of shadow fell across her face.

She was about six feet from the blazing fire.

A piece of wood seemed to crack under the weight of a human foot.

She clutched her fowling-piece.

"Did you see anything?" said Phineas, in a low, fearful voice.

"No."

"Hear anything?"

"N—no."

"You are quite sure."

"Yes," said Jessie, who now thought it was a delusion.

"You intend to marry Henry Haddington, do you not?"

"I do."

"Well, Jessie, if I restore you to your friends —if I render your father and mother thoroughly happy—if I disarm Mrs. Treherne, that bitter and revengeful woman who first enticed me to evil, would they not all forgive me?"

"I think they would. But, Mr. Bristowe."

"What?"

"This is not repentance."

"Why?"

"It is a bargain."

"What would you have me do?"

"Make no bargain. Do what you say; throw yourself on their mercy, and trust to their generosity," she cried.

"I can trust no one," he said, moodily; "Henry hates me."

"And has he not cause?"

"How so?"

"His father!"

"Hush!" gasped Phineas Bristowe, blanched with terror. "Hush! whisper not that awful event to any ears. I say I did not do it. Whatever of evil happened to him, living or dead, was no doing of mine—so help me, heaven!"

"Whose then?"

"His bitter, everlasting enemy."

THE RED INDIAN.

' Who—who ?''

" Mrs. Treherne.   She told me—I know not what to believe—that the dead body found in his clothes was not him—that she had secured him in a madhouse,   But who can believe her ?''

Jessie made no reply.

She sat open-mouthed with horror and astonishment.

In the bright light of the fire she saw an awful face close behind Bristowe.

It was the Indian.

In his eyes gleamed the fire of insanity.

In his hand was a gleaming knife.

Bristowe saw her gazing over his head.

His lips were steeped in falsehood and guilt, and, like most wicked men, he was superstitious.

He was afraid to look round.

" Eh ?—what—wha—wha—wha—what is it ?'' he stammered forth.

" The Indian !'' gasped Jessie, with clasped hands.

Bristowe leaped to his feet, turned, and confronted the Indian with his hand held out.

" Good night, brudder.   Lost way—last night —sorry—much drink—lose head.''

Utterly helpless with astonishment, Phineas shook him by the hand.

Jessie knew not what to say or think.

"Why come this way?" said the Indian, in a voice that thrilled to the very marrow of Phineas Bristowe's bones.

"I thought it the right way."

"False trail," continued the Indian, gruffly—"rest—show right—morning."

And sitting down, he lit his pipe, and sat for some time in silence.

"Rum," he said, after a considerable pause.

Phineas looked uneasy.

"Brandy."

Jessie and Phineas exchanged glances.

"Whiskey—fire-water," said the Indian.

Phineas hastened to hand him the bottle, from which the Indian drained a heavy draught, lay down, and was soon in a sound sleep.

Phineas and Jessie were not slow in following this example.

———

CHAPTER LIII.

THE CARAVAN.

THE Mormon elder, however, slept uneasily. Visions of past evil, the memory of the night before, vague apprehensions of he knew not what, made the visions of the night horrible.

He moaned, groaned, and turned heavily.

Smothered prayers and curses passed his lips.

At last he sat upright.

They were on the edge of a swamp, and what had partly prevented his slumbers was the infernal din which emanates from the least drowsy of all earthly monsters—the horned frog.

Jessie, however, slept still.

Ths Indian was nowhere to be seen.

But why does Phineas start, rub his eyes, and leap to his feet?

At no great distance, beneath the heavy shade of the trees, he beholds a camp fire.

He can see it plainly through a long vista of the forest.

An awful dread falls upon his soul.

It is a camp of Indians, and the man who came upon them so suddenly the night before was no doubt their scout.

But at that moment he heard a footstep.

Snatching the fowling-piece from beside Jessie, who woke with a wild start, he brought it to the charge.

"Who comes?"

"Friend," said the deep, bass voice of the Indian.

"Friend, be ——" began Phineas, cocking the murderous weapon.

Jessie thrust it up, and, with a stern glance, took it from his hand.

The Indian stood within the range of the camp fire.

"Pale-face—emigrants—out west," said the Indian, sententiously.

"The deuce they are!" said Phineas, with a strange glance at Jessie. "Suppose we join them?"

"As you will," replied the young girl, coldly, pulling down the cocks of the double-barrelled gun as she spoke.

The Indian looked at her with unqualified admiration.

He, however, said nothing, but took his way as guide to the party.

In a few minutes they could distinguish all the signs of a white encampment.

There were waggons, horses, mules, and several fires, round which and in the vehicles the whole body seemed to be sleeping.

One or two sleepy sentries reclined against trees.

"Speak," said the Indian, in a loud voice.

"Ho! the camp, there!" cried Phineas Bristowe, with a knit brow.

No answer.

"Hang you!—are you all asleep?" continued the Mormon elder.

"What's the row?" said an unmistakable English voice.

"Lost our way, friends," continued Bristowe. "Can we come in?"

"Come in, in Heaven's name!" said the sentry—"the more the merrier."

Bristowe advanced, followed by Jessie and the Indian.

"Bristowe, by the holy poker!" cried the sentry. "Hurrah! here's a lark!"

It was the Mormon caravan they were in search of, which had turned a little off the road to be sheltered from observation.

A general bustle now took place, and in a few minutes Bristowe was surrounded by all his old companions.

Paolo even advanced, though he scarcely ever left the side of the waggon which contained his treasure and Julie.

Rapid explanations ensued, and then Jessie joined Julie in the waggon.

"Where's that rascally Redskin?" whispered Phineas, as soon as Jessie had turned her back.

"Why?"

"I mean to give him goss. The vagabond nearly throttled me last night."

The Indian stood calm and serene among them, looking keenly around.

"Taking stock, eh? you tipsy Indian thief," said one of the Mormons.

"No harm look," said the Indian, with a cold and contemptuous smile.

"But great harm in throttling," observed Phineas, with a savage and ignoble grin, as he and Paolo caught him one by each wrist, and held him firm.

The Indian smiled scornfully.

Whenever he was at all excited, a strange light, as if of insanity, seemed to gleam in his eyes.

They took him, and lashed him to a tree, without a word emanating from his lips.

They lashed him solidly and firmly.

It now was break of day.

Every one began to busy themselves with their domestic duties.

Phineas Bristowe, in a stern and angry speech, addressed his Mormon brethren.

He told them the story of the unprovoked attack on him by the Indian.

He then significantly cut a hickory stick.

"Phineas Bristowe," said the Indian, in a tone

of terrible anguish, his brow covered with big drops of sweat.

The Mormon elder stood back aghast.

"How know you my name?"

"Did she not call you so?"

"True."

"Touch me not!" said the Indian—"touch not my body! Better hell ——"

"I will scourge the insult out of your hide!" cried Phineas, frantically.

He knew not why, but the Indian awed him. He gazed at him terror-stricken.

All the Mormons now approached with thongs and sticks.

"Hold!" cried a loud but lovely voice.

It was Jessie, who stood in front of the unarmed Indian.

"Get out of the way," said Phineas, hoarsely. "The fellow deserves hanging!"

"Strike me first." said Jessie, coldly, "since you are a coward!"

"Stand away!" cried the mob.

"Ha! ha! ha!" laughed a loud and maniacal voice as Jessie moved away.

And the Indian, waving a long and gleaming knife on high, bounded into the forest.

After cutting the cord which bound his wrists, she had placed the knife in his hand.

The camp was in utter consternation. They had yet a long road to go, and the Indians were rife in their passage.

"What have you done?" said Phineas, in an angry and stern tone of voice.

"My duty."

"How so?"

"I have prevented you from doing a base, cowardly, and dishonourable action."

Phineas turned away, with a bitter scowl upon his face, but he made no answer.

Meanwhile, the Indian had run, in the usual way of his tribe, to cover, and then halted.

"Ha! ha! ha! Noble girl! She saved me from the vilest degradation that can befall a man. She shall see all her desires fulfilled. But as for you, foul and hideous apostle of a new faith—you shall die—die—die! The flesh shall rot from off your bones!"

He wiped his heated brow.

"But I must be careful. My head is not quite right."

He paused.

A light foot was heard close at hand.

He looked round.

It was Jessie bringing him his rifle and his tomahawk.

"Thank you, angel of light," he said.

"You will not hurt them?"

"Not them—but him."

"Who?"

"Phineas Bristowe."

"How know you his name?" said Jessie, fixing her eyes strangely on him.

"I know it."

"I never mentioned it."

"Never mind—I know it," said the Indian. "Would that I could trust you, Jessie!"

"With your life you know you might."

"My secret?"

"You may."

"On your solemn word as a woman?"

"On my solemn word as a woman."

"You know I am not an Indian?"

"I know it."

"But I have joined the Indians for one sole purpose. I am the bitter, determined, and relentless enemy of the Mormons,"

"Indeed!"

"And more than that, Jessie."

"Well?"

"You will never breathe to living soul without my permission?"

"Never."

"I am—let me take your hand," he said.

Jessie took it.

He whispered two words.

Jessie fainted in his arms.

"Ha! ha! ha!" cried a sarcastic voice close to them. "A pretty idyl, indeed! A Red Indian and a white girl!"

They turned, and saw a gentlemanly-looking white man, in the garb of a hunter, close to them.

It was the Honourable Mr. Stanley.

"Judge not from appearances," said the Indian, coolly.

"I beg your pardon," replied the other, raising his hat, "but is your name Miss Jessie Treherne?"

"It is."

"I am, then, delighted to meet you."

"How do you know me?"

The Indian stood a little back, listening with marked attention.

"I am an acquaintance of Mr. Henry Haddington," he said.

"When did you see him, and where?" she gasped, in an eager, glad way.

Mr. Stanley told her.

He then eagerly enquired after the Countess Sidonia, *alias* Julie.

"I know her," said Jessie, casting down her eyes.

"But you know no good of her," replied the other, sadly.

"Well, she has been much sinned a : ." continued Jessie.

"That is enough. Will you oblige me, Mi : ' he added.

"In any way I can."

"Then tell her I am here—simply that more."

"I will."

At this moment a loud cry burst from the tents, and Jessie was compelled to return.

The Indian and Mr. Stanley buried themselves in the depths of the forest.

CHAPTER LIV.

JULIE AND PAOLO

WHEN Julie found that in the Mormon camp the influence of man was omnipotent, and that the voice of woman was raised quite in vain, she sank apparently into a most perfect state of apathy.

Paolo offered, on condition that she made over

to him a considerable portion of her vast riches, to grant her freedom, and allow her to return to England.

She sternly refused any compromise.

"You cannot always chain me up," she said. "The day must come when I shall be free, and fearful will be the revenge which I will take."

"I defy you woman!" cried the impetuous Levantine. "But, Julie," he added, in a caressing tone, "why cannot we be friends? Why not unite our fate for life? We need not live with these people. Let the nuptial knot be tied, so that no quibble can untie it, and we can go to Paris. There money is omnipotent. Not a question will be asked."

"Money with you is worse than useless," she said, with cold disdain.

"How so?"

"I love another, and am married to him," she continued.

He started back as if bit by a serpent.

He knew it, and yet each time he thought of it he grew mad with rage.

"But you were disappointed. I tore you away on your wedding-day."

Julie looked at him with an ineffable expression.

"Wretch, you do not mean ——"

"I do."

"Him? When?"

"The night of the burglary. More," said she, in a boasting tone—"he is after me."

"Is he?" said Paolo, in a cold and passionless tone. "What then?"

"He will take me away."

"Will he? Now do you know, if he comes—do you know what I shall do?" replied Paolo, with the most provoking self-possession.

"No."

"Ah! I will see that he does not take you away."

"How will you prevent him?"

"*By telling him the truth!*"

Julie turned ghastly pale. She had never thought of this. It was, indeed, a fiendish kind of revenge.

"You dare not, Paolo. This man is my last hope. I—I—I—love him!"

"So much the worse for you," said the supposed Viscount de Florac, turning away, with a cold and malicious grin.

At this moment Jessie glided into the tent, which was made by the aid of a waggon, the floor of which was transformed into a resting-place.

The busy hum of voices, the calls of the drivers, the cries of the teamsters, and all the usual sounds of a camp under weigh, began now to manifest themselves.

CHAPTER LV.

MRS. JOHN SMITH.

The caravan was composed of twelve or fourteen waggons, drawn in every case by either oxen or mules.

These contained the women, children, and other valuables.

There were above a hundred women.

There were thirty-seven men.

To conceal the preponderance of the female sex, whenever they approached a settlement, the waggons, which were covered, were closed.

In one waggon rode those who were as yet free—the unsealed women of the camp.

The men of the sect were noticed constantly to be hovering round this particular waggon.

Not one of them but had two wives.

And yet, such is the force of a bad and wicked custom, that those who had most wives were those who most hung about the last of the waggons.

In one of the front waggons sat a rather good-looking woman of about thirty.

She had entered the Mormon band from pure affection for a man.

She was a widow.

She loved John Smith, a man who, from being a dupe of the Mormons, had become one of their active agents.

He had wooed and won this woman, and though professing himself to have the strongest repulsion against the doctrines of polygamy, had fully explained them to her.

In the first intoxication of her love, she had thought little of this matter.

But now, the heat of passion having subsided, she had begun to reflect.

All the men in the camp but her husband had two or more wives.

Her husband appeared, hitherto, satisfied.

But Mrs. John Smith had a daughter!

Not her own daughter, but the daughter of her late husband.

Too near a relationship, we should think, in an ordinary case.

But nothing is too near or dear for the reckless apostles of Joe Smith.

She was about sixteen, and when, three months before, her step-mother had married, she was quite a child.

But imperceptibly she had ripened into a woman.

Now, the mother had not noticed this, so gradual had been the change.

But the man had.

Charlotte Davis was a rather bright-eyed girl, not excessively pretty, but very attractive.

There was a rich sparkle in her eye, a dimple on her cheek, and a smile upon her lips, which to such men was really irresistible.

And, then, she was very vain.

Her mother was very fond of her, and very kind to her, while John Smith was almost harsh in his way of addressing her.

Suddenly his manner changed.

He spoke in a soft, low tone, patted her cheek, pinched her dumpy arms, and was attentive in the usual way of a rough, uncultivated man.

Charlotte seemed pleased, and the mother-in-law laughed heartily.

Silly woman!

Then John would ride near the waggon twice as much as he used to do, and though tolerably attentive to his wife, was ten times more so to her step-daughter.

Still she suspected nothing—saw nothing.

One day, it was very fine, the waggons were toiling very slowly through a heavy prairie.

It was covered with tall grass, and richly dotted with flowers.

The earth was soft, and the wheels of the heavy carts stuck fast every now and then.

"Ain't you tired of sitting?" said John Smith, suddenly, addressing Charlotte.

"Yes."

"Come and have a run, then."

"Do—it will enliven the girl," added the step-mother, kindly.

Charlotte was down like a fawn.

The prospect delighted her.

John Smith fastened his horse to the waggon, and dismounting, began playing hide and seek with Charlotte.

She was only a child.

Very dangerous amusement, however, Mrs. John Smith, let me tell you.

He caught her.

The high grass concealed them from the caravan.

"Lotty," said the man, taking her arm in his and pressing her hand.

She blushed rosy red, and looked up into his face in an enquiring way.

She was sixteen.

He was eight-and-twenty, and very good-looking at that.

"Well."

"How pretty you've grown lately," he half stammered out.

"Am I."

"Yes, quite beautiful."

"You called me ugly little thing, the other day," she said, maliciously.

"I don't like little girls," he replied.

"Oh!"

"But then, Lotty, do you know you are no longer a little girl?"

"Ain't I—what then?"

"A woman."

"Indeed!"

"Yes, and a lovely woman too. Lotty, you will be too beautiful soon."

"Why?"

"Everybody will be wanting to marry you," he said, in a hushed tone.

"Marry," she replied, with a rich colour beaming up to her very eyes, "I'm o'er young."

"Lotty dearest," he said, in a softer and more insidious voice, "you must marry."

"Who will have me?"

"I will."

Lotty started back, in mute astonishment. She was surprised that the best-looking man in the caravan should love her.

Was that all?

We shall see.

"You love me," she gasped, speaking in a low, hushed, hurried way, for, really and truly, the idea of love was very new. "But mamma!"

"Lotty," said John Smith, with an impressive gravity which imposed wonderfully on the girl.

"I married your mother because it appeared

necessary to her happiness; but she is too old for me."

"Too old!"

"You know that our religion allows us several wives, but our hearts only one."

"I understand," she said, in a kind of hollow voice.

"Now, I loved you as a mere child."

A lie!

"I knew then what all these budding beauties meant; I knew how lovely, how perfect you would be one day, and to secure to myself the hope of such a dear treasure, I wooed and won your mother."

"My mother!"

"You must really understand, dear girl," said the insidious seducer, "that she is no relation of yours—really she is not."

"I have always fancied her my own mother; I never knew any other," gasped the young girl, half resisting, half convinced.

"But I tell you, dearest and loveliest of your sex, she is no relation."

"But—but though I have heard all you have said about spiritual wives, I don't like to be one of many wives."

"Charlotte—Lotty—you will be my real wife, the others will be only wife in name," he whispered, looking full into her eyes.

She bent them down and looked upon the ground.

"But what will mother say?"

"Your step-mother is a reasonable woman. She could never have expected that a man of my age could ever feel anything like a romantic passion for one older than himself. She is a very excellent person, and I have no doubt will play the part of housekeeper very well. But in a wife, a real wife, I need something to love, something to elevate my thoughts, something to look up to, adore, and worship."

"I'm afraid," said Miss Charlotte Davis, with that foolish giggle which some girls believe to be so becoming, "you've said all this very often."

"Never, I swear, my angel."

"Well, I'll think about it."

"Think about it!"

"Yes, about a month hence I may be able to give you an answer."

"A month hence!" said John Smith, with flashing eyes, as he caught her round the waist and pressed her to his beating heart. "I mean to make you mine to-night."

She tried to resist, to show firmness, to say that he must wait, but the iron of feverish passion had entered her soul.

She consented.

"But about *her*——"

"She must know nothing about it for awhile. When she knows it is done, she will no longer make any noise."

"I don't like that," said the girl, who had something of better feeling.

"Then you do not love me?"

"Why?"

"Because love does not hesitate—love thinks only of the one being loved."

"You mean that love is selfish."

" Very," said John, as he again kissed her warm and pouting lips.

And, after all, that is the best way of stopping a girl's mouth.

After some further parley, during which the girl seemed to shew a mock kind of resistance, it was agreed that that very evening, at the halting-place, the marriage ceremony was to be performed.

And this is no creature of the writer's imagination, but a fact.

What do Mormons, the fathers of adultery and lust, care for the ordinary relationships of society ? Their object is to fill their harems.

CHAPTER LVI.

JEALOUSY.

When the girl returned to the camp, she had schooled herself to appear calm and collected.

The man, the first who had ever shown any kindness to her, the first who had paid her those attentions which are so dear to the dawning woman's heart, had excited in her feelings of which she had never suspected the existence.

She began to have a vague idea of passion and all its fierce consequences.

She did not as yet see the horror of the deed she was about to commit.

She did not know that Nature, by the way she has balanced the sexes, has decided that if all are to have a wife, few indeed could have more than one.

She could not say with Julia :—

" Wedded she was some years, and to a man
    Of fifty, and such husbands are in plenty ;
And yet, I think, instead of such a one,
    'Twere better to have two of five and twenty,
Especially in countries near the sun ;
    And now I think on't, " Mi vien in mente."
Ladies even of the most uneasy virtue
    Prefer a spouse whose age is short of thirty."

When Charlotte, as the waggons reached the verge of a desolate plain, where, at all events, the wheels could turn with greater rapidity, approached to take her place in the waggon, the mother looked at her with a keen but almost glassy eye.

" You have been a long time," she said.

The demon of jealousy, the keenest torture a woman can feel, had entered her soul.

" Having a run in the prairies," cried Charlotte, tossing her head.

" A long run."

" It was so delightful," continued the other, angry at the tone of the cross examination.

" Was it ?" replied the injudicious mother. " Then in future we will go together."

" Why ?"

" I choose it."

" Do you ?"

Mrs. Smith stared at her step-daughter. The girl had utterly changed in an hour.

" Where is my husband ?" she asked.

" You," cried the girl, pointing forward.

He had just galloped past after a hasty glance at the two.

Mrs. Smith made no reply. Never before had

it struck her that Charlotte was anything but a child.

She knew the Mormon customs, but, like many another wronged and outraged woman, had believed that she could fix the affections of her husband.

As well seek to stay a foaming torrent as check a man's passions in a community where they are taught to go unrestrained.

A burning sense of jealousy, a feeling of hatred against him and her seemed to flood her very soul.

She spoke not.

But she determined to keep a keen watch upon them both.

She had seen and noticed Jessie. The pleasant face of Charlotte had won upon the warm heart of our heroine, who had shared with her some of the luxuries which the ill-purchased wealth of Phineas Bristowe procured her.

A halt was declared on the edge of the barren plain.

It was in a charming and scattered grove of trees, near a spring.

A settlement was at no great distance, and several farm-houses were scattered about.

Charlotte leaped to the ground, and joined Jessie, who had approached a fire.

Mrs. Smith was satisfied for the moment. She understood and appreciated the purity and innocence of out heroine's heart

Her character was written in unmistakeable characters upon her countenance.

She was a genuine-hearted girl

Her husband assisted her to alight, and fixed his own tent as usual.

He was kind and affectionate in manner. This reassured her. She was not aware of the fatal truth, that bad men are ever hypocrites, and can shew more kindness while meditating the deepest wrong than at any other time.

Wives of experience, unfortunately, are fully aware of this terrible and disgraceful truth.

Then, after bidding her prepare supper, he walked away.

Mrs. Smith prepared to execute his orders without the slightest dread.

She glanced, however, every now and then toward the group of the younger women.

She saw Charlotte in anxious conversation with Jessie.

The latter was bending close to her, and whispering in her daughter's ear.

She turned to attend to her household duties, determined as soon as possible to join the group.

When next she looked, Jessie was walking past her tent with slow and cautious steps, her eyes bent on the ground.

" What is the matter ?" said Mrs. Smith, in an anxious tone of voice.

She could not see Charlotte.

Jessie looked up. Her eyes were full of tears. Some deep emotion had sent the sparkling gems welling up from the fountain head.

" Speak—do—for heaven's sake !"

" Nothing—nothing but what was to be expected," said Jessie.

" What ?—anything about Charlotte ?" the poor woman gasped.

"Yes!"

"What is it?"

"She is going to be married, and I think, at her age, it is a pity," began Jessie.

"To whom," said the woman, in slow and hollow accents, "to whom is she going to be married?"

"She did not say."

"I know."

"Do you, then, approve?"

"No. She is about to be married to my husband," she half shrieked.

"Your daughter!"

"She is not my daughter," she gasped, "she is only my step-child. The villain—the wretch!"

"Be calm, Mrs. Smith. Are you sure of this?—I really cannot believe it."

"Come with me and you shall see."

She said no more, but, followed by the horror-stricken and terrified Jessie, she stalked along towards a large tent at the end of the camp.

It was crowded.

A Mormon priest stood at one end, in full canonicals.

As she expected, John Smith and Charlotte were standing before him.

The exasperated woman thrust her way in, and for a moment confronted them in silence.

Charlotte turned red, the husband, on the other hand, pale as death.

"So!" began Mrs. Smith, "not content with luring me from a happy home, you are about already to cast me off—and, what is more, to disgrace yourself for ever by marrying this child."

"Silence!" said, in a nasal voice, the officiating minister; "the ceremonies of the Saints cannot be disturbed."

"Turn her out—madwoman—maniac!" were the angry cries of the men.

The women listened in sullen silence.

"I will not be turned out. I am not a madwoman, though such deeds as these would almost make one wish to be insane. John Smith, are you coming away?—or is this farce to go on?"

"The ceremony is nearly concluded," said the so-called minister, severely; "and if this disgraceful interruption continues, I must use my authority."

"Authority! Is not this man my husband? is he not bound to cleave to me alone?"

"No. You speak as one of the Gentiles. You know that it is necessary for the salvation of the righteous and believing woman, that she should be sealed to one of the elect. Sister Charlotte, here, has manifested her desire to become one of us, and in token of her sincerity has given her hand unto a brother."

"Husband—John!" cried the maddened woman, 'is this to be? Do you abandon me?"

"Certainly not," he said, in a dogged, foolish, defiant way—"but ——"

"But you will give me a partner."

"Such is the custom."

"Foul and unnatural," she continued, despite the scowls and groans of the elect.

"Let this cease," said the minister, making a sign.

Two men caught her by the arms.

"Daughter—child, whom I have nurtured as my own, will you do me this great wrong?" she shrieked aloud.

Charlotte turned away. She had felt for an instant ready to yield, but Satanic pride, the curse of human nature, prevented her.

The poor woman was thrust forth, weeping and wailing, to where Jessie mournfully awaited her.

She was as one struck to stone. She moved now mechanically. Her eye had become glazed. Her skin was hot and dry.

Jessie led her away to her own tent, and, almost by force, made her lie down.

She was in a terrible and burning fever.

Soon the sound of music and revelry could be heard without in the camp.

"Ha! ha! ha!" laughed the woman, sitting up in the bed. "They come for me. Yes, I need them, it is my wedding-day. Will you put out the clothes? But why am I alone, and dressed in black? 'Tis indeed strange. Is that the wine-cup?"

Jessie poured a cooling draught down her parched throat and as she fell back, hurried away to procure medical advice.

There was a dissipated medical student among the apostles of the new religion.

As she passed the corner of the enclosure, she met the bride and bridegroom, preceded by a fiddler.

Casting a withering glance at the guilty pair, she accosted a man close to them.

"Mr. Jones."

"Miss."

"I want you to come and attend Mrs. Smith; she has a bad fever—she is insensible."

"Oh!" said the medical student, with a look of admiration, "is she? Well, I'll come."

The newly-married couple pretended not to hear. But Smith gave a peremptory glance to Jones, who, taking a small carpet-bag, which contained his medicines and instruments, followed Jessie. Her cold, severe, and haughty manner, at once chilled any attempts at gallantry on his part.

Really clever, when sober, he bled the patient, gave her a composing draught, promised to see her in the morning, and left to join the wedding supper.

And the abandoned wife remained alone, with Jessie as a nurse.

Such is our picture of the accursed evils of polygamy, and we beg and implore all those who shall, by the insiduous voice of the Mormon missionaries, be led to the brink of the dreadful precipice, to pause.

The first feeling of a true wife, is to win the pure and undivided affection of her husband.

They must love and cherish one another for all time, until death them do part.

Such is the true matrimony.

One, sole and indivisible.

No woman who really feels affection for a man, ever contemplates the possibility of sharing his affection with another woman—any more than she would herself think of breaking the ——

"Which commandment is't they break?
I have forgot the number, and think no man
Should rashly quote for fear of a mistake."

What, then, must be a woman's feelings, when, after a brief period of happiness, she beholds that love which has been all her own, and which she fondly believes to be her undivided possession, gradually fading away—and that in favour of a rival—another, perhaps younger and prettier, woman.

No poet, no writer, could ever paint the agonies, the doubt, the suffering being must endure, who first knows what it is to feel—jealousy.

Surprise, disbelief, a sinking of the heart, humiliation, a snapping of heart-strings, moral, mental and physical pain the most acute, all accompany the dread discovery.

No sophistry can extenuate, explain away, or in any way soften the force of the blow.

Now, among the Mormons this is of daily, of hourly occurrence, and the women are compelled to bear and put up with it.

This accounts for the apathy, pallor, and the dull, indifferent character and manner of the women in all the Mormon settlements.

No lying statements, no false assertions, no fabricated reports, can ever convince a reasoning English man or woman, that members of the great Anglo-Saxon stock have descended so low as to place themselves on a level with the be-fattened, be-dizened, and be-daubed inmates of a Turk's harem.

And they are not satisfied or content. Who has failed to read the best picture ever written, of the interior of the zenana of a Turk:—

" 'Tis said they use no better than a dog any
  Poor woman, whom they purchase like a pad ;
  They have a number, though they ne'er exhibit 'em,
  Four wives by law, and concubines *ad libitum* ;
  They lock them up, and veil and guard them daily—
  They scarcely can behold their male relations ;
  So that their moments do not pass so gaily
  As is supposed the case with northern nations.
  Confinement, too, must make them look quite palely ;
  And as the Turks abhor long conversations,
  Their days are either pass'd in doing nothing,
  Or bathing, nursing, making love, and clothing.
  They cannot read, and so don't lisp in criticism,
  Nor write, and so they don't affect the Muse,
  Were never caught in epigram or witticism,
  Have no romances, sermons, plays, reviews.
  In harems learning soon would make a pretty schism ;
  But luckily these beauties are no " Blues,"
  No bustling Botherbys have they to show 'em
  That charming passage in the last new poem."

But we must not be carried away by our feelings but rather, lay bare the monstrosity of polygamy, by fact and illustration.

CHAPTER LVII.

THOMAS HICKS.

THE camp had began to feel the want of a fresh supply of provisions. It was therefore resolved, partly in honour of the wedding, and partly because it was held by the elders to be necessary, to have a grand hunt.

Other members were to scatter themselves over the country, and obtain by purchase such provisions as were not already in stock.

A few men, who were not very enthusiastic for field sports, and who wished to keep their eye upon the doings in the camp, remained with the caravan.

Of these were Phineas Bristowe and John Smith.

Mrs. Smith was better in the morning. Her terrible state of excitement had been replaced by a calm, cold, callous demeanour, that boded no good to anyone.

She said not a word of her husband, or the girl he had taken to wife.

She appeared to have blotted the whole circumstance from her memory.

Jessie knew not what to think of this remarkable change in her demeanour.

She tolerably rightly judged that some fierce volcanic feeling was concealed beneath their seemingly calm exterior.

Still waters run deep.

She sat in her tent, brooding over her wrongs. Every now and then she would peer forth as if in search of something or somebody.

But the newly-married couple kept out of her sight. They might be intoxicated by their new happiness, or they might be ashamed to face the woman they had injured.

And yet, according to the received ideas of the Mormon tribe, they were ultimately to live together.

Charlotte, for a time, would be the pet of the Latter-Day harem—Mrs. Smith the drudge.

But how long could such a state of things as this be expected to last?

When a number of wives are content in the home of one man they must be utterly indifferent, or, otherwise, very profligate.

All the younger men of the caravan, with an intense love of excitement, especially of the chase, had gone out to hunt early.

Others scattered themselves over the plains and hills.

Among these was one Thomas Hicks.

He was a young man about five and twenty years of age. In England, he had been in a government office—then in a lawyer's. He had left England under compulsion.

Had he not eagerly joined the evil Mormon community, the chances are that he would have emigrated, by the advice of twelve respectable citizens, to the healthy and salubrious climate of Australia.

But a missionary of the Latter-Day Saints fell in his way.

The man had been ruined by his addiction to the society of the lost of the other sex.

On them he had lavished freely his money, his health, his time—and, above all, the money and time of others.

Now, the Mormon elder showed him a career exactly suited to his demoralized habits.

The man was without principle. He loathed the society of anything virtuous or good. His delight was to revel in the company of the abandoned of both sexes. He never spoke to a female of decent standing, but in the hope of dragging her down to his own standard.

He was of the foulest race that haunt and disgrace our streets and highways.

He was a wholesale and deliberate seducer of women—helpless women.

He had no consideration for anything. That he was about to break up and ruin a happy home,

THE TEMPTER.

was to him rather a subject of ribald rejoicing than of any other feeling.

His boast was of the hearts he had broken, of the young girls he had driven with ignominy to the streets.

Such men are commoner than would readily be believed.

They are the lepers of society. They are not to be found in droves, else were civilization a curse, but they haunt the saloons, night-houses, and ill-famed streets of our great metropolis.

He had got such a name that his own friends shunned him.

He had pretty well exhausted all his resources.

He had just been branded as a defaulter, almost as a thief.

There were things on his guilty conscience that must soon have driven him to suicide or some kind of expatriation.

He had heard of the Mormons. He went to one of their saturnalias.

The idea of a new country, a convenient and bestial belief, with a supply of wives, only limited by his own powers of cajolery and deceit, delighted him.

He joined them, and brought with him the wife and money of his too confiding employer.

He was not exactly handsome. The utterly reckless and evil never are.

No. 39.

But his was a strange, Satanic beauty.

He had black hair, regular features, a pale complexion, and dark, staring eyes.

He was a Satyr in ideas and propensities

This man mounted a good horse, took with him his rifle; and, dressed with extreme good taste and judgment, sallied forth to hunt.

What?

Not the wild beasts of the quarter. He had been told that in that part of the settlement there were girls, innocent, unperverted, and good; who, knowing no evil, could easily be seduced by the cunning and oily voice of the tempter.

He had laid an unhallowed wager that he would bring one of them into camp.

His companions in the morning tried to persuade him against an effort, which might set the whole of the population against them.

But he was determined to persevere in his desperate and villainous undertaking.

He had already two unhappy, miserable, wretched wives, whom he kept under by the sheer brutality and violence of his nature.

They feared, and of course, in their hearts, they hated him cordially.

He was now about to try and add a third to the list of his victims.

Are not these details revolting? And yet how else is it possible to expose the horrid malignity of the wretched apostles of this new and accursed creed?

CHAPTER LVIII.

COUSIN CHARLES

"I AM always more religious upon a sunshiny day, as if there was some association between an internal approach to greater light and purity, and the kindler of this dark lantern of our external existence. The night is also a religious concern; and even more so, when I viewed the moon and stars through Herschel's telescope, and saw that they were worlds."

Every one must agree with the writer of the above.

It was bright sunshine, and all living objects seem to seek for shelter in shady places.

A large farm-house rose from one bank of a river, while on the opposite side could be seen a lovely grove of trees, starting from a very lawn of rich and glossy verdure.

It seemed a scene of perfect content, and happiness, and peace.

Not so.

Gliding with quick and rapid step away from the house, comes a young lady.

She is well, even elegantly, dressed.

She is far too well dressed for the country she has chosen for her habitation.

She is an English girl, who, at the death of her sole surviving parent, had come out, by invitation, to the residence of an uncle, who had emigrated to America many years before.

She was a proud, haughty, self-willed girl; sound and good at heart, but eat up by the terrible demon, Pride, which shone radiantly from her countenance.

Had she been well off and prosperous, she would have been gentle, loving, kind to all around her—the Lady Bountiful of her home and parish.

But she was poor and dependent, and she thought it necessary to her dignity to be cold, haughty, and imperious.

Her uncle, was a plain, blunt, hospitable, worthy man, who had no sympathy with such tantrums—to use a favourite phrase of his.

He had loved his brother, as kind and affectionate brothers only do love.

When James Paulding died, and left nothing in the wide world but a daughter, as a legacy, Richard Paulding took her at once to his heart and home.

But Sarah did not see it.

She saw a gruff, jolly, rough backwoodsman, a prim aunt, with a pair of spectacles, and a great herd of rough boys and girls, varying from four to twenty, amongst whom she was as much out of place as a genuine Arab foal would have been with a lot of wild Mexican mustangs.

They were rude, uncultivated, and vulgar.

But they were ready to love, honour, and cherish their beautiful cousin.

Charles, the eldest born, a young man of stalwart frame, large heart, sound brain, but rude exterior, was, above all, devoted and attached.

But Sarah took everything in a converse sense. Her diseased imagination made her fancy that they were all protecting and condescending.

Her uncle asked her to drill and teach the girls, to polish their crudities.

She silently complained that she was treated as a common household governess.

He offered her money.

She defiantly refused it. Her father had left twenty pounds a year. That would suffice for all her wants.

If she was insulted she would go away.

With admirable, with generous and hearty forbearance, the old people bore with her, only moaning in secret over her obstinacy and self-willedness.

"Don't be in a hurry, dame," said the English backwoodsman. "She'll come round."

"Ain't sure of that. But, poor creature, we must take no notice—she's alone in the world."

And time went on, but Sarah Paulding did not get a whit better, more agreeable or sociable.

She taught the children patiently, she tamed much of the ruggedness of the girls, and even obtained an authority over the boys; but more by the exercise of stern decision than by that magic chord of love, which is the true way to the hearts of boy and girl.

Sarah was nineteen, and very, very beautiful.

On the morning in question she had set the children their tasks.

She then strolled into the large orchard, where cousin Charles was at work.

Tall, well formed, with a powerful frame for his age, Charles was really a model of manly beauty.

He wanted but the polish of society, and the assistance of his tailor, to be in appearance what he was in heart—a perfect gentleman.

But Sarah, fresh from the old country, could not fancy a gentleman in a blanket coat, souwester, and tou-linen continuations.

She had yet to learn the vanity and absurdity of mere outward appearance.

"Morning, cousin," he said.

"Good morning," replied the young lady, in a cold, stately way.

Charles was pruning trees, and left his pruning knife to join her.

"Are you in a great hurry to run away?" he said, in hearty tones.

"No—why?"

"Well, you see, miss, we are a precious large family now, and I'm thinking of keeping house."

"Indeed!"

"Now, father, and mother, and I've been talking over matters, and father says, he shall have a frolic, and build me a house yonder."

He pointed to a rude clearing on the other side of the river, where the charred and blackened stumps of the trees showed how recently the work had been done.

"Some day, I daresay it will be a nice situation," replied Sarah, coldly.

"First in the county. The trees round are maple, the land is magnificent. I mean to have a dairy, pigs, and poultry.

"A regular basse-cour," said Sarah, with a cold sneer.

Charles stared, as he always did at her French and Italian phrases.

"I don't know what you mean, cousin," replied Charles, quietly, but colouring up to the roots of his hair; "but I know what I mean!"

"Well?"

"Cousin, would you not like to have a home of your own?" he said.

She turned towards him with a look that might have changed some men into stone.

But he saw it not.

"Paupers cannot be choosers," she said.

"Sarah—cousin—pauper! How can you use such a word?—you who are the pride and hope of the whole family!"

A faint hectic flush covered her pale cheek, and something like a smile illumined her countenance.

"Indeed!"

"Sarah, why are you so cold? Do you not understand me? Must I speak plainer?"

"I like plain speaking."

"Then, Sarah, this is it. Next week neighbours will come over and build the house. Will be all done in a day. That will be Thursday. By Saturday the things will be all in. What say you to be married on Sunday?"

She turned upon him again, with a look, first of such blank astonishment, he could scarcely believe his eyes, and then the expression turned to one of such withering contempt, that he started back in amazement.

"Marry!" she cried. "marry, and after such an asking! Do you mean to insult me, cousin Charles?"

"Insult!" he stammered; "insult! No—you know I don't."

"I hope not. I would not stay an hour in the house if I thought so. I would sooner go to service as a house-maid than be jeered at. But I forgive you, cousin Charles. Let the subject never be mentioned again. I shall never marry until I am offered a home something like that which I enjoyed in England. I must marry a gentleman."

And the proud, self-willed and foolish girl turned away, with a scornful and rigid expression of countenance, which cut poor Charles to the very soul.

"Marry a gentleman!" he said, and sighed. "I should like to know what a gentleman is? I'm an honest, hard-working chap, and mean to be a big man some of these days. Well, let 'un marry a gentleman. I don't care a pea-chuck!"

And to show he didn't care, he wiped the big scalding tears away with the back of his great, rough, honest hand.

You don't know what a gentleman is, don't you, Charles Paulding? Why, you are one of the brightest and best specimens yourself.

CHAPTER LIX.
THE TEMPTER.

SARAH PAULDING, as soon as she was out of sight, flew rather than ran, crossed the stepping-stones of the river, and cast herself upon the grass, beneath the shelter of some umbrageous trees.

"I never was so insulted in all my life," she said, bursting into a passionate flood of tears. "Never! A great, hulking, ugly brute of a farm-labourer to ask me to marry him—to milk his cows—to feed his pigs—to look after his poultry—and," she added, with a savage, hysterical laugh, "to nurse his ugly children—faugh!"

And the young lady gave a ludicrous grimace of disgust.

"But what am I to do? After what has happened, it is impossible for me to remain here. Where can I go? With my miserable savings, how far can I travel? Heavens! that it should have come to this!"

And she bit her gloved hands with pettish rage and mortification.

The spoiled beauty knew that she was in the wrong.

"I want a friend—a congenial soul," she said; "but where to find one?"

As if some evil genius had been at her elbow, she raised her eyes, and saw before her the tall and graceful form of William Hicks. He had dismounted from his horse, and stood, hat in hand, holding the bridle of his steed by the left hand.

"I beg pardon, miss," he said, in insinuating and pleasant tones, "but having lost my way, and being a total stranger to these parts, I have ventured to disturb your meditations."

Sarah leaped to her feet, mentally comparing this polished gentleman with her uncouth lover.

"Any information I can give you are welcome to," she said, with blushing dignity.

William Hicks bowed.

A log was near at hand. He tied his horse to

a tree, and, as if to enjoy the landscape, seated himself, after begging Sarah to be his companion.

They soon began a serious and earnest conversation. He asked her questions about the neighbourhood, suggested that he might be tempted to stop, but soon finding that she gave him no encouragement, drew her out.

She told him her whole story.

There was a seduction in his voice, a witchery in his eye, a respectful demeanour in his whole manner, which was to her irresistible.

He was the first educated man of the world she had seen for one whole year.

She could not resist the power of his voice.

She told him all.

The ruffian's blood boiled—his heart bounded within him. He began to fancy his wager won.

He then told her that his name was Walter de Vere, that he was the younger son of a noble house, possessed of moderate means, but not sufficient for the old country.

"I have a large tract of land in Illinois, whither I am proceeding with my servants and some neighbours. Our caravan has halted for one day. We leave to-morrow. I shall do so with deep regret, as you are the only lady I have met since I have been in America."

"And you the only gentleman," faltered Sarah.

Poor, honest, worthy Charles Paulding—where is your good angel now?

"My dear madam," said the so-called Walter de Vere, in a deep, sad, impassioned tone, "this *is* a strange meeting. I shall look back to it with regret."

She cast down her eyes.

He took her unresisting hand.

"I am, however, going to say something very bold. You have been affronted. You are totally unsuited to the rude home you occupy. You have no fit society in those boors and labourers. Now, were you to receive from a gentleman, a man of honour and feeling, one who could appreciate such a treasure, the offer of his hand, his heart, his fortune, surely you could not be offended or affronted?"

"Oh, no."

"Then, lady, receive from me at once that offer. It is strange—it is sudden—it seems mad and wild; but, oh! believe me, this meeting is providential. But for your disagreement we should never have met. Soon, if you hesitate, we may be parted by hundreds of miles—I, full of bitter regret at not having rescued a bright and glorious flower from dull obscurity; you, sometimes thinking of the stranger who would have been proud to have devoted his whole life to making up for this sudden, strange, and seemingly indelicate proceeding."

She spoke not.

"Ere you spoke, bright and glorious vision of a happy hour," he continued, "I loved you. I felt irresistibly impelled towards you by one of those impulses which we cannot control, though our reason try never so strong to guide us. I thought it a privilege to speak. But when I found you—a diamond set in lead—a flower, wasting your sweetness on the desert air—I at once threw myself on your mercy; and say, lady—believe me,

that an acquaintance like ours has advanced as far as if we had known one another years; if we were to meet every day for months, we should not know one another better—will you not speak?"

"But ——"

"I know all you could say."

"But ——"

"There is a minister ——"

"Still ——"

"There are females—married and unmarried—in abundance in the camp who will gladly guard and protect you."

"But it is so sudden."

"Lady, I love you. I ask not for your love now," he continued.

"I have none to give."

"Still, I may hope."

"Hope as much as you please."

"Then ——"

"If I thought I could trust you."

"On my honour as a man—on my faith as a Christian!" he said.

The wretched, vile, and monstrous hypocrite!

"You must not misjudge me."

"I adore you ——"

"Cousin Sarah," cried a voice from the other side, "will you come in? Father wants to talk to you, and the children know their lessons."

This decided the struggle. It was the voice of coarse, ugly cousin Charles.

A look of ludicrous amazement on the countenance of *soi-disant* Walter de Vere carried the day.

She rose, and retreated behind the trees.

The steed he rode was a splendid one.

He vaulted into the saddle, and placed Sarah before him.

She thought the proceeding somewhat familiar, but had she not agreed, on an acquaintance of one hour, to become his wife?

What could she, then, expect?

Away they darted, the really thorough-bred horse scarcely feeling the weight of his double burden.

When he entered the camp he was greeted by a loud shout of applause.

"They are so glad to see me back," he said, with a peculiar wave of the hand to the Mormons.

He alighted at the door of the chief tent.

It was unused.

He ushered Sarah in, and then hurrying away to a place where all the men were congregated, begged them to be careful, as the maiden was skittish, and if not married right off to him in his new name of de Vere, might be troublesome.

All agreed to back him.

Even to going through the marriage service according to the ritual of the Church of England.

No blasphemy, mockery or villainy, was too great for these men.

The next thing was to select two of the safest of the young women to play the parts of attendants on her, until after the ceremony and consummation of the marriage.

Somebody suggested Jessie.

But she was nursing Miss Smith, as the wife of John Smith, in American phrase, was called.

There were two very sincere converts to Mormonism, who hitherto, though their husband had two wives, had lived in harmony.

Strange to say, they were sisters.

They had been always very loving and fond, and when the young man seduced one into the ranks of the new tribe, the other followed.

They formed the only tolerably happy instance of polygamy we ever knew of.

They were very young, and had not yet learned to be jealous of one another.

They were seated by a camp fire, close to the tent in which Mrs. Smith lay ill.

William Hicks approached them, and, in a laughing way, announced a new convert to Mormonism.

They, silly girls, laughed.

"Well now, you see, she ain't exactly a convert," he said.

"How so?"

"She's only converted to me. She's taken a frightful sudden fancy."

"You naughty man!"

"But I did'nt say a word about our being of the only true faith."

"Why?"

"I had'nt time. Besides, I think it would take weeks and months. She is of a very obstinate character," he added.

"A nice convert!"

"Well, the fact is, I have taken an irresistible liking to her. Now, I want you to help me. I mean to marry her to-night; in a day or two, I shall tell the doctrine of the Saints to her. You will, I am sure, give me every assistance."

"Well."

"Do. You are the prettiest girls in the camp. I want you to be my friends. You must'nt say a word about the Saints. I shall leave that for you at a future period."

"But Harry."

"He's to be my best man," said William.

"Then it's agreed."

And after some further instructions as to the false story which he had told, the girls started for the tent occupied by the stranger.

They thought they were doing a good action in bringing this lamb into the fold.

CHAPTER LX.

SARAH.

WHEN Sarah Paulding found herself alone in the tent where William Hicks had taken her, she began to reflect.

Had she repented, she knew that it was almost too late.

How could she return home after eloping with a handsome stranger?

Who would take her back?

No, she never thought of that.

But she began to reflect as to the future. She had never seen a handsomer, a more agreeable, or a more fascinating man, in her life.

She felt that it only wanted the consecration of the sacred tie to make her love him,

And how often is the love which is generated of marriage stronger than any other!

But it was all so bewildering, so sudden, so wild, so romantic.

But she did not repent.

The school teaching, the dependence, the feeling of outraged pride, the idea of being the wife of a rough, coarse farm-labourer was intolerable.

At least, she would shew them, that she was not reduced to such a necessity as that.

She was already planning in her own mind the bitterly-grateful letter she would write to them as soon as she was married.

Poor silly, ungrateful, lost girl, urged on by the fell demon, Pride!

Worst and most demoralizing almost of our evil passions, many as they are.

Then Walter de Vere, accompanied by the two sisters, the wives of one husband, entered the tent.

"Allow me, my angel," he said, "to introduce to you two married young ladies, who will be proud to attend to you in every way."

Sarah bowed affably.

"The minister will be ready at eleven o'clock," he said; "it would not be right to leave the neighbourhood without leaving notice of your marriage."

This suggestion silenced a rising objection Sarah was about to make.

Walter de Vere bowed and left the tent.

Sarah re-seated herself, and while one of the girls, Lydia, began to bustle about, on hospitable thoughts intent, entered into a conversation with the other.

"How do you like America?" said Sarah.

"Oh, I like it much," replied Amy; "it's a very nice country, but I shall like it better when we are settled. I'm tired of travelling."

"I adore travelling," continued Sarah, in a quick, reckless, nervous way, as if to drown thought. "Before I lost my father, I visited France, Switzerland, Italy, and I never was so happy as when looking about me."

"I daresay it is very nice. But for me, I like a settled home."

"Have we very far to go?" asked Sarah.

"Not very. I don't know much about America, only from school geography, and that ain't much—bounded on the north by the——I don't recollect," said the giddy-pated girl, and away she went off into a scream of laughter.

Lydia, who was the elder, held up her finger in an admonishing kind of way.

"Well, Harry says it's fine; he's seen the country," continued Amy.

"And who is Harry?" said Sarah, fancying that she must say something.

"Our—my husband," replied Amy, with a sudden fit of coughing.

"And what is his opinion?"

"Beautiful, overflowing with milk and honey," continued the other.

"It is a rich and fertile tract," said Lydia, who was of a slightly graver turn of mind than foolish Amy; "and my husband says——"

"Just what my husband says," observed the

younger sister, with a very peculiar twinkle of the eyes.

"Silence, there's a dear!" continued Lydia. "I have no doubt that we shall find it all we could wish."

"It must be a great change for Mr. de Vere," said Sarah, thoughtfully.

"A very great change," said Lydia.

"Very," observed Amy.

Sarah looked at them. But they were good actors, and whatever suspicion any little intonation of voice might have aroused within her bosom was completely eradicated by their innocent and simple faces.

Tea was now placed before her, and the conversation turned to England.

"What part of England do you come from?" said Lydia, suddenly.

"Devonshire."

"What part?"

"Deeping Dale," said Sarah, with a sigh.

The sisters exchanged a strange, odd, puzzled glance.

"May I ask your name?" continued Lydia.

"Sarah Paulding."

"I knew it! I could have sworn it!" cried Lydia. "Couldn't you, Amy?"

Amy was pale as death.

"But Miss Paulding does not recollect us."

She looked at them keenly.

"I have some recollection. But grief at the death of my dear father has so unnerved me that my memory fails me—and yet."

"Guess—remember——"

"Lydia—Amy—good heavens!—my Sunday-school teachers!" cried Sarah.

And she grasped both their hands, and then, despite their resistance, kissed them.

She told them then all her sad story.

They heard, with scalding tears—tears of such scorching sorrow, Sarah was amazed.

"Amy."

"Lydia."

"Let's go and speak to Harry."

It was quite dark now.

Sarah could see the hunters and others coming in and throwing down their burthens.

"We will not be a minute," said Lydia.

"Not a minute," said Amy.

"Why do you go?"

"We will tell you directly. Wait less than a quarter of an hour."

And they ran out.

At this moment her wrist was clutched by a firm little hand.

She turned and faced Jessie.

"Lady!" said our gasping heroine, "do you, in heaven's name, know where you are?"

"Yes, in an emigrant caravan."

"You are in a foul Mormon camp, and the man who in a false name has wooed you, has already two wives."

She stood utterly aghast and terror-stricken.

"But these girls, these sisters, I know them."

"They are the wives of one Harry James, as they themselves will tell you."

"My God! What have I done?" gasped the proud and haughty girl.

"Fly."

"Will they let me?"

"I know not—but try."

At this moment the sisters came running back, closed the entrance to the tent, and, without seeing Jessie, fell on their knees.

"Forgive us—pardon us!" they cried; "we will give our lives to save you from joining our sect against your own free will."

"Then what this young girl says is true?" replied Sarah, in choking accents.

"What young girl?"

They turned and saw Jessie. A frown and a pout was the only notice they took of her.

"What does she say?" cried Lydia.

"Yes, what?" said Amy.

"That this is a Mormon camp, that the wretched villain that has lured me here on false pretences has already two wives, that I am brought here to add another to the list of victims of man's vile deceit."

"Hush!" said Lydia; "we are willing to do anything to serve you, but do not speak against the tenets of our faith."

"Faith! and is it one of my school teachers who stands here and advocates a system, which is even the disgrace of a heathen land?"

The girls looked down.

"Did you never attend a marriage ceremony? where you never bridesmaid? Did you never hear these words :—

"'Will thou love her, comfort her, honour and keep her in sickness and in health; and *forsaking all others, keep thee only unto her*, so long as ye both shall live?'"

They did not answer.

"Will you not speak, girls? have you no tongues?" she continued.

"Miss Paulding," said Lydia, after a moment's pause: "we have chosen our path. We have not time to explain by what process of reasoning we have been brought to the true faith, and to a just conception of the real object of marriage, which is to save the woman through the instrumentality of the husband."

"Lydia!"

"Listen, Miss Paulding! You have been lured here—by falsehood and deceit—therefore, we are willing to help you to leave. But if you would enable us to serve you, let us drop the discussion."

"There is a stir by the fire," said Amy.

"Your address," whispered Jessie, drawing her on one side.

Sarah hesitated.

"You have no time to lose. You will never be allowed to leave the camp."

"Will they use violence?"

"Anything," whispered Jessie, "even to murder, to compass their unhallowed ends."

"Why are you one?"

"I will tell you when you are safe."

"Go!"

Jessie disappeared.

William Hikes entered. He had been drinking the amount of his unhallowed wager.

Both Lydia and Amy gave Sarah a terrified and admonitory look.

It told her to be cautious, for her own sake and theirs.

"Well, my darling" said the young man, who was, however, not too intoxicated to behave himself tolerably well, "how have you got on?"

"Very well."

"Have they been attentive, agreeable, and all that, eh?"

"Very."

"That's right—they are a couple of very good girls. To you, miss, I'm very sorry to announce a change; but our minister says he won't marry anybody after eight. So, if you please to accept these two young ladies as bridesmaids——"

"Can we not wait until to-morrow?" said Sarah, in as natural a voice as she could assume.

"Why?"

"It seems so hurried—so strange. I have been thinking," began Sarah.

He looked keenly at the two girls, but they met his searching examination by a calm and steady look.

"No, dearest. I must leave here at daybreak in the morning, and I could not think of going without sending up a certificate of your marriage."

Sarah seemed to hesitate.

"I am in your hands," she said.

"That is kind," replied the ruffian, who had began to feel uneasy.

Sarah spoke not, but, with one of her severe and haughty smiles, bowed him out.

"What is to be done?" she said, as soon as his back was turned.

"I don't know," cried Amy. "Harry will be very cross with us."

"Do you repent a good action," said Sarah.

"No; but we wish as much as possible to preserve what, to us, has been hitherto a happy home," said Lydia. "If we can serve you without injuring ourselves you cannot blame us."

"Certainly not," said Sarah.

"Well then, all we can do is to advise. When before the priest refuse to be married; ask for the presence of a qualified magistrate. Do, in fact, what your own impulse and feeling indicates to be right."

"Will you support me?"

"As far as in our power."

"That is all I require."

CHAPTER LXI.

THE ALTAR.

It was eight o'clock. Again the altar of the false prophet was erected to go through the blasphemous mockery of a marriage—this time according to the rights of the Church of England.

All the chiefs of the Mormon camp were assembled, and all the most contented of the women.

Walter de Vere was dressed out in a brave array. He had contrived to curb his drunken propensities for once, and stood on one side of the altar calm, collected, but very pale.

Sarah Paulding was ghastly.

Everybody whispered that they had never seen so unearthly-beautiful a pair.

Both had a strange gleam in their eyes, which was, to a keen observer, perfectly Satanic.

Nobody could make out, to see them, whether they were being united by great hate, or very great love.

They stood about two feet asunder.

One of the Mormon elders took up the prayer-book of the Church of England, and began to read its impressive "Form of Solemnization of Matrimony."

He turned to William Hicks, and asked him the usual question.

"Yes," was the ready reply.

"Wilt thou," continued the imposter priest, "have this man to be thy wedded husband, to live together after God's ordinance in the holy estate of matrimony. Wilt thou obey him, and serve him, love, honour, and keep him in sickness and in health; and forsaking all other, keep thee only unto him, so long as ye both shall live?"

"No!"

Had a thunderbolt fallen in among them, it could not have caused greater sensation than this single monosyllable.

"But Miss Paulding!" cried William Hicks, paler still with rage.

"What is the meaning you will not have him?" asked the astonished priest.

"False and outcast minister of God!" she said, "do you think, I, the daughter of a real servant of the Lord, would wed a forger, and thief, who has already dragged two wretched beings into the mire?"

William Hicks fell back as if stunned. The blow was so fearfully sudden, the charge so unexpected, terrible, yet true.

"Who has been calumniating me?" he cried, amidst the suppressed jeers of his companions.

They had all paid their bets.

His discomfiture was amusing.

But there were serious interests at stake, and to this it behoved them all first to look.

"No one here has said a word about you, except in your favour," replied Sarah, standing cool, collected, and firm, amid the excited mob. "But what I say I know to be true, Mr. Walter de Vere—alias Mr. William Hicks, for whose apprehension I saw many bills about, when I was last in England."

"By heaven's woman!" cried William Hicks, savagely, "whether you like or not, you shall be my wife. No one shall brave me with impunity."

"Proceed," said one of the elders.

"You dare not," cried Sarah, "you dare not violate the liberty of a poor woman. I will not wed this man, say or do what you will."

"Proceed," said the same nasal voice.

The ceremony proceeded, Lydia and Amy covering their faces with their hands, and weeping.

Two strong men held Sarah by the wrists, and had the reckless audacity to announce to the assembly, that Sarah had said "yes."

The villain had money, which, on an occasion like the present, he used freely to lavish on his comrades.

CHAPTER LXII.

AFTER THE WEDDING.

Then Sarah was taken to a tent by four women. Lydia and Amy were sternly told to stop were they were.

" You had better mind what you are at," said Lydia, wi.h a curl of the lip, which startled William Hicks.

" Why ?"

" Two hours ago, a mounted messenger started to alarm her friends and the settlement," replied Lydia, with a triumphant smile.

"D——n !" shouted several of the Mormons.

" Who went ?" said Harry, sternly.

" Why, Harry ?"

" Well."

" You are angry. If you knew all, you would not be. Miss Paulding was an old and dear friend."

" It matters not," said the young man, coldly, " the laws of the Saints must be obeyed."

" What mean you ?"

" And those who aid and abet traitors must be punished," he continued. " Who was the messenger ?"

" Jessie."

" By the foul fiend," cried William Hicks, " that girl will be the ruin of us !"

Phineas Bristowe, who hitherto had not said one word, groaned aloud.

" Let all the women return to their tents," said the elder, who had officiated as priest; " the Saints will enter into deliberation."

The women shuddered and obeyed. There was something in the tone of the man which terrified them.

William Hicks hastened to the nuptial tent, turned out the women, and remained alone with his so-called wife. She was seated on a box.

" But, dearest lady," he began, in husky and constrained tones, " what is the meaning of this change ?"

Silence.

" After all that passed this morning," he continued, in his old, seductive tones, " surely you cannot have forgotten all that was understood."

" You are a Mormon."

" Well."

" Answer me."

" I do, for convenience sake, take that name in order to travel with the tribe."

" You have two other wives."

" Well, according to the ideas of the Saints I have, but in my own idea, I have only one wife, and that is you, my own, dear darling."

" You are William Hicks, the forger and embezzler—the man who would, if caught, suffer at the Old Bailey," she continued.

" Woman, beware !" he cried, advancing closer to her, his eyes flashing, half with fury, half with passionate desire.

" Back !" she said.

As she spoke she rose, and showed a sharp knife, which hitherto she had concealed up her sleeve.

But William Hicks was nothing daunted by this display.

" Ah ! ah ! my Lady Macbeth. This acting will not do. Put down that knife, my dainty wife, or it will be worse for you."

" Worse for you, felon !"

" Use that word again," he said, with sullen and lowering brow, " and you will repent it the longest day you live."

" Would you strike me, coward ?" cried the exasperated girl.

A cold gleam of concentrated fury shot through his eyes, as, with a cry of frantic rage, he flew at her,

She drew back, and, cold and firm, stabbed right at him.

He fell to the ground, weltering in his blood, after giving one despairing cry for help.

" Murder—help !"

In they poured, to find her standing calm, resolute, firm, with the bloody knife held high above her head.

Men, women, boys, came rushing in until scared by the sight before them.

A man approached Hicks, while Sarah, without the slightest hesitation, allowed herself to be disarmed.

" Is he dead ?" she whispered.

" I know not, murderess—but dead or living, you shall shall die the death !" cried one of the elders.

" Anything better than his paramour," she replied.

" Bind her—let all leave but elders," continued the speaker, " remove the wounded man to his own waggon."

After some little difficulty and hesitation, this order was obeyed, and Sarah remained in the tent with the twelve elders.

A brief conference was held, in low, hushed whispers, and then Sarah was seized, blindfolded, gagged, and taken out into the open air.

She felt herself placed upon a horse; the clatter of other horses' hoofs could be heard around her, and then she was hurried away at a rapid rate.

Presently they halted.

They were in a dreary kind of dell, overshadowed by tall and wavy pine trees.

They ungagged her, took off the bandage from her eyes, without untying her hands, and seated her on the grass.

Two dark lanterns were placed upon the ground about seven feet apart.

Then a pickaxe and two shovels were produced, and three men, casting off their coats, began to dig.

Any one could at once see that they were digging a grave.

Sarah shuddered. It was hard thus to die in her unrepented sin. She had acted in self-defence, but her hands were red with blood.

It seemed a kind of retribution that she, too, should perish by a violent death.

The idea of past happy days came over her, and the thought forced itself upon her, that she had been a wicked and ungrateful girl.

Her uncle's character now appeared in a clear

BURIED ALIVE.

and vivid light—the light of truth and reason. How could she so have misjudged him?

But these ideas availed her no longer.

She was in the hands of men actuated by wild feelings of revenge.

She knew that she was going to die.

It was strange, but she looked on at the preparations with a strange, odd, wild kind of curiosity.

They were digging a mere hole in the earth; but, then, what a hole.

Not one spoke to her, reproached her, or alluded to the crime or the punishment.

She would have given something to have heard of *his* fate.

But no answer came in return for repeated questionings.

They were sullen, silent, and did not even speak among themselves. Whenever they glanced at the wretched girl, it was with looks of the most virulent hatred and scorn.

Up in the heavens not one of the starry lamps illumined the horrid, the fearful, and unparalleled scene.

Sarah had been to a certain extent religiously educated, though a fond mother had nurtured her pride.

She thought for a moment, and then murmured a prayer.

It was time.

No. 40.

Two of the men raised her and placed her in the deep hole, which was almost up to her beautiful cold neck.

Then, while these two held her with the rigidity of bars of iron, the others began to shovel in the earth.

Then the agonizing and maddening thought entered her brain that they were going to bury her alive.

This was too much for her, and she burst forth with the most awful shrieks that female throat ever uttered.

" Silence !"

" Never ! I will not be murdered. Let me have a fair trial. If you are men you will not thus illuse a poor girl."

" Gag her," said a sullen ruffian.

Again she gave a wild and horrible shriek. It resounded through the hills with fearful intensity. It was the agony of death.

But then they gagged her.

The men who were working did all they could, and in a few minutes the earth was up to her neck.

She struggled fearfully, but it was of no avail.

" Hark ! what noise is that ?"

All listened. It was the trampling of horses.

" Mount and fly. Smother the hell cat some of you," shouted one of the Mormons.

She had forced off her gag and had given another fearful shriek.

" Kill—slay—burn !" shouted a maddened and infuriated voice. " No quarter to the bloody heathen !"

Every Mormon shuddered, and abandoning pickaxe, shovels, and lanterns, they rushed to their horses, mounted, and flew.

Like a whirlwind, a body of mounted men sped by in chase. But two figures halted. One of them bounded to the grave, and casting himself flat on the ground, gazed in agony at the pale face of the girl.

" Dead ! dead ! my life, my soul, my own darling Sarah !" said a manly voice, in tones of fearful suffering.

" Not dead, but she has fainted," said Jessie, dismounting.

" Dig away the earth—quick. I will support her head."

The young man did as he was told, working with the strength and vigour of a young Titanic giant.

In a very brief space of time he had released her. A flask of brandy scattered over her face and pressed to her lips brought her to.

" Charles—dear Charles !" she said, clasping him round the neck and kissing his very lips, " was that a horrid dream ? No ! no ! no ! Take me away—I know I'm going to die—but take me home. Will you forgive me, Charley ? I am very sorry—I would'nt do it again. But you know that now. Let me die where aunt and uncle will be there to forgive me. I could'nt help it, he wanted to marry me—ah—I killed him !"

" Killed him !" gasped Jessie.

" Served him right !" said Charles, lifting her up in his arms ; " but do not die—you shall not, will not die. You shall live to be my happy, dear and honoured wife."

" You won't let them bury me alive ?" said Sarah wildly.

" B——t 'em, no !" shrieked Charles, who saw that her head was slightly wandering.

He raised her quite up now, and placed her on a horse ; Jessie mounted, and he walked.

In this way they reached the house, where none but women and children awaited them.

The men were all out after the Mormons.

At the entrance of the house Jessie paused.

" You will not go back ?" said Charles, anxiously.

" I must."

" But not directly. Step and see how she is. Besides, if the people muster strong enough, not a Mormon will leave the country alive."

Jessie sighed and went in.

They put Sarah to bed, and, under the judicious care of Mrs. Paulding, she so far recovered in the morning as to be able to converse rationally.

She did not recollect all that passed except as a kind of fearful dream or nightmare.

She got up to breakfast. The old man and Charles advanced to meet her with eager and sympathising looks.

" How do you feel, my child ?" said the uncle, kindly.

" Like an erring child seeking the pardon of her father," said Sarah, falling on her knees before the whole family.

" I will shrive you on one condition," said the old man.

" And that ?" said Sarah, rising and taking a chair.

" Is, that you become my daughter as soon as possible."

" Yes, Sarah—promise to be my wife, and all will be happy."

" If you are not afraid to take a weak, silly, and vain girl to be your handmaiden, Charles, I shall be too proud to have won your honest heart," she replied.

" Though I am not a gentleman," said the delighted lover.

" Don't say that again. I had enough of that yesterday. Have you heard ?" she said, with a shudder.

" The man is out of danger," replied Charles ; " the miscreants who abducted you have fled far away, and the whole Mormon gang have left our state—or else—"

" No message for me," said Jessie, sadly.

" A letter," replied Charles ; " but why, from a mistaken sense of duty, return to such infamous bondage ?"

" I have promised."

" But such promises—surely you do not hold them binding ?"

" All and every promise. Besides, those who love me are on the track. I know I am in no danger ; give me the letter."

Jessie read it, but made no remark. She took her breakfast quietly, and then wishing them all farewell, left—after a solemn promise to call if she ever passed that way.

Such is a portion of a Mormon episode of every-day occurrence, and which only did not end in the usual disastrous manner, because the woman had both a bold and valiant heart, and a sympathising friend.

To Sarah it was at all events at the time a severe and salutary lesson. But for it she would in all probability never have had her eyes opened to the sterling good qualities of her uncle and aunt.

Certainly she would not have learned to love cousin Charles as the apple of her eye, as she did from that day.

CHAPTER LXIII.

JESSIE'S RETURN—A SERMON.

MEANWHILE, Jessie, who had received a fawning letter from Phineas Bristowe, reminding her of all her promises, had started on her way.

He informed her, in his whining, hypocritical way, that the Saints had determined to travel as fast as possible towards Illinois. The ungodly disbelievers were determined to harass and worry the true Church.

The wounded man had been placed in a waggon, and sent forward to the next station.

The camp had escaped destruction only by denying all connection with the elders who had taken Sarah to the hills.

It would not, however, be safe to venture on remaining in the neighbourhood.

He, therefore, fixed upon a rendezvous where she could join him—promising at once on their arrival at the last station to communicate with her mother, father, and Henry.

Jessie would have hesitated probably, but she had given her solemn promise.

This, with her, was something peculiarly sacred.

Well supplied with provisions; armed with a small light gun, the gift of the grateful and humbled Sarah, she started on her way.

The trail of the waggon, he said, would be easily followed.

She was not to be uneasy. His influence and that of one or two other of the elders would prevent any reference to the part she had played in the escape of Sarah.

When Jessie thought of this, it seemed to her impossible that any amount of brutal fanaticism or false indulgence in a theory could drive men to the commission of such crimes.

She forgot the sanguinary instrument of Popery: the Inquisition.

She forgot the saturnalia of Romanism and royalty; the massacre of St. Bartholomew.

Men are demons when the fanaticism of party or religion is excited beyond measure.

But she tried to chase away thought by gazing about at the beauties of nature as they rose before her.

She took her way along a pleasant valley, with high hills rising on each side, and a slowly-moving river at her feet. Alone, save when birds kept her company, she seemed the new Eve of a most delicious and heavenly Paradise.

The heavy waggons, which had started on the previous night, and found their way by torchlight, had left marks it was easy indeed for her to follow.

She knew that, at this rate of travelling, she must soon come up to them with ease.

But she was in no great hurry. She loathed the companionship of the Mormons and of their dupes.

Above all, she shrank from communion with Julie.

It was about two o'clock in the afternoon.

Jessie had halted, to refresh her beast as much as herself. Her camp, to use an American phrase, was on the banks of the winding river.

Her short, light, elegant rifle was placed carelessly by her side.

She sat in a thoughtful and musing way.

Had Henry at last found her track—and if not, when would he? Or must she trust to the word of Phineas Bristowe for restoration to her friends?

Her horse, who was browsing to the length of his tether, pricked up his ears of a sudden, and looked towards a copse.

Jessie lifted up her rifle and examined the priming.

"What a deuced brave girl!" said a half sad, a half laughing voice, as Mr. Stanley, followed by the Indian, came out of the wood.

"All alone?" he cried, after a hasty glance all around.

"All alone," said Jessie, shaking hands both with him and the Indian; "but let us be moving."

Both nodded, and, walking one on each side of her horse, they escorted her along—while listening to her account of the adventures of the previous day and night.

They were horrified.

"And you mean to return to these men?" said Mr. Stanley.

"I have promised. You must not interfere," replied Jessie—"and now that I can see their camp fires in the distance, I must bid you both farewell."

The Indian, in whose eyes a kind of frenzy always rolled when he was talking, looked at her with a sort of sullen admiration. There were evidently times when he was madder than at others. It showed itself in sulkiness.

"Good bye—Good bye!" he said, without offering his hand.

Stanley stooped towards her and whispered a word.

Jessie nodded to both and rode off.

It was now at a smart trot that Jessie started on her way. She was anxious not to be seen by any of the scouts, who might be outlying on the skirts of the camp.

A ride of a mile brought her to where the waggons were drawn up in a semi-circle.

It was at the mouth of a savage kind of defile—and so arranged as to serve the purpose of a breastwork.

After the hideous tragedy of the night before, they were prepared for the worst.

Jessie was challenged several times by the sullen sentinels, who looked at her with no friendly mien.

They spoke not when she spoke, but only gave a kind of savage grunt.

Soon she found herself surrounded by the

women and elders. Phineas Bristowe was among them. He assisted her to dismount, and led her quickly into a tent.

"I wrote that letter by compulsion—be on your guard," said he, in low, tremulous tones.

"Let them beware! If any harm befalls me, an avenger you little imagine will be upon you," replied Jessie.

"I am your friend, you know," said Phineas Bristowe, in a deprecating tone, "but I am only one."

"What do they mean to do?" she said, coldly.

"I don't know. I suspect there will be a trial or something of that sort."

"And then?"

"It much depends on what humour they are in," continued Phineas, thoughtfully.

At this moment a loud trumpet sounded from without.

The Mormon elder hurried out to see what was the matter. He knew that it was a signal to be on their guard.

It often happened that, during their journey towards the upper country, the Mormons were assailed by those who believed them to be plentifully endowed with the riches of this world.

They had on several occasions been attacked by gangs very much of the same character as those which infest the Southern states, under the title of the Mustang Gang.

They came in the disguise of Indians and negroes.

We have already said that the Mormons had admirably chosen their position.

The waggons were placed in a circle, while the occupants had placed themselves in the midst.

Phineas hurried to where the men and elders were all collected together.

"What is the matter?" he said.

"We don't know. We've sent to see."

"Was not that our trumpet of alarm?" said Phineas Bristowe, anxiously.

"No. It was sounded by some one without."

Phineas looked very uneasy. Was it possible that he had been followed by the assailants of Dow's Creek?

Again the long winding blast of a horn was heard, though the scouts at the same time returned and stated that they could see no sign of anybody without.

The superstitious dupes began to look at each other with anxiety. What did this state of things portend?

The elders, though like most of their class, tainted by their own peculiar superstition, did not for one moment believe in any occult agency here.

They pretty well guessed that it was some signal arranged beforehand with some of their enemies.

Paolo went to the waggon occupied by Julie. He appeared to think that, perhaps, it might be an arranged thing between her and her husband.

She was utterly calm and unconscious.

He returned to his associates, and it was agreed to spend the night in watching.

Sentries were placed at every point likely to be attacked, and then a meeting of the elders took place.

As Phineas guessed, they discussed the conduct of Jessie and the punishment she deserved.

Opinions were divided. Some were for death, others for the brutal punishment of flogging, a favourite Mormon amusement, where the victims were women.

"That girl deserves death," cried Paolo, who had never got over the disappointment of his villainy.

"Why?" said Phineas.

"Has she not betrayed us?" cried Paolo.

"She is not one of us," continued the Mormon elder; "she is perfectly right to try and escape."

"But she knows too much," observed one of the others.

"She will do no harm, if we let her go quietly," said Phineas, who felt strangely anxious about the girl.

The Mormon elders exchanged glances.

"I rise," said one of them, with a grave and saturnine expression of countenance, "to reply to the suggestion of our worthy friend and coadjutor, Phineas Bristowe, who, very properly imbued with Christian charity and good feeling, wishes to screen the guilty. But in all cases of this kind there is a second class of person to be considered, and that is the innocent. Now this girl, filled with prejudice and hatred against us, will as much as possible misrepresent and blacken us to the Gentiles. I therefore propose that such steps be taken as will prevent her effectually from being any let or hindrance to the cause of truth and revealed religion."

"What do you propose?" said one.

"What? what?" cried several.

"Let her choose between the honoured position of wife of one of the Saints, and death."

A low murmur of applause greeted this proposition, while several at once made up their minds that they would take care to be the chosen one.

Mormonism means nothing else but—let us get together as many wives as we can; the younger, the prettier, the better. It is very easy to neglect the old ones and attend to the new; at all events, the old ones do for servants.

This is a fitting opportunity to introduce an episode in Mormon life, which will show the real character and amours of the race.

*   *   *   *   *

Mormonism is still in practical operation amongst us. A few months' since a tall raw-boned saint, with a complexion very strongly resembling that of tripe, arrived in one of the western cities of America, with a couple of wives; but deeming his flock too small to start Salt Lakeward with, held forth as follows to an admiring audience, at a house over a canal, with a view to the completeness of his domestic felicity. His text was—"Men is skeerce, and weemen is plenty."

"Brothers and sisters—pertickler the sisters—I want to say words to you about Mormonism, not for my own sake, but for yourn; for men is skeerce, and weemen is plenty.

"Mormonism is built on that high old principle, which sez that it ain't good for man to be alone, and a mighty sight worse for woman. Therefore, if a man feels good with a little company, a good deal of it ought to make him feel an awful sight better.

"The first principle of Mormonism is, that woman air a good thing, and the second principle is, that you can't have too much of a good thing. Woman is tenderer than man, and is necessary to smooth down the roughness of his character, and as man has a good many rough pints in his natur,' he oughtn't to give one woman too much to do, but set each one to work soomthin', some pertickler pint.

"Don't think I am over anxious for you to jine us, for I ain't. I'm not speakin' for my good, but [for yourn; for men is skeerce and weemen is plenty. I said that woman was tenderer than man, but you needn't feel stuck up about it, for she ought to be, she was made so a purpose. But how was she made so? Where did she git it from? Why, she was created out of the side-bone of a man, and the side-bone of a man is like the side-bone of a turkey, the tenderest part of him. Therefore, as a woman has three side-bones, and a man only one, of course she is three times as tender as a man is, and is in duty bound to repay that tenderness of which she robbed him. And how did she rob him of his side-bone? Why, exactly as she robs his pocket now-a-days of his loose change—she took advantage of him when he was asleep.

"But as woman is more tender than man, so is man more forgivener than woman; therefore, I won't say anything more about the side-bone, or the small change, but invite you all to jine my train, or I'm a big shepherd out our way, and fare sumptuously every day, in purple and fine linin.

"When I first landed on the shores of the Great Salt Lake, I wasn't rich in weemen—I had but one poor old yoe; but men is skeerce and weemen is plenty, and, like a keerful shepherd, I began to increase my flock. Weemen heard of us, and of our lovin' ways, and they kept a pourin' in. They come from north, and they come from the south; they come from the east, and they come from the west; they come from Europe; they come from Aishey, and few of 'em from Afrikey; and from bein' the miserable owner of the yoe, I became the joyful shepherd of a mighty flock, with a right smart sprinklin' of lambs, frisker and fatter than anybody else's, and I've still room for a few more.

"As I said before, I'm not talkin' pertickler for my benefit, but for yourn; for men is skeerce and weemen is plenty. Still, I'd a leetle rather you'd go along with me than not, perttickler you fat one with the kaliker sun-bonnet. Don't hesitate, but take the chance while you can get it, and I'll make you the bell-yoe of the flock. I'll lead you through green pastures and high grass—show you where you may caper in the sunshine, and lay down in pleasant places; and as you are in pretty good condition already, in course of time you'll be the fattest of the flock. Jine in—jine in—jine my train—jine in now; for men is skeerce and weemen is plenty!"

The appeal was irresistible. At the last account "the fat woman with the kaliker sun bonnet had jined in," and two or three others were on the fence, with a decided leaning toward the "keerful shepherd."

Such is a somewhat ludicrous exposition of what occurs every day. There is nothing too audacious for these men. They trade upon the ignorance and benightedness of their congregation, and rarely make converts except of the very lower order of the community, whose notions of religion and right or wrong are warped by a defective education.

Scarcely any of the Mormons can speak or write a correct sentence of English, while their addresses teem with vulgarity and coarse attempts at a low and blasphemous kind of wit.

As education spreads, these vampires will be driven from civilized society.

* * * * *

Phineas bit his lip until the blood came, as he heard the charms of Jessie discussed by the ruffianly assemblage; and he cursed the day and the hour he had brought her into such fearful peril.

CHAPTER LXIV.
AN ATTACK.

IT was midnight. The Mormon elders were still in council over a small fire of red embers.

The sentries dozed at their posts.

No sound broke the stillness of the night save the sighing of the wind.

Suddenly one of the sentries gave a sharp cry of mingled surprise and emotion, as a kind of beacon fire was seen to burst forth on the opposite side of the valley.

Though the distance was considerable, he could see two figures plying the flames with wood.

What could this mean?

Nothing else, he apprehended, but a general assault on the Saints by the exasperated country people.

A deep hush fell upon the camp as they watched the progress of the flames.

Then again was heard the sound of the solitary horn at no great distance from the camp.

The Mormons clutched their fire-arms, and then the whole party was placed on the *qui vive* by the explosion of a musket.

All ran toward the spot.

A faint, shrill cry followed the shot like an echo.

"What is it?" cried one of the elders to the sentry who had fired.

"I saw three forms gliding from our camp, and I fired," he said.

A general outcry testified to the rage of the Saints.

All rushed to examine their tents, with fear and awful dread in their hearts.

Three of the women were missing.

And these three were Julie; the wife of John Smith; and Jessie herself.

The exasperation of the Mormons was now something fearful to behold. They were frantic.

Three of their bitterest enemies were abroad, full of horror at their deeds, and ready to give the very worst interpretation of all their acts.

But there was no time to be lost. After a noisy and tumultuous debate, it was resolved to strike tents and start at once, while a small party remained behind to give chase to the fugitives.

This was no sooner decided on than it was carried out. The cattle were again harnessed, the tents struck, and the Mormon caravan, led by an experienced guide, started up the defile towards the mountains.

Paola, bursting with rage and fury; John Smith, angry, but rather glad of the riddance; Phineas Bristowe, anxious to be of use to Jessie, remained behind with four of the most active among the Mormons.

They were all well armed, and at once determined to discover the meaning of the fire on the hill top.

With slow and stealthy steps, they crept along the pathway until they came to a kind of ford.

This they crossed by the careful use of a small lantern to guide their steps.

The same means enabled them to discover that the fugitives had taken the same way. They, too, had seen the beacon, and made towards it—if, indeed, it had not been lit for their special guidance.

Suddenly it could no longer be seen, and the Mormons found themselves in total darkness.

A halt was declared, and a consultation held, which ended in their deciding on remaining where they were until morning.

Three inexperienced women must have left tracks by which they could easily be followed.

They were afraid even to make a fire, lest it should serve the double purpose of illumining their enemies and warming themselves.

The night was rather bleak, so they all huddled together in a small hollow overhung by trees.

None thought at first of sleep, but the power of nature soon shewed itself. All fell gradually off but Paolo, who, consumed by varied passions, lay awake despite all his efforts to obtain rest.

He sat up for some time, contriving to eke out the time by smoking.

Presently, however, he determined to make a serious effort at obtaining at least one hour's sleep and repose.

He accordingly laid his head on the ground, with a stone for a pillow, and closed his eyes.

No sooner did he do so than he gave a violent start. But he did not lift his head. He seemed glued to the earth for a minute or two.

He could hear voices, and those the voices of women.

The three unfortunate fugitives were camped near at hand. He, however, little suspected how far those voices came in the stillness of the night along the ground.

He raised himself up slowly, and then again listened.

He heard them plainly, but what of that? He must, on that dark and black night, continue to hear them, if he would track them with success.

He gazed around earnestly for a moment, and then made up his mind.

Taking his rifle in his hand, and slinging the dark lantern at his back, he began to crawl like some animal of the forest towards his prey.

He could in this way, by halting every now and then, distinctly hear the conversation of the three fugitives, who probably spoke a little louder than they otherwise would have done to keep up their courage.

The feelings of Paolo were those of unalloyed satisfaction. He was armed, and the women were not. Rather than they should escape, he would use his weapon.

One cry from him, and the sleeping Mormons would be upon the fugitives.

He chuckled with delight as he advanced.

He was crawling beneath some rather lofty trees without brushwood. This it was that enabled him to hear so distinctly.

On the prairies the tread of man or horse, the sound of voices, is carried prodigious distances, if the listener puts his ear to the ground.

On the water, on still and glassy lakes, that of Geneva, we have heard the voices of people coming across from Savoy before we could see the boat,— a distance of eight miles.

Of course, on a surface so much more uneven, Paolo could only hear a comparatively short distance.

And yet the journey, crawling like a snake, appeared to him terribly long.

He thought he should never get to the end.

In his impatience, he hurried forward, and unconscious where he was going, rolled suddenly down a deep acclivity, his gun being discharged as he fell.

In his ferocious desire to be ready for action, he had carried it cocked.

A wild cry followed his accident, a loud shriek arose to the heavens, and then all was still.

Paolo was stunned for a moment, but only for a moment. Leaping to his feet, he cast his light around.

He was on the edge of a precipice about twenty-five feet above the level of the river, on the opposite side of which he could hear the fugitives escaping.

His yells and execrations soon brought the Mormons around him. All seemed surprised that he had not met with his death, so fearfully near the edge of the precipice was he.

But their rage was all the more violent with the three refugees, who had contrived – how they could not conceive —to cross the river twice while they had only done so once.

They knew not what to do, and in idle discussion, menaces, and other talk, the night passed away.

CHAPTER LXV.

THE BIVOUAC.

WHEN the three women, including our heroine, Jessie, heard the solitary horn, and saw the beacon fire on the hill, the same idea of escape seemed to enter their minds.

Julie, the most active and enterprising, crept forth from her tent, and seeking that which contained Jessie, easily persuaded her to follow.

Jessie knew that her life was in danger, and this manifestly absolved her from all promises to Phineas Bristowe.

But she refused to move unless Mrs. John Smith was offered also the same opportunity.

The poor woman, who was utterly broken-hearted at the cruel conduct of her husband and step-daughter, readily agreed to accompany them.

While the Mormons were discussing the meaning of the beacon-fire on the hill, they crept between two of the sentries, and stooping as low as possible, contrived to get to a considerable distance before they were discovered.

Then the sentry fired, having just caught sight of their fluttering garments.

The shot, however, did not take effect. It hurried the movements of the three ladies considerably, but did not make them lose their caution.

Julie knew well that the Mormons never forgive an attempted escape of a dupe.

The many graves on the route to Utah, and the bleaching bones which lie on the hills which surround Salt Lake, testify to this.

Fearful are the murders committed to prevent the true state of Mormonism from being revealed by those whose eyes have been opened to the crude, wicked, and illiterate imposture.

Like the lords of Turkish harems, the poor victims of man's lust and villainy must die, if they would escape the foul contagion of the zenana.

Hence it is that so little is known of the real state of the case.

They soon reached the river, and walking slowly along its banks, came to what was evidently a ford. Their object was to reach the beacon light on the hills.

In their way towards it, they again came to the river, and, with some difficulty, crossed it.

They were now in a dense wood, and all sign of the fire had disappeared.

They could not make a forward step for the darkness. Their ears had already told them, that the Mormon camp had taken the alarm, and was hurrying away.

They did not think that anyone would venture to remain behind in a country so inimical to them, and where the fearful outrage on Sarah would soon spread over the length and breadth of the land.

They agreed then to sit down and wait under the shelter of the trees until morning broke.

They were too agitated to think of sleep. They preferred to lay down their plans for regaining Europe.

They knew, however, that Henry and Mr. Stanley being on their track, they would soon find friends.

Jessie averted her head.

"What do you mean?" whispered Julie, in a tone of earnestness, which went to the other's heart.

"Nothing——"

"Do not say that. You have some bad news for me."

"Henry and Mr. Stanley have met," said Jessie, in a low, hushed tone.

"Ah! and he has spoken," she gasped, "he has spoken and deprived me of the love of that man."

"But Julie—Captain de Lancy——"

"Ah!" she said, in a low tremulous voice; "They have set him against me. 'Tis well, ha! ha! ha! I did not think this of Henry. A woman's name is indeed a proper subject for the taunts and calumnies of boys——"

"Julie——"

"And ribald jests of sailors. But," she cried, in a loud angry voice, "I will be revenged—revenged—revenged—they know me not!"

It was now that Julie first realized the full force of the loss she had sustained when she had yielding herself up to unholy passions.

But she knew not what she had lost.

Oh women! women!—why have you not more faith in yourselves—in that strong inner purity, which alone can make a woman brave!—which, if she knows herself to be pure in heart and desire, in body and soul, loving purity for its own sake, and not for the credit that it brings—will give her a freedom of action, and a fearlessness of consequences, which are to her a greater safeguard, than any external decorum. To be, and not to seem, is the amulet of her innocence.

The consciousness alone that the free, happy innocence of maidenhood is gone for ever, and that the sacred dignity and honour of matronhood is not and can never be attained, surely must be the most awful punishment to any woman. From it no kindness, no sympathy, no concealment of shame, or even restoration to good repute, can entirely free her. She must bear her burden, lighter or heavier, as it may seem at different times; and she must bear it to the day of her death.

She remained silent for a few minutes, utterly overcome with thought and emotion. There was no repentance, no grief for what she had done, but the hope that she might be able to brazen out to Stanley that all that he had been told was false.

But she had yet to learn how difficult it is, to win back the love of a man, once disenchanted.

> "A weary chase and wasted hour—
> Then leaves him, as it soars on high,
> With panting heart and tearful eye;
> So beauty lures the full-grown child
> With hue as bright and wing as wild;
> A chase of idle hopes and fears,
> Begun in folly, closed in tears.
> If won, to equal ills betrayed,
> Woe waits the insect and the maid;
> A life of pain, the loss of peace
> From infant's play and man's caprice.
> The lovely toy, so fiercely sought,
> Hath lost its charm by being caught,
> For every touch that wooed its stay
> Hath brushed its brightest hues away,
> Till charm and hue and beauty gone,
> 'Tis left to fly or fall alone."

"Why did you not tell me this before?" suddenly said Julie, in hoarse, choking accents.

"I was told to say nothing."

"Then why have you spoken now?" asked Julie.

"Because, as you are soon about to see him, I thought you had better be prepared."

"I thank you for the consideration," said Julie, with a bitter sneer.

"I meant it kindly."

"I doubt it not. But all your calumnies cannot take away my wealth. I shall be rich and happy. What care I for love? If the man is a fool, let him go; at all events he is my husband. He cannot alter that, and I'll have him crawling at my feet, begging for my love, in less than a month."

Jessie made no reply. She was thinking of Henry, and how little she would have sought to reclaim his affection if once she had justly forfeited it.

Then came the attack of Paolo, and the discharge of the gun, as they fancied, aimed at them.

A sudden and very natural panic seized upon them. Without looking to the right or left, they fled.

When they regained their breaths, and heard no one in pursuit, they were scattered through the forest in various directions.

Julie, whose physical energies were beyond all comparison the greatest, stopped; she found herself almost at the top of the hill, on the opposite side of the valley, where she had seen the beacon fire.

She was quite alone, nor could she hear the slightest trace of her companions.

She gazed fearfully around, and for some time could see nothing to guide her steps.

Then a faint scintillation of light seemed to rise before her, and she found, on rapidly approaching the spot, that it emanated from the glowing embers of the beacon, which had excited so much attention.

Fearful to stir up the embers, and re-illumine the fire, she cowered over the glowing coals, and determined to remain there until morning.

She was now in a deep reverie.

Her first thought, on hearing that Henry had painted her in her true colours to the Honourable Mr. Stanley, was to betray Jessie back into the hands of the Mormons, and allow them to wreak upon her the vengeance which would be most sweet to her mind.

Nothing else but the dishonour of the girl he loved could satisfy the fiery hatred of her soul.

She loved, she passionately adored her husband. She had resolved to be faithful and true to him, and now, when she had made up her mind to cease her wild career; just as she had hoped for happy hours, this Henry Haddington had exposed her to the man of her choice, and blighted all her prospects.

Could any vengeance be too terrible for this?

"I never loved but this man," she said, clenching her two fists and raising them to the skies; "and these wretches have conspired to rob me of his noble heart. But I will have vengeance."

As she said these words aloud, a kind of blanket or horse cloth was cast over her head, while two powerful arms encircled her and dragged her forcibly along.

She made no resistance. She felt it was useless, but her busy brain was at work.

Presently her captor halted, and setting her down, took away the blanket.

To her astonishment, bewilderment, and partly to her terror, she found herself in a rude hut or cave, very commonly furnished—face to face with her husband.

CHAPTER LXVI.

HUSBAND AND WIFE.

THERE was a fire-place, a table, chairs, and even a bed in the place, while arms and accoutrements hung on the walls.

Mr. Stanley, who wore the dress of a backwood hunter.

"And," she said, gazing at him with eyes filled with astonishment and tears, "is it thus we meet after so cruel a separation? Why is this?"

"Madame," cried Mr. Stanley, in hushed and earnest tones, "you know best."

"For Heaven's sake explain yourself," she said; "I cannot control my fate. Under the influence of some strange narcotic——"

"Was it under the influence of a narcotic," said Mr. Stanley, "that you were seduced by Paolo, the galley slave?"

"Go on sir," said Julie, with a Sidonian start of horror,

"Or when you took his wife's place beside Captain de Lancy?"

"Hold sir!" cried Julie, rising to her feet, and speaking with a dignity, which, consummate actress as she was, she knew so well how to assume; "let me not hear the foul calumnies of men, who have, in revenge for my refusing their addresses, so horribly slandered me."

"Madame—all this is useless. These who gave me this information are men of honour."

"Indeed!"

"Men who cannot be capable of falsehood or deceit," he said, avoiding her sarcastic and bitter glance.

"Sir—you have married me; you have obtained sufficient of my fortune to make you independent—say so. But do not, as an excuse for a cruel and cold-blooded abandonment of her you professed to love and cherish, pretend to believe that which in your heart you know to be a falsehood."

"But madame ——"

"Hear me. I will not, after what has passed, ask to be your wife. If you need it, I will give you every facility for a divorce. But, as surely as I love only you—and never loved but you—you have been misinformed by those who are my enemies I am weary and exhausted—give me something to revive me, and then let me hear what your accusations against me are."

The Honourable Mr. Stanley, whose agitation in the presence of a woman he had so passionately loved, was dreadful, moved to a cupboard and drew forth a bottle of brandy. It was all his Indian friend, whose hut he occupied, had to offer him.

He poured out a certain quantity into two wooden cups. Julie dashed in some water, and drank the burning and acrid draught at one gulp.

Mr. Stanley did the same.

"Now, tell me all," she said, in something of her old caressing way.

He looked fixedly on the ground, and repeated all he had heard.

"Charles Stanley," she said, in accents of intense feeling and earnestness, "that man, the

HUSBAND AND WIFE.

Viscount de Florac, as he always called himself, did, when I was a girl, quite a girl, endeavour to win my affections, and induce me to marry him."

"Indeed."

"To avoid him, I fled to England to a boarding-school, where nearly ten girls were successively seduced by this man, and induced to join the Mormons. With me he failed, but in his great rage at being defeated, he maligned me all he could—he told others that I was one of his victims."

"But the mock marriage?"

"My father believed the slanderer, and compelled me to consent to the marriage, which he, in his ignorance of English custom, believed would be legal. I refused, however, to treat him as a husband, until our marriage was legally solemnnized—which I never meant it to be."

"Go on."

"As to the charge made against me by Captain de Lancy, it is a foul and despicable falsehood—unless it is a mistake. One of those forward girls who fell victims to de Florac may have played such a trick, but I did not. I am yours—only yours—and none but yours—in the past and in the future."

The Honourable Mr. Stanley wiped the heavy perspiration from his brow, and dashed off a neat glass of brandy.

He knew not what to think. Truly he believed Henry and Captain de Lancy—but then, he wished not to believe them.

He still loved Julie, his wife.

But he could not conceal from himself the fearful risk he was running.

He had made up his mind to kill her. That had been his daily, his hourly thought.

"Julie," he said, with a fierce gleam of something like insanity in his eyes, "do you know what I intend to be your punishment?"

"I care not. To whatever your erring judgment may condemn me, I submit beforehand."

"Cockatrice," he cried, "all this acting will not do. I know you to be guilty."

And rising, he snatched a long polished knife from the wall, while, with his disengaged hand, he clutched her wrist.

This was the critical moment, and Julie knew it.

She never flinched or stirred, but looked him meekly in the face.

"Charles," she said, "when I am dead, even those wicked men will do me justice. But before you accomplish your evil purpose, take charge of this."

And opening her dress, so as to expose all the beauties of her marvellous bust, she placed in his hands a sealed parcel.

But Stanley did not look at the parcel. His eyes were fixed on her glowing form.

Julie laid down the parcel and stood in an attitude of calm resignation.

"And you swear," said Stanley, "that you are innocent?"

"I swear it."

"By what?"

"By my love," she replied, gently.

"You are innocent and love me," he gasped,

"I am innocent, and I love you. To die by your hand is indeed happiness; for without your love, what is life?"

He opened his arms, she flew wildly to them, and all was forgotten but love, passionate love.

> "Full soon upon that dream of sin
> An awful light came breaking in;
> The shrine was cold at which I knelt—
> The idol of that shrine was gone.
> The humbled thing of shame and guilt,
> Outcast and spurn'd and lone,
> Wrapt in the shadows of my crime,
> With withering heart and burning brain,
> And tears that fell like fiery rain,
> I pass'd a fearful time."

"Julie," said Mr. Stanley, in the morning, when the sun was high in the heavens, and he spoke with a humbled and chastened mien, "I fear I have been very weak. But never from this moment shall whisper of mine call your attention to the past. I have forgiven and forgotten—but let the future prove to me that I have been misled by errors and calumnies."

"My own good dear, trusting husband," said Julie, tenderly—she was preparing breakfast—"never shall act or deed of mine give you pain or sorrow."

Stanley turned away. The very tones of her voice thrilled through his veins.

But he utterly despised himself, for in his heart of hearts he believed every word which had been uttered against her.

They had arranged to hasten as rapidly back to England as possible, their absence being laid to their having spent the honeymoon abroad.

Julie, or Mrs. Stanley, as we must call her, wished to avoid a meeting with Henry and Captain de Lancy. So did her husband, who, infatuated and mad as he was, knew yet the degradation of his position.

No man hoodwinks himself to his own follies or crimes.

We never do evil without being quite aware of the fact.

The Honourable Mr. Stanley would have cut the man who would have done what he was doing, and yet he could not find it in his heart to give up the woman.

He loved her, and this has been and always will be the excuse with some men for even such a miserable infatuation as that which urged him on now against his manhood's sense of right from wrong.

> "Thus, as the dove, to far Palmyra flying
> From where her native fonts of Antioch beam,
> Weary, exhausted, longing, panting, sighing,
> Lights sadly at the desert's bitter stream,
> So many a soul, o'er life's drear desert faring,
> Love's pure congenial spring unfound, unquaff'd,
> Suffers, recoils—then, thirsty and despairing
> Of what it would, descends and sips the nearest draught."

No sooner were their preparations made than they left the hut, descended the hill by a narrow path, nor halted until they reached a roadside inn, where one who had escaped from the horrid Mormons was courteously received.

CHAPTER LXVII.

ANOTHER VICTIM.

LEAVING Julie and her credulous and self-blinded husband to their fate, we follow in the footsteps of one in whom we hope all our readers take far more interest.

Jessie fled as fast as her footsteps could take her, when the explosion startled her and her companions.

Believing that the gun was fired on purpose, Jessie naturally tried to place a safe distance between herself and her pursuers, whose savage instincts she dreaded.

She knew that she had as much to fear from their love as from their hatred,

What would she not have given now for the protecting arm and agreeable companionship of Henry, her boy-lover?

Even that gloomy forest would not have appeared to her lonely or disagreeable.

As soon as she, on halting, heard no further sounds of any one in pursuit, she paused and seated herself under a wide-spreading beech tree.

She listened both with fear and hope.

What had become of her late companions? Little as she respected or loved Julie, she still hoped that she had escaped the ferocious grasp of the Viscount de Florac.

But she heard no sound to guide her.

In her hurry she had not the slightest notion which way she had come.

But she was utterly wearied and exhausted; and despite her utmost efforts, drawing her cloak around her, she fell into a sound sleep.

When she awoke it was with a violent start. Several shots were fired at no great distance. She gazed around, and on the other side of the valley saw a small body of men retreating before a more numerous body up a narrow pathway.

The Mormons had evidently been surprised and driven before the rifles of the indignant countrymen.

Jessie closed her eyes in awe, and, determined not to return to the society of the wretches she had so recently escaped from, turned to seek some pathway to an habitation of some kind or other.

She accordingly descended the hill towards the ford of the river.

She was soon about two hundred yards from the spot where they had camped on the previous night.

Suddenly she heard a deep groan.

She started, looked carefully around, and there lay, almost in the agonies of death, the wretched and unfortunate Mrs. John Smith.

Jessie flew to her side, kneeled by her, chafed her hands, and then rushing to the stream, came with a gourd full of water.

This seemed to revive her, though it was quite evident that her hour had come.

"Bless you!" she said.

"Where are you wounded?" asked Jessie, in her usual kind and gentle accents. "Are you much hurt?"

"Unto death," she said, "but I care not to live. He upon whom I had cast my affections has deserted me. Why should I exist to be a burden and a sorrow to him?"

"Nonsense!" said Jessie. "Don't think of him. I can see, by some smoke which rises yonder, that a house is near—I will go find help, and have you removed."

"It is useless, Jessie. I am ebbing fast. Do you take example by me—and let not your soul be subject to any man," she whispered. "Had I loved heaven more, and him less, I should not be a wretched deserted wife."

"You weary yourself with talking; rest your head here," she replied.

"Never be a Mormon, Jessie," said Mrs. John Smith, gently; "I see it all now. I have deserved it all."

"Never, so help me heaven!" said Jessie, in accents of unmistakable fervour.

"And then Jessie——"

"What, dear?"

"Tell him—that—that——" she gasped.

"What would you have me tell him?" asked our heroine.

"That—that—I forgive him—and—and—her—but Jessie——"

"What?"

"Let him be kind to her—and not leave her—nor take unto himself another wife to kill her."

"I will tell him."

"Tell him—I die—I die—happy—for I loved him, and could not have but half his love!"

She spoke no more, but bowing her head, her spirit passed away gently, quietly, without any evidence of suffering.

Jessie knelt and prayed fervently; then aware that alone she could do nothing, she rose and walked slowly away in the direction of the smoke on the other side of the river.

Her thoughts were sad. The death of the poor victim of a degraded and vile superstition had moved her deeply.

She had seen the former sufferings of the unfortunate woman, and while she could not hold her quite harmless for bringing her husband's child into the tents of the apostles of this abominable sect, yet had her punishment been more, a great deal, than the offence.

It was, indeed, cruel to be supplanted by a child she had looked on almost as her own.

It was the accidental discharge of Paolo's gun that had been the real cause of this terrible tragedy.

Crossing the river, and keeping her eye steadily on the smoke which served to guide her steps, Jessie soon came in sight of a clearing and log hut, which looked to her rather superior to any she had yet seen.

In front of the log was a man and woman, though she could not at that distance give much idea of their appearance and character.

CHAPTER LXVIII.

JOHN BUNT.

JOHN BUNT was the leading man in the band of neighbours who had come west together, not on account of being any richer than the rest of them, for he was not; but he had rather more education than the others, and a good deal of executive talent, and there had been a time when he was in easy circumstances. Joanna had snugly laid away in the old-fashioned bureau, which was one of the few articles of furniture they had brought with them, many relics of the former better estate of her parents; carefully preserved garments of that mother who died when she was a little girl.

There were linen sheets and pillow-cases, spun and woven by their owner for the bridal outfit; the wedding-dress itself of handsome brocade; a black lace veil, a set of silver tea-spoons, and three long spoons; a string of gold beads which Joanna sometimes brought forth on festive occasions.

The very white dress which she had worn to the camp-meeting had once been her mother's, and was the finest of old-fashioned India mull, tucked half way up the skirt, and with real thread-lace sewed around the neck. Other remains there were of those articles of dress and furniture common to the best class of eastern farmers, whose daughters rivalled those of their city cousins in solid education, if not in showy accomplishments.

Joanna's mother had been the belle of her county when she was a girl; she could paint in water-colours, write as handsome a hand as the writing-master, parse equal to the smartest young man, and dance better than any other girl in those parts.

Joanna was an only child, her mother had died when she was a little girl, and she had been left to the entire charge of her father—not always a fortunate thing for a young girl, but in this instance especially so.

"I'll tell you what it is, Joanna," said the father, as he stood looking out upon his clearing, which began to show signs of excellent cultivation, the result of hard work and industry, "I don't half like it."

"Like what, father?" she asked.

"These Mormons hanging about here," continued the farmer, bluntly.

"What are they to us?"

"Well, I don't know as they're much to us," continued John Bunt, "but we're a sight to them. Thee's a fine girl, Joanna, and thee knows it."

The girl blushed, but did not repel the soft insinuation.

"Now, lookee, gal. You like that George Parkinson?" he continued.

"I do, father."

"And so did I, once," continued the father, "but I've heard tell as how he's a colleaguing with them thieving Latter-day Saints, as they call themselves."

"But, father, they appear very harmless people to me. They have peculiar notions about religion, but that is all."

"Darn'd if I did'nt think it!—he's been talking thee over. Give me my goon—by the law, I'll teach him to come here any more. Why, child, I'd sooner see thee dead, than one of them pesky, infarnal varmints."

"Father, you should not decide too harshly," she began; "how do you know that these Mormons are——"

"They are murderers, assassins, and everything that is vile and wicked," said a soft voice close at hand. "Better perish than become one of their victims."

They turned and saw Jessie, travel-stained and sore-footed, standing close to their side.

"Say you so, girl?" cried the farmer; "then you know something about 'em. Come in, and tell us all."

Joanna seconded the proposition, for she saw that the girl was utterly exhausted. At the same time, her eager denunciation of the Mormons did not please her.

She looked upon them with very different ideas indeed.

But she was kind-hearted, generous, and in reality pure and good. So she took Jessie in, gave her hot coffee and corn-cakes, made her change her shoes and stockings, and was, in fact, as civil and kind as one girl could be to another.

Then Jessie, without entering much upon her own private history, told all she knew of the Mormons.

The farmer heard with horror; the daughter first with incredulity, anger, then with passionate sorrow and regret.

"And can I have been so deceived?" she cried, "Young lady, you would not deceive me?"

"I have not coloured one scene. Some of your neighbours will tell you worse tidings than this. A girl named Sarah Paulding was buried alive by them——"

"My cousin!" shrieked Joanna; "at least, my cousin's future wife."

"But he saved her," hastily added Jessie, and gave full details of the events of that terrible night."

"I would tear the dearest lover that I could have from my heart," said Joanna, wiping her eyes; "never again will I listen to a voice from these so-called Saints.

Right, girl! Whenever a young woman finds a man unworthy, better at once discard him and cry with the poet.

"Even from that hour, when first
My spirit knew that thine was wholly lost,
And to its superstition wedded fast,
Shrouded in darkness, blind to every beam
Streaming from Zion's hill athwart the night
That broods in horror o'er a heathen work—
E'en from that hour my shuddering soul beheld
A dark and fathomless abyss yawn wide
Between us two!"

So it would have been with Joanna, but at that moment George Parkinson entered the house.

He was pale as death, and walked with a hurried step.

"Farmer Bunt," he said, dashing his rifle against the wall, "ain't you going to make one?"

"Of what?" cried the other, gravely, while Joanna turned away and spoke to Jessie in an under tone.

"To hunt up these b——d Mormons," cried George Parkinson; "thee need'nt stare. I never knew till last night what infernal villains they were. But I know it now, and never shall a Mormon come to the end of this gun and escape alive."

"I'm glad to hear thee talk that way, boy," cried the farmer, eagerly, while Joanna turned round, smilingly, towards him and took his proferred hand.

An explanation then ensued. George had been one of those who had rescued Sarah Paulding from the clutches of the infernal elders, and in forty-eight hours his eyes had been thoroughly opened—where before he had been a complete and blind dupe.

Jessie's story of the previous night added to his utter hatred and detestation of the Mormons.

"This poor woman must be buried," said the farmer; "shut up the house, girl, and if you, miss, will show us the way, we will at once proceed to lay her in the ground."

Jessie willingly acquiesced, and in a few minutes the small party started on their way; the men carrying pickaxes and shovels, while Joanna had snatched up an old prayer-book, which had been her mother's.

The two men walked forward, conversing in an under tone, while Joanna and Jessie lingered a little behind.

They soon, however, reached the desolate spot, where the body lay calm and serene, asleep for ever in this world.

They gazed mournfully at it, and then, without

farther comment, a grave was dug, and the body deposited in it. Joanna, in a very solemn tone, read a few prayers for the dead, and then all was over.

Jessie now informed her new acquaintances of her desire to return towards the seaboard, but when she explained her reasons, they begged her to stop a few days, as an express could easily be sent to seek for Henry, who, no doubt, after the attack on the Mormon village had returned to the hospitable shelter of farmer Beckford's house.

Jessie, who was really overcome with emotion, excitement, and fatigue, agreed to rest a day or two with her new friends. In reality, she was incapable of progressing a single step.

The scenes of the few previous days had been decidedly too much for her.

The Bunts saw this, and looking upon her arrival as an almost direct interposition of Providence, they made her as welcome quite as the flowers in May. They talked no more of pursuing the Mormons. There were others to do that duty.

The best room was selected for her, and an ancient negress, who was Joanna's factotum, received strict injunctions as to nourishing and agreeable knick-knacks for her delectation and enjoyment.

But what kept her up was the hope of seeing Henry.

It could not be long deferred now, that much-coveted and happy meeting.

It was settled that George Parkinson should return on the back track of the Mormons, and by interrogating right and left, discover the whereabouts of Henry and his companions.

Jessie, in the dreadful excitement of the day, had utterly forgotten Julie. This was fortunate, though when she did think of her, it worried her very much.

Had she fallen into the hands of the revengeful Mormons?

If so, in all probability her fate was sealed, especially as they were baulked of their expected prey—Jessie.

CHAPTER LXIX.

A VISIT TO CHURCH.

At no great distance from the residence of the Bunts was a village, and as a matter of course a village church; for whatever the faults of American politicians and the vile propensities of the mob of the seaboard, the unsophisticated settlers up country are a noble and good race.

Of course the Bunts went to church.

The day after the arrival of Jessie in the neighbourhood was Sunday.

It was agreed that they should go to the house of God, to return thanks for the mercies vouchsafed to them.

Jessie had not a compunction in her heart about broken promises now. The abominable way in which they intended to treat her on her return was quite enough to justify her escape.

She was glad after all to be out of the clutches of that man, Phineas Bristowe.

She never believed him to be her own father.

She was quite sure of it now, for she had been told of it by one who never lied.

How she longed to know the wild, extraordinary and mysterious history of her father and mother.

Most likely she never will, but our readers will, as well as that still more inexplicable story of the heir to the Dukedom and Lotty.

When we come to that our readers will confess that no one in the world could have invented anything even half so extraordinary.

Joanna and Jessie had at once become great friends. Jessie always entered heart and soul into an attachment with the good, and Joanna was good.

The good farmer put on his go-to-meeting clothes, harnessed his nag to the old waggon, and seating his charges comfortably inside, drove on.

It was a tented waggon. The canvas roof kept out both sun and rain. In general it would have been called a market cart, but a very neat one in its way.

The road, like most others in that part of the world, was rather jolty and rough, but this only occasioned laughter.

Both Jessie and Joanna noticed that on the road they met very few men.

They were out after the accursed and fiendish Mormons.

They had gone forth to fight, leaving the old men and women to pray.

Several interchanges of courtesies took place, while in general the conversation turned to the excesses of the monstrous vagabonds, who took the men away a-fighting.

In this way the village was reached, where all entered the church, and listened to a very excellent sermon from the minister. He referred feelingly, and without bigotry, to the excesses and follies of the sect which made religion a bye-word and a laughing stock in the highways.

All listened with attention.

Not one present but had a deep interest in the matter.

Husbands, brothers, and lovers, were on the track of the ravishers and murderers.

At length the sermon, as usual very long, concluded with a blessing, and the congregation was dismissed awhile.

All went to seek refreshment, ere the afternoon service commenced.

A kind of way-side house, half farm-house, half inn, was always frequented by the Bunts. Here the old man took his daughter and Jessie to dine.

They were homely, pleasant people, and made everybody as comfortable as they could.

It was long after dark when the farmer started once more to return home. It was a fine, clear night, however, and they had nothing to fear, now that the Mormons had left the neighbourhood.

They were terribly and fatally mistaken.

On the road home the farm cart passed along a deep valley, crossed by a road which led up country towards the Mormon track—down, in the direction whence Henry would come.

By excess of precaution the farmer was armed.

He carried a blunderbuss and a pair of horse pistols. They were solemnly loaded every Sunday morning, and as solemnly discharged at night. No use had ever been found for them yet. In a new state of society, burglary and highway robbery are rarely in fashion.

The night was somewhat dark. Flickering shadows fell upon the road from tree and bush, while the wind whistled around them as if portending a terrible storm.

"Gee up, Jinny," said the farmer, gently castigating the venerable mare. "I calkerlate thee'll kotch it mighty quick if thee does'nt pull up lost time. A run of greased lightning 'ud hardly save us."

"Going to be very heavy," said Joanna.

"'Spect it is just," replied the farmer.

They were now entering the valley, and it was necessary to proceed with some caution as the shadows of the hills made advancing doubly dangerous.

There was a brook to be crossed, and as it was so dark, Farmer Bunt dismounted to lead the animal.

The rattle of eager horsemen now fell upon their ear, coming up the road from the seaboard.

"Heavens! can he have returned?" said Jessie.

"Perhaps," replied Joanna, eagerly.

"Mr. Bunt," cried Jessie, addressing the farmer, "will you wait one moment? I think friends are near."

The farmer made no answer, but the sound of a scuffle was heard. Jessie seized one of the old man's pistols, rose, and observing that Bunt was attacked by four men, fired.

"H—ll and d———n!" yelled a savage voice. "Down with him. Seize the girls, and come—"

Again Jessie fired, and again execrations followed, but before she could seize the blunderbuss both her and Joanna were dragged from the cart, gagged, and carried away by main force in the arms of powerful men.

Not five minutes elapsed ere several horsemen swept up.

"Bunt's team by thunder!" said the voice of the lover of Joanna. What's this?"

"Some new misfortune," cried Henry, eagerly dismounting, followed by Charles.

"Murder, by heavens!" said the horror-stricken youth.

"No, my boy," cried Bunt, raising himself up; "it ain't murder, but wuss. Them darned infernal long-shanked Mormons is just evaporated with the gals."

"Which way?" cried four voices, in tones of agony.

Bunt pointed to the hills.

"Follow up," he said. "Leave me here. I'm all serene now."

"Follow," cried Charles, wildly. "How can that be in this dark night? but we can try."

"Follow unto the death," said Henry, whose hopes having been raised to the highest pitch, were thus cruelly dashed.

CHAPTER LXX.

THE PURSUIT.

THE Mormon ruffians who, after the accidental murder of Mrs. John Smith, had collected together, had been ever since lurking about the neighbourhood. Despite his wish not to do anything injurious to Jessie, Phineas Bristowe was by no means desirous that she should leave his hands until he had made terms with her friends.

He had bound his companions by solemn promises—the promises of Mormons—to assist him in protecting Jessie against all violence.

"There's one easy way," said Paolo, with a grin.

"What is that?" asked Phineas Bristowe, sternly.

"I'll marry her," replied the ex-Viscount de Florac.

"I would slay her first. I have my reasons for all I do with Jessie—but no one shall hurt a hair of her head. So be warned in time!"

"Oh! just as you like. I don't want her. There's women enough about, for asking, Heaven knows."

This point thus amicably settled, the four men reconnoitred the country, and by spying about, asking a question here, and a question there, found easily out that nearly all the men were in active pursuit, and then that Jessie was at Farmer Bunt's.

They might have taken away Jessie openly from the worthy settler, but not without a struggle, in which one of their lives, at least, might be lost; so they determined to be careful, and to make sure of their prey without any personal danger to themselves.

They lurked about at a distance, hiding in thickets, behind trees, crawling through ditches, until they saw the party start for church. They then followed them actively.

The valley decided them.

Until evening they reconnoitred it in every part, and saw that it admirably suited their purpose.

They determined to attack the poor old farmer here, and to shoot him without mercy if he made any resistance. His alighting from his waggon enabled them to surprise him unawares, and to deal a dastardly and unexpected blow, which half stunned him.

They then grappled with him, and cast him senseless at his horse's feet.

Paolo it was who had been wounded by Jessie's pistol shot. He swore a savage oath of revenge, although the wound was a mere flesh wound in his arm.

Phineas, however, it was who, as soon as Jessie had been gagged, took her in his powerful arms and carried her off.

They did not follow the high road. The sound of approaching horsemen made such a proceeding too dangerous. Swift retribution would have followed their crime.

But their exploration of the neighbourhood had made them familiar with an easy way of escape.

The sides of the valley were lofty in the extreme

and rugged, but they had examined carefully, and found a path evidently used by hunters before them.

It led to the summit of the hills, and then by a very narrow bridge over a waterfall, that supplied the stream below, to the open country beyond.

It was no easy matter to ascend this hill in the dark, but desperate men in such an emergency will forget all peril. Paolo, whose assistance, with his wounded arm, was useless as far as the women were concerned, moved first to show the way.

They had a dark lantern, but they dared not use it.

Presently they heard the dash of the horsemen, and their execrations in the valley below.

They were now close to the narrow and treacherous ledge of rock which served as a bridge over the waterfall.

Paolo crossed first without any difficulty. Then came Phineas, carrying Jessie ; then John Smith, assisting the steps of the fourth Mormon, who bore the burden of Joanna.

At this moment the moon darted from behind a cloud, and the forms of all appeared clearly defined against the sky.

A terrible shout from below told them they were discovered.

Paolo sank out of sight. Phineas dropped Jessie, and fell beside her.

John Smith stood erect, bewildered and puzzled. That moment of irresolution and hesitation was fatal.

A sheet of flame, a loud crack—that of a rifle ; and, with a fearful cry of horror, he fell headlong into the valley below.

Mrs. John Smith truly had her revenge on her faithless husband and worthless daughter.

When the smoke cleared away, the Devil's Bridge was abandoned,

The pursuers advanced to examine the features of the victim. He was stone dead, shot through the heart.

But not a soul knew his features.

"What is to be done?" said Henry, turning in disgust from the senseless clay.

"Nothing to-night," replied Charles ; "but, sir, if you will listen to me, we shall be sure to find them. I know an old Indian in this neighbourhood, who will track them with certainity in the morning. I promise you rare sport, sir."

"But they will gain too much time," said Henry.

"My dear boy," put in Captain de Lancy, "we must be guided by those who know better than us. With the burden of those two haplesss girls they cannot go far."

"As you will, but fate is decidedly against us," said Henry, sadly. "I feel that I shall never see my dear Jessie more !"

"Never despair," replied Captain de Lancy, as, remounting their horses, they returned on their track, leaving the dead body to the vultures and the crows.

The night was spent at Farmer Bunt's, and at daybreak all were up and on foot. The Indian, a tall gaunt specimen of his race, with a keen restless eye and the usual loping walk of the red-

skin, appeared before them in his picturesque garb, and armed with tomahawk and fusil.

He appeared quite elated at the idea of following once more on the war trail, a thing unfamiliar except to his youth.

All were ready. The stern old farmer would have joined them, but by great exertions he was persuaded to stop at home.

He was not light of foot enough to keep up with younger men.

"I will bring her back, or you will never see me alive," said Charles.

Bunt wrung his hand, and the cavalcade departed on their way.

Their horses, however, only took them to the foot of the hills, where, by the advice of the Indian runner, they were left.

Though on foot, while they were on horseback, the Redskin had no difficulty in keeping up with them.

When the bridge was reached, the Indian waved to all his companions to keep back, following him at a little distance, that they might not disturb the trail, which, as a matter of course, began here.

It was wonderful to see the acuteness, the quickness of eye, the rapidity of decision, with which the Indian, like the avenger of blood, followed in the track.

Here a stone pushed from the damp earth, here a twig bent, here a blade or two of grass disturbed, a flower crushed, served to him as an infallible indication.

They watched him with extreme interest. All had heard of the instinct of the Indian race.

The party consisted of Charles, Henry, Captain de Lancy, two stalwart candidates for the hands of Rose and Blanche, and the guide.

All were armed with rifles, and all knew how to use them.

The trail lay for some time along a plain somewhat arid, but still with sufficient of soil and vegetable growth to enable the Indian to follow easily.

Then came a wood, where the track was equally easy. The girls were walking now.

The wood crossed, they came to a small farmhouse, in front of which sat a tall gaunt man, smoking. He wore a fierce and angry expression of countenance.

"Seen three cursed Mormons with two girls?" said Charles, eagerly.

"Guess I have——"

"Where are they ?"

"Don't know, thar."

"How long since you saw them ?"

"They kim last night—the eternal thieves. I gav' 'em bub and grub, and thin the almighty ungrateful vagabonds stole—what do you think ?"

"Your wife !"

"Yes, but that wasn't it—when they stole my wife, they tuk my waggon to carry her in—so !"

Quick glances were interchanged.

"Why don't you follow 'em ?"

"Look !"

They now remarked that his hands were in his breeches pockets, and that both his legs and arms were tightly fastened by ropes.

" Thunder !" he cried, as, after being cut adrift, he shook himself, " I'm ready."

There followed a brief explanation, after which some cider and other refreshments were freely indulged in.   The fact of the fugitives having a cart and horse was certainly in their favour, but then, the ground they had to traverse was heavy and difficult to work through.

" Go slow," said the Indian, pointing to the heavy ground.

The farmer, whose name, strangely enough, was Lemuel Sikes, took down a long rifle, loaded it, hung his pouch and powder-horn by his side, and proceeded, the moment the signal for a march was given, to keep up almost with the Red Indian.

" Humph !" said Lemuel, after they had proceeded some distance—" what the tarnation are they up tu ?"

" River !" replied the Redskin.

" Guess you're about right, my pipkin.   Well, if they gets my old woman afloat on any of them ere rafts as they can make, they'll be a mighty deal better coves ner I think !"

None of the others joined in the conversation. They were too full for words.   Presently they came to a wood, beyond which, Lemuel, stated was the river.

At this moment loud and long shrieks burst from just in front.   A dash was made through the thicket, and there, tied to the cart, was a stout woman, who rent the air with her exclamations.

" My old woman, by gum !" cried the farmer, rushing forward and letting loose his better half, who, as soon as she could explain, informed them that on reaching the banks of the river where they now were, she had made such a furious resistance as to render all hope of making her cross the water out of the question.

The others had constructed a rude raft, by means of which they had crossed the river, and were now quite out of sight.

Mr. Lemuel Sykes, after a brief private conference with his wife, determined that she should return home with the horse and cart, while he followed up the pursuit ; he was determined to have a slap at the niggers, he said.

" It's bad enough to steal away one's wife—it's tarnation bad to prig one's hoss; but, by the eternal pig as Moses made drunk, it's a tall thing to tie a man up at his own door, and make him a cocktail for neighbours to shy at."

None could help smiling at the scale of indignation which the farmer laid down, but all readily accepted his cooperation, as the Mormons were now fast approaching their own territory, and every rifle was of consequence.

But before they could even think of anything else, they, too, had to make a raft.

In this the Indian was of great assistance.   He pointed out the requisite trees to be cut down, and, when all were properly shaped, put them together in a very clever and scientific manner.

The raft was easily poled across the river, and, to their great astonishment, they immediately fell upon the trail.

The whole party, without any hesitation, threw their guns to the trail, and followed directly on the open track of the abominable fugitives.

It was evident that the girls were excessively wearied and fatigued by the way they walked. The others were, in fact, pulling them along.

About, however, a mile from the river, they fell across a high road, or rather, what is substituted for it in America, where in the back woods such things are done in a very rough and coarse manner.

The Indian examined the highway with a careful eye, and for some little time was at fault.

" Right," he said, and again fell into his long, loping walk.

About a mile ahead they found a small shanty, which was used by waggoners and others as a half-way house.   It was kept by an aged negress.

She could give them no other information, except that about an hour before three men had passed, dragging two girls with them, who wept bitterly.

" Heavens !" cried Henry, his eyes flashing with passion and anger, " when will this fearful trial end ?"

" Patience !" said Captain de Lancy, who almost feared for the reason of his young companion.

" Patience ! how can I have patience, when my very brain is on fire, when my soul is on the rack ?   Fancy her you love, she upon whom you have fastened your young affections, torn thus infamously through the wilds by demons in human shape !"

" Let us follow," said his captain, sternly.

Henry said nothing, but taking his place a little in the rear of the Indian, hurried forward.   The heavy pace of the Indian by no means tired him. He was too excited and exasperated to feel anything.

Suddenly, where the road opened on a wide and extensive plain, they were startled by the apparition of a large camp.   The persons to whom it belonged were evidently prepared for any emergency, having placed their waggons in a semicircle.

It was a very large camp.   Not less than thirty waggons were placed in a semi-circle. The animals were placed within, while behind all could be discovered the inhabitants.   Men, women, and children, were congregated round a large camp fire.

The Indian checked his companions, and made them draw suddenly behind a rock, and pointed to the fugitives, who were just entering within the precincts of the camp.

Henry snatched a telescope from the side of Captain de Lancy, and gazing for a moment in eager haste, let drop the glass, pronounced one word, and fell half fainting on the sward.

" Jessie !"

The eyes of love are keen indeed, and he had seen her and recognized her.

A few minutes sufficed, however, to induce a calm.   To do anything it was necessary to act with caution.   If they were seen from the camp there would be no hope but in flight.

They were far from all trace of civilization.

There was no legal authority in the neighbourhood.

They were six men against at least fifty.

But they had right on their side.

HENRY IN THE MORMON'S CAMP.

This was, at all events, to a certain extent satisfactory.

It was resolved finally, after some discussion, that they should camp on the spot, while one should enter the camp in the night in disguise, and discover if it were possible to do anything in the face of the overwhelming odds which were against them.

The Indian, as a matter of safety, was selected as the best agent, but Henry would not listen to this. Though he risked his life, he was determined to be a companion to the Indian.

"Paint," said the Redskin, with a grave and solemn smile.

"Anything you like," replied Henry, impetuously.

This being settled, a spot was selected from which a strict watch might be kept until darkness fell over the whole face of creation. They selected a spot surrounded by the prickly pear, and there, without a fire, and almost without conversation, the long weary day passed off.

The Indian slept. Inured to all the varied phases of war, the presence of the enemies they were in search of did not disturb his slumbers.

Towards dusk he rose, and, after joining in the frugal meal which had been prepared, proceeded to his somewhat difficult task of turning

Henry into such a Red Indian as should pass muster with the somewhat inexperienced Mormons.

They were to pass for two wandering and impoverished Indians, who, placed in difficult circumstances, entered the camp in search of such hospitality as the Mormons were able to afford.

The parting between Henry and Captain de Lancy was most affecting.

Once more his superior officer strove to persuade him against the danger he was about to encounter for a very small chance of any advantage.

But Henry firmly and solemnly declined to give up his adventure.

Once started on his undertaking, he determined to carry it through without flinching.

After an affectionate leave-taking, the two departed, after arranging signals with their somewhat doubtful and sorrowing companions.

The Indian and his companion, who was admirably made up as a lad attending on a warrior, walked deliberately and openly towards the camp. They walked slowly along without disguising themselves.

They wished particularly to be seen.

No sooner were they in the open plain, than a rush could be seen towards the semi-circle of the tents.

"Who goes there?"

"Fren," said the Indian.

"What kind of friend?" cried a sentinel.

"A poor Indian, want rest, tired."

"Indians be hanged! Come forward and let us have a look at you. We want no skulking ruffians about here."

In a few minutes more the Indian, whose name was Wild-horse, and his companion, who had adopted the patronymic of White Thorn, were caught rudely by the sentries, and dragged roughly into the camp.

The first man in whose presence they found themselves was Phineas Bristowe.

"Ah!" said that individual, after he had surveyed them carefully, "it is not the fellow I expected. But who are you, and what is your business?"

"Poor Indians, go to Illinois, want to travel with camp.

"Ugh!" said the supposed lad, who had been well tutored by his companion.

The Mormons, after a brief conference, selected a spot to which they sent the Indian.

It was next the hut which had been chosen as the prison to confine Jessie and Joanna.

Henry and his beloved future wife were within a yard of each other.

CHAPTER LXXI.

THE MORMON CAMP.

THE Mormons were now in no hurry to advance. They were in considerable numbers, at no great distance from that promised land which Joseph Smith had prepared for them, and were, more-over, being continually recruited by new accessions to their forces.

There are fools and knaves to be found in every community, however, simple or primitive.

Besides, they were on the track of every new caravan that arrived from Europe.

So weak or frail is human nature, that not all the exposure which has been given to their nefarious proceedings has yet succeeded in checking the progress of their teachers.

Mormonism must be put down by the strong hand of the law, just as prostitution and the recruiting for foreign brothels.

The Mormons were now on a debatable ground. It was hilly, slightly wooded, but not fertile enough for much settlement.

The friendly tribes of Indians camped in small villages about, while at times even hostile tribes came down in force, destroyed farms, carried off captives, and then disappeared.

But many of these outrages were well known to be perpetrated by white men, in the painted disguise of Redskins.

Then deeds were done at which Indians would have revolted.

It is impossible to express ourselves too strongly with regard to renegade whites. They are notoriously more vicious than the most uncultivated among the savages of the wilds.

When Henry entered the camp in the disguise of an Indian, the leaders of the Mormons, after secluding all the women in the tents and eliminating the doubtful among the men, were in deep conference.

An atrocious and abominable project had been laid bare to them by a leader. He had travelled that way before.

He had visited a certain locality.

He had been kindly and hospitably treated, and, as usual with such natures, he felt humiliated from that very circumstance.

The project was developed by him with infernal cunning, and that artful and dangerous eloquence which belongs to the class of men who make religion a means to an end.

All heard it with a suppressed murmur.

The affair was decided on at once. Not a man but applauded the decision.

There were women to be carried off, a great treasure to be divided, a treasure of gold, silver, and precious stones.

With men led on by lust and avarice, this was quite enough.

It was settled that a dozen men should be disguised as Indians, and under the guidance of this man led to the spot indicated.

The Mormons never travelled without ample means by which to disguise themselves. A large tent had been made round one of the larger waggons, and to this these slaves of their bad and evil passions retired.

About an hour later they sallied forth, and without breathing a word to any one, stalked across the camp in their war paint, and disappeared, marching in Indian file, led by the monster who had conceived the scheme.

We return to Henry.

The Mormons, who surrounded himself and his

companion, led them to a spot close to a fire, and motioned them to a seat.

"Hungry," said Wild-horse.

A young Mormon pointed to where some meat had been left by a party. It was nearly half a roasted sheep.

The Indian took it without a murmur, and began to eat heartily, motioning Henry to do the same.

Feeling that the eyes of several of the elder and more suspicious members were upon him, Henry forced himself to eat, even affecting to be exceedingly hungry.

The Mormons spoke apart. Evidently, after a time, they thought no more of the Indians, who, after eating, lit their pipes and smoked in silence. Then the elder Indian signed to his younger companion to lie down, which he did, wrapping himself in his blanket.

The Mormons took no notice of them.

They scattered in groups round the fire, and spoke of indifferent things. Two men took a place not far from where they slept. They were evidently continuing a conversation.

"I don't seem to see," said one, a young man, by his voice, "why the elders should have all the pull."

"How mean you?"

"Why, all the pretty young girls, while they turn over the old 'uns to us young men."

"Bah! when you get to Zion, you will have your choice of young ones. Old Joe, takes 'em like on trial, and, as about four in five don't suit, or he can't afford to keep them, you may have 'em for asking."

"Don't seem to see it," said the other.

"You ain't pleased——"

"Darned if it is," said the young man. "Do you see, there's a matter of six gals in the waggon yonder?"

"The unsealed waggon," laughed the elder.

"There's that tarnation fine gal, Jessie; there's a crummier one still, Joanna; there's John Smith's widder, as only wants to be consoled; and three others; and drat it! because they is pretty, some bald-headed old fool is to have the refusal of 'em, before they are offered to us."

"Respect age, my boy——"

"Respect my granny! Do you think the gals respect grey beards?"

"Curious fact in natural history, but they does. It's wonderful how uncommon fond they is of men of experience. You youngsters yare too flighty."

"Now, don't you talk none of your nonsense with me. I'm a young man. I've got an old gal for a wife, as is a first rate housekeeper, but when I joined these here blessed Mormons I was promised a whole tribe of beauties."

"And so you will have 'em," said the elder Mormon, who felt the necessity of conciliating the younger man—half dupe, half cunning.

"Just so," said he "you've been saying all this blessed time."

"Wait.

"Wait! Why now, to-night, there's a grand game on—a house and village to be pillaged—lots a gals to be stole—a mine of gold, and everyone as has gone is old 'uns."

"They have more experience. It will be no easy matter to trap Captain Isaac Cook, I can tell you—he'll die game."

Henry almost groaned aloud. He bore about him an energetic letter of introduction to the worthy pioneer of the desert, whose aid he had expected would have proved useful to him in his search after Jessie.

He tried to whisper to the Indian.

He was nowhere to be seen.

Henry knew not whether to be sorry or glad. He fancied, it is true, that he could depend on him; but why had he deserted him thus suddenly?

The men continued the conversation.

"I'm determined about one thing," said the younger man, whose name was John Jones; "that, when we have meeting to-morrow, if them old buffers brings in them six other girls, to propose that we young fellows has first choice."

"Are you tired of your life?" said the other, in a cold, sarcastic tone.

"Why?"

"If you talk that way, and contravene the laws of our society, you'll get goss, that's all, I can tell you."

"How?"

"You will find that things must be done in a regular way—that's all."

"Explain."

"Elders of the church first, and younger members after——"

"Deuced against nature," growled the aspirant for a plurality of wives.

The two rose, and lighting their pipes, walked away. This became very general shortly, and the camp was at rest.

Henry sat up slowly and methodically. Acting under the advice of the Redskin, he looked slowly round.

He had turned, however, carelessly once or twice, so as not to be in the shade of the fire.

He could see clearly without being seen.

Not a soul was visible in the camp.

One or two sentinels were posted around, but, as usual, they slept at their posts.

During the conversation between the two Mormons, Henry, by watching their eyes, had discovered the position of the tent occupied by the girls.

It was in the centre of four other waggons, and all but inaccessible.

But nothing is too much for the daring of devoted love.

Henry crawled slowly along until he found himself in the deep shadows of some of the waggons.

Then he crouched on his hands and knees, listening attentively for the faintest sound.

His ears were supernaturally keen.

Soon he approached the tent.

It was spread right round the waggon, and was closely pegged to the ground.

Again Henry listened. The breathing of many women could be plainly heard—it is different from the hard breathing of men.

At any other time Henry would have hesitated to enter the bed-chamber occupied by Jessie.

Indeed, the bed-room of any young girl.

But at this time there could be no hesitation. It was a mere matter of life and death.

He took a knife from his side, and cut a slit in the canvas.

He started back, for the sight was one, indeed, to have moved a stony heart.

Jessie had gone to sleep in the arms of Joanna, after weeping bitterly. Joanna herself was lying with her head thrown back, her eyes half open, though sleeping—while the other four were in various attitudes.

All were pretty, if not beautiful, and Henry could scarcely look at them unmoved.

CHAPTER LXXII.

INSIDE THE TENT.

For some moments Henry made no effort to move. He knew not what to do.

His eyes rested greedily on the form of Jessie, whom he had not seen for so long a period.

How to confer with her?

He did not forget his masquerade dress. He was afraid that a shriek at his sudden appearance might ruin all.

Then a young woman, restless and uneasy, sat up.

It was the guilty Mrs. John Smith the second, who, unfeeling as she was, did not receive the news of her husband's death without some little evidence of emotion.

She had wept herself to-sleep without receiving much sympathy from any of the others.

The woman she had supplanted had been her mother-in-law.

Certainly it was not so near, or dear, as a real mother, but it was next door.

She appeared to have been dreaming, for she passed her hand slowly over her eyes.

" What a fearful dream ! " she said ; " even more horrid than the truth. After all, it was a very wrong thing. Poor mother !—but, am I not punished ? I hate myself—I hate all the Mormons—I loathe, I detest them. Would that I could escape their fiendish clutches !"

Henry looked keenly at her.

" Never will I be deluded into believing in them again."

" Hist !"

The girl started and looked around.

" Girl," he said, " you can betray me if you like." •

" Who are you ?"

" A friend of Jessie's."

A dark frown passed over the girl's countenance.

" Indeed !" she said.

" Girl—I cannot explain now—but if you only knew ! I am rich, I am wealthy, I am powerful —aid my friends to escape, and there is no reward which shall be too great for you to claim."

The girl's eyes flashed.

Splendour she understood in all its accessories. But yesterday a girl, her first false step in life had made her voluptuous and greedy.

" You promise ? "

" On my sacred honour ! "

" Then will I trust you."

" Be cautious—wake Jessie and Joanna gently."

" All are of one mind here," said Mrs. John Smith, " so do not be alarmed."

She then touched Jessie on the arm. She awoke with a start, and sat up.

" What is it ? "

" What is it ? " repeated Joanna, who awoke at the same time.

" Hush !" said the young wife ; " a friend is near at hand."

" Who ? "

" You must be very cautious," continued Mrs. John Smith ; " the least noise, a single cry, and all will be lost !"

" Is it—I am quite calm—is it Henry ? "

" Yes ! " whispered our hero, who gazed at her upturned eyes and clasped hands with rapturous delight.

" And no one else ? " said Joanna.

" All friends are near," replied Henry, still in low, cautious tones.

The other girls now awoke.

We have known many of the dupes of Mormonism ; we have heard their enthusiasm as to the New Zion—but not one of the female sex but has deeply regretted joining them, not one but would have escaped if possible.

Shame, alone, keeps half of the neophytes.

They are ruined—lost—and cruel society would reject them.

But better face the cold, repellent feelings of the world, than wallow for life in a slough of hideous prostitution.

The three girls at once signified their intention to escape.

They had seen quite enough.

Not a young or old Mormon wife but would have done the same, if they could.

A whispered conference took place, and then Henry, after warning them of his disguise, entered the tent, where his handsome face, despite the paint, did not detract from the enthusiasm with which he was received.

He pressed the hand of Jessie, with tears in his eyes that sparkled like diamonds.

Jessie blushingly responded, and then all were ready.

Their worldly wealth was restricted to the clothes they wore.

But who cared, so that they escaped ?

Henry had cut a large hole in the tent, through which he was the first to pass.

The others followed in single file, holding their breath, and sending up a prayer to Heaven for mercy

Poor girls ! their lives had been bad enough ; now they were in danger of death.

The night was very dark, the clouds rolled in black sooty masses from the western hills, and not a shadow fell upon the ground as they walked.

The girls huddled together, except Jessie, who held fast by the hand of Henry.

It was a terrible, yet a joyous moment for the young girl.

Henry, in the buoyancy of his heart, was supremely happy.

Every now and then they halted to listen.

The girls spoke not a word—not a whisper passed through the little group.

They were half across the camp, when suddenly, by a most unfortunate accident, the clouds broke and the moon fell in a flood of light upon the scene.

Henry, at the same moment, fell over a half-sleeping sentry.

Shouts, execrations, shrieks, resounded through the camp. The girls stood still, spell-bound with speechless horror.

Henry clasped Jessie round the waist, clutched his tomahawk, and endeavoured to make good his retreat.

The girls surrendered without an effort. Even Joanna was paralyzed with fright.

They were driven, under a good guard, to their tent.

Savage threats warned them of the danger they had to expect.

Meanwhile, Henry was attacked by half-a-dozen Mormons.

They rushed headlong at him, but the first being felled by his bright little axe, they stood aloof a moment.

" Give up," cried one of them savagely, " or it will be worse for you !"

Henry made no reply, but whispering to Jessie which way to fly, let her go, drew a pistol from his belt, and stood at bay.

The Mormons drew pistols also, and a rapid discharge took place.

Four Mormons bit the dust.

Four rifles re-echoed in the hills.

The friends in ambush had spoken. But too late ; a perfect horde of the ruffians came up ; two secured the flying Jessie, while a dozen rushed savagely at Henry.

He was compelled to flee before overwhelming numbers.

Again, just as they appeared about to master him, a second volley of rifles checked their savage and impetuous career.

Then Henry, his heart broken with grief, rejoined his companions.

He told his melancholy story. Suddenly his eye flashed fire.

" Where is the Indian ? "

" Gone to warn Isaac Cook," replied Captain de Lancy.

" Then can we have revenge !" cried Henry. " They are a dozen—not one of the ruffians shall escape. In the Mormon camp, they must wait for their return. We may be able to rouse the country while they are expecting their leaders, but expecting in vain."

All readily agreed, and ten minutes later had started on their way by a route indicated to them by the Indian.

One thing which decided them more than anything else, was the wish to make the Mormons believe they had left the neighbourhood, and abandoned the chase.

CHAPTER LXXIII.
PUNISHMENT.

THE morning rose grey and cold in the Mormon camp. The men came forth sullen from their tents, the women looked alarmed and apprehensive.

Two of the warriors of the new sect lay dead, several were wounded.

An awful silence reigned during the morning meal.

The women looked up with terrified glances at their lords, but ventured no remark.

A fierce determination was on the brow of the Saints.

Directly after breakfast a council was held.

Then the women and children, and all who were not to be actors in the coming tragedy were placed in a half circle on the sterile plain.

The girls were brought pinioned.

Jessie and Joanna were fastened together.

" Loosen them," said one of the elders, sternly.

Their bonds were unfastened.

" Degenerate and base daughters of our holy faith, you would have deserted God and his people, to return to the accursed Gentiles.

" We would," said the girls, with one hasty and defiant accord.

Nothing could now make their position worse.

" You confess. That we might have visited with gentle chastisement. But, in the night when you were led away by the wiles of some monster in human shape, two of the Saints have perished, and four are badly wounded. What say you ? "

" We are very sorry."

" Sorry ! Will that restore life to Ebenezer Hatfield ?—will that give a husband to his three deserted wives?—will that bring to life Zebediah Ash ?—will that give a husband to his four wretched and disconsolate widows ? No ! "

The girls made no reply.

" It is my duty, as the leader of this fraternity, in the absence of the chiefs detached on special duty, to pronounce your punishment."

Jessie stood forward.

" Speak, and let it be speedy. Death, in in its most hideous form, is welcome—anything but the foul, unnatural consorting with a vile and wretched congregation of impostors, ravishers, and cold-blooded assassins."

She was magnificent.

Her colour had returned—her eyes flashed radiant—her arms were raised to heaven—and her lovely bosom beat with enthusiasm.

The men looked at her, despite their anger, half in admiration.

Not a woman looked at her with a jealous eye —they all felt that she had stood forward as a sacrifice to save the others.

" Silence, and return to your place !" said the elder, sternly.

" Sir— —"

" Silence," said Phineas Bristowe, who had advanced as near as he could—" silence, and I will create a diversion."

Jessie felt Joanna pull her by the arm.

A man advanced into the centre of the semi-circle.

"Two only will be punished. We wish no cruelty—we only wish to make example that shall warn neophytes and adepts from seeking to leave their tribe, and from betraying the secrets of the people of God."

A dead silence prevailed.

"There are two blanks in this hat," continued the man.

Four others now approached him.

"The two who draw the blanks will be punished —the others will be pardoned for the present," said the man.

The girls stood back, and refused to draw the —they were as pale as the still moon's rays on sleeping water.

"I will draw for you," said the man, with a sinister smile.

Still the girls moved not. They would have no hand in the punishment to which they looked with so much dread.

"Jessie," said the man, thrusting his hand into the hat.

It was number three.

"Joanna."

It was number four.

They were thrust apart.

"Mrs. John Smith—a blank," said the ruffian, with a fiendish grin.

She fainted in the arms of the two men who advanced to seize her.

"Esther Pride——"

It was number one. With a sad step, the girl moved on one side. The mysterious horror of the situation struck her with awe.

There were but two left, two good-looking, plump, naturally light-hearted girls.

They were now haggard, wan, and pale.

They were sisters—nineteen, and twenty-one. They were newly-acquired dupes, who were to be sealed to some burly brute on their arrival in Nauvoo—city of horrors, which we long to describe. They were heartily sick of Mormonism, and asked nothing better than to leave them.

Their names were Anne and Eliza.

They clung to each other wildly.

"Anne," said the implacable judge, "you too are free."

With a wild shriek, the sisters fell into each other's arms. They worshipped one another; they were devotees of sisterly love.

The two men separated them, and their shrieks rent the air.

Anne was removed to where the other culprits were held under guard.

The men coarsely tore off the shawls of the two girls, cut away their stays with knives, and in five minutes, Mrs. John Smith and Eliza were standing before the whole multitude, naked to the waist.

They were both very beautiful.

The women, without one exception, even old wives, who bitterly felt the loss of youth, because of the consequent loss of their husband's affections, gave vent to a cry of horror.

The men crowded round, jeering and admiring the fine forms of the victims.

They were tied up firmly by the waist, each to a separate tree.

To each advanced a man with a scourge in his hand. The two demons gazed with delight at the soft, plump flesh they were about to lacerate.

"Forty save one," said the brutal judge.

The lashes were raised.

"Stay!" cried the elder, who had been feasting his eyes on beauties rarely excelled in women.

The executioners paused.

The elder and judge advanced nearer, examining the girls as he would a fine horse, or a negro in the slave market.

"Ye are free, daughters! I have but two wives—say, will ye be sealed unto me? If so, I will remit your punishment."

He stood between them, casting his eyes alternately from one to the other.

They turned towards him a look of utter scorn and contempt.

They were heroines now.

"Too old!" said Mrs John Smith.

"Too ugly!" sneered Eliza.

A titter went round the circle.

"Mad! mad!" cried the infuriated elder.

"Proceed."

Then the horrid sound was heard of the lash, as it struck into the human flesh. The girls writhed in agony, but they did not cry out. They had roused themselves to that state of frenzy, half heroism, half madness, which has sustained so many martyrs through the hour of trial.

The blows were given with hearty goodwill, and soon the blood began to flow.

Women and girls fainted; others sobbed aloud; young men turned away in disgust.

Phineas, partly by coaxing, partly by the exercise of his authority, had removed Jessie from the scene; and, determined to outwit Paola, who was more and more in love with her every day, had glided from the camp, after leaving a message with one of his friends, and had hurried away on horseback to the next station, to convey the intelligence of the approach of a fresh body of elders and disciples.

The execution continued.

It was midday; the sun was hot in the blue and tranquil heavens.

The executioners, after some twenty blows, hit slower. Their arms were tired.

They might have saved themselves all trouble.

Both were utterly insensible to all pain.

Then the two scourgers fell back dead on the sward—shot through the heart by pistols close at hand.

A wild war whoop resounded over the plain, cries of awful vengeance rose on every side, and a perfect torrent of foes came bounding upon the horror-stricken Mormons.

It was a massacre, not a fight. The attackers gave no quarter. The wretched dupes and impostors fought feebly—some, in the confusion, fled behind the waggons, and escaped with difficulty to the hills.

Ere half an hour was over, the camp was in the possession of the assailants. Not a single Mormon man remained alive, save those, not a few in number, who had fled.

The two wretched girls had been taken down, washed, and conveyed to a waggon.

The victors and the women, and children, were alone on the field.

"Where is Jessie?" said Henry, who had been foremost in the fray.

Joanna told him exactly what had happened. He was frantic. Again was he foiled, and always by the vile Phineas Bristowe, the cold-blooded assassin of his father.

But so inured was the brave youth to this constantly recurring series of defeats, that it but drove him to be more desperate in his efforts for her release.

He wished to start in pursuit.

But not one would join him. They were utterly wearied and exhausted. A halt, refreshment, and rest, were absolutely necessary.

Henry yielded a reluctant consent.

The Mormon women, with the exception of those who were mothers, elected to return to the settlements

That day of horror sickened all.

The young women hailed their escape with rapture. The hideous execution even blinded them to the terrible nature of the retribution which had befallen their old companions—in many cases, their own husbands.

But there is no real love on the part of a woman, where she is one of a harem.

Such is the fearful scene known in Mormon history as the first Massacre of the Saints, on the great Illinois trail.

CHAPTER LXXIV.

CAPTAIN COOK.

WHEN dawn broke on that scene, Henry was nowhere to be found. His horse was also absent.

But how was it that they had come up in time to save the wretched girls from a part of their fearful and degrading punishments?

This must now be told.

At no great distance from the Mormon camp, not more than eight or nine miles, flourished an establishment, which, for a long time, was scarcely known beyond its own confines.

Some years before, a youthful trapper, by name Isaac Cook, had discovered, amid those arid and almost barren hills, a fertile valley, which he had hunted for months.

He found rich supplies of furs, and made it for a considerable time his habitation.

He loved the place.

It was well watered, a pellucid stream flowed through it, trees grew on its banks—and Isaac Cook thought that a lovelier situation for a settlement was not to be found on the face of the whole globe.

So he lingered for months, until his mules and horses were heavily laden with spoil.

Then he grew anxious and uneasy. The swarthy sun-burnt face of the trapper became sallow and pale. He did not seem to care about leaving at all. A strange mysterious spell made him hang about the place.

At length, he went away, as it were, reluctantly, with deep sighs and evident regret.

Years passed, and he was seen no more on that green and grassy spot.

At length—twelve years later—he entered the valley, this time accompanied by a large party. There were waggons, horses, cattle—and in one year, a handsome residence rose by the waterside.

Captain Isaac Cook was now married, with six children, two boys and four girls.

His wife had been spared to him.

A dozen huts, inhabited by labourers and their wives, rose within view of the habitation.

The valley began to assume the appearance of an old settlement.

All belonged to Isaac Cook. He had bought it of the state.

Not one of his labourers—English and German—seemed to have the least desire to become owners of the soil.

They were admirably paid, and in hard cash—so that, by a periodical visit to the lower settlements, they were enabled to obtain every comfort, almost every luxury.

The habitation was surrounded by a stockade, while on the solid roof were several ship carronades. They were the best defences against the Indians.

And such defences were necessary.

Captain Isaac Cook, who had made his fortune in a mysterious way, had fitted up his house, without regard to expense.

Carpets, mirrors, chandeliers, astonished the eyes of his visitors.

His daughters, who were taught by a most accomplished mother, had pianos and harps.

The sons painted.

This did not prevent them from being first-rate shots, indefatigable hunters, and bold horsemen.

When the eldest son was twenty-one, his sister was nineteen; then a brother eighteen; then three girls, twelve, fourteen, sixteen.

They were all exceedingly beautiful.

They were the adoration of their father, who was proud, when strangers came that way, to introduce them to their notice.

All went away admiring and wondering at the excessive wealth of Captain Isaac Cook.

Several rumours were afloat. He had discovered a treasure, he had married a fortune.

He had done both.

He had married an admirable wife, and she had brought him money.

This enabled him to carry out his life-long scheme. The valley was his hope and home.

There was a secret with regard to it, which he had confided to no one—except, indeed, his wife.

Ten years of exile was all he asked her to undergo.

Then he would return to the haunts of men, and resign his property to his labourers as tenants.

There were several outhouses fitted up within the stockade. Two of these were entirely devoted to bed rooms for casual travellers, of whom a great many came in search of hospitality.

If they were conversable people, officers, artists, or emigrants, they were invited to dine with the family, and initiated into the mysteries of the music-room.

They were, indeed, gorgeously entertained.

If they were rude drovers and coarse trappers, they were well fed in an appropriate dining-room, and given every accommodation.

All went away pleased, gratified, but wondering why had a man so wealthy secreted himself in that distant and secluded valley, when he could have commanded every comfort and luxury in a state of civilization.

Some whispered of crime.

Every hypothesis was exhausted, except, luckily for him, the right one.

That known, he would have been lost.

Then came, in the guise of a miserable, sneaking, and cold-blooded Mormon, the first dealer of desolation in the valley,

CHAPTER LXXV.

SILAS CRAIG.

SILAS CRAIG was a Mormon elder. He had been on a mission from Joe Smith, the arch-impostor, to his dupes and creatures on the seaboard; and he was returning home with good news for the citizens of Zion.

Money, women, and disciples, were on their way to the people of the only true Church; to the abomination of abominations, the sink of peerless iniquity, Nauvoo.

He was a sleek man. He wore, beneath his ample bear's-skin coat, a suit of black.

His feet were encased in black riding boots, with long black spurs.

He was a rubicund man, whose face told of indulgence in all pleasant vices, which are the vices which kill and brutalize.

Gluttony, drink, lust, were visible in every line of his cold, cruel face.

But, like all the teachers of his odious tribe, he was a hypocrite—he could conceal beneath a paternal smile all his viciousness.

Hypocrisy is the worst and most deadly of evil qualities, for you cannot guard against it.

This man, attracted like the vulture, by the odour of prey, entered the happy valley.

He saw—he coveted—he envied!

He rang at the gate, he sounded the conch; he was received with a hearty welcome.

He had ridden a long distance. A bath and change of raiment restored him.

He needed refreshment. Succulent viands and rich wines were placed before him.

He expressed himself fond of society. He was introduced to the drawing-room of the happy and hospitable Captain Isaac Cook.

The Mormon started. He had never entered such an apartment before, except as a servant. He had been an under butler; but having been taken with too great an affection for the family plate, he had been compelled to expatriate himself to America, where New York yawns to receive the scourings of the earth.

The room was lofty, spacious, and beautifully furnished. A rich carpet covered the floor, pictures hung on the walls, while two pianos and two harps indicated the musical tastes of the numerous inmates.

Mrs. Captain Cook was a handsome, elegant, and intellectual woman, of over forty.

The sons were fine youths.

But the girls—this was the thought on which the Mormon revelled.

They were in form and feature alike, but their hair was here black, there brown, there golden, and in the case of the youngest pure yellow.

They were four handmaidens of Paradise.

As the wretch bowed deeply to the wife and children of his host, the diabolical idea flashed across his mind, that they should all be his.

He was one of the elect, one of the chosen people of the land, and might indulge in his lustful propensities to any extent.

Besides, as the Saints coveted wealth even more than women, surely they would give him these four *houris* as his reward.

He would ask no more.

As he sat there, listening to the music, joining in the conversation, and making himself, by means of his infernal arts, as agreeable as possible, he was devising hideous schemes of destruction for the whole family.

The girls were excessively fascinating, artless, and devoid of guile.

They were glad to welcome a stranger, who brought them news from the settlements, for which they secretly sighed.

And quite naturally, for youth is the season of pleasure.

And what pleasure could young ladies find, suited to their own age, in such a wilderness as that?

They could play, they could fish, they could ride, they could dash over the hills in their pretty riding habits; but then, dear girls, they could'nt flirt, they could'nt go to balls—and they had no sweethearts.

Now, we know very well from the dreadful letters which young ladies write to the cheap periodicals, what foolish things some young girls will do to try and get sweethearts.

Now, these girls—intellectual, pretty, and amiable—were not at all melancholy at the fact that they had not yet found the men of their choice; but still, there can be no doubt that the golden valley would have been considerably enlivened by the presence of any suitable suitors for their hands and fortunes.

A great idea flashed over the mind of Silas Craig, as he gazed at Fanny Cook.

She was the eldest daughter.

He was a very young-looking man of six or seven and thirty. He was, when his bad passions did not disfigure his face, a very handsome man.

Suppose he gave up Mormonism, suppose he abandoned his three wives in Illinois, and laying siege to the heart of this solitary girl, obtain once more a footing in society!

She was highly romantic and very beautiful; she sang exquisitely—she played the same.

THE WILD HORSE

Before he went to bed, Silas Craig had made up his mind.

There was to be a great hunt in the hills the next morning, and availing himself of the host's hearty and hospitable invitation, he agreed to stop and witness it.

All retired at ten. They were a very early house, and Silas was himself shown to a comfortable bed-room on the ground-floor, where he fastened himself in, and, instead of going to bed, seated himself in a chair, to muse on his best course of action.

¶ He would have that girl, by fair means or foul.

First he would try fair means.

Then his vile imagination easily suggested to him how to compass his ends against her desires.

Even if it involved the destruction of the whole family, and the desolation of that beautiful and lovely habitation.

Not even the dependants should be spared.

Suddenly Silas heard suppressed voices, and hastily extinguishing his light, listened. Another light streamed through a little chink

Burning with curiosity, he removed a carpet which lay before his bed, and this exhibited a long crack from the warping of the wood.

Silas kneeled, and applied his eye to the unlucky orifice—unlucky for the host.

He had thus unwittingly betrayed his whole secret.

The habitation was built over the bed of the stream, leaving a kind of cavern beneath.

The river ran over a bed of sand, leaving about six feet on each side of the shore.

But that sand was a stream of gold.

This was the discovery that had made the trapper so loth to leave the valley.

The mountains washed down one steady stream of small golden particles.

A net of steel wire, as fine as gauze, had been placed right across the stream at the lower end.

A net, with meshes big enough to prevent any fish from passing, was at the other end.

Captain Isaac Cook and his two sons were working for gold. They shovelled out the sand, and carried it through troughs, sieves, and every now and then poured handfuls of the pure metal into small casks.

The younger son, every now and then, collected gold from the large net.

The mine was inexhaustible.

The Mormon felt the cold perspiration pouring from his face.

His limbs quivered, and had they not have been busy, they must have heard him.

His eyes almost started from his head. A vision of such mighty wealth almost maddened this lustful lover of voluptuousness and gold.

Now, in his inmost heart, he vowed that he would be heir to all this wealth.

He would be satisfied with *two* girls, with one, if the Mormons would give him a fair share of wealth.

Still, he did not give up all idea of winning Fanny Cook, the eldest daughter, by his cunning and diabolical arts.

That man knew every wile and trick by which to woo and win women.

But let us not, in our indignation against the systematic seducer, altogether absolve the almost equally guilty woman.

There must be error on her part—weakness, if you will—but only when the heart is wholly given to the guilty one.

But half the cases of seduction occur where there is no real love on both sides, but merely fierce animal passion.

We scarcely call these seductions. The fault is mutual.

Women, guard your own honour. If you will not, not all the mothers and duennas in the world can do it for you.

Silas Craig, fearful lest he should, by his agitation, discover himself, replaced the carpet and crept into bed.

But not to sleep—his agitation was by far too excessive.

Gold and girls!

Such is the Mormon cry—and both they will have, by fair means or foul.

CHAPTER LXXVI.

A HUNT.

" Up, up, my merry men !" was the loud cry of Captain Isaac Cook, as, after a hearty breakfast, the sons entered the court, followed by their sisters, all habited in a kind of masculine garb, which much resembled the knickerbocker dress of our children.

They wore jackets, very loose continuations, and gaiters tight from the knee.

To the great surprise of Silas Craig, they rode on horseback like men.

He, however, made no remark, but rode up alongside Fanny Cook.

By starlight they all had their breakfast, by starlight they started for the hunting ground—some three or four miles distant.

Ere the first streak of day had been seen in the East, they had ascended a hill about a third of the distance, and just as night and day seemed contending with about equal power for the supremacy, they were on the hunting grounds.

These grounds consisted of elevated plateaus of various sizes, divided by deep ravines or caverns.

There was a slight fall of snow, which had the effect to render the atmosphere of the mountains cold and uncongenial, and all knew that, in consequence, the deer would descend into the valleys out of the chilling wind, and take their positions on the plateaus, to sun themselves.

This fact had no little influence in deciding them to go upon the hunt in question at the time they did.

Once fairly on the ground, Cook drew his spy-glass, and from a favourable position, surveyed the surrounding country. About a mile off he descried a flock of some eighteen or twenty deer, quietly grazing.

Taking different directions, they separated, so as to approach the deer on four sides. The object and effect of those movements will presently be seen.

Of course great precaution was needed, in order to prevent attracting the attention of the deer by noise or scent.

The dogs accompanied them, and suffice it to say, that they succeeded in taking up their respective positions to their entire satisfaction ; Cook was to give the signal to fire, by blowing his whistle, which always has the effect to make the deer stretch up their necks, and gaze anxiously about them in all directions, affording an excellent opportunity to shoot.

At the proper time he gave a shrill blast, and instantly followed the reports of several guns. There were three deer down, and the fourth wounded, but the rest of the herd, instead of running, stood stupefied and bewildered.

The reports in all directions seemed to leave them no chance to flee ; and, in their fright, they remained as motionless as so many stumps. This gave them time to reload and fire again, each picking his mark as at first. This time two were killed and two wounded.

Still the deer remained motionless, and the third and fourth shots were given with like fatal effect.

Then the rest of the herd made a break for the mountains.

The dogs were let loose on their track, to overhaul and capture the wounded, while the rest of the party proceeded to cut the throats of those left behind ; and, when all brought in, they had twelve as fine fat deer as a hunter's eye ever need rest upon. But to return to Silas Craig.

Silas Craig had kept up with Fanny all the time. She was an excellent horsewoman, and an excellent shot.

But she confined herself to watching the sport. She took no part in it.

Silas had been speaking to her in his sly and insinuating way.

He had given her bright descriptions of life in New York, had spoken of balls and operas, of concerts, of Broadway, and of the every-day life of a woman of fashion.

Poor Fanny was musing.

Silas had a soft and impressive voice, one of the great stocks-in-trade of the hypocrite and imposter.

A loud, stentorian-voiced rogue has not half a chance with your oily one.

Silas said not a word of love, but he described a wedding with great gusto.

In this way, while the others were wrapped in the chase, mounting, dismounting, and riding backwards and forwards, they remained on a lofty hill, gazing all around.

"Why have you left civilized life?" suddenly said Fanny Cook.

"I was weary of it," replied Silas, "and longed with all my soul for a change."

"Indeed!"

"Your beautiful valley has delighted me; but I could not live here."

"Why?"

"Man requires bustle, activity, society. He must be doing ——"

"And woman?"

"Woman is made to adorn and render beautiful all nature, to be the charm of society, the worshipped of all, the glory and heavenly reward of man!"

Fanny smiled.

"You are enthusiastic."

"No."

"You admire the ladies?"

"I adore them!"

"Flatterer!"

"No, on my soul!"

"Ah, Mr. Craig, I know enough of the gentlemen, even up in this savage place, to put little faith in their words."

"Madam!"

"Are you married?" she said, abruptly.

"No."

"How is it that you have remained single, being such an admirer of the sex?"

"Because she died who was to have been my dear companion in life," said Silas, in a soft, hushed, and solemn voice.

Fanny made no reply. The emotion of the accomplished hypocrite awoke a strange feeling in her bosom. But she rebelled against it, for was he not old enough to be her father? —and her own father had strongly protested against any of his daughters marrying anyone much their senior.

The girl made no reply for some time, but appeared thinking deeply.

"You pity me," he said; "I can see that by the lustre of your dark eye."

"I pity all who suffer."

"And I have suffered. 'Tis ten years since she died—she, the heavenly and the good—begging and imploring me to find some other companion for my weary journey in life."

"And you did not obey her?"

"I did not."

"Why?"

"Because it seemed a desecration of her memory."

"There is something in that," said Fanny, riding on towards her friends.

There was a brief pause.

"And yet," resumed Silas, "now that ten years have passed—ten years of mourning and of sorrow—I begin to see my error. Because my early love has gone to those realms above, which we all hope to reach, should I deny myself for ever the joys of home, the glad voices of children, the sweet companionship of children?"

"Well, perhaps not; but here come the hunters—let us join them."

Merrily up came the chase; the labourers, who had come out with horses and light carts, having collected the spoil, which was, as usual, divided between master and servants.

Silas had no opportunity to renew his conversation. Indeed, to prevent any suspicion, he rode with the father and sons, and heard stories of their terrible encounters at times with bears.

They looked upon deer shooting as mere fun.

But bear hunting was serious work, as the beast was savage, and apt to turn and tear both dogs and men.

In this way the time passed rapidly, so that about three o'clock they reached the house, where a copious and succulent meal awaited them, to which all did justice.

After dinner, Captain Isaac Cook, who would not hear of his interesting guest leaving, at least not until the morrow, bade him amuse himself in the garden, while he looked about after his tenants, and dismissed some bales of furs and other things in a waggon for New York.

"Other things," muttered Silas Craig, to himself. "Barrels of gold; he must be awful rich! Well, well! at the worst, he must give his eldest daughter a good portion."

And musing on the best way of inveigling the innocent young girl, whose heart was not a bit touched, though her imagination was excited, he went out into the garden, where a black attendant told him she was.

CHAPTER LXXVII.

FANNY COOK AND THE MORMON.

It is a brilliant and joyous afternoon, when June, the loveliest month of the year, has thrown her mantle of surpassing beauty over hill and dale, tree and shrub—that Fanny Cook is seated upon a rustic seat beneath a lofty oak, whose luxuriant branches, bending gracefully, kiss the rippling surface of a noble stream that runs murmuringly at her feet.

Seldom does the eye rest upon more beautiful scenery than that which surrounds Fanny Cook.

In the background, upon an eminence, and gleaming from amid overshadowing branches of gigantic elms, stands the home of her childhood; across the stream are rich, verdant meadows; fields of grain, fast ripening for the coming harvest; luxuriant groves, and gently sloping hills, with here and there a white farm-house; and beyond is an expanse of living green, stretching to the far-off forest-clad mountains, that lean in calm repose against the western sky.

Not a single cloud casts its dim shadow upon the lovely landscape, and gentle zephyrs are playing amid the luxuriant foliage, making soft music like the rustling of an angel's wing, where here and there a feathered warbler is chanting his song in strains of untaught poetry; and as the fair maiden gazes upon the beautiful scene, listening, meantime, to the sweet, gushing music, her mind is filled with pure and beautiful thoughts.

Fanny Cook was beautiful; purity of thought had left its impress upon her brow, her hair fell in rippling golden ringlets upon an exquisitely-moulded cheek, and her deep-blue eye, ever glowing with an elevated expression, truthfully mirror the changing emotions of her true and gentle heart.

Slowly the sun is descending the western slope, and the lengthening shadows warn the fair maiden that the hours are passing, yet still she lingers. Of what, of whom, is she thinking?

Of no one in particular, but of love much. The stranger had dropped upon her virgin soul the first drop of poison.

Warily, carefully, gently, he had hinted at the joys of love.

She was thinking.

She had a vague idea that to be loved, and to love in return, was very delightful, but that was all—neither of its heartburns, nor its joys, knew she more.

She started, a step was near her, she looked up —it was Silas Craig.

"Your father has sent me to see the garden," he said; "this is an unexpected pleasure."

"The garden is very pleasant."

"'Tis like the garden of Eden."

"Why?"

"Because you are its Eve."

"A very strange sort of Eve!" said the young girl, with a laugh—which did not hide her genuine confusion.

"How so?"

"I don't know—I meant ——"

"Miss Cook," said the Mormon, seating himself beside her, "I am going to be very daring."

"How so?"

"I am going to speak to you, frankly and sincerely."

"What about?"

"This. I came here a sad and thoughtful man. The memory of the past was on me like a pall. I thought that never again should my eyes gaze on woman with thoughts of affection, and of love— but I was mistaken."

Fanny held down her head.

"I saw you, I heard you, I communed with you; and my soul was no longer my own. I love you!"

"Mr. Craig," cried Fanny, "this is very sudden!"

"I ask you not to decide. I am going further up into the country. I will return in a month, and seek your answer."

The girl remained thoughtful.

"And you shall have it," she said, "and you shall have it."

"Thanks."

"I do not really know my own feelings. You have interested me, you have made me, I must confess, discontented with this life, but I cannot say how much further my feelings will lead me."

"I hope and trust ——"

"Hope all," said Fanny, blushing; "I have never seen anyone I like better than you. But I cannot so suddenly decide my whole fate for life."

"My darling girl, I would not have you do it," said the wily Mormon, quite satisfied with the impression he had made.

He took her hand, impressed a kiss on her fingers, and led her to the house.

Next morning early he took his leave of the happy family, but not without leaving a sting behind.

* * * * * * *

In a month he returned, after settling his affairs in Illinois, quite prepared to leave the Mormons, if the fates were propitious.

He found Fanny engaged to be married to her cousin, Augustus Hartford, a dashing young artist, who had carried her heart by storm.

Silas Craig had only opened her thoughts to love—it was Augustus who warmed it into feeling the real true and passionate sentiment.

She blushed when she saw Silas, but that was all.

He did not show his fierce and passionate anger. But when he saw that man seated by his future wife, her hand in his, and now and then his arm round her waist, he grew mad.

He turned away, the demon of hate, disappointed love, and burning revenge, in his heart.

"You bear me no illwill Mr. Craig?" she said, following him to the door.

"No illwill."

"I was a mere child. You opened my eyes. I am now a woman. I regret if I have pained you."

Then she saw on the man's face a demoniac expression, which revealed his real character.

Fanny returned to the drawing room with a step which had lost half its elasticity.

Months again passed away. Fanny was the newly-married wife of Augustus Hartford, who had elected to stay with the family the allotted period of their self-elected exile.

They were very happy.

She adored her husband, and rightly judged how fatal a mistake it would have been to have given herself to one who, in a cunning and insiduous way, had sought to awake mere passion in her pure virgin bosom.

She was herself truly loved by her manly husband, now the companion of her brothers in all their sports, and in all their secrets.

He too worked at the never-ending gold mine.

It was evening. The party was the same as when Silas Craig entered the music-room, save that the husband was present.

They were all in conversation. There had been a bear hunt that day, and all were too tired to think of music.

But they were a happy family, and agreed together marvellously.

The younger sisters adored their elder sister's husband—as they generally do until they get one of their own.

Very pretty; but not always safe, be it known, even though you may not marry your wife's sister.

A law which the proposers do not seem to see strangely flavours of Mormonism.

Suddenly a conch sounded, and after some time, a servant came in, and said that an Indian, in the robes of a chief, desired to pay his respects to the family.

"Alone?" asked Cook.

"Yes, massa—entirely by his self," replied the negro,

"Let him come up."

A few minutes after, Silas Craig, admirably disguised, entered the room, with the haughty step of a warrior. He was gaudily dressed, and painted too, so that Augustus thought it a great treat, and determined to paint his portrait.

The Indian greeted them with a courteous bow, spoke a few words of explanation, said that he had missed his way, his tribe having probably followed a wrong hunting track, and then, by invitation, sat down.

Fanny looked keenly at him, and then at her husband.

She knew him as he entered, she knew his walk, she knew his figure, she knew his eye.

With marvellous courage and coolness, she schooled her countenance to express nothing but serenity, so that the wily ruffian was completely deceived—drank fire-water, smoked a pipe with Cook, and in a half Indian, half English dialect, spoke of big hunts and other incidents of the wild life of the mountains.

Again the conch sounded, and again an Indian entered, this time uninvited.

"Ah, Mastico!" said Cook, heartily. "How is this?—hav'nt seen you for an age."

"All right," laughed the Indian.

The first remained silently smoking, his eye apparently fixed on vacancy.

"Glad to see you, Mastico—sit down—but first let me introduce you to a chief.

"Dog—thief—Mormon—murderer!" yelled Mastico, as he flew at Silas Craig, and pinned him by the throat.

"He lies!"

"I say, him come here—rob, steal Miss Fanny and t'other girl——"

"Are you mad, boy?"

"He speaks the truth, father. This is the man who, as Silas Craig, came here, and while you were hunting, tried to steal away your daughter," said Mrs. Hartford.

"Good Heavens!" said Mrs. Cook.

"The scoundrel!" shouted the captain.

"Wipe him face," said the Indian. "Give me sponge."

Silas Craig was so utterly dumb-founded at the sudden assault of the Indian, that he was unable to speak, so that he was bound, and the paint was washed off his face, before he could say a word.

"And this is the hospitality of Captain Isaac Cook!" he muttered.

"Wretch!" began the irate captain.

"No time talk," said the Indian, "plenty more outside—all ready, take girl and *gold*," added Mastico, significantly.

Captain Isaac Cook started, looked uneasily at Silas Craig, and then drew Mastico on one side.

"Sir," said the gold-finder, after a short time, turning once more in the direction of Silas, "you are a scoundrel and a traitor, and you shall have the punishment of a scoundrel and a traitor."

"And pray what is that?" cried the other, in a blustering tone.

"Death," said the captain, sternly. "Let us retire," he continued, waving to all the females to remain.

Two caught the now pale and trembling Silas by the arm, and dragged him out. He saw that Captain Isaac Cook knew his secret was discovered, and he felt that to keep that a secret, he would be sacrificed.

They led him to the back of the house, where the lights, born by two coloured servants, could not be seen. A kind of court-yard was here surrounded by remarkably-tall palings.

Captain Isaac Cook spoke in a low, distinct, and very firm tone.

"This man came here not long since, foot-sore and weary. I made him welcome. I gave him all my house afforded. I treated him with the courtesy I extend to all travellers who call at my door. In return, he has tried to seduce away my daughter, and to pry into secrets which concern him not. Moreover, he is one of that accursed race of fiends (the Mormons) for whom I never have, and never will have, mercy."

"The people of the true church neither expect mercy nor justice from the Gentiles," said Silas, impudently.

"Silence, wretch! desecrate not the name of the Most High by such abominations. Say, all of you, do you see any just cause why this fellow should not die the death?"

"None."

"Cowards!" yelled Silas, when he heard how general was the outcry against him; "you think you can murder me with impunity. Beware! the valley swarms with my friends—one cry——"

And before anyone could check him, he gave a terrible shriek, which was speedily followed by the blowing of a conch at the stockade entrance.

Freeing himself from his captors, with a furious bound, Silas Craig made for the gate. Several pistol shots were fired after him, but in vain. He was swallowed up in the darkness.

"To the house," roared Captain Isaac Cook, dashing through a back entrance, barring it, and rushing to the front door to do the same—"to the house!"

It was time. The sham Red Indians, who had been admitted by Silas Craig, made a rush at the

portico, but finding no entrance, retreated as quickly as possible into the dark corners of the stockade.

Then upon the still night air came the sound of a large *tocsin*, or alarm bell.

"What's the meaning of this?" said one or two of the Mormons, in an angry whisper. "We were to surprise them without a struggle."

"I was betrayed," replied Silas Craig; "I could not help that—but think, boys, of the reward."

"A 'alter," said a cockney, who having been expelled an excellent society of Methodists, for being too fond of his pretty Sunday school teachers, had turned himself into a Mormon.

"I say, retreat!" added another.

"And I say fight!" cried Silas, barring the door of the stockade. "To seek to fly is useless. In a few minutes the whole valley will be up in arms. One rush, and we are masters of this house—see!" he said, pointing with his rifle.

In a room, faintly lighted by one window, a man was swaying to and fro, as he still pulled quickly at the bell. The echoes could be heard clearly from the distant hills.

As Silas spoke he fired, and a shriek and the falling of a heavy body shewed how true had been his mark. The Mormons, who now thought that they were in for it, began the attack in earnest. If they could secure the house and destroy the inhabitants.

A rush was therefore made once more towards the portico, against which they now began their attack by cutting away the wooden pillars which supported a balcony above. Then using as weapons these very pillars, they began battering down the powerful door.

But it was too thick, so that another mode of proceeding became necessary.

"Fire!" whispered Craig.

And fire was agreed on by all, as least dangerous to themselves, and most likely to compel the others to surrender quite at discretion. Wood was naturally abundant in the yard; which, being piled against the house, would soon have set it on fire.

Then a heavy something fell within the stockade; a light figure might have been seen gliding along and the door was opened.

Henry and his friends, with some dozen of the farm labourers came rushing in, and before the wretched Mormons could ask for mercy, they were to a man cut down, nor did any in that band feel the remotest compunction at thus destroying fellow-creatures.

Were they not Mormons, and in the disguise of their natural enemies, the Indians?

It is a question if, in their own hearts, Americans do not despise and hate the Red Indians as much as they do the black negroes.

Then a huge pile was made, and, to prevent any questions being asked—which was very unlikely in so out-of-the-way a district—the bodies of the marauders were consumed to ashes.

The rescuers were made heartily welcome by Captain Jane Cook, who, the moment he heard the story of the Mormon camp being near at hand, agreed to make one to rescue the unfortunate girls.

"If they had been daughters of mine, I should have expected you to give me a hand. I shall surely not deny you."

So, such a rest as could be snatched being taken, and refreshment freely administered to man and beast, the whole party were once more in the saddle at daybreak.

Their surprise of the Mormon camp, and the terrible resolution of Henry to follow up Phineas alone, is already known to our readers.

CHAPTER LXXVIII.

JOE SMITH AT HOME.

JOE SMITH, who had ever an eye to the main chance, certainly took care to select for his dupes and disciples places which were likely to be attractive and productive.

Mormonism, in its leading features, is lust and avarice. Women and money is the one want of its hierarchy.

But properly to get the dupes and workers of the hive into order, it was necessary to give them something for their money. Hence, Joe Smith, arch-impostor and priest, selected a spot for the habitation of the Saints, which flowed, as he himself, with milk and honey.

The Mormons were not, however, as yet collected together as one people. They were feeling their way; they were tracing the effect of their imposture on the minds of the weak and silly, on boys with large imaginations, and women with a natural tendency to be gulled by any religious pretence.

We trust and hope that women are the chief congregations of Spurgeons and Bellews.

The Mormons, however, despite their astuteness, could not keep themselves sufficiently to themselves. They roamed upon other people's ground, they marauded on rather too extensive a scale.

The first real Mormon village on the road to Nauvoo, was Smithville, which, being situated in a small valley a little to the left of the road, was not much visited by strangers. Its population was about two hundred—very industrious, cultivating the soil, and living by that and the product of the chase.

To the eye it seemed the abode of patriarchal happiness.

But it was a sink of social and moral iniquity.

Each man, as a rule, had three wives, and, as always is the case where polygamy prevails, women were pretty well in common. That this is not the case to any large extent in Turkey, is explained by the fact of their being under lock and key.

A mumbling, shuffling, greasy set of impostors, hypocrites, and knaves, were these same Mormon elders. They were not industrious. Hard work was left for the dupes and women, while the deacons, agents, and others, went about preaching, or prowling for fresh victims for their lust.

The houses of the village were scattered here and there, and in all cases were surrounded by neat gardens. In the background was a forest, behind which were vast—as yet uncultivated—plains, where the buffalo and wild h--- ---mustangs, roamed at will.

A party of young men had been out, and having lassoed three of these beautiful animals, had brought them in, and placed them in a kind of carrol or pound.

Phineas Bristowe was taking Jessie to this village, hoping that its peace and quietness might tempt her to forget a portion of the past, and to live a brief life of retirement, while he matured his plans.

He was willing to restore Jessie to her friends, if he was pardoned for the past, and well rewarded besides.

It is quite true that he was fond of Jessie, and would not, if possible, have had her injured.

But he loved himself most.

His second scheme was stupendous. The marvellous and exquisite beauty of Jessie almost excused the man in his belief. He hoped, once Jessie was surrounded by the influence of educated and cunning women, the aids of the chiefs in their imposture, she too might be converted.

He was about to tempt her with a crown.

In his wild and fertile brain he planned an empire above that of Joe Smith. The impostor was still to be the high priestess; but she would be empress of that mysterious centre of America, to which already the sons of Mormons looked with hope.

Jessie was herself, stunned, horrified, scarcely able to realize to herself all that she had seen, and beginning almost to doubt the justice of Heaven.

Away over savage hills, along dreary plains, avoiding, until very near the village of Smithville, all approach to the beaten road, they dashed for hours.

At length, however, the desired goal is reached, and below them in the valley is the peaceful village.

At this moment, turning a rock about a quarter of a mile in their rear, comes a horseman galloping wildly after them. He wears the dress of an Indian, but Phineas knows him.

On he dashes, descending a path, which should have been ventured on cautiously, with reckless speed.

Henry urges his horse to the utmost.

But Phineas is a-head of him, and Jessie, blinded by tears and sorrow, neither sees nor hears anything.

Several men began to come out from the houses, while several lounged round a rude kind of inn, kept in case Gentiles came that way.

"What cheer?" cried several, as Phineas rode up.

"The Saints have been attacked," replied Phineas. "I know not the result as yet. Charged with important dispatches, I have hurried on. My mission is with the prophet."

"Who comes?" said one, pointing to Henry.

"A bitter enemy. Take the girl in."

Scarcely had Jessie been led into the house, than Henry came dashing up. Behind him, descending the mountain pathway, could be seen two other horsemen.

Henry pulled in, and, going straight up to Phineas, laid his whip impressively on his shoulder.

"Murderer of my father, brutal ravisher, assassin, and thief; I arrest you in the name of the law. Where is Jessie?"

"Jessie who?" said Phineas, with a wink at the bystanders.

They laughed.

Henry looked keenly round. He had fancied that he had fallen on the settlement of quiet and respectable emigrants.

The lowering brow of the men, and the total absence of women, indicated his mistake.

Before he could say another word, several men flew to his horse's head, while others pulled him off the animal. Despite his protestations and threats, he was thrust into a small, dark, and secure room.

The other two horsemen were now at no great distance.

"Bad news," cried Phineas, "brothers Allen and Briggs."

A dead silence prevailed; a fearful dread came upon their souls. The caravan on its way up was one of the richest for many a long day—rich in wealth, in dupes, in women.

"What news?" gasped Phineas.

"All is lost," cried Briggs; "we are all that remain. The Saints have been foully murdered, women, children, and cattle taken away as prizes by the Gentiles."

"All!" gasped Phineas.

Another horseman was now seen in the distance. Phineas Bristowe, who had recognized him, gave a deep sigh. It was Paolo, Viscount de Florac, whom he believed to be dead with the others.

CHAPTER LXXIX.

THE NEW MAZEPPA.

A CONFERENCE was held on the arrival of Paolo, in which Henry was pointed out as one of the most ruthless and bitter of their persecutors. He it was who had hounded on this last dreadful attack.

The Mormons were beside themselves. They forgot the fearful provocation received by the inhabitants of the country they traversed.

They resolved, as there was open warfare, to do a deed that should startle, if not annihilate their enemies with terror.

They would make an example of Henry.

Paolo it was who proposed the fiendish and horrible plan.

Henry was dragged forth amid a storm of hooting and execrations. Two powerful men held him so that he could not move.

Then four youths, having secured the most powerful of the three mustangs, dragged him forth hoppled and secured by a muzzle.

A rude saddle was fastened round the kicking beast, so as to secure Henry the more easily.

"Inhuman wretches!" he cried, in a passionate voice. "What are you about to do?"

"To avenge our slaughtered brethren, and to teach the Gentiles a lesson they will never forget."

"Unhand me, barbarians, and hear me. I am rich, I am in my own country powerful. Give me back her in pursuit of whom only have I sought this country, and I will well reward——"

"Lies! falsehoods! Away with him!" shouted Phineas and Paolo, who saw some of the cunning and more grasping Mormons listening attentively.

"Lies!" re-echoed the younger members of the tribe, luxuriating in their promised treat.

At this moment Jessie rushed forth from the inn, and casting herself fainting on the breast of Henry—

"My own, my life, my husband!" she said.

"My darling——"

But Phineas and Paolo next instant tore them asunder, and, ere they could exchange another word, Henry was bound, his clothes almost torn off his back, upon the startled and mettlesome horse.

He was secured by waist, hands, and ancles, so that release himself he could not.

"Then, with a yell, and the cracking of whips, the affrighted animal was driven up the gully, the way that Henry had come. The frightened animal, furious at his burden, dashed away at full speed, amid loud laughter, cries, and shrieks.

No sooner, however, was their victim out of sight, than they began to think. Directly reason resumed its sway, they knew that they had done a deed which would rouse the whole country on them. There was no retreat, no escape, except in instant flight.

They would go to swell the army of the Prophet himself, and thus escape the fearful vengeance of the Gentiles.

CHAPTER LXXX.

THE ESCAPE.

CAPTAIN DE LANCY, and the rest of the party, followed in the track of Henry as rapidly as their own weariness and the fatigue of their animals would admit; but had not proceeded far before they were compelled to come to a sudden halt. They were completely worn out, and would have proved but poor adversaries to any of the Mormons who might have crossed their path.

Prudence, after all, suggested that they should not meet men with their senses and muscles all fresh, while they were really helpless.

So they camped on the edge of a stream, hoppled their horses, and eagerly stretched themselves beneath some willows that skirted the water, in search of that repose they so much needed.

All slept soundly. They were fearfully fatigued. Even the brain had been too much strained.

At length, however, the first heavy sleep was over, and then one or two awoke for a few minutes, turned, and prepared again to seek repose in slumber.

But a shrill cry, followed by low moaning, caught the attention of several.

They started to their feet, awaking as they did so the whole camp. A large fire had been made as a matter of course. Several handfuls of wood were cast on it. one or two resinous boughs held on high, and then the whole camp saw a horse kneeling exhausted on the ground.

It had fallen and broken a leg.

But on its back was a human being in a swoon, or dead.

"My dear boy!" shouted Captain de Lancy, rushing forward.

A dozen knives were drawn, the cords cut, and the insensible youth carried beside the fire.

Though much cut and bruised, he was still not injured in any vital part. But even with a copious application of brandy, it was very difficult to bring him to.

It was several hours ere his thoughts were sufficiently collected to relate what had happened.

Of his ride he knew nothing. He had remained all the time in a state of apathetic stupor.

The fall of the horse had, in all probability, saved him from madness.

They forcibly put him to bed, put heavy blankets round him, and gave him warm drinks.

Captain de Lancy added a soporific to his brandy.

He knew the other wanted sleep.

CHAPTER LXXXI.

NAUVOO.

BUT we must precede them in their pursuit of the Mormons.

Joe Smith was in full retreat on Nauvoo.

He dreaded the vengeance that had been roused, but he did not relax in his wickedness. He still employed his emissaries to search out and find all the women who could be duped.

Joe Smith was now in the height of his power. He was worshipped on all hands by his dupes, male and female.

He is thus described by one who went on a pilgrimage to see him:—

"The Prophet was now sixty years of age. He did not look more than forty-five. I had expected to see a venerable-looking old man; scarcely a grey thread appears in his hair, which is parted on the side, light-coloured, rather thick, and reaches below the ears with a half curl. He formerly wore it long. The forehead is somewhat narrow, the eyebrows thin, the eyes between gray and blue, with a calm, composed, and somewhat reserved expression. A slight droop in the left lid made me think he had suffered from paralysis. I afterwards heard that the ptosis is the result of a neuralgia, which has for some time tormented him. For this reason he covers his head, except when he gives audience, or at tabernacle. The nose, which is sharp and somewhat fine-pointed, is bent to the left; the lips close, like the New Englanders; the teeth, especially of the under-jaw, imperfect. The cheeks are fleshy, the chin somewhat peaked, and the face clean shaven, except under the jaws, where the beard is allowed to grow. The figure is somewhat large, broad-shouldered, and stooping when standing. His dress, all gray homespun, save cravat and waist-coat, was neat, and plain as a Quaker's. His coat

JESSIE IN NAUVOO.

and pantaloons baggy, of antique cut, buttons black. A necktie, of black silk with a large bow, was loosely tied round a starchless collar, which turned down of its own accord. The waistcoat of black satin, buttoned nearly to the neck, a plain gold chain was passed into the pocket. His boots were Wellingtons of American make. He is a well-preserved man, in fact, which is by some attributed to his habit of sleeping in solitude. He impresses a stranger with a certain sense of power; with his people his word is law. His manners are calm and cold; in fact, like his face, somewhat bloodless."

In this garb he sat in front of a small house at some distance from the city of Nauvoo, two mornings after the barbarous attempt on the life of Henry.

His women were scattered over the plain, the hillside and the forest, as much to conceal the fact of polygamy from others as to keep them apart.

A large harem of English women is simply impossible.

One or two might agree together, but not many.

Dreadful and terrible tragedies would be the immediate and certain consequence.

A late traveller, one just returned from Utah,

gives us some unwilling insight into the secrets of the prison-house.

What would a Christian traveller, with respect for truth and morals, have said?

Let us hear for a moment the latest arrival, Captain Burton, whose great fault seems that, being tired of all creeds, and quite ready to accept that nearest at hand, he should tell us that three-fourths of the world are polygamists, and evidently likes the institution. He has not told us that the polygamists are the basest and least humanised of all, and we quarrel with his assertions. Be it as it may, polygamy is the one subject of discussion at Utah, and many women are so subdued that they absolutely defend it. Emma, the wife of Joe Smith, never would submit to it, although Joe pretended to revelations. After his death she married a Gentile, and was formally cut off from the Saints. M. Remy and others found the women miserable, low, dull, and with the look of a beaten dog. The man becomes a Pope, the woman his slave. Hitherto the female sex is not denied education, but the time will come when polygamy will bear its results, and from being the helpmeet of man, woman will sink to his serf. Brigham Young has from fifteen to sixty wives: travellers' tales vary. Certainly he has very many. There are many ways of marrying a woman spiritually, and " sealing" and marrying for the dead ; but all ways meet in the common centre of a common passion, and cannot be discussed here. One thing is certain, there is no love there. Romantic young women may be here assured that in Mormondom, love, " that choice egotism of the heart," says Burton, is destroyed. There can be no tender tie where one, two, three, or fifty may share it. The first wife is always the head of the flock,—the sultana, no more. Brigham Young ridicules a man's love for his wife ; would act of his own accord only. Petticoat government is unknown.

The children take their mother's name before that of their father—thus, " had I married three ladies," says our author, " my child by Miss Jones would be Jones Burton ; by Miss Brown, Brown Burton ; by Miss Smith, Smith Burton ; and so on,—and are generally disagreeable, untaught, and carelessly bred. In this they perhaps do not differ much from the children of most colonists, especially of the Americans. A Mrs. Belinda Pratt has written a long letter in favour of polygamy. It is feeble and inconclusive. It would be better, if we must eliminate religion, to appeal to physiologists, such as M. Quatrefages, who, in his recent book on the unity of mankind, shows that polygamy is contrary to nature, and greatly arrests population. Paley had long ago perceived this, and stated it ; but Burton's Eastern experience gives him a bias in favour of it.

But we have left the Prophet too long.

Joe Smith, with that affectation of patriarchal manners which went so far with his dupes, sat in a large arm-chair, as if ready to hold a bed of justice.

His glance, from beneath his small, neat, white portico, was cast over the distant plains and hills. A telescope was by his side, which he continually used to watch the road which led towards Nauvoo.*

He was always, in this way, pretending to look out for the caravans that were advancing.

He often pretended to see the caravans arriving long before they did.

On this morning he was surrounded by several of his elders.

They were in solemn conclave.

A little way off were some rowdyish youths, rough and ready, with bright-hilted pistols, buckskin breeches, red-flannel shirts, half Indian, half alligator, with bowie-knives stuck in dandy sashes. These were the *jeunesse dorée* of the happy valley. Discharged soldiers, heavy mechanics, agricultural labourers, a few German students, farmers, and labourers, peasants from Scandinavia and Sweden, correspondents and editors, rogues, vagabonds, unsuccessful men—a very motley crew—filled up the rear.

Degraded, lost men, or weak and silly youths.

No news had arrived of the rich caravan which had been so long expected in Nauvoo.

Joe Smith was alarmed and impatient.

He had made up his mind to put Jessie at the head of his wives

Was she not the most beautiful creature he had ever seen?

Was any one of his wives to be compared to her?

" What can be the matter with the caravan?" said one of the elders ; Pope Smith, not having spoken for some time.

" Lazy, idle," said Joe, gravely.

" What comes?" cried one of the elders, ere his companions replied.

It was a courier, travelling full speed towards the Prophet's house.

" Hail, to the Great Prophet!" he cried, leaping to his feet; " the caravan has been massacred, the women and children taken into captivity, while the peaceful dwellers in Creek Valley are hurrying hither for protection."

Joe, Rigden, and several of the chiefs, started to their feet in deadly alarm.

If the Gentiles were beginning to deal thus with scattered parties of the Mormons, what was the larger settlement to expect?

Joe Smith was as pale as a sheet. He was never a brave man. Such impostors never are, unless they are also lunatics.

He thought deeply for one moment.

Was he defining the shape of that dread tragedy, which was soon to come, and which, by its unfor-

---

* Let the Mormon reflect on what he has to endure; at him reach St. Joseph, beyond all settlements, a difficult job just now. He will then have to join a wagon-caravan, and to journey for some twenty-three days, of forty-five acres, over prairie, swamp, stream, and waterless desert, or one thousand one hundred and thirty-six miles. Hunger, thirst, cold, rheumatism, many diseases, and every annoyance and privation, are found in this journey. The skeletons of teams of cattle, broken wheels and waggons, mark the road; and here and there a little hillock by the side shows where a poor deluded fool has fallen and died in his journey from Doubting Castle to the domains of Giant Pope Brigham. The pilgrim's progress is indeed full of doubt and misery, which, it is said, slay the young and the old in great numbers, the middle-aged and strong alone escaping.

tunate conclusion, did so much to advance the cause of Mormonism?

After a short pause, the Prophet summoned two or three of his chief supporters to enter the house with him, and there hold a conference.

Instead of thinking even of giving up his horrible and nefarious doctrines, his only idea was how to defeat and destroy his enemies.

In the course of that day the expatriated Mormons came up, making themselves out to be martyrs of the true church.

Their hypocrisy was fearful.

They spoke of themselves as of the new race of Israel.

No Tartuffe ever equalled the black and blasphemous deceit of this people.

These visionary and morally destitute rogues, formed the nucleus of the future new people. They called themselves Saints, they named their church, with an infinite impudence, the Church of the Latter-day Saints of Jesus Christ.

This alone disgusted the quiet and really religious settlers.

They were nothing but a desperate crew, panting for the New Jerusalem, and the wild license which they there hoped to meet.

It was late in the evening when Jessie and Phineas Bristowe reached the confines of Nauvoo.

CHAPTER LXXXII.

JESSIE IN NAUVOO,

JESSIE in Nauvoo! After all her trials, hairbreadth escapes, and hopes of being rejoined by Henry, she was now in the stronghold of Mormonism. How could she hope to escape?

Phineas Bristowe brought a letter of introduction to elder Kimble, one of the greatest arch-imposters of the whole tribe.

He, like Joe Smith and Young, made use of his high position with the dupes to trade upon their delusions.

His house was surrounded by an orchard, and large garden. This was encircled with a paling.

A portico admitted them to a large hall.

The house was two stories high.

To the right was a narrow staircase leading to the upper part of the house, wholly occupied by the women and children. We shall see, particularly when we reach Great Salt Lake, or Deseret, that the life of the Mormon women is precisely that of the Eastern harem,

The first wife may live with her husband and be treated as a wife; but the others are mere odalisques.

The back of the house extended a long way, with long walls facing east and west.

It was double storied, with the lower windows, which were barred, oblong; the upper were narrow, and shaded by a small acute ogive or gable over each. The colour of the building was a yellowish-white, which contrasted well with the green blinds.

Each odalisque had a separate bed-room, sitting-room, and closet.

But no Mormon woman was ever seen, no Mormon woman's voice ever heard.

Such is the life to which the sex is doomed by law and the prophet.

And yet we are told that English women, delicately-nurtured children of this land, approve and uphold the great imposture.

We shall see.

Jessie was taken to one of these apartments. She found it neat and comfortable. Everything was there calculated to satisfy mere material wants.

Wearied and exhausted, Jessie sought her couch, nor did anything happen that night to alarm or disturb her. Her terrible trials had made a bed indeed a comfort and consolation for once.

When she awoke and dressed, it was long since dawn, and scarcely had she dressed herself when a negress brought a tray into the sitting-room, with breakfast. There was none of the sociability of English life. How could there be? A man would find it difficult to get through his breakfast comfortably with two wives, much less a dozen.

Breakfast over, the negress asked if she would like a walk in the garden, as Phineas Bristowe was engaged, and could not see her until the evening.

As this appeared rather a command than a request, Jessie descended to the garden.

It was an extensive piece of ground, with fruit trees, ornamental trees, and flowers.

A number of children hung about, filthy, miserable, and disorderly.

They stared at Jessie as if she had been some new and singular wild beast.

What could be expected from children brought up in a harem, the true source of the degradation and low position of the Turks?

But it is when older that the Mormon youth becomes insufferable.

Every visitor gives one account. We are told that if they out-talk their fathers, out-wit their companions, whip their school teachers, out-curse a Gentile, they are thought to be promising greatness, and are praised accordingly. Every visitor to Salt Lake will recognize the portrait, for every visitor proclaims them to be the most whisky-loving, tobacco-chewing, saucy, precocious children, he ever saw—even on the continent of America, where all are precocious.

The women scarcely raised their eyes to gaze at her for awhile. Whatever their original beauty or ugliness, they were all gaunt and sallow now.

All were knitting or sewing during the hours of recreation, after which they would go to work, polygamy being a self-supporting institution.

All wore what is called a cottage or sun bonnet, with a long thick veil behind, which acted like a cape or shawl.

A loose jacket or petticoat, of coarse calico, completed their attire.

Jessie passed through them with downcast eyes, and sought a retired spot, near the very extremity of the garden. Here she had hoped to be able to gaze about her, but the wooden palings were too high. No indiscreet glances were permitted into an elder's habitation.

Not a man was anywhere visible.

Jessie seated herself on a bench at the foot of a tree, and gave way to deep thought.

Was there any escape now? She was so wholly in the power of the Mormons, that if Henry even penetrated to Nauvoo, he could not find her out. Even if he did trace her, and invoked the law, they would murder, rather than give her up.

Utter disrespect for human life, is one characteristic of the Mormons.

While Jessie thus sat in deep thought, she heard a sigh—a deep, heavily-drawn sigh, of utter despair.

She started, looked round, and saw, sitting close to her under the deep shadow of a bush, a young girl.

"Are you ill?" said Jessie, in her own soft, gentle, and winning voice.

"Not ill," replied the other, a beautiful brunette of seventeen, "but mad."

Jessie started, and would have drawn nearer.

"Do not move. If we are seen to speak, we shall be separated. Are you, too, a victim?"

"I am a prisoner."

"Then shall I meet with sympathy."

"Have you been here long—and who are all these women?"

"They are the wives of Elder Kimble. I have not been here long; but if I do not escape to-night, I shall be lost—lost for ever."

She looked keenly around, and then again addressed Jessie, sinking her voice in such a way as to be scarcely heard.

"If you are a victim—if you are opposed to this dreadful and odious system—let us act together, and we may escape."

"That is my dearest wish," replied Jessie.

"Are you," said the girl, with a bitter curl of the lip, "honoured by the preference of the same man who has kidnapped me from my home?"

"To whom do you allude?"

"To this Kimble."

"I know nothing. I am prisioner in the hands of one whose intentions I cannot fathom; but this I do know—death shall be my lot, ere I will submit to the loathsome union with any of these wretches."

"Death! death!" said the girl, "is very dreadful—but such life equally so. Look at those women. Do not believe that I came of my own accord here, but certainly the picture they painted of this place, did tempt me awhile; but now I know, now I see, my horror is great. All yonder women have children—hence do they cling, even to the semblance of marriage. But what a marriage! Love, or the semblance of it, for a few days, and then desertion and neglect. Some of these women have not seen their husband for months, while he has never seen some of his children. And this is called marriage!"

"How came you here?" asked Jessie, to turn the conversation.

"How came I here? You shall know if you will but listen. They are all going into work now. We are as yet free—but who comes yonder?"

"My guardian," said Jessie, with a shudder.

It was, indeed, Phineas Bristowe, but simply as bearer of a message to Jessie, that in the evening her presence and that of the other young lady was required at a dance given at the house of the Prophet.

Jessie bowed low, but made no reply.

"To-morrow there is to be a review of the Nauvoo legion," he continued; "a riding-habit will be provided for you. You will accompany the general."

And to avoid further explanations, he went away.

CHAPTER LXXXIII.

JESSIE AND SOPHIA.

SOPHIA'S story was a long one, but a brief outline will suffice for our purpose.

Her father and herself had emigrated from England some years before, and had brought with them an aunt, who was, however, not much older than herself.

Sophia was nineteen, Jemima twenty-six, and at the outset they were like two sisters.

The farmer in Illinois is generally successful, and John Purkiss was particularly so, and nothing could exceed his contentment and happiness.

He had been a widower from the birth of his daughter, and the only reason he had not married was, because he was too poor.

When, however, he left England, he left behind him a comely maiden of thirty, who agreed to share his fortunes whenever he could afford to come and fetch her.

Now, a near neighbour of John Purkiss was one Edward Merton, who combined in his person the farmer and the doctor, a not uncommon, and very wise conjunction in America.

Population is of rapid growth, but while waiting for population the doctor does not starve.

Edward Merton was a constant visitor, and soon made himself agreeable to both ladies; he was, moreover, a great favourite with John, with whom he smoked a pipe, and played backgammon of an evening.

Both Sophia and Jemima were very attentive to the young doctor, as ladies usually are to handsome members of that profession. He was exceedingly grateful for their attentions, but showed no peculiar partiality for either.

This lasted some time, when suddenly they became aware of a change.

John had suddenly made up his mind to go to England. He had heard of a small legacy, quite enough to pay his passage there and back, while it would enable him to marry comfortably. He publicly announced his intention, which all seemed to approve.

But Jemima, who had hitherto been mistress in the house, did not much approve of yielding up her authority.

She made up her mind, therefore, to sound the doctor. This sudden freak, as she called it, of her brother had decided her. She would marry, and thus end the question of supremacy.

Now, Jemima Purkiss had no more doubt that Dr. Edward Merton came to the farm on her account, than she had of her existence. She even admired his modesty in not venturing to declare himself without encouragement. But now this state of things could be allowed to exist no longer.

John was in conference with his daughter, who knew and esteemed her father's future wife—in that usual walk of the American farmer, his apple orchard—when Dr. Edward Merton made a morning call.

Jemima was all alone, occupied in some domestic way. She was a fine woman, very fair, and with a considerable amount of cleverness. Her passions were extremely violent, but this she as yet scarcely knew herself.

But here was too good an opportunity to be lost. Still there was a difficulty to be got over—how to pop the question.

But female ingenuity is something marvellous. When the dear creatures have made up their minds, they never fail—where there is a will, there is a way.

She hit upon an ingenious but an odd plan.

After some conversation upon indifferent subjects, Jemima had an opportunity.

"And where's my friend Purkiss, and Miss Sophia?"

"In the orchard. They are doubtless talking about the new ma'am."

"When does Mr. Purkiss start?"

"In four days. He expects to be away three months. It will be a great change for Sophia—"

"In what way, miss?"

"Hem—Sophia has been used to consider this her home—a new wife will make a change."

"True," mused the doctor; "she will not be quite so happy."

"Other people too may feel it. It's hard to have a happy and comfortable home, where you do as you like, and then to be under rule again."

"True," said the doctor.

"What do you think had best be done?" continued Jemima, with a side-long glance at the doctor, who was gazing down at his boots.

"Well you see, miss—I've been rather thinking about this matter," began the doctor, "and I thought just at the first, until you saw how things went, that a change might be desirable for both you and Miss Sophia."

"You are very kind," stammered the lady, with a roseate blush.

"So last night, I and Miss Sophia concluded to ask you——"

She turned slowly round. He was still looking on the ground.

"As we mean to be married as soon as her father comes home—if you would come and stay with us," he added, "for awhile, you know—just as long as it suited."

Oh! had he looked up, had he seen that ashen face, had he gazed upon those quivering lips, and seen the fierce, the awful agony on that face, he might have been warned,

But before he did so, with the wondrous power over their feelings possessed by almost every woman, she had calmed herself.

"This is sudden," she said, quietly.

"Well, her father's determination was sudden."

"Does he know it?"

"Well—I expect Sophia is telling him ——"

He had no time to add anything, for at that moment Mr. Purkiss came in hurriedly, and caught his friend by the hand.

"My dear fellow," he said, shaking hands heartily with him, "I am delighted, I'm only sorry the two weddings cannot be together—but I'll be back as quick as possible. Sophia, you sly puss, let us have lunch, and bring out the cherry-brandy; we'll drink the young people's health, old woman, eh!"

And in his jolly way, he slapped his sister on the shoulder.

She looked at him with an affected laugh, which concealed the rage and despair of a wounded heart.

And then she went out on some trivial pretence, and when she came in looked calm and collected, and was even cheerful. But behind those sparkling orbs of blue was all the fury of a woman scorned.

Jemima glanced at the happy couple from underneath her eyebrows,

"With an eye
Whose dark keen glance had power to wake
Both fear and love—to awe and charm;
'Twas as the wizard rattlesnake,
Whose evil glances lure to harm,
Whose cold, and small, and glittering eye,
And brilliant coil and changing dye,
Draw, step by step, the gazer near
With drooping wing and cry of fear,
Yet powerless all to turn away;
A conscious but a willing prey!"

CHAPTER LXXXIV.

A SNAKE IN THE GRASS.

JEMIMA loved Edward Merton. Arrived at maturity without her heart having once beat, she now had cast out the whole force of her affections on this man. Where now should she rest her wounded wing, where lay her bleeding heart?

During the days that preceded the departure of John Purkiss she was able to collect her thoughts, and prepare for the long-continued struggle which was to endure for three months.

What was her end and aim? To break off the match, even though she derived no advantage from it herself. But sweet is revenge to the heart of the ill-regulated.

Sweeter to none more than to an outraged woman.

She could not exactly say what would be the device she would hit on; but endure the sight of their happiness, she could not and would not.

Some of those who suffer from disappointments of this kind turn to religion, not to sour, repining, and groaning piety, but to the genuine consolations of true religion, which are never sought in vain.

Now, it happened that in the walks which Jemima constantly took alone, under pretence of visiting neighbours, she fell in with one of the wolves in sheep's clothing, who went about collecting recruits for their selfish purposes — a Mormon elder.

He was a good-looking, sleek man, of about thirty-five years of age. He had all the nasal twang and hypocrisy of his sect.

He was one of those described by Higbee, an ex-Mormon, "who stated his personal knowledge of the Mormons from their earliest history, throughout their hellish career in Missouri, which had been characterized by the darkest and most diabolical deeds which had ever disgraced humanity."

It was Kimble.

He at once marked Jemima for his own. He saw that she was a fine showy woman, with great personal attractions—what more did he want? Intellect, temper, good disposition, are of little consequence with one who has only to be the companion of a few occasional hours.

Of course he did not reveal himself at first. That was never the plan of the Mormons.

He, however, soon allowed it to be seen that he was a minister. He quoted Scripture, which every Mormon does, more or less glibly. But it was not long before Jemima discovered his true character.

Then a feeling of horrid joy spread through her frame.

They soon came to an understanding, and Jemima Purkiss agreed to become one of his wives, if he assisted her in destroying the happiness of Edward Merton and Sophia.

Kimble, who had caught one glimpse of the niece, turned away to hide a horrid smile.

The infatuation of the woman almost made him laugh. In order to be revenged on one who had unknowingly slighted her, she would throw a rival into his arms.

Kimble was introduced to the family home as a minister from the old country in search of a flock, and who, in the meantime, would try and locate himself in the neighbourhood, on some small plot of land.

He was received hospitably by Sophia, with some vague suspicion by Edward Merton.

A fortnight later, the happy home of the absent John Purkiss was entered by Indians, and having been pillaged, the two women were carried off.

But no one believed in Indians. This *ruse* was a common trick of the Mormons, who thus mischievously and wickedly increased the hatred of the Americans for the Redskins.

Edward Merton, among others, did not believe in the rapt by Indians; he at once hit upon the Mormons, and made up his mind to devote his life to the extermination of their race.

It was such deeds as these made the citizens of Warsaw, in meeting assembled, pass the following resolution.

"*We hold ourselves at all times in readiness to exterminate, utterly exterminate, the wicked and abominable Mormon leaders, the authors of our troubles.*"

Such was the story of Sophia Purkiss, with an allusion to the exact state of things.

Such outrages had been daily perpetrated, but one final and monstrous deed was required ere the public indignation was roused to the full pitch of rage and fury.

This we shall now have an opportunity of describing.

CHAPTER LXXXV.

A MORMON EVENING PARTY.

The house of the Prophet was extensive, a whole wing being devoted to a long and wide reception-room, supported by pillars, in which he gave his receptions.

The Mormons are inordinately fond of dancing. It is their great pleasure.

Dancing seems, indeed, to be an edifying exercise. The Prophet dances, the apostles dance, the bishops dance.

While any number of a learned profession might starve in Zion, a dancing-master would surely thrive.

None of your fashionable languid style for them. All is elaborate, with severe muscular exercise.

About four o'clock, Jessie and Sophia were escorted to the ball by several more elderly dames, amongst whom Jessie saw for the first time the scowling, haggard and wretched face of Jemima.

Already had the iron entered her soul, already did she begin to know what Mormonism meant.

None but elders and specially-trusted neophytes were admitted.

New arrivals soon find out how little they are trusted.

The elders brought with them, not only their Rachels, but their several Leahs, Zilphats, and Billahs.

There were six women to one man.

Jessie and Sophia were unquestionably the best-looking of the whole party, and many eyes were cast at them, especially among the neophytes.

About half an hour after their entrance, the Prophet entered amid profound silence. He at once ascended a raised platform, followed by some ten of his wives.

He then raised his hands, invoked a blessing, and descending from the platform, advanced straight up to Jessie.

She did not dare to resist.

Phineas had earnestly warned her to be cautious in her proceedings.

The Prophet, old fool as he was, insisted on her leading off the first cotillion with him, which Jessie, despite her disgust, did, with a grace and ease which defies description.

Then, having evidently attained his object, he led her to the supper table, where, amid the scowling looks, the covert sneers, and the affected smiles of some of his wives, he placed her at his right hand.

The repast was of the most substantial kind, including bear, elk, turkey, salmon, beavers, tarts, and other strange delicacies.

No sooner was the supper devoured, which it was with much alacrity, then all flew to dancing again.

Jessie and Sophia were left together. One or two important personages had arrived suddenly, and taken away the Prophet.

Some alarming news was afloat. The faces of the elders were unusually elongated. They were evidently in a state of great apprehension.

The Prophet turned pale as they whispered in his ear the news.

But the ball continued with unabated vigour ; songs and duets being sung between.

At five in the morning the company broke up, after thirteen successive mortal hours of dancing.

CHAPTER LXXXVI.

THE REVIEW.

JESSIE and Sophia slept until late. Though they had not joined much in the festivities, they were wearied and exhausted.

About twelve, however, they rose, breakfasted, and were instantly summoned to attend the President and Prophet.

Riding habits, hats and feathers, were provided for them ; and as they were prisoners, and resistance would have been simply useless, they tried to make the best of it.

It was a lovely morning, and soon the enlivening sound of fife and drum indicated the gathering of the Saints.

General Joseph Smith, little dreaming how he was hastening the great Carthage Tragedy, was about to review the Nauvoo legion.

When Jessie, who looked pale, but lovely as usual, in her riding habit and hat and feathers, came forth, she found herself one of a large and picturesque party of ladies.

They were all young and tolerably good-looking ; the *elite* of the whole Mormon body.

Jessie gazed with surprise and something like disgust at the whole party ; but reflecting by what insiduous means, by what arts and contrivances, they had been induced to join the sect, the state of her sentiments soon became that of pity.

There was a look of languor, of utter despair, in some of their eyes, which could not be mistaken.

Joe Smith raised his hat to Jessie as she approached.

He was habited in the full uniform of a field-marshal.

About a thousand soldiers, in a very plain uniform, were standing on the plain.

These men were brought from all parts, from every village and settlement of the great Nauvoo tribe.

They were well armed, and led by select and trusted chiefs.

General Joe Smith had already some premonitory hints of what was about to happen.

He determined, in case of things turning badly, on being prepared for the worst.

Around were the wives and children of such of the Mormons as were willing to allow them the recreation of such a sight.

But scattered here and there, in knots, were numbers of the Gentiles. Indians, too, were mixed up with the others, gazing on with an air of listless wonderment.

The general rode by one of these groups in order to survey the whole line. Jessie cast her eyes anxiously around, as if expecting some one. The amorous old general, who had resolved making Jessie his at any price, talked incessantly, but she heard him not.

Her thoughts were far away.

As soon as the legion had gone through its evolutions, it was ordered to march into the city, as a guard to the Prophet, who now was joined by Mr. Green, the city marshal ; Mr. Richards, the recorder ; and several of the council.

They entered the city, rode through several streets, and then halted in a small square. The soldiers at once, by previous directions, guarded every avenue.

It was the brutal *coup d'etat* of Louis Napoleon, on a small scale.

All despots are equally contemptible in their abuses of power.

They were opposite the offices of the *Nauvoo Expositor*, a paper which, from the beginning to the day it perished, fearlessly exposed the misdeeds, hypocrisy, and rascality of Mormonism.

The marshal entered the printing-office followed by a crowd of soldiers and civil officers, who, without any explanation, seized every man on the premises, savagely and inhumanly maltreated them, broke the presses and cases, and finally emptied all the type into the gutter.

Like all impostures and despotisms, Mormonism cannot exist with a free press.

This deed, the results of which were to be mighty indeed, having been performed, the whole crowd dispersed, and each family went to its respective home.

Jessie coldly declined to join the Prophet's ladies at lunch, and peremptorily told Phineas to take her home.

A scowl passed over the countenance of General Joe, as he heard her words. He resolved to be bitterly revenged.

And the revenge of such a man was to be feared.

Phineas Bristowe, who himself was not in the intimate society of the Prophet, was alarmed, and warned her to be cautious.

"I will not even tacitly encourage the gross insults of that bad man," said Jessie.

"What insults ?"

"What insults ? Does he not wish to degrade me to the level of his wretched wives, to add one more to the victims of a vile imposture."

"Hush !—walls have ears. The very air carries our sayings to the Prophet," cried Phineas, looking anxiously round.

He was right. By some mechanism beyond even the ingenuity of Louis Napoleon, or Russia's czar, the chief of the Mormons knew everything that passes even in the interior homes of the people.

The news of the outrage upon the liberty of the press, spread like lightning through the land ; meetings were held, indignation meetings, at which it was resolved to exterminate the Mormons.

First, however, it was privately determined to try the efficacy of the law, before appealing to Judge Lynch.

Jessie and Sophia were again companions, but on this occasion not for a very long period.

In the evening, Mr. Kimble invited his wives to tea with him.

They were eleven, and never did eleven more sad and doleful beings congregate around a board. Jemima, as the last new comer, and, as she fondly believed, the best beloved, was to his right. She smiled benignantly on all, and seemed to do so on Sophia, whose demeanour was cold and grave.

She sat by Jessie.

None spoke, unless addressed by the patriarch.

This affectation of imitating royalty was the custom in large families.

Kimble, a coarse vulgar man, related anecdotes, spoke of his services, and then began drawling about the church, quoting alternately from the Bible, and the Book of Mormon.

Then a negro servant came in and brought a letter. He opened it. It was an urgent letter of introduction from one of the Saints, for two Gentiles of great wealth and station, who were likely to increase the number of the Saints.

"Bring them in," said Kimble, who was in a good humour, and in whose eyes the possession of money was a perfect passport. "Ladies, allow me to introduce to you Messrs Grey and Lindel, two English travellers, who have kindly signified their intention of visiting Nauvoo, in a friendly spirit."

They were two strange-looking men, with long grey hair, grey beards and moustachios. Both wore spectacles, and despite their being English, had a strange, peculiar twang.

They had evidently been some time in America, time enough to catch the nasal intonation of Brother Jonathan.

Sophia whispered to Jessie, without moving.

"Heavens! 'tis Morton."

"And I know the other!" gasped Jessie.

Happily, in the hurry of introduction, the eleven ladies rising with one accord, the confusion and anxiety of the two girls passed unnoticed, nor did the excitement subside, when General Joe Smith and an armed guard were announced.

Jessie would have risen and left the room, but Phineas restrained her.

CHAPTER LXXXVII.

RED JACKET.

MEANWHILE, Henry lay at the point of death. He had caught a severe congestion of the lungs, and was generally in a dangerous state. As there was no possibility of removing him far, Mastico directed their steps to a valley at no great distance, where were camped a number of Pawnee Indians.

At that time the number of Redskins scattered over the different territories was very great.

But they were disrupted and disunited.

Now, a strange rumour was going through every tribe.

They were about to unite.

A mysterious messenger—no one knew whence he came, nor what he was—had gone from tribe to tribe, promising them empire.

A secret contract had been entered into between several of the tribes to retire towards the mountains, and there organize their forces.

The tribe of Pawnees received the whites with civility, especially as Mastico was an old friend, and a large tent was assigned to Henry.

Captain de Lancy tended him.

The poor fellow was insensible to all around. He was very weak, and still his cry was "Jessie."

Everything which affection could suggest, or forethought indicate, was done; but the terrible disease would have its way.

The Angel of Death hovered long over the tent.

Months passed ere Henry was even allowed to speak, as on two occasions a slight conversation had brought on a relapse.

There was all this time no news of Jessie, but terrible events had occurred, to which no reference was made in the presence of Henry.

Captain de Lancy, who alone remained in charge of Henry, the others having all dispersed to their several duties, was seated by the tent door.

Henry lay on a rich bed of skins. He had been pronounced out of danger, if he submitted to all the orders of his medical man, who came a long way to see him.

Henry, though enduring fearful mental torture, had to obey.

He was not allowed to speak.

It would throw him back.

Captain de Lancy was reflecting deeply. Though, by the kindness of his superiors, his leave of absence was indefinite, he was losing his chances of promotion. But what was to be done?

"How is the youth?" said a somewhat commanding voice, close to him.

De Lancy looked up. An Indian stood before him; an Indian who, however, spoke like a white man. His aspect was warlike and stern, while in his eye was a peculiar twinkle, which was suggestive of madness.

This was Little Red Jacket, the warrior, who was uniting the tribes.

"He is better," said de Lancy, "much better."

"Can I see him?"

"Certainly."

The Indian stepped into the hut. Henry, who was in a half doze, scarcely noticed him. The Redskin kneeled and peered in his face.

Captain de Lancy looked curiously on.

"It is him," muttered the other—"yes, there can be no mistake. But I may not speak—my oath—my oath! When will this agony end?"

Henry opened his eyes. A tear had fallen on his face.

The Indian rose hurriedly, and went out of the tent, followed by Captain de Lancy.

"You are not what you seem," said the young officer.

"I am Red Jacket, the scourge of the Mormons, whom I will sweep from the face of the earth," replied the other, wildly.

"You are——"

"Do you know me?" asked the Indian, speaking in a low and much calmer tone. "If you do, may Heaven bless you for your devotion to him; and now tell me—have you recognized me?"

"I have."

"He must not know it—or we must part. I have sworn that until the day, when I drive a dagger to the heart of mine enemy, I will remain what I am. A very different feeling from what

THE MARRIAGE CEREMONY.

burns in me now led me here, but now I have a motive—a great, a mighty motive. Can I trust you?"

Captain de Lancy assured him that he could, and the enthusiast, for such he seemed to be, opened up his plans, which had for object the total destruction, or at least dispersion, of the Mormons, against whom he had imbibed the most virulent hatred.

The other heard with intense wonder.

The man's story seemed a magical dream.

He must be the person he suspected him to be, and yet none of the Redskins seemed to hesitate to believe or follow him!

He belonged to no tribe. Here lay the secret of his success. There was no jealousy, and none could make out whence he came.

He, however, after a long conversation with the captain, appeared to tone down, and agree to more moderate measures.

The release of Jessie and the yielding up of Phineas Bristow was, however, an imperative ultimatum.

They were now about three days' march from Nauvoo, against which city, it was rumoured, a general attack was to be made.

The Indians were to join in this, and the chief announced that to-morrow, at latest, the Pawnees would march. A horse litter had been prepared for Henry.

Captain de Lancy agreed, on these terms, to allow him to be moved.

Next day, accordingly, the whole camp broke up, and started on their way. As the Pawnees are to be the comrades of Henry in his extraordinary chase after Jessie through the Rocky Mountains, some description of them may not be out of place.

CHAPTER LXXXVIII.

THE DEPARTURE OF THE INDIANS.

It was indeed a most interesting sight—an animated, shifting scene of warriors and braves, squaws and papooses, ponies dwarfed by bad breeding and hard living, dogs and puppies, straggling over the plains westward. In front, singly or in pairs, rode the men, not gracefully, but as if born upon, and bred to become part of the animal.

Some went barebacked, others rode, like the ancient chiefs of the western islands, upon a saddle-tree, stirrupless, or provided with hollow blocks of wood; in some cases the saddle was adorned with lead hangings, and in all a piece of buffalo hide, with the hair on, was attached beneath, to prevent chafing. The cruel ringbit of the Arabs was also not unknown to some.

A few had iron curbs, probably stolen; for the most part they managed their nags with a hide thong lashed round the lower jaw, and attached to the neck. A whip, of various sizes and shapes— sometimes a round and tattooed ferule, more often a handle like a butcher's tally-stick, flat, notched, one-foot long, and provided with two or three thongs—hung at the wrist.

Their nags were not shod with *parfleche*, as amongst the horse-Indians of the south. Their long, lank, thick, brownish-black hair, ruddy from the effects of weather, was worn parted in the middle, and depended from the temples, confined with a long twist of otter or beaver's skin, in two queues or pig-tails, reaching to the breast; from the poll, and distinct from the remainder of the hair, streamed the scalp-lock.

The parting in men, as well as in women, was generally coloured with vermilion; and plates of brass or tin, with bevelled edges, varying in size from a shilling to a half-a-crown, were inserted into the front hair. The scalp-lock—in fops, the side locks also—was decorated with tin or silver plates, often twelve in number, beginning from the head, and gradually diminishing in size as they approached the heels; a few had eagles', hawks', and crows' feathers stuck in the hair, and sometimes, grotesquely enough, crownless Kossuth hats, felt broad-brims, or old military casquettes, surmounted all this finery.

Their scanty beard was removed; they compare the bushy-faced European to a dog running away with a squirrel in its mouth. In their ears were rings of beads, with pendants of tin plates or mother o' pearl, or huge circles of brass wire not unlike a Hindoo tailor's; and their forearms, wrist, and fingers were, after an African fashion, adorned with the same metals, which the savage ever prefers to gold or silver.

Their other decorations were cravats of white, or white and blue, oval beads, and necklaces of plates, like those worn in the air.

The body dress was a tight-sleeved waistcoat of dark drugget, over an American cotton shirt; others wore tattered flannels, and the middle was wrapped round with a common blanket, presented by the government agent, scarlet and blue being the colours preferred, white rare; a better stuff is the coarse broadcloth manufactured for the Indian market in the United States.

The leggings were a pair of pantaloons without the body part,—in their palmy days, the Indians laughed to scorn their future conquerors for tightening the hips, so as to impede activity— looped up at both haunches with straps, to a leathern girdle; and all wore the breech cloth, which is the common Hindoo languti or bandage.

The cut of the leggings was a parallelogram, a little too short, and much too broad for the limb; it was sewn so as to fit tight, and the projecting edges, for which the light-coloured list, or bordering is usually preserved, answered the effect of a military stripe. When buckskin leggings are made, the outside edges are fringed; producing that feathered appearance which distinguishes in our pictures the nether limbs of the Indian brave. The garb ends with moccassins, the American brogues.

The braves were armed with small tomahawks, or iron hatchets, which they carried with the powder-horn, in the belt, on the right side, while the long tobacco-pouch of antelope skin, hung by the left; over their shoulders were leather targes, bows, and arrows, and some few had rifles; both weapons were defended from damp in deerskin cases, and quivers with the inevitable beadwork; and the fringes which every savage seems to love.

Their nags were lean and ungroomed; they treat them cruelly, yet nothing—short of whiskey —can persuade the Indian warrior to part with a favourite steed. It is his all in all, his means of livelihood, his profession, his pride; he is an excellent judge of horseflesh, though ignoring the mule and ass; and if he offers an animal for which he has once refused to trade, it is for the reason that an Oriental takes to market an adult slave—it has become useless.

Behind the warriors and braves followed the baggage of the village. The lodge-poles, in bundles of four and five, had been lashed to pads or packsaddles, girthed tight to the ponies' backs, the other ends being allowed to trail along the ground like the shafts of a truck; the sign easily denotes the course of travel.

The wolf-like dogs were also harnessed in the same way; more lupine than canine, they are ready, when hungry, to attack man or mule, and, sharp-nosed, and prick-eared, they not a little resemble the Indian pariah dog.

Their equipments, however, were of course on a diminutive scale; a little pad girthed round the barrel, with a breast plate to keep it in place, enabled them to drag two short, light lodge-poles tied together at the smaller extremity. One carried only a hawk on its back—yet falconry has never, I believe, been practised by the Indian.

Behind the ponies, poles were connected by cross sticks, upon which were lashed the lodge covers, the buffalo robes, and other bulkier articles. Some had strong frames of withes or willow basket-work, two branches being bent into an oval, garnished below with a network of hide thongs for a seat, covered with a light wicker canopy, and opening, like a cage, only on one side ; a blanket, or a buffalo robe, defends the inmate from the sun and rain.

These are the litters for the squaws when weary, the children, and the puppies, which are part of the family, till used for feasts. It might be supposed to be a rough conveyance—the elasticity of the poles, however, alleviates much of that inconvenience. A very ancient man, wrinkled as a last year's walnut, and apparently crippled by old wounds, was carried, probably by his great-grandsons, in a rude sedan. The vehicle was composed of two pliable poles, about ten feet long, separated by three cross bars, twenty inches or so, apart ; a blanket had been secured to the foremost and hindermost, and under the centre-bit lay Senex, secured against falling out. In this way the Indians often bear the wounded back to their villages. Apparently they have never thought of a horse-litter, which might be made with equal facility, and would be certainly saving work.

CHAPTER LXXXIX.

NAUVOO.

CAPTAIN de Lancy and Red Jacket, who had now resumed his gravity, rode beside the kind of rude litter in which Henry was carried, much to the surprise of the Indians.

The face of Red Jacket was stern and solemn. He seemed to have made up his mind never to loose his gravity in the presence of his followers.

He, however, continually conversed with the naval officer.

There was now a perfect understanding between the two.

But Red Jacket never gave any hint of a change in his intentions.

His hatred of the Mormons was unabated. The very mention of their names appeared to excite in him a morbid feeling akin to insanity.

He was decidedly under the influence of madness at times.

The march was slower than it would have been, but for the presence of Henry, to whom the Indians showed the utmost attention.

They camped in the mountains, in secluded and sheltered places, by springs known only to the Indians. Henry, though he fumed and chafed excessively, still abided by the decision of the doctors, that he was not to speak a single word.

The Captain and the Indian held a conference every night.

It was the evening of the third day, and they were within a few miles of Nauvoo.

They were on the hills which overlooked the city.

A great smoke had been rising from that direction all day.

Nobody could make out what it was.

That evening, Henry was able to sit up in the tent where Captain de Lancy and the Indian were having their supper.

He was ghastly pale.

They looked at him with the deepest interest. He made a mute appeal to their feelings.

" Speak, my dear boy," said Captain de Lancy, taking his hand, while the Indian began to eat with affected unconcern.

" Thank Heaven !" cried Henry. " And now what news ? I am dying to know ! Where is Jessie ?"

" She was safe when last we heard of her, began Captain de Lancy. " She has passed through many perils ; but still she is spared. Our spies have, until within a few days, brought us regular reports, but for a week we have heard nothing."

" And now ?"

" To-morrow, we enter Nauvoo ; and even if we slay the Prophet, Jessie shall be given up to us."

Henry smiled. Still, then, there was hope.

They now bade him rest, and Captain de Lancy and the Indian spoke in whispers.

Henry took the food prepared for him. After this, and a couple of glasses of wine, he retired to rest.

When he rose in the morning, he was so much better as to beg to be allowed to ride.

As he appeared exceedingly anxious on this point, they yielded.

They were about two miles from the crest of a mountain, which overlooked the city, and in this direction the whole party rode eagerly.

They did not, however, hurry too much, as Henry was pale and flushed by turns.

About ten, however, they came to the spot. They looked eagerly down upon the plain. The city of Nauvoo was at their feet. It was utterly abandoned, and many of its principal buildings were on fire.

A loud cry burst from the Indian chief, who then tore madly down the way which led to the city.

When he returned, his news was of the most terrible and disastrous character.

A tragedy, doomed to affect the whole future of most of our characters, had been perpetrated, without a parallel in American history.

But let us record it, so that it may be thoroughly understood by our readers.

CHAPTER XC.

THE ESCAPE.

WHEN General Joe Smith entered the sitting-room occupied by Kimble and his wives, the excitement was very great.

Such an incident was exceedingly unusual, as all the Saints were excessively jealous of their dignity, and more so of the privacy of their homes.

Such must always be the case where the infamous harem system is adopted.

No man who has not secured the affection of his wife, will trust her in the society of other men.

Defend polygamy as you will, the simple fact condemns it—that they love not one another.

Besides, they themselves acknowledge, that the great excuse for polygamy is economy.

Servants are rare and costly—*it is cheaper and more comfortable to marry them.*

Life in the wilds is a course of severe toil. A single woman cannot perform the manifold duties of housekeeping, cooking, scrubbing, washing, darning, child-bearing, and nursing a family.

So they take it in turns!

A division of labour is necessary, and so a man has many wives—that is, servants—of whom, perhaps, he may love one.

In the United States, society splits into two parts—man and woman—and each sex is freer and happier in the company of its congeners.

Amongst the Mormons there is a gloom.

That choice egotism of the heart, called love—that is, passion elevated by sentiment and not underrated by reason—subsides into a calm and unimpassioned domestic attachment.

There is none of the tenderness of home.

Womanhood is never petted.

But it would not have been wise for anybody to have shown the slightest disinclination to receive the Prophet.

He was, on the contrary, led to the seat of honour, and at once addressed with respect and deference by all present. After greedily devouring with his lustful eye the beauties around him, the Prophet looked meaningly at the strangers.

They were accordingly at once introduced. General Joe Smith, who disliked strangers, they invariably seeing through the sham of his sanctity, received them somewhat coldly, and asked for a song.

One or two of the wives, at the bidding of their husband, rose and went to a piano.

The Mormons, who care not for elevating pursuits, naturally love music, the resource of weak and feeble natures.

The Prophet made a sign to Jessie to come to him.

"Go," said Phineas, in a low, husky tone.

Jessie had to pass the two strangers.

"Keep a light burning, and do not go to bed," whispered the one she did not know.

Jessie made no reply, but pale, anxious, and careworn, moved up to where the Prophet sat.

"Well, handmaiden," said the unctuous old wretch, looking at her in a way to have disgusted even a not very modest woman, "have you become reconciled to the life in Zion?"

"No."

"Look around at this picture of happiness and bliss, of calm content, such as is unknown to the dwellers in the old land, which have not heard of the new dispensation."

"What dispensation, sir?"

Joe Smith looked at her, closed his eyes, and began to recite the abominable revelation on the patriarchal codes of matrimony.

It began :—

"Verily then, said the Lord unto you, my servant Joseph," and ended, "and ye shall abide by the law, or ye shall be damned, saith the Lord God."

Jessie turned away in disgust.

"Am I compelled to listen to this?" said Jessie, haughtily.

"What mean you?" cried the Prophet, purple with rage, as he turned upon her.

"Why?"

"Because in my opinion, it is rank blasphemy,"

"Retire, girl!" said Joe, in some confusion—the rogue was not fit for personal argument—"and we will confer with you again."

Jessie turned away with a look of ineffable scorn, and rejoined Sophia. In a few minutes after they glided from the room, and went up to the chamber they had contrived to have allotted to the two.

"That is my future husband!" gasped Sophia, clasping her hands—"is he not in fearful danger?"

"I know not—but this I do know, he is in the society of a bitter enemy of mine."

"Indeed!"

"I will explain presently. But now, Sophia, we must be calm and collected, for this night decides our fate. They will endeavour to effect our escape."

"How know you?"

"He spoke to me."

"Heavens!" said Sophia; "then there is still hope. I never thought to see him again!"

While talking, the girls were preparing for their departure. They selected such few things as they still possessed in personal property, and made parcels of them.

Then waiting until the dispersion of the party below, they sat at an open window.

They had still much to tell one another.

About eleven, the tea party broke up, and the Prophet might have been seen departing with his armed escort.

Then the two strangers left the house, but though they made their exit at the same time as the Prophet, they slunk behind.

Then they turned on their steps towards the house.

In a moment after they disappeared outside the high palings of the garden. A dull, heavy sound was heard, and they were in the garden.

From a short distance off they made signs to Jessie and Sophia to descend.

They had lighted their candles, and thus enabled the others to distinguish them.

Signals being exchanged, they again extinguished their tapers, and prepared to descend towards the garden.

CHAPTER XCI.

MORMON SECRETS.

WHEN the tea-party broke up, and General Joe Smith had taken his departure, Mr. Kimble, having first taken hold of the hand of Jemima, wished all the others good-night.

This was the delicate way the Mormon Pasha

used to signify that he had chosen his companion for twenty-four hours?

Does not this one thing at once prove the beastiality of polygamy?

And yet the Mormons pretend that women have been found to defend polygamy.

And they make a woman defend polygamy, on the ground that marriage is solely for the multiplying of our species, the rearing and training of children.

Why talk about slavers keeping fine blacks to breed slaves, after that?

What becomes of love, jealousy, and the other impulses of our nature?

"Polygamy," says Belinda Pratt, "as practised under the Patriarchal Law of God, tends directly to the chastity of women, and to sound health and morals in their offspring."

Why?

"Because, when once a woman expects to be a mother, she should be separated from her husband, as also while rearing her babe. During this long period woman's heart should be pure, her thoughts and affections chaste, her mind calm, her passions without excitement."

Then again.

"Where polygamy exists, a wealthy man need not keep a mistress in secret."

Of course not, when he can keep a dozen openly. But we shall, as we proceed, see the truth, and know if women really can be happy in this hideous and licentious state of existence.

The ten temporarily discarded wives having gone out, Jemima remained alone with Kimble, who was a very sturdy man of about forty.

His passion for Jemima, had not as yet palled, as such passions always must do, especially when they can have fresh victims at any time.

Jemima retired for a few moments to a side-room, and then came forth to the supper table in a dress which the Honourable Mr. Kimble particularly admired.

He opened a secret cupboard and took forth some very choice viands, with hock, champagne, and sherry.

Like certain teetotallers, the Mormon elders do not indulge in wine in the presence of others.

They reserve this enjoyment for their hours of privacy, when they persuade the favourite wife that once in a way, on great occasions, such indulgences are lawful.

And Mormon wives are bound to believe that all a Mormon husband says is true, for *Man is the head of the Woman.*

But Jemima was not one of those to be deceived. She thoroughly saw through the whole imposture and rascality of Mormonism, and was no more content to be the wife of an hour than any other woman of sense or decency.

But hate and jealousy will move a woman to almost any sin.

Jemima hated Sophia. She loved Edward Merton still; and this love it was that made her so hateful and wicked.

As if institutions and ideas could alter the nature of woman.

Jemima was essentially a voluptuous woman. She was magnificently made, and far more suit-able to a Mormon Sultan than an elegant or graceful girl. Her bust was magnificent, and the ingeniously contrived imitation of an odalisque dress, showed it off to great advantage.

It was open in front, revealing fully shoulders, neck, and bosom.

The eye of Kimble woke up at once. He had never seen a woman like her.

Her countenance was, too, very expressive. She feigned to love him from her very soul.

"You are the most beautiful woman I ever saw!" said Kimble, as she seated herself next to him, and passed her arms round his neck.

"So you will say to some one else to-morrow night," cried Jemima, pouting.

"Certainly not, for no woman can ever be like you," he added, warmly.

"Then I wonder you want to have so many," said Jemima, laughing.

She knew better than to seriously attack polygamy as yet, and yet she meant to try, as many other Mormon women have tried, and succeeded.

Apostacy, indeed, is so common, that many of the new Saints form a mere floating population.

"My dear," replied Kimble, "you must not joke about things serious. You know the law?"

"What law?"

"If any man espouse a virgin, and desire to espouse another, and the first gives her consent, and if he espouse the second, and they are virgins, then he is justified; and if he have ten virgins given unto him, he cannot commit adultery."

"Ah! you are a wicked sinner, Kimble. You men have made this law to suit yourselves. I dare say it is very right; but how can you love me and love others?"

"That is an abstract question into which, my dear, I decline to enter. Believe me, I really do love you, and what can you ask more?"

"Well—what about Sophia? Do you mean to seal her to yourself, or to some one else?"

"Well, I've hardly looked at her yet, my dear; but, really, just as you like."

"It must be done soon!"

"Why?"

"She is in league with that girl, Jessie. There is a self-satisfied look about her which alarms me!"

"Humph!"

"She smiled and looked defiant as she left the room," said Jemima, still entwining her arms around the other's neck.

"This must be seen to. These rebellious girls are dangerous; but once married, they cannot leave, while as single girls they have no dread."

Once married! because after that they are looked on in civilized America as prostitutes.

"I would rather you found her another husband," said Jemima, after some thought.

"Why?"

"She is very beautiful," said the unthinking aunt.

"Is she, my dear?" replied the Mormon husband, as he played with his wife's beautiful hair. "Very beautiful, is she?" he said, with a peculiar look.

Jemima saw her mistake, in the wicked, snake-like glance of the man's eye.

She coloured up, and tried to change the subject.

"How old is she?" said Kimble, after a few moments of silence.

"Twenty-one."

"It would be a pity to part you."

"I hate her!"

"But she is your relative."

"Kimble," cried the woman, warmly, "do not in this, the honeymoon of our love, turn me against you. I love you! I am prepared to devote myself to you, to forgive a peculiar institution which, I tell you, every woman loathes; but do not take to your bosom one who is to me a viper, who already once robbed me of the affection of one man, and would soon do so of another!"

Had she not have been too excited to hear anything, she would have heard a faint exclamation.

*   *   *   *   *

Jessie and Sophia had left their rooms, and, with a small taper in their hands to guide them on their way, had descended the stairs.

But here an unforseen difficulty occurred.

The hall door was locked, and the keys removed by Kimble himself on the departure of the guests.

But there was a back door to the garden, which was only on the latch.

To reach this they had to pass through the very room now occupied by Kimble and Jemima.

The door into the passage was open, and all that passed could be seen and heard.

Jessie, who had no motive for listening, retreated to the stairs, and sat down. One glance had been quite enough.

But Sophia had a deep interest in knowing the real position of her aunt.

She had never for one instant suspected her before.

Now she thoroughly understood the motive of all that had transpired, and knew that her aunt was her real enemy.

Her blood ran cold at the prospect of sharing the caresses of this hideous and impure Satyr.

Her eyes were at once and for ever opened to the wicked licentiousness of the Mormons; but though her blood boiled at the indecency of the scene, her earnest desire to know all made her go through with it.

Then, when the supper was over, and the two had indulged freely in wine, they retired to the nuptial chamber, and closed the door behind them.

Then Sophia turned towards the still pale and anxious Jessie, and signed to her to advance.

Sophia was of a robust and hearty nature, as courageous as a man, and as resolute.

She went to the cupboard, and drawing forth a bottle, filled two tumblers.

She gave one to Jessie, and then drank up the other herself.

This done, she led the way towards the garden. Still she carried the small taper, and by its means passed through the kitchen, and thence into the garden.

They could see no one.

They crept out towards the end of the garden, where they had seen their friends.

Not a sign of them was to be seen anywhere.

"Edward!" said Sophia, in a loud voice.

No answer.

"Edward!" she repeated, in a still louder tone.

Then there was a rush, and the two strangers were seen defending themselves against some dozen of the Mormon guards, who blew a conch.

The cry of Sophia had betrayed them.

The Danites had been prowling about in the usual way, and had remarked the removal of the plank in the wall of Kimble's house. They had at once determined to watch carefully.

The two men had concealed themselves the moment they had heard the approaching Danites, who are the watchers of the Mormon city.

They are men from seventeen to forty-nine, and were originally termed Daughters of Gideon, Destroying Angels or Devils, and finally, Sons of Dan, or Danites—from one of whom it was prophesied that he should be a serpent in the path.

They were originally organized under Captain Fearnot, for the purpose of dealing as avengers of blood with Gentiles; in fact, they form a kind of death society, desperadoes, thugs, assassins.

The Mormons deny this, but it has been proved by their own seceders.

Edward Merton and his companion drew both bowie-knives and revolvers, and firing at the Danites, endeavoured to make a passage for the girls, who, despite the horrors of the scene, tried to follow.

But suddenly they were caught behind.

Merton and his companion saw that all was lost, and made a fierce rush at their attackers, and passed through.

"Harm those girls, at your peril!" shouted Merton, "and your city shall be razed to the ground."

By this time Kimble had come forth, followed by his wife, who had assisted in the capture of the unfortunate girls.

Without a word, they were thrust into a dark room, and left to their own reflections.

CHAPTER XCII.

THE SEALING.

GENERAL JOE SMITH had long been aware that Nauvoo was a mistake. To carry out his nefarious practices, and indulge in the luxury of polygamy, it was necessary to be far away from civilization.

Hence the plan for emigrating in a body to that Great Salt Lake which is now the centre of these operations, and where the great Scarlet Lady of Adultery and Fornication has set up her temple.

When the time comes to transport ourselves to Deseret, we shall see Mormonism in full swing—polygamy in all its natural hideousness.

But Joe Smith, in his impatience, was preparing a tragedy he little expected.

The valley of Nauvoo was soon to be the Valley of the Shadow of Death.

There came rumours to the Prophet and his

advisers that a storm was brewing; strange faces were seen in the city and its outskirts, examining the approaches; friendly warnings were given to the less notoriously profligate among the elders, but in their blindness they believed not.

Their missionaries were still sent to scour all Europe and the States, in search of money and women.

Men they could find plenty of, until it became pretty well known that the juvenile male members of the sect found great difficulty in getting married at all.

But despite their blind confidence, it was quite clear that Illinois would soon be too hot to hold them.

And yet they had erected a city, and commenced a temple scarcely equalled in the world.

General Joe, the day after the review and *coup-d'-etat* against the unfortunate newspaper, resolved upon a grand show, and subsequently on a ceremony of unusual importance.

The Prophet was about to take unto himself a wife.

And it was known that this wife was Jessie.

Joe Smith sent in the morning for Phineas Bristowe, and very severely catechising him as to the backsliding of his pupil, informed him that he, the Prophet, had determined to put an end to any further escapades on her part by marrying her himself."

" But ——" said Phineas, retreating with horror.

" But what ?" replied Joe, severely.

" I have other views—I intended—I wished—indeed, I have promised, on certain conditions, to allow her to return to England."

" Indeed !" said Joseph Smith, with a savage and threatening scowl. " Are you aware of the consequences ?"

" How so, sir ?"

" I shall be obliged to hand you over to the Danites, to deal with you as a backslider," said the Prophet, sternly.

" But, sir !"

" Yes or no. This girl has been trusted in our homes; has had constant access to our secrets, and she must not go to England."

" Her word is her bond."

" I would rather have her person in safe custody," replied the Prophet, with a cold and cynical smile.

Phineas Bristowe wiped the sweat off his brow. He knew not what to do. With all his cold-blooded villainy, he really loved Jessie.

Her pure and innocent soul had won gradually on his affections. Though his assumption of being her father—one of those extraordinary things which it will take us some time to explain in its proper place—was a sham, no evil thought entered into his seared soul with regard to this girl.

She was his last buckler against the Evil One.

Joseph Smith eyed him with a cynical and suspicious glance.

" Perhaps you have thought of her for yourself," he said, with an assumption of humility.

" No, no !" stammered Phineas Bristowe; " in fact she is——"

" Not your wife !" said Joe Smith, slowly and emphatically. " Not your wife !"

" No; but my daughter."

" Sit down," cried Joe, rising; he had left Phineas standing all this time. " I am proud to hail you, then, as my father-in-law. From this day your fortune shall be my care. This day, at two, the girl will be sealed unto me. She is already in one of the cells at the temple, being prepared for the ceremony."

Phineas tottered out. He could not walk straight. His face was haggard. This, then, was the end of all. Jessie, who alone could save him, was now in the remorseless hands of the Prophet.

As a guardian, as a hostage, she could be of no use to him now, while those in pursuit would call him to a fearful account for what he had done.

He knew not what to do. In that abject state of things, which Captain Burton looks upon as the perfection of human government, there was no appeal from a decision of the Prophet.

Besides, was not Jessie already in his possession, and would the wolf, on any terms, give up the tender lamb?

He was lost, utterly lost, without hope of escape or redemption.

He had heard of there being mobs about, ready to attack the Mormons.

He felt half inclined to run round the country and state, until he met one, and beg them to come and rescue Jessie.

But it was too late ! too late ! too late !

In his despair, he decided at last to go to the Temple, and there devise some means, however violent, of preventing the sacrifice.

CHAPTER XCIII.

THE TEMPLE.

MEANWHILE, the two unfortunate girls, after the escape of their rescuers, had been thrust, as we have said, into a kind of dark hole, where they had but the consolation of weeping.

Before day-light, their prison-place was entered by several men in masks, who bound and gagged them; after which they were taken into the open air, and placed inside a small light van.

This then started at a tolerably rapid pace, and in less than ten minutes halted.

They were in a small court-yard, surrounded by very high walls, in one of which was a vault-like entrance leading to steps.

The girls were taken down there, dragged along a stone corridor, and thrust into a large square stone room, at one end of which was a large iron grating.

Behind this were chains, stocks, large wooden collars, and whips with many thongs.

A fearful museum of instruments, such as are usually found in the chambers of the Inquisition.

They were in the torture-room of the Temple, which contained the secret of as many dark deeds as ever were revealed by the turning out of the Bourbons from Sicily and Naples.

Before the sacking of the Temple, the Mormons

contrived to destroy some evidences of their guilt, but enough remained to show what they had been guilty of.

"Jessie!"

"Sophia!"

"This is too horrible. These hideous men are about to avenge themselves upon us."

"Impossible. No men, however degraded, can condescend to scourge the bodies of women. This is only done to terrify us."

"I don't know. There is that in the face of Kimble would make me believe in any villainy—while I believe, from Joe Smith's face, he revels in infamy."

"Still—not torture—not scourges."

The door opened, and two men, clothed from head to foot in black leather, with masks upon their faces, advanced towards the terrified and shrinking girls.

Behind them were several black girls, carrying piles of dresses on their arms.

Jessie and Sophia looked enquiringly at the hideous executioners and their sable and mute attendants.

"Choose," said a thick and hollow voice, "between punishment and robing yourselves for the ceremony."

"What ceremony?" asked Jessie.

"Marriage!"

Jessie looked scornfully at them, in a way peculiar to herself.

"I have chosen," she said.

"What have you chosen?"

"Retire," she cried, loftly, "and I will dress. Better be above ground than here," she whispered; "we shall then find somebody to sympathise with us."

Sophia nodded, and the black girls at once opened the door into a kind of dressing room very different from the stone chamber they had been originally confined in.

It was a well-furnished apartment, with all the appurtenances of the toilette.

The girls made no remark, but allowed the negresses to attire them in gorgeous array.

The dresses were rich and expensive, such as brides would have been likely to wear.

Jessie, though pale, looked magnificent.

Then she heard the swelling voices of some hundreds of men and women taking up a hymn, in the Temple above.

As soon as they were dressed, one or two pale and sickly-looking women came in and bade them follow.

They were some of the elder wives of the Pope—women who, having lost all hope, had descended to be the handmaidens of his will.

They indoctrinated and taught his younger helpmeets in their duties.

They were not such duties as we comprehend by those of a wife.

The Prophet expected peculiar reverence and obedience. No woman was to speak to him except humbly and lowlily.

Perhaps the dogged obstinacy with which his first wife refused to recognize his supremacy, may have led to his partiality for slaves instead of real partners in his joys and sorrows.

They bowed with a marked affectation of respect, and then, as if Jessie had been a princess, begged to be allowed the honour of leading her forth.

With a haughty bend, Jessie motioned them to advance.

They threw open a door and entered a passage, at the end of which was a carpeted staircase.

At the top of this, the whole view of the Temple burst upon them.

It was full of people, who had assembled to witness the ceremony.

Round the altar were the twelve apostles in their robes.

They were all to join in the theatrical and blasphemous copy of genuine Christian marriage.

The Prophet, in his robes as High Priest, sat in a large arm-chair.

The people generally were plainly habited, especially the women, as the Mormons repudiate their fair sisters making any display of their charms, except to their lords and masters.

Jessie was led to a vacant space in front of the altar.

Every eye was fixed upon her. At no great distance, through the crowd, peered the ghastly face of Phineas Bristowe.

He was perfectly hideous to behold. His skin was yellow; his eyes started out of his head.

General, or rather Prophet, Joseph Smith, rose to greet the new bride—the elect lady of his heart and home—she who was to supersede and upset all others.

A loud song from unseen choristers welcomed her approach.

Without pretending to see General Joe, Jessie advanced to the altar, and, turning round to the people, spoke in a loud, clear voice.

"Why am I dragged here? Why have I had to choose between scourging from the hands of brutal ruffians, or this costume?"

A loud murmur arose. There were very many Gentiles in the Temple, while even the Mormons were taken by surprise.

General Smith turned pale with rage, while a number of women and apostles surrounded Jessie, and drew her back.

One or two cries of shame burst from various quarters of the building.

A slight colour revisited the visage of Phineas Bristowe as the murmurs arose.

"Hear her! hear her!" said he, standing back so as not to be recognized.

Then up rose the oily, unctuous, cunning head of the Great Imposture, that man whom some have dared to compare with Him whose life was a pattern to the world—a joy to every noble heart and soul—a consolation to every sinner.

This man, who dared to assert that he had seen God, uprose in his place.

"Listen to me," he said, joining his hands together, and casting up his eyes to Heaven; "this poor misguided sister of ours is afflicted with a devil, which presently I will proceed to cast out. But yesterday, in an interview with me, having come to a thorough understanding relative to the future, and being made aware that no woman can enter the kingdom of Heaven, except through her husband, she implored fervently to be sealed unto me, that her soul might be saved!"

ARREST OF JOE SMITH.

"Wretched and abominable falsehood!" cried Sophia; "last night we were endeavouring to escape. Elder Kimble, there, can tell if I speak truth—when I say that for hours I listened to his conference with his new wife, my aunt Jemima."

"Sinner, beware!—lest you be caught in your guilt," cried Joseph, angrily; while Elder Kimble coloured up to the very roots of his hair.

Jemima turned deadly pale.

Not a sound was heard in the vast building.

"May I be heard?" asked Jessie.

"Not until I have cast out the devil," said Joseph Smith, sternly. "I shall not allow you to lose your soul. Hush!"

And he raised his hands as if to begin a prayer.

A terrible outcry arose at this moment at the entrance of the Temple.

It was announced that a body of constables and other officers were outside, and about to enter to effect the arrest of the Prophet.

CHAPTER XCIV.

ATTEMPTED ARREST.

THE apologists of Mormonism, among whom may be reckoned Dr. Mackay and Captain Burton, endeavour to portray them as a preeminently industrious, frugal, and painstaking people—

above all, moral. The truth of these assertions will be made manifest as we advance.*

We have now to deal with the events which preceded the great tragedy of Nauvoo.

A great clamour arose when it was announced that the constables were at the entrance of the Temple.

They were accompanied by the publishers of the *Expositor*.

They had a warrant for the arrest of the Prophet, and though their numbers were small, protected by the majesty of the law, they advanced boldly into the Temple.

Joseph Smith, who was for a moment pale, gave some whispered directions to a follower, who disappeared.

"I arrest you, general, and mayor of Nauvoo, in the name of the law," said the first constable.

"What!" exclaimed the Prophet, "think you the Prophet of God acknowledges the authority of the Gentiles?"

"But, Sir?"

"Begone, lest Heaven destroy you, for presuming to lift your hand against its servant."

"The man is mad," said the constable; "we shall have to take him by force."

A loud murmur arose, during which Jessie tried to demand the protection of the constables, but was forcibly held back by a mob of women, the wives of Joseph Smith, and other elders.

Jessie appealed to their merciful and womanly feelings.

She appealed in vain. Had she known more of human nature she would have been less hopeful.

Some one has said that fiends are the souls of fallen women, and I am inclined to reiterate the assertion; for then woman as far excels in hardened wickedness as she did, in the days of innocence, in tenderness and virtue.

The hour of agony and despair when they wept, prayed, and shrieked for help, but no hand was extended to save, had faded from a memory that was now calloused and seared, and they only thought of the gulf of infamy into which they were plunged, and over whose murky banks, far above them, they saw their pure sisters moving serenely in the atmosphere of innocence, their cares soothed by the hand of tenderness and love, sheltered from danger by the devotion of a father's and husband's unremitting attentions; while they, the playthings of an hour, were thrown aside for a new and more beautiful rival, whose cries of distress were like so much music to their ears; for in her despair they were revenged on the beauty that alienated their destroyer's thoughts from them.

Meanwhile the scene between the constables and General Joe Smith was going on.

"Raise but a hand against me," said the Prophet, arrogantly, "and my legion will cut you to pieces. Be off, nor never dare again to molest the servant of the Lord, who, in all he does, only obeys his master's will."

* Numerous correspondents are pressing us for a description of the Great Salt Lake. In No. 53, will be commenced a full and extraordinary description of the discovery and settlement of Deseret or Utah, with secret revelations of Mormonism.

"Which master is the devil," said a bystander, the Temple being now crowded with Gentiles.

The Prophet was listening. His sole object was to gain time.

"Do your duty officer," said the editor of the *Expositor*. "He dare not carry his threat into execution."

"Back!" shouted Joe Smith; "I stand upon my rights. If I were arrested by Gentile hands, I should be compelled to call down the maledictions of that great power you all should dread. Hearken, oh, people! Crape the heavens with woe, gird the earth with sackcloth, and let hell mutter one melody in commemoration of fallen splendour, for the glory of America has departed; and God will send a flaming sword to guard the tree of liberty, while such mint-tithing Herods as Benton, Van Buren, Boggs, Calhoun, and Clay, are thrust out of the realms of virtue, as fit subjects for the kingdom of fallen greatness."

Such are the exact words he used.

But the officers, tired of his rant, advanced nearer to execute their warrant.

"To arms!" shouted the Prophet, who had received an expected signal.

Then arose a furious clamour of drums, of trumpets, and of bells, mingled with the execrations of men, and the yells of women and children.

Then armed men of the Nauvoo legion, began to pour into the Temple.

The officers were hustled and pushed about.

"This opposition is uncalled for," remonstrated the officer. "Your arrest is a mere form, as you, no doubt, can clear yourself from the accusation: and if you accompany me in peace it may save trouble for yourself and me in future."

"The day is passed when the Gentiles can drive me from place to place, and imprison me. God has placed in my hands the means of defending his Saints from Gentile persecution, and bade me use it, and I dare not disobey, if I desired."

What the constable might have said can never be known. His voice was drowned in the outcries of the mob, and after an ineffectual attempt to obtain a hearing, during which he and his party were assailed by foul epithets, and then by stones, he retired with his party.

Joseph Smith then called for silence, and ordered the legion to assemble for review once more.

In the meantime directions were given to clear the Temple of all but a select few.

By his whispered directions, Jessie and Sophia had been gagged and transferred to the light cart which brought them to the Temple.

CHAPTER XCV.

THE LAST REVIEW.

Nauvoo city was unrivalled in situation. It stood on a high bluff on a bend of the Mississippi.

In the centre was the Temple.

Around were clustered the long, low ranges of the Saints' harems.

The city was of great dimensions, well laid out.

The streets were wide, and crossed each other at right angles.

But there was one object which was far more noble to behold, and far more majestic than any other yet presented to the sight, and that was the wide-spread and unrivalled father of waters, the Mississippi river, whose mirror-bedded waters lay in majestic extension before the city, and, in one general curve, seemed to sweep gallantly by the beautiful place.

On the farther side was seen the dark-green woodland, bending under its deep foliage, with here and there an interstice, bearing the marks of cultivation.

A few houses could be seen through the trees on the other side of the river, directly opposite to which is spread a fairy isle, covered with beautiful timber.

The isle and the romantic swell of the river soon brought the mind back to days of yore, and to the bright emerald isles of the far-famed fairy-land.

The bold and prominent rise of the hill, fitting to the plain with exact regularity, and the plain pushing itself into the river, forcing it to bend around its obstacle with becoming grandeur, and fondly to cling around it, added to the heightened and refined lustre of this sequestered land.

It was a kind of terrestial paradise in that land of great wonders and extraordinary scenery—America.

Nowhere, indeed, is nature viewed by man upon so grand a scale.

In the hands of a people who had been satisfied to live under the dispensation of truth, of a body of men who should not have made themselves obnoxious by their wicked seduction of girls and women, their rapts and abductions, the spot would have been a paradise.

When General Joe Smith left the Temple he was in a reverie. He knew that he had taken a very dangerous step, one that might lead to most tremendous consequences, and he was weighing the issue.

But he allowed no one to perceive his pre-occupation.

He feigned to be elated at the termination of the affair, and went into the privacy of his harem, to take his lunch.

Everywhere, as he passed, he scattered invitations to a ball, for which he gave instructions immediately on his return.

The parade-ground was at the foot of the bluff, and was approached by a broad smooth way that had been built and beautified by the Saints.

The ground itself was admirably adapted to its use, and was as hard and smooth as a floor.

Immediately the review was announced, the excited crowd began to collect.

A holiday in Nauvoo was what the Saints especially liked.

Before the hour thousands of Saints and Gentiles congregated at the foot of the hill.

Then the sound of martial music was heard—drums and fifes and other instruments, after which the troops, with quick measured step, rounded the bluff and descended into the plain.

They were an athletic set of men, erect, and well equipped in elegant uniforms.

But what did Joe Smith want with such a force ever increasing, ever practising?

This is a question often asked, never answered.

Well might the accusation of high treason have been brought against this ambitious schemer.

Well might the people cry out, as they did, "What does all this mean? Why this exact discipline of the Mormon corps. Do they intend to conquer Missouri, Illinois, Mexico?"

The designs of the would-be Napoleon of the West were thus rightly judged.

It is true, they were part of the militia of the State of Illinois, by the charter of their legion; but then, there were no troops in the States like them in point of enthusiasm and warlike aspect, yea, warlike character. Before many years this legion would be twenty, and perhaps fifty, thousand strong, and still augmenting. A fearful host, filled with religious enthusiasm; and, led on by ambitious and talented officers, what may not be effected by them? Perhaps the subversion of the constitution of the United States; and if this should be considered too great a task, foreign conquests will most certainly follow. Mexico would fall into their hands, even if Texas should first take it.

These Mormons were accumulating like a snow-ball rolling down an inclined plane, which, in the end, becomes an avalanche. They were enrolling among their officers some of the first talent in the country, by titles or bribes, it didn't matter which.

No wonder that the law being powerless to check them, the mob stepped in.

Then again strains of music were borne upon the breeze. Then came the band, with their notes ringing clear and harmonious, then dying away in melting cadences.

Then came the standard-bearer, his flag flung to the breeze, which, playing with its silken folds, spread it out in a daring mood, then let it fall gracefully downward, as if to display its rich folds and gorgeous dyes, a shame to the world, a disgrace to human nature.

Amongst the spectators were the two men who had been introduced to the Honourable Mr. Kimble, they had resumed their disguise.

They were conversing in low whispers, and watching the procession with eagle eyes.

"If they are among them, I will try the temper of the people," said Merton.

"How so?" asked the other, who called himself Fletcher.

"I will demand them at the pistol's point. There are friends enough about."

"Be cautious. Joseph Smith is a perfect demon. I know by his eyes."

"I will wrest my affianced wife from him at the pistol's mouth," said the other, sternly.

"Hush! here he comes."

It was, indeed, the sublime hypocrite. He was mounted on a magnificent black horse, with rich crimson and gold housings that glanced back the sunlight as it fell upon their brilliant surface.

He wore, as usual on such occasions, when he aped the Napoleon, the uniform of a general officer, faultless in all its appointments, and bore his accumulated honours of Prophet and general with an affected calm and grave urbanity that showed itself in the curve of his short upper lip, and small glittering eyes.

Nearest him rode a lady, probably the last favoured sultana, whose palfrey was also richly caprizoned, while she wore a robe of invisible green, fitting her full form with an ease that lent charming grace to the rider.

Its long folds nearly swept the ground.

Her head was surmounted by a hat similar to that worn by fast young ladies.

Behind, mingling with the staff, were other blooming beauties.

But neither Jessie nor Sophia. The two men examined every woman as she passed, but were convinced they were not there.

And the music played, and the banners waved, and the horses pranced, as Joseph Smith raised his hat, and his attendant sultanas exchanged quick and lascivious glances with favourite friends.

And Joe Smith neither heeded nor saw anything that passed. His mind was far away in the deep darkness of the Valley of the Shadow of Death.

He saw not the soldiers filing, he saw not the menacing, abhorrent looks of the Gentiles; he heeded not his harem; but slowly, coldly, mechanically, went past his troops, and then away back again to his own residence.

"I like not his look," said Merton. "That man is meditating some daring deed."

"Of what nature, think you?"

"He is fearful of the devil he has raised," continued the young man. "I fancy he will fly, and abandon the Mormons to their fate."

"Rather, that he will induce them to remove hence, as he has already been advised, to some distant region, where he will not offend society by shameless polygamy and prostitution."

The young man pressed Fletcher's hand.

"We are invited to this ball. Let us go; we may there get a clue."

CHAPTER XCVI.

THE LAST BALL.

THE Prophet had, on his return to his residence, retired for awhile to his most private and secret apartments, where he remained alone for above an hour.

These apartments communicated with a garden which no one was ever allowed to enter uninvited.

What passed can only be surmised, though after events will indicate the nature of his occupation.

But now night had gathered in, and his presence would soon be required in the ball-room.

It was illumined by a perfect flood of light.

Waving branches of trees draped the walls, while festoons of evergreens adorned the ceiling, dependent from hooks.

The raised dais had but two seats now, one for the Prophet, and another for his favourite sultana.

Chairs were ranged for the less favoured ladies, the Elect Lady, his only real wife, scorning to make an exhibition of herself.

Long benches round the room were provided for the guests, while the orchestra occupied an upper gallery.

In a very short time the room was full.

Then, with a burst of trumpets, the Prophet entered, and was received with loud applause.

But he was gloomy and thoughtful. Several couriers had arrived, warning him of what was about to happen, and calling upon him to prepare to defend Nauvoo by the sword.

There was, indeed, an uprising of the whole state against them, which can only be explained by their own evil actions.

In fact, despite the weak assertion, that the energetic Western farmers were jealous of their industry, it was the lawless acts of the Mormons that had brought them into antagonism with the citizens of the state. Husbands, whose wives purity had been poisoned or their delicacy insulted; fathers, whose daughters had been stolen or seduced; brothers and sisters, who had lost a mother or sister; farmers, who had lost their cattle and grain; merchants, who had depredations committed on their goods—all joined in the cry for the extermination of a band of parasites who lived and preyed, ghoul-like, on their fellows.

It was usual for the Prophet to open the ball, but on this occasion, he bade Brigham Young set an example to his fellows.

This elder—whose career, properly described, is far more curious than that of Joe Smith—nothing loth, selected one of his harem, whose graceful form, in all the abandonments of a Cyprian, was robed, not clothed, in the softest tissue, the gossamer folds of which exhibited every undulation of her voluptuous charms. She looked ethereal as she floated in the mazes of the waltz, her form enfolded by the coarse arms of the debauchee; but oh, how fallen! You saw it in the abandonment of her step, the curve of the dimpled arms, bared to the shoulder, where the tissue sleeve was scarcely an inch deep, and that inch tied back with a gauze ribbon, gathering down in its nœud the bodice from the swelling bust. In the glance of those sloe-like eyes, and careless smiles of the pouting mouth, the coarse jest and rude laughter, was revealed the defiled soul within.

It was about this time that Merton, and the man who passed as Fletcher, crept into the ball-room unnoticed. Everybody was watching the voluptuous spectacle before them, and they were able to scan the apartment, glide among the groups, and institute their search.

Merton could scarcely repress his disgust, but the other looked on with something like admiration. Many of the women were splendidly made, and their ball costume revealed their limbs to perfection.

But no Jessie and no Sophia.

"Fletcher," said Merton, in the tone of one determined to act firmly, "I am certain that my Sophia and your friend Jessie are in the hands of this man. They are concealed in the temple or here. Everybody is busy. We can easily explore the whole house, and assure ourselves of their being or not being here."

The other whispered assent, and once more they made their exit unperceived.

The long suite of apartments occupied by the women were, to all appearance, untenanted, for as they passed down a dark corridor, they could see the doors open, and the disorderly results of a hasty toilette.

Not one was inhabited.

They returned, made their exit from the building, and looked around. There was no evidence as to the place—not a solitary position or hidden nook.

They were in desperation. What could they do but watch, or return to their residence, and wait the arrival of the force which they knew would come the next day to attack the devoted and doomed city, city of abomination, like the ancient city of the plains?

Their inn overlooked the Prophet's garden, and being both too full of agony to speak, they sat at an open window.

The sound of the music was wafted to their ears.

Then they suddenly saw lights in the Prophet's private garden. Several persons were seen holding up torches, while others carried packages. A sudden idea illumined both their minds.

The Prophet was flitting unknown to his people. Both Merton and Fletcher, who had stout horses, descended to the stable, saddled their horses hastily, and then fastened them in the yard.

This done, they sallied forth to the open ground behind the Prophet's house.

A very large light waggon, drawn by three horses, was standing at a private entrance.

It was guarded by a dozen mounted and *masked* Danites.

They groaned aloud.

" What is to be done ?" said Fletcher.

" Alarm the Mormons, charge the Prophet with deserting them, and in the scuffle claim our own."

" It would be dangerous. I know a better plan."

" What is that ?"

" Crape is plentiful—cover our faces, button up our great coats, and ride with the Danites."

" It shall be done."

And away they sped to where their horses were waiting, entered the house, in ten minutes altered their disguise, and then again went out. The Prophet was mounting his horse. In the confusion that ensued they had no difficulty in mingling with the group.

The packages were placed in the waggon in front, and then the word was " forward."

The Prophet rode in front.

Not a word was spoken for some time, the Prophet setting the example ; but as soon as they were out of the city and on an unfrequented road he summoned one or two of the Danites to his councils.

" Precious quiet them mams is," said one of the Danites, with a coarse laugh ; " suppose them's the same as we kippered the other night."

" Esacly. General Joe's been and bagged 'em on his own account. Artful old possum, General Joe——"

And the Danites laughed in a low, cautious tone, and then relapsed into silence. They were evidently paid servants of the Prophet, not believers in his mission, and probably were the authors of many of those atrocities which so exasperated the population against them.

But apart from a single theft, abduction, or rape, it would have been impossible for Nauvoo to have existed in the centre of a civilized community.

People who claim to be the only recipients of truth, and whose habits and necessities require a plurality of wives, must be apart.

Nothing could induce decent men and women to live in continual dread of the seduction of their daughters.

Besides, the filthy example could not be allowed in a community which prided itself especially on the chastity of their women.

No one can, therefore, blame even the wild lawlessness of the mob which finally rooted out Mormonism from Illinois.

" I guess," continued one of the Danites, " that General Joe 'ull have to absquaterlate from these here parts. It's a getting too almighty hot."

" He will take us," said a deep grave voice, that made the two companions start, " to that long since promised land of which he has spoken thus,—" I will lead you over the Rocky Mountains to the fertile valleys of the Pacific, where a white man has never before trod. We will take with us our wives and our children, our cattle and our grain, our implements of labour ; and there, in the fastnesses of the West, we will rear for ourselves another Temple and home, which shall far surpass that we leave to be desecrated by the hands of the Gentiles. There we will be secure in our rock-begirt home, and defy the powers that refuse to us here the heritage which our God took from the unworthy and gave to us, to be ours and our children's for ever."

Again the old story came true. He could prophecy for others but not for himself.

Gradually the Danites, satisfied, as it appeared, that there were two to keep the rear, got to the front.

They remained alone.

" They are inside," gasped Merton, " but Heavens ! in what state—bound and gagged."

The other spoke not, but drawing forth a long glittering knife, of the kind called Bowie, ripped up the back canvas.

Yes ! there on a mattress, their feet and hands tied together, in the light of the glittering moon they saw two female forms, whose heads were covered by cloaks.

During the din made by the clatter of horses' hoofs ahead it was easy to act.

Each drew a girl gently from the mattress, and laying them on their horses in front, stood still.

" Not a word, on your lives !" whispered Merton ; " speak not, breathe not, and you are saved."

As they spoke they first cut the cords which fastened the gag in their mouths.

Where systematic seduction, abduction, and rape are the custom, gags become to be very scientific instruments.

As soon as the girls were free they halted, retreated to the cover of a rock, nor moved or spoke until they could no longer hear a sound of the van or Danites.

Then they were about to start, when they heard the quick returning gallop of several horsemen.

But, burdened as they were, they did not attempt to fly.

A pine grove stood hard by. To this they retreated.

Then they saw four or five of the Danites rush past, their horses' hoofs striking sparks of fire from the stony road, their bodies reeking in sweat, their tongues throwing back the foam, while the men urged them on even to increased speed.

CHAPTER XCVII.
DR. FOSTER.

Our sins find us.

The sins of the Prophet were lust of power and women.

He had ventured his soul on these two cravings of his insatiable nature.

He is described by some, who wish at least to remove from him the charge of imposture, as being a dupe of some clever man who fabricated the Book of Mormon.

His whole career disproves the possibility of this interpretation. His own words show how deliberate and solemn was his imposture.

Can anything surpass the cool effrontery of his own words?—

"While we (Joseph Smith and Oliver Cowdery) were thus employed (in the work of translation), praying and calling upon the Lord, a messenger from heaven descended in a cloud of light, and having laid his hands upon us, he ordained us, saying unto us, 'Upon you, my fellow-servants, in the name of the Messiah, I confer the priesthood of Aaron, which holds the keys of the ministering of angels, and of the gospel of repentance, and of baptism by immersion for the remission of sins; and this shall never be taken again from the earth until the sons of Levi do offer again an offering unto the Lord in righteousness.' And he commanded us to go and be baptized, and gave us directions that I should baptize Oliver Cowdery, and afterwards that he should baptize me. Accordingly we went, and were baptized. I baptized him first, and afterwards he baptized me. After which I laid my hands upon his head, and ordained him to the Aaronic priesthood; afterwards he laid his hands on me, and ordained me to the same priesthood; for so we were commanded. The messenger who visited us on this occasion, and conferred this priesthood upon us, said that his name was John, the same that is called John the Baptist in the New Testament, and that he acted under the direction of Peter, James, and John, who held the keys of the priesthood of Melchizedek, which priesthood, he said, should in due time be conferred on us, and that I should be called the first elder, and he the second."

No dupe could have made this deliberate statement. To all persons of sane and unprejudiced minds it decides the question.

But we must now precede the Prophet in his visit to one who, perhaps, influenced his fate more than any man in the whole of his extraordinary and chequered career.

The intentions of Joseph Smith, on leaving Nauvoo, was to take refuge in Iowa, and thence to send emissaries forward to that land of promise which he felt must now be the refuge of the Saints.

Thence he could in safety issue his manifestoes to his own people and to the Gentiles, as the officers of one state have no power in the next.

Several miles to the south of Nauvoo, on the banks of the Mississippi, was a pretty village, which, like Nauvoo itself, was young in years, but old in energy and thrift, for these qualities were transplanted from the Eastern States to this emporium of the West—the great Mississippi valley, which even now gives promise of rivalling the borders of the Atlantic in commerce and the wealth its deep, broad waters bear on its bosom. This village was, like similar ones that cover the Union from its farthest recesses to the heart of its interior, composed of all classes of America's hardy yeomanry, who, leaving the populous districts, chose a home in the wilds of the West, where they could, unmolested by party strife or jealous rivalry, carve for themselves at once a name and competency.

On the outskirts of this village, but scarcely within sight of its scattered houses, was the residence of one Foster, a name familiar to those who have studied the history of Mormonism.

He was a young medical student who, having passed his examination, had come out West to settle as a physician or medical practitioner.

But just then nobody was sick, so he bought some land, cleared and planted it, and, to his joy, found it the first year yielded him a better income than he had ventured to hope his profession would. On the slope that rolled away until it terminated on the bank of the river, he built a neat cottage, and surrounded it with all that could minister to the gratification of the eye and charm the senses.

The slope between the cottage and river was thickly studded with forest trees, which, cleared of the smaller growth of vegetation, and the surface converted into a greensward, made a natural grove of rare grandeur and beauty. The favourite sitting-room of the happy couple opened out on this grove, and they were wont to sit here and watch the restless waters as they moved on to the ocean, the tall waving trees hiding a full view, but leaving enough to make its fitful glimpses like gleams of silver through them.

To follow a profession is pleasant enough when success crowns our efforts, but it is the early stages which dishearten and discourage.

Not so, Dr. Foster, who cared not that the people hurried to call him in as long as he had fields waving with ripening grain, fat sheep filled his pasture, cows nightly were gathered in their pen, and sleek, high mettled horses filled his stables; while the fingers of his household god, assisted by the one maid, kept his cottage in order, and made the most exquisite dishes to grace his table out of the products of his land, and the most comfortable of apparel for his wear.

Now, in addition to all his other wants, Dr. Foster had a wife, a pretty, amiable, and loving woman, upon whom all the affections of his soul were centered.

For her it was he had studied, for her it was he had founded a home, and in her society he hoped to spend the remainder of his days in happiness and peace.

He counted without the Mormons, whose leprosy spread wherever there was a pleasing and fascinating woman to be found.

The Prophet had scouts who scoured the country, like the valets of profligate lords and gentlemen in a bye-gone age, in search of innocence, youth, and beauty.

It was evening, the hearth was swept, the tea was smoking on the board, the hot cakes were just taken from the iron girdle, and Mrs. Foster summoned her husband from poring over books to partake of the pleasant evening meal, which is rarely seen to greater perfection than in the newly-settled states of the American continent.

It was a delightful picture, and only wanted the addition of some younger and merrier faces to make it even more beautiful.

Married life is but half marriage without children.

They are the golden links which bind humanity to home and domestic comforts and enjoyments.

Foster put away the dry medical book which he pored over regularly for half an hour after dinner, and selecting a lighter and more amusing book, put it convenient to his hand to read out to his wife after tea.

They used to take it in turns. While he read, she sewed, while she read, he smoked.

At this moment a knock came to the door. A shade of vexation passed over the face of the wife. She had looked forward with particular satisfaction to the enjoyment of that evening — and ladies never like to be disappointed.

Dr. Foster himslf rose with an impatient shrug, and opened the door.

Three men, of tolerably respectable exterior, entered. They were sleek, and even sinister looking. There was about one of them, indeed, a self-satisfied look which was peculiarly offensive.

It bespoke a man who was, beyond everything, satisfied with himself and the world.

"Pardon me," he said, bowing, "if I intrude; but while wandering about admiring the prospect, we have become belated, and indeed have lost our way."

"Enter," replied the doctor, courteously, while his wife retired to the larder, and, summoning a tall, rawboned Irish girl to assist her, began copiously to replenish the board.

The men entered, and, as requested, took their seats.

The conversation began about the condition of the neighbourhood, its capabilities, its requirements, its beauty and fertility. The head stranger showed himself a competent judge, and as the young doctor was also learned in agricultural topics, the talk was pleasant enough.

"Have you been long here sir?" said the chief of the strangers.

"More than two years," replied Dr. Foster.

"Strange that, though a neighbour, I have never heard of this location before."

"Well, you see," laughed Foster, "perhaps I'm too young for a doctor, so I stay at home and work until I'm sent for."

"Charming location, sir-r," said the other, with the usual American burr; "fine meadows—pretty cattle."

"Tolerable," replied the doctor, modestly.

"Quite first-rate, sir-r," continued the other—"have a pretty picking myself. Heard tell of General Joe Smith, I suppose."

"I have," said Doctor Foster, with a dry cough, and a strange sense of impending evil.

"Ever seen him?"

"No—and ——"

"Allow me to introduce myself. I am General Joe Smith. But, doctor, if the presence of three humble apostles of the true faith be unpleasant—if you have prejudices ——"

"Oh no," said the doctor, rousing himself, and fully alive to the danger of making an enemy of one who had at his command the bloody Danites; "in fact, I know so little of your people in this, my seclusion, that it is rather a gratification than otherwise."

The Prophet bowed loftily.

"Alice, my dear," continued the doctor, "will you let us have tea? These gentlemen have had a long journey."

There were now on the table buckwheat cakes, loaves of bread, cold turkey and ham—universal food of the out-west—deer's meat, bacon in every form, molasses, and both tea and coffee.

The three Saints, powerful and corpulent men, made instant havoc with the viands.

Mrs. Foster sat at one end of the long deal table, which had been substituted for the cosy round mahogany one which contained their own tea. Her husband occupied the other end.

By this means the Prophet, who was to the right of the husband, was able to carry out his purpose of gazing at the young wife, which he did cautiously, but with a keen and critical eye.

Of this Doctor Foster was unaware.*

But so at the time was the wife, who, however, had awful reason to remember the circumstance.

After tea a conversation arose about Mormonism, in which Smith, assisted by his coadjutors, contrived to make out as good a case as possible for his doctrine.

Dr. Foster mildly, but with common sense and sound sterling eloquence, demolished every argument of the arch imposture.

No allusion was made to spiritual wifedom, as this was a delicate subject.

After awhile a case-bottle was introduced, and having been partaken of by all, the Mormons rose.

Doctor Foster made no attempt to prevent their departure. Had they been less obnoxious to him, he would certainly have asked them to remain the night.

---

* The Mormons, in their defence of the Prophet on this particular charge, speak of "one Foster, a Mormon, and member of the Danite band." They hope thus to weaken his evidence by making him a double renegade.

They shook hands, however, and Foster felt a cold shiver go through him when he saw his little wife's plump hand held tightly by the Prophet.

In a few minutes, however, they had left.

"Curses light on them!" he said, falling back in his chair, and filling up an unusually strong glass of brandy.

"What is the matter, dearest?" cried his affectionate wife, tenderly.

"No more peace—no more happiness!" he replied. "Those villains came here with a deliberate object!"

"What object, my dear?"

"That of stealing away my best, my most beloved treasure!" he replied.

"What treasure?" she innocently asked.

"You," he said.

The wife remained silent a moment. A faint blush came to her cheeks.

"That explains," she whispered.

"What?"

"That man's horrid looks—the wicked glance of his eye," she said.

"Heavens! we must leave this place,' cried Foster, hurriedly.

"My own dear husband, you have nothing to fear. Have you no confidence in your wife?" she added, proudly.

"Every confidence. But you know not these hellish Mormons. There is no art, however atrocious, no cunning, however base, which they will not put in practice. Violence is as nothing to them. But I will guard you, my treasure—none shall hurt you."

CHAPTER XCVIII.

THE PROPHET'S VISIT.

Two powerful dogs, and two brace of revolvers,* were added to the contents of the house.

Doctor Foster taught his wife the use of the latter, and sternly bade her shoot the first who dared to molest her.

Alice vowed she would.

But for some time nothing was heard of the Mormons, and they began to hope that they had forgotten the way to their house.

Mrs. Foster was fair. Some said she was really beautiful, and they were among the number of those who knew her best; for hers was the peculiar beauty that lay calm as starlight upon her smooth open brow, until the soul within was aroused to action, when sparkling light flashed from the soft eye, a sweet smile wreathed the mouth, and the soul within spoke in every curve of that fair face.

No wonder Foster was proud of her; for she was as good as she was beautiful.

The record of this phase in the Prophet's life we take from the joint narratives of his friends and enemies.

Alice was a woman, or rather, despite her marriage state, a girl of rare courage, inflexible purity;

* As we write we receive news of the death of Colonel Colt, who invented the revolver in 1829, and after great vicissitudes, died worth five millions of dollars.

and would brave any danger, rather than be intimidated by evil.

This gave Foster courage, though he had heard too much of the Mormons not to fear violence.

Still, as they came not, he began almost to laugh at his own fears, and, when one day he was sent for by a lady on an interesting occasion, he rode away without fear.

The summer was now almost gone, and the first crimson-tinged leaves of autumn strewed the ground.

Beautiful, sad autumn, in which the summer children go home, and in their departure warn their brethren that so must they follow!

Among the fallen leaves of the forest children on the lawn, Alice was walking, and as was her wont she bent her steps to the bank that overlooked the Mississippi. Here she paused gazing out on the waters, the opposite bank, and the clear blue sky; she stood drinking in the changing beauty of the scene, so rapt and so unthinking of molestation, that she saw nor heard not the approach of anyone, until her name was softly whispered by her side, and, with a startled exclamation, she turned and confronted the Prophet.

Alice felt no fear, but still, at the same time, she could not repress altogether the rising of the tell-tale blood to her forehead.

"Pardon this intrusion," said Joe Smith, with a soft and benignant smile; "I went up to the house to thank your husband for his kind hospitality the other evening, and finding both out, ventured to search for you in this pleasant retreat."

"My husband required no thanks for what he would have done for any other chance stranger," said Alice, as coldly as she could.

The Prophet bit his lips.

"How chances it," he replied, affecting not to notice her repellant manner, "that this beautiful spot was never located before?"

"It was," said Alice, turning towards the house.

"Then your husband bought it?"

"He did."

And still she moved towards the house. The Prophet, with a sinister smile upon his countenance, followed. There was a wicked look in his pig-like eyes which boded no good.

The house was now in sight.

Alice entered. The Prophet was close behind her.

"Sir," said the young woman, turning round upon him in all the pride of her glorious and womanly beauty, "if you wish to see my husband, you can wait here. My servant will see to your wants."

And she turned to go.

The Prophet was too quick for her.

"Madame," he said, hoarsely, "you must not leave me thus. I have travelled far for one glance at your beautiful eyes. I love you; do not say anything rash. You are married—so am I, you would say; but why be blinded to the truth? Polygamy is the most sacred institution of God. Did not the Almighty visit Abraham, the husband of many wives, and go into a discussion with him on his family and domestic concerns? Did he not virtually say unto Abraham, 'I find no fault with

JOE SMITH AND MRS FOSTER.

your taking two wives, but on the other hand, I bless you for it, and bless you in doing it, and I bless them in becoming your wives, above all the women of the earth ?' "

Alice was confounded, she could not speak.

" Jacob had several wives, and by them were born unto him the twelve patriarchs ; now, mam, one of these wives was honoured by being the lineal mother of——"

" Hold, foul blasphemer !" said Alice, disengaging herself ; " we are not Jews, but servants of Him who has prohibited, as adultery, taking a second wife. But go—lest in my passion I do or say that which I may regret."

Joe Smith fell upon his knees, and clasped his fat, oily hands.

" Beloved creature !" he began.

" Another word, and I let loose the dogs——"

At this moment, Doctor Foster entered, and, without saying a word, proceeded to administer to the kneeling Prophet such a cow-hiding as probably he felt the effects of for the rest of his career.

" And now, sir," said the doctor, drawing a revolver, " you may go. But let me catch you anywhere about my premises again, and no consideration shall save your wretched and miserable life.

With an awful scowl, the Prophet slunk out ;

and afraid to show himself in Nauvoo in his present state, slunk away to hide himself in a small farm-house, at no great distance, but, at the same time, on the frontiers of Illinois and Missouri.

CHAPTER XCIX.

OBADIAH JONES.

THE place selected by the Prophet for his temporary retirement (we must apologize for keeping the two men on horseback, on the road, all this time) was Dixon, in Illinois, but so close to the frontier line of Missouri as to render it somewhat of a dangerous residence.

The Mormons had been expelled from Missouri, with ignominy.

They were the utter detestation of the whole community, and the Prophet especially had several writs out against him.

The people, whose property had been pillaged and destroyed by the Mormons, had brought actions against their General, Mayor, and Prophet Smith, and obtained severe damages.

Up to this time they had not been able to take him, as the Missouri officers had no power to act in Illinois.

This strict law between the states was productive sometimes of most ludicrous results.

The several states made their own laws, and many men with Mormon tastes and habits had thus been able to gratify their lustful whims.

A man once married several wives, taking care, however, always to marry a fresh one in each state.

The law could not touch him.

He married a wife in Missouri, and after six months of wedded happiness, deserted her for another girl at Dixon.

Now, Dixon was on the frontier of Missouri, though in Illinois.

A conference was held. The man was arrested, and the jury found that he had been guilty of bigamy in the State of Missouri, *the township of Dixon being declared, for all legal purposes, in the State of Missouri.*

The Prophet Smith could have known nothing of this story, or he would have given his friends in Missouri a wider berth.

But those whom heaven has condemned, it first sends mad, says the proverb.

The friend of the Prophet Joe Smith, near Dixon, was a man of singular character. He was of unknown origin. He had come, nobody knew whence, and had established himself on the borders of Missouri, as near the line of demarcation as possible.

He had his reason for this.

Obadiah Jones was a coiner and dealer in forged notes, which rendered him anxious to have always the benefit of a doubt.

Fifty feet on one side of his cabin was Missouri.

Fifty feet on the other was Illinois.

If the sheriff of the latter came to pay him a visit—and he always kept a good look-out—he slipped into Missouri, and *vice versa*.

Thus, with the exception of a stray whipping,

one ride on a rail, and two tarrings and featherings, Obadiah Jones had come off pretty well—he kalkerlated!

Smith had known him years.

He was a first-rate purveyor and spy.

He could do a little in any line from abduction to burglary.

This man was just the unscrupulous agent the Prophet required.

"Do you know Doctor Foster?" said the Prophet Smith, as he sat down to forget his troubles over a stiff glass of grog and a pipe.

"Guess I do."

"Like him?"

"Kalkerlate I don't."

"Well—I hate him!"

"What's he been and done, gin'ral?"

"He's got a pretty wife ——"

"Oh!"

"Now you know, Obadiah, all I have told you of the desire I have that female souls may be saved and not cast out ——"

"Liquor up!" groaned Obadiah, "and none of your gammon with this here child."

"My glass is empty."

"That's it; brew it right hot—and then tell us hall about it. The gal takes yer fancy."

"She does."

"Just so—hit it on the nail. Well."

"I was just talking to her this morning, telling her of the gospel of truth, and trying to prepare her mind for the true faith, when ——"

"In kimmed the boss," said Obadiah Jones, with a most ludicrous glance.

"Just so, Obadiah."

"And kicked yer starn-post out of the diggens," grinned the outlaw.

"No, sir."

"What then?"

"He took a mean advantage of me, and, having a whip in his hand, I had to go."

"That air accounts for the oneasy way as you sits, general. Knows all about it—rode on a rail once mysel'. Don't reckon it just exactly good for the constertution. But d'ye see, friend Joe Smith, these trifles aint worth speaking about."

"Trifles!"

"Yes, general—trifles! But about that ere Doctor Foster—he's powerful rich, and got a mighty tall crop of hosses. Now, if there's one thing as Obadiah Jones kin do bang up and no mistake, it's hoss."

"Take all you like, so I have the woman and my revenge!"

"Wull, gin'ral, whin shall it come off?"

"When I can move without showing that I am sore."

"As soon as yer like."

It was a log-hut, with one room, and a half loft reached by a ladder. This was used by the outlaw as his look-out; but on this occasion he was too jolly and busy to trouble himself about such trifles.

Joe Smith again filled his glass and loaded his pipe.

"Let's take a look out—it's a mighty fine night," said Obadiah Jones.

And he threw open the door.

As he did so, in rushed four men with cocked revolvers, and before the astounded outlaw and his companion, the Prophet, had time to make the slightest resistance, they were each caught by two men.

"By what authority?" said Joe Smith.

"This!" said a sheriff's officer, shewing a writ.

"But this is Illinois."

"Is it?" grinned the officer; "then it's mighty nigh. But if you don't like the writ, these here dokements will do."

And they put their revolvers to his breast, and said these were their authorities. They refused, he says, to let him go and get his hat, and forced him into a waggon; they struck him over the head and back with the butt ends of their pistols, and, as he alleged, otherwise abused, insulted, and threatened him in the cruelest manner. He was retained in custody by these men for several weeks, but ultimately obtained his release on a writ of habeas corpus, and was sent back to Illinois. He thereupon commenced an action against them for false imprisonment, and for using unnecessary force and violence towards him. Though the case was clearly proved, he only obtained the small damages of forty dollars, and from first to last had to pay upwards of three thousand five hundred dollars, for legal expenses.

Such was the abhorrence of the people of him and his doctrines, that the jury which found in his favour had to be protected.

There are occasions when the *vox populi* is the only means of eradicating some pestilent evil.

But the damage done to Joe Smith by three weeks of imprisonment was more than he expected. In the interval the *Nauvoo Expositor* had been published, with a letter from Foster, and the affidavits of sixteen women to the effect that Joseph Smith, Sidney Rigdon, and others, had endeavoured to convert them to the "spiritual wife," doctrine, and to seduce them under the plea of having had especial permission from Heaven. This was somewhat too daring to be allowed in their stronghold; and Joseph Smith, in his capacity of Mayor of Nauvoo, immediately summoned the alderman, councillors, and other members of the corporation, to consider the publication. They unanimously declared it to be a public nuisance, and ordered the city marshal to abate it forthwith.

CHAPTER C.

ALICE.

HAVING thus recapitulated the events which caused the attempted arrest of Joe Smith, we will, after mentioning one fact, continue our narrative.

Foster, Law, and others it was who had obtained the warrants for the arrest of Joe, and some twenty other Mormon chiefs.

But the majesty of the law having been defied, they had retired to Carthage, to complain, and to demand from Governor Ford the assistance of the militia to enforce the warrants.

He had resolved to make one solemn appeal to General Smith, to surrender and take his trial, ere he risked the shedding of blood.

Having attended to this business, and being promised a final decision in forty-eight hours, Foster and his friend Law rode home attended by several armed comrades.

Their way was the same as that by which the Prophet had escaped.

Presently they heard the furious clatter of the Danites.

"Who comes?" they cried, as they approached.

The Danites halted, and a hasty whisper passed round the body.

"Only a spree," said one, with a drunken laugh.

And they turned back the way they had come.

"Strange," thought Foster, aloud.

"Danites," said Law.

"Ha! then there is mischief afloat," shouted Foster; "come!"

And he set spurs to his horse.

They had not gone very far before they came to the grove of pines.

"Who comes?" said a hollow voice.

"Good neighbours—enemies to all Mormons," cried Foster.

"Then take us somewhere where we may get help for two of their wretched and dying victims."

"This way," cried Foster, once more; "in a quarter of an hour you will be at my house. Come."

And leaving Law to guide them, he hurried forward at the very top of his speed.

Then loud and thrilling shrieks filled the air, and Foster knew that the spoiler was in his home.

A high fence divided him from his own ground, a fence his horse could not take.

But he has not three minutes' gallop to reach his house.

Away! away! at the utmost maddening speed to which he can urge his horse. Round the corner he darts; his house, his lawn, lay before him.

Up! up! he rises in the saddle; and clearing a high hedge, jumps from his horse, fires a revolver, and falls headlong to the ground.

His foot was caught in the stirrup.

When he came to himself, his wife was chafing his head, and embracing him tenderly.

"Where are they?"

"Who, dear?"

"The Mormons."

"Gone, dear."

"You recognized them?"

"I believe it to have been the two men who accompanied the Prophet, and some others."

The whole party now came up, and mutual explanations took place.

Foster heard all in moody silence.

"This cannot go on any longer," said Law.

"Let daylight come," cried Foster—and his words are on record, as having in the main been fulfilled—"so that I can place Alice in security, I swear by the Heaven above me, I will shoulder my rifle, and never lay it down until Nauvoo is razed to the ground. It makes me feel like a demon, to think they should dare raise their polluted thoughts to my wife; but they shall rue the deed, for devastation shall follow them until there shall not be one left in a week's travel from Nauvoo.

"Everybody is of the same opinion," returned Law, fiercely. "No one is safe."

"Come in; we forget these fainting sufferers."

The two half-insensible girls were borne into the kitchen, where the Irish girl lay moaning, and their faces brought to the light.

It was Sophia, but not Jessie.

It was a girl as beautiful, only with chestnut hair, and dark complexion.

Fletcher gazed at her for a moment in deep thought.

"I don't know her," he said, after awhile.

But Mrs. Foster and the doctor lost no time. They hurried them into a bed-room, and by chafing their wrists, and administering sal volatile, soon brought them to.

They had already a vague consciousness of their having escaped from Smith.

Sophia looked strangely at the strange companion who lay beside her. She was scarcely eighteen years of age, of full rounded form, and complexion that rivalled the peach, when ripened by the Southern sun; lips of the cherry, and eyes liquid and blue as the heart of violets. Now her long, shining hair was in disorder, her dark lashes drooped over the liquid orbs, and her rounded arms hung listlessly by her side, as the fair young head sank in despair upon her bosom.

"Where can Jessie be?" asked Sophia.

"If you mean our unfortunate companion," said the girl, in a soft, silvery voice, "she was in front of the waggon, less rigorously treated than us, being in custody of an old woman."

"Poor, poor Jessie!"

"I cannot say," said the poor young girl, "I am really and truly sorry for being saved; but I deeply regret that the state to which we were reduced prevented my giving warning."

"It cannot be helped, poor girl!" said Sophia.

"Will you join the gentlemen now, and have some supper?" said Alice, whose well-regulated mind had recovered its tone.

"Yes," said Sophia, blushing; for she knew to whom she was indebted.

The other girl sighed. She had not a friend in the world that she was aware of.

The hospitable table of Dr. Foster again groaned with the weight of victuals and drink.

Merton and Fletcher had removed their wigs.

They were now two handsome young men.

No wonder, when Sophia threw herself sobbing and weeping into Merton's arms, that the Unknown shook hands warmly with her own rescuer.

He was dark, with eyes which beamed with expression and something more.

There was something in his manner that rendered him nearly as dangerous as a Mormon.

They would have used violence. This man was deeply versed in the ways of sin.

It was Lord Thynne, in pursuit of Jessie.

Mrs. Foster sat at the head of the table, surrounded by her husband and neighbours.

Merton sat next to Sophia, who was telling her adventures since she left home.

Merton was scarcely surprised at anything which the girl told him, as he had his strong suspicions of her aunt from the moment that he had proposed.

Lord Thynne, throwing into his voice that low thrill which makes the hearts of young girls beat so wildly, begged the young brunette to tell her tale.

"Not now," she said; "not now. I am not sufficiently well. But I will soon."

"But I must continue the pursuit of Jessie."

The girl, whose name was Pauline, looked down upon the ground.

"She is," continued Lord Thynne, "the affianced wife of a dear friend of mine, whose life trembles in the scale."

"You are very generous," she whispered.

"No. But this so adventure has endeared you to me, that I know not what to do."

The girl did not answer.

Lord Thynne watched her keenly.

"Will you rise early and take a walk?" he said.

She consented.

The conversation soon became general, and then the ladies retired. On such occasions, in hospitable America—the finest country in the world where you have to deal only with the agricultural population—when the house is small and thus overcrowded, the ladies have the bed-rooms, while the men "pig" together in the public apartment.

Grog of all sorts was now placed upon the table, with cigars and pipes; and a plan of campaign entered on, by which to drive out the Mormons from Nauvoo and the state generally.

The whole state was in a furious mood, so that, in all probability, there would be a terrible and bloody conflict.

CHAPTER CI.

OBADIAH MYSTERIOUS.

THE fury of the Prophet, when his satellites returned without Alice, knew no bounds.

He had already foamed with rage at the loss he had sustained in Sophia and Pauline.

He looked on these two—Jessie and Alice—as the lights of his harem, around whom all the others were to shine.

At least in a Turkish harem there is a legitimate wife. The rest are *odalisques*, or slaves.

But now what was he to do? Doctor Foster, having gone the lengths of publishing his insult upon his wife, would publicly join in the persecution of the Saints.

Then he recollected Obadiah Jones.

The constables of Missouri would not venture to attack him again.

Thither then, with all speed, he took his way.

To his astonishment, he found Obadiah had just finished a much smaller and neater hut beside the other, as is often the case in America.

It was separated by a narrow passage.

The backwoodsmen do this in many cases, to have their wives and children apart.

Obadiah was standing smoking at his door

when they came up. It was two in the morning, but the fellow had odd ways.

"Can I have shelter for the night?" said General Joseph Smith.

"Dunno."

"Why not, my old friend?"

"How many on you?" grunted Jones.

"Two ladies and myself, the rest can sleep in your waggon."

Jones drew the Prophet on one side, and looked keenly at him.

"None of yer ma'ms?" he said.

"Why?"

"Look you here, Joe, I knowed you in other days, up in the New York hills, when we did *some* smashing. And I knows yer ideas of the female critters—and I wouldn't have one of your ma'ms enter thar—no, not if——"

Joe Smith looked at him. There was a remarkable change about the man. Something had elevated and made him better.

"The girl is a hostage—a prisoner," said Joe, "if you will let her go in there—she must be watched."

"There arn't no windows, except in the roof," replied Obadiah, "and I keeps the key of the gate."

"Bring her in."

In five minutes more Jessie, *not* gagged—not bound, but led by an aged negress, came in.

She was ill, but still could give a defiant glance of scorn at Joe Smith.

"A glass of water," she said, faintly, turning at the same time to the rough backwoodsman.

He gave her one look, and his once ruffian glance softened.

"Come this way, gal, go in thar," he said as he opened a door; "and you'll maybe find better nor water."

Joe Smith eagerly followed her with his eye. All he caught sight of was an elegantly furnished apartment.

Then the door closed.

The wearied Danites hoppled their horses, and retired to a barn-like shed of recent erection.

Decidedly there was a change in the circumstances of Obadiah Jones.

They made a fire, heated some water, drank a quantity of grog, and went to sleep.

Joe and Obadiah remained alone in the log-hut. They were seated at the fire; they had their brandy-and-water and pipes.

"Change come over you, Obadiah?" said Joe.

"There is."

"What's up?"

"Everything."

"How do you mean?"

"Gin up everything—coining, smashing, forgin—eh! Going to try work. Bought four hunder acre of land. Got cattle and labourers all a-coming to-morrow, and——"

"What?" said Joe, seeing that the other hesitated.

"Well, never mind. Are you flying at last?"

"I am a martyr. The Gentiles are thirsting for my blood," said Joe.

"I knows it," replied Obadiah, musing. "They means to sack your town, destroy your temple, and drive you to lands beyond the Rocky Mountains. Well do you know, Joe?"

"What?"

"*I means to jine 'em.* I gives you four and twenty hours law, Joe Smith—and then, why look out. This here child 'ill go in slick with the Regulators."

"Good heavens, Obadiah! what do you mean?"

"General Joe Smith, I've got a little fortin, which I wishes to enjoy in peace."

"Do you?"

"And, General Joseph Smith, I've got a darter —thar!"

A cold smile passed over the face of the general.

"And I've got this here fust-rate revolver," said Obadiah; "and if you moves a step, or tries to communicate with them darned Danites, here goes!"

And he rose, barred the door, and turned a key in a padlock.

"Here you stays until my friends come in the morning," continued Obadiah. "Don't be alarmed. I guv you four and twenty hours' law—and you shall have it. So drink away, old boy. We needn't part enemies, especially if yer going away."

Joe Smith made no reply, but sullenly drank and smoke; Obadiah Jones keeping his eye upon him all the time.

And thus the time passed until it was an hour past dawn, when the old negress began to bustle about, and, under the directions of Obadiah, prepare breakfast.

Then the backwoodsman, having seen to his long six-foot shooting-iron, threw open the door.

A number of labourers and friends were coming down a distant slope.

His daughter, his promise to amend after a frank confession of his evil ways, and the fact that he had inherited money, had induced many to forgive his past history.

"Give me my hostage," said Joe Smith, hoarsely, "and I will take your twenty-four hours' law."

Obadiah knocked at the door.

Receiving no answer, he opened and entered.

He stood a moment, utterly dumbfounded. Then he burst into a loud fit of laughter.

"Sloped, by gum! Been and 'listed Dora's feelings and hooked it."

Joe Smith rushed after him. A table had been dragged into the middle of the room, a chair placed on that, and then the sloping window of the roof removed.

"Them gals! them gals!" said Obadiah, screaming with laughter. "I thought I'd fixed her. Wull, p'raps I mout one, but tu's the devil. Clean gone, bolted, obsquatulated."

Joe Smith cursed and swore awfully.

"Riled are you, old 'un?" said Obadiah. "Well, if you likes to fight, I'm yer man, considering my gal's gone."

Joe Smith turned away, pale with rage.

He roused his men, had the horses put to, and intimated that he would breakfast at the first convenient spot on the road.

Then he hurried away, all the blackest passions of his heart gleaming through his eyes.

No sooner was he out of sight than two girls entered the house from a small wood, the one laughing heartily, the other grave, yet smiling

"You puss, you witch you devil, you!" said Obadiah Jones.

"Now don't talk nonsense," said Eudora, who was, without exception, the finest girl of her age—sixteen—perhaps ever seen; "I wasn't going to allow that old seven-leagued ogre to run away with the beautiful princess, I can tell you."

"Getting your father into precious scrapes, you witch, you," he replied; "but here come neighbours to finish the barn. Get up, you lazy one, and let us have some breakfast."

We will presently tell our readers how this escape had occurred, and how Jessie had been able to win the co-operation of Eudora Jones.

She now, in gratitude to her magnificent and beautiful young friend, hurried, after they both had made a hasty toilet, to lay out the breakfast.

You may be sure the neighbours stared to see *two* such lovely specimens of female humanity.

"What, Obadiah!" said a huge Kentuckian, "another wench—eh—not turned Mormon?"

"No—jist turned Joe Smith and his Danites out, with a flea in their ears."

"Law, sakes, have you, though? Du tell how it war—hearn tell there's goin' to be a great stir."

"There is," said a stout neighbour; "they're going to be exterminated. I recollect when they came. They worked hard enough. They had a printing press, and bank, and schools. There were large fields of grain, which grew, and were garnered; and the city, late a wilderness, was ringing with the busy throng of active, earnest, civilized life."

"True," said a bilious-looking Englishman, "and I fancied they would be good neighbours."

"So did I—but then came the Prophet, who found that they were harassed by us Gentiles, as they call us, who had sold 'em grain, vegetables, cattle, merchandize, and timber."

"Aye! aye!"

"They guv'd notes," said Obadiah, with a merry twinkle of his eye, "about as good as some others used to was."

"Good for you," grinned the farmer.

"Well, what does Joe Smith do, but has a visit from his angel, who says,—

"Behold, thou art forbidden n my laws to get into debt to thine enemies; but behold it is not said, at any time, that the Lord should not take when he pleases, and pay as seemeth to him good; and, wherefore, as ye are agents, and are on the Lord's errand, and whatever ye do according to the will of the Lord, is the Lord's business—He has sent you to provide for them in these last days, that they may obtain an inheritance in the land of Zion."

"That's too good," said the Englishman.

"Well, the Mormons no longer dared to make bargains with us Gentiles. But the Gentiles' fields, barns, and granaries were overflowing, while they had no money to buy, and were in want of those ores with which they were surrounded. Smith's devil here came to his aid—perhaps he

remembered the resources of his family of old in such a dilemma, for their peculiarities here burst out to an alarming extent. Oxen, cows, horses, and sheep by droves disappeared, while granaries some thirty farmers had at night left loaded with plump, ripe grain, in the morning were found to be entirely empty—while bogus coinage flooded the district for a hundred miles around."

"And, golly!" said Obadiah, laughing, "did'nt you lay some on it to me as was as innocent as a lamb?"

By this time the breakfast was ready. Coffee, tea, beer, were flanked by large quantities of every kind of solid food which is usually to be found in the richly-favoured Western districts of America.

Everybody did free justice to the meal.

Then came work. The barn had to be finished off and roofed.

This, as usual, was done with rapidity and alacrity. Such neighbourly attentions are universal in the backwoods. It is a fine trait in modern American civilization.

About one there was a dinner, and after that work.

Then came evening, and now began the fun.

CHAPTER CII.

A BACKWOOD FROLIC.

Now if you never have been in the backwoods of America, and never seen what is called a frolic, you ought to.

We have, and never in all our born days shall we forget the emotions of delight and fun with which we entered into the scene.

If you want to see girls and boys enjoy themselves, that's the real ticket.

It is a relief from the fearful tragedy of Carthage, which is coming, to pause a moment, and compare the honest settlers with the dissolute and crafty Mormons.

About six the girls began to arrive. Of course a frolic was nothing without them—and such girls! It made your eyes wink to look at them.

None of your pale-faced, quiet, demure city girls, who cast their eyes down upon the ground when spoken to by a strange man, who answer in a faint, lisping voice, and condescend to dance when very much pressed; but rosy, hearty, laughing girls, who were, to use their own expressive language, death on to a dance.

It was a bold man who began, for as sure as he did, he never left off.

There was a black fiddler, too, no other man of mortal make being fit for the work.

The tables were cleared away, the floor swept, partners chosen, and then amid shouts of laughter, such as only come from really happy natures, the dancing commenced.

We recollect the first frolic we were at. It began at six in the evening, and ended at eight in the morning. That was a frolic. But, then, it was eighteen years ago; heyho! how the time passes.

The first request made upon that occasion made us laugh unreasonably.

" Please, sir, take off them heavy boots, and dance in your stockings. I have."

And, as we glanced at our partner's feet, we discovered that she had taken off her shoes, and did *not* wear stockings."

But during all this merriment and fun there were more serious matters in hand.

A man came in and drew Obadiah Jones on one side.

He had the appearance of a townsman, but was dressed in the garb of a farmer; a portly and striking looking man.

He drew Obadiah out of hearing.

" Stranger," he said, " is your name Obadiah ?"

" Yes."

" Jones ?"

" Yes."

" Ever hear tell of a *posse comitatus* ?"

" Think I have."

" Well there's one a coming."

" Is there ?—Wull, d'yer know what I'll do with yer *posse comitatus* ?"

" No."

" Turn him out."

" But," said the stranger, fixing his eyes in surprise on the other's face, " has'nt you several warrants against you ?"

" I ayre had once," said Obadiah, kissing his hand to Eudora, who was handing round the whisky punch in a somewhat original manner.

Jessie, who was now full of merriment, carried the bowl in her hands. It had luckily a couple of handles, for the punch was reeking hot.

Eudora had one ladle, and one glass.

With this she served the company.

There had been one of those terrible shake-downs, during which we scarcely knew which to admire most, the energy of the dancers, or the patience of the fiddlers.

Everybody was seated, the swains were rubbing themselves dry wherever they were uncovered, and looking very much as if they wished custom allowed them to uncover a deal more.

The girls were mostly looking mighty red in the face—fanning themselves with their pocket-handkerchiefs or anything else they could get.

The whisky punch—of which each had a large tumbler—was very welcome.

The bold ones went up to a table and helped themselves. The timid ones waited their turn.

Eudora made as much haste as she could, for she wanted to give her father a glass.

The stranger's back was turned to her.

Jessie's load was lightened every moment.

There remained not more than two or three tumblers in the huge bowl.

" Now, father !" said the magnificent Eudora.

The stranger still turned his back.

" Liquor up, stranger ?" asked Obadiah Jones.

" Well," said the other, still looking in the direction of the door, " if I must, I must—but I'm not particularly given to drinking."

Eudora coloured up to the very eyes.

Jessie let fall the bowl, and sank on a wooden block that served as a chair.

The whole company rose as one man, and rushed to her assistance.

Eudora, however, waved them off, and supported Jessie in her arms. She was herself rosy red. The sound of the man's voice had startled her almost as much as it had Jessie.

" What's the matter ?" asked Obadiah, waving the others to stand back.

Eudora pretended not to hear.

" Do you know that man ?" she said, addressing the half-fainting girl.

" Know him," shrieked Jessie, standing up and glaring wildly around, " know that fiend in human shape !"

" My affianced husband," said Eudora, coldly.

" What—great 'Heaven forfend ! Rather die, and have the worms gnaw your body, than be the wife of one lost to all sense of shame and decency —the man of forty wives, the impostor only second in wickedness and deceit to Joseph Smith himself—the Archdeacon of Mormon infamy—Brigham Young !" *

All turned round. He was nowhere to be seen. But the galloping of a horse was distinctly heard.

This announcement seemed to strike the whole company dumb for a moment.

Then out poured a flood of maledictions, curses, and oaths.

Some ran to the door, just in time to catch a glimpse of the arch-impostor, the successor of the first Mahomet of Mormonism, Brigham Young, escaping at the full speed of his horse.

The repentant Obadiah Jones was ghastly with passion.

" Do you know him ?" he said, hoarsely— clutching his daughter by the arm—while he himself shook as with the palsy.

" Know him ?—yes. The wretch crept into our school at New York, as the friend of a French teacher. He told me he was an exiled Irish patriot, and working on my imagination, made me believe that I cared for him."

" The monstrous villain !"

" But I do not," said Eudora, who was very calm and very white ; " I never did. This, however, I do know, that I will not be thus insulted, and this man shall pay dearly for his levity."

" That he shall," cried Obadiah Jones, looking significantly at his rifle.

" I devote one year of my young life to revenge," continued the other, loftily.

" In the meantime," said Obadiah, " we've just got to kalkerlate what's to be done. This ere ruffian ain't alone—so what says you, gals and boys—will yer make it all night ?—and then I shuts up, puts Dora in safety, and hey falutin for Nauvoo !"

" Hoorah !" said the men.

" Fust chop," said the girls.

" Mighty good," said Obadiah, gravely, " so now kick up, and you, Dora, no puling—fill a pail full of grog and liquor up. But we'll have a sentinel outside to watch as them varmint don't kim on us unawars—and I'll begin."

Loud shouts of applause greeted this decision, and in a few minutes more the negro fiddler was at work ; the men were taking out their partners, the girls were mincing and giggling and laughing,

---

* Now Prophet. His career and the story of Eudora, will be narrated in second volume. The Salt Lake mystery has never yet been told.

and everything went on merry as a marriage bell, just as if no Mormons had been in existence at all.

Eudora took Jessie on one side, and they held a conference.

Eudora's self-love was wounded. She had never liked the man in the way a woman does who surrenders the whole devotion of her heart for life; but the artful cunning of the man had excited a feeling of pity—which is akin to love—in her bosom which cannot be easily eradicated in one moment.

The heart is not a machine which can be wound up and let down like the wheels of an ordinary watch.

It takes time to be toned down and calmed.

The plan of revenge fixed on by Eudora was so romantic and singular, that it startled and even revolted Jessie, who was herself too gentle to conceive the idea of vengeance.

But Eudora was eloquent, and pleaded her wrongs with energy and vigour.

Jessie refused to co-operate actively, and with this Eudora was compelled to be satisfied.

CHAPTER CIII.

ARREST OF JOSEPH SMITH.

GREAT was the consternation in Nauvoo among the elders and the disciples when it was known that General Joseph Smith had fled.

They looked at one another in dismay, and shook their heads. After all, the Prophet was human, and was afraid of facing his enemies.

Equally great was the fury of the people of Illinois when they found that the majesty of the law had been outraged, while the offender had, after insulting the officers of justice, fled to Iowa.

Meetings were held in every town, county, and village, and then the state rose as one man.

They informed the governor, that if he did not execute the law, the people would call in Judge Lynch.

The governor held council with his advisers, and it was determined, in the face of the indignation of the people, to call out the militia, and execute the warrants against the Prophet and his patriarchs.

The news reached Nauvoo, and the Mormons immediately began fortifying the city.

They announced their intention of defending themselves to the last.

The governor all the more quickly hurried out the militia, and with a large force marched on the Mormon capital.

But he found that the rage, fury, and hate of the populace had preceded him.

He rode on in front of his men, slowly and thoughtfully talking with his staff.

A mounted soldier came galloping up, and halting, touched his hat.

"What is it, Barker?"

"Two thousand armed citizens are now around the city, which bristles with bayonets. There will be a bloody conflict, general, if you don't make haste."

"Follow me, gentlemen," said the governor; "hurry up the men. I will ride forward."

And at a sharp trot the puzzled officer dashed onward, until he found himself surrounded by a wild, infuriated, and angry mob.

Loud shouts and murmurs greeted his approach. He held up his hand for silence.

"The law is strong enough to punish. Why this lawless assembly? Who has dared to take upon himself the collecting together of these illegal forces? I have come here in the law's name to arrest General Smith and his co-accused. He shall be tried by the law."

"No trial—hang him! Down with the bloody, thieving Mormons!"

"I will have no mob riots," cried the old governor, firmly. "Silence! I say."

At this moment the head of his column of troops debouched on the plain, and the mob, after some time, agreed to leave the matter in the hands of the general.

Then a flag of truce was sent into Nauvoo, with a demand that the accused should be given up.

The answer was, that General Smith and the others had retired from the city.

Governor Ford gave them forty-eight hours to surrender, after which he declared that he could answer for nothing.

He knew that if the hourly-increasing mob were to precipitate themselves on the city a terrible slaughter must ensue.

He knew that the Mormons would fight—but that would make matters worse.

He then sent a firm message. The accused must surrender, or Nauvoo would be sacked and razed to the ground.

The Mormons knew that they had no hope, so the leaders, who were in the secret of the Prophet's hiding-place, sent word that he must surrender, the more readily that he was certain of acquittal.

But the Prophet had no such hope. His whole life of crime would be laid bare.

But he had to choose between surrender and the utter loss of all hold over his deluded followers.

Had Joe Smith now have fled, Mormonism would have been extinct.

He surrendered, and was taken to the prison of Carthage, a name for ever memorable in Mormon history.

CHAPTER CIV.

THE PLOTTERS.

ABOUT half-a-mile from Carthage was a small inn, which once had been the place of meeting of all the horse thieves, coiners, forgers, and other loafers of the State of Illinois.

It was situated in a gloomy dell, sheltered by funeral looking pines.

It was a large wooden frame house, with stables and outhouses.

A narrow road, fit only for foot passengers and horsemen, led from the main highway to the Golden Bough.

In some days the inn had been unfrequented, but now there was an air of bustle and activity about it which showed that business was looking up.

MORMON VENGEANCE.

The large room was set out for a large company.

All day, however, everything was still and quiet; but no sooner did evening set in than they began to arrive.

They were all stalwart men, well armed, and grave and solemn in manner.

They all exchanged a password with the tall lanky incumbent of the inn, and then went into the public room.

Among those who came was, Obadiah Jones, Foster, Law, and others who had been injured by the Mormons.

There were some thirty in all.

As soon as the muster was satisfactory, liquor was ordered, and the door closed.

That which they had to discuss admitted not of publicity.

It was the first act in a horrible tragedy.

The men collected together in that place were all of powerful and energetic frames, or at least, of energetic and powerful minds.

They felt deeply on the Mormon question, and were determined to put up with no more of their misdeeds.

They would be satisfied with nothing less than their total expulsion from the state, if they would avoid extermination.

But all were thoroughly agreed upon one point, and that was, the punishment of Joe Smith.

That charlatan and impostor who had carried desolation into so many families, who had broken so many homes, and gained for himself such a fearful reputation, must be punished.

But how?

Nobody could exactly make up their minds.

Foster was put into the chair, and the question was discussed in an animated way.

At length it was decided that the law should be allowed to take its course, but that at the first sign of weakness on the part of the executive, the people would take the law into their own hands.

With this view the meeting resolved itself temporarily into a secret society for the protection of the country against the evil-doers.

It was resolved unanimously that they should disperse to their several homes, and collect from all parts such a force as should enable them to awe the militia if they sided with the Mormons, which, to a certain extent, they were likely to do.

The rendezvous was Carthage, at twelve o'clock, when the prisoners would be taken before a magistrate, and discharged or finally committed.

This agreed to, the party of Regulators, as the supporters of Lynch Law always called themselves, dispersed to their several homes.

Obadiah, Foster, and Law, took the same road. They had strong reasons for detesting the Mormons, and were the main movers in the plot against them.

Obadiah Jones had told Foster quite enough to convince the latter that the squatter was a useful associate. His deadly hatred against Brigham Young was such that he could scarcely be advised against a solitary foray into Nauvoo, to put the future Prophet to death.

But they induced him to bide his time, until the fate of Joseph Smith had been decided on.

About three miles from the house occupied by Obadiah Jones, they parted, and the squatter started on his solitary walk.

The greater part of his journey was to be performed under the shadow of trees. It was the remains of one of those vast forests which still remain to attest the magnificent character of American vegetation.

Obadiah had a long shooting-iron, as he called it, and a brace of revolvers. It was not likely, however, that he would require to use them, as highway robbery was not common.

Horse thieving, coining, forging notes, and petty larceny, were common enough; but, strange to say, violence towards the person, unless in the way of sudden quarrels, was unusual in those parts.

Obadiah walked at a rapid pace. He had left Eudora and Jessie alone. It is true, that they had locked themselves in, were well armed, and would open to none but himself. Still he was anxious to be with them.

The road was wide. It had been made by cutting trees down, and burning the stumps, so that though well enough for foot passengers, it was but ill-suited to vehicles.

Obadiah knew it well, and moved along in the gloom of night as easily and quickly as if it had been broad day.

Suddenly he halted, and stood still in the act of listening. He heard voices in the woods.

"My! if thar aint *some* down in Juke's dell. What on airth kin it be?" and then he added, after a pause, "hope taint none of the old pals. I've guv 'em up now, but don't want to sell 'em neither. It aint manly. Still I'm bound to see."

CHAPTER CV.

THE MUSTANG GANG.

HE had halted at the mouth of a narrow gully so thickly overgrown by huge pines and yew trees that it gave it the air of a dark cavern. Within this Obadiah Jones entered cautiously, halting at every step, holding his breath, and listening with the deepest attention.

Then he saw about fifty yards off, under the arches of the forest, the reflection of a fire.

"The Mustang Gang, by the Etarnal!" he muttered.

Then he paused and wiped the cold perspiration off his brow.

The Mustang Gang is a name given in most parts of the South and West to parties of horse thieves and other vagabonds, who prowl about on a half-settled community, taking care to rob in one state and sell in another a very long way off. Their depredations and rascalities were in every mouth, and whosoever was proved to belong to their set was lynched without mercy.

There was no effective protection against them. The vast continent, the forests, the caves, the means of flight by water, were so many sources of wealth to these thieves, who preferred running any risk and peril to working properly for a living.

There is something fascinating to certain organizations in lawless occupations, which utterly unfits them for honest labour.

The Mustangs, a gang of which Obadiah Jones had once belonged to, had no fixed place of residence. They were here to-day and fifty miles off to-morrow. Their means of existence were varied in the extreme. They stole horses, drove them off to a distance and sold them; they gambled with unwary travellers in inns and on board steamboats; they got rid of bad money and forged notes; and sometimes, in the disguise of Indians, plundered a solitary farm-house, doing deeds that Indians would have scorned to do.

Many an inoffensive Redskin has suffered for the infamies of these ruffians, who knew no shame.

Obadiah Jones felt a cold shudder over his whole frame, as the truth burst upon him. He wiped the big drops of perspiration away.

What did they want? Had they heard of his change of life, and knowing by what oaths he was bound, had they come to rebel against his joining the respectable class of society?

But Obadiah had made up his mind. His was a coarse and rough, but heroic nature. He would not rejoin his partners in crime. He felt the responsible position of a father.

Obadiah Jones had been married young to a charming woman, but quick tempered and a flirt. They quarrelled and she fled. He took to evil ways. He never heard from his wife until six months before the present time, when he received a letter.

It was to announce her death. But it contained also a letter from herself.

She left him a moderate fortune, some few thousand dollars, and informed him where his child was.

For her sake who on her death-bed implored forgiveness for her errors, she begged him to be a good father.

And Obadiah swore to be worthy of his dead wife's confidence and repentance.

All these memories flashed across his mind, as with the stealth of a serpent he crawled on. He now stooped low until he reached the summit of a slope that gave him a full view of the gang below.

They were not the Mustang Gang, for he knew none of them.

This alarmed Obadiah Jones more than ever. What were these men doing in that out-of-the-way place, with no house, save his own, within many miles?

They were about a dozen in number, seated round a large camp fire, smoking and drinking.

Their faces were all blackened.

Obadiah drew his breath cautiously. A terrible dread was on his soul.

Then he heard footsteps in the wood at no great distance. One of the gang started up.

"That you, Johnson?" he said.

"All right, my hearty," replied the other.

And a man of diminutive form and figure stood within the flame of the camp fire.

"What news?"

"Wall; the old man's out, and whosomever is in the hut won't answer. We must smoke 'em out."

"Dangerous work," said a huge ruffian, rolling himself lazily round. "Fire is seen a distance. Aint some on you seen this Obadiah Jones?"

"I huv," cried a stout man whom the squatter had not hitherto noticed.

"Kud'nt yer make the gals think it was him a hailing?" asked the giant.

"Spect I kud—but if that don't do, I can cut a hole in the log as will. When shall we start?"

"Soon I suspect," said a sanctified-looking ruffian; "that Obadiah has gone to join a band of villains leagued against the Saints. His object is the abomination of desolation. When he returns he shall find that we can heap coals of fire on his head."

"Darned pretty darter!" said the man who knew Obadiah.

"So I hear—but remember, you are to be well paid for your work, only if the two girls are given up unharmed to our chief and elder."

"You set of almighty cusses!" said Obadiah, in a fearful passion, as he fired into their midst. "Kim on, regulators—here's a whulle bilin uv Mormons. Kill 'em, flay 'em alive!"

And the squatter, using his gun as a club, rushed down the declivity with a fearful plunge, which sent him sprawling headlong into the middle of the camp.

When he rose to his feet and looked around, he was alone.

The fellows in their panic had fled without once looking behind, so taken aback had they been at his startling outcry.

Obadiah stepped back out of the light, loaded his gun, and then made tracks for his own home, taking good care, however, not to fall again into the hands of the Mormon ruffians.

Obadiah knew the men he had to deal with, unscrupulous, reckless, with all the cunning of the fox, and the morals of bullies, those professional outlaws of human nature, who live on the degradation of womankind.

He therefore moved along with extreme caution until he came almost within sight of his own house.

CHAPTER CVI.

DESOLATION.

OBADIAH Jones halted on the skirt of the forest, and looked towards that home which to him was a little paradise, for it contained within itself the germs of a better nature, such as he had already shown to exist.

All was still. They were calm within, in utter unconsciousness of the evil that lay without.

Obadiah looked behind him through the dark vista of the forest, and then ran like a greyhound.

"Open!—open, girls, for your lives!" he shouted; "the wolves are on my track."

Yells of fury and rage burst from the Mormon gang, who, surprised in their camp, had hurried to complete their villainous work.

They had seen Obadiah Jones, and were after him.

"Open!" he continued to cry, as he took terrific strides.

And they did open the door, and more than that, out they came with rifles cocked and presented them at the advancing gang.

"Back!" said the clear bell-like voice of Eudora; "if one advances, he dies."

Before they recovered from their astonishment the three were again inside the hut, and the door closed, while the discomfited Mormons halted at a little distance.

"Who are they, father?" asked Eudora, as soon as they were safe inside.

Obadiah stared at her with mute surprise. She wore the hunting-shirt, cap, leggings, and trousers of a backwoodsman, and a most elegant and accomplished hunter she looked, too.

"Riptyles," cried Obadiah, when he had slightly recovered from his astonishment; "Mormons—rascals."

"And what do they want?"

"You."

"And what for?"

"For Brigham Young?"

Eudora stepped back, drew her hunting knife, and showed its sharp pointed edge to her father.

"I fear no Mormon while I have this," she said, with a cold smile,—"not even Brigham Young himself—perjured traitor as he is."

Obadiah smiled, examined his rifle and pistols, and then approached the door to listen.

He could hear nothing.

Now there could be no doubt whatever that the Mormons, being in such overwhelming numbers, would make an attack; but how was it going to begin?

Not a sound.

Obadiah peered through the chinks of a wooden shutter.

"Creation!" he shouted; "stand back gals—and if yer valers yer life and honour, fight."

As he spoke, he handed his rifle to Eudora, seized a huge axe, and stood beside the doorway.

"Load," said Eudora coldly, as she pushed Jessie behind a press, and took up a gun.

At the same moment there came a terrific crush at the door.

The Mormons had got a beam of wood, and used it as a battering-ram.

The door gave way.

But no one entered. Having made an opening there seemed to be a hesitation about rushing to certain death.

Then a parley was called.

"Now thin, Obadiah," said the voice of the diminutive ruffian, "it's no use—you must give in."

"Never!"

"If you surrender now no harm shall happen; but if yer draws blood, you know the law of the wood."

"I know you to be a pile uv sneaking catamounts—uv ruffians as I'd kill like rattlesnakes; and if you comes near me, I'll skin yer alive. Kim on like men, and I'll fight the lot."

A volley of rifles followed, which, however, did not touch anybody.

All was still in the hut.

Then two or three dark forms were seen peering into the doorway.

Eudora fired.

A rush took place at once, with the idea that there would be no time for reloading; but another flash, another report, and the crashing of a body by the fall of an axe, proved how fearfully they were prepared for defence.

Obadiah Jones, as yet, had not used his revolvers. These he kept for a last emergency—well aware that his axe was a weapon of such a terrible character as to deter most men from approaching him.

During the halt that took place after the deadly rush, Obadiah Jones spoke two words to Eudora, and then, erect as a statue, and as silent, awaited further attack.

There was a pause, and then again they rushed forward, and again the axe fell; but this time the rush continued, and Obadiah fell to the ground.

"Secure him," shouted a voice in the rear, "and bring out the girls."

Some torches were now lit; three men kept Obadiah in a sitting posture, while the rest hurried to secure the girls.

"Hell cats!" shouted Obadiah; "you'r done – done brown."

They rushed about, into the back hut, but nowhere could a girl be seen.

A fearful chorus of shouts proclaimed the rage and fury of the Mormons.

"If you don't give 'em up," said one who appeared a leader—though, under pretence of being a priest, he had not fought—"you shall die the death."

"You rampagious, all fired, sneaking coward—fust, I don't know; next, if I did, wouldn't tell."

"They've gone to raise the country," whispered one."

"Likely," said another.

"Drag him out. Pile up all his rubbish, and set fire to it."

The order was instantly obeyed. Obadiah, overwhelmed by physical force, and despite his threats—intermingled with promises of pardon—was led forth, and tied, gagged and helpless, to a tree in front of his door.

To this he was lashed securely, while the busy fiends began the work of destruction.

They revelled in it like so many fiends.

They had lost the rich prize they were in search of, and gloated in the idea of foul revenge.

Such is the nature of some men, and of such are the Mormons.

Obadiah glared at them with a fiendish glance, as if he could gladly have destroyed them all; but being helpless in act, he gave them all he could in words.

CHAPTER CVII.

THE FIGHT.

THEY stood gazing at the fire until it seemed to have advanced to such a state as rendered it certain that the log-hut would burn, and then they turned to the squatter.

"Well, what shall we do with him?" asked the chief.

"Shute away, yer dogs. Obadiah don't care a dump, now. You've done your worst, yer unkenneled curs!"

"Have we?" said one, with a sneer. "Maybe you think we shan't git at yer darter."

"No, yer wont, for she knows yer."

"There is no time to be wasted in words," said the chief. "Just spear a knife into him, and let's a-done with it—thar."

The nearest man to Obadiah drew a long glittering blade, and without remorse thrust it into his bosom.

At the same instant, the Mormons, as if some new element had entered into their calculations, began to move off at a rapid rate.

A sound of horses had startled them.

Obadiah Jones was alone.

His head was leaning on his breast. He was either dead or insensible, it was difficult to say which. The blood trickled down to his feet.

In front of him was the crackling, furious, blazing hut.

Next instant, up rode four or five horsemen, the foremost of whom was Eudora, who, with a terrible shriek, leaped from her horse, and with her knife cut her father's bonds.

The body fell inert and heavily to the ground.

With clenched teeth and lowering brow, Eudora rose.

"Once more to the destruction of this hideous gang I devote my life. No love will I know—no husband acknowledge—no children own, till this foul crime is revenged!"

A faint groan made her stoop.

Her father had opened his eyes and was gazing at her, unable to speak.

Two experienced backwoodsmen raised him up, staunched his wound, and gave him brandy.

But he could not speak.

The back hut was not on fire. By the exertions of the backwoodsmen the connection of the two huts was broken off.

The fire was then soon extinguished.

And then the wounded squatter was carried and placed on his daughter's bed.

One of the men, who had a rude knowledge of surgery, examined the wound.

The knife had been stopped by a bone, and the wound was not dangerous.

But he had lost a considerable quantity of blood.

It now remained to be seen what was to be done. The girl could not be left without attendance and guardianship.

The only thing to be done was to get a cart, and remove Obadiah Jones to the farm-house where Jessie had been left.

One of the young farmers mounted a horse, and galloped off at full speed.

In about an hour he returned with a cart, on which a feather bed had been placed and a number of blankets. On these, the bedding out of Eudora's room was laid, and the wounded man placed thereon.

Eudora kneeled up and supported his head in her lap.

They rode round the cart, well armed and holding up torches.

After a toilsome and wearisome journey, they reached the farmer's house.

Doctor Foster was already in attendance.

He examined the wound with a critical eye.

"He will live with care,' said the doctor, " but he will require constant attendance."

Jessie and Eudora came forward, and took their station by the bed-side.

They were hopeful, but very exhausted and excited at what had passed.

The men went out, leaving the girls in attendance on the wounded squatter.

They determined to have a second conference as to what was to be done about Joseph Smith.

He was a prisoner on a charge which did not affect his life.

Now, nothing but the death of the evil-doer could satisfy any of those who had suffered from his rascality.

It was a terrible resolve to make, but the circumstances were such as to render calm reasoning and reflection out of the question.

When a wolf is at the throat of your wife and children, it is not easy to think whether it be wiser to capture the beast or to kill him.

You kill such noxious vermin.

CHAPTER CVIII.

CARTHAGE.

THE city of Carthage was not a large place, but it was a county town.

There was the gaol, the court-house, and the residence of the officials.

It was a scattered number of log-huts, shanties, and frame-houses.

The streets were wide and generally laid out regularly, but very many had only one house within their precincts.

It was a town that was to be, and was not yet. It was in its chrysalis state.

The gaol was a large wooden two-storied building, erected by means of large logs of wood.

Carthage was not, like many similar towns in the western states, in no need of a jail.

Illinois was flooded with horse thieves, forgers, and other vagabonds, who found temporary lodgings in this establishment at the public expense.

On the morning of the day after the attempted murder of Obadiah Jones by the emissaries of Brigham Young, Carthage was in an uproar.

The prison was guarded by two hundred militia men under the command of an officer named Sidney Brown.

They lined the road from the gaol to the court-house.

At ten the magistrate arrived.

He took his seat on the bench, with Governor Ford by his side.

The prosecutors and witnesses filled nearly the whole court, leaving but a very small space for the public.

But the public, in the shape of a constantly increasing and excited mob, crowded round the court-house, while arrangements were made to signal to them the proceedings within.

The day was rather hot, and the windows were wide open.

A number of men, chiefly those who met at the road-side inn to confer as to the mode Joe Smith should be dealt with, climbed up to the windows, and nearly blocked them up.

Thence they could hear what was going on.

The crowd was dense, stern, and even savage in its determination.

There were outraged husbands, men who had lost the daughter they loved as the apple of their eye; and others who had suffered in a more worldly way; but all angry and wrathful.

The door of the prison opened, and Joe Smith, followed by the other prisoners, came forth.

He gave a quick, frightened look at the mob; but perceiving the array of soldiers, plucked up courage, and advanced with a firm step.

The hooting and yelling was something terrible to hear.

Some shook their fists right in his face, but the soldiers stood firm, and drove them back.

These men hated the Prophet and his disciples as much as the others; but then, discipline had to be observed.

They were soldiers, and they acted as such.

The court-house was soon gained, and then the Mormons disappeared from view.

They were placed in the dock and the proceedings commenced.

The magistrate called upon the prosecutors to give evidence, which they did amid universal stillness.

"Mr. Smith," said the magistrate, "what have you to say against these charges?"

"Nothing," replied General Joe, "save that they are false. Some of the inhabitants of Nauvoo, indignant at the libels on myself published in a foul-mouthed journal, may have taken redress into their own hands; but with that I have nothing to do."

"But it is stated that you not only ordered the deed, but stood by when it was done."

The Prophet shook his head.

"It is false!" cried Law, one of the proprietors of the paper; "for I saw him there on horseback surrounded by his pack of ——"

The Prophet's eyes flashed, but he made no reply.

"Prisoners, it is my intention to commit you for trial," said the magistrate; "but I am willing to admit you to bail to answer the charge at the sessions."

The men in the windows telegraphed to the mob outside. A roar of reprobation and disgust arose from the mob.

A scuffle was heard outside.

"I shall send you back to prison," said the magistrate, firmly, "and there will visit you with my clerk to take your bonds. Remove the prisoners."

A number of soldiers and officers surrounded the Mormons, while the militia on the line between the court-house and the gaol, pressed the furious mob as far back as they could.

But suddenly a rush took place towards the court, and, amid the terrific applause of the mob, Higbee, a bitter enemy of Joe Smith, thrust his way in, followed by a fresh posse of constables.

In his hand he waved a warrant.

"What is the meaning of this disturbance?" said the magistrate, sternly.

As he spoke, he touched General Ford, the governor of Illinois, on the shoulder.

"I depend on you, sir, to support me against the lawless mob."

"Certainly," replied General Ford.

"I bring," said Higbee, "a warrant signed by *three* magistrates, with orders to arrest Joseph and Hyrum Smith, with their accomplices."

"On what charge?" asked the somewhat angry magistrate.

"*High Treason!*"

A loud cry was with difficulty repressed.

"Which is not a bailable offence."

Terrific was the shout of joy and satisfaction as Higbee handed up the warrant to the magistrate.

He handed it to the governor.

"Prisoners at the bar, it is my duty," said the magistrate, "now to commit you to prison, on the capital charge of high treason against the state. I advise you, under present circumstances, to say nothing. You had better take the advice of counsel."

Joseph Smith, who was very pale, bowed low, and, without a word, moved from the bar, and, in a few minutes, amid joyful shouts from the populace, was again within the walls of the prison-house.

And thus ended the first act of this terrible and gloomy tragedy, which will never be forgotten in the history of Illinois.

But were the people justified in their subsequent acts?

CHAPTER CIX.
ON THE MORMONS.

To answer this question, we must say a few serious words about the Mormons.

All who know anything of the Mormons have one opinion.

The ablest adventure novelist of the day—Captain Mayne Reid—has depicted them in the light they deserve.

His heroine is supposed to have eloped with a Mormon elder.

"Not by words can I express the suggestive hideousness of this thought. To understand it in all its cruel significance, the reader should be acquainted with that peculiar sect known as the Latter-day Saints—should have read its history and its chronicles. Without this knowledge, he will be ill able to comprehend the peculiar bitterness that, in that hour, wrapped and wrung my soul.

"Accident had made me acquainted with the Mormon religion; not with its tenets—for it has none—but with the moral idiosyncrasy of its most eminent 'apostles,' as well as that of its humbler devotees—two very different classes of 'Saints.'"

In the animal world we seek in vain for the type of either of these classes. The analogies of the wolf and the lamb, of the hawk and the pigeon, of the cat and the mouse, cannot be employed with any degree of propriety—not one of them. In all these creatures there are certain traits either of nobility or beauty. Neither is to be found in the life and character of a Mormon—whether he be a sincere dupe and neophyte, or a hypocritical apostle.

Perhaps the nearest antagonistic forms of the animal world by which we might typify the extreme conditions of Mormon life—both social and religious—are those of fox and goose; though, no doubt, the subtle Reynard would scorn to be compared to such creatures. Nor, indeed, is the fox a true type, for even about him there are redeeming qualities—something to relieve the soul from that loathing which it feels in contemplating the character of a "ruling elder" among the "Saints."

It would be difficult to imagine anything further removed from what we may term the "divinity of human nature" than one of these. Vulgar and brutal, cunning and cruel, are ordinary epithets, and altogether too weak to characterize such a creature. Some of the "twelves" and the "seventies" may lack one or other of these characteristics. In most cases, however, you may safely bestow them all; and if it be the chief of the sect—the president himself—you may add such other ugly appellations as your fancy may suggest, and be sure that your portraiture will still fall short of the hideousness of the original.

Perhaps the most striking characteristic of these fanatics is the absolute openness of their cheat. A more common-place imposture has never been offered for acceptance, even to the most ignorant of mankind. It appeals neither to reason nor romance. The one is insulted by the very shallowness of its chicanery, while its rank plebishness disgusts the other. Even the nomenclature, both of its offices and office-bearers, has a vulgar ring that smacks of ignoble origin. The names "twelves," "seventies," "deacons," "wifedoms," Smiths (Hyrum and Joseph), Pratt, Snow, Young, Cowdery, and the like—coupled as they are with an affectation and imitation of Scripture phraseology—form a vocabulary burlesquing even the Sacred Book itself; and suggesting, by their sounds, the true character of the Mormon church—a very essence of plebeian hypocrisy.

I have used the word "fanatics," but that must be understood in a limited sense. It can only be applied to the "geese"—the ignorant and besotted *canaille*—which the apostolic emissaries have collected from all parts of Europe, but chiefly from England, Scotland and Wales. The Welsh, as might be expected, furnish a large proportion of these emigrant geese; While, strange as it may sound, there is but one Irish goose in the whole Mormon flock! There are but few of these birds of native American breed. The general intelligence, supplied by a proper school system, prevents much proselytism in that quarter; but it does not hinder the cute Yankee from playing the part of the fox; for, in reality, this is his role in the social system of Mormondom. The President, or High Priest and Prophet himself, the Twelves and Seventies, the elders, deacons, and other dignitaries, are all, or nearly all, of true Yankee growth, and to call these "fanatics" would be a misapplication of the word. Term them conspirators, charlatans, hypocrites, and impostors, if you will, but not fanatics. The Mormon fox is no fanatic; he is a professor in the most emphatic sense of the word, but not a believer. His profession is absolute chicanery; he has neither faith, dogma, nor doctrine.

There are writers who have defended these apes of religion; and some who have even spoken well of their system. Captain Stansbury, the explorer, has a good opinion of them. The captain is at best but a superficial observer; and, unfortunately for his judgment, received most courteous treatment at their hands. It is not human nature to speak ill of the bridge that has carried one over; and Captain Stansbury has obeyed the common impulse. In the earlier times of the Mormon Church, there were champions of the Stansbury school to defend its members against the charge of polygamy. In those days, the Saints themselves attempted a sort of denial of it. The subject was then too rank to come forth as a revelation. But a truth of this awkward kind could not long remain untold, and it became necessary to mask it under the more moderate title of a spiritual wifedom. It required an acute metaphysician to comprehend this spiritual relationship,

and the moralist was puzzled to understand its sanctity.

During that period, while the Saints dwelt within the pale of the Gentiles' country, this cloak was kept on; but after their exodus to the Salt Lake settlements, the flimsy garment was thrown off, being found too inconvenient to be worn any longer. There the motive for concealment was removed, and the apology of a spiritual wifedom ceased to exist. It came out in its carnal and sensual shape. Polygamy was boldly preached and proclaimed, as it had ever been practised, in its most hideous shape, and the defenders of Mormon purity, thus betrayed by their pet *proteges*, dropped their broken lances to the ground.

The "institution" is even more odious under Mormon than Mahommed. There is no redeeming point—not even the "romance of the harem"—for the zenana of a Latter-day Saint is a type of the most vulgar materialism, where even the favourite sultana is not exempted from the hard work-a-day duties of a slave.

Polygamy? No! the word has too limited a signification. To characterize the condition of a Mormon wife, we must resort to the phraseology of the bagnio.

Still, with all the villainy of the Latter-day Saints, we think the law should have been allowed to take its course.

But so it was not to be.

CHAPTER CX.

A CONFERENCE.

EVEN when the people of Illinois found that the Mormon Saints were committed to the safe custody of a prison, they were not satisfied.

Their blood was up.

Their dark, lowering countenances—their muttered threats, like the whisper of a coming tempest, spreading from rank to rank—warned the officials.

Governor Ford accordingly placed a strong guard of soldiers round the prison, with strict injunctions to defend it from assault.

The soldiers made a kind of camp round the prison, and while some slept on the bare ground, with their arms beside them, others kept watch.

The duty was a peculiarly distasteful one.

It placed them in antagonism to the rest of the citizens.

Still, with few exceptions, they were resolved to obey the commands of their superior officers.

There is a powerful magic in the word "discipline," which is felt by all of Anglo-Saxon origin.

Meanwhile, however, those whose feelings towards the Mormons had been worked up to an excess of fury which could not be restrained, retreated to a certain distance from Nauvoo, and there held council.

The members of the secret society for the extermination of the Mormons, met under a rocky bluff close to the city.

They came silently, slowly, in twos and threes.

They were about two hundred in all.

Foster was called to the chair.

The noise, the cries, the appeals, were incoherent

enough at first, but when Foster had inculcated silence and order, a debate commenced in regular earnest.

A venerable man, a stern old pioneer of the Borne and Brady school, spoke first.

"My friends and brethren—I am quite sure that no one detests and loathes these here Mormons more than I does. But law is law, and seeing they is to be tried by a jury of citizens, I think as how we ought to let the law take its course. Listen! He is sure to be punished—he cannot escape; and if this is the case, a proper verdict and example inflicted on them by those in authority will put an end to Mormonism quickly and for ever. If you yourselves, acting under the influence of passion, take away his life, the effect will be bad—that's my opinion."

"No," cried another speaker, surprised at the effect produced by these simple words, "it cannot, it shall not be! They have swelled their cup of iniquity to overflowing, and stung the hand that was reached out to succour them when other states had driven them forth as so much poison on their soil; and shall we longer sit down and let them prey upon our honour, our property, and our lives? The other states have long cried out shame upon us for countenancing a system of iniquity which shames alike our manhood and humanity, and is a foul blot on our nation!"

"I deny nothing that can be said against them," cried the other; "I only think that if no rash act be done, we may now get rid of the villains once for all by legal means. If we make martyrs of them, they will increase in power and numbers."

"There is something in this," said the president, sternly, "if we could count on the law. But these men will be detained in prison for a short time, and then let loose again, like wolves seeking whom they may devour."

This speech seemed to meet the views of many.

Let not our readers suppose that these men, because they were enraged against a foul ulcer on the body politic, were without regard to law or reason.

They believed that they had a duty to perform, and were determined to do it.

Still, they were willing to take as calm a view of the matter as possible, and a very general idea went about, that the appointment of a committee of Regulators, representing the state, to watch the progress of the legal proceedings, would best answer the necessities of the times.

This opinion would in all probability have been adopted, but for a new event.

While the discussion was going on in knots rather than in a general meeting, while men were gradually toning down to a rational state of reflection, the sound of a horseman galloping over the plain adjacent was heard.

Then Eudora, in the costume of a backwoodsman, leaped to the ground.

"Vengeance! vengeance!" she cried. "While watching over my dying father, some of these villains stole my friend and sister. My father sleeps, and I have galloped here to tell you."

There was a dead silence for a moment.

"You mean Jessie?" said Foster, in a hoarse, choked voice.

"I do," replied Eudora.

"Go—return to your father's bed," said Foster—"leave action to us. She shall be avenged—aye, avenged—how fearfully, you shall know to-morrow!"

"I thank you," continued the girl; and mounting her horse, she again rode over the plains.

CHAPTER CXI.

AMY.

THIS is what had happened.

With the dawn of day all men capable of bearing arms within many miles of Carthage, started to that city to hear the result of the examination of Joseph Smith, the false Prophet.

Neither young nor old could resist the temptation.

The inhabitants of the farm-house were of the same mind as the rest of the people.

They could not wait for the evening report.

They let loose a couple of fierce dogs, and went away, leaving the sick man, Eudora, Jessie, and the farmer's daughter, Amy.

The two girls, Jessie and Amy, had had a little sleep, Eudora none.

As soon, then, as a hasty breakfast was over, they persuaded Eudora, her father being in a heavy sleep, to take some rest, while they attended to the household duties.

Eudora, who was really worn out with exhaustion and fatigue, consented on condition that if her father woke, she was instantly to be roused.

She lay down upon a wooden bench, with a rude cloak under her head.

In five minutes she was sound asleep.

Jessie and Amy, who was a pretty girl of about fourteen or fifteen, went out into the kitchen, to look after the household duties.

Everything had been left in the same state that the hunters had left it when they had their breakfast.

They cleared away, placed a cauldron of water on the fire, and did what was necessary to make ready for a large party of hungry men on their return that night.

Then they went in front, and gazed out upon the green prairies and the flowing stream.

Amy was a child in appearance, and having heard much of the adventures and dangers that Jessie had passed through, looked up to her with perfect awe.

She was a wonder of wonders to the little girl.

To please her, Jessie related such events as were not likely to wound her youthful susceptibility, at the same time that she guarded her strongly against the Mormons.

They were seated on a rude bench in front of the house.

The day was glorious in the extreme, and the two girls were glad to be still under the wavy shade of the forest trees.

"Are they all so wicked?" said Amy, with sad and downcast eyes.

"All, child."

Amy made no reply. She was thoughtful.

EUDORA.

The very imaginings which filled her soul in regard to these monsters of iniquity had done her no good.

It is evil to talk of crime which is sure sorely to defile the talker.

Amy gazed out upon the grassy fields and the flowing stream, and her eyes flashed and her cheeks flushed, and her bosom heaved with febrile excitement.

Jessie did not notice her.

Her thoughts were far away—away with that young lover to whom she appeared as a kind of mirage.

She did not notice the emotion of Amy.

Certainly, it did not arise from anything that Jessie had said.

Still, something that Jessie had let drop, some faint allusion to love, had awakened in her a dreamy thoughtfulness.

It is a fatal and painful characteristic of American women, that in the same way that they fade away prematurely, do they become marriageable earlier than in England.

They are often mothers at fifteen, which is a fearful blow to beauty.

Woman's most lovable hour is when she clasps in her own arms a tiny image of herself and of another, but it is a terrible responsibility for one child of fifteen to be the mother of another child.

And a girl of fifteen is a mere child fit for the school-room and the nursery.

But Amy, though her father and mother thought her a child, did not think so herself.

She believed herself a woman !

Why ?

A man had told her so ; a youth not much older than herself—at least, not many years.

He had met her thus,—

Amy, when her father was at home with her brothers, had little to do, except to prepare the breakfast. After this she did pretty much as she liked. Her favourite practice was to go down to the neighbouring stream, and there, under the shadow of a tree, to pass her time in knitting or reading.

One afternoon, hearing a rustling near her, she raised here eyes, and saw, fishing in the stream, a rather good-looking youth.

He was about twenty, with long, oval face, regular features, and a pale complexion.

His hair was jet black and long.

His eyes sparkled with a light that was perfectly dazzling.

He did not appear to see Amy, though he was looking at her from the corner of his eye.

It was such a look as Mephistopheles might have given to Margaret.

Amy looked at him sideways, and felt her heart beat as she did so.

He moved slowly towards her, still all the time looking at the water.

Suddenly he stumbled, started, and pretending to see Amy for the first time, apologized for his intrusion, in such a soft and insinuating voice, that no woman could have done anything but forgive him.

"I have been fishing all day, and have caught nothing," he said, with a laugh.

"Indeed."

" I am quite tired of such unprofitable employment," he added. "May I sit down?"

"Yes," whispered Amy.

And so he seated himself, and began talking about the country and the weather, and the pretty location her father had, and so on.

Then he spoke of travels in foreign parts, and, being a man of wit and ability, quite delighted the simple and confiding girl.

They sat together an hour.

Then a conch sounded, and Amy leaped up, rosy and blushing.

"I must go. It is dinner time."

"I am very sorry."

"Wont you come in ?"

"Well," said the other, hesitating, "I do not care if I do. No—on second thoughts, miss, excuse me. I am in search of a location, and will wait before introducing myself, to be able to say I am a neighbour."

"But father would find you one," said the artless girl.

"No ; I will choose for myself. It will not be far from here, I can assure you."

Amy held down her head and blushed.

"Do you often come here ?"

"Yes."

"Will you be here to-morrow ?"

"I cannot say."

"I should like to let you know how I am progressing," he replied, in low, earnest tones.

"I will come."

"Don't say anything about me until I have got my house."

Amy acquiesced, though she could not see what reason there could be for it.

"Thanks. You will understand me better, soon. I may as well confess at once, that I came to these parts to search for a wife as well as a home."

"Indeed !"

"I have not found the home yet. But——"

She looked up curiously in his face.

"I have found the wife."

Amy coloured slightly.

"Do I know her ?" she faltered.

"That is, I have found a wife to my satisfaction—but then the question arises, will she have me ?"

"Oh !" said Amy, eagerly, blushing a little in her enthusiasm, "she must be a very strange girl if she does not."

The young man looked into her deep blue eyes, and a strange expression crossed his countenance. Was it hesitation ? was it compunction ?

"Do you think so ?" he said.

"I do."

"Amy," he continued, taking her two hands in his, "then it shall not be a secret. I love you—you have enchanted my soul."

A conch was heard again.

But Amy did not move.

She was spell-bound.

"I love you. I cannot help it. I cannot explain how it has come about ; but this I know, that I could not live without you. I do not wish you to decide now. But meet me to-morrow—come to the trysting-place."

"I will," said Amy, blushing, and crying, and laughing.

"Thank you."

He looked into her eyes.

"I may——"

What ? Well, never mind, next minute Amy ran away confused and happy.

The other remained behind, looking very much like Satan in the garden of Eden.

They met again, and often, until the youth entirely subjugated the simple maiden, who, for this young lover, forgot friends, kindred ; and allowed herself to be guided by him in everything.

He did not visit her friends.

He had always some ready excuse to explain his conduct.

Poor Amy, like most very young girls when they love, easily believed everything he said.

This faith in the loved one is one of the most beautiful characteristics of real and true passion, but it is a great pity that it is so much abused.

Better, girls, therefore, be a little suspicious than too confiding.

I am quite sure many of my female readers will sympathize with my words.

But Amy was a mere child. She loved the man, and she believed him.

CHAPTER CXII.

A SECOND MEETING.

WHEN she saw him standing before her father's house, she started with pleasure.

At last he had come home.

She little suspected that he knew the men were out.

"Oh, John!" she cried, "how glad I am to see you."

No reply.

"What is the matter, John?"

She followed his eyes. He was staring at Jessie, with open mouth.

"I want to speak a few words with you," he said, in a low whisper.

Amy took his arm and retreated behind a wood-pile.

"Any bad news?" she said, noticing that he was very pale and agitated.

"Very."

"Anything happened to father?"

"No."

"What then? Why do you speak so fiercely?"

"Have I not a right? Here have I lived a quiet and honest life—kept myself aloof from all, resided in my lone hut, with no companion save my gun, no friend but you; and now, because a lot of bad money and notes, doubtless the work of that old sinner, Obadiah Jones——"

"Hush!"

"Why?"

"He is in there."

"What?" cried the other, with a fierce and angry start.

"Dying," repeated Amy, putting her hand gently on his arm.

"Oh!—but never mind. I have been accused as the author of these crimes, on no other evidence than that I live alone."

"But the law——"

"Law! These border ruffians know no law. They will not allow me a fair trial."

"What will they do?"

"Murder me."

"You must fly!" cried Amy.

"I know that; I must hide myself in Iowa until I can prove my innocence."

"But you will not be gone long?" said Amy, tenderly and reproachfully.

"These backwoodsmen are hard to persuade. They take ideas into their heads, which stick like burrs."

"But then?"

"If they won't believe my word now, they may not bye-and-bye."

"I hope they will, John."

"My dear Amy, it is no use mincing the matter. Unless you assist me, I shall stay and face it all out."

"What can I do?"

"Amy, you love me—I love you. Now I happen to know that, prejudiced against me by falsehood and deceit, your friends will never consent to our union."

"What then," asked Amy, in a trembling tone, "am I to do?"

"Go with me. The instant we cross the border I will make you my wife."

Now marriage in America is very easily settled. As everybody makes up his mind to the comfort of a wife, old folks are not much consulted. A daughter thinks little if, during a walk, they turn aside to the house of a magistrate, and are married.

Then they walk home, and, for the occasion, the youth occupies her room, or she his, as the case may be.

That this prevents a very large amount of immorality, there can be no doubt.

Did such a law exist in France, the whole fabric of society would be changed, and France might become a moral country.

"You'll bring me home some day?" murmured Amy, very nearly conquered.

"I will."

"Never," said a firm voice close to her.

They turned, and Jessie, pale but resolute and earnest, stood before them.

Both were so surprised they could not speak.

"Amy," said Jessie.

"Yes."

"Do you see yonder waters?"

"I do."

"Go and plunge headlong into them; commit your soul to the keeping of the demon, but not to this wretch—Simon Yackley, surnamed Captain Fearnot, chief of the Danite band!"

"Woman," said the young man, with a fierce and malignant glance, "you have sealed your own fate and hers. Had you not have betrayed me, she would never have known."

"What?" gasped Amy.

"The man has a dozen wives!" cried Jessie, who turned to alarm Eudora.

"Stop," said Simon Yackley, with a fiendish laugh, as he clutched her arm—"not so fast, my prying and inquisitive lady!"

And as he spoke he gave a shrill whistle.

Four ill-looking ruffians, who for some time had been peering from behind some bushes, now came out and waited for orders.

"Take this madam with you. Secure her, gag her if necessary."

A loud shriek from Jessie, wild, despairing, and prolonged, was the answer.

Amy sank fainting in the other's arms.

"Quick," said Simon, fiercely, "away, or we shall have that hell-fire fellow, Obadiah, at our heels."

A shot from Eudora, who came rushing forth, quickened their pace.

CHAPTER CXIII.

OUTSIDE CARTHAGE GAOL.

SUCH was the scene which caused Eudora to leave her wounded father and repair to the rendezvous of the Regulators.

We must now relate what followed.

Carthage slept. The peaceful inhabitants had long since retired to rest, convinced that the arch-impostor Smith was in safe custody.

A strong body of soldiers were camped round the prison.

It was twelve.

The moon fell in rich and radiant refulgence on the scene.

The guard nearly all slept, save one or two who surrounded the camp fire, ready to relieve the sentinels, who, being militia, and very much like volunteers, were quite satisfied with one hour's watch.

They had ceased to talk of Joe Smith, and were telling stories round the camp fire.

Two sentinels, one towards the country, one towards the town, kept a look-out.

The one towards the town had noticed for some time a suspicious movement about a beer-shop at no great distance.

Its being open so late was of itself an event.

But then, the citizen-soldiers had themselves been the cause of this. Nothing helped to pass away the night so cheerily as beer and tobacco.

They could not quarrel, then, with others who availed themselves of the same privilege.

But though the sentinel noticed a great many go in, he failed to discover that any came out.

A couple of soldiers were detached to report as to what was going on.

They returned to state that there were only some half-dozen topers hanging about the bar, chiefly Germans, who could not resist the fascination of lager beer.

So, on this hand, all was quiet and satisfactory.

Then there was a report that knots of men were collecting on the edge of a wood about two hundred yards from the town.

The captain in command rose, and hastily took a survey of the coming party.

They were Indians, in their panoply of war paint, armed with guns, pistols, and tomahawks.

"To arms!" said the officer.

The whole body was in five minutes under arms.

The advancing body was calm, not a sound rose above the low hum; but there was an ominous sternness, that brooded on every brow, and flashed from every eye, that told plainer than words that this calmness was more to be dreaded than wild, noisy disorder.

Again a body of men came in sight.

These were the armed citizens of Carthage, who had collected in a field behind the beer-shop; and there, incited by messages from the Regulators, had agreed to march on the gaol.

The soldiers seemed not to know what to do.

An eye-witness says, that though many murmured, there was no idea of joining the mob.

They saw the turn things had taken, their cheeks blanched, and their lips closed firmly; but it was not the emotion of cowardice—an American soldier knows not the meaning of such a word. They had fathers, brothers, friends, and neighbours among that throng of outraged citizens; and their hearts recoiled when the thought came over them, with its fearful reality, that they would soon be called to defend their prisoners against them; for though they revolted at the thought, it never occurred to them to betray the trust. No! the thought of dishonour was a stranger to their hearts. They were soldiers; and, as soldiers, were called upon to throw aside all other considerations, and to do their duty.

The officer in command stood at the head of his column.

The Indians joined the other party, and then a halt took place.

The accounts given of this fearful scene vary considerably.

Some date the tragedy at night, some in the morning.

One says distinctly that it was dark.

Hour after hour went by, and still there were no signs of attack on the gaol, and hope that the law would be allowed to take its course was fast rising in many hearts; but in others it only augmented anxiety, for they knew these western borderers too well to believe they would quietly return to their homes—which only reminded them of the guilt of a lawless band in their midst—without wreaking a fearful retribution on the prime movers of the crimes of which they were the sufferers. Night was drawing near; and the guard looked on the declining sun, and wondered, in their hearts, how many in that village would ever again look upon its rising. Yet no fears were spoken; only the rifles were grasped the more firmly, the troubled eye slowly scrutinized every joint and crack of the building they guarded, as if to determine the amount of resistance it was capable of sustaining should they fall.

Others are equally certain that it was morning.

This, however, does not alter the facts of the case.

Meanwhile, what was passing within the prison?

CHAPTER CXIV.

INSIDE CARTHAGE GAOL.

MEANWHILE, from the Mormon narratives, and from the confessions of one who left the tribe, let us tell what was passing inside the prison.

There were ten rooms.

In the front were Generals Joseph and Hyrum Smith, Mr. Taylor, and one Willard Richards.

The others were in other rooms.

General Joseph, from the moment that he was brought back to the prison on the charge of high treason, spoke little.

He knew that the enemies who were opposed to him would not relax in their vigilance. They would be sure to bring things to a crisis as quickly as possible.

When popular passion is concerned it is easy to press on a case of high treason.

Now General Joe had, since his boyhood, necessarily read a good deal.

Among other things he had a small smattering of law, and was trying to recollect precedents suited to his case.

He was also maturing his plans for his defence.

This was an opportunity for display not to be thrown away.

He had a pencil and some paper; the Mormons being supplied by the Governor with everything they required.

"Brother Willard," said Joe Smith, after some time, "what think you of this case? How long shall we be detained here?"

"We shall be fortunate if we ever leave," replied Willard.

"How so?"

"I doubt if we shall ever be tried."

"How so?"

"The mob will never wait for the form of law. They will murder us."

"Surely not," said Smith, rising in great trepidation, and stalking about the room.

His eye fell on their pistols, which were on a rude sideboard.

"We can defend ourselves."

"But not against hundreds."

"Ring that bell for the head turnkey," said Joe Smith, in a voice of authority.

Willard Richards obeyed.

The turnkey came up, and civilly asked what was wanted.

"I want to see Governor Ford; I have reason to believe that an attack will be made on the jail—that we are to be murdered this night."

"The prison is strong."

"Nothing is too strong, sir, for a lawless mob. If you would not aid and abet a murder, you will send for the governor. Is he gone?"

"No; he is dining with the magistrates."

"Then, sir, I ask you as a man to do me this service. Whatever I am charged with I never hurt you."

"I will go, sir." replied the turnkey.

While he was absent, Joseph Smith, who began for the first time to feel the reality of his position, walked up and down, evidently in great agony of mind.

The idea of death had never before been thought of.

Now the naked truth stared him in the face—gaunt—terrible—awful.

They might kill him!

Large pearly drops of cold sweat poured down his face, which, always flabby and white, was now terrible to look at.

In that fearful hour of danger, that which was comic in his face disappeared, leaving such a countenance as one might expect to see on a condemned murderer's face on the morning of his execution.

Did Joseph Smith, at that dread hour, regret his mighty imposture?

His friends say not.

They assert that he never was more energetic in his denunciation of his enemies, never more earnest in his assertions as to the truth of his revelations.

Most impostors have done the same; witness the other teacher of polygamy, Mahomet.

Presently the governor was ushered in. He was surrounded by several of his aides-de-camp and officers.

"What can I do for you, sir?" said the governor, blandly.

Joseph Smith reiterated his complaints, or rather, recorded his terrors.

"Never mind, sir," said Governor Ford, in a curt, positive way; "I have seen to that. I shall

have a guard here that shall terrify any gang or mob that may come here. If you have nothing else to fear, make your mind quite easy. I am responsible until the day of trial."

"I thank you, sir," responded Smith.

"Would you like to look out, sir?" said the governor.

"I should," said General Joe, hurriedly.

At a sign from the governor the wooden shutter was removed from the window, and General Joseph peered out into the street.

It was dark.

There he saw surrounding the prison the array of the militia forces.

"I am satisfied. Thank you," said the Prophet.

General Ford at once retired, and, mounting his horse at the gate of the prison, rode off to his own residence.

The Mormon chiefs now felt somewhat relieved, though still not without apprehension.

The shutter had not been replaced. There were sentries enough down below to prevent any attempt at escape.

And thus some hours passed away, during which some rest was taken on the truckle beds provided by the state.

But no one slept much. All felt too much in awe of what might happen to venture on lying down altogether.

When the several alarms were given, the anxiety of the Mormons was intense.

They knew not what to do.

They were armed, but what availed arms against angry multitudes?

When the furious and sanguinary mob which hoped to obtain a monopoly of the guillotine rose against Robespierre and St. Just, those two men most deeply deplored the weakness which made them allow such horrible executions in their name.

Joe Smith and his comrades must have felt how much better it would have been to have lived honest lives, and earned their living fairly, than to have founded a system which raised such bitter emotion.

The Mormons reply, that as much may be said of one whose name is too sacred to be quoted in these pages.

He, too, was reviled, and yet afterwards, all his sorrows and sufferings were productive of good.

But the end was coming.

About half-an-hour after sunrise a noise was heard.

The day was hot and sultry. All leaped to their feet.

Of what now passed, we have none but Mormon accounts.

Willard Richards is the speaker.

"A shower of musket-balls were thrown up the stairway against the door of the prison in the second story, followed by many rapid footsteps; while Generals Joseph and Hyrum Smith, Mr. Taylor, and myself, who were in the front chamber, closed the door of our room against the entry at the head of the stairs, and placed ourselves against it, there being no lock on the door, and no catch that was usable;—the door is a common panel—and as soon as we heard the feet at the stairs head, a ball was sent through the door, which passed between us, and showed that our enemies were desperadoes, and we must change our position.

"General Joseph Smith, Mr. Taylor, and myself, sprang back to the front part of the room, and General Hyrum Smith retreated two-thirds across the chamber, directly in front of and facing the door.

"A ball was sent through the door, which hit Hyrum on the side of his nose, when he fell backwards, extended at length, without moving his feet.

"From the holes in his vest (the day was warm, and no one had a coat on but myself), pantaloons, drawers, and shirt, it appears evident that a ball must have been thrown from without, through the window, which entered his back on the right side, and, passing through, lodged against his watch, which was in his right vest pocket, completely pulverizing the crystal and face, tearing off the hands, and smashing the whole body of the watch; at the same instant the ball from the door entered his nose. As he struck the floor he exclaimed emphatically, ' *I'm a dead man!*' "

CHAPTER CXV.

OUTSIDE AGAIN.

WE now return to the acts of those who were on the outside.

A little after daybreak the soldiers were again on the alert.

It was rumoured that a band of some two or three hundred men, headed by the Red Indians, were approaching.

Those who were not disguised as Indians had blackened their faces, so that whatever occurred they might not be recognized.

They came in solid ranks, with a firm, determined front, before which the stragglers and idlers who had collected around retreated in dismay.

They were soon close up to the guards and the gaol.

Not a word had hitherto been spoken, except by the commanding officer, who sent off express after express to the Governor of Illinois.

An attempt was made to convince the soldiers that they were real Indians; in which case they would have fired without difficulty. But they knew better. They were fully aware that, though dressed and painted in war costume, they were their own fathers, brothers, friends.

It was an awful position.

The officers in command felt keenly the fearful responsibility which fell upon them.

" Soldiers !" cried the commanding officer, in a loud and firm voice ; " stand your ground, and give not an inch."

He saw that the object of the Indians was to get between him and the jail.

Several of those at the head of the column now cried out to him to give way.

" Never !"

" Then shall we treat you as aiders and abettors of the accursed Mormons."

" We hate and detest them as much as you do," cried the officer ; " but our duty is plain."

" And that is ?"

" To guard them until such time as they are given up into the hands of the law."

" The law ! a mere quibble ; it is not intended they should be punished."

A loud shout from the mob proclaimed that this was the general feeling.

" The prisoners are well guarded ; they cannot escape the punishment our laws have provided for such crimes as they stand charged with. Return to your homes in peace, with this assurance, that all annoyance from them will henceforth cease," urged the captain.

" Will that wipe out the stain of foul dishonour with which they strove to stamp my name ?" demanded the Indian chief, angrily.

" Or restore to life and honour my murdered sister ?" cried one of the braves.

" Or give me back my squandered wealth, which they obtained by treachery and false pretence ?" said another.

" Or the cattle and grain they forcibly, in the name of the God they profess to worship, wrested from my hands ?" demanded still another.

" No !" exclaimed the chief, " husbands, it will not wipe out dishonour—fathers, it will not restore your daughters they have defiled and slain, neither to life nor virtue—return the gold out of which you have been swindled ; nor the cattle and grain stolen in the name of a deity they mock by deeds forbidden in His sacred law. The time is past when we can be cajoled by sophistry into tolerating such wickedness. Now we will put in force the laws they have violated, and execute a just sentence that their crimes have called down upon themselves ; and it is death ! Warriors, follow your chieftain !" and with a bound and a whoop the chief, bending low, darted forward, and striking up the rifle of the nearest soldier, sprang past him, followed so closely by his comrades, that the soldiers had no room to fire, for they were pressed and crowded by the Indians, who threw themselves recklessly upon them, striking up a rifle whenever it was attempted to be levelled.

A charge with the bayonet would have been worse than madness—it would have been murder breast to breast, and shoulder to shoulder.

It was only for a moment, for though the soldiers stood on the ground where they had been stationed, the Indians were between them and the gaol closely surrounding it. Chagrined at the maneuver that outwitted him, the captain drew his guard before the most salient point of the Indians, and endeavoured to regain what he had lost ; and a rough-and-tumble struggle ensued, when the guards were overpowered, many of their arms being wrested from them, and in a few moments they were powerless.

This accomplished, the chief, sounding the Indian savage war-cry, which, being taken up by his braves, rolled over them with the fierceness of the howl of a pack of hungry wolves attacked the door that barred the entrance into the building. A rail was brought forward, the door falling beneath the repeated blows, and the chief and his braves entered. And as a part were left without to guard the gaol, while others entered, in a moment a hundred rifles were levelled up the stair-way at the head of which was the prison, and discharged without aim or object.

The demon of retribution which the Mormons' lawless acts had aroused was now past control, and in the frenzy of exultation, on gaining the lower hall, they had levelled their rifles at the senseless walls that contained their foes, and fired.

CHAPTER CXVI.

THE EVIL NEWS.

MEANWHILE the people of Nauvoo were in sore plight. Some of the masses began to doubt whether they had acted with wisdom in adopting a system so utterly abhorrent to all civilized beings as Mormonism.

They were overpowered with dread ; fear paralyzed every heart.

Quivering, whispering lips, terror glancing eyes, and noiseless steps, proclaimed the intensity of expectation.

Spies kept them aware of all that was going on.

They were well aware that Joseph Smith was incarcerated in Carthage gaol on a charge of high treason.

They also knew that the infuriated populace were congregating on all sides to take the law into their own hands.

The Nauvoo legion, would, if called out, have been amply sufficient to guard against any act of mob-vengeance.

But Nauvoo was divided.

Certain of the head men were already speculating on the chances of who was to be his successor.

Brigham Young, Sidney Rigdon, and others, were closely closeted with their private adherents, canvassing the chances which might accrue if Joseph Smith perished.

The apostles were afraid to take upon themselves any combined action.

Everybody was giving advice, nobody taking it.

One or two of the Prophet's wives ran through the streets, wailing and shrieking, and calling on the people to save the great teacher of the new word.

At this moment a party of mounted Danites entered the city, bringing with them as prisoners, Amy and Jessie.

Captain Fearnot was hailed as a deliverer.

Hastily placing the two girls in a safe asylum, he hurried to mix with the terrified and excited groups.

He knew the danger of the Prophet, and understood the feelings of the people.

"Let us march to his rescue, let us destroy utterly his enemies!" shouted some of Joe Smith's most determined partisans.

"Let us hold council," said Captain Fearnot —as Simon Yackley was always called. "Where are the elders ?"

No one knew.

"Come to the Temple, and I will summon them," cried the captain.

Several of his Danites were near him. He started them off to the elders to announce a great meeting of the people.

The Mormons flocked in droves at once to the Temple, where soon after the elders began to congregate.

In half an hour the vast expanse of that huge building was full, and yet no one ventured to suggest anything.

The elders, particularly Brigham Young, Sidney Rigdon, William Smith, and Lyman White, had scowling and perturbed faces.

They had been disputing about the course to be pursued, if anything fatal happened to the Prophet.

They knew that a successor to the Mormon Pope must be possessed of audacity, cunning, and ready wit.

That they cared nothing for the cause may be seen by their grasping and savage ambition.

But none dared, in public, hint even at the thoughts which were uppermost in the minds of all the elders.

None ventured to hint that they were basing calculations on the possibility of the Prophet's death.

Brigham Young, however, knew that something must be said or done.

Accordingly, he rose and, in the usual rambling and disjointed style, he adopted in his sermons and speeches, began to pray that this great trouble might pass away from them.

The more ervent responded "Amen"; the lukewarm would have rather liked to have discovered the best course to pursue to pacify the infuriated mob, who were daily threatening to raze Nauvoo to the ground and slaughter its people.

Sidney Rigdon then rose.

Brigham Young looked at him askance. He knew that Rigdon was in all the secrets of Smith, and, under the influence of a threat to expose the mummery of the Book of Mormon, had obtained from the Prophet a written acknowledgment that he alone was capable of fulfilling the high offices of Prophet, chief, and guide of the Mormons.

But Brigham Young also knew that Joe Smith only gave this from fear that Rigdon would be a formidable enemy, if suffered to become estranged from the superstitious fanaticism had wound round him.

The Prophet had often in secret expressed his opinion of Rigdon.

This man, from having been a Methodist preacher once, had got a knack of speaking.

His proposition was a bold one.

The Prophet was in prison. Until his trial was over, he was, as it were, dead in the eyes of the law.

The Mormons were without a head or ruler.

During the interregnum, which must endure until the trial was over, why not choose a vice chief who should lead the Mormons now without a head ?

"Whom shall we choose ?" cried some.

"Lo!" shouted Sidney Rigdon, in a loud and

nasal voice, 'the angel of the Lord came unto me this morning, and said,—' Go forth, my son, and be unto me a prophet in the place of my servant Joseph, whom the Gentiles have taken prisoner. Go before my people, and guide them in the path I shall direct thee; then when thou layest down thy life, thou shalt sit on my right hand, by my servant Joseph, and wear a crown and bear a sceptre like unto the one with which he shall be crowned. Moreover, I charge thee to go out in battle with my legion against the Gentiles; and I will cause thee to be victorious over my enemies; then shalt thou enlarge my borders around thee, and dwell in peace all the days of thy life.'"

A terrific shout of applause caused Brigham Young to quail, and a personal altercation would have ensued, if a man had not ridden up to the door of the Temple, and forced his way in on horseback.

"What means this intrusion?" cried Brigham Young, in a stentorian voice.

"I come with news which will send a chill to the hearts of the faithful. The Prophet of the Lord is dead!"

"How?"

"Murdered—foully, abominably, murdered!" said the messenger.

Then arose a wail, or rather, howl of anguish from the whole massive crowd, followed by shrieks, yells, and cries, which demonstrated that some, at least, were deeply affected by the news.

"Let all disperse to their homes; let every man prepare his arms; the Patriarchs will hold council," said Brigham.

He was obeyed, and with one accord the whole vast multitude moved out to prepare for the dreadful struggle which seemed to them to be impending.

CHAPTER CXVII.

THE DANITE DWELLING.

SIMON YACKLEY had several residences. He was not one of those who approved of the peculiar form of polygamy which placed several wives under one roof.

He had his own private house, and then other smaller ones scattered over the city.

In each of these was one of his wives.

Without exception, they had an occupation of some kind, and entirely supported themselves.

There was no danger of anyone molesting them, though they were pretty; the reputation of the young, but ferocious, chief being well known.

Besides, as chief of the Danites, his power was terrible and irresponsible.

Woe to him upon whom the lord of the Avenging Angels looked with an evil eye!

The place in which Jessie and Amy had been placed for safe custody was the private residence of Simon; where he was attended by a negro boy and an old woman, who looked upon him with an awe which caused them to obey his faintest behests with painful alacrity.

A harsh and cruel master was Simon Yackley.

In his sitting-room—a luxuriant and comfortable apartment, where only his nearest friends were admitted—it was that Amy and Jessie were locked up; the former, bewildered, terror-stricken, and sorrowful—the latter, calm, resolved, and hopeful.

Amy seemed to regret the discovery as much as she did the course of events.

She was one of those simple and somewhat feeble minds which are content, so that they are loved, to ask no questions as to whether that love be shared.

There must be many such among the resigned and believing female Mormons.

But they are of a different mould from any women it has been our lot to know.

"Are you quite sure of what you assert?" she said to Jessie, when they were fairly housed in the dread retreat.

"Quite sure. I have seen the man often among the Mormons."

"But may he not be one of the Latter-day Saints, and yet a good man?" said Amy, casting down her eyes, and speaking in the tone of a petulant, spoiled child, whose toy has just been taken away from it.

"No, he cannot be a good man and a Mormon. Listen to me, Amy."

And she told her everything she could of the men of whom she had, unfortnately, seen so much.

"Besides," she added, "have you not a father and brothers, to whom you will be for ever lost if you remain with this man?"

"True. But we are told to cleave to our husband."

"Yes—a true and lawful husband; but we are equally commanded to leave a false and wicked betrayer."

"I should be married," said Amy, with a pout.

"How can you be married to a man who has already many wives? Amy, you are a mere child, and do not understand what you are talking about—else, would I never forgive you. You have been kind and affectionate to me, and I like you."

"I worship you, Jessie; but all cannot be like you."

"You can be good and firm. It is painful to give up all hope of one upon whom you have lavished the young affections of your heart; but remember how much more painful it will be for your poor father to give up all hope of you— never to see you again ——"

"Why should he never see me again?"

"Amy, I shall be angry with you soon. It is my intention to escape from here."

"How?"

"I don't know. Now, if I succeed, will you come with me?"

Amy made no reply, for at this moment both the negro woman and boy entered with a tray of refreshments, sent by order of the chief of the Danites.

The door of the room was left ajar.

Quick as lightning a light figure passed through the doorway, and, with the blow of the butt of a pistol, felled the boy to the ground.

DEATH OF JOE SMITH.

The black woman dropped on her knees.

"Come!" said the voice of Eudora—"they are approaching! We have not a moment to lose!"

Jessie quickly obeyed, and followed her into the street, which was at no great distance blocked up by a crowd.

"Where is Amy?" suddenly asked Eudora, who still wore her picturesque dress as a smart backwoodsman.

"Left behind," cried Jessie.

"I will go back!"

"See!" said Jessie, pointing to several men, who were approaching quickly. "Besides, I fear me, Eudora, the infatuated girl has stopped behind of her own accord."

"You amaze me! What can be the reason of such madness?"

"She loves Simon Yackley, the chief of the Avenging Angels of the Prophet Joe Smith."

"Who is Prophet no more!" said Eudora, hurrying her along at a rapid pace.

"How so?"

"He is dead! But walk quietly now. Turn down this lane; it leads to the woods. If we are pursued we may double on our enemies," but we must be cautious.

Jessie made no reply, but did as she was told.

They had as yet, they knew, attracted no attention.

The mob were intent upon the news which had been promulgated.

Everywhere the cry went through the city,—"The Prophet is dead! Woe has fallen on Zion!"

Still there was alarm and dread.

Many began to make secret preparations for leaving the city, and abandoning the false and cruel faith which had roused so much hatred on all sides.

Others stood wildly at the corners of streets, singing Mormon hymns.

One of these will give a better idea of the characteristics of Mormon devotion than anything else we can lay before our readers—

I'm a Saint, I'm a Saint, on the rough world wide,
The earth is my home, and my God is my guide!
Up, up with the truth, let its power bend the knee:
I am sent, I am sent, and salvation is free.
I fear not old priestcraft, its dogmas can't awe:
I've a chart for to steer by, that tells me the law,—
And ne'er as a coward to falsehood I'll kneel,
While Mormon tells truth, or God's prophets reveal!
Up, up with the truth, let its power touch the mind,
And I'll warrant we'll soon leave the selfish behind.
Up, up with the truth, let its power bend the knee,
I am sent! I am sent! dying Bab'lon to thee,—
I am sent! I am sent! take this warning and flee.

The arm of the tyrant fell terror may spread,
Yet, tho' they oppose us, their strongholds we'll tread;
What to us is the scorn of the selfish and vain?
We have borne it before, and we'll bear it again.
The fire-gleaming bolts of oppression may fall,
And kill off the body, death can't us appal!
With Heaven above us, and all Hell below,
Thro' the wide field of error, right onward we'll go!
Come on, my brave comrades! now's the time you
        should speak,
The storm-fiend is roused from his long dreamy sleep.
Our watchword, for safety in Zion, shall be,
I am sent! I am sent! dying Bab'lon to thee,—
I am sent! I am sent! take this warning and flee.

There was a rude eloquence about these singers, who were sincere dupes—not impostors—which was very striking.

In many cases where Mormons have been entirely sincere, there can be little difference seen between them and any other sect of extreme and rather eccentric dissenters.

Others again disbelieved the report of the Prophet's death, particularly as there could be no doubt of the murder of Hyrum Smith, his brother.

Many hoped and trusted that there was some mistake; for, as usual with all such impostures, opinions were divided as to the merits of Joseph Smith.

There were those who worshipped him as a real and true divinity.

Then once more the gates of the Prophet's harem flew open, says the eye-witness of this terrible scene; and the Cyprians within—this time headed by the Sultana—rushed forth, with savage cries of rage and despair, demanding vengeance on the murderers.

"Hang them higher than Haman!" shouted the Sultana, as she tossed her arms in the air; while her long, unbound hair floated back from her girlish face, bathed in tears.

The sight of the Prophet's mistresses, wailing in frantic grief, caused a reaction in the city.

Their wailings were taken up by his followers, and the sounds of grief and woe rose in one long cry from those who had looked upon him as little below the Deity.

Closely following in its train, arose a fierce, vindictive cry for vengeance; for the distress of the beautiful favourite touched their hearts, and her impassioned appeals for retribution on the murderers of her lord and master roused them to action.

"Shall the Lord's best-beloved Prophet," continued the Sultana, "His chosen messenger to fallen man, be thus robbed of a life more precious than those of a million of other men's, and we not rise up to avenge it? Let the legion he loved so well go forth, and slaughter the murderers by thousands and tens of thousands! It is not meet he should die thus like a dog, and his death not carry with it a retaliation that shall redeem the impious act."

The chief of the Danites—who, in case of the reality of the death of Joe Smith, had quite made up his mind as to which master he should serve—hurried to his home, to put on his uniform and be prepared.

He found his door open, his negro bleeding on the ground, and Amy kneeling, in the act of staunching his blood.

She looked up at him with a half-terrified, half-affectionate look.

Amy explained, without mentioning the name of Jessie's saviour.

"And why did you not fly?" asked Simon Yackley.

"Do you ask me, John?" she said.

"Do you still love me?" he eagerly asked.

"I do—I care not what they say, or what your faults may be—I love you still!" she said, with a kind of savage enthusiasm.

"By heavens, Amy, you shall never repent it!" said the Danite, turning away to hide his emotion.

"I believe it."

"Now, Flora, just you pick up, and look alive. See this young lady wants for nothing. I shall be back soon, Amy."

And he hurried out.

He now recollected having seen a couple in the distance, who very much resembled Jessie and some young man.

He soon summoned a couple of his friends, and, heedless of public events, started off in pursuit of the fugitives.

CHAPTER CXVII.

FLIGHT.

As long as they kept in sight, Eudora and Jessie made no manifestation of an intention to fly.

While casting behind them glances, which revealed extreme anxiety, they spoke not a single word.

Eudora was pale, but grave, earnest, and solemn.

At the back of the house was a lane, leading to a gulley that passed through a remnant of one of those forests which modern civilization has destroyed.

"Now run awhile," said Eudora.

And she set the example.

They were soon under the shadow of some trees, and Eudora halted.

"One moment."

"Why?"

"Jessie," said Eudora, "you are a brave and a good girl, and I only regret that scruples which honour you prevent your joining with me in my great scheme of revenge against Brigham Young and the Mormons."

"I know no such feeling as revenge," replied Jessie.

"I understand; but you are brave."

"I think so."

"Take this pistol. These men will be sure to pursue us. I know it—I feel it. We must defend ourselves. Will you?"

"I will," replied Jessie, calmly.

"That is a brave girl. I can feel that your hand is firm and steady."

She turned sharply round.

"They come—follow me!"

A sharp descent brought them to a narrow bridge, which was extremely dangerous.

It was a single plank over a swift rushing stream.

"They come!" whispered Eudora—"not a moment is to be lost!"

Eudora took Jessie by the hand, and assisted her to cross.

"Now," she added; and marking where a beaten path led within the trees, the masculine and brave girl led the way.

But no sooner was she out of sight of her pursuers than she crept under some bushes, and began a retrograde movement towards the little stream.

Jessie obeyed implicitly.

She thoroughly understood and believed in Eudora.

They heard the Danites passing close to them, vowing the most awful vengeance.

In a few minutes Eudora and Jessie were again on the banks of the stream, and close behind the town.

A small dug-out was at their feet.

"Enter," said Eudora.

They both seated themselves in the frail embarcation, and Eudora began paddling swiftly towards the great Father of Waters.

She had a small rifle in the boat, and, strange to say, she felt for the first time some hope of escape.

"You will, at all events, never betray me?" said Eudora, continuing the conversation which had been commenced awhile ago.

"Never!" said Jessie, "though I may not exactly agree with the means adopted, I am deeply grateful, and nothing could make me betray you to any living soul."

"Not even Henry?"

"Not even Henry," replied Jessie, blushing rosy red.

They were now approaching a spot where great caution was required.

The river was narrow, swift, and overhung by trees that cast all into shade.

The trees were, however, on one side only, while on the other were bare rocks.

Eudora, during the six months that had elapsed since she left New York, had taught herself to paddle, shoot, and fish.

She was doomed to become one of the best trappers of the Rocky Mountains.

She, however, now was obliged to be very careful.

"Sit quite still," she said, "for we have to pass a rapid—and, as poor father says, I kalkerlate it's a stiff one."

Jessie looked grave, and immediately did as she was told.

The river ran swift and strong.

Next instant they were in the current, and, before Eudora could dip her paddle in the right direction, were being whirled round in the first vortex of the rapid.

But Eudora was not to be defeated.

She fixed the broad short oar in the water, and in a moment the canoe was still.

"That was well done," she said, with a quiet laugh."

"Don't do it again," replied Jessie

Before they could exchange another word, the dug-out swept beneath the trees, and would next instant have been through the rapid, when Jessie uttered a sudden cry.

Eudora turned, and on the edge of a small projecting space of land fifty yards distant saw Captain Fearnot and his Danites.

A deadly pallor whitened the face of Eudora, and then, quick as lightning, her course of action was decided.

CHAPTER CXIX.
THE CROWN OF MARTYRDOM.

THE soldiers were in a terrible state of mind. To fight hand to hand with their own fathers, brothers, and friends, was a contingency they little approved of, while to allow the majesty of the law to be outraged was equally unpleasant for faithful citizens.

Still, their chief officer would not stand by and behold the illegal proceedings.

No governor had yet come to approve or disapprove his proceedings.

He accordingly drew off his soldiers, and allowed the Regulators to act just as they pleased.

Our hostility to the Mormons is unqualified and intense, our dislike of Joseph Smith and his imposture, genuine and real; but we cannot approve either of the conduct of soldiers or mob.

Several of the painted Indians and members of the mob, with blackened faces, ascended the staircase leading to the floor where Joseph Smith was confined.

A quick discharge of rifles and revolvers was heard.

Then the shutter of the upper window opened, and the Prophet appeared, gazing in a bewildered way at the mob below.

A volley of execrations greeted him.

Then, how or why no man could tell, he fell almost headlong out of the window, sprawling on his hands.

He was evidently quite stunned by the fall.

Then two or three raised him up against the stonework of a wall.

Four men, with loaded muskets, advanced to the front.

The Prophet opened his eyes, and appeared about to speak.

A volley, however, checked him.

When the smoke cleared away, Joseph Smith no longer lived in the flesh, but remained a martyr on earth to the great glorification of his sect.

Bad as he was, the evil he did was not so great as that perpetrated by the second Prophet Brigham Young, who, sheltered by the impunity of his wondrous Salt Lake, is able to set public opinion and laws at defiance.

When we come to Utah we shall find Mormonism *as it is now*, in all the fearful nakedness of its cynical immorality.

But what had passed above since Hyrum Smith was shot ?

We have this solely on Mormon authority.

Joseph looked towards his brother, and responded, " *O dear brother Hyrum*," and opening the door two or three inches with his left hand, discharged one barrel of a six-shooter (pistol) at random in the entry, from whence a ball grazed Hyrum's breast, and entering his throat, passed into his head ; while other muskets were aimed at him, and some balls hit him.

Joseph continued snapping his revolver round the casing of the door into the space as before, three barrels of which missed fire, while Mr. Taylor, with a walking-stick, stood by his side and knocked down the bayonets and muskets which were constantly discharging through the doorway, while Willard stood by him, ready to lend any assistance, with another stick, but could not come within striking distance without going directly before the muzzle of the guns.

When the revolver failed they had no more fire-arms, and expecting an immediate rush of the mob, and the door-way full of muskets—half way in the room—and no hope but instant death from within, Mr. Taylor rushed into the window, which is some fifteen or twenty feet from the ground.

When his body was nearly on a balance, a ball from the door within entered his leg, and a ball from without struck his watch, a patent lever, in his vest pocket, near the left breast, and smashed it in " pie," leaving the hands standing at 5 o'clock, 16 minutes, and 26 seconds—the force of which ball threw him back on the floor, and he rolled under the bed which stood by his side, where he lay motionless, the mob from the door continuing to fire upon him, cutting away a piece of flesh from his left hip as large as a man's hand, and were hindered only by Willard knocking down their muzzles with a stick ; while they continued to reach their guns into the room, probably left-handed, and aimed their discharge so far around as almost to reach the Mormons in the corner of the room to where they had retreated ; and then Willard re-commenced the attack with his stick again.

Joseph attempted, as the last resort, to leap the

same window from whence Mr. Taylor fell, when two balls pierced him from the door, and one entering his right breast from without, and he fell outward exclaiming, " *O Lord my God !*" As his feet went out of the window, Willard's head went in, the balls whistling all around.

He fell on his left side a dead man.

At this instant a cry was raised, " *He's leaped the window !*" and the mob on the stairs and in the entry ran out. Willard withdrew from the window, thinking it of no use to leap out on a hundred bayonets, then around General Smith's body.

Not satisfied with this, Willard again reached his head out of the window, and watched some seconds, to see if there were any signs of life.

Being fully satisfied that he was dead, with a hundred men near the body, and more coming round the corner of the gaol, and expecting a return to their room, Willard rushed towards the prison door, at the head of the stairs, and through the entry from whence the firing had proceeded, to learn if the doors into the prison were open.

When near the entry, Mr. Taylor called out " *Take me.*" Willard then pressed his way until he found all doors unbarred ; returning instantly, he caught Mr. Taylor under his arm, and rushed by the stairs into the dungeon, or inner prison, stretched him on the floor, and covered him with a bed, in such a manner as not likely to be perceived, expecting an immediate return of the mob.

Thus perished Joseph Smith.

Various have been the opinions expressed as to this man. Dr. Mackay thinks he was half impostor, half visionary ; others believed him to have had a mission ; others, to have been a godless hypocrite.

His mission we shall judge by its fruits in Utah.

That he was a remarkable man, there is no doubt.

Not thirty years have elapsed since a band, composed of six persons, was formed in Palmyra, New York, of which Joseph Smith, junior, was the presiding genius.

Most of these were connected with the family of Smith, senior.

They were notorious for breach of contracts, and the repudiation of their honest debts.

All of them were addicted to vice.

They obtained their living, not by honourable labour, but by deceiving their neighbours with their marvellous tales of money-digging.

Notwithstanding the low origin, poverty, and profligacy, of the members of that band of mountebanks, they have augmented their numbers till more than 100,000 persons are now numbered among the followers of the Mormon Prophet, and never were increasing so rapidly as at the time of his death.

Born in the very lowest walks of life, reared in poverty, educated in vice, having no claims to even common intelligence, coarse and vulgar in deportment, the Prophet Smith succeeded in establishing a religious creed, the tenets of which have been taught throughout the length and breadth of America.

The Prophet's virtues have been rehearsed and

admired in Europe; the ministers of Nauvoo have even found a welcome in Asia; and Africa has listened to the grave sayings of the seer of Palmyra.

The standard of the Latter-day Saints has been reared on the banks of the Nile, and even the Holy Land has been entered by the emissaries of this wicked impostor.

Reasoning from effect to cause, we must conclude that the Mormon Prophet was of no common genius; few are able to commence and carry out an imposition like his, so long, and to such an extent.

And we see, in the history of his success, most striking proofs of the gullibility of a large portion of the human family.

What may not men be induced to believe?

BOOK IV.

CHAPTER I.

AFTER THE FUNERAL.

EUDORA, during her wanderings about the neighbourhood, had become well acquainted with the accidents and peculiarities of the land. She gazed for one moment at the rapid, and then gave a whirl of her paddle, and they were not only concealed from view, but in total darkness.

Jessie looked curiously about, and saw that she was in one of those dark and gloomy caverns which are so common in America, and which have in their day been the refuge of Red Indians, wild beasts, and modern thieves—chiefly coiners and horse-stealers.

Eudora checked the dug-out just in time to retain a glimmer of light from the opening.

"Sit quite still," she said, "I know the place well. I will land."

"But they saw us."

"I think not."

"But if they did?"

"We have our resource."

"What?"

"To fight."

Jessie shook her head.

"It is our duty," said Eudora, warmly. "I look upon these men as wild beasts. If they take us they will have no mercy—why should we?"

Jessie shook her head.

"I will fight—and fight unto death," said the Amazonian girl, with great energy."

"I will defend myself against outrage," replied Jessie.

"It is your duty," cried Eudora, and then she added, with a spice of sarcasm, "it is your duty to Henry."

"Why do you laugh?" asked Jessie, quietly.

"Because men are so very particular about their virtue! The hypocrites! With a grave and solemn face, they enquire into the propriety and conduct and chastity of their future wives—but if we, on the other hand, were to inquire into theirs——"

"I am sure I could safely enquire into that of Henry," said Jessie, with her fearless confidence and love.

"Hem!"

"You doubt. Ah! you do not know my Henry."

"All men are alike; but I will not tease you since you have faith in this man, but rather think of what measures we are to adopt to escape."

While talking thus they had landed upon a ledge of rock, and Eudora, who never went unprovided, had taken from the boat a torch, which she held on high.

The vault was twenty feet above them, and went some distance into the mountain.

The ledge reached to the very edge of the stream which supplied the subterranean pond.

But Eudora thought it best to wait some time before they ventured to peer into the open air.

Thus passed an hour, when Eudora, clutching her light but deadly rifle in her hand, crept slowly along the ledge, glancing with keen eyes in every direction as she did so.

Then suddenly she halted and stood still.

Their presence in the cavern was known. Above and below the cavern, seated on the banks of the stream, leisurely smoking, sat two of the most ruffianly of the Danites.

Captain Fearnot was nowhere to be seen.

He had probably been called away to the excited and terror-stricken city, where his presence was more than ever necessary.

The Patriarchs had assembled in council, and there, more than ever, Rigdon felt the effect of the powerful, calm, calculating will of Young.

Boldly he displayed the document which yielded to him the office of succession to the Prophet. In a commanding tone he called on all to yield him that trust and obedience that had been accorded to the Prophet.

He said he came before them at the command of Jehovah, who had ordered him to restore peace among his chosen people by chastising the Gentiles, and then tender the revelation, as given by the Prophet Joseph to Queen Victoria.

Vain, self-sufficient man! whose reason totters before the casual glance, and he forgets all in the vile passion that mounts the usurped throne, and rules with a rod of iron, where it should have been the slave, not the master.

The Patriarchs listened to the vagaries of Rigdon with gloomy brows, and when he had ceased, James J. Strong, one of the twelve, arose, and, in authoritative tones, pronounced the revelations of Rigdon as proceeding from the evil one, who sought to distract the faithful in this perilous hour, declaring he had been appointed by God to seize the vacant post, and fulfil the divine mission the dead Prophet had begun!

William Smith likewise arose in indignation, and in choice vituperation denounced both competitors, and claimed, as the natural successor of the Prophet, the office of Prophet and Seer, denouncing all other aspirants as dissenters and fomenters of evil.

He was interrupted by Lyman White, another of the twelve, who proclaimed himself a Leader and Prophet; and in consternation the assembly broke up, for the vacant seat was likely to find as many contestants as ever, at one time, did the chair of St. Peter.

They had resolved to raise an army to defend themselves, but a conciliatory message having been received from Carthage, their ardour was somewhat cooled by the stern, steady hand of Young, who had assumed the leadership while others were quarrelling about it.

He did not intend to dispute the claims of others; all he did was quietly to assert his own, and on the twelve being again convened, he, by cajoling and intimidation, obtained the assent of the convention, and henceforth, Brigham Young, the second to the Prophet in the number of his harem, became the second leader of the Mormon fanaticism.

Rigdon, indignant at the injustice done him, thundered his anathemas at their devoted heads, and they, in turn, excommunicated him from the Church, and sent him adrift on the world.

Young knew not the secrets possessed by Rigdon, or he would have courted, instead of exasperated, so formidable an enemy.

The Prophet had stood in fear of a man who could thus injure his cause; but Young, ignorant of this, found, when too late, the mistake he had committed; for Rigdon made a grand *exposé* of the imposture, and from this *exposé* much of the early history of Mormonism has been gathered.

Friends, by hundreds, flocked around the would-be Prophet, and, placing himself defiantly at their head, he led his little colony away by themselves to Pennsylvania, where he settled with them, well pleased that he could rule a few, if not all. White led away another large party to Texas, where he settled with his adherents, also well pleased that he had a share of the subjects over which he had aspired to rule.

William Smith, the only surviving brother of Joseph, the Prophet, published some revelations, which made Mormonism still blacker to the argus-eyed Gentiles; and Young, in order to get rid of so dangerous a rival, cut him off, and turned him loose on the world also, greatly to his indignation.

The pruning hook was applied with no sparing hand by Young, who resolved to free himself of all who would be likely in future to dispute his absolute sway.

The Mormons then all submitted to the sway of Brigham Young.

Captain Fearnot, of the Danites, was the first to give in his adhesion.

The Patriarchs, except the excluded ones, then followed.

It was more like a jubilee, except on the day of the funeral of Joe Smith, which was grand in the extreme. The following is the description given by one present.

Early on the following morning the Nauvoo Legion was called out and addressed by Mr. Phelps, the editor of the Mormon paper, and other leading members of the community, who severally urged the legion and citizens to be peaceable. The legion remained under arms from ten in the morning until three in the afternoon, awaiting the arrival of the bodies of Joseph and Hyrum. " About three o'clock," says the *Times and Seasons*, published in Nauvoo three days afterwards, " the bodies were met by a great assemblage of people, east of the Temple, under the direction of the City Marshal, Samuel H. Smith; the brother of the deceased; Dr. Richards; and Mr. Hamilton, of Carthage. The waggons in which the bodies were conveyed were guarded by three men. A procession was formed behind them, consisting of the City Council, the Staff of the Lieutenant-General, the Major-General, and the Brigadier-General, of the Nauvoo Legion, the commanders, officers, and men, and the citizens of Nauvoo, to the number of from eight to ten thousand. These followed the bodies to the Mansion House, amid the most solemn lamentations and wailings that ever ascended into the ears of the Lord God of Hosts, to be revenged of their enemies!" An oration was pronounced over the bodies by Dr. Richards, and addresses were also delivered by four other Mormons, in which the multitude were strongly urged to remain peaceable. " That vast assemblage, with one united voice," said the *Times and Seasons*, " resolved to trust to the law for justice for such a high-handed assassination, and if that failed, to call upon God to avenge them of their wrongs. Oh, widows and orphans!" it concluded, " Oh, Americans, weep! The glory of freedom has departed!"

This matter settled, the Mormons began packing up, loading their waggons, and starting on their journey to Great Salt Lake.

But they were not allowed to part in peace.

A regular siege was laid to Nauvoo, and the saints expelled.

CHAPTER II.

THE CAVERN.

We left Jessie and Eudora in the cave.

Rapidly retreating, the latter communicated the fact that they were watched to Jessie, and added that their only hope of escape was to wait until night came on.

Jessie shuddered.

Her troubles seemed never over—always begun, never ending.

When should she find that best of all havens of rest—a husband's bosom?

She almost began to despair in the solitude of her heart.

But it was of no use despairing. On the contrary, in the circumstances in which she was placed, what she needed was courage.

" As soon as night comes," said Eudora, " we will creep out of the cavern, and before these wretches are aware of it, will shoot through the lower rapids. They are perfectly safe."

" I am in your hands—I trust you implicitly," said Jessie.

Then they spoke in whispers for some time, though gradually they were getting very faint and hungry.

" You don't feel well," said Eudora, suddenly, as seated in the dark with Jessie's hands in hers, the latter's head fell wearily on her shoulder.

" Are you ill ? " said Eudora, with a start.

" Faint and hungry," replied Jessie, with a low laugh.

" What a moony individual I am," cried Eudora, laying the other against the rock.

" Why ? " asked Jessie, in her dulcet tones.

" Because I have plenty of provisions in the boat, and never thought of it ! " she cried, as she stooped over the dugout.

In a few minutes she had lit a little spirit-lamp, placed it on the ledge, and producing a supply of the usual backwood fare—of which travellers complain so much—wild turkey and ham, made Jessie drink first a drain of buckeye.

It is a very repulsive kind of raw brandy, but in this case it revived Jessie.

Then she sat up and began slowly and quietly to eat of a kind of food, which, until the palate palls over it, is delicious.

But, as the great Boccacio says—*toujours perdrix* won't do.

If you want to know the origin of the tale, look in Boccacio. It will not suit our columns, which never violate the strictest decency, excepting when the revolting acts of the Mormons compel us to be explicit.

They sat some time over their welcome meal, not the last by many they were to take together.

Then, having recruited exhausted nature, they resumed their watch.

" Of what were you thinking," asked Jessie, in a stronger voice and more cheery tone, " that you forgot our dinner ? "

Here we may remark that novelists and romance writers rarely allow their heroines to have appetites ; they are like those knights of chivalry, who wander for weeks and months through pathless forests in search of adventure, but who never, by any chance, think of eating or drinking.

We object to this, and make it a rule to mention such sublunary matters, as a proof that our characters are real flesh and blood, and not shadows that pass like those of a magic lantern.

" I was thinking of Brigham Young," said Eudora, in low tones.

" In what way ? " asked Jessie, caressingly. " Do you forgive him ? "

" Forgive the man who has robbed me of my faith in human nature, who has made love odious to me, who has taken away my virgin innocence of thought, and left me a wreck of what I was ? "

" Still, believe me Eudora," began Jessie, " you are wrong. There are noble and good men in the world—and many of them. Forget this man—leave the very land which he burdens with his monstrous villainy, and come to England——"

" No."

" I don't say there are many Henries in the world," continued Jessie, naively. "I don't know."

" My dear girl, to you there can only be one Henry."

" I don't know. I think myself unprejudiced," said Jessie.

" No woman is who loves. She thinks him on whom she has bestowed her heart, the noblest and best of created beings ; *his* eyes are brighter, *his* mouth more expressive, *his* tongue more dulcet

than any others—and to be clasped in *his* arms is the great happiness of life."

" I have been clasped in his arms," said Jessie, faintly.

" How ? " said Eudora, with a start of astonishment.

Jessie explained.*

" I tell you this to show what Henry is. Alone at night—by some trick the companion of my chamber and of my bed—he respected me," said Jessie, whose roseate blushes were concealed by the darkness of the night.

" He is a noble fellow," replied Eudora, in a husky tone.

" You seem affected," replied Jessie, gently and tenderly.

" I am. Listen, dear, and I, too, will tell you a story.

Eudora paused, as if to collect her thoughts, and then began her narrative.

CHAPTER III.

EUDORA'S NARRATIVE.

" I was little more than fifteen when I first saw Brigham Young.

" He was then a very fascinating man, and obtained a post in our school ; with what motives I now see.

" He was a villain, if ever there was one.

" Considerable liberty was allowed us girls, at times, with the masters, because they were men of tried character and repute.

" How Brigham Young entered the school is a mystery, which I cannot unravel.

" He must, most certainly, have forged certificates.

" He must have deceived the worthy Mrs. Turner, for she was goodness and purity itself.

" I was as innocent as a new-born babe ; my mind was wholly given to my studies. I thought only of men as teachers of languages and accomplishments.

" I now know that teachers in girls' schools should all be women.

" Until such a reform is established, no girl of mine shall receive her education in a boarding school.

" At the very best, it is a mistake — a temptation.

" Brigham Young was not handsome ; but he had a soft, seductive, oily voice, which no woman can hear unmoved.

" He was engaged as Mr. Verdi, of Italian origin, but born in the United States of North America.

" Nobody for one moment thought of doubting him.

" He was a favourite with the mistress, that sufficient.

" He was often asked to dinner, because he condescended to look after us in our hours of recreation.

" The wolf was left in charge of the flock of lambs.

---

* See previous No.

"It was a hot summer's day, and I, who was verging on womanhood, was seated—as I believe most girls are at the age I then was—thinking of the mysterious future.

"As the dawn of womanhood breaks, we invariably think of the other sex—why are we kept separated from them?

"What is that mysterious intercourse of the sexes called marriage?

"Our imaginations are vivid, and we cannot help thinking.

"Few schools are without their devouring novel readers, who inoculate the whole body.

"I had some novels lent me, which spoke of love.

"I read them, and they naturally excited my curiosity.

"I thought a great deal about love, and wanted, in my heart of hearts, to know what it really meant.

"They were innocent books enough; but nothing is innocent to the mind of a young girl when it talks of love.

"The sight of such a miserable caricature of the passions as the conventional Cupid, is of itself enough.

"I was prepared to receive the sweet and delicious poison in my soul.

"I was alone, under a tree. A book was in my hand. I was holding it upside down. I could not see a line.

"'What are you thinking of?' said a soft voice near me.

"'I don't know,' replied I, with a start.

"'You dont know!' continued the other, while my eyes were obstinately bent on the ground.

"'I do not,' I said, in a silly, confused, terrified way.

"A deep sigh was the only response I received to my words.

"I now firmly believe that the wretch had been prowling about the ground until he found one girl in the right humour—that dreamy state of the soul when you are prepared to receive any new impressions.

"I looked up. It was M. Verdi, whose snake-like and glittering eye was fixed upon me.

"I looked down again.

"'You are very beautiful,' he said, taking my hand in his.

"A strange sensation ran through my veins.

"'And the beautiful always think of love.'

"He had watched me cunningly. I had been thinking of love.

"'Ah, Miss!' he continued, 'you know not the harm you have done with those beautiful eyes of yours.'

"I could not help laughing—his tone was so melancholy.

"'You laugh, because your innocent heart knows neither the pains nor the joys of love.'

"I don't know that I was so ignorant of the pains, as he called them, for I felt my face flush, and my heart began to beat with unexampled violence.

"He held my hand firm in his.

"'Eudora,' he said, again pressing my hand to his lips, 'I love you! I adore you! I have sought the position in which I am solely that I might be near you.'

"'Indeed!'

"'It is so. But we are watched. I cannot say all to you that I could wish, and still it must be said, as my fate trembles in the balance.'

"'How so?' I said, in half-real, half-affected surprise.

"'Eudora, queen of my heart's soul! I love you—love you to distraction. If you respond not to my affection—if you cannot love me, I leave for ever. If you do, I will seek out your parents, and they shall take me as a son-in-law.'

"I could not speak. I was dumbfounded.

"'Will you see me—alone—to-night?'

"'But how?—where?' I said, somewhat alarmed at his vehemence.

"'To-night—here—in this garden.'

"I made no reply; but, as he afterwards said, my silence gave consent.

"'Thanks! What time do you retire to your dormitory?'

"'I have a room to myself," I said, pointing to one which opened out upon a terrace.

"And then, as if instinct told me I had done wrong, I withdrew my hand and ran away to the school-room.

CHAPTER IV.

EUDORA'S NARRATIVE CONTINUED.

"That night I retired to my room with feelings which were quite new to me.

"I knew then I was doing wrong, but alas! like many other daughters of Eve, I felt a strange, wild, and fascinating satisfaction in the act.

"My heart beat with terrible violence.

"I waited for the coming hour with wild delight.

"Was I not like a heroine of a novel at her first rendezvous?

"Of harm I knew none—and could therefore fear none.

"It was beyond my ken. I had read no French novels.

"The school was all silent at ten—at eleven, was the rendezvous.

"I unfastened my window and opened it.

"It was a French window, and served therefore as a door on to the terrace.

"He advanced quickly towards me, as I now think, in order to enter my bedroom, but I had closed the window.

"He took my arm, after kissing my hand.

"He led me back to the seat where he had first spoken to me, and we were again side be side.

"Gliding his arm round my waist, and taking hold of my hand with his other hand, he began.

"What did he say to me? What arguments did he use?—how he persuaded me that our future was for ever intertwined, I know not—but he did.

"Then he wished me to fly at once.

"'My angel, you know all that you need know, your education is finished—a minister will unite us, and then away to the place where your father

ATTACKED BY DANITES.

lives—and where he will receive us with pride and joy.'

" ' My father communicates with me through a banker.'

" ' My angel, any way we can find him. But oh, my darling !' and he drew my head to his and put a kiss upon my lips.

" A strange fire awoke in my bosom—my eyes were closed, my blood seemed to run like molten lava, through my veins—he pressed me tighter to his heart, and——

Jessie looked keenly at her in the gloom to which their eyes were becoming gradually accustomed.

" Do not look at me so strangely. I was saved from the degradation of that man's awful passions.

" A door opened, and one of the school teachers, a young girl with whom I was very intimate, entered.

" She was of a romantic and melancholy disposition. I have reason to think now, from the tone of her conversation, even given to sensuality and vice.

" When I began to think of love, I let fall certain words — and her eyes flashed, her cheeks flushed, and her bosom heaved at the very word.

"She looked warily and cautiously round the garden.

"We were partly concealed by bushes, partly by the shadow of the wall.

"He caught me round the waist and drew me away.

"But terror at the sight of my governess had chased away all other thoughts.

"I was calm, and only thought of the pain of discovery.

"'Let me hide,' I cried.

"'I will advance and speak to her. She *must* be on some errand of love,' he said, 'a fellow feeling will make her wondrous kind. You escape to your room.'

"'I will.'

"'To-morrow night—here,' he continued.

"'Yes, anything you like—only let me go now. I should die if I were found out.'

"And I ran away. I feel no doubt now that if I had looked back, I should have been cured of my passions. Several concurrent circumstances combined to assure me that it was for him she had come.

"But next day a messenger from my father, by great and almost miraculous good fortune, came, and in the most peremptory manner proved the necessity for my removal.

"I never saw the man again until he presented himself at my father's house, and you were good enough to expose his real character."

Eudora ceased.

"You have had a great and merciful escape," said Jessie, "and were I in your place, I should be content."

"No. I will have revenge. It is indeed a sweet and hopeful thought."

"Revenge is not of man or woman either," said Jessie.

"My way is not your way. Be satisfied. I will not implicate you; but I could not rest in my grave until I am revenged."

Jessie sighed, and made no reply. She could not understand it.

CHAPTER V.

THE DANITES.

NIGHT gradually fell, and Eudora thought it time to prepare for their departure.

She was extremely anxious to return to her father, and learn what progress he had made.

It was now a week since the outrage by the Mormons.

He would, with his strong constitution, be nearly well.

He would gladly make one of the party in pursuit of the Mormons.

It was now generally known, that the Mormons were about wholly to abandon the abodes of civilization, and take up their residence at the Great Salt Lake.

A proper situation for them.

They should have had an island cut off from the whole human race, to play their pranks in.

They could there have lifted up their temple of polygamy and prostitution to the skies, without outraging the feelings of decent, honest, and Christian people.

But to support an imposture, it is necessary to have a good supply of dupes.

The boat, which was close to Eudora's hand, was now slowly impelled towards the mouth of the cave.

Eudora's plan was to run the gauntlet of her enemies, in the hope of being able to shoot the rapids.

"Now is our time," she said. "Are you ready, Jessie?"

"I am."

"Move along the ledge then."

Jessie followed.

"Hold the boat—no, lie down," suddenly whispered Eudora. "They come."

At the same moment, two of the Danite gang of Destroying Angels appeared in the mouth of the cavern.

One carried a heavy gun.

The other lifted a torch on high.

"Now thin," cried one of them, "we ain't a going to stand this here conduct no longer. Come out, or we're bound to shute."

"Back," said Eudora, in tones of deep determination, "back! or, by the Heavens above, it will be the worse for you both!"

The Danites looked at one another. The man with the torch showed a tendency to back out.

"Why," cried his companion "it's only a gal; but gal or no gal, here goes!"

And with his gun to the charge, he rushed at Eudora, whose figure he could dimly make out in the darkness.

Eudora delivered her fire with a steadiness which was miraculous in one so young.

The Danite fell back with a groan, his gun falling into the water.

The second Danite fled with the utmost precipitation.

Then Eudora, without a moment's hesitation, hurried Jessie into the boat, and carefully following the dug-out, glided forth next instant from the cavern.

No one interfered with their flight.

Eudora conducted her boat with consummate skill through the rapids.

In half an hour later they were within sight of the log hut to which Obadiah Jones had been removed by the disconsolate parent of Amy.

On his return he had learned of her abduction, and, in a moment of irritation, had sent Obadiah Jones away.

The farmer was not a hard, was not a cruel man, but he was extremely passionate, and unable to control his temper.

Eudora hurried into the house. Obadiah Jones was seated in an arm-chair, with an old woman near him, who had volunteered to be his nurse.

The meeting between parent and child was fervent in the extreme

Eudora easily explained the reason of her absence.

Her father was satisfied, and readily agreed to join her in her designs against Brigham Young.

Jessie now put in her claim to be allowed to return home. She was absolved from her promise to Phineas Bristowe, she could not make out the silence of Henry, and the only way, therefore, was to return to England.

They could not deny the truth of this.

But Eudora begged her to stay a few days longer. She had laid out a plan for her journey, so as to give her father as much rest as possible.

This could only be done by travelling by water.

She had also certain preparations to make, which could not be executed in less than three days.

During that brief period, tragic scenes took place.

Nauvoo was bombarded for three days. At length, after an obstinate defence, the Mormons surrendered, and were driven out with fire and sword.

A traveller reached the spot next day.

His outline of the scene would not have been ill-placed in the "Arabian Nights' Entertainments."

Let it have a chapter to itself.

CHAPTER VI.

AFTER THE SIEGE.

I WAS descending the last hill-side upon my journey, when a landscape, in delightful contrast, broke upon my view. Half encircled by a bend of the river, a beautiful city lay glittering in the fresh morning sun ; its bright new dwellings, set in cool green gardens, ranging up around a stately dome-shaped hill, which was crowned by a noble marble edifice, whose high tapering spire was radiant with white and gold.

The city appeared to cover several miles : and beyond it, in the background, there rolled off a fair country, chequered by the careful lines of fruitful husbandry.

The unmistakable marks of industry, enterprize, and educated wealth, everywhere made the scene one of singular and most striking beauty.

It was a natural impulse to visit this inviting region. I procured a skiff, and, rowing across the river, landed at the chief wharf of the city.

No one met me there.

I looked, and saw no one.

I could hear no one move : though the quiet everywhere was such that I heard the flies buzz, and the water-ripples break against the shallow of the beach.

I walked through the solitary streets.

The town lay as in a dream, under some deadening spell of loneliness, from which I almost feared to wake it ; for plainly it had not slept long.

There was no grass growing up in the paved ways ; rains had not entirely washed away the prints of dusty footsteps.

Yet I went about unchecked. I went into empty workshops, ropewalks, and smithies.

The spinner's wheel was idle ; the carpenter had gone from his work-bench and shavings, his unfinished sash and casing.

Fresh bark was in the tanner's vat, and the fresh chopped lightwood stood piled against the baker's oven.

The blacksmith's shop was cold ; but his coal heap and ladling pool, and crooked water horn, were all there, as if he had just gone off for a holiday.

No workpeople anywhere looked to know my errand.

If I went into the gardens, clinking the wicket-latch loudly after me, to pull the marygolds, heart's-ease, and lady-slippers, and draw a drink with the water-sodden well-bucket and its noisy chain ; or, knocking off with my stick the tall heavy-headed dahlias and sun-flowers, hunted over the beds for cucumbers and love-apples—no one called out to me from any opened window, or dog sprang forward to bark an alarm.

I could have supposed the people hidden in the houses, but the doors were unfastened ; and when at last I timidly entered them, I found dead ashes white upon the hearths, and had to tread on tiptoe, as if walking down the aisle of a country church, to avoid rousing irreverent echoes from the naked floors.

On the outskirts of the town was the city grave-yard ; but there was no record of plague there, nor did it in any wise differ much from other Protestant American cemeteries.

Some of the mounds were not long sodded ; some of the stones were newly set, their dates recent, and their black inscriptions glossy in the mason's hardly-dried lettering ink.

Beyond the graveyard, out in the fields, I saw, in one spot hard by where the fruited boughs of a young orchard had been roughly torn down, the still smouldering remains of a barbecue fire, that had been constructed of rails from the fencing round it.

It was the latest sign of life there.

Fields upon fields of heavy-headed yellow grain lay rotting ungathered upon the ground.

No one was at hand to take in their rich harvest.

As far as the eye could reach, they stretched away—they sleeping, too, in the hazy air of autumn.

Only two portions of the city seemed to suggest the import of this mysterious solitude.

On the southern suburb, the houses looking out upon the country showed, by their splintered wood-work, and walls battered to the foundation, that they had lately been the mark of a destructive cannonade.

And in and around the splendid Temple, which had been the chief object of my admiration, armed men were barracked, surrounded by their stacks of musketry and pieces of heavy ordnance.

Such was the end of Nauvoo the beautiful, of which even the Temple was soon after destroyed by fire.

CHAPTER VII.

JEALOUSY.

AT the junction of a beautiful stream with the Mississipi, and on the summit of a hillock, over which waved two or three trees, sat, a few days after the events recorded in the last chapter, three persons.

One was a powerful backwoodsman.

The second was a youth of elegant appearance, in the costume of a trapper of the Rocky Mountains.

The third was a young girl.

We need scarcely say that the party was composed of Obadiah Jones, Eudora, and Jessie.

And this is how Jessie had accompanied them.

On the morning of their departure, Jessie went with them to the landing place to see them off.

She was then going to take the stage to New York.

But parting had been deferred to the very last moment.

Like everybody else who came near her, they dearly loved Jessie.

The boat selected by Eudora was one well fitted to navigate the stream.

It was sharp, with a deep keel, and a tall mast and lateen sail.

It lay close to a landing, with nothing to attach it to the shore but a painter.

A man, who professed to have something to do with the coach office, had driven them up to the place in a cart, and was waiting to take her back to the office.

He was an ill-looking, downcast-eyed ruffian; but they being busy in talking, and carried away by the sweet luxury of a sorrowful parting, did not pay much attention to him.

"Why not change your mind?" said Eudora, as she stood in the boat, holding Jessie's hand.

Jessie was on the shore.

"No, I must return home," replied Jessie; "imagine the sufferings of my poor mother and father."

"Come one day's journey. The scenery is splendid; it will be a change."

Jessie caught a quick, startled glance in the man's face.

"Can I get back?"

"Plenty of return boats," said Eudora.

"I have half a mind."

"Now, miss," cried the driver, in a gruff and half commanding voice, "time's up, and I'm wanted at home."

"But I have half changed my mind," said Jessie.

The man gave a shrill whistle, and as he did so, three men darted from a thicket.

Jessie leaped into the boat, Obadiah Jones and Eudora covered her with their rifles.

The Mormons, baffled and furious, stood still.

The boat swung out into the stream, and in a few minutes was out of reach.

And so, until some means was found of Jessie being sent back under safe guard, she was to accompany them.

Outlying journeys in a dry and beautiful climate like that of this part of North America, are pleasant enough.

A small tent and some cooking utensils, are all that are required, as the river gives abundance of fish, and the shores plenty of game.

They had been two days on their way, and Jessie had written several letters home.

She had been rowing that day to help Eudora, as Obadiah was still unable to do anything but steer; and she was tired.

She had laid herself on the grass, and rested her head in the lap of Eudora.

She played with her ringlets.

Jessie held her hand.

It was a ravishing picture. They looked like a couple of young lovers.

They were conversing in whispers.

Obadiah Jones was examining a distant route by which the Mormons were in the habit of moving on their way to the Salt Lake.

It was marked by the heavy ruts of the waggons.

Here and there were poles, indicating the scenes of violent deaths, or deaths from the hardship of the road.

Some of them were the victims of their own passions. They had been waylaid and murdered by some of the parents, lovers, or husbands of some of their victims.

A number of bushes close at hand shielded the camp from the wind.

Presently a head might have been seen peeping forth from these bushes.

Then the head was withdrawn.

At this moment a flock of geese rose on the wing from the shore, and Eudora, who was extremely fond of sport, rose and followed them.

Jessie did the same.

Obadiah Jones remained alone.

But his backwood instincts were not forgotten. He had heard a rustling in the bushes.

He turned, and saw Henry, his face pale with agony, rage, and despair.

"Who is that youth?" said Henry, in a choked voice.

"Wall, stranger, that are a cute question," said Obadiah Jones, "and if I may be so bold as to ax—who is you?"

"The affianced husband of that unfortunate girl!" cried Henry, who was beside himself with passion.

"Ha! ha! ha!" roared Obadiah, holding his sides with laughter.

"Sir," said Henry, clenching his fist and clutching his rifle, "what means this ill-timed merriment?"

"So, youngster, you'r kinder jealous, are you?" said Jones.

"I am bewildered, disgusted, mad!" cried Henry.

"Wall—tu be sure, it are unpleasant, but look you here, youngster—there's no harm done; that ere young cove is my daughter."

"Daughter!" cried Henry, the blood rushing back to his face.

"Yes, sir—r—r!" continued Obadiah Jones, "she is my daughter, and for reasons best known to herself, she chooses to dress so; have you anything agin it?"

"No," cried Henry—"no, my dear sir—you make me the happiest and proudest of men. Your daughter, sir—I shall be happy to know her. Come on!"

He turned, and called apparently to some one behind, but no one answered.

Then two shots were heard.

"I will follow them," said Henry, pointing in the direction of the shots.

Obadiah Jones looked at him, leaped up, and caught Henry by the arm.

"What is the matter?" cried Henry, at once fearing some fresh disaster.

"Hell, is the matter! furies is the matter! Them shots was fired in anger," said Obadiah.

At the same moment, Eudora tottered up, threw her rifle on the ground, and then fell herself.

"What is the matter?" shouted Obadiah, in a voice of thunder.

"The Mormons!—Jessie!—gone!" murmured Eudora, faintly.

At the same moment, Captain de Lancy and the Indian chief appeared in sight.

The Paunee Indians had gone forward to way-lay the Mormons.

Henry staggered to them, and told his story.

Eudora, revived by brandy, sat up and told her story.

She had ran, laughing merrily, with Jessie, towards the spot where the geese had settled.

It was a small pond, surrounded by reeds and bushes.

Eudora bade Jessie hide behind a tree, while she crawled.

The geese had descended in the pool, and had settled.

Eudora knew well that she could kill four or five.

As she cocked her rifle, now loaded with several shots, she heard a scream.

She turned and saw three men, whom she knew to be Mormons, with Jessie in their arms.

Without a moment's hesitation, she levelled her rifle, and fired.

One of the Mormons was too quick for her—firing, and inflicting a flesh wound in the arm.

Then they mounted horses, and Jessie, being insensible, was placed on a horse and carried off.

Eudora fled in search of her father's assistance.

She found herself, when she came quite to, in Henry's arms.

"You are the lover of Jessie!" she said, abruptly.

"I am her destined husband," said Henry, quite blushing.

"You are worthy of her, I think, from what she has told me;" and as Eudora spoke, she fixed her eyes upon him with a strange, magnetic glance.

She did not mean it as such. She merely meant it to be arch.

But it was poison.

From that hour until the day of his death, Henry would never have forgotten it.

Never did a look produce such terrible and fatal results.

"Do you think so?" faltered Henry, scarcely able to speak.

Eudora looked keenly at him, sat up, and spoke.

"We will find her—she is a noble girl—I will die before she shall come to any harm."

Henry—the others were speaking in a low tone to Obadiah Jones—stooped and imprinted a kiss upon her lips,

It was returned, and not very coldly either.

Henry, for the first time, had been unfaithful in thought to Jessie.

It was a very venial fault, and one that, perhaps, Jessie might have forgiven, but these venial faults very often end badly.

A sip from a sweet and pouting lip is wondrous tempting. It makes us wish to drink deeper.

Eudora gently pushed him away, her eyes lowered on the ground, her cheeks rosy red.

"Are you better?" he stammered, taking her hand.

"I am," she replied; "but let us lose no time. A caravan of Mormons has passed this morning. How many friends have you?"

"Three days' journey forward, hundreds—here, two!"

"Three days, great heavens! we must rescue her to-night."

Henry lowered his eyes. Was it treason or was it not? But he hardly wished to overtake Jessie that evening.

Eudora's heart beat wildly, and with strange emotions.

This was not how she had felt with Verdi, *alias* Brigham Young.

Then the whole party joined, and after some delay, it was arranged to follow the Mormons, keeping them close in sight until they came to the spot where the ruthless Paunees were encamped.

CHAPTER VIII.

MISERY.

As they could not start until next morning—to give Eudora time to recover from her wounds—Henry, who had a splendid horse, rode into Nauvoo, in search of medicine.

It was yet early, and he arrived there before dark, and procured what he wanted.

He was guided by the stream and returned at a rapid pace.

He struck the stream about a mile from Nauvoo, and came upon its bank suddenly.

Here, among the dock and rushes, sheltered only by the darkness, without roof between them and the sky, he came upon a crowd of several hundred human creatures, whom his movements roused from uneasy slumber upon the ground.

Passing these, on his way to the light, he found it came from a tallow candle, in a paper-funnel shade, such as is used by street vendors of apples and pea-nuts, and which, flaming and guttering away in the bleak air off the water, shone flickeringly on the emaciated features of a man in the last stage of a bilious remittent fever.

They had done their best for him.

Over his head was something like a tent, made of a sheet or two, and he rested on a but partially ripped-open old straw mattress, with a hair sofa cushion under his head for a pillow.

His gaping jaw, and glazing eye, told how short a time he would monopolize these luxuries; though a seemingly bewildered and excited person, who might have been his wife, seemed to find hope in occasionally forcing him to swallow, awkwardly, sips of the tepid river water, from a burned, and battered, bitter-smelling tin coffee-pot.

Those who knew better had furnished the apothecary he needed; a toothless old bald-head, whose manner had the repulsive dullness of a man familiar with death scenes.

He, so long as Henry remained, mumbled in his patient's ear a monotonous and melancholy prayer, between the pauses of which he heard the hiccup and sobbing of two little girls, who were sitting upon a piece of driftwood outside.

Dreadful, indeed, was the suffering of these forsaken beings; bowed and cramped by cold and sunburn, alternating as each weary day and night dragged on, they were, almost all of them, the crippled victims of disease. They were there because they had no homes, nor hospital, nor poor-house, nor friends to offer them any.

They could not satisfy the feeble cravings of their sick; they had not bread to quiet the fractious hunger-cries of their children.

Mothers and babes, daughters and grandparents, all of them alike, were bivouacked in tatters, wanting even covering to comfort those whom the sick shiver of fever was searching to the marrow.

These were Mormons; but who could pity them?

CHAPTER IX.

THE CAMP.

HENRY was in a compassionate humour. Perhaps he felt that he himself wanted consideration, for, before leaving, he scattered a handful of dollars among these unfortunates.

Their blessings pursued him. Though followers of a misguiding and detestable imposture, they were still human beings.

Rather relieved by this act of charity, Henry rode onwards.

He soon came in sight of the camp. It had been removed for the night to a more sheltered place than that occupied during the day.

A fire had been made on the skirt of a thick grove of cotton wood.

A kind of awning was erected over the men; a tent of boughs, green leaves, and soft grass, had been made for Eudora.

She suffered much from her wound. At all events, she uttered continual groans.

Henry hastened to produce not only medicine, but various delicacies, which his amply supplied purse had enabled him to procure.

Eudora had selected the spot for her hut at some distance from the fire, quite out of its rays.

The men were in earnest conversation as to their future plans.

Captain De Lancy had obtained two years' leave of absence, to be counted as two years' service.

He was, however, anxious to return home as soon as possible.

Naturally enough, he did not like his separation from his wife. No man of any proper feeling does.

He was planning with the Indian and the backwoodsman how to end the chase most rapidly.

Jessie was now, doubtless, in the hands of a large party of Mormons.

It would have been folly to have pursued them unreflectingly.

But the Indian had his plans, and when he discovered that Nauvoo was no longer peopled by Mormons, at once sent forth his warriors to an appointed place.

There they were to disturb and attack every party that came up.

The sufferings of both dupes and knaves was something awful.

The pioneer band suffered most. It was chiefly composed of those who had reasons for getting away.

It was very imperfectly supplied with necessaries.

The cold was intense.

They moved in the teeth of keen-edged northwest winds, such as sweep down the Iowa peninsula from the ice-bound regions of the timbershaded Slave Lake and Lake of the Woods; on the Bald Prairie there was nothing above the dead grass to break their free course over the hard rolled hills.

Even along the scattered water-courses, where they broke the thick ice to give their cattle drink, the annual autumn fires had left little wood of value.

The party, therefore, often wanted for good camp fires, the first luxury of all travellers; but to men insufficiently furnished with tents and other appliances of shelter, almost an essential to life.

After days of fatigue, their nights were often passed in restless efforts to save themselves from freezing.

Their stock of food, also proved inadequate; and as their systems became impoverished, their suffering from cold increased

Sick with catarrhal affections, manacled by the fetters of dreadfully acute rheumatisms, some continued for awhile to get over the shortening day's march, and drag along some others.

But the sign of an impaired circulation soon began to show itself in the liability of all to be dreadfully frost-bitten.

The hardiest and strongest became helplessly crippled.

About the same time, the strength of their beasts of draught began to fail.

The small supply of provender they could carry with them had been given out.

The winter-bleached prairie straw proved devoid of nourishment, and they could only keep them from starving by seeking for the browse, as it is called—a green bark and tender buds—and branches of the cotton-wood, and other stinted growths of the hollows.

But we have left Henry and Eudora in the camp.

The wound on her arm had been rudely dressed, but Henry had obtained from one of the militia surgeons, all that was proper and needful.

He would dress her wound as it should be dressed.

It was necessary, for this purpose, to take off the kind of tunic she wore.

Henry assisted her.

He thought he had never seen anything so beautiful.

The wound was only a flesh wound after all.

Henry raised the plump arm to his lips.

Eudora did not prevent him.

Then, very slowly and deliberately, he dressed the place.

It took several kisses, as the children say, to make it well.

Then Eudora must surely thank him, especially when from a little basket he produced a cold collation, a fowl, some fruits, and a bottle of wine.

This once spread out before her, he returned to the fire.

The backwoodsman had brewed for each a stiff pannikin of grog.

They were drinking it in solemn conclave.

Henry glided beside them like an Indian warrior, saying not a word, but readily imitating their example.

About half-an-hour later the men all lay down, in search of that repose so necessary previous to the exertions of the next day.

Their plan of action was decided on.

About half-an-hour later, Henry sat up and looked keenly at his companions.

They all slept the sleep of hunters.

He rose, yawned, and again looked down.

Not one moved.

Next moment he was within the hut occupied by Eudora, where, truth compels us to relate, he was rapturously received.

It was an hour before dawn ere he returned carelessly to his own sleeping place, took his gun, and went out in search of game.

An hour later he returned with several wild geese and turkeys, which were very welcome additions to the provender of the camp.

No one welcomed him more quietly than Eudora, who bustled about, making coffee.

Meanwhile, what of poor Jessie?

CHAPTER X.

FEARNOT'S RESOLVE.

WHEN Captain Fearnot heard of the escape of the two girls, which news was brought to him by the two Danites, one of whom was severely wounded, he vowed to be revenged.

But it was necessary, in the first place, to see to the departure of the Mormons.

The Danites were to be their escort until they got beyond the precincts of civilization.

He, however, selected three men to carry out his scheme.

His idea of revenge was truly diabolical.

Nothing short of the utter ruin of Jessie and Eudora would satisfy him.

But he did not know the real character of Jessie.

She was worthy to have been named with Lucretia.

The failure of these men to trick Jessie is already known.

But the reward offered was one which made them determined not to be baulked.

They were to be promoted in the ranks of the Danites, besides receiving a gratuity from the hands of the keepers of the Mormon treasury.

These men laid in wait for Jessie. When they saw that Eudora was armed, and knowing that Obadiah was near at hand with his terrible rifle, they were glad to seize Jessie.

They would have made off without disturbing Eudora, but Jessie gave a fearful scream before they could gag her.

Then they mounted their fleet horses, and in a few hours had joined the head Mormon caravan.

Their steeds enabled them to outstrip all the waggons.

Jessie, as soon as she was out of reach of her friends, was allowed a horse to ride on.

No one spoke to her.

At length the waggons were reached, and Jessie confined within that of Fearnot.

Here, flaunting and satisfied, she found Amy.

Captain Fearnot had as yet been kind to her.

But Jessie would not speak.

Now began the fearful trials which were to decimate the Mormon exodus.

They were making for the Rocky Mountains.

The thermometer fell.

The open winds of March and April brought with them more sickness than the sharpest freezing weather.

Many died of want, starvation and suffering.

The frequent burials made the hardiest sicken.

On the soldier's march it is matter of discipline, that, after the rattle of musketry over his comrade's grave, he shall tramp it to the music of some careless tune, in a lively quick step.

But, in the Mormon camp, the companion who lay ill and gave up the ghost within view of all, all saw as he stretched a corpse, and all attended to his last resting-place.

It was a sorrow, too, of itself, to simple-hearted people, the deficient pomps of their imperfect style of funeral.

The general hopefulness of human—including Mormon—nature, was well illustrated by the fact that the most provident were found unfurnished with undertaker's articles; so that bereaved affection was driven to the most melancholy make-shifts.

The best expedient generally was to cut down a log of some eight or nine feet long, and slitting it longitudinally, strip off its dark bark in two half cylinders.

These, placed around the body of the deceased, and bound firmly together with withes made of the alburnum, formed a rough sort of tubular coffin, which surviving relations and friends, with a little show of black crape, could follow with its enclosure to the hole, or bit of ditch, dug to receive it in the wet ground of the prairie.

They grieved to lower it down so poorly clad, and in such an unheeded grave.

It was hard—was it right thus hurriedly to plunge it in one of the undistinguishable waves of the great land-sea, and leave it behind them there, under the cold north rain, abandoned, to be forgotten?

They had no tombstones, nor could they find rocks to pile the monumental cairn.

So, when they had filled up the grave, and over it prayed a *miserere* prayer, and tried to sing a potehlu psalm, their last office was to seek out landmarks, or call in the surveyor to help them to determine the bearings of valley bends, headlands, or forks and angles of constant streams, by which its position should in the future be remembered and recognized.

The name of the beloved person, his age, the date of his death, and these marks, were all registered with care.

This party was then ready to move on. Such graves mark all the line of the first year of the Mormon travel—dispiriting milestones to failing stragglers in the rear.*

The chiefs did all they could to keep up the spirits of the people, but they were not always successful.

The women, chiefly the young and beautiful, were kept from the knowledge of all this.

They were the valued treasures, and travelled, like eastern harems, in covered cars.

Jessie was ill. Amy, whose chief fault was a weak head and a love of admiration, nursed her kindly, and, by her influence with Captain Fearnot, kept her from being persecuted.

But this could not last for ever.

At length they arrived near *Point aux Poules*, where a halt was declared.

CHAPTER XI.

POINT AUX POULES.

This was a halting place fixed on, to repose all the members of the camp, both human and the brute creation.

They had a vast and wild territory to cross.

They were in the Pottawatamie country.

The hills of the High Prairie came down to the water's edge.

They overhung the Missouri in an unusual and commanding way.

From time immemorial these have been called Council Bluffs.

They are well known to the overland traveller to California, and Mormon overland travellers.

To the south of them, a rich alluvial flat of considerable width follows down the Missouri, some eight miles, to where it is lost from view at a turn which forms the site of the Indian town of Point aux Poules.

The landing and the large flat or bottom on the east side of the river, were crowded with covered carts and waggons.

Each of the Council Bluffs opposite was crowned with its own great camp.

They were gay with bright white canvas.

Captain Fearnot and his party—his harem had all this time been concealed from Amy—moved over to Point aux Poules.

He desired, for purposes of his own, to keep separate from the rest of the party.

This was easily managed.

None cared to intrude on the privacy of the Danites.

Some dozen tents and ten waggons were guarded by a band of as ferocious ruffians as ever were collected.

* This is Colonel Kane's account. He saw them on their journey. But he is very favourable to them.

The tent and waggon occupied by Jessie and Amy was at one end. The rest of the wives were placed quite at the other end of the little village.

It was on the edge of the water, and at no great distance from the Indian village.

The scene was lively enough, and every day became more so as the flying Mormons came up in droves.

No Gentiles were here to interfere.

Despite all the hardships of the way, the elasticity of the human mind overcame every obstacle.

In the clear blue morning air, the smoke streamed up from more than a thousand cooking fires.

Countless roads and bye-paths chequered all manner of geometric figures on the hill sides.

Herd boys were dozing on the slopes; sheep and horses, cows and oxen, were feeding around them.

Along a little creek were lines of women washing and ironing all manner of white muslins, red flannels, and parti-coloured calicoes.

It was an extraordinary exodus, and would have been magnificent, but for the abominable doctrines of the chiefs, subversive of all morality.

Jessie and Amy were allowed to walk about on the land side, under the guardianship of the negro boy.

They were not such friends as they had been before, but still Jessie could not wholly forget Amy's kindness during her illness.

She had ceased to persuade her against Mormonism, as, for as long a time as Captain Fearnot showed love towards her, she knew it to be useless.

She spoke, then, of other things.

The boy kept them in sight. He had not forgotten the knock on the head he had received from Eudora, when she effected Jessie's escape.

This made him vicious.

The camp on the side occupied by Jessie and Amy skirted a wood.

Towards this the two girls walked. Captain Fearnot was away, arranging the march of the caravans over the stupendous plains of the great American wilderness.

But he left trusty men in charge of the camp, with orders to shoot skulkers.

The Danite chief had no wish to have the secrets of his family pryed into by strangers.

Jessie and Amy sat down upon a fallen tree.

The negro laid down upon the ground, and watched like a faithful dog.

His master was tolerably kind to him.

And then, he had his knock on the head to avenge.

"And so, Jessie," said Amy, thoughtfully, "you think the day will come when he will cease to love me?"

"I am sure of it. Why am I brought here?"

Amy lifted up her eyes and stared. This was an idea which had never entered her head before.

A slight contraction of the muscles, and then a somewhat scornful glance, was her only reply.

"I will tell you."

"Speak."

THE ROBBERY.

"This man does not love me, but he would have me as his mistress. Who are those women yonder, by the river, from whom we are secluded?"

"I don't know."

"His wives."

"Jacko!" cried Amy, imperiously.

The negro rose and approached the two.

"How many wives has your master, now do not hesitate, I must and will know?"

"Golly, missee, how I know?"

"Will you answer me? Your master gave you to me—I will have an answer."

"Me say what you say."

"How so?"

"Wish me say massa one wife, say one wife; wish me say ten, twenty wife, say ten, twenty wife."

And the boy grinned from ear to ear.

"Go away," said the petulant Amy, who was white with passion.

"Amy—this man is no different from the other Mormons. He has many wives, and will have many more. Perhaps, however, he may love you —hope for the best."

"He has never passed a night away from me," said Amy, holding down her head and blushing crimson.

"You are new—you are the last toy," replied Jessie.

"If he deceives me, he shall rue the day."

"Jessie," said a voice close to her, "don't start, don't turn. That negro's eye is on you. Answer me in a whisper."

"Who speaks?"

"Phineas Bristowe, who has come to save you, and leave these accursed Mormons."

"Who is it?" said Amy, who looked keenly at the recumbent negro.

Jessie made no direct reply. She was thinking.

"Can Jessie Treherne trust Phineas Bristowe?" she said.

"So help me Heaven, she can! I am ill, weary, of this life, disgusted with the Mormons. But I cannot go to London without Jessie."

"Where is Henry?"

"He is not far off. For months he has been very ill, but now he is better."

Jessie felt a mist before her eyes.

"Is he far off?"

"No!" replied Phineas. "If you will come with me, I will take you to him. You will secure my pardon."

"I will if you are honest and true," replied Jessie.

"As I hope to be saved—as I hope my sins shall be washed out—as I deeply regret the past—as I know that I have not many months to live—I will lodge you in safety in the hands of those you love."

"Agreed. When do you wish me to start?"

"Now, this instant; the brutal, the licentious, the hawk Fearnot returns with a minister, to wed you this very day. He has boasted that you will make up the twelfth—and such a set of beauties, he says!"

Amy spoke not, moved not, stirred not.

"The negro may give the alarm," said Jessie, quickly.

"Come here, Jacko," exclaimed Amy, in a hollow tone.

The negro rose and came close to her.

"Which is the taller of us two?" said Amy, in a strange, jocular tone.

The negro grinned and opened his eyes.

"Stand against that tree, and I will make a mark."

Jacko advanced to the tree, and, with a gratified grin, prepared to make the trial.

It was the tree behind which stood Phineas Bristowe.

Amy made a sign to the Mormon elder.

Next minute a cold pistol-barrel was pressed against the negro's head.

"Move, speak, even look," said a hoarse voice, "and you die!"

The negro was too startled to speak.

They bound him to the tree.

Then Amy ran quickly towards the waggon, and brought away some necessaries.

She did not forget to take a casket of jewellery which the Danite, in a moment of enthusiasm, had given her.

Then she returned to the place where she had left Jessie and Phineas.

"Are you coming?" said Jessie, in an earnest tone.

"Would you have me stay and commit murder?" replied the girl, in hoarse tones.

"No! Come with us; you will never repent it."

"Is what you say true?" asked Amy, addressing Phineas.

"Fearnot has more wives than any man save Brigham Young," replied Phineas, who was haggard and ill.

"I will come," cried Amy.

A waggon of a light character, with two horses, awaited them.

They entered without a word, and then Phineas Bristowe whipped them up, and started to the southward.

Jessie suggested that he was going in a wrong direction.

"I know it," said Phineas, who spoke in a strange, moody way, that looked very much like insanity.

"Then why go?" asked Jessie, laying her hand on his arm.

"Because I know the infernal cunning of the wretches we have to deal with. They will miss you in a few hours, and to miss is immediately to pursue."

Jessie bowed her head. Fresh dangers, fresh sufferings.

"You know not the infernal devils—I do. I have gone too far into the very depths of their frightful secrets to be allowed to depart in peace."

"Why did you ever join them?"

"Ah, why—why have I done many things?"

"Why have you called yourself my father?" asked Jessie.

"You shall know all, before I die," said Phineas.

Amy sat silent in the back of the waggon. She was already almost sorry for what she had done. At all events, to her ideas, Simon Yackley or Captain Fearnot, was her husband.

What if he had other wives?

Did he not treat her as a wife, and had he not been very kind?

What would be her fate now?

At all events, she would not be pointed at. If she did return home, it would be as a victim, not as a willing sectary, of the Mormons.

Indeed, it is generally observed, that young men and women are almost always lukewarm Mormons.

The plurality of wives does not please them.

When the United States army went to Utah, they found the young men, flash, fiery fellows, characterized by a defiant air and independent spirit. Between these and the elders feuds and jealousies have already arisen in many cases, and we cannot doubt that similar causes will produce the same effects, with still more gratifying results in the time to come.

That the elders should monopolize the youngest, most beautiful, and wealthy women, must, of itself, be sufficiently displeasing to the young men, without further aggravation from the fact, that, as brothers, they must witness the humiliation and unhappiness of their sisters, added to the dishonour and domestic annoyances of their mothers. Many young fellows were heard to anathematize the whole Mormon system on this account, while others would run off to California with their sweethearts, and there abide, in order to preserve the objects of their love from falling beneath the libidinous influence of those they hated.

Brothers frequently urge their sisters to depart for California, and escape the contamination of living in a Mormon harem.

A young man by the name of Brian, a Mormon in sentiment, yet independent, and, for a back-woodsman, uncommonly intelligent, said, that he had a sister who n Elder John Tayler had married for his sixth wife.

That he considered such connexions abominable, and no marriage at all; that he told his sister so, and offered to bear her expenses wherever she wished to go, if she would only abandon the paramour.

"And did she accept your offer," he was subsequently asked.

"No; she said that here she was as good as the best," he answered; "but anywhere else she would certainly be despised, and her child called by an opprobious epithet, which she could not bear."

A young man, whose parents were from Oneidas County, in the State of New York, expressed a bitter aversion to polygamy. He had been wounded in the tenderest point.

His affianced bride, within one week of the time appointed for their marriage, jilted him in favour of one of the elders, an old man of fifty years, whose house was already shared by four wives.

In consideration of her youth and beauty, he promised the fifth a separate establishment, which, however, she never obtained.

Another young man, with who the officers conversed, had suffered severely when a child, from the persecutions of his father's second wife.

These women, it seems, are even more cruel and selfish than step-mothers are reported to be, and the helpless children of their rivals are made the subjects of their concentrated jealousy and rage.

This, however, must materially depend on the natural dispositions of the females, and would, by the Mormons at least, be referred to the faults of the individual, rather than the system.

A young Mormon says—"Our females can never take the rank and position among us that properly belong to them while polygamy is tolerated. Deprived of their legitimate influence as wives and mothers of families, they lose that self-respect which is one of the strongest safeguards of female virtue, become indolent, careless, and reckless; and it is needless to say that the consequences to the whole community are most disastrous."

And again :—

"The experience of ages may be trusted. Polygamy is a curse, a mildew that has blighted every region it has touched since the creation of the world. It presents no new phase, but from the first to the latest periods it has been destructive of the happiness of individuals, the peace of families, and the welfare of communities."

Amy felt all the degradation of her position, but her soul still felt the power of the Danite leader.

In her sensual and peculiar way, she loved him.

Meanwhile they were making their way across a stony plain.

The object of this maneuver was to leave no trail.

The Mormons had learned to track a fugitive with all the cunning and accuracy of a Red Indian.

It was a necessary part of their education.

There were very many indeed of their dupes who, when thoroughly aware of their character, were glad to escape.

Very few, however, succeeded in returning to civilization.

Phineas was not communicative. The man seemed to be terribly weighed down, and to prefer quiet thought to words.

Jessie examined him anxiously.

He was haggard, his eyes blood-shot, and his expression wild.

Presently they came to a stream skirted by cotton-wood.

Here he pulled up, and cried a halt.

CHAPTER XII.

THE NIGHT HALT.

THE spot was not one which promised any very great degree of comfort.

On the side where they had stopped, the ground was arid and dreary, though for a few yards along the river there was grass enough for the horses.

On the opposite bank rose steep cliffs, not exactly from the river, but a little way off.

A fissure revealed the entrance to one of those canons which are so common in that part of the country.

A canon is a narrow valley with precipitous sides.

The place seemed an excellent one for shelter and concealment, but as it was Phineas Bristowe's wish to follow the banks of the stream to the Missouri, he did not think it worth while to wade over.

The horses were carefully hoppled, lest they should stray from the camp.

Then, by the assistance of the waggon, a tent was made for the purpose of sheltering the suffering Phineas.

The girls were to sleep in the waggon.

Phineas Bristowe, in the expectation of a long journey, had loaded his waggon with food of all kinds.

The girls prepared coffee, girdle cakes, and toasted some jerked meat.

They ate with appetite; Jessie, because she saw a chance of returning home, Amy, because she was always a hearty eater.

Phineas sipped his coffee, and scarcely ate at all.

Then he advised them to retire to rest, as he should start with daybreak.

There was a fearful sullenness about him, which made Jessie very uneasy.

But she did not venture to make any remark upon the subject.

That he should be so eager to return to the haunts of civilization pleased and gratified her.

He must be sorry for many things that he had done.

This was a state of mind she had long hoped to see him come to.

But the realization of her hopes, at this particular time, was as fortunate as unexpected.

The camp-fire was on the edge of the tent, so arranged as to be sheltered by the canvas.

Phineas took great precautions not to make much smoke.

Then he took up a pipe, cast it down again, and finally lay down to rest.

Soon nothing was heard but the breathing of the sleepers.

Jessie was the first to wake just as the dawn broke.

She hastily leaped out of the waggon, and, descending to the river, made her ablutions and said her prayers.

Then she returned to the camp.

Phineas Bristowe lay still and motionless on the ground.

To wake him, she shook him with her fair and pretty hand.

He made no response.

His eyes were starting from his head.

She hastened to loosen his cravat, which was tied rather tight.

Then he drew a long breath.

Jessie gave him a pannikin of water from the stream.

Phineas Bristowe repelled it.

" Brandy !"

Jessie knew the bottle, for Phineas had drank from it the night before.

She gave him a small quantity by means of a metal spoon.

Again he breathed more freely, and opened his eyes.

He glared wildly at Jessie, as if he did not know her.

" How do you feel ?" she said, in her gentle tones.

" Ah ! that voice, I dreamed that she would come. Away—I will confess everything—I will confess all !"

" There are none but friends here," cried Jessie.

Phineas Bristowe appeared to rouse himself by a great effort.

" I have had some horrible nightmare," he said.

Jessie explained about his tight neckcloth having nearly choked him.

" That added to my sufferings," he replied ; " but I am ill and out of sorts."

" Will you have some coffee ?"

" No. I should like some hot brandy and water ; and then we will start."

Jessie made some water hot in a pannikin and gave him the grog, which he drank off eagerly, and at once fell into a deep sleep, from which no effort of theirs could rouse him.

He slept until evening, during which time the girls either watched him or walked about to pick up dry wood, or cut fresh boughs.

At sundown he awoke with a nervous start.

" I dreamed it," he said, hurriedly.

" What ?" asked Jessie.

" That you would betray me," he replied, trying to rise.

" I betray you !" cried our heroine, in a tone of surprise.

" What are you putting wet wood on the fire for ? They will see it miles off."

" I didn't know."

" Of course not," said Phineas Bristowe, in a whining tone. " But it can't be helped now. Be careful and select dry wood."

Amy went out to pick up a few dry sticks.

" Will you give me some dinner ?" continued Phineas ; " my sleep has done me good. I hadn't slept for four days."

" How so ?"

" Never mind ! never mind !" cried Phineas, with a terrified and startled look ; " I have my reasons."

Jessie took up a piece of meat and began to broil it.

Phineas watched her with a hungry look, and when she gave it him on a biscuit, ate it like a famished wolf.

" Brandy !" he cried, pointing to the bottle.

Jessie gave it him, and after drinking some, he tried to rise.

" Malediction !" he said, as he sank down, " I am not yet fit. We must remain here to-night—only in the morning can we move."

It was now quite dark. The night had fallen suddenly, as it will do in America.

" Jessie."

" Yes, sir."

" Will you stand at the door of the tent and tell me if you see anything ?"

Jessie went out as he told her, and cast her eyes round.

" Can you see anything ?" he said, in a hurried tone.

" No," said Jessie, who was gazing round on the horizon.

" Look again. Go further out," he replied.

Jessie obeyed, and again exercised her utmost keenness in examining the edge of the distant plain.

" I see a faint column of smoke, a long way off to the north, rising against the sky."

" But to the east—to the east," said Phineas, eagerly.

" Ah ; yes ; another column of smoke, equally distant."

" Put out the fire," he said, in a husky tone. " That may save us ; and then catch the horses. The river is fordable, and we can hide in the canon."

Jessie made no remark. The man was evidently suffering the most intense and acute agony of mind and body.

The horses were easily caught. They had had a long feed, and by the use of a little corn in a bowl they were induced to stand still while Amy unhoppled them.

Amy was almost sullen. She seemed to repent her flight from the habitation of the profligate Danite chief.

She was a girl fond of luxury and creature comforts, sensual and lazy.

This kind of life was utterly repugnant to her feelings.

"Where are we going at this time of night?" she said.

"In the canon, yonder," replied Jessie, quietly.

"Why? if I may be allowed to ask," said Amy.

"To escape our pursuers," replied Jessie, somewhat surprised.

Amy looked hastily round, with a flush on her face, and Jessie pointed out to her the two rising columns of smoke, probably ten miles distant, and equi-distant from each other.

Amy made no reply, but assisted in saddling the horses.

CHAPTER XIII.

THE CANON: A TRAGEDY.

WHEN the horses were to, Phineas Bristowe, aided by the two girls, climbed into the light waggon.

Jessie took the reins.

She had examined the river in the daylight, and even crossed it, without having water above her knees.

She knew exactly in which direction to drive the waggon.

The horses pranced and reared at first, but one pull of the bridle and slash of the whip, and the half-fed creatures were quiet.

The crossing was effected without difficulty.

Then Jessie alighted, and led the vehicle up the canon, which was wild and dreary enough, but completely sheltered.

The horses now, by the direction of Phineas Bristowe, were staked, and kept back out of sight.

Then all was still.

Ere we follow the fortunes of Jessie, let us explain the flight of Phineas Bristowe from among the Mormons.

Ever since his meeting with his well-to-do and happy brother, Phineas had been afflicted by qualms of conscience.

There was a furious struggle going on in his mind between his good and his evil genius.

The one prompted him to repent, to give up all his ill-gotten gains, to restore Jessie to her friends, without any conditions; the other, to make terms, to enrich himself, and to remain with the Mormons.

When the enemies of Mormonism rose against Nauvoo, he and certain other of the cautious ones retired to a village in the hills.

It was composed of Mormons, who devoted their whole time to wood cutting and money-making.

They were a very hardy and hard-working set, who were satisfied to chop timber, send it into Nauvoo, sell it, and live on the proceeds.

Few of them had more than one wife, for they were not rich.

The place was in a deep valley, surrounded by hills, covered with pine forests.

A narrow but deep stream enabled them to convey the logs close to Nauvoo.

On one side of the valley, however, where the poorer men had cleared an open space, some richer Mormons, with their flocks and herds, had collected.

Of course, being rich, they had also many wives.

Here came Phineas Bristowe, alone and unattended.

This was the end of all his scheming. He had been obliged to conceal himself in a wood-cutters' village.

But then, Phineas Bristowe was rich. He carried about him gold and notes to a dangerously large amount.

He would not have escaped the hands of some of the poorer Mormons had this been known.

But he was well acquainted with this fact, and boasted not of his wealth.

He determined, on retiring to this out-of-the-way village, to do something that should induce people to think he had to work for a living.

The natural avarice of his character at once broke out.

The people all made money, and, as yet, saved it.

So Phineas Bristowe built a large shanty, with the assistance of one or two of the more industrious wood-cutters.

It had two counters, and a snug back room.

On one counter he placed all kinds of dry goods. On the other he laid out a tempting stock of rum, brandy, buckeye, and whiskey.

There had been no store in the village, all the men fetching their things from Nauvoo.

Now all was changed. Everything could be had for money, and, by just turning round, a glass might be quaffed to seal a bargain.

Phineas Bristowe began to make money.

Hitherto, only the wood-cutters had patronized Phineas.

One morning, however, when his shop was empty, a gaudily-dressed lady, driven by a negro, stopped at his store.

She alighted, and entered with a haughty step.

She stood with open mouth, staring wildly at Phineas.

"Phineas!" she cried.

"Eliza!"

It was the girl who had lived with him in England as a servant.

"What are you doing here?" she asked.

"Keeping a store," replied Phineas, drily, "as you see."

"Are you alone?" said Eliza, inquisitively.

"I am. Not a soul is here," he replied.

"Drive about, and call in an hour," said Eliza, addressing her servant.

"Ees, missa," said the negro.

Then Eliza walked deliberately into the small parlour occupied by Phineas.

He stared at her, but offered her a chair, placed two glasses and a bottle of brandy on the table. Then he seated himself.

" And pray who are you living with now ?"

" Christian Whitmer."

" Ah !"

" Yes.   I have stuck to him.   I mean to do so until I am avenged,"

" You hate him," said Phineas, with a saturnine glance.

" I do," she replied, with stern emphasis.

" And pray may I ask why?" sneered Bristowe.

" Bristowe, that man has a house full of women, young and beautiful. He keeps me with him only as a kind of head over his house."

" Indeed ! And yet you are still very handsome," he said, in his quiet, sneering way.

" I know that," she continued, with a flushed face ; " but men like novelty. They weary of a woman in a month."

" I should never have wearied of you, Eliza," he added, filling up her glass with brandy.

" Which means that you would take me back," she said, abruptly, after draining off the brandy.

" Well," said Phineas, with a peculiar twinkle in his eye, " I rather think I would. I am alone. I am getting old—and we have been friends for years."

" I know we have, and until I was deluded by that wretch we were very happy."

" We were, Eliza," said Phineas ; " I often dream of those black eyes."

Phineas was drinking brandy very fast.

" Do you ? Now, mark me, Phineas. That man has so robbed and pillaged his dupes, has picked up so many widows and girls with money, that his treasure is very great.

" Ha !"

" I know where it is," continued the wicked temptress.

" You do?" cried Phineas, his eyes flashing with the old green covetous light.

" I do. And now, Phineas, if you will promise to leave the Mormons, to fly with me to England, and there to marry me, I will share the treasure with you."

" Eliza, with all my faults, I have been true to your memory. Whatever you wish me to do, I will do."

" Done ! Your hand. Christian Whitmer has heard of your being here—I see it now. He sneered when I said I was coming here. He will likely come to-night. Be cautious, be friendly, and to-morrow you shall hear from me. And now for coffee, tobacco, and sugar, and such like."

They embraced with something of the fervour of old times, and then Phineas was behind his counter, serving the head lady of Christian Whitmer.

And this is how that Mormon elder's name does not figure in the catastrophe of Nauvoo.

He was a wise and cautious man in his generation.

———

CHAPTER XIV.

THE CANON.—(Continued).

THAT evening Phineas Bristowe was very busy. He seemed to take dollars, notes, and shin plasters, with a rapidity quite delightful.

But he was uneasy and uncomfortable.

He expected every minute to see Christian Whitmer come in.

He had made acquaintance with a young man of the name of Sandy Edward.

He appeared a decent, honest young fellow, with a very hard-working wife.

There had been a talk about transferring the business.

This day Sandy had come round, at his request, to help, and Sandy was astonished to see the way the money came in.

It was to his mind a delightful prospect.

Sandy had money in the bank at New York, and he resolved at once to secure the business.

But Phineas put off all talk on the subject until the next day.

As he expected, about eight in the evening, Christian Whitmer came down.

Phineas started, burst into a cry of enthusiasm, and rushing forward, shook him by the hand.

" Sakes!" cried Sandy, " so you know one another !"

" Right you are," said Phineas Bristowe. " Will you mind the store, friend Edwards ?"

" Sartin."

And Phineas Bristowe led the way into the little parlour.

He knew Christian Whitmer well. He would not like to drink much before his women ; but there was nothing he enjoyed so much as a cosy pipe and glass.

Phineas placed a bottle of brandy before him, and filled up two glasses.

" Well," said Christian, " this is jolly. But how came you here ?"

" Things are going on wrong in Nauvoo. I am afraid there will be a rising against the Saints—and as I am a non-combatant, I thought it best to be out of the way."

" Between you and me, Phineas, exactly my opinion. Now, as I have bought this location, and have some eleven wives, and enough to live on, I don't see why I should risk my neck, because Joe Smith is an obstinate old fool."

" Exactly my meaning," cried Phineas, warmly.

" I don't mean to run my head into a noose, I can tell you."

" Don't mention it," said Phineas, with a shudder—he could never bear the faintest allusion to hanging.

" Not if you don't like it," replied Christian, grinning.

" I don't like it," cried Phineas; " so drop it. What say you to a game ?"

And he threw the cards upon the table.

That night they did not part before twelve. Phineas declared that he had not enjoyed himself so much for a long time.

Christian Whitmer was taken home considerably intoxicated.

Next day Eliza called round. She was in a wonderful humour, full of hope and excitement.

" You must make up your mind," she said. " He gives a grand supper to night, to which you will be invited."

" I ?" cried Phineas Bristowe, with a start. " I won't come."

"You must. He will drink himself stupid. Then, under pretence of showing you out, I will pass you into my room."

"Yes! yes!" said Phineas, with something of a shiver.

"His sitting room, in which is his iron box, is next to my room. It can easily be forced. Then we will fly together."

"Fly together," repeated Phineas Bristowe, mechanically.

"Shake off this stupor—here comes the boy with the invitation," she added.

A negro lad stopped, dismounted from a pony, and entered the shop.

Phineas Bristowe read the note.

"Say—master—highly honoured—come," he said.

One hour after he sold his business to Sandy Edwards, who transferred to him a sum at his bankers at New York, by means of a cheque.

Then he prepared for his departure.

He would ride up to Christian Whitmer's house, put up his horse, and as soon as the suggestion of the wicked woman was carried out, he would fly.

But he was quite resolved to fly alone.

He had had enough of Eliza. Her conduct to Christian Whitmer utterly disgusted him.

CHAPTER XV.

A FROLIC.

It was past dusk, when, hoisting a small portmanteau on his horse— a portmanteau that contained all his worldly wealth—he rode up towards the Pine Clearing, as Christian Whitmer's place was called.

He hid the portmanteau in a dense thicket, and then presented himself at the house.

Christian Whitmer, in full dress, received him himself, and introduced him to his bevy of wives, who were of ages varying from sixteen to twenty-five—none older.

The man had already unsealed one or two who were older, on various pretences.

The profligacy inaugurated by these elders is difficult to be described. Whitmer and his gang were more unblushing than any.

They abrogated all moral and civil law, set at defiance customs that we learn to view as sacred as law, and the common codes of decency. Mothers and daughters sought to win from each other the preference of some bashaw, who, loathing those he already had debased to the most loathsome servitude, looked with longing eyes upon the unappropriated frail sisterhood to fill the imaginary vacancy, while those thus left revenged themselves by shameless coquettings which matched their keeper at his own game. Sealings became promiscuous. Thus, a husband became privately the husband of as many of his neighbour's wives as he chose, provided they acquiesced in the private arrangement; and in *all things*, except publicity, they were identical with ordinary marriages.

Though middle-aged and ugly, Phineas Bristowe was a man.

The women had seen no one for a long time, but Christian Whitmer, and this, considering that they were eleven, was certainly monotonous.

What say you, fair and gentle reader, who, if your husband but looks at another woman, are uncomfortable, how would you like to be one of eleven?

There is a very delicate question with regard to polygamy, which we should like to ask the ladies, but dare not.

But if you guess it, we wish you would answer it.

The supper was ready laid, and a very abundant one it was.

They all sat down; Christian at one end, Phineas at the other. He had two dark-eyed beauties of five-and-twenty by his side.

Eliza sat at some distance from him. She was quite indifferent to this matter.

Suddenly she started to her feet.

"What is the matter?" said Christian Whitmer, severely.

"We are thirteen! I am not anxious to die before the year is out."

All pushed back their chairs, Christian swore, and Phineas Bristowe turned very pale.

"Fetch Julia," said he, with an affected laugh; "it is all nonsense, but still, I won't spoil your appetites."

A pretty girl of eight, the sister of one of his wives, and a doomed victim to the loosened passions of this luxurious sect, was brought in.

The festival went on, but all were dull.

Christian Whitmer made them all fill bumpers, proposed a toast, and soon started the feast again.

The supper was hearty, even luxurious; there were fish, flesh and fowl, and hot sauces, and all that inflamed the blood and roused the passions.

Soon their eyes began to glisten, their laughter to resound, their lips to be opened to give vent to songs, not of the Mormon kind we have already quoted, but drinking and amatory songs.

Then the sound of the fiddle was heard, and the Mormon passion for dancing broke out.

The floor was cleared, the tables and chairs removed, and full swing given to waltz, polka, and country dance.

Christian Whitmer and Phineas Bristowe were, of course, in great demand.

The latter did not much approve of it, as he was rather stout and podgy.

But still, under the influence of wine, he could not refuse.

As much as possible, however, he sat down and conversed.

The lady with the black eyes made desperate love to him.

This answers the question we have above propounded—where a man has eleven wives, each of the eleven wives has a *private* husband.

A resident in Utah has, in simple words, explained the practice.

"Under this system, some of the immortal twelve Apostles that the Prophet had chosen from among all his followers, as worthy of being admitted into all the enormity of his imposture, had, in addition, from twenty to forty acknowledged as wives, an equal number sealed, *and vice versa with the wives.*"

But, despite the effects of the wine, Phineas Bristowe was in no humour to make love to the wives of his quondam friend and companion, Christian Whitmer.

He was thinking of his treasure in the iron safe.

CHAPTER XVI.

THE CANON: A TRAGEDY—(Continued).

It was about twelve. All the wine provided for the festival was exhausted. A bowl of punch had been made and handed round.

Then Eliza, who had danced once with Phineas and whispered directions in his ear, wished them all good night.

Christian Whitmer, who was very far from sober, shook him by the hand.

Phineas shook hands all round, and left them all having an indiscriminate romp with the patriarch.

Then he glided out, opened and again closed the door, and then was, in a moment more, in Eliza's bedroom.

In ten minutes she came with a light, but a finger placed on her lips.

She pointed to the next room, and made signs that the patriarch was there.

Then she kneeled on the ground and removed slowly a rude panel.

Through this they both crept, and pushing it, were in the elder's sanctum and study.

It was a small room with a table, two chairs, and on the ground a large wooden box, enclosed by iron straps.

To this Eliza pointed with her finger, and stooped to hold the candle.

Phineas Bristowe drew forth a powerful chisel, and proceeded to remove the iron bands one by one.

They easily gave way, and nothing but a small lock remained.

This was next forced off, the chisel being good, and the hand of Phineas strong.

At this moment, a noise made them turn.

Eliza clutched the casket containing diamonds, gold, notes, and securities.

The door flew open, and in tottered Whitmer, who, with a tiger glance, flew at Phineas.

He received him with a blow of his terrible sharp chisel, and Christian Whitmer fell a bleeding corpse.

"Fly!" said Eliza, still grasping the casket.

"Not without that!" cried Phineas Bristowe, hoarsely.

"Touch it, and I will shriek!" she said, in gasping tones.

Phineas glanced at her furiously. With one hand he snatched the jewel-case, with the other he struck her to the ground.

And then, like Cain, he fled precipitately.

His horse was handy. He took his portmanteau, put the casket into it, and fled.

He rode until daylight, when he washed and removed the stains from his clothes and body.

Then he made headlong for Nauvoo, bought some new clothes, and then fled into the hills.

Here he heard of the murder, or martyrdom, of Joe Smith.

This made him venture to show himself, as he thought the hubbub and hue and cry about Christian Whitmer would be drowned in the great wail.

At length he heard that the women of Christian Whitmer had descended to Nauvoo, in search of the murderer.

Also in search of fresh husbands.

He bought a light waggon, and fled.

* * * * * * *

We left him in the canon, nursed by Jessie and Amy.

He was half delirious with fear and terror. He knew that if he were captured by the Mormons of the wood village, his would be a short shrift.

It will be seen that real repentance had not much to do with the change in his resolutions. He felt worse off in America than in England.

In England he would, at all events, be tried by a legal tribunal. In America he would be hung to the first tree, if he were not roasted alive.

Like a sensible man, he preferred trusting to the mercy of the law.

They could not even kill a slaver the other day without making a hideous scene.

But now he was struck down, annihilated.

His sin had found him.

This man was profligate, sensuous, a voluptuary. The first advent of moral and physical suffering had utterly prostrated him.

He felt he was going to die.

It was night. Amy was in the waggon asleep. Jessie sat by the sick man.

He was asleep.

Suddenly he awoke.

He looked wildly around him and saw Jessie. She gave him something to drink.

"Jessie," he said, suddenly, "do you know I believe my illness to be mortal?"

"No; you are feverish—ill; but you will get over it."

"I think not. But never mind. Would you like to know the story of your mother?"

"I should."

"It is a terrible one."

"Never mind. I wish to know it."

And Jessie's beautiful eyes flashed fire.

"You shall hear it. Suppose we call it the story of Esther and her four lovers?"

Jessie started.

"It is so. But do not believe I mean anything against her fair repute. No. She was good and pure. Still you must nerve yourself to hear something indeed strange."

"Very little can be strange to me!" said Jessie, hoarsely.

Phineas looked at her as if he would have liked to have asked her a question. But he did not. Before, however, we begin his extraordinary story, let us bring Henry to the Mormon camp.

JESSIE AND AMY.

CHAPTER XVII.

MORMON WORSHIP.

THEY did not travel very fast, we are sorry to say.

They both appeared so unwell that their companions would not hurry them.

They were both simply guilty.

But the longest journey must end, so at last they reached Point aux Poules.

The elder men remained on the outskirts.

But the other two resolved to venture into the camp.

They heard that solemn worship was to be performed, during which they might, unperceived, examine all that passed.

A rude temple of upright poles, with cross beams and boughs to protect the congregation from the rays of the sun, had been erected under the rocks, and hither Henry and Eudora wended their way, having taken considerable pains to disguise themselves.

They were in earnest in their search for Jessie; Henry especially.

He was heartily ashamed of having failed in his faith, but such is the weakness of human nature that he could not cast away the cause of his error.

Eudora had been seized by one of those wild

and savage impulses of passionate love which deprive a woman wholly of her reason.

But she had as yet no idea of supplanting Jessie.

The future was a sealed book, and she knew not the misery, the fearful tragedies, which her one deflection from duty, would bring about.

They followed the crowd, and soon stood on the skirts of the Temple. Unlike the Eastern polygamists, the Mormons did not attempt to confine their wives, or keep them secreted from the gaze of others.

All entered the church promiscuously, and sat just as it happened, though generally the husband placed himself in the midst of his wives. It was a strange assemblage ; yet who could expect anything better?

The rites of the Mormon worship open with singing and a full band of music.

Many of the females had good voices, and the strain was solemn and impressive.

When this was concluded, Brigham Young offered up a prayer for " Zion in the tops of the mountains " in particular, and for the Saints all over the world in general. The Gentiles, of course, were excluded from the benefits of this petition.

His discourse was short, yet pertinent.

He exhorted them to obedience and union, and reminded them that many females were unprovided with husbands, who ought to be married, and giving children to the church. " I think," he continued, " that I have set you a good example. My wives outnumber those of David, and children, like olive plants, gather about my table."

Eudora breathed thickly as she heard this, but made no remark.

He finished, and sat down, when the music struck up " Bruce's Address," followed by " Auld Lang Syne." It ceased, and elder Cumming arose. He was a tall, remarkably strong-built man. While surveying his athletic form and sinewy limbs, joined to a countenance not particularly expressive of intelligence, they thought how much better he was adapted to agriculture, or some useful mechanic art, than in dealing out harangues on subjects of which his audience were quite as well qualified to judge as himself.

His discourse abounded in anecdotes, all relating to what seemed of chief interest to them—taking new wives.

He rated those women soundly, who, having the opportunity, neglect to get married ; and said that a brother was deserving of hell-fire if he permitted a woman to remain single without making her an offer.

"Who cares if she is old, and ugly, and deformed? Her child will be young, and probably beautiful. If she has no child, why God has ordained it, and you have done your duty. When walking along the streets, I make it a practice to inquire of every woman I meet whose wife she is? To this, many of my sisters here can testify. If she tells the name of her husband, I bless her, and say, ' Go on your way rejoicing, have children, and rear them up for Zion!' If she has no husband, I bid her be gone, and get one."

There was no evidence of a devotional spirit, though much that was said elicited the boisterous mirth of the audience.

While listening to these discourses, none could help thinking that the Mormons seemed to regard marriage, not as a means for promoting social happiness, but solely as a method for the most convenient propagation of the race.

Yet this view is not novel, and has been frequently entertained by restless and aspiring spirits.

Augustus, after devastating the earth to promote his schemes of ambition, sought to replenish it again by recommending, and even in some cases enforcing, marriage ; and complained bitterly of the dancing-girls and other women who refused to give children to the republic."

Yet why did he wish this? To increase the sum of human happiness, or promote the welfare of the race ? No such thing ; but that his empire might be replenished with taxable subjects, and his armies filled with new soldiers.

The great desire of the Mormons to have children, and increase in population, displays some ulterior motive. They are looking forward, down the long vista of the future, to wealth and power, to independence, rank and distinction, among the nations of the earth. The examples of Moses and Mohammed are before them, and the lessons of ages have not been lost.

But the service was yet unfinished, and another speaker was on the floor. His words were as follows :—

" Now, my dear friends, what a dreadful thing it would be if, after all your trials and afflictions, your perils in crossing the deep (for many before me have come from countries beyond the sea) — after all this, and your difficulties and dangers in the howling wilderness—what a dreadful thing it would be to lose your inheritance among the Saints !

" Other sins are venial, other transgressions may be forgiven ; but there is no hope for him who, having once known the good way, has turned back. And, my sisters, I hear strange reports of you, which it grieves me to mention. I hear that some of you have become dissatisfied with the institution of our holy religion, and have dared to refuse a brother in marriage, because he had already a wife. My sisters, it is nothing to me— you must not imagine that it makes a particle of difference with me—whether you are married or not ; but it does make a difference to you, and that a very great one. Why, know you not that unless a woman is sealed or married to a man, and that man a true disciple, there can be no hope of salvation ?

" Consider well, then, that if you lose your souls—your precious, immortal souls—by remaining single, you have nobody but yourselves to blame. I have told you. You know that. And the good brothers are ready and willing to assist you, if you will only let them. Let them ! Why a woman, rather than remain unmarried, should ask some elder or saintly brother to bestow on her the seal of salvation.

" And, my dear sisters, there are other subjects on which I wish to speak. I have been informed that some of you have laid stumbling-blocks in the way of your husbands when they have proposed to seal other females. You have tried, by tears and protestations and rebellion, to hinder them from performing such duties—know ye not that these things are deserving of damnation? know ye not that in all things your husbands are your superiors—that they stand to you in the place of God, and that obedience—unqualified, unquestioning obedience—is your first, I had almost said your only, duty, as in that all others are comprised?

"Now, my sisters, an important thing for you to remember is this: if your husband wants more wives, you must help him to get them, and then you must be peaceable and not quarrel and lie and filch from each other, but live in harmony, with all loving-kindness and charity. What a dreadful thing it would be if the soul of one woman, through your opposition to her union with your husband, should be lost; and being in torments unspeakable, would she not for ever cry out against you?

All this to Henry was very painful indeed, though his heart smote him that it did not affect him so much as it ought.

But in all this assembly, though they walked about and peered wherever there were any young women, they could see no sign of Jessie.

What was to be done?

They dared not ask any questions. But Eudora knew this much.

They had been taken away by the chief of the Danites. To his quarters, therefore, they determined to go.

A ferry boat soon took them across the river.

They found the camp in a great uproar. Two of the women of the camp had eloped, and a man, in a towering passion, was lashing a negro boy, who he said had been their accomplice.

Then he stalked away, leaving the other crouching on the ground in an agony of pain.

Henry, as soon as the lad was alone—he was on the ground behind the waggon—went straight up to him.

"Boy," he said, gently, "tell me all about these women, and I will pay you well."

"Will you take me away, massa?"

"I will."

The boy leaped to his feet. He was of the true negro breed. He had not felt much pain from the severe infliction he had received—at least, not such as a white lad would have felt.

He then, in a hurried way, told his story.

He pronounced the name of Phineas Bristowe sufficiently near to be recognized.

Again was Henry puzzled.

What could this persistence of hers in following the Mormon chief possibly mean?

But something must be done.

Eudora advised a return to their own camp, where they could consult with the Indian and the other elder and more experienced people.

The negro followed them without a murmur.

He was promised a handsome reward and liberty. This meant in his eyes a happy and idle life.

But though the negro was positive as to the direction which the fugitives had taken, Henry could not make it out.

CHAPTER XVIII.

THE CAMP.

CAPTAIN de Lancy, Obadiah Jones, and the Red Indian, had remained in a picturesque spot on the borders of the Missouri river, while Henry and Eudora, who could more easily disguise themselves, ventured into the camp of the Mormon exodus.

It is not to be supposed that this step was viewed without apprehension, but in such emergencies it was necessary to risk something.

Still the hours which intervened between the departure and the the return of the two young people, were quite hours of torture.

The spot chosen for the camp was a very beautiful one.

It was at the mouth of a creek.

On one side of the bayou was a pine forest, on the other a grove of elegant cedars.

Beneath these the outlying warriors had made their huts, where, while waiting for some signal, they smoked almost in silence.

No lively talk, no stories, no anecdotes, no discussion.

They all seemed taciturn as Indians; but, strange to say, the Indian was most anxious.

Several times he rose and peered out upon the waters.

But the red sun went down on the mighty river, and they came not.

Obadiah Jones clutched his rifle with a convulsive movement.

Captain de Lancy curled his mustachio, which, since he had been in America, had become very long.

The Indian rose and went to the water's edge.

At this moment a bark canoe shot out from the cover of the trees.

A black lad was in the bows.

"Who goes?—speak!" said the Indian.

"Friends," replied the negro.

Next instant Henry and Eudora were on shore, and, after a few congratulations, relating their experiences and discoveries.

The Indian and Obadiah listened, with an earnestness which evidenced deep thought, to that part which alluded to the track taken by Phineas Bristowe.

"I have it," said Obadiah; "he's gone to the Canon Uraldi. He was afraid, if he took the direct trail, he would be caught by the Danites. I will find him before to-morrow sundown.

And with this assurance, the wearied and exhausted watchers were bound to remain content in the dark.

Had it been possible to make their way, they could not have started, from sheer fatigue.

We return to the canon.

CHAPTER XIX.

CORNELIA AND HER FOUR LOVERS.

THIS is the story which Phineas Bristowe, in an unconnected, disjointed way, told to his listener.

Some details he was obliged to soften, but we

cannot do the same.   It must be told with all its naked wickedness.

We must go back to events already alluded to.*

Sir Henry Haddington was a rich and wealthy man, and before the misfortunes which fell upon his house—before the diabolical schemes which alienated him from his wife—kept a most hospitable board.

This he did because he was a man of genial parts and warm disposition, and because he had a sister he was attached to living with him.

A popular man, too, was Sir Henry Haddington, not only because he was good, but because he was rich, and riches go a long way as regards men's popularity.

Do they not, young ladies?

And Sir Harry was exceedingly rich, for his was a noble and wide domain—far away over the distant hills stretched the broad lands which owned the boy-baronet as master ; far away over those bare, bleak ridges, that crowned the barren downs, there was many a snug homestead and substantial farm-house in which the rent was put by after the haymaking, or the harvest, or the pig-killing, or the sheep-shearing, to pay at the half-year's end to Sir Henry Haddington, baronet.

You might wander for miles through over-shadowed country lanes, and long, flat, white high-roads ; through woods of low, stunted fir-trees ; through tiny villages, lying so hidden under the shadow of the great hills, that you looked down into them from the high ground as you would have looked into a well : but inquire where you would, as to the proprietor of the shady pathway, shut in by hazels and wild roses ; or the fertile meadows behind the roadside hedges; or the little row of tumble-down cottages, that looked as if ready to fall upon the first incautious traveller who ventured to walk under their shadows ; inquire where you would, you would hear the name of Sir Henry Haddington.

Well, one feature in connection with his almost baronial position was that visitors came to see him far and wide.

Miss Haddington was a beauty, but her fortune was small.

Great as were the domains of Sir Henry, they were all strictly entailed.

But though he did not save much money, he could give his sister a portion, and he meant to do it.

She was now about eighteen.

She was dark, tall and commanding in person, but slightly scornful in manner.

But this depended on the persons to whom she addressed herself. She was never scornful to young men with good prospects or large fortunes.

She was ambitious.

But besides being ambitious, this young girl was passionate and headstrong.   Though pure in person she was utterly debauched in mind.

A library shelf on which rested, unnoted, some of the impurest of the literature which preceded the French Revolution, had fallen into her hand, and the contents been devoured with an eagerness which seems incredible.

But it has been discovered that it is women in a respectable class of life who have been the chief supporters, in secret, of a certain class of literature.

Miss Haddington gloated over these books.

Then came Mr. Treherne, as a visitor to her brother's house.

With him came his brother, who was a dwarf.

Treherne was a man of good estate, of great consequence in his county.

Leopold Treherne was a younger brother, with a small fortune.

The elder brother came more to go out shooting than anything else.

Leopold, of course, was debarred from any such amusements,

He devoted himself to music, painting, and the fine arts, and was a great favourite with the ladies.

Miss Haddington noticed him, though from the first day of his arrival it was evident that she was slightly encouraging the evident advances of the admiring and wealthy elder brother.

We will repeat what we said when alluding to this strange tale.

There is a strange and perilous beauty in cripples. The younger brother of Mr. Treherne, relative to whom we have a most astounding and tragic story to tell, was not more than four feet and a half high.   He was a dwarf and a hunchback.

His face was perfect as that of Apollo ; his golden hair fell over a massive brow of dazzling whiteness ; his soft blue eyes spoke of the most pure and yet passionate love ; his mouth had the smile of an angel.

So humble, so gentle, so conscious of his infirmities.

His soul was as noble as his face was beautiful. There was not an atom of the crookedness of his body in his soul.

Mr. Treherne was a jolly, fox-hunting country gentleman, of good estate, but without any of those fascinating qualities which a woman desires who is not satisfied with an honest man who looks to his home and children, without depriving himself of those amusements native to his sex and character.

But Mrs. Treherne, at that age, lived only for love.   Her soul burned with the most ardent passions ; and the frank caress of a husband who looked upon her with pride as the head of his house, sufficed her not.

She wanted some one to whisper soft nothings in her ear, to paint passion in glowing colours, to talk of forbidden joys, and woo her to them.

Her bosom was a volcano.

All this she thought she had found in the poetic soul of the hunchback.

She took occasion, whenever the elder brother's back was turned, to be tender and gentle to him, but he was too modest and timid to understand.

There are men who are very blind, are there not, young ladies ? We could never ourselves be made to believe that we were loved, unless the dear creatures directly told us so.

So with Leopold, and Miss Haddington soon saw that it was so.

What was to be done?

CHAPTER XX.

CORNELIA AND HER FOUR LOVERS (*Continued.*)

IT was a day in September, a real fine splendid day, and Sir Henry Haddington and Mr. Treherne had gone out shooting.

Everybody had dispersed somewhere or other. Leopold Treherne, who always sought an opportunity to improve himself, had collected his drawing materials.

He was passing across the hall, when by *accident* the library door opened, and Miss. Haddington came out.

He bowed, and was about to pass on with a smile.

" Whither so fast ?" said Miss Haddington, cheerfully.

" To follow the only out-door amusement for which I am fit," he said

" And pray may I ask what that is ?"

" Certainly. Sketching."

" How delightful ! Where are you going ?"

" To the fall."

" Beautiful—my favourite walk ! Do you know, Mr. Leopold, I feel half inclined to go with you, if I shall not be intruding."

" Intruding, Miss Haddington—do not say so ! When beauty smiles on the poor cripple he should be but too proud. If it will not weary you, I shall be proud of your society."

Miss Haddington, strangely enough, was dressed ready to start.

She tripped down the stairs and across the lawn.

She knew the soul of Leopold.

She knew that it contained treasures of love, devotion, and real passion.

But she also knew that he was not only pure, but highly romantic. She knew that the faintest inkling in his mind of impurity in thought or word would revolt his very soul.

She must be also purely sentimental and romantic.

She had read oceans of poetry, but not of the most purifying or elevating character.

But she was brilliant and a good talker.

That woman had talents which, if utilized, would have been heard of in the world.

But every energy of her soul was given to ambition first—and then to illicit passion.

They talked of flowers, of the stars, of the pleasures of study, music, pictures and then——

They did not talk, but he did, and began to feel the effects of the sweetest flattery known to man— the best compliment a woman can pay—that of being listened to by a beautiful and lovely woman.

To see two beaming eyes looking up at us with admiration, or better still, cast down upon the ground in virgin humility, sends to the soul of man one of the most joyous and delicious of known sensations.

He is aware, or thinks he is, that he is admired if not loved.

Leopold had read and thought deeply, and as he walked along, Miss Haddington thought how hard it was that one so gifted by nature should be so hardly dealt with by fortune.

She saw not his defects, she only saw the wondrous beauty of a countenance which was really and truly glorious.

But she did see that he was without fortune, and would never do for her husband.

What then was to be done ?

This man would never be her paramour—and yet does a young, passionate, and beautiful woman ever doubt her own power ?

They reached the chosen spot and Miss Haddington assisted him to arrange his materials'

In so doing their hands came in contact.

Leopold Treherne blushed violently.

It was the first time he had felt the contact of a woman's hand.

His eyes fell on the ground. Those of Miss Haddington flashed with triumph—with wild and delighted triumph.

She saw at once the prodigious power that any woman would have over that heart, who once had won it.

And she determined to win it.

Now, there are few things that a woman who is determined, cannot do.

And what think you, reader, this young girl of eighteen, in her wicked heart of hearts, had resolved on?

To marry one brother, while loving the other—and then——

But our pen refuses to write the dark imaginings of her impure and evil mind.

They remained for hours on that spot; and when that evening Mr. Treherne took Maria Haddington down to dinner, he thanked the blushing girl, in a grave and manly tone, for her kindness to his brother.

" Who can help being kind to him, poor fellow ?" said Maria, with a smile.

Treherne, who was the most unsuspicious of men, pressed her arm in his.

Though only thirty, Mr. Treherne had long since made up his mind to be a batchelor.

He had reasons for it—reasons of a most peremptory and extraordinary character.

Reasons, which not a soul living knew of but himself.

But many a man has made resolutions of the most positive kind, which the eye of a woman have broken through.

Mr. Treherne felt himself weak in the presence of Maria. How could he, when it was clear so beautiful a girl loved him, as he really felt sure she did, condemn himself to celibacy.

There had been no love passages, so far as words, between them yet, but there seemed to be a tacit understanding.

Now for several days Mr. Treherne had been combating with himself.

Should he fly, or should he remain?

Should he say the word that should make a bound man of him for life, or should he go ?

That evening a game of chess, which Maria herself proposed, settled the matter.

Somehow or other her hand got clasped in his, their eyes met, and explanations would have been exchanged, but that some *importun*, as the French say, came up and asked some questions of the sportsman.

But both felt that it was only adjourned.

Next morning Mr. Treherne rose early.

He had something on his mind, it was quite evident, for he went out into the garden before anyone was up. Perhaps he hoped to meet *her* there, perhaps he didn't.

Whichever was the wish he had felt, it was not to be gratified.

He met his brother Leopold.

A flush crossed the face of the elder brother. He had for a moment forgotten him.

But now he at once made up his mind.

" Ah, Leopold," he said, in his old hearty tones, " as usual, an early riser."

" I like to see Nature in her fresher moments."

" Always a poet, and always poetical. But what say you to a stroll and a chat on business ?"

" On business ?"

" Yes, on business, my dear Leopold ; and very serious business, I assure you."

The handsome dwarf looked up at his brother rather anxiously, but saw nothing to alarm him.

" I am at your orders, brother."

" Well, Leopold, the fact is, I'm going to change my name—bah ! I'm confused—change my state."

" How so ?"

" What, boy, cannot you guess ? "

" Going into the army ?"

" Nonsense, brother mine ; if you must have it plain out, I'm going to marry."

Leopold started, stopped in his walk, and looked up at him with a look of ludicrous surprise.

" You, brother ! the woman hater ! the confirmed bachelor ! impossible ! "

" We all change."

" So I see. But who is the fair lady ? I really cannot for a moment suspect."

" Really ? "

" No."

" Just think of all the charmers we have here."

" Miss Vaughan ? "

" No."

" Miss Temple ? "

" No."

" But who then ? "

" What say you to the lovely, beautiful, and accomplished Maria Haddington ?" said the elder brother, with something of pardonable pride.

A wonderful self-command had that dwarf, for he neither cried out, nor blushed, nor looked flurried, no matter what he felt.

" You are a very happy man," he said, with a low bow.

Not for the world would he have hinted that she was a heartless coquette, who had striven to win his own heart ; who had, the day before, made evident and unmistakeable love to him.

No, he would do nothing of the kind.

" You mus'n't think, Leopold," continued his brother, " that this will make any difference to you. I have always felt the injustice of my having so much and you so little. Some means must be found by which you shall not lose—neither you nor your children."

" My children ! What woman would marry me ?" said the dwarf.

" Nonsense, Leopold ! In the first place, money."

" I would *never* marry a woman who did not love me."

" You are right, Leo, quite right. I would not marry Maria if I had not positive assurance that she loved me ; but you are handsome, Leo ; much better looking than I am. You have talents too—a thousand talents. Find the true-hearted woman to love, and I will see that you are comfortable."

Leopold thanked him warmly, and they now returned to the house.

The first breakfast-bell had rung.

Maria was looking curiously at them out of window.

She had been watching them for some time.

She knew not what to think of their conference.

The countenance of Mr. Treherne showed her that all was right.

She did not venture to look at Leopold, who had slightly coloured when he saw her.

How easy for her woman's wit to persuade him that he had been wrong on the previous day, even if he ventured to show the slightest, the faintest, displeasure.

The elder brother sat next to her at breakfast-time, and was sufficiently attentive to cause notice to be taken of his manner.

Sir Henry Haddington smiled benignantly.

He was not at all certain that there would be anything come from it ; but, at all events, he had no objection whatever if there did.

There could be no possible doubt about Mr. Treherne's position and character.

About twelve—by that peculiar manœuvring which lovers are always up to—the two found their way on to a magnificent terrace overlooking the park.

Mr. Treherne, who was rather nervous, was at last compelled to speak out, in a sudden, sharp way that quite astonished Maria.

She was astonished, surprised, flattered—yes, very flattered—but it was so sudden, so quite unexpected—really, did he think that he could put up with such a giddy girl?

" My dear Maria," he said, " you have too much good sense ever to be giddy."

" Well, I suppose I shouldn't if I were married. But it's so very sudden—to give up all girlish ways—to be——"

" Mistress of my heart, my fortune, my life ! " said Mr. Treherne, with energy.

Maria looked at him keenly. He was not a man to be trifled with.

" If you will dare venture on the trial, I will try and be a good and faithful wife," she replied, with deep and burning blushes.

Next instant he was clasped in her arms and, in a month after they were married.

Not a word passed between her and Leopold Treherne, whom she thought her slave.

Ah ! Mrs. Treherne, you did a false thing when you even looked with an eye of affection on that young dwarf.

The reader will soon see.

CHAPTER XXI.

THE MARRIAGE.

AND so they were married, and after a wedding tour, went home to the splendid edifice inhabited by the Trehernes.

Leopold had remained at home, and superintended the renovations in the family mansion, which was usual on wedding occasions.

The old oak panelling, dating from the reign of an early king, had been repolished and relieved by gilt mouldings, and emblazoned armorial bearings; exquisitely carved sconces, in gold and bronze, silver and ebony, ormolu and steel, glittered before oval mirrors, in frames of marvellous workmanship.

The great library, fitted entirely in black oak and gold, had been lighted by an oriel window of stained glass.

The frames of all the portraits upon the wide staircases, which led from either side of the great hall, and met in a landing place opening into two galleries running the entire length of the house, had been regilded, and the pictures themselves cleaned and restored.

The long drawing-room had been furnished in the modern style; the hangings were of white watered silk and delicate rose-tinted fringes; the walls were of the palest cream-coloured panelling, the cornices and mouldings in white and silver; the carpet of a white ground, upon which, here and there, half-open blush rosebuds had fallen; the luxurious sofas were covered with the same delicate white and rose-hued silks and fringes; the deep easy chairs were of a polished white wood, resembling ivory, and ran noiselessly away from your hand, if you touched them ever so lightly, on the soft velvet pile of the rose-bud bestrewn carpeting.

All this and more had Leopold done during the time that intervened between the wedding and the return.

But very gloomy were his ideas on the subject of his brother's marital happiness. He knew Maria too well to believe in it.

He had seen her on her marriage day. He had seen her turn first white, then red, and he had seen her great lustrous eyes directed towards him with a tenderness which to him was perfectly horrible to witness.

He began to have an awful dread of this woman, a perfect and almost intense horror.

He could not believe that anyone who could marry his brother while affecting to love him could be one calculated to make anyone happy. But he would not have said so for the world.

Still it was his determination to watch his sister-in-law keenly, and see, at least, that she committed no sin against her true and proper allegiance to the man who had been weak enough to choose her.

But Maria—Mrs. Treherne—was as happy as the day was long, and seemed to love her husband.

And this lasted six months.

But then, during this six months, Leopold took care to avoid every opportunity of being alone with her.

And thus it was how the terrible tragedy came about.

Leopold continued his old studies. He painted as much as ever.

He would gladly have gone abroad to have improved himself, but his brother was wilful. He treated him like a son, and would not part with him.

Leopold was too fond of his elder brother not to give way to him.

He felt he could refuse him nothing.

And then he was so kind to him, took such pleasure in his studies, admired all he did so much.

Mr. Treherne's park was full of lovely scenery, especially small lakes and ponds.

There Leopold delighted in painting at all times.

There was one spot called his bower, where he had in reality made himself a complete studio.

Here he would retire and study for whole days.

And here, one day, Maria Treherne followed her brother-in-law.

She burst upon him suddenly, unexpectedly.

"So," she cried, with a merry ringing laugh, "you are still the art student."

"Yes, madam," he said, coldly and sternly, rising as he spoke.

"Leopold," she replied, "have you forgot?"

"What, madam?"

"Our old excursion to the favourite painting studio of a young artist," she continued.

"I have forgotten nothing, madam."

"What, then, do you remember?"

"I remember that a young girl, whom I thought ingenuous, gentle, incapable of deceit, made love to a poor cripple, tried to act upon his affections, and when she thought she had succeeded, went and accepted his elder brother the same night."

"Accepted!" said the clever actress, in a tone of deep passion—"accepted—no! Obeyed to order to accept."

"Whose order?"

"Leopold, as soon as I left you, I went to my brother. I told him my affection. He spurned me from him with scorn—I should never marry a younger son."

"So then, madame, you accepted the elder brother?"

"Because I was compelled. I am wholly dependent on my brother; I was menaced with penury—what could I do?"

"Have told my brother the truth!" said Leopold.

"And been left where I should never have seen you again."

"But, madame, now that you are the wife of another, you are far more surely divided from me than by a thousand miles."

"No," said the profligate young woman, her eyes flashing fire, her cheeks crimson red; "we are together every day, and though you so strangely shun me, I see you."

"Are you not my brother's wife?" he cried, horrified.

"I am; but surely where there is mutual love ——" she began.

"Silence, madame! My brother would not for

his soul do me a wrong—I know he would not;
he is the soul of honour and goodness.   Let me
never hear these words again, and I may both
forget and forgive—though it will be a hard task."

"You scorn my love," she said, with terrible
flashing eyes.

"I do."

"You even threaten me," she added, furiously
and madly.

"I do not; but rather than this should continue, I will throw myself at my brother's feet,
and confess all," he said.

"Dare to do so," she replied, with flashing
eyes; "and I will indeed be most fearfully
revenged."

"Revenged on me?" he said, calmly.

"Yes."

"How so?"

"I will say you have made love to me, and I
have refused you," she cried, with flashing eyes.

Leopold, quite pallid with horror, started back.

"Woman," he said, "in God's name! who and
what made you so wicked?"

"Disappointed love!" cried the furious young
woman.

He turned away.

"But listen, Leopold. I still love you, love
you to distraction, and will wait. I will not injure
you, I will give you time, ample time; but if in a
month you do not respond fully to my affection—
why then, who can say what may happen?"

And she left him mad—furious; she was a
woman scorned.

There is nothing equal to it—only as men
seldom do scorn women, we do not see many
instances of the case.

CHAPTER XXII.

THE CONFESSION.

THAT very night Mr. Treherne was taken
seriously ill.

It was a very sudden attack, and, but for the
deep love and devotion of Leopold, might have
ended fatally at once.

But he sent messengers in every direction, and
in an hour had two experienced doctors.

Mrs. Treherne had fainted at the news, and
been carried off in dreadful hysterics.

Her place, as that of every wife, should have
been by her husband's bed.

But she was another Madame de Laurens.*

She had no mercy or pity in her soul. She
hated and loathed her husband; but what could
she expect from his death?

After what Leopold had told her, surely
nothing.

But at all events, she could not bear the sight
of the man she had betrayed—murdered.

The attack with which Mr. Treherne had been
struck down, was apoplexy, and apoplexy of a
very dangerous kind, not immediately dangerous,
but very likely to prove so in the end.

* See Three Red Men, in London Herald, for this
hideous character.

So after some hours of assiduous attention the
patient came to.

He glared wildly round, saw Leopold, smiled,
held out his hand, and took it.

"How long have I to live?" he said, in a
sharp, quick way.

"Really, sir," began the most eminent of the
physicians.

"Doctor Robson, I have much to do; my will
to make; justice to be done—have I time to do
it in?"

"Certainly, sir—the attack has subsided; the
only danger is a relapse."

"Thank you, will you call to-morrow?"

"There must really be no excitement."

"There shall be none, if I have my own way
entirely." And the sick man, who seemed half
mad, pointed to the door.

The doctors, who revered their patient, went
out after a few directions to Leopold.

"Now, Leopold, close the door," said the
patient.

The dwarf obeyed.

"Lock it, and let no one enter."

"But your wife?"

"My wife—I have no wife."

"But Mrs. Treherne?"

"There is no Mrs. Treherne—if Mrs. John
Smith comes to the door, turn her away."

The dwarf looked at him with a pitying glance.

"Sit you down, Leopold, and listen. You
think me mad. I am only too sane. But first
you must promise me solemnly, on your oath to
a dying man, that you will obey my last injunctions to the letter."

Leopold Treherne swore without the slightest
hesitation.

There was a strange light in the invalid's eyes.

"And now everything shall be made clear, dark
shall be light, and light shall be dark. I have
been wrong, wicked unjust; but I will repair
everything."

"My dear brother," said Leopold, "you are
exciting yourself—you will make yourself really
and truly ill."

"No. I shall be ill if I do not speak out."

"But what is the matter?—what has happened?"

"Leopold, I just now overheard all that occurred
between yourself and my wife," he said, with a
rare bitterness of tone.

Leopold remained silent for a moment or two, to
collect his thoughts.

"You heard nothing that I am ashamed of
John."

"No, my dear brother—all was well on your
part; but hers!"

"She was mad," said Leopold, trying to
soothe him.

"When there is such method in madness,
'twere better one were sane," said Treherne.

Leopold dared not reply.

"You have sworn."

"I have."

"I believe you, Leopold. Now will I reveal
to you a secret which has been burning my very
soul for years. You said to her just now that I
was just and honourable."

MRS. TREHERNE AND THE COLONEL.

"I did, and said it from my soul!" cried Leopold.

"You are wrong. I am an unmitigated scoundrel and villain, Leopold!"

"John!"

"A wretched and silly coward."

"John!"

"You will understand me by-and-bye, Leopold."

"Never, my brother."

"You will. When my father died he confessed to me his sin and wickedness."

"John!"

"I was born out of wedlock," cried John, "and my mother's name was Smith. Do you begin to understand?"

"Merciful Heaven! can this be true?" gasped Leopold.

"It is. He proved it to me, as I will prove it to you."

"My dear brother, it is a dream."

"It is no dream. I will tell you all."

And he did, by that flickering light, tell the story.

"And now," he said, "by your solemn oath, I require you to keep your promise!"

"And what is that, my poor, poor John?"

"That one year after my death you will cause my wishes to be published."

"I will," said Leopold Treherne, gravely and solemnly.

And the lawyer was sent for, and, in the absence of Leopold, one short and one long will was made.

They were sealed up.

Next day, in the presence of his wife, whom he did not recognize, and a few friends, John Treherne died.

And there was a grand funeral, and much sorrow expressed.

A short will was read, which ordained that the final decision of the deceased's affairs should be put off for a year, until it was decided whether Mrs. Treherne was or not a mother.

This she at once announced herself to be in the way to be.

And so passed three months, and then she was indeed a gay widow.

Mrs. Treherne soon convinced the neighbouring families that she was not going to spare her husband's purse. She filled the great house with company, till there was not a garret in the roof untenanted by valets and ladies' maids, who grumbled and groaned at the lack of accommodation.

She surrounded herself with noise and gaiety. She gave *fêtes champêtres* in the park, and lighted the long avenues with myriads of coloured lamps in the dusk of the summer's evening.

She superintended in person the building of a range of new stables, with wonderful thatched roofs, and filled them with hunters, to be ready for the coming season.

She built a riding-school at the back of the house, in which she rode half the morning, flying over leaping-bars, and executing all kinds of alarming equestrian manœuvres.

A tennis-court, which had long been disused, was put into repair by her orders, and the balls were flying about half the day amongst a group of noisy players, with her ladyship, perhaps, at their head.

And Leopold, with a sad and bleeding heart looked on.

But how did she behave to him?

She never overstepped the bounds of delicacy, but she allowed him clearly to see that he had but to speak to be received with open arms.

But he would not speak. He preferred to wait and watch.

And she watched him, like a cat might a mouse.

There were many visitors at Treherne Hall, because in all parts of the world there are people who will overlook anything for money.

Amongst others who came, no one knew how, and was introduced no one knew by whom, was a Colonel Hooper.

He was a monstrous pleasant fellow

He was tall and stout, fresh-looking, and rosy.

He had blue eyes, that flashed and glittered with the radiance of their smile, and the lids of which opened and shut so often that his light eyelashes emitted transient flashes of light even in the sunshine.

His teeth were so white that they glittered almost as much as his eyes; his lips were as rosy, and his complexion as fair, as a woman's; his pale auburn moustachio exquisitely trained, and the forest of bright curls clustering round his white forehead were shot with golden hues ; and the mingled effect made his face seem all gold and glitter, so that you could scarcely look at him long without having your eyes dazzled nearly as much as if you had looked at the reflection of the sun upon a burning glass.

He was dressed in a loose, careless, style, which became him wonderfully.

He wore a bright-coloured handkerchief round his throat, a braided velvet collar, a lemon-coloured waistcoat, and a quantity of golden ornaments, that shivered and scintillated at his watchchain.

His hands glittered with rings.

From head to foot he was all flash, glitter, and dazzle ; and wherever he went he seemed to shed twinkling rays of golden light about and around him.

No sooner was he in the hall than his purpose became evident.

He would be master of Treherne Hall and its handsome widow.

Leopold Treherne saw this as plain as anybody, but he took no notice.

His oath kept him back.

His mission was to keep watch and ward.

He had enough to do at the same time.

But he too had, by this time, fallen upon an affair of the heart.

CHAPTER XXIII.

CORNELIA.

THE dwarf, though he kept his eye constantly on Mrs. Treherne, still found time to have a few strolls in the park.

During one of these he met with a remarkable adventure.

He was still, as always, sketching.

He was this time taking in a small and elegant cottage, which had recently been erected for the new curate.

A cry behind him made him start and look round.

A lovely creation of female beauty was gazing with admiration at the sketch.

" Pardon," she said ; " but it is so like, and I should so much like papa to see it."

" And your papa is——" cried Leopold, with admiring eyes.

" The new curate, Mr. Vaughan," continued the girl.

" Then it is at his service," said Leopold, gallantly.

" Thank you, but——"

" Let it be Mr. Leopold Treherne's introduction and apology for not calling sooner."

The girl blushed rosy red.

" May I have the honour of calling now?" said Leopold.

" Certainly," she said, in some confusion ; " too happy."

They had spoken to her of a hideous dwarf.

She thought him superhumanly beautiful.

And we have reason to know that the belief was mutual.

Leopold Treherne followed his beautiful guide with feelings which were quite new to him.

He had never felt such sensations in his life before—sensations so sweet, so charming, so exquisite.

He found Mr. Vaughan at home, who received him with the proud courtesy which so well becomes a man in his situation in life.

He appeared pleased that his daughter should have made such an acquaintance.

Leopold enjoyed his conversation immensely, and made no difficulty in accepting an invitation which was given.

"We dine early, Mr. Treherne," said the curate, "because it suits my health. I know it is your lunch time, but if you will join us, I can, without egotism, promise you a good glass of wine."

Leopold's eyes sparkled. He meant to have invited himself.

The dinner was neatly served, and well cooked. The wine was excellent; the plate, old family plate.

"I daresay now," said the Rev. Mr. Vaughan, "that you are surprised to find a curate so well appointed."

"Well," began Leopold, with an apologetic smile.

"I will explain. I have a small fortune. I like the Church—and have few friends. Your brother was kind enough to promise me the reversion of the rectorship if I would do duty for one whose health entirely incapacitated him from work. Your brother's sudden and untimely death does away——"

"Not at all sir," cried Leopold, so warmly as to raise a smile on the curate's face, and a blush on that of the fair and lovely daughter.

"I have no written promise, and should not presume to trouble Mrs. Treherne."

Leopold's eyes were bent down on his plate, in deep and anxious thought.

"My brother," he said, "has left me absolute power during my life over all such matters. I repeat the promise—you shall have the living."

How her eyes beamed, and how amply he was repaid!

"You are very kind," replied Mr. Vaughan, "and I accept, with thanks. Cornelia, my dear, let me have that bottle of sparkling moselle—we will drink to our better acquaintance. By the way, my dear, we must dine an hour later to-morrow. When I am rector, you know, I shall have to *obey* invitations to dinner."

"I would urge you while curate," said Leopold, "but I have reasons for not wishing you to come much to the Hall just now."

Mr. Vaughan bowed and smiled, and soon after, from a sense of duty, Leopold left.

But his visits were often repeated, and ere three months had passed they were engaged—the lovely, accomplished, elegant Cornelia to the dwarf.

Mrs. Treherne being now within two months of her confinement, was more quiet and reserved. It was only as mother of a male child that she could hope to reign at Treherne Hall, which otherwise became Leopold's.

Great anxiety was felt by her and by another intriguer.

The colonel had obtained great mastery over her mind.

She had promised him marriage out of pure pique, because Leopold scorned her.

But he would only marry the mother of the heir of Treherne; so he hypocritically suggested that he ought to go away until such time as she was up after her confinement.

She acquiesced, and promised to be careful.

But she was not still. She had her spies.

So one day she unexpectedly asked Mr. Vaughan and his daughter to dinner.

They could not well refuse.

So they came to dinner, and Mrs. Treherne saw that what she suspected was true. Leopold was loved, and loved wildly and passionately and gratefully in return.

Like the snake in the grass, she kept her discovery to herself.

Then, amidst great rejoicings, a male child was born seven months after the death of Mr. Treherne.

A month after—the child being handed over to a wet-nurse, a head nurse and a doctor, who were all promised large rewards if the child lived—the colonel returned.

CHAPTER XXIV.

MRS. TREHERNE AND THE COLONEL.

IT was in a small boudoir, at no great distance from the library.

The colonel and Mrs. Treherne were alone.

She sat in a *bergère*, he in an arm-chair by her side.

They had all the appearance of lovers.

He held her hand in his, she looked admiringly at him.

"Now, most charming and lovely of widows, why am I to suffer this long delay?" he said, coaxingly.

"The world! the world!" she replied, tapping him on the knuckles with her fan.

"The world! why should two loving hearts be separated by the world?" he urged, in soft, persuasive tones.

"I shall be blamed enough for taking you at all, my dear colonel," she said, with a strange, cat-like smile.

"My dear——"

"I shall; therefore let us not be in a hurry to seek blame. On the fourth of March, my husband died, on the fifth of next March, I will be your wife, if——"

"If!" said the colonel, elevating his eyebrows.

"My dear colonel, I want a proof of your devotion."

"Ask me anything," he said, in low and earnest tones.

"What I ask is difficult; but unless it be done, I will never—never marry," she continued.

"Excruciating widow, speak, that I may know my fate."

"There is a person I hate," she began, slowly.

"Sits the wind i'that quarter—Monsieur Leopold?"

"No," cried Maria, with a deadly pallor; "I do not hate him; but the woman who loves, and is loved by him."

The colonel frowned and looked offended.

"My *dear* colonel," said Mrs. Treherne, "allow me to observe, in the most delicate way in the world, that I am fully aware how far you are influenced by your very natural desire to share with me the arduous task of administering my son's property until he comes of age."

"My dear madam—I protest——"

"Oh, yes! love in a cottage. Well, I don't believe it. Now, the plain English is, I once loved Leopold Treherne; he scorned my love, and I have vowed he shall be happy with no other woman."

"Oh! oh!"

"This marriage must be prevented."

"How?"

"That is your affair."

"You surely don't want me to kill her?"

"As you like. But I would rather you would kill her honour," said Maria Treherne, with gleaming eyes.

"And to be revenged on him, you would allow me to do a little intriguing," said the colonel, with a strange, cynical smile.

"You are a single man. I have no right to call in question your deeds before marriage. Do, therefore, what you please," said Maria.

The colonel looked decidedly as if he intended she should not interfere with him very much afterwards.

"I will do all you wish," he said.

"I will then for ever be your obedient servant," she replied.

"Seduction is out of the question. That spoony of a girl loves the dwarf."

"Don't call her spoony; I loved him," she said.

"I beg pardon; well, she does love him, so my chance is very poor. Still, there is something to be done."

"Don't tell me your plans. All I want to know is that her heart is broken, and he is deserted."

"It shall be done."

So promised the colonel, and immediately set about his plans.

He had a valet, a man of considerable nerve, of some tact, enormous impudence, and nothing in the shape of scruples.

His name was Alfred Buster.

His lingo was a study. He always spoke through his nose.

"Shnow Mish Shvaun shvrel vel," he said, when his master began to lay his plans.

They were fully explained, and next day Alfred Buster was transformed into Septimus Jones, Esq., an angler who had come down to Treherne in search of sport.

Mr. Vaughan was a great angler.

With his shooting jacket and other appurtenances, he cast off his mode of speaking. He was now a bluff and jolly disciple of the reel.

Mr. Vaughan was in the habit of spending one day a week upon his favourite sport.

Septimus Jones, Esq., selected that day, took a rod, and strolled down to the stream.

It was a trout stream.

As Alfred Buster was an inveterate poacher, just returned from transportation, he was a very good hand.

His basket was nearly full when Mr. Vaughan appeared.

"Ah!" said that gentleman, "a brother of the reel?"

"Yes, sir, my favourite sport."

"A very delightful one," added the curate.

"I have been passionately fond of it all my life."

"Hum!" said the curate; "I don't speak quite so warmly as that; but it is a very pleasing amusement, especially to one whose life is sedentary. I study a good deal."

"I never had time, I am sorry to say," said Septimus Jones, Esq.; "my father started me to sea too early for that; but I have seen a deal of foreign parts."

"Travel is, next to books, the best mode of opening a man's eyes, and teaching him what the world contains, both of good and evil," continued the parson.

And thus they continued in friendly chat for some time—now together, now apart.

The valet was a shrewd, cunning fellow, had lived in many families, and could always suit himself to his company.

With his own master, he was saucy and vulgar, but with a gentleman of taste he would have been as civil and polite as a young girl.

He had really travelled a good deal, especially in France; and finding out the parson's taste for information, gave him plenty of it.

The Reverend Mr. Vaughan was enchanted.

He found out where he resided, and, being a cautious man, first invited himself to a bottle of wine at the very respectable village inn.

Septimus Jones, Esq., was not at all abashed. He trusted, by great caution, to make himself agreeable to the Rev. Mr. Vaughan.

Then, of course, it was all plain sailing with him.

He knew he should be asked to the house if he were only to make himself agreeable.

He ordered a very neat little supper; and there was no man who knew how to order one better than he did.

The worthy innkeeper had been once a cook to a nobleman, and it quite delighted his heart to undertake the pleasant task.

Then, about a quarter of an hour before the time when the Reverend Mr. Vaughan was expected, the innkeeper dressed himself.

He received the somewhat surprised parson in a suit of black, with "white choke," as Mrs. Grey's fast girls would say.

"Well, Morris, what's the matter? Anybody dead? Funeral, christening, or marriage?"

"No, sir; only a supper."

"And you going to wait yourself, Morris?" said the astonished curate.

"Yes, sir; highly honoured to wait on such customers."

"Indeed !" laughed the parson ; " and, pray, may I ask who these very distinguished and highly-honoured visitors are ?"

" Yourself, sir, and my guest, Mr. Jones."

The curate stared, then laughed, and, finally, was pleased.

" Nice sort of person, this stranger," he remarked.

We are all sensible to flattery.

" Very, sir—excellent taste—never knew a gentleman so well able to order supper since I lived at Lord M——'s."

" Indeed !" said the curate, who, however, now thought it right to announce himself.

Mr. Jones hurried to come down and receive his guest.

" Really, Mr. Jones," began the curate, " I only came here to have a chat with an old angler ; and I understand, my good sir—— "

" What, sir ? "

" That you have prepared supper for me."

" Well, sir, a mere *bagatelle!* I dined but indifferently. Morris, we are quite ready when you are."

And Morris ushered in the supper with considerable alacrity. He was proud of his handiwork. He had done nothing of the kind for so long a time that he had almost grown rusty. But now came the triumph.

There are few men in this world—and, we conscientiously believe, few women—who do not know the value of a good dinner. If their appetites are not depraved—if their minds are not warped—it makes them more cheerful, better, and happier.

Don't tease a man before dinner ; neither ask for his daughter, nor his signature, nor his patronage.

He will be sulky and disagreeable.

But after—when the dreamy sense of satisfaction and security is on him—when the glass of generous wine has warmed him—when he feels at rest with all the world—ask him for his daughter, his purse, or his signature, and you may possibly succeed.

Now the Rev. Mr. Vaughan was neither a greedy man, a voluptuary, nor a gourmand.

But he was a judge of what was good, and had a keen appetite, and an excellent relish for good cookery.

He quite enjoyed himself.

" Upon my word, sir," he said, " you have performed a wonder in this, our humble part of the world. I don't know that I can promise you anything half so good ; but if you will come up to-morrow to dinner, at three, we will try."

Septimus Jones, Esq., bowed low, and no more was said on the point.

CHAPTER XXV.

DINNER PARTY.

THE Rev. Mr. Vaughan was never taken by surprise. He was one of those people who never have to hide themselves for five minutes to get ready for company.

Cornelia was as ready to receive visitors at eight o'clock in the morning as she was at three in the afternoon.

An extra person to dinner did not surprise her at all.

Not even the hint of something peculiarly extra astonished her.

Leopold was coming, which made this care quite agreeable to her.

Had Septimus Jones been aware of this fact, he might, probably, have hesitated to dine in such company.

But he had no occasion to be afraid.

Leopold Treherne was too intent on watching the master to care, in the slightest degree, about the servant.

Besides, the fellow moved about with such a stealthy and cautious pace, and was so cunning and astute, that nobody ever thought of noticing him much.

Then, dress, a false whisker and moustache, and a wig, with the total change in voice, quite transformed him.

He did not look like a gentleman—education and early association are generally required to produce that result—but he appeared a bluff man of travel.

He was, to all intents and purposes, an admirable sportsman.

When, however—having arrived first—Mr. Leopold Treherne was announced, he gave one hasty glance at an open window, which, fortunately for him, was lost upon the clergyman, and then resigned himself even to discovery.

He could only be kicked out.

He had been served this way so often that he was always prepared for the indignity.

It was unpleasant, but then, like hanging, it was soon over.

Besides, unlike hanging, you were none the worse after.

But Leopold—unsuspicious, except were good reasons existed for his being otherwise—bowed low, greeted him in his gentle, pleasant way, and began to talk about angling.

He, too, was fond of that quiet sport, which only a man like Johnson, who preferred Fleet-street to Greenwich-park, would ever have thought of anathematising.

This passed the time very pleasantly, till Cornelia, who had been overlooking the cook, came in fresh, and blooming, and happy, to join them.

Septimus Jones very nearly gave expression to a cry.

Something had shot to his very heart.

That hard, cruel, and profligate man had never known love.

He had never even faintly understood what it meant.

He now was utterly dazzled, astounded, and overwhelmed.

Before dinner was over the emissary of the colonel was over head and ears in love with the very girl he had come to betray.

Did this check him in his vile and atrocious plans ? Not a bit.

He reasoned thus: "Money I must have, and I cannot afford to offend my master.

"But, probably, if there is any scandal, somebody will be wanted."

He would offer himself, like the marine in "Percival Keene," as a husband for the lovely Miss Vaughan.

He was bad enough for anything.

But what he endured as he saw and understood the looks which passed between Cornelia and Leopold can scarcely be told.

He was bitterly, furiously jealous.

But, to avoid the least evidence of the fact, he conversed all the time with the father.

With a peculiar art, which was his own, he made as if he were talking, while, in fact, the reverend gentleman was telling him a very long story.

How he hailed the retiring of Cornelia after dinner!

For a moment only.

Leopold rose with her, as a matter of course, and went out into the garden.

Septimus Jones ground his teeth.

It was with difficulty that he could restrain himself, but he did, and presently was deep in an abstruse discussion on the merits of some particular flies.

That night he wrote a long letter to his master, for further instructions.

Cornelia was neither to be dazzled by money, nor ambition, nor flattery.

She was irretrievably and over head and ears in love with the dwarf.

This unsatisfactory report drove the colonel to his wits' end.

It was necessary, after all, to have recourse to some diabolical scheme in order to carry out his designs.

Maria Treherne was positive in her refusal to marry unless her wishes were carried out.

The colonel was frantic, when a sudden idea came into the head of that lady.

"I tell you what it is, colonel," she said, languidly.

"What is that?" exclaimed that worthy, rather drily.

"We must leave this place and move to London town."

"Why?"

"If anything is to be done, we had better be far away."

"How so?"

"We had better be in London, to all appearance, while anything is going on."

"I understand. There is a new opera—will that be an excuse?"

"There are a hundred new things. Besides, my brother and this new wife of his are in town. I can surely visit him."

"Humph! he won't fancy me much," said the colonel, who had no very overweening idea of his own merits.

"Well, never mind that. When we are married, who knows what may happen?"

The colonel looked keenly at her.

"My brother has no children as yet."

"Well."

"My son might inherit ——"

"But Sir Henry's younger brother—your younger brother?"

"A boy who has ran away to sea. Who ever speaks of him?"

"But I know him to be alive," said the colonel, quietly.

"You are very inquisitive."

"I never omit anything which regards my own interest," smiled the colonel.

"Well—all right. But to-morrow I shall start for London, bag and baggage."

"Kid and all?" laughed the colonel.

"Is he not our most valuable possession?"

CHAPTER XXVI.

JOURNEY TO LONDON.

WHEN this determination of Mrs. Treherne was come to, Leopold was lost in astonishment, and filled with extreme vexation.

What was to be done by him in this most perplexing predicament?

He could not give up watching his sister-in-law, according to a solemn pledge to her deceased husband; nor could he leave Cornelia.

But she soon put an end to all difficulties.

She had never been to London in her life.

Nothing was more easy than to persuade her father to go there for a month.

He was a very obedient father, was Mr. Vaughan, as fathers with only daughters generally are.

Ought they not to be so, young ladies?

It was resolved at once, then, that Leopold, Mr. Vaughan, and Cornelia should take up their quarters at a well-known hostelry near Covent Garden.

As soon as everything was settled, Leopold Treherne announced the determination at breakfast table.

It was the very day of Mrs. Treherne's departure.

She and the colonel exchanged a hasty glance. Leopold appeared not to see.

They made no opposition—they were really delighted.

So they said.

Probably what they intended to do was easier done in London than anywhere else.

So the whole party started for London on the same day.

But not together.

Mrs. Treherne travelled with her child and the two nurses.

The colonel went off by the coach with his servant, Alfred Buster.

Mr. Septimus Jones had, since the dinner party, been no more heard of.

Leopold, Cornelia, and her father, travelled slowly up in a private carriage.

The journey, to them, was something really charming.

It was quite an epoch in their lives.

Never had the dwarf been so really and truly happy. He was all day with Cornelia, and then again all the evening.

They halted at inns every night.

Mr. Vaughan had some books with him, and rarely interfered in the lovers' secrets.

Strange to say, they had never made any, the faintest, allusion to their engagement.

They thought it unnecessary. They thought everybody knew all about it.

One day, he laid down his book, and seemed to think.

Suddenly his eye caught the hand of his daughter in that of the dwarf's, while his hand was round her waist.

They were utterly, like all true lovers, lost to everything around them.

The clergyman frowned darkly.

"Hem!" he said, rather drily.

Cornelia looked up, and blushed a rosy red. Leopold Treherne smiled, but did not look at all abashed.

"Won't she make me a handsome wife?" he said, pleasantly; "only too good."

"Wife!" cried the clergyman.

"Didn't you know, papa?" said Cornelia, with a laugh and a smile

"Know what, my dear?"

"That I and Leopold have long been engaged?" she added.

"To be married on the fifth of March," put in Leopold.

"Well, really," said the clergyman, with a smile, "you seem to have gone very far with your arrangements. I think I ought to have been consulted."

"Well, sir," said Leopold, with a puzzled look, "I suppose you ought. But we thought, of course, you knew all about it."

"Indeed, I thought so too!" added Cornelia, merrily.

The clergyman laughed outright, and the others followed suite.

"A very extraordinary and original couple, upon my word!" said Mr. Vaughan.

They smiled.

"But Mrs. Treherne," continued the clergyman, "what of her?"

"I neither have consulted her, nor do I intend," said Leopold, drily.

"Why not have done so, my son?" asked Mr. Vaughan.

"Do not ask me," cried Leopold; "I am under a solemn promise to my brother not to speak until a certain date. You shall know in good time."

And so, devising of the future, talking, making plans—the too often sorrowful employment of humanity—they reached London.

They put up at the —— hotel, close to Covent Garden.

The first person they saw in the hall of the house was the colonel himself, who bowed and passed on.

Their luggage had been taken out; but for all that, Leopold would have gladly changed hotels, but that he did not like to show such open dislike of the colonel.

He accordingly secured three bedrooms, and a private sitting-room for Cornelia.

The servants were left to make their own arrangements.

But before we even describe the position of the apartments, so essential to the right understanding of this most extraordinary part of our history, we must again introduce Sir Henry Thornley Haddington to our readers.

CHAPTER XXVII.

SIR THORNLEY.

WE were anxious not to interrupt the thread of of our narrative, so made no allusion to the Haddington family affairs in what may have seemed to be the proper place.

Scarcely had his sister Maria left his house, than, to the great astonishment of everybody, the young baronet started off on a journey to Brighton, and without fuss, ostentation, or previous announcement, got married to a charming woman.

She was the only and lovely daughter of a half-pay officer.

He was rather afraid of his sister Maria, whose temper was no secret to him.

He preferred his marriage to be over before she even heard of it.

She would certainly have opposed it, if it had lain in her power.

Not that she cared who her brother married, so that he married at all.

Ambitious in the extreme, she had vague ideas that, if he did not marry, her child might prove to be his heir.

She cared little for the brother, who seldom or ever wrote.

Sir Henry Thornley Haddington had come to town for the advice of medical men.

His wife was expected some months later to make him a father.

Sir Thornley was intensely anxious as to the result.

His wife was extremely delicate. She had not quite recovered a residence in a hot climate when Sir Henry first met her.

Still, she was getting more robust and hearty every day.

They were in the drawing-room, alone. They received very little company.

Sir Thornley, at his wife's earnest desire, gave bachelor parties downstairs.

She would not, for the world, have deprived him of his usual amusements.

Sir Thornley, who loved her with a deep and earnest affection, felt deeply grateful for this mark of attention and devotion, and loved her only all the more.

On this occasion he had invited a party to dinner, downstairs, and, therefore, devoted the day to his wife.

She had just come in, having taken a slight carriage airing.

She was richly dressed in brocaded silk, of shining silver grey, with glowing violet fringes and ribbons.

An immense shawl, of thick black lace, fell about her, not as a shawl, but as a drapery, hanging loosely from one shoulder, and trailing in artistic folds over the skirt of her dress.

She had thrown off her bonnet, and her dark-brown hair fell carelessly about her shoulders.

It was not fastened or dressed, like anybody else's hair, but seemed to be thrown back from her low forehead, to fall, in clusters of ringlets, where and how it chose.

Her face was perfectly oriental; the nose small and aquiline; the eyes black as night, almond shaped, languid, half veiled by long and inky lashes; her pouting lips a vivid crimson; her complexion a pale olive.

But to this glorious splendour of feature and of colouring, she added the still more winning loveliness of an exquisitely child-like and gentle countenance.

Her husband, who had hurried from the library on hearing her knock, rose to receive her.

At the same moment, there came a quick knock at the front door.

The moment the attendant answered the knock, a ringing voice was heard.

"Is my brother at home?"

Sir Thornley flushed crimson, and would have gone down-stairs.

But she stopped him.

"Your brother should come up here," said Lady Mary Haddington, gently.

"As you will, my dear; I am afraid he is rather a rough customer."

But this long-absent brother did not hear him, fortunately.

There he stood in the doorway, the very image of a polished gentlemanly sailor; his dark-bronzed face, his jet black eyes, his smiling face, giving promise of a character highly creditable to the family.

He stood irresolute a moment, and then entered the room.

"Thornley!"

"Marmaduke!"

And they shook hands heartily. All that might have separated them was forgotten.

"Lady Haddington, I suppose?" said Marmaduke, with a profound bow.

She advanced, and gave her hand warmly and kindly.

"I am delighted to see you so happily married," said Marmaduke, with all the ardour and fervour of his sailor nature.

Sir Thornley saw that he was in earnest, and wrung his hand with strong affection.

"You must come down to the park, Marmaduke, and you must renew our old ways. Won't we have some glorious shooting?"

"Won't we!" said Marmaduke. "I've done a deal of lion shooting, buffalo hunting, and elk stalking in my life; but, egad! I like my first of September."

"I'm glad to hear it. To-morrow is Sunday, Marmy—you must dine en famille. To-day, I have a bachelor party, Mary not being so well as I could wish."

"I will be with you at six."

"Where are you going, brother?"

"To my hotel."

"Why?"

"To dress."

"To fetch your traps, Marmaduke."

"But I have an Indian servant."

"Half-a-dozen, if you like, Mary will find room for them all."

"This is very jolly," said Marmaduke, in a cheerful and happy tone; "but I shall be very troublesome."

"Not at all, my dear fellow; not another word—you must come."

And so Marmaduke was domiciliated in the house of his brother Thornley.

CHAPTER XXVIII.

LADY MARMADUKE.

LADY HADDINGTON was, we have said, very delicate, and as she neither liked to trust wholly to hired nurses, nor even old servants of her husband's,* she had prevailed on her loving husband to send for a dear cousin of her own, who had been educated as a governess.

Her name was Mary Dawson.

She was a little fat plump girl, of nineteen, with a profusion of dark curls, and brown eyes, and a good little affectionate heart.

She came, of course, the moment she was invited.

That grand old house in Grosvenor Square quite staggered her at first; it was so different from anything she had been used to.

It awed her.

Then she became used to it all at once. Everybody was so kind to her, so considerate, so friendly.

Sir Thornley Haddington thought her a perfect angel.

What Marmaduke thought he did not say, but he became peculiarly absorbed in his own thoughts; and apparently reckless as to the opinions of the outer world, he strolled in the March sunshine up and down under the overarching branches of the leafless trees in the great avenue of Kensington Gardens, smoking his cheroots, and followed by a huge black Newfoundland dog. Sometimes he paused at the great iron gates which shut the park from the dusty high road, and looked out through the bars and the filigree work into the world beyond. There was something of the caged lion in the glance of the dark sailor, as he gazed through the ornamental grating—something of that far away, restless, hopeless look, which poets tell us they see in the eyes of the eagles shut up in the four-feet-square cages of a Zoological collection.

It was quite a certainty that he was in a very bad way.

Mary Dawson did all the shopping, saw all the tradespeople, superintended the baby clothes; so that she was a great deal out.

Sometimes the dark sailor is with her; but sometimes, when Sir Thornley is out, he will stop and entertain his sister-in-law.

She is somewhat irritable and fanciful, and does not like to be alone.

And then she and Marmaduke begin to have a great secret together.

* To comprehend all this explanation, it is necessary to refer to Nos. 1, 2, 3.

LEOPOLD AND CORNELIA.

They whisper a good deal, and they laugh, and they look sly; at all which good Sir Thornley laughs heartily.

They won't tell him a word about it—of course not they.

It is true that Marmaduke looks rather rueful sometimes.

He has nothing scarcely but his pay in the navy, and, Heaven knows, that is not much !

Then comes an entirely unexpected event.

" Brother of mine," said Sir Thornley, one day, " how would you like to give up the sea, live at home, and be, as you ought, my best companion and friend ?"

" It is my most ardent wish," he replied, with flashing eyes ; " but it cannot be."

The baronet remembered that glance long afterwards.

" Why ?"

" I cannot afford to live on shore."

" Pshaw ! The estate is damnably tied up, it is true, and I have been discussing with Morris and Jones, how to manage it, but I can't. But this I can give you—the Dower House and a thousand a year."

Marmaduke took his hand, and was about to say something; but he hesitated.

Unfortunate error !

Had he spoken, this history would never have been worth writing.

"Not a word," said the baronet, heartily, and left him, ere he was sufficiently recovered to make any reply.

He went out.

Mary Dawson was also out, so that Marmaduke had no one to whom to tell his story, save Lady Haddington herself.

She heard him with a smile of most extreme pleasure.

It was the dearest wish of her heart that the hopes of the young man should be realized.

In the immensity of her own happiness, she wished everyone else to be happy.

Indeed, she would not herself have been so, if she had believed anyone near her unhappy.

They talked for about half-an-hour.

"I tell you what it is," she said, suddenly; "you spoil me almost as much as my husband does. I declare I have not done a bit of work to-day!"

It was a kind of religious idea of that gentle woman to make her young baby one suit of clothes.

Marmaduke smiled, and looked out, of the window.

"She won't be here just yet!" said Lady Mary, laughing.

"Why, so?"

"She has to go to half-a-dozen places for me, before she comes back," replied Lady Mary, smiling.

"Shall I go meet her?" he said, speaking rather ruefully.

"No ; come and make yourself useful."

And she pointed, merrily, to the unwound skein of silk.

Marmarduke, like an obedient boy as he was, came to her side, and did exactly what he was told.

Lady Mary told him he was drilling for matrimony himself. He laughed, but shook his dark and shining curls.

It was in this state that Maria Treherne found the household of her brother on her arrival in town.

Maria had never before this seen her sister-in-law.

She had written a very clever letter to her brother; but her married life, her widowhood, and subsequent state, excused her calling.

But now she was in London, a visit to Grosvenor Square became, of course, absolutely necessary.

She drove round the first day with her child and nurse.

Sir Thornley was not at home, but Lady Haddington was upstairs.

Sir Thornley had gone out with his steward on very particular business.

But the servants knew Mrs. Treherne, and without hesitation showed her up-stairs.

Lady Haddington was dressed as we have seen her in the last chapter.

Marmaduke, in uniform, was standing by her, unravelling a skein of silk.

She was laughingly rapping his knuckles for his extreme awkwardness.

Mrs. Treherne gave one puzzled glance at them, and then a most fiendish idea crossed her wretched soul.

"Mrs. Treherne," said the servant, at last getting in front.

They started up. Lady Haddington looked both confused and alarmed.

Marmaduke, who, for a moment, had really forgotten the very existence of his sister, turned towards the window.

He had caught a glance at the woman, and did not like her.

Lady Haddington, recovering herself, received her visitor with a strange mixture of coldness and kindness.

She had evidently disapproved of her marriage.

"Sir Thornley is out," she said, "but will soon return."

"But I have come to see you, my dear," replied Mrs. Treherne, at the same time glancing meaningly at the officer.

"In the meantime, Marmaduke, this is your sister, Maria," Lady Haddington thought proper to add.

Mrs. Treherne started back deadly pale.

He turned round, and stared in a stupid kind of way.

"I went to sea so early," he remarked, vacantly, "that I really do require an introduction to my sister."

And somewhat coldly, he shook hands, and handed a chair.

Maria vowed in her heart of hearts that he should repent this slighting manner.

When Sir Thornley Haddington returned, and Mary Dawson came in, they made up quite a family party.

Sir Thornley was very kind to his widowed sister, and having no engagements, arranged for them all to dine together.

Mrs. Treherne gladly acquiesced, as she wished to lay the foundation of another of those fiendish plots, which were so peculiarly her own.

She saw at once the state of the case between Marmaduke and Mary Dawson.

Lady Haddington, of course, expected to have a son.

Marmaduke would be married, and, probably, have lots of children.

In this case, where were the chances of her child, which, having been duly shown, had been sent up to a room always called the nursery in that establishment ?

But Mrs. Treherne's fancy was that both these things might be prevented.

There was, evidently, a very strong affection between her brother and sister-in-law.

Might this not be improved into something criminal ?

At all events, Mrs. Treherne resolved to be very cautious. One plot was really quite enough at a time.

But one fact decided her.

"I tell you what it is, Maria," said the baronet, "we all go back to the hall in ten days. Come and spend a month with us. Your little boy will be a treat, and you can give good advice to Mary."

Lady Mary Haddington—not Miss Mary Dawson.

Mrs. Treherne at once agreed; and as they were all going down there, made up her mind to put off the realization of her other infernal plot as well.

CHAPTER XXIX.

HAMPSTEAD HEATH.

Mrs. TREHERNE lived in apartments in Harley Street. She had her own servants, and one in particular, who was her ordinary confidante in every scheme.

Her name was Louise—a thorough French *soubrette*.

This woman was about the height and size of Mrs. Treherne—a very convenient arrangement for a grasping maid and an intriguing mistress.

The evening after the events recorded in the last chapter, the mistress went in a close carriage to the opera.

So it was said; but anybody who had been exceedingly observant would have remarked that the opera visitor was Louise, in her mistress's clothes.

Then Louise glided out for the evening, to all appearance; but it was Mrs. Treherne.

She had already, on many occasions, been induced by the colonel to give him an evening in this way.

On the present occasion they had arranged to drive to a well-known hostelry in the north of London, where they could have a private room and every attendance.

They supped without conversing on any but the most ordinary topics of the day.

Then, the colonel having been supplied with wine and cigars, and Mrs. Treherne with coffee, they were left alone.

"Well, colonel, what progress?" she said, flippantly.

"None."

"How so?"

"They refuse every attempt at acquaintance-ship. The wretched little dwarf is perfectly insolent, the father cool, the girl actually supercilious."

And the colonel looked vastly irritated and annoyed.

"Ah, ah!" said Mrs. Treherne, with a laugh, "you like her!"

"She is a very beautiful girl, and your task is not an unpleasant one," he said, stroking his moustache.

"Colonel," said that awfully wicked woman, "I am willing you should do anything to wring his heart and break hers; but when we marry I shall allow no such freaks."

The colonel bowed low, and kissed her hand in a very passionate style.

"And now," she added, after some little circumstances which have no particular connection with this history, "let me tell you some other plans of mine."

"And what are they, beauteous lady?" he said, gallantly.

"In addition to the broad lands of Treherne, I mean to have those of Haddington—in all, fifty thousand a year."

The colonel flushed right up to the roots of his hair.

"Fifty thousand a year!" he exclaimed. "Prodigious! Really, Maria, you are a wonderful woman."

Since she gave him *rendezvous* and *petit soupers*, he called her, as a matter of course, Maria.

"Perhaps I am—but, at all events, I do not mean to be played with, colonel, nor trampled upon either."

The colonel seemed to think that she did not at all look like anyone to be played with.

"I mean to play what the French call *le tout pour le tout*—and have all or none. How advances your little game?"

"Well I don't know. She is a very peculiar girl. Everybody seems to like her."

"Including yourself," sneered Mrs. Treherne.

She knew all about this before, but it was a subject she liked to dwell upon.

The colonel poured out a glass of champagne, looked most fondly in her face, and then kissed her.

She was, or pretended to be, satisfied, and then spoke of their two most disgraceful and infamous plots.

They must go together.

To do this, it was necessary once more to return to the country.

Haddington Hall was not thirty miles from Treherne Place.

While Mrs. Treherne carried out her plot, the Colonel would be free to execute his.

But as there was still a week, he thought he would try at the hotel.

CHAPTER XXX.

A HORRIBLE PLOT.

The —— hotel was large, old-fashioned, with many a dark and gloomy passage.

The rooms were of various sizes, according as they were occupied by families, ladies, or single men.

The clergyman slept on the first floor, at the very end of a very dark passage.

Cornelia slept to the right, Leopold to the left, in two rooms of less size.

The colonel and his man slept on the second floor.

Cornelia's maid, a stout country girl, was very fond indeed of her mistress, and always waited upon her.

It was the custom of the Rev. Mr. Vaughan, not taking supper, to indulge himself in a glass of warm negus at bed-time.

He always sent one also to his daughter.

Cornelia used to take it, to please the nurse or waiting woman, either before going to her room, or when she was in bed.

The colonel watched keenly all their habits, and soon, by the aid of Buster, found them all out.

He determined to make use of his infernal knowledge to destroy and ruin her for ever.

But to do this, the wine-negus must first be drugged.

Nothing, however, is beyond the reach of cunning and villainy backed by money.

Buster contrived to make friends with all the servants.

The port wine-negus was sent upstairs already mixed.

Now, on the night on which the fiendish plot was to be carried out, a whole series of events occurred, which materially interfered with the plans of the colonel.

Cornelia went to the theatre with Leopold, who, knowing the colonel to be at the hotel, relaxed something of his vigilance.

Besides, Maria was incessantly at her brother's house, and this of itself was a good sign.

After the theatre, they had supper; and when, at midnight, Cornelia retired, having sent her maid to bed, Leopold and Mr. Vaughan sat up.

They had commenced a discussion on some point of deep interest to themselves.

They were very warm on the subject, and sat up till about two.

They had, we must confess, several glasses too much of wine.

Mr. Vaughan was certainly, to some extent, under the influence of the generous wine.

Not intoxicated. There is a happy medium between the two extremes, which may not be described as drunkenness.

He went along the passage with a sage look, and passed into his room.

The dwarf, who felt that he was a little advanced in liquor, hastened to conceal himself in his bed room.

His door was ajar.

Surprised, but not suspecting anything, he entered, undressed rapidly, and got into bed.

A warm body met his touch.

There was a woman there; that he could at once tell by the form.

He had been drinking wine, he forgot everything; his vows of chastity, which hitherto had required no very great effort to keep, were violated.

He could not make out who it was.

He had come to bed in the dark, and the person, whoever it was, pretended to be asleep.

Towards morning, also he went off asleep himself.

If he had not done so, he would have heard some one trying the door.

Then they went away.

There were three in the plot: the colonel, the man, and an under-cook.

This girl was a creature of Buster's, but had gone into this atrocious plot with considerable reluctance.

She was herself weak and unchaste, but she pitied the glorious creature.

She knew that Cornelia was the victim of a drug.

Towards daybreak, fully aware that the girl would not as yet be awake, she crept downstairs; and wishing, at all events, to avoid discovery as long as possible, she made use of a key she had in her possession, and entered the room.

She crept cautiously to the bed, and was astonished, on opening the curtains, to recognize the dwarf.

With the energy of a man, she lifted him up, and carried him to his own room.

She began to understand; and, woman like, chuckled over the idea of the colonel having been deceived, and the rightful lover being in his place.

She put him in his bed, and there she left him.

Next day, Cornelia awoke, utterly unconscious that she had passed the line which separates girlhood from womanhood,

Leopold either thought he had been dreaming, or that one of the chambermaids had taken a fancy to him.

Naturally enough, Cornelia was utterly unmoved and unconscious; and all the colonel was aware of was a defeat.

The under-cook utterly refused to have any further to do with the disgraceful and infamous plot.

She had had quite a severe fright enough.

The colonel, who was furious, not only at the utter failure of the whole plot, but at the severe disappointment he had experienced, saw that the affair must be deferred.

He began to see that both he and Mrs. Treherne must defer their little arrangements until they were able to plot together without interference.

The cookmaid declared that if anything were attempted against Cornelia while in that hotel, she would betray him.

And the colonel, with his friend Buster, were, for the time being, quite put out of court.

They did not dare even to threaten revenge.

But they were not going to remain long in town

Sir Thornely had intimated his intention of returning home as soon as possible.

The doctors were unanimously of opinion that all Lady Haddington now required was quiet and country air.

And then, the proud and happy baronet wished his child to be born at Haddington Hall.

It was a whim, but a very pleasant and harmless one.

It is a whim which we believe is shared by most country gentlemen in this country, and by most crowned heads out of it.

And no queen could have been treated with more love or consideration than was Lady Mary Haddington.

The fiendish soul of Maria Treherne treasured up the love and tenderness of the husband as so many more subjects of hate.

There are people who cannot bear to see others happy.

And Mrs. Treherne was, indeed, one of these.

She watched her own brother with a perfectly fiendish cunning, which might, if noticed, have betrayed her.

He somehow or other saw through her leprous soul.

He was coldly polite, nothing more; and when he one day met her with the colonel, passed her as if she had been a stranger.

This inflamed them both with furious rage.

The colonel was a vulgar man, despite his being of a good family. Every family has got its black sheep.

The colonel was one of them.

And this is why he had been sent abroad, to be polished, while he still had a fortune of his own.

But continental travelling had done very little for him.

If there is any peculiar polish to be attained by contact with the more refined inhabitants of foreign cities, the colonel had failed to attain it.

Perhaps this foreign polish, whatever its nature may be, requires a certain smoothness in the surface upon which it is to be spread, and may refuse to adhere to the coarser texture of certain cross-grained woods.

If there is any refining influence in the contemplation of beautiful and sublime scenery, in the sight of perfect and unapproachable works of art, in the sound of music, in the gorgeous colouring of Italian skies, the innocent faces of lovely peasant women; if, we say, there is in all these a refining influence which rarely fails to improve the most ordinary mind, that influence had no effect upon the sullen nature of the colonel.

He returned to England, if possible, a greater boor than he had been when he left his native shores. His dress, which had been before his travels generally chosen for him, was now in the most execrable taste.

He had picked up a coat here, a hat there; a gaudy waistcoat in one city; a pair of jingling spurs, a coloured cravat, and an embroidered smoking-cap in another. Parisian jewellery hung about his waistcoat, and glittered in his shirt front.

The Rue de la Paix and the Palais Royal had been ransacked to find him emeralds and rubies, opals and turquoises, amethysts and sapphires. The fingers of his clumsily-shaped hands were loaded with rings.

His watch-chain was heavy with the useless ornaments hanging to it. "I'll show them that I could buy up the best of 'em," he said sometimes, when he imagined himself not sufficiently admired or respected by the natives of some city through which he passed.

He abused and swore at the innkeepers, in shrill torrents of his native Saxon; and then swore at them again, because they could not understand him.

He blundered and vociferated, declaring that he'd make himself understood, or he'd know the reason why.

He abused the thin German wines; but drank so freely of those vintages as to travel through the whole of the Belgian, Prussian, and Austrian dominions in a state of semi-intoxication.

He yawned at the pictures, and talked aloud in the cathedrals.

He openly showed his contempt for the quiet worshippers kneeling at time-honoured shrines, and jingled his gilt spurs in the holiest recesses of the sacred fanes through which he scampered.

Even the courier shrugged his shoulders, and abandoned his master to his fate.

CHAPTER XXXI.

AT HOME.

"In the country," the colonel reasoned, "if this man dares to treat me thus, I will call him out."

"I am going to marry his sister—he must know me."

But the colonel did not know Marmaduke Haddington. The reader does. He has seen him in the first chapter of this strange narrative.

He was a man of singular determination, but eccentric in the extreme.

His eccentricity will be understood bye-and-bye.

He loved Mary Dawson, and she loved him. But when will the old trite saying cease to be true—that the course of true love never did run smooth.

He was poor, and she was poor.

Now, Marmaduke was proud, and did not like to be beholden for everything to his brother.

His sister-in-law laughed at him.

He ought to know his brother better. He had become acquainted with Leopold, and he too, who at once saw to the very depths of his character, advised him to speak out and abide by his brother's decision.

Marmaduke hesitated.

It was about a fortnight before Lady Haddington expected to be confined.

It was morning.

There was an old-fashioned habit in that house, which might be adopted everywhere.

That was, to take a stroll before breakfast.

Sir Thornley, who, young as he was, was slightly gouty, did, however, always carry out this plan.

Mrs. Treherne, from early association, found it easy to rise early.

The most saturnine observer would have described that garden as an earthly paradise.

There was Lady Haddington leaning on the strong and manly arm of her brother-in-law.

Maria rather supported *her* brother, than was supported by him.

"What a strange thing it is," began Mrs. Treherne, "that Marmaduke should so dislike me?"

"Nonsense, Maria!"

"It is no nonsense. You should have seen him shake hands with me when he first came home."

"My dear Maria," said Sir Thornley, "Marmaduke is rather shy."

"Shy!" laughed Maria, in a sharp, disagreeable, acrid way; "he is not shy with Mary."

"Why should he be, Maria?" said the baronet, rather tartly.

"Brother!"

"I believe there is a mutual affection, but I don't like to interfere."

"What a very peculiar husband!"

"Maria!"

"Thornley!"

"What the devil does the woman mean?"

"That you are very blind and very good," sneered Maria.

And she pointed to where Marmaduke was helping his sister-in-law over a style.

"Maria," said the baronet, stopping short in his walk, and speaking very severely, "I give you half-an-hour to think over this matter, and apologize—if you do not, you must leave my house. How dare you asperse my wife—my brother? Maria, I begin to think you a very bad woman."

And he walked away in a passion.

But the worst of these fiendish and diabolical insinuations is that, despite all you can do, they stick.

Even good Sir Thornley, as he joined his wife and brother, could not help thinking they were very affectionate.

But his manly heart came to his rescue, and he repulsed the idea.

Still, that day and other days, he could not help thinking of what his sister had said.

"A bad woman!" said Maria, aloud. "If I don't convince you that she is bad woman, my name is not Maria Treherne. I would sell my soul to defeat her hopes.

"Would you?" said a voice close to her.

Maria Treherne turned, and saw a smirking face close to her, that she knew she must buy or defy.

If she bought its owner, she might hope to succeed.

If she defied him, she must fail.

"Beckford!" she cried.

"Yes, madam. Why do you hate Lady Haddington?"

"Because, Beckford, she will deprive my son of his inheritance. Why should that woman's child take away the estate of the Haddingtons?"

"Why?"

"Beckford, I know, after what you have heard, I am in your power. You can sell me to my brother—now hark! what is your price to join me, and defeat her?"

"Money, and that which I asked for long ago," he said, with a strange look.

She started back. We knew him as Phineas Bristowe, and he was not very lovable.

"Beckford," she replied, with a look of ineffable scorn, "what was my answer last time?"

"You struck me in the mouth with your riding-whip," he said, coldly,

"And I will do it again."

"You won't."

"How so?"

"If you do, you shall leave the house in an hour," he continued.

"You would——"

"I would expose your plot against her and against Cornelia," he said, very coldly.

She started back.

"What is your price in money?"

"Money alone will not do," he continued.

"But you do not love me?"

"I don't love you as I did; wildly, frantically, with the love an archangel might feel for a fallen angel; but I desire to possess you."

"Why?"

"Because I once said I would."

"And then——"

"I will love you as well as ever, and be your slave, your servant, your drudge."

"And betray me after?" she said, with a strange light in her dark eyes.

"No; I will be your devoted slave for ever."

She held out her hand. The woman was, above all, voluptuous.

And then the colonel was absent; and as the French proverb says, *les absens ont toujours tors*, (the absent are always in the wrong.)

"When?" he asked.

"To-night."

The steward turned away with a smile of rapture.

CHAPTER XXXII.

AT HADDINGTON HALL.

THAT day, Leopold, Mr. Vaughan, and Cornelia came to dinner.

It was the first time that Beckford, *alias* Phineas Bristowe, had seen the mother of Jessie.

He fell in love with her there and then.

He contrived to conceal the fact from Maria.

But the sudden passion was, nevertheless, wild and sincere.

He would have given his soul to call Cornelia his.

She was to stay some days.

Now, Beckford and Alfred Buster were great friends, and had no secrets from one another.

The colonel, who always liked to look after his "dear Maria," was staying at an inn about ten miles off, where, on occasions, Mrs. Treherne visited him.

Beckford had told Buster his love for Maria, when the other revealed his passion for Cornelia.

They then mutually explained.

Beckford had laughed at Buster, but now he clearly understood.

But how could he hope to win any such glorious creature?

She had no weak point like Maria.

Leopold was very happy. His love for Cornelia was boundless; he even reproached himself bitterly for his infidelity to her.

Cornelia was sad and thoughtful.

She was not well.

A rich voluptuous beauty beamed from her eyes.

She spoke little, and scarcely ever addressed Leopold.

She had been drugged; but human nature is human nature. She had a vague memory of that night.

Leopold did not remark her gravity.

That night there was a dance, and as Leopold never indulged in such exercises, he played.

Beckford had been asked to dinner. He always was every quarter-day.

He followed Maria with his eyes for some time. He had dared not even to glance at Cornelia, for fear of betraying himself.

Leopold thought him strangely familiar with Maria; but, bound by a solemn oath, he made no remark.

Maria played the part of injured innocence with him.

She never even allowed him to see that her passion for him was unabated.

But her intense hatred of Cornelia was still the same.

Upon her she would surely be revenged.

It was a strange idea ; but Leopold did not like the looks interchanged between Maria and Beckford that night.

There was a strange meaning in their eyes, as they shook hands.

That night he watched. It was his duty, however painful, to the dead.

His companion, unwittingly, was Marmaduke, who at first was watching him.

When Lord Byron wrote his celebrated "Don Juan," he must have been describing something he himself had experienced.

Some such words might Phineas, who had been drinking, have uttered when he came out in the passage, and, in the dim light from a distant candle, saw a draped figure coming along.

" The ghost stopp'd, menaced, then retired, until
He reach'd the ancient wall, then stood stone still ;
Juan put forth one arm—Eternal powers !
It touch'd no soul, no body, but the wall
On which the moonbeams fell in silvery showers,
Chequer'd with all the tracery of the hall ;
He shudder'd, as no doubt the bravest cowers
When he can't tell what 'tis that doth appal.
How odd, a single hobgoblin's nonentity
Should cause more fear than a whole host's identity.

But still the shade remain'd, the blue eyes glared,
And rather variably for stony death ;
Yet one thing rather good the grave had spared—
The ghost had a remarkably sweet breath,
A straggling curl show'd he had been fair-hair'd ;
A red lip, with two rows of pearls beneath,
Gleam'd forth, as through the casement's ivy shroud
The moon peep'd, just escaped from a grey cloud.

And Juan, puzzled, but still curious, thrust
His other arm forth—Wonder upon wonder !
It press'd upon a hard but glowing bust,
Which beat as if there was a warm heart under ;
He found, as people on most trials must,
That he had made at first a silly blunder,
And that, in his confusion, he had caught
Only the wall, instead of what he sought.

" Why are you here ?" hissed Marmaduke in the ear of the dwarf.

" I am here by my dead brother's orders," replied Leopold.

" Have you seen enough ?"

" No."

" What need you more ?"

" I must see her enter his room, and close the door," replied Leopold.

" And what are your intentions ?" said Marmaduke, when they were in his room smoking cigars.

" I may not say," replied Leopold. " But this I tell you: unless she seeks it, there will be no public exposure."

Marmaduke pressed his hands. They were friends.

CHAPTER XXXIII.

POPPING THE QUESTION.

NEXT day the gravity of Cornelia became such, that, walking as they were in the park, Leopold could not but notice it.

They were in a most secluded spot, and, as they thought, without an eye to watch them.

But there was the double eye of hate and love.

Mrs. Treherne on one side, Beckford on the other.

They were both ignorant that the other was watching.

Guilty wretches as they were, they had arranged a meeting in order finally to deceive Sir Thornley.

Their plot was almost too wicked to be believed.

They hoped to kill the mother and child.

" Cornelia!" said the dwarf, gravely.

" Leopold!"

" Have you repented our engagement ?"

She turned sharply round, and looked him full in the face.

" What makes you think so ?" she said, in husky tones.

" You are so grave and thoughtful," he replied.

" Then, as you speak about it, I will tell you the truth. I have repented our engagement."

" Heavens !" gasped Leopold, starting back as pale as death. " Why ?"

" Because, Leopold, I am unworthy!".

They were close to a bench beneath a spreading oak. They sat down.

Mrs. Treherne glided behind it.

" Unworthy!" said Leopold ; " my dear girl, say rather ——"

" Leopold!" cried Cornelia, solemnly, " as Heaven is my judge, I am innocent, but I am in the way to become a mother !"

Mrs. Treherne smiled infernally. Then the colonel had deceived her.

Leopold sat annihilated, half scornful, half incredulous.

" I am a ruined, lost girl !" she gasped, bursting into tears, " and can never marry. I know not, and yet I have a vague idea that I was drugged and placed in the wrong bed ; and yet—no, I awoke in my own."

A radiance of summer light crossed the countenance of Leopold.

Mrs. Treherne saw it, and began to understand.

" It was at the —— Hotel, the night you sat with father," she sobbed.

Leopold was too happy to speak.

" Cornelia," he said, kneeling at her feet, " you are innocent as a babe unborn. Say no more. What occurred was not your fault. Ask me nothing—make no excuse—but be my bride."

" Leopold !—and reveal my shame to your sister-in-law ? " she gasped.

" My sister-in-law is criminal to the last degree. Let her dare even to look awry at you!" he began.

Mrs. Treherne did not hear this. She had seen Beckford, and had hurried away.

" Oh, Leopold ! Leopold ! will the day never come when you will repent this ?"

" Never ! " and he clasped her wildly, passionately in his arms.

Why did he not tell the truth ?

He was ashamed to confess that he had been even in thought unfaithful.

And so they were again plighted ; the poor girl

too amazed at the other's generosity to be able to express herself.

Leopold was happy beyond all power of expression.

The next day they were married.

By the expenditure of a sum of money which was perfectly fabulous, the ceremony was dated back two months.

The fury of Maria was awful, but she did not dare to speak.

"You have dared to marry this chit, who is not worthy of your brother's wife."

"Did you ever see her go in her night-dress to Beckford's room?" he said, coldly.

She fled in utter consternation.

Then came the other fearful blow.

Beckford walked into the library of Sir Thornley.

He was reading; but anyone could see that he was uncomfortable.

He did not like his wife's familiarity with his brother.

"What is it, Beckford?"

"Sir Thornley," began the villain, who had just got the letter from Mrs. Treherne which Lady Haddington afterwards found.*

"Well?"

"I deeply regret——"

"What?"

"The painful necessity I am under."

"Of what?"

"Leaving your service, Sir Thornley."

"Indeed!—and why?"

"I would rather not say."

Sir Thornley turned deadly pale. The awful sensation of jealousy that came over him, the sense of degradation, was terrible.

"Speak, man! look not so scared. Speak out! or by the heaven above——"

"I really cannot stand quiet by, while my lady ——"

"Scoundrel! liar! ruffian!" he exclaimed, rising.

"Sir Thornley, I am not the man to assert——"

"Give me proofs," cried the infuriated baronet, flying at his throat.

"Come," said Beckford coldly.

Schooled by the demon he obeyed, he had determined to risk all.

The baronet, tottering, followed him to where Marmaduke and Lady Mary were in the picture gallery.

She was at an open window, in an arm-chair.

Marmaduke was playfully kneeling on a foot-stool at her feet.

"And now, my own dear Mary, be generous."

"Marmaduke, be a man."

They were speaking of Mary Dawson. She wished him to speak to his brother; he wanted her.

"Ah, Mary, if you only knew how much I love you!"

"I would do anything for you, Marmy; but do, my dear fellow, recollect that my husband——"

"Is no longer a dupe to the infamous conduct

* See page 5, No. I.

of a woman, who, risen from the dregs—but go! go!" gasped Sir Thornley, striking at his brother. "Go, beggar! outcast! leave my house ere I ring to have you expelled."

Marmaduke, never suspecting the truth, left the house—not without seeing the steward's face, which lived in his memory for years—in company with Mary Dawson, to whom he was soon after married.

Then they went to America.

Lady Haddington was taken ill, and all hopes of an heir to the house of Haddington were at an end.

From that day Sir Thornley never spoke to his wife.

He knew her to be innocent, but he believed that she had loved his brother.

He never would listen to any explanation from his wife.

And so Maria Treherne triumphed.

But not for long.

A fearful retribution was coming on her.

CHAPTER XXXIV.

THE COLONEL.

BUT before we tell how this came about, let us explain the colonel's true position.

In London he was a regular man about town. He had his club, his acquaintances, his debts; of the latter, many.

And his creditors were getting very impatient. He told them of his marriage.

They were pacified, and, for a time, even obliging.

But then he was so fearfully reckless.

One of his largest creditors was a money-lender, named Joe Galpin; a man of whom it might be said that he was everything.

He dabbled in almost everything.

His resources were supposed to be inexhaustible.

This man, after verifying for himself the reality of Mrs. Treherne's fortune, lent him four thousand pounds.

About a month before the marriage-day, which was fixed for the 5th of March, the colonel was in his chambers.

They were very splendid, but very fast.

The colonel was alone. Though overwhelmed with debt; though he had judgments without end against him, still he felt perfectly satisfied with himself.

Was he not going to marry a rich wife, and did not all his creditors know the fact?

Of course he had nothing to fear.

But Colonel Hooper little knew his friend Joe Galpin.

It was breakfast-time. The colonel was luxuriating over the *Times*.

Alfred Buster was bustling about.

A ring came to the door.

Alfred Buster, in the most *nonchalant* way in the world, opened.

Two men, flasby Jews—horrid race!—forced their way in.

Behind, on the staircase, stood Joe Galpin.

THE COLONEL AT HOME.

Alfred Buster knew them at a glance.

"Levy, sir," he said, turning to the astonished colonel.

The colonel gave them one glance, and rose haughtily.

"What is the meaning of this intrusion, sir?" he said.

"Shorry! s'help me," began the first bailiff; "debt and costs, four thousand and forty pounds."

"Where is your rascally employer?" thundered the colonel.

"Outshide."

"Bring him in, and clear out," continued the irate officer, seizing a heavy stick.

Joe Galpin, bowing and scraping, with his hat in his two hands, came in.

"Wish to see me colonel," he said; "very sorry."

"Now, if you dare to say a word until those men are out of my sight, Joe Galpin, I'll kill you."

The Jews grinned a horrid grin; but at a sign from Galpin, they went out.

"Go with them," said the colonel, sternly, addressing Alfred Buster, "and give them what they wish."

The *soi-disant* colonel and Joe Galpin remained alone.

"Now, then, you rascally, contemptible scoundrel, do you intend to explain your meaning?" he began.

"I want my money," said Joe Galpin, doggedly.

"But did you not agree to wait until my marriage?"

"I did."

"Why, then, do you turn round upon me in this way?"

"Colonel, when you have the game all in your hands, don't you make all you can?"

"Of course I do."

"Well, and that is my little game."

"Will you speak out? or, by Heavens, I will strike you."

"I will speak out."

"A good job, if you do."

"I have you in my power, colonel. If I arrest you, most likely your marriage will be broken off. Now, I am willing to let you free, on certain conditions."

"What conditions?"

"You owe me four thousand and forty pounds."

"So it appears."

"Double it, and you shall have it for six months longer"

"Double it—how dare you speak of such a thing?"

"The King's Bench, colonel."

"And suppose I agree to give you eight thousand, you unmitigated rascal, where is your security?"

"Just what I want—I want the widow as security," said Joe Galpin.

"I'll see you — "

"Must have it, colonel."

"Do you think that I am going to expose my affairs to a worldly cunning woman like her?"

"Colonel, you do not seem to me to be so fly as you usually are. All I want is her signature. She need know nothing about it."

The colonel looked him full in the face.

"Joe Galpin, you are a most unmitigated rascal. Eight thousand pounds! How much loose cash have you got about you?"

"Why?"

"Answer me!"

"A thousand pounds."

"Hand it over."

"What for?"

"Do you think that I am going to let you rob me of four thousand pounds, and not have my share of the swag?"

Joe grinned, and drew out the stamped document.

"The money!" said the colonel.

The money-lender placed the notes on the table, and the colonel drew the bill and accepted it.

The signature to the acceptance was *Maria Treherne.*

The gallant colonel had committed forgery. Joe was quite satisfied. He was sure the dear widow would not allow her darling colonel to be transported for life.

He handed the money over to his friend, and,

refusing to play cards, went his way and discharged his followers.

The colonel remained behind, thinking how he would get the bill back again out of the hands of the money-lender.

Joe Galpin went away satisfied that he had done a good stroke of business.

CHAPTER XXXV.

4TH MARCH.

THE marriage of the colonel and Mrs. Treherne had been fixed for the 5th March.

Had she been as clever a woman as even *she* thought herself, nothing could have been better contrived.

Her husband's will was to be read on the 4th.

Mr. and Mrs. Leopold Treherne returned from the Continent on the previous day.

Cornelia's three lovers, the colonel, Alfred Buster, and Phineas Bristowe, were frantic with rage.

Her beauty had developed into something superhuman.

Leopold Treherne went to the house of his father-in-law.

But on the morning of the fourth he came over to Treherne with his wife and Mr. Vaughan.

There was the colonel and Mrs. Treherne, as bold as brass.

They had now no reason for keeping their affection a secret.

Their marriage was, of course, officially announced.

Sir Thornley was too occupied with his own sorrows to come.

Mad with conflicting emotions, he knew not what to do.

Mrs. Treherne was haughtier and more insolent even than usual.

Leopold was very grave and thoughtful, even unto sadness.

"Ladies and gentlemen," he said, "I deeply regret the painful duty which devolves on me."

The colonel turned deadly pale. His teeth actually began to chatter.

Mrs. Treherne curled her lip.

"Pray, Leopold, what does this exordium mean?"

"That I am master of this house, and you are penniless."

Not a soul but started to their feet in pure astonishment.

"D——" said the colonel.

Mrs. Treherne began to feel alarmed.

"Listen," said Leopold.

Mr. Vaughan began to read.

"I, John Smith, commonly called John Treherne, do solemnly confess that I was not born in wedlock. My father was absent in India; and although he travelled as fast as money could enable him to do so, arrived in England too late to marry my mother. I enclose the certificate of my birth, the attested statement of nurse and doctor, and the certificate of my mother's marriage subsequent to my birth. There can be no doubt about the matter.

"I never intended to marry, to the detriment of my brother born in wedlock.

"But I met the beautiful demon whom I call wife.

"On my death-bed, I confessed all to my brother, and his wish was, to let things remain as they were to the world.

"But I made him swear that everything should depend on her own conduct——"

"And that"—she gasped——

"Has been infamous," said Leopold, sternly; "my wife—the colonel—Phineas Beckford."

Mrs. Treherne sank in a chair, to all appearance dead.

"My brother and I broke up the entail," continued Leopold, "so that as everything is left to me, the true state, of the case need not be known to the world.

Mrs. Treherne did not, could not, speak.

The colonel looked as if he had been struck by apoplexy.

It was utter ruin, hopeless and fearful.

Worst of all, the forgery in the hands of Joe Galpin.

"What mean you, sir," gasped Mrs. Treherne, "about not being known to the world?"

"You can preserve the name of Mrs. Treherne, you can reside where you please, and I will take care that your child wants for nothing; but all personal contact must cease."

Mrs. Treherne rose tottering, and, aided by the colonel, left the room.

That night she posted to her brother's house, where she told a very simple story.

She had been deceived into marriage with an impostor, and, with her child, had been turned out of doors.

Sir Thornley was astounded, and all his indignation was poured against the family of the man who had deceived him.

The colonel fled to Boulogne, while Mrs. Treherne raised money to assist him.

Marriage was out of the question.

When Joe Galpin heard the truth, he came to terms, and gave up the bill for a moderate sum.

The colonel had saved something for a rainy day, and with this disappeared.

It was generally supposed that he had gone to America.

Leopold and Cornelia were now perfectly happy.

They had not a single dread or fear in the wide world.

But they little knew two of their enemies—Mrs. Treherne and Phineas Bristowe.

CHAPTER XXXVI.

A CONSPIRACY.

Mrs. TREHERNE had many failings, but her chief were grasping ambition and utter want of chastity.

A frail sister may be very good in all other ways, as it often is caused by extreme good nature and weakness of character; but where it is but one of many faults it helps to make the others much blacker.

Mrs. Treherne had no colonel now to waste her leisure hours upon.

Beckford, whom we have known all along as Phineas Bristowe, was handy to her.

He lived on the estate, and was often at the house.

Since her arrival, the baronet had gladly handed everything over to Maria to manage.

He and his wife never spoke.

Mary Haddington had once or twice gently intimated her wish to have an explanation.

The stern husband had refused.

His life was now almost wholly spent in his library. As the living had disappointed him, he would abide with the dead.

Thus it was that Phineas Beckford and Mrs. Treherne were thrown into contact.

They did what they liked with the large property of the infatuated baronet.

Lady Haddington was no one in the house, which wore a gloomy and painful aspect.

The servants walked about as if they had been undertakers and mutes.

Mrs. Treherne was a stern tyrant, and as all knew that she was entire mistress over everything, she was blindly obeyed.

No one presumed to watch her.

She had organized a system which defeated the attempts of any watchers.

Her apartments were those which had been originally appropriated to Marmaduke, and had their own door of communication with the lawn and grounds.

Mrs. Treherne professed to be very studious, and as everybody retired very early, always took her supper—a meal she was particularly partial to —in her own boudoir.

No sybarite of the Roman empire could have been more particular than was Mrs. Treherne.

She selected a cook herself in London, and even Sir Thornley, who seemed weaned from all earthly vanities, felt the difference.

He made no remark, but he certainly enjoyed his dinner.

Sir Thornley took a great deal of horse exercise, but always late at night.

Now, there were very few evenings that Beckford had not something to say to Mrs Treherne, and, then, he too was excessively fond of dainty suppers.

Thus it was there was nearly always two at the meal.

A trusted servant of Mrs. Treherne's always cleared away.

The cook thought that the man must assist the mistress in making away with so much of his cookery.

And thus for a long time not a suspicion was entertained of what was going on.

"Inherit the estates of Haddington my boy shall," she said one night; "and even, I hope, the title."

"But Marmaduke lives, and is married," said Phineas.

"Lives, and is married! and why do I now hear of this for the first time?" she asked.

"It never occurred to me to mention it. I found it out by mere accident——"

Mrs. Treherne's *eyes* flashed.

"You should have no secrets from me," she said.

"I thought it would only annoy you," he continued. "Marmaduke wrote, announcing his marriage to Mary Dawson, and absolving Lady Haddington. I waylaid the letter, and destroyed it."

"Married!" she mused.

"Yes."

"Where is he?"

"Gone to the backwoods of America. Very likely we shall never see him again."

"Nonsense! A baronetcy and fifteen thousand a year is not usually given up in this way. We can't keep the death of Sir Thornley out of the papers. Rely upon it, when that takes place, he will turn up; but we must be prepared."

"I don't see what we can do."

"If he dares to come home, he must die."

Beckford looked rather sharp at her. It was not very safe to be leagued with such a terrible and violent woman.

"It is very easily said, but not so easily done," he remarked.

"It shall be. I will not fall, now I have learned to reign," she said; "but of that another time. What of Treherne Hall?"

"Mrs. Leopold Treherne is expected shortly to give an heir to the old place."

Mrs. Treherne glared furiously at him.

"That was a very strange marriage," she said, as soon as she had recovered herself.

"Very," said Beckford, with an odd, dry, wicked smile.

"You know something, you wretch," said Mrs. Treherne; "speak, or, by Heavens, you and I will quarrel!"

"I think the heir will follow the marriage very quickly."

"Why, man, they have been married five months."

"Not three."

"Man, what do you mean—have you taken leave of your senses?"

"They were married less than three months ago," repeated Beckford: "I happen to know it. The date which, for some cause or other, they put to the marriage papers must have cost them no end of money. I have examined the book: the interleaving necessary to the fraud is not to be detected."

Mrs. Treherne mused.

"There must be some mystery under all this," she said; and then she added, with a laugh, "poor colonel!"

Then she told the story of the plot at the hotel near Covent Garden.

Beckford smiled.

"Rely upon it they made a blunder, and Leopold slept with her, instead of the colonel."

"Very probably. But I see something looming in the distance, Beckford. Go to town, bully or bribe the girl who was in the plot, and get the truth from her. Then we shall know how we shall have to act."

Phineas bent low to hide his delight. His pride made him the lover of Maria Treherne; but his love for Cornelia was intense.

He started early the next morning, and easily induced the girl to give every detail.

With these he returned to Haddington Hall.

Then these two infamous conspirators devised a scheme for the ruin of the happiness of Leopold Treherne and his wife, such as fiends might have envied them the invention of.

CHAPTER XXXVII.

HADDINGTON HALL.

BUT other events were brewing.

Mrs. Treherne, we have said, had with Beckford the entire management of her brother's affairs.

Now, they both knew that to make secure of fortune, they must take two views of the case.

Either Marmaduke would never turn up, and the son of Mrs. Treherne would inherit the property, or Marmaduke would defeat their machinations.

In this case, their only chance was to save money.

Sir Thornley was so absorbed in his studies, as well as misanthropical, that from him they had nothing to fear.

Living as they did, there were immense savings out of the estate every year.

"Invest them in the funds," said Sir Thornley, impatiently.

And they did, but in the name of Beckford. The crafty villain looked forward to cheating his accomplice.

This lasted some time, when one day a grave and sedate gentleman came down from London, and, calling at the hall, insisted on seeing Sir Thornley Haddington.

Beckford and Mrs. Treherne saw him come.

Sir Thornley was in the library.

Lady Mary was indisposed.

The two conspirators were at breakfast.

"It's Picton, the London solicitor," he said, with chattering teeth.

"Well?"

"He's here for no good. He's solicitor to the chief cashier of the Bank of England."

And Beckford rose, and walked towards his hat.

"Beckford!"

"Maria!"

"Don't be a fool. If my brother has found anything out, you must see him, confess everything, and throw yourself on his mercy. Leave the rest to me; but, whatever you do, betray not me."

"But he will have me arrested."

"No—go to the steward's room. Leave all to me."

Beckford backed out as Mr. Picton entered.

"Pray be seated," said Mrs. Treherne, in her most gracious manner. "Will you take breakfast?"

"I should be most happy," said the lawyer; "but my business with Sir Thornley admits of no delay."

"Let me beg you not to be too hasty," said

the lady, " with my brother. He is in a very poor way. I will have him into breakfast. You can then explain your business by degrees."

The lawyer bowed, and took his seat.

Mrs. Treherne sent in his card to her brother, who in a few minutes came out.

These two men were sincere friends, as well as lawyer and client.

"My dear Picton, who would have thought of seeing you?" said the baronet, with unusual animation.

"Well, my dear Sir Thornley, I regret to say I come on some very unpleasant business."

"How so?"

"Well, I come to unmask a confounded rascal of the name of Beckford, who is feathering his nest pretty handsomely."

"Beckford!" screamed Maria.

"Beckford," said the baronet, faintly; "what, all false?"

"A false hound he is. He has been investing large sums in the three-and-a-half per cents."

"By my order."

"Not twenty thousand pounds in his own name?"

"Is he not in the house?" asked Sir Thornley.

"I believe so," said Mrs. Treherne.

"Let him come in."

"But, first, what do you mean to do?" said the lawyer.

"How so?"

"Recover your money, or hang him?"

"Picton, my health is bad; I hate excitement; let him give up all, and go and be hanged elsewhere."

"As you wish. Now then we will have him in, if you please."

Maria rang, and requested his presence.

Beckford came in with a blanched face, that was pitiful to look at.

"Now, you unmitigated rascal," said the lawyer, hotly—at the same time, pulling out a roll of papers—"you know perfectly well why I am here. Forrester is outside. Sign this transfer of *all* your investments back to your too-indulgent master, or I will put in force the warrant I have for your arrest."

Phineas stood still, annihilated with terror and surprise. They knew all.

He said not a word, but signed the bond mechanically.

"And now," said Sir Thornley Haddington, turning slowly round, "let me never hear of you again. Go away, change your name, disappear; but, if ever you cross my path, beware! You are a wretched scoundrel, ungrateful and bad. Would that I could tear from my heart the thought that this was not all the evil you have done."

Beckford looked humbly on the ground. Maria busied herself with the breakfast.

"You had better go," said Picton, drily.

Beckford hurried away, and left the house by the back stairs.

He had no wish to face the detective.

Thus it was that he took the name of Phineas Bristowe, instead of that of Beckford; choosing, too, a neighbourhood to reside in, which, though close to Haddington Hall, was not inhabited by people who knew him.

He wished to be near Mrs. Treherne, though, of course, now he had to use the utmost caution in all his movements,

They had not done with their infernal plots.

CHAPTER XXXVIII.

A CALUMNY.

A HAPPIER home than Treherne Hall, and a happier couple than Leopold Treherne and his wife, could not be conceived.

It was impossible to think upon the young man, so intellectual and good, as upon a deformed little dwarf.

He was beloved by everybody.

His servants looked up to him with deep respect, and were only too delighted to have such a master in preference to Maria Treherne.

He was as kind and gentle as he was good.

He seldom left his wife, but there were occasions on which he was compelled to do so.

On these occasions she would take strolls in the park alone; always, however, keeping in sight of the house.

What had she to fear, however, from any enemies?

She was herself too good to suspect evil in others, or to understand the deadly nature of the hatred of such women as Maria Treherne.

She little suspected that she had once loved her husband.

She then might have suspected the nature of the hatred felt by Maria Treherne.

There is a fearful hatred which follows upon love, which is difficult to be described.

Still, Cornelia Treherne was at that time, too timorous by nature to venture far.

There was a favourite spot of hers, an elm tree overgrew it, and a rustic seat had been erected by her husband.

Here she would wander when alone, because she knew that her husband would look for her there.

One afternoon she strolled down with a book in her hand.

She was calm and happy as all women should be in the situation in which she was placed.

As she came near the seat, she saw that it was occupied.

To her utter astonishment, she found it occupied by a man.

No one was ever allowed in that division of the park.

But who was this, then, seated so gravely on the seat, deeply occupied in a book?

In truth, he looked like a methodist parson.

And so he was.

An enterprizing builder in a neighbouring town, having spare time on his hands, built a chapel.

But having built his chapel, and having furnished it with an imitation mahogany pulpit, in form very much like a wine-glass, and having further divided it into small square pews, with seats hewn out of the hardest wood he could find in his yard,—having done all this, the builder looked about him for a congregation out of whose pockets could be extracted, in consideration of the privilege of sitting in the hard-seated pews, an emolument which should remunerate the speculator.

After due deliberation, the builder decided that the best way to get a congregation was first to get a preacher.

For a preacher he accordingly sought, and was not long in finding what he wanted, for in three weeks from the completion of the building the denizens of the immediate neighbourhood were startled by hearing the gruff thunder of a bass voice resounding out of the varnished wine-glass.

People went to hear the new preacher at first out of curiosity.

Many went away disgusted before he had finished the rambling discourse, which he called a sermon.

Some were so malicious as to talk about blasphemy, profanity, and vulgarity, and to say that this man should be forbidden to desecrate the Holy Word which he pretended to teach.

But on the other hand, a few servant-girls, a fat tallow-chandler pretty well to-do in the world, and two or three old women with annuities, pronounced the preacher to be a great man, a new light. The servant-girls, indeed, went so far as to call him a ' pious dear.' "

There were, of course, numerous reports set afloat in the neighbourhood of Little Beulah as to where the builder had met with the minister of this deal and plaster tabernacle. Some said he had picked him up in a public-house; others, that he had found him fulfilling the onerous duties of supernumerary at the Victoria Theatre; others, that he had discovered him as a Cheap John.

None of these versions were true. He had found him wanting to hide himself, and his name was Phineas Bristowe.

Mrs. Leopold Treherne knew him, and would have retreated; but he was too quick for her.

"Madame," he said in a whining deprecating way, "I have not dared to come up to your house, though what I have to say is of the deepest importance."

"What can Mr. Beckford have to say to me?" Cornelia spoke rather haughtily.

"Madame, I am a wretched sinner. I have left the service of Sir Thornley, and have found grace enough to assume the calling of a servant of the Lord."

"Indeed!"

"And having done so, I have repented of my sins."

"I am very glad to hear it—but in what way can that concern one who scarcely knows you?"

"In many ways. You knew that Mrs. Treherne hated you."

"I did."

"But you never knew the extremity of her hatred."

"No, I did not. She was a bad, wicked woman."

"She was and is. I deeply regret to say that I was one of the guiltiest of her instruments."

And he bowed his head with deep humiliation.

"In what way?" she said, a strange terror in her soul.

"You remember a certain night at the —— hotel?"

Cornelia sank in the seat, with the most intense horror depicted on her countenance.

"What know you of that night?" she gasped.

"Everything."

"Then, in the name of Heaven, who was the villain?"

"I was the unfortunate wretch," he replied.

She did not kill him, she did not try to touch him; but she became annihilated with horror.

There was something in the man which was peculiarly horrible.

There was scarce a being on the face of the earth whom she would not have selected in preference.

"I never meant to have revealed myself unto you."

"Then why have you done so foul a deed?"

"Because I hear that there is likely to be a child."

"Well, sir," she gasped, "and what then?"

"The child is mine," he said, with a sinister look in his small, green, glassy eyes.

Cornelia bowed her head upon her hands.

What was to be done? Her husband, if told this fatal, horrible and vile secret, would feel an intense hatred for the child; while if she kept the secret, the man, she was quite sure, would trade upon it, and make her very existence a curse.

It was an awful, a terrible position.

What should she do?

"I am ill—overwhelmed—and must return to the house," she said. "I must think. What want you?"

"That you should come to me. The child is mine, surely the mother is also."

What a fearful, vacant look of horror there was on her face just then!

"Go. I must think," she said.

"I will be here to-morrow," he replied, in quiet tones.

"I will come."

And she fled to the house, scarcely able to support herself as she went.

This was an agony beyond everything that she could have imagined. Strangely enough, she never doubted a moment.

How could he know what he did know?

It was too horrible. It was the acme of all the misery she could have imagined possible.

What was she to do?

Tell her husband, she would not—no, rather would she die.

And what became of all that strong maternal love which hitherto had filled her soul?

On reaching the house she went to bed.

A severe sick headache was the immediate consequence of her adventure.

During this time Leopold Treherne returned home, sad, down-hearted, and in mental anguish of mind.

————

CHAPTER XXXIX.

LEOPOLD'S TRIALS.

His adventure had been of a very different character.

He had received an anonymous letter.

Now, there were few men more disposed to treat such documents with contempt.

But this was so essentially circumstantial.

"*You were married on the —— of ——. Now, your certificate bears date —— of ——. This is a punishable offence. Your not having been married on the day certified can be proved. Unless you are married again, the whole matter will be exposed.*"

He wrote to the clergyman.

He had accepted the charge of a foreign mission. What he had done for Leopold was with a good object.

What was to be done?

Marry over again he must, or the fraud in the certificate might invalidate the birth of his future child.

It was a terrible alternative.

But what was his intense horror when, on alluding to the subject to Cornelia, she became frantically delighted!

"I can't help it!" she said, wildly; "I am very glad I am not your wife!"

"But, Cornelia, my dear love, our child ——" he began.

"Our child—ha! ha! ha!" she cried, and turned away.

He could get nothing more out of her.

Then began a new life for Leopold Treherne. He took it into his head that Cornelia had taken a dislike to him on account of his dwarfish stature.

This was a terrible blow to him.

He was determined, however, that he would not endanger the legitimacy of his child.

He would follow the clergyman, and secure from him an attested certificate of her marriage.

And then what should he do?

There was no more happiness in store for him in this world.

But he would, at all events, secure the happiness of his child.

Then a wild, terrible, and mad resolve came into his head.

He made his will, and appointed trustees to manage his property until his child should come of age.

Cornelia was confined to her room, or the carrying out of his plan would have been impossible.

He had four servants on whom he believed he could depend thoroughly.

His scheme would be to die!

That is, not to die really and truely, but to sham death in such a way that he could always return to life when satisfied of his wife's affection.

Into the plot he admitted as counsellors four men—Matthew and John Pierson, Edward Brown, and Fred Watts.

He began by having a severe cold, which confined him to his room.

Cornelia had not as yet recovered from her stupor.

She had had no opportunity of seeing anything of Phineas Bristowe.

He had abstained from persecuting her, because he heard that she really was ill.

But he kept good watch.

There were very few nights that he was not prowling around the park, until he knew every hole and corner of the place.

He soon remarked that the four men we have mentioned seemed to be always together, as if plotting something.

But of this he did not take particular notice, as his thoughts were elsewhere.

At last it seemed to him that Cornelia was taking a very long time to get well.

He determined to effect an entrance to the house.

At no great distance from the mansion was a roadside inn, which Phineas Bristowe made his head-quarters.

Here the domestics of the house were apt to congregate of an evening when not wanted at the hall.

Fred Watts was particularly fond of his pipe and his glass.

He became friendly with Phineas Bristowe, who easily wormed out of him a full description of the house.

He in this way became possessed of the fact as to which room was occupied by Cornelia.

Phineas had not taken any lessons in burglary, but he had been long dwelling on them.

He had purchased some excellent implements of the kind.

It was now his determination to use them. Once in the house, he felt sure that Cornelia would protect him against any fatal consequence.

"Am I not the father of her child?" he said, with a hideous and ghastly grin.

That night, when all in the hall seemed still and quiet, he crept to one of the drawing-room windows that looked out upon the lawn.

He was a ready-witted man, and soon managed the business he had in hand.

The shutters gave way, and then the window was pushed up, and the burglar crept in.

He was in a large room where the lights had been put out.

He moved on to the doorway, and opened it with stealthy caution.

He at once saw that there were still persons up in the house.

They were in the library, and the door had been left ajar.

Phineas Bristowe knew the value of secrets.

He crept up, therefore, and listened attentively.

CHAPTER XL.

A STRANGE PLOT.

There were five men in the room round the table.

They had a glass of wine each—that is, four of them.

"My determination cannot be altered," said Leopold Treherne, who sat at the head of the table.

"But she will be very miserable—that is, missus," said Matthew Pierson, an old retainer of the family.

"If I thought so this would not be done," he said. "But a truce to argument. I have made up my mind. You have sworn solemn oaths, I now call upon you to keep them."

They bowed their heads, drank their glasses of wine, had them refilled, and then sat still.

"These are my final instructions. This night I mean to die!"

Phineas Bristowe almost cried out.

"Oh, master, surely not to night!" said the eldest man.

"Why not?"

"Give us time to prepare our own and other people's minds for the sad event," he said.

"I will do as you wish," replied Leopold, "for you are my friends. I will delay it for some days."

"But how, master, is it to be done?"

"The doctor who has given me the powder will certify my death. Then when I have lain, to all appearance, three days, you will have me placed in the coffin. You understand?"

"I do."

"By the connivance of Roberts, it can then be screwed up with weights, and I can conceal myself in the upper lofts."

Bristowe listened with the most wrapt attention. He could not make it out.

"If I have been deceived, if she upon whom I have cast the riches of my love does repent her marriage, I shall soon know it—and I will remain dead."

"No, master."

"If she does regret me, if I am a weak and silly hypochondriac, I can easily return. I will not have my death bruited abroad more than is absolutely necessary—but I will take all the explanation on myself."

There was a strange light in his eyes which looked like madness.

It was a sort of madness compounded of jealousy, and doubt, and absorbing love.

Men have done such things under these influences as would in any trial have had them declared insane a dozen times over.

But love ever was, and ever will be, the ruling passion of the world, and under its influence men will do things that at other times they never would have thought of.

Leopold Treherne worshipped his wife, but her unexpected and inexplicable estrangement from him had roused his pride and jealousy.

His devoted adherents would have argued with him, but he would not be argued with.

As they had sworn to obey him in all things, they, however, finally acquiesced.

Phineas Bristowe rubbed his hands. He had news for Mrs. Treherne now.

Properly made use of, this mad determination would enable them to carry out all their plans.

But they wanted more details. Again they listened.

"Now, my friends, leave me. I wish to write to her, to explain. She will not have permanently to think me dead, because she might reproach herself—but I wish to let her be free."

The men rose to their feet, and Phineas Bristowe hastily retired.

The dwarf spent the whole night writing.

Phineas hurried away to his inn, and wrote to Mrs. Treherne, in, however, a very enigmatic way.

CHAPTER XLI.

GOOD NEWS.

THE intentions of Leopold Treherne were to write a confession of his one fault, and to follow that up by a history of the reasons which had induced him to become jealous and unhappy.

He would then deposit it in the coffin which would be supposed to contain his remains, and which was to be left in the vault for ten years before it was consigned into the deeper parts of the tomb.

Then he would leave a letter with one of his confidential adherents to be given to Cornelia after the birth of her child.

This would decide him as to returning to life or not.

In the meantime, he could, if he liked, retire in obscurity to the Continent, and there wait her decision.

Mrs. Treherne no sooner received the strange despatch from Phineas, than she pretended sudden business in town, and hurried across country to where her ex-lover resided.

They met at the lonely house in which Phineas Bristowe afterwards resided.

"What is the meaning of all this?" she said, as soon as she had seated herself by a pleasant sea-coal fire.

"That I have made a most extraordinary discovery."

"Useful?"

"Which will enable you, in all probability, to regain Treherne."

"Speak, man! Do not keep me in suspense," she cried.

Phineas Bristowe told the story,

"Ah!" said Mrs. Treherne, drawing a long breath, "at last he too is unhappy. But let him once die—I will take care he does not come to life again."

"But Cornelia and her child?"

"That I leave to you."

"Madame, all these things are very dangerous and risky. You will pay me well if you succeed."

"I will make you a rich man."

Phineas hesitated.

"In what way can Cornelia be disposed of?" he said, after a while.

"That I leave to you."

"Well, I think you may leave it to me," he said, after some delay.

Had she guessed his plan she would certainly not have approved of it.

But then, she did not think him a man likely to devise any large scheme of action.

"But now," she said, "we must act with the

THE BOTTLE OF POISON.

most extreme caution. A slight false step would ruin all."

"I am always at your order. Command, I obey."

"You must visit the ball every night, and watch."

"I will."

"You must somehow secure any letter or will he may leave behind."

"I will do my best"

"You must not fail.

"As soon as he is reported dead, you will take an opportunity of securing his person and——"

"What then?"

"I leave that with you. He must never reappear."

"I like not blood," said Phineas Bristowe, thoughtfully.

"I would the colonel were here."

"Do you, madame?—was he so very successful in what he did?"

"No. But he was bold and brave, and would have done anything to satisfy me."

"I don't know that. But let us not dispute, madame. I will act as is best for us all. Leave the details to me. He shall never annoy you again."

"Will you give me no hint?"

"I suppose you have heard of madhouses?" said Phineas.

"Ha!" cried Mrs. Treherne, "you are a clever fellow."

In her excessive excitement she embraced him warmly.

"What's easier than, on a statement of the truth, to get two doctors to sign?"

"Certainly."

"But to prevent fuss and bother I had better do it secretly."

"Certainly."

"The doctors will have to be heavily feed."

"I can spare two hundred pounds," she said, after some thought.

"That will do. But will you sign the necessary affidavits?"

"I will with you. We must be strictly accomplices."

"Certainly. And now is your ladyship disposed to leave off business and think of pleasure?"

"How so?" she said, with a strange smile.

Phineas threw open a door and showed a brilliantly lighted room, with supper laid out

"You are a very clever fellow," she said, rising, and taking his arm.

There was no pride about Mrs. Treherne, when it suited her purpose.

CHAPTER LXII.
BIRTH OF JESSIE.

CORNELIA continued ill, but was able once more to receive visitors.

Leopold went up.

He was rather cold and distant in his manners, which only served to make her worse.

She had the fatal idea, that now the time of her trial approached he repented.

It had been her earnest wish to have denied him the position of husband until after the birth of the child, but his arguments had prevailed over every scruple.

Now one word from either side would have set every doubt and scruple at rest.

But that word was not spoken.

There was a strange scruple on both sides not to be the first to begin.

And still they conversed in an assumed friendly way.

But each doubted the other.

"You look better, Cornelia," he said.

"I am better. You are not looking well."

"I am not well."

In such unmeaning talk the time passed, when each would have gladly, on the slightest hint from the other, fell into the other's arms and wept for joy.

And then they parted, the doctor and nurse insisting on extreme quiet for her.

Now we have no excuse to offer for Leopold, except that he was raving mad with love and jealousy.

His physical defects made him peculiarly sensitive.

He could not bear the agony of calling that lovely woman his wife, and yet being evidently and clearly displeasing to her.

It was beyond his powers of suffering.

That night, when he took to his bed, he was really ill.

Two of his faithful adherents watched him.

Every arrangement had been made to simulate death.

At great expense, a drug had been procured which would give him for twenty-four hours all the appearance of a man who had died of apoplexy.

Leopold had the drug in his possession.

It was concealed in a bureau between the windows.

But his two watchers were determined he should not take it while in his present state of illness.

But he was equally positive that he would.

He was slightly delirious, and even under this form of madness men are very cunning.

He knew that the two men selected from his four faithful adherents to sit up with him were fond of wine.

He would indulge, and tempt them.

He ordered up two bottles of the strongest port wine in his cellar.

They were placed on the table, and one opened and drank slowly, without ceremony.

For a little while the dwarf chatted freely with the men.

At length he affected to yawn, drew his head under the clothes, and pretended to be asleep.

The men produced a pack of cards.

Leopold ground his teeth with rage.

This would make it longer about. He was perhaps mistaken, for unknown to him they were inveterate gamblers.

And gambling always makes one feverish and thirsty.

They were not long finishing the first bottle.

"Shall we open another?" said one.

"I think not."

"These cards make us devilish hot."

"But this wine is heady."

"One glass!"

"Well, one glass be it—but no more."

Leopold closed his eyes, and chuckled to himself. He knew that once the bottle was opened it would in a very short space of time be finished.

They went on playing cards; gradually they became heated, and glass after glass was poured out.

Leopold ventured to open his eyes. They were both flushed in the face and drowsy.

Soon they began to yawn.

The cards fell out of their hands.

Next moment they slept the heavy sleep of weariness and semi-intoxication.

Then Leopold crept out of bed, moved across the room towards where the bureau was placed, and opened it.

The powder was in a secret drawer he knew full well.

In a moment it was in his hand, and he had got back to the table.

A small quantity of wine remained, with which he mixed the white powder.

He drank it off.

In ten minutes, two sleeping men appeared to be watching a corpse.

It was dawn of day when they awoke.

They rose, rubbed their eyes, and peered at the bed.

A glass convulsively clutched in his left hand aroused their suspicions.

They glanced fearfully at the bureau.

It was open.

"D——! he has done it!" cried one.

"Heaven grant it may not be too much for him!" gasped number two.

Then they gazed wistfully at the calm but deathly pale countenance of their master.

"We must obey him," said one.

"We must," responded the other, very sadly.

"By his directions we are first to send for Apothecary Jones, who will at once say that he is dead."

"Then we must alarm the house."

"Send James—he will suspect nothing. Say our master is worse and we are afraid to trust to ourselves."

"All right. While I am gone, put away the bottles, and wash the glasses out. Be very careful."

And so he went out.

An hour after, the fussy little village doctor came in, examined the patient's eyes, felt for his pulse, and shook his head.

"Not so bad as that," said Matthew, alarmed.

"Worse."

"What do you mean?"

"Dead."

The two men turned deadly pale. Suppose that he was right!

"What is the matter?"

"Apoplexy."

"Indeed."

"Can nothing be done?"

"Post-mortem examination."

The two men exchanged most terrified glances. This was a climax they had little expected.

"Won't that be very unpleasant to the family?" said one.

"What about Mrs. Treherne?" urged the doctor.

"Heavens!" gasped the man, "she knows nothing. How lucky you were here, Doctor Jones."

The apothecary looked pleased.

"I had better," he said, "communicate the circumstance to her myself. How is she?"

"Poorly. There is a nurse in the room."

"I had better see her and judge for myself," added Jones.

He felt the dwarf's pulse once more, and then let fall his hand.

Knowing the ways of the house, he easily found the bed-room occupied by its unfortunate and bereaved mistress.

He knocked gently at the door.

The nurse appeared.

"Lawk, Mr. Jones, is that you? Anything the matter?"

"Something dreadful," he said, with a shake of the head.

"Master ill?"

"Very ill."

"Dying?"

"Worse."

"Dead."

A cry almost unearthly in its tones, a heavy fall, and all was still.

Cornelia—her suspicion excited by this early visit—had risen from her bed, and approached the door.

She had heard every word.

They lifted her up, carried her to bed, and some hours later Jessie was born.

CHAPTER XLIII.

THE FUNERAL.

WHEN Leopold came to himself he was horrified at the fright which his wife had received.

But his somewhat disordered state of brain still continuing, he could not bring himself to confess his deceit.

The orders were given for the funeral to be quite private, in consequence of the precarious state of Mrs. Treherne.

She saw her fatal error in not confiding in her husband.

The only thing that saved her from madness was the little babe by her side.

But still she wept all day, and would not be consoled.

Then the awful preparations for this fearful mockery of death commenced.

To deceive the undertakers, Leopold was compelled to take another dose.

He was screwed down.

But the coffin had holes in its sides and was ventilated.

In ten minutes more it was unscrewed, the body taken out, the documents placed inside with sufficient weight to deceive the bearers.

Then Leopold went up to a suite of rooms in the summit of the house, which had not been used for years, but which had been prepared for him by the confederates.

The funeral was conducted with the utmost privacy, not a stranger was invited, and soon the whole affair became a nine days' wonder.

But to Cornelia it was something so dreadful that she could scarcely realize it to herself.

At the end of a month she was up; but so wan, pale, and sad, that nobody expected her or the child to live.

Then came Phineas to execute his part of the plot upon her.

* * * * *

In the meantime, what had happened?

Leopold confined himself wholly to his room in the day-time, reading, writing, studying, and preparing himself to endure, if necessary, the life of a hermit, to which he thought himself for ever condemned.

The confederates waited upon him attentively.

They allowed him to want for nothing.

But Leopold was as temperate as an anchorite.

At night he would dress himself in a cloak and slouched hat, dive down a back stairs, and creep into the shrubbery.

As this was done long after twelve there was not the slightest danger of detection.

Nobody in that household was out of bed at eleven o'clock.

We except Leopold Treherne, and one or more of his adherents, who had all been retained in the establishment.

His will placed the estate in the hands of trustees ; his wife, a solicitor, and Marmaduke Haddington—the first to have entire sway until his child was of age.

This will ordered the adherents who had aided him to be perpetual charges on the estate.

Had any servant met him at the midnight hour in the gloomy fir-thicket to which he generally confined himself, they would surely have taken him for the ghost of the ex-master of the house.

But there were those who did see him, and who wickedly availed themselves of his folly.

Phineas Bristowe was a master in villainy and rascality.

This is why we have not allowed him to tell his own story.

CHAPTER XLIV.

THE HUNTER'S REST.

At some little distance from Haddington Hall there was a small wayside inn, very much used by the common people, and where not the very best of hours were kept; while its company was not very select.

You had only to enter the house with money, and no more questions were asked.

On a windy, gusty, dark, and gloomy night in the month February, there was very little company in the house all the evening, and about nine, none at all.

But through the red blinds could be seen the cheery light of the fire, attracting the eyes of anyone who came within reach.

And very attractive it is, on a dark and gloomy night, or perhaps on a wet night, when your legs are plastered up to the knees in mud, very cheering, and very jolly, and very pleasant, to see "mine inn" in the distance, and to know that for a consideration you can take your ease, and eat your meat, and drink your cup in comfort.

Teetotalism would reduce us to a level with the worst form of psalm-singing Yankeedom.

Well, mine host of the Hunter's Rest was uneasy.

He was a little, funny, odd man, who was great in the parlour—great anywhere, in fact, except in the eyes of his wife, who looked upon him as very small, and let him see it pretty freely, which Samuel Billow did not consider at all conjugal.

Perhaps it was not, but it's a way nearly all women have, if you let them.

My advice to married men is, read " Katherine and Petruchio," and act accordingly.

Mrs. Billow was a termagant—a woman who, when anybody spoke of the landlord of the Hunter's Rest, laughed.

As to the landlord of the Hunter's Rest, it must be here set down that there was no such thing.

Waiters there were—chambermaids there were—ostlers there were—but landlord there was not.

He was so entirely absorbed in the splendour of his large and dominant spouse, that he had much better have not been at all; for what there was of him was always in the way.

If he gave an order, it was, of course, an insane and utterly impracticable order ; and if by any evil chance, some domestic, unused, perhaps, to the ways of the place, attempted to execute that order, why, there was the whole internal machinery of the Hunter's Rest thrown into confusion for an entire day.

If he received a traveller, he generally gave that traveller such a dismal impression of life in general, and the Hunter's Rest in particular, that nine times out of ten, the dispirited wanderer would depart as soon as his horse had had a mouthful of corn, and a drink of water out of the great trough under the oak tree before the door.   There never were so many highwaymen on any road as on the roads he spoke of ; there never were going to be such storms, as when he discoursed of the weather ; there never were such calamities coming down upon poor Old England as when he talked politics; or such bad harvests about to paralyze the country as when he conversed on agriculture.

But still Samuel Billow, when standing with his back to his own fire, talking to his own guests, was quite another man to Samuel Billow behind the counter, or in the bar-parlour, or in his own bed-room.

The clock struck nine, and Samuel Billow shuddered as he peered out.

Now what did Samuel Billow shudder at ?

He could see nobody coming.

Now if no one came into the house in a few minutes, he would be compelled to sit down to supper alone with his wife, when he knew that all the pent up wrath gathered in business hours would be poured out on him.

When Mrs. Billow was busy, she of course let him alone. Sewing and taking money was her delight.

But if she caught Billow giving trust, then it was that things went cross.

Again Samuel Billow sighed, and was about to turn in, when he heard, yes, a carriage coming swiftly along the road.

But what mattered that to him ?   If it had been a waggon, a cart, a heavy coach, it might have been likely to stop.

But this was a post-chaise, and coming along too with four horses as hard as it could gallop.

What is this ?

They are slackening their speed, they are walking, they have halted at his door.

Here is an event which never happened before in the memory of man.

The clatter and the stoppage roused Mrs. Billow, who pushed her husband ignominiously on one side.

The house, which had been so quiet five minutes before, was now all bustle and confusion. First and foremost, there was worthy Mistress Sarah Billow alternately bewailing, shouting, and scolding at the extremest altitude of her voice. Then there was Samuel, her husband, pale, aghast, and useless, getting feebly into everybody's way, and rapidly sinking beneath the combined

effects of inward stupefaction and universal con-
tumely.

Then there was the ostler, and a rosy-faced
but frightened-looking chambermaid clinging to
the waiter.

There were two postillions, and on the box two
men, as ill-looking ruffians as you would wish to
see even on the stage.

The door opened, and out came first a man of
unpleasant exterior.

But instead of describing him, we will only say
that he was Phineas Bristowe in person.

Then came out a lady closely veiled.

Then two men with a solemn petrified aspect,
who looked like doctors.

And all of these people were about to enter the
house.

They sailed in like people who have been used
to be waited on.

"A private room for four, supper, and the best
wine you have."

Billow staggered back. Not that he had not
wine, and very good—he supplied the rector—but
he had not heard such a command for many a
long day.

"Get out of the way, you fool!" cried Mrs.
Billow, "and let the lady and gentlemen pass.
Sally, open the parlour door."

Sally did as she was told, the ill-looking men
and soon after the postillions entering a large
room, half tap-room, half kitchen, which was
accounted a rare comfortable room in those
parts.

Then everybody went to work with a will to
prepare the supper.

Mrs. Billow could not be taken unawares that
way. Her custom was so good that there was
always a supply of eatables ready.

So on a snow-white cloth a ham, a round of
beef, two roast fowls, with pickles and other con-
diments, were soon laid out.

Then some bottles of beer and wine were placed
at hand, when both landlady and Sally retired at
a sign from Mrs. Treherne.

"Rather jolly this," said Phineas, rubbing
his hands.

They all acquiesced.

"Strange," said Mrs. Billow to herself, "what
can she want here?"

"Who is she?" ventured Samuel, glancing in
an undecided way at his wife.

"Mind your own business, you fool!" said
Mrs. B.

Billow held his tongue, but slily drew himself
a glass of beer, which he equally slily imbibed.

"Havn't seen her for a long time, but knew
her directly," she continued, addressing Sally,
rather than her husband.

Sally said nothing.

"I only saw her once—but I never make
mistakes. It's Mrs. Treherne, she who went
away so strangely when young Mr. Treherne came
into the estate."

"Poor fellow!"

"You may well say that," cried Mrs. Billow,
"we've lost a good man."

This conversation continued some time, but in a
low tone, so as not to catch the ears of the men in
the kitchen.

Meanwhile, other guests began to arrive, and
soon the place was full.

CHAPTER XLV.

THE OUTRAGE.

It was midnight. As a rule, the house was
closed at this time, but neither Mr. nor Mrs.
Billow were very particular if there was plenty of
custom.

That with them was the *sine qua non*.

The guests in the parlour were very quiet.
They conversed in whispers.

At all events, not a sound came through the
doorway.

In the kitchen they were very merry—postillions,
ill-looking ruffians, and strangers.

The clock struck twelve.

Phineas peered out of the parlour.

"Mrs. Billow," he said.

Putting down a glass of grog which she had
intended to imbibe, she hurriedly obeyed the
summons.

Mrs. Billow entered the parlour.

Years after she recollected every detail.

"You are the landlady of this house?"

"Yes."

"Can we stay all night?"

"Lawk, sir, yes!—why didn't you say so
before?—the beds——"

"The beds will not be required, but you can
charge them in the bill."

Mrs. Billow could not help curtseying.

"When do you close?"

"Lawk, sir, we ain't particular!"

"But we are," said Phineas Bristowe, drily.

"About what, sir?"

"Well, the fact is, we expect somebody here
on business, urgent private business, and should
like to be private. If we interrupt your business
we are willing to pay."

Again the astonished Mrs. Billow curtseyed.

"Here are twenty pounds, they are yours if the
house is cleared in ten minutes."

"In five," cried Mrs. Billow, her face now
rubicund in the extreme.

And clutching the money, she hurried out.

"Not a drop more," she said, in her shrill or
criarde voice; "you drunken idle vagabond! I
wonder you ain't ashamed of yourself."

Poor Billow was helping a customer to a pint
of fourpenny.

The man looked astonished.

"I've only come in to drink my pint," he
said; "my horse and cart are at the door."

"Well, make haste. I've got quality in the
house and they must be attended to. Not a drop
more in the kitchen to-night."

In this way, alternately coaxing and threatening, Mrs. Billow contrived at last to clear her
house of all save the postillions and the two ill-
looking fellows.

Then Mrs. Billow coolly sent her servants to
bed, while she and her husband retired to the little

snuggery called the bar-parlour, to be in readiness to serve and watch.

In ten minutes more, Phineas Bristowe came out of the parlour, summoned his two rascally followers, and went out.

Mrs. Billow sat musing in her chair.

She could not make out what was going on, but she was quite sure it was no good.

True, this woman was very fond of money, but then her heart was in the right place after all.

She would not willingly have been mixed up in anything wrong.

What could they be doing?

What fearful mystery did all this conceal? Mrs. Billow could not make out, but she determined to discover.

But we must follow Phineas Bristowe and his bulldogs to the plantation of the dark firs.

That night, as usual, Leopold Treherne, who at this time was decidedly insane on one point—doubt of his glorious wife's love and devotion—came out to wander in the thicket, where he felt sure he was secure from observation.

He could gaze up at the windows of the room which was occupied by his wife and child.

Ought that not to have made him relent?

But the madness of love is something awful; it is pitiless to itself as to everybody else.

He folded his arms, he gazed up at the windows, he sighed deeply; he would have given half his life to have clasped her once more in his arms.

But what had he to do with love, what had he, an ugly dwarf, to say to youth and beauty such as hers?

There is an awful pleasure in lacerating one's own heart, in torturing one's own bosom.

Everybody who is jealous is painfully afraid of being in the wrong.

For this reason the casuistry of the heart is brought to bear on one's self.

Leopold Treherne had moments when he doubted. Then he suffered awfully.

If he were mistaken, and she really loved him, what then?

He had in that case thrust a dagger into her heart.

It was about twenty minutes past twelve, and Leopold, who from sheer loneliness had taken to pipes, seated himself on some timber and began to smoke.

It was, after all, a companion.

Suddenly he heard a footstep and looked up, expecting to see one of his confidential servants, who often came to fetch him.

"What is it?" he said, peevishly.

"Ha! ha!" cried a well-known voice, "so we are not dead after all!"

"Who are you? what mean you? by what right are you here?" gasped Leopold.

"Ha! ha! ha! a dead man talking of rights."

Leopold stood up transfixed with horror.

But his servants were near, he could hail them in a minute, even if all were discovered.

Perhaps even he hoped that all would.

He coolly drew forth a pistol.

"Stand back, man, or you will find a dead man a strange customer to play with," he said.

"Ha! ha! ha!" laughed Phineas, in a loud

hysterical kind of way which puzzled Leopold; "why, if you are not dead you must be mad!"

And he fixed his glaring eyes on the handsome dwarf.

The other dropped his hand as if he had been stung.

"Mad!"

Yes, he saw it all now as clearly as if he had known it all along.

He was mad. He had acted like an infuriated madman—he would confess all at once.

"I daresay my conduct may savour of insanity," he said; "but that is my affair, I have no account to give to you."

Phineas Bristowe saw that he was off his guard, and gave a shrill whistle.

At the same moment a cloak was cast over the face of the dwarf, and he was being carried swiftly along by two powerful men.

A quarter of an hour later Mrs. Billow saw an inanimate bundle carried into the parlour, which was then locked on the inside.

Mrs. Billow bounded from her chair.

In a minute her ear was to the keyhole.

The postillions had retired to a kind of loft-bed, over the stable.

She heard distinctly.

"Ah!" said the panting voice of Leopold Treherne; "I might have expected this. Mrs. Treherne is sure to be the instigator of every villainy.

"Pray sir, who are you?" she said, haughtily.

"You know well, I am Leopold Treherne, the brother of your late husband."

"Ha! ha! ha! Leopold Treherne is dead. Everybody in the county knows that."

And she laid the certificates before the doctors.

"But all the county knows me personally," he replied; "and the purpose for which I feigned death being answered, I shall resume my station in life."

"Doctors, if this be really Leopold Treherne, and he has been feigning death these three months, then is Leopold Treherne mad; but if it be, as I believe, an impostor, then is he equally mad to pretend to be one who is notoriously dead?"

"Certainly," said one doctor.

"Certainly," said number two.

"So you are doctors?" said Leopold, a cold sweat coming out all over his body—for he felt into what hands he had fallen—"and are leagued with this wicked woman, who, because I scorned her love, hates me."

"Ha! ha! ha!" laughed Mrs. Treherne, rather frantically, "do you not at once see that this man is very mad?"

"There can be no doubt of it," said number one.

"Certainly none."

"Gentlemen," said Leopold Treherne, gravely. "I can see through this hideous conspiracy. This woman has feed you well, but I can bribe higher than she can. Name your price."

"Sir," cried the elder of the two doctors, flushing up to the very roots of his hair; "this tone of speaking to professional men is insolent. It is the conduct, however, to be expected from a madman."

And he hastily signed the certificate, in which he was imitated by the other doctor.

Then Leopold Treherne knew that further resistance was useless.

"Woman," he said, coldly, "I am for awhile in the power of a female fiend, who is restrained by no sense of honour or justice, who will, for the sake of revenge, violate every law, divine and human, and even risk her soul. But the day of retribution will - must come! Remember that!"

"Remove him," she said, hoarsely.

"At once," cried Phineas.

"Yes certainly. The carriage waits a hundred yards on the road.

Then the door, from which the horrified and terrified Mrs. Billow had just time to retreat, opened and Leopold, gagged by the experienced attendants, was taken through.

Mrs. Billow had thoughts of a rescue, but then she had hoped that he would cry out, and thus give her an excuse for screaming for assistance.

But he went through the house without a word.

She scarcely knew what to think. In common with the whole country, she knew of the death of Leopold Treherne, and could not make out any object he could have.

It certainly did look very much like madness.

And, then, had not two doctors decided that it was?

And then it was very dangerous to meddle with rich and powerful people.

For the moment Mrs. Treherne was in the ascendant; and with a timidity she deeply regretted in after years, Mrs. Billow said nothing to anyone, but allowed things to take their course.

Towards morning the two doctors, Mrs. Treherne, and Phineas Bristowe left.

Leopold Treherne was an inmate of a madhouse.

The asylum to which he had been taken was one of those most cruel of all establishments where a medical man takes "a few nervous patients," and thus succeeds in evading the law.

If his premises are large enough, he can have a dozen, and, by a little management and contriving, keep himself clear of all inspectors and managers.

Dr. Growler was the man's name, and a very good name it was to represent such a man.

He bowed low as Leopold, quite free from gag or fetters, was ushered into his presence.

"Happy to see you, sir; hope we shall be great friends."

"Sir, if you believe me mad, a very short conversation will convince you otherwise; if you are paid to pretend to believe me mad, anything I can say will have no effect."

"My dear sir, you are a nervous patient, sent here to be cured by your friends. I never get angry with nervous patients; will you snuff, sir?"

"No. Show me my room. At least, as I tell you, I will when released pay well for good treatment; you will let me have every accommodation."

"Certainly—you don't snuff?"

"No, I do not."

He was a stalwart, broad-shouldered fellow, with rather a Jewish nose, black eyes, and a complexion that had grown almost copper-coloured by exposure to all kinds of weather.

He had been a navy surgeon. He wore a three-cornered hat, which was trimmed with tarnished lace, and perched carelessly on one side of his head.

His sleek hair was of a purplish black, and he wore a stiff black beard upon his double chin.

Gold earrings twinkled in his ears, and something very much like a diamond glittered amongst the dingy lace of his ragged shirt frill.

The bronzed, dirty hand with which he held open the box while he addressed Leopold was bedizened by rings, which might have been either copper, or rich barbaric gold.

"I am sorry for that; clears the head wonderfully," he said, tapping his box in the old scientific way.

Leopold made an impatient gesture. He wished to be alone.

He wished to be alone with his own thoughts.

He wished to ask himself if he were really and truly mad?

There were moments when he almost doubted himself.

There is nothing which acts so terribly on the mind as this kind of accusation.

It crushes brain and heart.

The doctor signed to a man to lead him to his chamber.

It had been prepared some days; and as Dr. Growler admitted only first-class patients, who could afford to pay handsomely, it was decently furnished.

Such things had happened as patients recovering.

Then they gave a good account of the house.

The windows, which looked out on a garden, had certainly iron bars; but otherwise there was nothing like a prison look.

And bars are used to keep thieves out at times.

Then they closed the door—it was morning—and informing Leopold that his breakfast would be brought up in a few minutes, he was locked in.

It was an awful sensation, that turning of the key.

And here, to wither and waste for years, we leave the young, the brilliant, the handsome Leopold Treherne.

They did not debar him from books, from paper, from pens and ink.

Doctor Growler liked little trouble, and studious patients were no trouble.

We return to poor Cornelia.

CHAPTER XLVI.

VILLAINY.

PHINEAS knew the great power he had gained over her by the means of the impudent and infamous falsehood which she had so readily believed.

She could not refuse to see him, much as her soul revolted from him.

It was horrible, a painful duty.

Jessie was two months old.

The widowed Mrs. Treherne was seated in the

nursery, with the baby asleep in the cradle at her feet.

Phineas came in, in his stealthy cat-like way, and was close upon her ere she knew it.

"Good afternoon," he said, in his oiliest tones.

"Good afternoon," she replied, so sadly, so humbly, the man must have been a fiend to have deceived her.

"The child looks well."

"Cornelia shuddered fearfully.

"What have you called her?"

"Jessie."

"Jessie what?"

"Jessie Treherne," replied she.

Phineas got up one of his hideous scowls.

"I expect you will be glad to change it."

"How so?" she gasped, in an agony of nameless horror.

"Is it not mine—has not your husband died rather than bear his shame?"

"What!" she shrieked, turning pale and white.

"I tell you the truth. Your husband died——"

"How mean you?—do you dare to come here and tell me that my darling Leopold——"

She could say no more.

"Gave out that he was dead, rather than live."

"Merciful Heavens! will the man drive me mad? Gave out——"

"I speak the truth. Lionel Leopold Treherne lives."

"My God! Is this man deceiving me? But no—no one could be so wicked. It is too dreadful—too horrible."

"It is true. If you will listen to me calmly, I will explain everything."

Cornelia sat down with a terrified and hopeless look, which was terrible to behold.

She was always very beautiful; but sorrow and maternity alters people much.

It was a very fair and girlish face upon which the fitful firelight trembled—now illumining one cheek with a soft red glow—now leaving it in shadow, as the flame shoots up or dies out of the scattered embers on the hearth.

A very fair and girlish face, with delicate features and softly dark-blue eyes, that left a sad shadow in their softness—a shadow as of tears long dried, but not forgotten.

There were pensive lines, too, about the mouth, which did not tell of an entirely happy youth—sorrow and Cornelia had met each other face to face, and had been companions and bed-fellows before. But, in spite of this pensive sadness, which shadowed her beauty, or, perhaps, even by virtue of this sadness, which refines the beauty it shadows, she was a very pretty girl.

It is difficult to think of her as a married woman; there is such an air of extreme youth about her, such a girlish, almost childish timidity in her manner that, as her husband—not too loving or tender a husband at the best of times— is apt to say, it is as difficult to deal with as with a baby, for you never know when she may begin whimpering like a spoilt child as she is.

But Phineas had not a spark of pity in his soul. He was cold, merciless, and selfish, or he must have pitied that poor girl.

For she was nothing else.

"I met your husband. He insulted me grossly, and in my rage I told him that I was the father of your child."

"And what said he?"

"Nothing."

"Go on."

"From that hour he resolved to die rather than live with you. Then he changed his mind, but swore never to enter upon this domain so long as you were in it."

"Merciful Heavens! what he must have suffered."

"He did. But now you know the truth, what do you mean to do?"

"To do? To go forth to the wide world—to beg, rather than except a mouthful of his bread."

"My home is a humble one."

"Sir!"

"I am the father of your child," he said.

"True, true," and she looked him full in the face. "But——"

He lowered his eyes.

"You will be my guest—but, to save appearances, must pass as my wife."

The man was even more covetous than he was lustful.

He knew that by Leopold's will Jessie was still the heiress of Treherne Hall.

Cornelia, after some hesitation, agreed to his terms.

"And now to leave here secretly, without exciting the most remote suspicion," she said.

"When will you go?"

"To-night; as soon as it is dark," she replied.

"I will be outside with a cart," he added.

"I will cross the park, and meet you at the gates."

And so she did, and thus for all these long years were these two parted, a pair made by nature for one another.

But though the villainy of Phineas Bristowe and Mrs. Treherne seems excessive, yet have worse things been done for the love of money by young and old.

This fearful passion, which knows no mercy, and more than love impels one on to crimes, which too often, the world forgives in success.

Louis Napoleon did worse than any of the sanguinary buccaneers of America.

But then he did it on a large scale, and is therefore now a great man and allowed to associate with our good queen.

Such is the policy of states and of men.

Louis demands and obtains applause when a minor villain would be hanged.

But to return to the story of Phineas Bristowe.

We left him in the Canon de Uraldi.

This was not the story he told to Jessie, but one very different.

When he had finished, he looked keenly at Jessie, to see the effect of his narrative upon her.

Her eyes were fixed upon vacancy.

She had guessed at much that he had left untold

She held him in the most unmitigated abhorrence.

"I am dying," he said.

"Yes," she gasped, "you are dying, and well for you is it that such is the case, or I would have killed you."

JESSIE, THE MORMON'S DAUGHTER.

HENRY AND HIS FATHER.

"Why, Jessie?"

"He asks me why—merciful Heavens!" she said, with straining eyes and bated breath; "this man who for all these years has ruthlessly doomed doomed my father and mother to so much endless misery!"

"But I have repented."

"Because you are dying."

"But your father and mother are perfectly happy now."

"Happy, when I am away from them?"

"Jessie, I know the full extent of my error. I know my faults and crimes, but I have confessed. May I not, at least, be absolved?"

He looked so utterly woe-begone, so pale, so gasping, that Jessie relented.

"May Heaven forgive you, as I do!" she at length said.

Phineas Bristowe closed his eyes, clasped his hands, and seemed in prayer.

Jessie and Amy went to the mouth of the valley to look out.

Scarcely had they done so, when four men armed to the teeth dashed across the valley, seized them rudely, placed them on some horses which were on the other side, and turning round a thicket, galloped off.

All was still and silent for a quarter of an hour, when another party came up.

They, too, were in search of Jessie.

They were the Indian, Henry, and the captain, with Jones and Eudora.

They entered the valley, which was still as death.

And death was in the valley.

"Good Heavens!" cried Henry, wildly; "gone again."

"But who lies yonder?" said the captain.

"Phineas Bristowe—dead!" cried Harry.

The Indian fell on his knees, with a wild and strange glance.

He placed his hand upon the other's heart to assure himself of the truth.

"Dead!" he cried; "then am I free. Come to my arms, my boy, for I am Marmaduke Haddington."

Henry looked wildly at him.

"I swore never to reveal my name, my rank, my hopes, until this man was dead. I had intended to kill him—but Heaven's bolt has at last reached him."

Henry, wild with astonishment and delight, fell into his arms.

The captain smiled.

"You knew it," said Henry, with a half-reproachful glance.

The captain nodded.

"Night is falling—my followers will soon be here," said Sir Marmaduke Haddington; "and once my braves upon the track, Jessie shall be found in twenty-four hours. I have two trackers, who will fetch her out of the middle of the Mormon camp."

Eudora gave a deep sigh, but she could not venture to look at Henry.

"During this time you shall become acquainted with my most marvellous and wondrous history."

They then removed to a distance from the body, which they intended burying in the morning, and the wondrous narrative of Marmaduke's life began.

CHAPTER XLVII.

OUT WEST.

WHEN Marmaduke fled his brother's presence, it was under the firm but delusive persuasion that he was angry with him for his proposed marriage with Mary Dawson.

His indignation was boundless, and he determined never again to have anything to do with one who could be so unjust and so unbrotherly.

But what to do he knew not. Money he had very little; and ask any of his unnatural relative, he would not.

His own funds were five hundred pounds—a poor pittance for the younger son of a wealthy baronet. Mary Dawson could add five hundred to this.

They determined to marry, and retire to the United States of America, where, in a border state, they might hope to conquer independence, and even wealth.

A capital of a thousand pounds, well employed, would do more in America than one of ten thousand here, where the rent of land is more than the purchase-money in the Land of Promise.

And the Land of Promise it has been, and will again be, despite the unnatural and fratricidal war which is now being waged over its vast continent.

Marmaduke Haddington was the more resolved on this course of action, that he wished to place the width of the ocean between himself and his unnatural brother.

So they were married in a quiet way, and about a month after sailed for the distant shores of America, to swell the many millions which are destined to carry the flood of empire over the whole of that vast continent from north to south, from east to west.

They reached New York in safety, but, without pausing to waste their money or time in this spendthrift city, made at once for the interior.

Out West was Marmaduke's idea—out West, where, without leaving a trace of the past, he might become a thorough citizen of the new land.

Out West, to the very uttermost verge of civilization.

The spot selected by him was a small clearing on the banks of a river, which he bought for a song of an old man, who, finding his neighbours closing up rapidly around him, was discontented, and wanted to go further West.

When the young couple reached the outskirts of civilization it was autumn.

The forest in autumn still bears its full frondage; the leaves resemble flowers, so bright are their hues; they are red, and yellow, and brown. The woods are warm and glorious now, and the birds flutter among the laden branches. The eye wanders delighted down long vistas, and over sunlit glades. It is caught by the flashing of gaudy plumage, the golden green of the paroquet, the blue of the jay, and the orange wing of the oride. The red-bird flutters lower down in the coppice of green pawpays, or amidst the amber leaflets of the beechen thicket. Hundreds of tiny wings flit through the openings, twinkling in the sun like the glancing of gems.

They took with them a sandy-haired Irish girl, whom they had picked up at New York, before she had got inoculated with that dislike to domestic service which is natural in a rising country, especially under a republican form of government.

They also succeeded in securing the services for one year of a powerful youth, who, though uncouth and rough in his manner, could use his axe with vigour, and, indeed, do any amount of rough work.

There was a miserable old shanty on the farm, which Marmaduke turned into a pigsty, as soon as he had erected a more fitting habitation for himself and wife, in the shape of a log-hut.

It was composed of two rooms—one a common room, in which the Irish girl slept at night; and an inner room, occupied by the young couple.

Hans slept in a barn, which was hastily run up on the little estate.

For a whole year did Marmaduke labour assiduously at his farm, until it began to assume a most pleasing appearance.

There were flocks and herds, and meadows quite

delightful to gaze on, almost reminding one of Old England.

Hans, who was a German, instead of leaving had hired himself for a year or two longer, until, in fact, he could stock a little farm himself, when he would marry the Irish girl, and retire.

A babe had been born unto Marmaduke—Henry, the hero of this narrative.

Was Marmaduke happy?

In a certain way he was—happy in the possession of a fine and rising property—of a loving wife and a child; but still restless and dissatisfied in another way.

He had been born for a life of action, and had followed it for some time, until love subdued him.

But as he gazed out upon the distant plains on the other side of the river, he would often sigh.

Hunting was his only amusement, but in his neighbourhood, both as an amusement and occupation, it was tame.

The approach of civilization had driven away all the larger game.

He longed to be away over those wild and savage deserts which lay beyond, under the setting sun.

He wished to do battle on the illimitable great prairie desert, where the earth is no longer level, but treeless and verdant as ever. Its surface exhibits a succession of parallel undulations, here and there swelling into smooth round hills. It is covered with a soft turf of brilliant greenness. These undulations remind one of the ocean after a mighty storm, when the crisp foam has died upon the waves, and the big swell comes bowling in. They look as though they had once been such waves, that by an omnipotent mandate had been transformed to earth, and suddenly stood still. This is the rolling prairie. Or he would visit the wild Rocky Mountains, where above, below, and around, are mountains piled on mountains in chaotic confusion. Some are bald and bleak, others exhibit traces of vegetation in the dark needles of the pine and cedar, whose stunted forms half grow, half hang from the cliffs. Here, a cone-shaped peak soars up till it is lost in snow and clouds. There, a ridge elevates its sharp outline against the sky, while along its sides lie huge boulders of granite, as though they had been hurled from the hands of Titan's giants!

A fearful monster, the grizzly bear, drags his body along the high ridges, the carcajou squats upon the projecting rock, awaiting the elk that must pass to the water below; and the bighorn bounds from crag to crag in search of his shy mate; along the pine branch the bald buzzard whets his filthy beak; and the war eagle, soaring over all, cuts sharply against the blue field of the heavens.

Such were his thoughts day after day as, leaning on his rifle, he gazed at the distant horizon, and sighed as he turned to shoot wild turkeys and racoons in the fertile bottoms of his own neighbourhood.

CHAPTER XLVIII.

REGRETS.

"MARMADUKE," said Mary, when the child was two months old, and she was walking with him in their orchard, that began to spring up in earnest, "why so sad and thoughtful?"

"Sad and thoughtful?" he said, with a start.

"Yes, my dear—you have got something on your mind, and if you don't tell me, I shall think that you have ceased to love me, and repent your foolish choice."

"Repent, my darling?" said Marmaduke, with a smile of sincere affection; "never!"

"Then why sad?"

"I am not sad; but you must know, Mary, what a dissatisfied being a man is. I am tired of steady work, and long for a roam over yonder desert in search of the deer, the buffalo, and the bear."

"Is that all?" she said, with a smile.

"All."

"And why have you never spoken before?" she continued.

"Because I could not leave you—even now."

"Marmaduke, a man should never be tied to his wife's apron-string. I wish you had selected some quieter occupation; but if you must do something more than home work, do not let me prevent you. In your absence I will take care of home."

His eyes flashed the delight he felt, and after thanking her warmly, he began his preparations.

He secured an excellent horse, of which he had now many, and took with him such provisions as were absolutely necessary, trusting to his powers as a hunter to provide himself with the rest.

He took a flask of brandy, and an ample supply of powder and ball.

His dress consisted of a hunting shirt of dressed deerskin. It was a garment more after the style of an ancient tunic than anything I can think of. It was of a light yellow colour, beautifully stitched and embroidered, and the cape, for it has a short cape, was fringed by tags cut out of the leather itself. The skirt also bordered by a similar fringe, and hung full and low. A pair of savers of scarlet cloth covered his limbs to the thighs, and under these were strong jean pantaloons, heavy boots, and big brass spurs. A coloured cotton shirt, a blue neck-tie, and a broad-brimmed guayaquil hat, completed the articles of his everyday dress. Behind him on the coutle of his saddle might be observed a bright red object folded into a cylindrical form. That was his mackinaw, a great favourite, for it made his bed by night, and his great-coat on other occasions. There was a small slit in the middle of it through which to thrust his head in cold or rainy weather; and so he was thus covered to the ankles.

It took several days and one or two journeys to the settlements before he was provided with all he required, and then he started amidst the cheers of his servants—he had now two negroes added to his establishment—and the smiles of his wife, changed to tears as soon as his back was turned.

But she knew his strange impulsive nature.

Wandering habits acquired in youth are not easily got rid of, and this Mary Haddington knew well.

But the love he had suddenly felt for her had been the means of temporarily stifling such desires, but they had returned afterwards with redoubled force.

She had seen this with great pain and sincere regret, but had at once determined to make the best of it.

Silent brooding over such wishes she knew to be extremely injurious.

It is such monomanias that often drive men mad.

It certainly was with something like pain that Mary observed how rejoiced the young husband was at the prospect of a solitary journey.

But it could not be helped.

He had caught the prairie fever.

I feel it now! Whilst I am penning these memories my fingers twitch to grasp the reins, my knees quiver to press the sides of my noble horse, and wildly wander over the verdant billows of the prairie sea.

It is useless contending against its influence. It will over-master the wisest and the most reserved of men.

And Marmaduke, though a good man and a clever man, was not wise with the wisdom of common sense.

But we must follow him in his adventurous career, and then explain how it is we suddenly find him in England with his boy and without his wife.

He crossed the river by means of a well-known ford, and then taking the sun for his guide, rode slowly along the mingled plains and woods which stretched out before him for miles illimitable.

That first day he did not seek adventures, as the hunters of the district had pretty well used up that region; but made the best of his way in the direction of the big timber.

His horse was a good one, and he might have made great progress, but it was not his wish to strain him the first day.

He might want him either for the exciting chase of the buffalo, or to escape the clutches of the more formidable Indians.

That night he halted by a cluster of willow trees, hoppled his horse, and made a small camp fire.

Large fires are always dangerous on the prairies, and always betray the inexperienced hunter.

Marmaduke was by nature of a wakeful disposition, so when he had supped, smoked his pipe, and looked around at the growing gloom, he wrapped himself in his blanket without much fear of being surprised by Indians.

His hearing was so keen, and his sleep so light, the slightest sound would have waked him.

But not being disturbed, and the day having been really a very tiring one, he slept the whole night, but woke at the very earliest sign of dawn.

That day was the first of his white ones; he was eminently successful.

While riding along, he observed a fringed head disappear behind a swell in the prairie.

He struck immediately for the spot where he had seen the object.

It appeared only half-a-mile distant, but was in reality much farther, a common illusion in the crystal atmosphere of these upland regions.

A ridge crossed the plain from east to west. A thicket of cactus covered part of the summit. Towards this thicket he directed himself.

Then he dismounted, and led his horse to a bush, and then crept cautiously through the cactus leaves towards the point where he fancied he had seen the game.

His labour was soon rewarded by the sight of two beautiful antelopes quietly grazing.

The wind was from them to him.

They were on a smooth, grassy slope, out of gun shot.

But there were numerous bushes between him and them.

He stooped on his knees and began to crawl.

In this way, by the exercise of marvellous patience, he came within shot.

His rifle hung at his saddle bow; he had now a double-barrelled English gun.

When he found himself within proper distance he took steady aim and fired.

The animal leaped into the air and fell lifeless. The buck it was which had fallen.

But the doe refused to move.

With something like a feeling of regret, Marmaduke shot the little fond animal, which would not stir from its companion's side.

There are drawbacks to the otherwise exhilarating and noble occupation of the sportsman.

But the deed was done, and before an hour was over Marmaduke was enjoying a meal with a zeal only known to the hunter.

For many days this success continued, and the young Englishman knew the wild delight of a prairie life. He shot buffaloes, turkeys, and cayote; but all this has little to do with our narrative.

We must hasten on, then, to events more immediately connected with our story.

CHAPTER XLIX.

A WONDERFUL ADVENTURE.

MARMADUKE had been out a fortnight, and the fever was on him still.

On! on! he went always following the setting sun, and with unvarying good fortune.

Game was plenty, water was abundant, and not the faintest trace of Indians had been seen.

But Marmaduke was not wearied of this life. He often thought of his happy home, and his wife and child, but still the excitement of this life was too much for him.

He could no more resist it than the confirmed drunkard can repel intoxication.

On! on! along that mysterious pathway which, ever moving westward, seems to belt the world.

At length the prairie grew more and more arid, and less fertile.

He was approaching a part which is so barren and destitute of water as to be avoided, it is said, even by the birds.

But Marmaduke was not repelled.

He determined to try the journey.

He had a stout horse, well fed and not very much over-worked.

He had food, and he had a good barrel of water, enough to last a man many days.

He filled it at a stream, gave his horse a good feed, made up a bundle of grass, put it on the crupper, and started.

Many a traveller has described this region, as the desert of desolation and death. One of the latest says, truly, it should be called the "Journey of Death."

Few travel far without discovering its desolate character.

Scattered along the path are the bones of many animals. There are human bones too.

That white rounded mass, with its grinning rows of serrated teeth, is a human skull.

It lies beside the skeleton of a horse, for horse and rider have fallen together, and the wolves have stripped them at the same time.

They have dropped down on their thirsty track, and perished in despair, although water, had they known it, was within reach of another effort.

There is the skeleton of a mule, with the alpajera still buckled around it, and an old blanket, flapped and tossed by every whistling of the bitter wind.

Again we see evidence of human misery and woe. Here is a bruised and crushed canteen, the fragments of a glass bottle, an old hat, a piece of saddle cloth, a stirrup red with rust, a broken strap, with many such like symbols, which, strewed along the path, speak a melancholy and foreboding language.

But such are the common characteristics of not only the great prairie waterless wilderness, but of the desert.

Nothing is wanting to transform these vast solitudes into fertile fields but water.

Irrigated, they would be rich and valuable plains.

Will it ever be done?

Yes. If the progress of the human race requires it, there is not a square inch of earth but will be made suitable for cultivation.

Marmaduke almost hesitated as he saw the nature of the ground he was travelling over.

But his was a brave and heroic nature. He was of the stuff of which conquerors and discoverers are made.

On! on! at rather a more rapid pace than he had hitherto adopted, in order to cross that arid plain, but it is not to be done in a day.

When night fell there was not a visible sign of tree or stream. All was desolation and woe.

Halting, the horse received his bundle of grass and a good measure of corn, which had been kept back for some such emergency.

Then Marmaduke collected together a number of bones of horses and cattle, with which and some parched shrubs he made a fire.

This is a very common practice.

A small fire of wood is made, a beast killed, its bones scraped and put on the fire, and the meat cooked upon it.

The air was chill, and Marmaduke was glad of a fire.

He had not much fear that any Indians would be attracted to him in that awful shadow of the Valley of Death.

He, therefore, collected everything he could to increase its volume, and at last seated himself beside it to enjoy his meal of jerked meat, hard biscuit, and water.

As he did so, his horse snorted and stood still, as a faint moan or sigh came to his ears.

Marmaduke withdrew from the shadow of the fire, and gazed around.

He could see nothing.

Then a faint and agonising cry, or rather sigh, came to his ears.

He looked in the direction, and saw something dark crawling along the plain.

Clutching his rifle, he hastened in its direction, and soon saw that it was a man crawling on his hands and knees, in an attitude not of menace, but of extreme suffering.

"Who goes there?" said Marmaduke, sternly, for he saw at once that it was an Indian, and knew their tricks and devilries.

"Brudder—water!" said a faint voice.

Water! the chief care, the ever present solicitude, the divinity to be worshipped by the voyager of the prairie.

Hunger he can stifle so long as a patch of his leathern garments hangs to him. Should game not appear, he can trap the marmot, catch the lizard, and gather the prairie crickets. He knows every root and seed that will sustain life. Give him water, and he will live and struggle on. He will, in time, crawl out of the desert. Without this, he may chew the leaden bullet, or the pebble of chalcedony; he may split the spheroid cactus, and open the intestines of the butchered buffalo, but in the end he must die. Without water, even in the midst of plenty, plenty of food, he must die. Ah! you know not thirst. It is a fearful thing. In the wild western desert it is the thirst that kills.

Marmaduke rushed back to the camp, filled a leathern cup with water, dashed a little brandy into it, and hastened back to where the Indian, now endeavouring to resume the stoicism of his character, sat up, without moving a muscle.

But he drained the water as only a famished, thirsty, dying wretch can.

"Ugh! good!" he said, drawing a long breath.

"And now get up," said Marmaduke.

"Leg broke," replied the Indian, gravely.

Marmaduke then understood the full extent of the misfortune which had befallen the unfortunate warrior.

He had, as he afterwards explained, been riding alone across the plain, when his horse tripping in a small hole, he fell to the ground, the horse breaking two legs, and he himself being stunned, and his leg apparently broke.

He had neither food nor water.

With great self-possession, he at once killed the horse, and seating himself near it, prepared to defend it against the turkey buzzard.

The pain he endured was intolerable, and thirst supervened.

At first the blood of the horse sufficed him.

But that failed him the second day.

Then for forty-eight hours he suffered the tortures of Pandemonium.

He could not eat. His throat was swelled and parched.

Then he laid himself down to die.

He would have committed suicide, but that is contrary to the creed of an Indian.

So he waited, with the agony of a brave man, the supreme moment.

Then he saw a flame twinkle in the distance, and knew that a white or redskin hunter was on the plain.

Then he resolved either to die in a struggle, or obtain food and water.

With this view, despite his weakness, despite the extreme pain and suffering he endured, he began to crawl towards the camp.

He had drawn his scalping-knife from his belt to be prepared for the worst.

He was, indeed, faithful unto death.

The unexpected conduct of Henry's father did away with the necessity for any further struggle.

He took him in his arms to the camp, and there again refreshed him with water, after which he gave him food.

It was like raising a man from the dead.

Another day, and the vultures and cawloe would have disputed for his carcase.

Marmaduke then next examined the Indian's foot, which, being something of a surgeon, he declared to be violently sprained, but not broken.

The Indian gave a guttural grunt of delight. He was a warrior once more.

They were seated beside one another at the fire. The Redskin appeared to be wonderfully revived, not only physically, but morally.

Escape from what appeared to be a slow, certain, and horrible death, was enough to produce a revulsion of feeling.

Then Marmaduke, who was in everything now a backwoodsman, loaded a pipe and handed it to the brave.

"Ugh!" said the other, in a deep guttural tone; and whiffed away with great delight.

There was dead silence for some moments.

"Brother," said the Indian, gravely, taking his hand, "the Manitou sent you to save me. Never, while the Wild-cat has breath, will you want a friend. I have spoken."

And he cast himself on the ground to sleep the first sleep which he had enjoyed since his accident.

It lasted over twelve hours, at the expiration of which time he awoke, and found Marmaduke waiting impatiently.

The Indian cast an upward look at the sun, and gave an expressive grunt at his own negligence.

He would have risen, but his foot rendered this impossible.

"Another day," he said, "and I shall walk."

"Not another hour," replied Marmaduke, tapping his water-barrel; "one drink, and we have no water."

The Indian shuddered; he had had one taste of what thirst really was, and that was enough.

"Leave me, good white man," he said, "you have already done too much."

"If I do," said Marmaduke, heartily, "may I be ——! Do you know the way?"

"The Indians' wigwam is not far off."

"Mount," said Marmaduke, bringing up the sleek and well-fed horse.

The Indian stared. He could scarcely believe his eyes. Marmaduke studied him attentively.

He was a man of about thirty years of age, and not much under six feet high. He was admirably proportioned, as are most of the genuine Indians of the mountains.

His features were somewhat Roman in type, and his fine forehead, aquiline nose, and broad jawbone, gave him the appearance of shrewd ability, as well as firmness and energy.

He wore a fancy hunting-shirt, leggings, and moccassins, but of a superior quality to those of ordinary Indian braves.

The shirt was made from the skin of the red-doe, bleached, and made remarkably supple.

The breast was copiously adorned with stained porcupine quills, while the sleeves were similarly ornamented, and the cape and skirts trimmed with the soft, snow-white fur of the ermine.

A row of skins of this animal hung from the skirt-border; while his hair, black, glossy, and luxuriant, hung in a flood down his back.

Marmaduke thought that he had seldom seen so splendid a specimen of manhood in the whole course of his travels. He was the true lord of the forest and plain before contaminated by traders and whiskey.

"Ugh!" he said, as he mounted.

Then, however, he requested to be led away to where his gun and other weapons had been left.

"Go," replied Marmaduke.

The Indian chief looked at him with admiration, and then galloped off, picked up his arms without alighting, and rode slowly back.

"No think Redskin run away?" he said, with a musical laugh.

"I did my duty to you as a man," replied Marmaduke, "and I expected you to do yours."

The Indian bowed gracefully, and then away they went in a perfect bee-line towards the distant mountains.

About two hours after midday they came upon a small oasis, where was green grass, three trees, and a muddy spring of water.

They halted, allowed the horse to crop his fill, and themselves again took refreshments.

Marmaduke again bared the Indian's foot, bathed it, and wrapped it in a bandage made from a pocket handkerchief.

The Wild-cat allowed him to do it, with a grateful and pleased glance.

There was, indeed, an eloquence in his eye.

Then by great exertion he contrived to get himself upright against a tree.

"How many hours ere we reach your wigwam?" asked Marmaduke.

"When the sun sets we shall be at home."

As Henry's father spoke he fed the noble steed he loved so well with the last remnant of the corn, which, with the grass he had been cropping, was enough to imbue him with renewed vigour.

Wild-cat then, assisted by Marmaduke, climbed to the saddle.

"Ugh!" he cried, as he did so, "mount, pale-face—mount."

His voice was so commanding that Marmaduke obeyed, and not until the gallant beast was flying over the plain in the direction of the distant mountains did he see that a whole cloud of mounted Comanche warriors were in pursuit.

It was a dreadful event, but it cemented the friendship of these two men in all perpetuity.

The Indian, with that splendid steed, would have easily escaped had he abandoned the long-knife pale-face.

But he was of the true-born gentlemen, the men of honour, who would rather die than do a dishonourable action.

Away! away! over that stony plain they sped at a fearful rate.

The horse was good and strong, and bore his double weight with an ease which was only explained by the gentle way in which he had been used during the journey.

But still it was a race for life, and though the distant sound of the war whoop showed that the Indians were a long way behind, still, in the end, they must overcome a horse so heavily laden.

"Pale-face," said the Indian, suddenly, in a stern whisper, "if you die I die. Can you trust me?"

"With my life!"

The Indian then in a few words explained that in ten minutes they would be behind a clump of cotton-wood, and near a small river. He wished Marmaduke to tumble off, hide, and await his return; which, as soon as the horse had his lightened load, would be easy.

Marmaduke required no twice telling.

He glanced back, however, until a turn of the trail hid the pursuing Indians from his sight, when he slid off the horse, and crawled into the bush.

He had scarcely done so when a cloud of cavalry came dashing past; he and they just seeing the flying horse's tail waving in the mouth of a canon.

The pursuers halted. To enter that canon was to enter an enemy's country, so that this helter-skelter mode of action would no longer do.

They sent forward scouts, moved with more caution, and entered the canon in military array.

Marmaduke kept close within the small thicket of bushes, waiting.

An hour passed; and then out of the canon came pouring the Indians—first one, then two, and then the whole body in the utmost confusion.

Shots were fired, arrows whistled, and then a vast and overpowering force rushed forth in their rear, chasing them like chaff before the wind.

The whole passed before Marmaduke's eyes like a dream; and then all he saw was one solitary horseman, who came straight for the bush with a magnificent led horse and a skin full of water, which the other freely partook of.

Then he mounted and watched the chase, which did not continue long, as they were fearful to be led into some dangerous ambush.

CHAPTER L.

VISITORS.

MEANWHILE, how had it sped with Mary Haddington and her babe?

For some days she supported the absence of her husband with a kind of calm resignation, which was painful to behold.

He had gone terribly against her will.

But she knew him so well as to fear a disordered state of mind if she did not compel him to follow his bent.

But as the wind whistled at night over the housetop, and Mary sat cradling her child, a shudder would pervade her frame.

And then a fortnight passed, and not a sign.

Mary began to be seriously alarmed.

She could scarcely believe this absence to be altogether voluntary.

She knew not the insatiable love of adventure which warms the bosom of the hunter.

She grew thin, and pale, and anxious.

She tried to keep her spirits up as much as possible, but it was a vain attempt.

The Irish girl who was to be married to Hans was her only consolation.

She could, at all events, talk to her of the departed.

Her household now consisted of Eliza, Hans, and two other hired hands, with some half a dozen negroes—not slaves, but well-paid field hands.

They lived in their own huts, adjacent to the house.

One evening, Eliza was nursing the baby, while Mary—desolate and hopeless—began to pen an epistle to her sister-in-law.

She felt an irresistible desire to pour out her sorrows to some one.

Then a knock came to the door. It was Hans. Three strangers—gentlemen on horseback—wished hospitality for the night.

The matter was unpleasant, but could not be avoided.

Hospitality is a necessity of this life, where there are no inns, and where houses and dwellings are so far apart.

"Ask them in," said Mary, "and then come and replenish the fire, Hans."

The men came in. They were respectably dressed, but ill-favoured.

They had evidently travelled far; and, in their haste to reach a resting-place, had not spared their horses.

Neither had they spared the bottle.

They were none of them quite sober, but Mary was too little experienced in these matters to notice this.

"We are sorry to intrude," said the eldest of the three, "but we have travelled many hours without food."

"You shall have all you need," replied Mary, quietly; "but I can offer you only this room."

"It will do amply."

"Hans," she continued, as the German entered, "let Phœbe stir herself and put supper on the table. Sit down, Eliza; I will give the gentlemen some wine."

She turned her back and went out. The three men—one about forty, another thirty, and the third not more than one and twenty—exchanged glances.

"Fine!" whispered the eldest.

"Scrumptious!" said the second.

"Divine! and wine, too!" said the youth, smacking his lips. "They must be rich."

Mary soon re-entered. They had changed the subject, and were chatting gaily.

The youngest member of the little party, and who was decidedly the most sober of the three, lounged with his back to the fire, and his elbow leaning on the mantelpiece; and was in the midst of some anecdote he was telling as Mrs. Haddington entered the room. His flashing black eyes, and his small white teeth, which glittered as he spoke, lit up his face; which, in spite of his evident youth, was wan and haggard—the face of a man prematurely old from excitement and dissipation—the hand of time having, during the last few years, drawn many a wrinkle about his restless eyes and determined mouth.

Heaven knows what there was in the appearance of either of the party to overawe or agitate the worthy mistress of the house; but, certainly, a faint and dusky pallor crept over Mary's face as she set spirits and glasses upon the table.

She seemed nervous and uneasy under the strange dazzle of this man's black eyes. They were not ordinary eyes; indeed, there was something in them that the physiognomists of to-day would have set themselves industriously to work to define and explain.

They were not only restless; but there was a look in them almost of terror—not of a terror of to-day or yesterday, but of some dim, far-away time too remote for memory—some nervous shock received long before the mind had power to note its force, but which had left its lasting seal upon one feature of the face.

"I have ordered supper," she said, in a somewhat timid way, "and have told my people to attend to you. Is there anything else you require?"

"Nothing," replied the young man, fixing his eyes on her all the while, "except your company."

"I am sorry to say," she said, "that I am unwell. My child needs all my services. Come, Eliza."

And, with a curtsey rather haughty than humble, she left the room, followed by the young nurse.

Then the bolt might be heard to shoot, and a bar to be let down.

"She is suspicious of us," said one.

"Not a word," remarked the youngest man, "until after supper; then we'll have a talk."

It was not long ere the viands made their appearance on the board.

They were both cold and hot, and in great abundance, as Phœbe was always proud to show her ability before strangers.

A huge black-jack of beer, and a large flask of buckeye, completed the repast.

"Thank you," said the eldest man, "we shall want nothing more. After supper, we will lie down in our blankets."

Hans retired, and for some time nothing was heard, save the clatter of knives and forks. The travellers were truly and really hungry, so that the meal to them was a magnificent one. They did it ample justice, washing their food down with huge draughts of cold water.

The Americans are in this very much like the Japanese. But the former swallow vast quantities of cold water, while the latter drink it warm.

The result of this was, that at the termination of the meal they were sober.

Then the eatables were pushed away, the beer and spirits brought forward, and pipes produced.

These three men, fiends in human shape, were three Mormon apostles, in search of dupes.

We know that Mormonism means lust of women and lust of money.

Both these seemed to be combined in this locality.

Mary was beautiful, and she appeared to be rich.

"I mean to have her," said Elder Robinson, the man of forty.

"Do you," cried the second, Elder Peters."

"I've got a word to say to that," remarked the youth, whose name was Hyrum Smith. "All's fair, but I mean to have a say. What shall it be—odd man out, or the bones?"

"The bones," cried the two.

Then Hyrum Smith produced a set of dice and a piece of chalk.

"Unto the chosen servant of the Lord, who is greater than the father or the son, will fall the right to this woman and her wealth."*

The two elders smiled. Their young friend was in the early or chrysalis period.

He was half a dupe of his own brother's imposture.

But not wholly, for none to whom Joseph Smith's early life was known could believe him to be anything but the gross, cunning, and ignorant impostor he was.

The dice rattled on the table, and for some time this disgraceful game continued.

Hyrum Smith at last gave a huge chuckle. He had won.

The others cursed their bad luck, filled up their glasses, and then promised to assist him in carrying out his nefarious design.

---

* The following, signed by Joseph Smith, will explain the above blasphemy. After this, let none dare say, that all exposure of these miscreants is not a full measure of justice:—

"What is God? He is a material organized intelligence, possessing both body and parts. He is in the form of a man, and is, in fact, of the same species, and is a model or standard of perfection, to which man is destined to attain, he being the Great Father and Head of the whole family. This Being cannot occupy two distinct places at once; therefore, he cannot be everywhere present.

"What are angels? They are intelligences of the human species. Many of them are the offspring of Adam and Eve—of men, it is said, 'being Gods or sons of God, endowed with the same powers, attributes, and capacities that their Heavenly Father and Jesus Christ possess.

"*The weakest child of God* which now exists upon the earth, *will possess more dominion, more property, more subjects, and more power and glory, than is possessed by Jesus Christ or by his Father*; while, at the same time, Jesus Christ and his Father will have their dominion, kingdom, and subjects, increased in proportion."

LEOPOLD IN THE MADHOUSE.

"I shall try soft sawder, first," he said; "she is a widder, I guess; and widders are rather fond of returning to the holy state of matrimony. She's pretty, she is—and so I tells you. You scatter about, and meet me at Juke's this day fortnight. If the soft sawder don't do, why then——"

And a wicked light flashed from his wicked eyes.

Soon after they took a parting glass, stretched themselves by the fire, and went to sleep.

They breakfasted without the presence of Mary; hers had been handed in at the window.

CHAPTER LI.

PREPARATIONS FOR DEFENCE.

WHEN the travellers departed Mary Haddington came forth.

She was very pale, very calm, very determined.

"Hans," she said, quietly, as she was having her breakfast., "I want you to put a strong oak shutter to my window, with bars."

"Yaw, mine frau," said he, "Hans do it first day he have time."

"You must do it to-day, at once," she replied, calmly.

"Yaw."

Eliza looked at him meaningly.

He went out to fetch materials at once.

"You may tell him all," said Mary, "but he must act as I tell him. If that man comes back, let none of you show the slightest suspicion. Leave him to me."

"Sure, and I'll do jist as you say," replied Eliza, who then stepped out to narrate all to her lover.

In a few minutes Hans came back with Eliza, to take his breakfast, which these two always did in the master's log-hut.

Mary took down a handsome revolver, which her husband was very proud of.

They were just invented then, though for many years after unknown in Europe.

"Will you show me how to load this?" she said.

Hans grinned, and did so with great gravity.

Then Mary put on the caps with extreme deliberation.

This done, she stepped out of the door, and took aim at a tree, at which she fired all five barrels.

Then she returned into the house and loaded the revolver herself.

"And now, Hans, mind you always sleep with your gun by your side. If you hear a noise in the night come to my assistance. But Eliza shall sleep with me for the present."

CHAPTER LII.

THE MORMON ELDER.

MARY sat in the porch that evening with Eliza; the boy Henry, our hero, slept in his cradle inside. The negroes were at work.

Mary was very thoughtful. Her husband's absence, joined with the abominable designs of the Mormons, made her extremely unhappy.

What should she do?

Was she, a lone woman left with her babe, to do battle with the world?

Suddenly she raised her head, a horseman was galloping down the valley.

She stood up.

It was an Indian.

Mary placed her hand upon her heart.

He came galloping straight for the hut, jumped from his wiry mustang, and presented a packet.

It was a letter from her husband.

"Give him food," she said, in choking accents.

Then she ran in, closed her bed-room door, and read.

Marmaduke told his story, and added that the gratitude of the Indians had been so demonstrative that he had been compelled to remain with them until he was formally received into the tribe as a brother.

Mary read every line through, and then sat down to write her answer.

It was brief, but to the purpose.

When she had finished, she went out into the kitchen, where the Indian was eating.

"How soon will my husband get this answer?"

"Hurry?" asked the Indian.

"Great. The wife of your chief's friend is in danger from wicked men."

"Good," said the Indian, with a grunt; "ride three days."

And he rose from his meal, took the letter, and prepared to depart upon his journey.

Mary would have offered him money, but he would have scorned it; she therefore contented herself with giving him a bag containing food, and a bottle of whiskey.

With a gratified smile the man went on his way.

Mary was much relieved, for, at all events, her husband was safe.

But would he return in time? This man would lose no time, but attempt to carry out his wicked designs as soon as possible.

What was to be done until her husband returned? She must temporize.

And thus days passed away.

Then he came. It was about midday when he rode over, and re-entered the house.

"Good morning, ma'am," he said, in his most insinuating way.

"Good morning."

"Good gentleman not back yet?" he continued, for he now knew that her husband was only temporarily absent.

"No—but I expect him every hour. I have had a messenger from him."

The man bowed to hide his confusion.

"Think of settling in these parts," he said; "I have seen a property I like about two miles off, so I thought I would consult your good gentleman about it."

Mary made no reply, but, calling Eliza, ordered lunch, excused herself in some way, and went out into the garden.

A dreary, heavy weight had settled on her soul. Would he never come back?

She walked up and down impatiently.

The garden, with its winding walks and beautiful shrubbery, close, high paling, that shut out all prying eyes, was a favourite haunt of hers, and here she wended her way, languid with the anguish that lay so heavily upon her.

But her queenly form was stately, her high regal brow as matchlessly beautiful as when first a bride and her heart was a stranger to grief.

The eye was a perceptible shade dimmer, the lip a tone more thoughtful than of yore, but this took nothing from her majestic beauty, it rather added to it a strange, undefined interest, that chained, but held in awe, the curiosity of others. Thoughtfully, pensively, she sauntered along, without object or aim, save the fresh breeze was grateful to her drooping spirits, when suddenly, from a clump of lilac, emerged the Mormon, who, stepping before her, made her start back in alarm.

"Be not alarmed, lady, you have no cause for fear," he said, in a deprecating tone, as he gazed boldly on the queenly beauty before him.

Quietly Mary turned to retrace her steps, when the Mormon cried, eagerly,—

"Stay one moment, madam. Why are you so chary of charms with which you drive men mad? Stay!" he added, as he sprang in the path in which she was hastening away. "I have spent weeks in endeavouring to speak with you, and I will not be thwarted now."

The majestic figure of the queenly young wife grew taller, the proud head was arched in scorn, while contempt hovered around the beautiful lips, as she surveyed the bold, impudent insulter before her.

Not one word passed her lips, but she stood, with her clear, calm eyes on him, until he cowered beneath the glance of scorn, and abashed, he stood irresolute.

His eye fell, and resting on a rose-bush, he broke a bud, and timidly but silently offered it to her, while she peremptorily but gracefully moved aside the hand that held it with a motion of her own, and passed on to the house, leaving the Mormon intruder completely baffled and cowed.

As her form receded, rage flashed from his eyes, and, muttering words of fearful import, he strode angrily away.

He did not return to the house for some time. His precipitation had ruined his hopes.

But endless is the generosity of woman, and he knew it.

Tearing out a leaf from his pocket-book, he wrote these words :—

"*Pardon, and receive me as if nothing had happened. I will never offend again.*"

A few minutes after Mary received him with a quiet dignity, which, under the circumstances, was sublime hypocrisy.

But what could she do?

The fellow was a villain, and had to be beat with his own weapons.

He remained about an hour in conversation, and once or twice referred to Mormonism, of which doctrine he spoke, while professing to be a Gentile, in the highest of terms.

Mary answered him by calm, cold arguments, taken chiefly from the Bible.

About polygamy he was very energetic.

Mary had scarcely patience to hear him calmly. She spoke like a woman, a true-hearted woman.

But Hyrum Smith could not understand her.

His reply was in the words of his brother. It is blasphemous and disgusting, but it shows Mormonism in its true colours.

He cited Abraham, who took to him wives with the sanction of the Lord, and then added :—

"'The Almighty actually visited this husband of many wives, and went into a discussion of his family and domestic concerns—concerns, by the way, more important to the progress of his kingdom, and to the everlasting happiness of the human family than many have seriously thought of. What did he say about his family matters? Did he say, Abraham, beware of a carnal mind—beware of the lust for woman? Did he say the first word of the kind? No; I repeat it—no; he said no such thing. Well, tell us plainly what he did say? Why, read it for yourself. He virtually said this to Abraham:—Abraham, I find no fault with your taking two wives; but, on the other hand, I bless you for it, and I bless you in doing it, and I bless them in becoming your wives above all other women upon the earth.

"'I will next call your attention to the mar-riage practice of Jacob, one of the most illustrious Prophets, and a grandson of Abraham. Jacob had several wives, and by them were born unto him the Twelve Patriarchs, after whom all the Tribes of Israel were named. Now one of these wives was honoured with being the lineal mother of Jesus Christ, according to the flesh. What! Jesus Christ descended from a man who advocated the doctrine of a plurality of wives, and actually had many wives? Why he was as bad Mahomet. I wonder, says one, that God ever kept a record of such a lineage, seeing it favours the doctrine of a plurality of wives. Why this was one object of keeping the record of Christ's lineage, that it might sustain this very doctrine. Another object was, that the promised seed might be accurately traced out. All the time that Jacob was labouring with Laban, for the purpose of getting his daughters for his wives, God was with Jacob, upholding him, and enriching him by his supernatural arm, in order that he might have ample means to support his many wives, and their numerous children, whereby he might become a king over a numerous and mighty nation, springing from his own loins. Did the Lord ever frown upon him for living with his several wives? No, never.

"'Well, I declare, says one, I did not know but this system of polygamy was the practice of some dark age, which God rather winked at through their ignorance, and in consequence of their being sprung from heathenish parents. But now it does seem that God really delighted in these polygamists and their practices, and wanted all generations to know it, and to know it distinctly, and never forget it. Well, says one, if this is the case, then surely the veil has been over my eyes in reading the Scripture; for I never discovered before that polygamy was a blessing and duty binding upon God's people.'"

Such is the coarse, vulgar, and indecent language of Mormonism on this delicate subject.

"Sir," said Mary, "I will not argue with you. The subject is a painful and disagreeable one. I have my child to attend to; good morning."

And she left him with a haughty bend of her head.

But he came again and again, until Mary began hourly to expect her husband's return.

Then she grew afraid of a collision between them.

"Sir," she said, one day when he came over, "I give you fair warning that I now expect my husband every minute. He will not be best pleased to find a stranger here."

"Indeed," said Hyrum, with a shade of displeasure on his countenance, "but I am not a stranger."

"You are to him," she replied, coldly.

"But not to you, love, best of women," he began.

"I have forgiven this insolence once," she said; "I will not do so again. Beware! Leave the house."

He slunk away like a beaten hound, ferocious passions, swelling his heart and impelling him to deeds of darkness and hate.

We know not ourselves. We may imagine, nay, positively assert, what would be the course we should pursue, if called to act under any peculiar circumstances; but let those same contingencies occur, not one out of a thousand would follow the bent of his judgment given in calmer moments. None but a heart that has been seathed by the lightnings that dart around the soul during the tempest of warring passions, can know or feel the agony of despair, the quivering of the heart's tendons as they are rudely torn from the trunk around which they have been taught to twine; the sickening of the soul as it recoils back on itself, while wrung with the agony of unavailing grief.

The wretched man really loved Mary Haddington to distraction.

Many a man has before loved a married woman to his cost, for love is involuntary; but a man of proper feeling and command over himself can conquer even the most devoted passions.

But Hyrum Smith had no restraint over his passions. Once he loved, he must win.

That evening Mary Haddington was very uneasy and miserable. The absence of her husband had been protracted for nearly six weeks. What could be the matter?

She went to bed as usual with Eliza in her room. But she could not sleep.

A vague dread was on her soul.

She seemed to fancy that there was something about to happen.

About midnight she rose and went into the kitchen.

Somebody was trying the door.

Mary listened close to the keyhole.

A man was trying to force the door with a chisel.

Mary went to the bed-room, fetched the revolver, and again returned to the doorway.

"Who is there?" she said, in a loud, quick tone.

"I—your devoted lover," replied Hyrum Smith, in a husky tone.

"What seek you?"

"Let me in. I cannot speak here—the night is cold and dark," he cried.

"Leave this spot," she said, in a loud tone, "or I will fire."

A violent kick at the door was the sole answer.

Mary put the barrel to the keyhole, fired, and fell in hysterics.

When she recovered there was another loud knocking at the door.

"Who is there?" she feebly cried.

"I—your husband," said a well-known voice.

With a bound like that of a wild animal, she rushed to the door, unbolted and unbarred it—and then fell fainting in her husband's arms.

Before they sought their nuptial couch that night Mary told her husband all.

His eyes flashed with fury and indignation, and he vowed that he would be avenged.

But this he did not communicate to his wife.

She had told him of the rendezvous at the inn, and this had suggested his mode of obtaining vengeance.

Marmaduke had hitherto only heard a little of the Mormons.

He heard them spoken of as hypocrites and polygamists.

He knew that the intrigues of the Prophet and

his Patriarchs were only samples which the more humble followed, with such additions and emendations as they chose to adopt; and extended from the hoary sinner of four-score years to the jacketed boy at school on the one side, and from the wrinkled hag bereft of every vestige of loveliness to the miss in pantalettes on the other. Cupid's missives flew thick, fast, and indiscriminately from the hoary head to the young miss, and from the old beldame to him who was yet unbroken by vice; from the husband and father to his neighbour's wife or daughter, and from the wife and daughter, wherever their wanton eye rested.

But now Marmaduke felt in his own person the curse of this infamous sect.

They would not even allow his obscure and happy home to be in peace, and from that hour he vowed mortal hatred to the whole gang.

Hyrum Smith and his two coadjutors were in the neighbourhood, with a view to collect dupes and to despoil the Gentiles of as much money as possible.

But they were also there to meet a band of their ruffianly companions on their way from Europe.

The rendezvous was to be at the inn above alluded to.

CHAPTER LIII.

FROGS' HOLE.

It was nine o'clock at night.

The usual customers of the inn had retired, and left the coast clear to the Mormons.

They were in a small parlour.

The arrangement of the shanty was peculiar. It was on the roadside, and was much frequented by western emigrants.

A stage coach also passed twice a week, when the passengers dined.

A room was specially set apart for this purpose alone.

The passengers had been there that day, and had left.

The Mormons now occupied the vacant dining apartment.

There were five, the three elders having been joined by two strangers from a mission to England.

They had not been there half-an-hour over their supper when a traveller came in.

He wore the dress of a farmer, of rather a humble class, while in his right hand was a heavy cow-hide.

He was rough in appearance, but still used to be waited on.

He at once entered a narrow slip of a room beside the parlour, and called for supper and a bottle of whiskey.

Then he withdrew a plug from the wooden partition, and sat with his ear to the crevice.

This crevice he had prepared on the previous day.

He could hear every word that was said; while leaning his shoulder against the hole when the landlord came in, he deadened the sound for the Mormons.

This is what he heard.

"So she nearly shot you, did she?" sneered one.

"She did, by Jerusalem!" said Hyrum Smith; "but, Jehosophat, I like her all the better. It will be a glorious triumph to hold her in these arms."

"Ha! ha! so you don't give up the idea?"

"Give up the idea! Sooner would I give up life itself. To fancy another possessing this idol of my soul is madness. We are five, well armed. Why should not the deed be done to-night?"

"Just as you like. You know our rules. Every man is bound to assist his neighbour. As soon as supper is over we'll start."

Much followed of a nature to horrify and disgust the listener, but nothing in any way connected with the events of this narrative.

About half-an-hour later the Mormons paid their bill, and rose to depart.

They got as far as the door.

It was a pitch dark night, so dark as almost to make them grope their way.

Then a small light might have been seen in the road, and then up flew the blaze of a dozen pine torches, borne by as many men.

The Mormons were caught, gagged, and led away to a thicket.

Twenty stout, powerful farmers and settlers were collected round.

Some ten or a dozen held up their torches, while others tied the Mormons to trees, after stripping off everything but their trousers.

Then five stalwart youths produced each a cowhide, and began.

Heavy and thick fell the blows, which were administered without a word of remark.

One hundred lashes on their bare backs.

Marmaduke Haddington commanded the execution.

"Now, scoundrels," he said, "perhaps this may teach you not to visit men's wives in the absence of their husbands, and insult them with infamous proposals. You will remember Marmaduke Haddington, and your own villainous plot awhile."

And untying the scarred and bleeding wretches, they moved away, leaving the Mormons to curse the ill-fortune which had made them cross the path of Marmaduke Haddington.

Two days after, Marmaduke, rightly judging that the vengeance of the Mormons might fall upon his wife, sold his improvements to a rich English speculator, and retired to a distant state, out of the line, as he hoped, of the Mormons.

Here he lived happy for many years, until, at length, he had the inexpressible grief of losing his wife.

Three weeks after her death a letter came from Lady Haddington, announcing the serious illness of his brother, and her suspicion that she now understood fully her husband's great error.

Then it was for the first time that Marmaduke understood his brother's fatal error, and determined to return to England.

He was comparatively a rich man, and could establish himself in England in respectability if even his brother did remain obdurate.

CHAPTER LIV.

HOME.

OUR readers will remember the murder in the opening chapter of our narrative, a murder which filled the whole city where it occurred with horror and astonishment.

This is what had occurred.

When Marmaduke Haddington, summoned by his brother's wife, who now understood the whole villainy of the plot, arrived, his first object was to seek out Beckford, alias Bristowe, and make him reveal the whole plot to himself.

When he came into the presence of the preacher, he little suspected that Bristowe was Beckford.

He knew that Beckford was a gambler and a roué; he, therefore, readily believed that he should find him at the gambling-house.

But things went very differently to what he expected.

The day was spent in making vain searches after Beckford, about whom no one save Bristowe appeared to know anything.

But he had an adventure which was rife in extraordinary results.

Marmaduke was now not quite forty years of age, though his travelled appearance made him look more.

He had to move about so rapidly that he did not take his child with him.

About five o'clock in the evening, after walking about Manchester all day, he turned homeward.

Suddenly an exclamation made him look up.

A man, very much resembling himself, was standing before him in mute astonishment.

Marmaduke held out his hand.

This man was an illegitimate brother, who had been provided for in a good business in Manchester, and with whom Marmaduke had been intimate.

They were both of roving habits, and when Marmaduke went to sea Edward accompanied him.

But now Edward was a thriving merchant.

"Who would have thought of seeing you?" cried Edward Markham. "Where have you been all these years?"

"In America."

"We must dine together. But have you heard of Sir Thornley?"

"What?"

"There is no hope for him," said Edward.

"Indeed! Then will I go down, and try and see him this very night. Come with me, Edward, while I order a post-chaise; we shall have time to dine."

"With all my heart."

They entered a tavern, told the waiter to order the chaise, and then sat down to a hearty dinner.

"Has my—has our brother been long ill?" said Marmaduke.

"Ever since you left."

"Great God!" cried Marmaduke, "how much have they not to answer for!"

"Of whom do you speak?" cried Edward.

"Of Mrs. Treherne and Beckford."

"I don't understand."

Marmaduke told the other all he knew. Edward listened with awe and horror to a story developing so much human wickedness.

"But you must go to Haddington Hall," he added.

"I must truly—but why do you make the remark?"

"What about the visit to the gambling-house to-night?"

"True—I had forgotten. But it will be only adjourned."

"But I can go for you," observed Edward, kindly.

"Many thanks," replied Marmaduke; "that would indeed be a great favour."

Then they entered into further conversation relative to their future plans, as Marmaduke had great confidence in his base-born brother, who was really a noble and generous-hearted fellow.

Soon after this they parted, never again to meet in this world.

Edward was somewhat eccentric, and lived in a neat house in the outskirts with a grave old house-keeper.

He had never married, being, perhaps, of too roving a disposition, or probably having been disappointed in his youth.

He took his tea with the old woman, sent her to bed, and about eleven o'clock let himself out and went slowly into Manchester.

Silver Street we have already described. By means of the pass-word, Edward easily entered the gambling house of which Phineas was one of the proprietors.

It was a large well-furnished floor, secluded from the street by iron shutters and padded planks.

In one room men played with cards, such games as whist, ecarte, and piquet.

In all Continental countries cards are allowed in all public places, and do not produce any evil result.

The prohibition of games of skill from our public-houses leads to the secret gambling-shop.

But the inner room was a regular hell.

There men played at a table where chance presided over all the money that was risked.

Edward, who was too respectable a man to let any of his fellow citizens recognize him, had not only dressed himself to resemble Marmaduke, but had dyed his skin dark, and put on false mous-taches.

The resemblance was wonderful.

When Edward entered he recognized many men who should have been ashamed to be in that den.

But then they were merely playing whist for moderate stakes.

These men were annual subscribers to the room.

But in the other room were regular gamblers. Still, nowhere could he see Beckford.

He sauntered up to the refreshment counter, where a man stood dispensing liquor.

Edward poured out a goblet of wine, and while paying for it, said

"I had an appointment with Mr. Beckford here to-night," he said, "but I do not see him anywhere."

"Mr. Beckford has been called suddenly to town," replied the man.

"Oh!—never mind—look in again in an evening or two;" and Edward sauntered round the room once more, and finally finding that Beckford was not there, descended the stairs and went out.

Let us repeat our own account of what followed.

*   *   *   *   *   *   *

It was a little past midnight, and that part of the town was as a city of the dead—not a coach or cart wheel, not a human footstep, not a voice, not a dog baying at the moon, not even a dissipated cock cheated by its brightness into crowing! One might have fancied one's self amidst the ruins of a deserted capital.

The street to which we more particularly allude was peculiarly dark and narrow. Its houses, doubtless in their day of some importance, were tall, and thus added to the gloom. They, too, appeared deserted; for not the faintest glimmer of a light was to be seen, which made the unearthly stillness almost awful.

Awful, yes!

In the placid meadow, in the calm seclusion of the country, such stillness would have been sublime; but in the vast emporium of commerce it was awful.

Suddenly a dark shadow appeared to flit along the wall, as if seeking to hide its form.

It was that of a man in a cloak and slouched hat, who kept his head all the time turned cautiously over his shoulder, as if he feared that some one was following him.

Not the faintest trace of his countenance could be seen.

Suddenly he halted, and disappeared as if by magic.

And again all was still, though had any one been present they might have felt that the spirit of evil was brooding over the place.

A keen and practised ear, too, might have heard a strange murmuring overhead, such as we have of a summer evening distinguished falling from the summit of a street in Venice—but then it was the whispering of lovers.

And this was not.

Then the click of a door might have been heard, a faint stream of light, and a man came jauntily forth.

He appeared to have no concealment about him, but strode along without hesitation as without fear.

But what is this phantom that crouches behind, creeping, crawling, like the slimy serpent of the forest?

It is the foulest spectacle that walks abroad, the hideous shadow of murder.

Thud!

The blow is evidently struck by one who understands what he is about.

The man fell upon his face, groaned, and lay utterly still.

*   *   *   *   *   *   *   *

CHAPTER LV.

TREACHERY.

In the meanwhile, what had happened to Marmaduke?

As soon as his orders relative to the post-chaise were given, he returned to the public-house where he had left his son.

He wished to be assured of his comfort and safety before he started.

Henry was all right, in great good friendship with the landlady.

It was about dusk when he started on his way to Haddington Hall.

He had twenty miles to go, partly over very heavy and bad ground.

That is to say, he had to take cross-roads.

The first half of the journey was performed in less than an hour, when the reeking steeds were pulled up, and fresh horses ordered.

There was some delay, as another post-chaise, going the other way, was being attended to.

Marmaduke felt hot, feverish and thirsty.

He went into the inn, and ordering a bottle of wine, passed into a small side parlour.

It was already tenanted by a lady, whose back was turned to him.

He bowed, and muttering some excuse, would have left.

But she turned slowly round, and exhibited the agitated countenance of Mrs. Treherne.

"Maria!"

"Marmaduke!"

He was cold, haughty, severe.

"Marmaduke," she continued, "this is no time to think of the past—on a terrible occasion like this we should forget all."

"What is the matter?" said Marmaduke, with a shiver.

"You are Sir Marmaduke. Your brother is dead; and at Lady Haddington's desire, I was on my road to summon you."

"Indeed—my brother dead—so suddenly!" and Marmaduke, overcome by his emotions, sat down.

The wine came in, though the waiter stared a little to see those two talking.

"It is late," she said, thoughtfully; "had you not better delay your arrival at Haddington Hall until the morning?"

"Perhaps so," he replied, pouring out some wine; "I am indeed overcome. Besides, on such an occasion as this my son should be with me."

"Son!" cried Mrs. Treherne.

"Certainly—the child of poor Mary Dawson," he continued, speaking almost mechanically.

A dark scowl came over the face of Mrs. Treherne, who turned away.

"I shall stay here as well," she continued, and rang the bell to give orders.

The landlord came in himself.

She ordered the horses to be put up until morning, while each wanted a bed-room.

Boniface bowed low. It was an unexpected pleasure.

Some slight conversation passed between the brother and sister, who supped together more for form than anything else, and then Marmaduke went to his room.

Mrs. Treherne wrote three letters and sent them off by special messengers.

About midnight all was still in the house; but not on all the premises.

In the yard over the stable slept one Jonas Slimby, a short, stout, strongly made, bull-necked ostler.

Midnight had long since passed, and all were still and slumbering.

The night was bright, and dark by turns, the full moon being now hidden by dark, dense clouds, which swept across the face of the sky—now reappearing in unveiled splendour.

Jonas Slimby, amorous, like all ostlers, was waiting impatiently for a kitchen wench, who had promised to console his solitude.

Then Jonas saw the shadow of a man passing swiftly along the face of the white-washed wall of an outbuilding, in the direction of the back entrance of the inn.

At that moment the moon was, as it were, blotted out of the heavens by a black opaque cloud; and the substance reflected by the shadow Jonas could not discern in the thick darkness, earnestly as he strove to do so.

But he would not alarm the house unnecessarily; so, tightly grasping a stout cudgel he had taken care to provide himself with, he stole quietly forward towards the spot where the gliding shadow had disappeared from the whitened wall.

Surely he must have been mistaken! Nothing was to be heard, and when the moon presently shone forth again, nothing having life was to be seen.

The door leading into the house was closed, and complete stillness reigned around, with the exception of the occasional rattling of ill-fitting windows, as gusty blasts of wind beat fitfully against them.

Still, Jonas fancied he could not have been mistaken, and that it was a man's shadow he had seen.

But after searching every nook and corner he gave up the task.

Then his mistress called him, and Jonas, on other thoughts intent, returned to the yard.

Next morning, when the house was up, Marmaduke was nowhere to be found.

He had disappeared, as if by magic.

Now, as the Boniface had recognized him, though not affecting to see through his incognito, he did not care.

He had no fear of the loss.

But why had Sir Marmaduke gone out so mysteriously?

Then it was rumoured that he had been murdered in Manchester.

How did he get there?

The landlord was a tenant of the family, and, though he could not make head or tail of the whole story, held his peace.

Jonas Slimby rubbed his nose, and looked wise; but as he could not make it out, he, too, held his tongue.

CHAPTER LVI.

THE MADHOUSE.

It was an old-fashioned building, with high gates and very high walls, and spikes and glass at the top, a little back from the main road.

A winding cross-road, darkly shaded by trees, led from the highway to the gates.

In olden time it had been a mansion.

It was now a mad-house.

Had Jonas Slimby for once allowed his fat and greasy kitchen wench to wait half-an-hour, he would have seen much more than he did.

Mrs. Treherne sent for the mad doctor and two experienced assistants.

As she dared not do the deed openly she resolved to act with rapidity.

She it was who let the men in one after another.

The bargain was soon made. Her son was notoriously the heir of Haddington.

Some money and large promises, and the thing was done.

Marmaduke slept heavily. His door was not fastened, and in crept these worse than midnight assassins.

They first gagged him effectually and then pinioned his arms and legs.

Then they carried him down stairs, went out by the back way, and bundled him into a carriage.

When the gag was removed Marmaduke Haddington was in a padded room.

And Marmaduke was mad.

Not a maniac exactly, but mad with rage, fury, and intense hate.

The taint remained with him until his death, though he in happy hours could always conceal it.

For some days he stormed and raved, until the doctor thought he would never recover.

Then came calm.

From that hour he raved no more. He even seemed perfectly reconciled to the change of life.

He asked to be allowed to take exercise.

As he uttered no threats, and was even civil in his deportment, his request was readily granted.

It was the game of Dr. M'Biffin to preserve his patients as long as possible.

He took none but those who were well paid for.

The grounds were extensive and even pleasant.

Marmaduke, with a book considerately lent him by M'Biffin, went out for a stroll.

There were shady trees at the end of the garden.

Marmaduke looked not to the right or the left.

He saw a seat, and mechanically took up his post there under an acacia,

" Good God !" said a feeble voice, " Marmaduke !"

He turned, and there close to him was Leopold Treherne—but Leopold Treherne so changed, so wan, so thin, so pale, as to be hardly recognizable.

He had been there for nine years.

Marmaduke cast a wild look round in search of the keepers, but none were near.

" Merciful Heavens !" he said, " what is the meaning of this ?"

" I am the victim of an infamous woman," said the dwarf.

" My sister ?"

" Yes."

" So am I, the victim of her and of that consummate fiend from hell, Beckford ; whom I doom unto the most cruel death that man can inflict."

" But we shall die here," said the dwarf, whose long imprisonment had cowed his nature."

" No. I will either escape in a week, or commit such a terrible crime as shall lead me to another place of confinement."

The dwarf's eyes sparkled.

Have you any plan ?" he said.

" No. But within twenty-four hours I will mature one. Do commissioners visit ?"

" Certainly."

" Why do they not release you ?"

" Because when visiting justices come here the inmates are all really mad."

Marmaduke started back, a settled horror on his countenance.

CHAPTER LVII.

THE ESCAPE.

"Marmaduke," said Leopold, in his soft and melancholy tones, "you have no idea what I have gone through. It is a wonder that I am not altogether mad.

"When first I came here my fury knew no bounds. I told the old villain who then kept this establishment such home truths that he hated me intensely.

"In my rage, I told him how I would expose him to the inspector.

"He gave a hideous grin.

"Little did I dream what he meant.

"They adopt the absurd plan of giving notice when they are coming.

"This is a premium to cruelty and extortion.

"On the memorable day when I expected to see a glimpse of hope I was confined to my room.

"About ten they came in, by a sudden jerk put on a straight jacket, and strapped me to the bed.

"Then two hideous ruffians tortured me by tickling my feet, which rendered me quite raving mad when the inspector came in.

"I heard every word that was said, but could make no remark.

"Rather than submit to this awful infliction again, I promised on my honour never to appeal to the examiners.

"I now feel that I shall die in this hideous den of crime, infamy, and iniquity."

"No ! said Marmaduke, " nothing of the kind ! We are wanted in the world, and we will escape to ruin and confound the villains who have sent us here."

" I wish that I could hope so."

" It will be so if we are cautious and wise. We must not appear to be great friends. But be ever ready when summoned."

" I will ;" and observing that a keeper was eyeing them from a distance they separated after a few common-place observations.

When Marmaduke was alone, he strolled listlessly about to all appearance, though all the while his attention was never diverted from the one idea in his mind.

THE ESCAPE FROM THE MADHOUSE.

Still no idea came to him.

This preyed upon him with fearful power; for had he not promised the dwarf to save him from all that he had suffered?

Fortune favoured him in a most unexpected manner.

He had taken a survey of the whole grounds, when he suddenly found himself near a thick hedge.

Voices fell on his ear.

One was the voice of Growler, the abominable mad doctor.

The other was that of a young girl.

"I swear to you," said the wretched proprietor of the establishment, "that my wife will not live a month."

"So you have said a long time," said a somewhat pert voice.

Marmaduke suspected that he was about to learn something which might give him a power over the doctor.

He stooped low, and both heard and saw all that passed.

Doctor M'Biffin, a man over fifty, and very ugly at that, was seated upon a bench beside a girl, bold and handsome, of not more than eighteen.

She was the daughter of a small farmer close at hand, who, having tasted of poverty, was extremely anxious to rise to wealth and consequence at any price.

Doctor M'Biffin who practised medicine generally had been an attendant on her father.

The stout, plump, rosy cheeked girl had taken his fancy. Now Lucy Jones had a lover of her own age whom she liked, but who was poor.

She therefore readily received the attentions of the doctor when he whispered marriage.

"But you have a wife."

"I have," said the scoundrel, casting his eyes upwards to the ceiling; "a woman much older than myself, and unsuited to me—she cannot live long."

Lucy made a feint of being indignant, but was by far too ambitious to feel any real dislike to the idea.

So she stepped, in imagination, into the living woman's shoes.

Thus much by way of preface.

"You angel of a darling," said the baboon-looking doctor; "you ducky of my soul, this is a charming condescension."

He had his arm round her waist, and was toying with her heavy brown locks.

"But if *she* were to see us——"

"She is in bed and cannot move," he continued.

"Adone," said the girl, repelling his too forward caresses; "or I'll scream."

"Lucy," cried the doctor, now speaking with an energy which had its source in his devouring passion, "you know that I love you—you are well aware of my intention to marry you—but it may be months before I can carry out my plans."

"I hope not."

"Now, dear darling—you will be kind, you will come this evening—I will have such a nice supper in the room next the surgery—champagne and cherry-brandy, eh?"

The girl looked down upon the ground. Her soul, bad as she was, revolted at the rendezvous. But if she should offend him? This at once decided her.

"I will come," she said, in a low tone.

"There is a good girl. You shall never repent your kindness."

"But how am I to get in, and when?" she continued.

"Wait till ten. I shall then have gone my rounds. Take this key, it will let you into the garden. I will be here."

Lucy took the key, like a naughty, bad, wicked girl as she was, and then went her way.

M'Biffin rubbed his hands, and an infernal chuckle spread over his countenance.

Then he went away to the sick bed of his suffering wife.

Marmaduke had listened with disgust, contempt, and yet with hope.

CHAPTER LVIII.
PREPARATIONS.

There was the door, and there was the key. Doubtless if the girl used it once, she would use it again, and by great good fortune they might be there to see.

Marmaduke returned into the garden, and looking keenly round, contrived to secrete some rusty nails.

As he now appeared quite resigned and harmless, he was allowed to walk about and poke his nose into almost any corner.

In this way he became possessed of an old chisel that he secreted about his person with the avidity of a miser who has found a mighty treasure.

He contrived to have Leopold's room pointed out to him, and then, when night came, allowed them to lock him in without a murmur.

No sooner was he alone than he began his work. It was a desperate resolve, but his situation was desperate.

The doctor he knew was busy, while the men had gone to supper.

With a long nail he easily turned the lock.

Then came the bolts, they were of iron.

But thrusting the chisel up and down he presently came to the bolts, which, by slow degrees, he was able to get at.

No sooner had he chipped away half an inch of wood than they yielded.

He was in a dark passage.

He groped along until he came to the dwarf's door.

It was fastened by three heavy iron bolts, which, however, was to him no impediment.

"Leopold," he said, in a low whisper.

"Who calls? Is it you, spirit of my beloved wife? I come, I come!"

"Hush! 'tis I—Marmaduke!" whispered the other. "Do not make a sound, but follow."

The dwarf came to the door in blank amazement. Astonishment deprived him of speech.

"Tread softly," said Marmaduke, who made for a spot where he saw a light.

It was the top of the carpeted stairs.

At the bottom were the library, dining rooms, and surgery.

The room which was to witness the *petit souper* was behind the surgery.

The kitchen and servants' hall were at some distance.

They could hear the men in Mrs. M'Biffin's room speaking to the sick lady.

They groped their way downstairs.

In the hall were some riding-whips. One of these Leopold clutched convulsively.

The hall door was a-jar, and Marmaduke, peering through, saw that some one was standing outside.

It was one of the keepers smoking his pipe.

Quick as lightning they turned down a narrow dark passage, leading past the surgery.

There was a door for poor patients at the end of this.

They were about to open it, when they were startled by the sudden appearance of a light.

They stood back and held their breaths.

Then they saw that it was the doctor, coming up from the cellar, with bottles of wine under his arm.

He had four—two of which were champagne, and two port.

They looked at him with mingled hatred and

contempt ; but, at the same time, they were not without apprehension.

He must pass within two yards of them ; although he only had a small tallow candle, that might betray them.

They were resolved to escape, if they felled him on the spot ; but as violence was no part of their plan, they drew back in the embrasure of a window.

The doctor passed into the little room, and came out rubbing his hands.

The clock struck ten.

The doctor hurried away, leaving the door open. Marmaduke hurried into the supper room, snatched up two bottles of wine, wrapped a fowl, tongue, and loaf in a napkin, and then gave them with two knives to Leopold.

He armed himself with a pistol which he took down off the mantelpiece, and found was loaded.

Then, after a slight search, he found some cord of the thickness of clothes lines.

This done, they hastily followed in the doctor's track, and caught up to him as he was closing the door.

"Speak—cry out—and you are dead !" said Marmaduke, presenting his pistol. "Secure that girl," added he, "and cut her throat at the first attempt she makes to move."

Then, with a vigour which was almost superhuman, he thrust the doctor against a tree, tied him to it, and effectually gagged him with his own handkerchief.

Then he did the same to Lucy, despite her whispered cries for mercy.

The key was in the door, and in another moment they were in a lane that led to the edge of a moor.

At the extremity of the moor were some hills covered with furze and trees.

For this the fugitives made with as much rapidity as possible.

They had not gone a quarter of a mile when they heard the piercing shrieks of a woman.

They took no notice, but hurried across the moor at a rapid pace.

Once in the hills they might hope to escape, as the keepers would be more likely to search the inns and ale-houses than to hunt all night in the woods.

The moor was about a mile across, and then came the steep hills.

Just as they reached them they caught sight of some distant lights.

It was the keepers in pursuit.

The shrieks of Lucy, who would not take the hint of the doctor to be quiet, alarmed the whole house.

M'Biffin was slowly getting his hands out of the coils.

He succeeded just as keepers and maidservants came rushing up, to stand there in speechless astonishment, which soon changed to a giggle.

"Two have escaped !" roared M'Biffin, in a voice of thunder. "After them ! If my wife hears of this, away you all go ; if not, a guinea each and a holiday on Easter Monday. Now go !"

Three keepers darted through the open door, the others went back to the house.

Lucy would have left.

"Not a bit of it," said the Doctor, "I don't care a curse. You'll be mistress soon and then they will understand."

Lucy rather reluctantly remained, nor was it until she had drank a good dose of wine that she recovered herself.

About midnight she retired to the library with the doctor, where they slept together in the bed made for Mr. Biffin ever since his wife's illness.

Whether she ever won the honoured title of Mrs. Biffin we cannot say.

CHAPTER LIX.

THE COPSE.

MEANWHILE the fugitives had reached a dense copse in which they contrived to secrete themselves by crawling on their hands and knees, until they were at least fifty feet in the heart of the wood, when they laid down, clutched one the pistol, the other a knife, and then waited.

Soon they heard the stamping, cursing and swearing of their pursuers, who were completely at fault.

Which way could they have gone ?

One said one thing, one said another, until at length their voices were heard in the distance, and then ceased altogether.

But these two victims of a system, too vile to be described at length, which reduces the freeman to the level of a slave, which invades every grade of society where greed of gold and lust of woman prevails, dared not move.

The dwarf had felt the iron enter his soul, but not so much as Marmaduke.

All the cunning he had exhibited during this remarkable escape, was the cunning almost of a mad man.

He felt a strange supernatural dread of Mrs. Treherne and Phineas Bristow.

He shuddered at the thought of once more falling into their power, and longed for the hour when he might be again free on the glorious prairies and plains of North America, where men hunt, and shoot, and fish without the restriction of game-laws, which so cruelly oppress the poor in what we call civilized countries.

They scarcely dared to converse even in whispers ; but aware that the whole country would be up in arms against them in the morning, under the pretence that they were escaped lunatics, they determined to take advantage of the very first dawn of day to creep off, obtain a vehicle at any price, and place themselves at a proper distance from the spot.

Then they proceeded to fortify themselves with a meal that was peculiarly grateful under the circumstances.

They had had nothing so invigorating for a long time.

Then they composed themselves to sleep.

There was little danger that sleep would invade them too long, though it does strangely under some circumstances.

It is not uncommon to hear persons attribute the sleeping of "guilty creatures" to hardness of heart, or recklessness. This is au error, referable to ignorance of the nature of sleep, and of the fact that all degrees of excitement in the parts of the brain and spinal marrow, associated with the nerves of the sensitive system, are followed by proportional exhaustion. The only limit to this law is a capability of bearing in those parts. Exhausted by mental excitement, the criminal is often awakened for his execution; and the soldier, both by mental and bodily excitement, sleeps by the roaring cannon.

It proved, however, with them, that fear of being again entrapped was far beyond anything which otherwise have influenced them.

It was just dawn when they rose to their feet.

They hastily finished the wine, bread, and meat, and ascended the hill.

The ridge at the summit was almost bare of trees, though a few stunted bushes grew upon them.

Before leaving the wood they peered out.

There was the doctor, with two keepers and a constable.

They hastily drew back and hid themselves.

It was useless their attempting to escape that way. They would be overpowered in a moment.

They hastily retreated into the wood again to hold a conference.

———

CHAPTER LX.

JOHN ROBERTS.

ABOUT half-a-mile from where they started they found a beaten pathway.

As this might lead them to some house, they determined to follow it at once.

But let us precede them.

About two miles further on was a farm-house, inhabited by one John Roberts.

A rare old curmudgeon was John Roberts.

He was a well-to-do man, with a wife and two children.

He ruled his house with a rod of iron.

His will was law, and his roaring voice might be heard from morning until night, if anything went amiss.

And everything did go amiss in a house where people are afraid of the most simple act.

They dared not ask him what he wanted.

It was a rule of that house that his people were to know what he wanted, without being told.

This, of course, caused many a terrible scene.

Mrs. Roberts was naturally, in return, crabbed and downcast, believing herself for ever unhappy and lost.

But there is no sorrow under heaven which is or ought to be endless. To believe, or to make it so, is an insult to Heaven itself. Each of us must have known one or more instances, when a saintly or heroic life has been developed from what at first seemed a stroke, like death itself—a life full of the calmest and truest happiness, because it has bent itself to the Divine Will and learnt the best of all lessons—to endure. But how that lesson is learned, through what bitter teaching, hard to be understood and obeyed, till the hand

of the Great Teacher is recognized clearly through it all, is a suoject too sacred to be entered upon here.

Still, scenes did occur in that place which would have suited an Irish public-house in St. Giles' on a Saturday night.

It was eight o'clock.

The breakfast was on the table. Mrs. Roberts, and a great stout, rosy girl, had been bustling about to get it ready, in a timid, terrified way; lest they should be a minute behind.

John Roberts and his two sons, Dick and Harry, were out in the fields.

Dick and Harry usually started out at daybreak to work with the men.

John Roberts rode out about seven, to see that there were no skulkers about.

There was little fear of that.

With his violence of temper John Roberts was a good and an honest man.

It was his fearful passions which came over him and which he could not control.

But for his real sterling qualities, his two sons would long since have left him to seek their fortune in the world.

But his good moments made up for his bad ones.

On the morning in question he had been unusually gracious.

He had asked Dick and Harry to ride out with him; and here they come all three riding slowly down the hill towards the house.

They are not tiring their horses, as they have much to do.

It is market-day, and a good store of cattle and pigs have been sent on, which they must rejoin by twelve o'clock.

The farmer is jolly because he expects this day to do a goodly trade.

And John Roberts loves money and moneys' worth.

He is a saving man, and will leave his wife and children independent of the world.

But John Roberts has a chance this day, which was worth all the business he could have done at market, and yet John did not see it.

The horses were sent into the yard to be kept ready saddled and indulged with a mouthful.

The father and two sons entered the house.

The wife glanced hurriedly at her husband, and saw that he was in a good humour.

Silly man; why not have been always so?

From conjugal love as from a fountain issues all the activities and alacrities of life.

Nobody sees it at first.

But the time soon comes, when the stern battle of life must be fought in earnest, and when a happy temper and a kind heart, in a husband or wife, are as oil to our wounds and marrow to our bones.

"Well, and how do the meadows look?" she said, in her mild and timid way.

"Bravely."

He sat down. A flash, which made everybody start, was in his eye.

"Why the devil," he began, "are my directions always disobeyed·"

"How so?" said his wife, in a timid, gentle way.

"What did I ask you to get for breakfast·"

This, with a fearful black frown, made everybody shiver.

"Potatoes, my love."

"Yes—" he began.

"Here they are."

"*Fried.*"

"Well."

"I said boiled," he almost shrieked, as at the same time he attacked the round of beef.

Now John Roberts preferred them fried, but the perverseness of his nature was that he preferred being obeyed to having that which he really liked.

Nobody said a word, but went on eating their breakfast in solemn silence, a state of things doubtless conducive to digestion.

"What, have you all fallen dumb?" he exclaimed.

"No my dear," said the wife, angrily; "but who is going to speak when you are in one of your tempers."

"Temper," he replied, laying down his knife and fork, and looking about with an air of vacant astonishment perfectly ludicrous; "temper; was ever man so cursed with people with tempers? a shrew of a wife, sullen sons——"

"We are not sullen," said Dick; "but we never wish to interfere when you are quarrelling."

"Quarrelling," screamed the farmer, "how dare you say I am quarrelling, sir?"

Dick held down his head and made no reply.

John Roberts, who was very hungry and had no time to lose, dashed half the *fried* potatoes into his dish, and began to eat them voraciously.

This was the signal that the storm was over.

Unluckily, as the devil would have it, a fresh cause of disturbance arose.

CHAPTER LXI.

THEY RISK THEIR NECKS.

THEY were breakfasting in a large front stone kitchen.

The door opened into the road.

It was hastily opened, and, presenting a very wild and unsatisfactory appearance, Marmaduke and Loepold entered.

"Well I'm d——d," shrieked the farmer, "if this aint cool."

"We have no time for explanation," said the dwarf.

"Then go——"

"We have escaped from the lunatic asylum of D——. We are sane and honest men, confined by cruel relatives."

"Escaped lunatics," cried Mrs. Roberts.

"What we ask is—lend us two horses. They shall be returned with a handsome present."

The farmer rose, and advanced towards a blunderbuss.

The escaped lunatics went out and closed the door.

"You'll be sorry, father," said Harry, the elder son, quietly.

"Why?" he said, with a fearful glare.

At that instant, the two fugitives swept by on two of the horses.

"Murder—thieves!" yelled the farmer; "I shall be sorry I did'nt load to horse-stealers."

"One is Mr. Leopold Treherne," said Harry, firmly.

"He's been dead, you fool, these ten years."

"Harry is right," cried Mrs. Roberts, starting up wildly; "that was Leopold Treherne, as I live."

The farmer wiped his head with a silk pocket-handkerchief.

At this moment, in rushed the doctor, two keepers, and a fellow who looked like a constable.

"What the—— do you want?" shouted John Roberts, who began to lose his head.

"Beg pardon," said the hideous doctor; "but two of my maddest patients have escaped."

"Oh!"

"Dangerous patients."

"Ah!"

"Have you seen anything of them?" continued Doctor.

"And if I had," said John Roberts, with a surly growl.

"I should be glad of information."

"Would you?" replied John Roberts, fixing his eyes upon the face of Harry with a meaning look. "Now, let me tell you, you white-livered, scoundrelly son of a—— female dog, who lock people up far more sane than yourself, in order to make money—do you know what I would do, if I had seen them——"

"What, sir?"

"First send my son after them to warn them——"

Harry disappeared.

"And then——".

He took up a cart-whip as he said this.

"And then," he repeated, "I would lash you all within an inch of your lives."

With his powerful arm he laid on his whip as he spoke, taking care to avoid the constable, and to give the most of his allowance of thrashing to the doctor himself.

As the discomforted pursuers issued from the doorway, they saw Harry gallop off on a large and powerful horse.

Then they understood.

Meanwhile, the fugitives, who had at least thirty miles to ride, and who were fully aware that they had been guilty of the crime of horse-stealing, still did not try to overwork their horses.

They had a long hill to ascend, and it was not before they had got nearly up to the top, that they heard another horse clattering after them.

They glanced back, and saw that it was one man only.

But everybody was bound to give him assistance if it happened to be one of their pursuers.

So they put their horses to their utmost speed, as soon as they got to the crown of the hill.

Still they heard the clang of this one powerful horse coming up behind them.

They saw at once that the rider must overtake them.

They looked around.

They were on a kind of common, with no other living soul in sight.

They determined to halt and face the rider.

They were two desperate men, and would stand no nonsense.

They halted, and Harry was soon beside them.

He took off his hat.

"I come," he said, "to say that you are welcome to the horses. We'll saddle my mare in the cart. The mad doctor has been to our house, and father horse-whipped him out."

"But," said Marmaduke, "your father was very uncivil to us."

"His bark is worse than his bite," replied Harry.

"Many thanks. The horses shall be taken care of," said Leopold; "when shall I return them?"

"No matter your honour," said Harry, with a laugh; "Harry Roberts knows where to find Mr. Leopold Treherne."

"Ha!" cried the dwarf, "so you have not forgotten me. I did not know you."

"I and mother knew you," replied Harry; "but now I must go back. We will keep them off your track as long as possible."

They shook him cordially by the hand.

"Have you any money, Mr. Leopold," he said with a blush.

"Well frankly we have not," replied Treherne, smiling.

Harry pulled out a purse, with some six or seven sovereigns in it, which he handed to them, and then galloped off to avoid any further thanks.

Leopold and Marmaduke, their hearts much lightened, hurried away.

Nor did they halt until two hours before sunset, when they entered a road-side inn, to refresh themselves and horses.

They were hungry as true hunters of the field or of the prairies.

As soon as they had refreshed themselves, fed their horses and thoroughly cooled them, on they again started.

They did not follow the main road.

They were too much afraid of being overtaken by the doctor and his gang.

So they went many roundabout ways known to Leopold.

As night began to draw on, the bridle path they were following narrowed more and more, till, running between two high banks, topped by hedges and trees, it was little better than a ditch.

Leopold, reining in his horse, had dropped in the rear of Marmaduke, who looked round laughing.

"I am mighty hungry," he cried; "how many more miles. When shall we get out of this dry ditch?"

"We have but a short way now," returned the other; "we shall soon reach the common."

Night had now arrived at that first stage which, succeeding to evening, gives just sufficient light for those without to see by, whilst, to one who should leave the house and the lights within, it would seem utter darkness.

The sky was covered by grey clouds, not a star was visible. A light fresh wind blew in the travellers faces, and whistled through the hedges about them.

The bridle-road now led them up a gentle rise, at the top of which spread out a large, sweet-smelling healthy common, desolate, little frequented, and not having a house within two miles of it.

The spot was well-known to Leopold, as indeed was every spot of that road, so often passed over by him from his youth upwards.

As they left the bridle road, he bent his hand on the crupper, and, turning his head, looked with piercing glance down the hill.

"What is it?" said Marmaduke.

"Some one standing under a tree yonder," replied Leopold. "By heavens! two!"

Marmaduke drew rein a moment.

"Our horses are still not blown. Do you draw your pistol—and if they strive to stop us, fire."

Leopold nodded.

In order to be more free, he pushed back his hat, lowered the collar of his short cloak, and holding the reins in his left hand, clutched the pistol with his right.

The two men sat motionless on their black-looking steeds.

They were not masked, and yet men could see that they were in truth gentlemen of the night.

Their collars were turned up, and their broad-brimmed hats brought over the forehead.

"Stand," cried one, as the two horsemen came close to them.

"On your lives, halt," added a deep, hoarse voice.

"Ha! ha! ha!" shouted Leopold, with a hollow laugh, "ha! ha! ha! the colonel and master Treherne."

"D——n" cried the colonel, firing, but without success, "shoot,—d——n you."

But master Treherne, with an unearthly yell, had leaped his horse into a field, nor could the other overtake him, until the others were out of sight.

"What made you run you whitelivered hound?" said the colonel, angrily.

"Because he knew me."

"And did you know him?"

"No."

"Your precious uncle, the dwarf, who has done you out of your possessions."

"Curses light on him," said Treherne, who had only been drawn into this dangerous pastime as a freak.

"It may be remedied," replied the colonel, "but let us return to the Rose and Crown. We will then decide as what is to be done."

We return to Leopold.

On they went.

As they rode through villages, they could see a light burning here and there, with tranquil ray, in small casements beneath the thatched roof.

Watch-dogs, disturbed by the clang of the horse's hoofs, barked long and loudly after them, their bark being the only sound that smote the ear.

Towards the morning they beheld the moon setting behind a clump of firs, and the beautiful morning star shining bright, clear, and cold, with white, pure ray in the high heavens. How different was the country, with its fresh, healthy air, and sweet smells, from the mad-house full of ghastly sights, despair, and death.

As night disappeared, and birds began to chirp and hop forth, whilst the rosy and saffron colours, that tinged the east, announced that the life-giving sun was at hand, they spied a distant and well-known wayside inn, and halted for ten minutes.

CHAPTER LXII.

TREHERNE HALL.

THEY were now fast approaching the end of their journey. They were nearing Treherne Hall, which we have hitherto omitted to describe, picturesque as it is.

It stands in a low situation, as most of such houses do. On three sides it is surrounded by a park that spreads over the adjoining hill; on the fourth, by meadows, which are watered by a river.

Close on one side of the house is a thick grove of lofty trees, along the verge of which runs one of the principal avenues to it through the park.

It is an irregular building, of great antiquity, and was probably erected about the termination of the feudal warfare, when defence became no longer necessary in a country mansion. Many circumstances in the interior of the house, however, seem appropriate to feudal times.

The hall is very spacious, floored by stones, and lighted by large transom windows that are clothed with casements.

Its walls are hung with old military accoutrements that have long been left a prey to rust.

At one end of the hall is a range of coats of mail and helmets, and there is on every side abundance of old-fashioned pistols and guns, many of them with matchlocks.

Immediately below the cornice hangs a row of leathern jerkins, made in the form of a shirt, supposed to have been worn as armour by the vassals.

A large oak table, reached from one end of the room to the other, might have feasted the whole neighbourhood.

The rest of the furniture is in a suitable style, particularly an arm-chair of cumbrous workmanship, constructed of wood, and curiously turned, with a high back and triangular seat, said to have been used by Judge Hepburn, in the time of "good Queen Bess."

The entrance is at one end by a low door, communicating with the passage that leads from the outer door in the front of the house to a quadrangle within.

At the other it opens into a gloomy staircase, by which you ascend to the first floor; and passing the doors of some bed-chambers, enter a narrow gallery, which extends along the back front of the house from one end to the other of it, and looks upon an old garden.

This gallery is hung with portraits, principally in the Spanish dresses of the sixteenth century.

In one of the bed-chambers which you pass in going to the gallery, is a bedstead with blue furniture, which time has now made dingy and threadbare; and as you pass through the other rooms, you find long corridors, little narrow passages, staircases of walnut or oak, with Gothic or Elizabethan banisters; and at the top, a great variety of little pigeon-hole bed-rooms.

During the reign of Henry VII., the country mansions of many of the gentlemen of the country were little better than cottages, being thatched buildings, covered on the outside with the coarsest clay, many of which are still to be seen in various parts of England, especially in that part of Suffolk called High Suffolk.

Some of the better sorts of these are inhabited by farmers, as at Kenton Hall; others are adapted for two or three labouring families.

In the servants' hall sat four men.

They were the sole occupants.

They were getting old in the service, but they looked well.

They were the four retainers to whom we have already alluded.

They had never left sight of the house, and sat there in the hope of his coming again.

They could not believe that he was dead.

During the whole of this period, by the terms of the will, they retained charge of the house.

A lawyer was deputed to invest the savings, but the four retainers were so honest that there was no necessity for any supervision.

They were faithful and true until the last.

They led a peculiar and regular but not monotonous life.

One always remained within on guard.

The other three would pay visits to the tenants, or spend their days in shooting and fishing.

They were hale and hearty, the more so that they had nothing to reproach themselves with.

They were at breakfast, when they heard the sound of horses dashing up to the door.

They exchanged glances.

Then came a knock and a loud peal.

All rose and went out into the hall. A kind of instinct seemed to tell them that at last the time had come when deliverance might be expected.

But they did not depart from their usual caution. They took fire-arms in their hands.

"Who is there?" said——

"'Tis I," cried Leopold Treherne, in a loud voice; "open."

He did open with a cry of joy and triumph.

He alighted rapidly and entered.

"You only here to receive me," he gasped; "where is my wife?"

They held down their heads.

"My child wife dead," he gasped; "have I escaped my torturers for this?"

Then closing the door and leading him into the library, they explained, that for all they knew, Mrs. Treherne and Jessie might still be alive.

Leopold drew breath.

"I see it all. There is some foul and dastard treachery under all this."

"I think so," said——"for two days before Mrs. Treherne fled, Phineas Bristowe alias Beckford was here."

"Ah!" groaned Marmaduke, between his set teeth, "then do I understand."

"And I," added Leopold, equally energetically. "But close and bar the door, let no one know of my return. I will set a watch on them. I will somehow unravel this mystery. The colonel is abroad, we will defeat them, yet."

And glad to gain repose, he desired that each should be shown to a separate room, to be called at dusk, when dinner was to be ready.

At dusk they dined, and then Leopold and Marmaduke, both amply supplied with money and mounted on splendid horses, armed to the teeth, and accompanied by——and——set out on their way to London.

There they proposed to set afloat inquiries as to the whereabouts of the villain, Phineas.

But on their arrival in London, Marmaduke, who had been sullen and wild in manner, parted company.

His terrible mad fit was on him.

CHAPTER LXIII.

ESCAPE TO AMERICA.

MARMADUKE's first idea was, to go down to Haddington Hall, and there find out the address of Mrs. Treherne.

But a wild, strange mania prevented him.

He was afraid of that fearful fiend, Mrs. Treherne.

He wandered about London streets, until his money was nearly spent.

Then he knew not what to do.

A sense of his own insensate folly, made him almost madder than he was.

He determined to go to America at any price, where, in the bosom of the tribe which had admitted him as a chief, he should be happy and quite safe from mad-houses.

He would never return, never own himself as Marmaduke Haddington until he was sure that Phineas Bristowe was dead.

But he had but little money.

What mattered that? He would find some way to escape the foul fiends from whom he was never free.

America—that was where he would wander and be for ever free.

He managed, heaven only knows how, through danger and difficulties, to make his way to Liverpool.

He watched, with the deep and acute cunning of a serpent, and semi-maniac, the ships.

He lounged round the ships.

He saw that one was being lighter loaded than the others, and that it was to sail with a great empty space in the hold.

But he also saw that great store of provisions was being placed in the hold.

More important than all, water and oil casks.

With his last few shillings he bought a lantern, a gimlet, and tin cup.

Then one night he crept into the hold of the ship.

Soon it was battened down and they sailed.

Then came that fearful *duel in the dark* which has been described in our third number.

We left him on the briny pathless ocean, alone in an open boat.

The vessel which had saved Phineas Bristowe never thought of examining a worthless boat.

Not an hour after the sails of the brigantine were mere gull wings in the distance; a slow sailing English brig passed.

They saw the boat, and for sheer humanity passed close.

They saw what appeared a dead body in the boat.

They however examined it and found that the man was living.

They also saw that hunger and thirst had nearly done their work.

But kind treatment saved him.

When he came too, he was very weak and quiet. All signs of madness was temporarily gone.

They provided him with clothes and money.

He merely said, that he and another had been left behind on board the ——, in the berths, and had lost all.

He landed at Boston, well dressed, with a good supply of money.

He knew that the other was going to New York, and there he made his way.

Our readers are aware how terrible was the scene between himself and Phineas,* and how vilely he was treated.

This scene affected his reason again, and once more joined the Pawnees, where, hunting and fishing, he slowly became himself again.

Then he persuaded his new friends to aid him in an onslaught on the Mormons who should endeavour to make their way to Salt Lake.

We have seen him at work.

We return to the dwarf.

CHAPTER LXIV.

FOKER.

It was sometime ere Leopold got the least trace of Cornelia and Jessie, and many adventures did they go through, ere they were on the track.

* See No. 12—In which we have painted some of the mysteries of Mormonism, of which it is truly said: The age is lost in wonder at the migrating stream of gold-seekers pouring in upon the El Dorados of California and Australia. A far more astonishing phenomenon is the emigration of thousands to the new holy land of Utah, seeking for a terrestial paradise amid the wilds of Deseret, and a New Jerusalem in the city of the Great Salt Lake. Ships sail from Liverpool laden with "Latter-day Saints," firm believers in the divine mission of Joe Smith, the literal inspiration of the Book of Mormon, the "hopeless corruption" of the Holy Bible, and the prophetic authority of Governor Brigham Young. Comfortable farmers, even small and unembarrassed proprietors, quit the homes of their ancestors and the scenes of their childhood, renounce an allegiance to the government under which they have safely and happily lived, and communion with the church of their fathers, to brave perils by sea and land for the sake of one of the grossest impostures and most transparent shams that ever deluded human credulity. Wonderful indeed must be the spell that can annihilate in the hearts of good homely men and women, not only all the elements of the Christian faith, about which they had never been taught to doubt, but even the ties, almost as sacred, by which their family life had hitherto been regulated. The converts to Mormonism—to a barbarous and bigoted false religion, to utter uncharitableness, and to polygamy—are not to be found among scoffers and sceptics, reprobates, and godless vagabonds, but among pious and well-conducted families, people against whom there is no slur, and frequenters of prayer-meetings. There must be something grievously wrong in the intellectual condition of the community amidst whom this strange form of fanaticism can take root. There needs no long search to discover the source of the evil,—in the want of enlightened education we can too plainly discern the cause.

LEOPOLD AND JESSIE.

They scoured London.

Leopold made himself known to his solicitors, who were astounded, and gladly assisted him in all his designs.

They were delighted to see a hope of his restoration to his wife and family.

Detectives were at last suggested.

Leopold was too well known for him to attempt to act.

But he was introduced to a Mister Siphoss Foker, one of those peculiarly cunning gentlemen who never allow anything in the shape of crime to escape them.

He was a stout, burly man, with a red necker-chief, and a smiling countenance, who listened to all that Leopold had to say, with deep attention.

The two retainers from Treberne Lodge were present.

"Do they know the person of the colonel?" asked Mr. Siphon Foker.

Dick nodded.

"Then I tell you what: you and I must set about this matter. I rather think I know the gentleman myself."

This agreed upon, Leopold gave the detective a certain sum of money, with which he and Dick departed.

Much to the amazement of Dick, he would have to play the gentleman.

Foker was to be his tiger.

The colonel, if in London, which, after his recognition by Leopold, was very likely, would frequent certain places, where men could only be admitted by means of money.

So they hired a cabriolet, and drove about to gambling-houses, or to those low night houses near the Haymarket, upon which the police make a sham onslaught now and then, in order to disguise the real fact that they tolerate them.

But they found him not.

One evening they were returning from the Haymarket rather late.

The night was dark—dark with the melancholy mysterious blackness of a winter midnight, and so still, that distant sounds seemed near at hand.

Snow fell lightly, quickly, and silently on hill and vale; on plains, and on frozen rivers, streams, and pools.

The earth was white with it; and every hour added to the depth thereof; as it fell, fell, fell, throughout the livelong night.

Everybody knows what London is on such a night.

It was slush, slush, slush, and the horse went slowly.

Dick was leaning back smoking a cigar.

Foker was driving.

They were going towards Westminster.

"By heavens, there he is!" suddenly said Dick.

"Where?"

"I saw him go up yonder alley."

They looked about anxiously. A boy was shivering at the corner of a street.

A policeman was at no great distance.

They alighted.

"Hold this horse," they said to the boy, "and you shall have a shilling. And you, Sharman, keep your eye on him."

With these words to the momentarily astonished policeman, they moved on, and went slowly up the alley.

"You must be careful here," said Foker, in a whisper; "it's a regular thieves' den. They know me. Do you look, and keep your ears open. Drink and smoke while I keep watch. Do not seem to take any notice of the colonel—*and don't know me!*"

Dick nodded assent, and they soon found themselves in a low public house, such as can scarcely be found out of Westminster.

And such as this are not even to be found in Westminster nowadays.

The public room into which Dick swaggered, with a kind of shudder at the night, was crowded.

Outside, the feathery flakes were falling in eddies upon eddies—while within, smoke was rising in clouds.

Those in the room were chiefly of the lower orders, and nowhere did Dick see the colonel.

But he knew he was not mistaken.

Taking up a position by which he could see if anyone left the house, he ordered a stiff shilling rummer of brandy-and-water and a cigar.

Then whiffing away with affected *nonchalance*, he glanced around.

A man opposite to him sat with an empty glass.

"Liquor up, my friend!" said Dick. "A terrible night—glad to get in anywhere."

As the other saw that he was a swell, he was not at all averse to accept his invitation.

They got into friendly conversation: and as Dick was a shrewd, clever fellow, he managed to draw the other out with great ability.

Most of the others were thieves, while he was really a distressed mechanic, who, having no work and no home, had come in, to earn the right to a shelter, for half a pint of beer.

Dick saw that he was hungry.

He was himself.

"Can I have anything to eat?"

"I think so," said the mechanic, with a curious flash of the eye.

"You," said Dick, bending over, "order something for two, I know you'll join me."

The other rose with good will, and obtained two plates of cold roast mutton, bread, and pickles, which they both ate with great relish.

"Where do you come from, my man?"

"T——."

"What!" said Dick, with a start, fixing his eyes curiously on the other; "then your name is James Denton?"

The other started, blushed, and looked almost guilty. He was the son of a good man, who, while good times lasted, had given him a superior education—hoping he knew not what.

He almost dared, while an excellent parson educated him, that he might follow the ministry; for Walter Denton loved study and religion.

He loved to follow the "parson" in his tours of charity; to stand by him and listen to the advice, the comfortings, and consolations he gave to his poor flock; or to stroll with him through the green meads beside the glassy, winding river—noting the reflection of clouds, trees, and reeds in the water—viewing how fleetly the flying swallows skimmed along, dipping their wings, and leaving many circles to mark the spot where the tip of their pinion struck the silvery stream; whilst he learnt the while how good men had lived and tranquilly died, and how the wicked might flourish in life, but how their death-bed was a bed of agony—their minds full of fear and torment, crying out for the fleeting moments to tarry; whilst the moments hurried on, and the wicked died with frightened soul and face of grief and horror—startling the living, and leaving them a double weight of woe.

"Who knows me?" said the other, dropping his knife and fork.

"A friend! and one who can serve you. B how comes this change?"

"Father died—Mr. Leopold died—I had no friend—I was obliged to follow any trade I could get."

"Leopold Treherne is not dead," said Dick. "Nay, do not start. I am here in his service; and if you will but aid us, I guarantee you shall have your best wishes realized."

The other could scarcely repress a tear.

At this moment Foker came into the room, and touched his hat.

" Ready, sir ? " he said.

" No," replied Dick, who understood his glance. " I find this better than the snow, rain, and sleet. And Joe, I think you want something."

The landlord came in, smirking and bowing at the sight of a livery servant, though he knew well enough who he was.

Foker drank his stiff-one, and then they rose to go. Walter Denton followed, at a hint from Dick.

CHAPTER LXV.

WHAT FOKER HEARD.

WHEN Foker entered the house, he made himself known to the landlord; and after giving an assurance that he should not be hurt from anything that occurred, was allowed to follow the men up to a private room.

A convenient cupboard—by which the landlord had become possessed of many a valuable secret—admitted him to see and hear the three men, who were waiting for brandy and cigars.

They were the colonel, Joe Galpin, and Josh Rackstraw.

Three more awful villains never sat down at a table together.

Josh was on his road to Joe Galpin's crib when he met the colonel and that worthy.

The night was so vile, and Joe Galpin so mean, that they all adjourned to a place they knew so well as the Jolly Beggars.

They had not spoken a word when Foker took up his position as a listener.

Soon the brandy was placed before them.

Every man filled a glass and lit a mild Havana.

" Well," said Joe Galpin, who had been the colonel's agent in the matter, " what's the news?"

" Found her."

" The deuce you have! " cried the colonel. " And the brats ? "

" Found them, too."

" I knew he had good news," said Joe.

" I have found them. They are nice and snug ; and now what is to be done ? "

" What we want is possession of the children," said the colonel.

" And when you have them, what then ? " asked the conscientious old rascal.

" Now Mr. Josh Rackstraw," put in Joe, " that is no part of your business. Do you return this very night home, and we will follow. Never lose sight of them—that's your game—or if you can secure them, so much the better."

Josh Rackstraw acquiesced, and it was finally arranged that he should return the next night, and start by coach from the Blue Post.

The others were to communicate with Mrs. Treherne and follow.

This was enough for Foker who at once came down.

* * * * * * *

This was the news communicated to Leopold

Treherne, who, wild with delight and joy, determined to start for Bristol at once.

But there was no post-chaise would start on such a night.

They were compelled to wait until the next day.

Leopold at once agreed to take Walter Denton by the hand once more.

He then retired to bed.

Next day excitement had so fevered him, that he was prostrate and unable to rise.

It took the whole day and the next night to fit him to travel.

Then away they went as fast as they could, and arrived in Bristol in time to find Cornelia but not the children.

No trace could be found of them nor of the Colonel, when Leopold and Cornelia returned to London.

We have described how soon after, by means of the public papers, the position of Jessie and Henry was at last found, we have seen the joyous happiness of the united family living in harmony and happiness, and we have seen it again marred by the villainous atrocity of Phineas and the Viscount de Florac.*

We now find after all the pain, labour, and patience which they have endured to discover her, once more trapped, deceived, and taken away.

CHAPTER LXVI.

THE DANITE CAPTAIN.

WHEN the Captain of the Danites discovered the trail of Phineas Bristowe, he at once started in pursuit.

He was a determined man, and whether determined by love or hate, acted with rapidity and decision.

The great Mormon camp was on the move, and would not be delayed for so paltry a purpose as the escape of two women.

Out towards the plains of the west they went, over two thousand emigrating waggons, besides a large number of nondescript turn-outs, the motley make-shifts of poverty, from the unsuitably heavy-cart that lumbered on mysteriously, with its sick driver hidden under its counterpane cover, to the crazy two-wheeled trundle, such as our own poor employ for the conveyance of their slop-barrels, this pulled along, it may be, by a little dry, dogged heifer, and rigged up only to drag some such light weight as a baby, a sack of meal, or a pack of clothes and bedding.

But the Captain of the Danites was filled with rage, hate, and love.

He loved the women for their charms, he hated them for their manifest dislike of himself.

This is a point which a man never forgives.

This is especially true where on his side the passion is strong.

And the Captain of the Danites was never satisfied, unless he made an addition to his harem once a month.

* See No. 17 and No. 58.

There is one thing to be said in extenuation of Mormonism.

They do openly what too many do slily and secretly here—and yet are not severely blamed for.

Society acquits the man and blames the woman.

Vices, that chance to be fashionable, are treated as slight failings, and coloured over in common discourse with those soft and gentle names, which express no condemnation. We enter perhaps on the world with good principles, and an aversion to downright vice. But when, as we advance in life, we become initiated into that mystery of iniquity, which is called the way of the world—the practice of the multitude renders vice familiar to one's thoughts—and, instead of men's vices detracting, as they ought to do, from our good opinion of the men, our attachment to the men oftener reconciles us to the vices of which they are guilty. To acquire a full view of any danger to which we are exposed, is the first measure to be taken in order to our safety. No virtue is more necessary to a man, than that firmness of mind which can enable a man to maintain his principles and stand his ground against the torrent of custom, fashion and example. We imperceptibly slide into some resemblance of the manners of those with whom we have frequent intercourse. This often shows itself in the most indifferent things; but the resemblance is still more readily contracted, when there is something within ourselves, that leads to the same side, which is countenanced by the practice of others.

We have seen that the Danite captain, after many difficulties by the way, succeeded on coming on the track of the fugitives and in taking away his prisoners.

They had been put at fault several times by the circumstance of Phineas Bristowe having driven over stony places, where no trail could possibly be found.

But now he had them, and he would have his revenge.

The men who accompanied him were three.

Fortunately for Jessie two of them were fanatical believers in the Mormon doctrine, and would not allow any outrage.

The Danite Captain knew that he must be sealed to Jessie ere he could claim her as his bride.

The Mormons had gained three days march upon him, but he knew the country, having journeyed this way before.

He was determined to travel as the crow flies.

It was an arduous arid journey, but good horses must soon overtake lumbering waggons, and droves of oxen and sheep.

Fearnot by name and also by nature, he had no hesitation.

He was well aware that he was in an enemies country, but he cared not.

The Pawnees, who, instigated by Marmaduke, had become the foes of the Mormons, were prowling about in large numbers, were to be feared however.

This made him cautious in the extreme.

He travelled ahead of the party, and kept a good look out, while the others guarded the prisoners.

It was a hot and sultry day.

They were compelled to halt at mid-day to refresh themselves and horses.

Fearnot spoke not a word.

He had made a terrible discovery, and was musing whether to go backward or forward.

They were close to a noted trail of the Pawnees, which was being daily crossed by them.

He consulted with his companions.

Before leaving the halt, they had stripped the shoes off the horses, filling the nail-holes up with clay, so that their tracks would be taken for those of wild mustangs. Such were the precautions of men who know that their lives might be the forfeit of a single foot-print.

Then again they started on their way, still keeping a good look out.

At night they reached a defile in the mountains and rested in a thicket of nut pine.

Here it was determined to pass the night.

CHAPTER LXVII.

THE CACHE.

In front of them was a low ridge covered with loose rocks and straggling trees of the nut-pine. This ridge separated the defile from the plain, and from its top, screened by a thicket of the pines, they commanded a view of the waters as well as the trail, and the mountain stretching away to the north, south, and east. It was just the sort of hiding place they required for their object.

Before daybreak they were again on foot, and were about to lead their horses down to drink, when a loud cry from Captain Fearnot startled them.

It was still moonlight, and they saw, moving along in the distance a large mass of something black.

Was it Indians, was it buffaloes.

Buffaloes do not advance in this steady way, while Indians often march by night to repose by day.

The moonlight fades and the grey light of day takes its place.

It is a large mass of Indian cavalry

To say that the Comanche is the finest horseman in the world would be to state what is not the fact. He is not more excellent in this accomplishment than his neighbour and bitter foeman, the Pawnee,—no better than the "vaquero" of California, the "ranchero" of Mexico, the "llanero" of Venezuela, the "gaucho" of Buenos Ayres, and the horse-Indians of the "Gran Chaco" of Paraguay, of the Pampas, and Patagonia. He is equal, however, to any of these, and that is saying enough,—in a word that he takes rank among the finest horsemen in the world. The Comanche is on horseback almost from the hour of infancy—transferred, as it were, from his mothers arms to the withers of a mustang. When able to walk, he is scarce allowed to practice this natural mode of progression, but performs all his movements on the back of a horse.

So with the Pawnees, who are advancing steadily over the plain in all their bravery.

The glittering points of their spears can be seen

flashing in the sun, and their half-naked bodies gleam in the morning light.

They are evidently about to halt near the sparkling spring in front of the defile.

What is to be done?

To move while they are there would be to expose themselves, to lose their prizes and their lives.

Jessie and Amy would certainly betray that they are Mormons.

For a moment Fearnot thought of killing them, or leaving them to starve, and presenting themselves to the Pawnees as mountain trappers

But the captain of the Danites is a man too well known to be able to thus disguise himself.

He is better known than trusted.

All they have to do is to lie still and wait.

But what are the Indians doing?

They proceed to picket their horses in a wide circle far out on the plain. There the grama grass is longer and more luxuriant than in the immediate neighbourhood of the spring. They strip the animals, and bring away their horse-furniture, consisting of hair bridles, buffalo robes, and skins of the grizzly bear. Few have saddles. Indians do not generally use them on a war expedition.

They little suspected that here was the rendezvous to take place between Marmaduke and his Indian braves.

They are to spend the intervening time in hunting and other amusements suitable to warriors.

Fearnot began to feel his heart fail him as each man strikes his spear into the ground, and rests against it his shield, bow, and quiver. He places his robe or skin beside it. That is his tent and bed. The spears are soon alighted upon the prairie, forming a front of several hundred yards, and thus they have pitched their camp with a quickness and regularity far outstripping the chasseurs of Vincennes.

They seemed to have no idea whatever of resuming their march.

Many fires are soon blazing brightly. The savages squat around them cooking their suppers. We can see the paint glittering on their faces and naked breasts. They were of many hues. Some were red, as though they were smeared with blood. Some appear of a jetty blackness. Some black on one side of the face, and red or white on the other. Some were mottled like hounds, and some striped and chequered. Their cheeks and breasts were tattooed with the forms of animals—wolves, panthers, bears, buffaloes, and other hideous devices, plainly discernible under the blaze of the pine-wood fires. Some have a broad hand painted on their bosoms, and not a few exhibit as their device the death's head and cross-bones.

And when night came not a sign of the resumption of the march was noticed.

What was to be done?

They had little provisions and less water.

A whispering conference was held. They would wait that night, and then if the Indians did not move, they must resort to something desperate.

There was no escaping any other way. The defile into which they had ventured was no thoroughfare.

It was blocked up at the other end by massive rocks almost overhanging the fugitives.

There was nothing whatever in the defile but a few bushes with the yacca nut upon them.

A single pine of singular growth was perched on the side, and could be seen from the plain below.

There is nothing whatever for the horses to eat but cacti.

The only hope of the party, if the Indians remain long, is horse flesh.

But then what follows?

How can they travel across the arid plain which now intervenes between them and the Mormon camp without horses?

Somebody must be left behind.

A ferocious idea enters the mind of Fearnot.

One of the men is a reckless dare-devil like himself, neither fearing God nor man. He has joined the Mormons solely to obtain immunity for his past crimes, and to enjoy as many women as he pleases.

The defile is about a hundred yards long, and twenty wide.

The girls have a kind of tent under some bushes; the two fanatics are sleeping.

Fearnot and Bill Bennett are watching at the mouth of the valley.

Jessie and Amy, hungry and thirsty, cannot sleep.

They are having recourse to the last resource of the hungry and starving hunter.

They are skinning each one of the cacti.

They carefully pave off the spikelets—a cool, gummy liquid exudes from the opened vessels.

It is food and drink.

Then Amy lay down, and sought forgetfulness in slumber.

But Jessie cannot sleep—some excessive horror sits upon her soul.

A something—she knew not what—preyed upon her mind, and rising, like one under the influence of somnambulism, she creeps to the mouth of the valley.

There sits Fearnot and Bennett, cowering under a bush, and smoking.

The wind is up the valley, and there is no fear of the smoke reaching the nose of the Indians.

Nothing is too trifling to be taken notice of by Indians when on the war trail.

That the human nose is keen, may be deduced from a celebrated anecdote.

During the French revolution, a party of sans-culottes, in ambuscade in a marsh *up to their waists in water*, were thus addressed by their chief.

"Smoking might be dangerous, but you may sit down!"

The Indians would have discovered the scent if the wind had been the other way.

"Dull work this," said Fearnot.

"Darned dull."

"Them fokes makes it duller."

"Which are them fokes?"

"Hezekiah and Jabez——"

"How so?"

"We are short of provisions and water; but we've got two handsome girls."

Jessie shuddered.

Bennet gave a low, but very significant chuckle.

"They might as well keep us company," continued Fearnot.

"And why not?"

"Well, those two puling idiots think I might wait till I am sealed to them."

"Well, so you is to Amy."

"But I want the other proud little vixen."

"Oh!"

"Now, Bennett, one thing is certain. If we are to be shut up here long, a horse or two must go. Well, the riders might as well go to, for there's no escape from here on foot; so my ideas is plainly this: you shall have Amy, and I will have Jessie, if you will join in putting those snoring idiots out of the way."

"Now?"

"No."

"We will wait, then, until when?" asked Bennett.

"A reasonable time."

This was enough for Jessie, who retired with death in her heart.

Into the hands of what fiend had she fallen? It was horrible to think of.

But she could wait no longer to listen to their atrocious plans. She would retire to her hut and pray.

———

CHAPTER LXVIII.

THE PAWNEES.

AGAIN morning broke warm and delightful, and still the Indians stirred not; when, all of a sudden, a great uproar, and raising his head almost to an imprudent height, Fearnot saw that it was caused by a party of horsemen coming from the north.

They were about half-a-dozen in number.

The Indian seemed to receive them with delight, and escorted them into the camp with demonstrations of great joy.

About an hour after, the Indians were scouring the plain in every direction.

But still there remained one camp fire.

This is what had happened.

As soon as they were sufficiently rested, the party composed of Henry, Eudora, Obadiah Jones, Captain Lancy, and Sir Marmaduke, started to join the Indian rendezvous, with a determination to attack the whole force of the Mormons if Jessie was not found.

Henry and Eudora rode side by side.

They were very gloomy and thoughtful. Henry was thinking of his dear lost Jessie.

And Eudora knew it.

She was not unconscious of the fact that it was but nature.

Illicit passion always brings its own punishment if the guilty parties do not hate or despise each other they suspect.

The first use man makes of his affections is to sensualize his spirit. Yet he cannot be ennobled, except through those very affections. There is a ipening of the fruit, when it is more austere and acid than at any other time. It is not the time

of greenness, but the moment when it is becoming red—the transition state, when it is passing from greenness into sweetness.

Henry had shown no dimuinution of affection to Eudora. He still stole every night to her hut. But he loathed himself.

How long will it be before this feeling extends to her?

All ye women readers take ye timely warning.

The others armed to the teeth, road on a-head in conversation.

Marmaduke to beguile the time was giving them a full account of the Pawnees.

But every now and then he paused to watch for the trail of Fearnot and his gang.

At length it seemed to be lost, but Marmaduke cared not.

They did not proceed quickly as their horses were exhausted.

At length the Pawnees came in sight.

The meeting was rapturous on both sides, as the chief was as delighted as Marmaduke to meet his brother.

Then Marmaduke called for silence, and the whole tribe seating themselves on their hams on the ground, prepared to listen.

They first, of course, lit their pipes, while the white men did the same with their puros.

Puros are simply cigars manufactured in Mexico. The name serves to distinguish them from "cigarros de papel," or small paper cigarettes. The latter, however, are in much more general use among all classes of Mexicans, high or low, male or female. Havannah cigars are also smoked, but to no great extent. The little cartridge of paper is the favourite. There is also another kind in limited use, the "campeacheanos," or husk cigarettes—that is, those rolled in the husk of the maize plant. The "Mexican puros," are smoked extensively in London, under the name of "Pickwicks."

He then addressed the Indians in their native language, and told them how recently the Mormons had stolen away his son's bride.

He then introduced him to the Indians, who grunted applause and welcome.

This done, he asserted positively that they must be somewhere on the wide plains before them, and begged that his brother would start at once and hunt them up, while they remained and watched.

Every warrior rose to his feet, and giving the shrill war-whoop, leaped upon their horses, brandished their lances, and dividing themselves into numerous parties, started off to scour the plain.

In half-an-hour none remained.

Yes, one,—and that was the chief, whose life Sir Marmaduke had saved.

They were seated round the camp fire, in conversation.

They were also eating a juicy and pleasant meal of buffalo hump.

Henry was a little way off, in conversation with Eudora.

They were talking of Jessie.

In a subdued and low tone, Eudora deplored the infatuation of her own love.

"Eudora, say not so," cried Henry, "think not that I do not love you."

"You love me, I know—but with a love that will pass away—while what you feel for Jessie is real, permanent, eternal."

"I have been affianced to her since childhood," he said.

"I know! I know! But, Henry, when a woman loves, when she has given her all in all to a man, perilled her soul and honour, she cannot but wish to be remembered. I feel strangely to-day: promise me that when I am gone, you will never, never, forget me—"

"Never! But why so sad—"

"Sad—I know not that I am sad, and yet, do you remember the lines:—

Thou melancholy thought, which art
So fluttering and yet so sweet! to thee
When did I give the liberty,
Thus to afflict my heart?
What is the cause of this new power,
Which doth my fever'd being move,
Momently raging more and more?
What subtile pain is kindled now,
Which from my heart doth overflow
Into my senses?
Love! O, Love!

"Why quote them?"

"Because I feel, Henry, that my last day of happiness has come—that—*What is fluttering yonder?*"

Henry followed the direction of her finger.

"'Tis Jessie's scarf—" he cried.

"Said I not so," said Euroda, rising with him, and following him as, heedless of her, he rushed to join his companions.

It was indeed Jessie's scarf, fluttering from the one pine-tree of the valley.

In her desperation at hearing the atrocious project of Fearnot and Bennett, she had clambered up the hill side, and, at the peril of her life, affixed her scarf in a conspicuous way to one of the branches.

Then she descended, and joined the whole party.

It was just as the Indians were joined by the party of whites.

CHAPTER LXIX.

A SIGNAL.

A dead silence prevailed in the valley, until the Pawnees sallied forth.

"How many?" asked Fearnot, pointing to the camp-fire.

"Seven——"

"Too many," said Fearnot; "hampered as we are, we must wait until night, and then making a dash for it, trust to our horses."

"Rather," said Bennett, "steal away quietly, and cut and run when we're a good way off."

A discussion rose on this point, which lasted some time, when suddenly Fearnot swore a great and savage oath.

"They've smoked us—back, you women, and keep a still tongue in your heads, or, by God, you'll have your tongues cut out."

Jessie and Amy readily retreated out of sight, as the former was seriously alarmed lest the Mormons might discover her stratagem.

"Now, my boys," said Fearnot, "we have a hard fight. But we have the vantage ground, plenty of powder and shot, and are as savage as bars—aint yer?"

They nodded their heads.

"Now, do you two hide in yon cactus grove," he said, to the two converts.

They walked straight there. They were brave and determined men.

Fearnot and Bennett lay down upon a sloping rock, so that they could not be seen by any one below them.

Presently the footsteps of those who were advancing were heard.

They were taking advantage of every mound, bush, and tree, to advance to the attack.

They were fighting, as men should fight in the prairies, according to Indian tactics.

It was the avoidance of this, and the martinet observance of European rules, that caused us so many defeats in America.

No other sound was to be heard, when suddenly Fearnot raised his head about an inch over the rock.

Two rifle cracks were heard simultaneously.

But the shots were too hasty to cause any execution.

Obadiah Jones had fired from behind a tree. His bullet hit the rock; that of Fearnot hit the tree.

Then came a pause. No one knew how to act. A kind of hand to hand fight seemed that most likely to be resorted to at last.

Then came two quick shots from the cactus bushes, and a loud cry from those below showed that somebody was hit.

The blood of the combatants was up, but all the firing was nearly in vain.

Then the Mormons, who were suffering from extreme hunger and thirst, resolved to do or die.

They raised themselves a little, and each picking out a man, fired.

The others did the same.

Then there was a rush from Obadiah, de Lancy, Henry, and Eudora.

Marmaduke sat wounded against a tree. The Indian was out of sight.

At that instant Fearnot received a shot in his back.

It was but a flesh wound, and yet very painful. He turned and saw—

The Indian and the scarf!

The one was descending the rocks; the other was floating on the pine-tree.

"To your cover," he shouted; "we are betrayed."

And he discharged a pistol full at the advancing foe, and then fled.

He was resolved, at any cost, to be avenged on the girls, whom he believed to have betrayed him.

Once in the valley, they were without the reach of the Indian's rifle.

With a yell, snatching up their guns, he darted to the very depths of the valley.

But the girls were nowhere to be found.

Ferocious cries of vengeance filled the air, and their souls were one sentiment of hatred and revenge.

But what was to be done ?

Two of the party were wounded, and the Indian was in a position where he could not momentarily touch them.

They were not pursued.

They would trust to their horses.

Hastily they mounted, crept through the valley, and then, spurring their faint and exhausted steeds, passed their assailants at a trot.

But no one took notice of them.

They were too little able to defend themselves to seek the reason why.

CHAPTER LXX.

WHY ?

WHEN Fearnot discharged his pistol at the advancing foe, Eudora, who had not yet fired off her rifle, was taking aim.

But the rifle fell from her hands, and she fell on the ground, bleeding copiously.

All rushed to her side, her father wildly cursing the assassin of his child.

At the same moment, Jessie and Amy, who had crept through the bushes and watched the run of the Mormons, no sooner saw them retreat, than they came rushing to join the horror-stricken group.

Eudora was supported in the arms of her father.

" My own child," he said frantically, " speak to me."

" I cannot speak—but just two words," she replied. " I am dying. Is that you, Jessie—and you, Henry—yes ! I feel you—you—are happy —I am."

And she fainted ; nor did her lips ever again move, until the last shudder came, and then she murmured a word, heard only by one.

" Henry !"

They all rose to their feet to see the Mormons galloping off over the plain.

In vain.

A dozen painted warriors were at their heels.

Then all moved towards where Marmaduke sat. He was severely wounded, but not beyond cure, though his mind was deeply agitated at the sight of the fearful tragedy which had just been enacted.

Had he have only known.

Henry kneeled beside him.

" Be not alarmed for me, Henry," his father said ; " all I care is for the murderers of that poor girl."

" They are taken," said the deep voice of the chief, pointing over the plain, where the Mormons were already to be seen, bound and captive, in the hands of the Indians.

In their blind hurry to escape, they had fallen into the hands of the Redskin warriors.

No one took any heed of them for a time. They were brought to the mouth of the valley, and there tied to trees.

Then they began to dig Eudora's grave.

They were about to bury her where she had fallen. Her father was the most busy of all those who worked.

Not a tear fell upon his rugged and pallid cheek.

Henry, despite the presence of Jessie, was utterly overwhelmed with grief.

He made no effort to disguise his feelings.

He never moved his eyes from the face of Eudora. He was overwhelmed with his misfortune, but could not find words to express his feelings.

Grief acts differently on different people.

With some it produces a reverent feeling.

It is not easy to describe the sensation which the mind experiences on the first sight of a dead countenance which, when living, was loved and esteemed for the sake of that soul which used to gave it animation. A deep and awful view of the separation that has taken place between the soul and body of the deceased, since we last beheld them, occupies the feelings. Our friend appears to be both near and yet afar off. The features present the accustomed association of friendly intercourse. For one moment we could think them asleep. The next reminds us that the blood circulates no more ; the eye has last its power of seeing, the ear of hearing, the heart of throbbing, and the limbs of moving. Quickly a thought of glory breaks in upon the mind, and we imagine the dear departed soul to be arrived at its long-wished-for rest. Amid the solemn stillness of the chamber of death imagination hears heavenly hymns chanted by the spirits of just men made perfect.

But no such sentiments acted on the mind of Obadiah Jones.

He assisted to dig the grave, with the calm of a stoic. He worked harder than any of them.

" Shall I take your stick ?" (for they dug with roughly cut stakes).

These were the words of Henry.

" Have you not taken my daughter ?" said Obadiah, sternly. " Would you interfere with the last privilege I have ?"

Henry fell back abashed. Jessie *did not* understand.

It was, perhaps, a fortunate thing for her, just then, that she did not.

As soon as the grave was dug, he took off his great blanket coat, and with a sob, which made every one of them turn away to hide a tear, wrapped her in it.

Then reverently, as a mother puts a babe to bed, he laid her in her narrow bed, and looked at her.

She seemed to smile even in death.

" Bring up the Mormons," he said.

They, wondering why, brought the trembling caitiffs up.

He pointed to the grave.

" Who shot that ar shot ?" he said, drawing forth his pistol.

" You won't let us be murdered ?" cried Fearnot ; while the others clasped their hands in agony.

They turned away.

The Mormons were the property of the dread father.

The rough backwoodsman looked at them with a withering glance.

" It wud be justice," he said, gloomily. " If I had never seen their faces, I should ——"

And he sobbed aloud.

THE SOMNAMBULIST.

"But no! Death were too good for the mean ruffians."

He looked around.

There were four trees close at hand.

By his directions they were lashed to them firmly.

There was not a chance of escape.

The grave was not filled. The trapper intended to return alone, and fill it in when they were dead.

Marmaduke was mounted on a horse, and the cavalcade departed.

Save Fearnot, the Mormons yelled and cried for mercy.

He was a man neither to ask for nor take it.

He looked after them in a defiant and scornful way, threatening them with annihilation.

"Those who raise their finger against the Lord shall go to the devil," he said.

"Yes, truly," said Obadiah, solemnly, "it is so, and you shall see him."

And he retired.

The three inferior Mormons fainted from sheer terror.

Fearnot began to sing in a defiant voice.

But when he saw that there was no one near, he, too, lost his air of defiance, and peered round, in the hope that they were only playing tricks with him.

"Wake up, you brutes," he said, "and see if you cannot loose yourselves."

Groans, prayers, and outcries, were the only reply he obtained.

They were too overcome to help themselves.

Their eyes were fixed upon the body of the poor murdered girl.

Murdered, because there is no fair fighting where the cause is a foul one.

"Will you hold your row?" shrieked the exasperated Fearnot.

"What's the use of talking?" said Bennett, "that won't do any good."

"Nor more will howling, you cowardly vagabonds!"

"Cowardly yourself."

In this awful way the time passed. Now they prayed, now they cursed; but no help came.

The three Mormons were prostrated with fear, suffering, and thirst.

Fearnot was calmer. He, at all events, hoped that something would turn up. And yet what could happen? He gazed fearfully at the cold corpse.

As he continued to look up, an object attracted his attention. Against the sky he distinguished the outlines of a large bird; he knew it to be the obscene bird of the plains, the buzzard vulture.

Whence had it come? Who knows? Far beyond the reach of human eye it had seen or scented the slaughtered bodies, and, on broad silent wing, was now descending to the feast of death.

Presently another, and another, and many others, mottled the blue field of the heavens, curving and wheeling silently eastward. Then the foremost swooped down upon the bank, and after gazing around for a moment, flapped off towards its prey.

In a few seconds, the prairie was black with birds, which clambered over the dead bodies and beat their wings against each other, while they tore out the eyes of the quarry with their fetid beaks.

And now came gaunt wolves, sneaking and hungry, stealing out of the cactus, and leaping, coward-like, over the green swells of the prairie. These, after a battle, drove away the vultures, and tore up the prey, all the while growling and snapping vengefully at each other.

At this moment a light step was heard on the shingle.

Fearnot almost ceased to breath, so great was his surprise and joy.

It was Henry.

He had slipped away from the camp and ridden many miles to save them.

The hideous sight appalled him.

"Bury her," he said, in a choked voice, as he undid the Mormons.

They obeyed, and no sooner had they done so, than he turned away and galloped off at the top of his speed to join his companions.

Jessie alone knew or suspected what had happened.

Obadiah Jones was so prostrated with fever that, as soon as they reached the settlements, they were compelled to give him over to the keeping of some kind-hearted friends.

The others continued on their way towards New York, where it was their intention to embark for Europe.

We shall see how their expectations are realized.

CHAPTER LXXI.

NEW YORK.

THERE was indeed a happy meeting in New York. Not only did Jessie find her father and mother, but Captain de Lancy found his true and faithful wife waiting for him.

She never regretted the months during which she had been deprived of the society of her husband.

She was more than rewarded at seeing the glistening eyes of Jessie.

At the same time, she noticed the melancholy of Henry.

At first, she tried to dissipate it by taking Henry about everywhere.

This did not succeed.

They went to the opera—to public ball-rooms; and though Henry seemed proud to have Jessie on his arm, he seemed low and melancholy.

Mrs. de Lancy determined to solve this mystery.

She turned Jessie one evening over to her husband—who, as much in love with his wife as ever, was not altogether pleased—and took Henry forcibly away.

"You don't seem happy, Henry," she said, looking him fully in the face.

Henry sighed, and looked down.

"Are you sorry to find Jessie?" she asked.

"No."

"Henry, be a man, and tell me your story."

Henry glanced at the place where Jessie was walking.

"You have been unfaithful to her," said Mrs. de Lancy, with a quickness of manner quite foreign to her.

Henry blushed still more deeply.

"You bad, wicked man;" she said—but with such a sparkle of fun in her eye as bespoke a rather lenient nature; "but, then, it is *before* marriage. Tell me the truth, and I will absolve you."

And Henry told her all. Mrs. de Lancy listened with wrapped attention.

A woman likes a bit of scandal dearly. Pope says that every woman is at heart a rake. But this we do not credit.

Still a woman may be a very good, loving creature, and yet pardon an infraction against the laws of love—especially when the injured party is not herself.

And then Eudora—had she not been fatally punished?

"It this poor girl had lived," said Mrs. de Lancy, with a gravity which became a young matron, "there might have been some doubt as to the right course to pursue."

Henry sighed deeply.

" But for her sin and wickedness and folly, she has died. You may not be able to forget her; but listen to me, Henry."

" I am listening."

" You love Jessie."

" More than my life."

" You wish to make her happy?"

" That is my firm and unalterable intention," he said.

" Then take my advice. Cast off this melancholy, which, if noticed by Jessie, will make her ask questions. You will blush and have to confess. Then do you know what will happen?"

" No."

" She will verbally forgive you, because she loves you. But there will be a gnawing worm at her heart, of which you will never know."

" Heaven forbid!"

" A secret sorrow, which will prey upon her mind, and show itself when you are absent."

" She shall never know—I was a mad fool!' he cried.

"The girl was very beautiful, you were thrown together under very peculiar circumstances, and much may be forgiven you. At all events, as myself a young married woman, I absolve you. But do not forget yourself again, or I will not even be indulgent."

Henry smiled, and, like a youth as he was, promised solemnly that he would never offend again, at the same time pressing the beautiful young woman's hands to his lips with a fervour that made her blush.

" That will do, sir. I am afraid you are quite a Don Juan," she cried; " let us join Jessie."

And they did, exchanging partners to the satisfaction of all parties.

They had still a fortnight to remain in New York, as the only vessel which would have room for them all could not start before.

Henry made a faint suggestion that the interval might be passed in getting married.

But Leopold Treherne objected. They must be married in the open light of day in their own country.

St. George's, Hanover Square, was mentioned as the destined locale.

Jessie, of course, at once agreed to this, though we daresay, in her heart of hearts, she would rather have made her young lover happy.

There was no lack of amusements. A grand masked ball was announced to take place at one of the theatres. All agreed to go in such costumes as their fancy suggested.

Jessie, however, had only a domino and mask, while Henry, with something of the fatuity of youth, appeared in ordinary ball-room suit.

He had no reason for hiding his face—not he.

They were all there, except Sir Marmaduke Haddington, who shunned all public scenes.

Even now, though the death of Phineas Bristowe had lessened his hatred of his enemies, he was not at rest.

His bitterest enemy was his own sister, and that sister's child.

He could neither compass nor wish the death of Maria Trehene, the widow of the illegitimate brother of Leopold Treherne.

But would she be as forbearing as he was?

It is true, he had great power over her by the knowledge he possessed of her many iniquities; but how could he use this power, unless he exposed their family affairs to the world?

But Leopold Trehene informed him that she was already hard at work, endeavouring in their absence to obtain for her son and his wife the inheritance of Treherne Hall.

She had instructed her counsel to declare the will to be a forgery.

Its having been kept back a year did look suspicious.

Sir Marmaduke's time was taken up chiefly writing letters to his sister and her solicitors, giving minute directions as to all that was to be done.

One thing he insisted on, that his brother's wife should never leave that house she was made so well to adorn, but where, from the wickedness of others, she had had so much to endure for so many years.

With an abnegation which was part of his character, he devoted himself entirely to the interests and happiness of his friends.

But the young people, naturally enough, were not willing to deprive themselves of seeing the sights of a town which they fully intended never to see again.

Besides, those who knew better than themselves, were desirous that the few weeks which were to intervene before their marriage should not be spent in inaction; when, seated by one another's side, their emotions too big for speech, they would only become weary of themselves and others.

When genuine and honest passion fills the heart of man and woman, the last month before marriage is, indeed, a trying matter.

So to the ball, opera, and *bal masque*, they went every evening.

CHAPTER LXXII.

THE BAL MASQUE.

IT was given at the largest theatre in New York, then called the Opera.

Now, neither Henry or Jessie had ever been to such a place, and their expectations were much raised.

Few of our readers forget their first theatre, their first play. We do not.

We do not mean to say that we recollect where it was, or what was the piece; but we do recollect the loss of appetite at dinner, the impatience to get over tea, the eagerness with which we got to the doors before they were open, the awe with which we stared at the green baize, and the rapturous delight with which we at last saw the curtain rise.

The opera could be nothing to it. The opera is a fine thing, the only question is whether it is not too fine.

Every object is there collected that can strike the senses or dazzle the imagination—music, dancing, painting, poetry, architecture, the blaze of beauty, the glass of fashion and the mould of form—and yet one is not satisfied.

The powers of the mind are exhausted, without being invigorated.

But Harry and Jessie were too happy to analyze their feelings, so they listened to the music, and stared with excellent good breeding at all that took place.

They were not like the denizens of the boxes, the worn-out opera-goers, who gaped and stared, and affected to whisper and talk loud, to hide their weariness.

There was a clock in a prominent place near the refreshment room.

This was made the rendezvous of all parties every hour, when each couple would stroll up and relate their impressions, again to disperse.

Henry had easily opened an account at a banker's, his own and his father's vouchers being undeniable.

It was his intention to do the liberal, and he had contrived to secure on the stage one of the many bowers erected for the occasion to accommodate private parties.

They were to sup at twelve, or as soon after as a party who had engaged it at half-past eleven could leave.

At twelve, they politely requested until half-past. Henry, equally politely, gave them until one, and then again strolled away with his domino on his arm.

Now, for some time, Henry had noticed a man, in a superb costume, closely masked, who was following, or, rather, dodging the steps of a woman, superbly habited, and equally closely masked.

She had a rose silk domino over an evening dress, and the opening of the domino, every now and then, revealed the gorgeous splendour of a figure which must have been that of a young woman in the very prime of her voluptuous beauty.

Every now and then she cast a cautious glance at Henry.

She was evidently watching him, and did not desire to be noticed.

Clutched in her hand was a small *billet-doux*, which every now and then she appeared about to pass to him.

But something seemed to restrain her.

The eye of Jessie, whether from accident or design, seemed to be always upon her.

She was mistaken. Jessie had never, except casually, even seen her, and as her domino was like that of many others, paid no attention to her.

But Henry did. A kind of instinct told him that that woman had some reason for wishing to communicate with him.

He had not the slightest suspicion who she could be, which naturally made him all the more anxious.

But how could he communicate with her?

His curiosity was roused, and he almost felt he must gratify it.

But the hour of one came ere he could find an opportunity, and then it was supper time.

He could not look after his Domino Rose for awhile, but he determined not to be thrown off the scent.

After supper he would make an excuse to leave them, and take one turn in the house.

Why?

He could no more have told than why a child takes a fancy to one particular toy more than another.

But things were not doomed to turn out as he expected.

CHAPTER LXXIII.

THE SUPPER TABLE.

THE former guests had departed, and were once more mingled with the busy throng which came and went.

The theatre was immensely crowded, and only those who had taken early precautions stood any possible chance of a supper.

A bun, a cake, a biscuit, might by great good luck be obtained.

The luxurious supper which Henry had thought proper to provide was welcome to all the party, even to the young lovers.

Love is not generally supposed to add to the appetite. But this is a mistake. Tom Jones, after he has just parted from his mistress in deep despair, eating a shoulder of mutton, is much more true to nature than a sickly sentimental lover, who is represented as going without food for twenty-four hours.

Besides, the acme of perfection at a ball is a good supper, and that provided by Henry Haddington was in all respects good.

Soon the conversation became more animated. A glass or two of champagne or sparkling moselle will open the dear creatures' mouths.

It is not generally supposed that women want any stimulants to make them talk, but this is a barbarous and vulgar error.

Some women, especially young ones, are exceedingly shy in company.

But soon all in this bower were merry and chatty enough.

They were all happy. There was scarcely a shadow as light as a feather on their souls.

Only Harry was fidgety. He was trying to invent some excuse for getting away from Jessie.

"How that man stares at us," said Jessie, with something like a shudder, as the tall man passed once or twice before their bower.

"What man?" said Henry, with a start.

He, too, looked surprised when he saw it was the same man who had been following the Domino Rose.

"He seems to know us," he added, "but does not like to introduce himself. I will speak to him."

"Sit still, Henry Haddington," said a low, silvery voice close to his ear.

Harry sat down again, as if in obedience to a motion from the captain.

The stranger, who had noticed Henry rise, moved away in the crowd, but only to take up a position where he could see without being seen.

Henry filled the glasses to hide his confusion, and handed them round.

Jessie happened to be talking to her mother; the dwarf and Captain de Lancy were in conversation; Mrs. de Lancy, unknown to Henry, was watching him.

She saw that he was perturbed, but she could in no way tell why. His back was turned to the neighbouring alcove, and Mrs. de Lancey could scarcely suspect that anything there could interest him.

"Put your hand behind your back," said the soft voice.

Henry, with a strange tremour, did as he was told.

A note was placed in his hand, which he crunched up, and then slily put in his pocket.

"Attend minutely to what it contains—be careful, watchful, and brave—nothing evil will occur to you or yours. But, for Heaven's sake, trust in me."

Henry knew not what to do or say.

"If you mean to oblige one who has a deep and earnest claim on you, squeeze my hand," added the soft, sweet voice.

Henry squeezed the hand and then withdrew it.

The voice spoke no more, and as Henry turned he caught sight of the retreating figure of the *Domino Rose*.

Mrs. de Lancy looked half mischievously, half reproachfully, at him.

Henry hastened to summon Jessie for a dance, while the crowd was engaged at supper.

About an hour later they left the ball-room and returned to the hotel.

CHAPTER LXXIV.

THE LETTER.

THEY drove rapidly, everybody was tired and weary, so that they were glad to retire to rest.

Henry scarcely allowed himself time to lay down his candle ere he opened the letter addressed to him in his name in full.

"*You remember Lotty.* She it is who has spoken to you to-night. She is mad. Her secret is terrible. She must tell it to somebody. You are young, pure, innocent. You will not make me blush, because you will believe me. Come to my room, No. 22, and you shall know all. Then you can advise me.*"

Henry was astounded indeed. He had felt that the voice was a well-remembered one, but now he knew it well.

Our young hero, had, we are sorry to say, a spice of the Don Juan in him, and had hoped faintly for a slightly different denouement.

Was he sorry? was he glad? We would rather not analyze the secret feelings of his heart.

He never made us or anyone else his father confessor.

----

* See back to Nos. 20, 21, and 22, for the extraordinary story of Lotty.

His was the age of love:

> Love—our being's waking bliss;
> Spirit garb of Happiness;
> Heaven's halo, sent to shine
> O'er a world no more divine;
> Nature's heart, whose choicest measure
> Beats in time to promised pleasure;

But on the present occasion he determined to act as he had been directed, and at once opened his door to see that none were on the look-out.

All was still, the long carpeted corridors were lit up by lamps, whose rays shed a soft, religious light that was infinitely pleasing to behold.

He trod lightly. His own number was *seventeen*; the number *twenty-two* was not, then, far off.

He moved along almost like a guilty thing, for in the dead of the night was he not going to a lady's chamber?

Did Jessie but know it, what would she think?

But these reflections were now too late; he had started on his adventure, and he would follow it up.

After going about ten yards he came to a couple of steps, which he descended.

He then turned to the right.

As he did so, a man, tall, pale—deadly indeed in his hue—opened a door and peered out.

He had seen him pass.

He had also seen that Henry had dropped something, which he eagerly snatched up.

It was the letter from Lotty.

He read it without the slightest hesitation.

A dark frown crossed his countenance, and then a red flush that rushed to the very roots of his hair.

He followed slowly.

Meanwhile, Henry had reached number twenty-two and saw that the door was open.

He pushed it further open.

He was in a boudoir, very dimly lighted. But no one was there.

Before shutting the outer door, he determined to be sure that his summonser had come home.

He advanced to the bed-room door, which was also ajar, and knocked.

"Is that you, Henry?" said the well-known, soft voice.

"It is," replied Henry, pushing the door open.

"Have you shut the outer door?"

"No."

"Then do so quietly; for the world, I would not have your visit known."

While this short conference had taken place, the man who had followed him into the passage glided in and passed behind the window curtains.

Henry, not at all anxious to be interrupted, both closed and bolted the door.

"Impudent puppy!" muttered the tall man, poking his head through the curtains.

Henry entered the bed-room, where Lotty, still in her ball-dress, received him with a hearty shake of the hand.

He would have embraced her, but Lotty gently repelled him.

"Henry, I have called you here, because I am nearly mad, to tell you a story which burns my very soul—which maddens me—which will kill me. I wish you to hear it, and then to advise me. You are young, and innocent of the world's ways. My confession is painful, almost indelicate

—but if I judge you rightly, you may be the means of restoring me to home, to happiness, to rank and consideration in the world."

"I will do anything to serve you, Lotty," he replied.

"Do not look at me—almost turn your back —or I shall not dare to tell the most extraordinary story you ever heard."

Henry did so, but as Lotty did not herself know the whole of her own story, we must give it in our own words, premising, that strange and Don Juan like as it is, it is strictly true in every incident.

CHAPTER LXXV.

FIRST ADVENTURE.

(Letter of a young Marquis.)

"I HAVE reached Dole, after a long and interesting journey, which, however, would weary you to record, but here, while my people are preparing my carriage, I will tell you as extraordinary an adventure as ever happened, I believe, to mortal man.

"I dislike all public conveyances.

"But, first, why am I hurrying on?

"You know the ambition of my worthy mother. Not satisfied with the great and increasing wealth of our family, she is for ever seeking to increase it, which, considering that my sisters have but moderate portions, is allowable.

"Two months ago she began to assail me with descriptions of a young lady who combined the double attractions, of great wealth and exquisite beauty.

"At first, I paid no attention to these missives, eing very happy in Rome, where I had a *chere amie*, and being in no hurry to marry.

"But water will wear away a stone.

"My mother wrote once a week, and at last she sent me her history and portrait.

"Charlotte was of good family, but had been adopted by a rich old lady with fabulous wealth, who, by deed of gift, had made her her heiress.

"Up to seventeen she had been brought up in a French convent, but was now going to Paris to be brought out.

"The old lady, the Dowager Countess of——, the last scion of her noble house, was a friend of my mother's.

"By correspondence they made up a match, and from that hour I had no peace.

"The portrait was indeed tempting. It represented her in ball dress, and truly Charlotte was about nineteen, tall, full grown, and exceedingly voluptuous in form for her age.

"Her shoulders were magnificent, beautifully rounded, and shown off by a superb blue velvet dress, which she had hastily donned.

"Her hair was glossy black, and hung in massive curls around her head.

"Her low, white forehead surmounted eyes of vivacity and energy, swept and softened by long flowing eyelashes,

"Her face was faultless, her coral lips a bow, and her chin massive enough to be richly voluptuous.

"I began to fall in love with my intended wife.

"I determined at all events to see her, so packing up my traps, burning my love letters, and bidding adieu to my *chere amie*, I started on my way.

"I did not halt much, because once my mind is made up to a thing nothing stops me.

"I was all impatience, not to say all love.

"But I arrived late at Dole, put up my travelling carriage, and ordered supper.

"I enjoyed it very much and soon found myself by a cosy fire with a bottle of Lafitte and a cigar.

"Presently a knock came to the door.

"Come in, I said.

"In walked a buxom French landlady of about forty-five.

"'Pardon mi lord,' she said, ' but is it your intention to stop here?'

"'Certainly.'

"'But—'

"'Is there anything the matter?'

"'But, monsieur—only this, I have no bed.'

"'*Diable! Diable!*' said I, ' that is serious, especially as I have not slept in a bed for three nights—and am tired.'

"'Ahem,' said the landlady, 'poor young man. It is a shame—but I really cannot help it, unless your servant sleeps in the kitchen and you take his bed.'

"I shook my head. I knew the style of place into which servants are poked in France.

"'There is,' said the landlady, in a timid, hesitating kind of way, ' a bed—'

"'Well.'

"'But——'

"'What?'

"'It is double-bedded room.'

"'What of that?'

"'The other bed is occupied.'

"'That is a nuisance, because, I don't like sleeping in the room with every fellow.'

"'But, monsieur, it is not a fellow.'

"'Some English gentleman.'

"'No, monsieur. It is a beautiful young lady.'

"This was a poser.

"'That is awkward,' I said.

"'Now, Monsieur, she is an angel of light. For a whole fortnight she has nursed a sick aunt until she is quite exhausted. The aunt is better and the young lady is going tomorrow to R—— to fetch a great doctor, who won't come for messages. Now she is so kind, so beautiful, that I firmly believe if monsieur will promise to be very *sage*, she will allow him to sleep in the spare bed."

"I frankly state that I hesitated. The situation was piquant in the extreme, and I knew myself well enough to be aware that I should pass a disagreeable night.

"But I was very tired, and anxious for bed.

"'I am an English gentleman,' I said, rather haughtily, ' is not that enough?'

"'I will retire and consult with mademoiselle,' said the landlady, shaking her head.

"Soon she returned with a smiling face.

"'She has agreed,' I cried.

"'On certain conditions,' she replied, demurely.

"'Well let me have them.'

" ' Monsieur will undress in the dark.'

" ' Agreed.'

" ' I shall be present.'

" ' Well certainly if it is wished.'

" ' You will get into bed, close the curtains, and not speak a word.'

" ' I am quite agreeable.'

" ' That you rise when called at six o'clock, and dressing quietly come out of the room.'

" I agreed to everything. I was taken to the apartment, the light was blown out, I undressed, slipped into bed and drew the curtains.

" Now began my sufferings. To have a sweet girl so near you, to imagine her more beautiful than she is, even to desire only but to look at her, and yet not be allowed, was certainly painful in the extreme.

" But I could not forfeit my word.

" I tried to go to sleep, and perhaps might have succeeded but for a most remarkable event.

" ' Monsieur,' said a soft and mellifluous voice from the other bed.

" ' Mademoiselle,' I replied sitting up.

" ' I am sorry to interrupt your rest here, but should you hear talking, don't be alarmed, when I am not well I talk in my sleep.'

" ' Oh dont mind me miss. I dare say I shall only hear charming things.'

" ' You are breaking our conventions,' said a soft and charming voice.

" ' A thousand pardons,' I cried, and again the room lapsed into silence.

" Soon the regular breathing of my companion told me that she was asleep.

" I never in my whole life had the devil tempt me so much.

" She was good, her voice was charming, and I was quite sure she was herself lovely. A devouring curiosity filled my soul.

" Hush! what is yon sound? She is talking.

" Heavens!

" ' He must be a nice fellow,' she said, in the unmistakeable tones of one who is unconscious; ' I should like to have had a peep at him.'

" I could stand it no longer, I slipped out of bed, and in another minute was bending over her. I could not see but I had hands.

" I found she was charming.

" She awoke with a sigh.

" Monsieur! monsieur!' she murmured, as I stopped her breath with kisses.

" ' I forgot to tell you I was a somnambulist.' I impudently averred

" Well—the rest of my story need not be told. When called outside the door, I crept out of her bed—she was soundly sleeping—it was dark, and and dressing I went out—I never saw her again."

" I," said Lotty, to whom Henry's back was turned, she telling her story in her own way; " was the heroine of that adventure. I was so taken by surprise. If it is wicked to be passionate, I am wicked. Certainly in my calm senses I should have acted differently, but the night, the scene, the landlady's praise of the handsome youth. I don't believe I closed my eyes until the wretch came to my side pretending to be a somnambulist."

" It was a delicious adventure for the young man," said Henry, with a sly look at Lotty.

" You wicked man," said Lotty, angrily; " why you are as bad as the rest. Hold your tongue—dont speak."

" I wont."

" My next adventure was even more extraordinary."

CHAPTER LXXV.

THE SECOND ADVENTURE.

IT was a cold day, the ground was covered with snow, when a travelling carriage moving at a rapid pace came to the crest of a hill, about twelve o'clock in the day.

On the seat in front was a cunning-looking fox of a servant, who kissed his hand to every woman who appeared at door or window.

Few showed themselves on the high road.

Inside the carriage was a tall and aristocratic young man, who seemed wrapped in slumber.

The postillions were used to the road and wanted to get to the end of their journey.

Down the hill, despite the snow, they went clattering at a tremendous pace.

The young man woke up and looked out of the window.

" They are going a devil of a pace," he said; " I say William," addressing his servant.

His head was out of the window.

He could say no more, for at that instant the horses reared, the travelling carriage swayed and —luckily it fell on the contrary side—the traveller stood amazed and upright.

In a moment he had clambered out and was engaged in helping up the postillions, and then in cutting the traces of the horses.

They went of their own accord to the posthouse and after some little delay, the young English nobleman walked after them, leaving his servant in charge.

In an hour a dozen men, with a blacksmith, were busy at the carriage, while the young man was enjoying all the very best that the house could afford.

He was rather an epicurean young gentleman in his way.

They told him his carriage would require some hours to repair; in fact, that they could not promise it could be used before eleven at night.

The young man treated the matter very philosophically, and ordered supper at nine.

Then he strolled about in thick boots in the snow, even condescending to go and watch the blacksmiths, and chucking all the pretty girls of the village under the chin, which, as he gave them each a two-franc piece, became rather a bore.

When he had supped gaily, and, indeed, taken too much wine, he intimated his will to depart; and having paid his bill, walked out just as the great travelling carriage, with four horses, came up to the door.

They were rather in a hurry to get him away, as the diligence was hourly expected.

The carriage drew up to the door in the shadow of the great house.

The night was dark, but the young man noticed that a young and elegantly dressed girl was standing in the portico.

The steps of the carriage were let down.

The young lady advanced to enter. The other, with the utmost calmness, helped her in.

"It was very naughty," he wrote; "but the supper and wine—I could not help it."

Then away dashed the travelling carriage.

It was quite dark.

"What a very quick diligence," said the young lady with something of a start.

"Very!" said the young man.

"But surely," cried the young girl, "there is some mistake.

"How so ?"

"This is not the diligence—pray, sir, explain."

"It is not, mademoiselle."

"Oh, monsieur, how could you have allowed me to enter ?"

"You wished to. Besides, only mention where you want to be taken to."

"Monsieur! monsieur! if you are a gentleman, do stop."

He took her hands in his.

"Do not deprive me of the pleasure of so charming a travelling-companion," he said. "How far do you go ?"

She told him.

"You will be there in half the time the diligence would take," he urged.

"But——"

"Now let us be friends," he said, in the low insinuating, seductive voice of one who has had some experience of women.

She made no reply.

He passed his arm round her waist, and began to talk of his adventures, of his travels, of his residence in Italy, until his auditor grew interested, and gaily joined.

He could not see her face, but he knew by instinct that she was pretty.

"She was a charming creature," he said in a private letter to a friend, "and I only wished the night could have lasted twenty-four hours."

At dawn of day, still with her veil down, she was sobbing on his shoulder, but she was compelled to leave him, as they had reached the end of her journey.

He wanted to know all about her—to know her name—to see her again ; but she begged and implored him not.

The journey in his travelling carriage was already enough to compromise any woman.

With the reluctance of a regular Don Juan, he would have resisted, but it was in vain.

They parted.

"It was provoking," he wrote, "for I would have given anything to become better acquainted. But rogue la galere, there are plenty of women in Paris, and am I not going to be married ?"

"This second adventure," said Lotty, whose face was crimson with blushes, "found me more to blame, perhaps, than the other. Still, at the same time, it was in the origin purely accidental. I was this time alone with a young man, who, without the cunning of my first betrayer, was charming in his way, and then rather imperious.

It was of no use to call for assistance. The carriage went like the wind."

"This becomes serious," said Harry, who began to think the confession rather startling.

"It is," replied Lotty; "but this is nothing to what is to come."

"But," said Henry, whose eyes spoke volumes, "why these revelations to me ?"

"You will understand. Listen," she continued.

But we must now follow the young man, leaving Lotty for the present.

CHAPTER LXXVI.

THE YOUNG MAN'S ADVENTURES TOLD BY HIMSELF.

I AM not very vain, but certainly two such charming adventures in forty-eight hours, do not fall to the lot of everybody. At all events, it served me for reflection on the road.

Who were they? Should they ever fall in my way again, should I know them ?

Well, I suppose I should not.

The proverb says that all cats are grey in the dark.

Well, I daresay there is something in it ; but I do not exactly believe it.

Away ! away ! on to Paris—city of delight and pleasure—city of the aristocracy, and city of the demi monde ; there where pleasure waits the man who has money, and, above all, audacity.

I had never been there alone, always with the duke and duchess, and my father.

That you know, with a family like ours, means a sort of reticence and carefulness.

Now I was alone.

I had plenty of money, money in abundance, and infinite credit.

I had plenty of acquaintances, if not of friends, and that, under the circumstances was just what I wanted.

And had I not also my future wife to see ?

Well I arrived in Paris. Unfortunately I had lost both the letter of introduction to the Dowager Marchioness and her address.

This would not have mattered much but that I drove to the——hotel, and there fell in at once with a whole party of English fellows whom I knew.

I was drawn into the vortex of pleasure without the slightest difficulty.

Who would not ? There were masked balls, there were private parties, there was everything that could attract a youth.

"What are you going to do to-night ?" said one of the party.

"Dont know really. I ought to try and find the address of old Dower——"

"Nonsense, you are coming to see the Marquise de Cancan !"

"Vraié !"

"Not a bit of it. A marquise de commande. But you will come ?"

"Vive la bagatelle—I will—what time will you call ?"

"At ten. The fun is then at its best."

THE DUEL.

I was not sorry to be alone. I had played billiards, I had drank champagne, and I wanted rest, so I laid down, ordered dinner at eight, and at eight was called fully refreshed for the night's work.

At eight a succulent dinner was placed before myself and one or two acquaintances who honoured the son of the Duke of —— so much as to dine with him.

We again payed our respects to the champagne, and at ten sallied forth.

Carnival time, and in Paris, the last of the three days. It was so cold; so cold on the bridges, that the blind beggars, tootling dismally on their cracked flutes, and rattling their battered tin money-boxes had one and all decamped, that the itinerant cake and sweet-meat sellers on the quays were to be found nowhere. A piercing blast went along with this cold, which swept before its icy gusts little particles of frozen dust, which blew down your back and into your eyes, and made you generally miserable.

Carnival time, and in Paris; the last of the three days. It was so cold. So cold on the bridges that the blind beggars, tootling dismally on their cracked flutes, and rattling their battered tin money-boxes, had, one and all, decamped; that the itinerant cake and sweetmeat sellers on the

quays were to be found nowhere. A piercing
blast went along with this cold, which swept
before its icy gusts little particles of frozen dust,
which blew down your back and into your eyes,
and made you generally miserable.

The day cleared up wonderfully before dark,
but though the snow had ceased to fall, the sky
was even a tender, loving blue, the cold was still
almost intolerably intense. About four o'clock, or
so, some of the more inveterate Boulevard flaneurs
came out, wrapped up to the nose in furs and
woollens, to lounge for half-an-hour between the
Rue Vivienne and the Cafe de la Madeline, but
the great places of resort were the almost innumerable passages.

Have you ever been to one of those apocryphal
aristocratic parties, where all the men are pretty
well first-rate, and all the women are—well, it
would be harsh to use a good old Saxon word, but
it is the truth.

Now, between you and me, they are delightful.
Women in our circles are beginning to be a little
less prudish and solemn ; but these reunions, where
there is no indelicacy, where everything is conducted with decorum, but where you may laugh
and chat as much as you please, and tell stories
and hear them, and be natural, have a very great
charm about them.

There is no evident sign of the real state of
things, except the circumstance that no introduction is required, and that certain ladies have their
peculiar ways about them.

Of course the great object of these meetings is
both gambling and gallantry.

They were all busy at the green table when we
entered, and scarcely one looked round to take
any notice.

I didn't then care much for gambling.

There was something much more attractive for
me, and that was the presence of these fascinating
women.

I glanced round.

There were a great many very ugly ones, made
ugly by gambling and vice, which never have been
known to beautify.

But there was one who instantly caught my
attention.

She was tall and slender. Altogether very
delicate in appearance. She was dazzlingly fair ;
she had large, light blue eyes, lovely in colour,
but perhaps rather wanting in expression ; a small,
straight nose ; a mouth which did not promise
much decision of character ; and long, loose
floating curls, of the palest flaxen hair. She
might have been a beautiful girl, but she was not
a beautiful woman.

But there was something strangely fascinating
about her.

She had an expression of face, which combined
to make up what is called the voluptuous.

She saw the effect she had produced on me,
and at once motioned me to her side.

The signal was almost imperceptible, but I saw
it. It was a glance of the eye, nothing more, but
it was irresistible.

You know me well enough, to be aware how
easily I am duped by anything with white
shoulders, and clear complexion, and bright eyes.

It is, I believe, bred in the family, and not
likely to be changed.

I seated myself on a couch beside her, she gave
an anxious glance round the room.

" You must introduce yourself," she said, " as
your friends have not done so for you."

I gave her my name and title.

Her eyes flashed ; I think she had never met
with a genuine English *milord*.

And let me tell you that a genuine *milord* is
not thought meanly of in France.

We began a conversation about poetry, flowers,
music, the drama, and all the nothings which
so peculiarly belong to French society.

She talked well, but, of course, superficially,
as do all French women out of the highly-educated
circles.

We were amused, that was quite clear, one with
the other.

And now, pray, thoroughly understand that I
am talking about France.

" I like you," she said, with a stabbing glance
of her eye.

I bent my head profoundly. What on earth
could I say ?

" Now," she added, " I am an odd woman—
you will say so—I am capricious."

" I should not think so."

" But I am, and you will understand better
when I explain."

" Will madame be kind enough to tell me ?"

" We shall probably meet once or twice before
you leave Paris."

" I hope so."

" Now, I daresay if we had met several times
you might have taken a fancy to me."

" Madame ——."

" Now, do listen. If you had, it would have
been unlucky, as probably by that time I should
have detested you, and loved somebody else. To-
night I find you are irresistible."

" Madame, you do me too much honour," I
replied.

" Do you wish to stop here ?"

" No," I said, " especially if more charming
company can be found elsewhere."

" Listen. I am a creature of impulse, and
always shall be. I married from impulse, and
hated my husband in a month. I ran away with
an officer from impulse, but hated him in a week.
I am now kept by a German baron. Well, I
utterly loathe him—but he has money, and I am
now poor."

I began to say something, intending to offer
my purse.

" Be silent, or I shall hate you," she said, impetuously. " I never like a man who gives me
money. I like you, because you are young and
unsophisticated."

Unsophisticated ! oh heavens !

" Madame, your kindness overwhelms me," I
said.

" Are you brave ?"

" Of course."

" You cannot enter my house by the door. I
live on the first-floor, No. 12, Rue du——; I
leave now. Be under my window at one o'clock.
The window will open ; a silken ladder will

be thrown down. I leave the rest entirely in your own hands."

And with a sly pressure of the hand, she rose and went her way.

Such, my dear ——, are the manners of that dear Paris, where all our young fellows so dearly love to dwell.

I daresay when I get into the House of Lords, I shall second the Bench of Bishops in doing away with the social evil.

But what young men of my age would not have done as I did?

I watched until I saw my friends all busily engaged, and then rose.

All were gambling, so my disappearance was not noticed.

I strolled along the Boulevards until I reached the Rue——.

It was quiet, retired, and the end was closed up; there was no thoroughfare.

The house to which I had been directed, was one of those large hotels which contain many families.

There was a magnificent garden.

A splendid balcony, with six windows, passed along the whole front.

I waited impatiently, not at all enjoying the promenade in the streets.

At last, a window opened. A silk ladder, with two pretty steel grapnels was placed upon the balcony, and thrown over.

In five minutes I was in the room where I was eagerly expected.

I cast my cloak and hat into a dark alcove, and was about to take a chair, while my *inamorata* was closing the window, when a scuffle was heard outside.

"Ter Teifel! I come in; madame, ish always visible for me, *if she be alone.*"

Madame pointed to the window.

"Wait five minutes, and I will get rid of the brute," she whispered.

And pushing me out into the balcony, she closed the window.

Here was an event. The night was cold. I was in evening costume. My cloak and hat were in the bed-room, or I verily believe I should have jumped over and given up the adventure.

Then the *garde* might pass, when I should look a pretty fool.

But I did not jump over, and the *garde* came not, so all I had to do was to walk up and down the balcony.

At last, twenty minutes having passed, I returned to my window, and leaning against it, listened—all was still as death.

Not a sound was to be heard within or without; I ventured to tap gently, and then waited. Suddenly I heard the window, a French window of course going from top to bottom, open slowly and timidly.

"Is that you, Minette?" said a voice.

I made no answer, but rushed in, closed the window, and turned towards my charmer, who was in something more than dishabille.

* * * * * * *

Half-an-hour later the following conversation took place:—

"Why do you cry, madame? I had every reason to believe——"

"Monsieur should have spoken. Doubtless——" this with considerable sarcasm—"monsieur thought he was in the chamber of the Baronne de——"

"And am I not?" I said.

"No, monsieur."

"Then where am I?" I asked, secretly delighted at the fact.

"Monsieur, are you a man of honour?" sobbed the charmer.

"I am a man of honour and a gentleman."

"Then, monsieur, you will leave."

"I will presently—not just this moment."

"Well, presently. And you will promise me, on your honour, never to seek to know who I am. Your mistake is bad enough, without dishonouring me in the eyes of the world?"

"Mademoiselle," I said, "I am so happy that a mistake has brought me to the wrong window, that I will never enter this house again."

She seemed pleased.

"You promise me that?"

"I promise you, upon my honour."

I remained until nearly daylight and then retired, watched for the first *fiacre*, and went to my own hotel.

Now, these anonymous intrigues may seem very well, but I didn't like them.

I was still as curious as ever to know who my three *inamoratas* were.

But to find out the two first was manifestly impossible, while honour forbade my in any way disturbing the tranquility of the last.

What was to be done? See my *baronne* I would not, as I knew the character of these women too well.

Besides, I next day received my cloak and hat at my hotel without a message.

If she had known I had been in the next room!

CHAPTER LXXVII.

COUNT DE PLICTON.

WHEN my mother wrote to me again, she intimated that I need trouble myself no more about the charmer whose description and character had so entranced me.

She was engaged to be married, having—at least, her guardian having—got tired of waiting for me.

This disgusted me, so I began to enter society, and made many excellent acquaintances of a different class to the above.

Among others was the Count de Plicton—a man of about thirty, who, though taciturn and uncommunicative, was a good swordsman, a capital horseman, and a most eccentric and amusing character.

He never told anyone his affairs, never made appointments, but always mysteriously came to join any party that was made up.

He seemed to hear of everything we did instinctively.

He was as brave as a lion, but awfully hot and passionate.

His great abhorrence was a young soldier who, by some influence, got into society.

As a rule, officers are not admitted into good society in France, except only by virtue of their civil rank.

A Captain Ledru was often of our parties. His relationship to a Minister procured him the *entrée* of many *salons*.

I saw very little of him, and scarcely ever near enough to recognize him.

But I had often heard of him.

He and the Count de Plicton never spoke. The captain tried to get introduced to the count, but the count would not be introduced to the captain.

He contrived this, too, in such a way that the other could not take offence.

But many said the captain was only biding his time, as he seemed to have some mortal cause of hatred against the count.

At last the count disappeared, and without giving the least notice to his friends.

I thought of going away. I was tired of Paris. I dared not visit the *cercle* where I had met the *baronne*—she passed me on the Bois with a look of scorn—and my intimate friends were spreading abroad.

I determined to go as well.

But the very next morning I was asked to join the wedding party of the Count de Plicton, which, in accordance with immemorial custom in his family, was arranged to take place at nine o'clock at night.

There would be a supper for all visitors, but the *mari* and *mariée* would retire after the ceremony.

It was a warm evening, the quarter I had to go was a distant one, so I took a *fiacre* to within ten minutes' walk.

Then I strolled.

It was a lovely night, though very dark, and I felt a strange pleasure in looking up at the old fashioned houses.

I was in the most remote part of the Faubourg St. Germain.

It was not considered in those days a dangerous quarter, so there were scarcely any patrols.

Suddenly I heard a *cliquetis* of swords.

I hastened on, and there in the street, alone, without seconds, I saw two men fighting.

I rushed forward.

It was the Count de Plicton and the Captain Ledru.

They paused a moment and looked at me in a surprised way.

"Here is an original," said Plicton, gravely, "who pretends to be in love with my wife."

"*En garde*," cried the soldier.

"One moment, sir. I was about to retire to the nuptial couch when I received a summons to say that if I was not a coward I would come down. Plicton was never a coward. So you see."

And, despite my remonstrance, they continued the combat.

The captain was decidedly in earnest, and suddenly, watching a hasty movement of the other, ran him through.

The circumstances under which he fought very likely made him less careful than usual.

I drew out the sword, and saw that he was dead.

"Bully and assassin," I began.

"Ah!" he cried, and flew at me with a fury such as I had never seen before.

Being a good swordsman, I only defended myself; but the man was mad.

He ran round me, about me, until at last in a paroxysm of fury he fell on the sword of his hated rival, and was killed at once.

I turned to leave, when a street door opened and a female voice spoke.

"Is that you, monsieur?"

In an instant every idea of duel, death, and desolation was over.

"Have you chastised him?"

"Yes."

"Then follow me. Fie! to leave the bridal chamber on the first night of your wedding," said the woman.

I know not what devil led me on, but I could not help it. I went up stairs. They were dark. The woman led me by the hand, giggling a little. I could tell she was a lady's-maid by the very tone of her voice.

She soon reached a landing, whence I could hear the joyous merriment of the guests in the *salle-à-manger*.

The *bonne* pushed open a door, and thrust me in without a word.

It was a charming chamber. It was fitted with all that *luxe* and style which is peculiarly affected in the chambers of young married women in France.

The floor was covered by a soft carpet.

All kinds of knicknacks were disposed of on all kinds of tables.

A delicious *souper* was laid out upon a small table, as the new married couple had retired previous to supper being served.

But I noticed nothing of this.

I hastened to look upon the bed.

There lay, with her face half concealed—there was only a kind of subdued lamp to give light in the room—a young person evidently lovely.

But her face was turned away from me.

Fearful, if I touched her, she might wake and discover the mistake, I turned down the lamp.

*   *   *   *   *

My dear, I daresay all this is very wrong and very wicked, but I could not help it.

In the morning I went away, and crept out of the house without making the slightest noise.

All Paris, an hour later, was ringing with the story of the duel.

The mistake they made on the evidence of the bride, *who said she could not be mistaken*, was that the husband had risen at early dawn to fight this fatal duel.

Sick of Paris, which was getting very empty, I left, and dashed away to Italy once more.

CHAPTER LXXVIII.

FIRST MEETING.

I TRAVELLED about, I saw sights, I climbed trees, I lived for weeks as a poor outcast in the woods, and was very happy.

But at last the old leaven began to act, and I wished myself once more in society.

I started for Naples. It was the English season, and there were there many people that I knew.

I had not been there a week, when my father, mother, and the whole tribe most mysteriously arrived.

They put up at the Hotel de ——.

I remained at the ——, as I always had a notion that at my age it was best to have a bachelor establishment.

My brother, Lord Thynne, was with my family.

We knew all the pleasant haunts in Naples, in which young men delight, and enjoyed ourselves thoroughly.

One night I remained at the Casino all night, and sallied forth only when the bright sun had risen in the sky.

I was perfectly sober, and walked with as much deliberation as if I had had a good night's rest.

The lazy Neapolitans were not up, but some English were, our nation being peculiarly early risers.

I did not feel inclined to go to bed, but took myself to a celebrated promenade, bordered with trees.

I sat myself down on a seat, and looked upon the surface of the glassy sea.

I was in a pensive mood, thinking over my strange adventures of the previous four months, and wondering if any such would ever happen to me again.

I should not have minded falling in with one of those whom I had so curiously made acquaintance with.

Presently I noticed that two ladies were walking up and down the promenade.

At a glance I saw they were English ladies, and listlessly cast down my eyes.

I knew no adventure was in store for me.

But presently, having to move to avoid the rays of the sun, I caught sight of their faces.

My heart beat violently.

I had never seen anything so marvellously beautiful in all my life, as was the younger of the two.

Young, almost a girl, there was a rich voluptuousness about her which suited my fancy.

I would have given the world to have spoken, but the etiquette of English society is imperative.

On a mountain, near a glacier, in any wild and picturesque portion of the globe the thing might have been done—but not in Naples.

I watched them for an hour and was gratified to see that the younger lady, who was very grave and serious, looked at me once now and then with interest.

I determined to make her acquaintance, and by means of my rank obtain an introduction.

I, at all events, knew sufficient people to be sure of attaining my object.

But then both were in deep mourning, and perhaps lived in utter seclusion.

While I sat musing and tearing my frilled shirt with my fingers, trying to hit on a plan to make her acquaintance, they suddenly disappeared as quickly and mysteriously as if they had not been.

I hurried to my hotel, took a bath, got into bed, slept until towards evening, and then rising paid unusual attention to my toilette.

There was a reception at my mother's, where all the first-rate English were to be.

There I might expect to hear something of my charmer.

Somebody surely would know one whose dazzling beauty must have been noticed.

I dined leisurely, and well. It is an excellent way of preparing for an evening's amusement.

It makes you feel happy yourself, and desirous of imparting happiness to others.

About eight I drove to my mother's hotel. I had never, I knew, looked so well.

Why had I thus prepared myself for conquest? That is what I never could make out.

"My mother appeared delighted to see that I came early and looked well."

"One would have thought you had guessed why I have given this little soiree," she said.

"Why indeed."

"Do you know who is here?" continued my mother, with her charming smile.

"No."

"Your ex-affianced wife, the widow of the Count de St. Veran."

"Widow!"

"It's a most extraordinary and romantic affair," she said, smiling, "and some day you shall hear it."

"I have not the slightest wish to know anything about the countess," I said, coldly; "I am not partial to widows."

"My dear boy," exclaimed my mother smiling, "but such a widow—judge for yourself."

And she dragged me into another room, where the young widow, to be out of the gaiety and bustle of the general saloon, was seated alone.

"Madame de St. Veran," began my mother, "this is my eldest son."

She rose, and we stood gazing at one another in astonishment.

It was my lovely and incomparable beauty of the morning.

I not only bowed, but recovering myself, took her hand and made her sit down beside me on a couch.

My mother smiled and left us.

What a charming voice, the perfection of all that was beautiful.

It was familiar to me at once. It seemed to be the concentrated essence of all the beautiful voices I had ever heard.

I listened with rapture, and I was listened to with attention.

I neglected everybody else that evening, and took no notice of some slight sarcasms and innuendoes from my mother.

Before midnight I had reminded her of the family compact by which we were to be united.

I proposed now in person, and with an earnestness which left no doubt of my sincerity.

She turned away with a deep sigh.

"You are aware that I am a widow?"

"Certainly. I regret the folly which made me waste precious time that gave an opportunity to a rival—but let us forget the past."

"I cannot," she whispered, still with her head averted.

"Did you love him so very much?" I asked, anxiously.

"No," she whispered, very low.

"Then why hesitate beloved and charming creature, to make happy one, who when he saw you this morning at once made up his mind to win you."

"Pray," she faltered, "change the subject now, it pains me much. The day may come when I may be more explicit—do let us talk of something else."

I did. I saw that I had made an impression, and that was sufficient for one evening.

When everybody had retired, I remained alone with my mother,

"Well?"

"Charming."

"But——"

"Lovely!"

"But my dear boy——"

"If she won't have me, I shall do something desperate!" I cried.

"But she's a widow."

"She's an angel."

"I am very glad to hear you say so. The unfortunate de St. Veran was a man of excellent family, though from pride or some other feeling he moved little in society. His sudden death left his widow enormously rich. I am delighted to find you have taken to her—it is the dearest wish of my heart to see you married."

"I doubt if she will have me!" I cried.

"Why?"

"I have asked her."

"Proposed the first evening," said my mother, laughing, "no wonder you were refused. Women are not to be taken by storm in that way."

Now, in my own opinion, and from personal experience, I believed that women were to be taken by storm, but of course I said nothing.

"Are you prepared to lay a regular siege and win her to your heart?" she continued.

"I am."

"Now my dear boy, your father and I have settled in our minds that, the sooner this marriage takes place, the better. *There will be no heir to St. Veran*, so the marriage might take place very well in three months. No one knows anything in England, so when you present your marchioness, few will know that she is a widow."

I highly commended this idea, and then learned that a drive to P——, had been agreed on.

I had a splendid English pheaton.

"Ask her to trust herself to me?" I said, warmly.

"I will, boy," she said, laughing at my eagerness.

And then I went away, and was obliged to sit up smoking and drinking with my brother and some of his friends, in order to reduce my mind to a state that allowed of sleep.

———

CHAPTER LXXIX.

POPPING THE QUESTION.

IT was a magnificent day when I drove up to my mother's door, cast the reins to a servant, and alighting rapidly, ran up stairs.

Carriages and horses were standing round the hotel.

All the company were collected. The Countess de St. Veran was more charming in her morning-dress even than in evening costume.

My mother had won her over, and she took my arm with a sweet smile.

Her sadness, however, remained. It never seemed to leave her.

What could be the reason of it? She had told me she did not love her late husband. She could not then mourn for him.

There must be some secret source of sorrow at which I could only hope to get in time.

But I determined not to think of such things that day.

I would be perfectly happy.

If there is one thing more conducive to happiness than another, it is to sit behind two smart horses, spirited and full of life, on a glorious summer's day, when nature is robed in her best, with beside you that one being of all others you set a value on and love.

Soon the Countess seemed to feel the animation of the scenes and time.

She began to talk, with all the life and soul of a happy and joyous young girl.

I was delighted, and in order the better to enjoy myself, kept my horses at a rattling pace, which both kept us free from dust, and the bore of conversation with other parties.

It was a pic-nic in some ruins. What they were I have completely forgotten.

But it was glorious.

We had a ruined temple, covered with ivy, and bushes to shelter us from the sun.

As everybody began to suspect at once the nature of the tie which bound us, we were voted bores, and left to ourselves in a corner.

I am sure it was just what we wanted.

We did not talk all the time. Somehow or other, her hand got into mine, and there it remained.

A warm pressure from mine was quickly responded to. I saw that whatever might be her reasons for hesitating to marry me, that her heart was warming to me.

This was enough to intoxicate me with joy.

Towards evening the party began to collect once more, and start on their way home.

I and the countess had lingered to gaze at a beautiful sunset, hand in hand.

We had not spoken for a long time.

We were too full of thoughts to give utterance to them in words.

There is between man and woman a mysterious time, when both come to a certain knowledge that they love, when neither of them could speak their feelings.

We, I believe, had reached that happy, dreamy period.

Presently a faint flash of lightning and a distant roll of thunder warned us to be moving.

The carriage was ready. I handed her in, the grooms jumped in, the head was raised, and we were again upon the road.

I held the reins with my left hand, that I might have hers in mine.

Away! away! the horses apparently in a hurry to get home.

We literally galloped at times, and as darkness brooded over the earth, I was compelled to use both hands.

A cry from my servants checked me.

"We have taken the wrong road, my lord," they said.

I looked around. High rocks were on each side of the way; while, at the same moment, a crack of thunder and the sprinkling of rain told that the storm was on us.

But the flash of lightning had also revealed that we were close to a certain well-known grotto or cavern.

I told the men to alight, take out the horses, lead them into the depths of the cavern, and there keep them until the storm was over.

The carriage was drawn in about twenty feet into a kind of recess, where it was quite dark.

In another moment my arm was round the warm and lovely waist, and her head upon my shoulder.

I was proudly, gloriously happy, for had I not won unto myself a glorious prize.

We remained silently watching the lightning, which every now and then lit up the cave.

"I could live thus for ever," I said, as in my deep and earnest passion I drew her towards me, and imprinted a kiss upon her lips.

She gently but firmly disengaged herself. I verily believe it was time.

"My lord," she said, in a voice which was affected both by passion and sorrow; "I am acting very wrongly, very wrongly indeed."

"Why so my dayling?" I said, in considerable surprise.

"My lord, I can never be yours. Let me once, at any expense to my own feelings, give the reason why, and then oh spare me."

"Speak dearest—remove from me this suffering and doubt," I cried.

"My lord, I see at once how deep, sincere, and pure is your affection. To deserve that I should have been a pure and innocent girl, whereas I am——"

"A widow."

"Yes—but——"

"Not another word," I said; "I will not hear it. If you had been unmarried, if no other had ever called you his for an hour, of course it would have delighted me. But you have been married, your husband is dead—and the dearest wish of my heart is to call you mine. As we have gone so far, let me urge you at once to say the word that will make me a happy man or a desolate and unhappy being for life."

"My lord," she said, in low and touching accents, "I know you will repent."

"Never—my own dear darling angel—be mine."

"If you will—if your happiness is seriously

engaged—if you will never reproach me with the past—well" she could say no more.

I caught her to my bosom, and during a lull in the storm, nothing could be heard but the murmur of our kisses and my passionate declarations of love.

I should scarcely have dared so much with a young girl, but then you must know she was a widow.

We drove home about an hour later, to find everybody excessively uneasy about us.

The wrong road and the storm, and the grotto explained all, and after supper, which was a very comfortable way of changing our thoughts, my mother's delight was great to know that we were affianced.

CHAPTER LXXX.

THE WEDDING NIGHT.

WE were to be married at the British embassy by the chaplain.

All the English, of any rank were invited to do honour to the occasion.

It seemed strange to me, but my brother was the only person who did not seem pleased.

I spoke to him about it, but he would give no explanation.

I really began to think that he envied me being the elder brother.

But once he saw that I noticed his change of manner, he in the most frank manner professed to to explain the causes thereof, alleging that it made him melancholy to see me carry off a beautiful bride, when he, a younger brother, had no chance.

But in the society of my lovely and charming future wife, I completely forgot all minor considerations.

I was supremely and incalculably happy.

Once the countess agreed to be my bride, she never recurred to any of the objections which had influenced her before.

She devoted a certain number of days to her milliners and dressmakers, and the rest to me.

But for those tedious and insane considerations, called settlements, which of course the elder parties insisted on, I believe the marriage would have been materially hurried, but it was not to be.

Still we were together, and never tired of telling one another how much we mutually loved.

Now that we had spoken out, there was no reserve. We had arranged to spend our honeymoon at a small, obscure town on a charming lake in Switzerland.

But the wedding night was to be passed at a road-side inn, about twenty miles from Naples, which I had furnished for the occasion – at all events certain apartments in it.

You may readily believe that no pains were spared by those I employed.

I did not spare money.

Well the settlements were made in a most brilliant style. I insisted on her keeping a very large proportion of her money for herself, only binding her down to leave it to her children, of which, as we were such young people, we might expect a goodly flock.

Then came the wedding day.

I won't describe it. I was in a dream, as are, I believe, most men who really love.

The wedding was over, the breakfast had been got through, and we were alone in the *Chaise de poste.*

She was mine.

Alas!

Away! away! the carriage tore, until we at length reached the destined point.

All the way she lay upon my breast. She appeared to me singularly thoughtful, and received my kisses in a strange passive kind of way.

I could not make it out.

I conceived it must be her way. She always said she looked upon marriage as a serious thing, and not one to be made anything like a joke of.

Well, I waited in a perfect dream of bliss unwilling to disturb her.

We reached the inn.

We were ushered into her apartments—we were alone.

With a passionate glance I sent her to her chamber, and bade her not keep her tiring women too long.

She did not detain them ten minutes.

I rushed to the chamber, which was to be witness of my nuptial night.

She was seated, dressed, in an arm chair, more serious, more thoughtful than ever.

"Are you ill?" I cried, as I rushed towards her.

"No!" she said, in a hollow tone "I am not ill. Be not alarmed my husband—my judge."

I started back, amazed.

"Husband—man whom I love beyond all conception—only being who has won my deep affections—hear me, I objected to marriage."

"If you did," I said, quite in a mechanical way.

"Because I had my reasons. I knew your character—I knew what you wished—a virgin bride."

"But have I not told you?" I cried, in a tone of almost angry expostulation, that I could not blame you for being a wife?"

"I knew! Heaven help me—that assurance blinded me to the truth. I thought if you could forgive other things. I have more to confess—when I married, I was not a virgin bride."

I started back aghast, fury was in my eyes.

"Listen," she said, falling on her knees, "listen, and you will see that I was not to blame."

I tore from her, called her by a fearful name, never to be forgotten or forgiven, and fled from the house."

Such was the substance of a series of letters written by the eldest son of the Duke of ——.

Such was the substance of the confession made by Lotty to Henry.

"I may have been weak, foolish, silly, but I was not designedly criminal. In each case I was carried away by an irresistible influence, each time the man seemed to be my fate. A power I could not resent led me on. I was guilty and innocent at the same time—for help me heaven, I always believed that it was my husband I held in my arms."

"And so it was," said a voice.

And her husband radiant with joy stood before her.

"And so it was," he cried, "even when you thought it was Count Plontin de St. Veran—for he was killed on the eve of your wedding-night."

Lotty gave one shriek and fell fainting in her husband's arms.

Henry, who was of a considerate nature, immediately rose and hastily retired.

CHAPTER LXXXI.
REUNITED.

THE next day about one, while the ladies were shopping, Harry called upon the reunited husband and wife, whom he found seated at breakfast, love and joy beaming from her eyes.

"You will keep our secret?" said Lotty.

"With all my heart."

"The more that I am Jessie's mother's cousin," she added.

"From all the world, I only called to ask you how you were?"

"Sit down, young man," said the heir to the dukedom, "chance has put you in possession of a strange secret, which from my knowledge of your character, I believe to be in good hands. You may as well know all the rest."

Henry bowed, sat down, and took a proffered glass of wine from the blushing marchioness, whose delight at the story of her first wedding night had known no bounds.

She had hated her first nominal husband, simply because he was forced upon her when the present one appeared to slight her.

To have, after all her trials, found that she never failed but with her husband, was a consideration indeed.

"When I hastily withdrew without hearing revelations that would have been so gratifying to myself, I was, as it were, mad. I ordered horses to be put to, and drove away to England like a madman. I wrote to my mother, to say that a strange mystery would separate me from my wife for ever.

"I declined any explanation.

"I travelled over all England, Scotland, and Ireland. I resided in London. I plunged into dissipation without enjoying it, and at length my doctors ordered me on the continent. A mysterious, and to all appearance fatal illness seemed destroying me.

"I tried the continent, all the while hoping, trusting that some explanation would come from my wife.

"None came.

"I loved the continent. Then I pined for the open prairies* of North America.

"I came here and found some advantage, I was returning home when I recognized Lotty, followed her to the ball—you know the rest."

"But you do not," said Lotty, in a somewhat sombre tone.

"Let me know all."

THE MARRIAGE OF HENRY AND JESSIE.

"Next day, the same man who has persecuted Jessie and Henry—your brother, Lord Thynne, halted at my hotel.

"He was surprised to find me alone and ill.

"He forced himself upon me, and demanded an explanation.

"I would not, and I could not give it to him, that I might be the mark of scorn.

"I told him you had supremely offended me by coarse allusions to my former marriage, and that I could never forgive you.

"I would be deeply, terribly revenged.

"He hinted at a kind of revenge so horrible, that I shrunk from him with horror."

"And what was that," said her husband, eagerly.

"That I should become what you thought me." The Marquis ground his teeth.

"I refused with perfect fury, but I told him if he would swear never to allude to the subject again, I would feign to be what he wished.

"I was mad with rage and despair, for I was a woman who loved with all the power of my soul, and I had been hastily condemned and cruelly scorned.

"I agreed, and we started for England in company.

"He placed me—that is, he feigned to do so—

in a cottage in St. John's Wood, though it was taken and furnished with my own money.

"It was my money I cared about, and that, in my delirium, I allowed him the free use of.

"He made my house his home.

"Then came Henry, and I had an object in view—to save my cousin's child, Jessie.

"I frustrated a dozen plans of his against her, and then weary of that life, I came over here in search of Henry and Jessie.

"Thank heaven I found you—our reconciliation is complete and no one knows our secret but one, who will, I am sure, be faithful."

"I will, not only because I ought—but for all you have done for Jessie and myself."

Lotty could hardly restrain a smile.

"And now," said the marquis, "simply say to your friends that we are in the house, shall be happy to see you at dinner and mean to be your fellow passenger to England on board the ——."

Henry bowed and retired.

CHAPTER LXXXII.
HOME.

"AND where have you been sir?" said Mrs. de Lancy, as the whole party sat down to lunch.

"Breakfasting with an old friend."

"And who is that?" said Jessie, looking up.

"Some old friends of your mamma; and not to keep ladies in suspense, let me say at once the Marquis and Marchioness of ——."

"Indeed!" cried Cornelia, with a meaning glance at her husband.

"Yes! By some trickery or misunderstanding they became separated. All has been explained, and they are now united never to part again."

"Do you know who she is?" said Cornelia, looking keenly at him.

"Yes—she is the daughter of your mother's sister."

"Yes—and it has pained me much that cruel rumours have separated us."

"It was the work of an enemy," said Henry, very gravely, "whom we have all reason to remember."

"Of whom do you speak?"

"Lord Thynne."

Jessie started and turned pale.

"Be not alarmed," said Henry, quietly, "he will respect my wife."

Jessie blushed, but smilingly. They had all really so accustomed her to the word, that she really was getting quite used to it.

Henry then gave the invitation which all gladly accepted.

Sir Marmaduke was glad, because it was a good introduction for Henry in life.

His son was very rich, was the sole heir to two mighty properties, and he wished him to have something to do.

For a man of wealth in England there is about only two occupations.

He must devote himself to agriculture or politics—even to both.

Now the Marquis of ——, could easily put his son into Parliament.

Cornelia was delighted to see the woman from whom she had parted, when being adopted by the rich dowager, a little wee thing, pale and sickly.

Cornelia was surprized to see the woman of twenty so fully and voluptuously developed.

She did not know and never did know of her peculiar adventures.

Jessie did—that is after she was married—for what husband ever keeps a secret from his wife.

The meeting between the cousins was very cordial, while Jessie blushed rosy-red at the recollection of the *very peculiar* circumstances under which they had once met.

Henry did the same at the same moment, and the blush was repeated.

A very joyous happy party they were that evening, talking of the past, present, and future.

Three days later they sailed for England, and after a very rapid passage reached home at last.

Their arrival was kept carefully secret, as they all wished to act before their enemies had time to prepare.

The Marquis, however, contrived to have his name put in the papers.

He then wrote to all his family, who in a few His will was law with his relatives.

His father, mother, sisters came together, and then Lord Edward Thynne with his good little wife, whom he loved despite himself.

They were in the drawing-room of the hotel, being introduced to our heroine and her friends.

Lord Edward Thynne avoided looking at Jessie. He had noticed that she was more beautiful than ever.

"I have now," said the Marquis in a loud tone, "to apologise to one publicly who in a moment of frenzy I deeply injured, and who has been kept apart from me by machinations to which I will no further allude than to characterise them as cruel, wicked, and disgraceful. Let not a word be said more. I forgive the past—let me have no cause to forgive in future. Mother, father, sisters, behold her whom I basely deserted from a causeless thought—my wife!"

And he led her forth, radiant in her beauty.

All rushed to congratulate her and him, Lord Edward Thynne whispering one word as he pressed his brother's hand.

"Forgive!" was all he could say, but his white face and quivering lip was more eloquent.

"Enough!"

CHAPTER LXXXIII.
THE FALSE HEIR.

THERE was deep sorrow at Haddington Hall.

The death of Henry Marmaduke Haddington had appeared in the papers with such circumstantiality of detail as to leave no doubt of its truth.

There was great rejoicing in a certain aristocratic hotel at the West-end.

The lawyers had decided that, Henry being dead, and Jessie utterly lost—though she never had been proved heir to Leopold Treherne—the son of Maria Treherne was heir to both estates.

The opinion was clear, and left no doubt except that it required legal proceedings to eject the present holders.

As soon as he was of age, then, the son of

Maria Treherne would be the happy owner of thirty thousand a year.

Imagine his delight and that of his mother. Even the colonel had ventured to turn up, and was staying at the hotel with them.

Money was no object. The solicitors—*upon whom a forged certificate of the death of Henry* had been passed—advanced any quantity of money.

A grand dinner was on the table. There sat down to the repast William Treherne and his wife —now quite a flouncing fine lady, but still good-hearted and affectionate; Mrs. Treherne, superb in her triumph; the colonel, stupendous in style and whiskers; the solicitors, Greed and Graball, calm, dignified, and pretentious.

There were six nobodies, friends of William and the colonel, who were glad to worship the rising luminary.

It was a stupendous affair, something perfectly glorious and wonderful, such a dinner as is not often seen.

It was put on the table regardless of expense.

You know what hotel-keepers will do under such circumstances for people who have a goodly estate and lots of ready cash.

Like all people unused to great dinners, scarcely any wine but champagne was ordered.

They were drinking it after the soup.

Now, why had Mrs. Treherne and the colonel done this?

Because possession is nine points of the law, and did Henry turn up, once in the house they could dispute his identity.

"To the health of the worthy heir of Haddington Hall and Treherne."

"Sir Marmaduke and Mr. Henry Haddington," said a loud voice, as the folding doors flew open.

Mrs. Treherne shrieked, all dropped their glasses, and rose to their feet.

There stood Sir Marmaduke and Henry, calm but stern—there was Leopold alone!

There was Cornelia and Jessie.

There were two gentlemen who were at once recognized as solicitors.

Behind were four rough-looking men.

"Villain!" cried Graball, collaring the colonel, while Greed did the same with William, "my money—you shall swing for forgery!"

"Silence!" said Sir Marmaduke, in a loud, stern tone, "unhand those wretches. I will see justice done, Messrs. Greed and Graball. Everybody shall be paid."

Messrs. Greed and Graball let go their hold and bowed respectfully.

Everybody shall be paid.

"I am Sir Marmaduke Haddington," he began; "this woman," pointing to Mrs. Treherne, "my most unnatural sister—failing in an attempt to commit murder, confined me in a madhouse."

"'Tis false."

"We have evidence to prove it."

"'Tis a lie, a cool deliberate lie," said Mrs. Treherne; "these are impostors."

"Another word of that kind and the law shall take its course—listen. I have been deeply wronged; I seek no revenge. But the happiness of my children," pointing to Henry and Jessie, "must be secured. They will never be safe while

you are near them. I give you twenty four hours. If in that time you have not left England, the law shall take its course."

"Where are we to go to?" said Mrs. Treherne, talking in an agony of hatred—without one spark of remorse.

"Where you please. When you have selected a residence write to me, and I will see that you have means to live decently—no more."

The colonel had already reached the door, which Mrs. Treherne trod with a haughty step.

"Young men," said Sir Marmaduke, addressing William, "according to the accounts I hear of you shall be my treatment. Treat your wife well, depart from your evil ways, and the past may be forgotten."

William made earnest protestations, and his wife joined in them.

"He is very good to me," she said.

"I am very glad to hear it," replied Sir Marmaduke, and turned away.

The friends of Henry and Jessie now bowed to the assembled and discomfited guests, and retired.

The exposure had been signal and complete.

They had no hope of resistance. The charge of forgery and the presence of the officers in plain clothes, was too much for them.

Henry personally would have shaken hands with his cousin, but his father restrained him.

The next night Mrs. Treherne, the colonel, with William and his wife, moved off.

They went to an obscure watering place on the continent, where Mrs. Treherne wrote abject letters to Sir Marmaduke and Leopold.

They never answered her.

There are things which cannot be forgiven.

But they remitted enough money to keep them

William settled down into a confirmed idler, but, his wife mastering him he did not descend so low as he otherwise would have done.

The colonel was the big man of the place, and spoke very confidently of his wealthy relation in England.

He married Mrs. Treherne on the strength of her dowry.

We shall hear no more of them.

CHAPTER LXXIX.

THE WEDDING.

TWENTY years since there stood (it stands now) in London town, an inconsiderable slip of a thoroughfare, which was (and is still), one of the channels of communication between the grand street that Nash, prince of architects, built for George the Fourth, and the grander square erected by some other Vitruvius or Palladio — whose name I never knew, but who was probably a German—for George the First.

The great street is all stucco, and the great square is all red brick, but my inconsiderable slip inclined (and flimsiness of the first).

This street (as it was, and is, and is to be, I presume, to the end of genteel time, I will speak of it in the present tense), is not a handsome street. It is not a wide street.

It has shops—shops both small and mean.

A grocer, who sells soup, lives at one corner.

He is not a wholesale grocer, not an Italian warehouseman, and his groceries are of so small a description as to warrant the suspicion that he was at no very remote period of time, a chandler's shopkeeper.

Nearly opposite to him there is a barber (he calls himself a peruke maker, but he shaves and for three half-pence; selling, also, valentines in the season; kites, penny canes, and cheap periodicals, all the year round.)

There was, when I first knew the street, a greengrocer's within its precincts.

There are yet several lodging-houses, a boot-shop, and two taverns, that flout its gentility.

Yet, with all these plebeian drawbacks, Little Maddox Street, Hanover Square, was in eighteen hundred and thirty, as it is now in eighteen hundred and sixty-two,—the most fashionable street in the greatest city of the world.

For in that formal, grey-stone, big-wig church of St. Georges's, right over against the street I have named, Fashion—ethereal, capricious, beauteous, glittering, happy Fashion—has for upwards of a century, erected a high altar to matrimony.

Since the death of Queen Anne, fashion has elected to be married at St. George's.

It signs its name in the register, its jewelled hand trembling, its peachy cheek blushing through the roseate cosmetics prepared by Mr. Atkinson, of Old Bond-street; it leaves an odour of mille-fleurs in the vestry; it comes forth, smiling and skirt-trailing, all lace and rich silks and gems, and perfect felicity (of course), down those fashion-worn, vestry-room steps, to where the tightly-hung chariots, with their gleaming wheels, and footmen in embroidery are waiting, to where the silky-skinned horses curvet in their armorial harness, pawing and stamping, and champing their bits proudly, yet not with such a grace and dignity as are the special gifts of those other long-tailed, long-maned, coal-black steeds, which Mr. Resurgam, the undertaker, who lives only next door to the vestry-room, in Mill-street, owns; steeds which, in the course of time and business, have not unfrequently to curvet and stamp at Fashion's door, when the shutters are up and the blinds are down, when there are to be no more marriages, or giving away in marriage, and when Fashion is no longer Fashion, but Mortality.

You know that the vestry-room is but the second entrance—the back door, in fact, of this aristocratic temple; that in stately George-street, with its tall shining windows, and red brick fronts with stone dressings are the portico of the fane, and the broad flight of stone steps. I could never justly understand why the wedding procession should, so to speak, sneak out of the back door, when, round the corner, it could come down to its chariots triumphantly, with room for coach and six to turn, with ample space for a crowd to admire, for the charity boys to be ranged in a line, for the beadle, in his scarlet and lace, to be seen to ad-

vantage, for the bride to shine forth in all her beauty, youth, happiness, wealth. But Fashion has said that it will come down those steps, and Fashion is an institution of so Eleusinian and inscrutable a nature, that it baffles reason and calmly crushes consistency. Its laws, whatever they may be, and whoever framed them, are as those of the Medes and Persians. It is not for us, plebeians as we are, to question them, and they will endure, my brother, long after you and I have done with the two first sections of the first column of the *Times* Supplement (obtaining, perchance, not so much as a fleeting notice in the third compartment of that column), and are out of Fashion altogether.

But enough of introduction, let us continue.

But our readers are all this time kept waiting to hear why we have described this church and quarter so minutely.

See where the carriages come, not one, not two, but a dozen.

This one contains Harry and his father, the former radiant with joy and happiness, the latter seriously and gravely happy.

Harry leaped out to gaze with perfect awe at the beautiful, blushing vision of Jessie, surrounded by her bridesmaids.

It was a sight never to be forgotten.

All the party seemed happy.

And then, the ceremony over, to see the young bridegroom come out with her upon his arm—

His own.

His own dear, darling, wedded wife at last, after all their perils and troubles by sea and land.

It was almost too beautiful to be true; it looked almost like a dream.

He was half afraid that he should suddenly wake and find himself alone.

But he heard the shouts of the people as, in a delighted way, they cheered the handsome couple, while Leopold scattered money right and left.

His Jessie was happy at last, under the care and guidance of a true-hearted husband.

They drove off, they breakfasted, and then the parting came.

Henry took her hand. Cornelia turned away to hide the tears which came like summer vision.

The young and ardent couple were gone on their way to Scotland.

But they did not go far that night. Henry halted at a famous inn, not twenty miles from London, and sent the horses away.

It was rather early; but had he not waited for years for the hour when this blooming and lovely creature was to be his.

They have now been married many years, they have grown up sons and daughters, but never have they had cause, one or the other, to repent the hour which made them one.

The baronet lived many years, his reason and intellect quite restored.

The memory of past sorrows only served to give a zest to present joys.

THE END.

www.ingramcontent.com/pod-product-compliance
Lightning Source LLC
Chambersburg PA
CBHW080944020726
47505CB00009B/2134